THE MASTER OF GRAY TRILOGY

Book One
LORD AND MASTER

Born into one of Scotland's noblest families, Patrick, Master of Gray, was a fascinating yet ruthless individual, winning all hearts by his strange personal magnetism. Involved in daring plots to free the imprisoned Mary, Queen of Scots, in the intrigues of the courts of Elizabeth I and James VI, in the Huguenot Wars and the Spanish Armada, he strode imperiously across the turbulent stage of sixteenth century European history.

THE MASTER OF GRAY TRILOGY

Book Two
THE COURTESAN

Unacknowledged daughter of the Master of Gray, the
young Mary inherited her father's spectacular good looks
and talent for intrigue. Her forbidden love for the young
Duke of Lennox proved she had also inherited Patrick's
passionate nature. Coming to maturity in a Scotland torn
by violent conflict, she was to engage in an extraordinary
battle of wits with her noble father, determined to
counteract his plotting and save Protestant Scotland from
the threat of the Catholic Inquisition.

THE MASTER OF GRAY TRILOGY

Book Three
PAST MASTER

With the end of Elizabeth I's long reign in sight, Patrick, Master of Gray, was determined that James VI should succeed to the English throne. Nothing could be allowed to stand in his way – not even his own daughter's happiness. And so Mary Gray and her lover, Ludovick, Duke of Lennox, were to be caught up in a savage game of power politics, shaped by personal ambition and religious bigotry.

The Master of Gray Trilogy

LORD AND MASTER
THE COURTESAN
PAST MASTER

Nigel Tranter

CORONET BOOKS
Hodder and Stoughton

First published as three separate volumes

Lord and Master © 1961 by Nigel Tranter.
First published in Great Britain in 1961 by Hodder and Stoughton Ltd
First published as a Coronet paperback in 1973

The Courtesan © 1963 by Nigel Tranter.
First published in Great Britain in 1963 by Hodder and Stoughton Ltd
First published as a Coronet paperback in 1973

Past Master © 1965 by Nigel Tranter.
First published in Great Britain in 1965 by Hodder and Stoughton Ltd
First published as a Coronet paperback in 1973

This edition 1996
A Coronet paperback

The right of Nigel Tranter to be identified as the Author of
the Work has been asserted by him in accordance with the
Copyright, Designs and Patents Act 1988.

10 9 8 7 6 5 4 3 2 1

A CIP catalogue record for this title
is available from the British Library

ISBN 0 340 66675 7

Printed and bound in Great Britain by
Cox & Wyman Ltd, Reading, Berkshire

Hodder and Stoughton
A division of Hodder Headline PLC
338 Euston Road
London NW1 3BH

Lord and Master

BOOK ONE

Lord and Master

BOOK ONE

AUTHOR'S FOREWORD

WAS the Master of Gray a devil incarnate? The historians say so. They unanimously portray him in 'colours so odious that, to find his parallel as a master of unprincipled statecraft, we must search amongst the Machiavellian politicians of Italy'. He was, we read, 'a young man of singular beauty and no scruples'. Again, 'He carried a heart as black and treacherous as any in that profligate age.' And so on.

Yet he was admittedly the most successful and remarkable Scottish adventurer of his adventurous age – the age of Mary, Queen of Scots, of Elizabeth, and of James the Sixth; of Reformation Scotland, the Huguenot Wars and the Spanish Armada, in all of which he had his finger. Moreover, he was accepted to be the handsomest man of his day – it was said, of all Europe – as well as one of the most fascinating, talented and witty. None, apparently, could withstand his charm – and though it is claimed that he betrayed everyone with whom he had any dealings, the same folk continued to trust him to the end.

What sort of a man could this be? What lies behind a man like that? Could so black a traitor be yet a lover of beauty, a notable poet and one of the closest friends of the noble Sir Philip Sidney? Or have the historians all missed something? Was the Master of Gray as black as he was painted – or even blacker?

What follows here is no more than a novel. Mere fiction. One writer's notion of Patrick Gray as he might have been; one man's attempt to clothe the bare bones of history with warm human flesh, however erring. In the process many liberties have been taken with historical characters – and to a much lesser extent with dates. Probably I have been less than fair to Chancellor Maitland, for instance, an able man and apparently more honest than most.

I have invented the important character of David Gray, the Master's illegitimate half-brother, in order to provide the necessary reporter close enough to highlight and interpret the latter's extraordinary career – so much of which, of course, must have taken place in secret assignations and behind locked doors, many of them bedroom ones!

5

Castle Huntly still stands, high on its rock, frowning out over the fertile Carse of Gowrie. It is perhaps no more than poetic if ironic justice that it now serves the purpose of a house of correction for young men who have strayed from the broader paths of virtue – and been caught.

NIGEL TRANTER

Aberlady 1960

PRINCIPAL CHARACTERS

In order of appearance

(Fictional characters printed in *Italics*)

PATRICK, MASTER OF GRAY, son and heir of the 5th Lord Gray.

David Gray, illegitimate eldest son of the same.

PATRICK, 5TH LORD GRAY, twice an Extraordinary Lord of Session, and a close friend of Mary, Queen of Scots.

Andrew Davidson, an agile cleric, former Abbot of Holy Church, now reformed, and Principal of St. Mary's College, St. Andrews.

Mariota Davidson, his daughter, duly legitimated.

ELIZABETH LYON, eldest daughter of the 8th Lord Glamis, Chancellor of Scotland – first wife of the Master of Gray.

SIR THOMAS LYON, MASTER OF GLAMIS, brother to Lord Glamis, later Treasurer of Scotland.

JAMES DOUGLAS, 4TH EARL OF MORTON, Regent of Scotland for the child King James the Sixth.

Hortense, Countess de Verlac, paramour and protectress of the Master of Gray, in France.

ESMÉ STUART, SEIGNEUR D'AUBIGNY, a cousin of Darnley and therefore second cousin of King James, later Earl and Duke of Lennox, and Chancellor of Scotland.

JAMES STEWART OF OCHILTREE, Captain of the King's Guard, later Earl of Arran and Chancellor of Scotland.

KING JAMES THE SIXTH OF SCOTS, son of Mary, Queen of Scots.

ROBERT LOGAN OF RESTALRIG, adventurer, cousin of the Master of Gray.

LORD ROBERT STEWART, illegitimate half-brother of Mary the Queen, and later Earl of Orkney.

LADY MARIE STEWART, daughter of above, second wife of the Master of Gray.

LADY ELIZABETH STEWART, notorious courtesan, daughter of the Earl of Atholl, and wife successively to the Lord Lovat, the Earl of March and the Earl of Arran.

SIR FRANCIS WALSINGHAM, Chief Secretary of State to Queen Elizabeth.

SIR PHILIP SIDNEY, poet, diplomat and soldier.

QUEEN ELIZABETH OF ENGLAND.

MARY, QUEEN OF SCOTS, prisoner of Elizabeth.

SIR JOHN MAITLAND, Principal Secretary of State to King James, later Chancellor of Scotland.

SIR WILLIAM STEWART, brother to Arran, assistant to Secretary Maitland.

In addition to the above, amongst the many historical characters, prominent during the colourful twelve-year period covered by this story, are the following:

JOHN, 8TH LORD GLAMIS, Chancellor of Scotland.

HENRI, DUC DE GUISE, Marshal of France, cousin of Queen Mary, and instigator of the Massacre of St. Bartholomew's Eve.

LOUIS, CARDINAL OF LORRAINE, ARCHBISHOP OF RHEIMS, brother to the above, international plotter.

JAMES BEATON, ARCHBISHOP OF GLASGOW, exile, and Ambassador of Mary in France.

WILLIAM, 4TH LORD RUTHVEN, uncle to the Master of Gray, later first Earl of Gowrie and Treasurer of Scotland. Chief actor in the Raid of Ruthven.

ANDREW, 8TH EARL OF ERROLL, High Constable of Scotland and Chief of the Hays.

SIR THOMAS RANDOLPH, English Ambassador.

M. CLAUDE NAU, Secretary to Mary, Queen of Scots.

ROBERT DUDLEY, EARL OF LEICESTER, favourite of Queen Elizabeth.

WILLIAM CECIL, LORD BURLEIGH, former Chief Secretary, later Lord High Treasurer of England.

SIR WALTER RALEIGH, diplomat and explorer.

SIR RALPH SADLER, of Wingfield, jailer to Mary, Queen of Scots.

GEORGE, 6TH EARL OF HUNTLY, Chief of Clan Gordon.

Chapter One

THE two young men were boys enough still to have chosen to await the summons to the great Lord Gray out of doors and in a favourite haunt of their childhood days – a narrow grassy platform or terrace before a little cave in the cliff-face, a sunny, south-facing, secure place, divided by a steep and narrow little ravine from the fierce and sombre towering castle that challenged earth and sky from its taller soaring rock opposite. Here, always, they had found their own castle, where they could watch the comings and goings to that other arrogant pile, close enough to see all that was to be seen, and to be hailed when required, distant enough to be out of the way and, when necessary, hidden in the cave – which was equipped with its own secret stairway, like the many within the thick walls of Castle Huntly itself, out at the back by a climbing earthy passage, up into the bushes and trees that crowned their cliff, and away. They had come here almost automatically, and without discussing the matter, when they heard from Rob Powrie the steward that my lord of Gray was not yet back from Dundee town, though expected at any time – and was expecting to see *them* when he did come. If this repairing to their cave and ledge was a harking back to childhood custom, it did not strike either of them that way.

For young men they were, even though for the taller slender one it was actually only his sixteenth birthday. The other was six months older, though frequently he seemed the younger. Young men matured early in the Scotland of King Jamie Sixth – and as well that they did, since so few achieved any length of years, what with one thing and another. The King himself, of course, was but eight years old, and his unhappy and beautiful mother Mary was already six years a prisoner of Elizabeth of England, at thirty-two – which all had something to do with it.

The youths passed their time of waiting differently – as indeed they did most things differently, despite the closeness of their friendship. Patrick, the slender one, paced back and forth along the little grassy terrace – but not in any caged or heavy fashion; in fact he skipped lightly, almost danced, every now and again in his pacing, in tune with a song that he sang, a song

9

with a catchy jigging air and words that were almost as grossly indecent as they were dangerously sacrilegious, while he twanged at an imaginary lute with long delicate fingers and laughed and grimaced and gestured the while, at David, at the soaring sinister castle opposite, at all the wide-spreading green levels of the Carse of Gowrie and the blue estuary of the Tay that lay below their cliffs. Patrick Gray was like that, a born appreciator of life.

His companion, a stocky plain-faced youth, with level grey eyes where the other's were dancing and dark, sat hunched at the mouth of the cave, and, stubborn chin on hand, stared out across the fair carselands and over the sparkling firth beyond to the green hills of Fife. He did not join in any of the ribald verses of Patrick's song, nor even tap the toe of his worn and scuffed shoe to the lilt of it. He was not sulking, nor surly, however heavy his expression might seem in comparison with that of the gay and ebullient Patrick; merely thoughtful, quiet, reserved. His heavy brows and jutting chin perhaps did David Gray some small injustice.

Each very much in his own way was awaiting the fateful summons, on which, neither required to be told, so much depended.

'He takes a plaguey time – eh, Davy?' the younger inter- rupted – not his jigging but his singing – to remark. He laughed. 'No doubt the old lecher requires to fortify himself – with a sleep, perhaps – after the exhausting facilities of Dundee! I have heard that the Provost's wife is exceeding sportive – despite her bulk. Tiring, it may be, for a man of his years!' They had observed my Lord Gray's return from the town, with a small cavalcade, fully half-an-hour previously.

'Houts, Patrick man – what way is that to speak of your own father!' the other protested. 'My lord was in Dundee on the business of the Kirk, did not Rob Powrie say?'

'And you think that the two ploys wouldna mix? God's Body, Davy – and you living in godly Reformed St. Andrews these past two years! Faith, man – the holier the occasion, the fiercer the grapple!'

David Gray considered his companion with his level gaze, and said nothing. He had a great gift for silence, that young man – of which no-one was likely to accuse the other.

Patrick laughed again, tossing back the dark curling hair that framed his delicately handsome features, and resumed his song – only now he inserted the name of Patrick Lord Gray into the lewder parts of the ballad in place of the late lamented Cardinal Archbishop David Beaton, of notable memory. And the refrain he changed from 'Iram Coram Dago' to 'Frown, Davy, Frown-oh!'

Even if he did not laugh in sympathy, the other did not frown. Few people ever frowned on Patrick Gray – or if they did, not for long. He was much too good to look at for frowns, and his own scintillating and unfailing good humour, barbed as it generally might be, was apt to be infectious. Beautiful, Patrick had been called, in face and in figure, but there was a quality in both which saved that beauty from the taint of effeminacy. From waving black hair and high noble brows above flashing brilliant eyes, a straight finely-chiselled nose over a smiling mouth whose sweetness was balanced by a firm and so far beardless pointed chin, down past a body that was as lithe and slender and graceful as a rapier blade, to those neat dancing feet, Patrick, Master of Gray, was all shapely comely fascination and charm – and knew it. A pretty boy, yes – but a deal more than that. Not a few had found that out, of both sexes, for he was as good as a honeypot to men and women alike. It was all, perhaps, just a little hard on his brother David.

For they were brothers, these two, despite all the difference in build and feature and manner and voice, in dress even – and despite the paltry six months between their ages. There were times when it could be seen that they might be brothers, too, in the lift of their chins, their habit of shrugging a single shoulder, and so on – attributes these, presumably, passed on by the puissant and potent Patrick, fifth Lord Gray, to his firstborn David, as well as to his seven legitimate offspring, and his Maker only knew how many others. Nevertheless, where the one youth looked a thoroughbred and a delight to the eye, as became a son of the late Lady Barbara of the fierce and haughty breed of Ruthven, the other, rather, appeared a cob, serviceable but unexciting, as befitted the bastard of Nance Affleck, daughter of the miller of Inchture.

The diverting song was pierced by a shout from across the ravine – pierced but not halted. Patrick, as a matter of principle, finished the verse before he so much as glanced over to the fore-court of the castle. But David stood up, and waved a hand to the man with the bull-like voice who stood at the edge of the other cliff, and promptly began to make his way down the steep slope of the gully, using roots and rocks as handholds. After a suitable interval, his half-brother followed him.

The climb up to that beetling fortalice was a taxing business, even to young lungs – and a daunting one too, for any but these two, for the place all but overhung its precipice, and seemed to scowl down harshly, threateningly, in the process. Castle Huntly, as well as crowning an upthrusting rock that rose abruptly from the plain of Gowrie, was, and still is, perhaps the loftiest castle in a land of such, soaring at the cliffward side no fewer than seven storeys to its windy battlements, a tall stern dominating tower, rising on a plan of the letter L in walls of immensely thick red sandstone, past small iron-barred windows, to turrets and crowstepped gables and parapets, dwarfed by height, its base so grafted and grouted into different levels of the living rock as to leave almost indistinguishable where nature left off and man began.

Breathless, inevitably, the young men reached the level of the forecourt, where horses stood champing, a level which was already three storeys high on the cliffward side, and found Rob Powrie, the castle steward and major domo, awaiting them in a mixture of impatience and sympathy. He was a friend of theirs, though only too well aware that his master was not a man to be kept waiting, especially when aggrieved.

'Why could ye no' bide decently aboot the place, laddies, instead of ower in yon hole, there?' he complained. He was a big burly man, plainly dressed, more like a farmer than a noble-man's steward. 'My lord's shouting for you. You'd ha' done better to cosset him a wee, this day, than keep him waiting, you foolish loons. Up wi' you, now . . . '

'My father has plenty to cosset him, Rob – too many for his years, I think!' Patrick returned. 'The Provost's wife, for instance . . . '

'Wheesht, Master Patrick – wheesht, for sweet Mary's sake! Och, I mean for whoever's sake looks after us, these days!'

'Ha! Hark to the good Reformed steward of the Kirk's holy Lord Gray!'

'Wheesht, I say! Davy – can ye no' mak him see sense? Get him in a better frame o' mind than this? My lord's right hot against the pair o' you, I tell you. It will pay you to use him softly, I warrant.'

'Come on, Patrick – hurry, man,' David jerked. 'And for God's sake, have a care what you say.'

The other laughed. 'Never fear for me, Davy – look to your-self!' he said.

'Haste you both. My lord is in his own chamber . . . '

12

They continued their climb, first up a light outside timber stairway, which could be removed for security, to the only entrance to the keep proper, past the great dark stone-vaulted hall within, where a number of folk, lairds and officers and ministers in the sombre black of the Kirk, set about long tables of elm, and up the winding stone turnpike stair within the thickness of the tremendous walling, David leading. At the landing above the hall, before a studded door of oak, he halted, panting, and waited for Patrick to join him.

Before the latter could do so, the door was flung open, and their father stood there. He frowned at them both, heavily, the underhung jaw thrust forward, but said nothing.

'My lord!' David gulped.

'Good day to you, Father,' Patrick called, courteously.

The older man merely stared at them head sunk between massive shoulders, rather like a bull about to charge. Lord Gray was a bulky fleshy man, florid of face and spare of hair. Though only of early middle years he looked older, with the lines of dissipation heavy upon him, from sagging jowls to thrusting paunch. The little eyes in that gross face were shrewd, however, and the mouth tight enough. A more likely father, it would appear, for the stocky silent David than for the beautiful Patrick, Master of Gray, his heir.

Equally without a word, the former stood before him now, stiff, wary, waiting. The latter fetched an elaborate bow, that was only redeemed from being a mockery by the sweetness of the smile that accompanied it.

The Lord Gray jerked his head towards the inner room, and turning about, stamped inside, the spurs of his long leather riding-boots jingling. The young men followed, with Patrick now to the fore.

It was a comparatively small chamber, the stone floor, that was but the top of the hall vaulting, covered in skins of deer and sheep, the walls hung with arras save where two little wooden doors, one on either side of the room, hid the cunningly contrived ducts in the walling which led down to the deep window embrasures of the hall, and by which the castle's lord could listen, when so inclined, to most of what was said in the great room below. Despite its being late May, a fire of logs blazed in the stone fireplace with the heraldic overmantel bearing the graven rampant red lion on silver of Gray. It was very warm in that room.

To this fireplace Lord Gray limped, to turn and face his sons.

'Well?' he said. That was all.

'Very well, I thank you, sir,' Patrick answered lightly – but not too lightly. 'I trust that I see you equally so – and that your leg but little pains you?' That was solicitude itself, its sincerity not to be doubted.

The older man's frown seemed to melt a little as he looked at his namesake. Then swiftly he shook his head and his brows came down again, as he transferred his gaze to the other young man. 'You, sirrah!' he cried, and he shouted now, in reaction to that shameful moment of weakness. 'You, you graceless whelp, you spawn of the miller's bitch – you that I've cherished and supported in idleness all these years! What have you to say for yourself, a' God's name? What do you mean by permitting this to happen? Fine you ken that I only sent you to St. Andrews College to keep this simpering poppet here out o' mischief. D'you think I threw my siller away on a chance by-blow like yoursel', for nothing? Do you? Answer me! What a pox ha' you been doing, to fail me thus? Out with it, damn you!'

David Gray drew a long and uneven breath, but his level gaze was steady on his father's purpling congested face. 'My lord – I have worked at my studies, and waited on Patrick here, as you ordained.'

'Waited on him! Fiend seize me – held up the lassie's skirts for him, mair like!' the older man burst out coarsely. 'Is that it? Is that the way you carried out my charges? Speak, fool!'

'No, sir.' Heavily, almost tonelessly, the young man answered him. He was used to being the whipping-boy for the Master of Gray. It was so much easier to pour out wrath upon himself than upon his fascinating and talented brother. Not that he enjoyed the process. 'I have done as you ordained, to the best of my ability . . .'

'God's Passion–*your* ability! Your ability means that the pair o' you are sent down from the University as a stink, a disgrace to the name and honour of Gray . . . and Master Davidson's daughter with a bairn in her belly!'

David stared straight in front of him, and said nothing.

'Speak, man – don't stand there glowering like a stirk? Give me an answer – or I'll have the glower wiped off your face with a horse-whip!'

David could have pointed out that it was not really the pair of them that had been expelled from St. Mary's College, but only Patrick. Likewise, that Mariota Davidson's bairn had not been conceived as a joint operation of the brothers. But such objec-

14

tions, he knew, would be as profitless as they were irrelevant. He had no illusions as to his position and what was required of him. Inevitably there were handicaps in the privileged situation of being foster-brother, squire, bodyservant and conscience for the winsome Master of Gray. 'I am sorry,' he said simply, flatly – but less than humbly. David Gray was in fact no more humble at heart than any other Gray.

'Sorry. . . . ' Lord Gray's face contorted and his fists clenched beneath his somewhat soiled ruffles.

Patrick, misliking the sight and the ugliness of it all, stared away out of the small window, and sought to dwell on pleasanter things.

David thought that his father was going to strike him, and steeled himself to stand the blow unflinching – as he had stood many another, when younger. But the head-turned stance of his other son seemed to affect the nobleman – possibly also the fact that he could thus look at him without having to meet the half-mocking, half-reproachful and wholly disarming glance of Patrick's fine dark eyes.

'You, you prinking ninny! You papingo! Does this not concern you, likewise, boy?' Lord Gray looked down as the younger man turned. 'And these clothes? These mummer's trappings? This fool's finery? Where did you get it? How come you dressed so – like a Popish whoremonger? Not with *my* siller, by God!' He gestured disgustedly at his heir's costume. 'How dare you show yoursel' in a godly household, so?'

Certainly Patrick was dressed very differently from his father. He wore a crimson velvet doublet with an upstanding collar piped in gold thread, reaching high at the back to set off a cascading lace ruff. The sleeves were slashed with yellow satin, and ended in lace ruffles. The shoulders were padded out into prominent epaulettes. The waist of the doublet reached down low in a V to emphasise the groin, and the breeches were short, ending above the knee, slashed also in yellow and padded out at the hips and thighs. The long hose were of yellow silk, and the shoes sported knots of crimson ribbon. Lord Gray, on the other hand, as became a pillar of the new Kirk, was soberly clad in dark broadcloth, the doublet fitting the body and skirted, in the old-fashioned way, with only a small collar, and the ruff a mere fringe of white. The breeches were unmodishly long enough to reach below his knees and disappear into the tops of his riding-boots. The only gesture towards richness was the heavy sword-belt of solid wrought gold. As for David, his patched doublet and breeches of plain brown homespun, darned woven hose and solid but worn shoes, were all clean enough and as neat as they might be – and that was about the best that could be said for them.

Patrick glanced down at himself with no indication of shame or dissatisfaction. 'An honest penny may always be earned in St. Andrews town, at a pinch,' he said. 'Learning, I have found, does not always damp out lesser delights. Even ministers of your Kirk, sir, can be generous, on occasion – and their ladies still more so, Heaven be praised!'

'Lord – what d'you mean, boy?' his father spluttered. 'What is this, now? Do not tell me that . . . '

'I shall tell you nothing, my lord, that would distress you – God forbid! Indeed, there is little to tell. Is there, Davy? My lord of Gray's son is inevitably welcome in many a house. You would not have him churlishly reject such . . . hospitality?'

The older man swallowed, all but choked, and almost thankfully, if viciously, turned back to David. 'This . . . this, then, is how you guided and looked after your brother! You'll pay for this – both of you! I'll not be used thus. To drag my name in the dirt . . . !'

'Never that, Father,' Patrick assured. 'The reverse, rather. Indeed, always your name meant a great deal to us, I vow. Is that not so, Davy? And your honour, sir, of value above, h'mm, rubies!'

The Lord Gray opened his mouth to speak, shut it again almost with a snap, and went limping over to a desk. He picked up a paper there, and brought it back to them, and waved it under the boys' faces.

'Here is how you valued my name and honour,' he exclaimed. 'A letter from Principal Davidson apprising me . . . *me*! . . . that he must banish you from his University by reason of your filthy lewdness, naming you as father of his daughter's unborn bairn, and hinting at a marriage. God's death – marriage! With Gray!'

Even Patrick faltered at that *cri de coeur*. 'Marriage . . . ?' he repeated. 'With Mariota? The old turkey-cock talks of *marriage*, i' faith! Lord – here is madness!'

'Madness? Aye, by the sweet Christ! But whose madness? With all the other trollops of St. Andrews to sport with, you had to go begetting a bastard on the worthy Principal's daughter! Why, man? Why?'

Patrick mustered a one-shouldered shrug. 'I have it on good

authority, sir, that the daughter herself was a bastard of the worthy Principal, until a few years syne – when he was the holy Lord Abbot of Inchaffray.'

'What of it, boy? Can we no' all make mistakes?' my lord asked, and then coughed.

'Quite, Father.'

'Aye – but there are mistakes and mistakes, Patrick. Mistakes o' the flesh can come upon us all unawares, at times. But mistakes o' the wits and the mind are another matter, boy.'

'Which was good Master Davidson's, Father?' Patrick wondered innocently.

'Tush – his mistakes are by with. Yours are not. Principal Davidson saw the bright light o' Reform in good time . . . and so wed a decent woman in place o' the Harlot o' Rome. So he now can decently own his lass, and call her legitimate. Moreover, he is a coming man in the Kirk, and wi' the ear o' the Regent and o' Master Buchanan, the King's Tutor. He is no' a man to offend, I tell you.'

'Must Gray go in fear and respect, then, of a jumped-up coat-turned cleric, my lord?'

'God's Splendour – no! But . . . laddie, you ken not what you say. My position is no' that secure. The country is in a steer, and Morton the Regent loves me not. He and the Kirk rule the land – and I am known as a friend o' Mary the Queen, whom the Kirk loves not. Where the Kirk is concerned, I maun watch my step . . .'

'But you yourself are one of the leaders of the Kirk party, are you not?'

'Aye . . . but I have my unfriends. In the same Kirk. Why did you bring the Kirk into this cantrip, boy? I'm no' so sure o' Davidson. You heard – the man hints at marriage. And if he talks that gait loud enough, it will surely come to the ear o' my lord of Glamis. And how will you fare then, jackanapes?'

'Glamis?'

'Aye, Glamis. I have, God aiding me, arranged a marriage contract between yoursel' and the Lady Elizabeth Lyon o' Glamis. After much labour, and but a few days past. What will my lord say when he hears o' this, then? Glamis is strong in the Kirk party. None shall shake *him*. 'Twas the best match in the land for you. And, now . . .'

Patrick was not listening. 'Glamis!' he repeated. 'Elizabeth Lyon of Glamis.' Those fine eyes had narrowed. The speaker leaned forward, suddenly urgent, his voice altered – indeed all of him altered, as in a moment. 'This . . . this is different, I think,' he said slowly. 'My lord – I knew nothing of this.'

'Think you I must inform you, a stripling, of all I plan . . . ?'

'I am old enough for the injury of your plans, sir, it seems – so old enough to be told of them when they concern myself, surely? Old enough for marriage, too . . . '

'Aye. Marriage to a cleric's mischance in a college backyard – or marriage to the daughter of the Chancellor, one of the greatest lords of the land . . . and the richest!'

Patrick smiled, and swiftly, as in a flash, was all light and cheer and attraction again. 'Elizabeth Lyon, as I mind her, is very fair,' he said. 'And notably well endowered . . . in more than just her dowry!' And he laughed.

'Aye – she has big breasts, if that is what you like,' his forthright father agreed. 'A pity that you ha' thrown them away, and what goes wi' them, for this strumpet o' Davidson's. Devil damn it – I had set my heart on this union between our two houses . . . '

'She is no strumpet.' That was quietly, levelly said.

Both Patricks, senior and junior, turned on David who had so abruptly but simply made that announcement. The elder's glance was hot and angry, but the younger's was quick and very keen.

'Silence, sirrah!' Lord Gray said. 'Speak when you are spoken to.'

'Davy likes the gentle Mariota well enough, I think,' his brother observed, significantly.

'I carena who he likes or doesna like – or you, either,' their father declared, 'What I care for is the ruin o' my plans, and the welfare o' our house and name. That you have spat upon, and cast aside . . . '

'I think you do me wrong, Father,' Patrick said quietly.

'Eh? Wrong? A pox – *you* say so? You mincing jackdaw!' Lord Gray took a wrathful step forward.

Patrick held his ground. 'Only because I judge you to be misinformed, sir. Your plans are not ruined, yet.'

'How mean you . . . ?'

'I mean that it is not I that should be the object of Master Davidson's ambitions – but Davy, here! Heigho, Davy is the culprit, I fear!'

There was little of difference between the gasps of breath drawn by each of his hearers. David turned swiftly – and found Patrick's gaze urgent upon him.

'Is that not so, Davy? Dear Davy! You have hidden your

light under your bushel for long enough, eh? The bairn is yours – faith, all yours!'

'But . . . !'

'God be good – what is this?' Lord Gray looked from one to the other. 'Are you telling me, now . . . ?' Davidson says in his letter . . . '

'Master Davidson, no doubt, would liefer have the Master of Gray for possible good-son than just our Davy! But he will be disappointed. Mariota's bairn need not claim me for father.'

'You mean that it was Davy . . . ?'

'Just that. We both found her . . . friendly. But Davy, I swear, found her kindest! You heard him. He is a deep one, Davy. I did not mind bearing the honour of it, or the blame, to save him, when it mattered less than a groat. But now, with the name and honour of our house at stake, in the matter of the Glamis match . . . '

'Yes, yes. Aye, so. I' ph'mmm. This is . . . altogether different. I' faith, yes.' The older man looked at David, his shrewd little eyes busy, calculating. As the latter started to speak, his father held up his hand peremptorily. 'Here, now, is a different story, altogether. Why did you not tell me this, earlier? I see it all, now – the rascal Davidson saw his chance. He would catch a fine fish with his little trull. He would hook Gray, would he? We shall teach him different.'

'Ah, but do not name her trull, Father,' Patrick put in quickly, smiling. 'Davy's feelings are to be considered, are they not? He would not have her named strumpet, recollect!'

'Aye, aye.' The Lord Gray actually chuckled. It was extra-ordinary the change that has come over the man. 'Davy's feelings shall be considered – houts aye. Davy will have his reward – our right lusty eager Davy! Boy – maybe we will make a church-man o' you yet . . . with Principal o' St Andrews, and like to be one o' Morton's tulchan bishops, for goodfather! We will have two marriages – aye, ye shall both embrace the holy estate o' matrimony. Embrace it right firmly. What could be more suitable? I will write me a letter to Master Davidson. No, better – I will ride and see him tomorrow, myself. I would not miss seeing his godly countenance at the good tidings I bring! Ha!'

'My lord,' David managed to insert, at last. 'Have I no say in this?'

'None, boy. None,' his father assured promptly, finally, but almost genially. 'You have done your part – and done it right notably, it seems. The rest is my affair.' He actually patted

David's shoulder. 'Now, off with you. Away, the pair o' you. There are folk awaiting me, below.'

'Sir – the lassie. Mariota. She, at the least, must needs have her say . . . '

'Houts – off wi' you! The lassie will do what she's told. And lucky to be made into a middling honest woman, by God! Now – off wi' you, I say. And, Patrick – in the fiend's name, get out o' those magpie's clothes before any o' my sainted callers see you!'

'Yes, Father.'

As the two young men went down the stairs, David leading, it was the other who spoke first. 'Was that not featly done, Davy?' Patrick asked, laughing softly. 'Was not there the dexterous touch? The storm taken at its crest, and calmed! The bubble burst! I flatter myself I wrought that not unskilfully.'

The other neither looked at him nor answered.

'I saved the day for us both, did I not? It got us out of there with smiles instead of tears. You cannot deny that I spared you a horse-whipping, it may be – or worse, man?'

Still his brother did not reply, but went stolidly on down the winding stairs.

'Davy!' Patrick laid an urgent hand on his companion's arm. 'You are not hurt at me? Man, Davy – you did not take it amiss? I acted all for the best. For all of us. You saw how it was. It had to be so. The honour of our name – aye, and the safety of our house, even – demanded it. You heard what my father said. I could do no other.'

They had come to the bottom of the stairs, and hurried past the hall. At the little guard-room that flanked the castle door-way they found Gilbert and James, two of Patrick's legitimate brothers, and Barbara his eldest sister, and these, mere bairns of ten and twelve, they brushed aside despite their eager admiration of Patrick's costume. Down the outside timber steps they went. Their own room was in one of the smaller corner towers that guarded the enclosing courtyard of the great keep on the landward side. Instead of heading thereto, however, David, still in the lead, made straight across the cobbled yard, past the tethered horses and lounging men-at-arms, to the great arched entrance under its embattled gatehouse, Patrick, still explaining, at his side. At the gateway itself, however, the latter paused.

'Where are you going, Davy?' he said. 'Not out there – not yet. I must be out of these clothes.'

'Later,' the other jerked, and kept on walking.

'No. You heard what my father said. About taking them off. We have him in kindlier mood, now. We should not offend him more.'

They were through the gateway now, past the main guard-room, out of which a woman's skirls of laughing protest issued unsuitably. David strode on, unspeaking.

'You are being foolish, Davy – stupid,' Patrick declared. There was more than a hint of anxiety in his attractively modu-lated voice now. 'Where . . . where are you going?'

His brother had swung off the castle's approach road, to plunge down the gentle grassy slope to the west. Below were birch trees, open woodland, reaching round the sides of the towering rock to the level carseland.

'Down yonder,' David told him briefly. 'Where we can speak our minds.'

'No!' the other cried. 'Not there. We . . . we can speak in our room. Anywhere, Davy . . . '

His brother's hand reached out to grip his arm fiercely, jerk-ing Patrick on. 'Come, you!'

Patrick looked back at the castle, glancing sidelong at his com-panion, bit his lip, but followed where he was led, silent now.

Slanting down through the trees they came presently to a grassy hollow hidden amongst the birches and the tall bracken, out of sight of castle and road and spreading fields below – a haunt of theirs less popular than their cave and ledge perhaps, but useful in its own way. There, roughly, David unhanded his brother, and faced him.

'Time we made a reckoning, I think,' he said levelly.

'No, Davy – no!' Patrick's fine eyes were wide. 'This is folly. No way to behave. To settle differences. We are men, now – not bairns. See you – I can explain it all. If you will but heed me, Davy. If you will but listen . . . '

'I listened,' the other interrupted him, harshly. 'You had your say back yonder. Now, I will have mine! You are a liar, Patrick Gray – a liar, and a cozener, and a cheat! Are you a coward too?'

His brother had lost a little of his colour. He drew a deep breath. 'No,' he said, and seemed to find difficulty in getting the word out.

'Good, I was feared you might be – along with the rest. And you can run faster than me, yet!'

Patrick's head lifted just a degree or two, and his chin with it – and for a moment they looked very much alike. 'No,' he repeated

21

quietly. 'I do not think I am a coward. But, Davy – my fine clothes?'

'The fiend take your fine clothes! This is for your lies!' And David Gray exploded into action, and hurled himself upon the other, head sunk into wide shoulders, fists flailing.

Patrick side-stepped agilely, leapt back light-footed, and lashed out in defence. Of the first fierce rain of blows only two grazed his cheek and shoulder. But David was possessed of a swift and rubbery fury of energy that there was no escaping, though the other was taller, with the longer reach, and hit out in return desperately, as hard as he knew. The driving, elementary, relentless savagery of the elder was just not to be withstood. Short of turning and running, there was no escape. Patrick knew it, from of old – and perhaps the knowledge further invalidated his defence. In less time than it takes to tell, his lip was split and his nose bleeding.

Panting, David leapt back, tossing the hair from his face. 'That for your lies!' he gasped. 'This, for your cozening!' And plunging into the attack again, he drove hard for the other's body in crouching battering-ram style. Despite himself, Patrick yelped with sudden pain, hunched himself up in an effort to protect his softer parts, and was driven staggering back with a great pile-driver, to sink on one knee, groaning.

'That for . . . the cozening! On your feet, man! This for . . . your cheating!' David swung a sideways upper-cut at Patrick's chin, which all but lifted the other off his unsteady feet, and sent him tottering back to crash all his length on the greensward, and there lie moaning.

Swaying over him, grey eyes blazing with a cold fire of their own, David suddenly stooped and wrenched up a turf of long grass and roots and earth. On to his brother's beautiful face he rubbed and ground and slapped this, back and forth, into mouth and nose and eyes, before casting it from him. 'And that . . . for Mariota Davidson!' he exclaimed.

Straightening up, then, he looked down upon the writhing disfigured victim, and the cold fire ebbed from him. Panting he stood there, for long moments, straddling the other, and then slowly he shook his head.

'Och, Patrick, Patrick!' he said, and turning away abruptly, went striding off through the further trees without a backward glance.

The Master of Gray lay where he had fallen, sobbing for breath.

Chapter Two

My lord of Gray was as good as his word, and allowed no grass
to grow under his feet, either. He rode to St. Andrews the next
morning, and was home again the same night – and in excellent
mood. He made no comment at all on Patrick's battered features
and gingerly held frame, nor questioned the young men further
on what apparently was now little business of theirs. A busy man
of affairs, of course, he was not in the habit of wasting much
time on any of his offspring. His orders, however, were explicit
and peremptory. He and Patrick would ride on the morrow for
Glamis Castle, to fix the date of the wedding, before the
Chancellor went off to Stirling for his monthly meeting with the
Regent. The other marriage date was already satisfactorily
fixed, it seemed – even the disillusioned Principal Davidson
agreeing, presumably, as to the need for some haste in this
matter. It only remained for David Gray to go and pay his
respects to his future father-in-law. The nuptials would be
celebrated, if that was the apt word, as discreetly and quickly
as possible before the month was out and before the lassie
became mountainous.

The brothers were to go their different ways, then, for almost
the first time in their lives.

So the day following, early, the two parties rode away from
Castle Huntly, in almost opposite directions and contrastingly
composed. My lord's jingling company of gentlemen, chaplain,
and score of men-at-arms were finely mounted, their weapons
gleaming, plumes tossing, the red lion standard of Gray fluttering bravely in front of father and son; both were soberly clad in
dark broadcloth but with rich black half-armour, inlaid with
gold, above. They headed north by west for the Newtongray
pass of the Sidlaw hills and Strathmore of the Lyons. David,
sitting his shaggy long-tailed Highland pony, and dressed still
as he had come from St. Andrews two days before, trotted
off alone eastwards for Dundee town and the ferry boat at
Broughty.

As they branched off on their different roads, David looked
back. He saw only the one head in that gallant cavalcade turned

23

towards him, as Patrick's steel-gauntleted arm was raised in valedictory salute. David lifted his own hand, and slowly waved it back and forth, before sighing and turning away. They were brothers, yet.

Five miles on, avoiding the climbing narrow streets of Dundee by keeping to the water-front and the boat-shore, David rode further to Broughty, another three miles eastwards, where the Firth narrowed to a bare mile across and a ferry plied. Here rose the soaring broken mass of another Gray castle, still proudly dominating land and sea despite being partly demolished after its bloody vicissitudes during the religious wars of a few years earlier. David sat waiting for the ferryboat beneath the frowning river walls, and cared nothing for the fact that his own great-grandfather had first built them, his grandfather had betrayed them to the English, and his father had gained his limp and almost lost his life in seeking to retake them.

The ferry eventually put him across the swift-running tide, at Ferry-Port-on-Craig, where still another castle glowered darkly on all but friends of Gray, and which, acting in conjunction with that of Broughty over the water, could in theory defend the estuary and Dundee from invasion by sea, and in practise levy toll on all shipping using the narrows – thereby greatly contributing to my lord's income.

A ride of no more than ten miles across the flat sandy links of North Fife brought David thereafter, by just after noon, to the grey city of St. Andrews, ecclesiastical metropolis of Scotland, with all its towers and spires and pinnacles adream by the white-flecked glittering sea. The young man viewed it with mixed feelings as he rode in by the Guard Bridge and the narrow massive gateway of the West Port. The blood of martyrs innumerable did not shout to him from the cobbles, nor did the sight of so many fair and handsome buildings in various stages of defacement and demolishment, eloquent witness to Reforming zeal, distress him overmuch; but here he had passed the two most free and happy years of his life, here he had studied and learned and laughed and sported, here he had met Mariota Davidson – and from here he had been expelled with ignominy, because he was the Master of Gray's shadow and dependent, but two days before.

He rode down the narrow kennel of South Street, where pigs rooted amongst the mounds of garbage that half-filled the causeway outside every door, squawking poultry flew up from his pony's hooves, and the wooden house gables that thrust out

24

on either side all but met overhead, enabling wives to exchange gossip above him from one side to the other in their own windows. Many of these timber houses were being pulled down, and the new stone ones being built by the Reformers out of the convenient quarries of the Cathedral and a score of fine churches, priories, nunneries, seminaries and the like, were set further back from the cobbles, so that one day the street would be wider, undoubtedly. But meantime the transported stone-work lay about in heaps everywhere, along with defaced statues, smashed effigies and shattered marble, greatly adding to the congestion and difficulty of passage. The smells and the noises and the sights of St. Andrews, though all familiar, were not without their effect on the banished student.

David turned in at the arched entrance of St. Mary's College. He dismounted, left his pony loose amongst the cattle which grazed on the wide grassy square within, and made for the corner of the great quadrangle where was the Principal's house, a handsome edifice, formerly the college chapel. He approached the door, and rasped diffidently on the tirling-pin. Needless to say, he had never before used the front door of this august establishment, whatever he may have done at the back – but his instructions for the occasion, from his father, were positive.

An arrogant man-servant answered his summons – and would have sent him packing with a flea in his ear, as one more pre-sumptuous and threadbare scholar, had not David declared that he sought Master Davidson on an errand from my lord of Gray. Grudgingly, suspiciously, he was admitted, and thrust into a dark and book-lined room to wait.

He had to wait, indeed. Though he could hear the Principal's sonorous and slightly nasal voice echoing, now from the room next door, now from the hall, it came no nearer than that as the minutes passed and lengthened into an hour. Undoubtedly Master Davidson had more important matters to attend to than such as he represented. David waited as patiently as he might. After a while, greatly daring, he glanced at some of the books on the shelves, and found them dull stuff, in Latin. He went to the window, and gazed out. He paced round and round the peri-meter of the stone floor, avoiding treading on its precious covering, one of the fine new carpets such as even Castle Huntly could not boast. Sometimes he listened, ear to the crack of the door, not for the well advertised presence of the Principal, but for the possible sound of Mariota's voice. She must be some-where in the house. He would have liked to see her before he

spoke with her father – though liked hardly was the word to use –
but he did not see how this was to be achieved.

It was nearer two hours than one before the door opened to
reveal the impressive figure of Principal Andrew Davidson. He
was less lean and hungry-looking, was less hairy, than the generality of the Reformed clergy, being amply and comfortably made,
and of an imposing presence. His beard, indeed, was only wispy
– which must have been a sore trial to him, with the Old
Testament prophet as the approved model – and it was said that
the large flat black velvet cap, which he was rumoured to keep
on his head even in bed, was to hide the tonsure which painfully
laggard nature was failing lamentably to cover up. He was
dressed in the full pulpit garb of black Geneva gown and plain
white bands, now as always – though once again scurrilous
student whisper had it that if the wind off the North Sea waxed
more than usually frolicsome around a St. Andrews street
corner, and the voluminous gown billowed up, much silken and
ungodly coloured apparel might be glimpsed beneath. He swept
into the room now, and the door slammed shut behind him.

'You are David Gray, for want of a true surname,' he declaimed, in his stride as it were, as though in continuation of a
previous discourse, hardly glancing at his visitor. 'A whore-
mongering idler and a trifler with women, whom it seems, God
pity me, I must accept as good-son because you have taken gross
and filthy advantage of my foolish daughter. I cannot and shall
not welcome you to this house that you have presumptuously
defiled and outraged. God is not mocked, and his righteous
wrath shall descend upon the heads of all such as yourself. Nor
shall any dowry come to you with my unhappy and ravaged
daughter, upon whom the Lord have mercy – think it not! Such
dowry as she had, you have already lasciviously possessed, in
fornicating shameful lust!' The resounding well-turned words
and phrases slid in sonorous procession off what almost seemed
to be an appreciatively savouring tongue. 'The carnal appetites
of the flesh shall not inherit the Kingdom of Heaven, nor any
goods and gear of mine. *Jacta est alea!* What provision has my
Lord Gray made for you both, boy?'

David was so overwhelmed by this flood of oratory and part
mesmerised by the ceaseless and remarkable perambulations of
the dignified speaker, that it was some moments before he
realised that a question had been flung at him, and that the last
sentence had not been merely one more rhetorical pearl on the
string of eloquence. He gulped, as he found the other's

imperious if somewhat protuberant eyes upon him, *en passant*, as it were.

'I . . . I do not know, sir,' he faltered.

'Almighty and Most Merciful – grant me patience! Grant a ravaged father restraint! Hark at him – he does not know! He knows how to steal a helpless lassie's maidenhead! He knows the sinful antics of the night! He knows the way to my door, with offers of marriage! But he does not know how to support the creature whom he hath got with child! What is my lord thinking of? He fobs me off with you, *you* – dolt, bastard and beggar – and sends no word of what he will pay! You have no letter, sirrah? No promissory token . . . ?'

'None,' David answered. 'My lord said that . . . that all was arranged.'

'Arranged! Aye – arranged is the word for it, I vow! Arranged to cheat and defraud me! All a plot, a trick! By the holy and blessed Saint Mar . . . h'mm . . . by the Sword of the Lord and His Kirk – does he esteem me a babe, a puling innocent to be foxed and duped? You are sure, knave, that there is no letter coming, no privy word?'

'I do not know,' David reiterated. 'All my lord told me was that all was arranged. That you would be satisfied – satisfied with me as good-son. And that the marriage was settled for ere the month's end, before, before . . . '

'Aye – before yon fond fool through there thrusts her belly's infamy in the face of all who walk St. Andrew's streets, to make me a laughing-stock and a by-word before all men!' The reverend Principal had noticeably increased the pace of his promenade, in his agitation, so that now his gown positively streamed behind him. 'Father in Heaven – was ever a humble servant of Thine so used! Was ever the foul fiend's work so blatantly . . . boy – you did say satisfied? Satisfied was the word? My lord did declare that I would be satisfied with you as good-son – God help me! Aye – it must be that. Mean that I should be satisfied . . . receive due and proper satisfaction. Aught else is unthinkable. Perhaps I have done my lord some slight injustice? 'Fore God I hope that I have! Tell you my lord, fellow, that I await his satisfaction eagerly. You have it? Eagerly. Aye. Now . . . weightier matters await me, boy. You may go.'

David gasped. 'Go?' he repeated. 'But, sir . . . that is not all, surely? That is not *all* I came to see you for?'

'All, fool? Enough and enough that I should have spared you

27

thus much of my time. I am a man with great and heavy tasks upon me. I have the care of hundreds of souls in this place on my hands and heart. I have to see that God's will is done in this University and city. How much more of my time would you have?'

'But the marriage, sir? What of that? When is it to be? My lord said that you would arrange all . . .'

'Arrange all? Arrange what, in the name of the good Lord? Think you that this unseemly union, devised under some back stair, should be ceremoniously celebrated with pomp and display? I vow not! A shamed and ungrateful wanton's mating to a nameless bastard! Faugh, sir – *me* arrange it?' Davidson had his hand on the door latch. 'Wed you where and how you will – so long as wed you are. And before due witnesses – but not before me, I warrant you!'

'I see, sir.' David's voice was level, set, now. 'And when? When is this to be?'

'Should I care, man? When you like. Today if you have the wherewithal to pay the chaplain's fee. Wed the baggage now if you wish – so long as you take her away out of my sight, out of this house and this my city of St. Andrews! But . . . see you have it lawfully witnessed . . .'

That last was tossed over a black-gowned shoulder, as the ornament of the Kirk, fount of learning, and one-time prince of the Holy Church strode out into the hallway and was gone, leaving the door wide behind him.

For long the young man stood in that dark room staring after the cleric with unseeing eyes.

At length, sighing, David went in search of Mariota Davidson. He moved warily through to the rear of the house to the great kitchen. A serving wench there greeted his appearance with sniggers and giggles, but in answer to his enquiry pointed to an inner door, leading to a pantry. Nodding, he moved over, and opened the door.

The girl sat by the window of the small room, her hands on her lap, staring straight before her. At sight of him she rose to her feet, and stood waiting, wordless, wide-eyed.

'Mariota!' he said, his voice thick. 'Och, lassie, lassie!'

She bit her lip, lowered her eyes, and drew a deep quivering breath.

Quietly David closed the door behind him.

Mariota Davidson was not notably mountainous, nor even

too obviously pregnant – only somewhat thicker about the middle than her usual. At fifteen, she was a well-built girl, almost as tall as David, a gentle fawn-eyed creature, bonny, auburn-haired, her burgeoning womanhood glowing for all to behold. Only, today those normally easily flushed and dimpled cheeks were pale and tear-stained, and the great hazel-brown eyes red-rimmed and a little swollen. Even so, she was bonny, warm, appealing – to David Gray perhaps the more so for her so evident distress. She was dressed in a short sleeveless homespun gown of dark green, almost black, as became a daughter of the Kirk, even an outcast one, the skirt split down the front and gathered back to show an underskirt of saffron linen, with a white linen sleeved sark or blouse above. She wore a brief apron also, at which she tugged and twisted.

David came near to her, but not too near. 'I . . . I am sorry, Mariota,' he said. 'You have been crying. I am sorry. Do not cry, lassie.'

She shook her capless head of reddish-brown curls, unspeaking.

'You are well enough?'

'Yes,' she said, small-voiced. 'Where is . . . where is Patrick?'

'He is not here. He is . . . he is with my lord.' David looked down at his feet. 'He sent you greetings. He wishes you very well,' he lied.

The girl did not answer. She was twisting and twisting that apron. 'Davy – oh, Davy – what is to become of me?' she exclaimed, her voice catching.

He swallowed. 'It is . . . we are . . . has your father not told you, Mariota?'

'He tells me nothing. He will not even speak with me. None must speak with me. None must deal with me at all, in this house. He has ordered it. No soul has spoken to me for three days. Oh, Davy . . . !' She choked.

He took a step forward, to touch her, to take her arm – and then hesitated, withdrew his hand. 'You know . . . you know nothing, then?'

'Only that I am lost, lost,' she wailed. 'God will not have me, nor man either. None . . . '

He clutched at that. 'I will,' he said. 'I will have you, Mariota.'

She did not seem to hear him. 'I would kill myself, if I knew how,' she went on, tonelessly. 'I have tried – but it is not so easy . . . '

'Och, hush you!' the young man cried, shocked. 'What way is

that to talk? Wicked, it is.'

'Aye – but I *am* wicked. I wish that I was dead, Davy.'

'Lord, lassie – never say that! Never. You will be happy yet. I swear it. I will see to it – believe me, lassie, I will.'

'You are kind, Davy. Always you were kind. But what can you do? It was kindly of you to come and see me . . . after what I have done. I wonder that you came. But there is nothing that you can do, you see . . . '

'I' faith, girl – I am to marry you!' Almost he shouted that, to get it out. 'Marry, d'you hear? I am to marry you!'

Her breath caught, as she stared at him. She put a hand to her high young bosom. She opened her lips, but found no words.

David took her arm this time, earnestly. 'I am sorry, Mariota. I should not have bawled at you, that way. Sorry for everything. Sorry about Patrick. He would . . . do not blame him too much, lass. My lord would not hear of it. He has other plans for Patrick. I . . . well, I am the best that you can do, I fear. I am not Patrick . . . but I like you, lassie. I like you very well.'

The girl seemed not so much to be listening as searching, searching his eyes with her own, huge, alight, but fearful. It was her turn to reach out, with both her hands, to grip him. 'Davy,' she whispered, 'you would not cozen me? You would not do that to me? Not now?'

'No,' he agreed. 'I would not do that, now or any time. See you, Mariota – it is best this way. The child shall be my child. Folk will not question it – not in the Gray country, anyway . . . '

He got no further. Mariota threw herself upon him, her arms around his neck, suddenly laughing and sobbing in one, and near to hysteria, her full weight upon him, head hard against his shoulder.

'Davy, Davy!' she cried, panting. 'My dear Davy! Is it true? True? You will marry me? *You* will! Oh, Davy lad . . . God be praised!'

All but choked, throttled, by the vehemence of her, the young man struggled for air, blinked – but patted her heaving back too. 'Och, mercy!' he exclaimed. 'There, there. Of course it is true. That is why I am here – why I came. But . . . och, wheesht, lassie. Do not cry. Wheesht, now – wheesht!'

The tears were welling up fast now – but they were tears of joy and thankfulness and relief. He put her a little way from him, and took the corner of her twisted apron gently to wipe and dab at her cheeks and nose, whilst shining-eyed, trembling, she gazed at him through the glistening curtain of them.

30

Then abruptly, her lower lip fell, her eyes clouded, her whole face seemed to crumple. 'My father . . . !' she quavered.

'I have seen your father,' he told her. 'I have just left him. It is all right. He will have me as good-son. He will have me – if you will . . . ?'

'Oh, Davy – he will?'

'Aye. He would liefer it was Patrick, mind – as I swear would you, lass. But . . . '

'Patrick!' she cried. 'Patrick – never! I think . . . I think that I hate Patrick, Davy!'

'Eh . . . ? Och, no – how could that be? After . . . after . . . ?'

'Aye – after what I did! With him!' The colour had come flooding back to Mariota's cheeks. 'Nevertheless, I hate him – for what he made me do. Do to you, Davy. Thank God it is not him that I am to marry.'

'But, lassie – I thought . . . ?' David floundered. 'Why did you let him do it, then?'

'Well may you ask, Davy! Sweet Jesu – how I have asked myself! For it was not Patrick that I liked. Och, I *liked* him well enough, sometimes – but not . . . ' She shook her head vigorously. 'It was *you*, Davy – always you. But Patrick is . . . Patrick is . . . well, he is Patrick!' She stopped, biting her lip.

'Aye – he is Patrick!' his brother said. But it was his eyes that were shining now. 'Och, my dear – forget Patrick!' he cried. 'Here's you saying that you like me, like me well enough to . . . och, Mariota lassie – here is a wonder! Here is joy – for I like you fine too! Just fine. And we are to be wed – you and me, just. Man and wife. Dear God – I just canna believe it!'

Laughing, if somewhat brokenly, unsteadily, he took her to him – and she came to his arms eagerly.

So they clutched and clung to each other in that pantry, her tears wetting his face, her urgent body pressed against his, the lips tight fused together. For them a blessed miracle had been wrought.

But at all the commotion the child within Mariota kicked, and when the girl could free her lips, it was tremulously to form that taxing question. 'The baby?' she faltered, her face turned away from him. 'The child? Patrick's child! Do you . . . can you . . . oh, Davy – what of the child?'

'I told you – it shall be *my* child. I care not, lass – you it is that I love. And I shall love your bairn. *Our* bairn. Call it Patrick's never again – do you hear? I . . . '

A sound from beyond the pantry door caused them both to

start, and jump apart, fearful, frightened, uncertain yet. They faced that door, hand in hand. But it did not open. There was no further sound. Probably it had been only the kitchen wench leaning close, to listen. The urgency, the anxiety, the sense of danger to their new-found joy did not leave them, however.

'Take me away, Davy,' Mariota jerked, breathlessly. 'Now – I beg of you. Away from here – from this house. Anywhere. Quickly. Before . . . before . . .'

'Aye – I will do that, lass, never fear. But first we will be wed. Here and now. At once. Yes, we can. We may. Your father himself said it. He would . . . he wishes you . . . och, well – he said it should be done swiftly, see you. He would have it so.'

'Davy – can we not do it some other where? Not here. Not before my father. He will change his mind. To punish me. He will not allow it . . .'

'He will, my dear. He will. The fact is, he wishes it done and over. And he will not be there himself, he said. He is . . . is busy, with affairs. We can be wed now, by the college chaplain. Before two witnesses, he said. And then we can go.'

'Are you sure? That it is no trick? That he will not stop us . . . ?'

'Never doubt it. See – I will go to find the chaplain. Go you and make ready. Whatever you have to do. Make a bundle of some clothes . . .'

'No – after. I will not leave you. Not until we are wed. Nor then, either.' She clung to his arm. 'Do not leave me, Davy. The clothes matter nothing.'

'Very well. We shall seek the chaplain together.'

'He will be in his house. I know where it is. He sleeps every afternoon. He is a dirty, foolish old man – but belike he will serve. Come, Davy – and pray that we do not meet my father!'

Hand in hand they went through to the kitchen and out of the back door of the house, into the lane beside the West Burn. And turning along this, whom should they meet but the shuffling unkempt figure of Master Grieve himself, chaplain domestic of St. Mary's College and pensioner of the Principal. Many were the rumours as to the reasons for Andrew Davidson's patronage of this curious broken-down scholar with the rheumy eyes and trembling hands – whispers even that he might be the Principal's own father – but these mattered not to the two young people now. Master Grieve, in fact, declared that he had been coming to seek them, the godly Principal apparently having actually called at his humble lodging and given instructions to that effect

32

only a short while before.

This evident confirmation of David's confidence that her father would not interfere, greatly comforted and encouraged Mariota. They turned, with the dirty and shambling old man, back to the house which they had just left, impatient already that the chaplain must go so slowly.

So there, in the great kitchen of her home, before her father's bold-eyed bustling housekeeper and the arrogant man-servant, more scornful-seeming than ever, as witnesses, with the giggling maid thrown in as extra, Mariota and David were wed, with scant ceremony, no ring, a deal of gabbling, sniffing and long pauses – but at least somewhat according to the lesser rites of the Kirk – even with a certain kindliness on the old man's part also. Bride and groom had no complaint to make. Only the calling of the banns had been omitted – but it would be a bad business if a great man of the Kirk could not arrange a small matter like that, afterwards.

When all was over, and the fee settled, Mariota was persuaded to go to her room and make up her bundle. She took but a few minutes about it, and no doubt her father at least would have approved the scantiness of the dowry which she took away from his ravished establishment. With only the kitchen-maid bidding them God-speed, they left the house thankfully, collected the pony from amongst the cattle in the quadrangle, and with Mariota mounted pillion behind her husband, set out by back ways through the streets of St. Andrews. They made a fair burden for even the sturdy Highland garron.

'Where . . . where do we go, Davy?' the girl asked, at his ear, her voice uneven, throaty.

'Home,' he answered simply. 'Where else? To the castle – Castle Huntly.'

'Must we go there? To . . . to Patrick?'

'Patrick will not be there. Patrick is at Glamis, with my lord. But never heed for Patrick – never heed for anything now, lassie. You are safe. You are the Mistress David Gray!'

But still she faltered. 'You will keep me safe . . . from Patrick, Davy?'

'Aye,' he said – but he frowned as they turned out of the West Port, northwards.

Chapter Three

PATRICK'S nuptials were of a very different order, as befitted the linking of two of the greatest and noblest houses in all Scotland. The matter could not be rushed, of course, in any unseemly fashion – even though Lord Gray was somehow possessed of an urgent itch to see the said link swiftly and safely forged. The Lord Chancellor Glamis, being a busy man and much immersed in affairs of the state, was not averse to a certain amount of expedition in the matter, so long as a minimum of responsibility for the business, bother – and incidentally, expense – fell upon himself. His lordship, though reputed to be the wealthiest baron in Scotland, was the reverse of extravagant, and with two other daughters nearing marriageable age, was inclined to look twice at his silver pieces. Gray accordingly, and contrary to normal custom, suggested that the ceremony and festivities should on this occasion take place at Castle Huntly and at his expense – and Glamis, after only a token protest, agreed.

Father and son, therefore, came home after four days in Strathmore, with the matter more or less settled, and Lord Gray, at least, in excellent spirits. The wedding would be held in one month's time, three weeks being required for the calling of the banns, and since my lord looked for much as a result of this union – especially as, so far, Glamis had no son, and Elizabeth was his eldest daughter – the arrangements should be on a scale suitable to the occasion.

Patrick himself, however, was just a little less ebullient than might have been expected. He confided in David right away – and he allowed no shadow of their recent clash of interests and temperament to cloud their companionship; Patrick was like that – he confided that he was more than a little disappointed in Elizabeth Lyon. Her breasts were as good as he had remembered them, admittedly, and she was a handsome piece in a strong-featured statuesque fashion, undoubtedly; indeed, as a statue, Patrick declared, she would be magnificent. But somehow she seemed to him to lack warmth; he feared that she might well prove, in practice, to be distinctly on the cold side – though needless to say he had done his by no means negligible best to melt her, in such opportunity as had presented itself. She had

34

shown him no actual hostility, or really repelled his advances – better, perhaps, if she had done, as a titillation and indication of spirit to overcome – but had just failed to respond satisfactorily, much less excitingly. This was a new experience for young Patrick Gray in his relations with the opposite sex, and he was a little piqued and concerned. He confessed to David, indeed, that he preferred the next sister, Jean, a more adventurous nymph, with whom he had tried a fling or two; even the third one, Sibilla, though ridiculously young, was more enthusiastic in her embraces, he had ascertained. He had gone the length of suggesting to his father, in fact, the third night, that they should transfer their assault to the Lady Jean, in the interests of effectiveness and posterity, but my lord would not hear of it – had been quite shocked, indeed. Elizabeth, at seventeen, was the elder by quite three years, and there would be no comparison between the scales of their marriage portions.

Even David was only briefly and superficially sympathetic, Patrick felt.

In contrast, Patrick was quite delighted, and demonstrably so, at unexpectedly finding Mariota already at Castle Huntly. He sought her out at once when he heard the news, in the sheltered walled garden where Meg Powrie, the steward's wife, had set her to the light work of household sewing and mending, at which she could sit – and promptly caught her up to kiss her long and comprehensively, laughing away her struggles and protests. He was genuinely amused at her tantrums of outraged modesty, when David came hurrying to her aid, vowed that her mock wrath became her mighty well, heightening her colour, and forgave her entirely the long scratch her nails had made down his own fair cheek.

'Davy! Davy!' she cried breathlessly, her great hazel-brown eyes wide with an unreasoning fear that verged on panic. 'He ... he ... you promised! You said that he would not ... that you would not let him ... '

'Och, lassie – do not take on so. He was but welcoming you to the castle, I doubt not.'

'No! No!'

'But yes, yes, my dear Mariota! Exactly!' Patrick assured genially. 'Here is a most happy occasion – my first good-sister. How would you have me greet you? Stiffly? Formally? I' faith, no. After all, we are old friends, are we not?'

She bit her red lip, looking from one young man to the other. Then, snatching up her needlework she turned about and went

35

hurrying away up the path between the blossoming fruit trees.

'Wait, lass,' David called after her, starting forward. Then he paused, and looked back at his brother. 'She is not herself. The bairn, it is – but two months to go, she says. But . . . ' His brows came down, in a fashion that Patrick knew well. 'You will kindly keep your distance from her,' he said. 'It is her expressed wish – and mine!'

'Well, now – here is no kindly way to usher the lass into the family, Davy . . . '

But his brother had swung about, to go hurrying in pursuit of his wife. Patrick looked after them both, thoughtfully.

Lord Gray's reception of the news of Mariota's presence in his castle, thus early, was of a different nature. Indeed, he showed very little interest, having so many more vital matters to attend to. He did not, in fact, see her for a couple of days, by which time his affability over the successful progress of the Glamis business was wearing a trifle thin as the full realisation of the expense of his wedding plans was increasingly brought home to him. Consequently, the fact that he had acquired even one more unproductive mouth to feed seemed to strike him with a force at first glance unlooked for in a man who constantly employed a resident bodyguard of between twenty and thirty men-at-arms, with little better to do than quarrel and procreate, not to mention the unnumbered other hangers-on that the dignity of a nobleman's household seemed to demand. It was David, rather than Mariota, who bore the impact of this realisation, in an unsought meeting with his father in the castle courtyard on the second day – for that young man had long made a habit of keeping out of my lord's way as much as possible, a practice at which Patrick was almost equally proficient. The lecture that followed, on expense, idleness, irresponsibility and bastardy generally, encouraged David to put forward, albeit tentatively, a suggestion of his own. Might he not be allowed to earn his daily bread, and perhaps his wife's also, as tutor to the younger members of his lordship's household? He had never had any urgent desire to become a minister of the Kirk, as had been part of Gray's intention in sending him to St. Andrews with Patrick, but at least he had done reasonably well with his studies, and almost certainly would have graduated Master of Arts in a few months' time, had it not been for the unfortunate clash with the Principal. Consequently he felt himself quite fitted to teach the young – and indeed would like to do so. He suggested, moreover, that as well as the nine Gray children, he might instruct others; some of the neighbouring lairds might well be glad to have their offspring taught, and be prepared to pay for the privilege – thus lightening his lordship's burden.

His lordship saw the point of this without any great deal of persuasion, and ordered David to proceed with the matter forthwith – especially the enrolling of his neighbours' idle and ignorant progeny. He further agreed to the allocation of the little-used north-west flanking tower of the courtyard as schoolroom, where wretched children would be well out of the way of his own feet. This arranged, he was able to wash his hands of David, Mariota, and all bairns and brats soever, to his considerable satisfaction.

David, therefore, thankfully took possession of the little north-west tower, set aside the vaulted ground floor for a storehouse and stable, the first floor as a schoolroom and the top storey as a home for Mariota and himself, and moved in with such plenishings as he could beg, borrow, or contrive.

Only Patrick appeared to find this arrangement not wholly to his taste. He and David had shared a room, and usually a bed, together all their lives, and though this proximity had its drawbacks in the realm of privacy on occasion, it had had many advantages also for someone of Patrick's sunny and congenial temperament. The addition, moreover, of an attractive young woman, pregnant or otherwise, to this pleasantly informal little sodality was an advantage so obvious as to call for no stressing. David's reminder that Patrick would veiy shortly have a wife of his own to bed down with, and be translated to a fine room in the main keep for the purpose, had an only lukewarm reception.

Not that Patrick moped or sulked, of course; he was not of that kidney. Never at any time short of friends, or at a loss for amusement, he now had leisure and freedom to make the most of life – and life, for the Master of Gray, in the Gray country of the Carse of Gowrie, could be full indeed. He left the marriage arrangements happily enough to his father, and wore out a succession of horses dashing about Perthshire and Angus, in the joyous freedom of a man about to become a husband. His only expresssed regret was that David was not with him to enjoy the sport and observe his triumphs – but he sought to make up for this by frequently invading his brother's room in the little tower, usually in the small hours of the morning, to deliver gay and uninhibited accounts of the day's and night's excitements to a sleepy and protesting David and a tense and shocked Mariota. When reproached that this was no way to behave on

37

the eve of matrimony, he countered with the reverse assertion –
that it was in fact of all times the most apt and essential for such
recreation.

So the weeks passed. Mariota grew thicker and heavier, and a
little less nervy and wary, the schooling progressed, and the preparations for the linking of Gray and Glamis went on apace.

For one reason or another, Patrick never managed to see
Mariota alone throughout.

Castle Huntly was transformed for the wedding-day – and not
only the castle but the entire countryside round about. Contrary
to common supposition, the Scots are essentially a demonstrative, spectacle-loving and colourful race, with a distinct flair
for extremes, however well they manage to disguise the fact
under a screen of dour gravity and curtness. Given the opportunity, they will kick over the traces more wholeheartedly than
any of your Latins or Irishry, and opportunities for such
jollifications had been sadly lacking in sixteenth-century
Scotland since the godly Kirk had successfully banished the old
religion with all its disgraceful though colourful mummery and
flummery. Consequently, any legitimate occasion for public
holiday and celebration, that the ministers could not very well
ban, was apt to be seized upon avidly by gentles and common
folk alike, and made the most of. And undoubtedly this was such
an occasion – and with both lords high in the Kirk party, the
ministers, however much they might frown on principle, could
hardly interfere.

From the battlements and each tower of the castle, banners,
pennons and streamers fluttered; stern parapets and machicola-
tions for the hurling down of boiling oil, lead, and the like, were
hung with greenery, and snarling gunloops spouted flowers and
blossom. On the topmost turret a beacon was erected, ready to
blaze and to spark off a line of similar flares on all the other Gray
castles and strengths on either side of Tay. On every hill around
the Carse bonfires were built, and the chain of them would
stretch right back across the Sidlaws to Strathmore, twenty
miles away. The Castleton and the Milton were almost buried
under fir-boughs, evergreens and gean-blossom, and the
villages of Longforgan, Inchture, Abernyte, Fowlis and the rest
were garlanded, walls whitewashed, and preparations made for
the public roasting of bullocks and broaching of ale-barrels on
greens and market-crosses that had so recently lost their crosses.
Dundee itself was to have its Law ablaze, and the bells of the

great four-churches-in-one, St. Mary's, St. Paul's. St. Clement's' and St. John's, were to ring out – by special gracious permission of the reverend Master Blair, who was indeed to officiate at the wedding – a thing they had not done even for the birth of an heir to the throne, who had a Popish mother of course.

It was all thoroughly inspiriting, and a mere month was all too short a time for proper arrangements.

The day dawned at last, and Patrick greeted the said dawn in an alehouse in the Seagate of Dundee, in riotous company – although the ride back to Castle Huntly through the fresh young morning cleared his head wondrously. Certain guests, with long distances to travel, had already reached the castle the previous night, and by mid-forenoon the stream of arrivals was resumed. There was no room for all, of course, in the fortalice itself, nor even within its courtyard, and pavilions and tents of coloured canvas had been erected on the grassy former tilt-yard before the main gatehouse, in a circle to enclose a wide arena. Here, to amuse the earlier comers and the crowding local folk during the long period of waiting until the actual nuptial ceremony in the early evening, sports and games, archery, trials of strength, and the like were organised. There were jugglers and tumblers and acrobats, too, musicians and dancing bears, horse-races on the level flats below the castle rock. Food and drink and comfits, in bulk rather than in variety or daintiness, were heaped on trestle-tables out-of-doors. My lord, once having taken the grievous decision to put his hand into his pocket, was reaching deep therein – he hoped, of course as a sound investment.

The castle staff, needless to say, were deeply involved in all this, and for once even the lounging loud-mouthed men-at-arms had plenty to do. David was allotted the highly responsible task of separating the sheep from the goats – that is, meeting and identifying the parties of guests as they arrived, well out in front of the tented area, and directing them to their due destinations. Only the great lords, powerful churchmen and notabilities, and certain relations, were conducted to the castle itself, where they were greeted by either their host or his heir, and their retinues led off. Lesser lairds and ministers and gentry were taken to the courtyard, where one of Lord Gray's brothers did the honours before sending them down to the tilt-yard. The rest were ushered straight to the tents and the food, to be welcomed by Rob Powrie, the steward. Obviously the initial separating was a duty where any mistake made could be serious in their repercussions, in the matter of injured pride, and where tact as well as a quick wit was required. Perhaps my lord thought rather better of his first-born bastard than he was inclined to admit, in selecting him for the work.

David, dressed for the occasion in some of Patrick's cast-offs – that was always the source of his wardrobe, but today he did rather better than usual – required all his wits. One of the first problems that he had to cope with presented itself in no less august a shape than that of his own new father-in-law, Principal Davidson, who arrived in the company of half-a-dozen other divines and scholars from St. Andrews, and who undoubtedly would have completely ignored the existence of David had he not been supported by three or four men-at-arms, in the Gray colours, in the capacity of escorts and guides. It fell to David to point out that whilst Master Davidson himself was expected at the castle door, his companions should not proceed beyond the courtyard – a rather delicate division, especially as one of the ministers had only recently been his own tutor in elementary philosophy, a subject that might well have commended itself to the said professor there and then, but unfortunately did not. David's polite but firm instructions, indeed, were not very well received at all, and only the jingling and impatient retinue of James, Lord Ogilvy of Airlie, queuing up behind, got them on their way without unseemly dispute. Master Davidson had no questions to ask anent his daughter – not of David, at anyrate.

More than one thorny problem to be settled concerned the vital matter of prededence: as, for instance, when the Master of Crawford's party and that of my Lord Oliphant came clattering up to David's gateway precisely at the same moment, one from the east and the other from the west. Like lightning, the coincidence developed into a major crisis. The Master, as heir and representative of the Earl of Crawford, premier earl of the kingdom, demanded that he should be admitted before any upstart baron, Oliphant or otherwise, whereas the Lord Oliphant insisted that as a Lord of Parliament, and Sheriff of Forfar, he took precedence over the heir of Crawford or Heaven itself. Angry words were exchanged, and hands sought sword-hilts as supporting gentry pressed forward to uphold these important points of view, when David hurriedly declared, at the pitch of his young lungs and in the name of my Lord Gray, that of course both noblemen should ride side by side up to the castle, as was seemly and proper, their followings likewise. Heads high, and frowning bleakly in diametrically opposite directions, the guests thereupon spurred on in what quickly developed into a race for the gatehouse.

The bridal party arrived promptly at noon in an impressive cavalcade of over fifty horsemen and as many laden pack-horses. My Lord Glamis, stern and noble-featured, and his dark-browed and hot-tempered brother, the Master, led the company, under the proudly fluttering blue lion on silver of their house, and it was not until the rearward passed him at the trot that David perceived the women of the party. Which was the bride he could not tell, for the six or seven of them were all wrapped in their hooded travelling cloaks – indeed, only of their legs and hose did he gain any admiring view, since they rode astride and at a pace that made primness difficult to maintain.

It was well into the afternoon before the last of the important guests put in an appearance, by which time David was not only weary of the business but fretting to get down to the entertainments and sports, especially the wrestling at which he excelled. Nor was he alone in this anxiety to be finished; my lord himself, fine in black velvet slashed with scarlet, came down from the castle to limp about and gaze impatiently westwards. The pompously important but self-conscious contingent of the Provost and Bailies of Dundee had just come up, with the Provost's markedly non-pompous and substantial wife interrupting her husband's official speech of congratulation and greeting with chuckles and ribald stage-whispers from the background, when the high winding of horns and the growing beat of hooves turned all heads – and turned them westwards.

The glint of sun on steel flickered amongst woodland to that side. Then out into the open came pounding a tight-knit column of heavily armed men, all gleaming breastplates, helmets and tossing plumes, led by a herald in spectacularly coloured tabard, four trumpeters with their horns at the ready, and two standard-bearers with streaming banners.

'A Douglas! A Douglas!' The chanted savage cry came on ahead of the riders, a well-rehearsed and ominous litany in the land for three centuries and more. David's back hairs lifted, despite the occasion, at the sound of it. He noted that, of the two great flags, that slightly to the fore, the larger, and set on the longer pole, was the Bleeding Heart of Douglas; the other was merely the treasured Red Lion on gold of Scotland.

As this hard-riding cohort bore down upon the waiting throng at a full gallop, the Dundee burghers scattered right and left alarmedly, women skirling. Even Gray drew back involuntarily from his forward-paced position. Without the least

41

slackening of pace, the phalanx came thundering on, still chanting, turfs flying from drumming hooves. Douglas indeed usually travelled thus. Past the shrinking assembly at the gate they swept. David had a brief vision of a hulking man in a flying crimson-lined cloak, red-faced, red-headed, red-bearded, hot-eyed, who glanced neither left nor right, hemmed in by steel-clad horsemen. Then they were past, the echo of the antiphon 'A Douglas! A Douglas!' floating back to the welcoming group, punctuated by the shrilly imperative summons of the horns' flourish.

My Lord Gray, left standing and staring after, spat out profanity, his face congested, his frown black. Never had he loved Douglas, nor Douglas him. Only because of Glamis would that man darken his doorway, he knew. Cursing, he went hastening on foot in the wake of the column. The Lord Regent, the Earl of Morton, ruler of Scotland in the name of the helpless boy King James, had deigned to honour the occasion. The marriage might go forward.

The success or otherwise of the afternoon depended upon the point of view. Counting heads, certainly, the vast majority found it entirely to their taste, whatever might be the case with the smaller group that centred round the host, Lord Glamis, and the Regent; or, again, the black-clad and numerous concentration of the professionally disapproving ministers. Patrick, for one, indubitably enjoyed himself, winning both the important horse-races, out-swording all competitors at the rapier-play – for gentlefolk only, this, of course, so that David for instance might not compete – coming third in the archery, friend of all, particularly those he defeated, laughing and talking his way into all hearts, the ladies' more especially. David did none so badly himself, coming second to his brother in one of the foot races, being worsted at the wrestling only by a black-smith from Inchture of twice his own weight, and making a respectable showing at putting the cannon-ball. Even Mariota ventured shyly out amongst the crowd, from the cherished seclusion of her tower-room, found herself caught up in the good-humoured excitement, and was the better therefore. The bride, of course, did not show herself; her time would come.

Two broken heads and a growing animosity between the Douglas men-at-arms and Gray's own retainers, rather than the ill-concealed impatience of the ministers, at length caused my lord to bring this stage of events to a close, around six o'clock.

Trumpets sounded from the topmost battlements, and all the important guests flocked into the castle, while the lesser gentry, the men-at-arms, and the commonality disposed themselves about the many long trestle-tables laden with food and drink. The serious part of the proceedings was at hand.

In the great hall of the castle, order gradually emerged out of chaos, the ministers, harsh-voiced, autocratic but notably efficient, now taking charge. Guests were herded six deep around the arras-hung stone walls, and, God having no use for precedence, except presumably amongst those ordained to preach the Gospel, no nonsense about position or prominence was permitted for a moment. Save, that is, around the doorway, where Lord Gray, the Lady Glamis and the Master thereof, the Regent and one or two others were grouped, with rather more elbow room, facing into the cleared centre of the hall, where the solid body of ministers stood behind a simple table covered with a severe white cloth on which lay a massive Bible, and nothing else.

David, with the Gray children, peered down at the scene from an inner window of the circular stairway, just under the springing of the high vaulted ceiling.

The trumpets sounded again, and a hush fell upon all in the hall – not on those outside, unfortunately, though the ten-foot-thick walling helped to deaden the noise of uninhibited jollification. Pacing slowly through the lane opened for them came two figures: the stooping ungainly person of Master John Blair, High Kirk minister of Dundee, whose plain loose black gown only partially shrouded his twisted and torture-scarred frame, hirpling but strangely dignified; and a few yards behind, Patrick Gray, resplendent in white satin padded doublet and trunks, slashed with gold, a white velvet short cloak slung negligently over one shoulder, and long golden hose of fine silk. The gap of admiration that was almost a moan indeed, with which the women at least greeted his appearance, was fully merited, for never had he looked more handsome, more beautiful, and at the same time more lithely if slenderly virile. Never, also, were trunks cut so short, or shapely legs so long. His expression schooled to a suitable sweet gravity, his gait so infinitely more graceful than that of the hobbling man of God, he came slowly forward, glance downcast. Only once did his eyes lift, as, when he passed the family group, the Regent Morton turned to stare from his curiously round, pale and owl-like eyes, hawked strongly in his thick throat and almost seemed as though

43

he would spit – but restrained himself to swallow instead. Patrick's dark eyes flashed and his step faltered, but both only for an instant. Then he paced on to the table, at which Master Blair had turned. The minister stood, eyes closed, hands together, seemingly in prayer. Something like a shiver ran through the crowded hall.

David caught sight of Master Davidson's face as he watched Patrick, and did not like what he saw.

A new sound reached them, the thin melodious singing of young voices, accompanied by the gentle twanging of a lute, that ebbed and flowed as the singers obviously came down the winding stairway of the castle. The chant was mere psalmody, a simple canticle; nevertheless, an almost universal frown spread over the faces of the waiting clergy at this dangerous toying with Popish folly – spread and remained as into sight came a youth with the lute, and six maidens, dressed all in white and singing clearly, angelically – however venturesome and eager their glances. These included the Ladies Jean and Sibilla Lyon, and Patrick's elder sister Barbara. Behind them walked the sombre stern-miened Lord Chancellor Glamis, in unrelieved black save for the high white ruff and sword-belt of heavy linked gold, and on his arm, his daughter.

The bride did not do her family or her groom injustice. A tall well-favoured young woman, fair, high-coloured, and comely rather than beautiful, she drew all eyes. She wore a handsome gown of quilted palest yellow taffeta, wide-skirted and wired, and overlaid by open silver lacework, beaded with pearls. The bodice was tight, with a lengthy pointed stomacher reaching low to her loins, but cut correspondingly low above, in a wide square neck, to reveal much of the high and prominent breasts that rumour had spoken of, and with a ruff, rimmed with pearls, rising from either shoulder rather like incipient wings. Over her long flaxen hair she wore a crescent-shaped jewelled coif of silk. She drew all eyes, yes – but, strangely, not the gasping tribute that had greeted the Master of Gray.

'What think you, Davy? Will she serve our Patrick?' young James Gray whispered.

' 'Tis Patrick will do the serving, I warrant!' his senior, Gilbert, crowed from the experience which twelve years had brought. 'Have you no eyes, Jamie?'

'Hush, you,' David reproved. 'They're about to begin.'

This seemed to be so. The Lady Elizabeth stood beside Patrick now, before the minister, with her father a pace behind.

44

Lord Gray had stepped forward alongside Glamis. The maids, under the battery of frowns from the divinity, had backed away into the mass of the congregation, the lute-boy vanishing quite. All waited. Master Blair, however, seemed in no hurry to commence. Or perhaps he had in fact commenced, and was already engaged in silent wrestling with his Maker. He stood, head bent, hands clasped, and if his lips stirred, that was all. People fidgeted, shuffled and whispered, and the Regent sniffed loudly, hawed and muttered in his red beard. At last the celebrant abruptly raised head and hands heavenwards, and launched immediately, strikingly, into the full fine flood of eloquent and passionate assault on God and man. In a voice harsh but extraordinarily strong for so meagre a body, declamation, exhortation and denunciation poured from his thin lips in a blistering, resounding, exciting stream. The fidgeting stopped – as well it might. The Kirk was getting into its stride.

This introductory invocation and overture – it soared far above the realms of mere prayer – on the rich themes of man's essential and basic wickedness, filthiness, lust and sinful pride; woman's inherent shallowness, worldly vanity and lewd blandishing cajolery; the Scots people's painful and inveterate proneness to backsliding and going a-whoring after strange gods; the blasphemous and idolatrous life of that wanton Mary Stuart, chamber-wench of the Pope, for the present, God be praised, safely immured within godly walls in the South – this with a sudden lowering of the eyes and a hard stare at Lord Gray – and strangely enough, the excellence and maidenly virtuousness of that daughter of the Lord, Elizabeth Tudor; this all led up to the sound and sublime allegory of God's true Kirk, as the Bride of Christ, vigorously trampling into the mire of damnation that other Harlot of Rome who had so long defiled the sanctity of the Marriage of the Lamb.

This emotional crescendo suitably prefaced the actual nuptials, into which Master Blair plunged after quarter-of-an-hour of impassioned harangue – a tribute surely to the undimmed spirit within the twisted body that the Cardinal Archbishop had racked for his faith twenty-five years ago. The slightly bemused and abstracted gathering was, in fact, not quite prepared for the sudden transition and change of level in the proceedings, taking a little while to adjust itself. As well that Patrick himself was quicker-witted, or he might not have had the ring out in time, for this central and less edifying, but of course necessary, part of the ceremony was got over at high speed and with an almost scornful brusqueness. Protesting fervour had so purified and pruned the unseemly mummery of the Old Faith's marriage rites that there was little left save the affirmation of the exchange of vows signified by the clasping of hands, the fitting of the ring, and the declaration of the pair as man and wife. That did not take long. On the exhortation to the newly wed, of course, a minister of the Word could spread himself rather. Master Blair did that, dwelling at some length and detail on the pitfalls of the flesh into which the unwary or wilfully disobedient couple might so easily fall.

Patrick listened to this with an access of interest, and out of the corner of his eye sought to observe the effect on his bride. She did not blush, he noted.

The celebrant paused, now. All this was merely the warming up, the ushering in of the vital business of the day. He walked round behind the white-clothed table, took a deep breath, put one hand on the Bible, raised the other on high, and commenced the Sermon.

It was a good sermon, too – that was evident, if by no other indication than the rapt attention and shining-eyed regard of the ranked and hypercritical divines at the preacher's back. Frail body or none, cracking vocal chords, sore throat, spells of dizziness where he had to hold himself up by the table, James Blair thundered and besought, blazed and wheedled, shouted and whispered and quavered, painting equally clear roads to salvation and to fiery and eternal torment. The increasing hubbub from outside, largely drunken singing and bawling now, only urged him on; swooning weakly females within the hall did not stop him – there was no seating for this multitude, of course; when the Lady Glamis collapsed and had to be carried out, he did not so much as pause, and only a scornful flashing eye acknowledged the fact that many of his hearers, even supposedly strong men, had felt themselves compelled to crouch down on the rush-strewn stone floor. With my lord of Morton snoring loudly from one of the few chairs available, and Patrick supporting his bride around the waist, one hour and ten minutes after commencing, the preacher brought the notable and inspiring discourse to a triumphant close, and croaked a perfunctory benediction.

The Master of Gray and the Lady Elizabeth Lyon had been well and truly wed, the houses of Gray and Glamis were united, and the Kirk had struck another blow against the forces of Babylon.

46

Dazed and stiff and glassy-eyed, bride and groom and relatives and guests staggered out, to order the trumpets to be blown, the fires and beacons lit, and the bells to be rung.

'Wine!' they shouted, 'wine, in the name of God! Possets, punch, purled ale, belly cheer, for sweet mercy's sake!'

The wedding feast thereafter was on as generous and memorable a scale as the religious contribution. In no time at all that hall was cleared, trestle tables were erected, one transversely at the top for the principals, and the others lengthwise, forms dragged in for seating, and the long procession of smoking meats, cold flesh, comestibles, cakes, confections, and flagons of every sort of liquid cheer, brought in at the run, while torches were lit and the musicians set about their business. Fortunately perhaps, clamorous stomachs outrumbled the usual difficult demands of precedency in most instances, and earls and barons, masters and lairds, elder sons and younger, and their ladies likewise, were prepared meantime to sit down almost anywhere, thus greatly easing David's task, who, under the steward, had been allotted this second unpopular duty of seating the guests.

There were some notable dishes, apart from the normal succession of roast ox quarters, gigots of mutton, haunches of venison seethed in wine because they were somewhat out-of-season, kippered and pickled salmon to encourage a thirst, howtowdies of fowl, herbs and mushrooms, cabbie-claw codfish, and so on; half-a-dozen peacocks made a brave show, roasted still in all the pride of their spread tails; swans swam in ponds of gravy, their long necks cunningly upheld by skewers; and the *pièce de résistance*, an enormous platter requiring six men to carry it in, containing a young sow in milk and her eight suckling piglets, cooked to a turn and all most naturally arranged at her roasted dugs.

To all this the assembly did ample and appreciative justice, the clergy by no means backward.

My lord allowed the banquet to proceed for rather longer than usual before calling for the toasts. He did this, with his eye on Morton, lolling on the bride's left. As Regent and most important man in the kingdom, he could not be overlooked for the principal toast of the bride and groom, without insult. Yet Gray knew not what he might say, and feared the worst. The red stirk had the name for speaking his mind, and unfortunately could afford to do so. Consequently, the host waited for two hours after they had sat down to eat, in the hope that the

Douglas would be too drunk to say anything. In this he was disappointed, however, for though Morton was indubitably drunk, he had by no means lost the use of his tongue; indeed he was growing ever more vocal, singing raucously, cursing the musicians because their tunes were not his, bellowing intimate appraisal or otherwise of all the women in sight, including the shrinking Elizabeth – who, being within arm's reach, received more than mere verbal compliments, to the sad disarray of her finery – and generally displaying the non-impairment of his judgment and faculties. Reluctantly, Gray at last rose, signed to a trumpeter to quell the din, and announced the noble representative of the house of Douglas, Lord High Admiral of Scotland and Viceroy of the Realm, to propose the health of the happy couple.

Morton clapped his high hat of the new mode more firmly on his red head, wiped beard, ostrich-plume and gravy-soiled ruff with the back of a ham-like hand, sought to rise, found it for the moment beyond him, and made his speech sitting down.

'My lords,' he said thickly, belching hugely, 'reverend sirs, masters all – aye, and ladies too, bonnie ones and, *hic*, the other kind – hear me, James Douglas. Here's a, *hic*, fine match, 'fore God! Glamis stooping to Gray! A bonnie sight. Hech, hech – not so fast, my lord. Keep your bottom on your seat! No' so hasty, man. Think you I'd spit in the face o' the provider o' all these goodly meats? Na, na. But stoop my friend Glamis here does in this matter . . . for Lyon was Thane o' Glamis when Gray, my lord, was but some scullion o' yon Norman butcher! A pox – you canna deny it, man – so why fash yoursel'? Eh – Douglas, did ye say? God's wounds – what said ye o' Douglas?' Suddenly the gross torso of the Regent was no longer lolling, but leaning forward over the board, crushing Elizabeth aside, glaring with those hot pale eyes along at his host, massive, menacing.

No sound was raised within the hall save only the hounds cracking bones beneath the tables, the hiss and splutter of the resinous reeking torches, and the deep open-mouthed breathing of the Earl of Morton.

'Aye.' He sank back as, tensely, Gray stared directly ahead of him, down the hall, his face a graven mask. 'Aye, then. Douglas, I'd remind all here, was lording Clydesdale before this Scotland knew a king, aye or a puling priest either! Forget it not, I charge you! Aye. But, hech me – here's the toast, my lords. Glamis stoops, aye – but then he'd stoop, *hic*, to you all! Have to, by God!' A stubby thick finger jabbed and pointed down and around the tables. 'All – save maybe Crawford, there . . . the fox! And none o' you the worse o' the stooping, I warrant! Even Gray! But what's a bit stoop amongst friends? We'd no' do well to keep the best blood in the land bottled up, when there's so many who could do with, *hic*, a droppie o' it! Och, keep your seat, my lord – like I do! The best's to come! I said it was a fine bonnie match, and it is. The realm o' this Scotland will be the better, maybe the safer, for it. I'm thinking – for we need leal and well-connected folk around the throne, godly men with no taint o' Popery, no stink o' the skirts o' that foresworn wanton Mary Stuart about them!'

Again the brittle silence.

Morton chuckled throatily. 'You'll all agree, I jalouse, that this match could strength further that goodly cause – the cause o' Christ's Kirk, forby. A bonnie union! The lassie's bonnie, none will con- controvert. Enough to make an auld man hot, hot – aye, and a young one scorch, heh? Aye, burn and blaze . . . if he's no' a prinking prancing ninny! If our pretty lad here canna bairn her this night, it's no' a toast he's in need of, but a horning! I'd teach him – eh, lass? Here's to their health, then – and may the blood joined tonight run for the weal o' this realm, for once! Aye – amen!'

Morton drained his heavy silver goblet in a great single draught, and hurled it from him vigorously, right down the lengthwise table that faced him, along which it went crashing, scattering and spilling flagons and broken meats.

After perhaps ten pulsating seconds, those who could rose to their feet and pledged the fortunate pair.

All eyes were now on Lord Gray, who had risen last of all and had not sat down again with the others. Patrick however jumped up, waving a jaunty hand for silence, and smiled disarmingly on all around, particularly on the sprawling Regent and on his father. Angelic, almost, he looked after the last speaker – but a gay and debonair angel.

'My lords and ladies, good friends all,' he called, 'my re- spected and noble sire undoubtedly should speak first – but I vow that you have all had so much eloquence of late that I mis- doubt if you can digest more, however fine. Moreover, I would hasten to relieve my Lord Regent's mind that I am indeed impatient to exchange even this fair room and company for another, higher in the house! Hence, forgive, I pray you, this cutting short of . . . compliments! Heigh-ho!'

A gust of laughter swept the hall. Lord Gray sat down.

'I cannot go, of course, without, and in the name of my wife also, expressing profound gratitude to you all for your good wishes, and especially to the noble lord of Morton for the delicate and typically droll fashion in which he expressed his kindly sentiments in your name. Ah, happy Scotia, blessed to have such a paragon, such a mirror of wit and wisdom, to preside over her destinies, Christ's Kirk abetting . . . in the name of His gracious Majesty, of course, upon whom the good God have mercy!'

Only the very drunk saw fit to applaud that, and laughter had died on all faces save that of the speaker.

'I am overcome, my friends – overcome with gratitude, with appreciation. It ill becomes a sprig of so humble a house as Gray to raise his voice in the company of the head of the house of Glamis, not to mention that of an illustrious, though alas junior, branch of the house of Douglas . . . !'

The sudden indrawal of scores of breaths was like a gust of wind in the trees. Morton was not chief of his name; Douglas, Earl of Angus, a mere youth, held that honour – though few indeed would have mentioned it in the presence of the Regent.

'However, I am at least a male, a son, Gray or no – thanks to my worthy and potent father – an attribute which has its advantages, especially on occasions such as this, and in present company!'

What started as a laugh died abruptly, as listeners perceived that there was more here than pleasant bawdry. Neither Lords Morton nor Glamis had a legitimate son to their name.

Patrick's own laughter was of the enduring sort, and music itself. 'So, my friends, I now go, with your blessing, my Lord Regent's urging, and the envy of not a few, I swear, to prove the said attribute to this fair bride of mine! My love – your hand, I pray.'

A great uproar broke out. Men shouted, women skirled, goblets were banged and sword-hilts beaten on tables. The Earl of Morton, bellowing, sought to rise, but liquor and Glamis's restraining hand held him down. Older men plunged into hot discussion with their neighbours, but younger men and women, from the lower end of the hall, were more active. They know their cue, and took it promptly, to come surging up to the top table. This was the signal for the bedding – and they had waited for it overlong. A rush of men grabbed Patrick, and propelled him at a run down one side of the hall, already tugging and pulling off his splendid white satin, while at the other side squealing girls did the same, and only a shade less vigorously, with Elizabeth.

David, who had watched all from the doorway, and quaked in his borrowed shoes towards the end, stood aside to let the loud-tongued parties past. He noted that Patrick was still smiling – but his bride was not, was weeping, in fact.

Up the stairs the laughing clamorous coadjutors of holy matrimony stumbled, almost half their principals' clothing already off.

David followed on, doubtfully.

At the bridal chamber two storeys higher, the disrobing process went on a-pace, only hampered by too many fumbling hands at the task – though now it was noticeable that it was mainly the men who gave of their services to the bride and the women to Patrick. Soon, stark naked, Elizabeth was carried over sobbing to the great bed and tossed thereon, and a few moments later Patrick was steered and pushed on top of her.

Thus went the custom, hallowed by years.

In the midst of all the advice, guidance and encouragement that followed, David suddenly and angrily decided that the business had gone far enough, and quite fiercely turned on the company and drove them from the bedchamber. Despite protests, he insisted, and far from gently. His only gentleness was when he closed the door behind them and himself.

Below, part of the great hall was cleared for dancing, but those who preferred to go on eating – or, more popularly, drinking – could do so at the top end of the apartment. David, still acting as assistant to the steward, was kept very busy. Lords, overcome by wine, had to be guided or carried into convenient chambers set apart for this necessary purpose; fights required to be discouraged as tactfully as might be; ladies were to be escorted to retiring rooms – no light or simple task this, sometimes; and early leavers, such as most of the ministers, and the Dundee burgesses, had to be led out to their horses, not infrequently needing a deal of help. Outside, too, a certain amount of surveillance became ever more necessary, as unlimited ale, good fellowship and high spirits had a cumulative effect, and hilarious uproar reigned. The crackling of bonfires, the wild music of bagpipes, the mass lovemaking, the shouting and singing and screaming were all very well – but fires in the wrong places had to be quenched, unofficial horse-races by firelight, with visiting lords' mounts, had to be stopped, and the large amount of expensive tentage spared as far as possible from damage.

It was a spirited evening, but taxing on those with a responsibility for oversight. Never had my lord's men-at-arms been so busy – or so many of them missing or unfit for duty.

It would be nearing midnight when, in the pandemonium caused by some young bloods' introduction of the dancing bears into the capers of the castle hall, and the consequent driving out of the animals into the courtyard and beyond, David, weary and dishevelled, heard a silvery laugh which he thought that he recognised, followed by a high-pitched whinny of feminine giggling. It seemed to come from the open doorway of his own schoolroom tower. Frowning, he paused for a moment, and then hurried thereto, to peer in. In the vaulted basement chamber, only dimly illuminated by the reflection of torchlight and bonfire-light without, were two people in close embrace. One was undoubtedly Patrick Gray, no longer in his white satins, and the other almost certainly was the young Lady Jean Lyon, his wife's sportive second sister.

Shocked, hesitant, David stood in the doorway, toe tapping the ground. The girl's laugh rang out again, part protestingly, part encouragingly. It had a penetrating and distinctive quality. David was turning to sign away the two men-at-arms who were his faithful shadows that night, when he caught his breath. Three more men were there, close behind, and the tall gaunt one who raised his voice now was the quarrelsome and haughty Sir Thomas Lyon, Master of Glamis. He and Robert Douglas, Younger of Kilspindie, with another Douglas, a mere boy, had come out in the train of the bear-ejectors.

'That was young Jeannie's voice, I'll swear,' he cried. 'She neighs like a mare in heat, that niece o' mine! Let's see who is playing stallion, eh?' And the Master came lurching forward, two parts drunk.

Desperately, almost unthinkingly, David turned and plunged into the tower to warn his brother. The Master of Glamis, a difficult and dangerous man, was known not to have favoured the match in the first place, and was close to Morton and the Douglases, closer than his brother the Chancellor.

Patrick and Jean sprang apart, the former cursing, the latter all guilt and disarray.

'It's the Master! Of Glamis,' David gasped. 'Quick – up the stair, Patrick, out on to the wall . . . ' A door from the schoolroom above led out on to the parapet-walk that crowned the enclosing curtain-walls of the courtyard.

He turned back, to delay the oncoming trio. But they were

52

close up, pushing aside the men-at-arms, young Kilspindie having snatched a torch.

'Out of my way, fellow!' the older man ordered, curtly.

'No!' David cried. 'This is my place, sir – my tower. My wife ... she lies upstairs. A-bed, awaiting a bairn. Wait, you ... '

'Aside, fool!' the Master shouted, one hand on his sword, and thrusting David back with the other. 'Think you I do not know Jean Lyon's voice?'

David was pressed against the door-jamp as the three gentlemen pushed inside. The flaring torch revealed Patrick standing waiting in mid-floor, unmoving, dressed in that same crimson velvet which he had worn on the day that they were sent down from St. Andrews. It also revealed the Lady Jean crouching away in a corner, white-faced, biting her lip. It revealed something else, too; her gown was now torn open down the front, baring her small bosom – though it had not been that way a few moments before, David would have sworn.

For seconds on end no one moved in that stone-arched chamber. Then the Master of Glamis let flow a furious stream of oaths and obscenity.

The girl raised her cracking voice. 'He ... he tried to force me. He dragged me in here. He did this!' She pointed a trembling finger at Patrick. 'He did, Uncle Thomas! He did!'

Patrick opened his mouth to speak, and shut it again.

Sir Thomas Lyon, the Master, breathing deep and unsteady, tugged his rapier out of its sheath – and made but a clumsy job of it. 'Devil burn you!' he roared. 'You foul lecherous blackguard! By God's eyes, you'll pay for this, Gray! With your worthless life!'

'No! Stop, sir – stop!' David exclaimed, and hurled himself on the Master's sword-arm.

'Off – a pox on you! Off, sirrah!' Lyon shouted, and sought to fling the younger man away, unsuccessfully.

The two Douglases were drawing their swords now. Recognising that he could achieve nothing thus against three armed men, however drunk, David loosed the Master and leapt for the doorway where the two astonished men-at-arms stood gaping. 'Your swords!' he yelled.

The men were slow. David knocked aside one fumbling hand and himself whipped out the fellow's weapon. As the other got his half out, David snatched it in his other hand, and turned.

Patrick was dodging about behind some of the stores kept in that vault, eluding the wild thrusts and pokes of the Master of

Glamis. Jean Lyon crouched further back, her hands over her face.

'Shut the door,' David commanded, to the men behind him. 'Patrick – here!' he called urgently, and as the other glanced towards him, he sent one of the swords spinning through the air, hilt first, to his hard-pressed brother.

Patrick tried to catch it, missed, and it fell with a clatter – fortunately behind an empty barrel. In a trice he had it picked up, and flickering wickedly in the torchlight. 'My thanks, Davy!' he sang out, above the imprecations of his assailants.

And now the entire situation was reversed, for though they were three to two, the three were all drink-taken, one held the torch, and the younger Douglas was obviously no sworder. Whereas, whatever else Patrick Gray had neglected at St. Andrews, it was not rapier-play; indeed, he had been reputed the swiftest and deadliest blade in the University and the city. And David had all along been his sparring partner and foil. These were no rapiers, but heavy cutting swords – but in the hands of experts they served very well. In almost less time than it takes to tell, Lyon was pinned against the stairway with Patrick's blade through the padding of his doublet, young Kilspindie was disarmed, and the other was pleading for mercy. The assistance of the men-at-arms was not required.

'You are impetuous, Sir Thomas,' Patrick declared, easily. 'And loud of mouth. You remind me grievously of my lord of Morton!'

David was panting. 'You are wrong, sirs,' he told them, eagerly. 'About that girl. The Lady Jean. Patrick was not forcing her. She was very willing. I saw them. You heard her laughing, yourselves. Did that sound like a forcing?'

'Foul fall you – what of that?' Lyon answered thickly. 'Willing or no, it was not Jean that this mincing daw married tonight! He is a filthy fornicator who has besmirched the honour of our house.'

'Not so, sir,' Patrick assured lightly. 'I merely found one member of your house exceeding cold and unrewarding. And listening to all of Scotland enjoying itself below me, thought why not I? It is *my* wedding, after all! So I came down discreetly – and lo, another of your good house was ... warmer! All, as it were, within the family, you see!'

David stared at his brother, biting his lip – though his sword-point wove a constant pattern between the two Douglases.

The Master of Glamis cursed loud and long.

'What now, then, Patrick?' David asked, at length.

'A choice for our friends,' Patrick said readily. He corrected himself, bowing. 'Our guests. Either we can all march from here into the hall, as we are now – dear Jeannie with us – to explain the entire matter to the assembled company, with possibly another little demonstration of sword-play there! Or else our guests can retire from here quietly and suitably, their swords in their sheaths, their mouths shut. For their own sake, for Jean's sake – and Elizabeth's. For everybody's sake, indeed. And I will retire equally discreetly and quietly to my bedchamber . . . and see if my wife has missed me! None need know what has happened within this room – for I shall see that these two men of ours do not talk. How think you, Sir Thomas? The choice is yours.'

There was no choice, of course. Not there and then. The reputation of the three gentlemen and the fame of the house of Glamis demanded silence on this matter. Angrily, sourly, they gave their words, were given back their rapiers, and went stamping out into the fire-lit night. Jean Lyon slipped out after them, her clothing held tightly in place, none halting her. Patrick spoke strongly, significantly, to his father's men-at-arms, and sent them packing.

When all were gone, the two brothers eyed each other.

'Thank you, Davy,' Patrick laughed, clapping the other's shoulder. 'I vow I do not know what I would do without you!'

David was less quick with his tongue. At last he spoke. 'Sometimes, Patrick, I think that you are the Devil himself!' he said levelly.

'Tut, lad – you exaggerate!'

'That poor lassie – Elizabeth . . . !'

'Ah, yes. Thank you for reminding me. I will return to her. But . . . och, Davy, I'd liefer it was our Mariota! Goodnight to you!' And he ran light-foot up the stairs and out on to the battlements.

It was still some hours before David himself was able to mount those stairs finally that night. He did so a deal less light-footedly than had his brother, and with little lightness in his heart either. He stood at his own window for a minute or so, staring out at the red fires that crowned every hill in sight, dying down now, but still a stirring sight, flaming beacons near at hand, mere pinpoints of light away to the north. The Master of Gray was wed.

Sighing, David turned and tip-toed to the bed where Mariota lay.

Chapter Four

IF Patrick Gray did not know what he would do without his half-brother, he very soon started to find out. Word of the affair in the schoolroom tower was not long in reaching his father, who, in a stormy interview, expressed himself forcibly and to some purpose. He pointed out that not only had Patrick jeopardised the entire accord between Gray and Glamis and risked undoing all his father's careful work, but he had made for himself a dangerous enemy in Thomas Lyon, whom all knew as a vindictive and unforgiving man, and influential. Made enemies, too, of the Douglases, which most in Scotland were heedful not to do. And of the Regent himself, in his reply to that toast. A notable achievement for one brief night's work! Morton, drunk or sober, would not forget.

Patrick's contribution, though prompt, was of the light-hearted sort. He observed that probably he should have been more discreet – but that discretion had not been greatly in evidence in anybody, that night. Must he be the only discreet one – on his wedding day? And had his reply to the unseemly toast not in fact preserved his noble sire himself from major indiscretion? His lordship had looked distinctly as though he might explode at Morton's insults.

Lord Gray was not to be sidetracked. The matter was serious. Patrick's life, indeed, might be in danger, for the Master of Glamis was not one to overlook a slight. Moreover the man need fear no serious retribution to come from Morton. His castle of Aldbar, at Brechin, was much too near for safety; the Douglases were much too thick on the ground in this area, too, to be provoked with impunity. If Patrick could not show discretion at the right time, he should show it now. He would be better out of the Carse, out of this part of Scotland altogether – and as far away as possible from that little jade Jean Lyon, at Glamis! He was to be gone – and right away. This very day. To the south, to Berwickshire. That was the place for him – Fast Castle, where his Aunt Agnes had married that ruffian Logan of Restalrig. He would be safely out of trouble there for a while, till tempers cooled. It was no unusual custom for the newly-wed to betake themselves off to other parts, after all – though in this case, the more prolonged

56

the stay away, the better.

Patrick went, since he must – and cheerfully enough. It did not fail to occur to him that pastures new, and life out from under his father's eye, might have attractions. It was only a pity that he had to take Elizabeth too. She was not consulted in the matter. She preserved a frozen-faced silence, which my lord assured would doubtless thaw in time.

David, not being important enough to incur the hatred or vengeance of noblemen, stayed where he was, schooling the children and aiding Rob Powrie. He missed Patrick.

Mariota, curiously enough, blossomed out like a flower in the sun. Even my lord noticed it, for her lightsome singing was apt to be heard when anybody crossed the courtyard, and vowed that never had he known a wench that looked forward to her lying-in so blithely. He even visited her at times, in her turret, and once went so far as to inform David that he was a fortunate man. David did not deny it. But still he missed Patrick. They had never been apart for more than a few days before.

Three weeks later Mariota was brought to bed of a girl, tiny, dark-eyed, exquisite.

When my lord saw the child, his small eyes widened, he whistled soundlessly, glanced at David, and said nothing. He came back twice that same day to look at her.

Very quickly David came to love that bairn. It had never occurred to him that it would not be a boy. He had decided that he would be a good, a just and affectionate father to the boy. But this tiny jewel of a girl, lovely from birth, quite overwhelmed him. He found her utterly absorbing – which was strange, for he never had taken any notice of babies hitherto. Indeed, Mariota railed at him a little jealously, vowing that the child had him bewitched. He would have had her named Patricia had not Mariota burst into tears at the suggestion. They called her Mary in the end – curiously enough on Lord Gray's urging. He said that he had had a sister of that name of whom he had been fond, who had died young. David had never heard of this – and wondered, in fact, whether it was not the lovely imprisoned Queen whom my lord was remembering.

Gray, indeed, to the wonder of all, grew swiftly and marvellously enamoured of the infant – unlikely in one who had spawned infants unnumbered and betrayed but little interest in any of them. In the hot sunny days of that fine summer, it became a commonplace to see my lord sitting in his castle courtyard rocking the cradle, tickling the mite's chubby chin, even carrying the creature about, pointing out flowers and bees and the strutting fantails from the doocote – a sight to make men-at-arms goggle and gape. Moreover, David was seldom behind-hand in the same silly business, so that not infrequently the two all but came to blows as to who should pat the brat for wind, or wipe her clean. Unseemly, Mariota called it – a shameful sight. The frowns which she bent on them, however, were scarcely black, and her reproofs dissolved in smiles. She smiled a lot those days, and sang a lot, and grew bonnier every week.

That was a good summer and autumn at Castle Huntly, the happiest that its grim walls had seen for many a year. If only Patrick had been there . . .

My lord, of course, was much from home, and when he came back he was apt to be black-browed and ill-tempered, until Mariota and Mary between them had him gentled again. For outside the castle, all was not so happy. Morton's hand was heavy on the land, and those who were not his friends must walk warily; the Kirk was squirming under the nominal bishops he had imposed upon her – Tulchans, or stuffed calves, they were called, to milk her of her revenues, most of which went straight into the Regent's bottomless pockets. Kirkcaldy of Grange, the best soldier in the land, and Mary the Queen's staunchest remaining supporter, was executed like a common criminal. Mary herself was moved by Queen Elizabeth to closer confinement in Sheffield Castle. And with all this, the south wind carried hints of Patrick's doings that set his father scowling. He was not confining himself wholly to Fast Castle and its cliff-girt surroundings on the Berwick coast, apparently. All the wide Borderland seemed to be learning the name of Gray.

The winter brought still darker clouds – storms, indeed. Morton was proving merciless to all who sought to thwart his ideas of government. He led an army to the Borders to impose his will upon the unruly clan chiefs there – and Logan of Restalrig, Gray's nephew, was no gentle dove, to do what he was told. Patrick perhaps would have been better at home, under his father's eye, after all. It looked as though full-scale civil war might break out once more in blood-stained Scotland, for the Kirk was gathering itself to resist Morton's harshness against its ministers, who were being banished the realm in large numbers – in order, it was believed, to assist the Regent's economical policy of one minister to four churches, which of course left the revenues of the other three available for confiscation. January brought word of Patrick being involved in no fewer than three duels in the closes and wynds of Edinburgh, in two of which his opponents were killed; and one of them was named Douglas. The next month, Elizabeth Gray arrived unexpectedly back at her home of Glamis Castle, and declared unequivocally that she had come for good. And when, a few days later, Sir Thomas Lyon, Master of Glamis, was appointed Lord High Treasurer of Scotland, and third most important man after the Regent and his brother the Chancellor, my lord saw the writing on the wall all too clearly. He sent for Patrick to come home, secretly but without delay.

It was in fact the first real morning of Spring, and the cradle was out in the courtyard in the March sunshine, sheltered from the east wind, when Patrick rode in under the gatehouse of Castle Huntly. He made a dazzling figure in white and scarlet, with cloak of chequered black and gold, and one of the new high-crowned hats with an enormous down-curling ostrich plume.

My lord, who had just helped David carry the cradle down the twisting turnpike stairway – for no servitor was to be trusted with its precious freight – turned to stare at this gallant sight. Even the mettlesome black mare was new.

'My God!' he burst out, interrupting Patrick's gay greeting. 'Look at him! What a Fiend's name is this? A pageant! A guizard, by the Rude! A posture-master!'

Patrick sketched a bow, from the saddle. 'On the contrary – your very devoted . . . !'

'Devil burn you – is this where my siller has gone? What way is that to travel, man, through the Kirk's Scotland? And Morton's? I told you to come secretly – and you ride here in broad daylight gauded to outshine the sun!'

His son laughed, dismounting, and pressed a hand on David's shoulder, who had hurried forward to welcome him. 'I' faith, my lord, you would not have your heir slink into Gray country like some whipped cur? Not so do I esteem your honour . . . and mine!'

'*Your* honour! God's passion – you talk of honour! You? I . . . I . . . ' His father gobbled, at a loss for words.

Not so Patrick. 'Heigh-ho!' he exclaimed. 'It is good to be home. My lord, you look uncommon well. Er, vigorous. Davy – you are getting fat, I vow! Fatherhood, it must be – eh? And this . . . ?' He gestured towards the cradle. 'This can be none other than the cause of it! My . . . h'm . . . niece!'

'I sent for you, sirrah, to come home in haste,' Gray said

angrily. 'Three weeks agone! And secretly. For good reason. And here you come, unhurried – and thus!'

But Patrick was not listening. He was bending over the cradle, gazing down at the dainty wide-eyed creature within, so brilliantly breath-takingly, like himself. And for the moment the smile had left his comely features, and his lips moved soundlessly.

'D'you hear me?' his father demanded. 'A pox on it, man – think you that my orders are to be thus lightly . . . ?' He gulped, and started forward, hands outstretched to the cradle. 'Keep your hands off the bairn!' he cried. 'Can you not see that she is new settled?' And he grabbed his side of the cradle, and jerked it away violently.

At the jolt, the child was thrown to the side, and bumped her head. The great dark eyes widened still further, filled with tears, and the rosebud lower lip trembled as a tiny wail arose.

'Sweet Jesu – look what you have done!' Patrick charged, and he reached inside to pick out the infant.

'I . . . I have done!' my lord spluttered. 'Put her down. Do not touch her, I tell you . . . ' He reached out to snatch back the baby.

Patrick swept the whimpering bundle out and away, stepping, almost dancing, backwards with it. He pressed the little face close to his own, and began to whisper in the shell-like curl-framed ear, backing further from his father the while. He chuckled and wrinkled his nose and grimaced – and in only seconds Mary's whimpers had changed to fat little chuckles also. Pink diminutive fingers clutched his own dark curls, and crows of pleasure mingled with his nonsense.

At sight of the two smiling faces, so close, so lit with the same light, Lord Gray halted, tugging at his beard, muttering. David watched, still-faced.

Patrick skipped about that cobbled courtyard as though it was a dancing floor, crooning a melody to the laughing mite in his arms, beating time before them with the ostrich-plumed hat. Right round the circuit of it he went, and came back to the cradle. But still he held the child.

'Here is a joy, a delight, a darling, a very poppet!' he declared. 'Why did you not write to me that she was . . . so? I swear, this one is fairer than any that kept me in the tall wynds of Edinburgh! Or otherwhere! I' faith – a beauty! And a rogue, too, I'll warrant. With a . . . a strong family resemblance, eh?' Patrick held the creature at arm's length, examining her. 'Remarkable!

Who would have believed that . . . !' He paused. 'Her mother?' he said. 'Always I esteemed the fair Mariota as most worthy of, shall we say, acclaim? Now, as mother of this cosset, this sweet-heart, I love her the more! Where is she – Mariota?'

He looked up. At the tower window two floors up, and looking down on them, Mariota stood, still, motionless, save that her features were working strangely.

Patrick bowed as best he might, laughing, and held up the babe towards her. 'Greetings, my dear – and felicitations!' he called. 'You have done well. Passing well. Here is a very fair achieve-ment. I vow, if I had known that you had it in you . . . !' He smiled, and shrugged one shoulder. 'And you are bonnier than ever. Which of you is the bonnier, would be hard to say . . . '

He stopped. The girl had turned abruptly away from the window, out of sight. Then he laughed again, and set the infant gently down in its cradle, to turn towards the tower doorway. 'I must go pay my respects to my good-sister!' he said.

'That can wait,' his father announced, shortly, sternly. 'Bide you a wee, my mannie. *I* have waited your pleasure for long enough. You will hear me, now. You have disobeyed my orders. You have squandered my money. You have made the name of Gray a by-word, going whoring about the land so that the poor lassie your wife is away back to her father. You have killed men . . . '

'Only in fair fight, sir – who would have killed me, else.'

'Quiet! You have endangered not only your own life, but the safety and well-being o' my house. You have offended needlessly the highest men in the land, so that I, *I*, Gray, may not walk the streets o' Dundee or Perth for fear o' meeting a Lyon or a Douglas! Aye, or even a minister o' the Kirk! Foul fall you, boy – is it crazed you are?'

'I think not, sir. I left here, when you sent me, and came home when you recalled me . . . as soon as affairs permitted me. Is that disobeying your orders? Can I help it if women favour me? As for Elizabeth Lyon, she is as warm to lie with as a fish – and smells something similar! Her father is welcome to her. Davy got the better bargain, 'fore God!'

'Silence, sir! You are speaking of your wedded wife . . . and the Chancellor o' Scotland's daughter! And worse, the new Lord Treasurer's niece!'

'Does that make her a better bedfellow? I will not go begging to Glamis for her . . . '

'No, sir – that you will not! You will do quite other than that. You go to France!'

'France . . . ?'

'Aye. And at once. You are better out of this Scotland for a while. It is a dangerous place to play the fool in! Perhaps in France they may teach you some sense. At least you will be out o' the way o' Morton and the Douglases and the Master o' Glamis. And maybe the lassie Elizabeth will like you the better for a year or two's parting. It has happened that way, before.'

'God forbid!' Patrick said, piously. 'But . . . France! My lord, this is a surprise indeed. I do not know what to say . . . '

'What you say, Patrick, is immaterial. You are going, whether you like it or no. Until you are of age, you will do as I say. We sail tonight.'

'Tonight? And *we* – you are going, too?'

'Only to Dysart, in Fife. A shipman there sends a vessel, each fortnight, to Le Havre. You missed the last one, by your delay – you'll no' miss this one. Wednesday she sails, if I mind aright. We'll go by boat from Dundee – I'll have Geordie Laing put us round to Dysart. I'm chancing no riding through Fife with you, with the Lindsays so thick with Glamis.'

'France,' Patrick said slowly, thoughtfully. 'France should be interesting, I think.'

'Aye, I daresay,' his father observed, grimly. 'But it isna just for interest I'm sending you there, you'll understand! You've a deal to learn, boy, that they didna teach you at St. Andrews. One day you'll be Gray, and a Lord o' Parliament. The Kirk's all very well – but you'll no' learn statecraft in Scotland these days. And statecraft is going to be important, especially foreign concerns, with the Queen of England having no heir but our poor Mary and young Jamie. Which way the cat jumps, Catholic or Protestant, is but a toss o' the coin. It behoves a wise man to take precautions, to be ready for either. Myself, I am deep thirled to the Kirk, these days – but you, lad, are young enough to keep, shall we say, an open mind. Such might prove valuable in the next year or two – who knows?'

'I see.' Patrick smiled. 'So I will be more valuable to *you*, my lord, in France, should the wind blow from Rome . . . is that it?'

'Something o' the sort. They say that Elizabeth Tudor is sickly, these days. Certain it is she'll no' marry now. Philip o' Spain kens that, and is casting eyes on our Queen Mary again. If Elizabeth died – and there's a-many who might help her that road – England could turn Catholic again almost overnight.

And it would be Mary on the two thrones of Scotland and England then, not young Protestant Jamie. It would be an ill thing if both Grays were so deep on the wrong side that our house would gain no advantage, see you.'

'I do see, very well, sir.'

'It will be kittle touchy work, mind. Work for no preening jackdaw. You'll have to watch your every step – for we want no ill tales coming back to the Kirk's Scotland. Warily you'll have to tread, and with your ear well to the ground. I have a sort o' a cousin, one Friar Gray, a Jesuit, at Blois. You'll go to him first. It is near Orleans. He is a man of James Beaton's, that was Archbishop o' Glasgow, who is Mary's ambassador. They will see you on the right track . . . '

'And Davy? Does he come with me?'

'He does not. D'you think I am made o' siller, man? Davy is fine here.'

The brothers' eyes met.

'A pity,' Patrick said.

'Come away up to my room, now, and I'll tell you something of what you must know if you are going to walk in step with the Guises. I was in France myself, at the Scots College in Paris, mind. Come, you . . . '

Regretfully Patrick glanced up at Mariota's window, sighed, shrugged, and turned to follow his sire.

Chapter Five

DAVID GRAY stood in the soaring plunging bows of the *Leven Maid*, of Dumbarton, shading his eyes against the April sun's dazzle off the heaving waters of the Bay of Biscay as he gazed eastwards, landwards. A pity, Patrick had said that time, those many long months ago, when he heard that his half-brother was not to go to France with him. A pity it may have been – and even Lord Gray had come to admit as much, in time, with increasing rue and regret. A pity – and here was David coming to France at last, three full years after that Spring day of 1576, not to undo the pity of it, since that might not be, but at least to cut short the sorry course of my lord's travail. David had come to France to fetch Patrick home.

Lord Gray had, in fact, miscalculated, and was paying the price thereof. Elizabeth of England had not died, nor even maintained her sickliness, and was indeed most notably and upsettlingly alive – even though still husbandless; Mary Stuart, poor soul, was still a prisoner, and seemingly further from the throne than ever – and owing to a succession of fairly feeble plots in her name, some instigated it was said by Elizabeth herself, was even more harshly warded than before; Protestantism remained unshaken in Scotland as in England, with the Kirk stronger than ever, and though Morton had resigned the Regency as a gesture to still the increasing clamour of the ministers, he retained the young King Jamie secure in his hands and ruled the country as before. All of which meant that Patrick's apprenticeship in statecraft was being worked out on the wrong side.

It was not this, however, that had brought my lord to the point of desperation, so much as that unfailing and chronic pre-occupation of all Scots lords, however powerful – money, or the lack of it. Patrick, in France, had proved to be a positive drain, a very sink and gulf, for money. What he did with it all, the Fiend only knew – he did not vouchsafe such details in his letters, only requests for more and more. Indeed, he gave little indication of what he was doing at all, in his deplorably light and frivolous writings, despatched from Rome and Florence and Cadiz and the like, as well as from various ducal courts all over France.

But they all ended with the inevitable demand for the due maintenance of the honour and dignity of Gray – money. My lord had ordered him home more than once – but in return Patrick had pointed out the extreme costliness of the voyage, and that he could not move without cash – as it would be a scandal to their name to leave a host of debts behind him. More money sent, and he still did not return. At length, at his wits' end, my lord had sent David to fetch him back, with the necessary silver and no uncertainty in his instructions.

The port of La Rochelle, protected by its screen of islands, lay ahead of the wallowing vessel. It was a far cry from Castle Huntly, and a long way round to reach Patrick at Rheims – but of late, with the increasingly savage treatment of the French Protestants, Queen Elizabeth's relations with France had deteriorated, and the English captains were so active in the narrow waters of the Channel that Scots ships were avoiding the northern French ports and taking the west coast route unless in convoy. So David had sailed from Dumbarton on the Clyde, the *Leven Maid* heading well out to sea around Ireland, to avoid Elizabeth's busy pirates. La Rochelle, being a Huguenot stronghold, was apt to be spared the latter's attentions.

David, now just past his twenty-first birthday, had attained very definitely to manhood in these last years. Still only of medium height, he had become broad of shoulder and stocky of build, though slender-hipped and light-footed as became a swordsman and a wrestler – not that he had partaken much of such sports since Patrick's departure. He had become a solid sober family man, indeed, and asked for no better. Leaving Mariota and the little Mary had been a wrench, greatly as some part of him longed to see Patrick again.

Impressed by the fortifications of La Rochelle, which had only a year or two before withstood successfully the attacking fury of the Catholic forces under the Constable and de Guise, and by the wider streets and fine buildings, which he esteemed as on the whole superior to Dundee, David made his farewells to the shipmaster at the busy quayside, and sought to learn the approximate frequency of vessels sailing back to the Clyde.

'You're no' feart, man, to ask that,' the other said. 'With all these fell Englishry scouring the seas like a pack o' hound-dogs, pirating who they will! The wonder is that any honest shippers put to sea at all – for no trading vessel's safe.'

'But there is no war between us,' David objected. 'No war with Scotland. Or with France, either.'

'Think you that matters, lad? They do it for the sport, they say, these fine English gentry – bloody murder and robbery. And their dried-up bastard of a queen knights them for the doing o' it, they say! Each voyage we make could be oor last. You'll just have to take your chance o' getting back, and that's a fact. You may be lucky, and you may not. It's Rheims you're making for, you say?'

'Yes. At least, that is where the Master of Gray was when last he wrote a letter. At the court of Guise.'

The seaman spat on the stones of the quay. 'Aye. I' ph'mm. It' a gey long road you have to ride, then – right across France. I've no' been to Rheims, mind, but I ken it's in the north-east o' the country. Calais would have been the port for it. Och, I ken, I ken – beggars canna be choosers. But, see – it's no' that far frae the Netherlands border, I'm thinking. If your friend's close to the Guises – foul fall them! – he'd likely get you a safe-conduct through the armies o' their friends the Spaniards in the Low Countries, and you could win through to Amsterdam, and home frae there. Better than coming back the long road here. But . . . certes, man, you have chosen an ill time to go traipsing alone across this Europe! God – you have! A brave man you must be – or a gey foolhardy one!'

David Gray, in the days that followed, came to appreciate something of the shipmaster's point of view. As he rode north by east, on the very ordinary nag that he had economically purchased in La Rochelle out of my lord's silver, it was through a land where few men rode alone, or rode openly at all, save in clattering dust-raising armed bands, a sunny fair fertile land, rich to his Scots eyes, that should have smiled indeed – but did not; a land that cowered and looked over its shoulder at ruined villages, deserted farms, burned castles, close-walled unwelcoming towns, neglected fields and rioting vineyards. When David had left Scotland the buds had just been beginning to open and the snow still streaked the hills; here the leaves were full out, blossom decked the land and flowers bloomed. But not only blossom burgeoned on the trees; men hung, and women and children too, from so many of the poplars and limes that lined the long straight roads, and no one was there to cut them down; almost every village, burned or no, had its fire and stake in the market-place; scarce a duck-pond or a mill-lade was not choked with bodies of men and beasts. The smell of death hung over a goodly land; the hand of tyranny, misgovernment and sheer savagery was everywhere evident. Over all these fair provinces, of Poitou, Touraine, Blois and Orleans, through which David rode, the tides of religious war had ebbed and flowed for years. The traveller had been used to religious intolerance in his own country, but nothing had prepared him for this. He was shocked. Patrick, in his infrequent letters, had not mentioned anything of it.

Poitou, the province of which La Rochelle was the port, was the worst, for it had been a strong Huguenot area. Possibly still was, though first impressions were that the land was now all but deserted, save for the walled towns; closer inspection, however, revealed that there were still people living in the devastated countryside – only they tended to keep out of sight of travellers, even lone ones, hiding in woods and copses, peering from behind ruined buildings. Some of them David hailed, trying on them his halting St. Andrews French, seeking directions and food – but with scant results. The first night, after looking in vain for an inn that still functioned, he spent in the barn of a deserted farmery near Niort – that was not, perhaps, quite so deserted as it seemed. He slept but fitfully, fully clad and with his sword at his hand, and was away again, hungry, with the dawn.

Thereafter he bought food in the towns, and always carried a supply with him, humble enough fare of bread and cheese and sausage and the light wine of the country; but then, David Gray was a humble man himself, and looked it, in his plain well-worn broadcloth doublet and trunks, dented breastplate, patched thigh-length riding-boots, and flat cap devoid of jewel or feather. As well, perhaps, that such was his aspect, for none were likely to suspect the store of Lord Gray's silver coin that he carried amongst the modest bundle of his gear and provender. Possibly the length and quality of his rather prominent sword helped to discourage the ambitious likewise – however ill it matched the rest of him, save it may be the level gaze of his grey eyes and the jut of his chin.

Not that his long journey across France lacked incident entirely. The third night out, on a low-browed inn under the Abbey church of St. Martin at Tours, he was eyed interestedly during the evening by a pair of out-at-elbow fellow-guests, probably temporarily unemployed men-at-arms, and approached more directly later in the night on his straw pallet in the communal sleeping-room; fortunately however, neither of them proved to be really swordsmen, daggers being their preference for this indoor interviewing, and David, a light sleeper when not in his own bed, had them out of the door in the space of a couple of active minutes, to the marked relief of the other sleepers – though, less happily, the offended landlord forced him to follow them shortly afterwards, lest he bring the hostelry into bad repute with the watch. Since the gates of Tours were not opened until sunrise the rest of the night had to be passed, in drizzling rain, wrapped in his cloak in the Abbey graveyard.

It was only the next afternoon, still in fair Touraine, that, riding up the fertile but war-ravaged vale of the Loire, David heard a drumming of hooves behind him, and turned to see a group of half-a-dozen horsemen pounding along the track at no great distance behind. They had not been in sight when he had looked back a few moments before, so that they must have emerged from woodland flanking the road on the north. France was theoretically at peace from her civil wars, since the Edict of Beaulieu a month or so earlier had provided for concessions to the Huguenots, but David recognised military-type urgency when he saw it, and prudently turned his horse aside from the road and rode down towards the river-bank, to be out of the way. The band, however, swung round and came after him, with loud cries, which though unintelligible to the Scot, had their own eloquence. Without awaiting interpretation, he drove his reluctant cob straight into the Loire. The beast proved to be a better swimmer than might have been expected from its bony appearance, but the Loire is one of France's greatest rivers and the current was powerful, carrying the struggling horse quickly away downstream. The pursuit presumably decided that this trick lay with the river, for they contented themselves with hurling a mixture of fist-shakes, catcalls and laughter after the swimmers, and turned away after a little to ride on eastwards. David fairly quickly perceived that French rivers were not like Scots ones, all splatter and foam, and turned his mount's snorting head back towards the northern bank, which he was perhaps fortunate to regain after a hard struggle and fully half-a-mile downstream.

Chastened and wet, he rode circumspectly towards Blois, deciding that probably a very fast horse, equally with a nimble sword, was a prerequisite for travel in Henri Third's France.

Two evenings later, David crossed the Seine at Melun, and the Marne a day afterwards at Château Thierry without further incident. Rheims, and, he hoped, journey's end, lay but ten leagues ahead.

*

David was much impressed, riding into Rheims. There had been but few signs of devastation or ruin in the rich Champagne country through which he approached it, for this was the territory of the aggressive and powerful family of Guise, that rivalled even the royal house in wealth and influence. Here were the dual courts of the Duke of Guise and of his brother, the Cardinal of Lorraine, Archbishop of Rheims.

It was a handsome city, dominated by the huge twin-towered cathedral, that some said was the most magnificent Gothic building in Europe. Great abbeys and monasteries and churches abounded – for here were no Protestants; splendid palaces and the handsome mansions of the nobility were everywhere, there was a university – not so large as the three colleges of St. Andrews, however – and even the merchants' houses were notably fine. David had never seen anything like it, though he imagined that Edinburgh might be of this sort. The streets of course were crowded – unfortunately with the usual swash-buckling hordes of idle men-at-arms and retainers that formed the inevitable train of the nobility, and the bold-eyed women who in turn could be guaranteed to follow the soldiery. It behoved a discreet traveller to ride warily and offer nothing that could be magnified into provocation.

After considerable searching, David found a very modest hostelry in a narrow back street, whose proprietress, after summing him up keen-eyed, agreed to squeeze him in – for the city was swarming like a hive of bees. As soon as he was cleaned and fed he began to ask about the Master of Gray. He might as well have asked for the man in the moon; Rheims was so full of dukes and marquises, bishops, abbots, counts and the like, that the whereabouts of a single Scots visitor was neither here nor there. The only *Ecossais* that the good lady knew of, was poor M. de Beaton, who called himself Archbishop of Somewhere-or-other. The unfortunate gentleman lodged in the Rue St. Etienne. If monsieur was to ask there . . . ? This advice was made with a nice admixture of sympathy and scorn, which made David wonder.

It was already evening as he made his way to Rue St. Etienne by no means one of the most handsome streets of Rheims. Not to put too fine a point on it, the district might almost have been described as mean, and the house pointed out, though fairly large, had seen better days and was in fact partly warehouse.

The door was opened by an elderly servitor in the worn relics of a fine livery. A single glance at the long sternly-disapproving features and greying sandy hair established him as a Scot, and David forsook his halting French.

'This, I am told, is the house of the Archbishop of Glasgow?' he said. 'I seek the Master of Gray. Can I learn here where I may find him?'

'Ooh, aye,' the man answered, looking his caller up and down interestedly, critically. 'The Master, is it, my mannie? I' ph'mmm' He sounded as though he did not think much of the enquired-for, or of the looks of the enquirer either. 'Well – you'll no' find him here.'

'No, I had hardly expected that,' David admitted. 'But do you, or your master, know where he is?'

'I wouldna hae thought you'd hae needed to ask that!' the other rejoined, with a sniff. 'He used to bide here, aye. But no' now. Och, no' him!'

'Indeed? Where, then?'

'Man, you must be gey new to Rheims to ask that!'

'I am but new arrived from Scotland. Today.'

'Is that so? Wi' messages? Wi' word o' affairs?' That was suddenly eager.

'For the Master of Gray,' David said pointedly. 'Where may I find him?'

'Och, well – you better ask at yon bedizened hizzy's, the Countess de Verlac. Aye, you ask there.'

'The Countess de Verlac? Will I find him in this countess's house, then?'

'Mair'n that – in her bed, man! In her bed, the fine young gentleman!'

'Umm.' David blinked. 'And where do I look for the . . . the lady?'

'In the Hôtel de Verlac, of course – where else? D'you ken him, this young gamecock?'

'We are, h'm, related.'

'D'you tell me that?' The servitor pursed thin lips. 'Well, if you're in a hurry to see him, you might as well just go to the Cardinal's palace, right away. He'll be there. They'll all be there, all the bits o' lairds and counts and sik-like, wi' their painted women. It's the usual high jinks, a great ball and dancing, to celebrate one o' their outlandish saints. They're aye at it – any's the excuse will do. There's one near every other night.'

David smiled faintly. 'You sound, I'd say, but little like an archbishop's henchman!' he said.

The other snorted. 'He's awa' there himsel' – the auld fool!

I tell him he should have mair sense.' He made as though he would shut the door in disgust – and then turned back. 'What's ... what's auld Scotland looking like, laddie?' he asked, almost shamefacedly. 'Where are you frae?'

'The Carse o' Gowrie, above Tay. And it was cold when I left.'

'Och, well – I'm frae Melrose, mysel'. Aye, Melrose, snug on the banks o' Tweed. Bonny, bonny it'll be yonder, now, wi' the yellow whins bleezing on every brae, and the bit lambs skipping. I've no' seen it in fifteen year, fifteen year – and I'll no' see it again this side o' the grave, either. No' me. Good night to you!'

The door all but slammed in David's face.

He went in search of the archiepiscopal palace.

It was not difficult to find, being near to the towering cathedral, a great and splendid edifice standing in formal gardens, with fountains playing in the forecourt, and statuary, naked and to David's mind surpassingly indelicate, scattered everywhere. The huge gates, though they were guarded by halberdiers in most gorgeous liveries, stood wide open, and David was surprised that no attempt was made to question his entry. Indeed, half of Rheims seemed to be passing in and out of the premises, grooms, personal servants, ladies' maids, men-at-arms, pages, even priests and monks. The sound of music drifted out from the great salons, but it had difficulty getting past the louder noises of laughter and shouting in the forecourt, a hubbub which centred round a couple of fountains there. Men, and women too, were pushing and jostling there, and drinking from cups and tankards and even scooped hands. It was only when looking at the second fountain that David perceived that the water was purplish-red in colour – that it was not in fact water at all, but wine, red wine in this, white in the other. Almost incredulously, he pressed forward, to reach out and dip a finger in the flood, and taste. It was real wine, as good as any that he had had the good fortune to taste. Amazed, he stared. Admittedly most of what was not drunk ran back into the cistern below and would be spouted up again through a dozen nymphs' breasts and worse – but even so, the quantity expended must have been enormous, and quite appalled David's economical Scots mind. And this, apparently, was for the servants, the soldiers, the hangers-on, some of whom already lay about on the ground, young as was the night.

The contrast of this de Guise munificence, as against the harried and war-torn want of the provinces through which he had come here, was rather more than David's stomach would take. He forbore to join the beneficiaries.

He moved forward to the palace itself. It was quite unlike any building that he had ever seen, not only in its vast extent but in the profusion of its terraces, balustrated galleries, pillared arcades and porticos, at various levels, merging with the far flung gardens, and with huge windows opening on to all these. David, brought up in a tall stone castle, noted that it would be an impossible place to defend.

No attempt was being made to bar anyone's entrance thereto this night, at any rate. Lavishly clad figures danced out on the terraces, embraced in every alcove, and strolled and made love in the formal gardens, so that it was a little difficult, in the creeping dusk, to distinguish coupling guests from the profusion of statuary. In and out amongst them all went servants bearing trays of viands, sweetmeats, goblets of wine, fruit and the like. David's fear had been that he might not gain access to the palace; now it was rather the problem of finding Patrick in the throng.

As it happened, that was not too difficult, either. Edging his way through one of the great windows that opened off the magnificent main salon, he stared in at the brilliant scene. Under the blaze of thousands of candles in huge hanging candelabra, a splendid concourse of dazzlingly dressed men and women stood and circulated and talked and laughed, watching a comparatively few couples who gyrated slowly in the stately but archly seductive measures of the pavane, at the farther end of the vast marbled room, to the music of players in a gallery. The clothing of these people took David's breath away. Never had he seen or conceived of such splendour and ostentation, such a scintillation of silks and satins and gems. Never had he seen so many long and graceful legs coming from such abbreviated trunks, so many white shoulders and bare bosoms, such fantastic head-dressing and outrageous padding of sleeves and hips. Nor had his nostrils been assailed by such a battery of scents and perfumes, or his ears afflicted by such din of high-pitched clamour. For a while he could only gaze, benumbed.

It was the part-contemptuous, part-angry gesture of a handsome and statuesque woman who dominated a group quite near to David, and who kept drawing the latter's somewhat guiltily scandalised eyes by the cut of her all black jewel-encrusted gown, that eventually turned his glance whither she pointed. It was towards one especial pair of the dancers.

David's breath caught.

Though he could scarcely believe his eyes, there was no doubt that it was Patrick. But how different a Patrick. Gone was the beautiful youth, the fresh-faced if mocking-eyed stripling, even the dashing young galliard of his duelling days in Edinburgh. Instead, here was a man of such elegance, superb bearing, confidence, and extraordinary good looks, as to draw all eyes, whether in admiration, envy or sheer malice, a man of such sparkling attractiveness and at the same time mature and easy dignity, that it was hardly believable that he had barely reached his twenty-first year. Dressed entirely in white satin and gold lace – and seemingly the only man in that salon to be so – save for a black velvet garter below one knee, a black dagger-belt, and the black lining to the tiny cape slung from one padded shoulder, his dark gleaming hair swept down sheerly to his shoulders in disciplined waves and unusual style, curling back from neat jet-jewelled ears. He had grown a tiny pointed beard and thin scimitar of black moustache, outlining the curve of his lips. His hose were so long and his trunks so short as to verge on indecency, front and back, and he danced with a young woman of swarthy fiery beauty clad in flame-coloured velvet, with such languid grace albeit naked and unblushing intimacy and touch, as to infer that they might well have been alone in the lady's boudoir – no doubt the reason for the disgust of the statuesque woman in black.

David watched, biting his lip.

In a little, almost imperceptibly, Patrick steered his voluptuous partner towards one of the open windows at the top end of the salon. David saw the woman in black start as though to leave her companions and hurry in that direction, then shrug and change her mind. He himself, however, slipped back through his own window, and moved up the terrace. He was waiting within the topmost window when Patrick and the young woman in red came out, laughing. They would have pushed past him without a glance had David not put out a hand to the other's arm. 'Patrick!' he said.

His brother turned, haughtily, angrily shaking off the touch. Then his eyes widened and his lips parted. 'My God – Davy!' he gasped.

'Aye, Davy. None other.'

For a long moment they gazed at each other. Patrick's fine nostrils flared, almost like those of a high-spirited horse. His dark eyes darted glances right and left. David read more than

73

mere joy and affection therein. He nibbled at his lower lip. Then, abruptly laughing again, he strode forward to fling his satin-padded arms around his brother's dull and well-worn broadcloth.

'Davy! Davy!' he cried. 'Here's a wonder! Here's joy indeed! My good dear Davy – here!'

David's own throat was sufficiently choked with emotion as to render him speechless.

'Patrick! Patrick! What, *tête Dieu*, is this?' The young woman had turned back, astonished. 'Have you taken leave of your senses?'

'Eh . . . ? No, no, Elissa. This . . . this is . . . my good friend, Davy. And secretary. From Scotland, you understand . . . '

'Friend?' That was as eloquent as the raised supercilious eyebrows, as the swarthy girl looked David up and down.

'It is . . . you could call us foster-brothers. It is a common relationship in my country. Foster-brothers . . . '

'I do not think that I congratulate you, *mon cher*!'

Patrick laughed. 'Elissa is jealous, I think, Davy!' he said lightly.

David looked at the young woman doubtfully – and hurriedly looked away again. Of all the low-cut gowns of that palace, that of this sultry ripe Italianate beauty was surely the lowest – so low indeed that the point of one thrusting prominent breast was showing. David's embarrassment stemmed not so much from the sight itself, for it might have been assumed that the dancing had disturbed the lady's attire, but from a second glance's perception that it was in fact painted flame-red to match the dress – and therefore that it was meant to be thus on view.

Keeping his eyes averted, he bowed perfunctorily. 'The Countess de Verlac,' he said, more to cover his discomposure than anything else. 'David Gray at your service, ma'am.'

'Lord!' Patrick exclaimed.

'*Dieu de Dieu!*' the lady cried. 'That old war-horse! That, that dragon! Fellow, you are insolent!'

'*Mort de Diable*, Davy – you mistake! The ladies are, h'm, otherwise. Quite otherwise! This is the Viscountess d'Ariège from Gascony.'

But his partner had swirled round, the Spanish verdingale under her billowing skirts buffeting David in the by-going. She swept on towards the steps that led down into the gardens. Patrick looked after her ruefully, and made a face that turned him momentarily into a boy again.

74

'Forgive me, Davy,' he said. 'Give me but ten minutes. Less. You trod on delicate ground, there! Wait for me here.' Smiling, and patting his brother's shoulder with his perfumed-gloved hand, he went after the Viscountess – but sauntering, not hurrying, a picture of exquisite masculine assurance.

David, frowning, and cursing his own blundering awkwardness by comparison, not for the first time but now more feelingly than ever before, withdrew into the shadows behind a pillar, to wait.

In much less than ten minutes Patrick was back, casually, unhurrying still. He took David by the arm. 'We cannot talk here,' he said. 'There is an ante-room that I know of, round here.'

Another terrace gave them access to a smaller room, full of cloaks, riding-boots, swords and the like, less brilliantly lit than the salons. One of the Cardinal's guards stood sentinel over it, but made no attempt to bar their entry. Patrick turned to consider his brother.

'*Pardieu*, Davy – the trouble I am to you, eh? Heigho – so you have been sent to fetch me home!'

David cleared his throat. This had seemed a simple enough errand back at Castle Huntly, however responsible, lengthy and expensive. But, now . . . ? Of old, when really necessary, he had always been able to impress his own personality and will upon this brilliant brother of his, by some means or other, even if it was only his fists, at least briefly and for a limited objective. Probably because he had seemed to be the elder. But now, this confident gallant in front of him had grown so far beyond him, had changed in these three years into a man, and a strong and determined man most obviously, whatever else he might be. What impression could he, David, the humble schoolmaster and rustic, hope to make on this dazzling nobleman now?

If David had perhaps considered well, in one of the many mirrors of that room, the man that he himself had grown into those three years, he might have looked a little less hopelessly on his chances. All he did, however, was to eye his brother with that level gaze of his, and sigh.

'Aye,' he said, 'I am sorry about the lady, Patrick.'

The other laughed with apparently genuine amusement. 'Say it not,' he declared. 'You showed me a side of Elissa that I had not seen before . . . difficult as one might think that to be! But . . . here is a surprise, Davy. You have a come a long road – which is the measure of our father's concern for me, is it? Or for his precious siller, eh? Our fond parent believes that he is not getting a sufficiently good return for his money – is that it?'

'Can you blame him, Patrick?' David asked briefly. His hand's gesture, to include all his brother's gorgeous appearance, and the magnificence of his surroundings, was eloquent enough.

'Fine, I can, Davy! Think you that his small grudging doles pay for . . . this? The Gray lands are wide, and my lord's treasure-chest less bare than he would have us think. As heir to one of the greatest lords in Scotland, I will not live like any starveling exile. He sent me here, did he not? But . . . enough of such talk, for the nonce. You look well, Davy . . . and very stern! An upright stubborn bear of a man – or should it be a lion? A lion of Judah, rather than of Gray, eh? You mind me of some of the stauncher pillars of the Kirk! I'll never dare cross you again, Davy – I'd be feared!'

The other shook his head. 'Man, Patrick – you've changed, your own self,' he said.

'You think so? It may be that I have had occasion to. But . . . och, Davy – it does my heart good to see you. Like a breath of fresh north wind you are, with the scent of heather and bog-myrtle to it.'

'Yet you prefer *this* scent, I think?' his brother said, and touched those elegant perfumed gloves.

Patrick laughed. 'In Rome, as they say, one lives like a Roman. In Rheims, likewise.'

'Aye – what *are* you doing here, Patrick? What keeps you here? Living thus. These women . . . ?'

'Women never keep Patrick Gray anywhere – however useful they may be!' he was assured lightly. 'I have affairs here, that is all. Affairs that are not yet completed.'

'What affairs?'

'The old Davy – ever blunt as a cudgel! Affairs of some moment, shall we say? When a man has a father such as mine, Davy, clearly he must make his own way in the world, if he would not live on bannocks and ale – for which, unlike yourself, I have but little taste. I . . . '

He stopped. An inner door had opened, and framed therein were three men. Patrick made a profound obeisance. David, after a quick look at his brother, bobbed a brief bow, and waited.

The first two gentlemen were very similar, in build, in appearance, in expression, tall hawk-faced exquisites, dressed in the height of extravagant fashion; they might well have been brothers. The third was very different, older, a plump but sagging man, with a tired and heavy-jowled face, clad in the florid and flowing, if distinctly tarnished, splendours of a prince of Holy Church.

One of the pair in front, a spectacular thin figure garbed wholly in crimson – doublet, cloak, trunks, hose, jewelled cap, ostrich-feathers, even sword hilted and sheathed in crimson and rubies, spoke, crisp-voiced. 'Monsieur de Gray, I was told that you had come to this room with a stranger, obviously a messenger. Who, and whence, is he?' This was curt, with little attempt to disguise a hint of suspicion.

'No messenger, Your Eminence, but merely my, er, my secretary, new come from Scotland,' Patrick assured, quickly.

'Secretary?' The speaker looked sceptical. 'He seems no clerk, to me. Since when have you aspired to a secretary, Monsieur?'

Patrick smiled, brilliantly. 'Only since tonight, Eminence. Formerly, Davy was my close companion and body-servant. Indeed, we were foster-brothers. My father, the Lord Gray, has sent him to me now, believing that he will be useful. In the matters in which we are interested. Davy is very . . . discreet.'

'I trust so,' the other observed, bleakly. 'If he is direct from Scotland, at least he will have news for us? For us all. What has he to tell us?'

Patrick shot a glance at his brother. 'I have not asked him yet, sir – save only of family matters. David – here is His Eminence the Cardinal of Lorraine, Archbishop of Rheims. Also his brother, my lord Duke of Guise, Marshal of France. And my lord Archbishop of Glasgow. They would have news of Scotland – of affairs there.' David felt a dig at his side from Patrick's elbow.

He bowed again, but still not deeply. David could not bring himself to bow low to any man. 'My knowledge of affairs is slight,' he said, in his stilted French. 'But such as it is, it is at their lordships' disposal.'

'How is it with Morton, lad? Is his grip of the young King weakening?' That was the rich and fruity voice of James Beaton, exiled Archbishop of Glasgow, traces of his couthy Fife accent still evident beneath the French. 'What of Huntly and Herries, the Catholic lords? Are the people making clamour for the Queen's release, God pity her?'

'Not that I have heard of, sir. The Kirk is not so inclined, and teaches otherwise. My lord of Morton still rules, yes. He is no longer Regent, but . . . '

77

'We know that, fellow!' the Cardinal exclaimed, impatiently. '*Mortdieu* – we are not years old in our information! News we desire – not history, sirrah! We have sent good money to Scotland, to stir up the people to demand Mary Stuart my cousin's release. Do not you tell us that it has been wasted?'

'No, no, Your Eminence – not that, I am sure,' the other and lesser Archbishop put in hurriedly. 'It takes time for the leaven to work. This young man, belike, is not from Edinburgh or Stirling . . . '

'He comes from the Carse of Gowrie only,' Patrick amplified. 'A country district. Where the Kirk is strong. Your Eminence need not fear . . . '

'I hope not,' the Cardinal said, thin lips tight.

'You carry no messages from our friends at the court of your king?' This time it was Henri, Duke of Guise, as crisp as his brother but a shade less keenly shrewd in aspect, however intolerant of eye as befitted the man who had instigated the Massacre of St. Bartholomew's Eve.

'No, my lord duke. I have not been near the court, at all.'

'Then, *cordieu*, we are wasting our time, Louis!'

'Perhaps. Fellow – your blaspheming renegades of the Church, these heretics of the so-called Kirk,' the Cardinal went on. 'How fond are they of Morton, now? What say they to the doles he takes from Elizabeth of England? Are they still as much a league of the damned as ever – or does *our* gold begin to do its work there? Even a country clodhopper will know that, surely?'

David took a deep breath, and felt Patrick's urgent elbow in his side again. 'The Kirk, sir, is not concerned with gold, I think,' he said, as evenly as he might. 'The Lord Morton, I daresay, is otherwise. Certainly the Kirk and he are not the best of friends.'

'Ha! Relations are worsening between them?'

'Morton was never popular, sir – but he is strong. He has not sought to make the Kirk love him. It is its revenues he desires.'

'And the other heretic lords?' the Duke asked. 'Glamis? Ruthven? Crawford? Gowrie? Monsieur de Gray's father? They are ready to turn against Morton?'

'I cannot tell you, my lord. They do not honour me with their confidences!'

'Sir . . . !'

'My . . . my secretary's French, my lord duke, is but that of a St. Andrews tutor,' Patrick interposed hastily. 'He means no offence, no incivility . . . '

'*Mort de Diable* – he had better not!'

'Patrick is right, gentlemen,' the Archbishop of Glasgow agreed smoothly. 'There is little in looking for a silk purse out of this sow's ear! I think that we have had as much from him as we are likely to gain. Perhaps, hereafter, I may question him in his own tongue, and see if he knows aught else of interest to us.'

'Very well, Monsieur de Beaton,' the Cardinal of Lorraine said shortly. 'See you do it.' He glanced at Patrick. 'Monsieur de Gray, I conceive that Madame de Verlac will be quite desolated if she is deprived of your sparkling company for much longer. Which would be a pity, would it not?' And without a further look towards David, his crimson-clad Eminence turned and stalked out of the ante-room, his ducal brother following.

Patrick fetched a deep genuflection. David did not. He, however, caught the swift and significant glance that passed between his brother and James Beaton, before the latter quietly closed the door behind him.

David expelled a long breath, and looked at his companion. 'You have a deal of explaining to do, I think, Patrick,' he said.

'Perhaps. But not now, Davy, not now. You heard what His Eminence said? About the lady. And such, in Rheims, from its Cardinal-Archbishop, is no less than a royal command. I must go. Later, we will talk.'

'When? Where?'

'It, h'm, may be difficult tonight. Yes, a little difficult, Davy – much as I would wish to see you. It will have to be in the morning. Tomorrow – not too early, though, I pray you! Lord – do not frown so, man. In Rome, as I say . . . !'

'Your lodging, Patrick – shall I call there, then?'

'Er . . . no. No, that would be inadvisable, I think.'

'But I am your secretary, it seems . . . !'

'Och, Davy, what's in a word? No – I will call on you. Where are you lodging? Ah, yes – undistinguished, but it will serve well enough. I shall call on you there, then, at noon shall we say? Yes, yes – noon will be amply early. Till then, dear Davy, go with God!'

'And you?'

'I . . . I do not aspire so high!' Patrick laughed, touched his brother's shoulder, and slipped out through the same door as the others had used.

Brows knit, David Gray turned back to the open windows.

*

79

'And how is the Countess de Verlac this morning?' David asked. 'Or this noontide!'

'Somewhat smothering, I fear – distinctly overwhelming, for the time of day! Despite her years, she is a woman of great energy and determination, I find. Fine to look at, mind you – at a modest distance. But . . . demanding.'

'Then why in Heaven's name bed with her, man?'

'For three good and sufficient reasons, Davy. One – she esteems me highly, and has a delightful house. Two – she is the richest woman in Rheims, in all Champagne it may be. And three – her late husband was a Huguenot, and her own leanings towards the true faith are not considered to be quite whole-hearted.'

'And how should this concern you?'

'Ah, that shows how little you understand the French scene, Davy. The Guises are most anxious that the lady should remain devoted to Holy Church – in particular her resources. And I am of some small value to them, in this regard.'

'But why, in the name of mercy? What is it to you what her faith may be?'

'*Pardieu* – as a good adopted son of our universal Mother in Rome, I cannot remain unaffected – especially when my lord Cardinal is so concerned!'

'Patrick – you? Rome? You are a baptised Protestant. Received to the Breaking of Bread . . . '

'Ah – in Scotland, yes. But do not shout the glad tidings aloud, so, Davy, I beseech you! For this is not Scotland, see you – far from it. And I would remind you – in Rome, do as . . . !'

David stared at his brother. Today, he was dressed all in plum-coloured velvet, slashed with silver, the long plumes of his high-crowned hat falling down one side to balance the long thrusting rapier at the other. 'You . . . you have become a Catholic!'

'Only insofar as it was necessary. And only in France, my dearest Davy.'

'Only in France! Does God take note of borders, then?'

'I sometimes wonder! I wonder, too, whether the good Lord cares more for the Protestants who damn His Catholics, or for the Catholics who burn His Protestants! But . . . a pox, it matters not to me, either way. It was necessary, I tell you.'

'Necessary for what? Patrick – what deep game are you playing here in Rheims? With these arrogant Guises? All that questioning, last night? By the Cardinal. What does it mean?'

His brother glanced around him. They were in David's unsavoury tavern, but the only other customer, for the moment, snored in a far corner. 'Surely you can guess?' he said, still easily but his voice lower set. 'You know why my father sent me here, in the first place. Apart from getting me out of the way of the Douglases and Thomas Lyon – to learn statecraft and foreign affairs, you'll mind. Well, I am learning fast. To ensure that if so be the Catholics should triumph in this stramash, in Scotland and in England, both Grays should not be notably on the wrong side.'

'I heard him, yes – and liked it not. But surely my lord did not intend that you should go the length of turning Catholic yourself!'

'What he intended, Davy, is not of the first importance. To me! As I told you, I have my own way to make. I cannot live in my father's tight pocket – nor wish to. There are ample means for an agile and clear-headed man to make his way in this naughty world, and I see them palpably. Whilst most men are blinded by passion and prejudice, less handicapped souls may gain considerable advantages. Hence, the Guises, or good Beaton, and Mary Stuart.'

'What has Mary Stuart – what has the Queen to do with it?.'

'Everything, my dear brother. Don't you see – here is what our late lamented Master Knox called The Honeypot? She is that still. Even imprisoned in an English castle for years, she remains a honeypot, the lovely Mary; and the bees – and still more, the wasps – buzz around her everlastingly. There is, h'm, honey to be gleaned there in plenty . . . for the clear-headed beekeeper, don't you see – who is not frightened of a sting or two!'

'I cannot say that I do see, Patrick.' David's voice was more level even than usual, cold even. 'Mary the Queen, poor lady, is in dire need of the help of honest men, I think. I cannot see where your honey comes in.'

Patrick was quick to note that chilliness of tone. 'Of course, man – that is just it!' he exclaimed. 'She needs help. She needs friends who will work for her – who will guide affairs in the right direction. No harm if they better themselves in the process, is there? By using foresight and wit? That was my father's game, and it is mine likewise. Only, I play it rather more subtly, and for bigger stakes.'

'Your father was known as Mary's friend. Still is, even in the Kirk.'

'Precisely – a belief that has been of the greatest advantage to me, whatever it has been to him! See, Davy, I have made my way deep into the councils of the Marian party here in France. The Archbishop Beaton is Mary's personal representative – and he and I are close. The Guises are behind it – for Mary's mother was their aunt – and the ruling house of Valois against it. Or, at least, the woman Catherine de Medici and her nitwit son, King Henri. France and Spain together can get Mary out of Sheffield Castle if they will, and if Scotland plays her part in the north. Elizabeth dare not challenge all three at once.'

'Aye. But Scotland is Protestant – as is England. And France and Spain are Catholic – and would impose that faith on us.'

'That is the difficulty,' Patrick agreed. 'But not an insuperable one. Religion is not the only thing worth fighting over, Davy!'

'The Kirk, I think, will not agree with you. Nor Scotland itself . . . '

'That is where I believe you are wrong. Properly handled, suitably shall we say encouraged, in the right places, I think Scotland – even the Kirk – can be made to see where her advantage lies.'

'And yours?'

'And mine, yes.'

'You do not suffer from over-modesty, Patrick – not that you ever did, of course.'

'I do not. It is a fool's attribute – with all due respect to yourself, Davy! But I have good reasons for my hopefulness, I assure you. It is no mere day-dreaming. I am not, in fact, a day-dreamer at all, you know.'

The other sighed. 'I do not know, really, what you are,' he admitted. 'I . . . I sometimes fear for you, Patrick.'

'Save your fears, brother, for others who need them more.'

'I still do not see what you hope to gain?'

'Leave that to me, Davy. I can surely serve Scotland, and myself, at the same time?'

'Others have said as much – and forgotten Scotland in the end!'

'I will not forget Scotland, I think – not with you as my watchdog!'

'Aye – I think you will not forget Scotland yet awhile, at least!' David agreed grimly. 'Since I am to take you back there, forthwith.'

The other laughed. 'Poor dutiful Davy!' he said.

'They are my lord's sternest orders.'

'Poor my lord!'

'I tell you, he is deadly earnest in this. Moreover, Patrick, he has given the money wholly into *my* keeping, the silver you asked for, to pay your debts and bring you home. There is sufficient – but *I* spend it, not you! On my lord's strictest command.'

'My dear good fool – think you that carries any weight now? I have made other arrangements for such matters! I thought that I had explained that? Moreover, do not forget that I reach the notable age of twenty-one in but a month or two's time. Coming of age may not have made *you* your own master, Davy – but it will me, I assure you! And it is quite inconceivable that we should be able to tidy up our affairs and arrange the difficult business of travel to Scotland in a few brief weeks! No, no, I fear that you must reconcile yourself to a further stay in *la belle France*, Davy-lad.'

David's glowering set expression was more off-putting and determined than he himself knew.

'Not too long a stay, of course,' Patrick went on, quickly. 'Indeed, I have hopes that it may be quite brief. I have affairs in train, with Beaton, that should take our cause a great step forward – and soon. We only await word from Paris – we wait the arrival of the key, the golden key, that may well unlock Mary's prison doors eventually. Until then, of course, I cannot leave France. But when that does arrive – heighho, I am at your disposal, Davy. You will not be able to get me back to Scotland fast enough!'

'So, you refuse to obey your father's express orders, Patrick?'

'I do, Davy, since other people are relying on me, now. Father's own friend Queen Mary, it may be. And you can keep his precious silver. It will not take up a deal of space in your baggage, I warrant!'

'I have no means of forcing you, but I shall make it my endeavour to see that we do go, and very soon, nevertheless.'

'Do that, Davy – if you can! Meanwhile, we must find you somewhere better to live than this kennel.'

'I will not come and roost with you in your aged Countess's houes!' David told him stonily.

'*À merveille!* I had not planned that you should!' his brother laughed. '*Pardieu* – that would be most upsetting! I would not trust the old lady with you, and that's a fact. No – I think my former lodgings with Archbishop Beaton will be best – hardened Calvinist as you are! You will be able to talk theology and ethics with him, Davy, to your heart's content! Come you – the stink of this place offends my nostrils. *Allons!*'

Chapter Six

AND so David was installed in the house of the exiled Archbishop of Glasgow, at the very centre of the web of plot and intrigue which was being assiduously spun around the future and fate of the lovely and unfortunate Mary Stuart, Queen of Scots. He came to look upon James Beaton as an old hypocrite and inveterate schemer, but sincere in his love of his unhappy mistress – and not nearly such a formidable character to deal with, in fact, as his gloomy and lugubrious manservant and mentor, Ebenezer Scott from Melrose, who ruled the seedy establishment and disapproved of all comers.

David saw Patrick irregularly and less frequently than he would have wished, but he saw a lot of others who frequented the house in the Rue St Etienne at all hours of the day and night, especially the night; largely English Jesuit priests and improverished Scots adventurers, few of whom won his regard. As a consequence of all this, he found himself to be adopting, at times, a cloak-and-daggerish attitude, entirely out of character and quite uncalled-for. He fretted and chafed at the waiting, idleness, and delay – and could do nothing about it, that he could see.

All Rheims, of course, lived in an atmosphere of intrigue, suspicion and duplicity, under the surface splendour and gaiety. The Guises seemed to attract plotters and schemers like magnets; perhaps it was her Guise blood that was responsible for Mary Stuart's fatal attraction for such folk. Only, the three Guise brothers were themselves the most active plotters of all, with a catholicity of interest, range and ambition that knew no bounds. Beside this Stuart one, their schemes embraced the Catholic League, their advancement in the Spanish Netherlands, the affairs of the Swiss Federation, even the destination of the Crown of France itself – and well the Queen-Mother, Catherine, knew it. Patrick had chosen richly troubled waters in which to fish.

At least he seemed to enjoy his fishing. Without appearing to be in the least secretive, he did not confide very deeply in David as to his comings and goings, his plans and exchanges. He was evidently adequately supplied with money, and his wardrobe was as extensive as it was handsome; if he did not inform his brother as to the precise source of all this, neither did he once approach him for a penny of my lord's silver. He was always cheerful, if occasionally slightly rueful about Madame de Verlac's excessively exclusive demands, though admittedly he did not let such cramp him unduly. He talked happily of his growing intimacy with Charles, Duke of Mayenne, the third Guise brother, and where this might lead, and more than once referred confidently to the awaited arrival of the golden key that was to unlock Mary the Queen's prison doors. This latter much intrigued David, but being the character that he was, he could not bring himself to question his brother more urgently on the subject than Patrick was disposed to tell. It might indeed have seemed a moot point, sometimes, which was the prouder Gray – the heir to the title, or his bastard brother and supposed secretary.

This role of secretary appeared to David to be so ridiculous and obviously false as to arouse the immediate suspicions of all who heard of it. That no such doubts were in fact expressed, at least openly, may have been a tribute to Patrick's exalted friends, his known skill with a rapier, or merely the fact that Rheims was so full of curious flamboyant characters, furtive conspirators, and people who were fairly obviously not what they seemed, that one modest addition was quite unremarkable.

David had no gift for idleness, and found time to hang somewhat heavily, even though, as the weeks passed, Patrick took him about with him more and more, declaring him to be something of a protection from designing women, bores, and once – in a dark alley returning from a clandestine meeting with Leslie, Bishop of Ross, in Mayenne's palace – protection from unidentified masked bullies whose swords proved to be but a poor match for those of the two brothers.

To salve his conscience in some measure, David wrote a letter to Lord Gray, informing him that they both were well, that the difficulties of getting home from France were however formidable, that the financial situation was better than had been anticipated – a cunning note, that – and assuring my lord that they would be travelling back just as soon as it might be effected. That was true, in some degree, too. The shipmaster of the *Leven Maid* had not exaggerated. It was no easy matter to arrange a passage to Scotland. Elizabeth's gentlemen-adventurers, so-called, had more or less closed all the Channel ports, and were increasingly turning their attention to the trade of the

86

west coast harbours, like Brest, Nantes and La Rochelle. Practically the only open route from France to Scotland now, save under strong convoy, was by the Low Countries and Amsterdam. With the Netherlands occupied by Philip of Spain's conquering armies, access to Amsterdam must be by their permission. The Guises undoubtedly could obtain that for whomsoever they would, but for the unprivileged traveller, the journey was next to impossible. David was wholly in Patrick's hand, in this. He wondered indeed how this letter would go, and how long it might take to reach its destination, but it seemed that Archbishop Beaton had his own curious channels of communication, and assured that, for a considera- tion, it would travel safe and fast along with more important missives. The writer's concern for its speedy delivery was, to tell the truth, mainly in the interests of getting news of his safety to Mariota his wife.

Patrick's twenty-first birthday was celebrated by a great entertainment and rout, given in his honour by the doting Countess de Verlac. All Rheims was invited that was worth inviting, and in the usual fashion of these affairs, it was practic- ally open house. The Hôtel de Verlac was not so large and magnificent as the archiepiscopal palace, of course, but it was even more sumptuously equipped and plenished, and the Countess, for so important an occasion, stinted nothing. There were two score of musicians from Savoy; performing dwarfs from Bohemia; a curious creature that was both man and woman, very rare, borrowed from the Duke of Lorraine; and a series of tableaux, cunningly devised and most lavishly mounted, depicting classical scenes, with a climax of the Judgment of Paris, showing Patrick himself, clad only in a vine-leaf, in the name part, producing swoons of admiration amongst the women guests, and Hortense de Verlac, naturally, as Venus, even the most prejudiced having to admit that for her age her figure remained extraordinarily effective – though perhaps if more candles had been lit it would have been a different story.

It was just after this exciting interlude, with Patrick newly returned in a striking costume, wholly black on one side and pure white on the other, from the two sides of the ostrich plumes of his hat down to the buckles of his high-heeled shoes, that an alternative diversion developed, quite unscheduled. The dukes of Guise and Mayenne had been present from the start, but now their brother the Cardinal-Archbishop was announced, with the usual flourish of trumpets. Dressed as ever in crimson, but in the extreme of fashion, he stalked in, to the deep bows of all the assemblage save his brothers and David Gray – who was here merely as a sort of a supernumerary to Patrick and not really a guest at all. For once however, it was not His Eminence who drew all eyes, but the man who strolled smilingly in his austere wake.

Involuntarily, David looked from this newcomer to his brother. For, somehow, the two made a pair; were sib, as the Scots phrase has it; came from something of the same mould. Not that they were alike in feature. Where Patrick was darkly and sparkingly handsome, this man was goldenly fair, and glowed. Patrick was the more tall and slender, the more youthful; the other was a man nearing forty, perhaps. Though also dressed in the height of fashion, and richly, his costume did not challenge the eye as did the younger man's. But he had a similar personal magnetism, a similar smiling assurance, an ease of bearing and grace of manner that were the counterpart of Patrick's Gray's. David considered them both, thoughtfully – and was not the only person in that chamber so to do, for the affinity and similitude were such as must strike all but the least observant. Men so well-matched, so essentially alike apparently, do not always commend themselves to each other. The reverse is indeed the more likely.

Patrick showed no signs of anything but intense interest, however. David was standing close behind him, having brought in a lute on which his brother proposed to accompany himself while entertaining the company to a rendering of romantic Scots ballads. Patrick spoke out of the corner of his mouth to him, softly, without taking his eyes off the new arrival.

'It must be,' he said. 'It can be none other. Yonder, Davy – yonder is the key, I'll swear. The golden key I told you of. Yonder enters our fortune, if I mistake not. I had not known that he was . . . thus. So well favoured!'

The Cardinal held up his hand for silence. 'It is my pleasure to announce the Sieur d'Aubigny,' he said in his thin chill voice.

The visitor bowed gracefully all round as the buzz of comment and admiration rose, smiling with seeming great warmth on all, and came forward to meet his statuesque hostess, who had just appeared, rather more fully clad than heretofore, from her boudoir.

'Yes, it is he,' Patrick murmured. 'Esmé Stuart. Methinks I schemed even better than I knew! That one will open many doors, it strikes me – and smoothly. Heigho, Davy – I see us on our way home to Scotland soon enough even to please you!'

After a word or two with the Countess, the Cardinal brought the Sieur d'Aubigny over to Patrick. 'Here is your colleague-to-be, my friend – Monsieur de Gray, from whom we hope for much. The Sieur d'Aubigny, Patrick.'

The two men's eyes met, and held as they bowed. In that great room, indeed, there might have been only the two of them. Then Patrick laughed.

'Esmé Stuart is as peerless as is his fame!' he declared. 'I stand abashed. Scotland, I vow, like Patrick Gray, is to be esteemed fortunate indeed!'

The other's glance was very keen. 'I, too, believe that I have cause for congratulation,' he said, and his voice had a delightful throb of warmth, of patent sincerity. 'Indeed, yes. I also have heard of the Master of Gray – and am nowise disappointed.'

'I am happy, sir. Happy, too, that you have so nobly with-drawn yourself from the dazzling regard of Majesty, to come here!'

The other smiled faintly. 'Queen Catherine's embrace was ... warm!' he said, briefly.

'We heard as much – and honour you the more.'

The Cardinal, who had been joined by the two dukes, took each of the speakers by an elbow. 'We must find somewhere more private than this to talk, gentlemen,' he said. 'You will have much to say to each other. We all have. The Countess will excuse us for a little, I think, Come.'

All the room watched them go – and more than one figure slipped quietly out of that house thereafter. Here was news of which more than one source would pay well to have early word. David was left, with the lute in his hands.

He knew something of this man d'Aubigny, though not enough to account for all this interest. He was in fact one of the Lennox Stewarts, though he spelled his name in the French fashion, which had no letter W, as did Queen Mary. Nephew of the old Earl of Lennox, the former Regent, he was a cousin of Darnley, and therefore second cousin of King Jamie, who was Darnley's son by Mary the Queen. His father had succeeded to the French lordship of d'Aubigny, that had been in the family for five generations, had settled in France and married Anne de La Quelle. The son's reputation as a diplomat and statesman had of recent years grown with meteoric swiftness, and yet most people spoke well of him – no mean feat in such times. D'Aubigny was considered to be one of the most notable and adroit negotiators in an age when dynastic negotiation was involved and intricate as never before. He had only recently returned to Paris from a successful but particularly delicate embassage, in the name of the Estates of France, to the Duke d'Alençon. He was namely as a poet, as well.

Patrick was aiming high, undoubtedly – and presumably with at least some initial success.

David did not see his brother again that night, and the Countess's guests for his birthday party had to do without their ballads. The next morning, however, Patrick was round at Beaton's house in the Rue St Etienne most notably early for him, and was closeted thereafter with the Archbishop for over an hour. When he emerged, it was to summon David to ride with him to the Jesuit headquarters at Château St. Armand, a couple of leagues from the city. What his business was with the Jesuits, he did not divulge.

As they rode, Patrick waxed eloquent on Esmé Stuart. 'There is a man, for you!' he declared. 'Accomplished, witty, excellent company – but keen as a knife. I had not thought to be so fortunate when I proposed this project, Davy. The Devil assuredly, looks after his own!'

'Is it you that the Devil is looking after, Patrick – or Mary the Queen?' David asked.

The other laughed. 'As always, Davy, the doubter! Say, both of us! Perhaps it is his turn to do something for poor Mary – for the good God, you must admit, has not done much for her! Whichever it is, however, this time I think that there is some hope for her.'

'There have been projects and plots before, in plenty.'

'Aye, but this is no mere plot, man. This is a diplomatic campaign – statecraft, as my father would call it – a different matter altogether. I have put a deal of thought into it – and was not that what my lord sent me to France for?'

'Your golden key . . . ?' David prompted.

'Just that. See you – here it is. Morton is no longer Regent, though he still rules Scotland through young James, and the Privy Council which he dominates. But the difference is important, for whatever document has King Jamie's signature is now the law, whereas before it was Morton's signature that counted. Now, James is a sickly boy, and there is no accepted heir to the throne, save only his imprisoned mother – which means that the forces against Morton have no figure round which to rally. Provide that figure, and the country will round on the man who has battened on it for so long . . . with a little encouragement!'

'Provide an heir to the throne! A tall order that, surely?'

'Who better than d'Aubigny – Esmé Stuart? He is the King's cousin. First cousin to the late lamented Darnley.'

'But not of the royal house of Stewart. Of another branch, altogether. Henry Darnley was no true king – only given the Crown Matrimonial by Mary his wife.'

'Yet d'Aubigny is the King's near male relative. There is none nearer in Scotland, I think. And he has royal Stewart blood, too, for he is descended from a daughter of James the Second, on his father's side. He is legitimate – there are plenty otherwise, 'fore God! We could hardly do better, man.'

'You go too fast for me, Patrick,' his brother admitted. 'I do not take you, in this. What has it all to do with getting poor Mary the Queen out of Sheffield Castle, out of an English prison?'

'Plenty, man. Do you not see? Two things are necessary before Elizabeth can be made to release Mary. First, our Scotland must demand it, and seem at least to be prepared to back that demand with an army – Spain and France threatening the same. Scotland will never do that so long as Morton rules, for he is Elizabeth's tool, accepts her gold, and moreover hates Mary. Second, Elizabeth must no longer fear that Mary is planning to take her throne – that they do say is her constant dread, for Mary has more legitimate right to it than she has. But if Mary is no longer apparent heir to the Scottish throne – if our d'Aubigny becomes that – then she is no longer the same menace to Elizabeth. You must see that? Indeed, in order to keep Scotland divided, as is always her endeavour, Elizabeth might well agree to send Mary north to contest her rights against those of Esmé Stuart. If that could be arranged . . . !'

'Lord, Patrick – are you proposing that this d'Aubigny should rob Queen Mary of her right to her own throne, and England's too? For though she abdicated under threat, in favour of James, she is still in blood and before God and man, true Queen of Scots. A high price for her to pay, indeed, for opening her prison doors!'

'*Cordieu*, Davy – let me finish! That is not it, at all. There are more ways of getting past a stone wall than by butting your way through it with your head! Esmé Stuart has no wish to be King of Scots – or of England, either. Nor I to see him that. He is strong for Mary. It is all a device to bring down Morton, and to effect the Queen's release. Once that is gained, he will be Mary's loyalest subject. Think you that the Guises, Mary's cousins, would support my project otherwise?'

'Mmmm. As to that, I do not know,' David doubted. 'But . . . how is all this to be brought about? I have not your nimble wits, Patrick. You must needs explain it.'

'Easily. We work on King Jamie, first. The boy has had an ill life of it – dragged this way and that between one ruffianly lord and another, Moray, Mar, Ruthven, Morton, without father or mother or true friend. Morton treats him no better than one of his own pages, they say. But they also say that the boy is affectionate, if shown a kindness. And shrewd, too, in a way, despite his quaking and drooling. Now, introduce Esmé Stuart, his own cousin, to his Court, to make much of him, flatter him, offer him the affection that he craves – Lord, Davy, don't you see? Jamie will be eating from his hand like a tamed bird, ere long, I'll warrant. We will see to that, the two of us!'

'And Morton?'

'Morton's grip is loosening. James is nearly fourteen. Morton will halt us if he can – but I have plans for that, too. Morton was deep implicated in Darnley's murder. Everyone knows that – but there was never any proof. In Edinburgh that winter, howbeit, I found a witness! Aye, I have a bone to pick with my lord of Morton, you'll mind! I think we can match him.'

'Faith, you fly a high hawk, Patrick! Is nothing too high for you?'

'I use my head, Davy. I told you – where most men are blinded by prejudice and passion, those who can preserve a nice judgment and a clear head may achieve much. Give Esmé Stuart – and your humble brother – a month or two with young Jamie, and we will have a declaration out of him nominating Esmé, his dear cousin, as his heir. And with that in our hands, the rest will follow as night follows day.'

'D'Aubigny is a Catholic, is he not? The Guises would never support him, were he not. Scotland – the Kirk – will never accept a Catholic as heir to the throne.'

'In the first instance, probably not. But we have considered that also. Esmé I am happy to say, is like myself – no fanatic in matters of religion! He is prepared to turn Protestant. This for your ear alone, of course, Davy – for our friends here might not like the sound of it too well!'

David looked with wondering eyes at his handsome brother, sitting his horse like a centaur. 'I do not know that I like it overmuch my own self!' he said.

'Shame on you, man – a good Calvinist like you! *Mortdieu*, you ought to rejoice at another brand like to be plucked from the burning – and such a notable brand, at that!'

The other did not reply to that.

'You will see now, Davy, why I could not just leave all and go home with you, at my father's whistle. Great things are toward, and since it was I who set them in train, I could not well abandon them to others.'

'So nothing now prevents us from going home to Scotland, with this d'Aubigny?'

'Nothing . . . save a letter. A scrap of paper. We cannot reach a king's Court, even such a king as our Jamie, without a royal summons. It is always so. And this has had to be sought with great secrecy, lest Morton get wind of it. We expect it any day now, however, for we have a friend at Court, who is privy to our project . . . and whom Morton himself appointed to be the King's watch-dog!'

'A gey slender thread that, I'd say, to hang your hopes on!'

'Not so. For James Stewart is an ambitious man, likewise – that is his name, a namesake of the King, James Stewart of Ochiltree, Captain of the King's Guard. He perceives that Morton is growing old and will not live for ever, and recognises that it is a wise man who makes due provision for the future! Moreover, he it is who was the witness that I spoke of, to Darnley's murder, and Morton's part therein. Why Morton advanced him, indeed! He was a page of Darnley's, then. A useful man, as I think you will agree.'

'And a traitor too, it seems!'

'The more useful for that, perhaps. But you are over-squeamish, Davy. We must use the weapons that come to our hands. Stewart has sent us word that he is confident of gaining the King's signature to our summons. We await it, daily.'

'So-o-o! You have been busy indeed, Patrick. I wonder how my lord will like it all?'

'My lord may like it, or otherwise, Davy – I care not. I am of age, and my own master now, do not forget.'

'And the siller?'

'Leave the siller to me, lad. I flatter myself that I have quite a nose for the stuff!' Patrick whistled a stave or two tunefully, and then turned to his companion. 'Dammit, Davy, you are a surly dog today! I vow you're no better than a crabbit auld wife.' Even so, he said it with a rueful smile.

David waited for a moment or two before he answered. 'Sorry I am if that is so, Patrick,' he said at length. 'I would not wish it that way – I would not. I daresay it is true. It is but . . . but my fondness for you, see you. You have started on a queer road, a gey queer road, that is like to be long and that we canna see the end of. I'd ask you to think well, Patrick, before you go further on it – out of the fondness that I have for you, I ask you. It is a road I'll not say that I like . . . '

'Whether you like it, or no, Davy, it is *my* road, and I am taking it. I am Master of Gray, thanks to our good father's curious tastes in women – not you! So be it – the Master of Gray will follow his own road. If you will follow it with him, so much the better – for we make a pair, Davy, and that's a fact. But if not, he takes it alone, and none shall stop him. Even you, brother! Is the matter clear?'

The other drew a long sigh, as he looked away from the brother that he loved so well, admired so greatly, and feared for so increasingly – and profoundly regretted, amongst other things, that the days when he could, as a last resort, drive some sense into that beautiful head with his two fists, were most patently gone for ever. 'Clear, aye,' he agreed, sad-voiced.

'Good. And do not sound so doleful, man. I promise you much diversion on our road – oh, a-plenty of it, 'fore God!'

'*Your* road, Patrick – not ours!' the other corrected, levelly, tonelessly. 'Is *that* clear?'

'I am sorry,' Patrick said, after a few moments.

They rode on in silence towards the Château St Armand.

Wherever their chosen roads were to diverge, at least the brothers' road home to Scotland was the same, and that road proved to be no smooth one. In the first place they had to wait for another two weeks before the hoped-for letter from Stewart of Ochiltree arrived. When it did, happily, it enclosed a not very impressive document, signed in an unformed hand by JAMES R, summoning his dear and well-beloved cousin Esmé, Lord of Aubigny, to his Court and Presence at Stirling, this fifteenth day of May in the fifteen hundred and seventy-ninth year of our Lord, together with his right trusty Patrick, Master of Gray, and such others as the said Esmé might bring in his train. Then, a further delay was caused by the non-arrival of six matched Barbary black horses, which the Guise brothers were contributing to the project as a gift for d'Aubigny to present to the young King, who was known to have a fondness for horseflesh, which no doubt he had found more to his taste in his short life than was the human sort. These brutes, though undoubtedly they would greatly help in producing a welcome reception at the Court of Scotland, were considered by the travellers as a major nuisance, not only for the delay, but because of the complications they must inevitably add to an already difficult journey.

Just how difficult it was to be, only began to dawn on David when, one day, Patrick informed him that they would be leaving the next afternoon. Not in any straightforward fashion, however. No farewells were to be taken, and thei baggage was to be sent on secretly ahead of them. The Jesuits were looking after that; they apparently had their own efficient methods. Patrick and David would, in fact, ride almost due south, without d'Aubigny, supposedly on an evening visit to the château of the Duke of Mayenne, and only at dusk would they turn away north-eastwards towards the Meuse and Ardennes and the Low Countries. Meantime, d'Aubigny would have ridden, likewise without baggage, north-westwards towards Picardy, and would also turn east at dusk. Both parties would ride all night, changed into inconspicuous clothing, meeting at Sedan the next day, where their baggage would be waiting them. Sedan, on the border of France and the Netherlands, was in the centre of a Huguenot area, and so should be safe.

David thought all this was quite extraordinary, and taking the Guises' conspiratorial mentality altogether too far. Patrick explained, patiently. The Queen-Mother, Catherine, who still ruled France in the name of her feeble son Henri, was known to be against this project – and devilishly well-informed. She was automatically against any ambitious scheme of the Guises, though they were too strong for her to take open steps against them and she had to play them off against other divided forces in her kingdom. But in this instance she was particularly hostile, because of her abiding hatred of her former daughter-in-law Mary – and, it was suggested, of her personal predilection for Esmé Stuart's delightful company. At any rate, she had frowned on the entire Scottish proposal, forbidding d'Aubigny to leave her country. Catherine de Medici was not a woman to offend lightly, and Esmé was taking a serious risk in this matter. It was presumed that the Queen-Mother would not omit to take further steps to prevent him leaving France.

David thought that, surely, in this Guise country, an escort of the Duke's men would be sufficient to solve this problem?

It was not so easy as that, his brother assured. The Guises could not afford openly to challenge Catherine either. A clash between their soldiers and the royal forces was not to be considered at this stage. The Duke and the Cardinal were not going to embarrass their already delicate position over it – they had too many other irons in the fire. The start of the journey, they insisted, must be secret. That was one reason why the wretched horses were such a nuisance. Magnificent brutes, and six of them all matched, they would draw attention everywhere. So they must be split up. He and David would ride a pair; d'Aubigny and his man would take two more; and the remaining couple would be ridden separately by Guise minions to Sedan. Sedan had been chosen as the meeting-place because, being Protestant, the royal spies were less likely to infest it. Had it not been for the splendid horses, they might all have travelled as Jesuit priests, under the Spaniards' protection, right to Amsterdam.

God, forbid, David declared.

So, the following afternoon, nine weeks less a day after David's arrival at Rheims, he left it again, riding a very much more handsome and spirited mount, and only the Archbishop Beaton and his censorious servitor knew that their heretical guest would not be back again. With Patrick ridiculously over-dressed for travelling, they rode southwards quite openly. Patrick indeed sang tunefully, and for once David joined in occasionally. Though heading in the wrong direction, they were on their way home.

At dusk, they hid in a wood, and Patrick changed out of his gaudy clothes into more suitable attire for riding, of excellent quality still but quiet and sober – David, of course, requiring no such metamorphosis. Thereafter, they rested their mounts for a while, and ate of the good fare provided by the kitchens of the Hôtel de Verlac.

'What does Madame the Countess say to the departure of her
. . . her guest?' David asked, from a full mouth.

'Do you think I informed her?' his brother exclaimed. 'Lord, I would not wish to be in that house when she learns the truth, and that's a fact! Hortense is a woman of somewhat strong emotions, tête Dieu!'

'She has given you much, has she not?'

'Out of her plenty, yes,' he answered lightly. 'And I, for my part, have given her, of my modest store, more than I would!'

'I grieve for you,' David said.

They rode eastwards by north all that night, unchallenged,

through the low foothills of the Ardennes. It was more than twenty leagues, direct, from Rheims to Sedan, and by this route almost half as far again. Their horses were mettlesome and of fine stamina, however, and were not over-taxed. Patrick had had his route very carefully described for him, avoiding centres of population, choosing easy fords for the many rivers, and following roads which even in the summer dark they would be unlikely to lose. By sunrise they had crossed the Aisne, and by mid-forenoon were in Sedan, a strongly-defended city that allowed them entry as a pair of good Scots Protestants, Patrick's silver crucifix consigned to his pocket.

They found a modest tavern near the famous seminary that was already a place of pilgrimage for the Protestant world, and lay quietly there all day, resting themselves and their horses. In the late afternoon David slipped out on a reconnaissance, on foot, as the least conspicuous, and duly returned with the satisfactory information that he had located the Three Feathers Inn, that Aubigny and his man Raoul were there, with all four black horses. The city gates shut at sun-down, so they must all leave fairly soon, and by different gates. It was arranged that they should join up a couple of kilometres upstream where there was a passable ford over the Meuse during the dry summer months, that was not likely to be guarded. For this was the frontier. Once across the river, they were in the Netherlands.

Since to leave Sedan for open country immediately before the gates were shut might seem suspicious, they rode out, by the same gate through which they had entered, in the early evening, and turned southwards, unquestioned. There was considerable woodland along the riverside in that direction, in which they could wait until the shades of night made an approach to their ford as safe as might be.

While they waited thus, Patrick, after a certain amount of throat-clearing, came out with an intimation. 'Davy,' he said, his glance elsewhere, 'now that we are to be travelling in company with the Sieur d'Aubigny, I will have to ask you to address me with, h'm, less familiarity than is our usual, I fear. In his eyes, in the eyes of the world, you are but my secretary and . . . and attendant. I have told him that we are foster-brothers, but that is not a relationship that is much understood outside Scotland, I find. For the Master of Gray to be overfriendly with a . . . a retainer, might seem strange, you see . . . '

'You could always tell him the truth,' David mentioned, stiffly.

'I do not think that is necessary, or advisable.'

'I see. You do not wish me to call you my lord, or Excellency, by any chance?'

'Do not be stupid, Davy! Sir will be adequate. And another small matter. Since undoubtedly d'Aubigny's man will ride a little way behind him, not beside him, it will look a little strange if you do not do the same. So, hereafter, we shall ride two by two, myself with d'Aubigny, and you with his man. You understand?'

'Perfectly . . . sir!'

'It means nothing, Davy – between ourselves. You see that, surely? Just a . . . a convenience.'

'It means a deal, I think – the end of a chapter, brother. But so be it.'

When, a little later, they rode out of that woodland on their way through the gloaming, up-river, Patrick remarking that it looked like rain and a dark night, turned to find that his brother was not at his side. He was riding fully three lengths behind. When the former reined up, so did the latter.

'There is no need for this – yet,' Patrick said, frowning.

'Practice, they do say, makes for perfection,' the other observed. 'It would be a sorry matter, later, if through habit, I . . . inconvenienced you, sir.'

They rode on in silence thereafter.

It was David, however, who presently broke that silence. 'I think that they are behind us – the Lord d'Aubigny,' he said. 'I think that I heard the sound of hooves.'

They halted, and listened, but heard nothing save the murmur of the river and the rustle of leaves.

A little further, David again spoke. 'I heard it again. Or not so much heard, as sensed the beat of hooves. Many hooves.'

'It matters not,' Patrick decided, peering back into the gloom. A thin smirr of rain blew chill in their faces. 'The ford must be no more than a kilometre or so ahead. We will wait for them there. It may be that they are riding further inland.'

'Or others are,' David suggested.

However, when they reached the ford, easily identified by a ruined castle which had once guarded it on the French side, d'Aubigny and his servant were already there. They had all the baggage with them, loaded on the two extra blacks as well as on a pair of other beasts. D'Aubigny was a little anxious, for while waiting they had thought that they had heard the drumming of hooves, likewise. Patrick, however, was not of the anxious sort, and pointed out that there could be other parties than their own travelling war-torn France by night. But let them get across the ford, at once, by all means.

The crossing, in fact, was not difficult, for though the river was wide, the bed was of gravel, and the water never came higher than the horses' bellies.

At the far side there was a broad flood-belt of reedy level water-meadows, dotted with heavy foliaged trees that loomed monstrously out of the gloom. It was raining now fairly heavily, but there were no complaints on that score; the consequent darkness of the night was the more welcome. D'Aubigny, at least, let out a sigh of relief as they left the river behind.

'We are clear of the beloved France, at any rate!' he declared. 'Safe now, I think – if, *mort de diable*, there was ever any danger, in the first place!'

It was on the tip of David's tongue to remind him that what had been so easy for them to cross, was not likely to present any insuperable obstacle to possible pursuers – but he recollected his due place in the company, and kept silence.

It was only a few moments thereafter, however, before the Seigneur's satisfaction was rudely shattered. A rumbling pounding sound from over to their left turned all heads. The noise grew, and out of the mirk a dark solid mass seemed to thunder down upon them, across the grassland, on a broad front, the ground shaking under its approach.

'*Mortdieu* – back to the river!' d'Aubigny cried, tugging out his sword. 'It is an ambuscade!'

'No – forward!' Patrick shouted, 'This way!' and began to spur in the opposite direction.

David, behind with the man Raoul and the led-horses, peered, cursed, and then, straightening up in his saddle, laughed aloud.

'Mercy on us, it's just stirks!' he called out. 'Cattle-beasts, just. Come back, will you . . . sirs!'

Distinctly sheepishly the two noblemen reined in and returned, from their alternative directions. The meadowland, it seemed, was dotted with grazing cattle, and a group of them, as often happens at night, had come charging over inquisitively to inspect the new arrivals, and now stood a few yards off in a puffing, blowing, interested line.

In dignified silence the travellers moved on, David and the other attendant well in the rear, with an escort of lowing livestock behind.

'Drive those brutes away,' Patrick shouted back. 'We do not want the whole world joining in!'

Beyond the meadows, the track eastwards rose up a gentle hillside through thick woodland. It was very dark in there.

After making a brief effort to discourage the cattle, David and the man Raoul were riding after their principals, when, mounting the first rise, David in the lead, abruptly drew rein. Before them, the track dipped down fairly steeply through a slight clearing, and this suddenly came alive with movement and noise and the clash of steel. Here were no cattle, but armed men assuredly, converging on both sides upon the two noblemen.

'Halt, in the name of the King!' rang out a peremptory command. 'Stand, I charge you!' The skriegh of drawn swords, many swords, was very audible.

David's hand flew to his own sword-hilt as Raoul came pressing forward.

'*Allons*!' the other cried. 'It is the Valois! *Peste* – come! Quickly!'

Almost David dug in his spurs to charge forward also – but on an instant's decision, his hand left his sword-hilt to grab at Raoul's arm instead. 'No!' he jerked. 'No – not now! It is useless. There are a dozen – a score. Too many for us. Better to wait. Wait, man! They will not see us here, in the trees. Wait, I say!'

'*Mon Dieu* – fool! They need us. Can you not see? Are you a coward? Come – *avant*!' And shaking off David's hand, the other spurred forward, drawing his sword.

Tight-lipped, David watched him go. But only for a moment. Then, tugging at his reins violently, and dragging his mount's head right round, he went clattering off whence he had just come, perforce pulling the four led beasts behind him.

Back down into the meadows he galloped, to the cattle which he had so lately driven off.

That main group was still fairly tightly bunched nearby, but many others were scattered in the vicinity. In a wide sweep David circled these, whooping, driving them inwards. Times innumerable, as a boy, he had herded my lord's cattle thus on pony-back, amongst the infinitely larger levels of the Carse of Gowrie. Skilfully he rounded up the startled snorting brutes, sword out to beat flatly against broad heaving rumps, the four led-horses by their very presence assisting. How many beasts he collected he did not know – possibly thirty or forty. There were more available, but he had no time to gather them. Back to the track through the woods he drove the protesting herd, and the steaming stench of them was like a wall before him.

Up the track between the tree-clad banks the cattle steamed, jostling, stumbling, half-mounting each other's backs, eyes gleaming redly, hooves pounding, and at their backs David Gray rode and beat his way and yelled.

At the top of the slope, he redoubled his efforts. Through the mirk and steam he could just make out the horsemen still clustered about the track below him, presumably staring up. Onwards down the hill he drove his plunging herd, in thundering confused momentum, and at the pitch of his lungs he bellowed in French, above their bellowing.

'God and the Right! God and the Right! A Bourbon! A Bourbon! A Condé!'

He kept it up as though his life depended upon it, straining his voice until it cracked. These were Huguenot slogans, he knew, heard on many a bloody field; the King's men below would know them all too well.

Whether indeed the soldiers down there were deceived into thinking that here was a large squadron of Huguenot cavalry bearing down upon them, in the darkness of the wood, or recognised it merely as a concentrated charge of many angry cattle, is not to be known. Either way, however, it was no pleasant thing to stand and await, in a narrow place. Right and left and backwards, the horsemen scattered, bolting in all directions to get out of the way. Shouts, vaguely heard above the thunder of hooves and the bellowing of beasts, sounded confused and incoherent, pistol-shots cracked out – but David's bawlings undoubtedly were the loudest, the most determined.

Down over the site of the ambush he came pounding, behind his irresistible battering-ram of stampeding cattle. 'To me! To me!' he shouted, now. 'Patrick! D'Aubigny! To me!' He yelled it in English, of course, in the excitement.

Peering urgently about him in the darkness and steam, David sought for his companions. He saw vaguely three horsemen struggling together part-way up the bank on his right, and glimpsed flashing steel. If they were indeed struggling, one of his own people must surely be included? Swinging his black off the track, and followed inevitably by the impressive tail of four laden pack-horses he headed up the bank, sword waving.

One horseman broke away from the little group as he came up, and went off higher, lashing his mount in patent anxiety to be elsewhere. The two remaining horses were very dark, and to his great relief, David discovered their riders to be d'Aubigny and his servant, the former supporting the latter who was evidently wounded. Both were disarmed.

'Quick – get down to the track! After the cattle!' David ordered. 'Hurry, before they rally. Where is Patrick?'

'I think that I saw him bolting – away in front,' d'Aubigny told him. 'In front of the cattle. Raoul's hurt. Run through the shoulder . . .'

'I . . . am . . . well enough,' the man gasped, clutching his shoulder.

'Can you ride? Without aid?' David demanded.

'Yes. I can . . . ride.'

'Quickly, then. After the cattle.'

Back down to the track they plunged, to go racing after the herd. Another horseman joined them almost immediately. In the gloom, assuming that it was Patrick, David was about to exclaim thankfully, when he perceived that the horse, though dark-coloured, had white markings. Thereafter, a slash of his sword in front of the newcomers' face was sufficient to discourage him as to the company he was keeping, and he hastily pulled out in consequence.

David began to shout Patrick's name, now, again and again, as they pounded along. His cries were answered, here and there, from the wooded banks – but none were in the voice for which he listened. It was not long before they made up on the cattle, the momentum of whose rush was beginning to flag.

The creatures slowed down still more notably as they came to an open glade, wide and comparatively level, where there were no banks to contain the track. Right and left many of the leading beasts swung off, others plunged on, others again wheeled and wavered, In a few moments all was a confusion of veering uncertain bullocks, snorting and panting, forward impetus lost. And at last, above the din, David's calling was answered. High and clear, from their right front, could be heard the cry 'Davy! Davy!' The cattle were not alone in pulling aside off that trench of a track, at first opportunity.

Swiftly David answered his brother's call, and, urging the others to follow him, pressed and beat a way into and through the milling mass of beasts.

Some few of the bullocks still went plunging before them, but the riders won through the main bulk of the bewildered animals – and there, in front of them, to the right, was a group of apparently four horsemen, waiting. Directly at these they charged – and the group was scarcely to be blamed for breaking up before them promptly, for though they were but three men, one armed and with one wounded, the others would be likely to perceive only a menacing mass of mixed cattle, horses and shouting men bearing down upon them. Moreover, Patrick, swordless, took a hand, kicking at other horses' flanks and lashing out with his fists.

Chaos seemed complete – but was not. The four re-united men, with the pack-horses, at least had purpose and a kind of order to them. David in the lead, they bored onwards through the trees unhalting, lashing their mounts, trending back towards the track and shedding their remaining bullocks, one by one, as they went. Thankfully they felt, presently, the beaten firmness of the roadway beneath their horses' hooves, and turned north-eastwards along it.

Only hard riding remained for them now – and they were almost certainly better mounted than would be any pursuers, on these Barbary blacks. The wounded Raoul was their weakness, but the sturdy Breton snarled that he was well enough, and would ride to hell if need be. Crouching low in their saddles, they settled down ot it.

Whether or no they were in fact pursued, they never knew. They had covered many kilometres of that road, and passed through a couple of either sleeping or deserted villages, before they deemed it safe to pull up, to attend to Raoul's wounded shoulder. About them, when they did halt, the night was wetly silent. Dismounting, David put his ear to the ground. No hint or throb of beating hooves came to him.

'*Dieu de Dieu* – we are safe, I think!' d'Aubigny panted. 'The King's men – or, rather, the Queen's – will not dare follow us far into this Namur, surely? *Peste*, but we were not so clever, Patrick!'

'I' faith, we were not!' Patrick agreed. 'Who would have thought that they would have followed down *this* side of the river? They must have known of our ruse, all along, but not dared to touch us near Sedan itself.'

'Or else got word of us in Sedan, and sent parties to watch the far sides of all the fords of the Meuse. It would be them we heard while waiting for you. *Pardieu*, Catherine is well-served, Patrick!'

'Aye – and so are we, I think! Davy – my thanks!'

David, examining the man Raoul's wound, shrugged. 'That

is unnecessary, your honour,' he said briefly. 'A mere exercise in farmyard tactics. I was, as it were, born to such!'

Patrick bit his lip.

David turned to d'Aubigny. 'My lord, I think that this hero of yours will survive. The bleeding is almost stopped. A clean thrust, I'd say – painful, but with no serious damage done.'

The Breton muttered something beneath his breath.

'Good. As well, praise the saints! Raoul, *mon ami*, it was a gallant attempt . . . though lacking in finesse, perhaps. Though who am I to judge, who did naught but lose my sword! Here is the paladin! Patrick, your Davy is a man of parts, I swear. That was notably done. He has a quick wit and a stout heart, damned Calvinist or none!'

'He is my brother,' the Master of Gray said slowly, deliberately. 'My elder brother.'

'But, of course!'

'No – not just my foster-brother, Esmé. My father's eldest son – only, conceived the wrong side of the blanket!.

'As though I did not guess as much, man! All Rheims, taking a look at the pair of you, said the same.'

Patrick's breath seemed to take the wrong route to his lungs, somehow, and all but choked him.

'He has my gratitude, at all events,' d'Aubigny went on. 'Here is my hand, Master Davy Gray. I shall not forget.'

'I thank you, sir. Do you not think that we should be riding on, nevertheless . . . if your lordships will forgive my presumption?'

'Davy, let it be, man!' Patrick all but pleaded. 'I am sorry.'

'He is right, Patrick. If Raoul is fit enough, we should no longer linger here. We cannot be sure that they will not follow us. This town, Montlierre, can be no more than a league or two ahead, where we are to place ourselves in the hands of one of Philip's captains. Until then, we cannot be assured of our safety.'

Getting started, thereafter, was difficult, with Patrick holding back so that his brother might ride alongside, and David doing likewise so that he should lie suitably behind – d'Aubigny looking on, eyebrows raised.

That, indeed, was to be the pattern of their subsequent journeying through the Low Countries to the sea at Amsterdam. The Guise letter of credentials, and the noble travellers' Catholic eminence and charm, might be sufficient to gain them safe conduct from Philip of Spain's occupying forces, but more than anything of the sort was necessary to soften entirely a stiff Gray neck.

Possibly the miller's daughter of Inchture had had almost as good a conceit of herself as had my lord of Gray.

The Scots are like that, of course.

Chapter Seven

THE brothers' long road homewards together finally parted at
the port of Leith, in the estuary of the Forth and in sight of the
great rock-girt castle of Edinburgh. Patrick, to the end, urged
that David should stay with him, pleading the need, both of
himself and d'Aubigny, for a secretary and esquire in their
ambitious project. But David was adamant. His road was not
Patrick's; he had to render the account of his stewardship to my
lord, who had sent him; moreover, he had a wife and a bairn
awaiting him at Castle Huntly, from whom he had been parted
overlong already. He had no desire for a life of courts and cities
and intrigue, anyway – his schoolroom and country affairs were
amply to his taste. It was Castle Huntly for him, forthwith.

Patrick could have gone to Castle Huntly also, with d'Aubigny,
and from there prosecuted the very necessary spying out of the
land and enquiries before they descended upon the Court of
King James at Stirling – for of course their appearance must be
very carefully arranged and timed, with prior secrecy vital, lest
Morton and his friends should take steps to nip all in the bud;
but Patrick preferred to avoid his father's house meantime, and
claimed with some reason that Castle Huntly was too remotely
placed for gaining the essential gossip and information about
the Court and the Douglases, and for making contact with the
right people, to enable them to make their move at the best
moment. He fancied rather his cousin Logan's house of
Restalrig, between Leith and Edinburgh, for a start at least,
where they could roost incognito meantime. Surely, never did
two more incongruously and conspicuously eye-catching
incognito-seekers land on a Scottish shore, Barbary blacks
and all.

So David bade God-speed to his brother, with urgent but not
very hopeful requests that Patrick watch his step for sweet
mercy's sake, and offer as few cavalier challenges to fate as in
him lay, and thereafter transferred himself to a coasting vessel
which would sail for Dysart and Dundee at the next tide. He
frowned a little as he went, for in his baggage he now carried an
expensively handsome jewelled clasp for Mariota and a
brilliantly dressed Flanders puppet for little Mary, just handed

to him by Patrick, which must greatly outshine the length of cambric and the roll of ribbon that were to be his own humble gifts.

David rode on a very third-rate horse next day, after the Guise blacks, through fields of ripening corn in the fertile Carse, into a sinking golden early August sun, and his heart was full. Here was his own colourful matchless land, so much more beautiful and diversified than any that he had seen on his wanderings, with the blue estuary of the Tay, the green straths and yellow fields, the hills everywhere as background, rolling or rocky, cloaked in woods or decked in bracken and heather, and beyond all, the blue ramparts of the great mountains. He had scarcely realised how much he loved it all. Even the tall frowning castle on its jutting rock had its loveliness for him, the raw red stone-work mellowed by the sunset; or perhaps it was only what lay within its massive walls that made it beautiful for him.

He clattered into the courtyard, under the stern gatehouse, flung himself off his mount, and went racing up the stairway of the little schoolroom tower, to hurl open the door of Mariota's room – and find it empty, deserted. Not even their bed was there. As though an icy hand had clutched him, he ran back, down into the yard. A single man-at-arms sat in a sunny corner, cleaning harness. Of him he demanded where was his wife, his daughter?

'Och, they bide up in the main keep noo, Davy,' he was told. 'They're fine, man – fine. My lord's had them up there beside him a couple o' months syne, for the company, ye ken. Sakes – no' so fast, Davy. They're no' there, the noo. They're doon below – doon in the fruit garden, pulling berries . . .'

David was off hot-foot, through the postern-gate and down the steep stepped path cut in the side of the rock to the little hanging garden, dug out of a flaw in the cliff-face, with soil laboriously carried up from the plain below. The woman stooping over the berry-bushes, and the child at play beside her, made a pleasing picture in the chequered gold and shadow of the sunset.

Mariota heard him coming, and turning, stared. Then, with a cry, she dropped her basket, sadly spilling the fruit, and came running, arms wide. 'Davy! Davy my heart!' she sobbed.

Hungrily, joyfully, he took her to him, swinging her up off her feet, kissing away the tears of gladness, murmuring incoherent broken endearments, follies, questions. Tightly they clung, the man's fierce possessive strength a haven, a benison to her, the woman's warm rounded comeliness an exultation and a promise to him – until the insistent tugging at the top of his dusty riding-boot made David look down, to sweep up the child in one arm, laughing to her chuckle as she thrust a fat raspberry into his mouth. So they stood, under the towering walls, for the moment in bliss that the angels might envy.

Still holding the child, David put Mariota from him, a little. 'My dear,' he said, considering her. 'You are the fairest bonniest sight that my eyes have seen since I left this place, and that's a fact!'

'Not . . . not bonnier than the fine French ladies, Davy?'

He snorted. 'Them! The brazen painted hizzies! None of them had the looks of you.'

That was true. Mariota, at nineteen, was grown a very lovely young woman, fresh-coloured, gentle-eyed, tall and well-built, with nothing meagre or skimped about her. Something of this last, indeed, drew rueful comment from her husband now.

'At the least, lass, you have not dwined away for missing me! You are getting fat, I swear!'

She coloured, and dropped her glance. ' 'Tis . . . 'tis just that you . . . that Patrick is not the only . . . that you will be a father indeed, Davy . . . '

Here was further cause for embrace and joyful acclaim, more vehement on David's part, perhaps, than he realised. But in the midst of it, Mariota's gaze was over his shoulder, raised to scan the castle rock.

'Patrick?' she asked. 'Is he here? You have brought him?'

'No,' he told her briefly. 'He is at Edinburgh. My dear, my pigeon, my heart's darling – here is cheer indeed! Och, lassie – it's grand! I did not know . . . '

'He is not come, then – Patrick?' she said. 'But .. he is well? There is nothing wrong . . . ?'

He let go of her. 'Aye. He is well enough, never fear.' Rather abruptly he raised high the child whom he had still held within an arm. 'And see this fine lady! Is she not a fondling, an amoret? And as fat getting as her mother!'

Little Mary Gray was now four years old. She was a tiny laughing jewel of a creature, all lightness and beauty and dainty taking ways, and so uncannily like Patrick as to catch the breath. Though face and hands were stained with raspberry juice and her clothing was far from fine, she yet presented an extra-ordinary impression of grace and breeding and delicate enchantment. Emotions chased themselves across David's blunt features as he studied her.

'She is a cozener and a charmer, that one. Like . . . like her Uncle Patrick! Davy – why has he not come home with you? Is he coming soon? How does he look, now?'

'Older.'

'Aye, no doubt. It is three years and more since I have seen him.'

'And then, were you not only too glad to see the back of him?' David had not intended to say that.

'Yes, yes. Of course. I . . . I hate him!'

'You do not,' David said, heavily. 'Any more than do I? He sent you many good wishes – both of you. And gifts, too.'

'Ah – he did? Gifts, Davy? For me? For us?'

'Aye.' Her husband sighed. 'They are up there. Come you up, and get them.' A grey cloud seemed to have come over the face of the sun.

Up in the courtyard again, David handed over Patrick's jewel to Mariota and the doll to Mary – and neither having ever received such a present before, or dreamed of such a happening, their delight and excitement knew no bounds. In the circumstances, David let his own humbler gifts of cambric and ribbon more or less go in as make-weight, not even emphasising that they were from himself and not just more of Patrick's largesse. He was not good at this sort of thing.

The shadow passed, of course. Soon smiles and laughter were back.

David would have preferred to be back in their own little room in the corner-tower rather than in the fine chamber in which Lord Gray had installed the pair, but Mariota declared that it was a great improvement and that my lord had insisted on the move, saying that they must not be lonely whilst David was away. It was Mary, of course, who was at the bottom of it all. She and her grandfather were inseparables, and the child could do what she would with the irascible nobleman – which was more than could anyone else alive.

Lord Gray came back from Perth later in the evening, somewhat drunk, but loud in his demands to see his chicken, his little trout, his moppet Mary. The sight of David, however, especially minus Patrick, sobered him rapidly, and his son was haled into my lord's sanctum above the hall forthwith, the door shut, and questions hurled at him, thickly, incoherently, but with no lack of point or vehemence.

When he could make himself heard, David sought to explain.

He did his best for Patrick. 'He sends you all respectful duty and greetings, my lord – all reverence. But his affairs make it necessary for him to bide near to Edinburgh, for the nonce . . .'

'*His* affairs! A pox – *I* sent for him to come here, did I no'?'

'Aye, sir, but . . .'

'But nothing, man! I didna have him brought home to idle and bemischief himsel' in Edinburgh. You were to bring him here . . .'

'My lord, I brought him nowhere. Patrick is a man, now – of age, and, and his own counsellor. He came back to Scotland at your request, not at my bringing.'

'But with my siller, burn him!'

'Not even that.' David unbuckled the heavy money-belt that he had worn around his middle for so long, and put it down on his lordship's table, the solid weight of it thudding thereon significantly. 'There is your siller back, my lord – or the most of it. What has been spent of it was spent on *my* journeying – none on Patrick. He spends his own moneys now.'

'How may that be? Whence comes his siller – a young jack-daw with no penny to his name?'

David cleared his throat. 'He is that no longer, my lord. The years in France have changed him, almost beyond recognition. You will scarce know him. He has not wasted his time. You sent him to learn statecraft, and he has done it. He is very close to the Guises and Archbishop Beaton, and deep in their affairs. They trust him, wholly. He bears their despatches to the King, from the Duke and the Cardinal . . .'

'The more fools them, if they sink their money in Patrick, 'fore God!'

David did not comment on that.

'To the King, you said? To the Council, you mean, man?'

'Not so, sir – to the King. To young King Jamie, himself. And he has brought back with him the King's cousin. The Sieur d'Aubigny.'

He heard his father's breath catch. 'D'Aubigny? You mean . . . John Stewart's son, that was brother to old Lennox? Whe-e-ew!' All traces of intoxication were gone from Gray now. He stared at his informant. 'That man–some Frenchified outlandish name he has . . . aye, Esmé – that man, in Scotland, could be gunpowder, no less! He is ower near the throne, for safety.'

'I think that is why Patrick brought him. Patrick, I'd say,

finds gunpowder to his taste, my lord!' David told him, a little grimly.

His father took a limping turn or two about the room. 'I' faith, this requires thinking on, Davy,' he said. Then, swiftly, 'Does Morton know?'

'We hope . . . Patrick hopes not.'

'God's Body – *I* hope not, likewise! For if he does, he'll have the heads off both o' them! The young fool – to have brought that man here! It is as good as treason – or so Morton will have it! Don't you see it, man? This d'Aubigny, in Scotland, is like a dagger at James's throat . . . or a poison in his cup, more like! There is none nearer to the Crown's succession, in blood, save only that child Arabella in England. Morton will see him as a threat to his power over the King – and no man is that, in Scotland, and lives!'

David bit his lip. He had not realised what great danger Patrick had thrust himself into, with d'Aubigny. Put thus, he saw it clearly – and the picture of Morton that rose in his mind's eye, hurling that goblet smashing down the length of the table in the hall below, did nothing to soothe his new perception. 'He is as strong as ever – my lord of Morton?' he asked. 'Now that he is no longer Regent . . . ?'

'Foul fall him – of course he is! Who else, think you, rules? That slobbering thirteen-year-old boy, Jamie? Others who have tried are in their graves – Atholl, Mar, Lennox himself, Hamilton, even Moray. Morton's hand, if you look for it, you will find in the deaths of them all. He has the Council in his pocket still. Me, I havena dared show my face in the streets o' Edinburgh or Stirling for three years, man – no' since yon wedding-night. I never ride abroad with less than fifty men, for my life's sake. And I – *I* have done nothing against the man, save draw breath! And be a friend o' Mary the Queen, whom he hates. And now – this! Patrick hurt Morton sore, that night. Bringing this d'Aubigny to Scotland, I tell you, is as good as his death-warrant! The young fool!'

'I . . . I hope not, sir.' David shook his head. 'I misliked it, my own self. I said that he was flying too high a hawk . . . But I had not realised . . . Patrick believes, see you, that through d'Aubigny he may clip Morton's wings – aye, and gain Queen Mary's release also . . . '

'Precious soul o' God! Does the nestling clip the eagle's wings? What harebrained folly is this? What bairns' game have

III

they been teaching him in France? Statecraft he was to learn . . . !'

'The plot seemed to be well worked out – with the Cardinal and the Duke and Beaton. The Jesuits, too, were in it, deep. They have sent money with him – much money, I believe . . . '

'Eh? Money? In Patrick's white hands? God be good – they must be lacking their wits!' But my lord's tone of voice had altered a little. He limped to the table, and picked up the heavy money-belt, weighing it in his hand, abstractedly. 'Jesuit money, you say? So that airt the wind blows! That is why he didna need his auld father's siller! Our Patrick's found bigger fools than himsel', eh?'

'Patrick is no fool, my lord, believe me. These years have done more for him than you realise . . . '

'Nevertheless, Davy, he has run his fool's head into a noose, here and now, by bringing this d'Aubigny to Scotland. Morton, with the power o' the Crown and the help o' Elizabeth's gold, holds the land fast.' Gray had dropped the money-belt and resumed his anxious pacing, and in that gesture David thought that he read proof that my lord, harsh-tongued and scornful as he might seem, was in fact fonder of Patrick than he cared to admit, more concerned for his gay and handsome son and heir than for the silver that he talked so much about.

'Morton has his enemies,' David said.

'Aye – in plenty. But they are powerless, disunited. That I ken to my cost.'

'That is one reason, I think, why Patrick has brought d'Aubigny – to give them someone to rally round . . . '

'A headless corpse will no' rally that many!' the older man declared, shortly. 'And that is what he'll be – and Patrick with him. As a threat to the Throne – treason . . . '

'Can Morton claim that? They have a letter from King James, summoning them to his Court.'

'They have?' Gray halted. 'Lord, how did they win that?'

'Through one, James Stewart of Ochiltree, Captain of the King's Guard – a friend of Patrick's.'

Unwilling admiration showed itself on Lord Gray's sagging face. 'So-o-o! Young Stewart? Old Ochiltree's son, and good-brother to John Knox! He is one o' Morton's own jackals.'

'One who is prepared to turn on the old lion, it seems.'

'Or to sell Patrick to him!'

'M'mmm. At least, he got the summons out of King Jamie.'

'For a price?'

'Presumably. Patrick did not inform me. But the summons to Court will make it difficult for Morton to accuse them of treason to the Crown, surely?'

'Maybe. But Morton has more than treason to his armoury. Poison, the dagger, a troop with swords, the cudgels o' a mob – it is all the same to Douglas. And there is no Glamis now, to lift a hand to help save Patrick, as Chancellor – even if yon business of his Elizabeth hadna scunnered him. He's dead. Slain, a year back. He left a new-born heir, thank God – so at the least the Master is no' the lord . . .'

'What is to be done, then? Patrick must be warned. I think that he does not understand all this, perhaps.'

'Warned, aye – if it isna too late. You must go to him at once, Davy. Bring him back here, secretly. Safer here, until we can make other plans.'

'And d'Aubigny with him?'

'A pox – no! Do you want us *all* brought low? Besieged in this castle? No – yon one must leave the country again, forthwith. Back where he came from, on the first ship for France. The only way for Master Esmé to come to Scotland is at the head o' five thousand French soldiers. God's name, I'd welcome him then!'

'I do not see them doing it, my lord – not after coming thus far . . .'

'Then you must convince them, Davy. Show them the truth. I think maybe this d'Aubigny will take heed for his own neck, if Patrick doesna. I will write you a letter for them.'

'Even so . . .'

'Davy, man, would you have your brother die, and no' lift a hand to save him?' It was not often that my lord referred to their brotherhood.

'No,' David sighed. 'As you will, sir.'

'Tomorrow, then. You'll be off in the morning. And pray sweet Jesu that you are in time.'

'And if they will not heed me? If Patrick will not come?'

'You will send me word at once, and bide with him to try to keep him out o' the worst trouble. Thank the good God that you at the least have a sensible level head on your shoulders, Davy.'

'Much good it does me!' that young man declared, sombrely, and went back to his wife. One night only, they were to have.

That was the homecoming for which David Gray had waited months.

Chapter Eight

'MY lord is getting old, I think,' Patrick laughed. 'He was
bolder once, if reports do not lie. Mary's friend in more than
mere name! We must not encourage his unworthy fears, Davy.
But we could nowise do as he says, in any case, for all is in train.
Events move – they move. Or are moved! And, faith, we cannot
turn them back, if we would!'

David turned heavily, determinedly, at his most levelly bull-
like, to d'Aubigny. 'You, my lord – you have heard. My lord of
Gray believes that you may have more regard to your own neck
than perhaps has Patrick here. He bade me tell you that Morton
is bound to win – and the penalty for losing will be your head.
The heads of both of you. Morton still rules here – and kills.'

'Yes, Esmé, pay your due heed to our good sober councillor!'
Patrick mocked.

D'Aubigny smiled. '*Mon cher* Davy, I appreciate your care
and thought for us. And that of my lord of Gray. But we do not
esteem your terrible Morton quite so terribly as do you. An
angry vengeful savage, *vraiment* – like a bear. But even bears
may be baited – when they provide sport for folk with more wits
than themselves. I think Morton may well provide that sport.
Mortdieu, even now, he begins to chase our ban-dogs, rather
than ourselves!'

Patrick nodded. 'You see, we have not idled, Davy. We hope,
before nightfall, to have a messenger from the Borders bring us
the word that the bear has struck – at thin air. Then, heigho – it
is Stirling for us, and the sunrise of youthful majesty!'

Mystified, David looked from one to the other. They were
closeted in a room of the small but strong tower-house of
Restalrig, the home of Patrick's cousin Logan, above its little
loch, a mere mile from the royal but empty palace of Holyroodhouse. From its windows they looked in one direction upon the
long smoky skyline of Edinburgh, climbing up its spine of hill
from palace to stern dominating castle; in the other, out over the
smiling fields and woods and links of Lothian, down to the green
cone of North Berwick Law and the scalloped sandy bays of the
silver Forth. It was five days since their arrival from France, for
it had taken David longer than he had hoped to make his return

passage from Dundee.

Patrick explained. 'A well-lined pocket, I have found, will achieve much, Davy – especially in a land where so many men hate Morton. Two days ago, Cousin Rob Logan headed south for the Borders, where he has friends as you know – and Morton has both unfriends and lands. Lands in upper Teviotdale – Hawick and beyond. Around those parts are many Scotts and Turnbulls and the like – mere Border freebooters and rapscallions, but with a grudge against Morton for the Warden of the Marches he has set over them . . . and grievously short of siller, as ever. Last night, sundry houses of Morton's would be burning, I fear – so barbarous are the natives of those parts! This morning, at anyrate, Morton rode southwards hot-foot from his palace of Dalkeith – that we know from an eye-witness. Since it is his own Douglas lands that smoke, he has not just sent some underling. We but wait to hear that he is safely chasing Scotts and Turnbulls over the moss-hags south of Eildon – then Stirling and the King!'

'Our bear, Monsieur Davy, is decoyed, you see.'

'For how long?' David asked.

'Until, no doubt, he hears from the Master of Glamis, or other, that King Jamie has taken into his royal arms his dear cousin Esmé Stuart. Then, methinks he will come north again without undue delay! And by then, Davy, I hope that we will have a right royal reception awaiting the good Morton – with the aid of the Captain of the King's Guard. You see, we have not been entirely laggard, or as innocently witless, as our potent sire believes.'

David nodded slowly. 'I see,' he said. 'You will not give up your ploy, then, Patrick? You will not do as my lord says, this time either?'

'I fear not, Davy. Would you?'

'I do not know,' David admitted, honestly.

Patrick laughed, and jumped over to clap his brother on the back. 'Good for you, man – that from you is encouragement indeed! All will be well now, Esmé – for our Davy does not know! So usually, he knows all too clearly – and always against what I desire! It only remains for you to come with us, Davy, to Stirling, and our cause is as good as won! Be our secretary, guide, and mentor – aye, and our fervent intercessor with Scotland's Protestant God – and who can best us?'

David eyed his gay and beautiful brother steadily. These were my lord's own orders also, should he fail to get Patrick to abandon his project. It seemed that there was to be no connubial bliss for him at Castle Huntly yet awhile. 'I'll come with you if I must,' he said. 'Though, God knows, I'd rather be otherwise.'

'Bravo! Esmé, you hear? The flagon, man. We'll drink to this, *tête dieu!* And now, Davy – what of the fair Mariota? And of that exquisite daughter of yours . . . ?'

D'Aubigny and David sat their mounts before the main gate-house of the great fortress of Stirling, with all the grey town in steps and stairs beneath them, the winding Forth, a mere serpent of a river here, coiling below, and the soaring ramparts of the Highland mountains filling the vista to north and west as though to make but doll's fortifications of these man-made ramparts nearer at hand. The six Barbary blacks, gallant, groomed and gleaming, sidled and stamped at their backs, for now, advisedly, the travellers bestrode less splendid beasts. The massive gates stood open before them, guarded by bored and insolent men-at-arms clad in the royal livery of Scotland – King Jamie's gaolers. The noon-day sun shone down on them, and on a fair scene. David wondered how many more such noons they might live to see.

At length Patrick came back down the cobbled roadway within the castle, strolling at ease and laughing, and with him a tall and resplendent figure, richly clad in gold-inlaid half-armour, with the red Lion Rampant enamelled on the breast-plate, and on his head a magnificent plumed helmet with the royal arms in gold embossed thereon. A handsome arrogant swaggering man this, a full head taller than Patrick and of a very different sort of good looks – bold, sanguine, aquiline, of age somewhere between Patrick and d'Aubigny. He looked the latter up and down, now, with undisguised interest if scant respect – and then his glance passed on to the horses behind, and more esteem was born.

'All is well, Esmé,' Patrick cried. 'Here is our good friend Captain Stewart of Ochiltree. The Sieur d'Aubigny, Captain. I suppose that, far enough back, you two are probably related?'

Stewart shrugged, but d'Aubigny was very gracious, assuring the other of his pleasure and satisfaction at the meeting.

'Our friend has arranged all,' Patrick went on. 'With notable effect. His Highness awaits us. He has arranged a formal audience, as being the safest plan in the circumstances – the more open our arrival at Court, now, the better. Not that there seems to be much danger . . . '

'None,' the newcomer announced curtly. 'I control the guard, and the King's person. My men are everywhere. No man in this castle will quarrel with James Stewart, and no message leaves but by my permission.' Stewart had strolled past d'Aubigny and David casually, and was stroking and running his eye over the black horses, but his fleeting glance flickered swiftly towards the two visitors. David, of course, he ignored entirely. 'A pair of these beasts will suit me very nicely,' he mentioned. 'This one, I think – and this!'

D'Aubigny stiffened, but Patrick caught his eye and an eloquent glance passed between them.

'His Highness may well so decide,' the latter said, quickly. 'It is most fortunate, is it not, Esmé – the Treasurer, my old friend the Master of Glamis, was at Court but two days agone, and is now returned to his castle in Angus. The Chamberlain is here, but he is elderly – next to a dotard, the Captain says. My Lord Ruthven is but new arrived from Perth – but happily, though one of Morton's men, he is also my mother's brother. The only other great lord in the castle is Glencairn, but he apparently is always drunk by this hour. So, *allons*!'

Sauntering with exasperating slowness, Stewart led them in under the gate-towers, up the cobbled roadway and through the inner walls, skirting the Douglas Tower and into the Palace quadrangle. At a strongly guarded doorway on the north side, the horsemen dismounted. Stewart was giving curt orders for the beasts to be led away and stalled, when Patrick intervened, explaining that they would prefer the blacks to be left where they were meantime.

Stewart frowned, but Patrick met his glare with an easy smiling firmness, and after a moment, the former shrugged again, and stalked on within. The three vistors followed.

Stewart was heading straight for great double doors, guarded by gorgeously apparelled men-at-arms, beyond the wide vestibule, and d'Aubigny realised with a shock that they were being taken directly into the presence chamber forthwith, just as they were. Hurriedly he protested, pointing out that they could not come before a monarch dressed thus, in riding attire, dishevelled and dust-covered after a forty-mile ride.

The Captain tossed a brief laugh over his shoulder. 'It matters nothing. He is but a laddie. There is no one here this day worth the dressing up for!' And he strolled on, to throw open the door.

D'Aubigny looked at Patrick, and then at David.

Stewart, with a perfunctory nod rather than an obeisance into the great room, spoke a few words to an elderly man stationed just within the doorway, and then beckoned forward the callers. For want of any instructions to the contrary, David moved onwards behind Patrick.

Their door opened half-way down a long high narrow chamber, somewhat dark because of the smallish windows of a fortress, the dusty arras-hung wood-panelling of the walls, and the smoky massive timbering of the lofty ceiling. To their left a number of people stood and talked and circulated in the lower end of the stone-flagged hall, at the base of which a wide fire-place held, even on this warm August day, a large fire of splutter-ing hissing logs – perhaps with reason, for it was a gloomy, chilly place within the thick stone walls. To their right were only three persons; two, halberdiers in royal livery and helmets, guarded two doors in the far wall; and near a raised dais bearing a throne of tarnished gilt with a sagging purple canopy, an ungainly youthful figure stood, in nondescript clothes, nibbling at a finger-nail and glancing nervously now towards the new-comers, now out of the nearest window.

The old man at the main door thumped with his staff on the stone floor. 'Your Highness,' he declared, in a high cracked voice. 'The Lord Esmé, Seigneur of Aubigny in France, to answer Your Grace's royal summons. The Master of Gray, likewise.' The Chamberlain looked doubtfully at David, sniffed, and added 'Aye.'

There was a pregnant silence, save for the spitting of the fire.

D'Aubigny and Patrick swept low in profound obeisance, graceful, elaborate. At their side, Captain Stewart grinned mockingly. Behind them David bowed as comprehensively as his stiff nature would permit.

The youth up near the throne made no move, other than to hang his head that was distinctly over-large for his mis-shapen body, and stare at the visitors from under lowered brows. He continued to bite his nails.

Straightening up, d'Aubigny and Patrick bowed once again, a little less low, but in unison, and then began to pace forward, Patrick a pace behind the other. David stayed where he was near the door.

James, by the grace of God, King, shambled over to the Chair of State, and sat uncomfortably on the very edge of it, where the stuffing was escaping from the torn purple cushion. At first glance he was quite the most unprepossessing boy that might be met with on a long day's journey, and the contrast with the two superlatively handsome, graceful and assured gallants advancing upon him was fantastic. Without being actually undersized, he had a skimped twisted body, thin weak legs and no presence whatsoever. His mouth was large and slack, but even so it was not big enough for his tongue, which was apt to protrude and slobber. His nose was long and ill-shaped, his hair was thin and wispy; moreover, he did not smell altogether pleasantly. Only his eyes redeemed an otherwise repellent exterior – huge, liquid dark eyes, timorous, darting, expressive, but intelligent.

D'Aubigny went down on one knee before him, kissed the grubby nail-bitten hand that was jerkily extended towards him. Still kneeling, he looked up, and smiled, warmly, brilliantly, kindly.

'Your Majesty,' he said, low-voiced. 'Here is the greatest pleasure of my life – that I have travelled five hundred miles to enjoy. I am your very humble servitor, subject . . . and friend.'

'Ummm,' James mumbled. 'Oh, aye.'

Still d'Aubigny knelt and smiled, looking deep into those great frightened eyes. He saw therein the child who had been, a couple of months unborn, at the brutal murder of Rizzio; who a year later had screamed to the explosion at Kirk o' Field that blew up his father Darnley; who was taken from his mother the same dread year, when she ran off with Bothwell, and had not seen her since; who had known in this thirteen years no true friend, scarcely an honest associate or a kind action; the child who had been torn between ruthless greedy nobles, kidnapped, scorned, bullied, preached over, the pawn of power-seekers – yet the true heir of a line of kings that was the oldest in Europe, stretching back over a thousand years.

'May I rise, Cousin?' he asked, gently.

James had never been asked such a thing, before. He had never been spoken to in a voice so intriguing, so melodious, yet so friendly. He had never been smiled to, thus; he was used to being smiled *at*, mocked, when smiles came in his direction at all.

'Y-yes, my lord,' he said, jumping up himself.

'Do not call me that, Sire. I am your own true cousin, you know. Esmé. Esmé Stuart.'

'Aye. You are son of the Lord John who was brother to my grandfather Lennox.' That came out in a little gabbled rush.

Rising, d'Aubigny nodded. 'You have it exactly. I am much honoured, Cousin.'

'And you . . . you are legitimate. No' like the others.' Half-scared, half-defiantly, the boy blurted out. 'That's different, eh? You . . . you're no' after my crown, man?' A nervous snigger finished that.

The other's own eyes widened as he looked into those deep young-old brown eyes of the boy, and saw therein more than just intelligence. He raised a perfumed lace handkerchief to lips and nose, to give him a moment's grace. 'It is not your crown I seek, Cousin – only your love,' he said.

James stared at him – or rather, at the handkerchief. 'Yon's a right bonny smell,' he declared.

'Yours, Sire.' d'Aubigny said, and handed the trifle to him, bowing.

The boy put it to his big nose, and sniffed, and smiled over it, a fleeting smile at once acquisitive, cunning and simply pleased.

D'Aubigny turned. 'Here is my good friend and companion Patrick, Master of Gray, Highness,' he announced. Patrick, who had been standing back a little, sank down on one knee like-wise. 'Another who wishes you very well, and can serve you notably, I think.'

'Aye – he's bonny, too,' Majesty said, and thrust out the grubby hand again. 'You are both right bonny.'

'Your most humble subject, Sire – as was my father to your lady-mother,' Patrick murmured.

'Much good it did her!' the boy jerked, with a strange half-laugh. 'And you are Greysteil's nephew, are you no'?'

Rising, Patrick darted a quick glance at this strange youth, who was so uncommonly well-versed in genealogy. 'The Lord Ruthven was brother to my mother, yes, Highness – though I have not had word with him for years.' Something about the way that James had enunciated that ominous nickname of Greysteil, one of the men who had butchered Rizzio, warned him to go cautiously.

'Better no' let him see yon wee crucifix peeking out o' your doublet then, Master Patrick – for he's here in this room, mind! Or the godly Master Buchanan, either!' James said, low-voiced, giggling. 'Or they'll give you your paiks, I tell you!'

'H'mmm.' Patrick hastily moved a hand down the front of his doublet, which had opened slightly with his elaborate bowing, and tucked away the little silver cross that hung there. Only a tiny corner of it could have shown – which meant that those limpid dark eyes were as keen as they were expressive. He gave a little laugh. 'I am entirely grateful . . . and at Your Majesty's mercy now, more than ever!' he declared, but conspiratorially, almost below his breath. 'You can let me serve you – or tell the Kirk, to my sad ruin!'

He could not have chosen a surer road to the boy's heart and sympathy – and vanity. For James to hold power over someone was almost a unique experience, and delightful – especially over a handsome gentleman such as this – as was the thought of deceiving his dour Calvinist gaolers. 'I'll no' tell, Master Patrick – never fear!' he whispered. 'And I'm no' so much assured, mind, that the use o' symbols and sacred ornamentation is altogether contrary and displeasing to the mind o' Almighty God. For, see you, the Crown itsel' is a symbol, is it no', o' the divine authority here on earth. Aye.'

Both visitors blinked at this extraordinary pronouncement from the suddenly and pathetically eager youth, shifting from one foot to the other before them.

'Er . . . quite so,' d'Aubigny said, clearing his throat. 'Exactly, Your Highness.'

'I am greatly indebted to you, Sire,' Patrick declared, still in a suitably intriguing whisper.

Entering into the spirit of the thing, d'Aubigny murmured,
'The fiery men of God's true Kirk, in ire,
See in his Cross but timber for their fire!'

James stared, his eyes alight. 'You . . . you are a poet, sir?' he gasped.

'Say but a versifier, Cousin.

The name of Esmé, in the Halls of Fame
Shall ne'er be writ,
His Muse is lame
– and there's an end to it!'

'Och, man, that's grand!' the boy exclaimed, quite forgetting to whisper. 'I write poetry my own self,' he revealed. 'I . . . I canna just rattle it off like yon, mind. It takes me a whilie . . .

'True poetry comes only out of sweat and tears,' d'Aubigny nodded. 'That is where I fail, unlike yourself . . . '

He paused. The murmuring and whispering and stirring from the lower end of the chamber was growing very noticeable. Undoubtedly men there were becoming restive at this prolonged *tête a tête.* The elderly Chamberlain made no move to check the unseemly disturbance – indeed, his own glance at the trio up near the throne was distinctly suspicious as he strained his old ears to catch some hint of what was being said there. David, standing nearby, noted it all, perceived the hostility amongst the waiting throng – and also that the Captain of the Guard, for all his insolent-seeming lounging stance, was more tense than he appeared. As Patrick swept a glance around the room, and it met his own, David raised a hand, warning forefinger uplifted.

King James did not seem to notice; no doubt he was used to noise and hostility. 'I will write you a poem, Cousin Esmé,' he said. 'About you – aye, and Master Patrick here. Bonny men. And bonny France. The sun, they say, shines there a deal more than it does here?' He sighed a little. 'It will take me a whilie. I'm no' quick at it. And Master Buchanan gives me my paiks if I waste my time. Though poetry shouldna be a waste o' time, surely? You'll no' be gone, sir? You'll no' be away, that soon, before I get it done . . . ?'

'Indeed we will not, Your Majesty. We have come a long way, in answer to your royal summons. Until you send us away, we are at your disposal, Highness, and esteeem your Court to be our greatest joy.'

'Fine, fine. Give me but a day or two, sirs, and I'll have it ready. I vow I will. It will maybe be no' that fine, mind – no' in the French fashion . . .'

Patrick coughed, as James sought words for his over-large tongue. 'We must not weary His Highness, Esmé,' he said, almost imperceptibly jerking his head towards the other end of the presence chamber. 'We must not monopolise too much of his royal time. And there is yet the matter of the horses.'

'But, yes. Sire, we have brought a small gift for you from the illustrious Duke of Guise and the Cardinal his brother. A horse or two. They are without. If Your Majesty will deign to come inspect them . . . ?"

'Horses? For me?'

'Yes, Cousin – all the way from France. From Africa, indeed – from the Barbary coast.'

'Barbary! Eh, sirs – Barbary horses! For me!' The boy's excitement swelled up within him in slobbering incoherence. Then suddenly he began to chew at a slack lower lip. 'I canna,' he got out. 'I canna come. No' just now.' That was almost a wail.

'Cannot, Your Majesty . . . ?' d'Aubigny wondered.

'I'm no' allowed, man. I'm no' let to the stables until after my studies. Master Buchanan is right hot on that. He was hot against this audience, too. He wasna for letting me come – but Captain Jamie said he must.'

'I see. This Buchanan . . . ?'

'His Highness's tutor,' Patrick explained, one eye on the other end of the long apartment. 'The renowned scholar, Master George Buchanan, a pillar of the Kirk and lately Principal of Glasgow University.'

'And something of a tyrant, it seems?'

'He's a right hard man,' the royal student agreed, feelingly.

'Still, Sire, the audience is not yet over, is it?' Patrick asked. 'You can include therein the inspection of the presents that we have brought from the high and mighty princes of Guise, your mother's cousins, surely? It is a matter of state, I'd say.'

'I'm no' allowed, Master Patrick,' James repeated, miserably. 'I'd like it fine. But they'll no' let me out. I have to bow to them, and then go out the wee door at the back here. Master Buchanan's man is waiting for me behind there to take me back. I'm never allowed out the big doors.'

'*Mortdieu*, I think that you have not your Court entirely well arranged, Cousin!' d'Aubigny declared. 'I have visited many princes, and never have I seen it this wise!'

'Have you no', Cousin Esmé?'

'You are the King, Sire. You can do as you will,' Patrick put in.

'I wish I could, sir – but I canna . . .'

'I suggest, Esmé, that we prove to His Highness that his powers are greater than he thinks,' Patrick said, and laughed softly, easily, lest the boy be further affrighted.

'I agree. Sire, it is time that you asserted your royal self, I think. After all, you are nearly a man, now. You rule this Kingdom, for the Regency is at an end. Moreover, Cousin, I fear that their Graces of Guise might be much offended if they were to hear that you had not taken note of their gifts for hours.'

'Would they? Och, but . . . look – there's that Greysteil glowering at me, now! He aye glowers at me. He doesna like me, yon black Ruthven man. He'd no' let me past . . .'

Patrick laughed again. 'Leave you my uncle to me, Sire. Leave you it all to us. Just walk between us . . . and remember that you are the King of Scots in your castle of Stirling, and that fifty generations of your fathers have had their boots cleaned by the likes of William Ruthven!'

The King gulped, and looked from one to another, as they

took place on either side of him. Each lightly touched a bony elbow.

'We go look at your Barbary nags,' Patrick said. 'And there is no hurry, at all.'

So, together, the strangely assorted trio came pacing down the chamber, the two men at smiling ease, the boy in shambling lip-biting alarm. Great now was the stir at the fire end of the room. Men stared at each other, nonplussed – for there were no women present in this Court. The Chamberlain started forward, tugging at his beard and all but falling over his staff of office. Stewart of Ochiltree, all lounging past now glanced swiftly around, and especially over in the direction of one man at the front of the uncertain throng. That man did not look uncertain. Tall and lean, and hatchet-faced, in clothing more suitable for the hunt than a Court, of middle years, stooping a little, hawklike, he stepped forward determinedly. At the sight, the two escorts felt the boy between them falter and hold back.

Patrick spoke quickly. 'Sire – my uncle,' he declared loudly. 'We have not met with each other for years. Has the Lord Ruthven Your Highness's permission to greet me?'

Into the sudden hush that followed, the King's uncertain voice croaked. 'A-aye.'

'We are well met, my lord,' Patrick said immediately. 'His Highness has been speaking of you.'

'I am glad to hear it, Nephew,' Ruthven answered, in a voice like a rasp. 'I wouldna like to think that he would forget me! Nor you either, my cockerel! Where are you going?'

'The Sieur d'Aubigny, of the house of Lennox,' Patrick gestured. 'My mother's brother, the Lord Ruthven, one of the King's most faithful supporters, Esmé.'

D'Aubigny bowed, but Ruthven scarcely glanced at him.

'I said where are you going, Nephew?'

'His Highness is minded to inspect a gift of horseflesh sent to him by the Duke of Guise and the Cardinal of Lorraine. The suggestion is that you, Uncle, as a renowned judge of a horse, accompany the King and give him the benefit of your knowledge.'

There was a tense pause. Ruthven, who was a man of violent action rather than nimble wits, stared at his nephew from under beetling brows. Patrick gazed back, and meeting the other's fierce eye, lowered one eyelid gently but distinctly. Then, smiling, he turned again to James and pressed his elbow.

'Come, Sire,' he said. 'There is nothing that my lord does not know about horses.'

It was as easy as that. They moved on towards the door, and the terrible Greysteil, finding himself moving along behind, hastily strode forward to stalk alongside. The Chamberlain, at the sight of the four of them bearing down on him, hesitated and backed. Other men, with none of the great lords amongst them, stood irresolute. But Captain Stewart at least did not misjudge the situation. He raised his voice authoritatively.

'Way for His Grace!' he called. 'Aside, for the King's Highness!' And though on the face of it, his orders were for the guard at the door, none questioned the generality of their application. Men stood aside and bowed the quartet out.

David and Stewart fell in behind, and after a moment or two the flustered Chamberlain came bustling along also, to be followed by the entire throng.

Out in the quadrangle the horses stood where they had been left with the guard, the three nondescript saddled beasts and the six magnificent unsaddled blacks. At sight of them, James forgot his alarm, forgot the company he was in, forgot all save his delight in those splendid gleaming animals. He burst away from his companions and went running forward.

'Six!' he cried. 'Six o' them! Look – the bonny beasts! Och, they're bonny, bonny! And for me! You said they were all for me?'

Smiling, d'Abugny went strolling after the boy, calling reassurances.

Patrick elected to direct his attention upon Ruthven, however. 'A pleasant sight, is it not, Uncle?' he said. 'So much youthful enthusiasm! And enthusiasm in a prince, properly directed, can achieve much – can it not?'

Greysteil looked at him, broodingly. 'You're no' blate, Patrick – I'll say that for you!' he declared. 'You've a glib tongue in your head. But how long, think you, will you keep that head on your shoulders, man, playing this game?'

'I shall keep my head, never fear,' his nephew laughed. 'I use it, you see. As, I have no doubt, you are using yours. You know more than just horseflesh, I think?'

'I ken who rules Scotland, boy!'

'Who *ruled* it,' Patrick amended. He pointed. 'Yonder is the rule in Scotland, hereafter – the pair of them. The King and his cousin Esmé. Or shall we say Esmé and his cousin the King? It is a wise man who recognises a fact like that in good time!'

His uncle snorted. 'What think you Morton will say that that?'

'What he says is of small matter. What he *does* depends on who supports him!'

'The whole Council supports him, laddie.'

'Does it? Does Huntly support him? Does Erroll, the Constable? Does Herries, or Montrose, or Balmerino, or Sutherland . . . ?'

Ruthven spat on the cobble-stones. 'Papists!' he exclaimed.

'Are they? But still of the Council, even though they have not attended it of late! In letters to me, they indicate that they are thinking of taking a greater interest in their duties, Uncle!'

Greysteil said nothing to that.

'And the Kirk?' Patrick went on. 'Is the Kirk united in support of my lord of Morton?'

'The Kirk will no' support any Catholic Frenchie, I'll tell you that, boy!'

His nephew coughed. 'I have it on the best authority that Esmé Stuart has h'm, leanings towards Protestantism!' he said.

'God!' the older man commented, simply.

'The Guise brothers have been extraordinarily generous,' Patrick added, as though on another subject altogether. 'Not only in horses. They have entrusted me with considerable gold. As have . . . others. In the interests of amity and peace in Scotland, you understand. A noble cause, you will agree?'

Ruthven licked his thin lips.

'Elizabeth Tudor, I have heard, is finding her dole to Morton waxing unprofitable. She is thinking of cutting it off, they do say.' The younger man sighed. '*Pardieu* – the problems of steering the galley of state!'

His uncle was staring ahead of him, but not seemingly at the black horses. He appeared to be thinking very hard indeed.

THE conspirators could scarcely have chosen more effective means of gaining the young King's regard and confidence. He doted on horses, and hitherto had been allowed only a small stocky pony. He esteemed poetry as god-like, and d'Aubigny, no mean practitioner, had him enthralled. He was new enough to flattery, too, to be more than amenable to it; and Patrick never failed to remind him that, owing to the small matter of the crucifix, he held him as in the hollow of his royal hand. James was quite overwhelmed.

Indeed, the boy became almost embarrassing in his fondness, affection-starved as he was. He would scarcely allow either of them out of his sight – which had its disadvantages. He took a parallel delight in David also, whose plainness in appearance and manner no doubt came as something of a relief to the unprepossessing youth after the dazzling looks and scintillating converse of the other two.

But success for their plans depended on so much more than young James's reaction, vital as that was. On the whole, they were fortunate. In the absence of the youthful Earl of Mar, Hereditary Keeper of Stirling Castle, the Lieutenant-Governor, who might well have made difficulties, was not inclined to assert himself. He was a plain soldier, with no urge to meddle in politics or statecraft. He was undoubtedly impressed by the high birth of the visitors, and their authoritative manners. That he would not wish to offend Morton went without saying – but he was much under the influence of the strong-charactered Captain of the Guard, whom hitherto he had looked upon as a tool of Morton's. In the circumstances, he did not interfere.

The Chamberlain was actively hostile, but his duties were purely formal and gave him no executive power. The famous and scholarly George Buchanan, the King's tutor and Keeper of the Privy Seal, was crotchety and censorious, but at seventy-three, and ailing, was not in a position to challenge the new-comers. Moreover, he was known to hate Morton; their relations for long had been that of an uneasy truce.

As for Lord Ruthven, he disappeared from Court forthwith, with remarkable speed, discretion, almost stealth, for so spectacular a nobleman. There was no lack of suggestion as to where he had gone or what his errand might be. Patrick, however, was not greatly perturbed on that score.

It was, in fact, Stewart of Ochiltree who was the trouble. D'Aubigny disliked him from the first – which was scarcely to be wondered at, since the other made no attempt to be civil, much less respectful.

'That one is a surly dog, and too ambitious for our comfort. I think!' he told Patrick, whenever they were alone that first day. 'He has sold Morton – he will sell me, at the first opportunity ... and yourself likewise, *mon ami*.'

'I would not deny it,' Patrick agreed. 'But not until it is to his advantage to do so. We must see to it that his interests lie with us – and suffer him meantime. Unfortunately, he is all-important to us. I like him as little as do you, Esmé – but we must have patience. We could not have done what we have done without him – nor do what we hope to do.'

'Then let us pray the Blessed Virgin that his manners improve!' the putative Protestant convert observed.

David, who was present, put in a word. 'Stewart is not just as he seems, I think. He is less confident, less sure of himself, than he would have you believe. I was watching him while you talked with the King. At the first, yon time. He was in a sweat, despite of his insolent airs. In especial, over the Lord Ruthven.'

'Say you so? That is worth knowing. Keep you your keen eye on him, Davy – watch him always.'

'If he is in a sweat over Ruthven, what will he be when Morton comes?' d'Aubigny wondered.

Always it came back to that – when Morton comes.

They were fortunate in being allowed five days of grace. Logan of Restalrig had done his work well – as indeed he might, considering the gold he had received. A courier from him reached Stirling the second day, saying that most of Teviotdale was alight, and the Armstrongs of Liddesdale had taken the opportunity to join in on their own account, as too good an opportunity for booty to miss. Morton was busy ranging the Border valleys, hanging men – ever his favourite pastime – though a little less spry about the ranging, if not the hanging, than in the past.

In Stirling no time was wasted. While d'Aubigny insinuated himself ever more deeply with James, Patrick wrote and despatched urgent letters, interviewed modestly retiring individuals in back-street taverns down in the grey town, and made one or two hurried visits further afield. David was sent secretly and in haste on the most important errand of all – across wide Perthshire indeed to the head of their own Carse of Gowrie. At Erroll he delivered a message to Andrew, eighth Earl of Erroll, head of the Hays and Hereditary High Constable of Scotland, and was closely questioned by that Catholic nobleman who, because of his religious convictions, had lived to some extent in retirement for years. David was less eloquent, undoubtedly, than were his brother's letters, for he had gained no noticeable enthusiasm for this entire project, and the thought of deliberately using his fellow-countrymen's religious beliefs against each other far from appealed to him; he had seen whither that could lead in France and the Low Countries. Thereafter, it was only with a real effort of will and no conviction at all that he turned southwards again, for Stirling; Castle Huntly and Mariota lay but a mere ten miles eastwards along the Carse.

The visitors from France were installed in a suite of rooms adjoining those of the King's own, in the half-empty palace wing of the fortress, where James could reach them and be reached at any time – gloomy old-fashioned quarters, of scant comfort, but the best available. They sent for their baggage from Restalrig, and even in their third-best French clothes made an enormous impression on the excessively dull Scots Court. D'Aubigny came to an arrangement with Master Buchanan whereby the royal studies were not to be too drastically interrupted; the tutor was grimly acquiescent, giving the impression that he found it hardly worth while to argue, when only a little waiting would resolve the matter.

Indeed, that was the general attitude, in Stirling. All men waited.

Then, on the fourth afternoon, Logan of Restalrig himself rode into the town at the gallop, with a score of tough Border mosstroopers at his heels. Only after a considerable clash of wills did Patrick prevail upon Stewart to allow this party, of what he named freebooters, within the castle precincts. Logan, a coarse, foul-mouthed, gorilla of a man, but namely as a fighter, brought the word that he had been racing Morton north from Teviotdale, and reckoned to have beaten the old sinner by half a day at least. The cat was out of the bag, at last. There would not be much more waiting.

There was no hiding the tension in the castle of Stirling that night. Patrick sent out hurried messages north and south.

According to Logan, Morton rode with his usual close escort of a hundred Douglases, only. He could raise a score of times that number if the occasion seemed to warrant it.

Despite the obvious need for closing the ranks, Stewart of Ochiltree was at his most arrogant and unco-operative. Perhaps he was merely frightened; perhaps he was beginning to doubt the wisdom of his change of sides? Even Patrick allowed himself to be a little put out by this. He came to James, down at the royal stables, where he was spending a deal of his time, with d'Aubigny, admiring, exclaiming over, even grooming, the six Barbary blacks.

'Your Grace,' he said, seeking to hide the urgency in his voice. 'I fear that it is necessary to make a gesture towards your Captain Jamie. To, h'm, bind him closer to your royal side. To indicate to him that your Highness's favour is . . . important.'

'Eh? Captain Jamie isna that much interested in my favour, Master Patrick.'

'He should be, He can be, Sire. It is essential . . . with my lord of Morton on his way here.'

At mention of that name, the boy seemed to shrink in on himself. 'He . . . he will send you away? The Lord Morton will no' have you here? He . . . he will give me knocks, again – hard knocks . . .'

'Knocks, Sire?' d'Aubigny raised his brows. 'Surely you cannot mean that Morton could strike you? Your royal person?'

'Aye, could he! Often he has done it. Hard knocks.'

'By the Mass, then he will do it no more, the ruffian! We shall see to that, Cousin.'

'And one way of seeing to it, Your Grace, is to ensure that Captain Jamie is your good friend, since he controls your guard. You should give him a present, Sire.'

'Eh? A present? What have I that Captain Jamie might want . . . ?'

'Plenty. For instance, Your Highness might give him a couple of these black horses. He has already expressed his admiration . for them.'

The boy's eyes widened, became huge. 'Eh? Give . . . my blacks! No! No – I'll no' do it!' The thick uncertain voice rose abruptly almost to a scream, as James started forward to the nearest horse. 'I'll no' give them!' he cried. 'They're mine, mine!'

Blinking, Patrick looked at d'Aubigny. 'Just two, Sire. You will still have four left.'

'No! Never! You'll no' take my bonny beasts! No, no, no!'

D'Aubigny hurried over to slip an arm around the boy's heaving shoulders. 'Never fear, Cousin,' he soothed. 'If they mean so much to you, no one will – no one *can* – take them from you. Forget it, Sire – it is all right. There are plenty of other gifts that you can make, after all.'

James had pressed his tear-wet face against the gleaming black flank of the horse. Sidelong, now, he peered up and round at his cousin. 'I'll no' give him my horses,' he declared, with tremulous stubbornness. 'But . . . but I havena anything else, Cousin Esmé. I've no other presents that I could give him.'

D'Aubigny laughed. 'You do not realise what you have to give, Cousin. You have more than anyone else. You are the King. You have lands and houses and castles and titles to give. Offices and privileges and honours. All yours, and yours only.'

'No' me. Yon the Lord Morton gives.'

'No more, Sire. He is no longer Regent. Nothing can be given without your signature. And anything given *with* your signature, stands.'

James turned round to stare at the speaker now, doubts, ideas, hopes chasing themselves across his ugly expressive face. 'Is that . . . true?' he asked. And he turned to Patrick to confirm it.

'Absolutely, Highness. All that is needed is Your Grace's signature on a paper, and the thing is done. Anything is done.'

'And . . . and I have lots o' . . . these things that I can give?'

'You have all Scotland.'

'Then . . . then, Cousin Esmé – I could give *you* a present!' That came out in a rush. 'Master Patrick, too. And Davy Gray, of course. What would you like, Cousin? Eh, man – what would you like?'

The two conspirators could not forebear to exchange glances. David, standing in a cobwebby corner by the hay-forks, did not fail to read momentary naked triumph therein. But when d'Aubigny spoke, he shook his handsome head.

'No, no, James – nothing for me.' That was the first time that he had called the King merely James. 'Nor for Patrick either, I think. We are your true friends – we do not need gifts. Just for Stewart, the Captain. Give him something that will hold him fast.'

'I'd liefer give *you* something.'

'Another time, then. Later, perhaps . . . and thank you, James. Now – what for Stewart?'

Patrick spoke. 'The Master of Glamis,' he said, smiling brilliantly. 'The Treasurer. He has been amassing overmuch treasure of late, I hear. They tell me that he had Morton appoint him Commendator of the Priory of Prenmay, a year back, with all its fat lands and revenues. I suggest that you transfer the Commendatorship to Captain Stewart of Ochiltree, Your Grace.'

'C-can I do that?'

'Most certainly. It is all in your royal gift.'

'You wouldna like it for yoursel', Master Patrick?'

'I would much prefer, Sire, that Stewart had it. If I write you out a paper, will you sign it?'

'Aye.'

'Excellent, Your Highness. I think that we may rely upon Captain Jamie, hereafter!'

Late that night the uneasy fortress awoke to the clatter of horses and armed men, and shouts for admittance at the gatehouse. Patrick, fully dressed and unsleeping, was quickly down at the portcullis chamber – but only a few moments before the new Prior of Prenmay. They exchanged quick glances, in the gloom.

'Is that the Lord Morton?' Stewart demanded, of the guard. A large body of horsemen could be made out, beyond.

'No, sir. It is the High Constable, my lord of Erroll, demanding admittance to protect the person of the King's Highness. He says that it is his duty.'

'As so it is!' Patrick ejaculated, with rather more vehemence than was necessary. 'That is . . . well.' He sought to hide the relief in his voice.

Stewart turned to consider him, narrow-eyed. 'I had not known of this, Master of Gray,' he said slowly. 'I congratulate you. It seems that you have not idled.'

'Idleness has its delights – in due season, Master Prior. Time for that will come . . . for all of us,' the other answered lightly. 'Can I request you to have the drawbridge lowered?'

Stewart gave the order.

The Earl of Erroll, a grave middle-aged man of impressive appearance but few words, had brought with him seventy men and a dozen Haylairds. It was his hereditary privilege to keep the peace around the King's person, and so was the only man who might legitimately bring armed men into the near presence of the monarch – however many did so otherwise. His clinging to the old religion had cost him dear.

Patrick and Stewart, with David in attendance, had barely seen this contingent settled in quarters, when a further hullabaloo from the castle approaches brought them hurrying back to the gatehouse, wondering whether Erroll had arrived only just in time. It was not Morton yet, however, but the Lord Seton, with forty retainers, who had ridden hard from East Lothian on receipt of a message from Patrick. Seton was no Catholic, but he had fairly recently been ousted from the enjoyment of the revenues of the rich church lands of Pluscarden in favour of James Douglas, one of Morton's illegitimate sons. He was therefore in a mood for reprisals. He had been, of course, one of Mary the Queen's most staunch supporters, suffering banishment for her failing cause, and of late years living quietly at Seton Palace, taking no part in state affairs.

Stewart fingered his pointed beard as this company rode in under the portcullis. 'You cast a wide net, my friend,' he said to Patrick. 'I wonder at the diversity of your friends. Think you that they will make good bedfellows?'

'All unfriends of Morton are friends of mine, this night,' Patrick told him. 'And I would suggest that you consider not their diversity but that they come at all! Men who have not moved for years. Think you that they would be here if they believed that the tide ebbed against them?'

The Captain did not argue that. 'Are more to come?' he asked.

'One only, I think. There are others, but they lie too far off to reach here in time.'

'Your noble father?'

Patrick laughed. 'Where is my Lord Ochiltree?' he wondered. 'Fathers are safer kept in the background – do you not agree?' He did not require to amplify that, to point out that it was a short-sighted house which committed both chief and heir to the one side. 'what I wonder is . . . where is the Master of Glamis?'

Stewart frowned at that name – as he was meant to do.

It was a crisp autumn sunrise, however, before the red-eyed weary guardians of Stirling Castle saw the final company come climbing up the hill through the morning mists. No great cohort this, a mere score of riders perhaps – but the banner at their head widened Stewart's heavy eyes.

'So-o-o!' he declared. 'You fly yon carrion-crow, Gray! Beware that it does not peck your Frenchie's pretty eyes out!

133

It and its foul brood. They are nearer the blood, mind, than is your Monsieur.'

'My Frenchie is protected by a fine paper from such as these,' Patrick pointed out. 'The pen is mightier, as someone has said, than . . . h'm . . . than the implement that banner represents! What a blessed thing is holy matrimony, duly witnessed! Man, the Kirk and the Crown are united in love of it!'

The flag that they saw bore indeed the royal arms of Scotland – only with a black bar sinister slashing diagonally across it. Under it rode the Lord Robert Stewart, illegitimate son of King James Fifth, half-brother of Mary, uncle of the boy in the castle behind them. Rapacious, untrustworthy, fickle, he represented trouble. He was not long out of Morton's gaol, where he had been held by the Regency on a charge of treason, for years. He could bring no long tail of fighting men, since he had not the wherewithal to pay them, but he did his best with sons innumerable. Of the seventeen with him this morning, none were born in wedlock, and it was their father's boast that none claimed the same mother. They all required properties, lands, inheritances.

'A hungry ragged crew!' the other Stewart observed scornfully.

'Aye – but there is the witness to Elizabeth of England's doles, see you,' Patrick said. 'So the Guises assured me – and they are knowledgeable. He it was who brought them, at the first, they say. Heigho!' That was laugh and yawn mixed together. 'Now I am ready for the Douglas!'

They had plenty of warning – Logan's scouts saw to that. Morton had spent the night at Linlithgow Palace. The long presence-chamber, so much fuller of people than it had been for years, heard the distant echoes of the ominous cry, that had terrorised Scotland for so long, come drifting up from the town, and few there could repress a shiver at the sound. 'A Douglas! A Douglas!' the fell slogan rang out, and behind it the thunder of furious hooves throbbed on the warm air of noontide. In the long apartment hardly a man spoke.

Stiff, still, they waited as the noise grew and drew closer. Ears straining, they followed its progress, up out of the climbing streets, over the wide forecourt, drumming over the lowered drawbridge. Stewart the soldier had said keep the drawbridge up and the portcullis down – keep the man out; but the Master of Gray said rather let the man in, or he will turn at the closed gates, go and collect his thousands, and come back to batter them down. Doors open, therefore, they waited.

They heard the great clattering on the cobbles of the quadrangle outside, the shouts of men and the clash of steel. Patrick pressed a hand on the trembling shoulder of the boy on the Chair of State. No sound came from the entire room.

A hawking and a spitting came first. Then an angry bearlike growling, and heavy deliberate footsteps with the ring of spurs.

'Way for Douglas!' someone shouted outside, and from beyond scores of hoarse voices took up the refrain. 'A Douglas! A Douglas!'

Morton strode into the presence-chamber, scene of so many of his triumphs, took a few paces forward, and stopped dead, to stare around him. At his back came half-a-dozen Douglas lairds, and the Master of Glamis. No Lord Ruthven.

Quietly David and Stewart closed the double doors at their backs.

Morton had grown stouter, even more gross, since last David and Patrick had seen him, but lost nothing of his appearance of bull-like vigour. Clad carelessly in tarnished half-armour and dusty broadcloth he stood wide-legged, straddling, stertorously panting. If there was silver amongst the red of his flaming bushy beard, it did not show, nor in the untidy hair that stuck out from under his tall black hat. He glared about him, head and chin forward.

'Davy, request my lord of Morton to uncover, in the presence of the King's Grace.' Patrick's voice rang out clearly, pleasantly – the first words spoken in that room for some time.

David, needless to say, did not take that seriously, but as a gesture. He stood where he was, being a man of common sense. Morton emitted a sort of choking roar, and reaching up both hands, wrenched down the hat more firmly.

'A stink for the King's Grace!' he said, and spat on the stone flags.

Round all the great chamber he glowered – as well he might. Never before had he seen it thus. Armed men lined every inch of its lower walling, so that no space for another remained there, right round the throne-half of the chamber as well as the fire end. Some were in the royal livery of the guard – well spaced out, these, for Patrick did not altogether trust them – some in the red and white colours of the High Constable, the red and gold of Seton, others in the nondescript rusty morions and bucklers of Logan's mosstroopers, two hundred men at least. Silent, tense, armed to the teeth, they stood, their hostility like a palisade.

Morton's little pig's eyes darted on, ignoring the people at the lower end of the chamber, over those nearer to the throne – Erroll, Seton, Oliphant, Logan. At sight of the Lord Robert Stewart, they paused, and then passed on to where James, cloaked specially in the royal purple and wearing a chaplet of gold for crown, sat on the Chair of State and quaked. With an open sneer, he jerked his red head, to bring his lowering stare finally to the two brilliantly clad gallants who stood one on either side of the throne. Dressed in the lavish height of the French mode, d'Aubigny in golden satin, Patrick in white velvet with black, they looked like a couple of birds of paradise in a rookery.

Morton hooted, belched coarsely, deliberately, and then turned right round to look at Stewart, near the door. 'Clear me this rabble!' he snapped.

Stewart gazed straight ahead of him, motionless, wordless.

It was Patrick who spoke. 'Lord of Morton,' he said clearly. 'You have come unbidden into the King's presence – and remained covered deliberately. As a former Viceroy of the Realm you know the penalty for such. The Lord Constable is here to enforce His Grace's royal commands . . .'

'I do not talk with pap-suckers, nor yet prancing clothes-horses!' the other interrupted harshly. 'Erroll, you Pope's bottom-licker – this is rebellion!'

The Constable stared through and past him, and said never a word.

'Seton, you crawling louse – I ha' better things than you in my body hair! Is it banishment again for you – or the clasp o' my fair Maiden at the Tolbooth o' Edinburgh? Eh, creature?'

Silence.

'Robbie Stewart – whoreson! Fool's get! Beggar at my table! Was my last cell no' deep enough for you? Is it below ground you'd be?'

There was no answer.

'Precious soul o' God!' the Earl roared, and the entire room vibrated to the volume and the fury of it. 'Think you that you may remain dumb when Douglas bespeaks you? A fiend – I've plenty steel outby there to loosen the tongues o' you! Aye, a plenty. Will I have my lads in – eh?'

'Earl Morton, is that a threat of force in the presence of the King's Grace? Force and fear?' Patrick enquired, even-voiced.

'If so, you must know that it carries the punishment of immediate death, without formality of trial. And here is ample power and authority to enforce sentence – at once. Twice as many as your Douglas bullyrooks without!'

Morton drew a long quivering breath – but muttered only into his beard.

'Do we take it, then, that no threat was intended?' Patrick pressed, silkily.

'Not to Jamie, damn you – not to the King!' the older man spluttered.

'Ah! Good! Excellent, my lord. Nevertheless, I would counsel you to be more careful in your speech, in the royal presence, lest an unfortunate mistake is made – too late to be rectified!'

'Misbegotten whelp . . . !' the Earl began, when Patrick held up his hand.

'Silence, in the King's name!' he cried authoritatively, 'His Highness has something other against the Lord Morton than mere threats.' He drew a folded paper out of his doublet. 'Sire, is it your royal wish that I read this indictment?'

Dumbly James nodded.

'Hear you, then – by the command of the gracious and high prince James, King of Scots, King of Man, High Steward of Scotland, Lord of the Isles, Protector of Christ's Kirk – this! It has come to our royal knowledge that James Douglas, Earl of Morton, formerly our Viceroy and regent of our Realm of Scotland, has on occasions many received from our excellent sister, the well-beloved princess Elizabeth, Queen of England, certain moneys and treasure intended for the comfort and well-being of our royal self and person, it being inconceivable that the said princess should treat with and constantly enrich a subject not her own. And that the said James Douglas has wrongfully and treasonably retained the said moneys and treasure unto his own use and keeping . . . '

'It's a lie! A barefaced lie!' Morton bellowed. 'Jamie, they cozen you! It is lies – all lies!'

' . . . thereby grievously injuring both our sister Elizabeth and our royal self,' Patrick read on, without change of voice. 'Whereof we have witness in the person of our right trusty and well-beloved Lord Robert, Sheriff and Bishop of Orkney, who will testify . . . '

'Aye, I will!' the Lord Robert cried, stepping forward. Though dissipated, he had the typical Stewart good looks that had so woefully escaped his royal nephew. 'It is all true.'

'You forsworn lying bastard!'

'I was twice the courier who conveyed these moneys from Queen Elizabeth. Believing them for His Highness's Treasury . . .'

'Judas! Such as didna stick to your own accursed fingers!'

Patrick signed to the Lord Robert not to answer. 'This treasure, ofttimes repeated, amounting to many thousands of gold crowns, is therefore required at the hands of the said James Douglas, to be delivered without delay into the hands of our Lord Treasurer . . .'

'God's Passion! Are you all crazy-mad . . . ?'

'Furthermore, it being evident and assured that such ill measures against our comfort could not have been taken lacking the knowledge and agreement of our Realm's Treasurer, the said Treasurer, Sir Thomas Lyon, called Master of Glamis, is hereby indicted as being art and part in the said mischievous conspiracy . . .'

' 'Fore God – it is not true!' the Master of Glamis exclaimed, from behind Morton. 'I swear I know nothing of the matter, Your Grace!'

'Silence, sir! This is in the King's name. Accordingly it is our royal will and declaration that until such time as this indictment is duly and lawfully examined by our Privy Council, the said James Douglas, Earl of Morton, shall hold himself in close ward in his own house, nor enter our royal presence, under pain of treason, forthwith. Also that the said Sir Thomas Lyon, Master of Glamis, shall do the same, and is moreover hereby relieved of the office of Treasurer of this our Realm. Signed this day at this our Court of Stirling. James.'

For a few moments Morton's furious mouthings and trumpetings were quite incoherent, however alarming. At length he won consecutive words out of the chaos of his wrath. 'Jamie – Your Grace!' he cried. 'I demand speech with *you*. With your royal sel' – no' this fribbling babbler, this scented ape! It is my right – as an earl o' this realm . . .'

Patrick stooped, to whisper something in James's ear.

In a high-pitched nervous voice, the boy spoke. 'We cannot have speech with our royal . . . with any who remain covered in our royal presence.'

Cursing foully, Morton reached up and snatched off his hat, hurling it to the floor. 'It's lies about the money, Jamie,' he cried. 'It wasna for you, at all – never think it. A wheen gold pieces Elizabeth has sent me, now and again – but only for friendship's sake, see you. I did her a service once. Write and ask her yoursel', Jamie . . . '

Patrick was whispering again.

James stood up, having to hold on to the arms of his throne to keep himself upright. 'To accept doles from a foreign prince . . . within our Realm is in itsel' a, a treason,' he squeaked. Patrick prompted. 'Our Council shall debate o' it. Meantime our . . . our royal will is declared. You are in ward. Both o' you. You will leave our presence . . . no' to return. This . . . this audience is over.'

'God save the King's Grace!' Patrick called.

There was an answering vociferation from hundreds of throats. 'God save the King's Grace! God save the King's Grace!'

'Jamie . . . !' Morton exclaimed as the surge of sound died away – and there was pleading in that thick voice, for once.

Patrick, touching the boy's arm, James turned right about, to present his back to the room. 'My Lord Erroll,' he shrilled. 'Your duty!'

The Lord High Constable raised his baton of office. 'Earl of Morton . . . ' he began, deep-voiced – and at the sign every armed man in the great room took a jangling pace forward. It was not a very exact manoeuvre, for so close were they placed together already that the contraction in the ranks inevitably resulted in jostling and stumbling. But the effect was forceful and significant enough. The very walls of the presence-chàmber seemed to contract upon the threatened figures.

Morton darted swift glances all around from red-fringed eyes. Already Patrick and d'Aubigny, their arms linked with the King's, were strolling towards the farther doors. 'Christ!' he said, and whirled abruptly around, almost knocked over the Master of Glamis, elbowed aside his gaping Douglas lairds, and went striding to the double doors. Captain Stewart opened them for him – and was rewarded by a stream of spittle full in his face. The Earl stormed out, shouting for his horses, shouting for many things.

When he and his had passed from view, all men in that room as it were froze in their places, silent again, listening. They heard a great confusion of voices, the well-known bull-like roaring, but no shouting of the name of Douglas. Then they heard the clatter of hooves, many hooves.

A great sigh of relief escaped from throats innumerable.

'*Magnifique! Splendide!* My congratulations, Patrick!' d'Aubigny exclaimed, laughing a little unevenly. 'You were quite impressive. Most dramatic, I swear. Our bear is baited . . . and retires to lick his wounds. Personally however, *mon ami*, I would have preferred our bear to be locked up – or better still, despatched forthwith. I would have had him on my cousin Darnley's business, right away. And saved time.'

Patrick shook his head. 'We are scarcely ready for that. Time is needed, there. Moreover – whisper it – I was not sure that our two hundred stalwarts would be so sure a match for his Douglases out there! Patience, Esmé – little by little is the way with bears. Anyhow, I vow he will never be the same bear again! Ah – but what is this, Sire . . . ?'

Majesty, between them, had burst into blubbering tears.

Chapter Ten

MORTON was not beaten yet, of course; it was not so easy as that. But he found it expedient to retire to his own great palace at Dalkeith – The Lion's Den, as it was called. And all Scotland rang with the word of it, in a surprisingly short time; all Scotland indeed, in consequence, seemed to flock to Stirling – or, at least, all that counted in Scotland – to see the new star that had arisen in the land, to test out the new dispensation, and to try to gauge for how long it might last.

A sort of hectic gaiety reigned in the grey old town under its grim fortress.

King James was by no means overwhelmed by this gaiety. Perhaps, having been dominated all his young life by the red shadow of Morton, he could not conceive of it being ever removed. Morton, and the fear of his vengeance, was at the boy's narrow shoulder day and night. Many of those who now thronged Stirling Castle had been Morton's friends, he swore – and doubtless still were. They were only spying out the land for the Douglas's return.

Only d'Aubigny could sooth him – Cousin Esmé, dear bonny Cousin Esmé, whom he had grown to love with a feverish and frightened and rather sickeningly demonstrative affection that caused titters, sniggers and nudging leers on all hands, but which David Gray, at least, found heart-wringing.

It was Patrick's idea, but Cousin Esmé's suggestion and advice, that a move would be the thing – a change of scene and air and company, a clean sweep. Let His Grace get out of this gloomy ghost-ridden prison of a fortress. Let him go to Edinburgh, to his capital. Let him set up his Court, a real Court, in his Palace of Holyroodhouse. Let him start to reign, call a Parliament, be king indeed. Let them all go to Edinburgh.

'Edinburgh . . . !' James quavered. He had never been to Edinburgh since he was a babe in arms, never been more than a few miles from this rock of Stirling. Clearly the notion was a profoundly radical one for him, full of doubts and fears as well as of intriguing possibilities and excitements. He stared. 'Edinburgh . . . Edinburgh is near to Dalkeith, where my Lord Morton lives, Esmé!' he got out.

'A fig for the Lord Morton, James! He will be the nearer, to keep an eye upon, *mon cher*. Edinburgh is the heart of your kingdom. If you will reign, it must be from there.'

'*Must* I reign, Cousin Esmé? Yet, I mean? Would you not reign for me . . . as my Lord Morton did?'

D'Aubigny moistened his lips, and could not resist a flashed glance at Patrick. 'Never, Sire,' he said. 'I am but your most devoted and humble servant . . . and friend.'

'But you could serve me best thus, could you no'? I wish that you would, Cousin Esmé.'

'How could that be, Your Majesty? I am but a lowly French seigneur – think you that your great Scots lords would bear with your rule through such as myself?'

'I could make you a great lord also, could I no'? I could, I could! I'd like to, Esmé.' Urgently, James came shambling over, to put an arm around the other's neck, and stare wistfully at his friend. 'I'd *like* to give you something – I would that! You said yon time that I had lots to give – titles and lands and honours. Will you no' let me give you a present, Esmé? I could make you a lord.'

'You are kind, James. But a title without lands and revenues to maintain it is but a barren honour. I am better as your humble d'Aubigny . . . '

'I could give you an earldom . . . wi' the lands and revenues. Could I no'?'

'Dear boy! But . . . ah, me . . . though I am humbly placed, I have my foolish pride, James. I come of a lofty line, all unworthily – your own father's line, the House of Lennox. Some new-made earldom might well suit many. But for me – ah, no! Leave me as I am, Sire.'

Those great liquid eyes lit with shrewder gleam. 'It is the earldom o' Lennox that you want, then, Esmé?'

'H'mmm. That would be . . . interesting. But . . . ah, no! Too much!'

'Unfortunately, there is already an Earl of Lennox,' Patrick mentioned, level-voiced for him. 'Esmé's uncle Robert, to whom Your Highness gave the earldom but last year.'

'Yon was my Lord Morton's doing, no' mine, Master Patrick. I but signed the paper . . . '

'A pity. Though, I suppose that a paper could be unsigned?' D'Aubigny yawned delicately. 'Not that it is a matter of any importance.'

'Aye, I could – could I no'? Unsign it? He is but a donnert

auld man, my great-uncle Rob. If I gave him something else . . .'

'I daresay that another earldom would serve him just as well,' d'Aubigny admitted, judicially. 'But . . . *il ne fait rien.* It is a trouble for you, Jamie.'

'No, no. I would *like* to do it – fine I would, Cousin. You shall be Earl o' Lennox, I swear it.'

Again Patrick spoke, in the same cool tone. 'Parliament's agreement would be required to revoke an earldom already held, I think, Your Grace. It is not the same as making a new creation.'

'We were suggesting a Parliament, anyway, you will recollect, *mon cher* Patrick. In Edinburgh,' d'Aubigny mentioned lightly. 'Though the issue is hardly vital.'

'But it is, it is, Esmé. It is the first thing that I have ever done for you – you that have done so much for me. We shall do it. It . . . it is our royal will!' James darted glances around like a dog that has barked out of turn. 'And then you can really rule for me!'

David Gray, from his corner, saw his brother consider the Stewart cousins long and thoughtfully.

And so, since Cousin Esmé, who was to be Earl of Lennox, advised it, the Court of the King of Scots was moved to Holyroodhouse.

David would have taken the opportunity to return to his own life at Castle Huntly, but Patrick was urgent that he should stay with them. He needed him, he said, more than ever, for the good Esmé was beginning to grow just a little bit lofty and difficult, and someone close to himself Patrick must have. David insisted on at least returning home to inform their father on the situation, since he considered himself still to be Lord Gray's servant, not Patrick's.

At Castle Huntly, however, my lord was just as determined as was his heir that David should remain at the Court; he did not for a moment believe that Morton had shot his bolt; he believed that Patrick needed his brother's level head more than he had ever done; moreover, it appeared to Lord Gray that the cause of the unhappy Queen Mary was tending to be lost sight of – and David should keep the urgency of that matter before his brother constantly.

After only a couple of halcyon autumn days with his Mariota and the little Mary, therefore, David turned his nag's head reluctantly westwards again for Stirling. A more unwilling courtier would have been hard to find.

The first snows were whitening the tops of the distant blue

mountains to the north when, on October the twentieth, the royal cavalcade approached the capital from the west. A dazzling company, for Scotland, they had passed the night at Linlithgow and now, thankful that, despite their escort of three hundred miscellaneous mounted men-at-arms, no assault by massed Douglases had materialised, they looked at the crowded roofs and spires and towers of Edinburgh, out of the blue smoke-pall of which the fierce and frowning castle, one of the most famous and blood-stained in all the world, reared itself like a leviathan about to strike. King James was staring goggle-eyed at this, declaring fearfully that it was still greater and more threatening than that of Stirling, when a crash as of thunder shattered the crisp autumn air, and set the horses rearing, all but unseating the boy on the spirited black, who cowered, terrified, as the crash was succeeded by another and another.

'Fear nothing, Sire,' Patrick called out, above the reverberating din, laughing. 'Those are but the castle guns saluting you in right royal fashion.'

'It's no' . . . no' my Lord Morton . . . ?'

'No, no. Those are *your* cannon.'

'But . . . but who are they shooting at, then?' James demanded, clinging to his saddle. 'Where go the cannon-balls?'

'No balls today, Highness – only noise. Blank shot.'

'A barbarous din,' d'Aubigny declared. 'But fear nothing, James – here is no danger, save to our ear-drums! But, see – folk await us before the gate, there.'

Pacing out from the archway of the West Port, and dwarfed by the soaring Castle-rock, came a procession of the Provost and magistrates of the Capital, bare-headed and bearing a great canopy of purple velvet and gold lace, under which Majesty, after listening as patiently as he might to a long speech of welcome, rode into the walled city. Crowds lined the narrow streets to see this strange sight – a king in Edinburgh again, after all these years. But they did not cheer. Edinburgh's crowds have never been good at cheering. The guns up at the Castle continued to make din enough for all, however – to the confusion and distress of the two ladies who, in allegory, contended for an unfortunate child before this youthful royal Solomon, who had to shout his judgment at them in between bangs. At the West Bow, a great globe of polished brass was suspended from the archway, and out of this descended a shivering child, as Cupid, naked but for sprouting wings, to present the keys of the city to the King. The infant's chattering teeth, fortunately or otherwise, prevented any speech, and the royal cavalcade pressed on. At the Tolbooth, in the long sloping High Street, however, Peace, Plenty and Justice issued forth, and sought to address the monarch suitably in Latin, Greek and Scots respectively, to the accompaniment of the incessant gunfire – which greatly upset James, who desired to answer back in the appropriate languages, and even, later, in Hebrew, when Religion, personified by a graver matron, followed on; for James, King of Scots, curiously enough, in bookish matters at least, was possibly the best educated youth in Christendom, thanks to the good if stern Master George Buchanan. There being no apparent means of stopping the loyal cannonry, frustrated, the royal scholar had to move on to the High Kirk of Saint Giles, where at least thick walls slightly deadened the enthusiastic concussions – though, before the ninety minutes sermon by Master Lawson the minister was finished, explaining, demanding and emphatically setting forth the royal duty of protecting the reformed religion of Christ Jesus, with thumps and bangs on the Bible to under-line his points, James and his entourage were almost grateful for the explosive punctuations from the Castle.

Dazed and with splitting heads, the glittering company staggered out of church, to be led to the Market Cross, where a leering Bacchus in painted garments and crowned with garlands askew, sat on a gilded hogshead distributing slopping goblets of exceedingly bad wine, and an orchestra seemingly and necessarily composed largely of drums and cymbals, competed with the clamour of gunpowder. Almost in hysterics, James was conducted from these down the packed High Street again to the Netherbow Port, or east gate, where a pageant representing the sovereign's birth and genealogy, right back to the supposed Fergus the First at the beginning of the Fifth Century, was presented – and took some time, naturally, since each monarch in a thousand years was represented. The cannonade stopped abruptly, after some six hours of it, in the middle of the reign of Kenneth MacAlpine – presumably having at last mercifully run out of powder; though the entire city seemed to go on pulsing and throbbing to the echo of it for long thereafter.

At last, with sunset past and the figures of history becoming indistinct in the gloom, genealogy died a sort of natural death about the times of James the Second, and the bemused and battered and benumbed Court – or such of it as had not been able to escape long since – lurched and tottered in torchlight procession down the Canongate to the Palace of Holyroodhouse, and presumably a meal. Edinburgh had done its loyal best.

'My God!' d'Aubigny gasped, as he collapsed into a great chair in the banqueting hall, that happened to be the royal throne. 'My God, *c'est incroyable! Détraqué!* What a country . . . !'

'Would you prefer to return to France?' Patrick wondered.

'No! No – never that!' James cried. 'Och, Esmé – are you tired, man?'

'Our good Esmé is paying for his earldom!' Patrick observed.

Life at the great Palace of Holyroodhouse, under the green pyramid and red crags of tall Arthur's Seat, was very different from that in the cramped quarters of Stirling Castle. There was room and opportunity here for men to spread themselves, and Esmé Stuart, already being called Earl of Lennox though not officially so by ratification of the Council, saw to it that they did. He had James appoint him Lord Great Chamberlain and a member of the Privy Council, the former an office long out of use but which raised him above the elderly Court Chamberlain and put him in complete charge of the entire Court. And this was a very different Court from that of Stirling. Only those might attend who were specifically summoned – and the summons were made out by the Lord Great Chamberlain. Until the Council agreed to the appointment of a new Lord Treasurer, that vital office was in the hands of a deputy, a mere nobody, who did what he was told in the King's name; therefore the Treasury, such as remained of it, was available. Balls, masques, routs and banquets succeeded each other in dizzy procession – if not on the French scale, at least after the French pattern. Women appeared at Court in ever greater numbers, not just as the appendages of their lords, but in their own right, and frequently unaccompanied, a thing that caused considerable scandal and set the Kirk railing. The ladies all loved Esmé and Patrick, whatever they thought of the slobber-mouthed James – and Esmé and Patrick loved the ladies, but of course.

Patrick, however, in all this stirring Court reformation and improvement, devoted most of his efforts elsewhere. To Esmé's motto of 'a fig for Morton, *mon cher*,' he did not wholly subscribe; and he spent the majoirty of his time and energy at this stage seeking to circumvent and forestall any move on the part of the Douglas faction. Considerable funds were required for this purpose, since major persuasion was necessary in more directions than one; for while it was one thing to attend the new Court and enjoy the King's hospitality, as dispensed by the new Lennox, it was altogether another actively and publicly to turn against Morton, who sat like a lion ready to pounce from his den at Dalkeith six short miles away. Certain of the most essential personages in Patrick's plans demanded very substantial inducement indeed to throw in their lot with a régime which, on the face of it seemed unlikely to last overlong. The moneys which he had brought from France dwindled away like snow off a dyke – more especially as a gentleman at Court had to be adequately clad and appointed. Yet d'Aubigny – or my Lord of Lennox, as he preferred now to be called – was markedly unsympathetic, not to say niggardly, in this matter, making light of Patrick's fears and failing to put before the King the necessary papers for signature that would have opened the royal Treasury to his friend.

The fact was that now, Patrick – nor David either, for that matter – never saw James alone. Always Cousin Esmé was with him, delightful, amusing, friendly, inescapable. Both Esmé and Patrick had been appointed Gentlemen of the Bedchamber; but while the former's room adjoined, indeed opened into the King's bedchamber, Patrick found that he and David had been allotted rooms in the opposite wing of the palace, ostensibly on the King's command.

David not infrequently smiled grimly at the situation, and suggested to his brother that both of them would be safer and happier back at Castle Huntly.

Patrick and Esmé never quarrelled; they both needed each other and understood each other too thoroughly for that. It was rather that they seemed to be moving in different directions, their sights set at different targets, perhaps.

Patrick accordingly wrote urgent letters to the Guises, Archbishop Beaton, the Jesuits. Money he wrote about, but not only money.

More than once David spoke to his brother about the imprisoned Queen. Was poor Mary any nearer to her release, for their coming, or for all this expenditure of money? *Her* money – for it was largely the Queen's own French revenues that were being disbursed thus generously. Had Patrick not planned this entire project with a view to convincing Queen Elizabeth that Mary was no longer a menace to her throne and life, that Esmé Stuart was to be James's heir-apparent instead of his mother – at least on the face of it? Patrick admitted all that, and declared that it still stood. Only, Esmé now felt that it would be more practical to gain power in Scotland first, real power, which would make any announcement about the succession the more telling. This was not an issue that could be rushed . . .

The projected meeting of the Estates of Parliament was summoned at last, and on the eve of it Esmé Stuart arranged a great ball at Holyroodhouse, to which all those summoned to the Parliament were invited. No effort or expense was spared on this occasion, for it was important that all concerned should feel beholden to and enamoured of the young King and his new Earl of Lennox, in view of the nature of the enactments which the said Parliament was expected to pass the next day. Esmé, with Patrick's co-operation, excelled himself, and it is probably true that Scotland had never seen the like before. Nothing was stinted; decorations, illuminations, fireworks, musicians, entertainers, tableaux – at some of which the Kirk's representatives present all but had apoplexy – viands, wines, and bedchamber delights for those so inclined. In imitation of the archiepiscopal palace at Rheims, Mary the Queen's fountain in the forecourt spouted wine – and good wine at that, even though such as men-at-arms, grooms and ladies' maids were not made free of it. The Treasury lid had been opened wide, this time.

The evening was well into its high-stepping stride, and the tableau which had been such a success at the Hôtel de Verlac, The Judgment of Paris, was just breaking up after a noisy reception composed almost equally of rapturous appreciation and howls of offended modesty, when there was an unlooked-for interlude. Patrick, in his brief and rather shrivelled vine-leaf, as Paris, was laughingly strolling off, with an arm round the delectable middle of Venus, and a hand cupping one of her fair breasts – suitably or otherwise, according to the point of view; Venus was not quite so authentically undraped as had been Hortense de Verlac – but on the other hand she was very much younger, and of a figure more slender and only slightly less magnificent. A Stewart, the Lady Elizabeth, daughter of the Earl of Atholl and new widow of the Lord Lovat, she was almost certainly the ripest plum yet to grace the remodelled Court, a bold-eyed, high-coloured voluptuous piece.

Down upon this charming couple strode a tall, handsome, and angry figure, unceremoniously cleaving his way through the cheering throng. It was the Captain James Stewart, of the King's Guard, and Commendator-Prior of Prenmay. Reaching them,

148

he smote down Patrick's pleasantly engaged arm in most ungallant fashion.

'Unhand this lady, Gray!' he barked. 'Here is an outrage!'

All innocent amaze, Patrick stared at him. 'Eh?' he exclaimed. 'I' faith, Stewart – what's to do?' That was said into a sudden hush.

'Damn you – keep away from her!' the other jerked. And abruptly whipping off his short cloak which he wore in the fasionable style hanging from one padded shoulder, he cast it around Venus's upper parts.

Patrick gazed from him, downwards, and gulped. 'Mon Dieu – you . . . you have turned her into a pretty trollop now, at any rate! Venus into . . . into Messalina lacking her skirts!' he gurgled. 'Oh, dear Lord!'

There was some truth in that. Venus's round pink hips, even with their wisp of net, and her long white legs projecting beneath the waistlength crimson velvet, somehow did indeed look supremely indecent.

The banqueting-hall rang to comment, delighted or scandalised, but all was outdone by the loud peals of clear laughter from the lady herself.

'Och, Jamie!' she cried. 'What a fool you are! Do you . . . do you think me cold? If so, you are wrong, I vow!' And she laughed again.

'You see,' Patrick said. 'You have mistaken the lady's requirements, Captain! She merits your apologies, rather than your cloak, I think!'

Wrathfully Stewart's hand fell to his rapier-hilt. 'Foul fall you, Gray, you Frenchified monkey!' he raged. 'Mind your tongue.'

At sight of that dropping sword-hand, David Gray, from his discreet corner in one of the great window-embrasures, started forward – to be restrained unexpectedly by a hand that clutched his sleeve quite firmly.

'Let them be, sir,' a cool quiet voice advised, at his side. 'Let them be. I know yon tall lad – and he is dangerous.'

'So I think!' David tossed back, jerking his arm free. He took two or three more paces, and then paused. Esmé and the King were hurrying over to the curiously clad trio in mid-floor, and everywhere men were bowing and women curtseying. David stayed where he was, meantime.

At the sight of the King, Stewart pulled himself together, and bowed stiffly, though his face still worked with passion.

Patrick sketched a graceful but capering obeisance suitable for a Greek hero, and the Lady Lovat, starting to curtsey, glanced downwards at her so spectacularly vulnerable lower parts, and then at the blushing faltering monarch, and tossing off the cloak, struck an attitude. James gobbled.

'Captain Stewart,' Esmé said coldly. 'I think that you forget yourself. Your duties in His Grace's protection do not require such dramatics!'

Stewart looked only at the King. 'I was carried away, Sire, by what seemed . . . offensive before Your Highness.'

'Och, it was naught but mumming, Captain Jamie,' James mumbled, keeping his thin shoulder turned on Venus. 'Master Patrick wasna meaning anything . . .'

'Besides, the Lady Lovat is affianced to my lord of, h'm March, is she not?' Well might the former d'Aubigny hesitate over that title. The earldom of March, like his own, was not yet ratified by Parliament; it was one of things to be done tomorrow. The lady's betrothed was indeed the elderly uncle of Esmé's, Robert Stewart, up till now Earl of Lennox, who had been persuaded to resign Lennox in exchange for this other title of March. 'What is she to you, *Monsieur?*'

The other did not answer that, though the lady giggled. He sketched another bow to the King, 'Have I your permission to retire, Sire?'

'Och, aye, Captain Jamie – but no' that far away, mind.' Majesty flickered his eternally anxious gaze around the crowded hall. 'You'll keep us safe guarded from the Lord Morton . . . ?'

Back at his window, David looked interestedly at the young woman who stood there alone, and who had sought to restrain him. She was dressed much less impressively than were most of the ladies present, but simply, tastefully, in ash-grey taffeta embroidered in silver, that went very well with her level grey eyes and sheer heavy golden hair.

'Your pardon, lady,' he said. 'I intended no discourtesy.'

'And I no presumption, sir,' she answered gravely. 'I but feared that, unarmed as you are, you might have fared but poorly with that long fellow. He is Captain of the Guard and an ill man to cross. And . . . and the Master of Gray can look after himself very well, I think!'

'He was not, h'm, clad for such encounter!' David mentioned.

She smiled, fleetingly. 'Perhaps not. Yet I think that the Master is fairly well appointed, however he is clad!'

'Umm.' He considered what that might mean. Both of them

had the same sort of level grey eyes.

'I was watching you, during yonder fool's-play,' she went on. 'I saw that you were concerned – and not for Captain Stewart, I think. Can it be that you are a friend of the beautiful Master Patrick?' Her glance, encompassing his own severely plain and inexpensive attire, seemed to question the possibility of such a thing.'

'Aye,' David said briefly. 'You could call me that.'

'Then, I think, my estimation of Master Patrick rises a piece,' the strange young woman declared.

Warily David eyed her. He had not seen her before, he thought. By her dress she might be a daughter of one of the country lairds attending the Parilament, or even the attendant of one of the great ladies; yet not in her style and manner, which was calm, assured, and spoke of breeding. He could not deny liking what he saw, whoever she was, and the cloak of secrecy and restraint, which he had come to wear like a second skin, drooped a little.

'I should not call myself his friend,' he amended then, rather stiffly. 'He names me his secretary. His servant would be more true, for I am no clerk.'

'Yet you do not look like a servant – nor sound one!'

'I am the Master of Gray's half-brother – but in bastardy. David Gray is the name.' He could not have stated why he told her.

'I see,' she said slowly. 'That accounts . . . for much.'

Mistaking her tone and pause, he flushed a little. 'I am sorry,' he said tartly. 'You should not be talking, Mistress, with a servant and a bastard. I . . .'

'And something of a fool!' she interrupted calmly. 'Who am I to look askance at bastardy or poverty, Master David Gray? Not Marie Stewart – even with her Queen's name.'

'Stewart? Another . . . ?'

'Aye. We are a prolific clan. In especial my branch of it! And not always over-particular – like yonder naked hizzy whom Master Patrick and Captain Jamie seem to find to their taste! I am the daughter of Robert Stewart, who tomorrow, for some reason that I have not divined, is to be made Earl of Orkney.'

David swallowed. 'You mean . . . the Lord Robert? The Bishop of Orkney? The . . . the King's uncle . . . ?'

'In bastardy!' she reminded, smiling.

'And you, you . . . ?'

'No,' she told him, gravely. 'By some chance I was born in

wedlock. One of the few! But that makes me no better – nor richer – than my bastard brothers and sisters.' She snapped slender fingers. 'So much for legitimacy! And now, Master David, since you are so close to the dazzling and all-conquering Patrick Gray, perhaps you will tell me why my peculiar father is being given an earldom tomorrow?'

'I . . . m'mm . . . I do not rightly know, lady. Save, it may be, that he testified against the Lord of Morton over the English bribes.'

'Rich recompense for biting the hand that once fed him!' she observed dispassionately. 'I believe that there must be more to it than that. Could it be that, bastard as he is, my father is near enough to the throne to rival . . . someone else? And so has to be bought off?'

David moistened his lips, uncomfortably. 'I do not know, your ladyship. I cannot think it.'

'There is talk,' she went on, 'of someone being named successor to our sorry young King – someone who has none of the royal Stewart blood. Could it be that since my father has the blood, even though illegitimate, he is to bought off with this earldom?'

'I do not know,' David repeated.

'And tell me, sir, should such indeed be true – about the succession – how long is my poor feckless cousin the King likely to live, think you?'

Shocked, David stared at her. 'You do not mean . . . ? You are not saying . . . ?'

'I but asked a question. I thought that the Master of Gray's secretary might have been able to answer it.'

This alarming conversation was interrupted by the arrival of the Master of Gray himself. Patrick, clad now in his silver-gilt satin, came sauntering up, smiling brilliantly right and left – but David knew, from something about his bearing, that he was upset.

'Davy,' he said, low-voiced. 'Where is Stewart? The Captain? I cannot see him. I must have word with him.'

'I would have thought that you had had words enough with him . . .' David began.

'Tush – this is serious. Stewart is too important a man to us to quarrel with – yet. And he is aggrieved already.' Suddenly Patrick became aware of the young woman at David's far side. He bowed, all smiles again. 'Ah, fair lady,' he said. 'Here is Beauty herself! And I am ever Beauty's most humble servant.'

'I doubt it, sir,' Beauty said briefly.

'Eh . . . ? You flyte me, madame. Beware how you flyte Patrick Gray!'

'I do not flyte you, sir. I do nothing for you – save prevent you seeking the Captain! He passed through yonder door into the ante-room, not long since.'

'Oh. Indeed. I see. Thank you. As I say, your servant. Come, Davy.'

'Fare you well, Master David,' she said. 'Though I doubt it . . . in the company that you keep! And trust not my father, earl or no earl!'

David shook a worried head, and hurried after his brother.

'Who was yon sharp-tongued jade?' Patrick wondered, making for the ante-room.

'The Lady Marie Stewart, daughter to Lord Robert, that's to be Earl of Orkney.'

'So-o-o! The beggar-man's brat – or one of them! So that is who she is? But she's handsome – I'll admit she's handsome.'

'May be. But I do not think that she likes you, Patrick.'

'Say you so? We'll see about that! You wait, Davy – wait and see!'

The Captain was not in the ante-room. They sought him in the long corridor.

'You said that Stewart was aggrieved?' David mentioned. 'Other than over the woman. What meant you by that?'

'There is bad blood between him and Esmé – our noble lord Earl of Lennox! You know that. Tomorrow Parliament is to assign the forfeited Hamilton lands that Morton has been enjoying, to Esmé, and h'm, in a small way, to my humble self. It seems that the Captain is something of a Hamilton himself – his mother was daughter to the Earl of Arran – an unlovely scoundrel to claim as grandparent! So now our warrior mislikes the dear Esmé the more!'

'With some reason, perhaps?'

'Reason, Davy, and the game of statecraft, are not related. Come, we must find our friend and soothe him with good words. Possibly even with some small Hamilton property somewhere. A pity – but we cannot afford an open rift. Not yet. Tonight's affair was folly – quite stupid. Over that strumpet! Already I have heard people whisper. We walk too delicately to seem to fall out. Or all is lost.'

'All being . . . ?'

'Why, Davy – the cause of the Queen. And the Master of Gray! What else?'

'I am happy that you remembered the Queen!'

'But of course, lad. Now, you take yonder stair, and I'll take this. We must find him, and quickly. He is a headstrong fellow . . .'

'*You* find him, Patrick – not I. Do your own soothing. I have better things to do, I think.'

'You have? You are going back to that wench of Orkney's?'

'Not so. To my bed. And I would to God that bed was at Castle Huntly!'

The next day, after a record short sitting, the Estates passed some godly business of the Kirk, redistribution of the Hamilton lands, ratification of the three earldoms of Lennox, March and Orkney, and the appointment to the Privy Council of the Lord Great Chamberlain and the Master of Gray. The Lord Ruthven, Greysteil, had arrived at Court unbidden, but coming to his nephew, attained entry – if not an enthusiastic welcome. He was a reformed man, it appeared. Now, most suitably, the Council appointed him Treasurer – a man with a good sound respect for money. Patrick, who undoubtedly arranged the nomination, declared that he lent the new régime both respectability and continuity, as well as a sound Protestant flavour – even though James and Cousin Esmé were less impressed. Morton, even if his shadow flickered constantly across the proceedings, was not once mentioned by name, even by Ruthven.

In a day or two, David did indeed return to Castle Huntly, to see his wife delivered of a fine boy. Almost without discussion and by mutual consent, they named him Patrick. In due course, even though he had promised himself otherwise, the proud father returned to the Court. He could not help himself, it seemed.

Chapter Eleven

MORTON was ill. Morton was dying. Morton was shamming ill, seeking to lull his enemies to carelessness. Alternatively, Morton was not ill but was planning to depart secretly to England, there to raise an army with Elizabeth's help, and return on its swords to power in Scotland. Morton planned to kidnap the King, send him to join his mother in an English prison, and rule as Regent again. Morton had attempted to poison the Earl of Lennox, who had the stomach-ache. The English Lord Hunsdon had arrived at Berwick-on-Tweed to organise the invasion of Scotland, to put Morton back into power . . .

So the rumours swept Scotland in the months that followed. Men did not know where they stood, where to place their allegiance. In the hectic gaiety of the Court at Edinburgh, uncertainty, fear, doubt, were always just below the surface. Yet Morton made no open move, lying omniously quiet at his Lion's Den at nearby Dalkeith. He *must* be ill. Or just waiting for his supplanters to destroy each other, or themselves, for him?'

The Earl of Lennox still claimed to care not a fig for Morton – but he had special secure quarters made ready for himself and the King in Edinburgh Castle, and the fortress stocked up to withstand a siege, plus a carefully worked out and secret method of escape from palace to castle, should the need arise. Moreover, a ship was kept in readiness at Leith, provided and crewed. That was the background to as brilliant a season as the old palace of Holyroodhouse had yet experienced.

The Master of Gray was somewhat better informed than most on the subject of Morton – as he ought to have been, considering the French moneys he disbursed for the purpose. He admitted once, of all people, to the Lady Marie Stewart, that the Douglas had indeed been ill, confined to his bed – to the young woman's prompt query of poison he made no comment. He admitted also that Morton had been sending couriers to Elizabeth, certain of whom had apparently called *en route* at a discreet house both going and coming back, with nteresting revelations. He agreed that Hunsdon had arrived at Berwick, and troops were being levied from the North Country English lords, for purposes unspecified. But when the Lady Marie had asked where all this was leading, Patrick only laughed, and advised her not to be over anxious – indeed, to leave anxiety to others, to whom it would do most good.

These confidences to the grey-eyed and calm Marie Stewart were not isolated, and represented 'an unforeseen but notable development. They coincided with a distinct and continuous cooling of relationships between Patrick and Esmé Stuart, also, with a parallel divergence of sympathies on the part of his brother David. Patrick, in fact, had to have a confidant always, and where one failed another had to be found. Why he should have chosen the Lady Marie is debatable; certainly she did not encourage him. Indeed, from the first she kept him at arm's length, not attempting to hide her hostility, distrust, and cool mockery – and obviously much preferred David's company. Perhaps that was part of her attraction: she represented a challenge, in her unaccustomed antagonism, and her curious partiality for his brother. Moreover, she was intelligent, discreet, and of a highly unusual quiet magnetism that served her better than the more obvious and spectacular charms of other of the Court beauties. And, because of her father's comparative penury, with the revenues of the Orkney Isles not yet fully organised, he and at least some of his multitudinous family had been granted quarters in the palace itself, and so she was fairly readily available.

Patrick appeared to feel himself compelled to lay siege to her, which might seem strange, since he not infrequently referred to her to David as 'the beggar man's brat' and 'that woman Stewart.'

David, for his part, liked her very well, and came to consider her simply as his friend – which, curiously enough, provoked Patrick into mocking mirth and barbed wit. He declared that simple friendship between a man and an attractive woman was a fable – and what would Mariota say?

Patrick did more than rail and confide and hint and laugh, of course. He was very busy, though even David knew but a tithe of all that he did. Especially in the vital matters of the Earl of Morton. A new subsidy from the Guises enabled him to subvert many who were very close to the Douglas himself – and Patrick had an undoubted nose for traitors. It was said that he had more spies in and around Dalkeith Palace than Morton had men-at-arms there – and many of these also were said to be bought, though rumour could lie. He enrolled large numbers of men to increase the size of the Guard, Captain Stewart co-operating – possibly with his own ideas as to their ultimate usefulness. This was before the days of standing national armies, but Patrick, by judicious friendships, favours and promises, provided at least the nucleus of an army, theoretically at call, from the armed bands of selected lords in Lothian and the borders – in the King's name, of course. He said – whatever he believed – that within twenty-four hours he could assemble four thousand men in Edinburgh . . . or to surround Dalkeith.

Esmé, Earl of Lennox, was busy too, though in rather different directions. He wooed the Kirk, publicly announcing his conversion to Protestantism, and humbly asked the Assembly to appoint one of their ministers to instruct him fully in the true and reformed Evangel of Christ Jesus. Master Lindsay, of Leith, was nominated for this important task. He hunted with James – well escorted – hawked with James, and wrote poetry with James. He produced masques from the compositions that he encouraged James to concoct, refurnished and refurbished the palace, personally designed the King's clothes and stocked the King's wardrobe. Nothing was too good for James, nor too much trouble – nor did the cost matter, for what else was the Treasury for?

As a consequence, James's love for his cousin grew and deepened, until it was the greatest factor in his life. Nothing could be done without Esmé, nothing decided, nothing even contemplated. And curiously, inconveniently, undoubtedly, if unforeseen, the accomplished elegant man grew fond of the shambling awkward boy. The lovers, they became known as – and tongues wagged unkindly, inevitably. Patrick was not concerned for James's morals, leaving that to others; but he was concerned for Lennox's usefulness to himself and his projects. He spoke to the other about the dangers of this so obviously burgeoning affection between man and boy, more than once – and earned no access of affection for himself thereby. To him the matter spelt complications, trouble – and he said so.

Incidentally, as another consequence of affection, Esmé gathered unto himself the rich abbacy of Arbroath, sundry royal and Hamilton estates in Lothian, Lanark and Carrick, the revenues from harbour dues at Leith, and the Keepership of Dumbarton Castle, most powerful stronghold in the West.

Not all of Scotland greeted these tokens of affection with acclaim.

Captain James Stewart, in especial, found the royal generosity excessive. His dislike of the Earl of Lennox waxed even stronger and more apparent – not that he ever had attempted to hide it. Scarcely a day passed without some incident between them – much to the King's distress, for he seemed to have some regard for his brusque and soldierly Captain Jamie also. Nevertheless, the latter would have lost his appointment and been banished from the Court long since had not Patrick insisted otherwise, that until the threat of Morton was finally removed, one way or another, Stewart's adherence was vital for them. After that, it might be different. The Captain, with great reluctance on Lennox's part, had been granted the Hamilton property of Kinneil, near Linlithgow. It markedly failed to satisfy him.

In the handsome new tennis-court at Holyrood which Esmé had installed for summer amusement, on the first sunny day of a wet July, a curiously mixed company sat in scattered groups watching a foursome in which Lennox partnered the King against Patrick and the Earl of Orkney – the former winning consistently, of course, for James did not like to lose. David was there, new back from a journey into the Highlands on the King's behalf, sitting on a bench beside the Lady Marie. Her elder legitimate brother, the Master of Orkney and Abbot of Kirkwall, sat with the Master of Mar, Keeper of Edinburgh Castle, waiting to play the winners. The Reverend Lindsay, Esmé's chaplain and preceptor, uncertain whether or not to disapprove of tennis, talked with Mr Bowes, Queen Elizabeth's new resident ambassador. And over in a far corner, part hidden by the shrubbery, Captain James was fondling the Countess of March – once Venus and Lady Lovat – whom marriage in no way incommoded.

'So you have come back, after all, Davy,' the Lady Marie was saying. 'You did not go home to your Mariota, as you threatened?'

'I had letters to bring back to the King,' David said, sighing. 'But I will go – and soon.'

'If Patrick will let you.'

'Patrick shall not, cannot, stop me.'

'Patrick can do most things that he sets his mind to, I think.'

'Most, perhaps – not all. As you yourself have shown him, my lady!'

She looked at him, in her grave way. 'No – I suppose that I

am the only woman at Court that he has not bedded with . . . as yet!' At David's frown, she smiled a little, 'You do not like the Court, the life of it, or the people at it, do you, Davy?'

'No,' he admitted, simply. 'Only you, of them all.'

'Thank you, sir – I am flattered! But you would be away from me to your Mariota, like a hawk released!'

He did not answer.

'You do not like what Patrick is doing, either, do you?'

'I do not.'

'And yet you love your brother, I believe.'

'Aye, I daresay. But that does not make me love his works.'

'No.' She paused. 'I do not think that you should go home yet awhile, Davy,' she said, at length. 'Even for your Mariota's sake. I think that you should stay – for Patrick's sake, for Scotland's sake, may be.'

'Eh . . . ?'

'Aye – if you love Patrick. If you love Scotland. I have watched you both, Davy, and I believe that you alone have any influence with Patrick. For he loves you also, you know. He is an extraordinary man, our Patrick. He is capable of great things – for evil or for good. He will do great things – already he is doing them. He is two men in one – and I fear that the evil may triumph. To the hurt of himself, and many.'

David turned to stare at her. 'You . . . you see deep, lady,' he said, trouble in his voice. Often, often, had he thought the same thoughts.

'I see a great responsibility on the broad shoulders of one Davy Gray!'

'What can I do?' he demanded. 'Patrick will not change his course one step, for me! Think you that I have not tried, reasoned with him? All my life . . .'

'And achieved more than you think, belike.'

'Achieved mockery and laughter . . .'

'Look, Davy, here is not time for small thoughts, small offence. Patrick is not engaged in small things – that is clear. He needs you at his shoulder. You may keep him from . . . from great wickedness. You may save him, as none other can.

'I . . . ? I am a mere servant, a humble attendant, no more . . .'

'Spare us the humbleness, Davy, for you are no humbler than I am! Less, I think. They say that we cannot escape our destiny.' She pointed into the tennis-court. 'Yonder is yours, is it not? Stay with him, and help him, Davy.'

He glowered straight before him, from under frowning brows.

159

'You . . . ,' he said. 'You have a great interest in him, in Patrick!'
That was roughly said, accusatory.

'Say that I have a fondness for his brother,' the Lady Marie
declared, even-voiced, and rising, moved over to speak to her
brother.

David sat still, biting his lip.

The Earl of March came bustling into the garden, a foolish
red lobster of a man. At sight of him, though his Countess did
not still her squealing laughter, Captain Stewart arose, and
came sauntering from the shrubberies. Seeing David alone on
his bench, he came over and sat beside him.

'The Master of Gray plays a losing game out yonder,' he said,
after a moment or two. 'If he takes not care, I think he may play
a losing game elsewhere also!' That was ever the Captain James,
blunt, scornfully to the point.

David made no reply.

'He rides the wrong horse,' Stewart went on. 'Yon prancing
jennet is due for a fall – and will pull your fine brother down
with him, man. He rears high, the Frenchman – over high.
Your brother would be wise to bridle him . . . or find another
mount!'

'You should tell that to the Master of Gray, sir, not to me,'
David said.

'I will, never fear. And he would do well to heed me!' Stewart
sat still, stretching out his long legs, and yawning.

The game was over shortly, in a handsome win for the
cousins, and Patrick, after congratulating the King, came
strolling over to David's bench, mopping his brow with a
perfumed handkerchief – at which Stewart sniffed crudely.
He sat down between them.

'Lord, it is warm!' he said. 'You look devilish cool, the pair
of you. You should be warmer in His Grace's service – and play
tennis!'

The Captain snorted. 'I like to win my games, Gray!' he
jerked. 'Not play second to a French mountebank!'

'Hush, Captain! Can it be that you speak of my lord of
Lennox, High Chamberlain of Scotland, Abbot of Arbroath,
Keeper of Dumbarton?'

'Aye, none other. Mountebank, I said, and mountebank I
mean! What else is his play with the King? What else is his
trifling with the Kirk? He is no more a Protestant than is the
Pope of Rome! He plays the part of a convert – but all the time,
privily, he is bending the King towards Rome and France. I

160

know – I have heard him at it.'

'Is that so? You must have good ears, then!'

'Aye, almost as good as your own, Gray! But maybe the Kirk's ears will grow sharper, too!'

'You mean – you might tell them? Enlighten them?' That was entirely easy, casually conversational.

'I did not say so – though the man makes me spew!'

'It might do no harm,' Patrick observed, smothering a yawn. '*Pardieu* – this heat! A little gossip amongst the fathers and brethren might enliven even the chill bones of the Kirk ... to our dear land's benefit!'

Both his hearers looked sharply at the lounging elegant speaker, who now produced a comb to discipline his damp dark curls.

'*You* say that?' Stewart, the explicit ever, asked. 'How strong is your own zeal for the Protestant faith, Gray?'

'Need you ask, friend? Here at the grey heart of reformed Scotland, it all but eats me up!' Patrick assured, but lazily.

The Captain frowned. 'I doubt if I understand you, man,' he said.

'I am desolated.' Patrick gestured with his comb towards the tennis-players, who were commencing the second game. 'Dear Esmé – he is indefatigable. I hope that ... he may not do himself an injury, with it all!'

Again the sharp glance. 'He well may!' Stewart said, grimly. 'He offends all the old nobility. He intends to rule Scotland – all can see that. Observe if he does not soon displace Argyll as Chancellor! Then he will make us all Catholic again – for I believe him to be, in fact, a Jesuit agent. I think that he plans an alliance with Spain and France ... which means war with England.'

'So? You ... er ... think quite a deal, Captain, do you not? For a soldier!'

'Aye. And so do you, Gray. I do not believe that any of these thoughts of mine are new to *you*!'

Patrick smiled, and nodded towards a corner of the palace garden. 'A picture of connubial bliss are they not? The Lady March and her husband!'

The other did not rise to that. 'This is not what I aided your return from France, to the Court, for, Master of Gray,' he said heavily. 'As I understood it, you planned that Queen Elizabeth should hear of a new successor-designate to the Scots throne, and so fear our Queen Mary no longer – not that this Frenchman should take Scotland for his own!'

'Something of the sort,' Patrick agreed.

'If Elizabeth should come to hear of what is indeed toward, here,' Stewart went on, slowly. 'I think that she would take steps to set it otherwise.'

'That is possible. Then . . . why not tell her, Captain?'

'Eh . . . ?' Stewart looked not only at Patrick this time, but round at David also, as though seeking confirmation that his ears had not deceived him. 'Tell Elizabeth . . . *tell* her?'

'Why not? Her Mr Bowes does not strike me as a very intelligent man. It would be a pity if the good Protestant lady was misinformed, would it not? If the position concerns you, write to her, man. There is a great traffic of letters to her from these parts, anyhow!'

'And d'Aubigny – your Lennox?'

'A little . . . correction would no doubt be a kindness to him. As a bridle gentles too spirited a steed! A touch of the knee here; a pull on the bit, there – and a straight and useful course results for all, does it not?'

'God, Gray – you astonish me!'

'Why? 'Tis but common sense, my friend. When your mount veers to one side, you tug to the other, do you not?'

'But . . . why not write to Elizabeth yourself, then?'

'Ah, no. That would be unwise. Her Grace of England knows well, I am sure, that our Esmé and myself are close, that together we set this course. In any letter from me she would assuredly smell . . . jesuitry! Which would be unfortunate, would it not? No, no – you wield the pen instead of the sword, for once, Captain . . . in the good Esmé's best interests!' Stretching, Patrick rose to his feet. 'Now – I see the Lady Marie Stewart wasting her favours on her reprobate of a father! That will never do. Your servant, sir.' And with a bow of pure mockery, he sauntered off.

The Captain stared after him. 'Yon is a strange man, I vow!' he said. 'Deep. Deep as the Nor' Loch – and with as little knowing what is at the bottom!'

'Yes,' David said, level-voiced.

'Aye, an unchancy brother to have, I'd say!' Stewart rose, and stalked away abruptly, without farewell, as though he had just recollected something that he required to do.

David sat still, unmoving. The Lady Marie was right, it seemed – dear God, how right! He had not realised that it could go this far. The Queen of England, now . . . ! Troubled, seeing nothing of the gay and colourful scene about him, David gazed ahead. Almost, he was saying goodbye to Mariota and little Mary and Castle Huntly.

Chapter Twelve

'THE Douglas has played into our very hands, I tell you, Davy!'
Patrick declared. 'A Yuletide gift, in truth! My waiting game is
proved the right game. Here is the proof of it.'

Seldom had David seen his brother so openly, undisguisedly
elated – indication, if such was needed, of the weight of menace
that had hung over all about the King for so long, however
lightly Patrick, for one, had seemed to bear the burden.

'He is coming to attend the Council next week, unbidden. My
information is sure. He has decided that the time is ripe to move
– that with most of the lords offended in Esmé, he can sway the
Council, and with a few hundred Douglases around the Parliament Hall and a street mob worked up to yell against Popish
Frenchmen, the day will be his.'

'As may not he be right?'

'I think not, Davy. Something on this sort is what I have
waited for. There is more than my Lord Morton can make
plans!'

The meeting of the Privy Council, an important one, was to be
held on the afternoon of Hogmanay, the last day of 1580. Only
an hour before it was due to start, the venue was changed from
Parliament Hall, up near St Giles, to a room in the Palace of
Holyroodhouse itself, at the King's command. When the
Councillors – or such as had not already been warned – thereafter came riding down the long High Street and Canongate,
on a chill dark day of driving rain, jostled by a clattering escort
of hundreds of Douglas men-at-arms, it was to leave the No
Popery crowd behind, their ardour notably damped. And at the
great forecourt of Holyrood, and all around the palace, rank
upon rank of armed men stood, mounted and afoot, pikemen,
hagbutters, mosstroopers, Highland broadswordsmen, waiting
silent, motionless in the rain, five or six times outnumbering the
Douglases. No lord might bring with him more than ten men
into the palace precincts, the Captain of the Guard declared – by
the royal command. Morton, who obviously had expected to be
forbidden to enter anyway, snorted a scornful if somewhat
disappointed laugh, and strode within.

He was still smiling grimly amongst his red whiskers when he stalked into the Council Chamber. Men greeted him uncertainly, but there was nothing uncertain about James Douglas. He marched straight for his accustomed place at the right of the empty throne, where he had been wont to sit as Regent, and sat down at once. He produced from a pocket the small Regent's baton – to which of course he had not been entitled for two years, but which made a potent symbol nevertheless – and rapped it sharply on the great table.

'Sit ye down, my lords,' he commanded, in the sudden silence. 'Let's to business, Argyll, you are still Chancellor, are you no'? We'll have the sederunt.'

At the other end of the table, the Earl of Argyll, dark, thin-lipped, fox-faced, still stood. 'We await the King's Grace, my lord,' he said.

'The laddie can come in and signify the royal assent when we're done, man,' Morton snapped. 'Here's no bairn's work!'

'His Grace has intimated his intention of presiding in person.'

'Has he, 'fore God! Then let word be sent him that we are ready.'

David, sitting at another table at the far bottom end of the room, along with other secretaries and clerks, took in all the scene–the uneasy hesitant lords, the watchful Chancellor, and the assured dominant Morton. He was perhaps a little thinner than when David had last seen him, but had lost nothing of his truculent authority and sheer animal powe₁. David noted that, though summoned, his father, the Lord Gray, was not present.

A fanfare of trumpets marked the royal approach. Preceded by heralds in the blazing colours of their tabards, the Lord Lyon King of Arms, and the Earl of Erroll as Constable, King James came in, robed in magnificence, but anxious-eyed and chewing his lip. He looked both older and younger than his fourteen years. At his right and left paced the Earl of Lennox and the Master of Gray.

Such as were seated, rose to their feet, bowing. Even Morton, sniffing and hawking loudly at all this display, perforce raised his posterior some way off his chair in a mocking crouch.

'We bid you all welcome to our Council, my lords,' James got out thickly, as he sat down in the throne, beside Morton unavoidably, but not looking at him. 'Pray be seated.'

As Morton, still crouching, opened his mouth to speak, Argyll the Chancellor banged loudly on the other end of the table. 'Is it Your Highness's declaration that this Council is

duly constitute?' he asked quickly.

'Aye, it is. But ... but first I ... we oursel' would, would make announcement anent our dear cousin Elizabeth ... Her Grace of England.' James was trembling almost uncontrollably, continually glancing over his shoulder and upward, where Lennox stood behind the chair which Morton had appropriated. 'I ... we do hereby declare ...'

He was interrupted by a loud rat-a-tat from without. The doors were thrown open, and the Captain of the Guard strode in, in full armour, plumed helmet, hand on sword-hilt. Straight for the King he hastened, an imposing martial urgent figure.

'Sire,' he cried. 'Your life is endangered!'

'Eh ... ?'

'Sirrah – what means this unseemly entry?' the Chancellor croaked but with little conviction.

'Treason!' Stewart exclaimed, and sank down on one knee at the side of the throne. 'Sire – I say treason!'

At that dread word fully half the men in the great chamber were on their feet.

Two distinct table bangers beat for quiet, the Chancellor's gavel and Morton's baton. 'Silence!' the latter bellowed – and no voice could be more effective. 'What fool's cantrip is this?'

He got his silence and his answer. 'Sire, take heed!' Stewart declared. 'As Your Grace's guard, I charge you – take heed! This man at your side, the lord of Morton, has designs upon your royal person.'

'Belly-wind!' Morton scoffed.

'I ... we will hear of our trusty Captain of the Guard,' James quavered. 'What is this, of treason, Captain Jamie?'

Still kneeling, and pointing directly at Morton, Stewart cried, 'Treason I said – high treason it is! I accuse James Douglas, before Your Grace and this whole Council, of the cruel slaying of Your Grace's royal father, King Henry Darnley!'

Uproar followed. A dozen lords were shouting at once. No amount of baton banging would still it. Not that Morton was trying. He was on his feet, in towering rage, roaring his loudest.

Terrified, James cringed on his throne, with Cousin Esmé's arm protectively around his shoulders. Patrick signed to Stewart to rise to his feet, and together they interposed themselves between the wrathful Morton and the boy. Stewart part drew his sword; he was the only man who might lawfully wear arms in the presence of the monarch.

Morton raved on for minutes on end, a furious foul-mouthed

166

tirade of such sustained violence and vibrant force as to set the
nerves of every man in the room aquiver. Only when speechless
through sheer lack of breath, was there a pause, and Stewart
was able to resume.

'Such denials abate nothing of my charge, Sire. I charge this
Council, for the King's safety, to bring the Lord Morton to his
assize, when I will testify on oath that all is truth. I was but a
page then, but I bore the confidences between this lord and his
cousin and familiar, Archibald Douglas of Morham – whose
was the hand that slew the King. The same whom this Earl
Morton made a Lord of Session and judge of this realm, for
reward!'

'You snivelling puppy . . . !'

'Where is Archie Douglas?' somebody demanded. 'Produce
him, to testify. Produce Archie Douglas!'

'Aye!'

'The Senator Archibald Douglas fled last night, south of the
Border and into England!' Stewart announced grimly.

That clinched the matter. When Argyll, perceiving his
moment, demanded whether or no they, as the Council, would
heed the plea of the King's Captain, there were a score of ayes.
Any who thought to say no, looked hastily around them, and
discreetly held their tongues.

Morton himself almost seemed to be stunned – or it may have
been the first stages of apoplexy. He mouthed and all but choked,
staring. 'Lindsay!' he managed to get out, at last. 'Ruthven!
Glamis! Glencairn!'

But the aged Lord Lindsay gazed at the floor, and twisted his
claw-like hands; Ruthven, the once terrible Greysteil, now considering events afresh, and in consequence the new Treasurer,
looked out of the window at the beating rain; the Lord Glamis,
that sober man, was dead, killed in, of all things, a brawl in
Stirling street, and his brother the Master was banished the
Court and sulking in the north; Glencairn indeed was there, but
drunk, as ever – only, maudlin drunk where once he had been
fiery drunk. The fact was, the old lion had outlived his jackals.

'God's curse on you all, for puling dotards and tit-sucking
babes!' Morton almost whispered. He spat. 'That for you – each
and all! I will see you in hell . . . '

'Captain Stewart,' Erroll said stiffly. 'You will see the Lord
Morton warded securely. In this palace until late tonight. Then
you will convey him straitly to the Castle of Edinburgh, where
you, Master of Mar, will answer for him with your life. In the

167

King's name! Take him away.'

Stewart signed forward guards from the doorway.

Morton, of a sudden, assumed a great dignity. 'No man's hand shall touch Douglas!' he declared quietly, finally, and without a glance or a word to anyone, passed from the chamber, surrounded by the soldiers, Stewart following.

'The Council will resume,' the Chancellor called out, before chatter could begin, his gavel now unchallenged on the table. 'Silence for the King's Grace.'

James, however, was too overcome to do more than blink and wag his head. Argyll nodded.

'In the matter of Her Grace of England her letter to His Highness . . .'

So fell James Douglas, harshest tyrant that even Scotland had known in a thousand years, who had waited too long in the waiting game. Neither the Earl of Lennox nor the Master of Gray had so much as said a word, throughout.

Morton was taken after dark, by devious ways, to Edinburgh Castle, and though his leaderless men-at-arms rioted throughout the city and did immense damage, they could neither assail the palace or storm the castle to free their lord. In due course he was removed to Lennox's distant castle of Dumbarton, for greater security.

It was six months before the red Earl was brought to trial – if trial it could be called. One thousand men, no less, were sent to convoy him back to Edinburgh, and a Douglas attempt at rescue *en route* failed. By a jury of his peers, all his enemies, he was tried on June the second, and on the testimony of Stewart, Sir James Balfour, one of his own Douglases turned renegade, and letters from the imprisoned Queen Mary, was found guilty of being art and part in the murder of Henry Stewart, Lord Darnley, the King, fourteen years before. No one witnessed in his defence; those who might have done were either dead or had ill consciences and no desire to swim against the tide. He was condemned to die that same day.

The Maiden, set up at the Market Cross, outside St Giles, was Morton's own invention, and had long given him a great deal of pleasure and satisfaction. It was a somewhat clumsy contrivance, of a great knife counterbalanced by a heavy weight, all set within an upright frame, that was designed to whisk off heads with mere fingertip control – a forerunner of the guillotine, in fact. Now the Maiden took her begetter to herself right lovingly, to his own grim jests as to her well-tried efficiency. He faced her mockingly, declared as his last testament that none should know what so many wished to hear – where his vast accumulated treasure was hidden, since he had let none into his secret and made sure that the servants who had helped him stow it away had not lived to reveal its whereabouts; and as his dying prayer, mentioned, grinning, that if he had served his God as well as he had served his King he might not have come to this pass. Then, puffing, he got down on his thick knees, to lay his red head in what he called his Maiden's bosom – and the knife fell.

Set on a spike on the topmost pinnacle of the Tolbooth thereafter, the said head grinned out for long over all the capital that its owner had so long dominated. James the King trembled every time that he passed beneath.

Chapter Thirteen

'Is it not as good as a puppet show, Davey?' the Lady Marie asked, nodding her coifed golden head forward. 'An entertainment, no less. Even here, on the high top of Lomond, they're at their mumming . . . with Patrick pulling the strings.'

'Aye,' David said briefly. 'I see them.'

'One day, Patrick is going to get his strings entangled!' she added.

He companion made no comment, but shook his horse into a trot, to keep pace with their leaders. The young woman did likewise.

They were high on the green roof of Fife, on a crest of the long ridge of the Lomond Hills, far above the tree-level, with the land dropping away below them on either side in great brackeny sweeps, northwards into the strath of the Eden, wherein Falkland nestled amongst its woods, and southwards over rolling foothills and slanting fields to the sandy shores and great glittering estuary of Forth, beyond which Lothian smiled in the noonday sun and Edinburgh was discernible only because of its soaring castle. They had been hunting, from the Palace of Falkland, almost since sunrise – for James loved hunting, and was but a poor sleeper into the bargain. They had raised and killed three times in the forested foothills of Pitlour and Drumdreel, and then had put up a notable fourteen-point woodland stag, and all else was forgotten – at least by the King. For two hours they had run it, as it twisted and turned and sought sanctuary ever higher up out of the glades and thickets of the wood, up through the birch scrub and the whins, on to this high bare ridge where the larks sang and the curlews called, James and Lennox ever in front because of the fine Barbary blacks which they alone rode. And on the very crest they had found the hunted brute dead, its poor heart burst – for woodland life makes a stag heavy if nobly headed – and James had wept in vexation, for he had thought to shoot the killing bolt himself. Now they rode back along the heights, seeking a spot where they might water the horses and eat their picnic meal, a colourful and gallant company – though not all of them as fond of this sort of thing as was their monarch.

It was extraordinary how James had changed in the months since Morton's death. He was a different youth altogether, like some plant long hidden under an obstruction which blossoms up and swiftly spreads itself whenever the obstruction is removed. Not that all held that the transformation was for the better. He had taken to asserting himself, erratically rather than consistently; he would have no more of Master Buchanan; he indulged in sly tricks and devised cunning traps for all but his beloved Esmé; he sought to spend as much of his time as he might in the saddle, where undoubtedly he made a better showing than on his spindly knock-kneed legs. Morton's shadow had been potent indeed.

More than James burgeoned, of course, under the smiling sun that the Douglas's lowering threat had for so long obscured – in particular Esmé Stuart, Captain James, and the lady who had been Venus, the Lady Lovat, and Countess of March, and now was none of them. Unfortunately, to a large extent their burgeoning was mutually antagonistic. The Captain had blossomed to best effect, most assuredly. He was now James, Earl of Arran, Privy Councillor and Gentleman of the Bedchamber. He had known the price to ask – and when to ask it. On the very day before Morton's trial he had announced his terms: the Hamilton Earldom of Arran and the rest, or he would not testify. Since all depended upon his impeachment, at that late hour there could be no denial, Patrick had pointed out – though Lennox would have risked disaster fighting him. So the legitimate holder of the title had been hastily and judicially declared to be insane, and the honours and lands transferred to his illegitimate third cousin. And on the same happy day that his patent of nobility was signed, the Captain had the Court of Session declare the Earl of March to be frigid and incapable of procreating children, with the fortunate consequence that his marriage of less than a year earlier to the Lady Lovat was esteemed to be null and void. The pair were married the very next day – which enabled the lady's child by the Captain to be born legitimate a couple of weeks later – excellent timing, as all had to admit. The Earl and Countess of Arran were riding high – and would ride higher.

And yet, the Lady Marie Stewart suggested that it was Patrick Gray who pulled the strings.

Esmé, Earl of Lennox had not looked on entirely idly, of course. James, with a little prompting, had gladly created him Duke of Lennox, almost the first non-royal Scottish dukedom in history; moreover he had convinced Argyll that he was getting too old for the tiresome duties of the Chancellorship, and could well transfer these to the elegant shoulders of the new Duke. So now dear Esmé was Chancellor of the Realm, President of the Council, and first Minister of State. Also, he had taken over Morton's magnificent palace at Dalkeith.

David, for one, doubted whether these were strings of Patrick's pulling.

Such were the puppets that the Lady Marie exclaimed over on West Lomond Hill.

Admittedly they had been behaving ridiculously in front there, all morning, Lennox and Arran bickering with each other when they thought that James was not looking, very civil before the King's face and aiming slights and insults behind his back, ever jockeying for position, seeking to pull the boy this way and that. And the Lady Arran made her own contribution, ogling the King – and indeed all others so long as they were male – managing to have her riding-habit slip aside with marked frequency to reveal great lengths of hosed, gartered and well-turned leg, fetching a lace handkerchief regularly in and out of the cleft of her remarkable bosom with much effect, and laughing in silvery peals the while.

The Master of Gray, smiling, debonair, equable, but watchful always, rode beside and amongst them, occasionally coming back to where the Lady Marie chose to ride with David, but never leaving the principals for long.

An entertainment, that young woman called it; she had, perhaps, a mordaunt sense of humour.

The chief huntsman had found a suitable hollow, with a bubbling spring, and had come back to guide the royal party thereto, when the drumming of hooves drew all eyes northwards. Up out of the low ground rode a single horseman on a gasping foam-flecked mount. It was Logan of Restalrig, red-faced, rough, untidy as usual. He doffed his bonnet perfunctorily to the King, but it was at Patrick that he looked.

'Sire two embassages have arrived at Falkland, for Your Majesty, misliking each other exceedingly! One is from Her Grace the Queen, your mother. The other from Her Grace Elizabeth of England. I left them nigh at blows!'

'My, my mother . . . ?' James faltered, biting his lip.

'From Elizabeth!' Arran cried. 'An embassage you said, man – not a courier?'

'Sir Thomas Randolph himself – one o' the Queen's ministers.

Yon one who was once ambassador to our Queen Mary. Talking exceeding high and hot.'

Arran glanced sidelong at Patrick.

'And the other? From Queen Mary?' Lennox demanded. 'How comes it that she can send . . . that she . . . ?' He paused. 'She is not released? From her prison?'

'I think not,' Logan answered. 'It is Monsoor Nau, Her Highness's secretary. But he has my Lord Herries with him, and a troop o' Catholic Maxwells. They have ridden neck and neck frae Edinburgh – and are no' speaking love to each other!'

'Sire, with your permission, I shall ride fast to Falkland to welcome these, er, notable visitors,' Patrick proposed. 'To see to their entertainment until such time as Your Grace is pleased to receive them.'

'Aye. Very well, Master Patrick . . .'

'I will come with you,' Arran announced briefly.

'As Chancellor, it is meet, surely, that *I* should greet the Queen of England's envoy, James,' Lennox put in. 'Ascertain his business . . .'

'No need,' Arran interrupted. 'I am acquaint with Randolph.'

'I rather feared so . . .'

'Let us all go, Your Highness,' Patrick said quickly. 'You can outride us all, anyway, I doubt not.'

'Ever the one who minds his mark,' the Lady Marie mentioned, low-voiced to David. 'Observe how much attention poor Queen Mary's embassy receives! I wonder why Arran is so anxious to see the Englishman first?'

David did not put forward any suggestions.

So they all rode hot-foot, without stopping for a meal, down through the miles of woodland to Falkland, that most remotely rural of the royal palaces. James this time did not attempt to outdo his supporters. Always the mention of his mother's name set him in fear and alarm.

In the end, all three contestants for the duty saw the two ambassadors together in the great hall of Falkland, prior to the formal interview with the King – and for makeweight Patrick invited a fourth, his Uncle William, the Treasurer, never now called Greysteil, Lord Ruthven no longer, but Earl of Gowrie, so created by a grateful monarch who still feared the sight and sound of him. William Ruthven was another who had burgeoned and blossomed since the fall of his old colleague Morton; having once chosen the right course, he pursued it single-mindedly,

173

and being the darling of the Kirk and idol of the godly, his nephew found him exceedingly useful on occasion. The fact that neither Lennox nor Arran liked nor trusted him by no means always invalidated his usefulness. As now.

The two ambassadors, with their trains, were already waiting at opposite corners of the hall, eyeing each other like packs of angry dogs, when James's representatives filed in. Immediately there was an unseemly scramble as to which should be first received. Monsieur Nau, small, dapper, excitable, claimed the right as his, as representing the sovereign lady of this realm of Scotland approaching her own son. Sir Thomas Randolph tall, dyspeptic, disapproving, asserted that as representing the reigning Queen of England, he took precedence over all others soever, especially one whose principal was a mere guest of his lady.

'Her prisoner, shamefully, monstrously held, you mean, *nom de Dieu*!' the Frenchman cried.

'Watch your words, sirrah, when you speak of my lady!' Randolph exclaimed.

'Your lady is a . . .'

'Your Excellencies,' Patrick intervened, smiling. 'My lord Duke of Lennox, my lord Earl of Arran, my lord Earl of Gowrie, and your humble servant, bid you both welcome in the King's name, I am sure that matters of precedence may readily be resolved by receiving you both at the same time. Then . . .'

'Not so, by the Mass – not so!' Nau contradicted. 'The Queen of Scots shares place with none, in Scotland!'

'The Queen of Scots is abdicate,' the Earl of Gowrie said bluntly. He certainly should have known, for he had been one of those who put the abdication papers so forcibly before the hapless Queen at Loch Leven, seventeen years before.

'*Jamais*! Never!' Nau declared. 'That was done by force. It is of none avail. My mistress is Queen of Scots, yet.'

'Then what is her son, man?' Gowrie demanded.

'He is the Prince James, Her Grace's heir and successor in the thrones of Scotland and England both, and . . .'

'My God!' Randolph burst out.

'Och, you're clean gyte, man!' Gowrie asserted.

'Fool!' Arran muttered. 'Does he take us all for bairns?'

Even Lennox looked alarmed and uneasy, and glanced swiftly along at Patrick.

'Monsieur Nau,' that young man said courteously. 'These are matters for debate, are they not? How are your credentials addressed, may I ask?'

'To James, Prince and Duke of Rothesay, from his Sovereign Lady Mary, Queen of Scots,' the other answered promptly.

'Then, Monsieur, I fear that they are in error. I would respectfully advise that you withdraw to yonder chamber and amend them. Amend them, Monsieur to James, by God's grace, King of Scots.'

'Tête Dieu, that I will never do, sir! Never! By Her Grace's command.'

Patrick shrugged one shoulder, sighed, and nodded along the line. Lennox took him up.

'Then, Monsieur Nau, I regret that you cannot be received,' he said firmly. 'It is impossible.'

'But Monsieur . . . my lord Duke! C'est impropre! The Prince's own mother . . . !'

'It is impossible,' Lennox repeated. 'If James is not King, then, then . . . No, no, Monsieur, you leave us no choice. Sir Thomas Randolph, you are accredited to King James, I take it?'

'Naturally, Your Grace.'

Lennox bowed. Nobody in Scotland had yet been brought to term him Your Grace, which here was awarded only to the monarch or his regent. 'And have you aught that you would say, h'm, privately, before you see His Highness?'

'No, sir.' ..

'Very well.' Lennox signed to the hastily summoned herald, who threw open the double doors and cried,

'His Excellency the Ambassador of Her Grace of England, to the high and mighty James, King of this Realm and of the Scots. God save the King!'

'You failed the Queen – Queen Mary,' David repeated heavily, stubbornly. 'The Queen whose cause you came to uphold – and for which you have received moneys in plenty! Failed her just as surely and as openly as though you had slapped her face!'

'Tush, man, I told you! Do you not see? I could do no other. She is foolish, headstrong, the beautiful Mary – always has been. To have accredited her envoy only to Prince James . . . for us to have accepted that, in front of the English Ambassador, would have been to accept her as sovereign still, and her son as no King. And if he is not King, then nothing that has been done or signed in his name since his crowning is lawful and true. I am not of the Privy Council, Lennox is no duke, Arran

175

no earl!' That would signify little – but what of greater affairs? What would the Kirk say? What would Elizabeth say?'

'I have not thought, of late, that you cared deeply what the Kirk said, Patrick! And should Elizabeth of England shape Scotland's policies!?'

'Lord, but she does, man! There's the rub–she does. So long as she holds in her hand the gift of the succession to the English throne, with Mary and James as the first heirs, so long can she take a part in shaping Scotland's policy. There is no avoiding it.'

'Tell me, Patrick,' his brother said quietly, deliberately. 'Would you rather see James on Elizabeth's throne, and you, his minister, wielding the power of England – or Mary released from her bondage and back in her own country as the Queen she rightly is?'

Patrick frowned – and he did not often frown. The brothers were standing on the parapet-walk outside Patrick's room in the south round tower of Falkland, on the evening of the ambassadors' arrival. 'Fiend take you, Davy – that is no question! You talk nonsense. I am pledged to the Queen's interests – but her best interests, not such folly as this. Besides,' he laughed again, 'I see Elizabeth's cunning hand in all this, anyway!'

'Elizabeth . . . ?'

'Aye. Elizabeth's hand. Or the heads of her two minions, Burleigh and Walsingham, the two cleverest brains in Christendom! How think you Monsieur Nau comes here in open embassage? Hitherto, Mary has been able to send to her son only letters smuggled secretly out of Sheffield Castle, these thirteen years. But now her secretary is permitted to leave her openly, to travel to Scotland. Elizabeth knew what his errand was, that is why – and wished it accomplished, I swear.'

'M'mmm. And you know what that errand was?'

'Aye. I saw Nau later, privately – and soothed him somewhat. Though he is not to see the King – that we cannot permit. He has come to propose an Association – a sharing of the Crown between Mary and her son. That they should rule as King and Queen together – or rather, as Queen and King, for she will grant the honour and be the senior.'

'As is only right and proper,' David said. 'An excellent purpose, I would say.'

'Aye,' his brother commented dryly. 'I daresay you would!'

'But . . . what of the religious differences? What is purposed there?'

'That the Kirk remains supreme, with James as its head –

as now. But that Mary remains Catholic, and there shall be full freedom of worship.'

'As there should be. Surely these are good proposals – if Elizabeth can be made to release the Queen. You say that you think that Elizabeth knows of this, and would have it so?'

'I did not say that – quite. Knows, yes, I think – and would have Scotland consider and desire it. So, heigho – she sends Randolph at the same time, threatening war!'

'Eh . . . ? War, do you say? War with England?'

'Just that. Such is Randolph's embassy. Threats of war, fierce railing over Morton's death, thunderings of vengeance. She does not like losing money, does Elizabeth – and she invested much in Morton, I fear!'

David shook his head. 'I do not understand. You have just said . . . How can she both approve of Nau's errand, and also threaten us with war?'

'We are dealing with clever folk, Davey – folk who understand statecraft as yon tranter down there understands falconry. They want James, and Scotland, to grasp at this Association with Mary, and the threats of war are to frighten him into doing it.'

'But why?'

'Why does Elizabeth hold Mary prisoner? For a good purpose, you may be sure – all that woman does is for good reason. It is to have a hold over Scotland. To prevent Scotland joining her ancient ally, France, or Spain either, against England. Her nightmare – Burleigh's nightmare – is a war on two fronts: Scotland in the north and France in the south. This proposed Association would play into her hands, so long as she holds Mary. Scotland would want something from her, must woo her, to get Mary back. She would dangle promises before us, and the hope of the ultimate succession – but that is all. Mary she will hold on to – and Scotland will not align herself with France. We beg our Queen back from her, and while we beg, Elizabeth and England are safe.'

'What then if *we* made the war? To get our Queen back.'

'Elizabeth is no fool, Davy. And she is well served with spies. She knows that we are in no case to invade England. We could mount a sally over the Border, yes – in conjunction with a French invasion across the narrow seas and perhaps a Spanish attack from the Low Countries and Ireland. But war, by ourselves, no. And would not the first Scot to fall be Mary the Queen?'

David shook his head. 'It is too deep, too murky for me,' he declared. 'Who may resolve such a tangle, the deil knows!'

Patrick bowed mockingly. 'Why, your younger brother may, Davy!' he said, smiling, 'if only Esmé Stuart will keep his meddling fingers out of it, and the gallant Arran confine his undoubted abilities to his bedchamber . . . and if perhaps Davy Gray does not carp and cavil quite so determinedly!'

'You . . . *you* would set yourself up against Elizabeth of England? And Burleigh and Walsingham? At your years, Patrick?'

'Why not? What have years to do with it? In such a case, a clear head, a nimble wit and a sure goal are worth many grey hairs!'

'And you believe that you have all these in sufficiency?'

'Thanks to God – and none at all, I think, to our esteemed father – yes! Have I failed hitherto?'

'Failed . . . whom?'

The two looked each other directly in the eye.

'I think that you can be too nice, too delicate, brother!' Patrick said softly.

'And I that you can be too clever . . . and too much forsworn!'

'So-o-o!' Then, at the least, we know where we stand, Davy. I thank you for all your somewhat negative advice. Meanwhile, I fear, we must send the ambassadors home – both of them . . .'

'Saying . . . ?'

'Ah, me – Nau telling his mistress that *King* James will consider her proposals fully, dutifully, and, h'm, at length. And Randolph, Randolph telling *his* that we shall do no such thing, that James alone rules Scotland, and that his mother is very well where she is . . . and that threats of war ill become so gracious a princess – who dares not carry them out anyway!'

'So it is out, damn you, Patrick – you admit it! Mary is very well where she is! There is our Queen's doom pronounced!'

'To your mind, it may be. To mine, it is the speediest way to win her home – if Elizabeth thinks that we do not want her. Go sleep on it, man!'

Chapter Fourteen

THREE people strolled by the sylvan banks of the River Eden, the noise of the chase long lost in the far-flung woodlands. Only the sounds of the forest were there; the river gurgled and chuckled, the finches chirped, cuckoos called hauntingly, endlessly, from far and near, and now and again a mallard duck would go quacking off in over-done alarm, seeking to draw attention away from her brood. For it was Spring again, the late and lovely short Spring of Scotland, and King James had returned to his beloved Falkland, where, even though the stags were not yet out of velvet, none could say that the King must not hunt them.

Of the three strollers, only David Gray, leading the horses, appeared ill at ease. The other two sauntered on ahead in apparent content – but only a very little way ahead, for the Lady Marie kept hanging back to include David in the desultory conversation. Nor did Patrick give any sign that he was otherwise minded, laughing, humming snatches of song, rallying them both, at his gayest, most relaxed, most charming.

David realised now, however, that Patrick had deliberately contrived this interlude – and presumably not for *his* benefit – urging Marie Stewart to take a shortcut with him to head off the stag, away from the main hunt, but soon finding themselves at the river and slowing down unhurriedly to proceed thus along its banks, dismounted. David had automatically followed his brother, since that seemed to be his destiny. Now he could have wished himself elsewhere, for he enjoyed acting neither groom nor gooseberry – though neither of the others gave the least indication that they considered him as such; indeed, it might well be that Marie was glad enough of his presence.

The three of them bore a strange relationship. Marie and David were now very good friends in their rather difficult situation, understanding and trusting each other, looking at many things in the same way. With Patrick the young woman was very different – provocative, highly critical, often downright unkind. Yet her interest in him was as undisguised as her frequent hostility. As for Patrick himself, he had pursued her in a casual and intermittent sort of way since that first meeting at Holyroodhouse, without letting it interfere with more urgent conquests or politic wooings. Something always seemed to bring him back to her – perhaps the fact that she refused to succumb to his wiles. David, for his part, recognised that she could be an excellent influence with Patrick, but liked her too well to wish to see her just another of his brother's playthings.

A faint call, rather different from that of the cuckoos, reached them from afar – the winding of a hunting-horn.

'Another kill,' the Lady Marie observed. 'Majesty is insatiable for blood. I suppose that we should be thankful that it is only deer's blood. Myself, I quickly have enough of it!'

'Aye, men's blood may come later!' Patrick said. 'James, God help him, has much to wipe out in his twisted mind. Kings often do such, bloodily.'

'He is a strange youth,' she agreed. 'He could scarce be otherwise. He will not thank us for deserting his beloved chase.'

'There are better things to chase than out-of-season deer!'

'Meaning, sir?'

'Meaning that the company of a beautiful woman is to me the more potent lure.'

'I have noticed that,' she said coolly. 'Many times.'

'Do you condemn me for that, Marie? In every sport does not practice make for perfection?'

'A comfort for those practised upon!' she returned. 'Like the King's poor stags!'

Patrick shook his dark head over her, ruefully. 'She has a curst quick tongue, has she not, Davy? She speaks *you* a deal more kindly, I've noted! How do you do it?'

'Davy does not practise on me. Or on every other woman that he sets eyes on!'

'I should say not! He has no need, you see. For our Davy is a practised galliard already. He has a most faithful wife . . . and two bairns born most undoubtedly in holy wedlock! Eh, Davy?'

'And you? You have the Lady Elizabeth Gray, once Lyon, have you not?'

A shadow, like a tiny cloud passing over the sun, darkened Patrick's face – but only for a moment. 'Have is scarce the word, I think,' he answered, lightly. 'A marriage to a painted picture or a marble statue would reward as well! I have not so much spoken to her for three years.'

'Yet she is your wife.'

'Wife! Is that a wife? Does marriage mean so much to the daughter of Robert Stewart!'

Steadily she looked at him. 'I wondered when that would out,' she said.

Patrick bit his lip. 'I am sorry,' he declared. 'That was ill said. Unworthy. You – you cause me to act the fool, always. It is those grey steadfast eyes of yours, I think. Accusing. So like Davy's. Always accusing. Christ God – you make a pair! It is not that . . .' He stopped. 'But why do I babble so – to you?'

Neither of them answered him.

They walked on along the riverside path, in silence, and the cuckoos came into their own again. Marie had fallen back alongside David, to take her own horse's head.

Abruptly Patrick turned. 'A plague on you both!' he exclaimed. 'You . . . you have spoiled a bonny day, a bonny lightsome day!'

David moistened his lips to speak. That was not like Patrick. But the young woman forestalled him.

'I am sorry, Patrick,' she said, gravely. 'I would not have wished that.'

He looked at her searchingly, at all the slender, riding-habited, coifed grace of her, and then at his brother – for him broodingly. Then, jerking a laugh at them, he turned forward once more to his pacing.

So they continued, beneath the young green canopy of the trees, in their strange walk, thinking their own thoughts to the mocking murmur of the river. Presently the surprising Patrick was singing again, an Italian air of pathos and pride and poignancy, the notes and words dropping singly like pebbles into a deep pool, a sad thing but somehow gallant. The girl behind him nibbled at her lower lip.

Coming to a grassy bluebell-painted bank at a bend of the stream, loud with the hum of bees and the heady scent of the wild hyacinths, Patrick suddenly sat down. 'Sit here,' he invited, indeed commanded. 'These bluebells, mayhap, will warm those eyes of yours, for me. Tell me, Marie – will you come with us to France?'

In the act of sitting down, she stared at him. 'France . . . ?' she repeated. David still standing, had turned to look as sharply.

'Aye, France – fair and sunny France. I find that I must needs go there. Come you with us, Marie. You would bloom richly there, I vow!'

'But – I cannot do that, Patrick . . .'

'If it is your reputation that concerns you, my dear, bring your father with you. A sister likewise, if you wish. But Davy will be there . . . to look after you, never fear!'

'I think not,' David said, from the background. 'I have had sufficient of France. Why go you there again, Patrick? This is sudden, is it not?'

'I go because affairs require it.'

'Your affairs? The Queen's?'

'Shall we say Scotland's affairs!?'. .

'You go on the King's business? As ambassador?' Marie asked.

'Not exactly. Though something of the sort may be arranged, no doubt.'

'I cannot think that the Master of Gray would be a very welcome ambassador at the Court of France, of Catherine de Medici!' David mentioned. 'Not after our last hours on French soil! I'd jalouse that his errand is rather to the Duke of Guise and the Archbishop of Glasgow? Though, to be sure, I had thought that with his increased closeness to Scotland's Treasurer, my Lord Gowrie, he would have but little need of the gentry at Rheims!'

Lazily, Patrick turned to survey the brother who spoke so formally. 'Do I detect more accusation there, Davy? Man – you are so righteous, I wonder it doesna choke you! A painful affliction, it must be. Be warned, Marie – or you may grow as bad as Davy, scenting wickedness in my every move!'

'You will be spared my troubling you in France, at the least!'

'Not so, Davy. You must come. Life without you would lack all savour, I vow! Besides, Marie, I feel sure, will desire your sober guardianship . . .'

'Patrick, do not be foolish!' the young woman said, almost sharply. 'I cannot go to France with you – even if I would.'

'Why, my dear? What keeps you here? This Court is plaguey dull getting, you must admit. Nothing but Esmé posturing and duking, Arran strutting and quarrelling, and deer being chased! Even Elizabeth Tudor has decided, it seems, that we are too dull and harmless for her concern. I' faith, Scotland will be a good place to be furth of, this hunting season, I swear.'

'Even so, I cannot go with you, Patrick.'

'Ah, me – your womanly repute wins the day, eh?' He sighed, gustily. 'Then there is nothing for it – I must marry you!'

The young woman's intake of breath was sharp enough to be audible. David's shock was almost as great. Together they gazed at the elegantly lounging speaker, wordless.

'Come – it is not so ill a thought as that, is it?' Patrick went on, smiling. 'It has been done before!'

'You . . . you are not serious?' Marie got out, at last.

'But, yes. Why not? For Patrick Gray to propose matrimony, after his former experiences, is serious indeed. As a last resort, you will understand! Will you not be the Mistress of Gray, my dear Marie, if you will not be my mistress otherwise?'

Marie turned to look at David, as though for aid, where he stood with the horses. That young man shook his head helplessly. This was quite beyond him. With Patrick, one never knew what might be in his mind; but surely he would not have made the suggestion thus, in front of David, if he had not been in earnest?

Presumably Marie thought along the same lines. 'And your wife?' she faltered. 'Elizabeth Lyon . . . ?'

'There is the blessed dispensation of divorce or annulment. You will have heard of it? If Arran can undo a knot but ten months old, what might not Patrick Gray achieve!'

She shook her head dumbly, Marie Stewart who was not usually dumbfounded.

'Come, you are a young woman who knows her mind,' he declared. 'You have spoken it to me times unnumbered. Now is the time for it – for, see you, it will be necessary to work fast. I . . . we must be furth of Scotland within the month, at the latest.'

The young woman took a deep breath. 'No,' she said.

'No? Think well, woman. It is not every day that Patrick Gray proposes marriage.'

'No,' she repeated. 'I thank you, Patrick – but no.'

Patrick leaned forward, his nonchalance for the moment forgotten. 'See, Marie,' he said. 'For your own sake, for your father's protection, you would do well to come with me, married or other. And your father with you.'

At his changed tone, she searched his face. 'I do not understand you, Patrick. How comes my father and his protection into this?'

The other paused, and then sat back, smiling again, half-shrugging. 'We all walk but delicately at this Court,' he told her. 'There are pitfalls a-many. Your father has his . . . unfriends.'

'Always he had those. But that is not what you meant, I think?'

He leaned over, to pat her hand, himself again. 'I meant that I would constrain you to marry me, anyhow! And you could do worse, you know, my dear. Look around you at Court – and admit that you could do worse!'

'I grant it, Patrick. But . . . you must go to France alone, nevertheless. I am sorry. You must be content with Davy for company.'

'No,' David declared firmly. 'I will not go to France again. I go back where I should never have left.'

'A pox – would you have me go alone, the pair of you? With none to advise and chide me?'

'Does not my lord Duke return with you?'

'Indeed, no. My lord Duke will be otherwise occupied!' Patrick rose to his feet. 'It is not in me to plead with you – with either of you,' he said. 'But perhaps you will change your minds. Women particularly are said to be good at it. And our esteemed Davy has sometimes a likeness to a scolding old dame! Heigho – I hope you do. But it will have to be soon, I warn you – it must needs be soon.' He held out a hand to aid Marie rise. 'Come, I am tired of these cuckoos' mockery. Whom do they mock – your or me? Or just mankind?'

'I am sorry, Patrick,' the young woman said.

Chapter Fifteen

THE hay, though late, was abundant and of good quality, thick with clover. All the Carse smelt of the sweet but vital scent of it, as everywhere men, women and children laboured with scythe and sickle, fork and rake, to cut and dry and stack the precious harvest, so much more important even than the corn and bere of autumn to this predominantly cattle-rearing country, on which the breeding stock would depend throughout the long winter months. My lord of Gray's herds were the greatest in all the Carse, and therefore his servants, and his tenants likewise, must grow and harvest a deal of hay in the reedy water-meadows and rich flood-plain of the Tay beneath and around his towering castle. Always David Gray had loved to work at the hay. This summer of 1582 he could do so again.

And, tossing tirelessly with his two-pronged hay-fork at the endless wind-rows of scythed and drying grass and clover, this was a totally different character from the somewhat morose, guarded, watchful man who walked so warily, uneasily, through the gilded life of court and palace. Here was the real David, who laughed and even sang as he worked – albeit tunelessly – joked with his fellow-harvesters and laboured prodigiously in sweating bare-armed satisfaction. None would have called him dour and humourless, now.

Nearby, Mariota worked almost as effectively under the July sun, her brown arms rhythmically flexing to the steady play of her fork, her deep rounded bosom and strong shoulders all but bursting out of the brief shift that was all she wore above the short skirt kilted to the knee. Red-cheeked, bright-eyed, Mariota clearly throve on motherhood. Her glance swung, almost as regularly as did her fork, between her husband and the coles of hay, flattened and scattered, where the baby Patrick rolled and staggered and clambered, chuckling, whilst around him young Mary danced, hurling clover-heads at him, covering him with grass, trilling her laughter, in her eighth summer of fascinating roguery.

It seemed a far cry from Falkland or Holyrood – or indeed, from the Principal's house at St Andrews.

'You go too hard, Davy,' Mariota protested, as he shook the

sweat off his brow with a toss of the head. 'You will have no strength left for, for . . .' She left that unfinished; it would have been hard to say whether she blushed or no, pink-faced as she was already with exertion.

Without halting in his stroke, David turned to grin at her. 'Try me!' he panted. 'Now, if you care . . . or tonight!'

She glanced down, not to meet his eye. Defensively she threw back at him. 'You work . . . as though this hay, was Patrick . . . and you were tossing the Devil out of him!'

This time his fork did falter and pause. He did not require to be informed to which Patrick she referred. Never a day passed without his brother's name being mentioned – and usually with just the hint of criticism of himself implied somewhere. Poor gallant Patrick! A strange thing, for Mariota made a most loving, happy and uncomplicated wife, and obviously rejoiced to have her husband home with her, even though, like his father, she had held that he really ought to have gone to France with Patrick, to look after him. Patrick – always Patrick! He laid a spell upon them all.

'I would it were so simple!' he said, shortly.

They worked on in silence for a while. Soon however David was at his singing again, and tossing occasional forkfuls of hay at the children.

Again it was Mariota who next interrupted their labours. 'Two riders,' she said suddenly, nodding towards the castle on its rock half-a-mile away across the flats. 'One of them a woman.'

David raised his hand to shield eyes from the sun's glare. 'I see them,' he agreed. 'But how you may tell that one is a woman, at such distance, I do not know.'

She looked at him pityingly.

She was right. As the riders drew closer it could be seen that the better mounted of the pair was dressed in a flowing riding-habit, the hood thrown back from coifed hair. The other looked to be an ordinary man-at-arms. They pulled up beside Tom Guthrie the land-steward, obviously asking a question. Then they came directly towards David and his wife.

It was the Lady Marie Stewart, and an attendant. She rode up to them, and drew rein, to sit looking down at them, un-smiling. 'Davy Gray . . . being Davy Gray at last,' she said, in her grave way. 'And Mariota. And young Mary. And little Patrick, too.'

David, suddenly very much aware of his sweat-soaked shirt and old darned breeches, hastily wiped the back of a hand over dripping brow and tousled hair, thereby smearing the hay-dust the more notably. 'My lady . . .' he began. 'I . . . here is a surprise. How come you here?'

'From Erroll. Where I am staying with the Constable.' She dismounted with a lissome grace before ever David could think of assisting her and shook out the dust from the folds of her habit. 'It is not far. A mere ten miles. But . . . will you not acquaint me with your wife, Davy?'

'Aye. Mariota, this is the Lady Marie Stewart, whom I have told you of. Daughter to my lord of Orkney, the King's uncle.'

'Yes.' Mariota bobbed a brief and stiff courtsey, whilst retaining a firm hold of her hay-fork.

'I hope that he has told you well of me, Mistress Mariota. Even a tithe as well as he told me of you! For I esteem your Davy's regard highly.'

'Yes, m'lady.'

The other smiled then, so faint a smile, yet sweet. 'Call me Marie, surely,' she said. 'Then perhaps we may be able to win Davy round to doing the same! I have been trying, these many months.'

Mariota did not answer that. She was seeking to draw together the gaping front of her shift to hide the deep cleft of her breasts from the admiring scrutiny of the mounted man-at-arms.

'You find us at something of a disadvantage,' David jerked. 'This hay . . .'

'Not so,' Marie corrected him, quickly for her. 'I find you making better use of your time than I have made for many a day. Would that these useless hands of mine could wield a fork as do your Mariota's! I envy her – and in more than that!' She spoke to the mounted man. 'Go back to the castle, Willie, and await me there. Take the horse, too.' Then, turning to the interested Mary, she took a couple of paces forward and sank down on one knee in the cut grass before the child. 'So this is . . . this your firstborn. The charmer that all the Court has heard of – even the King! I can see why, too.'

Woman and child eyed each other steadily, directly. Mary showed no hint of her elders' unease and uncertainty. She never did, of course. Great-eyed, but sparkling, assured, she considered the visitor. 'You have bonny hair,' she said, and reached out a grubby hand to touch the heavy golden tresses that escaped from the coif.

'Mary!' her mother exclaimed, shocked.

187

But the Lady Marie remained kneeling, and nodded agreement. 'It is the best of me,' she said, seriously. 'We cannot all have . . . what you have got, Mary. See,' she drew a necklace of tiny pink shells from a pocket. 'I have brought you these. Once they were the only gauds I had. And a comfit for your little brother.'

'Thank you,' the child said, and bending down she plucked one of the little heart's-ease flowers which grew everywhere low in the grass, and presented it to the other with the most natural dignity. 'For you.' A royal gesture of bestowal could not have been more gracious.

Marie leaned forward to kiss a sticky cheek, and stood up. 'You are better blessed than I knew, Davy,' she declared, looking from daughter to mother. 'I do not wonder that the Court could not hold you.'

'It has not held you either, it seems, Lady Marie!'

'Me – I have only escaped for a little while. Seeking a breath of fresh air. Patrick was right – it is plaguey dull, and a good place to be furth of. Lennox and Arran and Gowrie all bickering round the King . . . and Arran's wife lying with all three, they say!'

'So – do you wish that you had gone to France, after all?'

She raised her grey eyes to look at him levelly, calmly. 'Do you?' she said.

David frowned. 'By God, I do not!' he asserted, with more vehemence than seemed necessary.

Gravely she nodded. 'Perhaps you speak for me, also. Who knows? We think alike on many things, I would say, Davy.'

Mariota looked from one to the other, and bit her red lip.

The visitor examined her little wild pansy. 'Have you any tidings . . . from Patrick?'

'A letter, a week ago. From Seville, in Spain. What he does there, he did not say – save that the climate and the women were hotter even than in France, and the statecraft colder!'

'Spain . . . !' she said. 'What deep game is he playing, Davy? Is it the old religion? Statecraft cold, he said? That could mean – what?'

'I do not know – save only that he is Patrick. And since he is, his going there will not be out of any whim . . . or mean what may appear on the face of it.'

'No. No – I fear that is true . . .'

'Why must you always be so hard against Patrick?' Mariota exclaimed abruptly. 'Why must he ever be judged so sorely?

Davy is ever at it. My lord, too. And now, you! You are unkind
– all of you! I . . . I . . .' She stopped, undoubtedly flushing
this time.

The other young woman considered her thoughtfully.
'Perhaps you are right,' she said. 'It is too easy to judge, may be.'

David opened his mouth to speak, and then thought better
of it.

'He . . . Patrick is well, at least?' Marie asked, after a moment.
'He did not say . . . anything else?'

'He did not say that he missed my company.'

'Nor mine?'

'Nor yours, no.'

'I see. Why should he?' Without change of expression, Marie
turned to the other young woman. 'A new light is beginning to
burn brightly at Court,' she mentioned. 'A supporting luminary
of my lord Duke's . . . that burns with the sweet odour of
sanctified oil! A notable and godly influence, I am sure.'

Mariota, hurriedly stooping to tend the baby, looked both
surprised and mystified.

'The new Lord Bishop of St Boswells. Better known as the
learned Principal of St Andrews, Master Davidson. A cause for
congratulation?'

'Bishop . . . ?' Mariota faltered.

'Did you not know? Ah, yes, Lennox has had the old lapsed
bishopric of St Boswells, in the Borders, revived for him . . .
with its revenues of Kelso, Dryburgh and the rest. He has
become the Duke's spiritual adviser, in place of the mournful
Master Lindsay. A worthy bridge between Kirk and State,
don't you think?'

David barked a single mirthless laugh. 'So – he has achieved
more through the new religion than the old, after all! Morton
made him Principal . . . and Lennox a bishop! A man of parts,
'fore God!'

'Indeed, yes. A man not only with the cure of souls innumerable and a sure seat in Heaven, but with a seat in the Estates of
Parliament likewise, the income of three abbeys, and through
Lennox the ear of the King! And you are his only child, are you
not, Mariota? We soon will all be curtseying to *you*, my dear!'

Mariota's comely features were working strangely, her bosom
heaving. 'No!' she cried. 'I am no child of his! He told me so, the
last time that we spoke together. He said that I was none of his
hereafter, that he hoped that God would spare him the sight of
me! And I . . . I wish never to hear his name again! I am Mariota

Gray – that, and that only!' She gulped, and bobbed the sketchiest of bows. 'With your permission, m'lady . . .!' Bending, she snatched up the baby, grabbed Mary's hand, and turning, went hurrying at half-a-run across the hay towards the distant castle, without a backward glance.

Marie started as though to hasten after her, but David restrained her with a hand on her shoulder.

'Let her be,' he counselled. 'Let her be. Better so.'

Go you after her, then, Davy. Tell her that I am sorry. I did not mean to hurt her – it is the last thing I would have done! You must tell her so. I did not know that she was thus with her father . . . '

'I should have told you, perhaps. He . . . he did not think highly of me as good-son! He injured Mariota cruelly.'

'And now – and now my talk has upset her. I am a fool! I should not have come, Davy. I thought twice before coming, but . . . I pined for the sight of your honest face . . . '

'And word of Patrick,' he added heavily.

'Yes – that also,' she admitted, quiet-voiced. 'What is it that Patrick does to us all, Davy?'

'I do not know,' he said, and sighed.

In their own room later, with Marie returned to Erroll, Mariota, tense and fretful, turned on David as soon as he came in.

'That woman,' she cried. 'Why did she come here? What does she want of us? What does she want of *you*?'

'I think that she but wanted word of Patrick . . . '

'Aye, that was easily seen! But she wanted more than that, I think. I saw her – the fine lady with her sly looks and hints! I saw the pair of you, and your quick glances . . . '

David jerked a laugh. 'Sly, of all things, I would not call the Lady Marie! She is honest and straight, Mariota – the only one such that I ever found at the Court . . . '

' "We think alike on many things, Davy!" ' the young woman mimicked unkindly. 'Oh, aye – a fine honest loose Court hizzy, with her mocking slow ways and yellow hair! She knows how to twist men round her little finger, yon one – great foolish men, who believe that they turn the world over in their hands!'

Perplexed, he stared at her. This was not like Mariota the gentle, the mild. What had come over her? Surely the mention of her father's advancement was not sufficient for all this? 'You have it all amiss, my dear,' he told her. 'Far from twisting men around her finger, she it was whom Patrick asked to marry him.

And she would not. I told you . . . '

'Aye – and so twisted him the tighter! He thinks to run away to France to escape her, no doubt, to Spain – into dangers and trials without number! Poor foolish Patrick . . . !'

'I' faith – poor Patrick indeed! Lassie, you do not know what you are saying. Patrick uses women as he uses all else – for his own advantage and amusement, and that only. As once he . . . he . . . well, as he always has done. She – the Lady Marie – would not be so used . . . '

'There you are – ever traducing him! You can think no good of him – your own brother! A shame on you, David Gray! And she – she must cozen him to his face, and speak ill of him behind his back! Aye, and when she cannot have *him*, she comes here to lay her soft white hands on you . . . !'

'Lord! Are you out of your mind, girl? I think that she is fond of Patrick, yet sees his faults . . . as only a bemused and gullible ninny would not! And because she knows that I am fond of him likewise, though no more blind than she is, she is drawn to me a little. That is all. We are friends . . . '

'Friends!'

'Aye, friends. Is that so strange? But fear nothing – you will see no more of her! She will not come back, after the tantrums you have shown her, I swear! I do not know what has come over you, and that's a fact!'

'There is a lot that you do not know, I think . . . ' she began, with the first glistening of tears in her eyes. And seeing that gleam, David Gray, as became a man of some discretion, turned and stamped out of the room, and down the winding stone stair-way; better causes than his had been lost in the flood of a woman's tears.

David was wrong about Marie Stewart not coming back to Castle Huntly. It was almost five weeks later before she did, but then she came in some urgency, in late August. She arrived, again with a single escort, just as Lord Gray was setting out for Dundee, at noontide on the twenty-fourth of the month. My lord greeted her, in the courtyard, with the somewhat ponder-ous gallantry and comprehensive leering inspection that was standard with him for attractive ladies. He was a little bit put out that it seemed to be David whom she had come to see, not himself. He delayed his departure, however, while that young man was fetched down from his tower school-room, to entertain the caller.

191

'Here is the Lady Marie of Orkney speiring for you, Davy,' he announced. 'A right bonny visitor, too, for a damned bookish dominie! A wicked waste, I call it!'

David bowed, unspeaking, and Marie appeared to be in no mood for badinage.

'In this pass, a dominie at his books may have the best of it!' she said coolly.

'Pass? What pass is this?'

'You have not heard, then? It is the King. He has been taken.'

'Taken . . . ? What do you mean – taken?'

'Taken. Captured. Held, my lord,' she answered, though it was at David that she looked. 'Laid violent hands on, and abducted. Whilst hunting, from Falkland. Taken to Ruthven Castle.'

'Fiend sieze me – captured! The King! And taken to Ruthven, you say . . . ?'

'Aye. By your good-brother, sir – my lord of Gowrie, the Treasurer. And others.'

'Christ God!'

'When was this?' David demanded. 'Is the King harmed?'

'I think not. Though he will be frightened. He must be, for, for . . . ' She paused. 'But two days ago, it was. Word reached the Constable at Erroll last night. I came as soon as I might.'

'Gowrie did this,' my lord burst out. 'Is the man mad? Here is high treason!'

'No doubt. But successful treason, may be. And carefully planned, it seems. There are many more to it than Gowrie. All of the Protestant faction. The Earl of Atholl, Arran's own good-brother; the Earls of Angus and Mar and Glencairn. And March, too. My lords Home and Lindsay and Boyd, and the Master of Glamis . . . '

'That black rogue!'

'What of Lennox? And Arran? Where are they?' David asked.

'It was carefully planned, as I say. My lord Duke had gone to his palace of Dalkeith but the day before, to meet the new French ambassador, when he comes to Leith. And Arran was conducting justice-eyres in his new sheriffdom of Linlithgow. He – Arran – has been arrested and held, by Gowrie's command. My father likewise! And . . . the Bishop of St Boswells!'

'Waesucks – here's a pickle!' Gray declared agitatedly, tugging at his greying beard. All this, indeed, touched him much too closely for personal comfort; not only was Gowrie his brother-in-law, but most of the other lords mentioned in the plot were close associates of his own in the Kirk party.

'I am sorry about your father,' David said. 'You have no word of him? His welfare . . . ?'

'No. But I do not fear for him greatly. Most of his life has been spent in custody of a sort, and he has survived well enough.' She smiled faintly. 'He said that this present prosperity was too good to last! He survived Morton's spleen – I do not think that Gowrie's will be so harsh.'

'M'mmm. So Greysteil has become Greysteil again! I wonder . . . ?' David looked at her thoughtfully. 'You said that the King must be frightened. He must be indeed, for he is easily affrighted. But you meant more than that, I think . . . ?'

'Yes. For the Ruthven lords have extorted a royal warrant from him, ordering the Duke of Lennox to leave the country within two days, on pain of death!'

'Lord! He signed that? He was more than frightened, then. Such means terror, no less! His dear Esmé! The apple of his eye! Och, the poor laddie!'

'God be thanked, at the least, that Patrick was safe away in yon Spain,' Lord Gray asserted. 'Or it would have been himself, as well.'

David slowly looked up – to find Marie's eyes on his. Their glances locked. Neither spoke.

'You are sure of the truth of all this?' the older man went on. 'It is no mere talk? Hearsay . . . ?'

'No. The Lord Home himself was sent from Ruthven Castle last night, to Erroll. To order the Constable to keep his house. Under threat. Being a Catholic. He it was who told us. He said much – gave many reasons for the deed. He said that they had proof that the Duke meant to turn Scotland to Catholic again. That he planned to have James sent abroad to be married to a Catholic princess, and meantime he would rule Scotland alone. Lord Home had it that James would never return to Scotland – that he would be assassinated. Then a secret paper would come forth, with the King's signature, naming Lennox as heir to the throne. Then we should have King Esmé!'

'Soul of God!' Gray swore.

'Oh, there was much else. That Lennox had applied for foreign soldiers, Papal or Spanish, to land in Scotland. The Duke of Guise was to land in Sussex, and Elizabeth was to see her nightmare come true, and have to fight north and south. Home said that Bowes, the English ambassador, had told them that Lennox planned to have all the Protestant lords arrested on a charge of treason . . . '

'That does not ring true, at any rate!' David said. 'He could not have dared that. Wild charges.'

'May be. But they are the excuse, whether they believe them or no.'

Lord Gray took a turn or two up and down the flagstones of his courtyard, spurs jingling. 'This needs a deal of considering,' he muttered. 'You say that Angus and Atholl and Mar are in the conspiracy? Powerful men. And what of the Catholic lords – other than Erroll? Huntly, Herries and the others?'

'No doubt they are being attended to, likewise.'

'Aye. I . . . I must see Crawford. And Oliphant. I . . . '

'The Master of Oliphant was another of those whom Lord Home mentioned as in the endeavour.'

'Say you so! God's death – Oliphant too! I' faith – I must be hence. I must talk with, with . . . You must excuse me, ma'am. Davy, see that the Lady Marie receives all attention. That my house does not lack in anything for her comfort. I must be away. I was in fact on my way when you came . . . '

'I understand, my lord. Go you.'

As they watched him ride clattering out under the gatehouse, solid phalanx of men-at-arms at heel, the young woman shook her head. 'There goes a man with much on his mind, I think.'

'Less than his son and heir, I would say!' David amended.

She turned to him. 'Davy – you think the same, do you?'

'I do not know what to think. Save that it all falls into place damnably neat!'

'Yes. I see it thus also. He said . . . that the Court, Scotland, would be a good place to be furth of, this summer.'

'Aye. And that you would be wise to take your father with you!'

'He could not wait. We must be furth of Scotland within the month, he said. He must go to France, then. For what reason he never told us – or me, at any rate.'

'All he said was that, it was on account of Scotland's affairs. But not on the King's business, I gathered.'

'No.'

'And he has been wearying of Lennox for months.'

'You, you think, then, that he could have arranged all this beforehand? Plotted this conspiracy, left his instructions – and then sailed from Scotland in good time, so that none could hold him in anything responsible? All to bring down Lennox? Without seeming to have a hand in it?'

David drew a hand across his brow. 'I do not know. I do not say that he did it. All I say is that it looks as though he knew that it was to happen – and when. Not to a day, perhaps – but when-abouts. Knew – and did nothing to stop it!'

'Remember – when we asked whether the Duke of Lennox would be returning with him to France, he said – how was it? My lord Duke will be . . . will be otherwise occupied! That was it. That was three months ago.' She shook her head. 'And Patrick is not one to know of plots and intrigues and take no part.'

'No. And William Ruthven – Greysteil – my lord of Gowrie – is not the man to have plotted this. Always he has been a fighter, and not a plotter. Patrick thought but little of his wits – his Uncle Steilpate, he called him! Though they have been mighty thick together, since Morton fell.'

Man and woman looked at each other blankly. What more was there to say?

'Your Mariota would berate us sorely for so thinking of Patrick!' Marie said at length.

'Aye, she would.' Involuntarily, David glanced up at the main keep windows. Nobody seemed to be looking down there-from. The young faces of scholars peered out from the corner-tower, however. 'Come – you must need food. Rest. Or will you be staying here, with us? You will not wish to go back to Erroll? A Catholic house . . . ?'

'No. I thank you – but no. I have a sister, natural but dear to me. Married to an Ogilvie laird deep in one of the Angus glens. I will go there until this trouble is past. I can be there in but a few hours.'

Much as he liked her, David hoped that his relief at this announcement did not show too plainly.

'If you have word of Patrick, you will send to me, in Glen Prosen, Davy?'

'Aye. You still . . . would wish to hear of him? After this?'

'Yes,' she said simply.

'Very well. I am sorry . . . for it all.' He said that with difficulty.

'Yes,' she repeated, and looked away and away. 'I wish . . . I wish . . . ' Shaking her yellow head, she left that unsaid.

Esmé Stuart, the Sieur d'Aubiny, Duke of Lennox, was dead. The news reached Castle Huntly quite casually, at the tail-end of a letter to Davy, sent from Rome. Patrick mentioned a dozen other matters first – the interests of foreign travel, kind enquiries for friends, and his amusement over reported events in Scotland. In this connection, he added, he had just had sure word that poor Esmé had died of a broken heart within a few weeks of his return to France. Personally, he was apt to be suspicious of fatalities from this disease – but since Esmé's lady-wife had refused to see him on his somewhat hurried and informal arrival from Scotland, it might be true . . . though they had got on well enough apart for three years. Heigho – women were the devil, were they not? All of them – even the mature Queen of France herself, Catherine de Medici, who pettishly so seldom forgot old scores! How thrice-blest was his good old Davy, with his so reliable and amiable Mariota, whom the gods preserve . . .

For long David conned and considered that letter, and sought to fathom what lay behind it, before sending the gist of it off to the Lady Marie in her Angus glen.

Meanwhile Scotland seethed, but did not boil over. The King remained a prisoner in Ruthven Castle – though, officially of course, he had merely elected to set up his Court there – and many were the rumours as to his treatment that circulated through the land. Arran, too, was held fast, in various strengths, though his wife, who was free to come and go, did so to some tune, working mightily on his affairs, or at least on affairs of some sort, so that she was as much at Ruthven Castle as she was with her husband. A consortium, with Gowrie as its nominal head, ruled Scotland in the King's name. No major effort was made to release the unfortunate James. Relations with Elizabeth, however, were better than almost ever before, and her Mr Bowes' voice spoke loud in the land. The Kirk gave its approval to the godly lords' doings.

So the winter passed. The Earl of Orkney was released, apparently none the worse for his immurement and very ready to co-operate with all concerned. The Bishop of St. Boswells likewise. Marie Stewart stayed on in Glen Prosen.

Patrick's next message, months later when the snows were all but gone from the high blue mountains to the north, did not reach Castle Huntly in the usual fashion, via a Dysart shipmaster, but by the hands of Robert Logan of Restalrig. Patrick's – and for that matter, David's – roystering, fierce, but cheerful cousin arrived in the Carse in person one late Spring day almost a year after Patrick's departure, and after a drinking session with

my lord his uncle, slipped a sealed letter quietly into David's
hand. It read thus:

'My fine D.,
I think that it is time that our poor J. had a change of
company. Do you not agree? It could be arranged with no
great difficulty. J's present companions think not highly of
his spirit, and overlook him but scantily, I am assured – no
doubt with excuse. The lad pines, and would well do with a
change. Moreover, his habits are in need of reform, for he still
hunts unseasonable deer. I charge you to see to his improvement. Cousin Robert is in a good situation to assist you,
because of his mother. But dear Robert is rash and lacks your
sober wits. If you see to it, with his aid, all will be well, I have
no doubt.
They tell me that Saints Boswell and Andrew are now again
in heavenly embrace. Were J. to join them, at the time of the
justice-eyres, it would be justice indeed.
Salutations, my good and upright D!
P.'

If David had perused the previous letter long and carefully,
this curious epistle set him frowning more fiercely still. Not that
its contents and wording mystified him; he perceived the
allusions readily enough. Patrick wanted King James rescued
from Ruthven Castle, considered that the time was ripe for the
attempt, and proposed that it should be done during a hunt –
and at the justice-eyres period in late June when so many of the
lords, because of their hereditary jurisdictions, must be holding
courts in their own baronies and sheriffdoms, just as Arran had
been doing a year before when the Ruthven raiders had struck.
Apt justice indeed. Cousin Robert's usefulness, because of his
mother, must refer to the fact that the Lady Agnes Logan,
formerly Gray and my lord's sister, had as a widow married the
Lord Home, now so prominent at Ruthven. Through his stepfather, no doubt, Logan could learn much that would be
necessary for the success of any rescue attempt. Lastly, the
picture of Saints Boswell and Andrew in heavenly embrace
could only mean that Master Davidson, Bishop of St. Boswells,
was back in St. Andrews town, and this, for some reason, would
be the place to take the released King. Obviously, however far
away, Patrick was kept very well informed.
But none of that was what wrinkled David's brow.
The question was – what was he to do about it? Could he

accept this task, lend himself to this new plot? Patrick, in his lordly way, just assumed that he would do it. But why should he dance to Patrick's tune always? He was no plotter, no schemer. Indeed, he hated it all. Yet Logan assuredly would be in favour of it, whether he himself took part or no – and headstrong as he was, might well end it all in failure. And that could bear hardly on the King. Indeed, he had to consider James in all this – his own loyalty to his King. Was it his plain duty to help to free him, if he could? The boy had been a captive for nine long months. Was it no one's duty to rescue him?

Was the thought that it might well have been Patrick who first arranged that capture, relevant to his own decision about freeing him? It was difficult . . .

David cudgelled his head over it all, and eventually took his problem upstairs to Mariota, who saw it as no problem at all. The King should be freed, she said. Patrick, hundreds of miles away, could see that clearly enough, and had shown how it could be done. It only remained to carry the business out. But carefully. She wanted no trouble, no dangers. And Davy must keep that horrible Logan man in order . . .

So are the major affairs of men settled.

David, doubtful still, went later that night to Robert Logan's room. He wished that he had had time and excuse to visit remote Glen Prosen first.

Chapter Sixteen

On a heavy sultry morning of late June, leaden and grey, David sat his horse and fretted. Below him, one of Logan's uncouth mosstroopers squatted amongst the young bracken, paring his nails with a naked dirk. Also in the bracken, beside him, a poor unhappy stag lay on its russet side in panting wide-eyed alarm, its long graceful legs bound together at the hocks so that it could only twitch and jerk them. David was sorry for the beast; it had had a bad two days of it. But nobler game than this was to be chased today; moreover, it was to be hoped that the creature would soon regain its freedom, now.

David gazed northwards, over the rolling green Perthshire landscape that sloped down gently towards the River Almond. Down there, a couple of miles away, Ruthven castle's twin towers and grey walls could just be seen against the background of trees. He was waiting to catch the first glimpse of the hunt – the hunt which he hoped would take place, and which had not in fact taken place yesterday. He fretted because there was so much that could go wrong, even though they had taken every precaution that they could think of. A hunt was planned, certainly; Robert Logan had attached himself to his stepfather's entourage at Court for the past two weeks, and had sent the word. But then, a hunt had been planned for yesterday too, and had just failed to take place – why, they knew not – after they had made all their difficult arrangements. It might be the same today – and this wretched stag could not be kept thus captive and shackled indefinitely, without dying on them . . . whatever might be the case with the King. And yesterday had been an ideal day for the attempt, whereas today it was threatening rain. Rain now would ruin everything, washing away the vital scent.

Though the morning was still young, David and his assistants had been busy for hours. The captive stag, procured at considerable cost from a forester, and brought to the district secretly and with extreme difficulty by night, they had taken down to within half-a-mile of the castle while it was still dark, and then led back here, hobbled. At least the scent that it left should be strong and evident, for the unfortunate brute had been in a sweating panic all the way, leaping against its bonds, falling time and again, in direst danger of breaking its legs. It was supposed to be a tamed stag, but it looked as though their forester had deceived them with a fairly newly-caught wild one. a broken leg would have confounded their whole attempt. At last, however, they had got the creature here, and Gowrie's deer-hounds should have no difficulty in picking up the scent – if it did not rain.

Ensuring that the hunt came in an exact direction had been no simple problem to solve, and David had spent much time in the district, and dodging the Ruthven foresters, before he chose this spot. Fortunately, with Ruthven Castle sited as it was, hunting must start out in a southerly direction; for eastwards lay the populous lands and Perth town, to the north the Almond curved round in its deep trough, and to the west was Ruthven village itself. South lay the rising open woodlands, mile after mile of them, lifting to the long ridge of Lamberkine. Many were the routes that could be taken approximately southwards, however. Hence the need for this hot scent, fairly close to the castle. It was to be hoped and prayed that no other wandering deer would stray across their track, meantime, to confuse the issue – though that was surely unlikely, with the man-smell so prominent also, inevitably.

Well might David fret. Why had he ever agreed to this crazy enterprise?

They heard the hunting-horns sounding before ever they spied riders, but that only meant that indeed the hunt was on today, and presumably a scent had been picked up – not necessarily that it was the right scent, and coming in the right direction. A smirr of thin rain chilled David's face, and set him cursing.

The horn sounded a few times again, and significantly louder, before at last horsemen became visible – three of them riding hard, and over a mile away, emerging from denser woodland. David gave a sigh of thankfulness. They were on the right line. The huntsmen, they would be. He could not pick out hounds at this range.

A tightly-grouped knot of four or five riders appeared fairly close behind the first trio; Gowrie with the King, no doubt – and, it was to be hoped, Logan of Restalrig. Then, just coming into view, the mass of the hunt, strung out behind. A small company compared with the Falkland hunts.

From his vantage point, David could see most of the ground

between the riders and himself. A spine of wooded ridge ran down almost half-way towards them. It was vital that they took the western side of that. The scent was there to lead them, but he dare not assume that the project would go forward until he saw the leaders past that fork.

He jerked a few words to his seemingly careless companion. 'You are ready, man? They are nearing the parting of the ways – half-a-mile away. When I see them take the right route, I leave you.'

'Aye,' the Borderer said, nonchalantly.

'Be ready, then, in mercy's sake! When they reach yon dead tree – the huntsmen see you – cut the brute's thongs. And quickly. No moment of delay, then – but no moment before either. If the creature seems like to bolt the wrong way, wave your arms, scare it – but do not shout, or the huntsmen will hear you. Then, up after me to the others. You have it?'

'Aye.'

'Do not let yourself be seen – that is . . . Here they come to the parting. I see the hounds now. Aye, Glory – the hounds have taken the right road. Praises be! The huntsmen too. One is holding back, to guide the hunt. I'm off! Play your part aright, and you shall be well rewarded, I promise you!'

The other grinned white teeth in a dark gypsy face, and said nothing. Presumably Logan knew his men.

Forcing his way through the thick tangle of undergrowth and brushwood immediately behind them, David spurred his mount uphill, pushing it urgently up over the littered difficult slope. In a half-circle he climbed, to get well above and ahead of the line of the approaching hunt – and to remain unseen, of course. Timing was everything, now – timing, and the instincts of an ill-used deer.

The immediate wooded slope that he was on ended in a secondary ridge, wooded but fairly sharp. Through this a fast-flowing stream had cut a deep ravine, steep, almost precipitous. It was towards the eastern lip of this that David rode in not too wide an arc. At the summit nick of it, he drew up beside half-a-dozen men who waited there, more of Logan's mosstroopers.

'They are coming. Is all in train?' he panted.

Axe in hand, their leader nodded. 'Gie us the word, Maister, and we'll hae them doon before you can spit!'

David glanced at the three wind-blown Scots pines that over-hung the grassy ride rimming the edge of the ravine. They looked secure enough. As well that there was no wind today to blow them. 'Right – to your places. We shall not have a deal of warning.' He slipped a mask over his face. This, and the rusty breastplate that he wore, was Mariota's idea, that she had made him promise to use, in her preoccupation with being careful.

The green ride that the scent, and therefore the hunt, followed, continued right on up to this point, and beyond, bordering the very rim of the gully. David had selected this spot with infinite care, after days of prospecting. The entire endeavour depended upon the known instinct of a frightened deer to run uphill, always. When their captive stag was released, the chances were ten against one that it would bolt up here. The other slope that it might use would be barred by its late captor. With the hounds in view, it would choose a clear run up the ride rather than any battling with thickets – that was almost equally certain. Strange factors on which the fate of a king should hang.

The men were moving over to the three pine trees, where heaped brushwood would screen them, and David, feeling distinctly foolish behind his mask, was making for a slightly higher spot where he would gain a better over-all view, when the sudden baying of hounds rang out. Without a doubt that meant a sight; the long-legged shaggy-coated grey deer-hounds ran silent on a scent, and only gave tongue on a sight. Immediately afterwards as though to confirm it, a horn wound ululantly, proclaiming to the hunt behind that a deer was seen. The stag had been released, and was running. But running where?

That question was answered only moments later. Into sight round a bend in the lip of the ravine the creature came bounding swiftly, seeming to drift over the ground, no longer the awkward ungainly captive of the past two days but the epitome of grace and speed, long neck outstretched, velvet-clad antlers laid back along rippling shoulders, nostrils distended wide. Up and past the hidden watchers it raced, on over the crest, and down beyond.

The baying sounded close behind, but it was quite a few seconds before half-a-dozen rangy hounds came, in a tight group, noses down, slavering in hot pursuit. If they caught the man-scent, at the crest of the ridge, it did not deflect them for a moment from their quarry. They disappeared down into the dip beyond, clamantly implacable.

The beat of horses' hooves throbbed on the still air now. Round the bend in the green track rode two huntsmen, almost neck-and-neck, horns in hand, leather jerkins already flecked with spume from their galloping mounts. David watched them pass, frowning. It was a pity about the third one; he might possibly complicate matters a little.

There was an interval now, with David beating a tattoo on the pommel of his saddle with his finger-tips; Patrick and others had called him stolid, but he was in fact nothing of the sort. Then the drumming of hooves, many hooves, began to drift uphill towards them again, a jumbled sound that precluded any individual identification.

The third huntsman seemed long in coming. When at last he rounded the bend into view, he came only at a trot, looking back over his shoulder. Worse, at the very summit of the ridge, directly below the group of hidden mosstroopers, he halted his slavering horse, and sat looking back. David shrank in on himself, and felt as obvious as a beacon amongst the bushes.

But after an agonising half-minute or so, the fellow raised his hand and waved – an unnecessary signal surely. Then he turned and rode on.

Now . . .

Into view rode four horsemen, one, two and one – colourful people these, not russet-garbed huntsmen. In front rode the youthful figure of King James, on one of his black Barbaries. Just behind were the Earl of Gowrie – whose justice-eyres of course need not take him from home – side by side with young Johnny, Earl of Mar, who as still a minor could not yet act as magistrate. Then, close on their tails, came Robert Logan. Logan's eyes were busy.

David drew a deep breath. Seventy or eighty yards to go – and no sign of the next group of riders behind. The King, superbly mounted of course, always led at a cracking pace – his one accomplishment.

The mosstroopers' eyes turned on him. David waited.

With the King just below the hidden group of Borderers, David suddenly raised his hand.

Immediately, the half-dozen men were furiously active, pushing and heaving with all their might. The three tall pine trees, their shallow roots already cut through and supported only by props, swayed, almost imperceptibly at first. Then, ponderously, one toppled, its boughs catching in those of its neighbour, expediting its fall. With a great crash it came down, right across the grassy ride below, its dark topmost branches well out over the lip of the ravine – and a bare horse's length behind Logan of Restalrig. The second tree crashed three or four seconds later, and the third, toppling somewhat askew, fell slantwise down the ride in a shower of twigs and cones and snapping wood. The entire ridge seemed to shake and tremble to the fall of them.

Round the bend in the ride, farther down, the first of the next group of horsemen appeared.

David did not wait to see more, but brushing aside his cover, spurred his mount downwards.

At the sound of the crashes behind them, the leaders had sought to rein in their horses in alarm, James gobbling in fear, Gowrie and Mar shouting. Logan whipped out his sword, and rode straight at the two earls. From up the bank his moss-troopers came leaping down, yelling.

David, naked sword in hand likewise, made directly for the King. 'Your Grace,' he cried. 'Fear nothing. It is a rescue. A rescue!'

It is to be doubted whether the youth heard him. He sat his plunging black, petrified with fear, only hanging on by instinct. Cold steel always had that effect on James Stewart.

Gowrie and Mar had little time to spare for reassurance of their monarch. The former, an old soldier, was not long in getting out his own sword, but young Johnny Mar, not very much older than James, was making a fumbling botch of it. Scornfully leaving him to his minions, Logan bore furiously down upon the other, weapon weaving. The clash of their steel rang out above the shouting.

David, eyes busy, ranged his horse right up against the King's Barbary, and grabbed its bridle. 'Come, Sire!' he jerked. 'Nothing will harm you. All is well.' He saw that the Borderers were dragging Mar off his horse, well practised in the art as they were. Through and beyond the barrier of fallen trees, he could just glimpse agitated riders milling around, unable to get their mounts past, veering away from the steep drop into the ravine, and continually glancing up the steep bank to their left as though expecting further attacks from thence. He was wondering whether it was fair to leave Logan, good sworder as he was, to battle it out with the veteran Greysteil, when the sudden appearance of another horseman, halberd couched and levelled, ready to charge, clinched the issue. It was the dark mosstrooper whose task it had been to release the stag. Seeing him directly above him on the bank, and presumably recognising the folly of argument with a seven-foot long halberd, Gowrie sought to back his horse, to disengage. He threw down his sword to the ground, and folded his arms across his broad chest.

David, letting out a sigh of relief, reined his own horse right round, dragging the black with it, and urged them both to a trot southwards along the ride, after the stag, the hounds and the huntsmen. At the same time he whipped off his mask from his face.

'It's . . . it's you! Davy! Davy Gray!' James stammered. 'Och, man – it's just yoursel'!'

'Aye, Sire, none other. We had to get you away from the Ruthvens some way. We're Your Grace's friends, never fear.'

'Friends, aye – friends,' tremulous Majesty repeated, pathetically eager to believe it.

'This way Sire – and quickly. See – down here. It is a steep track, but there's no danger in it. And you are a good horseman . . '

A little way along the ride David swung the horses off sharply to the right, into a tiny track that seemed to plunge right over the edge of the ravine. Daunting it looked, and David heard James's gasp as he eyed it, zig-zagging away down dizzily amongst the bushes and ferns, a deer-track of the woodland stags, no doubt. David led the way into it, but the King was still hesitating on the brink when Restalrig came cantering up, and more or less bustled him over the edge and down. Robert Logan did not know the meaning of either tact or caution.

Sandwiched between the two of them, James was forced down into the ravine, and at no laggard pace. Most of the way his eyes were tight shut, undoubtedly. Fortunately horses do not seem to suffer from vertigo, and have an instinct for the surest road. The foot was reached without mishap.

There was still a lot of shouting from above, but it sounded incoherent, undirected.

'Your men?' David called to Logan. 'Will they get away, well enough?'

Restalrig hooted. 'God's eyes! Think you a wheen Court jackdaws could hold my callants? Never heed for *them*, Davy. It's oorsel's we hae to look after. Yon Greysteil will no' give up that easy.'

At mention of that name, James gulped, his big eyes rolling from one to the other. 'Wh'where are you taking me?' he got out.

'Up the bed of this burn, for a bittie, Your Highness – then an easy way out that I know of. Then across the Earn, and make for St Andrews.'

'St Andrews? Man, Davy – that's a long way . . . '

'It is, yes. But you will want to win a long way from Ruthven Castle, do you not?'

'Aye. Aye – but . . . '

'Come on – there's nae time for idle blethers!' the forthright Logan declared.

They went, splashing up the bed of the stream, screened from above by the overhanging trees. The going was reasonably good, though there were some steps and stairs over which tiny rapids poured. But at a larger waterfall they had to leave the burn to climb the far side of the ravine, by no path but a milder slope. Whether there was yet any pursuit they could not tell, by reason of the intervening woodland.

At the summit they paused for a few seconds, searching the prospect, near and far. Nowhere was there any sign of movement – though the echoes of shouting floated to them across the valley. Away to the east the land began to fall to the wide strath of the River Earn.

'So far, I think, Sire, we are not followed,' David announced. 'But it is a far cry to St Andrews. A long ride before we can consider that we are safe.'

'Safe . . . ?' the King repeated. 'Will I be safe at St Andrews, Davy? Will I ever be safe, man?'

David bit his lip. 'Assuredly, Sire,' he said – and hoped that he was not a forsworn liar.

They were down into the wide trough of Strathearn near Aberdalgie before they perceived that they were in fact being chased. Looking back, they saw coming down off the high ground a long strung-out trail of horsemen, fully a mile away, but riding hard. It was too much to hope that they were unconnected with themselves. Sheer neck-and-collar work was now all that remained for them.

That they did, taxing their beasts to the utmost. With this situation very much in view, David had borrowed the longest-winded horse in his father's stables – a big rangy roan. Logan, who was probably as much interested in horseflesh as he was in anything, was always well-mounted. Even so, the King's Barbary had the heels of them. He at least would take a deal of catching.

They splashed across the shallows of the Earn at a point where it spread wide around a shoaling island of sand and pebbles. Then up and across the rolling northern foothills of the Ochils, with the Tay estuary beginning to open before them to the north and east. High above the woods of Rossie and the tall tower of Balmanno they galloped, and looking back, decided that the leaders of the chase were no nearer, and the majority of it further off.

Keeping to the heights, they drove their steaming foaming horses esatwards. Over the glen of Abernethy and above the shattered Abbey of Lindores, they could only distinguish five horsemen still in pursuit.

'We have them outridden,' Logan panted, grinning. 'Your Grace needs swifter gaolers!'

It was not until they were well crossed into Fife that James accepted that they had indeed shaken off the chase, and the paralysing fear seemed to leave him. Suddenly he was a changed youth. He remembered that he was the King again, and said 'we' instead of 'I'. He laughed and gabbled somewhat, referring to 'our good Davy' and 'our worthy Restalrig', and hinted that superb horsemanship, his own more especially, had won the day. He also pointed out that it was only a few days after his seventeenth birthday, and that hereafter he intended to rule his realm sternly, as Scotland should be ruled.

Nevertheless, as they rode in a more leisurely fashion through North Fife, David came to the conclusion that James had changed fairly radically since last he had seen him – as perhaps was scarcely to be wondered at. He was bitter, suspicious, now childishly and unnaturally cynical, now naturely astute. More than once he startled his rescuers by the penetrating shrewdness of his questions and comments. He asked after Patrick and Arran and his Uncle Robert of Orkney, as well as of March and Bishop Davidson. He cursed Gowrie and the Master of Glamis and Johnny Mar and the other Ruthven lords. The one name, significantly, that he did not mention was that of Esmé Stuart.

David perceived that the boy whom he had rescued was almost a man. A strange man he was going to be. He doubted whether he would like to trust him as a friend; as unfriend, he imagined, he might well prove to be implacable.

Even as the crow flies it is forty long miles from Ruthven to St Andrews – and as the fugitives rode it was half as far again. Accordingly, it was three very weary travellers who eventually spied the towers and pinnacles of the grey university city by the eastern sea, and gave thanks, Logan profanely.

'To where do you take us, Davy?' James asked. 'To the castle? Does not my lord of Moray hold the castle now?'

'That I do not know. My instructions are to bring Your

Grace to Master Davidson, the Bishop of St. Boswells.'

'Eh, so? A godly man – but canny. Is he in this, Davy? Did he plot it?'

'No, Sire.'

'I thought no'. He's ower canny, yon one. Who, then? No' you two? You're bold enough – ooh aye, I'll gie you that. But a longer heid plotted it, I'll swear.' James recollected himself. 'We'll swear. Who?'

A little ruefully, David rubbed his chin. 'It was the Master of Gray, Sire. From France,' he admitted.

'Man – is that a fact! Waesucks – our good Patrick! Frae France. Aye, but it is like him, like him! He has a long arm, the bonny Master o' Gray, has he no?' Time he was back wi' us. What is he doing away in yon France, man? He should never have gone. All this ill that's come to us might never have been, if he hadna gone. What for did he leave us, Davy?'

'I do not rightly know, Sire.'

Logan snorted a laugh. 'As well ask that o' Auld Horny himsel'!'"

They rode into St Andrews town that evening by the same West Port out of which David had taken his new bride eight eventful years before, and which he had never since darkened. In the narrow streets none knew the dusty tired travellers. Though he would, in fact, rather have gone to any other premises in that city, David made for the Principal's house of St. Mary's College, for Master Davidson had managed to retain the office of Principal, and its revenues along with his bishopric, at the trifling cost of appointing an underpaid deputy.

The cattle were gone from the grassy quadrangle, and gardens were being laid out therein, more in keeping with the enhanced status of the establishment's master. David rapped resoundingly on the former chapel door, beside which three horses already stood tethered.

The same supercilious man-servant, now the more so out of his advancing years and much more handsome livery, opened presently, to stare. It was at David that he stared, in undisguised astonishment and hostility, though his glance did show some slight glimmering of respect at the quality of Logan's hunting clothes and general air of authority. The youthful King he ignored completely.

'We would see Master Davidson – the Bishop,' David said. 'Is he at home?'

The other pursed his lips, frowning.

'Quickly, fellow!' Logan barked, and the man, blinking, turned and went within. But he closed the door behind him.

'Curst lackey!' Logan cried. 'Sink him – he'll no' keep Restalrig standing at some jumped-up cleric's door, like a packman!' and he thumped loudly on the door-panels with the hilt of his sword.

James was too tired to do more than pluck at his lower lip, and mutter.

The servitor came back in a few moments, his expression a nice mixture of triumph and alarm. 'My lord Bishop canna see you,' he said. 'He is throng wi' important folk. If you have a message frae the Lord Gray, you can leave it.'

'God damn your scullion's soul!' Logan roared. 'Stand aside, fool!' And striding forward, he knocked the fellow reeling backwards with a violent back-handed blow, and stalked within. To the servant's wailing protest, the others followed him.

Logan was marching hugely down the arched lobby, but David heard voices from the same front room in which he had once waited for so long. Without ceremony, he opened the door.

Bishop Davidson was perambulating to and fro on the carpet, his purple cape and cassock flowing behind as once a black Calvinist gown had done. He was holding forth to three men who looked like country gentry or prosperous merchants, and who were listening to him with due respect. At sight of David, he halted in his episcopal steps.

'Sweet Mary-Mother – what insolence is this!' he demanded. 'Get out of my house. I told you – never did I wish to see your face again. Now, go – before I have my men take their whips to you!'

David ignored all that. 'I request word with you, in private, Master Davidson,' he said. 'In the King's name.'

'The King's name! Are you mad, as well as insolent and depraved, fellow?' It was dim out in the lobby, with the evening light, and David stood in front of the King. 'Out with you!'

'These men with you – who are they?' David turned low-voiced to Logan. '*You* had better ask him. We cannot hazard the King's safety.'

'With all the pleasure in the world!' Restalrig cried. 'I will prick this overblown priestly bladder!'

But James asserted himself, for once. He shambled from behind David. 'Good Master Bishop,' he said. 'I . . . we are tired. We have ridden far. And apace. You receive me . . . us but ill. We require comforts . . . food . . .'

'Merciful soul of God – Your Grace! Your Highness! Sire
– I . . . I . . .'

'Aye, you quivering bag o' lard, get down on your fat knees?'
Logan shouted. 'Or where's your fine bishopric, eh?'

And strange to say, there before them all, the Bishop-
Principal did just that. Down on the carpet he sank, in prompt,
hearty and urgent supplication, clasping white hands. 'Your
Majesty, I crave your most royal clemency! Humbly I seek
Your Grace's pardon. I did not know . . . I have been much put
about . . . I thought that Your Highness was . . . I meant no
discourtesy. All that I have is yours, Sire . . .'

'I ken that fine, aye.' Catching David's eye, James leered a
sidelong grin. 'Oh, aye. I'm glad to hear you say it, my lord.'

'But of course, Sire. All, all. If I may have your gracious
pardon. I will prove it – prove my enduring devotion and loyal
service. By all that is holy, I swear it!'

'I'ph'mmm. Is that so, Master Bishop?' Most evidently
young James was enjoying having this august personage
grovelling before him. Thanks to Master George Buchanan's
tutorship and the Kirk's fiery orators, he had an imbued respect,
if no great love, for learned divines. To have one thus before
him, was sweet.

It was David who called a halt. 'Sire,' he said bluntly.
'What is important is not Master Davidson's contrition, but
your safety. First we wish to know that these three gentlemen
are to be trusted? And then to know where in St Andrews you
will be safest disposed?'

The three earlier visitors, who had been standing in appalled
amaze, forthwith broke into incoherent protestations of
loyalty. Davidson, seeing the attention transferred from himself,
got to his feet. 'Majesty,' he interrupted earnestly. 'These are
sound men – but of no importance. The Provost of this town,
just, and his brother and friend. They shall be gone, this
instant . . .'

'Wait!' David ordered, briefly. 'We do not wish word of the
King's arrival in the town bruited abroad – yet. Who holds the
castle?'

'It is part-ruined, since the troubles of . . . of . . . But my
Lord of Moray, the Commendator, has a Lieutenant therein
. . .'

'Is it still a strong place? His Grace would be safe there?'

'Indeed, yes. My men will guard His Grace to the death . . . !'

'*Your* men!' Logan jeered. 'Mouthing acolytes and scribbling clerks! Have we no better warriors than that, in St Andrews?'

'They are good men, and true, my lord,' the Bishop assured, humbly. 'Well founded and lusty. I have two-score of them. And there is my lord Earl of March, his men ...'

'March!' David and Logan cried in unison. 'How came March to St Andrews? And when?'

'But two weeks agone.' When the Bishop answered David, he did not look at him, but addressed himself as to the King. 'Why he came, I know not. He lodges at the Priory, with full three-score men-at-arms. Did he know, perchance, that Your Grace was to be here?'

David and Logan exchanged glances. This looked like more of Patrick's work, March, the Countess of Arran's deposed husband, and a simple bumbling man, had been used by Patrick before for his own purposes, being rich and gullible.

'Aye,' Logan said, heavily. 'It falls out powerfully convenient.'

David nodded. 'Your Grace, we will send the Provost to request my Lord March to attend you here forthwith. And another of the gentlemen to the Lieutenant of the castle, with orders to have it open to receive Your Highness at once. Will that serve?'

'Aye, Master Davy. But I'm right hungry, mind ...'

'Master Davidson will surely see to that, while we wait.'

'It is my joy and delight, Your Majesty.'

And so it fell out. The King of Scots, fed, refreshed and to some degree rested, attended by the Earl of March, the Bishop of St. Boswells and the Provost of the town, was installed in the part-demolished but still powerful castle of St. Andrews, seat of former Archbishops, on its sea-girt rock, and the gate locked and barred. And in the safety thereof, he made one of his lightning-like changes of character. Of a sudden he was in command, arrogant, boastful. The admiring courtiers learned a version of the escape from Ruthven in which the King himself was the hero and main protagonist. He damned and cursed the lords Gowrie, Mar, Glencairn, Master of Glamis and the rest, in impressive fashion for a youth of seventeen, and commanded their immediate arrest on a charge of highest treason. He ordered the citizens of St. Andrews to provide for his every need, and to raise an adequate force for his sure defence. James was the King, and no one was to forget it ever again. From now on, he would rule this realm with a strong arm, as a king should. And let the good Captain Jamie, Earl of Arran, be brought to him forthwith.

David decided that it was high time for him to go home to Castle Huntly, whatever Logan might elect to do. He requested permission to retire from Court the very next day, and His Majesty was graciously pleased to grant it.

Chapter Seventeen

PATRICK did not return home just yet. Perhaps that was as well for a peace-loving man like himself, for the Ruthven lords had not quite shot their bolt. Resisting somewhat half-hearted efforts at arrest, they seized the town and castle of Stirling – of which of course Johnny Mar was Hereditary Governor – and manned and munitioned it against the royal forces. This situation at least gave the newly-freed Arran what he wanted – *carte blanche* from the frightened James to take whatever measures he required to restore order, as the only soldier of any experience in the King's present company. Captain Jamie had learned his soldiering in the hard ruthless school of the Swedish wars, and nothing could have pleased him more than to be given the opportunity to demonstrate something of what he had learned – especially against the men who had kept him a prisoner for the best part of a year, wife or no wife. With a force consisting mainly of the followings of the great Catholic nobles, Huntly, Montrose, Herries, Erroll and the rest, he marched on Stirling – and the Ruthven lords, deciding discretion on this occasion to be a distinct improvement on valour, melted away before him, without a siege, into the convenient fastness of the Highlands. The Kirk kept very quiet; James sported a crucifix; Elizabeth thundered from Whitehall; Arran stretched himself in all directions; and the Master of Gray, in response to repeated urgent summons from his monarch, at last arrived back in his homeland at the end of August, a bronzed gallant and carefree figure in the most dashing of the new French modes, a joy and a delight to all who saw him. This was made the more striking in that he brought with him a snub-nosed, freckled and awkward ten-year-old boy, whom he seldom let out of his sight, even for a moment. What ever malicious tongues might say, however, this boy was with him apparently also at the King's express command. He was Ludovick Stuart, second Duke of Lennox, Esmé's son. How Patrick had convinced Esmé's Duchess, who had refused even to see her husband, to allow him to bring away to hated Protestant Scotland the apple of her eye, is something that he alone could tell.

He rode in, unannounced, under the gatehouse at Castle Huntly, one golden first day of September, with the boy at his side, both mounted significantly on black Barbaries. If anything could indicate high royal favour, that did. The pair did not have even a groom as escort.

In all the wide courtyard only one small figure happened to be there to greet them – the petite and self-possessed person of Mary Gray. She curtseyed prettily, and then stood regarding them with headcocked speculation.

From his saddle, Patrick gazed down at her for appreciable moments, his handsome features unusually thoughtful. It was nearly two years since he had seen her. 'My dear . . . Mary,' he said, and for once forgot to smile. 'You grow . . . you grow more . . . in fact, Mary, you grow marvellously!'

'I do not think that I am very big, sir,' she answered. 'I am nine years old, you know.'

'Aye, 'fore God – so you are! Nine years. But . . . you know me, child?'

'But of course. You are my Uncle Patrick, come from France. Uncle Patrick – who makes my mother look strange, and my father frown. I know you fine. But I do not know this boy. Is he a new son that you have got?'

'H'mmm.' Patrick drew a hand over his mouth. 'No, Mary. Not so. This is Vicky. Ludovick Stuart. He is also my lord Duke of Lennox, but I do not suppose that you will think much of that. He is just near your own age – a few months older. You will be good friends, I am sure. But he speaks very little of our language, as yet . . .'

'I can speak French,' Mary assured. 'My father has taught me. My father went to France, too, long ago. *Bonjour, Monsieur Garçon*,' she said, curtseying again. '*Je parle français. Un peu.*'

The stocky boy on the black horse stared down at her owlishly.

Laughing again, Patrick dismounted, and went to help down the boy from his tall perch. 'Vicky is a littly shy, lass. But you will soon remedy that, eh? Do not be too hard on him, Mary! ! . . .'

'Patrick!' Mariota came running down the timber steps from the main keep, skirts kilted high, a picture of flushed, bright-eyed loveliness. Almost she seemed as though she would throw herself straight into his arms. Then, recollecting herself, she came to a teetering halt in front of him in breathless, attractive confusion. Behind her, David appeared in the iron-grilled doorway, displaying less forthright rapture.

Patrick had no qualms to recollect. He swept up Mariota –

though a little less high than once he had done, for she was a big well-made woman now and no slip of a girl – kissing her comprehensively and enthusiastically.

'My splendid and adorable Mariota!' he cried. 'How beautiful you are! How kind. And generous! What a form! Aye, by God – and what a weight, too!' And he set her down, panting.

'You are home then, Patrick,' David greeted, his voice coming thickly. 'It has been a long time. More than a year. You look . . . as though you throve!'

'Aye, my good stern Davy! He who frowns! It does me good to see you all. You have all grown, I swear – Mary more bewitching, more ravishing; Mariota more beautiful, more desirable, more rounded   and Davy more like Davy than ever!'

'Aye,' David said 'And the laddie?'

'That is Vicky,' Mary announced

'Why yes, so he is. This is Ludovick Stuart, Duke of Lennox . . who resembles his father but little, I think.'

'Lord! You . . . you have brought him here? D'Aubigny's son. *You* . . . !'

'Indeed, yes. On the King's express command. He is, after all, Scotland's only duke!'

'He is the son of the man . . .' David paused.

'The man whom we both knew so well. Surely we can do no less than show him kindly welcome, brother?'

David bit his lip, but Mariota stooped quickly, arms out to the boy, who eyed her but doubtfully.

Mary took him by the hand. 'Come with me,' she commanded. 'I have a hedgepig with babies. In my garden. Come.'

Without enthusiasm, the Duke went with her.

'Patrick!' Mariota exclaimed, rising. 'You are thinner, I think. You are well? Where have you come from? Have you ridden far?'

'I am perfectly well, my dear. We do not all have the facility for growing fat! And have ridden only from St Andrews, of blessed memory! Where James insists in keeping his Court, meantime. A chilly place in autumn mists, as I think you will recollect. We must move him before the winter, I vow! I came thither from Rheims only two days ago.'

'You are not come home to stay, then . . .?'

'I fear not, my dove. Much as I would relish life here with you . . . and with Davy, of course!'

'Have you not done enough? At the Court?' David asked,

pointedly. 'You have a fair heritage here . . .'

'God forbid! Would you have Arran and his . . . lady ruling all Scotland? Save us from that!'

'James himself aspires to rule his realm, I think.'

'One day, no doubt. James will need to rule himself before he rules a kingdom. Meantime, a loyal subject's duty is to aid and guide him, is it not? For the good of that kingdom!'

David began to speak, and then held his tongue, meeting his brother's eye steadily instead. Patrick changed the subject.

'Where is the noble and puissant Lord Gray?' he asked, lightly.

'He is at Fowlis Castle. Has been for some days.'

'Ah! With a new lady, I'll be bound!'

Mariota led the way indoors for refreshment.

Later, with the young woman gone down to the gardens for the children, Patrick manoeuvred his brother out into the courtyard again, where none might overhear. 'The Lady Marie?' he said, abruptly for him. 'She is not at St Andrews. None there know her whereabouts. Do you, Davy?'

David did not answer at once. 'What if I do?' he said, at length. 'Why should I tell you?'

'Why not, brother?'

'It could be that she were better off lacking your company.'

'So-o-o! Are you her keeper, then, Davy?'

'I am not. Only her friend.'

'Ah. And I? What then am I?'

'Aye – well may you ask! It is a question that I ask myself frequently! What are you? Whose friend are you – save your own?'

Looking at his brother, it was Patrick's turn to be silent for a little. 'This is . . . interesting, Davy,' he said presently, 'Aye, interesting. What makes friendship? Judgment? Criticism? Or trust? Understanding? Sympathy?'

'Something of all, it may be. But the trust and the sympathy must be two-sided, I think. Whom do you trust, Patrick? And who may trust you?'

'Heigho – you I hope, Davy! And Marie likewise. Where is she man?'

'If I tell you, will you make me a promise!?'

'I will, of course. Anything that is in reason.'

'It is in reason, certainly. It is just this – that you will not use her in any of your intrigues. That you will use her kindly, and not knowingly hurt her.'

216

'Lord, Davy – of course I promise it. But . . . this, from you! What does she mean to you man?'

'Just that I will not see her hurt. You understand, Patrick?'

'I hear you, anyway!' Patrick glanced sidelong at his brother, knowing that grim tone from of old. They had walked out beneath the gatehouse into the wide and grassy forecourt. 'You have my promise. Where is she?'

'In Glen Prosen. With her natural sister. who is married to Wat Ogilvie, a lairdling there.'

'Glen Prosen? In the wilderness! I see. Has she been there long? Was she there when . . . when . . . ?'

'No,' the other said briefly. 'She went afterwards. Her father was held, and her brothers scattered.'

'But . you saw her?'

'Aye. She came here. She it was who first told us of it. Of the King's capture. And what followed.'

'I see.' Patrick kicked a fallen twig out of his way, casually. 'How did the matter appear to her? How did she take it?'

David almost imperceptibly edged his brother over the greensward towards a little path, all but overgrown with long grasses. 'I think that she took it as I did,' he said slowly. 'Took it but ill. Took it that a clever hand was behind it all – a hand that did not appear.'

'Indeed.'

'Yes, a ruthless hand that played with men as though they were but puppets on strings – whilst itself remained safe hidden in a sleeve!'

Patrick laughed. 'A pretty conceit, Davy – but improbable, I think. Was that her invention, or yours? She has a level head on her, that one. I would not think her so fanciful.'

'No?' He took his brother's arm. 'This way, Patrick.'

The other suddenly perceived whither he was being led, guided. He halted, and made as though to turn back. David's pressure on his arm was strong, however. They were on the start of the little track that led down into the birchwood, where once and more than once criticism had taken a physical form.

'I am not dressed for woodland walking,' he said, a little strangely.

'Are you ever? Come you, Patrick.'

'No. This is folly. I have not the time . . .'

'Come, you. We have all the time that there is. I only wish to speak with you, brother.' David said softly. 'Did you think . . . ?'

Patrick mustered a laugh and a one-shouldered shrug. 'We are

217

grown men,' he said. 'Bairns no longer. I am Master of Gray, of His Majesty's Privy Council, Master of the Wardrobe, Gentleman of the Bedchamber, Commendator of St Vigeans – did you know that? – Knight of the White Cross of Castile.'

'Aye. And I am just Davy the Bastard, still! So your lord Councillorship need have no fears. Come, you.'

In silence, nevertheless, and wary-eyed, Patrick paced down the path, through the brushing brackens, beside his brother. 'Well, man?' he said at length. as though it was forced from him. 'Out with it. What is this talk you would have?'

'Wait,' David advised, mildly. 'We are nearly there.'

'But . . .'

They came down to the little green amphitheatre amongst the trees, that Patrick at least had not visited since that day when he had laid the blame for Mariota's pregnancy upon his brother – and had paid some sort of price therefor in battered features and bleeding nose. There David halted.

'Why did you betray Esmé Stuart to his death?' he asked levelly.

Patrick raised finely arching brows in astonishment. 'Betray . . . ? I? Why Davy – what are you thinking of? What foolishness is this . . . ?'

'Why did you betray Esmé Stuart to his death?' the other repeated inexorably. 'You plotted his downfall. encompassed his ruin and banishment, and assured his doom, as surely as though you had stabbed him with your own dagger. Whether you arranged his final death also, is small matter. Why did you do it, Patrick?'

'Christ God, man – are you crazed? Am I responsible for what Gowrie and Lyon and Angus and the others did?'

'I think that you are, yes – since it was you ensured that they did it!'

'You talk of you know not what. Lennox died in France, while I was in Spain.'

'What does that prove? The power of silver – Jesuit silver, perhaps? And a far-seeing eye. How was it that you put it, one time? "Most men are blinded by passion and prejudice. Those who can preserve a nice judgment and a clear head may achieve much." I have never forgotten your creed, Patrick!'

'This is not to be borne!' the other cried, his handsome features flushing. 'So much will I accept from you – but only so much!' And he swung about on his high-heeled shoe.

David's hand shot out to grip his brother's shoulder, and

whirl him round to face him again. 'Not so fast, Patrick,' he remarked evenly. 'This is the place where always truth was spoken, in the end. Let us have the truth, now. That is why I brought you here. Or must I beat it out of you, as I used to do, with my bare hands? We are bairns no longer as you say. Tell me then, why you betrayed your friend. It is important to me, who have been your friend also. For he *was* your friend. You brought him to this land. You helped to make him ruler of all Scotland. If he offended, and went too far, you could have corrected him surely, brought him down a little? But to ruin him entirely, and from a distance . . .'

'That is only your vain imagining, I tell you.'

'Can you deny that you knew that it all would fall out so, before ever you went to France? That is why you went – to let others do your ill work, while you went safe, and retained the confidence of the King? You gave yourself away, to the Lady Marie and myself, yon day by the Eden. You admitted then . . .'

'I admit nothing! You forget yourself, man. I thought that you loved me, Davy?'

'Aye – but does that mean that I must love the evil treacherous ways of you? That I may not try to save you from your own lust of betrayal? And others, too . . . ?'

'Aye – and others too! There we have it! Marie Stewart! It is Marie Stewart you would be the saviour of! *You* talk of lust and betrayal! It is her that you lust for . . .'

Like a whip cracking David's hand shot out and slapped hard across his brother's sun-bronzed features. 'Say that again, and I will make your beautiful face . . . so that you dare not show it . . . to Marie . . . or your maggot-blown Court!' he jerked.

Patrick shivered strangely, fine eyes glittering. 'You whore's-get!' he breathed. 'For that, any other man would die! For you – this!' He spat contemptuously, full in the other's face.

David was stepping forward fists clenched, jawline tense, when a new voice broke in, and turned both their heads.

'Davy! Davy – stop it! Stop it – do you hear?' Mariota came running down to them through the turning bracken, in flushed disarray. 'Oh, how can you! How can you!'

The men stood staring, panting, wordless

'Do not dare to strike him again!' the young woman cried. 'I saw you. You struck him. Oh, that it should come to this, between you!' She halted before them, tears in her eyes. 'Fighting! Fighting like wild brute beasts!'

David said nothing, but Patrick managed to fetch a smile of

sorts. 'Not fighting, my dear,' he protested, fingering his burning face. 'Surely not fighting. Just an argument . . .'

'Fighting,' Mariota insisted. 'And think you I do not know what you were fighting over? It is that woman! The two of you were fighting over that Stewart woman! I know . . .' Her voice broke.

David started towards her, but she plunged away from him. 'Do not touch me!' she cried. 'Do you think that I will come second – to her!?'

'But, Mariota lass – it is not so!'

'Can you deny that it was of her that you talked? When you came to blows. I heard her name . . .'

'Her name, yes. We spoke of her. But . . .'

'My dear, do not distress yourself. It was nothing,' Patrick declared, his assured and smiling self again. 'We but spoke of Marie in relation to the Court. Did you not hear that, also? The Court and its h'm, factions and loyalties. Eh, Davy?'

His brother did not answer.

Patrick took the young woman's arm. 'Surely you know that men may become incensed over statecraft and the like, Mariota my dove? It signifies nothing.'

She twisted away from his clasp. 'Leave me!' she exclaimed. 'Leave me alone. Both of you. She turned, and began to hurry back up the slope, whence she had come. 'You are both nothing but a hurt to me – a hurt and a shame! Both of you!'

Patrick would have hastened after her, but David pulled him back, urgently. 'Let her be,' he said. 'You heard her? She wants neither of us this moment. Not even you!'

The other looked at him, searchingly. 'So-o-o!' he said. 'That is it! Poor Davy!'

Abruptly, his brother swung about and went striding off through the trees, away from the direction of the castle. Patrick looked after him.

'Davy,' he called. 'At the least you saved the King for me . . . after the other matter. Why, if you so mistrusted me?'

David threw no answer back.

'My thanks for that, at any rate,' the Master of Gray said. 'I am sorry, Davy – sorry for both of us!'

He sighed, and then went slow-footed up the hill.

Chapter Eighteen

How strange, frequently, are the things that drive men to a change of course, to active intervention in this cause or that – small unimportant things, it may be, where greater issues have failed to do so. Thus it was with David Gray When the Court of the King of Scots moved to Stirling for the winter of 1583 – where Arran had obtained the Keepership of the Castle, in room of the forfeited Johnny Mar, and even had himself appointed Provost of the town, so that he had all things under his hand – Patrick wrote to his brother apparently anxious to forgive and forget all, requesting that he come thither to be with him again, as secretary, where he would be most useful. He promised that he would find life at Court more amusing than heretofore.

David refused.

Thereafter, the Lady Marie wrote, also from Stirling. She had been weak, she admitted, and had returned to Court. Should she have been strong, rather, and remained to be snowed-up for the winter in Glen Prosen? Was hiding oneself away strength? Anyway, here she was, back with her father and brothers. She was no politician, but even to her it was evident that the course which the new régime was taking boded ill for Scotland, a course in which her father was becoming deep implicated – Arran's course. Arran was acting Chancellor of the Realm now, claiming that Argyll was too sick and old for his duties. He was behaving disgustingly with James, corrupting him blatantly, unashamedly, before all – and accepting bribes, through his wife, from any and every man who had a favour to gain from the Crown. He was attacking the Kirk, selling more bishoprics, and giving the bishops power over the presbyteries, bolstering their authority by getting the Estates to declare James, and therefore himself, supreme in matters spiritual as well as temporal. Refusal to submit to the bishops, appointed in the King's name, was branded as treason. So Arran sought to hold more power in his hands than any man had ever done in Scotland. Free speech was being put down everywhere, the Catholics were being advanced, and there was talk of leagues with France and Spain and the Pope. And all the while, Patrick, whom she was convinced could have greatly affected events for the better, sat back and smiled and played the gallant – and did nothing. It was maddening, she wrote. The man who could, if he would, save the King and the country, scarcely lifted a hand, save to bedeck himself, toss dice, organise a masque, or pen a poem. Would Davy, whom she was assured had more influence with his brother than anyone else alive, not come to be with him again? There had been a quarrel, she believed – and could guess the cause. But Patrick loved him, she was certain, and wanted him at his side. Needed him, she declared. What good might he not achieve there, Patrick being as he was? Would he not come?

Briefly, firmly, if kindly enough, David penned his refusal.

At Yuletide, Patrick, laden with gifts, came again to Castle Huntly, in his sunniest mood. To David he could not have been more kind, more friendly, bringing him a handsome and costly rapier as present. He urged that he return to Court with him, where the King himself, he averred, frequently asked for him, and where undoubtedly, if Davy so desired, some office or position could easily be procured for him. Lord Gray, privately, added his own plea – indeed, it was more like a command – declaring that he would feel a deal happier about Patrick's activities if David was apt to be at his shoulder. David, dourly setting his jaw, declared that he hated the idle artificial life of the Court, with its posturings and intrigues. He preferred to continue as dominie, and assistant to Rob Powrie, the steward.

And then, a mere remark, a casual reference made by a passing visitor to my lord, changed it all. This caller, a minister of the Kirk, on his way from Stirling to his charge at Brechin, mentioned amongst other gloomy forebodings and wrathful indictments, that that Jezebel, Arran's Countess, now went brazenly bedecked in the jewels that belonged to Mary the imprisoned Queen, the King's mother.

Within twenty-four hours thereafter, David's mind was made up and he told Mariota firmly, determinedly, that he must leave her for a while. Mary Queen of Scots reigned yet, in some measure.

It would have been difficult satisfactorily to explain David's intensity of loyalty and regard for the unhappy Queen, to his wife or anyone else. He had never seen her. Most of what he had heard of her had been ill, critical, indeed scurrilous. She had been Elizabeth's prisoner now for fifteen years, all his understanding life, and her legendary beauty could hardly have survived. He was strongly Protestant though not bigoted, where she was insistently Catholic. Yet David, as well as many another in Scotland, still accorded her his unfailing loyalty and deep sympathy. He looked on her infinitely more as his true sovereign than he did her son James. All her hectic life – and ever since, indeed – Mary had that curious faculty of arousing and sustaining devotion in men, a devotion quite unaffected by her own morals, behaviour or follies. She was of the same mould as Helen and Deirdre and Cleopatra. At the word that the Countess of Arran had appropriated her jewels, the sober and level-headed David Gray overturned his oft-reinforced decision, packed his bags, and left wife and home to seek to do he knew not what. Perhaps it was but the last straw? Perhaps it had required but this? And was it so surprising? In Scotland, men had died for her by the score, the hundred, and even her enemies had been driven to their most virulent spleen for fear of themselves being lost in complete subjection to her allure. John Knox himself was half-crazed with desire for her. And in England a steady stream of devotees had gone to the block for her, some the highest in the land, ever since the fateful day of her immurement. Hence, partly, Elizabeth's cold hatred and fear.

It was a blustery day of March when David rode over the high-arched bridge across the stripling Forth, and into Stirling town. A very different Stirling this from formerly, with every house full with the overflow of the Court, bustle, gaiety and extravagance on all hands, soldiers everywhere – for Arran, as newly-appointed Lieutenant-General of the royal forces, was enlisting manpower determinedly – lordlings, hangers-on, men-at-arms, loose women. It reminded David of the Guises' Rheims.

He made his way up to the great fortress that soared above the town, and had less difficulty in entering therein than he had anticipated. The Master of Gray's name opened all doors.

He found the Court in a state of excitement and stir that surely could not be its normal even under the new régime. Enquiries elicited the startling information that Walsingham was on his way, no further away than Edinburgh, in fact – Sir Francis Walsingham himself, the most feared name in England now that Burleigh was growing old, Elizabeth's cold, ruthless and incorruptible principal Secretary of State. What his visit boded, none knew – but that he had come himself as envoy could only indicate that the matter was of the gravest importance. None could deny that.

Patrick, when David ran him to earth, writing letters in a pleasant tapestry-hung room with a blazing log-fire, and facing out to the snow-clad Highland hills, did not seem in the least perturbed. He jumped up from his desk, and came forward, hands outstretched.

'Davy! My excellent and exemplary Davy!' he cried. 'How fair a sight is your sober face! I am glad to see you – I am so!'

That sounded genuine enough. David nodded dumbly, always at a loss for words on such occasions.

'What brings you, Davy? Love of me?' He did not await an answer. 'Whatever it is, you are welcome. For yourself – and also for this. Look!' He gestured at the littered table. 'Letters, letters. My pen is never idle.'

'Aye. But even so, there are letters that you would never let *me* write for you, I think, Patrick!'

'What of it?' his brother shrugged. 'There are plenty that I would. What brought you here at last, Davy?'

The other did not answer that. 'They say, out there, that the English Secretary. Walsingham, is coming here. Is it so?'

'Aye, true enough. What of it?'

'Elizabeth must have something strong to say, to send that man!'

'No doubt.'

'It does not concern you?'

'Should it, Davy? It is not I who have to answer him.'

David looked at his brother, brows puckered. 'I do not understand you,' he said, shaking his head. 'Even yet – after all these years. To be in so deep, yet to care so little. Ever to move others, and always to remain yourself untouched. What is it that you want, Patrick? What do you seek, from your life?'

'Why, Davy – why so portentous? Should I tear my hair because others do? Because the King bites his nails and pleads not to have to see Walsingham? That is Arran's business, not mine. *He* acts the Chancellor . . .'

'Aye – what *is* your business, then? Once I believed that it was to save our poor Queen. To get her out of Elizabeth's power. That is why I aided you. But what have you done for her? For Mary? In all these years when your hand has been behind so much that goes on in Scotland? Nothing! Nothing, save to write her letters, and spend her money! Aye, and prevent her envoy from having audience with her son! And all the while she rots there, in prison, while you who were to succour her, grow rich, powerful. And now, 'fore God, even this painted woman of Arran's struts and prinks, they say, in the Queen's jewels! It is not to be borne!'

'I' faith, Davy – here is an outcry indeed!' Patrick said softly, staring at the other. It was not often that David gave himself away so quickly, so completely. 'I do believe that is it! That is what has brought you. The Honeypot still draws, attracts – eh? Astonishing! Our staid and sensible Davy . . . !'

'My lord says that you have brought back a further six thousand gold crowns of the Queen's revenues, from France!' David interrupted him harshly. 'That means that she still trusts you – or her servants do.'

'So – our father has heard that, has he? And passed it on. How . . . inadvisable! I wonder whence he got it?'

'Why did they give you it? What do you intend to do with it, Patrick? Apart from lining your own pockets . . . ?'

'Have a care, Davy – have a care! I do not like your questions.'

'Nor I. But that is what I came to ask, nevertheless. Someone, it seems requires to ask them. Someone who is not afraid of you . . . '

'So you are the Queen's champion – self-appointed? Davy Gray is to be accounted to, for the Queen's moneys? De Guise and the Archbishop and Morgan her Treasurer trust me to expend it aright, for Mary's best interests – but not Davy Gray!'

'These others do not know you as I know you, Patrick . . . '

'Do you know me? Have you not just finished saying that you do not! That you do not understand me, do not know what it is I want? Yet you would interfere in what is no concern of yours . . . '

'She is my Queen, as much as yours, brother. If I can do aught for her, here at your shoulder . . . '

David stopped as the door burst open without warning. King James himself came shambling into the room, rich clothes untidily awry, big eyes unsteadily rolling and darting. 'Patrick, man – what are we to do? What . . . ?' At sight of David, he halted, his slack lower jaw falling ludicrously. 'Guidsakes – it's you again, Master Davy! Davy Gray. I didna ken you were in Stirling. What brings you, Davy . . . ? Och – but no' the now. No' the now.' James turned back to Patrick. 'What are we to do with the man, Patrick? With this Walsingham? I'll no' see him. Jamie says I must – but I'll no'. I willna see him, I tell you!' The slurring voice rose high. 'He's a terrible man. They say he's like any blackamoor. Yon woman's sent him to glower at me. I'll no' be glowered at! I'll no' see him . . .'

The tall figure of the Earl of Arran appeared in the open doorway behind the King, frowning. He was somewhat more stout than when David had last seen him, and despite his campaigning and lieutenant-generalship, looking less the soldier. He showed no enthusiasm at David's presence, and did not trouble to acknowledge it.

'It is you that he comes to see, Sire, assuredly,' he said, as though in continuation of a discussion. 'Let him glower, I say – glowering will not hurt. It is his message from his Queen that must needs concern us . . .'

'No, I'll no' do it, Jamie!' The King beat a fist on the table. 'Man, Patrick – you will see him for me, will you no'? Yon Walsingham gars me grue! Sir Jamie Melville says he's no' human.'

'Tush, James . . . !'

'I shall be there, of course, Your Grace,' Patrick said easily, soothingly. 'But I would not dream of cheating my lord of Arran out of the honour that is his!' He turned to the other man. 'My lord, I think that His Grace has the rights of it. Better that you should see Walsingham, than His Highness. Undoubtedly Elizabeth has sent him to overawe us, to browbeat the King. It would be suitable and dignified, therefore, that His Grace should not see him, should keep him at arm's length, lower his English pride a little.'

'Aye, Patrick, aye. That is right.'

'He will demand an audience, Gray – it is his right. And stay until he gets it.'

'Not so. Not if His Grace is not here! A prolonged hunting-match, for instance? A tinchel. Into Atholl and the north. Under good and sufficient escort, of course. The deer are not in season – but, heigho, that has happened before, has it not? I think that Walsingham will hardly follow His Grace into the Highlands.'

'God be good – Patrick's right!' the King cried. 'Our Patrick's aye right, Jamie.'

'M'mmm,' that lord said doubtfully.

'When will I go, Patrick? Now?'

'Why not, Sire? The sooner the better. So soon as the escort can be mustered. If you go at once, Your Grace can be at Perth by the time that Walsingham gets here.'

'Aye, Perth. Yon's the place for me this night. Perth.'

226

'You will not, h'm, be lonely? Overnight, Sire?' Patrick asked solicitously, but with a wicked glance at Arran.

'No, no. I'll bide with Murray o' Tullibardine at yon Scone I gave him – Gowrie's Scone.' At the thought of Gowrie, James blinked. 'Man, Jamie, you'll get me a right strong escort? I'm no' for having more o' yon Ruthven business. Yon Gowrie's running free. Patrick got me to pardon him. I shouldna have done it . . . '

'Do not fear, Sire – I will see to your safety. If you go . . . '

'Oh, aye – I'm going. And you'll see to Walsingham, Jamie. Use him strongly, mind – strongly.'

'Exactly,' Patrick murmured. 'Strongly is the word.'

'But no' too strongly, mind,' James amended, nibbling his lip. 'We dinna want yon woman . . . we dinna want our good cousin Elizabeth ower put out, mind. We are her heir, mind, and . . . and . . . '

'Precisely, Sire – and she must be encouraged publicly to acknowledge you as such.' Patrick stroked his silky dark curls back from his face. 'I think that it should not be difficult for my lord of Arran to put Master Walsingham in his place, and at the same time avoid offending his mistress.'

'How, man?' Arran demanded bluntly.

'Her Majesty of England is greatly fond of jewels, Sire. As fond of jewels as she is of young and handsome men. She uses both alike – to toy with, and adorn herself!'

'Aye, but . . . '

'A superlatively handsome jewel, Sire, as a gift. Hand that to Master Walsingham to give to her, and I swear Elizabeth will overlook his humbling quite! Such a toy as, say, yon great ruby ring in your royal mother's casket.' Patrick glanced quickly at David. 'I do not think that my Lady Arran has it on loan, as yet! Used thus, I vow, it will serve a better purpose than lying in a box.' That undeniably was addressed to his brother, not the King.

'Aye. Fine, fine! Man, Patrick – you think on everything, I swear,' James exclaimed. 'Let it be done so. I . . . we give our royal authority. Now – I had best be off, had I no' . . . ?'

Arran tugged at his beard. 'You think that such will serve, Gray?'

'Assuredly. It is a most notable jewel. A gift of his late Holiness of Rome, if I do not mistake. Which should commend it the more to her Protestant Majesty of England! She will take it to her bed with her, I'll wager!'

'How know you Elizabeth Tudor so well, Gray?' Arran demanded narrow-eyed.

Patrick smiled. 'I have good friends who tell me . . . much, my lord.'

'Aye well – here's no time for blethers ' the King declared agitatedly. 'I must be awa'. Jamie – my escort . . . '

Arran looked at Patrick. 'You will be there, Gray, with me, when I receive Walsingham?'

'But of course, my friend – we shall all be there. Save only His Grace. All the Court. Receive him before all, at the ball tonight. So shall you humble him the more publicly – and therefore the more deeply.'

'Before all . . . ? Not a private audience?' Arran stared and then slapped his thigh. 'Aye my God – you are right! That is the way to treat Walsingham the black snake! A pox on him – I'll do it!'

'Aye, then. Come, Jamie . . . ' the King said, plucking at Arran's sleeve.

Patrick bowed low as the monarch hurried his acting Chancellor out of the room and down the twisting stone stairway.

As he straightened up, he caught his brother's eye, and one eyelid drooped gently.

'What . . . what did you there?' David asked moistening his lips.

'Me? I but preserved one of your poor Queen's jewels from the clutch of Lady Arran . . . for a better purpose. And ensured an amusing and instructive evening!' he replied lightly. 'It all ought to prove an entertainment indeed – and vastly improve upon the ball that I had planned. One ball is so plaguey like another, isn't it? You chose your day to return to Court well, Davy. Now . . . ' He shook his head over his brother's apparel. 'As usual, I must needs find something for you to wear. Where, in the fiend's name, do you get your clothing, man? Let me see . . . ' Patrick paused. 'But, first – I had forgotten.' He rang a silver bell that stood on his table. 'It will not do to neglect the ladies . . . '

In a few moments a youth came running down the turnpike stair from the floor above, a handsomely-clad page, who eyed David superciliously.

'Will, down to the town with you, and request Deacon Graham the goldsmith attend on me forthwith. Forthwith, you understand? Off with you. Oh . . . er . . . request him to bring

some of his trinkets with him, Will. Small things. Off.' Patrick
turned back to his brother. 'Who would not be a goldsmith?
The ladies, bless their hearts, ensure that such folk are ever
prosperous!' He sighed gustily. 'Ah, me – they cost me dear,
the darlings. But then, I have not your faculty for instilling
devotion by merely looking stern, Davy! Come, and we shall
see what the royal wardrobe can do for you . . . since I am its
Master . . . !'

A distinctly nervous and brittle gaiety filled the great
audience-chamber of Stirling Castle – the same vast hall in
which the brothers Gray had first clapped eyes upon their
King, and which had witnessed the first chapter in Morton's
downfall. It was packed, tonight, with a colourful and noisy
throng – if the nobility of Scotland could so be described. Few
had seen Walsingham, as yet, but all knew that he was in the
Castle somewhere, and his name was on every lip, the shadow
of the man who was reputed to have the largest spy system in the
world at his disposal lay over all the assembly. The fact that the
King had left in a hurry, for the north, was also known to all,
and two added promptly to two. Arran, dressed at his most
extravagantly gorgeous, was very much master of all – just so,
it might be said, his wife was mistress of all. Undoubtedly his
lordship had fortified himself from the bottle. Patrick, who had
arranged this evening's entertainment, like so many another,
strolled apparently at aimless ease, greeting all, yet was never
very far from Arran.

David watched the scene from a corner, and looked for Marie
Stewart.

Whoever else was concerning themselves with the impending
arrival of Walsingham, the Countess of Arran was not. Perhaps
she believed that she had the wherewithal to tame even him.
David eyed her, in astonishment. Once, in France he had been
shocked to watch his brother dancing with a woman, whose
dress left one nipple exposed. But this woman flaunted both of
hers. And deliberately, provocatively, using them to keep all
men's eyes turning her way. She was a much less beautiful
woman than many who were present there, though
magnificently built and shaped, but there was no question as to
who caused most distraction – in both sexes, though distraction
of a differing sort. It was not only the exposure of her body that
counted, but her entire attitude, carriage, expression – blatant
indeed yet potent too, and so assured.

David by no means escaped the impact, despite his disapproval. Presently the lady espied him in his corner, and came directly across to him, all smiles.

'Davy Gray!' she cried. 'I did not know that you were back at Court. You are welcome, I vow! All true men are welcome – and you are a true man, I think? Are you not?'

David rubbed his chin, and frowned. Perhaps he should have been grateful for this queenly welcome for a humble secretary whom the lady's husband had already completely ignored? He tried not to look at her, and if that was impossible, to concentrate on the glittering gems in her hair, at her throat and ears and fingers. 'Aye, ma'am,' he muttered.

Directly she eyed him, for she was almost as tall as he was, pink tongue-tip touching her full lower lip. 'You are one of the strong men, Davy, I am told? I like strong men. I am a strong woman, you see.' She came close to him, so close that her thrusting breasts brushed him, and the musky vivid smell of her came to him powerfully.

'I can believe it, ma'am,' he said, glancing around him in embarrassment at all who watched.

'You are very different from your brother, are you not? Of a less ready tongue, assuredly. But otherwise, perhaps, as active?' She laughed loudly, and raised her voice, so that many around must hear her. 'I wonder how you compare with your brother in bed? An interesting question, is it not?'

David looked appalled.

She laughed in his face. 'Patrick has his talents, I admit,' she added. 'But I think, perhaps, you may have the longer . . . wind! Wordless men often have, strangely enough! We must put it to the test, Davy. But not tonight, perhaps. No, no. It is . . . '

'What is not tonight, perhaps?' Patrick's voice asked pleasantly, close at hand. 'Do not say that you are trying to corrupt my good Davy, Bett? Both impossible and unprofitable, surely.'

Thankfully David turned to his brother, for rescue – an unusual state of affairs.

'Think you so, Patrick?' the lady demanded. 'If he is to be your secretary again, then, Lord, I might well win some profitable secrets out of him . . . as well as other satisfactions!'

'Away with you, woman! You should be thanking me, not threatening me. Have I not assured your husband to your bed, this night?'

The Countess made a rude gesture. 'Thank you for nothing!'

She tossed David a smile. 'Remember, Davy!' she said.

As she was moving away, Patrick called, quite openly, loud enough for any around to hear who listened – and undoubtedly there were many who did. 'Bett, you have come apart, down the front. Perhaps you have not noticed?'

She jerked one bare shoulder and breast at him in a gesticulation as flagrant as it was expressive, and strolled on.

'Lord,' David gasped. 'That woman . . . she is more apt to the stews of some sailors' town than a king's court! A common street-woman is nicer . . . '

'Not so, Davy – that is the daughter of a long line of Stewart earls!' Patrick corrected. 'An extraordinary family, the Stewarts, are they not?'

The glances of both of them slid round the crowded chamber, searching.

'She . . . the Lady Marie . . . will be here?' David asked.

'It is my hope. Her father, you will note, is drunk early tonight.'

'Aye. And Arran like to be joining him!'

'He but ensures a good courage to face Elizabeth's ogre, lad.'

'No doubt. Why are you not doing the facing, I wonder?'

Patrick shrugged. 'Why should I? There is a saw about making a bed and lying therein. Arran is good at beds – like his lady!'

'Yet, have you not had a hand in making this bed, also?'

'You get some strange notions, Davy – God, you do!' The other laughed.

'Perhaps *you* have a notion as to what brings Walsingham here?'

'That is easy. Fear. Fear that the delightfully so-called Reformation is in danger in Scotland – and therefore Elizabeth's Protestant throne is endangered. Fear brings Walsingham, bearing threats.' Patrick's eyes kept turning towards Arran's slightly unsteady figure, where he supported himself against the empty throne. 'Fear is the great spur to action, is it not? Fear sends James scampering off to Perth; fear sends Arran to the bottle . . . and his wife to throw her bed open to all and sundry. Even you! Ah, me, nothing would be done at all without fear, I fear, in this sad world!'

'And you? What do you fear, Patrick?'

'Me? I fear that one, Davy Gray, is about to give me one of his . . . '

He stopped. Marie Stewart was coming swiftly across the

231

crowded dancing floor towards them, not actually running but hurrying. For so essentially calm a person, her haste was notable.

Patrick took a pace forward.

Coming up, Marie passed him with a significant wave of the hand, which she then reached out to David. 'Davy!' she exclaimed, grey eyes warm. 'How good to see you! It has been so long. When did you come? I had not heard. Have you come to stay awhile? You look . . . just as you always look!'

David smiled, and nodded wordlessly.

'Faith – an Inquisition, no less!' Patrick declared. 'Torquemada could have done no better, I vow!'

'How is your wife – the fair Mariota?' she asked, ignoring Patrick. 'Am I yet forgiven? And the enchanting Mary? And small Patrick?'

'We all fare well enough,' David assured her. 'I thank you.'

'You have not asked *me* how I fare!' Patrick protested. 'I might have the plague, the pox and the palsy, but you would care naught!'

'You look to yourself too well for any such anxiety,' the young woman retorted. 'What brings you, Davy, in the end?'

'Not you, my dear – do not flatter yourself!' his brother answered for him. 'It was another Marie Stewart altogether. The Queen, your aunt. Davy aches for her plight – as do we all, of course – and in especial, interests himself in her jewels. He is . . . '

'Jewels! Davy does?'

'Och, never heed him, Lady Marie. He but cozens you . . . '

'Not so! I swear it is nothing less than the truth. In particular he would, I think, deprive the Lady Arran of her new-won finery.'

'And I with him!' Marie exclaimed. 'That woman is contemptible – beyond all shame. That she should assume the Queen's treasure . . . ! Look at her there – or, i' faith, do *not* look at her! Parading herself like . . . like a bulling heifer! She makes me ashamed of my kind! And to think how nearly she rules the land!'

'At the least, she knows what she wants, my dear – which is more than do some women that I might name! And as to ruling the land, she has her own felicitous methods of choosing the men to do it. First she samples deeply of their purses – which is a very practical test of their ability – and then she tries them in her bed. And if they pass both assizes, they are to be considered well-fitted for bishopric, collectorship or sheriffdom. You must admit that less effective methods of ensuring the continued virility of church and state have been . . . '

'Patrick, how can you talk so? Even you! But to jest of it is a shame – it shames you, and us all. And you – you pander to her!'

'Me? Heaven forbid! Marie, Marie, how can you even suggest it . . . ?'

'Of course you do. Think you I have not seen you at it? Aye – and *you* know her shameful bed as well as any!'

'Tut, lass, in statecraft one must use such tools as come to hand . . . '

'But you no longer play the statesman, you claim! You leave that to Arran and the others, you say – even to my poor silly father, there! You but pen verses and contrive masques and balls, and . . . and chase women!'

'A mercy – this is not Marie Stewart, surely? The serene and imperturbable! What has become of her tonight? Chase women, forsooth! What woman have I been chasing these many months – to no purpose? One woman only – and she a cold grey-eyed virgin whom no plea, no art or artifice will stir. Until tonight . . . '

'What of Eupham Erskine? And Lady Balfour? And Madame de Menainville, wife to the French Ambassador? What of these? Aye, and others! Under what head do you woo all these?'

David had never seen Marie Stewart so patently moved. And seldom his brother so palpably disquieted thereat, though he sought to gloss it over. David indeed found himself to be strangely affected. 'I think that Patrick may be engaged in more of statecraft than he would wish to appear,' he put in, in a jerky attempt to ease the tension. 'These ladies may well have a part in it. The French lady, in especial . . . '

Marie rounded on him with surprising vehemence. 'Do not *you* make excuses for him, Davy Gray!' she exclaimed. 'He is well able for that himself . . . '

She stopped. Indeed she had to stop. The music and dancing and the chatter of the great throng had all along necessitated raised voices. But none such could compete with the sudden ringing fanfare of the heralds' trumpets which sounded from the lower end of the hall, turning all eyes thitherwards. Talk died, dancing faltered and stopped, and the music ebbed to a ragged close.

'His Excellency Sir Francis Walsingham, Ambassador

233

Extraordinary of Her Grace the Princess Elizabeth, Queen of England!' it was announced into the hush as the flourish died away.

The hush was not complete, however, and resounding as was this announcement it was insufficient entirely to drown a single voice that talked on thickly and laughed loudly. The Earl of Arran, up at the Chair of State, chatting with the Earl of Orkney and others, did not appear to have noticed this development.

Mr Bowes, Elizabeth's resident envoy, stood in the great open doorway behind the heralds, biting his lip, frowning, and tap-tapping his foot. Suddenly he was thrust unceremoniously aside, and a tall, thin, angular man strode past him into the chamber. Stiff as a ramrod, soberly clad, Walsingham paced forward looking neither right nor left, while before him men and women fell back respectfully to give him passage. A man now of late middle-age, grey-haired and grey-bearded, he was of so sallow a complexion as to be almost swarthy, offering one explanation for Elizabeth's nickname for him of 'her Moor'; the other explanation went deeper, and referred to the man's cold, almost Eastern, ruthlessness, his unfailing calm and intense secrecy of nature. A fanatical Protestant, a man of utterly incorruptible morals and piety, and yet one of the greatest experts in espionage and subversion that the world has known, he had been Elizabeth's principal minister for the eleven years since Burleigh's partial retirement to the Lord Treasurership. But not her friend, as had been his predecessor. Faithful, efficient, unflagging, he yet did not love his Queen – nor she him. One look at his lugubrious dark face, hooded eyes and down-turning scimitar of a mouth, might instil doubts as to whether indeed the man was capable of love for any. All eyes now considered him urgently. searchingly, many fearfully, Patrick Gray's not the least closely. Or not quite all eyes those of the Earl of Arran, acting Chancellor of Scotland and deputy for the King, could not do so, for he had his back turned to that end of the apartment, and still joked in loud-voiced good humour with his little group of friends.

David and Marie both looked from Walsingham to Arran and then to Patrick. Other glances made the same circuit. The latter, lounging at ease, made neither move nor gesture.

Almost running behind Walsingham, Mr Bowes called out agitatedly. 'My lord! My lord of Arran! His Excellency is . . . ' A guffaw from the head of the room overbore the rest.

Walsingham never faltered in his jerky pacing. No sound other than the footsteps of himself and his entourage, and Arran's throaty voice, now broke the silence.

A few paces from Arran's broad back Walsingham halted, and stood stiffly, patiently. When Bowes commenced another outraged summons, his senior flicked a peremptory hand at him.

All waited.

It was Marie's father, the Earl of Orkney, who brought matters to a head. Affecting only just to have noticed the new-comers, he raised his eyebrows and turned to Arran, tapping his padded shoulder.

The latter swung round, a little too quickly. 'Ah! God's Eyes – what's to do?' he demanded. 'What's this? A petition? A deputation? Some favour besought?'

'My lord!' Bowes was not to be withheld. 'Here is Sir Francis Walsingham, my royal mistress's principal Secretary and Envoy Extraordinary . . . '

'To see your master, sir.' Walsingham's voice crackled dry, like paper.

'Eh . . . ? Walsingham, is it? Ah, yes. We heard that you were on your way. You travel fast, it seems, Sir Francis.'

'Aye. And with reason. I seek His Grace, your master.' Cold, impersonal, and without being raised, the other's voice carried more clearly than did Arran's.

Beneath his breath, Patrick murmured. 'Here is a cunning game. Do not tell me that Bowes' spies have not informed him that James is gone, long since.'

'The King is not here. He is gone to the Highlands, hunting.'

'In the month of March?'

'S'Death, yes! Our prince will hunt in season and out. There is no containing him. But that need not concern you, sir. *I* govern this realm, for His Grace. What you have to say, you may say to me.'

The corners of Walsingham's mouth turned down still further than heretofore. 'I am accredited to the King of Scots – not to you, or any other!'

'No doubt. That is the usual practice. But His Grace entrusts me to handle all affairs of state, in his name.'

'You are to be congratulated, my lord. But my mission is still with the King.'

'Then, Christ God – you'll bide long enough!' Arran cried coarsely. 'For James will no' be back for weeks, belike. Can you wait weeks, Sir Francis?'

Walsingham shut his mouth tightly.

Patrick Gray seemed to rouse himself. He strolled forward easily across the floor, his high-heeled shoes clicking out the unhurried nature of his progress. He bowed profoundly to both the speakers.

'My lord of Arran – your Excellency of England,' he said. 'My name is Gray – and your very humble servant. If I may be permitted a word . . . ?'

Bowes began to whisper in Walsingham's ear, but that stern man waved him away curtly. He looked directly at Patrick, however.

'It is to be regretted that His Grace should not be here to receive so distinguished a visitor, Your Excellency. But princes, as indubitably you are aware, are not to be constrained. May I propose a compromise? Your despatches, letters, from your royal mistress, are undoubtedly addressed to, and for the eye of, King James alone. They should be sent after him, forthwith – though they may take some while to reach His Highness. But the substance of any representations and proposals, being a matter of government, as between the monarchs' advisers, are surely suitably to be made to my Lord Arran and members of the Council?'

Unblinking, Walsingham eyed him. 'Young man,' he said thinly, 'I do not require lessons in the conduct of affairs. My information is that your prince was in Stirling but this day's noon. I think that he cannot have travelled very far to your Highlands. I have no doubt that either he may be fetched back, or else that I may overtake him tomorrow.'

'Impossible, sir,' Arran asserted. 'Your information will no doubt also have acquainted you with the fact that King James rides fast. It is his invariable custom – and he has the finest horseflesh in three kingdoms. Moreover, the King of Scots is not fetched back, for any man – or woman – soever!'

Seconds passed. 'Can it be that you intend that I do not see the King?' Walsingham said, at length, his voice entirely without emotion, but none the less menacing for that.

'The intention is of no matter, sir. The possibility is all.'

'Sir Francis,' Patrick put in. 'Our prince is young – a mere seventeen years. His rule is entrusted to his Council. Most of that Council is here present. In default of His Grace's presence . . . '

Walsingham ignored him. 'Do I return to my mistress then,

my lord, and inform her that her envoy was refused audience of your prince?'

'Not so. That would be false, sir. If you will wait, possibly for a mere sennight or so, His Highness my be back. Who knows?' Arran's sneer was but thinly disguised.

'Beyond this room, sir, is a Council-chamber,' Patrick mentioned. 'Your embassage could there be discussed, in privacy . . . '

'No, Master of Gray,' Walsingham interrupted him. 'The Queen of England does not treat with . . . substitutes! I shall return to her, and inform Her Grace of my reception. And I warn you all, she will take it less than kindly. Moreover she has the means to show her displeasure. Ample means!'

'Would . . . would you threaten us, by God?' Arran cried. 'You are in Scotland now, I would remind you, sir – not England!'

'I do not threaten – I warn. Your prince will, I fear, learn sorely of the folly of his advisers. I bid you goodnight, my lord.'

'As you will. If your message is of so little import. But . . . wait, man – wait.' Arran recollected. 'I have here a gift for your royal mistress. A jewel for the Queen. I understand that she is partial to jewels? You will give her this, sir, with our warm favour and respect.'

Walsingham hesitated. He was placed in a difficult position. Elizabeth's fondness for gems was so well known that any outright rejection of the gift on his part, and in front of all these witnesses, could be construed as a grievous slight to her interests. 'I think that my lady would liefer have your love and worship than your jewels,' he said sourly.

'She shall have both, Sir Francis,' Patrick declared genially.

Arran held out a ring on which an enormous stone redly reflected the light of the candles. 'Take it, sir,' he urged. 'Her Highness would not thank you to leave it!'

Grudgingly, Walsingham took the ring, and hardly so much as glancing at it, thrust it into a pocket.

Arran grinned. 'A good night to you, Sir Francis. And if you change your mind the morn, we'll be happy to treat with you!'

With the stiffest of bows, Walsingham turned about and went stalking back whence he had come. Lady Arran's high-pitched laughter alone sounded from the other end of the room.

Marie Stewart turned to David. 'If I had not seen that with my own eyes, I would scarce have believed it!' she declared.

'Has Arran lost his wits, to treat that man so? He must be more drunk than he seems.'

'I think not,' David told her. 'All was planned beforehand, you see.'

'Planned? Arran does not plan what he will say. Patrick . . . ?'

He nodded.

Though Walsingham left for the south again the very next morning, by midday all Stirling knew that his mission had been to complain to James about an alliance that he claimed was being negotiated between Scotland, the Guises, and the King of Spain, for a simultaneous invasion of England, to be touched off by the assassination of Elizabeth herself, and a subsequent restoration of the Catholic religion to both countries, with James, in association with his mother Mary, to sit on the thrones of both. Highly circumstantial and markedly unanimous were these dramatic rumours, most obviously representing an inspired 'leak', no doubt from Bowes. With them went sundry threatenings and slaughters and demands, plus the suggestion of an alternative pact, a Protestant alliance, with the removal of the King's present pro-Catholic advisers – the bait to be Elizabeth's long-delayed public recognition of James as her ultimate heir.

From half-a-dozen sources David and Marie heard approximately this story, in while or in part, next day. Patrick, questioned on the subject, laughed and declared that there were surely vivid imaginations about the Court these days. When it was pointed out that he himself had been recently in the neighbourhood both of the King of Spain and the Guise brothers, he protested, but amusedly, that he had gone to the Continent purely as a private citizen, with no authority to discuss pacts, alliances, and such-like. They ought not to take Mr Bowes' considered flights of fancy so seriously. Let them rather be suitably diverted by all this ingenuity, and recognise it as an attempt to stir up the Kirk and the Protestant faction to play Elizabeth's game for her. Was it not all as good as a play?

It took considerably longer than a day, however – weeks in fact – before the news travelled up from London that Elizabeth was very angry. Not so much annoyed at the reception of her envoy and minister, but incensed, outraged, over the fact that Arran had insulted her by sending her a ring with a great piece of red glass in it, instead of a ruby. The stone was a crude fake, it appeared – and the greatest and most impudent discourtesy shown to Gloriana in all her career.

Many were the interpretations put upon this extraordinary development. Needless to say, despite Arran's fervent expostulations that he knew nothing about it, and that it must have been either the former Pope who had sent a sham ruby to Queen Mary in the first place, or else Walsingham himself had done this thing in revenge for his reception – despite this, the most popular theory undoubtedly was that Arran had hit upon the ingenious notion of hitting at Elizabeth and at the same time enriching himself, by substituting the glass in the ring and retaining the great ruby. Most people, indeed, looked to see a large ruby, or a swarm of smaller ones, appearing on Lady Arran's person at any time.

David Gray did not altogether agree with this view.

Chapter Nineteen

THE rumblings of threat and wrath from Whitehall, the rumours of a great Spanish fleet being built to attack England, the reports of the Guise brothers' collection of a large army which was to co-operate with the Duke of Parma's Spanish forces in the Netherlands for the cross-Channel adventure, plus the Pope's comprehensive and violent denunciation of Elizabeth Tudor as an illegitimate usurper, an idolatress and a murderess, worthy of death by any and every means – with a dispensation in advance for any faithful believer who might effect her happy demise, and an absolution for all her subjects of any allegiance to her – all this tended to dominate Scots political life and discussion that summer of 1584. The sense of sitting on a volcano which was liable to erupt at any time was very prevalent. Nevertheless, sundry developments and activities took place at home to counter-balance the weight of foreign affairs, and enliven the Court, if not the nation.

The Earl of Gowrie, ostensibly pardoned by the King on Patrick's advice, when the rest of the Ruthven lords were banished the country, was arrested on a visit to Dundee, presumably on the orders of Arran, removed forthwith to Stirling, and there tried by a hastily assembled but carefully selected panel of his peers on a charge of high treason against the King's person, unanimously found guilty, and beheaded the same night. His servants manged to recover the head from its lofty spike on the Castle battlements, and having sewed it back on to the body, hastily gave the remains a form of burial. So ended the great Greysteil, second only to Morton as James's childhood bogey. Patrick made a speech in his favour, as became an affectionate nephew – but found surprisingly little of good to put forward in his defence. His faithfulness to the end, however, was in due course rewarded handsomely by large royal grants of the deceased's forfeited property, so that the estates did not altogether go out of the family, though Gowrie's widow and sons, of course, were reduced to penury.

Then the Estates of Parliament duly passed Arran's Black Acts, against the violent opposition of the Kirk – the Kirk as opposed to the Church, that is, for of course the new bishops and

240

commendators voted solidly for them. Under their provisions treason became the commonest offence in the land, the King was to rule the Kirk, and its revenues were made readily transferable – far-seeing legislation that even the Pope of Rome could scarcely have improved upon.

In May, Arran had Argyll declared officially unfit owing to ill-health, and became authentically Chancellor. A month or two later he had himself appointed Governor of Edinburgh Castle as well as Stirling, and for good measure, Lord Provost of Edinburgh. There were few more offices that he could usefully aspire to.

David watched all this with alarm, doubt and wonder. Alarm at what misgovernment and personal greed was doing to Scotland, was always doing to Scotland; doubt as to what, if anything, could be done to amend the situation, by such as himself; and wonder that Patrick seemed to be not only so unconcerned but so inactive, so passive, in the face of it all. As Marie had said in her letter, his brother seemed to interest himself in little but amusements, frivolities and gallantries of one sort or another. That this was not, in essence, his nature, David knew well enough. That he was behaving thus, therefore, must mean something. What, fell to be discovered. David, as secretary, spent most of his time transcribing a play that Patrick was writing, making copies of poems, and penning lists for masques and balls and parties. There were letters, indeed, also, to addresses near and far, but none of these, unless they were in a form of code, seemed to deal substantially in statecraft or intrigue.

Marie, of whom David saw much, was equally perplexed. Patrick was assiduous in his pursuit of her favours – but not exclusively so. She kept him at arm's length, yet by no means avoided his company. Indeed it is probable that many at Court presumed that they were lovers, Patrick's reputation being what it was, and their association being so open. David knew better than that.

David and Marie formed a league, purely involuntarily and spontaneously at first, but later deliberately and in collusion, to seek to advance the sadly neglected cause of the unhappy Queen Mary. Not that there was a lot that they might do, that anyone might do, indeed. But they kept on at Patrick about her, assured that somehow, some time, he could do something to aid her if he could be brought to it. Patrick, of course, expressed entire sympathy with their aims, but pointed out the insuperable difficulties in the way, more especially since the worsening of relations between Scotland and Elizabeth. What could he do? What even could James do, short of invading England for the purpose of freeing Mary – the first victim of which undoubtedly would be the imprisoned Queen herself? David insisted that he had sung a different song once, in France – and presumably Mary's own moneys and the Guise subsidies were given him only for this end? Patrick replied that it took more than money to open a Queen's prison-doors – and he was older now, and wiser, than he had been those years ago in France.

In this campaign for Mary the Queen, curiously enough, David and Marie had no ally in the lovely captive's son. James, in fact, had no desire for his mother's release; indeed undoubtedly he dreaded any such thing. Excuses could be made for him, for these unnatural sentiments. First of all, she represented a threat to his kingship, for free, she would assuredly claim the throne at once – indeed she claimed it now, and the idea of an association in the crown between them would quickly become such only in name; for she was all that James was not – charming, fascinating, lovely, vigorous, not such as would play second fiddle to anyone, least of all to her own diffident, awkward and uncouth eighteen-year-old son. Again, James not only had no love for his mother, but only knew her as a source of trouble and intrigue all his life. He would do nothing more than he was forced to do to encourage Elizabeth to cause him further trouble in this respect.

Equally curiously, it was in Arran that the campaigners found an ally, however unconscious of his role. Arran was not interested in Mary, or in anything much save his own aggrandisement. But he knew something of Patrick's ostensible link with her cause, and was becoming ever more rapidly jealous and resentful of the said Patrick. He conceived the idea of using one against the other. He obviously found Patrick's presence at Court increasingly irksome, his sway over the King annoying, and his growing influence with the Countess almost more so. Yet he was well aware of his usefulness in council, his intelligence, his undeniable capacity, and he did not wish to make an enemy of him. He therefore thought of the device of getting Patrick out of the way by having James send him as ambassador to London, ostensibly to seek an improvement of relations with Elizabeth, but also to try to gain an interview with Mary. The gesture towards Elizabeth was advisable, for relations had deteriorated alarmingly; there were constant incidents on the Border; moreover, Philip of Spain was blowing hot and cold, proving dilatory in the extreme, and the Guises consequently cautious – possibly as a result of Walsingham's machinations. Scotland was in no position to challenge the might of England alone, and some temporising appeared to be necessary. As for Queen Mary, if she could be induced to sign an undertaking to be only a nominal queen, a sort of junior partner in an association of the throne, then that problem might be fairly easily resolved, and possibly Elizabeth persuaded to release her, as being no longer a threat. This, with an agreement that Scotland should remain Protestant – meantime, at any rate; to Arran, religion was approximately as significant as, say, morality or heraldry.

Arran convinced James of the need for this embassy, but he had more difficulty with Patrick. The latter laboured under no misconceptions as to Arran's motives, and was in no hurry to conform. Moreover, it was highly probable that his own aims and objects in foreign affairs, as in other matters, were quite other than Arran's. Nevertheless he seemed to see certain advantages in a visit to Whitehall also, and clearly was prepared eventually to be convinced – though never forced – to go.

David only realised that he was seriously contemplating the assignment when Patrick asked him if he would accompany him to the South, baiting his suggestion with the lure of actually seeing and talking with the almost legendary Queen of Scots. This, of course, put his brother in a quandary. While he did not want to be away from Mariota and his own life for so long, on the other hand, the pull of Mary the Queen was strong. It might be nothing less than his duty, indeed, to go, to influence Patrick where and when he could in the Queen's interests.

In his doubt, he went to Marie Stewart. Her father, meantime an important figure as useful to Arran, had now a fine house in Stirling and a wing of Holyroodhouse in Edinburgh. The Court being at Holyrood for hunting in the Forest of Pentland that September, it was to the latter that David repaired. He found Marie teaching one of her young sisters to play the virginals, explaining that they had all been sadly neglected in such niceties during their years of poverty.

David came straight to the point. 'This whispered embassage to Elizabeth – it is true,' he told her. 'Patrick is going. He has asked that I go with him.'

'I know, Davy. Already he has asked me the same. But this morning.'

'He has?' Though he would never have admitted it, David was perhaps just a little bit piqued that Patrick should have approached the young woman first.

She nodded. 'He is very persuasive.'

'Offering marriage again?'

'Oh, yes. But that is all but a daily occurrence! This time he has been more cunning. He has arranged that my father shall go with him.'

'Your father! And . . . will he go?'

'Yes. The King is sending him. You know how it is the Scots custom to send two ambassadors – lest one betray his trust! Patrick has asked that my father be the second envoy here. It is an adroit move, for Arran and my father are close, and Arran will esteem him useful for watching Patrick. And, of course, my father would have me accompany him, if you please, like a dutiful daughter – for he would have me married off to Patrick if he could! Master Patrick has excelled himself, this time!'

'And . . . do you go?'

'I am sorely tempted. To see London – the Court of Elizabeth – even perchance to see Mary the Queen, my aunt, herself!'

'And for this you would be wife to Patrick?'

'No, Davy. When I marry, it will not be as part of any bargain. Anyway, how could he marry before he goes, when he has still made no move for a divorcement? That is a matter that I do not understand, Davy. He ever asks that I marry him – and yet, in all these years, he has never moved to end his marriage to Elizabeth Lyon. Is it to be wondered that I doubt his intentions?'

'It is strange, yes, I have asked him, many a time, and always he says that he made one foolish marriage; it is safer and more convenient to be a married man until he can make the true marriage of his life.'

'Aye! How like him – how like Patrick Gray! His own safety and convenience. Caring nothing for others' feelings . . . '

'But he does care for you, I think, Marie. Patrick is . . . Patrick. But I believe that he loves you truly.'

'You do?' Levelly she stared at him for a long moment.

Uncomfortably he looked away over the smoking Edinburgh roof-tops, nodding.

'So you would have me give myself? Overlook all, and . . . and . . . '

'No, no! I did not say that. God forbid that I should seek anything but your weel . . . !'

244

'I know, Davy. I am sorry. I am just a silly vapourish woman Forgive me.' She paused, and ran slender fingers over the keys of the virginal. 'You have not said whether or no you are going to London, yourself?'

'I go, if you go,' David said, simply.

'Very well, my friend – we will both go.'

Chapter Twenty

THEY made an impressive cavalcade as, in clear crisp October weather, they took the long road southwards. Since Scotland's ambassadors must travel in suitable style, there were no fewer than one hundred and twelve riders in the company – mainly men-at-arms, of course. but including also many aides, secretaries, servants and hangers-on, even their own heralds. The Lady Marie was by no means the only woman present, for the Earl of Orkney never went far without just as many high-spirited females as his means would allow; moreover he had brought along a couple of other daughters, doubtfully mothered, whom he hoped to marry off to suitable English lords. Since the object of the expedition was as much to impress as to negotiate – and since Patridk was the leader, and the Treasury had been made available – no expense had been spared in the way of fine clothes, trappings, horseflesh, gifts, and the like. Altogether the entire entourage presented a notable spectacle, which was a source of great admiration and wonder wherever it went, greatly embarrassing the over-modest David – and vastly complicating the problems of overnight accommodation throughout. Arran himself accompanied them for half-a-day's journey southwards, so thankful was he, it was thought, to see the back of the too-talented Master of Gray.

Patrick, whatever his earlier doubts about the necessity for this mission, was in excellent form, the soul of gaiety, hail-fellow with all, gentle and simple alike, apparently without a care in the world. Orkney was always a hearty character and good company within limits; moreover he got on exceedingly well with Robert Logan of Restalrig, whom Patrick had brought along presumably in the interests of the more active aspects of diplomacy. Marie, having decided to come, seemed her serene self again and ready to be amused; while her young sisters obviously looked upon the whole affair as an entertainment. There was a holiday atmosphere throughout, which David did not feel to be entirely suitable, in view of the gravity, for Scotland and its imprisoned Queen, of their mission; but which, recognising that he was too sober a fellow, he sought not to spoil.

Despite all this, Patrick did not dawdle. The first night out they spent at Logan's weirdly-situated Fast Castle, and by mid-day next were in Berwick-on-Tweed, where they gained a reluctant warrant of passage through England from the suspicious Governor, the Lord Hunsdon, Queen Elizabeth's own cousin.

For practically all of the party, save Orkney who had sampled English prisons also, it was the first time that they had set foot on English soil – though admittedly Logan had led many raids across the Border, in the interests of cattle rather than sight-seeing – and great was the interest. Almost as great was the disappointment at finding Northumberland, Durham and even Yorkshire not so vastly different from Lowland Scotland, with most of the people living in even more miserable hovels, when it had always been understood that the soft English all lived in palaces.

The Midlands and the southern shires approximated a little more nearly to the popular conception of England, yet even so it was all much below expectations. The great mansions, certainly, were larger and more splendid and frequent, but there were many fewer good defendable castles, and of ordinary gentle-men's stone towers, none at all. Presumably their lairds lived in these rambling lath-and-clay barn-like dwellings, which any good Scot could cut his way through with his sword. Their churches were more like cathedrals, and their cathedrals enormous – though this was assuredly a sign of decadence. But the common people appeared to be mere serfs, and their villages wretched in the extreme. The Scots came to the con-clusion that they had been considerably deceived by visiting envoys.

It took them twelve days to reach London, twelve carefree autumn days in which Patrick established a personal ascend-ancy over all of them, in which he was the best of company, the most thoughtful of masters. Marie and he had never been closer. David watched and wondered – and doubted his own doubts.

They came to London by Enfield Chase and Islington, and, distinctly affected by the size of it all, the seemingly endless spread of tight-packed houses and winding lanes – not to men-tion the stench, which, lacking the hill and sea breezes of Edinburgh, was worse than anything that they had so far encountered – reached the river in the vicinity of London Bridge. By then, of course, the narrow crowded streets had strung out their cavalcade into a lengthy serpent, the rear of which might be anything up to a mile back.

Enquiries as to the whereabouts of the Queen's palace brought forth stares, jeers and pitying comments upon strangers with outlandish speech who did not know that good Queen Bess had scores of palaces scattered around London. Which did they want – Whitehall, St Mary-le-Bone, Hampton Court, Richmond, Greenwich, Nonsuch, Hatfield, Windsor . . . ? Where was the Queen today? God only knew where she might be – Bess, bless her, was seldom still for two days on end. Folk, clearly, who asked such questions, were fools or worse. Catholics, perhaps . . . ?'

The problem was solved unexpectedly, and fortunately without the drawing of touchy Scots swords. A major disturbance down at the crowded waterside drew their attention, with considerable shouting and commotion. Inspection proved this to be something like a miniature sea-battle. Up and down the Thames reaches, uniformed guards in skiffs, pinnaces and gigs were clearing all other boats from the wide river – and doing it forcefully, ungently. The waterway obviously was much used for passage and transport – not to be wondered at, considering the congested state of the narrow alleys and wynds which were scarcely to be dignified by the name of streets – and all this traffic, from the wherries of the watermen to merchants' lighters and public ferries, was being protestingly driven in to the shore. Investigation produced the information that these represented new security measures for the Queen's safety. With the recent assassination of the Prince of Orange, the other Protestant stalwart, Parliament had grown exceedingly worried about Elizabeth's preservation, in view of the Pope's *pronunciamento*. The Queen apparently did much of the travelling between her numerous palaces by royal barge. She was now on her way back from Greenwich to Whitehall, and this clearing of the river was a precaution against any surprise attack.

Strangely enough, these tidings seemed to galvanise Patrick Gray into urgent action. Leading the way hurriedly a little further westwards along the waterfront, he pulled up at a cobbled opening from which one of the numerous flights of steps led down to a tethered floating jetty, and dismounted, signing to David to do likewise.

'I want one of those boats, Davy – and quickly,' he said, pointing down, low-voiced. 'Large enough for . . . say, six men. Aye, six. Do not question me, man – see to it. Hire one.

Any of these fellows should be glad of the earnings, since they may not use the boats themselves. An hour's hire. Less. Quickly, Davy.'

Mystified, David went down the steps. Half-a-dozen wherries were tied up there, and their owners standing by. The watermen looked at him strangely, began to laugh at his foreign attire and accent, thought better of it on noting the length of his rapier, and then stared in astonishment at his untimely request. However, the silver piece held out talked a language that they understood notably well, and with grins and shrugs a sizeable skiff was pointed out as available. He could have it to sit in, if he cared, to watch the Queen go by – but only that; no waterman was going to risk his skin by rowing out into the river meantime, not for even a gold piece.

Back at street level, David found his brother impatiently holding forth to Lord Orkney and the other principals of his party.

' . . . I tell you, it is a God-sent chance!' he was declaring emphatically. 'You know passing well the fear we have had that Walsingham will not allow us near to the Queen, after what happened at Stirling. Archie Douglas, our envoy, has written as much to the King. Here is opportunity to catch the eye of the Queen herself – and they do say that she loves boldness.' He turned. 'Davy, another boat we need, as well. For decoy. You got one?'

'Aye, easily enough. But they will not row for us. Not until the Queen is by.'

'Who cares? We can row ourselves.'

'Och, this is folly, Patrick!' Orkney objected. 'Yon guards will have us, and we shall end up in the Tower, no' the Palace! I'll no' be party to it.'

'Then wait you here, my lord, and watch.' Patrick turned to Logan. 'Rob, you'll be a bonny rower? You take the second boat. With some of your men. You will row out first – decoy the guards away from us. When I give you sign. You have it? I will see that no ill comes to you afterwards.'

'To be sure, Patrick.' Logan grinned widely. 'I'll lead them a dance. Just watch me . . . '

'No real trouble, now, mind – no broken heads or the like. Just a decoy. Now – where are those heralds? Get the two of them down into my boat. Aye, trumpets and all. Davy and I will row. Get the second boat, Davy . . . '

'Man – this is madness!' Orkney cried. 'You'll have us all undone.'

'Let us come with you, Patrick,' his daughter interrupted. 'A woman in the boat will look the better. I can row, too . . . '

'Lord save us, girl – are you out o' your wits?'

The faint sound of music came drifting up to them, through and above the more clamorous riverside noises.

'That must be the Queen coming,' Patrick exclaimed. 'Haste you, now!'

David ran back down the steps, to acquire another boat. Whether or not Patrick had given permission, he found Marie tripping down after him, riding-habit kilted high to the undisguised admiration of the watermen. There was no difficulty about hiring another wherry; they could have had all the craft there, had they so desired. Logan, who never travelled without some of his Borderers close, came down with three of his fellows. Then Patrick and the two bewildered heralds clutching trumpets and furled banners. Well might the bystanders gape.

They all piled into the two boats, Marie into the bows of the first, the heralds in the stern, and David and Patrick midships on the rowing thwarts. As yet they did not touch the oars.

The music was now much more distinct, punctuated by sporadic and ragged bursts of cheering. From their present position they could not see much to the east of London Bridge. The fleet of small craft bearing the guards had moved on further up river, but three or four heavier barges remained, more or less stationary, held by their oarsmen in the main stream. One lay about two hundred yards downstream of them, the bright liveries of its company making a splash of colour against the dirty water of the river.

Catching Logan's eye, Patrick gestured towards this barge. 'Heavy craft,' he commented. 'Upstream it will be no greyhound.'

Restalrig nodded, and spat over the side, eloquently.

'And you, my dear?' Patrick turned to look behind him, at Marie. 'What do you in this boat?'

'I give you an aspect of the innocent, the harmless. You may be glad of it.'

'H'mmm. At least you have a quicker wit than your sire! But you should not have come. This is no woman's work.'

'It is to impress a woman, is it not . . . ?'

'Here they come,' David jerked.

Into view below the arches of London Bridge swept the royal

procession First came a boatload of soldiers. Then a flat-decked lighter, rowed by hidden oarsmen, on which played a full orchestra of instrumentalists. Close behind was a huge decorated barge, with a thrusting high prow in the form of a great white swan with its wings swelling out to enclose the hull of the craft, ro ved by double banks of white oars, the rowers being garbed in handsome livery with large Tudor roses embroidered on ch:sts and backs. A great striped awning in the red-and-white colours of England covered all the after part of the barge, and u .der it, in the well, was a company of gaily-clad men and women. In the stern was a raised dais, and sitting all alone thereon, in a high throne, was a slight figure all in white. Nearby, a tiny negro page stood, bearing a laden tray. Some way behind were another two barges, filled with men on whom metal breastplates glinted and ostrich-plumes tossed – no doubt the celebrated Gentlemen Pensioners, without whom Elizabeth seldom stirred. Another boatload of soldiers brought up the rear.

David glanced at his brother. He did not know just what Patrick intended, but whatever it was, it must now have the appearance of a formidable proposition. He said as much, briefly.

Patrick smiled. 'Wait, you,' he said.

They waited, all save Patrick it seemed, tensely. Timing was evidently going to be all-important, whatever the venture. The watermen on the jetty close by were not the least of the problem.

As the Queen's squadron drew near, Patrick suddenly jumped up, rocking the wherry alarmingly, and leapt lightly back on to the floating timber jetty. 'Look! he cried, pointing away eastwards dramatically. 'Over there!'

As all heads turned, the watermen's as well, he stooped swiftly, and deftly unlooped the mooring ropes which tied both wherries to bollards. Gesturing urgently to Logan to be off, he leapt back into his own boat, the impetus of his jump helping to push it out from the jetty.

Logan and his men had hurriedly reached for the oars, but they had not fitted them into their sockets before some of the watermen, turning back, saw what was afoot and began to shout. Both wherries, however, though only a yard or two from the jetty, were beyond their reach.

After a splashing awkward start, Logan's crew got away in fair style, pulling strongly. Patrick, for his part, ignoring the shouts from the shore, sat still in the rocking boat, smiling easily, imperturbably, not reaching for oars. Up above, the Earl of Orkney sat his horse, tugging at his beard.

Logan was heading his craft straight out into mid-stream. It was not long before the guards in the stationary barge noticed him; the shouts may have warned them, though these could well have been taken as loyal cheers. There was a great stir aboard, and much gesticulation. Then the barge's long sweeps started to churn the muddy water, and it swung heavily round to head off the intruder.

Logan turned a few points to the west, upstream, his four oars biting deep, sending the light craft bounding forward.

From across the river another barge of guards, perceiving the situation, came pulling over to join in the chase.

'What now?' Marie demanded.

'Wait.'

When both pursuing barges were well upstream of them, with others joining in, and Logan's wherry twisting and turning ahead of them as though in panic, Patrick suddenly nodded, twice. 'Now!' he said.

The first of the royal procession, the soldiers' boat, was already past their position, and the musicians' lighter coming almost level. Grabbing up their oars at last, Patrick and David thrust them into the water, and sent their craft scudding outwards. The shouting on shore redoubled.

The brothers had rowed together hundreds of times, in the Tay estuary, in heavier boats than this, in rough weather and smooth. They knew each other's stroke to an ounce. They sent that wherry leaping forward like a live thing.

The Thames here was some two hundred and fifty yards across, and the Queen's array kept approximately in mid-river. The heavy royal barges were being pulled upstream against tide and current. With only a hundred yards or so to cover, in the light fast wherry, Patrick could judge his time and direction to a nicety. Rowing, with head turned most of the time over his right shoulder, he directed his small craft on a line directly astern of the musicians and just in front of the Queen's barge.

'Quickly!' he panted, to the heralds. 'The banners. Up with them. Hold them high. And your trumpets. Sound a fanfare. Aye – and keep on sounding. Hurry! A pox on you – hurry!'

The heralds were but clumsy in their obedience, fumbling between banners and trumpets. One flag was raised, somewhat askew – the red tressured lion on yellow of Scotland's king. A wavering wail issued from one instrument.

'Damn you – together, of a mercy! Together!'

The second standard went up, the red lion on white of the House of Gray. The second trumpet sounded tentatively.

Their presence had not passed unnoticed, obviously. There was reaction apparent in most of the barges. In that in the lead, the soldiers were pointing and shouting, seemingly in some doubt; the flags of course would give the impression of something official, unsuspicious, and probably their officers were more exercised about Logan's errant skiff in front. The musicians played on without any sign of concern, but there was a good deal of gesturing in the royal barge itself and in the boatfuls of gentlemen following on.

Rapidly the gap between the large boats and the small narrowed. The heralds had at long last achieved unanimity, and their high shrilling fanfare sounded challengingly across the water, quite drowning the orchestra's efforts and all but deafening the other occupants of the wherry. Both banners were properly upright now, and streaming, proudly colourful, behind the small boat, by their size making it look the smaller. The brothers' oars flashed and dipped in unison.

The slender white figure on the throne-dais out there, sat unmoving.

'The last boat! At the end. With the soldiers. It is pulling out.' Marie had to lean forward to shout into Patrick's ear, to make her report heard above the noise. 'It is coming up this side. To cut us off, I think. And . . . and on the Queen's boat, Patrick! Harquebusiers! They have harquebuses trained on us.'

'Never fear. They will not shoot. Not yet. Not on Scotland's colours. Nor with you here, Marie. I said not with *you* here. We have yet time . . . '

'Some gigs coming back, too. Down river,' David mentioned.

'Heed them not. We are all but there.' Patrick glanced over his shoulder again. 'Marie – can you hear me? You said that you could row? Will you take this oar when I say? In just moments. Row, with Davy. He will keep the boat steady. Alongside the barge. Can you hear me?'

She nodded, unspeaking.

They were no more than thirty yards from the Queen's craft, now, just slightly ahead of it, and roughly the same distance behind the bewildered orchestra, many of whose members had ceased to try to compete with the stridently continuous blasting of the trumpets' barrage.

Nudging David, Patrick suddenly began to back water,

whilst his brother rowed the more vigorously. The result was to swing the wherry round, prow upstream, on a parallel course with the great barge and less than a dozen yards or so from its rhythmically sweeping white oars.

'Hold it thus,' he shouted. 'Marie!'

She came scrambling to his thwart, almost on all fours, her riding-habit far from helping her. Even so the light boat rocked alarmingly. Patrick, handing his oar to her, squeezed past her, and stepped unsteadily forward to her place in the bows. The exchange was less graceful than he would have wished. Even this brief interval had been enough to bring the steadily-forging barge level and a little more than level, so that the wherry was now opposite the after part of the larger craft. As Marie's oar dug in too eagerly and too deeply, the small boat lurched, and Patrick, who had remained standing in the bows, all but lost his balance. Recovering himself, and grimacing and laughing towards the royal barge, he gestured to his heralds at last to cease their blowing.

The second soldiers' boat, after furious rowing, was now level with the first of the gentlemen's craft, but seemed to have slowed down its rush, doubtfully.

It took a moment or two for the prolonged fanfare decently to die away. In those seconds, Patrick considered the Queen. He saw a thin woman, keen-eyed, pale-faced, pointed-chinned, in a monstrously padded white velvet gown, whose reddish hair though piled high did not yet overtop the enormous ruff which framed her sharp and somewhat aquiline features. Glittering with jewels, she was regarding him directly, her thin lips tight, her arching brows high. Undoubtedly she looked imperious, most dauntingly so.

In the sudden silence, Patrick dofferd his feathered velvet cap with a sweep, and bowed profoundly, smiling. Then, raising his voice, and with a peal of his happiest laughter, he declaimed clearly.

> *Fair, gracious, wise and maiden Queen,*
> *Thy fame in all the world is heard,*
> *Thy beauty when to eyes first seen*
> *Bewilders, mutes, this stamm'ring bard,*
> *Yet peerless lady, withhold not now thy face,*
> *From stunned admirer of another race,*
> *Of charity so well renowned,*
> *Your Grace in grace towards him abound,*

Who in far Scotia heard thy virtues hymned
And now beholding them true limned,
Sinks low on knee, dumbfound!

He ended with a most elaborate obeisance, sinking with one silk-clad knee on the wherry's gunwale – no easy performance with the boat rocking to uneven rowing – and thus waited.

Almost immediately a fierce and authoritative voice started to shout from the forepart of the barge, from amongst the group of harquebusiers with menacingly levelled weapons, demanding to know, in the name of the Crown, the Deity and the various powers of darkness, who and what this extraordinary party might be, what they meant by disobeying the express commands of Parliament, thrusting themselves upon the royal presence, and making a fiendish noise fit to deafen the Queen's Grace . . . ? Undoubtedly the Captain of the Guard, recovering from his fright.

Patrick, still in his precarious stance, never for a moment took his eyes off the Queen. He saw her flick a beringed hand towards the shouting officer, and forthwith his shouting died on him as though choked off. Another regally pointing finger beckoned elsewhere, and an elegant and handsome youngish man dressed all in sky-blue satin leap lightly up on to the dais, bowed, and then turned towards Patrick.

'Her Grace would know, sir, who you are and whence you come, who thus address her in passable verse and yet assail her royal ear with execrable bellowings and blowings?' he called. He had a pleasant mellifluous voice and an easily assured manner.

'Why, sir, I am a very humble and distant admirer of Her Grace, Gray by name, who has come far to worship at her shrine.' Patrick smiled ruefully. 'But, good sir, if you have any influence with the fair and royal lady, will you beseech her gracious permission that I rise up off my knees – for I vow that this craft is plaguey hard and I am fast getting the cramps!'

They could hear Elizabeth's tinkle of laughter sound across the water. They saw her say something to her spokesman, who called out,

'My lady would have no man suffer for her in knees as well as heart! Rise, Master Graves, I implore you – for I ache in sympathy!'

'My thanks to your divinity – and mine, I hope!' Patrick declared, rising and balancing. 'I would that she could heal my heart as readily as my knees!' He made as though to strum a lute, and clear-voiced extemporised a lilting tune.

> *How harsh the pangs of suppliant feeling,*
> *Compared with those of suppliant kneeling!*
> *Oh, bones and gristle, more resilient*
> *Than heart smit sore at grace so brilliant!*

The other man, a score of yards off, waved a delightful hand.

> *Sir – almost I envy your Muse,*
> *Combined, 'fore God, with oarsman's thews.*
> *How comes a man who Fate so braves,*
> *With such curst churchyard name as Graves?*

The Queen clapped her hands, the rhymster bowed, and Patrick laughed aloud.

'Not Graves, Sir Poet – but Gray. Commonly called the Master of. But now the mastered! At your service – and at your Princess's every command. She may, I think, have heard it, but no doubt has rightly long forgot my humble name. The Master of Gray.'

Even at that range the change in the Queen's expression was apparent. She leaned forward, staring from under down-drawn brows. Clearly the name was not forgotten. She spoke rapidly to her courtier, and then, with another of those flicks of the finger, summoned a second and more soberly dressed individual up on to the dais. Those in the wherry were at least thankful to see it was not Sir Francis Walsingham. After a short speech with him, the young man in sky-blue called again.

'Master of Gray, your name is known to Her Grace. She asks your errand – other than boating and poesy?'

'Tell Her Grace admiration and worship, as I said,' Patrick answered promptly. 'And also an important compact proposed by my royal master, King James.'

Again a brief conference.

'Her Grace will receive you at the Palace of Whitehall, this night, Master of Gray.'

'I am deeply grateful for her gracious favour.' Patrick bowed. 'And for your courtesy, sir. May I know to whom I am indebted?'

'Surely, sir. My name is Sidney.'

'Not . . . not Sir Philip Sidney?'

'The same, alas. Do not tell me that my small fame has reached even as far as Scotland?'

'Indeed it has, sir. This, Sir Philip, is an honour, a joy . . .'

Like a whip-lash came the sharp rap of one of Elizabeth's great jewelled rings on the arm of her chair. Hastily, at her curt gesture of dismissal, the handsome Sir Philip Sidney stepped back, to efface himself before the suddenly cold draught of Majesty's frown. She jerked a word or two at the other and dark-clad man.

He raised his voice, and much less melodiously than had Sidney. 'Her Highness asks who is the muscular lady, whom you use so strangely, sir?'

For a brief moment Patrick bit his lip, glancing down at Marie. Then he laughed, shrugging one shoulder. 'She is a determined lady who refuses to marry me, sir, tell your mistress. So I bring her here that she may be dazzled and made jealous by my adoration of the Queen's beauty and grace!'

He heard Marie gasp – and something extremely like a snort come across the water from the royal barge. Plain to be heard was the Queens' crisp words. 'Bold!' she snapped. 'Over-bold!' And turning a hugely padded shoulder on the wherry, and her face the other way, Elizabeth Tudor waved an imperious hand forwards. Clearly the interview was at an end. As Patrick swept a final extravagant bow, the orchestra started up again in front.

'How could you, Patrick?' Marie panted, as he moved over to relieve her of her oar. 'How could you say such a thing – thus, before everyone? It was . . . shameful! Aye, and stupid, too!'

'Not so, my dear. It was salutary, rather.'

'Salutary? To shame me in front of all? And to rally the Queen?'

'Does it shame you that I should offer marriage? That I should have all men know it – and women? I should have thought otherwise.'

'To shout it forth, so! To make use of it for . . . for . . . !' She shook her head. 'Anyway, it was folly. You have but offended the Queen. After all that you had gained . . . '

'Offended, you think?' Patrick matched his oar's swing to David's. 'I wonder? Say rather that I provoked her, challenged her, dared her. And she is the one to take up a dare, I believe. She will be the kinder tonight, I swear!'

Marie stared at his elegant back, bending to the pull of the oar, as they rowed back to the jetty. 'Patrick,' she said, 'have you a heart, at all?'

Turning, he flashed a smile of pure sweetness upon her. 'You ought to know, beloved, for it is all yours!' he declared. 'Now – what has become of our good Rob Logan . . . ?'

Chapter Twenty-one

THE Palace of Whitehall was vast and sprawling – more like a town in itself than a single residence, containing within its precincts avenues of lesser lodgings, churches, barracks, gardens and orchards and ponds, even a bear-pit and a huge tilt-yard for tournaments. It flanked the river for a long frontage, and it was by boat that the Scots embassage approached it that night – and in more orthodox fashion than the afternoon's caper. Lamps and torches blazed everywhere, turning night into a lurid day of wavering, flickering colour and shadow. Never had the visitors seen so much glass, in windows and mirrors and crystal ornament.

The party numbered only six – Patrick, Orkney, the Lady Marie and David, with the two heralds in case they were needed. All were dressed at their finest, the latter colourful in armorial tabards displaying the royal arms of Scotland. Logan and his men had been rescued from the clutches of the Queen's guards, but it was felt that his qualities were not likely to be in demand tonight.

The entire palace area appeared to be alive with a gaily dressed throng that circulated around more than one centre of attraction. Enquiries from their escort, a marshal of the Court, elicited that the famous Robert Dudley, Earl of Leicester, was holding one great ball in his own extensive quarters next the Queen's, Robert Devereux, Earl of Essex, another in his, and Sir Walter Raleigh a third, the Court and multitudinous guests seeming to drift from one to another more or less indiscriminately, the Queen herself honouring them all at some stage during the evening. Elizabeth, it appeared, despite her love of display, had a strong streak of economy, and much preferred her favourites and subjects to pay for such expensive entertainments, rather than herself. King James had better not be told about this.

To the strains of different orchestras, the visitors were conducted through all this magnificence and gaiety, through a series of huge intercommunicating apartments, tapestry-hung, with much marble and lavishly-painted ceilings. The prevalence of silver and gold plate, of fine carpeting, the richness of the clothing worn, and all the aspects of wealth and luxury and prodigality, raised Scots eyebrows – though not Patrick's, who of course had but recently visited the Courts of Spain and France and the Vatican, and moreover himself was seldom outdressed by anysoever; tonight, in white and gold velvet, there was no more eye-catching figure present.

In the fourth of the great salons they were halted. Here the dignified and formal measures of a pavane were being danced – though not in every case too formally. It was disclosed to them that this was my Lord Leicester's assembly, and that was my lord himself dancing with the shepherdess in lilac.

Looking, they saw a tall, extravagantly dressed man, just beginning to incline to puffiness and thickness, with a flushed, dissipated, but still handsome face. He was dancing with a buxom, bouncing young woman, a mere girl, little more than a child, in fact, but a precocious one, holding her very close for such a dance and caressing her openly, expertly, comprehensively the while – yet looking slightly bored at her giggles and wriggles. The Earl of Orkney licked his lips in appreciation.

Patrick turned to their escort – and found Marie looking at him a little strangely. 'You are not shocked, my dear?'. he asked. 'You? After all, he is . . . Leicester!'

She shook her head. 'No. It was not that . . . ' She still eyed him almost searchingly.

Suddenly he understood the searching quality of her scrutiny, reading her mind. 'You wonder whether *I* shall look like Leicester, in a few years of time?' he put to her. And he frowned – but only momentarily. 'I think not.' That was almost curt. He turned back to the marshal. 'The Queen is generous, I think, to her favourites. A broadminded mistress!' He nodded towards Leicester.

'Her Grace has but to snap her fingers and my lord will drop all his pretty chits and come running,' he said. 'None knows it better than the Queen.'

Presently the music stopped, and the marshal went forward to Leicester.

'I do not see Walsingham here,' Patrick murmured to David. 'I do not know how this Leicester will serve us – but Walsingham is the prime danger.'

'Why? Surely this man is of the more importance? The Queen, it is said, has considered marrying him . . . '

His brother shook his head. 'Elizabeth, though a very woman, has a hard man's head on her shoulders in matters of state. Her favourites and her ministers she keeps far separate. To the Dudleys and the Devereux she gives honours, wealth, privileges and her favours – surprisingly close favours! But to the Cecils and the Walsinghams and Hattons she gives the power, great power. Would that our poor Scotland had a prince with so much wisdom!'

'And where would you be then, Patrick?' Marie, listening, asked – and received a grimace for answer.

The Earl of Leicester approached them with a sort of tired swagger, as though he only did it because he knew that it was expected of him. Dressed in purple satin, with a tiny cloak of olive-green lined with ermine, on which was embroidered a great Star of the Bath, his hair and spade-beard dyed a bright orange, he seemed to be covered with orders and decorations, from the Collar of the George down to the blue Garter below his left knee. Marie had never before seen a man with pearls threaded into his beard, nor wearing earrings large enough each to contain a tiny jewelled miniature of the Queen. His jaded glance took in Patrick's superlative good looks and striking costume, without evident pleasure in the sight, skimmed over Orkney ignored David, and came to rest on Marie. The disillusioned, slightly bloodshot eyes lightened then, somewhat. He bowed to her, disregarding the men.

'The Lady Marie Stewart, my lord,' Patrick mentioned pleasantly. 'Daughter of the Earl of Orkney, here. Who is uncle to our prince, King James. Myself, Gray – at your service.'

'Aye.' Leicester did not take his eyes off the young woman, examining all her fairness frankly, lasciviously. 'Indeed? I congratulate my lord of . . . where did you say? Orkney? Where the devil is that?'

'A larger province than Leicester, I'd think, my lord!' Marie's father chuckled.

The other shrugged, and turned to Patrick. 'And you, sir? I take it you are the play-actor who this afternoon played jester on the river?' He yawned. 'Aye, I can see that you might well arouse Her Grace's passing interest.'

'I am flattered, my lord, to hear it. Especially from you, who once were such your own self!' The slight emphasis on the word 'once' was just perceptible. 'It is Her Grace whom we seek now – at her express command.'

Leicester stroked his pearl-fringed orange beard. 'The Queen, like most women, is unpredictable,' he said. 'My advice, sir, is that you should remember it.'

'I thank you, my lord . . . '

Another brilliant figure came up to them, the sky-blue spokesman of the barge that afternoon, Sir Philip Sidney. Now he was dressed all in crimson, overlaid with silver lace, with long silver gleaming hose below puffed-out trunks. Marie decided that, though his features were not so perfect as Patrick's and his smile a shade less dazzling, he was very good-looking, entirely fulfilling the picture that his reputation had painted of the noblest figure of his day, poet, thinker, soldier, diplomat. She had not thought that he would look so young.

He bowed to her, very differently from Leicester. 'Fairest siren, sweet bargee!' he said. ' 'Tis said that Helen launched a thousand ships – but I swear that she never sculled a one of them! I do not know your name, but I heartily proclaim my admiration of the anonymous gondolieress!'

She curtseyed prettily. 'My anonymity need not trouble you further, sir – though my muscularity, as I think it was named before, is not so easily disposed of! My name is the same as that of *my* Queen – Marie Stewart.'

'M'mmm.' Sir Philip blinked. 'I see that I must needs tread warily!'

'Indeed you must, babbler – for *I* was before you in appreciating the lady's qualities!' Leicester declared. 'Lady Marie, will you step the next measure with me, and reject this windbag nephew of mine?'

Marie had not realised that this disparate pair were indeed uncle and nephew. She glanced uncertainly from one to the other.

Sidney smiled. 'It grieves me to deny you, Sir Uncle, but Her Grace has sent my humble self to bring the Scots party into her presence.'

'Her Grace, I think, is not so desperate anxious for a sight of them that she will fret over one measure of a dance,' Leicester said easily.

The young woman looked at Patrick for aid, but he only smiled, and nodded airily. 'To be sure, Marie, you must not disappoint his lordship. We shall await you.'

Surprised, David considered his brother. He had not expected this. Marie likewise seemed somewhat put-out. Even Sidney raised his eyebrows. But Orkney laughed, and pushed his daughter forward, with what was practically a slap on her bottom.

Leicester turned and waved to the leader of the orchestra, who, it seemed, seldom took his eyes off his patron. The music recommenced at once, and the Earl led Marie out on to the floor.

'Sir Philip, I esteem myself fortunate indeed in this meeting,' Patrick announced. 'It has long been my ambition to meet the author of *Arcadia*, and to pay my tribute to

> . . . *the ornament of great Liza's Court,*
> *The jewel of her times.*

I trust, sir, that this day's cantrip on the river did not cause you aught of embarrassment with Her Grace?'

'Lord, no, my friend! The Queen was smiling again in two minutes. You gave her more to smile at, than to frown at. Indeed it was an entertaining introduction to one whose name is not unknown here in London . . . as well as in the wider realms of Paris, Madrid and Rome!'

Patrick bowed, but he eyed the other keenly. 'You do me too much honour,' he returned. 'I fear that my poor repute cannot serve me so kindly as does *your* fair renown?' That was really a question.

'Your repute has its own . . . efficacy, I assure you, Master of Gray,' the other told him. 'The Queen will be much intrigued to speak with you. After your exploit with the boat, she is prepared to find that your speech will fully measure up to your letters. I feel convinced that she will be noways disappointed.'

David darted another glance at his brother. Letters . . . ? To Elizabeth?

Patrick cleared his throat. 'You are very kind, Sir Philip. Your guidance is appreciated. Tell me, if you will – is Walsingham with Her Grace?'

'No, sir. He is not yet returned from Theobalds Park, where he confers with my Lord Burleigh.'

'Thank the Lord for that, at any rate!' Patrick said, with one of his frank smiles. 'Your Lady's Chief Secretary is scarcely to my taste as sponsor!'

'I dare say not, sir – though mark you, he makes a surprisingly useful father-in-law!'

Patrick started. 'Dear God – yours?'

'Why, yes. I have the honour to be married to the daughter of Sir Francis.' Sidney laughed understandingly, and patted the other's padded shoulder. 'I have some devilishly awkward connections, have I not?' And he gestured to where Leicester danced.

'H'mmmm. I am . . . overwhelmed by your good fortune, Sir Philip!' It was not often that Patrick Gray was silenced.

They stood looking at Leicester and Marie. The Earl was holding her much more closely than was usual, yet not nearly so blatantly as he had done with his previous partner. She held herself, not stiffly, but with a cool and most evidently amused detachment that undoubtedly had its effect upon Leicester. Many eyes were watching their progress. David, who found himself as hotly indignant against Patrick as against Leicester over this, recognised now that his brother had deliberately used both Marie and the Earl's lecherous demand to give himself time for a feeling of his way with Sidney preparatory to the forthcoming interview with the Queen. As though he read David's mind, Patrick nodded easily, though he addressed himself to Sir Philip.

'Marie Stewart is well able to look to herself, is she not? A plague on it, I ought to know, whom she has held just slightly further off than she does now my lord, for years!'

The Englishman looked from the speaker to the dancers and back, thoughtfully, and said nothing.

When the dance was over, Marie came back to them alone, Leicester finding other matters to occupy his attention. His nephew, declaring still more profound respect, pointed out that it was not every day that a woman could put his Uncle Robert in his place. He asked them to follow him now, and he would conduct them to the Queen.

Since no one indicated that he should stay behind, David went with the other three.

Sidney led them down a corridor, through a handsome anteroom where gentlemen waited and paced, past gorgeously liveried guards flanking a door, into a boudoir wholly lined with padded and quilted pale blue silk, where four or five of the Queen's ladies sat at tambour-frame or tapestry whilst a soulful-eyed gallant plucked a lute for their diversion. Three doors opened off this boudoir, and at one of them Sir Philip knocked, waited, and then entered, closing it behind him. The lute-players twanged on with his slow liquid notes.

After a few moments, Sidney came backing out again, and signed to the Scots party to enter. Patrick went first, bowing the requisite three times just within the doorway, followed by

Orkney, Marie, and, since Sidney seemed to be waiting for him, David also.

They found themselves in a strange apartment that at first quite confounded them as to shape, size and occupants, for it was panelled almost wholly with mirrors, reflecting each other and the room's contents times without number. It was only after a moment or two that it became clear that there was, in fact, only the one occupant other than themselves.

The Queen sat on a centrally-placed couch of red velvet, a stiff, brittle-seeming figure, positively coruscating with such a weight of gems as to seem almost entirely to encrust her. In a padded, boned and rucked gown, so sewn and ribbed with pearls that it would have sat there by itself without body inside, she glittered and glistened, her now Titian hair, obviously a wig, wired with droplets and clusters and pendants, such of her somewhat stringy neck as was not covered by the enormous starched and spangled ruff being all but encased with collars and chains and ropes of jewels, her wrists weighted with gold, her fingers so comprehensively ringed as to be barely movable. So she sat, upright, motionless, alone, and the mirrors all around her and the crystal candelabra projected and multiplied her scintillating image to all infinity.

Whatever the first arresting and confusing impression of all this, however, it took only seconds for a very different impression to dominate the minds of the newcomers, produced by another sort of gleam and glitter altogether. Elizabeth Tudor was fifty-one, but her dark brown eyes, ever her finest feature, were as large, brilliant, searching and shrewd as ever they had been, seeming almost unnaturally alive and vital in the midst of that curiously inflexible and inanimate display. Thus close, she could be seen to have no other claims to beauty save those eyes. Long-headed, long-nosed, long-chinned, heavy-lidded, thin-lipped, her skin was so pale as to be almost entirely colourless, the patches of rouge on her high cheek-bones but emphasising the fact, her brows and eyelashes almost white and barely visible. But no one there, under the blaze of her eyes, might dwell upon her lack.

Almost imperceptibly she inclined her head to the obeisances of her visitors but there was nothing rigidly formal about her voice. 'The bold young man who looks too beautiful to be honest,' she said quickly, crisply. 'The young female who would like to play the hoyden but cannot. The second young man who is not so humble as he would seem. Who is the fourth?'

264

Patrick, glancing quickly over to Sidney, cleared his throat. 'He is the Lord Robert Stewart, Earl of Orkney, uncle to our prince, and ambassador to Your Grace with my humble self,' he said. Orkney bowed again.

'Ah – one of the previous James's brood of bastards!' the Queen said. 'Less of a fox, I hope, than his brother Moray, who cost me dear! Sent, no doubt, to seek keep *you* in order, Master of Gray – a task beyond him quite, I fear!'

As Orkney's mouth opened and shut, Patrick blinked and then smiled. 'The lady is his eldest daughter, Marie, Your Grace.'

'I believe he has a-many,' Elizabeth said baldly. 'Most of them natural.'

'*My* royal father married but one of his ladies, Highness,' Orkney got out, red-faced. 'Myself also. 'Tis a habit we have in Scotland!'

Patrick held his breath at this undiplomatic rejoinder, reflecting upon the matrimonial habits of Elizabeth's own father, Henry the Eighth. But the Queen only smiled thinly, briefly. 'Other habits you have in Scotland, less respectable,' she observed. 'And the young man with the obstinate chin, who scorns clothes and queens alike? Who is he?'

David caught himself frowning, bobbed a travesty of a bow, and stood hands on hips, wishing that he had not come, but more bull-like than ever.

'He is my half-brother and secretary, David Gray, Your Grace. He, ah, is that way always. But sound . . . and very discreet.'

'I would trust him before you, rogue, anyway,' Elizabeth announced. 'Stand up straight, man, and let me look at the renowned Master of Gray. So-o-o! And you call yourself the handsomest man in Christendom?'

'Lord, Madam – absolve me from that! You are well informed as you are well-endowed, I swear – but I would never say such a thing . . . '

'But you would believe it, natheless! Handsome men, I have found, are even vainer than handsome women – save only our good Philip here, whose vanity takes other forms! Think not that I shall price you at your own value, Master Patrick – any more than I believe your flattery of my own person.'

'Then you value me low indeed, Your Grace. Fortunately, however, our own poor worth is not the measure of our mission.

It is our privilege to represent the goodly Realm and Crown of Scotland.'

'Aye – if you can call that privilege! For me, I beg leave to doubt it! A Realm and Crown that can treat with my enemies, harry my subjects, mistreat my ministers and grossly insult my person . . .'

'Madam, you have been misled. I swear. You are mistaken . . .'

'I do not mistake glass for ruby, sir!' the Queen told him shortly, tartly. 'Does James, or the man Arran, take me for a fool, 'fore God?'

Patrick dropped his glance. 'Your Highness, that would be the primest folly of all time. Worse than the folly that played yon scurvy trick – but of which I pray you will absolve my prince, who knew naught of it. Let blame lie where blame is due.' And putting a hand within his white-and-gold doublet, he brought out a great red stone, which even amongst the competing brilliance there present, blazed and glowed with a rich and vivid fire.

Almost involuntarily the Queen's beringed hand came out for it. She took it from Patrick, and held it up before her, for the moment speechless.

David felt a jolt like a kick somewhere within him. In that moment, much moved into its due and proper place in his mind; he knew, suddenly, so much more than what he merely saw. He knew that here was infamy. He knew, as though Patrick had personally confessed as much, that it was not Arran who had exchanged the glass for the ruby in the Queen's ring; that it was for this that the Stirling goldsmith had been summoned to his brother's quarters that day when James had scuttled off to Perth to avoid Walsingham – and on Patrick's advice; knew now why Patrick had so advised; knew why he had urged Arran publicly to offend Walsingham. All was clear, Patrick was using them all, Arran, Walsingham, James, even Elizabeth here – aye, and Marie and himself also, undoubtedly – as a chess-player uses his pieces. To what end? That David could not yet perceive – save that the downfall of Arran almost certainly was involved. Did Patrick himself wish to rule Scotland? It did not seem as though he did. When he had brought Esmé Stuart low, he had not stepped into his place as he might well have done. Indeed, to some extent he had built up Arran, as indubitably he had built Lennox. To destroy him? Was it the destruction, then, that was Patrick's ultimate aim and object? Not position, power as such, statecraft, government – but just destruction? Was his winsome, talented, handsome splendid brother just a destroyer, a force for wreck and annihilation and nothing more? Could it be anything so horrible . . . ? In that extraordinary room of mirrors, before the great Queen whose word was life and death to so many, David abruptly knew fear, real fear. And it was not fear of Elizabeth.

The Queen was speaking now. 'Whence came this, Master Patrick?' she asked softly. 'And how?'

'I pray that you do not ask me that, fairest lady. So much would fall to be told, of others, in high places, where my lips must be sealed. Suffice it, Your Grace, I beseech you, that it is yours now as it should have been yours from the start, as my prince intended it to be. And who, in all the world, could adorn it, and it adorn, so well?'

'I see.' Thoughtfully Elizabeth looked from Patrick to the great red gem – which in fact belonged to her prisoner Mary – and back again. 'I see.'

'I knew naught of this stone, Madam,' Orkney put in, doubtfully, looking sidelong at Patrick. 'But we have brought other gifts . . . '

'No doubt, my lord – and no doubt a host of petitions and requests likewise! The morrow will serve very well for all such exchange. This is but a private audience.'

'For which we are deeply grateful, Highness,' Patrick assured. 'Perhaps, however, Your Grace would now accept the credentials of our embassage from our prince, and so save time . . . ?'

'No, sir – My Grace would not! In such matters of state, I prefer that my ministers be present. You would not wish it otherwise, surely?' Thinly the Queen smiled. 'You have met my good Secretary Walsingham, I believe? My Treasurer Hatton – no?'

Patrick schooled his features to entire equanimity. 'As Your Grace wills. The vital subjects which we have to discuss no doubt will interest these also – the possibility of a defensive Protestant league; the machinations of Jesuit plotters; the matter of our prince's eventual marriage; the question of a limited Association in the throne of King James and his lady-mother; the . . . '

'Never!' Elizabeth snapped – and then, frowning, held up a glittering hand. 'Not another word, sir! No matters of state tonight, I said. You shall not cozen and constrain me! Keep your tricks, Master Patrick, for innocents!' She rose briskly to her feet, no longer stiff. 'Now – my lord of Leicester, I understand, has a most fair spectacle for our delight tonight – apes that make a play, purchased from the Prince of the Ethiops. He but awaits my presence. I shall see you tomorrow, Master of Gray, and you, my lord, when, never fear, you shall have your say – and I mine! Come! Philip – the apes!'

Stepping aside right and left for her, the men bowed low. Passing David, the Queen raised a hand and poked him quite sharply in the ribs.

'Can you smile, man – *can* you?' she demanded abruptly.

David swallowed. 'When . . . when there is aught to smile at – yes, Ma'am.'

'I see. The honest one of the pair! Aye – then come you tomorrow with your brother, Master . . . David, it was? Tomorrow, to our audience. Then I shall be able to watch your face and know when Master Patrick is for cheating me! That is my command, and I call you all to witness.'

Elizabeth swept out, with Sidney holding the door for her.

And so when, the following mid-day, a Court marshal came to the Scots' lodging to conduct the two envoys to their official audience, David once again accompanied them. Embarrassed, he did not go with any eagerness; but though he would have expected Patrick to be still less enthusiastic, his brother in fact appeared to be perfectly pleased with his company. Davy had evidently taken the Queen's fancy, he declared, with his notably individual sort of Court manners – and with a woman, even Elizabeth Tudor, that was half the battle.

This time they were escorted to a different part of the palace altogether, with a minimum of fuss and display. They were shown into a smallish wood-panelled chamber overlooking the river, where, before a bright log-fire, the Queen sat at the head of a long paper-littered table, no scintillating bejewelled figure now, but simply though richly clad in dark purple grosgrain, with a moderately sized ruff, her greying reddish hair drawn back beneath a coif. David at least thought that she looked a deal better than on the night before. Soberly dressed men sat two on either side of her, first on her left being the grim-faced Walsingham. The entire atmosphere was businesslike, more like a merchant's countinghouse than a royal Court. Patrick and Orkney looked shockingly overdressed, like peacocks in a rookery. Here was no occasion, obviously, for heralds' trumpetings or flamboyant declarations. The contrast to the previous night was extraordinary.

Only a clerk at the foot of the table rose to his feet at their entrance. 'Your credentials, gentlemen?' he said.

Patrick, straightening up, and with a swift glance all round, handed over the impressively sealed and beribboned parchment. The clerk took it without ceremony, unrolled it, and read out its contents in a flat monotonous gabble, like a weary priest at his fifth celebration of Mass, thereby robbing the carefully chosen and resounding phrases of almost all significance. Not that any of the hearers appeared even to be listening.

Whilst this was proceeding, the newcomers eyed the sitters – and were not themselves offered seats. The Queen's expression was sternly impassive, revealing nothing; she might never have seen her callers before, nor be in the least interested in what they had come to say. Walsingham sat immobile, as though frozen, eyes almost glazed – though that was not unusual. On the Queen's right was a stooping, white-haired, elderly man, with a sensitive weary face, toying with a pen-feather; sitting in that position, he could be none other than William Cecil, Lord Burleigh, himself. Next to him sat a handsome, keen-eyed, stocky man of middle-years, who wore a great key embroidered on his dark doublet – one of the few decorations to be seen in the company; almost certainly he would be Sir Christopher Hatton, Keeper of the Privy Purse under Lord Treasurer Burleigh. The fourth man, sitting next to him, was younger, dark, wiry, with a quick intelligent face and darting lively eyes. He was different from the others in more than years – a man perhaps somewhat after Patrick's own mould.

When the clerk had finished, and rolled up the parchment, it was Walsingham who spoke, coldly, unemotionally.

'Master of Gray and my lord of Orkney,' he said, 'my princess treats your prince's envoys a deal more kindly than yours did hers. Can you name any reason why she should not turn you away unheard, or worse?'

'Only Her Grace's well-renowned clemency and womanly forbearance,' Patrick declared easily.

'You can stretch Her Grace's clemency too far, sir.'

'Not, surely, towards her youthful and fond cousin, who must learn kingcraft only by her guidance and favour? The fault lay not with my prince but with his advisers.'

'Of whom yourself, sir, and Lord Orkney are principals – by these credentials.'

'Alas, you do us too much honour, sir. King James has other advisers, and closer.'

'Aye,' Orkney agreed. 'A deal closer.'

'So that you accept nothing of responsibility of what occurred. Yet you both were present, and in close association with the Earl of Arran . . . '

The Queen coughed slightly, and Burleigh intervened quite gently.

'Master of Gray' he said. 'Your present mission treats of great matters. Are these matters according to the mind of your young prince, of the Earl of Arran, or of your own?'

Patrick's sigh of relief was almost audible. 'They represent the mind of the King in Council, my lord. As such they are authentic, the voice of Scotland. In their name we have full power to discuss and treat.'

Burleigh nodded his white head. The old eyes were washed-out and colourless, but shrewd still. 'Treat is a large word, sir. How far may you treat, for instance, under your first matter of a defensive Protestant pact? Are you not a Roman yourself?'

'On the contrary, I am a member of the Kirk of Scotland, born into it, baptised and communicate.'

'And wed,' the dark younger man mentioned, from down the table.

'Yet in every country of Europe you have acted the Catholic, sir,' Walsingham intervened harshly. 'At all times you have associated with Catholics. I am not utterly uninformed.'

'And you, Sir Francis, associate with Jesuit priests – Father Giffard, for instance. But I do not hold that such makes you a Catholic, or unfit to transact your Protestant lady's business! I, too, am not utterly uninformed, you see!' Patrick essayed a laugh.

David saw a mere flicker of smile cross the Queen's sharp features, and then she was stern again. Walsingham never changed his expression, but he sat very still, silent. Father Charles Giffard, a Jesuit missionary and agent of the Guises, had recently been serving as a counter-spy for Walsingham also. That this should be known to the Master of Gray, and therefore presumably to Giffard's Catholic employers also, must have been a telling blow to the Chief Secretary of State.

Again it was Burleigh who took matters forward. 'And your proposals anent this Protestant alliance are, sirs?'

'We propose that an alliance of our Protestant realms and Crowns of Scotland and England shall ensure and cherish Her

Grace's northern borders from all assault, shall act together against the attacks of all Catholic states and princes. We shall also send ships and soldiers to aid in your landward defence.'

Five pairs of eyes searched Patrick's face intently, wondering. David's also. Such proposals, indeed, seemed barely credible, in view of Scotland's traditional need and policy to play off her powerful southern neighbour against France and Spain; it was, moreover, the reversal of all the trend of Arran's, and indeed Patrick's, previous outlook. Well might they stare.

Patrick went on, easily. 'In addition, it is proposed that our prince shall agree not to marry for three years, during which time it is hoped that Your Grace will find a suitable English lady worthy to be his queen.'

Even Walsingham could scarcely forbear to look surprised at this extraordinary piece of conciliation. Elizabeth's known dread of James producing a son and heir was not merely the pathological jealousy of a barren woman who could not herself do the same; a son would make him more desirable as heir to her own throne, for nothing was more necessary to the stability and internal peace of England than the assurance and continuity of the succession. It was the Queen's fear that if James had a son, some might prefer to see this desired stability established sooner rather than later; it was not as though the threat of assassination was unheard of. This proposed concession, therefore, could mean a lot in security – and the selecting of a bride for the Scots king an opportunity to sway him and his country greatly.

'And the price?' That was Elizabeth herself, the first words that she had spoken in this audience. They were all but jerked out of her.

Patrick gestured magnanimously, as though any sort of bargaining was hardly to be considered. 'Only Your Grace's goodwill,' he said. 'Your continuing affection for our prince and people.'

'I would not wish to name you liar, Master of Gray! The price?'

'It is nothing, Madam – or little. Agreement to a limited Association in the Scottish Crown of our prince and his mother; your declared acceptance of King James as your eventual heir – which may Almighty God delay for a lifetime yet – and meantime a suitable annual pension, so that His Grace may worthily maintain a style apt for your successor. That, and the return to Scotland and their due trial, of the intransigent Ruthven lords, who now harass my prince's borders from your kingdom – the lords Mar, Lindsay, Bothwell, Master of Glamis, and the rest.'

Elizabeth's snort was undisguised and eloquent.

Burleigh spoke. 'A pension, young man? Is your prince a beggar, then?'

'Not so, my lord – but I think that you will agree that he has much to offer that you need.'

'Need, sir?' Walsingham said flatly. 'You mistake your word, I think.'

'Perhaps I do. You undoubtedly will know better whether or no you *need* a secure northern border. Or an ally against Spain, France, the Empire and the Pope.'

'How large a pension does King James look for, sir?' Sir Christopher Hatton asked.

'That, of course, he leaves to the generosity of Her Grace – who, to be sure, knows well what a crowned monarch may suitably give or receive.'

The Queen grimaced.

'Any Association in the Crown would require the return of the former princess, Mary Stuart, to Scotland,' Burleigh observed.

'Which is not to be considered,' Elizabeth added incisively.

'Queen Mary in Scotland would mean fewer plots and intrigues in England, Highness.'

'Think you that Mary, once in Scotland, would lose a day in snatching back her throne from under her son? Or another day in plotting to have mine from under me! God's death, man – do you take me for a fool?'

'I take you, Madam, for a great princess who knows wherein lies her own strength and others' weakness. It has been sixteen long years since Queen Mary became your . . . guest. In such time, undoubtedly, she will have changed much, learned much. But, alas, in that time also she has had little to occupy her save to plot and intrigue. Give her back work to do, her kingdom to part-rule, and she will have but little time for plotting.'

'You admit, then, that she plots and schemes against me, sir?'

'To be sure. Though not against Your Grace, but for her own freedom. It is inconceivable that a woman of spirit would not do so. I dare to suggest that Your Highness, in a like plight, would do no less.'

'You are very persuasive, Master of Gray, but I am not yet persuaded! This will all require much consideration.'

'In a defensive Protestant alliance, sir, how could a Catholic princess concur?' Burleigh demanded. 'Will Mary Stuart reform her religion?'

'Three years, I think you suggested, sir, that your prince would remain unmarried?' the dark younger man put in. 'Is this King James's own desire, or only his advisers'?'

'The banished lords of the Ruthven venture are all good Protestants,' Walsingham declared. 'In the event of a Protestant league, will they be pardoned and their estates restored?'

For a while Patrick answered a bombardment of questions as to details in his own skilful, quick-witted fashion, elaborating, explaining, reassuring, good-humoured and unflurried throughout despite the atmosphere almost of a trial that prevailed, with three prisoners at the bar, rather than the audience of envoys of an independent monarch. Orkney ventured one or two insertions, had them savaged by the trained and fiercely keen minds of the Queen's ministers, and was thereafter glad to leave all to his colleague. David, wondering at his brother's ability, wondering at what lay behind his proposals, wondering at the unfailing arrogance of these Englishmen's attitude, noticed the Queen's eyes often upon him, and sought to school his countenance to a determined impassivity in consequence – achieving in fact only an implacable glower.

At length, it was at David rather than to him that Elizabeth spoke. 'I have been watching your secretary, Master of Gray – and seldom have I seen a man less sure of his cause. You have been mightily eloquent, but I think that you have not convinced Master David any more than you have convinced me! You may retire now. I shall consider all that you have said, in council with my ministers, and shall inform you in due course. Meanwhile,' her eyes glinted, 'tomorrow being our Lord's Day, I shall expect to see you at good Protestant worship. At our Chapel of Saint John the Divine. Ten of the clock. You have my leave to retire, sirs.'

They backed out of a distinctly hostile and unbelieving presence.

Patrick spent the afternoon with Sir Philip Sidney, with whom he seemed to have struck up a spontaneous friendship, and it was evening before David saw him alone.

'You look even more gloomy that your usual, Davy,' Patrick declared gaily. 'Does the English food lie heavy on your stomach?'

273

'I cannot see that you have much cause for cheer, yourself,' David gave back. 'Your mission scarcely prospers, I think. The Queen and those others will have none of it. Nor do I blame them if they scarce believe what you now propose.'

'Do not tell me that *you* have become a doubter!' his brother mocked.

'Who would not doubt your Protestant alliance, man? Or King James's sudden desire for an English wife? It is only a game that you play. But a dangerous game, I think.'

'Heigho – but is not life itself a dangerous game also, Davy?'

'Is it a woman's life that you are playing for? Mary the Queen's?'

'I suppose that you might say so, yes.'

'Yet you admitted to Elizabeth that our princess was plotting against her.'

'Why not? Walsingham has spies in Mary's very household, amongst her own attendants. Think you that they do not know well all that goes on?'

'Yet you still hope to effect her release?'

'Hope, yes. That today was but a beginning, a formality. I shall be seeing the Queen again, later. In private. Philip Sidney is to arrange it. Then, it may be, I shall get her to sing a different tune.'

'By singing first another tune yourself?'

'Why, as to that, who knows? You would not have me to go beyond my mission, Davy?' He smiled. 'Have you seen Marie?'

'Aye – she is over in the Earl of Essex's precincts, with a host of English lordlings round her and her sisters.'

'That may please her father – but I think that I must go rescue her, nevertheless. It would be a pity if she was to become entangled, would it not?'

David did not answer.

Chapter Twenty-two

NONE sang the hymns more joyfully and tunefully, none made their responses or said their Amens more fervently than did Patrick Gray next morning in the Church of Saint John the Divine attached to the Palace of Whitehall. The Queen watched him shrewdly from her throne-like seat just within the Chancel; she had had the Scots party placed in the very front seat, a bare half-dozen yards from herself, where she could observe their every expression. David found her imperious yet inquisitive gaze frequently upon himself, and though he was a good enough Protestant, grew the more uncomfortable. Not so his brother, most obviously.

After the service, Sir Philip Sidney came up to Patrick, and David heard him say, low-voiced, that the Queen would see him privately that night. Marie Stewart, walking beside him, looked at David.

'You heard that?' she said. 'Tonight. Perhaps you will learn now the answers to some of the questions that we ask ourselves.'

But when Sidney came to conduct him to Elizabeth late that evening, Patrick did not ask his brother to accompany him.

This time Patrick was taken to a small library in the Queen's own wing of the palace, where Elizabeth sat alone before a fire. She eyed him coolly.

'Well, Master Patrick,' she said, unsmiling. 'It is not every envoy who requires three audiences! My good Philip here has persuaded me to see you once more. I hope that it is to good purpose!'

'I am grateful to Your Grace – and also to Sir Philip. I do not think that you will regret this condescension, Madam.'

'No? What is it to be this time, sir? Poetry, or child's stories?'

'Neither, Highness. Now you hear what was not to be said formerly.'

'But by you only, eh, my friend? Not my Lord Orkney, nor even in your brother's hearing?'

'That is so, Your Grace.'

'I see. Philip, leave us. I am not to be disturbed until I ring this bell.'

'Of course, Majesty.'

275

When Sidney had gone, the Queen made room for Patrick on the couch on which she was sitting. 'Come, sit here, my handsome liar,' she commanded. 'As well that you are so well-favoured, or even for Philip Sidney I would not have allowed this. But do not think that you can cozen me with your pretty face any more than with your pretty words, sir.'

'I would that I might, fairest lady – for other advantage than matters of state!' Patrick asserted boldly. 'It would be a joy – reserved alas for a prince or an angel!'

'But not a devil, sir, not a devil – in especial a Scots devil.' She leaned over closer, so that the white but no longer youthful bosom divided for him, and tapped him with her fan. 'Am I safe with you, Master Patrick – a helpless woman?'

'That is a difficult question, Madam,' he said cunningly. 'To which it would be difficult to answer yes or no. Shall we say that you are no safer than you would wish to be?'

'Clever,' she gave back. 'Too clever. Do not presume on your cleverness, Patrick. For I am clever, too!' Reaching out, she first caressed his ear – and then suddenly tweaked it, hard. 'You will remember that, will you not, Patrick?'

'Assuredly, my lady,' he told her, and smiled. 'It is not a matter which I could forget.'

'Good. Then we may get on very well.' The Queen took his hand in hers, and stroked it. 'And so, my friend – what have you to tell me?'

'First, lovely one, this.' Patrick drew from his doublet a fine gold chain on which hung a handsomely-wrought heart-shaped locket set with diamonds and amethysts. Carefully withdrawing his other hand, he leaned over to clasp this round the royal neck. The locket itself he guided gently into the hollow between the Queen's small breasts. When she did not stir, he allowed his hand to linger there.

> Happy the gift to be enbowered there,
> The giver sighs; such bliss he may not share!

he murmured.

'Very commendable, Sir Gallant,' Elizabeth acceded, brows raised. She rapped his hand sharply with her fan. 'But not all for love of me, I fear! What do you seek now?'

'Your kindness. Your esteem. And your belief that I speak true.'

'That I shall decide when I hear you, sirrah. What do you wish me to credit . . . for this bounty?'

'First, Madam, that you should know that your realm is in greater peril than even your Sir Francis Walsingham can tell you.' Patrick was all serious now. 'He no doubt informs you that ships are building in every harbour in Spain and the Netherlands for the invasion of your land. But he cannot know that there are plans to welcome the ships in Scottish ports; that Spanish soldiers are to land there, so as to attack at the same time as the others, over the Border. Also, French and Spanish forces are to land in Ireland, and to assail you from there. These plans are well advanced.'

'Christ God, man – and you come to me with a Protestant league! Is this true? Is this your James's true dealing? Is this the worth of your Scots Council?'

'Not the King, no. The King knows naught of it. Nor even the Council – or much of it. It is his . . . advisers.'

'The man Arran, you mean?'

'Alas, yes. My lord is misguided enough to see Scotland's place as with the Catholics.'

'But your Kirk . . . ?'

'The Kirk, my lady, is being ever weakened and brought low. Arran's new Black Acts make the King supreme in matters spiritual also, and all resistance treason. He has the power to silence the Kirk.'

'And James?'

'The King is young, inexperienced, and Arran holds him in the palm of his hand . . . '

'And in his bed, the catamite – so I am told!' Elizabeth interposed bluntly.

Patrick shrugged. 'That is as may be. But Arran will turn Scotland Catholic, if need be. And if James proves difficult, this Association in the Crown with his mother will solve all. Queen Mary will not prove backward in such an enterprise.'

'God's passion, she will not! And you ask me to free her – for this?'

'No, Madam. I do not ask it.'

'Eh? See you, Master of Gray – with what voice do you speak? Whose envoy are you? Where lies your loyalty?'

'To my prince and his realm of Scotland, lady. For that I work. I spoke yesterday as I was instructed, for the King and his Council. Today I speak in your secret ear, as Patrick Gray.'

'Then your embassage is folly, and worse – false!'

'Not so, Your Grace. It represents the expressed desire of my prince, and is true and wise in all respects save in this proposed

277

Association of the Queen and her son.'

'The *former* Queen!' Elizabeth corrected. 'You, then – *you* advise me not to release Mary Stuart?'

'Who am I to advise as between two crowned princesses, Your Highness? All I say is that if Queen Mary returns to Scotland, Arran will use her to further the Catholic encirclement of England.'

'Arran than does not agree to this Protestant league? Yet he is Chancellor.'

'Arran is cunning, Madam. He does not oppose it openly. But he works against it. Once he has Mary back in Scotland . . . '

'I see.' The Queen was looking thoughtful. 'There were two other proposals in your mission – James's marriage, and the return of the Protestant lords. Is Arran against these also?'

'No, not against them. They were, indeed, his own proposals. He would not have the King to marry, in especial with a Protestant princess, since that would strengthen James's position and weaken his own. So he proposes this stratagem – and for three years he is safe. And he would have the Ruthven lords back, that he may have them executed for treason, and so dispose of his rivals and gain their forfeited estates.'

'Aye, that is ever the way of it. A nice rogue, this Arran, of a truth. A fool also, if he thinks that *I* know not glass from ruby! It is time that he had a fall, 'fore God!'

Her visitor said nothing.

'Well, what do you propose, sir? Do not tell me that you have revealed all this to me for no purpose!'

Patrick shrugged one elegant shoulder. 'With the full weight of Your Grace's support, *I* could supplant the Earl of Arran. Already I have much sway with King James. I could have more. I could unite Scotland and your realm in an indissoluble league, and overturn all the secret plots of the Catholics.'

'I thought as much! You shoot a high shaft, Patrick. And so you would wish me to leave the banished lords in England?'

'Not so, Highness. Send them home, as King James requests – after I am back. Separately, one by one, in secret, I could use them to ensure the triumph of our Protestant cause – and Your Grace's.'

'You are a fervent convert, sir! And the princess, Mary Stuart?'

'The peace of Europe and the survival of the Reformed Church demand that she be kept separate from her son, Madam. Do you not think so?'

'I think that *you* have done a deal of thinking, Master of Gray! Who would have looked for it in that beautiful head! But . . . my good Walsingham assures me that you are one of Mary's men, trained in France to her service, and the recipient of her moneys. I cannot believe that he is entirely mistaken!'

'Your good Walsingham is not. But the fair unfortunate Mary's weal and good do not necessarily demand that she should rule in Scotland, and there cause bloodshed, religious persecution and war. I would help my princess otherwise.'

'God – you are frank, man!' the Queen declared.

'Such was my intention, in seeing you alone, Madam.'

'And how would you help her, if you could, I would ask?'

'I would have her, with Your Grace's permission, return to France. There, with England and Scotland united in a Protestant alliance, she could work no harm. And . . . the Queen-Mother, Catherine, who hates and fears the Guises, would see that she never set sail for Scotland again.'

Elizabeth's sharp eyes blinked. 'God's wounds, man, where did you learn your business?' she almost whispered. Then, in a different voice, 'And think you that she would go – Mary?'

'I believe that I might persuade her to it.'

'You? And you think that I would permit you to see her? You, of all men?'

'Why yes, lady, I do. Both as a wise ruler and a wise woman, I believe that you will.'

For moments on end Elizabeth stared at him, almost through him. 'One day, Master Patrick, you are going to take one step too far!' she said at length. 'And then that so fascinating smile will be gone – for ever!'

He smiled still, and said nothing.

Abruptly the Queen lifted to her feet. 'Leave me now, Patrick . . . before I . . . I forget myself,' she said, a little breathlessly for so great a monarch.

'Would that such were possible – even for a moment, sweet princess.'

'Enough! Enough, sir. Go!'

He rose, as she reached over to ring a little silver bell. 'I go . . . desolate,' he told her.

'So long as you go . . . '

The door opened, and Sidney stood there. 'Fair lady?' he said.

She looked from one to the other, frowning. 'Demons!' she declared. 'Limbs of Satan! Sent to tempt and try and mock me!

279

Both of you. Begone, begone – before I deal with you as you deserve.'

Sir Philip glanced quickly at Patrick.

That young man sighed, and bowed.

Elizabeth held out her hand to him. He stooped low over it, and then raised it to his lips. Slowly the hand turned over in his. He kissed the palm, the wrist, and was part-way up the forearm, before the Queen flicked him away.

'Off to your grey-eyed Lady Marie,' she ordered, hoarsely. 'I do not wonder that she will not marry you.'

'And the princess, her namesake, Your Grace? Have I permission to go speak with her?'

'We shall consider it, man. We shall see. But do not think it assured. Do not think anything assured.' She turned her slender back on them.

They bowed themselves out.

David waited for his brother in their lodging. 'Did you see the Queen?' he demanded. 'Did you find her more to our favour? Did you speak of the Queen – *our* Queen?'

'I did, Davy.'

'And what does she say? Will she release Mary?'

'Not so fast, man – not so fast! That will not be achieved in a day. But I think, yes, I think that I will convince her.'

'And the Association in the Crown? Will she agree to that?'

Patrick shrugged. 'That is less certain. Perhaps.'

'The banished lords?'

'I think, that she will send them back. Time, Davy – just a little time.'

'Time for Queen Mary has been long, long.'

'I tell you, I do not think that it will be long now.'

'Why are you doing this, Patrick? Urging the Protestant alliance, working for the English advantage? It is not like you, like all that you have done hitherto. Are you doing it all on behalf of Mary, of the Queen? At last?'

'I suppose that you might say so.'

David rubbed his chin. 'Then, Patrick,' he said stiffly, awkwardly, 'I would say that I love you for it. I have said many things ill of what you have done, spoken against your seeming forgetfulness of our poor Queen. But this – this is a great thing that you are doing now. To go so far, to harry Elizabeth herself, to change even the King's policy and risk all . . . '

His brother eyed him sidelong. 'I am overwhelmed, Davy!' he murmured.

'Marie . . .she will love you the better for this, also.'

'Indeed! That is, h'm, a consolation.' For once Patrick did not smile.

'When shall we know? Know whether Mary goes free? Know what is decided?'

'We can only await Elizabeth's pleasure.' Abruptly Patrick turned away. 'I am tired. I am going to bed . . . '

Chapter Twenty-three

WAITING on Queen Elizabeth's pleasure was not apt to be a static business, however protracted and uncertain. The waterman had been right when he said that the Queen changed palaces day by day. She was possessed of a great restlessness and nervous energy, which seemed to drive her on to incessant movement, constant change. And all her Court and those who circled in her orbit must move likewise.

On the Tuesday, apparently without warning or prior arrangement, she decided to go on one of her frequent progresses. These peregrinations around the houses of her lords and powerful subjects served the purpose not only of satisfying her restlessness but of seeing and being seen by her people, and incidentally helping to reduce any unseemly surplus wealth which the said lords might have accumulated, and at the same time conserving her own resources; indeed, she deliberately planned her itineraries so as to include those whom she considered most in need of such blood-letting. Since she travelled with anything up to three hundred of a retinue, and expected entertainment suitable for a queen, her descent upon an establishment for even a day or two could have a salutary effect.

They left Whitehall in fine style, the Queen driving in a white-painted glass coach drawn by six plumed white horses, their manes and tails dyed orange. Around her rode her gorgeously attired corps of Gentlemen Pensioners, splendidly mounted, led by Sir Walter Raleigh and Sir Francis Bacon. Then came her ladies-in-waiting, a blaze of colour, followed by her favourite courtiers – Leicester, Essex, Oxford, and the others, each surrounded by his own little court of admirers and hangers-on.

The Scots party rode with Sir Philip Sidney, who was rapidly becoming the inseparable companion of the Master of Gray, and quite soon they were joined by the dark, wiry, youngish man who had been one of the councillors at the official audience and whom Sidney introduced as Sir Edward Wotton, one of Walsingham's foremost deputies in the realm of foreign affairs. He was affable, charming, paying particular attention to Marie, and strangely enough, to David. Patrick was genially wary with him, as well he might be; anyone high in Walsingham's service was not a man to be underestimated, however delightful.

Progress was slow, for the narrow London streets were crowded with cheering people and the Queen's coach could only proceed at a snail's pace. The Scots were interested at the crowd's obvious affection for Elizabeth. This was something new to them. In Scotland the common people were not great cheerers, and seldom saw much to cheer about in their rulers. The visitors knew of the Queen's boast that her greatest strength lay in the love of her ordinary folk, but it had never meant more than a saying to them, a mere theory.

'Why should your Queen be so well-loved by these people?' Marie asked Wotton. 'What has she done for *them*?'

'She has given them much that they never had before, my lady,' he told her. 'She thinks for them, protects them from the fire and the gibbet of Rome, has paid back her royal father's debts to the city of London, gives them plays and spectacles, and lets them see her. No monarch before her has thought to do all this for the commonality. They love her because she loves them also.' He smiled. 'Your prince, I take it, is not so?'

She shook her head. 'No, I fear not. How could he be? He has never known the people, or they him – kept apart all his life. We had a king like that in Scotland once, who went about amongst the common folk – James Third. They called him the Gudeman of Ballengeich. But his lords resented it, and made constant trouble. Do your nobles here not do likewise?'

'Why should they? If the Crown is strong, the realm is strong, and they are secure therefore. It was not so under the late Queen Mary, Her Grace's sister, nor under previous monarchs. Only fools would change it now.'

Marie sighed. 'I wonder when it may be thus in Scotland?' she said. 'Our lords look for more than peace and the strength of the realm, I fear '

'If a Scots king could live and reign long enough to gain his full strength, it might be so,' David put in. 'For generations we have not had a prince who did not die young and leave a child as heir.'

Patrick, a vision of elegance, riding just a little in front, with Sidney, looked back over his shoulder, and smiled at them mockingly, saying nothing.

Once free of the congested streets they made but little faster progress with the heavy coach slow on the atrocious roads. A succession of lords and gallants were summoned up to ride for awhile in the royal presence, but no invitation came for Patrick

Gray. When Orkney and Marie were sent for to go forward, David drew the obvious conclusions.

'You have offended the Queen, Patrick,' he declared. 'I fear that you have gone too far with her. And on our Mary Queen's behalf. I am sorry.'

'Never think it, Davy. Give her time. She is a woman, and will act the woman. But she will act the princess also, never fear. I believe that I have convinced her what is the best policy where our Queen is concerned. Wait, you.'

When Marie came back, she spoke in the same fashion, lowering her voice so that none others should hear. 'She must be displeased with you, Patrick. I tried to bring her to speak of you, but she would not. I wanted to ask her about Queen Mary, but could not. I fear, Patrick – I fear the hopes for our lady are in vain, despite all your efforts.'

'Have patience, my dear. There is no reason for despair. It is a great matter, and Elizabeth must have time fully to consider it. That she may wish not to discuss it with me until she has done so, is but natural. I have just been saying the same to Davy – give her time.'

'You are wonderfully patient, Patrick. In all this you have ... surprised me. All who love my aunt will thank you for it.'

'Do you think that I do not love Mary also?'

'I do not know whom you love, Patrick. I have sometimes thought, only yourself. But now . . '

'Have I not told you a thousand times that I love *you*?'

'Told me, yes. But deeds speak louder than words.'

'What would you have me do, then? Must I force myself upon you, seduce you, to prove my love?'

'Even that might be preferable to merely using me for your *other* purposes, Patrick,' she said quietly.

He looked at her thoughtfully, and said nothing.

'At any rate, in what you are seeking to do now, Patrick, even though Elizabeth loves you the less, others do not.'

'That thought will sustain me in all my disappointments!' he declared. And at the cynical note in his voice, she bit her lip.

With the early October evening almost upon them, they came to Theobalds Park, Lord Burleigh's great red-brick house in Hertfordshire, down a mile-long avenue of cedar trees. They found it all lit up for them with coloured lanterns, fountains playing, and hosts of servants. Though a man of simple habits himself, Burleigh knew his mistress's tastes very well, and created this vast establishment largely for her entertainment.

It was a convenient day's journey by the coach from London, and most of her northern progresses started from here. Beside it, even Morton's fine palace at Dalkeith paled to insignificance.

Presumably Burleigh had had a few days' warning of this excursion, for he had an evening of ambitious feasting and amusement arranged. It was to be a 'ladies' night'; while the spectacle of musicians, dancers, tumblers and masquers went on, the Queen dined alone at a table at the top of the huge hall, waited on by her host and four earls – Leicester, Oxford, Essex and Warwick. Tonight she was ablaze with jewels again. Patrick did not get near enough to see whether she wore his locket. At a lower table were six countesses, served by lesser lords; at another the Queen's ladies-in-waiting with Raleigh, Sidney Bacon, Wotton and others in attendance; this table Marie was invited to join. Following the Queen's example, the ladies fed tit-bits and sips from their glasses to the gallant and noble waiters, who made extravagant gestures of gratitude and adoration. Frequently Elizabeth summoned up one or other of the gentlemen to be presented with a sweetmeat or a glass of wine. Orkney was so favoured, and almost all of her intimate courtiers. But not Patrick Gray. Anxiously the Scots party noted, and waited.

Later, when Marie went out through the gardens to the dower-house where their party were quartered with many others, and David would have accompanied her, leaving Patrick to the continuing festivities, his brother shook his head and insisted in going with her himself. England's Queen could well do without him tonight, he observed, apparently entirely care-free. David could squire Marie's sisters back, in the unlikely possibility of their requiring such – their father being already much too drunk.

For a while Patrick and Marie walked wordless between the shadowy clipped yew hedges and the pale-gleaming statuary, the man's hand at the young woman's elbow. At length, it was Marie who spoke.

'You are silent tonight, Patrick. It is a strange experience for you to be the outcast, rejected. Poor Patrick!'

'I am not rejected yet, my dear – save by you this many-a-day! Even so, and if I was, I would be blithe and happy if I could reverse your rejection with the Queen's.'

'I do not think that is the truth. But assuredly, Patrick, I do not reject you.'

'No? Here is joyful news, then.' He held her a little closer.

'Do not tell me that this cool, sober heart of yours is warming to me, at last?'

'My heart has never been cool to you. You are a difficult man to be cool to.'

'Do not say that you have been deceiving me, all this time?'

'There are more sorts of heat than one, to be aroused in a woman's heart.'

'Aye. I pray that it may be the right sort that I have aroused at last, then. Let me feel, and see.' Sliding his arm around her, he brought his hand to rest on her firm left breast.

They were walking very slowly now. She neither paused nor shook him off.

'It beats,' he murmured. 'It beats, undeniably. But what does it say?'

> *Beat, beat, cool heart, and speak me clear,*
> *Your beauty warms my hand so near,*
> *But truer glow than that I crave,*
> *The flame of love my heart to save!*

'Save your poetry and, and posing for Queen Elizabeth!' Marie told him, but with a faint tremor in that level voice. 'Myself, I prefer plain honest words that mean what they say.'

'You do not believe that I love you, Marie? Despite all the times I tell you?'

'I do not know – I do not know at all, Patrick.'

'Then let me prove it, my sweet.' Gently but firmly, he turned her round, to face him, and bent his head to hers.

She did not turn away as their lips met. Lingeringly, expertly, he kissed her, and, as her mouth stirred a little under his, strongly, ever more fiercely he bore down upon her. But she parted her lips no further, though he felt her bosom heaving against his own chest. At length he loosed her and drew back a little, to peer into her eyes in the gloom.

'That . . . proves . . . nothing,' she said, as even-voiced as she might. 'You do as much, and more, for any woman who takes your fancy – or who can serve some purpose of your own.'

Patrick sighed. 'You are hard, Marie – like flint. I had hoped . . . ' He stopped.

'I am not like flint, Patrick – I would that I were, I think.'

'So calm, so sober, so sure of yourself.'

'Not inside of me.'

'No? How may I reach that inside, then? My avowals of love do not reach there. Nor my offers of marriage. Nor my poetry,

286

nor yet my kisses. What may I do other than I have done?'
Abruptly he laughed in the darkness. 'You said that I would do
as much and more, for other women. Come you into this arbour
here, my dear, and we shall see how much more I shall do for
you – and you alone! And, it may be, I shall gain that inside of
you at last!'

She shook her head, but not angrily. 'That is not the way
either, Patrick. Not . . . yet.'

'Not yet! Then in God's good name – when, girl? And how?
I have been wooing you for years. How can I make you love me,
woman? Or must I ask Davy that?' In anyone else but Patrick
Gray his voice would have seemed to grate, there.

'No, Patrick, that is not your task. Not to make me love you.'

'You mean . . . ?'

'I mean that I love you already,' she stated simply.

For once the man was silenced. He gazed at her, gripped her
arms, and said nothing.

'Are you so surprised, then?'

'You . . . this is . . . for how long, Marie?' he got out.

'For all the same long years that you have said you wooed
me.'

'For years? Can that be true? Me – not Davy? Never Davy?'

'I love Davy, yes – but quite otherwise.'

'You love him? Then . . . then how do you love *me*? Otherwise from him?'

'I have never dreamed that I might marry Davy,' she said
quietly.

'So-o-o! Then, why? Christ God, Marie, why have you held
me thus away? Why injure me, and yourself as well, all this
time? If you did not doubt your love . . . ?'

'It was not my love that I doubted, Patrick – but yours.'

'Mine! But I have told you, assured you . . . '

'Telling is not enough, for me. Nor kissing. Nor that other you
propose. Before I marry a man, he must put our love before all
else. Before his ambition, his freedom, his convenience. He must
act as though to be my husband was the greatest project of his
life. Perhaps I am foolish and ask too much – but that is the
fashion of me. He must earn the right to marry me, Patrick.'

'And have I not earned that right, in all these years? I have
known other women, yes – but they meant nothing. Would you
have me a celibate, a recluse?'

'No – since it is Patrick Gray that I love, to my cost!' She even
smiled faintly there. 'These others – they may mean nothing.

287

I am prepared to believe that. But it is not of them that I speak. The truth is that you have no *right* to marry anyone, Patrick. You yet have a wife, already. In that fact lies the answer to your questions and my doubts. You still *have* a wife. In all these years you have taken no step to end your marriage . . . '

'But that was no marriage – never was, from the first. I am as much wed to any women that I have ever held in my arms, as to Elizabeth Lyon.'

'Yet she is still your wife. And her property is still in your grasp! And should her young and weakly brother die, she is the greatest heiress in Scotland! So she is still your wife – and I doubt, Patrick. I doubt.'

He stroked his small pointed beard. 'So – that is it! Elizabeth Lyon. For that you have repulsed me, always.'

'For that – and what it signifies of your mind, my dear.'

'Lord, if that is all, then I shall seek an annulment of that piece of folly – my noble father's folly more than my own indeed – forthwith, Marie. I do not require Elizabeth Lyon's wealth, now.'

Again that faint smile. 'Not now? Oh, Patrick – for so clever a man, you are a child yet.'

'If I do this, if I end this marriage that is no marriage, will you wed me, Marie? Have I your promise?'

'No, my dear, you have not. But come to me a free man, and I shall give you an answer, an honest answer. I hope that it may content both of us.'

He frowned, took a pace away from her, and turning, came back to hold her arm. 'And meantime, my love . . . ?' His voice had become a caress.

'Meantime you may take me to my chamber, Patrick. To the door of it, only. But I hope that one day that door will stand wide open for you. It lies in your hands to make it so.'

'Dear God!' Patrick Gray said. 'Come you, then.'

The next night and two days following, the great cavalcade stayed at the Lord Howard of Effingham's magnificent new house of Long Barnton. He had accumulated a vast amount of treasure through the naval activities of the privateers and sea-rovers under his command, against the Spanish plate fleets from the Indies, and no doubt his Queen felt that some attention might not come amiss. Certainly he showed no grudging spirit in her entertainment, far outdoing Burleigh's efforts. The first night there was a notable fireworks display, the next day a pageant in which most of the adjoining town seemed to take part, that night a mock naval battle on the large artificial lake, with Spanish galleons going up in flames; and the second day a tournament of jousting in which most of the gentlemen took part and in which the Master of Gray particularly distinguished himself. The Queen presented the prizes, and so Patrick must go up to her, with the others, to receive his awards; but it was noticeable that she said but little to him on these occasions and was distinctly cool about it.

David grew more and more depressed, even if his brother did not. Sidney, watching it all shrewdly, wondered.

By the end of the week, at Kirby, Sir Christopher Hatton's seat in Northamptonshire, with still no sign of favour from the Queen, David, with Marie, came to his brother just before retiring to bed.

'It will not serve, Patrick,' he declared. 'We shall never have our Queen Mary released thus. Elizabeth will have none of you, or of our mission. Do not say again to give her time. She shows her disfavour of you over-plainly. She will be sending us back to Scotland, with naught accomplished.'

'You are too impatient, Davy. Besides, much is accomplished already, I am sure.'

'But not the great thing – not the release of our princess. If we are to free the poor lady, we must use other methods.'

'You think so? What do you suggest?'

'I suggest that we stop profitless asking, and take.'

Patrick turned to stare at his brother. 'Lord, Davy – what is this? What do you mean?'

'I mean that our Queen deserves better of us than that we should only beg proud Elizabeth for her, patiently wait her pleasure, and humbly accept her decision.'

'Instead of which, brother, you would do – what?'

'Lift Mary out of her prison . . . by either guile or force. Or both.'

'But how, man – how? There have been a hundred plots to that end since she was imprisoned sixteen years ago. Think you that you can succeed where all others failed miserably?'

'Me? Should you not say we, Patrick?'

'You or we, it makes no difference. Mary is straitly guarded, held fast.'

'So was her son, at Ruthven Castle. Yet you planned his escape, from France – and I achieved it, with but a handful of Logan's Borderers.'

'That was quite otherwise, Davy. That was in our own country, where all might be arranged. Mary is held fast deep in the centre of this England.'

'We outwitted Catherine's soldiers deep in the centre of France.'

'He is right, Patrick,' Marie put in. 'We must do something.'

'I came to England only to aid our Queen. To see her if I might.' David spoke doggedly. 'I'll no' go home without attempting something.'

Patrick looked from one to the other thoughtfully. 'You have talked of it together, I see, the two of you. Have you any plan?'

'Of a sort, aye. Our Queen, since August, is held at Wingfield Manor, in Derbyshire. On our return journey to Scotland, we can travel that way. Mary goes riding and hawking and hunting under guard of Sir Ralph Sadler and Sir Henry Nevil and their men. I cannot believe that they attend her, on such occasions, with so many men-at-arms as have we as escort.'

'But, man, Derby is not on our true road to Scotland. Think you, that if we went that way, towards this Wingfield and not by the direct road, Walsingham and Elizabeth would not know of it within a few hours? Little indeed escapes Walsingham's spies. I have no least doubt that we are watched all the time. A large force would be sent after us, forthwith, and Mary confined to her rooms that same night.'

'There are gentlemen of Derby in this Court – Lord Fenby, Sir William Soames, and others. It should not be beyond your ability, Patrick, to make friends with one of them – to make excuse to ride north with him, to see his house, or his hawks or his cattle. Or his wife, indeed! Even your fine Sir Philip Sidney has a property near to Chesterfield, I have discovered. He is Walsingham's gudeson – none would suspect if he came with us. Thereafter, we can see that he does not inconvenience our project.'

'I would not wish to use a friend so, Davy.'

Brother eyed brother levelly. 'It is a deal better than you used your friend Esmé Stuart!' David declared bluntly. 'Is not your first loyalty to your Queen, rather than to your new English friends, man?'

Patrick seemed about to answer, frowning, but Marie intervened calmly.

'Better if it was not Sir Philip, perhaps. He has been very kind. But whoever we go with, need not be so hardly used, surely? Only allowed to know nothing of our plans.'

'Plans!' Patrick took her up. 'What plans can you have?'

'Few, as yet,' David answered. 'Until we see this Wingfield, and how it lies. But it will be a strange thing if our wits cannot devise a way to see our Queen once we are near her. You, Patrick, have solved greater problems than this, I swear.'

'H'mmm. And after?'

'Send the women and the baggage on before us, with a small escort. We are well mounted – as well as any that Walsingham can find to send after us, quickly. With our escort of nearly five score, we can ride for Scotland with Mary – and who shall stop us?'

'I think that you are too sanguine, Davy. It would not be so simple and easy as that.'

'Who would expect it to be simple or easy? But it is our plain duty.'

'I cannot see that it is mine – as King James's and Scotland's ambassador.'

'To save Scotland's monarch and James's mother?'

'But not this way, Davy.'

'We have tried your way. You did as much as any man could. But Elizabeth will have none of it. We have waited her pleasure for long enough. We have tried talk. Now we must use deeds, Patrick.'

'What Davy says is true, Patrick,' the girl asserted again. 'We have an opportunity, a great opportunity, with our strong armed escort. Never have plotters for my aunt's release had this – armed men who need not go secretly. I believe that it would be wrong not to take this opportunity.'

Patrick looked away, sighed, and shrugged. 'When do you propose that we attempt this . . . adventure?'

'Before long,' David declared. 'It is time that we went home. It lacks dignity thus to wait on Elizabeth's whim. Besides, the sooner we attempt it, the less the opportunity for Walsingham.'

'Aye. Very well, we shall see.'

'Restalrig had best not be told, as yet. He talks . . . '

In Sidney's room in the main house, the following evening, Patrick smiled. 'I think that you will find that she will see me, Philip. Tell her that I believe that it is necessary, and urgent. She will not say no.'

'My dear Patrick, perhaps, you are right. But no other man that I know would demand an audience thus. Do you have an understanding with her? In spite of how she is treating you this week? I think that perhaps you have, my friend.'

'I would not presume to name it that.'

'No? Very well. I will do what I can, Patrick.'

To the surprise of the attendant courtiers, in half-an-hour Patrick was shown into the Queen's private apartments – indeed into her bedroom. Elizabeth sat up in bed, in a state of highly elaborate undress, her head bound in a jewelled turban.

'Leave us, Philip,' she commanded, very much the queen despite her décolletage. 'The Master of Gray is showing more marked attention to his Lady Grey-eyes, so I think my maidenly virtue may be safe from him for a space!'

Patrick grimaced, as Sir Philip retired. Walsingham did not miss much, clearly.

'Well, sir?' the Queen said, suddenly business-like. 'What is it? What is this important matter which you must tell me?' She made no comment on her arm's-length attitude of the past days.

'It concerns our princess, Your Grace,' he told her.

'What of her?'

'May I be so bold as to ask, has Your Grace decided whether or no I may see her, and whether you will release her should she agree to renounce the Crown and retire to France?'

'Impertinent, sir! What the Queen of England has decided, and when, is not a matter for *your* enquiry.'

'Yet, dearest Madam, without knowing your mind on this matter, I cannot know what action to take in a new situation. A situation that affects Your Grace's interests as nearly as it does mine.'

'A new situation, Master Patrick? With regard to Mary Stuart? What is this? How can this be? Is it a new plot? My good Moor has reported none such.'

'I fear that even your well-informed Sir Francis cannot be apprised of this, Lady.'

'Cannot? Cannot is a large word, sirrah. What is this situation?'

Patrick offered a convincing display of hesitation. 'May I say, Majesty, that it makes the need for a decision on the matter of our princess urgently necessary. Else events may move beyond even Your Grace's grasp.'

'My God, sir, will you play cat-and-mouse with me? Out with it, man – or I shall find means to make you talk plain!'

Gustily the young man sighed, and spoke with every appearance of reluctance. 'There is a project to rescue our princess from your . . . hospitality, Madam. One that, for once, may well succeed. One that for once, also, is simplicity itself.'

'I do not believe in this marvel of a plot, sir.'

'If you know my brother Davy as well as I do, Highness, you would be the more ready to believe.'

'Your brother . . . ? The honest, unsmiling Master David? *He* plots against me?'

'Not against you, Your Grace, but *for* our Mary Stuart. He is her man, heart and soul. There are many in Scotland still, like Davy Gray.'

'Indeed. But not you, Master of Gray?'

Patrick shrugged. 'While I am devoted to the well-being of the unfortunate but headstrong lady, as has been my father, to his cost, I can take the wider view.'

'I see.' Through narrowed eyes the Queen inspected him. 'And this plot of your brother's, sir?'

'It is not so much a plot, as a simple plan of action. On our way home to Scotland, we make shift to go to Derby, to visit the seat of some lord. Near enough to Wingfield Manor to make a descent upon it, by surprise. With our escort of five score armed men. Mary goes hunting, hawking, riding – guarded indeed, but by sufficient to withstand our many Scots mosstroopers? I doubt it. Your people would pursue us, naturally, but we are well-mounted, vigorous . . . and the North of England is traditionally of Catholic sympathies.'

'Christ's wounds – they would attempt treachery! Such base ingratitude for my fond hospitality! Your graceless Scots would so outrage my trust? I shall know how to deal with such, 'fore God!'

'That is what I believed, Highness, and why I told you. That, and my love for you.' He essayed to touch her jewelled wrist, lightly.

Elizabeth snatched her hand away. 'You tell me, you betray your brother to me – if so be it this is true – only for some very good purpose, Sir. Good, for you! But do not think that you may bargain and chaffer with Elizabeth Tudor.'

'That would be unpardonable – and foolish, Your Grace. Also unnecessary. The sure and wise course is so evident.'

'The sure and wise course, with treason, is to the Tower and the block, sir! That is where your precious Davy and the rest should go, forthwith.'

Patrick actually laughed, though not disrespectfully. 'But that is not where the astute Gloriana will send them, I swear!' he said.

'No? Where then, sirrah?'

'Where but to Mary herself, Lady? To Wingfield. To speak with her – under due restraint, to be sure. To take strong measures against our company would set back Your Grace's relations with Scotland grievously, offend King James, and greatly rejoice France, Spain and the Pope. Yet this project was devised only because Davy and the others believe that you will not permit us to see Mary. Allow that, under what safeguards you desire, and there is no need for this desperate venture – no rift in Your Highness's relations with Scotland.'

Elizabeth drew a long breath, and then exploded into urgent speech. 'God's passion – I believe that you have devised it all your own self, Patrick Gray, in order to constrain me! It fits all too close, too snug by far. It is *your* work, you devil . . . !'

'Not so, dear Madam. For I have patience, and entire faith in your wisdom. My brother and his friends it is who are thus headstrong, not me.'

'Either way, you are a devil, Patrick. Why I permit you even to speak with me, I know not . . . ' she paused, and from the littered table at her bedside picked up the locket which Patrick had given her some days before, weighing it in her hand. Though he smiled gently, the young man watched that beringed hand keenly. 'I should return this bauble to its shameless giver,' the Queen went on. She dangled it back and forth. 'Should I not, Patrick . . . ?'

He leant over. 'If Your Grace wishes to break my heart,' he told her.

'Have you a heart, Patrick – or but a busy, black, scheming mind? And a honeyed tongue?'

'Feel you whether or no I have a heart, Lady. Feel whether it throbs,' he advised, and reaching out, took her hand and placed it against his chest.

'Lord – you are so padded, man, I feel naught but stuffing . . . !'

Smiling, he opened his white velvet doublet, and guided her hand therein.

'I think . . . yes, I think that you have a heart, Patrick,' Elizabeth murmured. 'I feel something. But . . . it beats but slowly, sluggishly, it seems. What dull cold message does it spell out, I wonder? Come nearer, lad, that I may listen.' She patted the bed at her side.

'If mine is cold and slow, yours must be hot and fast indeed fairest one,' he asserted softly, sitting down. He took the locket and chain from her other hand, and proceeded to settle it, as before, between her breasts.

'Rogue liar!' she said, but leaned the closer. 'Mary Stuart, they say, is growing fat. You must tell me, Patrick, when you return, the truth of it. Will you, boy – the truth?'

'Assuredly, dear lady – always the truth. As now . . .'

Chapter Twenty-four

WINGFIELD Manor belonged to the Earl of Shrewsbury, who had long been burdened with the expense of acting gaoler to Queen Mary in his various strongholds – for in her usual fashion, Elizabeth expected her faithful subjects themselves to pay for the privilege of entertaining her guests, voluntary or otherwise. In this instance, however, Walsingham had found a deputy for Shrewsbury – no doubt because he feared that the Earl might be growing soft where Mary was concerned – in the person of Sir Ralph Sadler, a stocky, square, impassive man in his early sixties, a soldier, stiff, unsmiling and a little deaf. The Manor of Wingfield was a large and compact house, standing in a strong position on a steep promontory, in foothill country about ten miles north of Derby, its only accessible side guarded by a moat.

As Sir Edward Wotton, Walsingham's deputy, introduced the four visitors to Sadler, under the fortified gatehouse, the drawbridge lined by his men-at-arms, he greeted them without betraying emotion of any sort, nodded to Marie rather than bowed, and turned away forthwith to lead them within. The choice of the unhappy Queen's gaolers-in-chief was always something of a mystery. Presumably Walsingham selected them for qualities which were no doubt of vital importance. Whatever their differing types, it was essential that they should be staunch Protestants, past the age of probable susceptibility to women's wiles, stern of heart.

'A single-minded gentleman, undoubtedly,' Patrick murmured.

'Necessarily so.' Wotton smiled. 'I would not play host to your princess for a dukedom! I would end in the Tower, I have no doubt – and very quickly.'

'I wonder!'

The house formed two squares, one within another, around a central grassy court where fantail pigeons strutted, ducks from the moat quacked, and women washed clothing at a trough beside a well. Wotton informed them that one of the internal wings was allotted to Mary and her small entourage, and another to her guards and Queen Elizabeth's respresentatives.

David's eyes were busy on strategic details as he followed Patrick, Orkney and the Lady Marie.

At the entrance to Mary's apartments, a thin saturnine stooping man, like a moulting crow, met them, and was introduced as Mr. Secretary Beal, a Clerk to the Privy Council and Elizabeth's 'envoy' to her royal cousin – in fact, her principal and very efficient spy. Behind stood Monsieur Nau, Mary's own secretary – he who had once been refused audience of James at Falkland – and also Sir Andrew Melville of Garvock, her most faithful attendant, styled Master of her Household, who had elected to stay with his mistress throughout the long years of her captivity, brother to the better known Sir James of Halhill and Sir Robert the soldier.

Beal spoke coldly, nasally. 'I understand, Sir Edward, that these gentlemen are to be permitted a short exchange with the former princess, Mary Stuart?'

'That is so, Mr. Secretary – in your presence and mine, naturally.'

'If Her Grace permits an audience,' Melville put in, valiant yet.

Beal sniffed, Wotton smiled, Sadler stared straight ahead of him, but Patrick bowed. 'Indeed yes, sir,' he declared. 'It is our humble desire and request that such audience may be granted to us, her loyal subjects.'

Orkney chuckled. 'Mary will see me, never fear. I am her brother – God help her!'

Melville, and Nau also, bowed and withdrew.

'The lady maintains this ... comedy,' Wotton observed, shrugging. 'She never wearies of it. Extraordinary.'

'Is comedy the word, sir?' That was Marie, eyeing him levelly. 'She is anointed Queen of Scots, and Queen-Dowager of France. Where is the comedy?'

'Your pardon, lady.'

They waited, in silence.

Presently Melville returned. 'Her Highness is graciously pleased to receive you,' he announced.

He led the way indoors, into and through a chamber where two ladies mended garments. At an inner door he glanced back at Wotton and Beal, who had come long behind the Scots party. 'Her Grace prefers to receive her Scottish subjects in private audience, sirs,' he asserted evenly.

'No doubt,' Wotton answered. 'But the Queen's command is definite, sir.' Never did Elizabeth or any of her servants accord

Mary her title of queen. 'Your lady may not see these, or any visitors, save in the presence of myself and Mr. Beal.'

Tight-lipped, Sir Andrew turned and resumed his walking.

They passed through a kitchen, and then up a narrow twisting staircase. Undoubtedly these had been the servants' quarters of Wingfield Manor. In the little corridor above, Monsieur Nau stood on guard outside a closed door. As the party came up, he turned solemnly to rap on its panels with his little staff, slow dignified knocks.

In marked contrast to this somewhat laboured and pathetic striving after royal style and ceremony, the door was flung open swiftly, and a woman stood framed therein, smiling. A rivulet of laughter, spontaneous, unaffected, silvery, seemed to cascade around the company.

'*Alors, mes amis* – visitors! True visitors, from Scotland!' a clear musical voice rang out. 'Happy this day! Ah, I am glad, glad!'

In front of her all were dumb – even Patrick, even indeed the insensitive and hearty Orkney, her unlikely brother. David, looking, found himself to be incapable of any coherent thought, only of powerful and conflicting emotions. He was aware of a quite shattered admiration, an eager and overwhelming sense of devotion, and a great pity.

He perceived, after some fashion, that though Mary Stuart was indeed lovely, beautiful, that was not the heart of the matter. Nor was her attractiveness, her fascination. These affected him, undoubtedly – or he would have been no man. But it was something other than all this, something of such extraordinary quality and radiant personality that held him transfixed, transported, so that he could neither have moved nor spoken had he been called upon to do so. It was was not he was blinded by emotion. He perceived well enough that she was not the ravishing girl who, sixteen long years before, had crossed the Border and thrown herself upon her cousin Elizabeth's mercy – saw even, with a pang at his heart, that the knuckles of the slim white hand that she held out to her brother were swollen with rheumatism. It was that he perceived that she had no need of the chiselled perfection of her small and delicate features; of the alabaster transparency of her skin; of the flaming glory of her red-gold hair, as yet barely touched with silver; of the amber-and-green translucence of her eyes; of all the vital grace of a slender and almost boyish yet supremely feminine figure that the years were only just beginning to thicken. Without all these she would still have been, for David Gray, the same glowing magnetic being that was Mary Stuart and Mary Stuart only.

Well might Elizabeth Tudor insist that she should never set eyes on her.

'*Robert*,' she cried, pronouncing the name in French fashion, 'You are an old man! What have they done to you, *mon cher Robert*? Your belly is enormous!'

Orkney guffawed, but even he was not unaffected. He could find no words. He looked at her – but later had to ask Patrick how she had been dressed. She was indeed all in black, save for white lace at neck and wrists, and wore no jewellery, the black velvet threadbare and mended. But how she was clad was quite unimportant, irrelevant, with Mary Stuart's beholders – however fond she was of clothes. What she wore was seldom noticed at the time.

Laughing warmly, the Queen turned to her niece. 'And this – this can be none other than *ma petite Marie*, my namesake? So fair, so true, so douce! My dear, let me kiss you. I swear that you are the prettiest thing that these eyes have seen for long years. Ah me, once I was like you. And behold me now!'

'You. . . Your Grace.' In face of that unlooked for sparkle and lively humour, the younger woman could only stammer. She curtsied, for her, clumsily. It seemed incredible that Mary should still laugh, after all the years of sorrow and prison.

The Queen's extraordinary eyes rested on Patrick, and changed expression. 'So-o-o! For once rumour has not lied,' she murmured. 'The Master of Gray is even more beautiful than has been told me. Is all else likewise true, I wonder?'

He sank down on one satin knee, to kiss her hand. 'Madam,' he said thickly. And again, 'Madam.' He bowed his head. 'Accept my . . . my devotion.' That was not like Patrick Gray.

'I do accept it, sir – for I need all such, direly. But that you know as well as I do.' She raised him up. 'I thank you for coming. For achieving what few others have done these endless years – this meeting with friends from Scotland.'

She turned to David. 'Who is this brave one who stands so surely on his two feet?'

'He is David Gray, Highness. Secretary to this embassage. Brother to myself as the Lord Robert is to you.'

'Ah. Another son of my good friend, your father. And a very different son, I vow! But, *pardieu*, I would not have thought him a secretary! Eh, Master Beal?' There was flashing scorn in that last – but not for David.

299

As in a dream he took her proffered hand. He did not sink down on his knee. He did not even bow. Nor did he speak, nor raise that hand to his lips. He merely stood and looked his adoration, his worship, lips parted.

Brilliantly the Queen smiled on him, and the hand which he clutched stirred and slid up to touch his face, briefly, lightly. 'Yes, very different, *mon cher*,' she repeated softly. And then, in another voice, 'Come,' she commanded.

They followed her into a sitting-room of modest dimensions and scant furnishing, where another lady sat stitching in the autumn sunshine at a window. The company all but filled the apartment. As though noting it, the Queen turned.

'Mr. Beal, and you, Sir Edward – you may retire,' she said, all regal suddenly.

'That is not possible, Madam,' Beal declared, in his rasping voice. 'We must stay.'

'Unbidden, sir? In a lady's chamber? *Any* lady's chamber?'

'It is the Queen's command.'

'The Queen? Ah yes, of course – the Queen. My sister is ever ... thoughtful.' She shrugged, Gallic fashion. 'The Lady Melville will entertain you, then, gentlemen.'

The woman at the window, Sir Andrew's wife, rose and came over to the Englishmen. Beal brushed her aside with a wave of his hand, however, and continued to eye the Queen.

'You have not long, Madam,' he warned. 'These gentlemen needs must return to Derby forthwith.'

Wotton had the grace to look uncomfortable, and to mutter apologies.

Mary ignored them both thereafter, as though they were not present. She turned to Orkney. 'How is my son, Robert?' she asked. 'How fares James – my poor James?'

'Och, the laddie does well enough,' her half-brother told her, grinning. 'He warstles his way towards manhood . . . o' a sort!'

'He grows the man? He is tall? Fair? Of a noble countenance? *Mortdieu*, to think that I must ask the aspect of my own son! Whom does he favour? Does he favour Henry, or rather myself?'

Orkney guffawed. 'God kens whom he favours, Ma'am. No' your own self, and that's a fact. Maybe he has something o' auld Lennox to him – yon slippit mouth and gangling gait . . . '

'His Grace is not tall, Madam, but his proportions are adequate,' Marie put in hurriedly, 'and his eyes are very fine – Stewart's eyes. He is the most learned youth in the land, and of great talents.' She knew that she gabbled, but could not help herself. Indeed, it seemed utterly impossible that this super-lative, radiant creature should be mother to the shambling, sly and frightened James. 'He reads the Latin, Greek and Hebrew. He writes poetry . . . '

'But not to me, alas,' the Queen interposed sadly.

'His Highness sent his most devoted filial greetings, Your Grace,' Patrick announced. 'He assures you of his duty and affection. And he would have you to know that he does all in his power for the easement of your situation and the improvement of your state.'

'I am happy to hear it, sir,' Mary mentioned, a little dryly. 'It would seem to be a prolonged process!'

'It is, yes, unfortunately, Madam – with the fate of realms in the scales. But, at last, the clouds open and the way becomes clear. Your Highness may take heart. Your long and weary vigil is like to be nearly over.'

'Do you say so, Master of Gray? Ah, how often have I heard that before! *Ma foi* – soon now, this one assures me. Wait but a little longer, another says. And I have waited – aye, *le bon Dieu* knows how I have waited . . . !'

'I also know it, Highness – we all do. But this time, it is different. I . . . we come direct from Her Grace of England. The King, your son, gave us full power to treat and negotiate. And at last we have something that Queen Elizabeth desires, something that Scotland may treat with.' Patrick's glance flickered over to where Wotton and Beal stood.

Mary looked in that direction also. 'But does Elizabeth desire that I ever return to Scotland? Indeed, does my son, sir?'

Patrick coughed. 'It may be that Scotland is not the next step for you, Madam. It may be that meantime you should look southwards rather than north, for your freedom. I believe that Your Grace loves France second only a little to Scotland?'

The Queen's lovely glowing eyes looked deep into Patrick's own. 'I think that you should speak me plain, Master of Gray – in especial if, as these gentlemen of England say, we have but little time. What is this of France? And what that my sister of England desires, which Scotland may give?' Though that was said calmly, there was no doubting the tension behind the words.

Patrick took a long breath. Seldom had Marie seen him less master of a situation, less at ease. He picked his words with obvious care. 'The King, Madam, proposes a, h'm, limited

Association in the Scottish Crown.'

'Limited? *I* first proposed such Association. Limited in what, sir?'

'A sharing of the style and address, Your Grace. Also of certain revenues – in a due proportion, of course. With mutual powers in the granting of titles of honour, appointments of patronage . . . '

'These are fripperies, sir – *pouf*, mere nothings!' The Queen interrupted, with an expressive gesture. 'What of the rule and governance of my kingdom?'

Patrick moistened his lips. 'That, His Grace and Council have decided, must meantime be left to himself. Neither the Kirk, nor Her Grace of England, will consider it otherwise. It is . . . '

'*Sacrebleu* – you come to me with this! This insult! I am to yield all my rights and powers as ordained monarch to my son, a youth not yet of age, at the behest of the ministers of the Kirk and the Queen of England? How think you of me, Master of Gray? How thinks my son of me? Do I seem a shadow, a ghost? Look at me, sir. What do you see? A cipher? Or a fool?'

'I see a very fair lady long held captive, Madam, for whom freedom of a surety must speak louder than any other word.'

'But not freedom at any price, Monsieur. One may pay too dear for even such bliss. I have taken solemn vows before God, at anointing and coronation. I cannot divest myself of them as of a worn-out dress. I am Queen, not of Scotland but of the Scots, I would remind you. I cannot un-queen myself, at the behest of others. Sometimes, but yes, in weak moments, I have wished that I could, *pardieu*. But it is not possible.'

'But . . . for sixteen years, Madam, you have exercised none of the powers and rights of monarch. You have been in all matters a prisoner. Surely, what now is offered is infinitely to be preferred? A release from this bondage. Your freedom. To live your own life again . . . '

'My life is not my own – it is my people's. If I forgot that once, I have paid sufficiently, have I not? I shall not forget it again. How shall I live amongst my people in Scotland, and take no hand in their affairs, do naught for their needs, leave their care, for which I am responsible before God Almighty, to other hands? How shall I, sir?' Mary spoke warmly, passionately.

Patrick cleared his throat. 'That trial would not arise, Your Grace, were you to dwell in France – in your beloved France. There you would be free in truth – free of this bondage, and of the affairs of state also.'

'To the satisfaction of my sister Elizabeth!'

He shrugged. 'To your own also, surely. The two are not irreconcilable, I do believe.'

Mary looked from Patrick to Orkney and the others. 'Whose device is this?' she demanded. 'Elizabeth's? Or the man's who calls himself Arran? Or your own, Master of Gray? For I swear it is not that of the son of my loins, to torment me with a freedom that I may not grasp.'

'The Association in the Crown is the policy o' the Council, Mary,' her brother averred. 'Adopted out o' your own proposal. This o' France I ken naught of.'

'The Association that I agreed to was to share the duties and responsibilities of the Crown equally, in partnership, Robert. This is quite otherwise – a travesty, a mockery!'

'Yet even this, Your Grace, has been hard won. Agreement to it by Queen Elizabeth has been achieved only after much entreaty and difficult negotiation,' Patrick declared. 'I beg you to consider it well.'

'And what choice favours did you promise Elizabeth, that she agreed to this so noble and generous gesture, sir?'

Orkney laughed coarsely. 'Waesucks – it cost us a-plenty! Spit on it not, Mary, for it cost the reversal o' all auld Scotland's policy. It cost a Protestant league, nae less.'

Patrick bit his lip as Mary's eyes widened.

'Mother of God – a Protestant league, you said? Scotland and England?' she cried. 'Against France? Against Holy Church? No – never! I'll not believe it. Never could I agree to such a betrayal!' . .

'I'm thinking you're no' asked to agree it, Ma'am,' her brother pointed out baldly. 'It's been agreed. By King Jamie and the Council.'

'But they cannot do such a thing. It is against all Scotland's interests, her safety. Her ancient alliance with France, that is her shield and buckler. James is a mere boy, led astray by evil self-seekers. He cannot do this . . . '

'He is King of Scots, and head of Scotland's Kirk, Madam – a Protestant Kirk. He can do it, and has done,' Patrick assured.

'And you? *You* tell me this, sir! You who were trained to my service, have dipped deep of my revenues! The Master of Gray, son of my old friend, bears me these tidings!'

Patrick did not answer. Nobody spoke. Even Beal and Wotton looked away, embarrassed.

The Queen gazed round them all, and though anguished, mortally disappointed, helpless, never could she have seemed more a queen. 'If this is your mission, gentlemen, then you have my answer,' she said, quietly now. 'The Queen of Scots does not purchase freedom so.'

David heard Marie sob in her throat. Then, almost surprised, he heard his own voice speaking.

'Your Grace – think for yourself,' he urged, the words coming thickly, unevenly. 'I . . . I have no right to speak. But think for yourself in this – not for Scotland, Scotland has thought but little for you. Go free, even on these terms. It is your right, your life. Forgive me . . . but you have suffered enough for statecraft, Ma'am. I . . . I . . . forgive me . . . '

Those glorious eyes considered him, closely, thoughtfully. She even mustered a wan smile. 'Thank you, Master David. There speaks a true heart. But think you, even if I forgot my kingdom and my people's weal, that in Catherine's France I should remain free? Think you that the Queen-Mother would tolerate another queen in her son's realm? *Parbleu* – I should fare not better with her than with Elizabeth! The Queen of Scots may only *be* Queen of Scots – or she is nothing, and less than nothing. Under God Almighty, it is my destiny.' Mary waved a sorrowful graceful hand. 'We shall speak no more of it. The issue is closed, finished.' She turned to the younger woman. 'Marie, my dear, tell me of Scotland. Do the folk still speak of me? Have they forgot me? Is the Kirk still as hot against the Harlot of Rome? Against the Scarlet Woman who would seduce poor Scotia to the Devil? And how fare my friends – my Maries, such as remain? Huntly? Seton? Herries? My lord of Gray, himself? Do the buck still run sweetly in my forest of Ettrick? And the wildfowl flight at dawn and dusk from the sea to Falkland marshes? Has the heather faded yet on the Lomonds, and the snow come to the Highland hills? Tell me, *ma chérie?*'

Marie Stewart could answer her never a word from between her quivering lips.

Mr. Secretary Beal spoke for her. Time was running out, he said. His orders were definite. If the Scottish envoys were nearly finished . . . ?

Mary ignored him. 'You bring me word of more than grudging policy and the like, surely, my friends?' she chided, but gently. 'Is that all that you will leave with me? I danced once in the halls of Holyrood; do any dance there now? Linlithgow, where I was born – I was building a water-garden at the loch,

304

and a new fountain in the courtyard; did they ever come to completion? In St Andrews by the sea, the grey northern sea, I planned a fair new college . . . '

'The new college is near finished, Your Grace. King James is very hot for learning . . . '

'But no' for Linlithgow. Jamie cares naught for the place, Mary. But Arran's lady finds it to her taste, so it's no' just deserted! Lord, she has . . . '

Marie again hastily interrupted her father. 'The Court is not a great deal at Holyroodhouse. The King prefers Stirling and Falkland, and even St Andrews. He does not dance, but is a great huntsman. He plays at the golf, also . . . '

'Enough!' Beal exclaimed, testily. 'Her Grace the Queen did not authorise this meeting for the exchange of tittle-tattle! Come, gentlemen.'

'I fear that we must insist,' Wotton agreed, if more civilly. 'It will be dark in no more than a couple of hours, and our strict instructions are that we must be back in Derby before nightfall.'

David looked over at the Englishmen thoughtfully. Could they possibly suspect some attempt at rescue, by night?

'We must go, then, Highness,' Patrick acceded. 'You will consider our proposals, I hope, with much thought, much care, since so much depends upon them. Has Your Grace no message, no word of hope which we may convey to the King your son?'

'Aye, *mon Dieu* – I have! I send him all a mother's love and devotion. Tell him that I remember him daily in my prayers, and beseech Our Lady and Her Son to look in mercy upon this unfortunate woman and *her* son, riven cruelly apart. I pray that my son may not be led astray by false councillors, of which I fear Scotland breeds a many, Master of Gray! Above all, tell him that I pray that he may remain true to his trust, to the people of Scotland whom God has given into our hands. To look not only to the immediate advantage, but to the continuing weal of our realm. An alliance with England, be it Protestant or other, for Scotland is but a marriage of lamb and wolf, of fly and spider. England is too close, and too powerful, too sure of her mission to lesser men. Such a compact must end in Scotland being swallowed up. Always it has been thus, always the cat has wanted to swallow the mouse. Always the first and surest foundation of our country's policy, if she would preserve her precious independence, is to keep England at arm's length, by cleaving to France and even Spain. Without that our small land is lost, I tell you. I am a Catholic, yes – but I do not speak as one, now. Only as Queen of Scots. Surely you know it – you all know it? Tell James that he must not proceed with this alliance, sir. You, Robert – tell him well. Promise me that you will assure him of it. Promise, sirs.' That was a command, passionately, fervently, but royally given.

Orkney mumbled, eyes on the floor.

'He shall be told, Madam,' Patrick said levelly, tonelessly.

'Then adieu, my friends. I thank all the saints for the sight of you. I thank even my good sister Elizabeth! If you see her, convey my gratitude for this at least, and my warm well-wishes. But view her not as the friend and ally of Scotland, at your peril and mine – for that she was not born to be. And . . . the good God go with you all.' The Queen's voice broke as she said that last, and swiftly she turned her graceful back on her visitors and walked unsteadily towards the window.

Bowing and backing, the Scots withdrew, Marie at least stumbling, unable to see where she went.

The two Englishmen were last out, face foremost, and Sir Andrew Melville closed the door on them.

'God damn you!' he said savagely. 'God damn and·flay you! God's curse upon you all!' To whom he was speaking was not apparent; he did not seem to be looking at anyone. But his face was twisted as with pain.

It was a silent company that rode across the reedy pastures and rolling slopes towards Derby. David, like Marie, was profoundly depressed. This surely should not, could not, be the end? But what to do, what to hope for, now – since all too clearly Mary Stuart would not change her mind? His thoughts had turned at once, of course, even whilst they were in the Queen's chamber, to his earlier idea of a rescue by force; but on riding out from Wingfield Manor again, he had glimpsed an encampment behind some woodland, an armed encampment of scores of men and horses, where tents were being erected. And later, on the road, they had passed another column of men-at-arms riding towards Wingfield. Most evidently, Mary's guard was being massively reinforced. Why, he wondered? A mere unfortunate coincidence? At all events, it would seem to rule out any attempt at a rescue, meantime.

Patrick, strangely enough, though silent also, did not seem to share the others' depression. Indeed, he hummed snatches of song to himself as they rode, and occasionally made cordial, even jocular, remarks to Wotton who still escorted them.

Patrick seldom acted obviously, of course. David, low-voiced, assailed his brother, at length.

'Could you not have done more, Patrick?' he demanded. 'Could you not have made it easier for her? Is this *all* that we can do? Are we so quickly defeated in our endeavour?'

'Who is defeated, Davy? What gloomy talk is this? Today has been one small episode, a mere chapter – not the end of the story. Indeed, I expected little else. We have but sown the seed. The fruiting will come later.'

'The Queen seemed certain enough in her decision. She will not change her mind, I think.'

'Minds are made to change, Davy – especially women's minds. She knows now that she *can* go free. That is a hard thought to live with, in prison. In her solitary days that will work as leaven in a dough. The fair Mary will come to it never fear.'

'And you think that is right, seemly? When it is against her conscience . . . ?'

'Lord, you cannot have it both ways, man! And what is conscience . . . but the flagellant courtesan we hire when we tire of the good wife of sound common sense?'

David stared ahead of him, and said nothing.

At Hampton Court Palace, where they eventually found Elizabeth and her Court the following night, Patrick had no need to seek to arrange a private audience. The Queen sent for him forthwith. He found her pacing alone with almost masculine strides up and down a long gallery. Courtiers watched her covertly from alcoves and doorways, but none shared her stern promenade.

'Well, sir?' she snapped, as he fell into step beside her. 'So you talked nonsense! You made me took the fool! Mary Stuart would have none of your proposals – or *my* generosity. You have wasted your time and my patience. I do not love bunglers, Master of Gray!'

Patrick affected to look at her with astonishment. 'What misconception is this, Your Grace?' he wondered. 'What distorted mirror of events has been held up to you? I had esteemed Sir Edward Wotton – since he it must be – to have more wit than this!'

'Do not wriggle and twist, sirrah! Do not blame others for your own failure. Mary refused what you proposed – no clever talk will alter that.'

'Of course she refused, Madam. I expected naught else. She could do none other, without renouncing her Crown for the second and final time. Nor could she swallow our Protestant alliance. That was clear. The one tied to the other made the issue certain.'

'But, man, this is not what you told me before! Have you been mocking me – *me*?'

'Far from it, Highness. But the questions had to be asked, put to her. That was essential.'

'But why? Why go to this trouble, 'fore God? Why make the offer, if you knew that it must be refused?'

'Because the offer is everything, Your Grace – the refusal nothing. The offer blesses you, honours you. And King James. And the refusal condemns Mary only. I have changed Mary Stuart for you, dear lady, from a millstone to a jewel. Do you not see it? Before – you will forgive me saying it – men criticised you for holding Mary fast all these years. They may do so no longer. You have offered her her freedom, and she has rejected it. James has offered her an Association in his Crown – and she has rejected that also. He is now free to do as he will – under your guidance, and I hope, mine. And you are justified before all men. Heigho – and you talk of my failure, Madam!'

Elizabeth had halted in her pacing, to stare at him. Smiling confidently if respectfully he returned her scrutiny. Never was a man more assured of himself. Tight-lipped she shook her bewigged head. It almost looked as though Elizabeth, Elizabeth Tudor, did not trust herself to speak.

'I will make so bold as to suggest that you will not deny the truth of what I say, Majesty,' he went on. 'In all modesty, I would claim to have earned some small thanks. King James's, also. Now, as regards Mary, your position is assured. No longer can you be blamed for holding her. And if she changes her mind, and agrees to the terms offered, Catherine de Medici will take over your burden, and she cannot upset your relations with James and Scotland. Is it not so?'

The Queen did not controvert him. Instead, she spoke wonderingly, obliquely. 'Whence comes a man like you, Patrick Gray? Under what strange star were you born? How came such a man of your father and yon long daughter of old Ruthven? God's death, but I think that I am frightened of you, Master of Gray!'

'You jest, Madam,' Patrick said shortly, almost abruptly, and despite himself he frowned.

Elizabeth eyed him sidelong. 'If I was James Stewart, sir, I think ... yes, I think that I would shut you up in the dread

308

bottle-dungeon of Edinburgh Castle.'

Recovering himself, he smiled. 'King James, Madam, I am sure has more wit than that! As indeed have you. Send me back to Scotland with Your Grace's sure support, as I have besought you before, and I promise you that Scotland will no longer be a thorn in your flesh.'

'No?'

'You do not doubt my ability?'

'I do not doubt your ability, Patrick.' Sombrely she said it. 'If I have doubts, they are . . . otherwise.'

'I shall prove them baseless.'

'Perhaps. I hope so. So be it. Go back, then, Master Patrick, and fail me not. For I have a long arm!'

'And a divinely fair hand at the end of it, Gloriana!' he whispered triumphantly, and raised her unresisting fingers to his lips.

Chapter Twenty-five

MARIOTA GRAY nibbled her lip and shook her head in indecision, her deep soft eyes troubled. 'What should we do in Edinburgh, Davy – in a great city? The children and I? We should be lost in the streets and wynds, choked amongst all those houses, in the stench. It would be worse than St Andrews, much . . . '

'It is not so ill as that, my dear,' David protested. 'Edinburgh is a fair town. We should have a house high in one of the tall lands, where we can look out far and wide. Patrick is generous with his money – wherever he gets it. We can pay well for a house such as we want.'

'What would my lord do without us?' Mariota shifted her ground. 'You know how he dotes on Mary. He requires me to look to his needs . . . '

'And do not I – your husband? My lord managed very well before you came to Castle Huntly, girl. He will again. You are *my* wife, not my lord's. We have been apart too much, I tell you. Do you not wish to be with me, Mariota?'

'Aye, to be sure, Davy – you know that I do. You know well how I have hated all this parting. But . . . *need* you go? Must you be off to Edinburgh, at Patrick's whistle? You are but newly back from England. Has he not used you sufficiently? Can you not stay at home, now? Is Castle Huntly no longer good enough for you?'

David ran a hand through his unruly hair. 'It is not that. I would that I could return now to my old life here. It is what I intended, and looked to do.' Even as he said that, he knew that it was both truth and a lie. While one part of his mind longed for the simple country life and the verities and satisfactions of home and family, another was appalled at the thought of spending the rest of his days teaching unwilling and uncaring scholars in this quiet backwater, after the excitements of life with his brother at the centre of events. 'But Patrick needs me. He insists that I stay with him, in his present need.'

'And is Patrick your keeper, your master, now? Must he rule our lives?' Mariota's voice quivered a little, strangely, as she said that.

'No. No – but . . . he is next to ruling Scotland, now.' David took a pace or two back and forth, in the room that was now theirs in the main keep of Castle Huntly. He had been back less than a month from the London embassage, and there was no hiding his restlessness. 'You know how it is, lass – how I am placed. I believe that Patrick *does* need me. Och, I know that it is little enough I can do, and that there is nothing so notable about Davy Gray. But the truth is that in some things I can affect Patrick, sway him. Not much, but a little. And, 'fore God, I need not tell you that often he needs the swaying! There's nights I canna sleep for thinking of what is in him, what devilish force, what power for ill. And good, too, I suppose – for he is the ablest man that I have ever known. But it is the ill that I ever fear will prove the stronger . . . '

'But is much of it not in your own mind, just, Davy? Always you have seen Patrick so, as though he was some sort of a monster. About him you are a little crazed in your mind, I think. Long I have felt that . . . '

He frowned, shaking his head impatiently. 'That is nonsense. I know Patrick – know him better than does anyone else. I tell you, I have *felt* the evil in him, again and again. It has done much harm, already. One day, I fear, it may destroy him – and God knows what else with him! If I can save him from that, even a little . . . '

'And so you must follow him, always, like a cow's calf? Oh, Davy – must you go?'

Stubbornly he jutted his jaw. 'Aye, I must. He is doing, now, what he has never done before – taking more and more of the rule of the realm into his own hands. Why, I know not – but he is. The King and the Privy Council are not stopping him. He needs a helper, a secretary, as never before. And there is still Mary the Queen to think of. If there is anything that I may do for her, it is with Patrick that I shall do it. That is certain. The Lady Marie says . . . '

'Aye – the Lady Marie says! She says aplenty, no doubt. And you heed her well, both of you! She . . . she is to be in Edinburgh also? Then – then perhaps I had best come with you, indeed!'

David smiled then. 'Och, do not say that you are jealous, lass? Of the Lady Marie! Save us – what next?'

'What next, indeed! You are ever speaking of her – and uncommon highly! I know her kind. Men are easily led astray by a pretty face . . . '

'Lord – then what about *your* pretty face, my dear? You are more beautiful than Marie Stewart, by far. Who are you leading astray? Only your poor husband, I hope?'

She still flushed like a girl when he spoke that way, and was the more lovely for her blushing. 'Do not think that you can cozen me, Davy Gray! Nor wheedle me into going to Edinburgh . . . '

'I neither cozen nor wheedle, woman – I command!' he declared, straight-faced, loudly. 'It is high time that I asserted myself, I see. You are my wife, and you will do as I say. You come to Edinburgh, and look after me, and warm my bed for me these winter nights, as is your plain duty . . . and keep me out of the clutches of the Lady Marie Stewart!'

She swallowed. 'Very well, sir,' she said.

And so, that winter, the David Grays were installed in three rooms high in a tall tenement in Edinburgh's Lawnmarket, near to the great house, former town mansion of the Earl of Gowrie, which his nephew Patrick had taken over. From their north-facing windows they could look out over lesser roof-tops and smoking chimneys, over an almost illimitable prospect, over the Nor' Loch and fields beyond, across the silver Forth to the green uplands of Fife, to the soaring Ochils and the blue bastions of the Highland Line. Directly between, if far behind, the thrusting breasts of the twin Lomonds, David pointed out, lay Castle Huntly beyond the Tay, and often Mariota gazed thitherwards and could feel that she was not so very far from her own place, after all. She did not love the city life, as she had feared, nor indeed did her husband, but she made the best of it; and the children revelled in it. They were all quite proud, moreover, of this, the first house that they had really been able to call their own.

David, at least, did not find time to hang heavily. Never had he been so busy. Patrick was responsible, of course. Indeed, ever since the day of his return to Scotland from London, Patrick had been a changed man. Gone, apparently was the idling gallant, the trifler with poetry and play and women, the dallier with only the graces of life. Instead he had swiftly and deliberately become the active man of affairs, the vigorous and tireless statesman, drawing the reins of government ever more tightly into his own hands. Circumstances aided him in this. The King was delighted with him and the results of his mission – particularly the pension, provisionally set at £2,000 a year, which Elizabeth had reluctantly agreed to produce. Also, privately, the fact that he need no longer worry about his mother coming back to take part of his kingship away from him. The Privy Council, as it was now composed, welcomed the improved relations with England and the Protestant alliance which Patrick had negotiated. They were more than ready to allow him to take on further responsibilities, for Arran's régime was lax, ineffective, appallingly corrupt, and growing ever more unpopular. His notorious Black Acts had turned the Kirk solidly against him, and much of the people with it; his boundless appropriations of lands and wealth, and his open contempt of the laws, were too blatant even for Scotland, while his wife's rapacious bribe-taking, office-granting, and wild orgies offended all save the utterly depraved. Arran was essentially a lazy man, however ambitious, and it seemed that he was well enough content for Patrick to pick his chestnuts out of the fire for him, to put right much that was going wrong, and to accumulate numerous offices of state. He himself remained secure in the key position of Chancellor and President of the Council – and in James's affections, and, as was generally assumed, his bed. Certainly no open rupture occurred between the two men during this quiet but steady transfer of power.

It was largely through Patrick that the Court became centred in Edinburgh, for he saw that efficient government could not be maintained from ever-changing localities. James and Arran still spent much of their time elsewhere, hunting, hawking and riding the kingdom, but more and more the capital city reverted to being the seat of government. In this, strangely enough, Patrick was aided by the Lady Arran, who disliked traipsing about where she could not surround herself with non-transportable luxuries. She quickly perceived that Patrick was infinitely more efficient in most respects than was her husband, and acted accordingly. There were not a few who suggested that she might well be preparing to switch husbands once more.

David watched all this extraordinary change in his brother with wonderment, for he could not believe that Patrick's ambitions really lay in garnering a multiplicity of offices, in the wielding of executive authority, in the daily management of affairs. If he was doing all this, he was doing it for some specific purpose, David felt sure. The fact that Patrick's closest companion, these days, tended to be Sir Edward Wotton, whom Elizabeth had sent north to replace Mr Bowes as English ambassador, worried his brother. Also the great sums of money which Patrick undoubtedly now had at his command, and which did not seem to come from the chronically threadbare Scottish Treasury.

Not that David had much time for worrying. Being Patrick's secretary, under this new dispensation, ceased to be a sinecure, a mere nominal position, and became an office of much responsibility in itself, demanding all his time and attention. He did not particularly relish the work, nor the mass of detail in which he became involved. Had he wished, undoubtedly he could have had a choice of lucrative and more or less permanent positions for himself, in some sphere of government with which he was in daily contact; but he preferred to remain free, his brother's secretary and left hand. That he was not his *right* hand, he knew very well; clearly there was a great deal that Patrick kept from him, particularly in his relations with Wotton and the English.

One of the English items with which David was not fully conversant, was the matter of the exiled Ruthven lords. One of the points of Patrick's embassage had been James's, or rather Arran's, request to Elizabeth to take steps against these nobles, who had settled just over the Border in Northumberland and constituted a constant threat; a plea that she would send them back to Scotland for trial. Elizabeth did indeed remove them, ostensibly out of danger's way, but only deeper into England. With this the King had to be content. And secretly, David knew, one of them, the Earl of Angus, Morton's nephew and head of the Douglases, had already returned home and was in hiding somewhere in his own Douglasdale. Patrick seemed to suspect that the others might follow at short intervals. As to the purpose of his manoeuvre, Patrick did not commit himself.

The Master of Gray did not allow his preoccupation with English affairs to prejudice other matters, of course; for instance, his good relations with the Guises. He kept up a regular correspondence with them, through the Archbishop of Glasgow and the Jesuit couriers – with not all of which was David conversant either. One letter which he did see, however, contained an extraordinary document – a Papal *pronunciamento*, no less, declaring Patrick Gray's marriage to the Lady Elizabeth Lyon to be null and invalid, on account of the ceremony being heretically and improperly performed. Patrick laughed at David's expression when he saw this. A precaution, he asserted – a mere question of providing for all contingencies. One could not be too careful where these divines were concerned, could one?

Arrangements for the annulment of Patrick's unfortunate

marriage were in fact going on through certain channels in the Kirk, Bishop Davidson indeed having the matter in hand, most suitably. Divorce being more difficult and apt to be prolonged – moreover requiring some small co-operation from the lady in the case – annulment seemed the preferable course. That the parties to the marriage had both been minors at the time was a great convenience. Patrick also claimed duress on the part of his father and Lord Glamis. If this failed, he could always assert that he had, in fact, been secretly married prior to the wedding, to an unnamed woman now fortunately dead. But he did not think that it would be necessary to go to such lengths. Elizabeth Lyon or Gray, it seemed, was now showing a certain interest in young William Kirkcaldy of Grange.

David did not have to wait long to hear further word of Mary Stuart. She had been moved to Tutbury Castle soon after the Scots visit to Wingfield, presumably as an added precaution. Then, one January afternoon, Sir Edward Wotton came strolling into the room in Gowrie House where Patrick worked amidst parchments and papers innumerable, and David with him. Sir John Maitland, the Secretary of State, was there also, brother to Mary's late Maitland of Lethington.

'Ah, you are busy, Patrick – always busy!' he said. 'You have become a very glutton for papers, I do declare. I had hopes of better, from you! I will see you anon.'

'I am just finishing,' Patrick assured. 'Davy, the blessed Davy, will do the rest for me. I believe that he actually *likes* handling pen and paper! And Sir John is just going – are you not, Mr. Secretary?'

Maitland, a thin, ascetic, unsmiling man, able but friendless, looked sourly at the English ambassador. He did not like him, nor anything to do with England. Yet he was accepting Patrick's money, David knew, as were many others – and not enquiring whence it came. He bowed stiffly, and stalked out.

Wotton came and sat on the edge of Patrick's littered table. 'I have despatches,' he said. 'Some of which will interest you, my friend. Your Mary Stuart is a great letter-writer – which is a great convenience.'

Patrick sat back. 'You mean that Walsingham has been reading her correspondence – and has intercepted something else of interest to England?'

'Exactly. She is remarkably explicit in her writings, the good lady.'

'I wonder that she does not realise that her letters will be

tampered with. If not herself, Nau or Melville at least. It seems
. . . elementary.'

'Ah, but she does, Patrick. We have allowed for her unkind
suspicions, however. Walsingham arranged for the brewer who
supplies the beer to her household to claim to be a fervent
Catholic and supporter of Mary, and to offer her the use of a
specially-contrived beer-barrel which should go in and out of
her quarters with a secret container within for letters. And so the
fair lady may now write to whom she will, with an easy mind –
and Sir Francis has a convenient inspection of the letters and
their answers. A truly useful barrel!'

David, head down over his papers, had to choke back his fury
and indignation. Patrick laughed, however.

'Very neat,' he admitted. 'And I take it that something of note
has now come out of your barrel?'

'Indeed it has. Many things. But in especial one in which you
will be interested. A letter written to Mendoza, former Spanish
ambassador to Elizabeth, and a friend of your Mary, as you
know. In it she tells of your interview with her and declares that,
to bring her son to his senses and to halt this Protestant alliance,
she proposes to name Mendoza's master, Philip of Spain, her
heir instead of James – heir to the throne of Scotland, and her
reversion to the throne of England likewise! How think you of
that, Master Patrick?'

'Lord!' Patrick was sitting up straight, now. 'This is . . .
fantastic! She would do this? The proud Mary would go so far?
To disinherit her own son – for the Spaniard!'

'To *say* that she would do so, at all events.'

'Aye. It is likely but a gesture, a ruse.'

'But a potent one, i' faith. For you will see where it leads. It
would give Philip what he greatly needs – the sure support of the
English Catholics. We know that he plans invasion. If he can
rely on our dissident Catholics to rise in his support . . . ! The
Pope has declared Elizabeth to be illegitimate and a usurper,
and Mary the true Queen of England – St. Peter roast him! If
Philip is her heir, and she a prisoner, then he will have all good
Catholics seeing his coming as a rescue, not an invasion. Our
good Queen's life becomes the more threatened. Ah, a subtle
and dangerous gesture, indeed. Who would have thought the
woman capable of it!'

'M'mmm,' Patrick examined his finger-tips. 'Extraordinary!
She is a fighter yet.' There was admiration in his voice, un-

doubtedly. 'And has Walsingham passed on the letter to Mendoza?'

'Dear God – no! Why scourge our own backs? The question is – to tell your King James, or no? It is left to my own decision, meantime. A little difficult, as you will concede I think. How would he take it? Would it move him for the alliance, or against, think you?'

Patrick toyed with his goose quill for a moment or two. 'I would advise that you do not tell him, Edward,' he said at length. 'James is easily frightened. He is firm enough for the alliance now. But this might scare him away from it – as is his mother's intention. The succession to Elizabeth's throne is his dearest ambition – to rule both realms. Any shadow that might come between him and that vision could terrify him into a folly. Better that he does not know. If Mary writes to him, therefore, to the same effect, I'd take it kindly if the letter comes to me.'

Wotton nodded, and glanced over at David, eyebrows raised.

Patrick answered his unspoken question. 'Davy is discretion itself,' he assured. 'All secrets are safe with him.'

Looking up, David opened his mouth to speak – and then shut it again, almost with a click.

'Very well – James shall not know.' Wotton lifted himself off the table, and moved over to the door. Then he paused. 'It may interest you to know, Patrick my friend, that Mary Stuart added an amusing footnote to this dramatic letter. She said that she believed now the Master of Gray to be a traitor to her cause, and that she would not trust him hereafter!' He laughed lightly. 'How misguided are women!' And nodding, he opened the door and passed out.

For a long moment there was silence in that room. David stared at his brother. Presently Patrick met his gaze, and sighed.

'Ah, me – you see how I am misjudged, Davy!'

'Are you, Patrick?' That was but a husky whisper.

'Need you ask?' There was sorrowful reproach in the other's melodious voice. 'You know the risks that I took for her. All that I have done, as you know also, I have done in her best interests. But . . can she see it, poor lady? I do not blame her, mark you, shut up there, cut off from her friends, from guidance and advice. But it is . . . hard.'

'Are you so sure, Patrick? So sure of your judgment? Her best interests, you say. Can you be so certain? So much surer than Mary herself? Do you never doubt yourself, man?'

317

'I leave the doubting to you, Davy – who have a talent for it! Myself, I use the wits the good God has given me.'

'Aye. But once you told me that, since most men are blinded by prejudice, and fettered by beliefs and misconceptions of religion and honour, a man who keeps his wits unfettered may go far, rise high on the weakness of others. You have gone far, brother, risen high by those wits God gave you. But . . . does the cost to others count with you? What of the cost to Mary, of your best interests for her? I have doubted often, yes – but have not turned my doubts into action. It may be that I have been weak. I have stood by and seen you undermine and betray much and many, in the name of clear wits and . . . '

'Have a watch what you say brother!' Patrick interposed, half-rising.

'That is what I am doing, yes,' David went on levelly, holding the other's eyes. 'I am warning you, Patrick. If ever I come to believe that you have betrayed Mary of Scotland, I will stand by no longer. I will act, Patrick – act! Forget you *are* my brother. Believe me, brother, you would never betray another! You have it?'

The other moistened his lips. 'Are you crazed, man?' he got out. 'What . . . what fool's talk is this, of betrayal? You know not what you say.'

'I may be a fool, Patrick – as well as weak. Indeed, I often judge that I am. But I mean what I say.' Heavily David spoke. 'See that you do not forget it.'

Patrick's glance fell before his brother's burning regard. He began to write.

That same night a courier rode into Edinburgh with other news for Patrick Gray – news which affected the man more notably than his brother had ever seen before. Sir Philip Sidney was dead. He had died heroically, of wounds, on the battlefield of Zutphen, on an expedition to aid the Protestant Netherlands. Dying, he had sent a message to Patrick, with certain of his unpublished poems.

Patrick wept. 'War!' he cried. 'War and bloody strife! The folly of it – oh, the damnable folly! It plucks the flowers and leaves the nettles to flourish! There lies the finest flower of this age, rotting on a foreign field . . . '

David had never known Patrick so moved, so hurt, so affected by anything. He had not realised how deeply he had felt for Sidney, that their friendship had been more than the mutual appreciation of two able minds. Himself he sorrowed now for his brother's pain and sorrow. But something in him was glad also – glad. For he had begun to fear that Patrick was perhaps incapable of such love towards any. He knew a great relief in this proof that he was wrong. Perhaps he was wrong in other matters also?

Chapter Twenty-six

DAVID rode hard and alone down the winding valley of the Gala Water, with the green rounded hills of the Borderland crowding in on every side. His body and his senses rejoiced in the freedom and exercise of it all, the scents of broom and pine and raw red earth, the colours of golden gorse, emerald bog and sparkling water under a cloud-flecked sky, the sounds of the trilling curlews, the screaming peewits and the baaing sheep. After the long months cooped up in Edinburgh, buried amongst parchments and books, this headlong riding represented a welcome release.

His mind was preoccupied with anxiety, however, and on a subject very close to his heart – Mary the Queen. The day before, a message brought by urgent courier from one of Patrick's trusted informants in London, had revealed that Walsingham had uncovered a new Catholic plot which was to involve the assassination of Elizabeth and the placing of Mary upon her throne – a plot for which plans were well advanced, the details revealed by the torture of a suspect. The English Parliament, informed, had exploded into great wrath, and amongst other measures, had demanded the immediate bringing to trial of Mary herself on a charge of treason. How one monarch could be charged with treason against another monarch was not explained – but the situation was fraught with danger for Mary, obviously. She had been moved once more, from Tutbury to Chartley, and was now little better than a felon in a cell. Representation on her behalf, action of some sort, was urgently necessary.

Unfortunately, the King and Arran, with much of the Court, had a few days before gone to hunt in Ettrick Forest, deep in the Borders, lodging at the Castle of Newark. For some unexplained reason, two days later, Patrick had followed them thither, which was not his usual practice, leaving David behind to deal with many unresolved matters. Hence the latter's hurried dash after his brother. At an hour's notice he had set out, and got as far as Borthwick that same night.

What Patrick might do, what the King might be able to do, in the circumstances, David did not know. But assuredly something must be attempted, some forceful representations made to Elizabeth. She wanted this Protestant alliance; pressure could be exerted over that, surely?

It was early evening before David reached Newark, in the fair valley of Yarrow – only to find that Patrick was elsewhere. The King was there, and most of his following, though Arran was absent too. He had gone to Ferniehirst Castle, near Jedburgh, where the laird was his close friend Andrew Kerr, Scots Warden of the Middle March. The seasonal formal meeting of the English and Scots Wardens of the Border Marches was to take place in two days' time, when all current Border disputes were discussed and if possible resolved, and it was presumed that Arran had gone to talk over certain outstanding issues beforehand. It was also presumed that the Master of Gray had followed him to Ferniehirst.

Though tired, after borrowing a fresh horse David set off again forthwith, cursing these delays which might mean much to his trapped and threatened Queen. He headed southeastwards now, over into the vale of Ettrick and on beyond, climbing into high ground, till the late summer darkness enfolded him and he slept briefly at the remote upland village of Ashkirk. Off early in the morning, once more, he rode through empty hills of grass and gorse, down to the great trough of Teviotdale at Denholm-on-the-Green, to turn eastwards, under the graceful peak of Ruberslaw, through the Turnbull country. He reached Ferniehirst's grey strength soon after mid-day.

Once again he was disappointed. Patrick was not here either, had never been here. Arran he saw, with Kerr and some of his cronies, and a new light-o'-love, the Lady Hester Murray. But the Master of Gray was neither present nor expected.

At a loss, David racked his brains. Where could his brother have gone? What errand had he been on? Where might he look for him now amidst these green hills, with his fateful tidings? He had no pointer to guide him, save for the fact that his brother had indeed called at Newark and on leaving there had been assumed to be coming here to Ferniehirst. Which meant that at least he must have started by turning in a south-easterly direction. So Patrick must have intended to turn up the Ettrick valley, or else cross over into Teviotdale as he himself had done. The Ettrick led nowhere, save by a high and difficult pass into Eskdale and the west; if Patrick had wanted to go in that direction, surely he would have taken the shorter and easier route up Yarrow? So the chances were that it was Tevoit. Back whence he had come David turned his horse.

It was late afternoon when, at Denholm again, after asking fruitlessly at tower and cot-house all the way up, the village blacksmith gave him what might be the clue that he sought. The man knew nothing about the Master of Gray, but Logan of Restalrig and a small troop had stopped at his smiddy the previous afternoon, with a horse that had cast its shoe. To David's eager description of his brother, the man had nodded and agreed that there had been a Frenchified gentleman with Logan – who was of course well-known in the Borders. They had left Denholm for the south, by the drove road which led through Rule Water.

And now David drove his jaded mount fast and free. The road before him plunged deep into the wild Cheviots, which constituted the Border between Scotland and England. Only two routes led out of Rule Water – both to high passes into England. One, to the east, was the well-known passage of the Redeswire, on Carter Fell; the other, to the west, was the lonely pass of the Deadwater, at the head of Tyne.

At a tumbledown herd's cabin where the drove-roads forked, many miles on, the savage-looking occupant admitted to David that a party of riders had taken the route to Deadwater early that morning.

What in Heaven's name brought Patrick to these lonely fastnesses? And in Robert Logan's company. When Restalrig came on the scene, violent action of some kind usually followed.

His route, the only route, now lay along an ancient Roman road, ever climbing across the desolate uplands which heaped themselves in heathery billows around the mass of mighty Peel Fell. This was the Debatable Land, where no king ruled, unless he be an Armstrong or a Turnbull chief, and the only law was that of cold steel and hot blood. Men seldom rode this country alone, and David loosened his sword in its scabbard uneasily.

Darkness overtook him high on the swelling flank of Peel Fell, but he still pressed on, the Roman road a clear straight gash in the shadowy hillside before him. And halfway down the long slope beyond, into the valley of the infant Tyne, he saw the red gleam of camp-fires. Weary horse and rider made for them, thankful, but wary also.

David was challenged fiercely by a heavily-armed sentinel while still some distance from the fires, and relievedly discovered the man to be none other than the dark mosstrooper who had once helped release a bound stag on the heights of

Ruthven in far Perthshire. Companionably he clapped the visitor's drooping shoulder, and brought him stumbling to the circle of the firelight.

Perhaps a score of men lay asleep, wrapped in cloaks and plaids. But around the fire a group still sat, in talk. His brother was there, and Logan. It was not at them, however, that David stared, but at the Lord Home, the Earl of Mar, the Earl of Bothwell, and – yes, the Master of Glamis.

The mosstrooper had not been the only link with Ruthven.

'Lord – Davy! What . . . what in the fiend's name is the meaning of this?' Patrick cried, starting up, and less than welcoming.

David felt like asking the same question. 'I have a message,' he said. 'An important message. On a private matter.' He said no more, for these men were the Queen's enemies. They looked at him suspiciously, inimically.

Patrick frowned, shrugged, and then bowed to his companions round the fire. 'Gentlemen – if you will excuse me . . . ?'

Patrick listened to his brother's tidings almost impatiently. As David stressed the seriousness of the Queen's case, the other interrupted.

'Yes, yes, man – but there is no need to come running after me with it, thus. She has brought it on herself. It can wait . . . '

'It cannot wait, Patrick, I tell you, the English Parliament is demanding her trial, for treason. Allow them to start that, and no protests will avail anything – for they must finish the business or be made to look fools. This folly must be stopped before it starts.'

'How think you that *I* am to stop it? Is their Parliament to listen to me? Halt their courses because I forbid it? What can I do? Or even the King?'

'You can do much – you *and* the King. I think. You have the means, in this alliance. You yourself negotiated its terms. Elizabeth wants it, and so no doubt does her Parliament. Send swift word that Scotland cannot proceed with it whilst her Queen is unlawfully charged with a treason which she could not commit . . . '

'But, Lord – she probably *was* deep in this plot! She has been in many another.'

'Mary would never countenance the assassination of Elizabeth. But even so – !'

'She countenanced the assassination of her own husband, Darnley!' Patrick asserted grimly.

323

'That was never proved. Do you credit the words of dastards like Morton and Archie Douglas? But that is not the issue, Patrick. Can the crowned monarch of one realm be accused of treason against that of another? It is impossible. Indeed, how can a king or a queen commit treason, at all? Treason is for subjects. This trial would be no trial, but a savagery. A savagery against a poor, defenceless lady. And an insult to Scotland, also.'

'Ah well, Davy – I will think of it. Consider the matter . . .'

David gripped the other's arm. 'Brother, you will do more than that!' he said, low-voiced, tense. 'And swiftly. You can and you will! You recollect what I said yon time . . . ?'

'Mary Stuart has smitten you crazy, man!'

'Call it that, if you will. But act, Patrick. For Mary. Or, in my own way *I* will act for her! And forthwith.'

His brother sighed, and shrugged that one shoulder. 'Very well. I should have done what I could anyway, of course . . . but without these dramatics! Now – these lords are becoming restive. I must go back to them. Tell them something to keep them quiet. But not this, of Mary . . .'

'No – for these are no friends of the Queen's! These indeed are her enemies. The King's enemies, too – the men who held him fast at Ruthven. You keep strange company, I think, Patrick, for one of the King's ministers? And a strange meeting-place!'

'Your comments on the matter must await another occasion, Davy,' his brother declared coolly. 'Meantime, I would prefer that you hold your tongue before them.'

'You need not fear – I wish no dealings with them. My wonder is that *you* do. The last time I saw the Master of Glamis, both of you had swords in your hands!'

'That was long ago – and some of us at least have learned some wisdom since then! These men are not the King's enemies. Indeed, they may be more than useful in the King's service. We want our Scotland united, do we not? How else shall the realm flourish? I could not speak with them, save thus in secret and just over the English march, for Arran would have the heads off each of them if he could.'

'Did not Elizabeth agree to remove these lords deep into her own country? It would seem that she failed in her under-taking . . .'

'Enough, man! I tell you, another time.' Patrick took a pace away, and then paused. 'How did you find me here?' he asked, of a sudden thought. 'None could have told you . . . ?'

'Say that I smelt you out. I have a good nose for some things, brother! But do not let me keep you from . . . your friends!'

David, with arrears of sleep to make up, did not awake next morning until Patrick roused him with the word that they would be off shortly. By which time the exiled lords had disappeared. The mist-shrouded desolate hills of the watershed where Tynedale and Liddesdale were born effectually kept their secret.

Patrick was almost his usual unruffled sunny self this morning. Indeed he was never the man to bear a grudge or to sulk, and David, less admirable in this respect, as usual grew to feel himself to be in the wrong, somehow. Riding north again, between the boisterously hearty Logan and his smiling brother, he contributed little to the good company.

Where the drove roads joined, near the headwaters of Rule and Jed, the company turned to the right, eastwards. To David's prompt query, it was pointed out that this was the way to Ferniehirst. Patrick required a word with Arran, and the Chancellor was reliably reported to be at present keeping company with Dand Kerr of Ferniehirst. To David's remonstrance that it was the King whom they should be hastening to see, on Mary's behalf, Patrick countered that James could be persuaded to any suitable course of action much more readily than could his Chancellor; and since any effective move would require the Council's backing, it was only elementary common sense to convince its President first.

When, at the lonely upland peel-tower and church of Southdean, they turned still further back into the south, to face the great hills again, David fretted. His brother explained patiently that, since this was the day of the half-yearly meeting between the Scots and English Wardens of the Marches, and Arran was almost certain to accompany Kerr the Scots Warden to the assembly place at the Redeswire, they would save time by seeking him there rather than awaiting him at Ferniehirst Castle. This, of course, sounded true enough. Perhaps David Gray was hopelessly suspicious by nature.

It was nearly noon before, climbing the long, long flank of Carter Fell, their track brought them out on to the level tract of tussocky grassland, high on the very roof of the Debatable Land where the River Rede grew out of a bog, and where tradition ordained the meeting of the two countries' representatives. Already the greensward was astir with men, and while from a distance it seemed no more than a milling crowd of men, horses and banners, closer inspection revealed that, though there was some small fraternisation, on the whole a long narrow gap split the two companies, so that one faced south and the other north.

The Earl of Arran was easily found, his banner fluttering near that of Kerr and indeed just opposite that of Sir John Foster the English Warden. As the newcomers rode up, the two Wardens were sitting their horses a few yards apart, and hearing the case of one Heron, an Englishman, who was claiming the return of certain cattle lifted from his land by a Turnbull of Rulehead; he was not objecting to the principle of cattle-reiving, since this was normal Border usage, but asserting that although he had paid an appropriate mail for his beasts' return, Turnbull had in fact retained the cattle. Turnbull, for his part, vowed that he had never received the mail and Heron's emissary must have stolen it. This hundrum case, of which no doubt there would be a score of others similar, was exciting very little attention from the throng of lairds, squires, farmers, mosstroopers and men-at-arms, though there was nevertheless a general watchful tension on all hands, for these brief truces on the Border by no means always passed off without violence, and only ten years before, on this same venue, a full-scale battle had developed, with numerous slain on both sides, known as the Raid of the Redeswire.

Patrick went to talk to Arran, Logan found numerous cronies of his own, and David, still starved of sleep, lay down amongst the tussocks a little clear of the crowd – and did not remain awake for more than a few seconds.

For how long he slept he did not know. He was awakened by a great hullabaloo – bawling, cursing, the clash of steel and the neighing of horses. Everywhere around him men were running, drawing swords and whingers as they ran, some already mounted, some afoot.

Rubbing his eyes, David stared. It seemed to be a general mêlée. The two Wardens were in the middle of it, the English one at least shouting, gesticulating, seeking to order his men back, but with little apparent success. Any spark was enough to cause a conflagration on such an occasion. The whistle of an arrow winging past his head and plunging into the soft ground behind with a phut, jerked David out of his dazed preoccupation. He ran for his horse nearby, and vaulted into the saddle.

Mounted, he could see better. Though a lot of swords were drawn, the actual fighting seemed to be confined mainly to a comparatively small group. In towards the centre of this Sir

John Foster, his standard-bearer at his side, was fighting his way, beating right and left with the flat of his own sword, ordering men apart. Kerr of Ferniehirst, however, his Scots counterpart, appeared less anxious to intervene, sitting his horse further back, grim-faced. Blood was already flowing. David counted three men squirming on the grass, transfixed by long-shafted arrows – all on the Scots side.

He looked about for Patrick, but could not see him amongst the tossing plumes, rearing horses and brandished swords and lances. Logan, he thought – Logan was the man to stop this, if he would, with his tough mosstroopers and strong Border reputation. Where was Logan . . . ?

Anxiously he searched for his brother and their cousin. He saw Arran, looking alarmed, shouting something to Kerr, and that man at length plunging forward with his bodyguard of men-at-arms to the aid of the English Warden. He saw Scott of Harden in the thick of it, striving to drive back his own folk. And suddenly, in the press of the English, he glimpsed another face that he knew and that gave him pause – that of Home of Bonkyldean. He had seen this man only the night before, at Patrick's camp, one of the exiled Lord Home's lairds and companions. What was he doing on the wrong side of this scuffle – and with blood on his upraised sword?

Then David perceived Patrick and Logan, with the latter's men in a solid phalanx, boring their way into the mêlée, shouting 'A Logan! A Logan!' and scattering men like chaff on every side. David spurred to join them, his sheathed sword drawn. Scot and Englishman alike they beat aside lustily, and none might penetrate their tight spearhead formation. These were the experts.

This vigorous if belated intervention, added to the efforts of Foster and Kerr and Harden, turned the tide. Indeed, in a few hectic minutes it was all over. Angry men were pressed back to their own sides of the score in the turf that marked the actual Border-line, nursing their wounds, shaking their fists, and hurling bloody threats. But these were mere echoes; the storm was past.

What had provoked it, nobody seemed to know for sure. There were half-a-dozen wrathful assertions. The Scots were unanimous that it was amongst their ranks that men had fallen first – shot by unheralded English arrows. Sir John Foster denied this, swearing that his friend, the Lord Russell, had been the first to fall, quite close to his side. And, sure enough, amongst the actually few slain lay the handsome son of the Earl of Bedford, with an arrow projecting from between his shoulder-blades. David, had his opinion been asked, would have said that he had been shot from behind, whilst facing the north.

By mutual consent the meeting broke up without more ado, even though its business was by no means finished; the atmosphere was no longer conducive to negotiation and sweet reasonableness. Not that anyone took the disturbance seriously, for on the Borders violence was the rule rather than the exception. It was just unfortunate that amongst the casualities should have been an earl's son, all agreed.

Just how unfortunate that fact was, few however could have guessed.

David himself, two days later, copied out the letter to be sent to Elizabeth, signed by James, protesting in dignified terms at the proposed trial of the Queen of Scots, insisting upon the impossibility of a charge of treason being levelled against a crowned monarch, and indicating that unfortunately, whilst any suggestion of such a trial remained, the Scots Privy Council would most assuredly refuse to consider the ratification of the proposed Protestant alliance. David indeed actually adjusted some of the wording himself, to his brother's mild amusement, for the King's signature, and helped impressively to seal and despatch by urgent courier the precious document. He did not see, however, the private letter which Patrick sent by the same courier.

It was while they awaited an answer from Elizabeth, David at least with much anxiety, that a quite different storm burst upon the Scottish Court from the south, all unexpectedly – at all events, once again, to David Gray, as to others much more loftily-placed. It came in the form of a furious letter from Elizabeth, a second from the Lord Burleigh, and vehement supporting representations from the English ambassador on the instructions of Walsingham. Like an explosion it rocked Edinburgh.

The Queen of England was enraged. One of her most gallant and favoured subjects, the excellent Lord Russell, had been savagely and barbarously done to death, whilst on an official mission and on English soil, by the minions of the Earl of Arran. Arran had indeed been present at the dastardly outrage. Assuredly nothing of the sort could have occurred in the presence of the Scottish Chancellor without his approval and instigation. Arran was therefore the murderer of one of the Queen's most beloved friends. She demanded forthwith that he be handed over to her Governor of Berwick, to stand immediate trial for his crime.

To say that James was appalled by this extraordinary communication, is to put it mildly. The young King indeed took to his bed, and at first refused to see anyone, Arran included. For Burleigh's supporting letter left no doubts as to the seriousness with which the matter was viewed in London, though nobody in Scotland had ever heard of Lord Russell being prominent at the English Court. Burleigh, repeating the Queen's charges, announced that should her demands anent the Earl of Arran not be met immediately, James's pension would cease, all diplomatic relations would be broken off, a punitive expedition would be despatched to the Border, and a Bill would be rushed through Parliament debarring James from any possibility of the succession to the English throne.

The King turned his face to the wall, and wept.

Well might Arran fume and curse and plead, mystified as he was wrathful. James would not hear him. The younger man was struck in his most vulnerable spot – his overmastering ambition for the dual throne of England and Scotland. He would hear nobody indeed, shutting himself away, while his Court wondered and questioned and debated. Never had a storm arisen out of so small a cloud. Border incidents were an everyday occurrence, and many more prominent men than this Bedford heir had died in them. What did this mean? And what would be the outcome? It was inconceivable that the King could hand over his Lord Chancellor and favourite to an English trial . . .

Yet, when at last a puffy-eyed, nervous and stammering James was brought to the point of granting the audience that the English ambassador demanded, it was on this impossible condition that Wotton insisted. Arran and Kerr of Ferniehirst must be delivered up, he declared. His instructions were adamant. James gabbled and shrilled and choked. Wotton would not budge – and reiterated the consequences. The English Parliament had never been so anti-Scots, he pointed out, especially with the other matter of Mary Stuart's plot and the threat of assassination against Elizabeth. They would debar the Scots succession without any urging from the Queen; indeed, it would undoubtedly require Elizabeth's active intervention on his behalf to save his claim now.

James's tears overflowed again. He wailed that he would that all the lords of his Borders were dead and the fine Lord Russell alive again.

It was the Master of Gray who, presently, suggested a compromise. While it was unthinkable that my Lord of Arran should be handed over to the Governor of Berwick like some English renegade, it might be advisable and acceptable that His Grace should confine him in some assured stronghold where he could be held secure until this unfortunate business was suitably adjusted and resolved to the satisfaction of all parties . . .

'Yes, yes,' James cried, clutching at a straw. Assuredly, that was the solution. His good sister Elizabeth would surely be satisfied with that! Captain Jamie should be shut up, at once. Let it be seen to. In St. Andrews Castle for sure. It was the strongest. Aye, right away. He would send a letter to Her Grace of England – a special envoy – explaining the matter. Ferniehirst should be punished, of course – hanged.

Wotton, professing serious doubts, withdrew on Patrick's pressing his arm.

And so, ridiculously, fantastically, for one of the few crimes that he had not committed, fell Captain James Stewart, Earl of Arran. Or commenced his fall, for his was a somewhat prolonged descent. He was immured in St. Andrews Castle, deprived of his high offices, and James mourned for him as though dead – but not quite as he had mourned for Esmé Stuart. And the Master of Gray ruled in his stead – though modestly he refused the style and title of Lord High Chancellor. He did however preside over the meetings of the Privy Council, even though in a determinedly unofficial and temporary capacity. No jealous earls or lords might say that Patrick Gray thrust himself into the highest office under the Crown.

Elizabeth Tudor informed her Parliament that she could not countenance the public trial of her erring sister Mary Stuart – meantime. But an Act passed, naming as liable to summary execution not only all who plotted against her life but those in favour of whom the plots were made, would be a sensible and just precaution. The Act was passed with acclamation.

Bishop Davidson announced to Patrick that he was now a free man. The Kirk, after due and devout consideration, had decided that he had in fact never been married at all to Elizabeth Lyon.

Chapter Twenty-seven

IT was always difficult to know whether there was some sort of large-scale entertainment going on in the Earl of Orkney's apartments at Holyroodhouse, or whether it was a mere domestic evening. Orkney was so prolific of progeny and so fond of a multiplicity of female company – as indeed were his sons – that he had always sufficient members of his own establishment respectably to fill a ballroom; moreover, apart from Marie, who was so out-of-type as scarcely to seem to belong to the same family, they were all of such hearty, lusty and extrovert nature that it was seldom indeed that their quarters did not sound as though either a rout or a rape was in full progress. More dull and sober members of the royal household had long given up complaining; only solitary confinement, it had been ascertained, would change the King's uncle.

Patrick was faced with the usual problem as he strolled round Orkney's eastern wing of the palace in the September dusk. Laughter, shouting and skirling, it seemed, issued from every window. Yet it was unlikely, surely, that here was an invited company, for would anybody at Court hold such a function without seeking the exalted company of the acting Chancellor, especially Orkney who had never made any secret of his designs upon the Master of Gray as a prospective son-in-law?

Patrick slipped in through a side door, looking for a servant to ask the Lady Marie's whereabouts. He could find none; Orkney's servants tended to take after their master. One room from which he heard voices, on his opening the door, was revealed to contain two persons grovelling on the floor in extra-ordinary and vigorous embrace. Another he did not trouble to look into, the sound of a woman's giggles and screeches being sufficiently informative. These were the servants' quarters. He mounted the first stairway that he came to, and was promptly all but knocked over by a laughing, uproarious, stumbling trio, a young girl in front, dishevelled and all but naked to the waist, one young man behind grasping her flowing red hair and another her torn chemise. One of the gallants, Patrick recognised as a son of Orkney's; probably the other was, also. Presumably they would not be disposed, meantime, to guide him to their sister.

Not for the first time, Patrick asked himself how in the name of all that was wonderful, Marie Stewart had managed to grow up such as she was in this atmosphere.

By following the music to its source in a long picture-hung gallery, he ran Orkney himself to earth – but not just as he expected. It was the Earl indeed who was doing the fiddling, sitting at a lengthy and almost empty table of broken meats and spilt wine, over which one or two figures still sprawled. Patrick had not realised that the man had this attribute. Though obviously drunk, he was leaning back, glazed eyes fixed on a frowning painting of King Alexander the Second, and playing the instrument with great pathos and sweetness. One of his current young women leaned against his shoulder, despite her clothing managing to look extraordinarily innocent because she was asleep, and further down the table an older woman beat solemn time to the music with a slopping goblet of wine. Marie was not there. Indeed, the only other sign of life was a large wolfhound which methodically moved up the table, forepaws on the board, selectively clearing the various platters of their débris.

It was in the garden that Patrick eventually found Marie, in an arbour – and with a companion. Though the pair were only sitting on a seat together, he was profoundly shocked – infinitely more so than by any of the scenes that had presented themselves within the house. He knew the fellow – a George Ogilvie, brother to the sister's husband in Glen Prosen in Angus. He had been hanging around the Court for a while . . . with this as attraction?

'I beg your pardon,' Patrick announced, coldly. 'I had not realised that you were thus engaged. I will retire.'

'Why, Patrick, there is no need,' Marie assured. 'It is good to see you. We are but seldom so honoured, these days. You are so important a figure . . .'

'Nevertheless, I will await another occasion, I think. With your ladyship's permission!'

At his tone, she raised her fine brows, and then smiled. 'Was it myself, then, that you came to see? Or Mr. Ogilvie?'

'I can conceive of no subject which I would wish to discuss with . . . this gentleman,' he answered. Ogilvie, on perceiving the newcomer's identity, had started up.

332

'I . . . I shall be off, Marie,' he faltered. 'A good night to you. And to you, sir.'

'No, no, George. Do not go . . .'

Ogilvie went, nevertheless.

For a while there was silence. Patrick paced to and fro in front of Marie's seat.

'If it is exercise that you came here for, Patrick, let us walk, for sweet mercy's sake!' the young woman said, a little tartly for her, rising.

He frowned, and halted. 'Not so,' he said. 'Unless you are tired of sitting? Perhaps you have been at it overlong? Perhaps you are chilled, now that he is gone?'

Unspeaking, she looked at him in the gloom.

'It may be that I should be grateful that at least you are but sitting, and not lying, as are most of your peculiar family, it seems! This Ogilvie – he is not lacking in the necessary virility, I hope?'

'Patrick – George Ogilvie is my sister's good-brother – and my good friend,' Marie said evenly. 'I would ask that you speak honestly of him in my company . . . if not of myself!'

'Of course, of course, my dear – I am all respect! My only hope is that I have not ruined your evening!'

'You are in a fair way to doing so, sir, I think,' she gave back. 'May I ask, had you any other purpose in your visit?'

'Nothing that need give you a moment's concern, no! Nothing that in the circumstances could do other than amuse you, Marie. I did but come once more to ask if you would marry me. So wearisome an errand, I must admit.'

She turned her head away, biting her lip.

'Undoubtedly I should have sent you warning. It is thoughtless to descend upon a lady unawares! Another time, I shall remember.'

'Do,' she said swiftly. 'As no doubt you do for any of your other women – the Lady Hartrigge . . . Eupham Erskine . . . Madame de Courcelles . . . or even Elizabeth Arran – though perhaps *she* does not require warning! We all deserve a like courtesy, surely?' She took a deep breath. 'Or is it too much to ask, now that you have become so great a man, so busy? Master of all Scotland, indeed – and therefore, of course, of all its women!'

Quite suddenly Patrick laughed – and amusedly, not sourly, harshly. 'Lord, what a fool you are, Marie!' he declared. 'And myself also. Like bairns, we are!'

'A bairn – the great Lord High Chancellor of the Realm! The Master of the King's Wardrobe . . .'

'Aye, there you have it! Think what you have just said, girl. Does it not sound strange in your own ears? For I am *not* the Chancellor, but I *am* the Master of the Wardrobe! There is a great difference, is there not? I could be the Chancellor – yes. I act the part, for the moment. But I do not seek to be the master of Scotland, see you – merely of the royal wardrobe! James has offered me an earldom, but I have refused it. I am well content to be Master of Gray. I do not seek any of these things. Aye, the Wardrobe suits me very well!'

She turned to look at him. 'What signifies the name?' she asked. 'You *are* the master of Scotland. You have made yourself that – and by no accident, I think. Does it matter what they call you, so long as all men do what you tell them? Even the King?'

'You dream, Marie – you dream!'

'It is true. Has not James shut up even Arran at your behest – his own favourite and familiar?'

'Only as a gesture towards Elizabeth.'

She said nothing.

Patrick sighed. 'I would, at least, that the women did as I told them – one woman in particular!'

'Enough do, I believe, to keep you from . . . discomfort!' She looked away again. 'And yet you . . . you deny me even George Ogilvie!'

It was the man's turn to be silent. He began to pace the garden path, and quite naturally she fell into step beside him.

'George tells me,' she went on, in another voice, 'that the Master of Glamis is back in Angus, at his castle of Aldbar. That my lord Bothwell has been seen in Dundee, and the Earl of Mar is said to be on Donside. None of them without your knowledge, I am sure?'

'Your George would seem to be notably well informed for a heather lairdling!'

'He says that the whole north country buzzes with it. All the Ruthven lords are back – and to some purpose, no doubt.'

'And does your knowledgeable Ogilvie suggest what these purposes may be?'

'He says – he but repeats the clash of the countryside – that it is *your* doing, Patrick. That you have brought them back, in order to constrain the King . . . without your hand seeming to appear.'

'Lord, was ever a man so detracted! Whatever ill is done in Scotland, it must be my doing, for some deep and sinister motive! And do you believe all this, Marie?'

'I do not know. I have long since given up trying to know what to believe of you, Patrick. Save that you will go your own gait, always.'

'And would have you go it with me, my dear. That, too, you know.'

'George Ogilvie notwithstanding?'

He shrugged. 'As you say, George Ogilvie, or the Devil himself, notwithstanding!'

'But this . . . this is most generous of you!' she exclaimed, though her voice broke a little. 'Am I to be almost as privileged as you are? Permitted the magnificent freedom of a man, plucking fruit by the way where I will?'

'Aye,' he said, heavily for Patrick Gray. 'If needs be. If that is how you would have it. For have *you* I must, Marie.' Wryly he smiled. 'You see how much means your talk of me being master of all!'

She was moved – but hardened herself. 'You conceive this as the only way to master me, perhaps?'

'I think that I shall never master you. I do not know that I wish to. Only to marry you, woman – and that is different.'

'Yes, Patrick, marriage is different, as you say. But you know my views on marriage, to be sure.'

'Aye. That is why I came here with some hopes tonight, Marie. Perhaps foolishly. But tonight I am a free man – save for *your* toils. Today, I had word that my marriage to Elizabeth Lyon is no more.'

He heard the catch in her breath, as she turned to him. 'Patrick!'

'Aye. Or better than no more – that it has never been. It is annulled, as void and invalid.'

'Annulled . . . ?'

'The Kirk, in its wisdom, finds this the better course. And who am I to question it? Moreover, I think that you will take it kinder than a divorcement . . .'

'Oh, yes, yes! I do! I do! Patrick – you did not tell me . . . ! This is . . .'

'You are happy, my dear?'

'Of course. Of course. Can you doubt it?'

'Then . . . does it mean . . . can I believe . . . that you will indeed wed me now? At last, my love?'

335

Brokenly she laughed. 'I cannot see . . . how I can refuse, any more! Can you?' Abruptly she swung round, to bury her face against his chest, clutching him convulsively. 'Oh, Patrick! It has been so long! A very lifetime. I can hardly understand it. That at last there is nothing to stand between us . . .'

'Save the Master of Gray?' he asked, holding her fast. 'This . . . monster who must rule Scotland and all men! The satyr who uses all to serve his own wicked ends?'

She looked up at him. 'Even he does not stand between us,' she said. 'Perhaps he should. Perhaps I am a fool, weak, sinful. But I love you, Patrick – all of you, the good and the bad. I am not so very good, my own self, And I will wed you as you are. Once I told you that, a free man, I would give you an honest answer. There you have it.'

'My beloved! And . . . your door that was to stand wide open for me, one day?'

She raised a hand to his hair. 'It stands open, my heart. I could not hold it shut, any longer. I am but a weak woman. But . . . I would esteem you the more if you would bear with me, and wait . . . a little longer. Until we are wed. Or is that too much to ask of the Master of Gray?'

He drew a long breath. 'I' faith, Marie Stewart, you drive a hard bargain! Is life with you going to be this way, always?'

'I think not, Patrick. But . . . if it is?'

'I will wed you, just the same – God help me!'

They were married on a grey November day, with great pomp and ceremony, at Holyroodhouse, in the presence of the King – who indeed gave away his cousin – and all the great ones of the land. Mariota saw her father there, for the first time since Patrick's earlier marriage; the Bishop was prepared to be affable, but his daughter was not.

James once more suggested that to celebrate the occasion he should make the happy couple earl and countess, but again Patrick declined. He was the Master of Gray. Let that stand. One day, God being merciful, he would succeed his father as sixth Lord Gray; until then he would serve his King very well as he was. He did, however accept the Commendatorship of the prosperous Priory of Culross as a small mark of his monarch's esteem – which at £5000 Scots a year, was always a help to a man taking on the burdens of matrimony.

Actually, Patrick had another and personal request to put to the King, that he humbly ventured to suggest might fittingly mark this joyful occasion. He pleaded that James might, of his royal goodness and clemency, see fit to transfer the unfortunate Earl of Arran from durance vile in St. Andrews Castle, to less rigorous ward in his own house of Kinneil – under due and strict guard, of course. He had had a word with Wotton on the subject, and he agreed with him that Queen Elizabeth was not likely at this stage to differentiate between the two forms of imprisonment. His Majesty was of course graciously, indeed eagerly, pleased to accede to this generous request on the part of the bridegroom. Indeed, everybody was pleased – fond monarch; Arran, who had himself written to Patrick suggesting the move and offering as inducement to his friend the great and influential Commendatorship of Dunfermline, the wealthiest church lands in all Scotland, which he had held for some time; and the returned Ruthven lords, who now knew where they could lay hands on Arran's person, that had been hitherto safe from them behind the impregnable walls of St. Andrews Castle.

Altogether it was an auspicious wedding-day, even though somewhat less dramatically celebrated than had been its predecessor eleven years before.

Patrick Gray had now reached the mature age of twenty-seven years. The bridal pair were still delectably engaged in the discovery of each other, in one of the remoter Gray castles of northern Perthshire, when the reunited and assembled Ruthven lords, with a following of almost eight thousand men, struck without warning at Stirling, where James was in residence. The move was well planned, the royal defence half-hearted in the extreme, the town fell, and the great castle surrendered with scarcely a blow struck. James, in dire agitation, and vowing that this could never have happened had his good Master Patrick been on hand, nevertheless found that his former harsh captors had adopted a new attitude towards him. Instead of hectoring and bullying, they knelt at his feet, swearing devotion and allegiance, and assured him that only His Grace's true good and the weal of the realm had moved them to act thus drastically in order to remove the traitors and scoundrels with whom the unprincipled Arran had surrounded his liege lord. For themselves they had no claims nor ambitions – only the triumph of the true Protestant faith and the King's gracious goodwill. In token of which they did not claim any hand in the government for themselves, suggesting instead that James chose some faithful, well-tried and experienced minister of his own whom his loyal Reformed subjects might support and serve in

337

the interests of all Scotland – for instance, the Master of Gray, if he could be persuaded to exchange his present blissful dalliance for the burden of state affairs.

Nothing loth and mightily relieved, James sent forthwith for the innocent Master of Gray with pleas, indeed imperative royal commands, to come quickly and take control of the rudderless ship of state.

Arran, warned, bolted from Kinneil, the royal guards conveniently looking the other way, and fled the country.

Patrick sighed, complained that they might at least leave a man alone to his nuptial exercises – and returned to duty, resolutely refusing to admit that he was now indisputably the master of Scotland, even to his wife.

Happy Scotland, that seldom in her long history can have known a ruler at once so able and so devoid of personal ambition.

Chapter Twenty-eight

FOR the best part of a good, peaceful and prosperous year, that of our Lord 1586, Patrick Gray largely controlled the destinies of his native land – whatever the names and titles of the nominees who carried out his policies, for he still rigidly refused the office of Chancellor, or indeed any other save that of simple Master of the King's Wardrobe, the holding of which seemed to tickle his fancy. For that year, the bribery of underlings all but faded from the life of Scotland; corruption, in the major courts at least, became a rarity; and the King's law, however uncertain and curious, prevailed in all but the wildest Borders and remoter Highlands. For one year even the great lords held their hands, sheathed their swords, and waited. For one bare year.

Then on the fifth of August, Walsingham reached out his long arm and arrested Anthony Babington, in Harrow Woods, and the peace of Scotland, the *pax Patricius!* was shattered quite.

Babington was a hot-blooded young Derbyshire squire and a Catholic. In concert with some companions of like outlook, he devised one more project for the dethroning of Elizabeth, the elevation of Mary in her place, and the re-establishment of the True Faith in England and Scotland. Unfortunately perhaps, he was more effective than most of his predecessors, more thorough-going and vigorous. His plans were not in the clouds, but realities. Unfortunately, too, he communicated the gist of them, by letter, to Mary the Queen, though taking the precaution to sign them with a cipher.

Warned, through Giffard the Jesuit counter-spy, Walsingham laid hands on Father Ballard, another Jesuit agent who was in touch with Babington. Tortured, he at length revealed the identity of the leaders of the plot. Babington and his colleagues were apprehended, and put to the rack. Their confessions, and the progress of their plans, shook England. The ports where Spanish, French and Papal troops were to be landed were listed; estimated numbers of local supporting forces were given; arrangements for the rescue of the Scottish Queen were detailed; and, worst of all, the identity was revealed of six gentlemen who were conjointly responsible for the assassination of Elizabeth, without which the invasion could not be assured of success – the names including Babington himself and even one, Charles Tilney, of the Queen's own Gentlemen Pensioners.

Mary was taken to Fotheringay, now under closest arrest, while Parliament screamed for her blood. It mattered not now whether she knew of the proposed assassination or no. The new Act naming as guilty any in whose favour a plot might be hatched adequately covered her position, from the point of view of England's law.

Babington and his companions died horribly, on the 20th and 21st of September, as a public spectacle and warning, Elizabeth's own commands insisting that their agonies be extended for as long as humanly possible, after mutilation and disembowelling.

Parliament, in London, set an early date for Mary's trial, and, prejudging the issue, vociferously demanded the death penalty.

The trial, held in indecent haste at Fotheringay, was a farce, a mere formality, and intended to be nothing else, the judges including even Walsingham himself. Mary, denied an advocate, defended herself with vigour and dignity, but Walsingham could produce letters to prove all that he wanted, genuine or forged. Although the judges held that it was legally unnecessary now to prove Mary's knowledge of and condoning of the assassination attempt, Walsingham produced a letter addressed to Babington from the Scots Queen, plainly supporting this course. Mary, whilst admitting the authenticity of most of the other intercepted letters, swore by all that she held to be holy that this was false, a forgery, that never could she countenance the violent death of her sister-queen, that the assassination of an anointed monarch was a crime against the Holy Ghost, the assenting to which would damn her own soul to everlasting torment.

The thirty-six judges, under the Lord Chancellor, the two Lord Chief Justices and Burleigh himself, were not impressed. They adjourned the Court for a week, and on the 25th of October found Mary Stuart, daughter and heiress of James the Fifth, late King of Scots, guilty, and sentenced her to death by execution at such time and place as appointed by the Queen's most excellent Majesty. God save the Queen!

Scotland boiled into a ferment. England could not do this to her Queen – even though many Scots had called her a whore and an idolatress for years, well enough content for her to linger a captive. Imprisonment was one thing, but death by execution quite another. Moreover, this was a national insult, since no English court assuredly had jurisdiction to try and condemn the Queen of Scots. Demonstrations and near-riots broke out all over the country. The Kirk itself was moved to protest against this unwarrantable attack on the sovereignty of Scotland. The Catholic north and the Highland clans blazed alight with ire. The Estates of Parliament met and demanded the anuulment of so iniquitous a trial and judgment.

All this might seem strange in the circumstances, if not positively ridiculous, but it could be argued that the Scots were always a particularly thrawn, awkward and disputatious race, and wickedly proud. Moreover, despite their determinedly dour and matter-of fact façade, they are sentimentalists, romanticists, almost to a man. But perhaps still more to the point is the fact that the Reformation had come late to Scotland. At this time, therefore, the majority of the population had been born Catholic, whatever faith they opted for later. If the Gaelic Highlands were taken into account, as was not always the case, probably more than half the Scots people still belonged to the Old Religion.

Scotland did not seethe alone, either. France, Spain and the Vatican, as might have been expected, sent vigorous protest, combined with dire threats, to London; but apart from these, practically every crowned head in Europe, every princeling even and petty ruler, sent envoys or urgent written representations to Elizabeth. All saw only too clearly, in Mary's sentence, a shocking and unthinkable threat to their own order – the judicial execution of a monarch. Accept that, and the entire principle of the divine right of kings was jettisoned, lost, their sheet-anchor gone.

Elizabeth neither confirmed nor rejected the death sentence. Elizabeth, indeed did nothing.

Not that she was entirely alone in that. Two others who might have been expected to be markedly active in this crisis seemed in fact to be almost entirely supine, passive. They were James, King of Scots, and his trusted mentor and minister, Patrick, Master of Gray.

James's state was, to say the least of it, curious. He made little comment on the situation, keeping his own counsel. When public opinion forced him to speak, he deplored the grievous assault on the idea of kingship, the injury done to Scotland's pride, the invalidity of the court and its judgment. He did not allow himself the luxury of a more personal statement – and certainly not once did he unburden his soul of the anguish that a son must feel for a mother in such dire straits. Not for kings was the exhibition of private griefs and anxieties, he asserted – and quoted a Latin tag to prove it.

Patrick Gray's attitude was as disciplined, and more calmly assured. Elizabeth would not endorse the death sentence, he declared firmly, unshaken by all urgent demands – David's and his own wife's in especial. She could not, without disastrously weakening her own throne, endangering her own crown. She would not put another queen to death – she dare not. There was no need for alarm, therefore. No move was better than a false move in a delicate situation.

From this considered attitude Patrick would not budge, in public or in private utterance.

Alas for statesmanlike calm and discipline. These admirable qualities were at all times somewhat scarce amongst the Scots nobility, and in a crisis of national sentiment such as this, they were notable for their absence. Indeed, they were even more unpopular than the idea of unity, which is saying something, in Scotland. Adversity, they say, makes strange bedfellows. This death-sentence on an eighteen-years-imprisoned queen did likewise. Sworn enemies made common cause, Catholic and Protestant lords spoke with almost the same voice, and men who had cursed and abused Mary for years suddenly became her vocal friends.

Patrick Gray, for once, had miscalculated.

The extent of his miscalculation was brought sharply home to him when, on the last day of October, he was abruptly commanded into the royal presence from his house in the Lawnmarket of Edinburgh. With David at his side, he strolled unhurriedly down the steep mile of tall lands and tenements to the grey Palace of Holyroodhouse, frowning occasionally. He was unused to such brusque summonses.

They found the palace in a state of considerable commotion, and thronged with men – the supporters of many great lords.

'Huntly's Gordons and Bothwell's Hepburns mixing – and not at each others' throats!' David commented. 'Here is something new in Scotland!'

Wondering, they made their way to the Throne-room. It was as thronged as was the courtyard. One swift glance was enough to establish that this was not just a spontaneous coming together of sundry lords that happened to be in Edinburgh at the time. This was an assembly, summoned and arranged.

That Patrick's sources of information had not advised him of it was interesting. The Ruthven lords, Angus, Johnny Mar, Bothwell, Home, Lindsay, the Master of Glamis and the rest, now the dominating force on the Scottish scene, were very much to the fore; but so were also the Catholic leaders – Huntly, Herries, Montrose, Erroll – along with men of neither faction, such as Atholl, Wemyss, Crawford, Seton and the Lord Claud Hamilton. The King himself, as so often the case, stood nervously in a far corner, a hunched shoulder turned against Sir John Maitland, the Secretary of State, who seemingly sought to convince him to some course.

At sight of Patrick, James's young but woebegone and sagging features lit up. He came across the floor at an ungainly run. 'Man Patrick!' he cried. 'You've been ower long. Where have you been? Could you no' have come quicker than this? Man, it becomes you ill – ill, I say! to treat your prince's summons thus. They have all been at me, Patrick . . .'

'Sire, I was so deep buried in the affairs of your realm that I fear I took a deal of digging out. It is a toil that I would be quit of, I do declare.' He smiled reassuringly, as James gripped his arm. Then his genial regard circled the entire great room, and he laughed pleasantly, amusedly, and waved a welcoming hand. 'I see many friends of mine here gathered, Your Grace – a great many. I applaud the happy circumstances that brings us all together, thus.'

'They've been at me, I tell you, man – all at me. Like hound-dogs!' the King declared. 'About . . . about . . . her! About Mary – my mother.' It was not often that James was brought to enunciate that word. 'They are all at it. They'll no' let me be. I have told them what you said, Patrick . . .'

'Master of Gray,' the brash young Earl of Bothwell inter-rupted. 'We fear that His Grace is not fully apprised of the danger in which our Queen is placed . . .'

'*Our* Queen, my lord?' Patrick commented, but mildly. 'I do not think that I have heard you name her that, before!'

The high-coloured, bold-eyed nephew of Mary's former paramour bit his lip. 'Nevertheless, sir, our Queen she is. Scotland's Queen,' he asserted strongly. 'Her life is sore threat-ened, and Scotland's name and honour with it. We are here to urge that His Grace take immediate and sure action.'

A strong chorus of Ayes came from the assembled company.

Patrick bowed his head to the strength of expression rather than to the fears expressed. 'I applaud your concern, my lords' he said. 'We all feel deeply for Her Highness. But I believe your dread to be ill-founded. I have said before – I do not accept it that Queen Elizabeth will endorse this sentence of execution.'

'*You* may not accept it, but Archie Douglas does!' the Earl of Angus declared. 'He writes to me that all about the Queen believe that she *will* sign the decree, that the bishops have advised that it is her duty, and that Leicester has sworn that he will have Mary slain in her cell if the execution goes not forward.'

The King and Patrick had received a like account, of course. Archibald Douglas, the Scots resident ambassador in London, was a sort of cousin of Angus, as of the late unlamented Morton.

'Master Douglas is a notable correspondent, my lord, but his judgment has been proved to be at fault ere this, where Queen Mary is concerned!'

None failed to detect a barb in that. The Reverend Archibald had been one of the principal parties to the murder of Darnley.

The Earl of Huntly spoke up – to James, not to Patrick. The Cock o' the North addressed no one less than his monarch. 'Your Grace's fair name demands that you protest in the strongest terms at this outrage against your royal mother. And more than protest...'

'But I have protested!' the King cried. 'Have I no' sent Sir William Keith to make protest against the wrongous trial . . . ?'

'Keith!' Huntly exclaimed scornfully. 'Think you, Sire, that Elizabeth will pay heed to such as Keith?'

'What else can I do, man Huntly?'

'You can annul and cancel your country's participation in the infamous Protestant League!' the Catholic Gordon chief roared. 'It is a work o' the devil, anyhow!' And he glared at Patrick.

There was a shuffling of feet and a murmuring, there. Unity might cost too much.

Another Douglas, George of Lochleven, the same who had once proved Mary's friend indeed and aided her escape from his own father's fortress, now raised his voice for her once more, and boldly. 'Your Grace would be well advised to listen to the promptings of your own heart, rather than the honeyed words of some who constantly counsel you,' he said. 'Some there are close to you, no doubt, who are but the pensioned slaves of Elizabeth! Their aim, I will swear, is but to create bad blood between Your Grace and your royal mother . . .'

'Quiet, man!' James squeaked, his eyes rolling and darting. 'How dare you speak me so!'

Patrick laid his hand on the King's arm. 'Sire, perhaps Lochleven will give us the names of these dastards whom Elizabeth has bought?' He smiled. 'It may be that in his remote tower, he hears whispers which pass over us here! And the House of Douglas, as all men know, has its, h'm, its own channels of information.'

The Earl of Angus, for his part, laid a hand on his kinsman's shoulder. George Douglas swallowed, but met Patrick's amused gaze squarely.

'Let it suffice, now, that His Majesty knows that such men there are, and in whose service they labour. The rest can wait.' He turned back to James. 'Your love for your mother must instruct you, Sire.'

The King frowned, staring at the floor. 'How is it possible for me to love her, man? Or to approve her proceedings? Did she no' write to the French ambassador here, that unless I conformed mysel' to her wishes, I should have nothing but my father's lordship o' Darnley? Has she no' laboured to take the crown off my head, and set up a regent? Is she no' obstinate in holding a different religion, man?'

There was a considerable stir at the King's outburst. Men, hardened men who had never hesitated to decry any cause but their own, to name Mary harlot and Messalina, to savage any who stood in their way, looked askance at each other in discomfort at the expression of these unnatural sentiments of a son towards his mother. Half-a-dozen lords began to speak at once. Strangely, it was the calm and measured tones of Monsieur de Courcelles, the French ambassador, that prevailed.

'My master, the Most Christian King, is gravely perturbed, Sire,' he said. 'He urges that you make the most vigorous, the most stern representations, the most vehement of which Your Grace is capable. Even to the moving of an army to your borders. I would remind Your Grace that the lady your mother is also Queen-Dowager of France. This threat to her life and affront to her name and state, is equally an affront to my royal master. I am to say that any failure on Your Grace's part to uphold her honour and assure her safety, must be looked upon as an attack upon His Most Christian Majesty – and indeed upon all Christian princes.'

Strangely enough, even the Protestant lords growled fierce

commendation of these strong sentiments.

James gulped, and looked unhappily at the Master of Gray, seeming even younger than his twenty years. 'But . . . but what can I do, sirs?' he gasped. 'She'll no' heed me. She's a hard, hard woman, yon Elizabeth. I canna put soldiers at her. She has more o' them than I have, Monsieur. What can I do, sirs?'

'You can denounce this shameful alliance!' de Courcelles said briefly.

'But, man – the cost! The cost o' such a process! I canna suffer it.'

Bothwell snorted. 'If Your Majesty suffers this other process to proceed, I think, my liege, that you should be hanged yourself the day after!'

A shocked silence fell upon the Throne-room. Only the slightly crazed young Hepburn, who was also James's cousin, could speak in such fashion – but even so, he had gone too far. Patrick judged that it was time to take a hand, a decisive hand.

'My lord of Bothwell is carried away, Sire, by his new-found love. You must forgive him. He misjudges more than the occasion, I think. Far be it from me to suggest that these good lords, His Excellency of France, and the most Christian King are all mistaken. Such would be unthinkable. This matter is all no doubt a question of degree, a question not of right and wrong, of statecraft or government – but of understanding character. One woman's character. I flatter myself that I can read Queen Elizabeth's character as well as any here present – even my Lord Bothwell and Lochleven! – having talked with her, debated with her, even danced with her. And I do believe that she will not warrant another Queen's death. It is not a matter of her hardness of heart, nor yet her anger and fear. It is much more than these – her whole life and outlook and situation. She is Queen of England. Dog, they say truly, does not eat dog. Queen does not execute Queen. Elizabeth will commute the sentence.'

'We know that is your opinion, Monsieur de Gray,' the Frenchman demurred, 'Others think otherwise. Is this lady's life – possibly the fate of Europe : to hang on so slender a thread as one man's opinion? Your Highness – is it, *mon Dieu*?'

Patrick answered quickly. 'No – indeed no. I would be the last to suggest it. I could be mistaken. His Grace would be unwise, wrong, to ignore the advice of so many good councillors, so great a weight of wisdom and experience.' He turned to the

King. 'Your Highness must send forthwith another envoy to Elizabeth.'

'Another envoy will win the same reception as the first – as Keith!' Angus objected. 'Elizabeth will not even see him.'

'I think that she will. More particularly if that envoy is myself, my lord.'

No one spoke for a few moments – a silence that was at length broken by James himself.

'Aye, Patrick – that's it, man! That's it!' he exclaimed. 'You go. You tell her. You tell Elizabeth of our feelings. That we are much perturbed. That we canna be unmoved by our royal mother's fate...'

'My God – you will have to tell her more than that!' Bothwell burst out. 'Tell her that if she does not denounce this monstrous sentence, we sound the call to arms!'

'Aye – tell her that I myself will lead five thousand lances across her march!' the Lord Claud Hamilton cried.

'Tell her that I will burn Carlisle!' Bothwell declared. 'Thousands shall die!'

'I suggest, my lords,' Patrick intervened, with his faint smile, 'that what I tell Queen Elizabeth is for His Grace's Privy Council to decide.'

'But when, man? There must be no delay.'

'Fortunately, with so many of the Council here present, we can meet forthwith. Today, if it is His Grace's pleasure.'

'Aye, aye, Patrick...'

'And when will you go to the south? The matter is of great urgency...'

'This very night, if it is the Council's wish.'

'Tonight, yes. That is straight talking.'

'To this Council then, gentlemen...'

Patrick Gray did not miscalculate twice.

After the Council, the King, with much secrecy and gesticulation, beckoned Patrick, and David with him, into a private room. Locking the door behind them, he listened at it for a few moments, and even went poking behind the hangings and tapestries of the walls.

'Ears,' he muttered. 'Ears everywhere. Aye, and eyes too. They're aye listening, aye watching me, Patrick. I've none I can turn to, but you. They took Cousin Esmé from me, and Captain Jamie. We'll have to watch that they dinna take you, man...'

'I think that Your Grace need not fear for me...'

'Aye, you've aye got Master Davy to look after you. Man, there's times I thank the Lord God for Master Davy – so sure, so strong! Never let him frae your sight, man Davy – d'you hear me? That's a command, mind – my royal command. Or they'll get you, Patrick . . . !'

'Do not fear. Your Grace is overwrought . . .'

'I'm no' overwrought. And I ken fine what I'm saying. Davy's to go with you to yon London, mind – to watch over you. The man Walsingham . . . and Leicester . . .'

David cleared his throat. 'I will see that my brother is enabled to fulfil his mission. Your Grace – God aiding me!'

Patrick smiled sardonically.

James shambled about the small room, throwing uncertain glances at the two brothers. 'After you have seen Elizabeth,' he said in a different voice. 'You must seek a private audience. Private, see you. Could you do that, Patrick? Think you could you win her ear, privily?'

Gravely Patrick nodded. 'I think that it might conceivably be arranged, Sire.'

'Aye, good. Good. Then, in her privy ear, man, you must tell her that this is a bad business and I must have my amends. My amends, see you. You'll tell her that?'

'Amends, Your Highness? You mean . . . ?'

'Aye – amends, man. Compensation. As is only just and suitable. The woman has laid a great insult upon me and my kingdom. A monarch canna do the like to another monarch, and no' pay for it! Na, na – she will have to recompense me. And richly. You will insist on that, Patrick. In her private ear, mind.'

Patrick stroked mouth and chin thoughtfully.

David was less controlled. He could not hold himself in. 'You mean *money* Sire?' he gasped.

'That would be best, aye. It is a matter o' principle. Just and fair indemnity for hurt done. Without the like there would be no decent commerce between realms and princes. It will need to be a goodly sum, mind – for our honour isna to be lightly spat upon. Or maybe an increase to our pension – a substantial increase.'

Patrick's glance flickered over to his brother. 'I shall essay what may be achieved, Highness,' he said solemnly.

'Aye, do that. And another matter. It is time that there was an Act of her Parliament naming me Second Person to Elizabeth, and successor to her Throne. High time. Tell her privily,

348

that if she will have siklike an Act passed, I will overlook yon other ill Act they passed. You have it?'

'M'mmm. I do not know, Sire, that Queen Elizabeth will bear with talk of that kidney – even privately. She is a woman of notable spirit. But . . . I will do what I may.'

'This is an opportunity, man Patrick – a great opportunity. And I have great faith in you. Aye, and in you, Master Davy, to look after him. There's no others that I'd trust with an errand o' siklike delicacy. No' a word o' this to Sir Robert, mind. He's gey thick in the head, yon soldier-man.' Sir Robert Melville, brother to Sir James and Sir Andrew, was the second envoy whom the Council had chosen to accompany Patrick on his mission, one of an honest family, and an uncompromising Protestant.

'It shall be as you say, Your Grace . . .'

Chapter Twenty-nine

THE Master of Gray's second embassage to Queen Elizabeth was a very different affair from his first. There was no pomp and ceremony, no splendid gifts, no ladies, no impressive escort; only the two principals, David Gray, and two or three armed servants. They made the four hundred miles to London, in consequence, in little more than half the time that it had taken the previous entourage.

Elizabeth made much play about not receiving them, keeping them hanging about for days in the ante-rooms of various palaces, while demonstrations of popular wrath against the imprisoned Mary were staged for the envoys' edification, undoubtedly on Elizabeth's own instructions, decapitating the Scots Queen in effigy with gruesome realism, with the help of buckets of ox-blood. Sir Robert Melville blustered and swore, David fretted, sick with anxiety, but Patrick was an example of all that such an envoy should be, imperturbable, courteous, amused even. Play-acting, he asserted, should be enjoyed, not taken seriously.

When, at last, at Greenwich, the Scots embassy was admitted to the royal presence, Elizabeth interviewed them, flanked by a glittering array of her nobles and ministers, including Leicester, Oxford, Essex, Burleigh, Walsingham and Hatton, and treated them, while they were still bowing their entry, to a full and stirring ten minutes of impassioned oratory, brilliant dialectic and vicious vituperation such as few of her hearers had ever experienced, and which left them all dumbfounded and almost as breathless as the Queen herself.

All, that is, except Patrick Gray – and perhaps old Burleigh, who had weathered so many storms in his Queen's service. The former bowed low again, and into the gasping hush spoke pleasantly, admiringly.

'Such eloquence, Your Majesty – such brilliance, such lucidity of utterance, leaves all men abashed and wordless. None may hope to prevail against such a tide of logic, wisdom and wit – least of all this humble spokesman from the north, with but a few uncouth words to jingle together. Yet speak I must, on behalf of your royal cousin, James, King of Scots, and his

Council, if all unworthily.'

'If you do . . . you waste . . . your breath, sir!' the Queen panted, her own breath all but gone, her superstructure of blazing gems heaving alarmingly. 'You . . . come to plead . . . for mercy for . . . that self-confessed murderess . . . Mary Stuart! You waste your time . . . and mine, sirrah!'

'Fair lady, can it be that you misapprehend?' Patrick asked, wonderingly. 'That you have been misinformed in this vital matter?' He cast a comprehensively reproachful glance on the serried ranks of England's advisers. 'We had thought Your Highness better served than this! For such is not the burden of our mission. I plead for nothing – save Your Grace's patient hearing. It is not mercy that we seek. Only justice.'

'Justice, sir!' Elizabeth cried. 'Have you the effrontery to stand before me and say that my courts do not dispense justice? In the presence of my Lord Chief Justice, who himself presided over that woman's trial! You can be too bold, Master of Gray – as I have had occasion to warn you ere this!'

'I speak but what I am commanded, Your Grace. Is it not one of the very elements of justice that the court which holds trial on a cause shall have due authority and jurisdiction so to do? Can your Lord Chief Justice, or any other, show that he had jurisdiction to try the crowned and anointed monarch of another realm – or even of *this* realm, indeed!'

'God's Passion, man – have a care!' the Queen exclaimed, jumping up from her Chair of State. 'Watch your tongue, sirrah, or you yourself will taste the power and authority of my courts!' Imperiously she waved aside the Lord Chief Justice who had stepped forward to speak, 'I myself will answer your ill-judged question sir. Mary Stuart is no longer Queen of Scots, nor crowned monarch of any realm. She abdicated eighteen long years ago, and voluntarily entered *my* realm as a private citizen, thereby placing herself under my authority and the laws of England.'

'Does not Queen Mary deny such abdication, Madam? And if an anointed monarch denies abdication, who shall declare her abdicate? How may you prove otherwise?'

'But . . . good God, man, if Mary did not abdicate, then your James, in whose name you speak, is a usurper! You have no authority to be here, troubling us!'

'Would you deny Scotland a ruler, because you have shut up her Queen these eighteen years, Highness? James and his mother are both anointed sovereigns of Scotland.'

'Lord, this is but wordy dissembling! Words, words, words! Mary, in England, has conspired the violent death of the Queen of England. And plotted the invasion and overthrow of the realm. For that she must pay the penalty required in law. That is all there is to it, sir. Tell you your prince that same.'

'But, dear lady, that I fear is not all that there is to it. I fear . . .'

'By God, it is not!' Sir Robert Melville burst out, unable to contain himself longer. 'If we tell that to our Prince and Council, Ma'am, Scotland marches! Hamilton leads five thousand lances against Newcastle. Bothwell burns Carlisle. The Scots, the Kerrs, the Turnbulls ride. Your border flames from end to end, and the clans march south! Is that nothing to you, Ma'am?'

An outburst of growling wrath and consternation arose from the great company – an outburst that was speedily silenced, however, by Elizabeth's own high-pitched neighing fury.

'Christ's Holy Wounds!' she shouted. 'You . . . you threaten *me*! Threaten me with force, with swords, with bloody attack – here in my own house! Fiend seize you, fellow – how dare you!'

Blinking a little at the storm he had unleashed, the blunt soldier yet held his ground. 'I but warn you what the Council declared . . .'

'God's curse on your Council, then! Think you they can speak so to me – Elizabeth? Yapping curs! Penniless savages! Lord – what insufferable insolence . . . !'

'Madam – good lady,' Patrick intervened – and it took courage indeed to interrupt Elizabeth of England in towering rage. 'Sir Robert may have used injudicious words, but he only intended to indicate that passions in Scotland are much roused in this matter. It would be wrong, improper, for us not to have you know it. The people *here* are roused, as you have rightly shown us. If the two realms and peoples are so equally roused, then, alas, blood may well flow, innocent as well as guilty. It becomes but the simple duty of all in whose hands are affairs of state, to act not only by law and rule, but with mutual care and compassion . . .'

'Shrive me – is that the Master of Gray preaching me a sermon, now!' the Queen broke in, impatiently. 'Are you seeking to teach me my business, sir? Have the pair of you come all this way but to insult and to preach? Have you nothing better than that to say? If not, 'fore God, you may go whence you came – and swiftly!'

Patrick, who indeed had but talked to gain time and a change of tune, nodded now. 'We have indeed, Your Grace. The compassion and care I spoke of, we do not seek only from your-self, noble as is your reputation. Our Prince suggests that his mother, if she were to resign her rights in the succession to your English crown to himself, would no longer endanger you, and so all might live in peace. He will vouch that she will so do.'

'What rights, man – what rights? Mary has no rights. She is a prisoner. She is declared "inhabil", and can resign nothing, convey nothing to her son.'

'If she have no rights, Your Majesty need not fear her. If she have, let her assign them to her son, in whom then will be placed the full title of succession to Your Highness . . .'

'What – by the Living God!' Elizabeth's voice actually broke, in her passion. 'Get rid of one, and have a worse in her place! Nay – never! That were but to cut my own throat, no less. For you – yes, *you*, Master of Gray – for a duchy or an earldom to yourself, you or such as you would cause some of your desperate knaves to murder me! And so secure your prince on my throne. No, by God, your master shall never be in this place!' And she banged her white fists on the wooden arms of her throne. 'The sentence stands!'

Patrick took a long breath. 'Even, Madam, if the League, the Protestant League which we so sorely wrought, were to be quite broken . . . through the passion of the Scots people?'

Tight-lipped Elizabeth nodded.

Patrick looked away from her, then, all round the rows of watching, hostile faces, and from them to Melville, and back to David who stood half-a-pace behind them. And one shoulder faintly shrugged.

David swallowed, noisily.

Sir Robert, at his colleague's gesture of failure, sank his grey head on wide old shoulders. 'Ma'am,' he mumbled, 'I beg of you . . . give us respite. Spare Her Grace . . . if only for a little. For fifteen days even. That we may have time to seek other instructions from our Prince.' The Melville brothers had always loved Mary.

'No,' the Queen declared.

'Then . . . for a week, lady. Eight short days . . .'

'Christ-God – no! Not for an hour!' Starting up, Elizabeth stood trembling. 'This audience is at an end!' she cried, and turning about without another glance at envoys or hurriedly bowing lords, she stormed out of the presence-chamber in a swirl of skirts and a glitter of diamonds.

*

'The woman is a monster!' David declared. 'Crazed with her power, and without human feeling, without sympathy or even conscience. This realm is ruled by a mad-woman, puffed up with belief in her own greatness, her invincibility. Lord – and for her blind pride, our Mary must die . . . !'

'Not so, Davy,' his brother denied. 'On the contrary, this realm is ruled by a very frightened woman indeed! A woman driven near to distraction, I believe. There lies the danger of it – and the doom of our hopes, I think. For there is no goad like fear, no surer barrier to break down than mortal dread. With aught else, I might yet achieve much – in private. But with this fear . . .'

'You think . . . ? You really believe that, Patrick? That it is fear that makes her thus? Not damnable pride? Hatred? Myself, I believe that Elizabeth hates Mary, envies her, and always has done. Envies her for her beauty, her grace, her motherhood, her way with all men – and her legitimate birthright to her own crown. All the attributes which she herself lacks. For that, I believe, she would send Mary to the block. Yet you say it is fear? Fear for her own life? Fear of assassination? Or of losing her throne?'

'Not for herself, no – not directly, that is. For she is a courageous woman. They both are that, these two queens. No, it is fear for her realm, Davy. Elizabeth believes that she alone can save England – and England is in grave danger, God knows. Indeed, she believes that she *is* England. Blame her if you will, for that – call it outrageous pride – but there is truth in it too. And she loves this England, I think, that is another form of herself, with all the passion that a woman has to give – and that our Mary has squandered on worthless men! She is the Virgin Queen – and England is her true lover. She sees that lover in dire danger, threatened within and without – and will do anything, everything, to save her love. Mary she sees as the heart of the danger. So long as Mary lives her crown is unsure. Therefore Mary must die.'

'I' faith, man, you sound as though you do believe that your own self!'

Patrick frowned. 'I believe that is what governs Elizabeth. I do not say that it need be so. I shall indeed seek to convince her otherwise. But . . .'

'She will never see you, Patrick. It is crazy to imagine that she will.'

'I think that she will, Davy. I have besought Raleigh to

354

approach her. He has her ear these days, I am told. Philip Sidney would have assured it – but Raleigh may serve...'

'But to what end, man? She is set in her wicked course. You say yourself that you do not think to move her. Better surely that we should spur back to Scotland with all haste, and set forward a march over the Border! Before it is too late. Perhaps she will pay heed to that, if not to your words.'

'Would you be for war, Davy? Bloodshed? Houses, towns, aflame? Rapine? The innocent dying? For one woman's life?'

Heavily his brother answered him. 'For right, truth, justice, the sword must be drawn, at the last. When all else fails. Scotland has drawn it oft in the past for less worthy cause.'

'Thus, sober Davy Gray! Thus, no doubt, noble Philip Sidney, at Zutphen! And so men die – and women and bairns – the many for the few. Myself, in this matter of dying, I'd liefer it was the few for the many, Davy! The rulers for the people – not the people for the rulers. But I may be mistaken. It seems an unpopular creed!'

Patrick was not mistaken in one instance. Late the same night, Sir Walter Raleigh rapped on the door of the Scot's lodging. The Queen's Grace would see the Master of Gray forthwith, secretly and alone, he announced. A brief private audience. Only the Master of Gray...

Elizabeth, crouched over a great fire, received him in a dark-panelled sitting-room, clad in a bed-robe, and looking older than her fifty-four years. She huddled there in silence, while Raleigh closed the door behind him, and Patrick straightened up.

'Well?' she said. That was question, challenge, reproof, all in one – and something else as well, something warmer, something that might even have been the glimmerings of hope. But she sounded weary, nevertheless – and looked it.

'Very well, dearest lady,' Patrick agreed, smiling. 'First of all, in that you have graciously consented to this meeting. Then, in the felicity of your warm and womanly presence. Also in the anticipation of your understanding. Aye, very well indeed!'

'God, Patrick, do you never tire of it?' she interrupted. 'Tire of such talk, such empty flattery and fulsome praise? I swear it oozes out of you like wind from a bladder!'

'Your Grace jests – for here is no flattery. Is gratitude flattery? Or a man's appreciation of a woman? Or recognition of intellectual worth? If these be empty things, then Patrick Gray is but a bladder indeed.'

355

'Very well, man – let it be. Let it be. I confess I am too weary to debate it with you! I am glad that I give you so much satisfaction, for it is more than I give myself, I promise you!'

He stepped forward to take her unresisting hand and press it to his lips. He had never seen Elizabeth like this. 'My satisfaction is beyond poor words,' he said. 'Would that I might translate it into deeds! And the more so that, tonight, neither of us need act a part . . . unlike this afternoon!'

Swiftly now she looked up at him. 'You think then that I acted a part, this day?' And, before he could answer, 'Was it so evident, Patrick?'

He schooled his features to calm understanding, and no hint of surprise. 'We both had our roles to fill, Your Grace, before the eyes of men. But now, please God, we may be done with dissembling, and speak plain.'

'Do you ever speak plain, Patrick? And to what end?'

'I do, Highness. As now. To the end that folly and weakness and confusion shall not always triumph, even in affairs of state!'

'Plain speaking indeed, sirrah!' Elizabeth's eyes flashed momentarily. 'Folly, weakness and confusion, forsooth! So that is what you think of my policies?' Even as his hand rose in protest, the Queen's turbanned head sank again. 'But it is true – God knows it is true, man. I knew this afternoon that you saw it – aye, and your precious bastard brother too! I watched you, you devil, even as I stormed and raved. I saw it in your eyes. You knew that I could not, dare not, sign Mary's death-warrant. The Master of Gray *would* know that, if none other did! And so you mocked me – and I hated you, man. I do not know that I do not hate you now – only, tonight, I fear that I am too tired for hate. I knew that you would seek this private audience, to tell me what no others are bold enough to do. And I . . . I granted it, lest I dare not face myself in a mirror again!'

Patrick Gray stood very still, but his mind was furiously active. For a long moment there was silence. 'You say . . . that you cannot sign? Dare not sign the death-warrant?' he got out, at last.

'Not without cutting my very throne from under me – as well you know! Not without executing my own queenship as well as hers! Think you that I do not recognise that to execute an anointed monarch is to destroy my own authority – the divine authority vested in all Christian princes? Christ-God – was ever a woman so trammelled, so enmeshed! Mary will have my life and my throne if I let her live – and I endanger my throne, all thrones, if I take her life! You did not need to come to tell me this, Patrick!'

'I did not come to tell you this,' he said, even-voiced.

'I have thought of it and thought of it – beaten my wits!' Elizabeth went on, tensely. 'Some way out of this toil there must be. Do not mock me with your talk of sending Mary to France, or of her resigning her rights to her son! You know that to be utter folly, as well as I do. Mary, while she lives, will resign nothing of her claims. And even if she would, or could, others would not, on her behalf. Every Catholic in Christendom would continue to plot to put her on my throne. You know that, man.'

'I know it,' he said.

'Why do I talk thus to you?' she demanded, heatedly. 'Admit my fears, my impotence – to you, of all men? A devil – and my enemy!'

'I am not your enemy, but your friend. I have been your friend since the first day that I saw you, in yon barge. Have we not acted friends, since then? Have you not supported me, in Scotland? And have I not done there what I said I would do?'

Eyes narrowed, suddenly she interrupted him, not listening to what he was saying, but recollecting. 'Patrick, you said . . . a little ago, you said that you did not come to tell me this. That I could not sign the warrant. What did you mean? Why then did you come?'

He spoke slowly. 'I came because I am indeed your friend. I came to bring you . . . this.' And drawing a folded parchment from his doublet, he handed it to the Queen.

Taking it, her eyes widened as she saw the scrawled signature at the foot, the cracked Great Seal of Scotland. As she glanced at the heading, the brief wording, already fading with the years, she gasped.

'But . . . man, this is . . . this is beyond belief!'

'It is true, nevertheless, Your Grace. You will know what to do with it!'

'But why, Patrick? Why? This is the key to all. Why give me this? You? I had heard that there had been such a document – a deed of abdication. But I never thought to see it. I was assured that Mary would have destroyed it, long since. Yet it is her signature – I know it only too well! Or . . . is it a forgery, man?'

'It is no forgery. Mary was . . . careless in such matters, shall we say?'

'This is the true deed of abdication, then? Signed by her own hand at Lochleven. In July 1567. Twenty years ago. And all these years this has existed – the proof that I needed! That she had indeed abdicated – signed with her own hand!'

'Under unlawful pressure, as she ever claimed,' Patrick observed dryly. 'Not that I think that need concern you now!'

'No. No – not with this in my hands! I have her now!' Elizabeth rose to her feet. 'I can prove that she abdicated her crown twenty long years ago. None may claim that she is any longer a crowned monarch. She has not been for twenty years, whatever she has claimed. God – what a notable writing is this! That signature is her own death-warrant!'

'I thought that you would perceive its value!'

'Where has it lain all these years? Where did you find it, man?'

'Amongst the ordinary state papers. Amongst her bills for silks, and appointments of sheriffs!'

'Lord! And to think . . . !' Elizabeth paused, parchment in hand, to search Patrick's handsome features. 'But why, man – why? You have not answered that. Why have you given this to me? Delivered your Mary into my hand, thus? After what you declared before all, this afternoon? What is the meaning of it, Master of Gray?'

He shrugged one shoulder. 'This afternoon, I said what I was commanded to say – played my part as you played yours. Scotland's envoy. Tonight I am Patrick Gray and my own man. And yours. I give you this, now, for good and sufficient reason – in addition to my love for Your Highness. You have declared that reason with your own lips. Whilst Mary lives, your life is in danger, your throne also. England is threatened, within and without, and all Europe stands on the brink of war – bloody war. It is too high a price to pay for one woman's life. There is no other issue from the tangle. Mary must die.'

For seconds on end Elizabeth stared at him in silence, at all the grace and beauty of him. Then her eyes fell before his calm, even compassionate, regard. 'Lord . . . !' she muttered.

'I told you,' he went on. 'Folly, weakness and confusion. It was not *your* policy that I condemned thus, but our own. Scotland's policy. Stupid maudlin sentiment instead of clear thinking. Scotland needs peace – not Mary Stuart, strife and war!'

'But, you said yourself that there would be war if Mary was

358

executed. That Scotland would march. Carlisle would be burned...'

'That was Melville. Tut – a few Border caterans may cross your March, yes, burn a few thatches, steal a few cattle. Nothing more. I know them – wind-bags, slogan-shouters all! In a month all will be forgotten.'

'But . . . but not by me!' The Queen sank down again. As though all of a sudden she seemed to realise what the paper in her hands meant for *her*, meant in personal decision. Her way was cleared, but she still had to travel that way. 'Not by me,' she repeated, her voice uneven – so unlike the voice of Elizabeth Tudor. 'If I sign that death-warrant, I shall see it before me for the rest of my life!' she whispered.

Brows puckered he looked down at her. 'At least Your Grace will be alive!' he said.

'Mary will haunt me,' she insisted.

'You have signed other death-warrants, Madam, in plenty!'

'Aye.' She raised her head. 'God pity me, I have! I perceive that you are a harder man than you seem. You see only a weak woman before you now, but perchance tomorrow I shall be Queen of England again – and hard as my name and reputation!'

'Just, say, dear lady – never hard.'

'It will require hardness to sign that warrant.'

He fingered his chin. 'It might just be possible, Madam, that fate might overtake Mary other than by the headman's axe?' he suggested. 'With no need of a warrant signed.'

'Think you that I have not considered that, man? But, with my court's sentence of death hanging over her, would the world acquit *me* of her death by other means?'

'Still, with proof of her abdication in your hands, the world's censure would be tempered. If you are so averse to signing the warrant.'

'I . . . I shall think of it. But, oh – if it did not have to be . . . death!'

'The dead do not bite, Highness. That is worth remembering, also.'

'Aye. I thank you for reminding me, sir!' The great Elizabeth, this strange night, was like a weathercock, blowing this way and that. 'And what of James?' she demanded. 'What of your master? How will he take this? He, who sent you to speak so otherwise!'

Patrick smiled faintly. 'I think that you need not fear for my Prince's fury, Madam! James is an indifferent warrior, but an excellent huckster. He would have his amends. A fair sum, he said, for the insult done to his realm by the trial and sentence on his mother – no doubt a slightly larger sum for her actual death! A small matter of adjustment between himself and your good Lord Treasurer!'

'Fiend seize me – money! Is this the truth, man?'

'Aye. He commanded me to seek a secret audience, especially to impress this upon Your Grace. May I assure him that his pension will be increased?'

'God be good! And this is the creature who would follow me upon England's throne!'

'No doubt he will nurture England's trade to unheard-of heights, Majesty!'

She stared at him. 'Does he know of this paper, then?'

'No. No one knows of that paper, save only ourselves. I pray you that you do not reveal whence and when you obtained it.'

The Queen smiled thinly, for the first time in that interview. 'I can understand your concern on that matter, Master Patrick,' she said. 'I can keep a secret better than most women, I believe.'

'So I judged – since it puts my life into your hands!'

'So it does, Patrick! So it does. And *that* you judged also, I have no doubt. Knowing something of weak women. Indeed, you know women too well, I think.' With a somewhat laboured return to her favourite coquettish pose, Elizabeth blinked weary eyes and simpered. 'Some day I shall perhaps consider how suitably to handle that life you have put within these hands of mine. Eh, Patrick? But . . . not tonight. Ah, no – tonight I am tired. Tonight I would sleep, not dally – if I may. Go now, Master of Gray – your mission well accomplished. Poor Walter will be asleep out there, I do declare – if he is not already bedded down with one of my Sluts of Honour!' She yawned elaborately. 'Off with you, man. I do not know whether to thank you, or no!'

He kissed her thin hand. 'Thanks I do not seek. Only and always, your esteem, lady.'

'M'mmm.' At the door, she touched his arm. 'Tell me, Patrick, what says your honest and beloved brother to this matter?'

Her visitor's whole visage, even carriage, seemed to change before her, his handsome features hardening strangely as though into stone, his fine eyes going almost blank, flintlike. 'A good evening to you, Madam,' he said, gratingly, and turning, without so much as a bow, he stalked out.

For long the Queen looked after his striding upright figure.

It was almost morning before Patrick Gray arrived back at

his lodgings. David, who had lain more or less awake and waiting all the night, heard him come in, reeling drunk. Never before had he seen his brother thus. It was, he adjudged, the final proof and evidence of the failure of the mission. Sick at heart, he got him to his bed, with difficulty but with a great sympathy.

The very next day, the Scots ambassadors, silent, depressed, rode north again for their native land. It was the first of February.

Chapter Thirty

THAT same first day of February, Elizabeth Tudor signed the death-warrant of Mary, Queen of Scots, in her Palace of Greenwich, in a state of near-hysteria. After snatching at her pen and signing, she dropped the paper on the floor beside her chair, and refused thereafter even to acknowledge its existence. Bitterly she compained that surely somewhere amongst her supposedly loyal and loving subjects was one with enough true affection for her to spare her the odium of this necessary task, to settle the matter of Mary without this unhappy warrant being needed? Davison, her Secretary, stooped to pick up the fatal document thankfully, even gleefully, and conveyed it with all haste to Walsingham.

There followed some delay. Walsingham, knowing his mistress only too well, to cover his own head put to Sir Amyas Paulet, Mary's gaoler at Fotheringay, Elizabeth's expressed wish that, now that Mary's fate was sealed, it would save a deal of trouble if her death could be achieved quietly, without fuss, and without further involving the Queen. As the only man with access to the prisoner, it would have to be done by himself – Sir Amyas – or at least with his connivance and arrangement. Undoubtedly, the Queen's gratitude would be very substantial for any such loyal help.

Paulet, however, could not be brought to see that this was his duty. Hard and unsmiling Puritan as he was, he insisted in putting private morals into public practice. The very qualities which made him a sure and incorruptible gaoler now turned him quite against this other service. He claimed stubbornly that he had lived an honourable life to date, and that though his heart was the Queen's and his head at her disposal, he did not propose to turn assassin at this time of his life.

That, however, was enough for Walsingham. Two men now stood between him and any monarchial second thoughts or scapegoat-making – Davison and Paulet. His own position was well secured. He gave the necessary orders for carpenters, witnesses, headsman and the like.

Mary of Scotland was executed on February 8th, the day that Patrick Gray and his colleagues rode across the Border into their own country. She died as she had lived for these last eighteen years, courageous, dignified, with spirit, even a trace of humour, professing the Catholic faith and her hope in God's mercies for her undoubted sins. The headsman made something of a botch of the first stroke – it was said, owing to tears in his eyes – but managed to sever her lovely neck at the second.

The church-bells pealed out joy and triumph all over England, thereafter; in London crowds sang and danced in the streets; bonfires were lit, largesse was distributed, loyal addresses were delivered, and Parliament sent a deputation to congratulate the Queen on her blessed and God-sent deliverance.

Elizabeth took to her bed and would see no one.

In Scotland, the Master of Gray and Sir Robert Melville reached Stirling and conveyed their fears to their royal master and his Council, informing that Elizabeth was sore set on carrying out her terrible intent, each ambassador vouchsafing for the other that all that could have been done to save the royal prisoner had been done – Sir Robert even pointing out that he believed them fortunate to have escaped with their own lives, such was the violence of Elizabeth's wrath. In private, Patrick assured the King that while utterly determined, Elizabeth was not quite so wrathful as she must seem publicly, and had listened with patience to his royal demands for amends; he thought that he could promise an increase to the pension, and possibly even an additional lump sum, but that, unfortunately, there was still no great probability of an Act naming James as Second Person and official successor to the English throne.

Scotland waited, therefore, and though James did so in nail-biting agitation, and members of his Council may have fretted in some alarm, by and large the country lay quiet, seemingly almost apathetic – readily explainable in the sheer disbelief of ordinary people that one queen could cold-bloodedly order the death of another.

Exactly one week after the ambassadors' return, another traveller, weary and unescorted, galloped over the Border – one Roger Ashton, an extra Gentleman of the King's Bedchamber, who had been in London on routine state business. He sought the King in private audience at Stirling. Mary, His Grace's royal mother, was dead, he reported.

Suspense over, James put a brave face on it. After ordering that, since this was a purely private and unofficial intimation, no word of it was to be publicly announced, he conferred with Patrick and Maitland about suitable steps to take, consonant with proper dignity and filial duty. Patrick had his advice ready, and Maitland agreed sardonically that it could hardly be bettered in the circumstances. Lord Maxwell Kerr of Ancrum, and young Ferniehirst, son of the late unfortunate Warden of the Middle March, were sent for, as two suitably fiery yet accessible and therefore disciplinable Border leaders – with orders to muster their clan.

Six days later Sir Robert Carey, son of old Lord Hunsdon, Elizabeth's own cousin-german, arrived at the Border at Berwick-on-Tweed, as official courier and envoy of his Queen. On the King's orders he was halted there, and required to answer whether or no it was true that the King's mother had been cruelly done to death. On his admission that Mary was dead indeed, but that he had a letter from the Queen explaining all, he was told that the King of Scots would on no account receive him, and was kept kicking his heels at Berwick until Sir Robert Melville and Home of Cowdenknowes were sent south to interview him and relieve him of his letter. Seldom had an official English ambassador been so scurvily treated.

Elizabeth's letter amazed even Patrick Gray. In terms of heartfelt sorrow and sympathy, it mourned Mary's death as a miserable accident that had befallen, far contrary to her own royal meaning. It was all the fault of her Secretary Davison, she declared, who had wickedly outstepped his responsibilities and given orders in her name, for which grave fault he was now confined to the Tower of London, dismissed his office, and his property confiscated. For herself, she was prostrated by this unfortunate incident, was overwhelmed with excessive grief, indeed had been made very ill and had eaten nothing for days. James would understand full well the problems of a monarch with untrustworthy underlings, of which she judged he had had rich experience. Suitable and tangible expressions of regret and recompense naturally would be forthcoming, but meanwhile would James accept the deep and sincere condolences of his devoted sister in God, Elizabeth R.

King James's first reactions, that this was a very suitable and proper letter, were rudely upset by the much less understanding and charitable reactions of his councillors and nobles. Bothwell, Angus, Mar and the rest of the Ruthven lords seemed to have lost all their previous fondness for Elizabeth. The Catholic leaders, of course, made a great outcry. On Patrick's advice, a strictly limited foray of Kerrs was dispatched over the Border, in a flag-showing gesture which was straitly enjoined to avoid

364

large centres of population and not to burn any important castles. A suitable letter of protest was also concocted, for transmission to Elizabeth – sufficient to show the deep hurt sustained, without of course disturbing international relations – and prayers ordered for the soul of the departed in Scottish churches, however contrary to Calvinist principles. More than this seemed scarcely feasible in the circumstances.

As the news leaked out, however, and spread abroad through the land, the Scottish people, lacking any understanding of statecraft or the predicaments of rulers and princes, blazed out into elemental and extraordinary fury. Without more than a rumble or two of warning, almost the entire country seemed to erupt in wrath. Highlands and Lowlands both gave tongue. Mobs formed in the cities and towns, demanding vengeance. The lesser lords, barons and lairds, insisted on the calling together of the Estates in Parliament. The Kirk was almost split in twain. Scotland, as distinct from the Scots nobility, seethed up as it had not done for centuries.

If the King and his immediate advisers were surprised, so, to some extent, were the great lords and the Council. It did not take these latter long, however, to grasp their cue. Soon they were heading up the popular clamour, arming men, demanding action. Every pass and road into England was closed by armed and angry companies. Six quite spontaneous and independent raids were made over the Border, causing the Kerrs' careful foray to seem like a puppet-show. Young Bothwell did indeed descend upon Carlisle, with nearly three thousand men, and while he did not manage to burn it, he created considerable havoc and alarm. Other raids by Home, Angus, Hamilton and others, penetrated much deeper into Cumberland and Northumberland, spreading terror and death, one particularly audacious joint effort by Scott of Buccleuch and Kerr of Cessford going the length of assaulting the English Warden, Sir Cuthbert Collingwood, in his own fortress of Eslington, burning him out, putting his men to the sword, and taking himself and his sons prisoner. Well might the English commander in the north write a piteous letter to Walsingham, describing the country as having been reduced to a desert, wasted with fire and sword and filled with lamentation and dismay.

All this, though stirring, did not satisfy Scotland – more especially as England, with highly unusual patience, refused t be drawn, and refrained from making any counter-moves worthy of the name. The King and his advisers were abused as faint-hearts, cravens and worse, and demands for outright war resounded. The name of the Master of Gray, in especial, came to be spat upon, as the King's closest adviser.

That man of peace, however, continued to smile confidently, imperturbably, even when he was hooted at in the streets of Edinburgh. He had never had any high opinion of the populace anyway, of course. The fact that his brother David sided rather with the popular clamour, seemed only to amuse him. His advice to the King remained the one stable and predictable element in a maelstrom of emotion, tumult and confusion.

Unfortunately or otherwise, all this was the ideal forcing-ground for that most fatal of all Scots weaknesses – the preference for fighting each other instead of a common foe, that has been the comfort and stay of the English from time immemorial. Gradually, as Patrick had foreseen that it would, the clamour for invasion, reprisals, war, faded – or was at least metamorphosed into internal dissention. The strong urge to violence, since James refused to go to war – recognising the end of all his hopes of the English succession if he did – found outlet in turning upon the King himself, on his ministers and Council, on the symbols and servants of authority. Near-anarchy gripped the land – not for the first time in such circumstances, nor the last. Terrified, James cowered in Holyroodhouse, afraid to show himself to an angry people, who named him matricide, coward, Elizabeth's toy and hireling. Patrick, who had been trying, since he attained authority, to build up a national army, so that the Crown should not have to rely upon the unpredictable levies of arrogant lords, had only sufficient men as yet to protect the royal person and palaces. The country at large he could not attempt to control.

The Catholic lords saw their opportunity, and sent out a call to arms, Huntly, Erroll and Herries sending an urgent demand to Philip of Spain for soldiers and support.

Three short months after the execution of Mary Queen of Scots, her mourning realm was on the verge of civil war.

It was in these circumstances that England decided that the time was ripe for playing a somewhat more positive role – but not blatantly or too obviously. Walsingham wrote a lengthy and interesting letter – not to the Master of Gray, but to Sir John Maitland, the Secretary of State. It was a very important letter indeed, nevertheless, for Patrick Gray.

*

Conditions made Patrick almost something of a prisoner in Holyroodhouse, along with his royal master, when in the capital, since his beautiful but unpopular features were only too readily recognisable wherever he went. He and Marie had therefore taken residence meantime in the palace itself, now considerably overcrowded.

Nothing of these complications, of course, applied to David, whose aspect and apparel were ordinary enough to escape notice anywhere. He continued to live with Mariota and the children in their lofty eerie in the Lawnmarket, and in consequence heard much of what went on in the city of which his brother remained ignorant.

David came to Patrick's quarters in the palace rather urgently one night in early May – an unusual procedure. Marie, who greeted him, remarked on it.

'How good to see you, Davy,' she declared warmly, taking his hand. 'You are as good as a stranger to me, this while back, I do declare. I believe that you avoid me, do you not? Confess it. Sorrow that it should be so – whatever the cause.'

He shook his head. 'Not so,' he declared. 'No, no. You I would never avoid, Marie.' But he looked away from her, out towards the dim bulk of Arthur's Seat, rising huge in the gloom.

'It is Patrick again, is it not? You are at odds with Patrick, Davy? Seriously at odds. Oh, I always know it, when you are. Patrick shows it, plainly enough...'

'Patrick!' his brother jerked. 'As though Patrick could care for any opinions of mine!'

'He cares more than you think. He considers your opinions more than those of anyone else – mine own included! Always I can tell when *you* are strongly against what he is doing, however little he cares for the opposition of others.'

'If he considers, then that is all that he does! Never has he let an opinion of mine change his course...'

'I would not be too sure, Davy. But ... you are against what he is doing now? You have been against his policies for some time?'

'I believe that he is in the wrong road, Marie. That is nothing new, of course! It has been my croaking plaint for years, as he seldom fails to declare. But this time it is different. Usually I have been afraid for the hurt that he might do to others. Now, I fear that he himself it is who will be hurt.'

'Hurt, Davy? How mean you – hurt? In himself? Not in his person...?'

367

'That is what I fear. I think that he is in danger. I have told him, warned him, that the country has turned against him ...'

'He cares nothing for what the people say, I know. But it could be that he is right, in that. They are so ignorant, he says – unthinking, swayed by gusts of emotion. Like a ship without a helm ...'

'Aye – perhaps they own to emotions like love and loyalty and faith and trust!' he asserted bitterly. 'And Patrick, with his statecraft and clear wits, is above all these! But ... it is not such poor honest fools that I fear. Not in themselves. It is the lords, their masters. They are frightened. The King is frightened. The Council is frightened at the way in which the country has risen. And I fear that all are going to turn on Patrick.'

'Turn on him? But why?'

'As the author of the King's policies. As the chief minister. As the man who can be blamed for their fright. As a scapegoat.'

'As the man who would not have bloodshed! Who refused to lead the country into war!' Marie added loyally.

'Perhaps. Though I think that there are two sides to that. But whatever the reasons, I believe Patrick is in danger. Not from the mobs who hoot him in the streets, but from men closer, much closer.'

'And you have told him, Davy?'

'Aye, I have spoken of it in a general way, many times – to his amusement. But tonight I have had more sure, more definite word. The danger is closer than I had feared. I must see him, Marie. Where is he?'

'Where else but as always – at his papers. Through in the small room, with Sir William ...'

'With Sir William, aye – always with William Stewart, now!'

'You do not like him, Davy? Patrick says that you are jealous of him! Can men be jealous, thus? I do not know ...'

'I do not trust him, anyway – and with reason.'

'But, then, you do not trust Patrick either, do you!'

Their grey eyes met, and held, for seconds on end. Then David shrugged.

'I must see him,' he said. 'But I do not wish to see Stewart.'

'I will fetch him for you,' Marie told him.

In a few moments she was back, with Patrick, a furred house-robe over his silken shirt.

'Here is an honour indeed!' he declared. 'Davy gracing my humble abode unbidden! To what mighty conjunction of the stars do we owe this felicity?' That was heavy, laboured, for

368

Patrick – presumably indicative of strain or preoccupation.

'Davy fears for your safety, Patrick,' Marie said urgently. 'He believes that you are in danger.'

'That Davy has been fearing all his life, and mine!'

'This is new. Only tonight have I heard of it,' David said evenly. 'And I beg you to spare me your mockery, this once. I have heard that you are to be impeached.'

'Impeached! Lord, man, are you crazy? Who would impeach the Master of Gray? Who *could*?'

'Many, it seems. Most of the Council, indeed. But specifically, one Sir William Stewart!'

'What! Save us, Davy – have you taken leave of your senses? Stewart is my own man. I trust him entirely. I have been working with him all this evening. He is but newly gone back to his lodging...'

'That may be. But none of it means that Stewart cannot impeach you tomorrow!'

'But... why should he? All that he is, I have made him.'

'He is Arran's brother.'

'What of it? What reason that for doing me injury?'

'Well may you ask! For the same reason, perhaps, that you have advanced him so notably, singling him out for preference – since his brother's fall.'

Patrick frowned. 'What nonsense is this, now? William Stewart is a man of talent. He has been of much service to me – and to Scotland. To what tales you have been listening, Davy, I do not know. But any talk against Stewart is manifestly ridiculous, close as he is to me. The work of enemies...'

'He is close to Maitland also, Patrick.'

'What do you mean?'

'I mean that Maitland sees more of Stewart even than you do. He is Secretary of State and Vice-Chancellor – and he has never loved you. As I heard it, he is behind this matter.'

'What matter, man? Out with it. Speak plain, for the good Lord's sake!'

'Very well. One of Maitland's own clerks, to whom I once did a favour, told me. This night. At tomorrow's Convention of the Estates, called in answer to this clamour, you are to be impeached on a charge of treason. The accuser being Sir William Stewart, acting on the instructions of Sir John Maitland of Thirlstane and the Council.'

Patrick stared at his brother. 'I do not believe a word of it!' he declared. 'The thing is absurd. And impossible. James himself

369

is to preside at this Convention. He would never permit it – even if the rest were true.'

'The King will permit it. He has been informed and per- suaded, and has given his agreement.'

'Tush, man – this is beyond all belief! Which is the greater fool, I know not – Maitland's precious clerk for concocting it, or you for crediting it!'

'They are frightened, Patrick – frightened. All of them. Even if you are not. James most of all. The country is torn with strife, the people are out of control, the Catholic lords are openly pre- paring to strike – and this Convention called for tomorrow is going to demand that heads fall, in consequence. It will be the most unruly of the reign, you yourself said. And yours is the head that has been chosen to fall! Maitland and your friends the Ruthven lords have selected you as scapegoat, that their own heads may remain. I have feared something of the sort for long...'

'And I have seldom listened to such folly!'

'Patrick, pay heed to him!' Marie cried, in agitation. 'You cannot be sure that it is not as he says.'

'Think you that I should believe the maunderings, or worse, of a knavish clerk, against my own wits and the words of my closest associates, Marie? Have I not been working all this night with Stewart, preparing the arrangements and agenda for tomorrow's Convention? Think you that he would be doing that if he intended to do this thing tomorrow? The man who is but new back from my business in France – for whom I have gained the appointment of Ambassador to King Henri? It is nonsense even to consider it.'

'Yet Davy believes it – and despite what you say now, you have never thought Davy a fool! At the least, you must enquire into it. Take precautions...'

'Enquire into it? What would you have me do? At this late hour? The King is retired to his bed, long syne. Stewart is away to his lodging in the town. Maitland is not in the palace. What precautions would you have me take, woman?'

'*I* would counsel you to leave this place forthwith – tonight,' David said heavily. 'At Castle Huntly you will be safer...'

'Fiend seize me – this is beyond all! To bolt like a coney because some grudging clerk whispers deceit...'

'You will not deny, Patrick, that Maitland has never loved you? With you out of the way, he can be Chancellor, not Vice-Chancellor, and rule the kingdom.'

'Maitland is not of that sort. He is not one for adventures – a canny able man who knows his own place. Besides, what has he to impeach me on? A charge of treason against such as myself demands much and damning evidence. What have they? Nothing. I have . . .' Patrick stopped himself there, shortly.

'That I cannot say,' David admitted. 'But was such necessary for Arran's fall? Or Lennox's? And you have taken many . . . risks, have you not?'

'These were, h'm, different. They were not impeached. Morton was – but there we had the proof, the evidence . . .' Patrick paused. Clearly some new notion had struck him. 'If there is anything in this clerk's tale at all, then it might be that Maitland, or others, may desire this very thing to happen – that I should take fright and run. A gobbledygowk to scare me away from tomorrow's Convention. Maitland could then steer the meeting, under the King. If he, or others, had some project afoot, which they believed I would oppose. It might be that. In which case, this whisper of Maitland's clerk in your ear, Davy, would be readily explained! Aye, that bears thinking on.'

David could not deny it. Just as he could not think of a charge of treason that could stand proven against his brother. He recognised that Patrick's suggestion made sense – a manoeuvre to keep the acting Chancellor away from the Convention. Stewart's name might have been taken wholly in vain. 'It could be,' he admitted reluctantly. 'Yet, even so, it smacks of trouble, of danger, with enemies moving against you . . .'

'Small men intriguing, mice nibbling! Of such is statecraft all the time, man – as you should know. Think you that, placed as I am, I can pay heed to such?'

'Pay heed, yes. At least you are warned. It may be more than this, as I still fear.'

'I am warned, yes. For that I thank you. At the Convention tomorrow, I shall be ready for any untoward move. But I still believe it nonsense . . .'

'You will attend then, Patrick, still?' That was Marie. 'Is it . . . wise?'

' 'Fore God – could I do otherwise? Have you joined the mice, Marie? I have not, I promise you! But enough of this. Davy – late as is the hour – some refreshment?'

'No. Mariota awaits me, anxiously. And the children. Ready to ride forthwith. For Castle Huntly, or otherwhere!'

'Lord – so seriously do you all take my poor affairs! The kind Mariota...'

Next morning, in the Throne-room of the palace, Patrick from the Chair had only just managed to still the noisy assembly of the specially-called Convention of the Estates of Parliament to welcome decently the King's entry, and had begun to read out the form of the day's business, when Secretary of State and Vice-Chancellor Maitland of Thirlstane stood up and in a loud voice addressed the Throne directly. He declared, into the hush, that before the important debate of the day should commence, it was proper that a matter which demanded the immediate attention of His Grace and the whole Convention should be brought to their notice. It concerned the fitness of the Master of Gray, in the Chancellor's seat, further to speak in their name. Sir William Stewart indeed accused the said Master of Gray of highest treason.

As Patrick, brows raised, lips curling, began to rule this out-of-order without due notice and warning, James from the Throne raised a trembling hand. They would hear his trusty and well-beloved Sir William Stewart, he declared in a falsetto squeak.

Stewart, a good-looking man though less boldly handsome than his brother Arran, rose, and in unimpassioned tones announced that out of his love for the King and the weal of his realm, he was in duty bound to declare that he knew of treason committed against the Crown by the Master of Gray. On no fewer than six counts. To wit: Having trafficked with France, Spain and the Pope for the injury of the Protestant religion in Scotland; having planned the assassination of Sir John Maitland, the Vice-Chancellor; having counterfeited the King's royal stamp; having worked for the alteration and troubling of the present estate; having sought to impede the King's marriage; and having, in England, failed in his duty in the matter of Queen Mary's death.

James hardly allowed him to finish before he stood up – and all men must needs stand up with him. They would not hear more of this just then, he stammered without once looking towards Patrick. This was not the time nor the occasion. The matter must be duly investigated. He repeated the word investigated. The Convention had other important matters to deal with. Sir William Stewart should have full opportunity to substantiate these serious charges, and the Master of Gray to answer them. He hereby fixed the diet of trial for four days hence, the tenth of May, until when both principals to the charges would be confined in strict custody, as was right and proper for the safety of the realm. He therefore ordered his leal Captain of the Guard to take and apprehend the said Patrick, Master of Gray and the said Sir William Stewart, convey them forthwith to his royal castle of Edinburgh, and to hold them both straitly there until the said day of trial, on pain of his life. Meanwhile his right trusty and well-beloved Sir John Maitland, Vice-Chancellor, would act as Chancellor of the Realm and look to the good ordering of this Convention. This his royal will. The Captain of the Guard to his duty!

The paper from which the King had gabbled this peroration slipped from his nerveless fingers to the floor, as the assembly erupted into uproar.

David, from the clerk's table, watched his brother led from the seething Throne-room under substantial and ungentle guard. The fact that Sir William Stewart was marched off with him deceived none.

373

Chapter Thirty-one

THE trial of the Master of Gray took place in the Council chamber at Holyroodhouse, not before any mere panel of professional judges, but in front of a very specially selected section of his fellow Privy Councillors – Angus, Bothwell, Mar, Hamilton, Home, the Master of Glamis and so on – in fact, the Ruthven lords, almost to a man. The King was present, though looking markedly ill at ease. David Gray sat amongst the other clerks and secretaries as was his wont, none ordering otherwise.

Patrick, though led in under guard, to find his accuser and supposed fellow-prisoner esconced comfortably beside the president and acting Chancellor, appeared to be quite the most coolly assured and confident person in the room, even though his clothing lacked something of its usual excellence.

The atmosphere, from the first, was strained, unreal. In all the company none seemed willing to catch the sardonic eye of the man who had so often presided over this same company in this same chamber, and who was now the accused. Unease and uncertainty clothed them all in an uncomfortable garment, which some wore with nervous posturings, some with brash noisiness, and some with glum silence. No single Catholic lord was present.

Maitland, sitting in the chair that formerly had been Patrick's, opened the proceedings as acting Chancellor, craving the King's permission to proceed. He at least spoke in the dull clipped pedantic voice that was his normal.

'Your Grace, my lords,' he said. 'I declare to you that Patrick, Master of Gray, Master of the King's Wardrobe and Commendator of the Abbey of Dunfermline and of many other priories and benefices of Christ's Reformed Kirk, stands before you charged with the most heinous and monstrous of all crimes, that of treason against his King and liege lord, in that, while he was himself accepted leader and preses of this most high Privy Council, did conspire to the injury of the realm, of the King's peace, and of Christ's holy Kirk. Sir William Stewart, whom all know to be an honourable and true servant of His Grace, has been the means of discovering for us this evil and base traitory. He has acted for the said Master of Gray

374

in many close matters, as all here are aware, and has but lately come to perceive that much of the said Master's works were and are contrary to the good of the kingdom and the King's honour. For the weal of His Grace, therefore, and the greater comfort of his own conscience and soul, the said Sir William came to myself, as His Majesty's principal Secretary of State, with the matter, that His Highness might be apprised and informed. Hence these proceedings, taken upon the command of our gracious liege lord. I therefore call upon the said Sir William Stewart to speak to his charges.'

Patrick, from the other end of the great table, intervened pleasantly, quite conversationally – for no air or impression of court or trial prevailed, what with the lounging confident attitude of the accused, the discomfort of his judges and, despite the grave wording of the charges, the unimpressive aspect and manner of the speaker.

'Your Grace, my lords and friends all,' he said, smiling. 'Interested as I am, but naturally – nay, agog to hear what poor doings of mine have so inconvenienced the conscience of my good familiar and assistant, Sir William Stewart, I would nevertheless seek to spare the time of this noble and notable company, by pointing out that any findings of this court of enquiry are already invalid, the presiding judge having thus early prejudged the issue by declaring my conduct to be evil and base traitory. You will note, gentlemen, that he did not specify that the charge was such, but that Sir William – whom God succour – had discovered such to be the case. In consequence, Your Grace, I request that this enquiry be dismissed, and the charges with it, or else a new hearing fixed.'

Various emotions chased themselves across the features of his hearers – astonishment, consternation, wrath, even relief.

Maitland hurriedly leaned over, stooping, to murmur something to the King, who blinked rapidly, pulled at his ear, wagged his head, and then nodded.

'Aye. A slip o' the tongue just, my lords. Och, nothing mair. Sir John but meant that the charges were thus, no' the deeds. No' the deeds, my lords. Aye. Let Sir William proceed. He has . . . he has our royal attention.'

Stewart rose, bowed, and addressed himself to a pile of papers. 'This first charge, Your Grace and my lords, refers to the traffic of the Master of Gray with the King of France, the King of Spain, the Duke of Guise and the Pope of Rome, for the injury of our true Protestant religion. I testify that he wrote letters – I was indeed the bearer of sundry of them – to these princes, proposing the invasion of certain portions of the realm of England by the forces of the said princes, to the hurt of the Protestant faith.'

Patrick nodded agreeably. 'That is not a charge, but a statement of fact,' he averred. 'It was done with the full knowledge of the King and of Sir John Maitland, to the end that it might weigh against Elizabeth in the matter of her sore oppression of our beloved Queen Mary, mother of the King. If most of the noble lords present do not know of it, that is because they were at the time unfortunately banished this realm and Court on a charge of treason, and dwelling in the said realm of England under the protection of the said Elizabeth. If charge there be here, surely it should be preferred by the Queen of England, whose realm was threatened, not by the King in whose name the threat was made!'

'Ummm,' James said. 'Och, well.'

Stewart cleared his throat, and went on hurriedly. 'The Master of Gray further sought to persuade His Grace to allow liberty of conscience and worship, in the matter of religion, to the admission of wicked heresy and contrary to the laws of the Kirk and the statutes of this realm.'

'Lord – is that treason? To seek to persuade! I am a traitor self-confessed, then! As, of course, are you likewise, Sir William – who sought to persuade the King, with my assistance, to alter the law passed forfeiting the estates and property of your unhappy brother the Earl of Arran! Indeed, each of you noble lords committed treason, in such case, when you pleaded with the King, through my own self as mediator, to overturn the sentence of banishment passed upon you all after yon ploy at Ruthven! Certes, when a minister of the Crown may not advise the King to alter a law, then there will be no more Ministers, and soon no more Crown!'

Angus cleared his throat loudly. 'Here is a minor matter, i' faith. Let us to the greater evils,' he declared.

'Indeed, yes,' the prisoner agreed affably.

Stewart, after a glance at Maitland, went on. 'Secondly, I charge that the said Master of Gray planned and intended the assassination, for his own ill purposes, of certain of His Grace's Ministers, to wit, Sir John Maitland, Vice-Chancellor; Sir James Home of Cowdenknowes; and the Collector-General, Master Robert Douglas, Provost of Lincluden. This was to be done at Lauder . . .'

'Wait a bit, wait a bit,' Patrick urged, actually laughing. 'Did I hear you to say planned and intended, Sir William? Man, man – have I not taught you better than this? This will never do. What a man may plan and intend is no crime – only what he does or attempts to do. Will Sir William tell us of any occasion on which I attempted, or occasioned to be attempted, the assassination of the good Sir John, Sir James and the Reverend Master Douglas . . . since it seems apparent, most happily, that the attempt lacked something of success?'

'I heard the plotting of it. In a room of this palace . . .'

'Heard, friend? With whom did I plot this intention, I wonder?'

'That I could not see. It was done secretly, behind a closed door.'

'Ah – you did not see! Then how do you know that it was I who spoke?'

'By your voice. I ken your voice full well . . .'

'Through a closed door, sir, you *thought* that you heard me expressing the intention to do way with these three gentlemen? A slender charge, my lords, is it not? Heigho – I can give you a better, here and now – and through no closed door! I say, may the devil roast and blister one, Sir William Stewart, who owes me the sum of 4,000 pounds Scots, which I intend to recover even if I have to wring his neck to do so!' Patrick's smile was wide, utterly inoffensive. 'There, my lords, you have plan, intention and dire threat in one! Yet I dare assert that none here will charge me with having committed any offence – much less a treason. So much for Sir William's testimony!'

Out of the involuntary laughter and comment, Bothwell spoke. 'You deny, then, that you plotted against Maitland's life?'

'There is no need to deny anything so flimsy, my lord. A charge based on the length of Sir William's ears, the depth of his pocket, and his interpretation of a supposed conversation with somebody unknown, represents no charge at all. Even Even if it was a crime to intend.'

'You will not deny that you have ever misliked me, Master of Gray,' Maitland interposed stiffly. 'That you have worked against my endeavours, and spitefully used me?'

'I do not deny, sir, that there are others of the King's Ministers for whom I have more personal esteem, with whom I would sooner spend a night! But do not take it to heart, Sir John – it is all a matter of taste, is it not?'

377

The Lord Home guffawed loudly, and not a few of his companions grinned or covered mouths with hands.

'Proceed with the charges,' the acting Chancellor snapped.

'Yes, do,' the accused nodded. 'Now that we all know why this peculiar impeachment has been brought!'

Stewart fumbled amongst his papers uneasily. 'It is thirdly charged, that the Master of Gray did counterfeit the King's royal stamp, and did employ the same to stay the King of France from his intention of sending an army of soldiers to Scotland on King James his royal mother's behalf.'

Patrick looked straight at James, who kept his head down. 'I have been using the King's royal stamp for many months, with the King's full knowledge and agreement – as must any of the King's Ministers . . . not least Sir John himself. I had a new stamp made, yes – since the old one was much worn and the imprint scarce to be made out. Do not you all, my lords, do the same with your seals as they wear out? But do you name the new a counterfeit of the old . . . or just a replacement?'

'It was done without the King's authority,' Maitland declared.

'Certainly. I conceive His Grace to have more important matters to attend to than the replacing of his stamps! As for the staying of the King of France his soldiers, my letter was to suggest that His Most Christian Majesty use his men for the invasion of England rather than land them upon this realm. It occurred to me, perhaps wrongly, gentlemen, that with the Catholic lords entreating the said King of France, Philip of Spain, and the Pope, to send troops here for their own purposes, it might be less than convenient to have some thousands of his Christian and Catholic Majesty's soldiers already secure on Scottish soil! Was I mistaken?'

There was no doubt as to what the Protestant Ruthven lords thought of that, however anxious they might be to dissemble their feelings.

'The next charge, man,' Angus jerked.

'It relates, my lords, to His Grace's proposed marriage to the Princess Anne, the King of Denmark's daughter,' Stewart went on. 'The Master of Gray, consistently and without due warrant, has sought to impede such marriage, to our liege lord's injury and the ill of his realm, in order that a Papist and idolatrous woman be chosen instead.'

'And the name of this Papist idolatress, sir?'

'What matters her name . . . ?'

378

'Much. Since you have named the one lady, you must name the other.'

'You cannot gainsay that you have been against the Danish match?' Maitland challenged.

Patrick shrugged. 'I have seen the lady's portrait, and conceive that His Grace might do better!' he answered lightly. 'Moreover, I have not heard that His Majesty of Denmark is so well endowed with possessions as to provide a dowry which will, h'm, paint the said portrait fairer! If such well-wishes for our dear prince's future happiness add up to treason, then condemn me out of hand, my lords. Off with my head!'

'You have other charges yet, I think, Sir William?' the young Earl of Mar said, impatiently. 'Let us have done with this play-acting.'

'Aye – enough o' this. Let us to the heart o' the matter.'

'Speak up, man.'

Stewart stroked his scanty beard. 'To be sure. There is my assured knowledge, through long and close working with the Master of Gray, that he has laboured for the alternation and troubling of the present estate of Scotland, in many matters which might have destroyed the King's realm. Which works, if they had taken effect, might have endangered His Majesty's person, thereby committing the crime of treason . . .'

'Might have . . . ! If . . . Might have . . . !' Patrick scoffed. He snapped fingers in the air. 'That for your further evidence! In your generalities, sir, you are as enfeebled as in your particulars. No word that you have spoken would convince of my guilt the most heather-toed sheriff in all this land – much less the lords of His Grace's Privy Council. Indeed, I am ashamed for you, man – I had thought that I had trained you in statecraft better than this!' He turned a scornful shoulder on his accuser, and squarely faced the ranked Council. 'As for you, my lords,' he said with easy authority, as though he still presided over them. 'I need not tell you that your time has been wasted quite, this day. Nothing that has been put before you represents other than the fact that at sundry times Sir John Maitland has disagreed with my policies for His Grace's realm. But disagreed within himself, mark you – not, as was his plain duty in such case, before this Privy Council. I submit that all that you have before you here is the evidence of the spite and spleen of a small and twisted mind. The mind not of Stewart, my lords, for he is but a poor paid creature, unworthy of your attention – a mere jackal where his brother once was something of a lion!

But of Secretary Maitland himself, who now presumes to sit in presidency over your noble lordships ...'

The acting Chancellor's gavel beat loudly on the table, but the Master of Gray spoke on, without so much as a glance towards the Chair.

'This dismal clerk, this knight of the scratching quill, now seeks to rule His Grace's Scotland! Mark it well, my lords! We have had many bonny masters in this realm, 'fore God – but never, I swear, such a gloomy piddling notary as this ... !'

'Highness! Your Grace . . . !' Maitland cried, his creaking voice cracking indeed. 'This is intolerable! I protest! You must ... I pray ... I pray that you silence this, this scoffer, this mountebank! To speak thus, in Your Majesty's presence ... !'

James, who had been alternately drawing off, sniffing at, and pulling on his heavily scented gloves, licked slack lips, and seemed to have difficulty in getting his tongue, once out, back into its due place. 'Ooh, aye. Just that, aye,' he said thickly. 'Belike it's no proper, Sir John. You must speak otherwise, Patrick man . . . er, Master o' Gray. In our royal presence. Aye.'

'Sir, I intend to speak no more. I have nothing to answer in these paltry accusations. They do not merit the name of charges! I deny any and every suggestion that I have worked to other than the best interests of Your Grace and your realm. I never sought the office of Chancellor – indeed I have refused it time and again – but while I have been Your Grace's Minister it has been my duty to advise on sundry policies. If these policies have been mistaken, then it was for this Privy Council to decide and pronounce thereon. There was no need for this absurd impeachment. I rest content in the assurance of Your Grace's and your lordships' wise judgment.'

'Wait a bit, man – no' so fast! Wait you,' the King mumbled. 'We are no' finished yet, Patrick. Are we, Sir John?'

'We are not Your Grace!' Maitland declared tightly, and smiled, actually smiled.

David Gray, at the clerks' table, sat forward, as indeed did most others in that great chamber. He had never before seen Maitland to smile, and the effect was somehow ominous, chilling, in the extreme. Hitherto his brother had dominated the entire proceedings. David had recognised it, better than any other, as a brilliant performance, perceiving all the innuendoes, the side-blows, the playing on weaknesses and prejudices of his hearers, the thin ice over which Patrick had skated with such apparent confidence and authority. David indeed had almost begun to believe in the possibility of an acquittal, despite the fact that he knew that this was a trumped-up trial, arranged beforehand not only by Maitland and Stewart, but by the King and the Council also; that Patrick had been selected for the role of scapegoat. The Master of Gray's personal ascendancy and consummate skill might have achieved, if not complete triumph and a reversal of the situation, at least a modified success. But, of a sudden, the entire atmosphere seemed to change at Maitland's thin smile and the King's unusual assurance and obvious knowledge of something vital yet to come.

'Aye, out with it!' Johnny Mar exclaimed. 'The matter o' the Queen.'

'Proceed, Sir William,' Maitland ordered.

Stewart leaned over the table, and raised a hand to point at Patrick. 'I further charge that, for sumptuous reward in England, the Master of Gray did, while especial ambassador for the release and saving of the King's royal mother, conspire, advise and consent to the death of Queen Mary of this realm!'

For long moments there was complete silence in the Council Chamber, broken only by James's heavy, throaty breathing.

Patrick's voice, when at length he found it, was strangely uncertain, almost breathless. 'That is . . . a lie,' he said.

'We have ample proof that it is not!' Stewart assured. 'From the most lofty and certain sources. I hereby charge the Master of Gray, not only with compounding the death of the Queen, but of urging it and working for it, in foullest treachery and treason!'

Patrick stared at his accuser, seemingly all but mesmerised by the still pointing hand. The difference in his aspect and attitude from heretofore was markedly evident to all.

The stout goose-quill pen which David held, snapped broken in his hand with a crack which sounded through the room, as he gazed at his brother.

'The proofs, Sir William – let us have the proofs,' the Master of Glamis demanded, into the hush.

Stewart held up a paper. 'I have a letter here, written to Sir John Maitland as Secretary of State, by Sir Francis Walsingham, principal Secretary of State to Her Grace of England. In it he declares that after making public protest against the sentence of death, before the Queen and her Council at Greenwich Palace, the Master of Gray did privately seek audience of Queen

Elizabeth, and there did urge and persuade her to the signing of the death warrant, which Her Grace was in doubts as to doing. He told her the words. "The dead do not bite!", and declared that while Queen Mary lived, Queen Elizabeth's own life must be in danger, thereby persuading Her Grace to the death. Moreover, he counselled that some other means might be found to encompass our princess's bloody fate, more secret and convenient than the headsman's axe, if this puked Her Grace. And he assured Elizabeth that there would be no uprising or commotion in Scotland over the said death, but only a few slogans shouted. That the folk cared not for their Queen, that the lords were hypocrites and windbags all, and that naught need be feared of fury from the King . . .'

'It is untrue!' Patrick cried. 'Lies – all damnable lies!' Curiously, he had turned around, so that it was at the clerk's table that he looked, not at his accuser, his King nor his judges. 'I tell you, it is false. Walsingham lies. He would divide us. He fears the invasion of his realm. He would have us fight each other, not England! It is ever the English way . . .'

David sat, eyes wide but unseeing, motionless, as though turned to stone.

'Do you deny that you had this private audience with Queen Elizabeth?' Stewart demanded, notably confident now.

'No. That I sought on our prince's direct command.' He turned to look at James. 'It was for another purpose, as His Grace knows well.'

'But you used the opportunity to press for the death of your Queen!'

'No! I deny it. I would never do such a thing. You have no proof – save the accusation of Walsingham who hates me, who hates Scotland.' That was said with violence but a certain lack of assurance, and Patrick's eyes now rested on the pile of papers in front of his accuser, tensely, as though his allegation of lack of proof held a question-mark behind it, and out from those papers one might materialise which would answer his question.

'We have clear proof, other than Walsingham's word,' Stewart nodded grimly. 'Is it your wish that it should be produced, Master of Gray?' In his hand, now, was a faded folded parchment, discoloured by years.

For seconds on end there was no sound nor movement in that chamber. Patrick Gray moistened his lips, but no words came. The silence became almost unbearable. That parchment, the accursed Deed of Abdication, had been Mary's real death warrant; now, it could equally well be his own. It could condemn him, utterly. Elizabeth had played false, in the end. But . . . why was Stewart not reading it out? Why this asking him if he wished it to be produced? Because, of course, if it was proof of his guilt, it was also proof that Mary at her death, and for eighteen years, had been no longer true Queen of Scots – thus lowering his offence from highest treason to something less. That reluctance to publish this lost and forgotten document might yet save him . . .

As Patrick hesitated, on the horns of this dire dilemma, Maitland shook his head at Stewart, almost imperceptibly, and looking along at the King, nodded.

It was James, therefore, who broke the throbbing silence, less than willingly it seemed. Swallowing loudly twice, he licked his lips, and after a false start, spoke. 'I . . . we ourself can testify to, to this matter. That the Master o' Gray willed our royal mother's death. He . . . he advised us that it would be best. Best for our Crown and realm. Mair than once, aye.' The King kept his lolling head down, looking at none.

Swiftly Maitland took him up. 'Your Grace – we are beholden to you. My lords, what need have we of further evidence? The King's testimony is final and cannot be overturned or questioned. The Master of Gray stands condemned of advising and contriving the death of His Grace's royal mother. If nothing else is accepted against him, this is sufficient indictment. How say you, my lords?'

'Aye, he is guilty!' Bothwell exclaimed. 'Guilty as Judas Iscariot!'

'After our command that he take sure and immediate action to save her, yon time!' Angus cried. 'He didna believe that Elizabeth would sign the warrant! *He* misnamed Archie Douglas for saying that she would! And all the time – this!'

The Master of Glamis spoke gratingly. 'Always the man was a dastard – have I no' told you so? A forsworn rogue. Away with him!'

'Aye, his guilt is assured. Manifest.'

'My lords,' Maitland began, primly correct. 'If this Council is duly . . .'

Patrick interrupted him urgently. 'My lords – hear me. Since His Grace has spoken, my lips are unsealed. Hitherto I could not speak you plainly, owing secrecy to the King's privy affairs. But now . . . ! You have heard His Grace's own testimony. How that I advised him for the good of his Crown and realm. I did so advise him, yes. That for Scotland's sake and his own, his mother would be better dead. I admit it. Indeed I tell you, assure you, that it is so. While Mary lived, she would not abate one jot of her claim to this throne. To her, His Grace was but a child, a princeling, usurping her Crown. No King. And you, my lords, therefore, no true Council. While she lived, Elizabeth's life and throne were in danger, and there could be no peace between Scotland and England. While she lived, our prince could never be named successor to Elizabeth's throne. While she lived, Philip of Spain stood heir to Scotland – she had nominated him so. With all inducement to invade and take, in Mary's name, what she had given him. While she lived, therefore, the Protestant cause, in which I was born and reared, stood menaced. It was Mary or war, my lords.'

'Away with him! He is a Papist rat himself!'

'Heed him not. He lies, as always.'

'It is the truth. Think, my lords – use the wits God has given you. You are of the Kirk, all of you – Protestant. You raised no hand to free Mary, all the years of her captivity. You were content. You called her the Whore of Babylon, the Pope's Harlot! You would have none of her. Why – if I am wrong . . . ?'

'Master of Gray,' Maitland said, hammering with his gavel. 'What you say is nothing to the point. You are impeached on a charge of treason in that, contrary to the express and solemn instruction of the King and this Council, when sent to strive and treat for the life of Mary the Queen, contrariwise you did advise and contrive her shameful and bloody death. Which infamous and treasonable deed you have admitted . . .'

'Not treasonable – no, sir. Since Mary was abdicate, and no longer Queen of Scots, how can it be treason?'

'Any act contrary to the King's interests and given command is treason, sir.'

'Even if His Grace knew and approved?'

'Silence, sir! How dare you drag His Majesty into your base treacheries!' Maitland exclaimed. 'Sire, we have had patience enough, have we not?'

'Aye. Oh, aye,' James agreed hurriedly.

'My lords, you have found the Master of Gray guilty of treason. The penalty of treason is death. Can any of your lordships state reason why the said penalty of death be not passed upon the said Master of Gray?'

'No! None!'

'Away with him! Send him after Mary!'

'If any man deserves to die, Gray does!'

James half-rose, and leaned over to tap the acting Chancellor's arm, hesitantly.

Hastily Maitland spoke, feigning not to notice the King. 'You judge well, my lords. Anything less than death, and our own heads would be forfeit, I do declare! The folk are roused, as I have never known them. They will have their vengeance on their Queen's murderer, that is certain. If we fail in our plain duty, they will not deal lightly with *us* – nothing is surer. With any of us!' He glanced at the King now. 'The Crown itself might not survive. A people roused is no' a thing to gainsay, I tell you.'

James subsided into his Chair of State again plucking at his lip.

Maitland stood up. 'I declare the findings of this most high Privy Council to be, then, that Patrick Master of Gray is hereby found guilty of the heinous and monstrous crime of treason against his sovereign lord King James whom God protect, and is in consequence worthy and deserving of the punishment of death. Which punishment shall be achieved, according to the law of this realm, by cutting off the said Master of Gray his head from his body, at such hour and place as the King's Grace shall command. And this is pronounced for doom. God save the King!'

'God save the King!'

'God save the King!'

'Captain of the Guard, to your duty. Take the prisoner away, and ward him in the castle of this Edinburgh, secure on peril of your own life!'

Patrick Gray was marched from the Council Chamber, looking neither to left nor to right.

Chapter Thirty-two

THE brothers faced each other at last, in a dim, damp, vaulted
cell of Edinburgh Castle, with the heavy door locked upon them
and the clank of armed men pacing outside.

'Thank God that they have let you come, at length, Davy!'
Patrick cried. 'I feared that they were not going to allow you to
visit me, for all my pleading. Man, it is good to see you.'

David stood stiffly, just inside the door, looking stonily
ahead of him. 'No man prevented me from coming to see you,
save my own self, Patrick,' he said evenly his voice flat.

The other searched his face urgently in the gloom. 'So-o-o!
That is the way of it, is it, Davy? I am sorry. But at the least,
you have come now, at last.'

'Only because I heard that the day of your your execution
has been set for Thursday. I take it that there will be matters
which you will wish to be arranged? Charges which I may
be able to carry out for you . . . ?'

'By God, there are! A-plenty! And but three days to do it in,
curse them! The folly of it – the utter senseless folly! Frightened
bairns, scared of their own shadows! It is hard, hard, to be so
trammelled by fools and paltry knaves, Davy. And now they
have left me so little time – so much to be done in so short a
space. They would let me see no one, Davy, ere this – not even
Marie. How is she, man? How does she take all this . . . ?'

'She is well enough. She bides with us. in the Lawnmarket.'

'Good. That is well. But . . . why have they let you in, Davy,
and not Marie?'

'I do not know. I came, and none hindered me.'

'They have not sent you with some message for me? Some
proposition, perhaps?'

'No. I came of my own accord. I have seen none in authority.'

'Ah well - it matters not so long as you are here.' Patrick
began to pace up and down his restricted floor. 'Listen well
then, Davy, here is what is to be done, and quickly. You must
win your way into the King's presence, and seek a royal pardon –
annulment of this ridulous death sentence. Have it reduced
to imprisonment, forfeiture banishment - anything. Any of
these I can deal with well enough, in my own time . . .'

'I cannot, Patrick.'

'Och, man, I know it will not be easy for you to gain James's presence, as matters lie. They will keep you from him, if they can. But it must be done, and it can be done. You must get one of the great lords to convey you in – one who has the King's ear. It will have to be a Catholic – for none of the Protestants will oblige you, I swear. It had better be Huntly – he is a far-out cousin of ours, and as Lieutenant of the North, the most powerful. Our Ruthven friends cannot prevent Huntly from seeing the King – and you with him. Not yet . . .'

'It is of no use, Patrick . . .'

'Tut – do not be ever so damnably gloomy! Huntly will do it, I promise you – if suitably induced. He is no different from other men, Cock o' the North though he be. Offer him, in my name, the Abbey of Dunfermline. It is the richest plum in all Scotland. George Gordon of Huntly will accept it, never fear.'

'That is not what concerns me, I tell you . . .'

'If it is the King, Davy, I think you need have no fear either. James's heart was not in yon business. He is not set against me, and cannot wish my death. He would have spoken against the death sentence, yon time, had not Maitland silenced him with fool's talk about the folk's wrath. Indeed, I cannot think what they used to turn him thus far against me. It was not the business of his mother, or Walsingham's letter, I swear . . .'

'*I* can tell you what turned him,' David said grimly. 'If your own conscience does not. The Ruthven lords told him who was truly responsible for Esmé Stuart's downfall and death.'

'Tcha – that! An old story, and no proving it. He was but a bairn then . . .'

'But James has never forgotten it. He loved his Cousin Esmé, Patrick, as he has never loved another. James never forgets anything.'

'Then he does not forget Ruthven either! He loves not these bullying Protestant lords, you may be sure, for what they did to him there. By the same token, he will not forget who delivered him out of their hands, yon time. He owed *you* his freedom then, and much service since. He will pay heed to you, Davy. If you plead for a pardon, he will not withhold it. They cannot stop him – the Protestant lords – from signing a royal pardon. And once in Huntly's hands, and given by him to Erroll the Constable, that will put all well, Secretly mind – for I do not doubt that they would have me despatched privily here in this cell, if they feared that their execution was going awry.

Poisoned food, or a slit throat...'

'Exactly as you proposed to Elizabeth for our Queen Mary! Pretty justice would it not be?'

'Tut, man – must you still harp yon tune? What's done is done. Here is no time for such talk, for recriminations and arguments on policy and statecraft...'

'As you say, Patrick,' David interrupted levelly, but strongly. 'Such time is past. As I have been trying to tell you. I did not come here to argue or to recriminate. Not any more. Only to take any last messages...'

'So be it. I am glad to hear it, Davy. Now – you have it about Huntly, and the Commendatorship of Dunfermline? That should be enough, and more...'

'No. It is no use, Patrick. You might as well save your breath. I will not see Huntly. Nor yet the King.'

'Eh...?' The other stared at his brother. 'What in God's name do you mean?'

'I mean that we have come to the parting of the ways, at last, Patrick.' Slowly, heavily, David brought out the words one by one his tone so flat as to be almost expressionless, his features as though carved. 'Too long I travelled your shameful road with you – God forgive me! It is finished now.'

'You mean...? Good Christ – you mean that you will not do this thing for me?'

'This – or any other that might save you from the judgment that you have so richly so terribly, earned'

'Merciful Heaven – it cannot be! You jest Davy – aye, you but jest?'

'Think you that I could jest at such a time? Was I a jester ever? You were the jester, Patrick – not me!'

'Then. God Almighty – it is beyond all belief!' Patrick strode forward and grabbed his brother's shoulders all but shaking them, staring into the grey steady eyes. You to do this! You Davy Gray to desert me, to turn traitor at the end! After all – you to betray me! My own brother. I'll not – I tell you I'll not believe it!'

Unwinking, unflinching, David's level regard held the other's blazing eyes. 'Betray...?' he repeated quietly. 'I wonder that you dare form that word, brother!'

'Brother! And you dare call me brother? You that could save me, but prefer to throw me to my enemies! You, who would have me die rather than lift a hand to save me! Brother, forsooth!'

'Perhaps you are right in this, Patrick. Perhaps never were we true brothers – only suffered under the accident of the same heedless sire! For 'fore God, I would not wish to be brother to the man who sent Mary Stuart to the scaffold!'

'As you would send me now!'

'As I . . .' David swallowed. 'As I would send you now!'

The other whispered. 'You . . . you want me to die, then?'

Stiff-lipped, slowly, David nodded. 'I . . . want you . . . to die.

'Christ God – this then is . . murder! The crime of Cain.' Glittering-eyed Patrick gestured towards his brother's head. 'Watch you your brow, for the mark coming! Cain's mark . . . !'

The other gazed straight ahead of him. 'So be it, if it be God's will.'

'God's will . . . !' Patrick flung away from him, to go pacing about the cell again. '*You* prate of God's will. Lord – this is not possible!'

'I warned you, Patrick. Have you forgotten? I told you, yon day after Wotton left, that if ever you acted to betray Mary the Queen, as you had betrayed so many others I would stand by no longer. I would act. I would forget that we were brothers. And you would never betray another. Do you not remember?'

'That woman! She was a witch, a devil! She turned your head, man. About her, you are crazed. What was she, man, to set above your own brother? A woman whom you saw for a few moments, once – near old enough to be your mother!'

'She was my Queen, and yours – and a helpless, sorrowing, gallant woman whom we had vowed to free and serve and cherish . . .'

'Tush – what is that but callow sentiment! And for such youth's dreams such pap. you would have me die under the axe?'

'For more than that. I would see an end to your destruction. For that is what you are, Patrick – a destroyer. All your life you have worked for destruction, setting up only that you may drag down, enticing and fascinating that you might betray. You betrayed Mariota, seducing her and then abandoning her with child. You betrayed *me*, to your father, asserting that the child was mine. So that you could have Elizabeth Lyon and her riches. You betrayed *her*, on her very wedding-night. Then, rising higher, you betrayed your faith, the Protestant faith in which you were baptised and bred, going over to the Romans – not for conviction, but for gain only, and that you might betray them in turn. You betrayed Esmé Stuart, your friend, to the death, after raising him high. Then Gowrie, your own uncle, also to the death. Arran you betrayed and brought low over yon business of the Redeswire, and Ferniehirst you threw to the dogs. Your King you betrayed to Elizabeth - and no doubt Elizabeth to de Guise and Philip of Spain. Mary Stuart was only your final and crowning infamy, dear God!'

Patrick had stopped his pacing to stare at him. mouth forming words but no sounds. He seemed to shrink in on himself, as he stood there, and for perhaps the first time in his life there was no beauty, no attractiveness, visible in those delicately moulded features. 'Are . . . are you finished?' he got out, at last, from ashen lips.

'Aye.' David sighed wearily. 'Finished yes.'

'Finished your smug, hypocritical, self-righteous litany!' That was a gabble.

'Aye. And making sure that you are finished your tally of betrayal, at last, also. Would to God that I had had the courage, and found the way, to do it sooner.'

Patrick was silent. He turned and went over to the bench that was his couch, and sat down heavily.

'So this is the end?' he said. 'I had never envisaged it... thus. David said nothing.

'I can see now why they sent you in to me - you, and only you! '

'They did not send me. I tell you, I came of my own accord.'

The other did not seem to hear him. 'I trusted you, Davy. I never thought that you would go over to my enemies even though you found fault with me. Ever you have done that. Is there nothing I can do, man - nothing that I can say to soften your heart? If you have a heart? No amends I can make?'

'None. Even if I believed you capable of amend.'

'Marie... ? And the bairn to come? For her sake... ?'

'I shall look after Marie as best I am able. You can rest assured of that. As for the bairn, it will be heir to Gray. My lord will see that it suffers nothing.'

'Aye. So. It is all decided. So simply. So nicely. And I thought that you loved me ... !'

'Simply!' David's stern armour seemed to crack. 'Lord, man - think you that aught has been decided simply, nicely? That I have not worn out my knees with praying, deeved the good God's ears to guide me, to help me to my duty? Think you that all these years I have not fought and struggled with this evil thing, cursing myself and my weakness - aye, and my love for you - as much as your fatal ...'

'Aye – so you prayed your iron Calvinist God – and He sent you here to comfort my last hours thus! My thanks, brother – my thanks! *I* pray now – pray that you will spare me more of your pious hypocrisy.'

The other seemed to bite his lips into stiffness again. 'I came . . . I did not wish to come. I came, as I told you, but to see if there were any last messages, final charges . . .'

'Ah, yes – fond farewells! You touch me deeply, Davy – i' faith you do! But I think that I can do without your loving services in this! Marie knows me well enough, without grave-yard messages. Mariota also. My beloved father never knew me – no words will change him now. Only . . . only young Mary, sweet small Mary, will, will . . . oh. for God's sake, get out! Go, man – go! If you have any heart left in you, leave me alone!'

'I . . . I am sorry.'

For moments brother looked at brother, starkly, nakedly, unspeaking, their tormented, searching, anguished eyes saying the goodbyes which their lips would not form. Then slowly, Patrick raised his hand and pointed, urgently, pleadingly, to the door.

Blindly, David turned on his heel and strode thereto. He had to rattle on the iron latch for it to be unlocked from outside, waiting wordless.

The door opened, and he stumbled out without a backward glance.

David Gray had taken only a few almost drunken steps along the stone-flagged corridor, when his arms were gripped strongly ungently, from either side. He looked up, blinking the tears from his eyes, seeking to see clearly. Two men in breastplates and morions, men-at-arms presumably, held him. Two more levelled halberds at his chest. Beyond them another man stood, of a different sort, seemingly richly dressed. Shaking his head to clear the weak tears away, David perceived that it was Sir William Stewart.

'Master Gray. you will come with me,' he was told curtly.

They led him out across the cobbled square. up a flight of steps cut in the naked castle-rock, and into another wing of the fortress – the Governor's quarters. In a richly furnished apart-ment therein, he found himself thrust before the presence of Sir John Maitland.

The Secretary of State and acting Chancellor eyed him with his usual dyspeptic and disapproving stare. 'You have taken some time to visit your brother, Master Gray,' he said, without explanation or preamble, in his dry lawyer's voice. 'It is eight days since he was imprisoned. I adjudge this to mean either that you have singularly little of brotherly affection for the said base and wretched traitor, or else that you oppugn and condemn his wicked treasons - as indeed must all His Grace's loyal servants. In either case, it seems likely that you will not fail in your duty to your King, now.'

David looked from the speaker to Stewart, to another who seemed to be an officer of the royal guard, and sought to jerk his arms free of the men-at-arms who still gripped him. 'I do not understand you, sir,' he said, frowning. 'Nor why I have been roughly handled and brought here thus. I have committed no offence. What means this, sir . . . ?'

Maitland ignored the other's protest entirely. 'Your duty to King James is plain. You will do well to remember it. By what means does the Master of Gray plan to circumvent the King's justice?'

Astonished, David gazed at the man. 'You mean .. ?'

'Tut, man - do not play the fool! You are not dealing with fools I assure you. Your precious brother is a nimble-witted rogue. He will not fail to take such steps as he may to save himself and overturn the true course of justice. And undoubtedly he has friends amongst the disaffected and the disloyal. He cannot achieve much in a prison cell without a go-between. You are the only one who has been permitted to visit him.'

'I see!' David's grey eyes smouldered, now. 'So that is why you permitted me to see him, without hindrance! You must have a poor opinion of me. I think, sir! You name him traitor - and adjudge me to be a traitor likewise, in that I would betray my own brother!'

'We give you the opportunity to prove that you are *no* traitor, rather, Master Gray,' Maitland said, but sourly. 'Less merciful and patient Ministers of the Crown might consider that since you were your brother's close confidant and secretary, you must be equally implicated with himself in his treasonable activities. You might well be in the next cell to the Master of Gray at this present, sir! You would do well to remember it.'

'If I am not, sir, it is not because of your love for me, I swear!' David returned. 'Rather, because you have no evidence which would condemn me - for I am as loyal to King James as I was to his gracious mother the Queen. As I have proved.'

'I rejoice to hear it. In that case, you will tell us what steps your wretched brother intends in this pass – since it is inconceivable that he will not strive to save his neck, contrary to the King's decree.'

David looked steadily at his questioner, and said nothing.

Maitland frowned. 'Master Gray, I would remind you that we have the means to loose halting tongues in this castle!'

'No doubt, sir. But they would avail you nothing. For though I would not reveal my brother's plans to you if I could, the truth is, there are none. I bear no messages from him, am committed to no projects.'

'Think you that we shall believe that, fool!'

'Whether you believe it or no, it is the truth . . .'

That ended in a wheezing gasp, as David reeled back and would have fallen had not the two men-at-arms held him upright. The officer had struck him hard full across the mouth with a gloved fist, at Stewart's nod.

Maitland went on primly, as though nothing whatsoever had occurred. 'We require the truth, Master Gray, and shall have it. Your brother is not one to accept his fate without lifting a hand. we have known that from the first, and have taken due precautions. He has already tried to bribe his guards. Your visit offered him his greatest opportunity. What would he have you to do?'

David licked the blood from his lips. 'I would not tell you – even if I knew.'

His head snapped back with a sickening jolt as the captain jabbed two vicious blows at him, to nose and eye, in swift succession.

'Yes, Master Gray? We are waiting.'

'Curse you . . . !' David, dizzy, reeling, yet struggled desperately with his captors, striving to free his arms. But the men-at-arms held them fast, indeed twisted them behind his back until the agony was excruciating. Even so, as the officer lunged forward again, David lashed out with his foot, to catch the man strongly below the knee-cap.

A hail of furious blows fell upon him, and the weight of his own body sagging against those twisted arms had him half swooning away.

Dimly, as though through a thick red mist, he heard Maitland's dry voice droning on. '. . . obstinacy is the attribute of a fool, Master Gray. I had not esteemed you that, ere this. Come, man – enough of this folly. What are your brother's wishes? To whom does he send you?'

Slowly David's swollen and bleeding lips moved, sought to form words, 'Do . . . your . . . worst,' he got out, at length, only just intelligibly. 'You . . . cannot . . . make me . . . speak. You cannot . . .'

He choked to silence then, as the edge of a hard hand slashed at the front of his neck, his adam's apple. The torment was exquisite. His throat filled with bile. Blind with pain and nausea, David was convulsively sick.

It was a little while before he realised that it was a new voice that was speaking through it all – presumably Sir William Stewart's voice.

'. . . that this is all we can do? That there is not the rack and the boot, the wheel and the thumbscrews? Och, we are well provided with such niceties here – my lord of Morton saw to that! You have a long way to go, fool, before we are finished with you!'

David sought to raise his splitting head. He did not know whether he achieved it or no, even whether the words which he so sorely formed were indeed enunciated. 'I'll . . . no' . . . speak,' he muttered. 'You've . . . got . . . the wrong . . . man!'

The hails of blows which followed that made but little difference.

For how long David Gray's tribulation lasted, he never knew. Looking back, it seemed an endless purgatory of searing pain. But at the time he was almost more obsessed, undoubtly, by a furious anger, an all-consuming rage of hatred at his persecutors, and an overwhelming ache of anguish, not for himself and his plight, but for his inability to hit back, the wicked injury to his pride in that he could not give as good as he got. The Gray in him undoubtedly was far from latent.

And presently there crept upon him a warm and grateful awareness that things were not quite as they had been, that blows were no longer really hurting him, that savage pain was ebbing, that nothing mattered so much. It was a good, an excellent feeling. A great and overpowering relief began to enfold him, and he embraced its warm drowsy comfort with all that remained of his reeling consciousness.

The final descent into blessed insensibility held no single lingering echo of hurt.

Chapter Thirty-three

THE ascent to pain and tribulation was gradual, also. Reluctantly, indeed, David came to himself. He kept his eyes shut, in
fact, deliberately, out of sheer shrinking unwillingness to accept
the grievous burden of it all, for quite some time – until,
indeed, he discovered that he could scarcely open them anyway.
One eye was in fact completely closed up; out of the other,
presently, he decided that he could see, after a fashion.

What he saw out of it took some time to register, for it had to
compete with other and very pressing perceptions and impressions, mainly of multiple and comprehensive hurt, of dizziness,
sickness, stiffness, and general physical misery. But at length his
eye told him, with some insistence, that the people standing
watching him not only were not belabouring him in any way,
but were not so inclined, at all. They were, indeed, small
children.

This knowledge, when it sank into his bemused brain, aroused
him. His mind suddenly began to function with a strange
clarity, even while his aching body remained inert, anxious
only to escape back into blessed oblivion.

He perceived that he was lying on the ground, out-of-doors.
Moreover, he recognised that it was raining. He seemed to be in
a narrow, confined place amongst damp stone walls – undoubtedly one of the wynds or closes that opened off the main
city streets. And only the children watched him, and a small
sniffing dog. He was no longer in the castle, then ...

As David lay there, eyes closed again, seeking to understand
this strange circumstance, his nose, though battered and very
sore, kept transmitting to him a message of its own. At length
he attended to it. Malt liquor – whisky – that is what it was. He
stank of it. Gingerly he opened his eye again. All the torn front
of his doublet was soaking wet – indubitably with whisky.

Groaning involuntarily, David stirred, sought to raise himself, got to his knees, staggered to his feet, leaning against the
wall for support .The children stepped back warily, but hooted
their merriment. Obviously he was thought to be drunk, very
drunk indeed.

Testing his joints, his muscles, cautiously, painfully, the man decided that no bones were broken. He took a tentative step or two, clinging to the wall – and though he winced with the stounding hurt of it, he perceived that he could walk. The dog began to bark, loudly.

Feeling his way, hand never leaving the masonry, and with the children chanting in his wake, he began to edge along. A dark archway opened ahead of him – no doubt the pend from the wynd leading out on to the street. Through its echoing vault he limped, tottering.

At the other end he paused, breathing deeply, trying to focus his unco-ordinated sight. Even so, it did not take him long to recognise his whereabouts. He was in the Lawnmarket, not far from his own house – even on the same side of the street. Thankfully, if with great care, he began to stagger up the cobble-stones. The children and dog deserted him.

How he managed to drag himself up the many steep stairs to his lofty eerie of a house, David did not know. Undoubtedly it took a long time. But one part of his mind was busy through-out, despite the physical stress – that clear, active part which pain indeed almost seemed to sharpen.

They had not put him into a cell, like Patrick, as they had threatened, then. Nor had they resorted to the rack and the thumbscrews. Why? They had brought him down from the castle, spilling whisky over him to make him appear to be drunk – to account for his unconsciousness and battered condition. Brought him near to his own house. Why?

Not out of any remorse or pity, that was certain. It could only be policy. What then? Why trouble thus? They wanted in-formation from him. Presumably they had decided that they would not get it in a cell or under torture – nor from an un-conscious man. They must still hope to get it out of him some-how, then, or they would merely have locked him up, or dis-posed of him out-of-hand. They must be going to watch him, therefore – keep him under observation, and hope that he would lead them to the information that they sought. No doubt they were watching him, now. The fools! If only they knew the truth, the terrible, incredible truth! Not that they would have believed him if he had told them . . . !

David Gray lurched into his own house, and collapsed part upon a settle, part against the table. Consternation gripped the little household. Fortunately both Mariota and Marie, who had stayed with them since her husband's arrest, were practical-minded women, not given to hysteria. However vocal their distress and urgent their demands for explanation and information, however vehement their denunciation of whoever was responsible for his state, they set about the loving care of David's injuries and provision for his comfort and needs, without delay. They both knew him too well to be impressed by the smell of liquor. Mary, now thirteen years old, stared in wide-eyed horror, whilst seeking to keep young Patrick quiet.

Speaking with difficulty through cut and swollen lips, David told them briefly what had happened after leaving Patrick's cell, dwelling mainly upon the fact that his assailants had but used him as a bait, allowed him unhindered access to his brother merely so that they might question him afterwards, and stressing that they undoubtedly would be watching him still, watching the house, hoping that he would lead them to what they wanted to know.

'The brutes!' Mariota exclaimed. 'The dastardly brutes! To think that they could sink so low – Maitland, Stewart! Men you have worked with ... !'

'It is but what Patrick would name statecraft, I suppose!'

'It is savagery! Barbarity ... !'

'It is shameful! They are no better than brute beasts!' Marie said. 'But ... but ...' Her voice faltered. 'If you are to be watched, Davy, as you say – then what are we to do? It is but three days until ... until ...' She bit her lip.

David cleared his throat, but said nothing.

'We shall find a way, never fear,' Mariota asserted stoutly. 'We shall win Patrick free.'

'But how? Oh, how can we? If they watched David thus, they will watch me also, Patrick's wife, without a doubt. And you too, Mariota ...'

'My lord – he would help. They would not dare to treat *him* so!'

'I would not be so sure. But Lord Gray is at Castle Huntly, still. He has not come – he has not come, though he must know well that Patrick is taken and condemned. I wrote to him, but ... he has not come! Anyway, to ride to Castle Huntly and back would take too long – four days.'

'The King, then. You must try to see the King again, Marie. He is your own cousin.'

'They will not allow it. I have tried – you know how I have tried. But they surround James – guard him like a prisoner himself. They will not allow me into the palace. Davy – what did Patrick say? What did he tell you to do?

397

David moistened damaged lips. 'He . . . I . . . ' He swallowed sorely. 'I cannot do it, Marie. I told you before. I am sorry – but I cannot do it. Would not, even if I could.'

'Davy! You do not . . . you cannot mean that! Not really mean it . . .'

'Aye. As God is my witness, I do!'

'But . . . your own brother!'

'Aye. My brother.'

'No, Davy – no! Oh, I know how he is at fault. That he has done shameful things. I know that you blame him – I blame him also. But . . . but not this, Davy. Not to . . . the death!'

'Has he hesitated at the death of others?'

'Perhaps not. But . . . that does not make us his judges.'

'You would have me to forget all the evil that he has wrought?'

'Not forget – but forgive!'

'Who am I to forgive him? The ill was not wrought against me. But I . . . I could have saved some of the ill from happening, had I been stronger, truer to my conscience, of a better courage. Do not talk to me of forgiveness, for I do not forgive myself!' David had sat up in his bed, in his vehemence, and now swayed dizzily with the effort, his features contorted with pain. 'Only . . . only of this I am sure,' he declared thickly, uncertain only in the enunciation of his words. 'It must not, it shall not, happen again.'

'Davy, lie down,' Mariota commanded. 'You distress yourself. Lie back, Rest – you must rest. You are not yourself. We shall speak of this again . . .'

'If you mean that I will think differently in the morning, woman, you are wrong,' he told her, sinking back.

'Tut, now, In your right mind, Davy, you would never condemn your brother to death! No, no. I tell you . . .' Suddenly Mariota turned, recollecting her great-eyed, watching children. 'Mary, take your brother ben the house. Quickly, now – off with you. Here is no talk for bairns . . .'

'I am sorry, Mariota,' Marie said, low-voiced, after the door had closed on them. 'I had forgotten the children. I hardly know what I am doing, or saying. I think that I shall go mad – if we are not all mad already!'

'Hush you, my dear. It will be better in the morning. Davy will think differently then, I swear. He is hurt, sick . . .'

'That is nothing to the point,' the man said, wearily. 'My mind is made up.'

'Oh, Davy! If not for his sake – for mine!' Marie besought

398

him, brokenly. 'We have understood each other, been good friends, always.'

Slowly, painfully, David turned his head away from them, to face the wall.

'Leave him, Marie – let him be,' Mariota counselled. 'He needs rest, sleep. We must let him be ...'

David did not sleep, nor scarcely rest. Tossing and turning on his bed, despite the hurt of it, he wrestled with himself, his faith, his conscience and his love, and knew no peace of body, mind or spirit.

Some time, how much later he knew not, he heard the door of his bedchamber open and shut. But he did not turn towards it, did not open the eye that was less painful closed. Indeed he had forgotten it when, after a while, some faint stir of movement near him penetrated the turmoil of his mind. Reluctantly he turned his head and looked.

Young Mary sat on a chair beside his bed, gazing at him silently. In her hand she held a cup.

'I have brought you a posset,' she told him. 'It is to help you to sleep.'

'It will require more than a posset to make me sleep this night!' he said. 'But ... thank you, lass.'

She helped him drink it down, so that he need not sit up. Then, still unspeaking, she sat down again at his side, to watch him, her eyes fixed on him, unwavering.

David would have turned his head away once more – but somehow could not. He would have shut his eye again – indeed did shut it often enough, but always opened it again. He could not keep his gaze away from her, avoid her eyes. It was those eyes that held him, burned in on him, ravaged him – deep, dark, lustrous, lovely eyes, so damnably like Patrick's. They never left his face, considering him, reproaching him ...

Mary Gray had more than fulfilled the promise of her early childhood. She was small still, but perfectly made and already well developed, thus early on the threshold of most lovely young womanhood. Always she had been a dainty, exquisite creature; now she was of an elfin beauty to take the breath away and catch the heart-strings. Only one other had David ever seen who touched her in beauty – and that her namesake Mary of Scotland.

He stood it for as long as he could. 'Why do you stare so,

child!' he exclaimed at length. 'Lord knows, I cannot be a pretty sight!'

Gravely she shook her dark head, but her great eyes never left his ravaged features nevertheless. 'Father,' she said, gently, but thoughtfully, 'Mother and the Lady Marie are weeping. Because my Uncle Patrick is to die, is it not?'

Swallowing, the man nodded dumbly.

'And you could save him, could you not, if you were well and able?'

David started up, aches or none. 'No, I could not! I could not, I tell you!' he cried, almost shouted. 'It is impossible, child.'

'Oh yes, you could,' she asserted, quietly, assuredly. 'You can do anything that you set your hand to. Uncle Patrick told me that, himself. Long ago. He told me that you were the finest, strongest man that he knew, and that he would wager you against any man or set of men in all Scotland. It is true. I know.'

David groaned. 'It is folly, girl – sheer arrant folly. I am weak, helpless, a broken reed ...'

'Only because you are sick and injured and beaten, by those evil men. But you *could* save him, if you were well.' She nodded decidedly. 'So *I* must do it, in your place.'

David choked, and the blood came trickling from a corner of his mouth. 'Lord child, – what ... what are you saying?'

'That I must do it, for you, Father. You will tell me what to do, and I will do it.'

'Och, Mary lass, Mary – you do not know what you say ...'

'I do, Father. These wicked men must not gain the mastery. And it is right that I should do it, I think – for Uncle Patrick is my true father is he not?'

Dumbfounded David gazed at her, peering from his watering eye. 'You ... you ... who told you that, child?' he got out at last, thickly.

'Many have said it. Often. Children about the Court. My grandfather, once, when he was drunk. I am so like my Uncle Patrick – all can see it. It is the truth, is it not?'

After seconds, wordlessly he nodded his head.

'So, you see, it is right that I should do it – for my own father. I love you best, of course. But I have always loved my Uncle Patrick, too.'

David drew a long breath. 'My dear,' he said. 'There is nothing that you can do. Nothing. I am sorry ...'

'I can go to the King. If you will tell me how I may win in to him. The King will hear me. He likes me well. He told me that I was a bonny lass. He thanked me, mind, for being kind to Vicky that is Duke of Lennox. He would pay heed to me.'

'But, lass, it is not so easy as that. Even if I could bring you into the King's presence.' He paused. 'Do you know for what your, your Uncle Patrick was judged and condemned?'

'That I do. Everybody knows that. It was for not saving poor Mary the Queen, when he went to London.'

'Aye – just that. For not saving Mary the Queen! A heavy charge, my dear.'

'Poor Mary the Queen! I hate that Elizabeth for killing her – hate her! But it *was* Elizabeth who killed her, was it not? It was not Uncle Patrick?'

'No, Yes. But, you see . . .'

'And you went to London with Uncle Patrick to try to save her too, Father, did you not?'

'Yes. I went also. But not as Patrick went – only as a secretary . . .'

'But to try to save the Queen. But you did not save her, either of you.'

David looked down, away from those glowing, searching eyes, at last. 'No,' he said. 'Neither of us.'

'But you did try – which is the main thing, is it not? Mother says that you did all that you could to save the poor Queen. Tell me what you did, will you? Did you try to save her, the way that you saved the King, at Ruthven?'

He did not answer.

'As you saved Uncle Patrick and Vicky's father in France, that time – with the cattle-beasts?'

He stared at the floor. 'No,' he muttered. 'It was not possible.'

'Then, Father, if you tried all to save her, and could not do it – how could Uncle Patrick? Always he told me that you could do anything that you set your hand to – and I know that it is true. Did you not set your hand to saving the Queen?'

He met her eyes now, and strangely his swollen lower lip was trembling. 'God help me, child – I do not know!' he burst out. 'I do not know.'

Gently she reached out to touch his clenched bruised fist. 'Do not worry, Father – do not worry,' she said. 'I am quite sure that you did your best. Like Uncle Patrick – whatever they say. Is that why these evil men beat you so cruelly?'

He made no reply, did not seem to hear her.

401

'They had no right,' the girl declared. 'Even though they loved the Queen, they had no right. For she said that all were to be forgiven. She said that all, all who encompassed her death, even the horrid man who cut off her head, and Queen Elizabeth who told him to do it – all were to be forgiven.'

'Eh . . . ? What was that? What did you say?' The man turned slowly, to lean towards her, as though hard of hearing. 'What did you say?'

'Have you not heard? Everyone speaks of it. The speech that she made. They have made a broadsheet of it. Mary the Queen spoke it before she died. She said . . . I mind not all that she said. But this she did say – might God, who alone can judge the thoughts and acts of men, forgive all those who have thirsted for her blood. Was she not good, Mary the Queen? Kind. I am glad that I am named Mary, too. She said all were to be forgiven. So, the King cannot be angry with Uncle Patrick, any more – nor with you either, Father. Can he?'

David Gray was not listening.

'If I go to him, I am sure that he will say that Uncle Patrick is not to die. So, will you tell me how I can come to the King, please?'

There was silence in that bedchamber for long moments, as Mary Gray waited, serious, intent. Only the man's deep breathing sounded.

Then abruptly, he brought his open hand down upon the quilt that covered him. 'Amen! So be it!' he said, and turned to her urgently. 'Child – you know my lord of Huntly's great house down the Canongate?'

'Huntly House – over the street from the Tolbooth? Aye, I know it fine, Father.'

'They will never think of you, a child . . . with a basket, maybe. Aye, a basket on your arm, when you go errands to the booths for your mother. In the morning. That is it . . . See, Mary – fetch me paper and quill and ink-horn from my desk. You know where they are – paper, quill, ink-horn. And quickly!'

Eyes alight, the girl ran to do his bidding.

402

Chapter Thirty-four

GEORGE, 6th Earl of Huntly, Chief of Clan Gordon, Cock o'
the North, principal Catholic of the realm – and now, curiously,
to be the Kirk's Commendator-Abbot of Dunfermline – red-
faced, haughty, arrogant, leaving his tail of five-score mounted
Gordons stamping and clattering in the forecourt of Holyroodhouse, strode past all wary-eyed and circumspect guards
and officers in the various palace doorways and corridors without
so much as a glance. Behind him his five bonneted and plaided
Gordon lairds were scarcely less proudly overbearing, hands on
their broadsword hilts, so that the sixth, David Gray, wrapped
in Gordon tartan and with bonnet crammed hard down over
his brow, stiff and sore as he was, had great difficulty in keeping
up with this fierce Highland stalking. And, Heaven knew, he
did not want to fall behind, to become in any way conspicuous,
to become other than just one plaid-wrapped supporter amongst
six, for keen-eyed watchers to consider. It was a blessing that
these Highlanders always kept their bonnets on, save when
actually in the royal presence; also that his face was still swollen
and discoloured enough to be barely recognisable.

Huntly's shouted demands as to the whereabouts of the King
brought them expeditiously to the library of the palace –
Huntly always approached his sovereign in this fashion, as a
matter of principle, considering himself practically a fellow-
prince. In the ante-room, the young Earls of Bothwell and Mar
sprawled at ease with tankards of ale, and deliberately did not
rise to their feet at the Gordon eruption. The older man snorted
loudly as he passed, but otherwise ignored them. Their mocking
smiles were discreetly kept below the level of laughter which
might reach Gordon ears. They did not bother to look at
Huntly's following.

At the door of the library, an officer of the guard stood on
duty. He made no attempt to halt the oncoming party, but on
the contrary threw open the door and announced that the noble
Earl of Huntly, Lieutenant of the North, sought audience of His
Grace. Reinforced by a growled pleasantry from the noble
suppliant himself, the party swept inside, David in the midst.
It was as easy as that. The last Gordon in, turned to close the

door with something of a slam in the face of the officer.

The King was sitting alone at a table in the musty-smelling, booklined room, surrounded by open volumes, pen in hand, scratching away at a paper. Next to the hunting-field James was happiest when in a library. He looked up, frowning, with no relish for being disturbed. Moreover, he had always been a little afraid of the potent and fiery Huntly.

'Ha, y'Grace,' the latter cried, doffing his feathered bonnet at last. 'At your books again, I see! Man, I would not let the books take a hold of you, see you. They are worse than women or the bottle for sucking the marrows out of a man!'

James rose, trembling with his earnestness. 'My lord, books are the finest gift of Almighty God to men!' he protested. 'Without them, we should be as the beasts that perish.'

'Bah!' the Gordon snorted. 'Without them, many men would be the happier. Many men now dead would be alive. Mother o' God – show me a bookish man and I will show you a rogue ... with due respect to Your Grace! Yon Maitland, for instance. William Stewart. The bladder o' lard, Davidson, whom you miscall a Bishop! George Buchanan, that fount o' bile – aye, and most of the rest of his Bible-beating kin!'

'My lord, you speak amiss! Och, man – yon's no way to talk. You should think shame o' yoursel' to speak o' godly men so. I'll no' have it. I'll no' listen to such ill speech. What ... what do you want with me, Lord Huntly?'

'For myself – nothing, Sire. Save maybe that you get rid of the pack of yapping lap-dogs of the Kirk that yelp around you, these days! No, no – for George Gordon – nothing. It is Davy Gray, here, who seeks your ear. Eh, Davy?'

David stepped out from behind his protective screen of Gordon lairds. 'Yes, Your Grace,' he said.

'Master . . . Davy!' the King gasped. 'Man – is it you? Waesucks – your face! Man Davy, how . . . what . . . what has become o' you?'

' 'Tis nothing, Sire. The methods of your new Chancellor Maitland, that is all! In search of . . . information, on Your Majesty's behalf! Heed it not. I seek Your Grace's ear on a much more important matter. In clemency ...'

'Na, na – I canna do it, Master Davy!' James interrupted him, pulling at his ear in agitation. 'It's no' possible, man. I canna do anything for Patrick – for the Master o' Gray. Dinna ask me to ...'

'But I do so ask, Your Grace. I ask you, of your royal clem-

404

ency, to pardon him. Or, at the least, to commute the sentence of death.'

'No. I canna do it, I tell you.'

'You can, Sire – if you will. For you are the King. You can sign a pardon if you will – and none can gainsay it.'

'They'd ... they'd no' allow it. They'd no let me. And they'd no' let him go, man.' James babbled, slobbering copiously in his distress. 'They watch me, all the time. I canna do it.'

Huntly growled. 'You are afraid of a coven of upstart clerks and lawyers, Sire – you, the King of Scots?' His scorn was undisguised.

'They need not know – not until it is too late to stop it,' David declared hurriedly. 'Keep the matter secret, Highness. Your signed pardon, in the hands of my Lord Erroll, the Constable, and presented to the Governor of Edinburgh Castle ... ! He could do no other than release Patrick. Then my lord of Huntly's men would escort him to a ship at Leith, within the hour. None could challenge them.'

'Challenge Gordon?' Huntly hooted. 'The Saints defend them, if they did!'

The King plucked at his lower lip. 'But ... treason is no' a thing I can pardon, man. Conspiring the death o' my royal mother ...'

Set-faced David eyed him. 'The Queen was sentenced to death, Sire, before Patrick ever went to London.'

'Aye. But you'll no' deny that it was an ill thing to do, Davy – to aid Elizabeth to the death ...'

'I do not deny it, Sire. It was a shameful and wicked deed. I only cast myself and Patrick's life upon your royal mercy.'

'Ummm. Ooh, aye – do you so, man?' Always, any implication that James was all-powerful and in a position to grant or withhold life or death, was apt to be well received. And clearly the frank admission of guilt left him at something of a loss. 'Well, well, now ...'

David sought to pursue his advantage. 'I do not ask for more than his life, Highness. He deserves to suffer much, I do not deny – though it may be true that he believed that he did what he did for the benefit of this realm. Punish him, yes – forfeit him, take away his offices and estates, banish him the realm. But spare his life, Sire, I beseech you.'

James moved round the littered table at his shambling walk, touching papers, frowning, darting, glances here and there. 'I ... I ... no, I canna do it, Master Davy,' he declared. 'Can

I, my lord? As ambassador o' this my realm, Patrick betrayed his trust. To pardon that would never do – never do, man. My ambassador speaks for me – he is my royal voice, see you. If thy tongue offends thee, cut it out, the Good Book says . . .'

'It also says forgive, until seventy times seven, Your Grace. Moreover, has not your own mother, Mary the Queen, ordained forgiveness on all concerned with her death, even with her dying breath? You would not have her noble wish made of no avail, Sire? You wrote kindly enough to Queen Elizabeth, who ordered the execution; can you not at least spare the life of him who but advised it?'

'Och, that is altogether different, Davy. Dinna harry me, man – I'm no' to be harried. You shouldna do it . . .'

'Sire, he is my brother. I will do much, say much, even that I should not say or do, to save my brother! *I* failed Queen Mary also, in England. I could have attempted her rescue. I spoke of it, once, but allowed myself to be dissuaded. I was weak. I believe, had I been strong, that I could have saved her. At Wingfield. I shall never forgive myself . . .'

'Mercy, man – what havers is this? How could you have saved her . . . ?'

'The way that I saved you, Sire, at Ruthven. By force and guile and fast horses. By deeds and not words . . . '

'Waesucks, Davy – are you crazed? Yon would never have done – never. Dinna speak o' it. In Elizabeth's England! Yon would have meant war!'

'I wonder. Now I look back on it, I think not. Sire. But . . . it is done now, past. I failed the Queen. My eyes are open to it, at last.'

'Never say it,' the King told him. 'Violence and swordery – yon's no' the way to conduct the affairs o' the realm, man.'

'It gained you your freedom, Sire, once.' David took a step forward. 'I pray you now, not to forget it. If it meant anything that I saved Your Grace then, spare Patrick now! I have asked for nothing – would have accepted nothing. But now, Sire, I do so ask. For Patrick's life.' He paused. 'It was a long time ago, but surely you owe me something for that? And for other services, since.'

Even Huntly frowned. 'Davy – here's no way to speak to your King!' he protested.

'I know it, my lord. I said, did I not, that I would do and say things for my brother – things that I should not do?'

James was biting his finger-nails. 'Aye, Davy – I was beholden to you for yon business. And for others, aye. I should have rewarded you. I've thought o' it, man – more than once. Oh, aye – it was featly done. A . . . a knighthood, man Davy? Eh? Aye, I could knight you. There's many a bastard been knighted. I could do it here and now – with my lord's braw broadsword, there. Sir David Gray, Knight . . .' James was almost eager, for the first time.

'No, Sire – I am not of the stuff of knights. Save that for Sir John Maitland and Sir William Stewart and their like! I have tasted their knightly prowess, and want none of it. I am just plain Davy Gray, schoolmaster . . .'

'A grant o' lands, then? Estates? An office under the Crown . . .

'Thank you, no, Sire. Nothing – save my brother's life.'

'A curse on you, Davy Gray!' the harassed monarch exclaimed. 'Hard, stubborn as a Hieland stot! I told you – it's no' possible. The folk, the people, would decry me, if I did. They would have my mother avenged.'

'Forfeiture and banishment would be vengeance enough for them.'

'Who rules in Scotland, then – people or King?' Huntly scoffed. 'Besides, Sire, the people will have other matters to think on! Very shortly.' That was grimly said. 'Good Catholics, in especial. And what did the other sort care for Mary?'

James's jaw dropped. 'You're, you're no' meaning, my lord . . . ? You wouldna, wouldna . . . ?'

'. . . Say that I would advise Your Grace not to fash your head about what the folk will say. They will be a deal too busy shouting for Christ's true religion!'

David frowned. He drew out a paper from his doublet within the plaid, and smoothing it out, laid it on the table before the King. 'Here is a pardon, all written out ready, Highness,' he said. 'It declares the Master of Gray forfeit, dismissed all offices, and banished from Your Grace's realm. But his life spared. These provisions may be amended with a scrape of your pen . . .'

'Master Gray, you exceed yoursel' – you greatly exceed yoursel'!' James declared, drawing himself up with a pathetic dignity.

'No doubt, Sire,' David nodded, and fixed the huge, limpid, royal eyes with his own direct grey ones, however red-rimmed and bloodshot. 'But you will mind that I was in yon small room, not so far from this, when you gave my brother his instructions, his secret instructions, as to what he was to say in private audience with Elizabeth! You mind? About the terms on which you would overlook certain matters relating to your royal mother?'

'Hey, hey – what's this, Davy?' Huntly demanded. 'What's this, in the name of God?'

James sat down abruptly on his chair.

'Just a small matter, my lord, that His Highness may have forgotten. That may lead him to think more kindly of my brother on the matter of his amends . . .'

The King croaked something unintelligible.

'Amends? What mean you, man? About Mary the Queen, you said?'

'Small matters, yes – but which perhaps were not irrelevant to Patrick's behaviour. If I had thought to mention it at his trial, perhaps His Grace might have judged . . . differently. I blame myself.'

'No!' James got out, in strangled voice, 'No.'

'What of the Queen, man? Stop speaking in riddles,' Huntly commanded. 'Are you seeking to say . . .?'

'Only that, if His Grace will not sign the pardon, at least he may grant a stay of execution. So that this matter may be brought before the Council. You, my lord, might consent to bring it?'

'Not, by the Powers, until I know what it is, fool!' the Gordon cried.

James reached out his hand for his quill, dipped it tremblingly in the ink, and scrawled JAMES R. at the foot of David's paper.

'My God . . . !'

'My sincere thanks, Your Majesty!'

Huntly looked hard at David. 'This matter was none so small, I think!' he said. 'Do not tell me that the King . . .?'

'It is not for me to tell you anything, my lord – unless the King so will it.'

'I do not!' James cried, his voice cracking. 'Nothing, do you hear? It was a, a private matter. Between Queen Elizabeth and mysel'. A matter relating to my privy purse. Expenses, just . . .'

'M'mmm,' the Gordon said.

'No' word o' this will be spoken – by any!' the King declared breathlessly, staring from Huntly to his five perplexed-looking lairds, and back to David. 'This is my royal command. D'you hear – my royal command? No' a word. And as for this . . .' James pointed a quivering finger at the signed pardon. 'It is for life. For life, d'you hear? Banishment for life. Put that in,

408

man – put it in. And no' to England. I'll no' have him in England, making trouble. I never wish to see his face again. Nor yours either, Davy Gray! You are an ill graceless breed, and I'll be quit o' you both! Begone, now – and mind, never let me set eyes on you again.'

David bowed stiffly, and picked up the paper. 'Your command shall be obeyed, Sire – most explicitly,' he said.

'Aye. See to it, then. And you, my lord – you have my permission to retire.'

'No doubt, Sire,' Huntly nodded. 'No doubt. And I shall not linger, for I do not like the smell o' this, by the Mass!'

'Go, then . . .'

So the tartan-clad party backed perfunctorily out of the royal presence, clapped on bonnets, and went striding through Holyroodhouse again, David Gray anonymous once more in the midst. Huntly exchanged no word with any of them.

Indeed he did not speak until, at the head of his mounted retinue, he drew rein outside his great mansion in the Canongate. He turned to David, at his back.

'It is done, then,' he said.

'Aye.' David drew out the pardon from within the folds of his enveloping plaid. 'Relays of your fastest gillies to get this to the Constable, my lord – riding day and night. We have less than forty-eight hours. When my lord of Erroll rides up to Edinburgh Castle, the deeds and charters of Dunfermline Abbey will be ready awaiting you.'

The Earl took the paper, but his eyes never left the younger man's battered face. 'Davy Gray,' he said slowly. 'You are a hard man to cross, I perceive. I'd liefer have you as friend than enemy, by the Rood! I vow you should turn Catholic!'

The other shook his head. 'You are wrong,' he returned. 'I am not a hard man, at all. Would to God that I was! It is just that . . . my, my daughter believes that I can do anything that I set my hand to. I had to prove it. Heaven forgive me, I had to prove it! A good day to you, my lord.'

Leaving Huntly to enter at his front door, David, with the rest of the clattering horsemen, rode down the side vennel to the stable entrance in the South-Back Canongate. There, dismounting, discarding plaid and bonnet and clad as just plain David Gray again, he slipped away by back-courts and wynds, to approach his own house in the Lawnmarket up the hill.

No song of triumph lightened his heart.

409

Epilogue

HUDDLED in shawls and plaids, the Grays sat their horses, all four of them, in the shadow of the dripping trees, waiting. The morning mists still rose from the Nor' Loch below them, and wreathed the battlements of the great fortress high above them, with the blue plumes of Edinburgh's breakfast fires beginning to add their daily veiling. They waited each in different fashion – young Patrick excitedly restless, vociferous, forever twisting and wriggling in his saddle; Mary in still quiet eagerness; Mariota flushed, strained, not far from tears; David set-faced, silent. All gazed in the same direction, up over the steep slope of grass and rocks to the high ridge-like causeway, outlined against the morning sky, which climbed up from the outer gate at the head of the Lawnmarket, right to the main frowning gatehouse of the castle, the lofty slender catwalk which formed the quarter-mile-long approach to the fortress, open to the eyes of all men and all the winds that blew. Sometimes, admittedly, David's glance turned elsewhere, making a swift survey of the broken slopes below and around them, and the window-pierced ramparts of the nearest tall houses – so many windows, so many eyes to watch them.

The high defensive causeway was some two hundred yards above them. Nearer than this, under the last of the scattered trees, they dared not go. They were taking all too great a risk even to be here, though probably only David considered that aspect of the matter. The pacing guards up on the castle battlements could hardly fail to see them, just as would a myriad eyes that might peer from all those windows at the other end of the causeway. Undoubtedly they would have been better, wiser, to have left Edinburgh before the city gates shut the night before. Waited somewhere on the road to Leith ...

The dense mass of horsemen that could be seen waiting up there outside the portcullis gatehouse was reassuring, of course – even though they had no interest in, represented no security for the little family, bunched, all packed and ready to ride, beneath the trees. They were armed Gordons, save for the few of Erroll's Hays, and the sound of their confident,

410

laughing, north-country voices came clearly down to the anxious group, so that David, beneath his breath, cursed all arrogant boastful Highlanders, who must thus draw attention to themselves and what was toward so early in the morning.

Would they never come? Had anything gone wrong, in there within the castle, where so much might well go wrong? Was the Governor refusing to release his prisoner, despite the royal pardon? Was he trying to get word out to Maitland or the lords – though how could he achieve that, past the barrier of Gordons? It could not be that they were, in fact, too late? That James had resiled, gone back on his signature – or revealed the whole matter to his Ministers? And Patrick already disposed of, in his cell? Surely, if that had been so, he himself would have been arrested and silenced before this?

Apparently stolid, steadfast, but inwardly seething, David wondered for how long he could prevent himself from snapping at his small son to be quiet, to be still; how far they might already have progressed on the long road to Stirling and Perth and Castle Huntly, had only Erroll and Huntly not lain so late in their noble beds? The city gates would have been open now for well over an hour...

For all his seeming inattention, young Patrick's keen eyes first perceived the increased agitation and stir up amongst the horsemen by the gatehouse, and his voice proclaimed the fact shrilly. The eddying of the riders around the end of the draw-bridge must surely mean that somebody had just crossed it, emerged from the gatehouse archway. The press of Gordons hid any actual view of this.

'There is the Lady Marie,' Mary's quiet but vibrant voice announced. 'See – her red cloak.'

Above the noise and commotion up there, a great laugh sounded clearly – Huntly's laughter.

'They have come out,' Mariota whispered. 'Is ... is Patrick there?'

David did not answer her.

The mass of Gordons was now circling round, manoeuvring, forming up into some sort of a column, all with infuriating leisureliness and lack of urgency. To see them, one would have said that nobody up there had a care in the world – or that it lacked only three short hours until the appointed time of Patrick Gray's execution.

Then, as the cavalcade began to string out, to ride slowly down the narrow causeway, not even at a trot, a great banner rose at the head of them – the three golden boars' heads on blue, of Gordon – and, to the horrified eyes and ears of David Gray at least, the reason for this deliberate and unhurried progress became evident, as a couple of strutting, puffing pipers came pacing out in front of all, blowing their shrieking, skirling instruments to the ears of all Edinburgh, and thus, to the challenging triumphant strains of *The Cock o' the North*, led the long procession down towards the city. A less discreet and expeditious rescue operation could scarcely be conceived.

They could see Patrick now, riding alongside, Marie slighter-seeming than most of his burly, plaided escort, hatless, his dark curls blowing in the breeze. A lump rose in David's throat at the sight. He seemed to be laughing and chatting vivaciously with Huntly, who rode just in front.

Slowly, in time to that most insolent Gordon march, they came on. Young Patrick was now singing his own monotonous version of the song at the pitch of his lungs.

As they came nearer, Marie could be seen to be pointing down the steep slope towards the little waiting party, drawing Patrick's attention. They saw him gazing, and then a hand rose in salute.

The boy shouted, Mary waved vigorously, Mariota's hand rose to her throat, her mouth.

They came on. Again Patrick raised his hand, looking down.

Mariota this time whipped off the kerchief that bound her hair. and flapped it. Her son all but fell off his horse in his enthusiasm. Mary was smiling, moist-eyed.

The cavalcade was at the nearest point of the causeway to the watchers, now, no more than a couple of hundred yards away. Patrick was half-turned in his saddle, leaning over, his eyes fixed on them. It seemed almost as though he was going to rein in his horse, to turn down to them – but the causeway had a vertical stone ramp, and was moreover protected by a formidable *cheval-de-frise* of iron spikes. The arm that had remained raised in salute, slowly sank.

Mariota sobbed in her throat, and turned to David. He sat still, immovable.

Patrick could not delay. All the Gordon cohort pressed on at his back. His mount, inevitably, moved on, away. He had to turn ever further round in his saddle. At his side Marie was waving and waving. He shouted something, and his hand half-rose again, but his words were indistinguishable against the bagpipes' shrilling and the beat of hooves.

'Davy – oh, Davy!' Mariota whispered.

Patrick was carried onwards, his whole slender body now twisted to face the rear. His handsome features were only a blur at that distance, but his entire posture and bearing were eloquence itself. In a few moments the riders behind him would block the line of vision between him and the group below. He raised both hands, not up as before but out, back behind him, open-palmed, towards his brother – and so rode.

David sat like stone, although the knuckles of his fists, clenched on his horse's reins, gleamed whiter than ivory. Then, gradually, one of those fists loosened, relaxed its grip, and slowly, quiveringly, lifted. It was as though it rose of its own volition, but hardly, against the man's will, until it was high above his head, open, no longer a fist, and so remained.

There was no drowning Patrick's shout, then, high-pitched, ringing, exultant, as his own hands shot up above his dark head, to clasp there, and shake, and unclasp and clasp again. They saw Marie's arm reach out, to her husband's shoulder. And then the horsemen at their back came between to hide them both.

In silence the family group sat now, watching as the front of the cavalcade reached the end of the causeway and was swallowed up amongst the high frowning tenements – or not quite silence, for Mariota was sobbing frankly, openly.

David moistened his lips twice, thrice, before he could find words. And even then his voice was curiously uneven, broken, for so stern-faced a man. 'Why . . . why are you crying, my dear?' he asked. 'What is there to weep for? All is . . . well, is it not?'

The strangled choking sound that Mariota produced might have signified anything or nothing.

David reached out his equally uncertain hand, to stroke her hair. 'Very well, is it not?' he repeated. 'He is safe, now. None will snatch him from Huntly's care, before Leith. He has his life. He will do very well in France . . . will the Master of Gray! She nodded, blowing her nose.

'And we . . . we shall do very well, too. At Castle Huntly, my dear. Very well. No more cities and courts and statecraft for us! You were right. I should never have left Castle Huntly. We shall do finely – leading our own life, at last.' His voice strengthened. 'Rob Powrie is past stewarding. I shall steward Castle Huntly hereafter. My lord promised it. We shall be very happy, Mariota my dear – the four of us. It is what was meant to be – for we are simple country folk, you and I.'

A sniff – but she put her hand out to grasp his.

'Whatever Mary Gray may be! Very well so – on our way to Castle Huntly, before anyone can say us nay. To the West Port with us ... and ... and no looking back!'

'Yes, Davy ...'

Postscript

THAT was not the end of Patrick, Master of Gray, of course – not by a long chalk. Indeed, he was back again in Scotland within two years, and suing the Crown for damages – and winning! But that, and a further catalogue of typical and highly doubtful endeavours is, for the moment, another story.

Enough for the day . . .

N. T.

The Courtesan

BOOK TWO

PRINCIPAL CHARACTERS

In order of appearance

(Fictional characters printed in *italics*)

Mary Gray: supposed daughter of David Gray, but actually of his half-brother, Patrick, Master of Gray.

David Gray· illegitimate eldest son of 5th Lord Gray; land steward and schoolmaster.

PATRICK, 5TH LORD GRAY: Sheriff of Forfar. Strong in the Kirk party.

Mariota Gray: wife of David, daughter of the Bishop of St. Boswell's; mother of Mary.

KING JAMES, THE SIXTH OF SCOTS: son of Mary Queen of Scots; became first monarch of the United Kingdom.

LUDOVICK, 2ND DUKE OF LENNOX: second cousin of King James; near heir to the throne, son of Esmé Stuart of D'Aubigny, former Chancellor.

JOHN, EARL OF MAR: Keeper of Stirling Castle; boyhood companion of King.

The LADY MARIE STEWART, MISTRESS OF GRAY: daughter of Earl of Orkney, wife to Patrick.

SIR JOHN MAITLAND OF THIRLESTANE: Chancellor of Scotland.

PATRICK, MASTER OF GRAY: son and heir of 5th Lord Gray; former Master of Wardrobe, and former Acting Chancellor; condemned for treason and banished, 1587.

The LADY JEAN STEWART: younger sister of Marie.

PATRICK LESLIE: Commendator of Lindores Abbey; later 1st Lord Lindores; married the Lady Jean.

Mr. ROBERT BOWES: Queen Elizabeth's resident envoy at Scottish Court. Later knighted.

MASTER ANDREW MELVILLE: Principal of St. Andrews University and Kirk leader.

LORD ROBERT STEWART, EARL OF ORKNEY: one of King
    James Fifth's many bastard sons. Former Bishop of
    Orkney; uncle of King; father of Lady Marie, Mistress
    of Gray.
GEORGE, 6TH EARL OF HUNTLY: Chief of Clan Gordon;
    principal Catholic nobleman.
JAMES STEWART, EARL OF MORAY: known as the Bonnie
    Earl. Son of another of James Fifth's bastards. Nephew
    of the Regent Moray.
The LADY ELIZABETH, COUNTESS OF MORAY: wife of
    above; daughter of Regent Moray.
SIR WALTER RALEIGH: courtier, diplomat and explorer.
QUEEN ELIZABETH OF ENGLAND.
FRANCIS HEPBURN STEWART, EARL OF BOTHWELL:
    son of one more of James Fifth's many bastards, and
    nephew of Mary Queen of Scots' third husband, Bothwell.
ANNE, PRINCESS OF DENMARK: wife of King James the
    Sixth.
MASTER DAVID LINDSAY: the King's chaplain.
Peter Hay: page to the Duke of Lennox.
GORDON OF BUCKIE: a laird of Huntly's, who struck down
    the Earl of Moray.
The COUNTESS OF ATHOLL: Lady-in-waiting, daughter of
    1st Earl of Gowrie, wife of Earl of Atholl.
The LADY BEATRIX RUTHVEN: Lady of the Bedchamber;
    sister of above.

Chapter One

THE girl picked up the much creased and battered looking letter, smoothed out the folds, and began to read the dashing, sprawling handwriting. She knew that she ought not to be reading it; but equally she had known that she was going to do so from the moment that she caught sight of the broken-sealed paper lying there on the table. She had seen the shipmaster from Dundee handing it to her father in the castle courtyard that morning – and had cried out then, was it from her Uncle Patrick? David Gray had turned away abruptly, thrusting the letter deep into an inner pocket of his doublet, jerking a rough negative. And few people ever found it in themselves to be either rough or negative with Mary Gray.

Her slightly pouting red lips silently formed the carelessly vigorous letters into words as she read – such different writing from her father's own neat and painstaking hand, so much more difficult to read. Yet how vividly it spoke to her of her Uncle Patrick himself; all the gallant, mercurial, laughing brilliance of him, casually masterful, shatteringly handsome – beautiful indeed, the only man that she had ever seen who could be so called and yet remain indubitably and essentially masculine. If there had been a mirror in that purely functional modest chamber in the north-west flanking tower of Castle Huntly – which of course was unthinkable in a room solely her father's – Mary Gray would have had little need to conjure up any mind-picture of the writer of that letter, as she spelled out the words, for what she would have seen therein would have served better than any such year-old memory, better than any painted portrait however expertly limned.

The girl knew that she was quite fantastically like the absent Master of Gray, and in more than mere features, colouring and expression – embarrassingly so to a great many who saw her, though never to herself. Mary Gray was not readily embarrassed, any more than was her Uncle Patrick.

7

Slightly but gracefully built, at fifteen she was nevertheless already showing more than the promise of a lovely and challenging young womanhood – for women as well as men ripened early in the vehement, forcing days of James Stewart the Sixth, and of Elizabeth Tudor. Dark, of a delicate elfin beauty, she was exquisitely made alike in face as in figure, great-eyed, lustrous, with that highly attractive indeed magnetic expression, unusual as it is apparently contradictory, which seems to combine essential, quiet gravity with a more superficial gaiety, even roguery. Mary Gray left none unmoved who saw her; that would be her burden as well as her guerdon all her days. Only some few women are born with that fatal stamp upon them – including that lovely and unhappy royal Mary after whom she had been named.

The girl read with a sort of still absorption.

'My good and respected D.,

Will you hear a sinner's plea? I write in all humility, not to say trepidation – for you did not answer my last. It is important that you heed me now, I assure you. Important for your upright self, for both dear M.'s, for whom – dare I say it? – you will not deny me some mede of devotion if not responsibility? Even for our noble progenitor – whom, however, God may rot if so He wills!

Heed then, good D. The glorious and utterly accursed lady whose price was above a ruby will, within a three-month, meet her deserts. This beyond a peradventure. The two most catholic have decided it at last, and all is in train. Your humble debtor has the ear of H.C.M., if not of H.H., and is satisfied that this time justice will be done. These eyes have indeed looked on the ready-forged sword of that justice, and are content. Here is no plot, no conspiracy, but invincible persuasion sufficient to the task. More than sufficient, craft replacing craft, *nota bene*. You have doubted my word times a-many, D. Doubt it now at your peril. You are a deal less dull than you seem, and it will not have escaped you, I vow, that H.C.M. is testatory heir to that other unfortunate lady, against whom the fates waged such unrelenting war. Now, great as must be our gratitude to this paladin, I judge that you will agree with me that an

8

overdose of good things is seldom a kindness. Moreover we have our errant young friend J. to consider. Accordingly certain precautions will be advisable.

Here they are. Inform our blustering northern cousin H. of all this forthwith. Urge that he brace himself, and swiftly. Likewise S. and the C. and others of that kidney. A month must suffice them. Then, only when they are ready, inform young J. But not his tutor and servitors, lest the lad be unduly distracted. J. to write to H.C.M. offering a mutual arrangement, satisfactory to both – pointing out, needless to say, that short of some such convenient understanding, it might be necessary for him to go to the thrice-damned woman aforementioned. He will take the point, I have no doubt.

This should serve, I think. See to it, D – and swiftly. Not for my sake but for all you hold dear – lest the office be set up on Castle-hill! Do not doubt the choice before you.

My own M. would send you all too much of love, I fear, if she knew that I wrote. She is well, as am I.

Do not withhold my worship and devotion from those whom I also hold so dear and on whom I pray God to smile – though your stern Reformed God never smiles, does He? Who knows, I may see them, and your own sober visage, sooner than you think. Salutations.

P.'

Mary Gray had worked her way once through this peculiar epistle, and, wide brows wrinkled slightly, was part-way through a second reading, when a sound from the open doorway drew her glance from the paper. David Gray stood there, frowning, lips tight, a more formidable figure than he knew.

The girl did not start guiltily, nor drop the letter. She did not even look discomposed. That had ever been the problem with her from earliest childhood – how to assert parental authority and suitable sway over one so strangely and basically assured, so extraordinarily yet quietly judicial, so patently quite unassertively master of herself and her immediate situation. Even my Lord Gray himself did not attempt to impose his imperious will on her; indeed, he had always spoiled her shockingly.

9

'What do you mean by reading that letter, girl?' David Gray demanded, jerkily. 'It is not for such eyes as yours. Is nothing private to me, even in my own chamber? Can I not leave my table for two minutes, but you must come prying, spying? I did but go to speak to the foresters . . .' He stopped. Not for him to explain to this chit of a girl. 'Put it down, child! Think you that all my affairs must be business of yours? I will have you know otherwise, 'fore God! I lock my door from such as you?'

He went on too long, of course – and knew it. Too much school-mastering, too much the petty tyrant as my lord's steward. At the clear and unwinking regard of those deep dark eyes, he cleared his throat loudly and rubbed his clean-shaven chin.

She ignored all that he had said – or perhaps not so much ignored as listened to it, considered it, and dismissed it as irrelevant.

'What does Uncle Patrick mean, Father, by the lady whose price was above a ruby? He calls her accursed. And the ready-forged sword of justice? I think that I understood some of his letter – but not that. Nor this, where he writes of craft replacing craft? What means that? And who is H.C.M. and H.H.? And all those others? "Both dear M.'s", of course, means Mother and myself. But these others? Tell me, if you please.'

There it was, the almost imperious demand, none the less infuriating for being quite unconscious, quite devoid of any undutiful intent, any impertinence, yet ridiculous, insuffer-able in a girl still in her teens. So might a born queen speak and look – not the bastard daughter of a bastard, however lofty the standing of three of her grandparents. Davy Gray's problem, self-assumed, for fifteen years. Or one of them.

The man stepped over to the table, and took the letter out of her hands. He was a stocky plain-faced youngish man – extraordinarily young-seeming to play the father to this bur-geoning beauty. At thirty-two, indeed, he showed no single grey hair, no sign of thickening about the belly, no physical corroboration of the staid man of affairs, the schoolmaster, steward of a great estate, father of three, the man who had shortly rejected King Jamie's proffered accolade of knight-hood but a year previously. Somewhat blunt-faced, heavy-browed, strong-jawed, grey-eyed, his hair worn short, and dressed in simple and well-worn homespun doublet and breeches and tall riding-boots, he looked perhaps a harder man than he was. Swordless despite his position of steward to the fifth Lord Gray, his father – and despite all the notable swording that was credited to him in days not so long past – he looked like a man who might be seeking the sober, the settled and the respectable rather before his time, and by no means always finding it.

'I shall tell you no such thing,' he said. 'On my soul, did you not hear me? I said that it was not for your eyes. It is naught to do with you.'

'It is from him. From my Uncle Patrick.'

'Aye.' For some reason his glance dropped before hers. 'Aye, more's the pity! But what he speaks is of no concern of yours, child. Nor . . .' David Gray sighed heavily, 'nor of mine either, indeed. Nor of mine!'

'Surely it is, Father? For I think that it concerns the King. 'Young J.' – that is King Jamie, is it not? Who else would he name our errant young friend J.? He is to be informed after these others. It is what he is to be informed that I do not understand.'

'God be good, Mary – I . . . I . . .!' Her father swallowed. 'Have done, girl, I tell you. Will you never heed what I say? You are too young. Fifteen years – a mere child . . .'

'At fifteen years you married my mother, did you not? Carrying me within her.' That was calmly, factually said.

David Gray drew a deep quivering breath, blinking grey eyes quickly, but found no words.

She went on, as calmly. 'I am not a child any more, Father. I am a woman now. You should know that.'

'I know that you are an upstart, saucy malapert, a hussy, a baggage! And that my letters are no concern of yours, d'you hear?'

'This letter greatly concerns my Uncle Patrick.' She paused on the name, and then repeated it carefully. 'My Uncle Patrick. Therefore it concerns me, does it not?'

David Gray opened his mouth to speak, and then closed it again. He turned away from her, and took a few paces across the bare wooden flooring to the window, to stare, not down

11

into the cobbled courtyard of the great castle, but out over the wide, grassy, cattle-dotted levels of the Carse of Gowrie and the blue estuary of Tay beyond, gleaming in the brittle fitful sunlight of a February noon stolen from spring. South and south he gazed, as though he would look far beyond Scotland, beyond England even, to sunny France or Spain or wherever his damnable, disgraced and yet beloved half-brother presently spent his banishment. And however hard he frowned, his grey eyes were not hard, at all.

In three light running paces, Mary was at his side, her hand on his arm, her lovely face upturned to his wistfully, all winsome tenderness now. And in such mood no man whom she had yet encountered could resist her.

'Forgive me, Father,' she said softly. 'You are my true father, my only father. And always will be. You have my devotion always. You know it. But . . . I must know of him. I cannot help myself, you see. What concerns him, I must know. Do you not understand?'

'Aye.' Licking his lips, David Gray turned to her, and his arm slipped up around her slender shoulders. His voice shook a little. 'Aye, lass. He is . . . what I can never be. Well I know it. And you are so like him. So . . . so devilish like him, child. Sometimes I am frightened . . .'

'I know,' she whispered: 'I know it. But never be frightened, Father. Never – for me. There is no need, I think.'

He considered her, all the quality of her that made him feel like a plough-horse beside a Barbary, a bludgeon beside a rapier; that made her unassuming country wear of scarlet homespun waisted gown, aproned and embroidered underskirt and white linen sark or blouse, in fact as simple as his own attire, apear as apt and as strikingly delectable as any court confection. He sighed.

'Aye, Mary – you are a woman now, in truth. Folly to shut my eyes to it. Yet, all the more you need guidance, counsel, protection, my dear.'

She nodded her dark-curled head, accepting that. 'But not from Uncle Patrick, I think?'

He hesitated a little before answering her slowly. 'I would that I could be sure of that.'

She searched his face intently. 'Mother says that you

12

always have been less than fair to Uncle Patrick,' she observed. 'Do you think that is true?'

'Your mother knows him less well than I do, girl.'

'And yet . . . you love him, do you not?'

'Aye.' Sombrely he said it. 'Although it might be better – better for us all, I think – if I did not.'

'No.' She shook her head decidedly, rejecting that. 'No.' Then she smiled again, in her most winning fashion. 'You love me, and you say that you love *him*, Father. Yet you will not explain his letter. To me. When he says not to deny me and Mother his worship and devotion. And responsibility also, does he not say?'

David Gray ran a hand over brow and hair. 'Och, Mary, Mary – the letter is an ill one, a dangerous one. Better that you should know naught of it . . .'

'But I do know some of it. Much of it, I think. I know that it concerns King Jamie, and therefore that it must concern us all, all Scotland. And if young J. is indeed the King, then will not the accursed woman be the Queen of England? Elizabeth? And will not that make the other unfortunate lady, on whom the fates waged war, our own good Mary the Queen, whom Elizabeth murdered? If I know all this, is it not better that I should know the rest? And I know that it is dangerous, for does he not say to doubt it all at your peril?'

'That is not the danger that I meant,' the man said. 'But let it be.' He shook his head over her again. 'I' sooth, you are shrewd, child. Quick. Sharp as a needle. Your . . . your father's daughter, indeed!' He shrugged. 'I suppose, yes, having gleaned so much you may as well learn all. Mayhap it will teach you something . . . something about the Master of Gray. That you ought to know.' He spread out the letter. 'But . . . this is for your ears alone, mark you. You understand, Mary? No one else must know of it. Do not discuss it, even with your mother. She knows of the letter, but not all that it portends. She has ever misliked secrets. Nor would she understand much of it, besides. She frets. Some things it is better that she should not know.'

'*I* do not mislike secrets,' the girl said simply. 'And can keep them.'

He glanced at her sidelong, almost wonderingly. 'That I

13

believe. Else I would not tell you this.' He tapped the much-travelled paper, soiled by the tarry paws of seamen and heaven knew what furtive secret hands in France or Spain or Italy. The missive bore no address.

'Patrick – your uncle – has not changed in a year,' he said heavily. 'Nor ever will, I believe. Ever he must dabble in affairs of state. It might have been thought, to be condemned to death for treason and only to have escaped with his life by the breadth of a hair, that he might have been cured of such folly. But, no. A few brief months after his banishment for life – eight months, no more – and he is back at it. I suppose that to have ruled Scotland in all but name is too much for him to forget, to renounce . . . although he said that never did he wish to bear the rule. And that I think he meant, in truth. And yet . . . I do not know. I cannot understand him, what makes him what he is . . . '

Gently she brought him back to the letter. 'He says that the accursed lady will meet her deserts within three months, does he not? What is this of a ruby? A price above a ruby?'

'That is Elizabeth Tudor, yes. The ruby was one that he sought to buy her with. A great gem. Elizabeth had ever a passion for such things. It was Mary's of course – our own Queen's. Sent her by the Pope, years before. First he used it to discredit Arran, when he was Chancellor, and then he took it to Elizabeth. She accepted it . . . but she did not keep her side of the bargain.'

'He bargained it – this jewel – for Queen Mary's life?'

David Gray looked out of the window again. 'No. That is not what Patrick bargained for, I fear. Something . . . other! But that is an old story. He mentions it here only that I should know for whom he speaks. This letter – I know not where he writes from. The last was from Rome . . . '

'And you did not answer him.'

'No. I . . . it was better that I should not. Better for all – himself also, I think.'

'You mean that it is dangerous? To deal with one who is convicted of treason? If the letter should come into the wrong hands? The King's hands? That then you would be endangered?'

'No, it is not that . . . '

14

'But that is why Uncle Patrick writes as he does, is it not? In this strange concealed fashion. So that you shall not be implicated . . . ?'

'It is not for fear of implicating *me* that Patrick writes so! Indeed, he means that I *shall* be implicated – very much so. He would avoid evidence – written evidence he fears. He has tasted of its dangers, already! Written evidence can condemn, where nimble wits and a honeyed tongue would otherwise save. It is himself that he seeks to spare – not me!'

'But he is safe. In France. Banished . . . '

'Aye – so it might be thought. So Scotland thinks. But . . . does he not say that we may see him sooner than we think? Where he may be, even now, the good Lord knows! I know not where he writes from – notably, he does not say. The last letter was from Rome – but clearly he has been in Spain but recently. And what he has seen and heard in Spain convinces him that Queen Elizabeth's days are numbered.'

'Spain? Not France? Always it was France, was it not, Uncle Patrick dealt with. The Duke of Guise and the Cardinal of Lorraine? Our Queen Mary's cousins. I thought that it would be these, perhaps, whom he meant by the two most catholic . . . ?'

'No. The two most catholic are just what he says – H.C.M., that is His Most Catholic Majesty, the King of Spain; and H.H., that is His Holiness the Pope of Rome. It is of these he speaks. They have decided it, he says – decided that justice, as he calls it, will be done, and that Elizabeth of England will meet her deserts.'

'For killing our Queen?'

David Gray's heavy brows lowered in a band across his face. 'I would not swear, child, that such is what *he* means by justice – whatever Spain and Rome may mean. Would that it was. Rather, I think, it is because Elizabeth betrayed *him*, broke their wicked compact over Queen Mary, and denounced his part in that vile execution to Chancellor Maitland and the Council of Scotland. For that, I think, he will never forgive her. Elizabeth, I vow, made a dangerous enemy the day she wrote that letter betraying the Master of Gray.'

The girl drew a long breath. 'You do not sound . . . as though you loved him,' she said.

15

'You do not understand, Mary. Indeed, how could you? Himself I love. Patrick, my brother.' His lips tightened. 'My half-brother. The noble brother of my lord's bastard! I cannot help myself. We have been very close, always. Strangely, for we could scarce be more different. Himself I love, then. But what he is, and what he does, I hate! Hate and fear, do you hear me? Hate and fear.' The paper was trembling a little in those strong hands. It seemed as though almost with relief he came back to it, back to the letter. 'In Spain, then, Patrick saw sufficient to convince him that Elizabeth's days are numbered. It can only have been the ships, the great armament, that King Philip is long said to have been preparing. Armada is the word that they use for it – a great fleet of galleons, and great armies of men, to invade and subdue England. There has long been word of it, rumours – but Patrick must have seen it with his owns eyes, and have been satisfied that it is great enough, powerful enough, to serve its purpose. The downfall of Elizabeth's England. Beyond a peradventure, he says. For him to be sure, the armament must indeed be vast and very terrible. And nigh ready to sail, since he says within a three-month. Unless . . . '

'Invasion of England – before the summer!' Mary said, with slight difficulty. 'So soon. Yet a year too late!'

'Eh . . . ?'

'To save Mary the Queen.'

'Aye. That is the truth. One short year. Or, perhaps . . . I do not know . . . but perhaps there is a reason for that. It may be that Philip of Spain prefers to invade England with Mary safely dead rather than invade to save her life. In her testament she named him, not her son James, as heir to her two kingdoms of England and Scotland, you will mind. She did it, I think, more as a threat to make Elizabeth keep her alive, than as her true desire – for when we saw her at Wingfield Manor only a year before her death, she spoke most warmly of young Jamie – warmer than he deserved, 'fore God! Still, she died leaving Philip of Spain her heir, by this testament – and now he is prepared to claim his inheritance!'

'And Scotland? Surely that could never be? Not here . . . ?' The girl's great eyes widened. 'Is that what Uncle Patrick means when he says that . . . ? Here it is . . . He says "you will

16

agree that an overdose of good things is seldom a kindness. Moreover, we have our young friend J. to consider". He means, then, that Scotland must be saved. Saved from King Philip and his invasion. That is it?'

David Gray nodded. 'Something of the sort, he suggests. Although not all would say, I think, that it was for the *saving* of Scotland! He would have me inform the Early of Huntly of all this – that is "our blustering northern cousin H." of course. With the Earl of Erroll, the High Constable, and the Lord Seton, and others of the like kidney. In other words, the Catholic lords. These to brace themselves – to muster their forces, to arm. Then, and only then, when they are ready and assembled, to inform King Jamie.'

'Why that? Should not he be the first to be told?'

Her father smiled, but not mirthfully. 'We are dealing here with the Master of Gray, child – not some mere common mortal! The King then to write to Philip of Spain – or to send an ambassador, belike – offering a treaty of alliance, to aid in the invasion of England. On the condition, need I say, that Scotland is left free. Assuring him that a Scottish army is assembled and waiting. And, of course, to add that if Philip refuses to agree, he, James, will be compelled to inform Elizabeth of all – even to join forces with her. Which assuredly would much distress His Most Catholic Majesty.'

The girl swallowed. 'I . . . I see.'

'That is your Uncle Patrick! That is what the letter means. Scarcely apt intelligence for a chit of a girl?'

'Perhaps not.' She took the letter and gazed down at its curiously untidy yet vital, forceful handwriting. 'But I do not see, Father, why you say that it is no concern of yours, either? Is it not of the greatest importance?'

'He would have me esteem it so, I agree.'

'But is it not, indeed? For us all? For all Scotland?'

'I do not know.' David Gray moved away from the window, to pace up and down the little bare room. 'It could be – indeed, probably it is – but one more of his many conspiracies. A plot for the furtherance of his own affairs. Like so many.'

'But . . . the invasion of England! That is no private plot!'

'No. But what he would have transpire here in Scotland

17

might well be, girl. He would have this done *now* – this of Huntly and the rest. Philip of Spain's armament, this Armada, may not be so near to sailing as he says. There have been rumours of it for long. He could be using the threat of it for his own purposes. To stir up trouble again in Scotland. He knows that Huntly is a firebrand, ever ready to rouse the north . . . '

'Yet he writes this not to my lord of Huntly, but to you, Father.'

'Aye. Huntly, the great turkey-cock, would not make head nor tail of such a letter! Patrick would use me – use me as he has done before, times without number. I had thought that we had done with such. I *have* done with such, by God! I'll no' do it – I will not!' The man thumped clenched fist on his table as he passed it.

Thoughtfully, gravely, the girl looked at him. 'How can you say that?' she asked. 'He declares roundly that this is no mere conspiracy. Not to doubt him. The King, and the whole realm, must be endangered if the Spaniards invade England. None can question that, surely? Uncle Patrick has pointed a way of escape, has he not? For Scotland. How can you refuse your aid? If not for his sake, as he says, for the King's sake. For all our sakes.'

'I can – and do! You hear?' Almost he shouted at her – which was markedly unlike David Gray: 'I will be entangled in no more of Patrick's plots and deviltries. I swore it – and I will hold to it. I have seen too much hurt and evil, too much treachery and death, come of them. No – I will not do it.'

She shook her dark head slowly, and turned back to the paper in her hand once more. 'What is this about an office?' she enquired. 'An office to be set up on Castle-hill? Here, does he mean? This castle . . . ?'

'No. He means the Holy Office, so called. The Spanish Inquisition. Set up on the Castle-hill of Edinburgh. He would chill my blood . . . '

'The Inquisition!' Mary Gray stared at him now, wide-eyed, something of the terror of that dread name quivering in her voice. 'Here? In Scotland? No – oh, no! That could never be! Not . . . that!'

Her father did not answer her.

18

She came over to him almost at a run. 'Father! Father – if that could happen, the Inquisition here . . . then . . . then . . . ' She faltered, gripping his arm. He had never seen her so moved. 'You would never stand by and see that happen? Anything would be better than that, surely? You – a true Protestant? You cannot stay your hand from what he would have you do – from what this letter says, if that could be the outcome? You cannot!'

'Mary – can you not understand, child?' he cried. 'Cannot you see? What Patrick here proposes could well *bring* that very evil about! Bring the devilish Inquisition to Scotland, to Edinburgh. You talk about saving Scotland – about Patrick saving Scotland, thus. Do you not perceive, lass, that this is in fact most like a conspiracy to overthrow the Reformed religion in Scotland? The Catholic lords are to muster and arm. Secretly. Not until they are assembled is the King to be told. Not even then the Chancellor and the Council – that is what he means by James's tutors and servitors. The Protestants around the King are not to know of it. Until too late. Think you that this Catholic army will do the young Protestant King's biding? He will become its prisoner. Then James is to make a secret alliance with Catholic Spain. Against Protestant England. Do you believe that the Kirk could ever agree to that? So the Kirk will have to be put down – by Catholic arms. What will remain, then, of Protestant Scotland? Would the Catholic lords keep out Philip's Inquisition? *Could* they? Do you not see what it means?'

She stood still, silent.

'It is not easy, straightforward,' he went on, sighing. 'Nothing about Patrick Gray is ever easy or straightforward.'

'Yet you cannot leave it thus, Father,' she said. 'You cannot just do nothing.'

'What can I do? Other than act as he demands? Which I will not do.'

'You could tell the King, could you not? Without telling the Catholic lords. He used to rely on Uncle Patrick's advice in matters of state. Is the plan itself not a good one? Apart from putting Scotland in the power of the Catholic lords. If it was the *Protestant* lords who armed and assembled instead? The King could still treat with Spain, with an army at his

19

back. It is a sound policy, is it not? The only way to preserve the realm in this evil pass? Uncle Patrick has the cleverest head in Scotland – often you have said it. Use it then, for Scotland's weal, Father. But . . . use your own likewise. Let it be the Protestant lords who arm – but otherwise the same.'

It was the man's turn to stare. Almost his jaw dropped as he considered what was proposed – and who proposed it. Was this the infant that he had petted and played with? The child that they had brought up? What had they nurtured, Mariota and himself?

'You . . . you do no discredit to your sire, I think,' he said, a little unsteadily.

'It is best, is it not? That you should go to the King?'

'It is not, i' faith! I cannot go to the King, girl. His last words to me, yon day at Holyroodhouse, were that he wished never to see my face again. Nor Patrick's either. An ill and graceless breed, he named us . . .'

'The same day that he would have made you knight?'

'Aye. But that was before I had abused him. I spoke him hard that day – as no subject should bespeak his prince. No base-born subject in especial . . . like Davy Gray the Bastard! I threatened him sorely. The King. For Patrick's sake. He will never forget it, will James Stewart. I have cut myself off from the King.'

'If you told him that the safety of his realm depended on hearing you? The safety of his person – for it is said that he is heedful for himself? Surely he would see you.'

'You do not understand, Mary. Kings are not to be approached thus. I cannot see him, or speak with him, without he summons me . . .'

'But, Father – even *I* used to speak with the King. He said that I was a bonny lass, and that he liked me well. He thanked me for being kind to Vicky – to the Duke of Lennox.'

'That was different, lass. Then your Uncle Patrick was a power in the land. Acting Chancellor of Scotland, and Master of the King's Wardrobe. I was his secretary. We were part of the royal Court. Ever about the King. Now . . .' He spread his hands. 'I cannot speak with James without he summons me. And that he will never do.'

'The King, it is said, is not one whose mind cannot be

20

changed . . . !' she began when her quiet voice was drowned.

There was a great clattering of hooves, clangour of armour, and the shouting of commands, from close outside. Man and girl moved back to the window. Through the arched doorway under the gatehouse streamed into the inner courtyard of Castle Huntly a troop of heavily-armed riders mounted on the rough garrons of the country, shaggy and short-legged but sturdy horses whose hooves struck sparks from the cobblestones of the enclosed square and echoed back and forth from the tall, frowning walls of great soaring keep and flanking-towers. Amongst them all, conspicuous because of the height of his handsome Flanders roan, rode a heavy florid man of middle years, dressed in richly embossed half-armour, black and gold, dark doublet and trunks, and long riding-boots. On his massive greying head was clapped a flat old-fashioned velvet bonnet instead of the more fashionable high hat and plume – the only man there not wearing a steel morion helmet.

Throwing himself down off his horse, this paunchy bull-like man started to shout as soon as his boots touched the cobbles – and at his bellowing, all other voices soever fell discreetly silent.

'Davy! Davy Gray – to me, man!' he roared. 'A pox on you – where are you? Where in hell are you skulking, i' God's name? Poring over dusty books and papers, I'll be bound . . . ' He glanced up at the round north-west flanking-tower, and perceived the figures at the window. 'There you are, damn you! Down with you, man. Would you ha' me stand waiting your pleasure like some carle frae the stables? Me – Gray! Did you no' hear my horn? Are you deaf, man – as well as heedless o' my affairs and well-being . . . ?'

'My lord sounds as though restored,' David Gray said to the girl, drily. 'His gout is improved, undoubtedly – and therefore he must needs burst a blood-vessel with his shouting!' But he raised a hand to the window in acknowledgment of the summons, and folding the letter, tucked it away carefully in his doublet, and turned to the stairway – but not in any urgent haste.

The fifth Lord Gray's voice neither awaited his arrival, nor lessened its volume. 'And where is my moppet? Where a pest's

21

Mary – my ain Mary? God's mercy – is this a house o' the dead, or what? Must Gray come to his ain, and naught but doos and jackdaws greet him? Mary!' he bawled. 'Mary Gray – haste you, lass. Would you hide frae me? Bairnie – where are you?' Although the noise of him had nowise diminished, the tone and tenor had altered significantly; almost there was a chuckling, wheedling note in the vociferation now, if that can be imagined, distinctly ridiculous in so notable a tyrant.

Smiling gently, the girl turned to follow her father down the narrow winding turnpike stair. And for all her curious calm and serenity of manner, she tripped lightly as might any child.

When she emerged, my lord was hectoring her father in front of all the fifty and more grinning men-at-arms. ' . . . trees down all along the Inchture road, dykes broken and beasts straying! But two nights gone, and I come back to this, Davy Gray! I make you steward o' half the Carse, the more fool me, and here's you roosting in your tower moping over papers . . . '

'Last night's storm was notably strong, my lord . . . '

'What of it, man? Must trees lie where they fall because o' a skelp o' wind? And my beasts stray, because you canna keep your nose out of books and parchments?'

'I have men clearing the trees and mending the dykes,' David declared, his voice flat, nor noticeably apologetic. 'I set them to the home parks first, believing that you would have it so.' His glance flickered over the ranks of armed retainers. 'If your lordship would travel with a wheen less of escort, more men there would be for clearing your trees!'

'Insolent, on my soul! *You* to speak me thus! You – a chance by-blow!'

'Exactly, sir. But *yours*! And with my uses – where secrets are to be kept!'

Father and son eyed each other directly, choleric yet shrewd pig-like eyes in that sagging, dissipated face, meeting level grey ones. This was an old battle, almost a formality indeed, something of a game to be played out.

'The godly business of the Kirk prospered at Perth, I hope, my lord?' the younger man went on, as evenly. 'Knowing its import, we scarce expected to see you home for a day or two yet. Or, should I say, a night or two?'

The other frowned, black as thunder, but before he could

22

speak, a trill of laughter came from the small tower doorway where Mary stood watching.

'Was the Lady Murray unkind, Granlord . . . or just unwell?' she called, dark eyes dancing. 'Or perchance did her husband come home oversoon from the Court?'

'God be good – Mary, you . . . you ill-tongued hussy! You shameless baggage!' my lord spluttered, but with the frown vanished from his heavy brows like snow before the sun. He went limping forward, all jingling spurs and clanking steel, arms wide, ridiculous. Into them the girl came, not running, indeed with a sort of diffident hesitancy of pace, so at variance with her dimpling, smiling assurance as to be laughable, and was enfolded, swept up off her feet, and chuckled and crooned over. 'Och, lassie, lassie!'

She gurgled something into his neck above the steel gorget.

'Lord – it's good to have a grip o' you! You're the bonniest sight these eyes have seen in a score years!' he told her, nuzzling his gross empurpled features in her hair.

Her laughter pealed out. 'Bonnier than the Lady Murray? Bonnier than the Provost's wife at Dundee? Or Mistress Moncur? I have not her great paps, Granlord!' And she kissed him full on the lips.

'Och, wheesht you, wheesht you, wench! The randy wicked tongue o' you!' her grandfather gasped. 'Damme, you're a handful! Aye, God – an armful is nearer it, eh? An armful getting, I swear!' And he squeezed her comprehensively.

She bit his ear, quite sharply, so that he yelped.

David Gray looked at his father and his daughter from under puckered, downdrawn brows. Always this was the way of it – always it had been. The child, conceived in shame, born in disgrace, fathered on himself, could do what she would with this bellowing bull of a man, one of the proudest, most arrogant and powerful lords of all the arrogant strutting nobles of poor Scotland, where none other could do anything. She alone, of all within his wide orbit, not only seemed to have no fear of him, no revulsion, but actually seemed to love him, taking outrageous liberties with him, as he with her. Sometimes he feared for her in this also – for David Gray cherished no illusions as to his potent sire's character and appetites, pillar of God's Reformed Kirk as he was. The great stot, drooling over

23

her, pawing her . . . aye, and letting her call him Granlord, that silly childhood name she had given him. Why did she never act so with himself, Davy Gray – who would give his right hand for her, his life indeed, any day? Who had cherished her and brought her up, and loved her as that sodden, whoring wind-bag of a lord could never conceive? Himself, her father – at least, in all but blood – she seldom hugged and laughed with and rained kisses upon.

Abruptly, the stern, sober, soft-hearted Davy Gray swung on the watching leering ranks of my lord's unmannerly and uncouth men-at-arms, and waved a peremptory hand at them.

'Off with you! Away with you!' he commanded. 'Gawping idle gowks! There are trees to be cleared. Dykes to mend. Cattle to herd. And see you look to those beasts, your horses. That they are rubbed down and baited. No watering till they are cooled, d'you hear? The brutes are lathered wickedly. Ridden over hard, and for no need. Horseflesh is scant and dear . . .'

'Hark at him!' my lord hooted. 'The right duteous steward . . . now!'

'He looks to your affairs very well, Granlord,' Mary Gray said, gravely, shaking the older man's arm. 'Well do you know it, too. Better than ever did old Rob Powrie.'

'As well he might! Did I no' pour out my siller to put him through yon college at St. Andrew's? Him, and that . . . that graceless, prinking jackanapes, that simpering Popish coxcomb who . . .'

'Hush, my lord!' The girl's voice went cool, aloof, and she sought to withdraw herself from her grandfather's embrace. 'That is an ill way to speak of one who . . .'

'Who has brought shame on my head and hurt on my house, girl!'

'Who is your son and your heir. And could a coxcomb and a jackanapes have raised himself above all others to be the King's right hand in Scotland?'

'Eh . . . ?' Lord Gray looked at her askance. 'What way is this to talk to me, child? I . . . I . . .'

'Your Uncle Patrick was never highly regarded in this his own home, Mary,' another voice said, tightly, from behind them. 'Save . . . save perhaps by me! You know that.'

24

Unnoticed by the others, a woman had come across the courtyard to them from the main keep, a very lovely woman, and still young. Tall, auburn-haired, high-coloured, a satisfying, well-made, deep-bosomed creature, she had fine hazel eyes that were wide and eloquent and anxious. Those eyes, ever wary, questioning, prepared to be startled, like the eyes of a deer, told their own story, despite the determined resolution of an appealingly dimpled soft round chin. Even yet they could turn David Gray's heart over within him, in an access of protective affection, however hard he might seek to disguise the fact. Compared with the inherent calm and composure of her daughter, Mariota Gray was essentially the child, the uncertain one. Lovely as they both were, indeed, mother and daughter resembled each other in little or nothing.

'Woman – hold your tongue!' my lord barked. 'How should you ken aught o' the matter? Who are you to judge – save, belike, between your legs!' He snorted coarsely. 'And there, nae doubt, Patrick's regard is high, high!'

Flushing hotly, and biting a quivering lip, Mariota turned to her husband, instinctively, those gentle eyes quickly filmed with tears. David Gray spoke harshly, set-faced.

'My lord – I'd urge you to mind that you speak to my wife!'

'D'you think I forget it, man? Waesucks, yon's no' a thing any o' us could forget, I swear!'

'Then I'd have her spoken to with the respect that is her due. And mine. Or . . .'

'Aye, then . . . or? Or what?'

'Or you can seek a new steward, my lord.'

'Ho, ho! So that's it, by God? Hoity-toity, eh? I can, can I?'

'You can, yes. Nor find one so cheap, who will save your precious siller as I do. Nor write your letters to certain proscribed and banished lords!'

His father's swiftly indrawn breath all but choked him.

Both women turned to him, as quickly – Mary keen-eyed in speculation, her mother unhappy, alarmed.

'No, no, Davy!' Mariota cried. 'Not that. Pay no heed to it . . .'

'I heard him. Not for the first time. And paid heed. As I urge my lord to do now!'

Mary spoke. 'Granlord – you are tired. From your journey.

And hungry. I can hear your belly rumbling, I vow! Come you. Mother and I will have your table served before you have your harness off. Come.'

Lord Gray looked from her, past her mother, to his son, and meeting David's eye directly, swallowed audibly.

'Och, be no' so thin-skinned, Davy!' he said huskily. 'You're devilish touchy, man, for a . . . a . . . Houts, Davy – let it be, let it be.' The older man flung his arm around the girl's slender shoulders. 'Aye, lassie – you have the rights o' it. As usual. Come, then – and aid me off with this gear. Aye, and feed me some victuals. Thank the good Lord there's one with some wits in her head . . . !' And muttering, the Lord Gray stalked off limping towards the guarded doorway of the great keep, Mary seeking to match her pace at his side.

David Gray muttered also – more to himself than to his bonny agitated wife. 'Patrick! Patrick Gray!' he whispered. 'Still you can do it. Set us all by the ears. Every one of us. Wherever you are. Still you pull the strings, be it from France or Spain – and we dance! Damn you – are we never to be quit of you?'

But that last was breathed on a sigh.

It was evening before Mary Gray saw her father alone again, with my lord safely carried to his bed in a drunken stupor, and the girl on her way to her own little garret chamber high within the keep's dizzy battlements. On the corkscrew stone staircase they met.

'I know how we must gain the King's ear, Father,' she said, without preamble. 'With Uncle Patrick's tidings. I had thought that my lord would be able to speak with the King. He is great with the Kirk and the Protestant lords. But he is so bitter against Uncle Patrick . . . ' She took David's arm. 'You have not told him, I think? Of the letter?'

'I have not. Nor shall. But what of it, girl? It is no concern of yours.'

She ignored that. 'Moreover if Granlord has been writing letters to banished lords – that is what you said, is it not? To banished and proscribed lords? Or, since he writes but ill, you wrote them for him? That could be treasonable, could it not? So my lord may not stand over well with the King, after all.

Any more than do you, Father. So . . .'

'Lord!' the man gasped. 'What has come into you, child? All this of statecraft and affairs of the realm! Grown men's work, lords' work – not lassies'. Put it from you, Mary. Forget that you ever saw yon letter. Off to your bed, now . . .'

'Somebody must do something, Father,' she insisted. 'And I know what to do.'

Uncertainly he stared at her, by the smoky light of the dip that he carried, flickering in the draughty stairway and casting crazy shadows on the bare red stone walls.

'We must tell Vicky,' she said. 'And he will tell the King. Vicky Stuart, the Duke of Lennox.'

David Gray blinked rapidly, and moistened his lips. He did not speak.

'Is it not the best way, and the surest?' she went on. 'Vicky liked me well. And King Jamie likes Vicky. He is closer to the King than is anyone else, he says – even the Chancellor. And he sides with the Protestants – though he knows not the difference in one belief from another, I vow! And he was brought up a Catholic, was he not?' She smiled.

The man pinched his chin. 'All this may be true, girl. But . . . the Duke is ever at the King's side. To reach him will be as difficult, belike, as to come to the King himself. And he is young, little more than a laddie – young even for his years . . .'

'Is that not all the better, Father? He will do as I say.'

'As *you* say! You flatter yourself, child, do you not? Lennox likes you well enough, in a way, I dare say. You are bonny, and you played together as bairns, yes. Although, then I mind, you thought him dull . . .'

'He still is dull,' she agreed, frankly. 'But he is kind and honest.' Mary Gray's dark eyes gleamed amusedly. 'And he says that he would die for me!'

Her father gulped. 'Die! For you? Lennox? What . . . what nonsense is this, mercy on us?'

'It is not nonsense, Father. At least, he swore it on his heart and the cross of his sword!'

David Gray sought for words. 'I . . . I . . . you . . . Dear God – he must be clean daft! Duller even than we knew! But this would be but child's talk – when he was a laddie indeed?

Bairns playing together.'

'Not so. It was not long since. And does he not write it anew, in each letter?'

'Letter . . . ? Lennox? The Duke writes letters . . . ?'

'Indeed, yes. He is a better writer than a talker is Vicky! He writes very well.' She laughed. 'As do I, of course, like-wise.'

The man shook his head, completely at a loss. 'You? How can this be? Letters! You . . . you are cozening me, child. How can you write to the Duke? 'Tis more bairns' make-believe . . . '

Almost pityingly she regarded him. 'It is the truth.'

'But . . . how could *you* send letters? Have you a messenger, a courier? You?'

'No. But Vicky has. Indeed, he uses the King's couriers, and so do I.'

'On my soul, Mary . . . you . . . ' Her father had difficulty with his respiration. 'You use the King's couriers? For your exchange of letters? You – Mary Gray – and young Ludovick of Lennox! Lord – this is beyond all belief!'

'Why should it be? It is very simple, Father. The King, or the Council, are ever sending couriers to the Master of Glamis, that is Lord Treasurer, at Aldbar. Or to the Sheriff of Forfar. Or to my Lord Ogilvie at Airlie. These must needs pass here. Vicky, who is on the Council likewise, gives the man a letter for me, also. He leaves it at the mill at Inchture. Cousin Tom there brings it to me. I leave mine at the mill for the courier to take up, on his way back. Could aught be more simple?'

The other's head wagged helplessly. 'I' faith, it is beyond me! Beyond all. Tom Affleck in it, too – and therefore his father. Whom I shall speak with, 'fore God!' David Gray's own mother had been Nance Affleck, the winsome daughter of the miller of Inchture. 'And does it . . . does it stop at writing letters, girl?' he got out.

'Oh, no. We meet. But only now and again. Not so oft as Vicky would have it, I assure you.'

'You . . . meet!' Easy simple words to make such a croaking over. 'He was here – Lennox was here – three months past, yes. On his way to my Lord Innermeath at Redcastle . . . '

'He was here last week,' the girl amended demurely. 'We

28

have an arrangement. The King is often at Falkland, hunting. Vicky can ride to Newburgh in little more than an hour, he says, from Falkland, cross the ferry to Erroll, and be here in another hour. He rides fast horses – the King's own. It takes him but little longer from his own castle of Methven, the other side of Saint John's town of Perth . . . '

'Damnation – will you be quiet, girl! I care not how long it takes him, how he comes hither to you! Do you know what this makes *you*, child? You – our daughter? Meeting secretly with the second man in the realm, the King's cousin? You, a common clerk's daughter – at least, in the eyes of men. A bastard's daughter. It makes you a . . . a . . . ' He stopped, regaining partial control of himself somehow – and it was seldom indeed that David Gray required to do that. 'You have not . . . ? He has not . . . ? Och, Mary lass – he hasna . . . ?'

Calmly, almost sadly, she met his urgent demanding gaze. 'He has not had me, no – if that is what you mean.'

'Thank God for that! But, the danger of it, the folly . . . '

'There is no danger, Father. He is gentle, simple almost. When we meet, *I* am master – not Vicky. Always it was so.'

His mouth opened, and then closed, as he considered her. She had David Gray silenced.

'So, you see – it will not be difficult. Whether the King is at Falkland or Stirling or even Edinburgh, I shall have a letter to Vicky in but a few days. We shall meet, and he shall bring me before the King. He will do as I ask, never fear. And so Uncle Patrick's warning shall not be lost. Nor the Protestant cause either. It is the best way, the only way – is it not?'

'God save us all . . . !' her father prayed.

'Yes. But we must do our own part also – so good Master Graham says, at the kirk. We cannot just leave Uncle Patrick's letter to God, can we?'

'Would that I knew, girl.'

'But we do know. You said yourself, did you not, that in Spain Uncle Patrick must have seen sufficient to be sure that Queen Elizabeth's days are numbered? Seen with his own eyes. Therefore Scotland is endangered also. And must act if this realm likewise is not to fall to the Spaniards. So that *we* must act. And quickly.'

29

'I vowed . . . ' he began, but wearily.

'Yes, Father – I know. But *I* did not. Is it not most fortunate?'

Chapter Two

THE four riders sat their fidgeting, steaming mounts within the cover of a thicket of scrub birch and holly, and waited. The cover was to shield them from view, not from the rain, for the shiny holly leaves sent down a cascade of heavy drops upon them with each gust of the chill wind. It was no better a day for hanging about in wet woodland than it was for hunting – but King Jamie cared nothing for the weather so long as there were deer to chase. In season and out of season – as now – day after day, storm or heat or snow, he must hunt the heavy woodland stags, in what had become little less than a mania with him – to the sorrow and discomfort of most of his Court, who would have preferred more seasonable and less active entertainment.

The riders looked out, across a broad grassy ride, to the reed-fringed border of Lindores Loch. Their stance was a strategic one, and had been as carefully chosen, at short notice, as the difficult circumstances would allow. All day they had been moving across trying and broken country, hill and bog and forest, seeking to keep in touch with the royal hunt, without being seen or scented thereby – no easy task, for James, with some reason, had a great fear of being ambushed or attacked on such occasions, by some coalition of his ambitious and arrogant nobles, and always sought to maintain a screen of armed guards in attendance. The watchers were now, wet and weary, on the skirts of rocky Dunbog Hill, in north Fife, fully seven miles from the King's palace of Falkland. The hunt had killed for the third time near Inchrye, and as the light was already beginning to fail, James would be satisfied. He did not like to be out in the dark, being much aware of the forces of darkness, human and otherwise. Almost certainly the royal party would return to Falkland this way. The steep hillside and Lindores Loch would confine the cavalcade to this woodland track before them. So declared the groom, sent by the Duke of Lennox. The man had been ferrying back and forth between his master and the little party of three all day, to keep them informed and to have them in readiness and available when and wherever the energetic monarch should make his final kill. It had been a testing time for all – and not least, undoubtedly, for Ludovick, Duke of Lennox.

David Gray glanced at his daughter. Tired she must be, inevitably, but she at least showed no signs of it. Upright, alert within her enveloping cloak, she sat her stocky mud-spattered garron, even humming a little song to herself, eyes gleaming like the raindrops that glistened on the dark curls escaping from her coif, eager and watchful still despite all the similar waits and false alarms of the day. Almost, she might be enjoying herself. Which was more than her father was doing – or either of the Duke's men, by the look of them.

The situation did not fail to bring to David's mind that other occasion, six years earlier and distinctly similar to this, when he had waited, hidden likewise, for another of James's hunts, near Ruthven in Perthshire, waiting to effect a rescue of his youthful monarch from his cynical captors of the Raid of Ruthven. The Master of Gray had been behind that venture also – had indeed planned it all from far-away France. He himself had been merely the fool, the poor puppet, who carried it out, with thanks from none! Nor did he anticipate either gratitude or satisfaction from this day's work – save perhaps in the mind of this strange girl whom he called his daughter and whom he now wondered whether he knew at all. David Gray waited by Lindores Loch, not only against his inclinations but really against his better judgment.

'Vicky said that the men-at-arms will come first, as they ride back to Falkland,' Mary declared. 'We are to let them past, before coming out – else they might attack us and the King be alarmed. I hope that he and Vicky are not too close behind the soldiers. It may be difficult, a little . . . '

Her father nodded grimly. He had never seen this entire project as anything else but difficult. At their early morning secret rendezvous with the young Duke, he had impressed

31

upon them the need for quite elaborate care and planning. James was as nervous as an unbroken colt, and sensed treason and violence in every unusual circumstance – as indeed he had reason to do. So many attempts had been made on his person, in his twenty-one years, as on his executed mother and assassinated father before him, that such wariness was only to be expected, and precautions highly necessary. The wonder was that he should persist with this incessant hunting, which provided opportunities for the very attacks that he dreaded.

'Let us hope that the Duke keeps his wits – and uses them,' David said. 'As well that he is less excitable than his royal cousin!' He turned to the other of the two attendants, Lennox's tranter or under-falconer. 'Your master is to have his hands bare, is he not, if all is well? As signal for you to ride out. If he is gloved, you are to remain in hiding?'

The grizzled servitor nodded. 'Aye. We dinna move if he is wearing his gloves.' These two men were known to the King, and dressed in the Duke's livery, bearing his colours of red and white. It was hoped that they would not alarm the apprehensive monarch as they issued suddenly from cover.

'I hope that we shall be able to see him clearly – and he us,' Mary said. 'That there is not a throng round the King, so that we cannot see . . . '

'Och, never fear, lassie,' the tranter assured. 'My lord Duke kens fine what's needed. He decided it, did he no'?'

'It is not what the Duke does, nor yet the King, that so much concerns me,' David Gray observed. 'It is the men-at-arms, in front. And people about the King. If the guards hear you, and turn back. Or if the others rush out from behind, fearing an ambush . . . ? I do not want the lass here embroiled in any clash or tulzie . . . '

'Na, na, master – dinna fret, man. They all ken the Duke's colours. Ken us, too. Dand, here, has been riding back and fore to the Duke all day, has he no'? They'll no' be feart at him and me and a lassie, just. Eh, Dand?'

The short dark groom appeared to be otherwise preoccupied. 'Och, quiet you!' he jerked. 'I heard them, I think . . . ' He was gazing away to the right, through the tracery of the dripping branches.

They all strained their ears.

Sure enough, the faint beat of hooves, and even the slight jingle of arms and accoutrements could just be distinguished above the sigh of the trees in the wind. Waiting was over, at last.

Riders appeared on the track to the right, northwards. They came at a jog-trot, two by two, for the track was not broad. Although dressed proudly enough in the red-and-gold of the royal livery, they looked jaded, weary, spume-flecked from the mouths of tired and hard-ridden horses. A score of them, perhaps, they rode loosely, slouched in their saddles, witness to the exhausting service of their restless and anxious master. None appeared to be examining the track before them with any great vigilance, much less scanning the flanking woodland.

In a few moments, they jingled past the hidden watchers without a glance in their direction.

The latter need not have worried about the King coming too close on the heels of his escort. There was a distinct interval before the next group of riders appeared – and then it was three huntsmen, leading each a garron on which was tied the carcass of a stag, their burdens jouncing about with the uncomfortable trotting pace.

'The kill coming *before* the King!' David exclaimed. 'Here is a strange sight! I hope that he comes. That he has not delayed. Or gone some other way, perhaps.'

The tranter pointed. 'Yonder's the reason, master. See yon last beast? The head o' him! Fourteen points if he has a one, I warrant! A notable kill. His Grace will be right pleased. He'll no' be able to keep his eyes off yon stag, will Jamie. Aye – there he is now. I've seen him do the like before, mind. He'll be proud as Auld Hornie! Aye – he'll be in good fettle this day, will His Grace.'

'Good!' Mary commented. 'See – Vicky rides beside him. And his hands are bare.'

Two horsemen came trotting no great distance behind the third and most heavily-laden garron, with, at their backs, the beginning of a lengthy and motley cavalcade emerging into view round a bend of the woodland track. They made a markedly different impression from that of the previous riders, this pair – or indeed from those who followed them. They looked very young, for one thing, little more than boys, beard-

33

less, slight, and with nothing jaded about their appearance. Richly dressed, though less than tidy, and superbly mounted on identical lathered black Barbary horses, they rode side by side, with nothing of the aspect of weariness that afflicted the men-at-arms in front or the generality of the straggling if colourful company behind, even though they were inevitably travel-stained, mud-spattered, with clothing disarranged, like all the others. Yet there was but little of similarity about themselves – indeed they contrasted with each other in most respects. Where one was trim and and slimly upright, sitting his mount almost as though part of it, the other sprawled loosely, in an ungainly, slouching posture that was as unusual as it was undignified. Neither youth was handsome, nor even conventionally good-looking; but the upright one was at least pleasantly plain, whereas the other's features were almost grotesquely unprepossessing, lop-sided and ill-favoured generally, only the great expressive, almost woman-like eyes saving the effect from being positively repellent. James, by the grace of God, King, was singularly ill-endowed with most other graces.

His companion, while paying respectful attention to the other's seemingly excited talk, was looking about him keenly, watchful. His glance kept coming back to the projecting clump of evergreens and birches ahead.

As the huntsmen and the laden ponies swayed and ambled past, the grizzled falconer raised his hand. The groom nodded. Together they urged their horses forward. Between them, Mary Gray was only half a length behind. As she went, her father muttered a brief God-be-with-you. He himself remained where he was.

James was not so deep in chatter as to fail to notice the trio the moment that they emerged into view. He jerked his spirited black in a hasty dancing half-circle, as quick as thought, sawing at the reins, his words dying away in immediate alarm. 'Vicky! Vicky!' he got out, gasping.

Lennox was almost as prompt in his reactions. 'My own lads it is, Sire,' he called loudly, reassuringly. 'Never fear, Cousin. It is but Patey and Dand, see you. And they have found a lady for us, by the Mass!' Ludovick Stuart seldom remembered to adhere to only Reformed oaths.

'Eh . . . ? Oh, aye. Aye. So it is. Patey, aye – Patey and yon Dand. A . . . a p'plague on them – jumping out on me, like yon!' the King gabbled, slobbering from one corner of a slack mouth. He had been born with a tongue just too large for his mouth, and had the greatest difficulty in controlling it, especially when perturbed. He was peering; James was not actually short-sighted – indeed he saw a deal more than many either desired him to see or knew that he saw – but he was apt to peer nevertheless. 'It's no' a lady, Vicky – it's just a lassie,' he declared. 'A lassie, aye – wi' your Patey and Dand.' That came out on a spluttering sigh of relief. Majesty drew up his thin, skimped and twisted body in the saddle. 'What . . . what is the meaning o' this, eh? They're no' to do it. I'll no' have it, I tell you. I . . . we'll no' abide it. Jumping out in our royal path like, like coneys! Who is she, man?' That last was quick.

'A friend of mine, Sire – and of yours. An old friend of yours,' the Duke assured, waving Mary forward. 'I crave your permission to present . . .'

'I ken her fine,' the King interrupted. 'She's no friend o' mine. She's the lassie o' yon ill man Gray!' He sniggered. 'I didna say his daughter, mind – just his lassie! No friends o' mine, any o' that breed o' Gray.'

'You are wrong, Sire.' Clearly, unflurried, the girl's young voice came to them, as she rode up, her attendants having dropped back discreetly. 'It is only because I *am* your Grace's friend, your true friend, that I am here.'

'Na, na. I ken the sort o' you – fine I do. Ill plotters. Treasonable schemers. *Both* your fathers!'

'Sire – what she says is true,' Lennox asserted urgently. 'It is to do your good service that she is here. I would not have countenanced it, else.'

'Aye – so *you've* countenanced it! This is your work, Vicky? I'm no' pleased . . . we are much displeased wi' you, my lord Duke. We are so. We had thought better o' you . . .'

'Do not blame Vicky, Highness. Do not blame the Duke,' Mary pleaded. 'I greatly besought his help. For your Grace's weal. For the weal of your realm. It is very important . . .'

'Does this young woman annoy your Grace? Shall I have her removed?' a deeper voice intervened. Behind them the

35

long cavalcade was in process of coming up and halting, not so close as to seem to throng the King but not so far off that the front ranks should miss anything that was to be seen or heard. The speaker, a big, red-faced, youngish man, too elaborately dressed for hunting, searched the girl's lovely elfin features boldly, calculatingly. 'You may safely leave her to me, Sire . . . '

'Not so, my lord of Mar!' Lennox said, his open freckled face flushing. 'The lady is a friend of mine. She has private business with His Highness.'

'That is for His Highness to say, sir.' The Earl of Mar looked slightingly at the younger man. Ludovick Stuart was just sixteen, and by no means old for his years, a snub-nosed, blunt-featured youth, not nearly so sure of himself as he would like to have been, and an unlikely son of his late brilliant and talented father, the former Esmé, Seigneur D'Aubigny and first Duke, Chancellor of Scotland. Mar, nearly ten years his senior, did not attempt to hide his disrespect.

James plucked his loose lower lip, and darted covert shrewd glances from one to the other. 'Oooh, aye. I'ph'mmm. Just so,' he said, non-committally. At twenty-one he was already an expert at playing his nobles off one against another, at waiting upon events, at temporising so that others should seem to make decisions for him – for which they could be held responsible afterwards, should the need arise. His survival, indeed, had depended on just such abilities. With the ineffable Master of Gray out of the country, Queen Elizabeth of England's astute and well-informed advisers, Burleigh and Walsingham, believed this extraordinary, oafish and tremulous young man, so often considered to be little more than a half-wit, to possess in fact the sharpest wits in his kingdom.

Mary Gray spoke up again. 'His Grace's safety is in no danger from such as me, I think, my lord,' she said. 'Could a girl drag her King to Ruthven Castle – even if she would?'

King James's suddenly indrawn breath was quite audible – as indeed might have been Mar's own. She took a risk in naming Ruthven Castle in such company and in such a place. But a calculated risk. It had been when out hunting, as now, from Falkland Palace six years before, that the King had been attacked, forcibly abducted to Ruthven and there held prisoner by a group of power-hungry Protestant lords. And John, Earl of Mar, had been one of those lords. The Ruthven Raid was not a thing that had been mentioned at Court for quite some time, James preferring not to be reminded of those days of humiliation – and others equally wishing them forgotten.

'M'mmm. Ah . . . umm.' The King peered at her from under down-drawn brows, gnawing his lip. His head was apt to loll at curious angles, seeming to be too big for his ill-made body, too heavy for the frail neck that had to support it. Now it drooped forward, and served His Majesty fairly well to hide those great tell-tale eyes of his. 'Ruthven, eh? Aye . . . Ruthven. Yon was an ill place. Aye.' He swung round in his saddle abruptly. 'Eh, Johnnie?'

'Er . . . yes, Your Highness. Indeed it was. Certainly – most certainly . . . ' The red-faced earl was assuredly redder.

'Aye. I mind it so – mind it well.'

'It was my father who gained Your Grace's freedom from that toil, was it not?' the girl went on, gently pressing her advantage. 'He was none so ill a friend then. And would be again . . . from another danger.'

'Eh? Danger?' The King's voice squeaked. 'What danger? Fiend seize me – tell me, lassie! What danger?' That word could ever be guaranted to arouse James Stewart.

'I would prefer to tell Your Grace in private.'

'Private. Aye, private. My lord of Mar – leave us. Leave us.' James waved a suddenly imperative hand.

Mar cast a narrow-eyed vicious look at Mary, curled his lip at Lennox, and bowing stiffly to the King, swung his horse's head around savagely and trotted back to the waiting throng.

'Ride on a little, Cousin,' Lennox advised.

'Now, girl – this danger. Speak me plain,' the King commanded.

'Yes. It is danger for your person, your throne, for your whole realm,' she told him earnestly. 'From Spain.'

'Spain, you say? Tcha, lassie – what nonsense is this?'

'No nonsense, Sire. It is the King of Spain's invasion. His Armada . . . '

'That for the King of Spain's Armada!' James snapped long, strangely delicate fingers. 'A bogeyman he is, no more! Yon Philip has talked ower long o' his Armada. Forby, his

37

invasion is no' for me.' He leered. 'It is for my good sister and cousin, Elizabeth – God preserve her!'

'Yes, Sire. Elizabeth first. But who thereafter? When King Philip has England? Mary the Queen, in yon testament, left him heir to Scotland likewise, did she not?'

James all but choked. 'That . . . that . . . God's curse upon it! Foul fall you – it's no' true! It's lies – all lies. A forgery it was, I tell you! A forgery.' Gabbling, he banged his clenched fist on the pommel of his saddle. 'Never say yon thing in my hearing – d'you hear me? I'll no' have it! She . . . my mother . . . she never wrote it, I swear. A plot, it was – a plot o' yon glowing fiend out o' hell Walsingham, Elizabeth's jackal! I ken it – fine I ken it!' The last of that was scarcely coherent or intelligible, as the King lost control of his tongue, and the saliva flowed down unchecked in a bubbling stream.

Wide-eyed, startled by this passionate outburst, even sickened a little by what she saw, Mary instinctively drew back in her saddle, glancing quickly at Lennox. That young man stared distinctly owlishly at his cousin, and produced neither mediation nor guidance.

The girl, small chin firming, did not further flinch. 'That may be true, Sire – but King Philip holds otherwise. We have word, sure word, that he intends to have Scotland as well as England.'

'Then the Devil burn him! Roast and seethe him everlastingly! Precious soul o' God, I . . . I . . . ' With an obvious effort James controlled himself, if not his twitching mouth and flooding spittle. 'Folly!' he got out. 'This is folly! D'you hear, girl? All folly. For Philip willna win England – much less Scotland.' He rounded on Lennox. 'You, Vicky – *you* ken it's folly! He shouts loud, does yon Philip – but he'll never reach London. Na, na – he's been shouting ower long, the man. His Armada's all but boggarts and belly-wind! For years he's been threatening it . . . '

'A great fleet of ships, Sire, takes long to build, does it not?' Lennox pointed out.

'Tcha! These ships are but spectres, I warrant. And didna the man Drake burn a wheen o' them no' that long past . . . ?'

'Drake could not burn spectres,' his cousin pointed out reasonably.

38

'Houts, man! Forby, doesna Elizabeth build ships, too? She is a hard woman yon – but she kens how to hold her ain. Soul o' God, she does! She builds fine ships, too – bonny ships . . . '

'Will they be ready in three months, Your Grace?'

'Eh . . . ?' James goggled, as much at the calm factual way that the girl asked it, as at the question itself. 'Three . . . three months?'

'Yes. For that is when they will be needed. So says my Uncle Patrick. The Master of Gray.'

'A-a-ah!' The King's breath came out part-sigh, part-snort. 'So that's it! Yon limb o' Satan! Yon apostate knave! Yon . . . yon arch-traitor!' His eyes darted and rolled with seemingly enhanced urgency, as though their owner looked to see the Master of Gray materialise there and then from behind some tree, from the very ground at his feet. 'So *he* is in it, eh? Where? Where is he? Here's a plot, then – a black plot, if yon one's in it. You'll no tell me otherwise . . . ' The royal gabble faltered and died in a harsh croak, as James abruptly raised a padded arm, and jabbed a pointing, trembling finger. 'Who's yon?' he demanded, out of his incoherences. 'Guidsakes – who's yon? There's a man in there – a black man in yon bushes. Watching me! Hiding! It's . . . it's a plot. Treason! God be good – treason, I say!'

He was pointing straight at David Gray in the thicket, as his voice rose towards panic. His questing glance was proved none so short-sighted: their move forwards, away from the throng of courtiers, had in fact brought the trio into a position that partly invalidated the cover of that thicket.

'No treason,' Mary said quickly, but quietly still. 'That is but my father. Davy Gray, whom you know well.'

'Davy Gray! Davy Gray! A rogue, then! A base-born limmer! A knave . . . watching me . . . !'

'Not so, Sire. But the same man who saved you from Ruthven!'

'He means no ill, Cousin,' Lennox put in. 'He but brought his daughter. That she might warn you of all this . . . '

'What does he hide for, then? Yonder. Peeking out at me? Spying on me?'

'He but waits for Mary, here. You have forbidden him your

39

royal presence, he says. So he could not come before you himself . . . '

'Have him out, then. Here wi' him. I'll no' be spied on, I tell you . . . '

At the Duke's wave, David Gray rode out from his bushes, slowly, reluctantly, set-faced. Doffing his humble blue bonnet, he came up to them, inclined his bare head stiffly to his monarch, and so sat. But not humbly. That was Lord Gray's constant complaint against this by-blow of his; he was never suitably humble, in any circumstance. Sometimes indeed he seemed to have more unseemly pride than even the nobly-born Grays, soberly stern as he was. He did not speak, now.

James seemed to find it difficult to look at him directly. 'Well, man – well?' he said impatiently. 'What's the meaning o' it? Hiding in there like a tod in a cairn?'

'Twelve months back, Your Grace – less – you said that you never wished to set eyes on me again.' David answered evenly. 'I would not seek to oppose your wishes – in that, or in any other matter.'

'Haughty-paughty yet, man! Aye, you were right ill-mouthed yon time – rude and unbecoming in a subject,' the King declared, plucking at lip and chin. 'You were aye a hard uncourtly man, Davy Gray – dour and frowning.'

'No doubt, Sire. But at least I was honest in your service. More than others who were . . . more courtly. And you used to trust me.'

'More fool me, maybe! When it came to the bit, Davy Gray – who did you serve? Your king or yon traitorous knave, Patrick Gray?'

'It was for my brother's life, Highness. In the end, a man must do his all to save his brother.' He paused briefly. 'Or . . . his mother! Must he not?' Directly his level grey eyes sought to meet and hold the other's liquid flickering gaze.

James however looked away, anywhere but at his questioner, his sallow features flushed. 'You . . . you presume, by God! Greatly you presume!' he stammered. 'As you did yon time. I could have had your head for yon, man. You threatened your king. Yon is . . . is *lèse-majestié*, I tell you. Aye, and it was misprision o' treason too, man!'

David swallowed. 'No doubt, Sire. Perhaps I misjudged my duty.' He managed to make his voice no less stiff than heretofore. 'Others have done that likewise – in the matter of Your Grace's royal mother in especial! But I am seeking to redress it now. Redeem my loyal duty. As is the Master of Gray . . .'

'Yes, yes – what o' this? Come to your point, man.' Hastily, the King interrupted him. 'What is this folly? The lassie prating o' His Majesty o' Spain and his ships. Some talk of three months . . . ?'

'That is the time that my brother says, Your Grace. I have just received a letter. From Spain, I take it. He says that within a three-month England will indeed be invaded. He says that with his own eyes he has seen King Philip's preparations, now all but ready, that they are enough. Beyond a peradventure, he says. Invincible, he calls this Armada. And all is in train. Within three months he assures, Elizabeth will be under attack.'

'Houts, man! We have heard that sort o' talk before. In plenty.'

'Not from the Master of Gray, Sire. Say what you will of him – did you ever know Patrick to make a mistake anent matters of fact? Was his information ever wrong – whatever his policies?'

James explored his nostrils with nervous fingers. 'Maybe no', maybe no'. You say he has been in Spain himsel', the ill limmer?'

'Yes. He has seen it all with his own eyes, he says. Satisfied himself. Spoken with the King of Spain, indeed, it seems . . . '

'Treasons, no doubt, then – treasons, for a surety!'

'At least he would have me warn Your Majesty.'

'Aye – but why, man? Why?' Shrewdly the King peered. 'He doesna love me, does Patrick Gray! He loves nane but himsel', I swear. If he's that close with Philip? And he's a Papist, as all men ken. And banished my realm for his treason. Eh? Why warn *me*?'

David hesitated, moistening his lips. 'I do not search his reasons, Sire – only the facts. That this invasion endangers Scotland as well as England.'

Mary Gray spoke. 'Is that not your answer, Your Grace? That he can still love *Scotland*?' she asked simply.

41

'Eh . . . ?' James frowned, wriggling in his saddle. '*I* am Scotland,' he said.

No one spoke.

Into the pause the beat of hooves sounded, as the escort of men-at-arms belatedly came pounding back along the track, to discover what had happened to their royal charge. James waved them away again, peremptorily. At the other side, the clustered seething company of his lords and ladies and courtiers kept up an unceasing hum of talk and conjecture as they gazed inquisitively, suspiciously, resentfully, at the little group beside the monarch. The Earl of Mar in especial looked and sounded angry, not minding who perceived it apparently. Undoubtedly he had not forgotten Davy Gray and his part in the rescue of Ruthven.

James grimaced at the colourful noisy throng and turned his puffed and padded shoulder on them. 'Forby,' he said, returning, with one of his lightning changes, to his former querulous, weasel-like probing. 'Why did he no' write these tidings to me, mysel', man? Tell me that. He's aye writing me letters, is Maister Patrick.'

David stared, at a loss. 'He is . . . ? Patrick? He writes to *you*? To the King? Still, Sire . . . ?' Incredulity was evident in every word of him.

'Aye, he does.'

'But what . . . ?' He bit his lip, pausing. A subject could scarcely demand of his King what even his half-brother might write to the monarch – though the brother had been condemned to death by the same monarch less than a year before, and only had his sentence reduced to banishment for life by a hair's-breadth, through certain unseemly pressure on the part of the present questioner. David wagged his head helplessly. 'Patrick . . . is a law unto himself, Your Highness,' he said.

'Aye. The last letter was from Rome. Wi' a message from the Pope himsel'. Ooh, aye – your Patrick rides a high horse, for a felon! Vaunty as ever! He sends me advices, whispers, intelligences, from a' the Courts o' Europe. Aye – and in return would have Dunfermline back! Guidsakes – he has the insolence, the shameless audacity, to demand the revenues o' Dunfermline Abbey be returned to him! For his decent upkeep and reasonable dignity, as he names it! God in Heaven – was there ever sic a man?'

Involuntarily, David Gray exchanged glances with his daughter – though whether she recognised the enormity, as well as the vital significance of this revelation, he could not know. The Commendatorship of the Abbey of Dunfermline, once the richest church lands in all Scotland, the prize plum for all the hungry Scots lords after the Reformation, had eventually and most skilfully been acquired by Patrick, Master of Gray at the downfall of Arran the Chancellor. At his own downfall, in turn, they had been the main price that had had to be paid for the necessary intervention of the powerful Earl of Huntly on his behalf, David acting as go-between. Huntly was now Commendator of Dunfermline, and held its rich revenues. That Patrick should be working to get them back, though a forfeited exile, and so soon, not only indicated an extraordinary impertinence and double-dealing, but showed that he was seeking to conduct a campaign against Huntly, his own relative, with the King. Yet, this letter that had brought them here to the Wood of Lindores, had as its ostensible purpose the saving of Scotland by means of Huntly and his Catholic colleagues. Or at least the implication of Huntly in a Catholic rising, to control the King, dominate the land, and engineer a strategic alliance with the Catholic King of Spain. Could it be . . . could it be, after all, only a conspiracy? A deep-laid and subtle device to discredit and bring down Huntly, and so win back the riches of Dunfermline? Good God, it was possible – so possible, with Patrick! David Gray, frowning blacker than he knew, sought an answer, racking his wits. He needed time – time to think this thing out, to winnow down through the dust and chaff to the secret inner core of his brother's intention. Heaven save him – he had to think . . . !

His daughter gave him a moment or two, at least. 'If Uncle Patrick wrote to you from Rome, Sire,' she said, 'then that would be before he went to Spain. Before he saw the Spanish ships. Therefore he could not tell you of it.'

'Houts, lassie – why write to *you* to warn me, then? Why no' send the letter to me, the King? There's an ill stink in this somewhere, I swear. I smell it . . . '

The girl looked from her father to Lennox, and received no help from either. 'Would your Grace have believed it?' she asked.

'A pox! If I believe not him, why should I believe you, with his tale, woman?'

'Because the Master of Gray knows that you will esteem my father honest. Whatever he said to you yon time. All men know David Gray as honest, do they not?'

So artlessly, apparently innocently, entirely naturally and yet authoritatively did she come out with that, that she left her hearers, somehow, with no option but to accept it. They stared at her – her father longest.

'So it is true,' she added, with a sort of finality. 'And there is little time. But three months.'

'Aye – three months. This three months . . . ?' Majesty nibbled his fingernail. 'Little time – if it is true. What can I do eh? What can I do in three months?'

David found his voice. Whatever his brother's real intentions, they must go through with this now. The substitution of a Protestant instead of a Catholic muster at arms would prevent any involvement of Huntly anyway – and so wreck Patrick's plot, if that indeed was his aim. 'The Master of Gray, Sire, has his suggestions to make,' he said. 'For Your Grace. Have I your permission to put them?'

'Suggestions, eh? From *him*? Aye, man – out wi' them. Waesucks – what does the rogue suggest?'

David cleared his throat. 'The project is simple – and, I think, the wise course in the circumstances, Sire. Possibly the only course that could save your realm in the event of a successful invasion of England. It is that you call upon the lords to muster their forces, the Protestant lords of course. Within the month. The Spanish ambassador will quickly acquaint his master of the fact. Then you send a message or an envoy to King Philip, suggesting a secret treaty of alliance against England. On the condition that Scotland is left free and unassailed. Offer a Scottish expedition over the Border at the same time as his Armada sails, to weaken Elizabeth's arms. And, if Philip should reject this – then the word that Your Grace would be forced to inform Elizabeth of all. And to send your assembled forces to join her own . . . in the

44

defence of the Protestant religion!'

'Good God in Heaven!' Lennox exclaimed.

King James seemed considerably less startled. 'A-a-aye!' he breathed out. 'So that's it! Guidsakes – it sounds like Patrick Gray, to be sure! Aye, i'ph'mmm. Here's . . . here's notable food for thought. 'Deed, aye.' Keenly he peered at David. 'But the Master's a Papist, we a' ken. Here's unlikely Popery, is it no'?'

The other looked away, in his turn. 'My brother, I think, has never taken matters of religion with . . . with quite the seriousness that they deserve,' he said.

James actually giggled. 'Aye.' He nodded the large top-heavy head. 'I can believe that.' He glanced over towards the restive throng of his followers in the hunt, growing the more impatient as the rain grew heavier. 'We'll have to think on this. Think closely. It's no' that simple, mind. The lords . . . they'll likely no' be that eager to muster their strength. It's costly, you ken – costly. No' without I tell them what's to-ward wi' Spain. And then yon woman . . . then my good sister Elizabeth would hear o' it in a day or two. She's right well served wi' her spies, is Elizabeth.' The great unsteady, luminous eyes narrowed. 'A pox – I canna ken which o' a' these pretty lords there will be writing to her frae my ain house o' Falkland this night!' And he gestured towards the overdressed company. 'Or how many! For she pays them better than she pays me, the auld . . . ' He swallowed, adam's-apple bobbing. 'How am I to get the lords to muster, without I tell them this o' Spain – and have Elizabeth champing at my door?' The King of Scots suffered under the major handi-cap of having no sort of standing army of his own, other than the royal guards, so that he must depend for any real military force upon the feudal levies of his haughty lords.

It was Mary Gray who answered him promptly, simply. 'Tell them that you fear a *Catholic* rising, your Grace. In favour of the King of Spain's plans.'

Her father caught his breath. Here was thin ice for even light feet.

'Aye. Uh-huh. Well, now . . . ' James paused. 'But . . . would they believe it?'

'They would, would they not, if the Catholic lords did

45

indeed likewise muster? If your Grace was to write to my lord of Huntly and the other, privily, that they muster quietly. In case . . . in case perhaps of a Protestant rising to aid Protestant England against Spain.'

All three of her hearers made strange noises. The Duke of Lennox's plain and homely face was a study as he stared at the girl. King James's high-pitched laughter burst out in a whinny. David Gray chokingly protested.

'Mary – be quiet, child!' he exclaimed. 'What fool's chatter is this? Have you taken leave of your wits . . . ?'

'Na, na, Davy!' the King chuckled. 'Leave her be. It's nane so foolish, on my oath! Sakes, it's easy seen whose daughter this is! I can see profit in this – aye, I can.'

'And dangers too, Your Grace. Dangers of civil war. With your realm an armed camp. Both sides facing each other, sword in hand.'

'Och man, if it came to that, some small blood-letting, a few lords the less, might no' be just a disaster for my realm, you ken!' The monarch licked his lips. 'But – och, that needna be. I could keep them apart. Huntly and the Catholics are mainly in the north. I could have the Protestants assemble in the south – along the Border.' James smote his wet knee: 'Aye – along the Border! And how would our good cousin and sister o' England look on that? Wi' Spain threatening? Guid lack – I might even win Berwick back! And never a shot fired!'

'Your Grace will do as you think best. But I would advise that you muster only the Protestant lords,' David said heavily. 'Lest you light a bonfire that you canna douse!'

'Aye, well. I'ph'mmm. We'll see . . . '

'Cousin, the lords would rise – the Protestant lords – fast enough, I vow, if it was to make a sally to avenge the Queen your mother's execution. Over the Border.' Young Lennox made his first contribution. 'Have I not been asking for such a thing this six-month past? *Ma foi* – I myself will raise and arm five score brave lads for such a venture! Marry that to this matter of the Spaniards, and do you not shoot two fowl with one arrow?'

'M'mmm. Well, now . . . '

'Why, yes,' Mary nodded. 'Then, with your army on the

46

Border, Sire, are you not well placed? No need, surely, to draw sword at all – to shed blood. If the King of Spain will treat with you, all is well and Scotland is safe. And you will have Berwick again, no doubt. He will know that you are assembled ready, and could march south to Queen Elizabeth's aid. So he will indeed treat, I think.' She paused for a moment. 'And so, I think, will Queen Elizabeth.'

'God's Body – you are right, girl! So she would, I swear.'

'Yes. But . . . ' Mary looked, with touching diffidence, at her father, and smiled, at her most winsomely appealing. 'I am only a lassie, I know, and understand little of affairs of state. But . . . would it not be wise to have my lord of Huntly and some of his Catholic forces with you, Sire – lest while you are away over the Border, maybe, with the Protestants, the Catholic lords should indeed arise and seize Scotland?'

The three men took some seconds to assimilate that. James found words first – or rather, he found a guffaw which rose and cracked into a less manly tee-heeing.

'Save my soul – here's a right Daniel! A bit female Daniel! Lassie – I should have you at my Court. I should so . . . !'

'No, Sire – you should not!' Harshly, almost in a bark, that came from David Gray. 'My daughter's place is in my house – not in any Court. I have seen enough of Courts! She is young – a mere child. However forward, malapert! She is but fifteen years . . . '

'Och, she's no' that young, man. At fifteen was I no' ruling Scotland? And without a Regent. And . . . and you could come wi' her, Davy. I'd owerlook yon time. I'd . . . we would exercise our royal clemency, maybe, and admit you back to our Court and presence. Aye . . . '

'No, Sire. I thank you – but no. I am a simple man. I do very well as a schoolmaster and my lord's steward. I know my place. And Mary's. *Her* place is in my house, with her mother.'

'But Master Gray,' Lennox exclaimed. 'Here is a notable opportunity . . . '

'For whom, sir?'

'For her. For Mary, *Mon Dieu* . . . '

Mary Gray silenced the Duke with a touch of her finger on his wrist. She looked at the King, however. 'Your Grace is indeed kind. But my father is right, I am sure . . . '

'Of course I am right, girl! God grant me patience! Your Grace – have I your permission to withdraw? We have done what we came to do – acquainted you with my brother's tidings and advice. The matter is no further concern of ours.'

'Aye, Master Davy – you may go. I . . . we are grateful. Grateful, aye. For your tidings. We shall consider it well. Closely. And take due action.'

'The Chancellor . . . ' Mary whispered to her father, but loud enough for the other to hear.

'Eh . . . ? Ah, yes – the Chancellor.' David frowned. 'Sire – my brother also has it that it would be best, safest, if Your Highness dealt with this matter yourself, without informing Sir John Maitland, the Lord Chancellor. Especially the letter to King Philip. I take it that he believes that the Chancellor would not approve.'

'Aye. Belike he wouldna, Sir John! The more so if he kenned that Patrick Gray was at the back o' it! They never loved each other yon two, eh? We'll see, man – we'll see. I canna promise you anything, mind. It's a matter o' state . . . '

'Exactly, Sire. For myself, I care not which way it goes. It is no more concern of mine. Nor of Mary's. Our part is done.'

'Just so, just so. Aye. Off wi' you, then. Time, it is. Johnnie Mar is glowering there black as a Hieland stot! Hech, Vicky – you'll hae to think o' some matter to tell him we've been discussing on. Some matter to do wi' Lord Gray, belike. Aye, maybe anent his Sheriffdom o' Forfar. That will serve . . . ' The King held out his not over-clean hand. 'Our thanks to you, then, Master Davy. And to you too, lassie. We are indebted to you, and . . . and shall weigh it generously against your former misdeeds. Aye. You may leave our presence.'

Stiffly indeed David leant over to offer but a token kiss of the royal fingers. Mary was more suitably dutiful, even warm. As she straightened up in her saddle, she said quietly. 'I greatly thank Your Grace for asking me to your Court. It is true that I am too young, as my father says. But . . . would you not be better served to have back my Uncle Patrick to your Court? Much better. He is a clever man . . . '

'A plague on him – too clever by half! Tush, lassie – enough o' that! Yon one will serve me better in France or

48

Rome or Spain itsel', than here in my Scotland. Be off wi' you.'

'Come, Mary.'

'I shall accompany you some way on your road, Mary?' Lennox suggested.

'Not so, my Lord Duke,' David jerked. 'Your place is with the King – not with my lord of Gray's steward and his brat! Besides, I am very well able to look after my daughter, I assure you – *very* well able!' Reaching out, he took the reins of Mary's garron, and pulled his own beast's head round hard. 'Your servant, Sir . . . and my lord Duke!'

'Farewell, Vicky!' Mary called, as they trotted off.

Her father clapped his blue bonnet back on his wet head.

Past all the staring supercilious courtiers they rode, northwards, the man gazing straight ahead of him, the girl eyeing the chattering fashionable throng with frankest interest, unabashed.

It was not until they were well past and on their way, alone, towards Lindores village and the Tay, that David spoke. 'I do not know what to make of you, Mary – on my soul, I do not!' he said.

'Must you make aught more of me than you have made already, Father?' she asked fondly. 'Some would say, I think, that you have wrought not ill with me hitherto – you, and Mother . . . and Uncle Patrick!'

David Gray uttered something between a groan and a snort. 'God help me . . . !'

Chapter Three

THE Lord Gray came home to Castle Huntly in a gale of wind and the worst of tempers. For three weeks, three solid weeks, he had been away kicking his heels down in the Borderland, along with many another Scots lord, whilst his wretched men ate and drank themselves silly in armed but pointless idleness, by royal command but at *his* expense – men who should have been hard at work rescuing the hay crop from the sodden far-flung grasslands of the Carse of Gowrie, hay for the vast herds of cattle that were the very basis of my lords prosperity. It was mid-July. The wettest and wildest spring and early summer in living memory. There would be the devil to pay for it next winter, in lack of forage and starving beasts, with the hay lying flattened and uncut, or rotten and mildewed – and the corn harvest like to be as bad. Seventy-five men of his, seventy-five able-bodied men, wasting their time and his substance amongst those damnable mist-shrouded bog-bound Border hills, on the commands of a crazy young half-wit King, who feared Catholic risings, Spanish invasions, and God alone knew what else!

Lord Gray had come home with fully half his force, king or no king. And those that he had left behind in Teviotdale were the most useless of his band, moreover – as was the case with many of the other feudal contingents, the majority of the lords being in a like state of impatience and fulmination, almost revolt. James, the young fool, had forbidden any worthwhile activity, even cattle-raiding, any forays across the Border – although that is what they understood that they had been there for – and nibbled his finger-nails instead, afraid of the English Lord Dacre's Northumbrian levies hurriedly raised to face them, afraid of the Governor of Berwick's garrison, afraid of the Catholics in the west under the Lords Maxwell and Herries who were supposed to be threatening the English West March, afraid of what the madcap Earl of Bothwell might do in these circumstances – afraid indeed of his own shadow. Waiting for his envoy back from Spain, it was said, delayed by storms; waiting for the supposed Spanish invasion of England; waiting for the gold that Queen Elizabeth had hastily promised him for keeping her northern march secure and denying his ports to Spanish ships; waiting, Christ God, for anybody and everybody to make up his royal mind for him!

In such case was the Kingdom of Scotland this deplorable summer of 1588, with its monarch a drooling ninny, the lords made fools of, and the so-called Spanish Armada a myth and a Popish fable. At least, such was my lord of Gray's profound conviction.

50

It required all of Mary Gray's soothing charms to make him even bearable company for the rest of his household and dependants at Castle Huntly in the next few days.

Those days brought tidings and rumours to the Carse of Gowrie that gave even Lord Gray second thoughts, however – whether he admitted them or not. First came the word that the Earls of Huntly, Erroll and Montrose had risen in the north, with, it was said, as many as five thousand men – though that might well be an exaggeration – and had taken over the direction of the towns of Aberdeen, Stonehaven, Banff and Elgin, expelling the provosts and ministers of the Kirk and installing Catholic nominees of their own. Then, only two days later, they heard that O'Neill, Earl of Tyrone, revolting against Elizabeth in Ireland, had landed in person in the Western Isles, and was there urging the Highland chiefs to raise a clan army to make cause with him – Catholic, of course – that was to link up with Huntly in the east. That this Irish move should have coincided so closely with Huntly's seemed unlikely to be mere chance – and the linking of the name of Logan of Restalrig with the business, no Highlander, no Catholic, but cousin and erstwhile bravo of the exiled Master of Gray, set at least some minds furiously to think. King James's reluctance to venture over the Border into England with his distinctly unruly force, was to be considered now in a new light. There were even whispers that the Crown had all along been privy to the entire business; it was noteworthy that it was the Kirk that whispered thus – and in far from dulcet tones. On the other hand, it could not but be recognised by all that, had not the Protestant lords been providentially assembled at this time, there would have been little or nothing to prevent the combined Catholic forces from turning southwards and taking over the kingdom. King Jamie might be owed some small thanks for this, accidental though it could have been. Even Lord Gray had to acknowledge that.

The next news made Lord Gray wish even – without saying so – that he had been perhaps a little less hasty. It was that the King, as counter to the northern situation presumably, and as something to occupy the remnant of his Protestant forces, had personally marched them westwards along his own Border, to attack, capture and destroy the great castle of

51

Lochmaben in Annandale, ancestral home of his heroic predecessor Robert Bruce and now held by the Catholic Lord Maxwell as hereditary keeper. As a politic gesture he had hanged its captain and six other Maxwells. Whatever the reasons for this flourish, James's first military exploit – and it was variously reported that it was to please Elizabeth, who, with no Armada appearing, it would be wise to keep well-disposed; that it was to keep the Kirk quiet; that it was to warn Huntly and the Northern Catholics not to move too far south – whatever the reasons, the Lord Gray could have wished to have been present, for Annandale was a rich land, and the sacking thereof could hardly have failed to be profitable for those engaged.

It was all difficult and confusing in the extreme. A man could scarcely tell which way to turn, to best advantage.

Then, on the very last day of the month of July, something more substantial than tidings and rumours reached Castle Huntly. All that boisterous day ships, great ships such as had never before been seen in Scottish waters, were to be observed all along the east coast, heading northwards in ones and twos and straggling groups, before an unseasonable south-easterly gale, weather-worn, battered, sails rent and shredded, top-hamper askew. One great galleon indeed, limped in through the gap in the long roaring sand-bar of Tay, and let down her anchor off Lord Gray's castle of Broughty which guarded the estuary, the rich colours and banners of Castile torn but still flying proudly from her soaring aftercastle and broken foremast. She sought provisions, water, care for her wounded, and time to effect repairs. My lord was sent for in haste the dozen miles from Castle Huntly. He found a Spanish marquis, a round dozen dons, and no fewer than two hundred soldiers of the Duke of Parma's Netherlands army aboard, as well as the crew, all armed to the teeth, though with many wounded and much damage apparent, not all of it caused by the storm. The *Santa Barba del Castro* had, it seemed, put into the Tay in error, mistaking the estuary and assuming that Dundee town was Aberdeen.

My lord was in something of a pickle. Nominally at least he was a staunch Protestant and a strong supporter of Christ's Reformed Kirk. These were notorious Papists, and therefore

52

anathema. On the other hand, he was not sure whether they were in fact allies of his King or enemies, at this precise moment – depending on whether Philip was treating with James or not. James admittedly was anxious to accept a large sum in gold from Elizabeth for denying port facilities to the Spaniards – but then it was well-known that the gold had not yet been paid, and the Tudor woman's promises were markedly unreliable. Moreover, this galleon mounted three tiers of cannon on either side – fifty-two guns, fully five times the number available on Broughty Castle's battlements – and disposed of more armed manpower than Gray could raise in a month. He compromised, therefore, very sensibly, supplying provisions and water, and timber for rough-and-ready repairs, but permitting no landing of wounded and only two days anchorage – thereby enriching his coffers by a sizeable quantity of gold ducats and some quite excellent silver plate.

So Scotland became aware that the long-delayed and much-dreaded Armada of Spain was in fact over, a thing of the past, a cloud dispersed – and unlike neighbouring England which went crazy with joy, did not know whether to be relieved or disappointed. As details gradually became known, and the size of the disaster to Spanish arms was assessed, so grew the realisation that England, the Auld Enemy, released at last from the bogey and spectre that had haunted her for years, was likely to prove a still more arrogant and dangerous neighbour than heretofore, and Elizabeth more interfering than ever. King Jamie saw his promised gold melt away for sure, and the English dukedom with which Elizabeth had also tempted him at the same time evaporate into thin air. Even the public and long sought-for announcement that he was evident, lawful and only heir to the said ageing Queen, now that Mary his mother was dead, was clearly postponed once again. The deceived and ill-used young man left his Borders and returned to Holyroodhouse and his capital in a state of deep depression.

At Castle Huntly, at least, there was no such depression. My lord had done better out of the Armada than most. David Gray heaved a profound sigh of relief, for not only was the threat of Spanish interference removed, but civil war likewise, for Huntly and his friends in the north promptly saw the light of reason and dispersed their rising as though it had never been. The Irish-Highland venture still went on, but that was far away. His brother Patrick's conspiracy, if such it had been, was surely brought to naught, exploded, blown away on the south-easterly gale – for which the good God be praised! And Mary Gray each night at her maidenly bedside thanked the same much-invoked God that the Holy Office and Inquisition would not be established on the Castle-hill of Edinburgh – but besought Him fervently at the same time that He would bring her Uncle Patrick home to Scotland just as quickly as it was celestially possible. Ludovick, Duke of Lennox was adjured likewise to entreat the Thrones of both Heaven and Scotland in the same cause. Patrick Gray it was who had brought the ten-year-old Ludovick from France to James's Court on his spectacular father's death.

Alas for the prayers and devotion of youth and innocence – the Master of Gray's stock had seldom been lower, his acceptability in circles of government more improbable. The Armada might almost have been entirely his own invention, and the unusual gales which had first delayed the fleet for six weeks, then harassed it in the narrows of the Channel, putting it at the mercy of the lighter and better-handled English ships, before finally breaking it up in major disaster and sending its dispersed vessels scudding north-about right round Scotland and Ireland as the only way of getting back to Spain – these gales might have been of the Master's personal devising. James, mourning his lost gold and duchy, even his unpaid pension from Elizabeth not received for months, was in no state to lend his ear to even Vicky's pleas. Instead he listened rather to the creaky voice of his wily lawyer-like Chancellor Maitland, who had lain notably low during all these alarms and excursions and now emerged again, like a tortoise from its shell, for the proper running and weal of the realm. And the King had spoken truly when he had declared that the Chancellor and the Master of Gray did not love each other. Sir John Maitland, as all at Court knew, never ceased to bewail that the beheading of the said malefactor had not gone off as planned – as *he* had so efficiently planned. And that was the bastard Davy Gray's fault.

Almost it seemed, indeed, as though God Himself was

against the unfortunate exile in foreign parts. Only a short time after the Armada fiasco, the powerful de Guise brothers, Henry the Duke and Cardinal Louis, Archbishop of Rheims, full cousins of the late Mary of Scotland, were assassinated by order of Henry Third of France. These had been Patrick Gray's potent protectors and supporters for years, the source of much of his influence, employment and funds on the Continent. Without their far-reaching Jesuit backing, Europe was going to be a very different place for their gallant and handsome protégé.

If the Reformers' stern God was going to take a denominational hand, of course, then the Master of Gray was not the one to fly in the face of destiny. Not even his worst enemy had ever suggested, however he might miscall him, that he was apt to do such a thing . . . once destiny made its intentions reasonably clear. Destiny might always be gently aided and piloted, however, along its chosen course, contrary though that might be, by a philosophical and agile-minded man. Such a man as Patrick Gray.

Mary Gray came to her father one golden morning that autumn, when he was superintending the placing and building of the numerous round oat-stacks of the belated corn harvest, in a sheltered stackyard nestling beneath the tall upthrusting crag out of which rose the red-stone walls of Castle Huntly, high above the flat carselands. It was the sort of work that David Gray enjoyed – much better indeed than schoolmastering; with all the local lairds, whose children he taught along with my lord's more recent brood, equally busy rescuing their corn and glad of even youthful help, lessons had been postponed with mutual relief. Her father now stood atop a round half-built stack, in shirt-sleeves, doublet discarded, hair untidy, face, chest and bare arms coated with oat-dust, catching the heavy sheaves that were tossed up to him from the laden two-horse wains, and building them into position on the steadily growing stack. He laughed and joked with the workers, and even sang snatches of song, as he laboured.

Mary looked up at him affectionately. This was as she loved best to see her father, working carefree and effective in the good honest toil of the fields and woods. Clearly he ought to have been a farmer; all his learning and experience of affairs seemed to bring him little or no satisfaction. He was more truly grandson to old Rob Affleck, miller of Inchture, than son to my lord of Gray. And yet . . . she knew also that he would have made a better lord for Castle Huntly than did Granlord, or even, it might be, than Uncle Patrick would make one day. She loved him, up there, all strong, confident, cheerful manhood. She felt loth indeed to interrupt and bring him down. But the matter might be urgent.

'Father,' she called. 'A lad from Kingoodie – Tam Rait, it is – came seeking you. With a message. There is somebody there asking for you.'

'Eh . . . ?' David paused in his rhythmic toil, and wiped back an unruly lock of hair from his brow with the back of a dusty hand. 'At Kingoodie? Sakes, lassie – if anybody wants me from Kingoodie, they can come here for me!'

'Yes. But . . . ' She moved closer to the stack, as near to her father as she could get. ' . . . this is a woman, Tam says. A lady.'

'A lady?' The man stared down at her. 'At Kingoodie? A few salmon-fishers' cots and a fowler's hut!'

'Yes. She is at Tam's father's cottage. And asking for Master David Gray. To go to her there, forthwith. I said that I would tell you.' Roguishly she laughed. 'I asked him if she was handsome – and by his face I deem that she is! And something more than that, maybe.'

'M'mmm.' He frowned.

'Tam said that she had told him not to tell anyone but your own self. But . . . well, Tam Rait could not keep a secret from me!' The girl's eyes danced. 'I did not tell Mother.'

Her father coughed. 'Well . . . ' he said. He jumped down from the stack, already rolling down his shirt-sleeves, and called for one of the men to take his place. He picked up his old torn doublet. 'I . . . I am but scurvily clad for visiting ladies,' he said doubtfully. 'Even at Kingoodie. But if I go home first . . . '

'Mother will undoubtedly be much interested,' she finished for him. 'I think that we should just go from here, do not you? It will save time, too.'

'We?' her father asked, brows raised. 'I can find my way

56

to Kingoodie, Mary, without your aid!'

'Oh, yes,' she agreed. 'But I promised Tam Rait that I would bring you myself. And at once.'

'Promised . . . ? Houts, girl – be off with you! I'll manage my business, whatever it is, without you. Or Tam Rait!'

'Would you rather that I went home to Mother?' she asked, innocently.

He looked at her, sidelong. 'You are a – a shameless minx! Yes, go home, girl. What should there be here to alarm your mother?'

'I do not know, Father. Only . . . Tam says that the lady who was asking for you so secretly is big with child!'

David Gray swallowed. He looked away, and ran a hand over his mouth and jaw – thereby smearing the sweaty dust thereon into still more evident designs and whorls. He moistened his lips.

Silently the girl took the scarlet kerchief from around her neck, and reaching up on tip-toes, wiped his features with it gently, before handing the silken stuff to him to continue the process. As she stood there close to him, throat and shoulders largely bare above the open-necked and brief white linen bodice, the man could not but be much aware of the warm honey-hued loveliness of her, and the deep cleft of her richly-swelling firm young bosom. Mary was indeed, beyond all question, physically as well as mentally, no longer anybody's child – and the sooner that he came to terms with the fact, almost certainly, the better for him.

Unspeaking they turned and walked side by side towards the stackyard gate where David's horse was tethered.

'I shall ride pillion at your back, very well,' Mary mentioned, as he made to mount the broad-backed shaggy garron.

Without a word he leaned down, and arm encircling her slender waist, hoisted her up behind him.

To the admiring grins of the workers – for the beast's broadness meant that the girl's shapely legs, long for her height, were much in view – they rode off.

They had to go a bare three miles across the reedy levels of the flood-plain of the Tay, marshy cattle-dotted pasture, seamed with ditches lined with willow and alder and the spears of the yellow flag. Taking a track which followed the

57

coils and twists of the Huntly Burn, they headed almost due westwards until they reached its outfall at the low weed-girt shore. Turning along this by a muddy road of sorts, presently they came to a few lonely cot-houses and turf-coated cabins, where there was a rough stone jetty, boats were drawn up on the shingle, and nets were hanging up to dry on tall reeling posts. Kingoodie, where my lord obtained most of his salmon.

Their approach had not gone unobserved, and a youth emerged from one of the houses and waved to them. As they rode up, behind him in the low doorway, a lady stooped and came out.

She made a strange picture, materialising out of that humble stone-and-turf windowless cottage that was little better than a hovel, a beautiful youngish woman, stylish, assured, dressed in travelling clothes of the finest quality and the height of fashion, carrying her very evident child with a proud calm. Grey-eyed, wide-browed, with finely-chiselled features and sheer heavy golden hair that was almost flaxen, she had a poise, an unconscious aristocracy of bearing most obviously unassumed.

'God be praised – Marie!' David Gray cried, and leapt from his horse in a single agile bound, leaving his daughter to slide down as she could – a strangely impetuous performance for that sober, level-headed man, rash indeed in front of witnesses.

'Davy! Davy! Davy!' the woman called out, part-laughing, part-sobbing, and came running, light-footed enough considering her condition.

Wide-eyed, Mary Gray stood by the garron, watching.

David halted before he reached the newcomer, seeming to recollect discretion. Not so the lady. She ran straight up to him, to fling herself against him, arms around him, to bury her golden head on his dusty chest. Something she said there, but what was not clear. He raised a hand, a distinctively trembling hand, to stroke her fair down-bent head. So they stood.

At length she looked up. 'Oh, Davy,' she said, blinking away tears from grey eyes almost as level and direct as his own. 'How good! How fine! To see you again . . . to feel you . . . good, strong, solid, unchangeable Davy Gray! Let me look at you! Yes – the same, just the same. You have not changed one whit . . . '

'It is but a year, Marie,' he said, deep-voiced. 'Fifteen months . . . '

'Ah – you count them also! Fifteen long months.'

'Aye. Long, as you say. I . . . I . . . ' He shook his head, as though consciously denying himself that train of thought and emotion. 'Is all well? How came you here? Patrick . . . ? And you – you are well, my lady?'

'Well enough, yes. Can you not see it, Davy? Larger than ever I have been! Well – and in the state all good wives long to be, so they do say! Do you not congratulate me?'

'Aye,' he nodded. 'I am happy to see it – happy indeed.' Gravely, unsmiling he said it. 'I was sorry . . . about the other.' The Mistress of Gray had miscarried in a storm-tossed ship on her way, with her banished husband, to exile.

She searched his face. 'No doubt,' she said. 'But . . . there is young Mary. Good lack – she is . . . she is liker . . . more than ever she is like . . . '

'Aye,' the man agreed briefly. 'How, and where, is Patrick?'

'Mary, my dear,' the woman called out, and leaving David's side moved over towards the girl. 'On my soul, you are lovely! A child no longer. A woman – and a beauty! Let me kiss you, poppet.'

Mary curtsied prettily before the other reached her, and then embraced her unreservedly, returning her kisses frankly. 'How nice you are, Lady Marie,' she declared. 'What a splendid surprise! And the baby – how wonderful! She gurgled delightedly. 'Will it be my cousin – or my brother or sister?'

'Mary . . . !' David Gray protested, shocked.

The Lady Marie Stewart, Mistress of Gray, laughed musically, mock-ruefully. 'Lord – I do not know, Mary! I do not. But, I vow, if it is like you at all, then I shall be happy.'

'Thank you. And how is my Uncle Patrick?'

'He is well, And sends you his love and devotion. As well he might! I left him at Dieppe, where he put me on a ship . . . '

'He put you on a ship?' David demanded, coming up, and dropping his voice heedfully, glancing around them for listeners. 'Patrick sent you here? Alone? From France?

'Yes. I suppose that he sent me. Though I wished to come. I was pining for home. And determined that my son should be born in Scotland. It is a boy, you know – I am sure of it. Do not ask me how I know. But . . . he will be called Andrew, and he will be heir to Gray. It is only fitting that he should be born here. Wise, too – that there be no doubts, with my lord . . . !'

'Even lacking his father?'

'Even so. Although . . . who knows, his father may not be so far away by then, God willing. And Patrick scheming!'

'M'mmm,' David said, frowning.

'But how did you come here, Lady Marie?' Mary asked. 'To Kingoodie?'

'I shipped on a Scots trading vessel. Bringing wines and flax. To Pittenweem, in Fife. Faugh – the smell of her! Hides she had carried before, from Scotland to France. Do I not stink of them yet? From Pittenweem I bargained with a fishing skipper to bring me round Fife Ness and put me ashore secretly in the Tay, as near to Castle Huntly as might be. I arrived last night, here. And these good folk have treated me full kindly.'

'Kindly! Dod Rait should have brought you straight to the castle. It is but three miles. Instead of keeping you, wife to the heir of Gray, in this cabin . . . '

'Not so, Davy. They know not who I am, for one thing. I could not come to Castle Huntly. My lord would scarce welcome me, I think! Would he? I am the wife of a condemned and exiled felon, banished the realm. I must go warily indeed. It was you that I had to see – you whom I knew would guide and help me.'

'Aye – that I will, to be sure. But . . . was it wise to come, my lady?'

'Wise! Wise! Is Davy Gray doubting already? Is that my welcome? Would you that I had stayed away?'

'No. But there are hazards – grave hazards. Patrick's credit is low, my lady. The Armada business . . . '

'There are hazards in living, Davy – in breathing! And it is to improve Patrick's credit that I am here, see you. But . . . am I to be my lady to you again? Would you keep me at a

distance? Was it not Marie that you named me, Davy when
first you beheld me? I thought I heard it. Am I not your
good-sister. And before I was that – your friend?'

'Aye. You are kind.' David Gray could look very grim at
times. 'But you are the Lady Marie Stewart, daughter to the
Earl of Orkney, and own cousin to the King.' That was true.
Her father, the Lord Robert Stewart, former Bishop and now
Earl of Orkney, was one of King James Fifth's many
bastards, brother on the wrong side of the blanket to the late
Mary Queen of Scots. 'You are a great lady. And I am . . . '

'Stop! We all know what you are, Davy Gray! The
proudest, stiffest-necked man in this kingdom!' She shook her
coifed golden head, but smiled at him warmly nevertheless.
'The man who bought my husband's life, when no one else
could, at great cost to himself. I have never had opportunity
truly to thank you for that, Davy.' She laid a hand on his arm.
'I do now. I do, indeed. And, alas, need your help once more.'

'It is yours, always.'

'Yes, Davy dear. I know it. Like, like a warm glow at my
heart that thought has been, many a weary day.' She mustered a laugh. 'Patrick says, indeed, that you are the only man
who could make him jealous of his wife . . . !'

David's face was wiped clean of expression. 'That is no
way to talk, your ladyship,' he said evenly. 'Nor this any
place to talk, at all. Come – can you mount my beast? In these
fine clothes? And in your, your present state? Mary can ride
behind you, holding you. And I will walk, leading the beast. It
will be quite safe, I think. I will send for your baggage later.'

'Lord – of course I can ride, Davy! I am not that far gone.
But five months. Do I look so monstrous? But . . . where will
you take me?'

'To Castle Huntly. Where else?'

'But I cannot go there. Surely you see it? Anywhere but
there. My lord always was out of love with Patrick. Now, he
will have none of him, or his, I swear. And I will not come
begging his charity. Or any man's. Save . . . save perhaps
yours, Davy Gray!' She shook her head again. 'Besides, it
would not do. Lord Gray is a notable pillar of the Kirk.
Though no Catholic myself, I will be held to be one for Patrick's sake. To harbour me at Castle Huntly could do my lord

61

much harm – you all, perhaps. I thought to go to my half-sister's house – Eupham, that is married to Mark Ogilvie, of Glen Prosen. If you could help me to win that far . . . '

'We go to the castle,' David interrupted her bluntly.

'But, Davy – what of my lord . . . ?'

'Allow me to deal with my lord! That Patrick's wife, bearing Patrick's child, should seek shelter in her need anywhere but at Castle Huntly is unthinkable. Leave my lord to . . . to his steward!'

'And your Mariota?'

David was a little less definite. 'Mariota will, will rejoice to see you,' he said.

'I hope so, yes. But . . . ' She shrugged and sighed. 'She is well? How does she, the fair Mariota?'

'She is well – and in the same state as you are!'

'Oh!'

'Yes. Now – we will take leave of the Raits here. How much of belongings have you . . . ?'

So presently the trio were pacing across the flats of the carse, the Lady Marie mounted with Mary Gray behind her and the man leading the garron. Ahead, the great towering mass of Castle Huntly reared its turrets and battlements above the plain like a heavy frown in stone, even in the golden sunlight. To its presumed future mistress it seemed less than beckoning.

'My lord has been away at Foulis Castle these two days,' David informed her. 'But he will be back tonight.'

'Then I had rather be gone by then,' she said.

The presence of a number of stamping, shouting men-at-arms in the castle courtyard, when they arrived, indicated that Lord Gray had in fact returned home earlier than anticipated. As David aided the Lady Marie to dismount, young Mary slipped down and ran on ahead, and in at the main door of the keep.

Mariota came hurrying down the winding stone stairway to welcome them, in consequence, greeting the newcomer with a sort of uneasy kindness, all flustered surprise, bemoaning her own unsuitable attire, that she had had no warning, my lord's untimely arrival, exclaiming how bonny was my lady, how tired she must be coming all that way from France, how sad to be parted from dear Patrick, and was he well, happy? All in a breathless flood.

Marie kissed her warmly. They made a strange contrast, these two, both so very fair to look upon, but so very different in almost every respect. David considered them thoughtfully, rubbing his chin. Into the chatter of exclamation and half-expressed question and answer, he presently interrupted, gently but firmly.

'Up with you,' he declared. 'Here is no place for talk. Let the Lady Marie in, at least, my dear. She will be weary, hungry. She needs seating, comfort, refreshment. Up the stairs with you. Our rooms are on high, but they are at your service . . . '

'Indeed!' a hoarse voice challenged heavily. The Lord Gray had appeared on a half-landing just above, a stocky massive figure, a furred robe thrown hastily over and only part-covering his dishabille. At his broad back, a hand tentatively within one of his arms, was his grand-daughter. 'In my house, *I* say what rooms are at whose service! Bring the lady into my chamber, Davy!'

Marie sank in a curtsy. 'Greetings, my lord,' she said. 'I hope that I find you well? I am but passing on my way . . . elsewhere . . . '

'Aye,' he answered shortly. 'No doubt.'

'I think not,' David put in quietly, evenly. 'Patrick's wife does not pass Castle Huntly!'

'Eh . . . ? Fiend seize me – who are you to speak?'

'One who esteems the name and honour of Gray, sir. And, since we are privy here, and all of a family as it were – your eldest son!'

'Damn you, you . . . !' My lord all but choked, unable to find breath or words.

Mary found them. 'We knew that you would wish to honour the King's own cousin, Granlord.'

'Ah . . . ummm.'

'And very beautiful, is she not?'

'Wheesht, child – hold your tongue!' her grandfather got out, but in a different tone of voice. 'A pox – but I'll be master in my own house, see you!' He jabbed a thick accusatory finger, but at David. 'Mind it, man – mind it, I say!' He turned on Marie. 'How came you here? And where is yon graceless popinjay that has bairned you? If he it was!'

'Yes, my lord – he it was,' Marie answered without heat, even smiling a little. 'I carry your heir. I would have thought that you would have rejoiced to see it. I am new come, by ship from Dieppe, secretly – where I left Patrick.'

'Thank the good God he's no' here, at least! Why are you come, woman?'

'I have good reasons, sir. One, that you would wish the heir to Gray to be born where you could see it, I believed. Not in some foreign land. Was I wrong?'

The older man grunted. 'A mercy that you came secretly, at the least,' he said, after a moment. 'None know that you are here, then?'

'None who know who I am.'

'My lord – the Lady Marie is tired. Unfit to be standing thus. In her condition. She must have food and wine . . . '

'I am very well, Davy. I seek nothing . . . '

'I said to bring her into my room, did I no'?' Gray barked. And turning about abruptly, he went stamping back up the stairs.

As David took Marie's arm, to aid her upstairs, she held back, shaking her head. 'No, Davy,' she declared. 'I had liefer go now. Away. It is as I thought. This house is no place for me. He is set against Patrick, and therefore me . . . '

The man did not relax his grip, and propelled her forward willy-nilly. 'You will stay in this house,' he said grimly. 'It is your right. He will do as I say, in the end. For he needs me, does my lord of Gray! I know too much. Come, Marie . . . '

'And do not take my lord too sorely,' Mariota advised, biting her lip. 'He has a rough tongue, and proud. But he is not so ill as he sounds. And . . . I think that he loves Patrick at heart, more than he will say.'

'Forby, he loves beautiful ladies!' Mary added, with a little laugh. 'So smile at him, Lady Marie – smile much and warmly. And he will not withstand you long!'

'Tut, girl . . . !' her father reproved.

They went upstairs together, three of them turning in at

64

my lord's private chamber just above the great hall of the castle, and Mariota proceeding higher to collect viands and refreshment for the guest.

The master of the house stood at the window of a comparatively small apartment, the stone floor of which constituted the top of the great hall's vaulted ceiling. It was snug, overwarm indeed, for my lord liked a fire here summer and winter in the fireplace with the elaborate heraldic overmantel showing the Gray arms of rampant red lion on silver, carved in stone. Skins of sheep and deer covered the floor, and the stone walls were hung with arras, again embroidered heraldically. Gray gestured towards one of the two chairs of that room without leaving the window, for Marie to sit down.

'Patrick?' he jerked, not looking at her. 'Is he well enough?' And lest that might seem too mawkishly solicitous, 'And what follies and mischiefs and schemes is he up to in France or Rome or whatever ill-favoured land he's plaguing with his presence now?'

'He is well, yes,' Marie answered. 'And as for his schemes ... well, Patrick is Patrick, is he not?'

'Aye!' That came out on an exhalation of breath that was something between a groan and a sigh. He turned round to stare at the young woman now. 'Why did he send you here?' he demanded directly. 'I ken Patrick, God pity me! You didna come without he sent you. And he didna send you just to drop your bairn in front o' me, where I could see it! Na, na. He doesna care that for me, or mine!' The older man snapped his fingers. 'Unless for my gear and lands.'

'I think that you wrong him, my lord,' Marie told him quietly. 'But at least credit him with the desire that there should be no doubts about the birth of the heir of Gray.' She smiled a little. 'And that not on account of your lands and gear! Believe me, sir, great as these may be, Patrick looks for greater.'

'Eh ... ?'

'He is determined to win back the Abbey of Dunfermline and its revenues, from the Earl of Huntly.'

'Christ God – the more fool he, then! The prinking prideful ninny! He'll never do that.'

'He will try, my lord, without a doubt.'

David, frowning, spoke. 'I mislike this,' he said. 'I mislike it, for many reasons. It is folly, dangerous, flying too high. But it is less than honourable, too. And it brings me into it. For he used me to offer Dunfermline to Huntly. I made the bargain for him – Dunfermline for his life. Dunfermline for Huntly to get me into the King's presence, so that I could bargain with James also! Now, to go back on it . . . '

'Faugh!' his father interrupted him scornfully. 'Save your breath, man! Patrick's no' concerned with honour, or keeping bargains, or aught else but his own benefit.' He swung back on Marie. 'But here's idle chatter. He'll no' get back Dunfermline – that's sure. And dinna tell me, woman, that he sent *you* here on such fool's errand? You!'

'No,' she agreed patiently. 'That is not part of my errand. That he must look to himself – if he can win back to Scotland It is to intercede with the King to permit his return – that is my duty.'

'Ha! Now we have it. And near as much a fool's errand as the other! You'll no' manage that, I'll vow! He's banished for life, is he no'?'

'What decree the King has made, the King can unmake, she asserted. 'And *I* am not banished. If I can come to my father in Edinburgh, he will bring me into the King's presence.'

'To what end, woman – to what end? The King's cousin you may be – in bastardy – but that winna serve to gain Patrick's remission. You pleading for him on your bended knees, weeping woman's tears? Think you that will move our Jamie? Or the Chancellor? And the Council? Condemned by the Council o' the Realm for highest treason and the death o' the King's bonny mother, think you that tears and pleas will bring him back? None want him here. You'll need a better key than a woman's snuffles to open the door o' Scotland again to Patrick Gray!'

'That key,' she told him calmly, 'perhaps I have.'

All gazed at her – and Mariota's entrance at this moment with food and wine was greeted with considerable impatience by my lord. It was pushed aside peremptorily.

'What mean you?' Marie was challenged. 'How can you have anything such? What is this?'

'The King's marriage,' she answered.

There was silence in that overheated chamber.

'Patrick has been busy,' she went on, but levelly, factually, almost wearily. 'He has not wasted his time abroad. He has been working for a match between James and the Princess Catherine, sister to King Henry of Navarre.'

'Patrick . . . ? The King's matching?' my lord gobbled. 'Devil slay me – what insolence! What effrontery!'

'Navarre . . . !' David exclaimed. 'But . . . what of the Danish match?'

'Patrick believes this better, of more worth. Henry of Navarre is the Protestant champion – whilst the Danish royal house is known to be unsure in its religion, inclining back towards the old faith . . . '

'God's Body – is Patrick concerned now for the Protestants! What next, woman?'

Marie ignored that. 'Moreover, Navarre will be heir to France. And Patrick believes the King of France to be sickening.'

She had them silenced now.

'And the King of Scots married to a sister of great France is a different matter to him married to the daughter of little Denmark'

That was not to be denied. David, somewhat abstractedly, began to offer refreshment to their guest, while his father hummed and hawed.

'This . . . this is scarce believable,' the latter got out. 'That Patrick should dare fly this high – a condemned man!'

'Flying a high hawk never troubled Patrick,' David said. 'No doubt we were foolish to believe that he would change just because he was banished. But . . . how much substance has this project, Marie? What says King Henry of Navarre? Does he even know aught of it?'

She nodded. 'Patrick has been closeted with him more than once. He is agreeable, it seems. The matter has reached the stage of considering the worth of the dowry . . . '

'Precious soul o' God – and King Jamie kens naught o' it, woman?'

'That is why I am sent, my lord. To apprise him of it. Of its . . . advantages.'

David noticed the tiny hesitation on Marie's part before she used that term.

'Aye. But what makes Patrick believe that this ploy will win him back into the King's favour?' his father asked. 'A big jump that, is it no'? Agile jumper as he may be!'

'Perhaps, sir. But Patrick does not seek to take it all in one jump, I think. He has kept all in his own hands, thus far – so that, if James is interested, it will be necessary for Patrick himself to come here to Court to discuss it. And once back in the King's presence, Patrick does not fear but that he will stay there. He swayed James before, readily enough; he does not fear that he cannot do so again.'

My lord could only wag his bull-like head. 'The devil!' he muttered. 'Cunning as the Devil himself! I' faith – he almost makes me misdoubt my own wife's chastity!'

'Marie,' David said carefully. 'We have heard the advantages of this project. But I think that there are disadvantages, are there not?'

She looked at him for a moment steadily, before she answered, level-voiced. 'Catherine of Bourbon is ugly, crooked and no longer young,' she said. 'Moreover, few I think, would name her chaste.'

'Oh, no!' That was a young voice, in involuntary urgent protest, as Mary Gray broke the hush. 'Not that!'

The Mistress of Gray looked down at the goblet of wine in her hand, and said nothing.

David considered her thoughtfully, rubbing his chin.

My lord produced something between snort and chuckle. 'Houts!' he said. 'No insuperable barrier to a royal match, yon! Forby, she'd no' be getting aught so different hersel' – save maybe in years! Jamie's no' that much o' a catch!'

'He is the King of Scots, Granlord,' the girl demurred in quiet reproach.

'Aye, God help him!'

'You will not acquaint His Grace of this? Of the Princess's . . . quality?' David asked, in a moment or two.

The Lady Marie's answer was to put her hand into a brocaded satchel-purse that hung from the girdle of her travelling-gown. From it she produced a miniature portrait, painted on ivory, within a delicately gemmed frame. She handed it to

68

David. It showed a young woman, oval-faced and pale, richly dressed and bejewelled, almost dwarfed within a high upstanding ruffed and pearled collar.

'She looks none so ill,' he said, passing it to his father.

Faintly Marie smiled. 'A Court painter may flatter,' she observed. 'And that was painted ten years ago, at the least.'

My lord was admiring the diamonds round the frame. 'Potent persuasion this!' he mentioned. 'And the dowry? What of that?'

She shook her head. 'Of that I have no knowledge. It would be necessary for Patrick himself to come to Scotland to discuss it.'

'Oh, aye. I'ph'mmm. No doubt. So he baits his trap, the miscreant!' Lord Gray took a heavy limping pace or two about his chamber. 'Cunning, artful, I grant you. If this match should take place . . . ! France! It would be a great matter for the realm. For Scotland. For us all. Aye – and for Patrick Gray!' He turned on Marie. 'How comes it that he is so close with Henry of Navarre?'

'Patrick has a nose for . . . for keys! Keys that will open doors. And a powerful colleague in Elizabeth Tudor. The Protestant lioness and the Protestant lion!'

'Elizabeth!' David exclaimed. 'The Queen? You mean . . . you mean that he deals with Elizabeth still? After all that has happened? Elizabeth, who betrayed him?'

'He writes to her, or to Burleigh, or to Walsingham, each week.'

'But . . . but this is scarce to be believed! He hates Elizabeth. She played with him, led him on, and then worked his downfall. With Maitland and James. Elizabeth, that monument of perfidy – his chiefest enemy!'

The young woman shook her head. 'That is not how Patrick views it, Davy. For him, it is all the game of statecraft. He does not cherish friends or enemies. He does not measure injuries done to him . . . nor that he does to others. He uses the cards that come to his hands – *uses*, you understand?' She sighed a long quivering sigh. 'Would it were not so! God – would he were as other men! But he is not. He is . . . Patrick Gray. And I am his wife. I married him knowing him. Elizabeth betrayed him, yes – but had he not betrayed her beforehand? They are of one kidney. But she is Queen of England, and therefore an important card in his game indeed, to be played if he can . . .'

'But the Armada of Spain! That was to destroy her? That he built his hopes on . . . ?'

'Did he, do you think? Another card in the same game, Davy.'

'A card that went sore agley, 'fore God!' my lord snorted. 'I'm hoping this new card o' his, this Navarre match, isna like to go the same way, eh?'

Marie looked at him coolly, directly. 'You hope . . . ? You approve of the venture then, my lord? Of the attempt that I am here for?'

'Me? I didna say that, did I, woman? *Me* approve? Na, na – I said no such thing,' the older man blustered. 'An unlikely day it'll be when I approve o' any plot o' Patrick's! But . . . if Elizabeth o' England is behind this match, it's no' to be taken lightly. And Navarre *is* heir to France, right enough. The French king is young. But if he is ailing . . . ' He coughed. 'And I am a good Protestant, forby!'

Marie smiled slightly.

'Aye, then.' My lord seemed to make up his mind. 'I'll see that you get to my lord of Orkney your father's house in Edinburgh. I'll no' take you, mind – for thanks to Patrick my credit's no' high at Court. But I'll see that you win there. Davy here will take you, belike. Till then, you can bide here.'

She inclined her golden head. 'Thank you, my lord. This is generous indeed. More generous by far than I looked for. Or Patrick either!' She met his shrewd little pig's eye. 'But I shall not burden you with my awkward presence for long, I assure you – for the sooner that I can reach the Court, the better. For this . . . this estimable royal project.'

'Aye. So be it.'

She turned to David, and found him eyeing her strangely, intently, almost sorrowfully, with little of gladness or elation in evidence over this happy change in her immediate fortunes. At his look she bit her lip, and mute appeal shot with some sort of pain clouded her clear grey eyes. She said nothing – nor did he.

It was Mary who spoke. 'May I see the picture, Granlord? she asked, and slipped over to take the miniature portrait from

70

her grandfather. She looked at it closely, and then from it to the Lady Marie.

'No!' she declared briefly, softly, but with a strange finality.

'I am sorry,' Marie Stewart said – and sounded as though she meant it.

Chapter Four

THE new heir to Gray was born in the icy mid-January of 1589 – not at Castle Huntly but in the somewhat raffish and ram-shackle establishment of the Lord Robert Stewart, Earl and Bishop of Orkney, in the old eastern wing of the Palace of Holyroodhouse which King James allowed his carefree but never debt-free, permanently impecunious, illegitimate uncle. No festivities were held, no bonfires lit on the hill-tops flanking the wide Gray lands in the Carse of Gowrie, as was normal on such auspicious occasions. The Lord Gray had reverted to his former attitude towards his daughter-in-law, and would have none of her.

Undoubtedly my lord was disappointed. The worthy, hope-ful and ingenious scheme for the Navarre match had come to nothing. Admittedly it was still being mooted in certain quar-ters and Queen Elizabeth had declared herself in favour. But James himself had become quite definitely opposed. Which was very strange, for at first it had been quite otherwise. When the Mistress of Gray had arrived at Holyroodhouse in October, it had not taken long for the entire Court to buzz with the exciting news that King Jamie was veering away from the pro-posed Danish match and was much intrigued with this new notion of marrying the sister of the man who was heir pre-sumptive to France and might very well shortly be king thereof. James indeed began drawing elaborate heraldic doodlings and designs incorporating the Lilies of France into the Royal Arms of Scotland, and calculating the shining possibilities of himself, or at worst his heir, succeeding eventually to the throne of France as well as that of England – since Henry of

71

Navarre, although married for seventeen years, had no legitimate children. James was even said to have made up a lengthy and romantic poem to dispatch to the lady.

Then, all of a sudden and without warning, all was changed. James lost interest. Word spread through the Court that the King had discovered that Princess Catherine was in fact old, ugly, crooked and of doubtful morals. Whence and how this intelligence had reached him was not known, although it was noted that the Duke of Lennox, who, being half-French himself, had at first been strongly in favour of the match, quite abruptly became as strongly against it, James following suit. Indeed so offended was the King that he went further, and promptly reverted to negotiations with Denmark once more – where, as it happened, King Frederick, having given up Scotland, had pledged his elder daughter the Princess Royal to the Duke of Brunswick in the interim; however, he still had his younger daughter, the fourteen-year-old Princess Anne available. She was prettier than her sister, too, he pointed out – though naturally the dowry would be smaller in consequence.

So Lord Gray's hopes of credit and profit through being intimately connected with a resounding Franco-Scottish union faded almost entirely.

The Master of Gray perforce remained an exile. But it was a very near thing. Letters of recall from the King and the Chancellor were in fact bringing him home to Scotland, when suddenly they were countermanded without explanation. Had bad weather not kept his ship storm-bound at Dieppe, he might indeed have beaten the ban. As it was, he did not allow receipt of the royal edict, which reached him actually on shipboard, wholly to demolish his plans, for by February information reached Scotland that the Master was in London, and apparently cutting high capers at the Court of Saint James.

The ageing Lord Burleigh, Lord High Treasurer of England, wrote a letter to Sir John Maitland, Lord High Chancellor of Scotland, to the effect that that realm would much benefit by the speedy return of the talented Master of Gray, and suggesting that the said excellent Chancellor should advise his royal prince to that effect.

The royal prince maintained, as so frequently was his habit, a masterly inactivity.

There was further correspondence – a deal of it now, a flood. Sir Frances Walsingham, Principal Secretary of State to Elizabeth, and the most sinister figure in Europe, wrote to Mr. William Ashby, English Resident at the Scots Court, desiring him to urge King James to countenance and receive back to favour the notable Master of Gray, whose love for His Majesty was as well known as his services were assuredly valuable. Archibald Douglas, lifelong enemy of Patrick's, and Scots Resident at the Court of Saint James, informed Chancellor Maitland by letter that he truly believed the Master to be far changed in his fashions and moreover filled with goodwill towards the said Chancellor to whom he might be of considerable use if he was permitted to return home. Sir Christopher Hatton, Lord Chancellor of England, wrote to the Vice-Chancellor of Scotland, Sir Robert Melville – he refused to have anything to do with Maitland – indicating that Patrick, Master of Gray had an excellent head for figures and that he had put certain financial proposals before himself which, if he was allowed to bring them to fruition might well greatly advantage King James and his realm. Lord Howard of Effingham, Lord High Admiral of England, wrote to the Earl of Bothwell, Lord High Admiral of Scotland thanking him for his belated congratulations on the defeat of the Armada, and in a postscript recommending to him the useful Master of Gray with whom he was sure he would have much in common.

Chancellor Maitland's prim lawyer's mouth was almost permanently down-turned these spring days of 1589, and his royal master nibbled urgently at his ragged nails, wagged his great head, and sought the patience of the Almighty God whose earthly vassal and vice-regent he was. Doing nothing can tax even the most expert, at times.

At the end of April, Queen Elizabeth herself had occasion to set her royal hand to paper. Walsingham's minions had been successful in intercepting letters from the Earls of Huntly and Erroll and other Catholic lords to the King of Spain and the Duke of Parma, lamenting on the defeat of the Armada and promising to share in another attempt against England, provided 6,000 Spanish troops were landed in

73

Scotland. Elizabeth's reaction was vigorous, clear and by no means restricted to diplomatic terminology. Was ever a realm plagued by such neighbours, she demanded? Was this to be borne? Good Lord, she wrote, her quill spluttering ink, methinks I do dream! No king a week could bear this! Was James a king indeed? Her last paragraph, however, ended on an abruptly different note. Obviously her well-beloved but youthful cousin of Scotland could do with more sage counsel and seasoned advice about his government and realm, and to such end she could not do better than recommend the return of Patrick, Master of Gray, of whose good intentions, probity, and agility of mind she was now heartily assured. With this admonition she committed James to God's especial care and guidance.

That young man, sorely tried, took himself away for a prolonged bout of hunting in Ettrick Forest.

Lastly the Master of Gray himself wrote to his monarch, privily, and enclosed the letter in one to his wife. Significantly, it was addressed from no farther away than Berwick-upon-Tweed. After assurances of his undying devotion and loyal service, he mentioned that while in London, having had some conference with Queen Elizabeth and sundry of her ministers, he had been deeply shocked to learn that His Grace's pension from that princess, negotiated by himself a year or two before, was much in arrears and moreover sadly inadequate to the situation. He had certain proposals for the rectifying of this deplorable state of affairs, consonant with the dignity of all concerned, and believed that he had convinced Her Highness and her Lord Treasurer in the matter. It but remained to lay his proposals before His Grace. Moreover, in a purely personal matter he craved the royal indulgence. His son and firstborn, whom as yet he had not had the felicity to behold, was now four months old and notably in need of christening. It was suitable that the boy should be received into Christ's true and Reformed Kirk of Scotland, for the eternal salvation of his soul, a ceremony at which he, the unworthy father, had perhaps understandable ambitions to attend. If His Grace would exercise his royal clemency so far as to permit the devoted petitioner to be present at such a humble ceremony, this would surely provide a suitable occasion to discuss the afore-

74

mentioned financial matter, and also the additional suggestion that he had made to the Queen of England that Her Highness might decently invest her heir and successor with an English dukedom as token and earnest of responsibilities to come. Etcetera.

No mention was made of the Princess Catherine of Bourbon.

James, by the grace of God, King of Scots, Duke of Rothesay, Lord of the Isles, and Defender of Christ's Reformed Kirk, saw the light belatedly – in the warm glowing reflection of English gold pieces as well as in the saving of an innocent young Catholic brand from the burning. He capitulated, inditing a note in his own intricate hand, permitting his right worthy and traist friend and councillor Patrick, Master of Gray to re-enter his realm of Scotland forthwith. He personally appended the royal seal – omitting to inform the Lord Chancellor – and despatched it by close messenger to Berwick-upon-Tweed.

It was exactly two years, almost to the day, since the royal sentence of beheading for high treason had been reluctantly commuted to banishment for life.

The great banqueting-hall at Holyroodhouse presented a scene of which Mary Gray, at least, had never seen the like. In the hall at Castle Huntly she had witnessed many an exciting and colourful occasion, but never on such a scale and with the atmosphere of this one. It seemed to her, from her point of vantage in one of the raised window-embrasures which she shared with her father and mother and a life-size piece of statuary, that there must be hundreds of people present – not one hundred or two, but many. Every hue of the rainbow shone and revolved and eddied before her, jewellery flashed and glittered in the blaze of a thousand candles. The noise was deafening, everybody having to shout to make themselves heard, so that the music of the royal fiddlers and lutists in the ante-room was almost completely drowned. The smells caught the throat – of perfumes and perspiration, the fumes of liquor and the smoke of candles. The cream of Scotland was here tonight – the Protestant cream, that is – by royal command and in its most splendid apparel. Chancellor Maitland, in sombre black, who must pay for it all out of a chronically impoverished Treasury, frowned sourly on one and all from beside the high double-doors at the top end of the vast chamber. Few heeded him, however, for his frown was part of the man.

The small Gray party was very quiet and dully-clad compared with the rest of the gay and confident throng, in their best clothes as they were although none would call dull the flushed and ripe comeliness of Mariota Davidson, a mother for the fourth time, all tremulous wide-eyed unease; and Mary's lip-parted, utterly unselfconscious excitement, wedded to her quite startling elfin attractiveness, drew innumerable glances, admiring, intrigued, speculative and frankly lecherous. As for David, his frown almost matched that of the Chancellor as he partly hid himself behind the statue that had been one of Mary the Queen's importations from her beloved France – for too many of the faces that he saw here tonight he knew, and had no wish to be recognised in turn. All this had been his life once, all unwillingly – and he had hoped, indeed sworn, never to tread the shifting-sands of it again. They were in Edinburgh, at the Lady Marie's earnest request, for the christening on the morrow; and here tonight only to please the urgent Mary, who had engineered a royal summons for them through Ludovick, Duke of Lennox.

Abruptly the din of voices was shattered as, from the top of the hall, a couple of trumpeters in the royal livery blew a fanfare, high-pitched, resounding, challenging. Chancellor Maitland stepped aside, and footmen threw open the great double doors. From beyond strode in the Lord Lyon King of Arms, baton in hand, with two of his heralds, brilliantly bedecked in their red-and-gold tabards and plumed bonnets. This, it appeared, was to be a state occasion.

Behind paced, preternaturally solemn and looking extraordinarily youthful, the Duke of Lennox, newly appointed Lord High Chamberlain, a position once borne by his father, not quite sure whether to wield, carry or trail his staff of office. Dressed in plum-coloured velvet, padded and slashed, he took very long strides and appeared to be counting them out to himself. At evidently a given number of paces, he halted, turned, cleared his throat in some embarrassment, and then thumped his staff loudly on the floor.

76

Mary Gray gurgled her amusement.

In the succeeding hush they all heard the King sniffing, before they saw him. He appeared beyond the open doorway presently, shambling in a hurried knock-kneed gait, almost a trot, peering downwards and sideways as he came, fumbling at the stiffening of his exaggeratedly padded trunks. He was over-dressed almost grotesquely, in royal purple doublet barred with orange, stuffed and distended about the chest and shoulders inordinately, pearl-buttoned and hung with chains and orders. His lolling head seemed to be supported, like a joint on a platter, by an enormous ruff, soiled already with dribbled spittle, whilst round and about all this he wore a short but necessarily wide cloak, embroidered with the royal monogram and insignia, edged with fur, and boasting a high upstanding collar encrusted with silver filigree. To top all, a fantastically high-crowned hat, fully a score of inches in height, ringed with golden chain-work and festooned with ostrich feathers, sat above his wispy hair. The effect of it all, above the thin and knobbly legs, was ludicrously like an over-blown and distinctly unsteady spider. It could now be seen that the reason for the regal preoccupation was the extraction of a handkerchief from a trunks pocket, less than clean.

A woman giggled, and somewhere from the back of the throng came a choked-off guffaw. Then, as the monarch came shuffling over the threshold, Lennox bowed deeply, if jerkily, and thereupon the entire concourse swept low in profound obeisance, the men bending from the waist, the women curtsying, remaining so until James spoke.

'Aye, aye,' he said thickly. 'I . . . we, we greet you warmly. Aye, warmly. All of you. On this, this right au – auspicious occasion.' His protruding tongue had difficulty with the phrase. 'You may stand upright. Och, aye – up wi' you.'

With a very audible exhalation of breath the noble company relaxed again, amidst an only moderately subdued murmur of comment and exclamation, not all of it as respectful as the occasion might have warranted.

'I do not like his hat,' Mary mentioned judicially. 'It is too high, by far.'

'Hush, you!' her father told her, glancing around uneasily.

'Yes. Is not Vicky ridiculous with all that padding?'

77

'Ssshhh!'

Servitors brought in a gilded Chair of State, on which the monarch sat himself down. The Chancellor moved up on one side of it, Lennox to the other, while the Lord Lyon stood behind. The music resumed, and so did the noise and chatter, while certain notables were brought forward by the heralds, and presented by either Lennox or the Chancellor. James, fidgeting, extended a perfunctory nail-bitten hand, eyed them all sideways, and muttered incoherences. He kept glancing from Lennox to the far end of the room, it was noted, impatiently.

Presently, while still there was a queue of candidates for presentation, James leaned over and plucked at his cousin's sleeve, worrying it like a terrier with a rat. 'Enough, Vicky – enough o' this,' he whispered, but loud enough for all around to hear. 'On wi' our business, man.'

Lennox nodded, waved away the queueing lords, and thumped loudly on the floor again with his staff. The musicians in the ante-room were silenced.

'My lords,' he said. Clearing his throat again, and as an afterthought, 'And ladies. His Grace has asked . . . has commanded your presence here tonight for a purpose. An especial purpose. A notable undertaking. His Grace is concerned at idle talk that has been, er, talked. About his royal marriage.' Ludovick ran a finger round inside his ruff. 'Unsuitable talk and inconvenient . . . '

'Aye – blethers, just. Blethers,' the King interrupted, rolling his head.

'That is so, Your Highness. To still such talk . . . ' Lennox swallowed. ' . . . such blethers, His Grace has been at pains to, to prove otherwise. Quite otherwise. In his, ummm, royal wisdom he has decided to seek the hand . . . '

Sir John Maitland, pulling at his wispy beard, had stooped to the King's ear. James, nodding vigorously, reached over to tug at Lennox's sleeve again. 'Heir,' he said. 'Our royal heir, man.'

'*Mais oui*—the heir. *Pardonnez-moi,*' the Duke observed, little harassed. 'His Grace, recognising the need for an heir, not only to this throne and realm, but that of England also, has decided that this matter should be arranged. Arranged and settled forthwith. Accordingly, he has chosen and elected to seek the hand of that Protestant princess Anne, daughter to the illustrious King Frederick of Denmark in, in . . . '

'In royal and holy matrimony,' James finished for him enthusiastically, producing a lip-licking leer that went but curiously with the phrase. 'I've wrote a rhyme . . . we have turned to the Muse in this pass, and have indited a poem. Aye, indited a poem, I say . . .' He began to search within his doublet, muttering.

There was an uncomfortable pause.

'His Grace has written this poem. To the Princess,' Lennox went on, far from confidently, as the search produced much but no papers. 'A, h'mm, noble poem, setting forth in verse, good verse, excellent verse, his royal offer for her hand. To convey this to the lady, it is decided . . . '

'Och, mair'n that, Vicky – mair'n that! I've expounded on her beauty – for she's right bonny, the lassie. And on her virtue and chastity – for she's but fourteen years, and no' like to be much otherwise!' The royal whinny of laughter tee-heed high. 'No' like . . . no' like . . . ' James gulped, and went on hurriedly.'As to her wit – och well, I'll teach her that mysel'.' He looked down, as at last he managed to extract some crumpled papers from his doublet, breathless now from the contortions inevitable in a hunt through his over-padded and stuffed casing. 'Here it's. Aye – this is it. I'll read it to you. To you all. For it's good, mind – as good as any I've done. Guidsakes – there's no' that many crowned monarchs could write the like! No – and fewer, I'll be bound, who could put it down in the Latin and the Greek as well, forby! You see, I dinna ken if the lassie kens our Scots tongue. Belike they dinna, in yon Denmark. So I've wrote it out in all three. Aye – well, I'll read it to you. I've named it *The Fond and Earnest Suite and Smoking Smart of James the King*. Aye. I'll read the Scots first . . .' Quite carried away, James got to his unsteady feet, smoothing out the crushed papers.

The great company did not actually groan, of course, but the restraining of such in a hundred throats, and the stirring of innumerable feet, sounded like the moaning and rustling of a lost wind in a forest.

Lennox at one side and Maitland at the other, moved in on the King, whispering.

'The Marischal, Sire!'

'The Ambassador . . . !'

'Eh . . . ? Ooh, aye. Uh-huh. I forgot. Aye.' Somewhat crestfallen, the sovereign looked down regretfully at his epic, tipped his tall hat forward over his brow to scratch at the back of his bulging head, sighed audibly, and sat down again. 'Hae them in, then,' he said.

The Duke resumed. 'In order that His Grace's intentions and royal suit be worthily and courtly presented before the Princess and His Grace of Denmark, it is the King's pleasure that an embassage carrying suitable gifts shall . . .'

'And the poem, man – the poem!'

'And the poem, of course, Sire. An embassage shall depart for Denmark forthwith. Tomorrow indeed, if wind and tide serve. This embassage shall consist of my lord the Earl Marischal and a noble retinue, with Master, er, Herr . . . with the Danish envoy. They now wait without. His Grace will now receive them, read to them his poem, entrust them with its delivery and the royal gifts, and wish them God-speed.' That all came out in something of a spate, as though a lesson learned and thankfully got over. Lennox thumped the floor loudly. 'In the name of King James – admit the King's guests.'

James himself, craning round his Chair of State, signed to the trumpeters to render a flourish.

At the far end of the great hall, double doors were thrown open. To the ringing echoes of the fanfare the colourful concourse seethed and stirred, as some pressed backwards to open a lane, an avenue, down the centre, and others pressed forward the better to see.

After a moment or two of delay, in through the doorway walked a single man, unhurriedly.

'Waesucks!' came a croak from the Chair of State. 'Christ God be good!'

Something between a shiver and a shudder ran through the entire chamber, electric, galvanic. Chancellor Maitland reached forward, gropingly, to steady himself against his master's chair. Lennox looked the merest boy, his heavy lower jaw dropped.

Silence descended, complete but throbbing.

80

In that silence the only sounds were the steady, deliberate, yet almost leisurely click-click of high-heeled shoes, punctuated at regular intervals by the tap of a stick.

All eyes were riveted on the walker – almost to be described as a stroller. As well they might be. Of medium height, slender but graceful, the man was dazzlingly handsome, with a radiance of good looks that could only be called beauty – redeemed, however, by a basic firmness of line from anything of femininity. Cascading wavy black hair, worn long, framed a noble brow above brilliant flashing eyes. The delicately-flared nostrils of a finely-chiselled nose matched the wicked curving of a proud scimitar of moustache, to balance a warmly, almost sweetly smiling mouth. A tiny pointed beard enhanced the firm but never aggressive chin.

If the tension in that great room was such that all seemed to hold their breath, the same could not be said of the spectacular newcomer, by any manner of means. Unselfconscious, urbane, confident yet with a sort of almost gently mocking deference toward the Chair of State, he moved without haste between the lines of silent watchers, dressed dazzlingly yet simply, all in white satin save for the black velvet lining to the miniature cape slung negligently from one shoulder, the black jewelled garter below one knee, the black dagger-belt, and the black pearls at each neat ear. His spun silk white hose, half as long again as any other in that place, lovingly moulded an excellently-turned and graceful leg almost all the way up the thigh, to disappear into the briefest trunks ever seen in Scotland, verging on indecency back and front; across shoulders and chest hung the delicate tracery of the chain and grand cross of some foreign order of knighthood.

Almost as much as the man himself, and his elegance, it was the staff that drew all fascinated eyes – and the manner of its use. Tall, shoulder-height indeed, slender as its owner, white as ivory save for its deep black ferrule and bunch of black ribbons at its top, it was as different from the Chamberlain's thick rod-like stick of office as it was from the Lord Lyon's short baton. Never had any of his watchers seen such a thing. Nor such casual but extraordinarily effective flourish as the way in which its owner walked with it, swinging its ribboned head forward in an eye-catching wide figure-of-eight movement at every second pace, so that its ferrule made one loud and authoritative tap to each of the two lighter tap-taps of the notably tall-heeled satin-covered shoes. It was impossible not to compare it with Lennox's awkward handling of his own stick.

Some few of the company, who had been close enough to notice the little Gray party in their alcove, turned now to gaze from the newcomer to Mary Gray, eyes wide. To say that Mary's own dark eyes were wide and shining would be a crass understatement. She stood on tip-toes, lips parted, bosom frankly heaving, one hand convulsively clutching David's arm. That man stood as though graven in stone.

It was a long apartment, with fully a hundred feet of floor to cover between the lower doors and the position of the throne-like chair. King James and his immediate supporters therefore had ample time to adjust themselves, to cope with the situation, to give orders to heralds and servitors, even to summon the Captain of the Guard standing nearby. That they did none of these things was strange, a token of the depth of their surprise perhaps, or an involuntary tribute to the calm assurance of the new arrival. James blinked owlishly, jaw going slack, lips twitching. He half rose to his feet, gripping the arms of his chair and crushing the papers of his poem, and so waited, almost crouching. Maitland tugged at his beard, glanced right and left uncertainly, and then, stooping, began to whisper agitatedly in the royal ear – and was completely ignored. Lennox merely stared – although something like the beginnings of a grin appeared at the corners of his wide mouth.

There was some slight commotion back at the bottom end of the room, where a group of gesticulating individuals, one actually bearing a sort of banner, had appeared at the still-open doorway – but no attention was paid to them. All eyes were fixed on the progress of the man in white. He reached a point two or three yards from the Chair of State, paused, and smiling brilliantly, placed his staff, with an elaborate brandish, slant-wise against his delectable person, and extending one foot behind him, sank low in the most complicated genuflexion King James had ever received. His smile advanced to what was almost silent laughter as he held this extraordinary stance, head up, regular white teeth gleaming, eyes dancing. He did not speak before the monarch.

James found words, if incoherent, ill-formed ones, as he sank, or rather shrank, back into his chair. 'Guidsakes, Patrick man . . . you shouldna . . . this isna right. It's no' correct. Where . . . how did you come here, this way? I didna . . . we gave you no summons, man – no royal summons. It wasna you we were looking for . . . '

'Alas, Sire – do I disappoint, then? Heigho – and me foolishly hoping, believing, that after all these weary months of absence from the sun of your royal presence, I might win the bliss of a regal smile, the kind accolade of your kingly generosity!' The Master of Gray's voice was in tune with the rest of him, attractive, warm, lightsome, musically modulated – and clear for all the room to hear as he straightened up. 'Ah, me – is it not to be so? Alack-a-day – must I return banished, Your Grace, to outer darkness? Where I have dwelt so long? When you so raised my poor hopes . . . ?'

'I didna. I didna do that, man. Na, na. You mistake me. You werena to come here. No' to our Court and presence. And I . . . we are employed, see you. Busy. Aye, transacting business. Important business. We were looking to see the Marischal. And yon manikin frae Denmark . . . '

'The Marischal, Sire? Why, I saw my Lord Marischal back there on the stairs. As I came up. Throng with business, he looked, too, i' faith! Laden with packages and merchandise, like any packman! Never fear, Sire – he is about your palace somewhere . . . '

'Yon were my royal gifts to Denmark,' James protested, spluttering. 'I'll thank you, Master o' Gray, no' to name my favours and offerings to the Lady Anne of Denmark as merchandise!'

Patrick Gray's laughter held a gay and carefree note. 'Is that what it was, Sire? Here's felicity, then – here's joy! Is it permitted for a most humble and unworthy subject to congratulate his sovereign on his happy choice?'

'Aye, it is, Patrick – it is,' the King nodded. He glanced up, risking a brief direct look. 'But it was no' *your* advising, mind! You were for a mare frae another stable, eh? Nor ower nice anent her parts and aspect, I'm told. In especial her teeth, man – her teeth!' James produced something between a snort and a snigger.

The other inclined his dark head. 'I but considered Your Highness's interests in the matter of a large dowry. And a notable alliance with the power of France. And the lady is . . . kind. But, Sire, 't'was only a notion. Your own choice must be the joyful choice of us all. And the Princess Royal of Denmark no doubt is a notable-enough match. Even for the King of Scots.'

'Aye.' James coughed. 'But . . . it's no' just the Princess Royal. No' now. It's her sister. The Princess Anne. Anne, it is.'

'Anne!' Something like consternation showed on the Master of Gray's expressive features. 'Only the *second* daughter! For you – king of a greater realm than Denmark. To be King of England, also . . . !'

'Och, well – it wasna to be helped, see you. He'd given the other lassie to Brunswick. Elizabeth, they call her . . . '

'Brunswick! A mere German dukedom! Dear God – on whose advising was this done, Sire? For but a second daughter! The dowry? What of the dowry?'

The King licked slack lips. 'The Marischal is to see to that, Patrick . . . '

The Chancellor came to the rescue of his master. 'Highness,' he broke in. 'Suffer not this insolence! It is intolerable. This man is a convicted felon, an arch-traitor, condemned for highest treason. Sentenced to the axe for the death of your royal mother. Of Your Grace's undue mercy rather than wisdom he was spared – but banished your realm for life. Here, against your commands and those of your Council, he has returned to Scotland. He has the effrontery to force himself into your royal presence. The dignity of your crown and throne, Sire, requires not only that he shall not be heard, but that he be warded securely forthwith. Committed to the castle, to await his further trial. Permit that I summon the Captain of the Guard to his duty, Highness.'

'Aye. Oh, aye, Sir John. Nae doubt you're right, man – nae doubt. But bide a wee – just bide a wee. Master Patrick's done ill to break in this way, to intrude – aye, to intrude. But it's maybe no' just necessary to ward him . . . '

'Sir John was ever a great one for the warding, Majesty,

was he not?' the younger man observed pleasantly. 'Like the laws of the Medes and Persians, he changeth not. Even when circumstances are notably changed. God keep you, my Lord Chancellor. I hope that I see you as well as you merit?'

'Highness – this is not to be borne!' Maitland exclaimed. 'The verdict of Your Grace and Council cannot be set aside . . .'

'Cannot, Sir John? Cannot, eh? Cannot is no' a word to be used to anointed monarchs, man. What we have said, we can unsay. What we decreed, we can un-decree. No' that I'm saying that we'll do that, mind. We shall hae to consider . . .' James darted glances between the two men. 'Consider well . . .'

'Exactly, Your Grace,' Patrick agreed. 'And there is so much to consider, is there not?' He lowered his voice confidentially. 'The matter of your royal pension, for instance. My negotiations with Her Grace of England.'

'Aye, Patrick – what o' it?' The King sat forward, eager now. 'How does she say, the woman? It hasna been paid – no' a plack o' it. No' since you left, man . . .'

'Sire,' the Chancellor interrupted heavily, harshly. 'It is inconceivable that this question, the matter of Your Grace's royal dealings with the Queen of England, should be traded and chaffered over by an outlawed miscreant! Her Grace would never countenance such a thing. This man but seeks insolently to cozen Your Highness . . .'

'You forget, Chancellor, that it was Master Patrick who arranged my pension with Elizabeth in the first place. Aye, maybe you forget it – but I dinna.' The King pointed a nail-bitten finger at the Master of Gray. 'Would you seek to cozen me, man? Would you?'

'Your Grace must be the judge of that,' Patrick declared simply. 'I would have brought the tokens and proofs of my, er, trade and chaffering with me into this your chamber, Sire – save for its weight. Gold, you see, is heavy stuff!'

'Gold!' James cried. 'Gold, you said. You have it with you, man? You brought me gold?'

'Only a token payment, Sire. Not the entire pension. I convinced the lady, I believe, that three thousand gold pieces would be a more suitable and worthy pension for her heir than two. It is but the extra thousand that I brought with me, I fear.'

The King gulped and swallowed convulsively – but even so the saliva flowed copiously down his doublet. 'A thousand gold pieces! Extra! God's splendour – the pension is increased, you say? You have a thousand gold pieces for me, Patrick man? Here? Is it the truth?'

'Outside. In your own palace, Sire. In my Lord of Orkney's lodgings. The rest is promised within the month.'

James was so moved that he got to his feet and reached out to grip the Master of Gray's white satin arm, his poem falling unnoticed to the floor.

Sir John Maitland's sallow features were wiped clean of all expression. He actually moved back a little way from the Chair of State. He knew when, for the moment, he was beaten.

Without seeming to fail in support of the royal grasp, Patrick stooped low to retrieve the fallen papers. To do so he had to use the long staff as prop, so that the ribboned top of the thing was just under the King's nose. James blinked at it.

'You've . . . you've done well, Patrick,' he said thickly. 'I . . . we shall accept the gold from our sister, gladly. Aye, gladly. It's no before its time, mind. But you've done well. And . . . and yon's a bonny bit stick, you have. I've never seen the like.'

'The latest folly at Versailles, Sire. His Grace of France uses one such. You admire it? Then it is yours. Take it.'

'Eh . . . ? Me?' Flushing with pleasure, the King reached for the staff. 'Thank you, thank you. Man, it's a bonny stick. But . . . ' He giggled. ' . . . I'll no' ken what to do wi' it, Patrick.'

'I will show you, Sire. Privily. It is very simple. When you can spare the time. There are other matters for your royal ear, also, when you can spare the time. This dukedom . . . '

'Ooh, aye – I'll spare the time. I've plenty time.'

'Perhaps then, Sire, you will graciously spare a little of it tomorrow? To attend the christening of my son?'

'M'mmm. Oh, well – maybe . . . '

'I was hoping, Highness, that you would consent to be godfather to the boy.' That came out a little more hurriedly than was usual in the utterances of the Master of Gray. 'Since he is, in blood, second-cousin to Your Grace. And in order that his reception into the true Kirk and Protestant faith may be . . . unquestioned. Alas, my own faithful adherence has been so oft and shamefully doubted by my ill-wishers! And you are God's chosen and dedicated Defender of the Faith, are you not?'

'Aye, I am.' James was very proud of that title.

'For the saving of the innocent mite's immortal soul . . . '

'I'ph'mmm. Ooh, aye. Well . . . maybe. Aye maybe, Patrick. We'll see.' The King was twisting and poking the staff this way and that.

'Your Grace – I am profoundly, everlastingly grateful!' Patrick bowed low, to kiss the royal fingers. And, straightening up, 'You dropped these papers I think, Sire.'

'Oh, aye. My poem. M'mmm. For the Princess Anne. I wrote a poem. For the Marischal to take wi' him to Denmark. Aye . . . my Lord Marischal. He's down there yonder waiting yet, the poor man. And the wee envoy frae Denmark. Vicky – my Lord Chamberlain – summon the Marischal again, man.'

The Duke beat his tattoo on the floor once more, and gestured to the heralds, who in turn moved down to usher in the impatient and injured party at the door. The buzz of excited talk and comment from the company hardly sank at all, now – although some laughter sounded.

James sat himself in his chair again, but clung to his new staff, which he laid across his knobbly knees. Patrick strolled over to Lennox, smiling warmly, to grasp the youth's padded shoulder.

'Vicky!' he declared. 'It does my heart good to see you again – I vow it does! And Lord Chamberlain too, i' faith! On my soul, you are a grown man, now!'

The Duke looked at the other with a frank, almost doting admiration. 'I thank you, sir,' he jerked. 'It is good to see you also.'

James, close by, did not miss the admiration in his young cousin's tone – and glowered his jealousy. 'Quiet, you!' he comanded. 'The Marischal . . . '

Patrick and the Duke of Lennox exchanged conspiratorial grins, and stood side-by-side waiting, as the little procession, that was the object of and reason for the entire assembly, approached. Indeed, the Master of Gray appeared to have become an integral and prominent part of the proceedings and royal committee of reception.

George Keith, fifth Earl Marischal of Scotland, a tall soldierly figure in early middle age, dressed it would seem rather for the battlefield than the ballroom, came first, looking angry, with at his back his standard-bearer carrying the red, gold and white banner of his house and office. Next strutted a tiny dark bird-like man, the Danish Envoy, richly but sombrely dressed. Behind followed perhaps a dozen lordlings, lairds and pages, bearing a variety of boxes, chests, parcels and bundles.

Coming near to the Chair of State, the Marischal bowed stiffly, his splendid half-armour creaking and clanking at the joints. The little Dane bobbed something remarkably like a curtsy, fetching titters from the body of the company. The others variously made obeisance.

At a cough from James, Lennox suddenly recollected his duty. 'Your Grace's embassage for Denmark,' he announced.

'Aye,' the King said. 'We greet you well, my Lord Marischal. And you, Master . . . er . . . Bengtsen. Aye, all o' you.'

'Sire – we are here by your royal command,' Keith declared, his deep voice quivering with ill-suppressed ire. 'We have been waiting . . . we were misled! Yon man Gray . . . he misdirected Master Bengtsen, here. Aye, and sent these others off. Down to your stables, Sire. His wife kept me in talk . . . '

'Ooh, aye, my lord – just so,' James acknowledged, head rolling but eyes keen. 'Nae doubt. A . . . a mischance, aye. A misadventure. But nae harm done . . . '

'But, Sire – it was very ill done. 'Fore God, it was! I am not to be made a fool of . . . '

'Na, na, my lord – never think it. The Master o' Gray wouldna ken what was toward. New come to the palace. You'd no' intend any offence – eh, Patrick man?'

'Indeed no, Sire,' that man assured, pain at the thought and kindliest bonhomie struggling for mastery on his beautiful face, in his whole attractive bearing. 'If I have transgressed against my lord in some fashion, I am desolated. I tender profoundest apologies. But . . . I must confess to be much at a loss to know wherein I have offended?'

'Damnation – you made a mock of me, did you no'?' the

Marischal seethed. 'You named Skene, here, a pedlar! You sent Master Bengtsen to the other end o' the house, and these others to the stables! Deliberately, I swear, in order to . . .'

James, leaning forward, banged his new stick on the floor reaching it out almost to the speaker's feet, and then made a poking motion with it at the earl's middle. 'Enough, my lord – enough!' he protested, his voice going high in a squeak. 'You forget yoursel'! We'll hae no bickering in our royal presence. Aye.' He rose to his feet. 'Now – to the business. I . . . we now, my Lord Marischal, solemnly charge you to convey these our gifts and liberality to the Court of our cousin King Frederick o' Denmark, in earnest and in kindly pledge o' our love an affection. Aye – that's towards himsel', you ken. But more especial towards his daughter, the Princess Anne, wi' whom it is our intent and pleasure – *pleasure*, mind – to ally oursel' in holy and royal matrimony. In token o' which, my lord, you will gie to the said lady this poem and notable lyric which I have wrote wi' my ain hand. Aye.'

With a curious mixture of urgency and reluctance, James thrust the crushed papers into the earl's hand.

Blinking, Lennox cleared his throat. 'Sire – are you not to read . . . ?' he wondered.

'No.' That was a very abrupt negative for James Stewart. His glance flickered over to the Master of Gray, however, and away. Poets were scarce indeed about the Scottish Court – but Patrick Gray was a notable exception.

The Earl Marischal, the arranged programme thus further disrupted, eyed the papers doubtfully, glanced around him, and then, for want of better to do, bowed again.

'Aye, then,' the King said, scratching. 'I'ph'mmm. Just that.' He seemed, of a sudden, desirous of being finished with the entire proceedings. 'Er . . . God speed, my lord. And to you, Master Envoy. To all o' you. Aye. God speed and a safe journey. You will convey the Princess Anne to me here, wi' all suitable expedition. Expedition, you understand. Tell her . . . tell her . . . och, never heed. You hae our permission to retire, my lords.'

'But . . . the gifts? The presents, Sire . . . ?' the Marischal wondered.

'Och, I ken them a'. Fine.' James waved a dismissive hand. 'You may go.'

Schooling their features to loyal if scarcely humble acceptance, the bridal ambassadors proceeded to back out of the presence – a trying business, with a long way to retire and all the gear and baggage to manoeuvre. James let them go only a bare half-way before he rose and hurried over to the Master of Gray.

'Man, Patrick,' he said, turning his back on the assemblage at large. 'This o' the dukedom? Think you . . . think you she means it, this time? Elizabeth?'

The handsome man smiled. 'I think that Her Grace meant it . . . when I left her, Sire,' he said gently. 'It is for us to see that she continues to mean it!' He gave just the slightest emphasis to the word us.

'Aye. She . . . she seems to think highly o' you, Patrick. Why?' That last came out sharply.

There was nothing sharp about the reply. 'Your Grace – I have not the least apprehension. Not a notion!'

'U'mmm.'

It was some little time before Patrick Gray was able to detach himself from the King and from the many others who came clustering round him – the ladies in especial. It was noticeable, of course, that quite as many others did not cluster around him, or greet him in any way, other than by hostile stares, muttered asides and coldly-turned shoulders – amongst these some of the most powerful figures in the land, such as the earls of Mar, Glencairn, Atholl, Argyll and Angus, the Lords Sinclair, Lindsay, Drummond and Cathcart, the Master of Glamis who was Treasurer again, and numerous black-garbed ministers of Christ's Kirk. One man who dithered betwixt and between, in evident perplexity and doubt, was the splendidly-attired Bishop of St. Boswell's, Andrew Davidson. Towards him, Patrick cast an amused smile, but by no means sought the cleric's company.

Dancing in progress, the Master of Gray threaded his graceful way through the throng, greeting and being greeted, all amity and cordiality, but not permitting himself to be detained for more than moments at a time. As directly as he might, he made for the raised window alcove wherein he saw his wife standing, with three others.

As he came close, those in the near vicinity moved aside, as by mutual consent, to allow him space. Scores of eyes watched, intently, curiously.

The newcomer's eyes were intent also. After a swift, searching initial glance up at all four occupants of that embrasure, he gazed at one and one only – young Mary Gray. For once his brilliant smile faded – which was strange, for the girl was beaming, radiant.

None in that circle spoke. Never, surely, were a man and a woman so alike – and yet so different.

'Mary!' the man got out, throatily, almost hoarsely.

'Uncle Patrick!' the other cried, high, clear and vibrant, and launched herself down off that plinth and into the white satin arms.

David Gray stared straight ahead of him, grey eyes hooded, lips tight. The Lady Marie reached out a hand to press Mariota's arm.

They kissed each other, those two, frankly, eagerly, almost hungrily, as though unaware of all the watching eyes. They were in no hurry. There was no pose here, no seeking after effect, no calculation. It could have been this, rather than anything that had gone before, that had brought the Master of Gray across most of Europe, moving heaven, earth and hell itself to make it possible. Long they embraced, elegant, magnetic man and lovely eager girl – as though magnets indeed held them together.

Then Patrick as with an effort put her from him, at arm's length. But still he could not take his dark eyes off her face. For once he had no words to speak.

'Oh, it is good!' Mary said, for both of them. 'Good! Good!'

He nodded, slowly, as in profound agreement. Then, still holding one of her hands, he turned to face the others.

'I rejoice . . . to see you,' he said, the so eloquent voice unsteady, uncertain. 'All of you.'

His half-brother inclined his head.

'Oh, Patrick – Patrick!' Mariota exclaimed, breathlessly. 'Thank God! It has been long. So long.'

'Aye, long,' he agreed. 'Too long. You are very beautiful, Mariota my dear. I had almost forgot how beautiful. And how warm. Kind. And Davy . . . Davy is just Davy!'

'Aye,' that man said. He stepped down, to hold out his hand. 'Aye, Patrick.'

Still holding Mary to him, the Master slipped his free hand from his brother's grasp and up around his wide shoulders, there to rest. 'God help us – what a family we are!' he murmured.

The Lady Marie laughed, though a little tremulously. 'You see, Mariota,' she said. 'Those three will do naught for us. We shall have to climb down from here as best we may – for these men scarce know that we are here!'

The ladies were assisted to the floor, and more normal greetings exchanged. Mary was agog, however, for information, for explanations, for secrets.

'Uncle Patrick,' she demanded, just as soon as she had opportunity, dropping her voice conspiratorially. 'How did you do it? You were not expected until tomorrow. How wonderful was your entrance here! How did you affect it? Did you know? Know that it was all arranged for the Danish mission? Did you?'

He touched her hair lightly. 'What think you, my dear?'

'I think that you did! I think that you conceived it all – and deliberately upset all the King's plans. So that you should be the one to whom all looked – not the King. And not the Marischal. I was sorry for my Lord Marischal. And the little Danish man. That was scarcely kind of you, Uncle Patrick. But . . . I think that you are very brave.'

'M'mmm,' he said. 'You appear to think to some effect, young woman. What else do you think, eh?'

'I think that King Jamie, though he may seem to have been won, though he smile on you now, will not love you any the better for this night.' She shook her head seriously, dancing roguery gone. 'He planned all, that he might read his poem for the Danish princess. To us all. For he esteems himself to be a notable poet, does he not? But then, you came. You upset all – and he dared not read it. For he knows full well that you are a much better poet than is he. I think that he will not readily forgive you for that, Uncle Patrick.'

'Say you so?' The Master of Gray fingered his tiny pointed

92

beard. 'It may be so. Perhaps you are right. It may be that
I was a trifle too clever. Who knows? I can be, you know.'

'Yes,' she nodded gravely. 'As in the matter of the Navarre
lady.'

His finely arched eyebrows rose. 'Indeed!' he said. 'Mary,
my heart – what is this? What has come to you? Here is
unlikely thinking for, for a poppet such as you! What is this
you have become, while I was gone?'

'I am . . . Mary Gray,' she told him quietly, simply.

Into the second or two of silence that followed, both Mariota
and her husband spoke.

'Do not heed her, Patrick,' her mother declared, flushing.
'She is strange, these days. Foolish. Perhaps it is her age . . .'

'She is no longer your poppet, brother – or mine!' David
jerked. 'What she has become, I know not. But . . . she
concerns herself with things a deal too high for her – that I do
know. Nonetheless, Patrick – she is right in this, I fear. The
King will not love you the more for this. And you have made
an enemy of the Marischal – when you have enemies enough.'

'The Marischal, Davy, is off to Denmark tomorrow – and
by the time that he wins back to Scotland, it will matter not.'
The Master, speaking softly, guided his little company into a
corner where at least they might not be overheard. 'It was
necessary, see you, that I should be received back at Court –
and be seen by all to be so received. Before my enemies could
know that I was here, and could work against me with the
King. James did not summon me to Court – only permitted
my temporary return to Scotland – and that reluctantly
indeed. For the christening. Tomorrow. So I wore out relays
of cousin Logan of Restalrig's horses getting here tonight. I
am here before the courier who brought me the King's letter
could himself win back! Think you that Maitland and the rest
of the Protestant lords would have permitted that I be received? By tomorrow night, I swear, my body would have
been floating in the Nor' Loch, rather! And an outlaw, none
could be arraigned for my death. But now – I am received,
admitted, one of the elect once more! They dare not touch me
now – not openly. I have the King's ear, the King's protection . . . for so long as he needs something that I can give him.
One thousand golden guineas! And, he is to pray, more to

93

come! A deal of good money – but cheap at the price, I vow!'

'Cheap . . . ? The price? What price? To you? It is Elizabeth's money . . . '

The Master's laughter was silvery. 'Why, Davy – I thought that you at least would know our Elizabeth better! That gold was hard-earned – but not from Elizabeth of England. It came from less lofty sources – at no little cost to me. Methinks that she will not deny credit for it one day, nevertheless! Heigho – we cannot have chicken-soup without immersing the chicken! Cheap at the price I esteem it, yes – and moreover have we not achieved a royal godfather for young Andrew! Which also may have its value, one day. But . . . enough of this whispering in corners. It looks ill, furtive. And I am never furtive, am I – whatever else I am, God help me! I see my lord of Mar eyeing me closely. He grows ever more like a turkey-cock, does Johnnie Mar.' The Master of Gray was of a sudden all smiling gaiety again. 'See – it is a pavane that is being danced. I am partial to the pavane. In good company. Now – which of you ladies will do me the honour . . . ?'

It was at Mary Gray that he looked.

A moment or two later they moved out together to the stately measures of the dance, eyes in their hundreds watching, dazzling satin and humble lawn. Mary Gray danced like a queen.

Chapter Five

A bare three weeks after Patrick Gray's dramatic return to Scotland, the country was in a turmoil. The Catholics had risen again. All of Scotland, north of Aberdeen, was said to be in revolt, and the Earls of Huntly and Erroll declaring that they would march south forthwith and would be in the capital to rescue their King in a week or so. The departure of the Earl Marischal for Denmark was said to be the immediate cause of this; he was the Protestant's strong man in the north, and co-lieutenant with Huntly for the King's rule in those vast and unmanageable territories. There appeared to be more than just this in it, however, for the madcap Earl of Bothwell, with the assistance of the turbulent and widespread Border clan of the Homes, had assembled what amounted to an army near Kelso, and threatened to march on Edinburgh from the south should the royal forces move north against Huntly. This was curious, for Bothwell and the Homes were no Catholics. What was their objective in this affair was not clear – though it was assumed that the downfall of Maitland the Chancellor and his friends from their positions of power around the King, must be the aim. There were those in Court and government circles, nevertheless, who did not fail to point out that, equally curiously, the Master of Gray, only two or three days after his son's christening, had disappeared off in the direction of the Borders, ostensibly to visit his disreputable cousin Logan of Restalrig and his aunt, the former Lady Logan, now married to the Lord Home – and had been away for a full week.

However, base suspicions on this score were lulled, if not altogether scotched, when, on word of Bothwell's threat reaching Edinburgh, Patrick, newly returned to town, sought audience of the King – and, strangely enough, of the Chancellor. He urged that a strong and vigorous gesture be made forthwith against the unruly Borderers, whereupon, he vowed, Bothwell would not actually fight. Moreover, he was able, loyally and almost miraculously, to warn King and Chancellor of a nefarious conspiracy to seize their persons, by certain ill-willed folk about the capital – who, when arrested and suitably put to the question, admitted that such had been their aim, and were thereafter satisfactorily hanged. Since James had an almost morbid dread of such plots, and Maitland was a deal more at home with clerkly administration than military action, the Master's advice was taken, if doubtfully, and a force of the levies of Protestant lords in the Lothians hurriedly assembled. And lo, as prophesied, Bothwell's force, which had meantime reached as near as Haddington, seventeen miles from Edinburg, promptly melted away, shrinking, it was reliably reported, to a mere thirty horse.

Flushed with this demonstration of the value of firm action, the King smiled upon the useful Master of Gray, and called upon all leal lords, the Kirk, and his faithful burghs, to provide him with a sufficiency of armed men to march north to deal with the much more serious threat of the Catholic rising, at the same time issuing a proclamation ordering all men to forsake the service of the Earls of Huntly, Erroll and Bothwell, on pain of treason.

This Catholic threat had indeed cast its shadow elsewhere than on the Court and Capital. Dundee was the nearest large Protestant city south of Aberdeen and of Huntly's domains. When reports of Catholic columns reaching as far south as Bervie and Montrose, and of raiding Gordon bands pouring down the Angus glens, began to reach Dundee, the Provost and magistrates and ministers of the kirk of that God-fearing city perceived the need for drastic action. Walls were hastily repaired, gates strengthened, citizens called up. Dudhope Castle, the town's fortress, was stocked and garrisoned, and a deputation sent hot-foot to call upon the Lord Gray to urge that Broughty Castle, the key to the city from the east and seaward, be likewise garrisoned and put in a state of defensive readiness forthwith.

My lord, in some agitation and with no little reluctance – for his castle of Broughty, for one reason and another, was not in a good state of repair – and the expense of doing what was necessary would undoubtedly fall wholly upon his own pocket – agreed to see what could be done. In no sunny frame of mind, and at the almost feverish pleadings of the Provost and Sir John Scrymgeour, the Hereditary Constable of Dundee, he set off for Broughty, hailing David Gray his steward along with him.

This was the distinctly involved and dramatic situation prevailing when, the very next morning, on a sunny and sparkling July day, the Master of Gray, with his wife and baby son, attended by only two servitors belonging to Marie's father, returned, unexpected and unannounced to his birthplace, onetime home, and presumably future seat of Castle Huntly, after an absence of years – for he had been estranged from his father for long before his trial and banishment. In the absence of my lord and Davy, Mary Gray greeted them, and joyfully, all laughter and delight. She explained that her grandfather and father had been at Broughty Castle since the day before, and it was not known when they would be back. Patrick announced that, much as he would have preferred to stay at Castle Huntly with herself and her mother, it was his father that he had come to see, and as the matter had some urgency, he would ride on to Broughty forthwith. Mary, despite the attractions of cosseting and cherishing the baby Andrew, declared that she also would ride to Broughty with him – her Uncle Patrick nowise objecting. The Lady Marie was glad enough, apparently, to remain with Mariota, having ridden from Megginch that morning.

Pensively the two women watched the man and girl ride off eastwards, thinking their own thoughts.

The larks carolled, the sun shone, the countryside basked, and Patrick Gray seemed to have not a care in the world this fine morning. He was barely out of earshot of the castle gatehouse before he began to sing. He had an excellent lightsome tenor voice, and plunged straight into some gay and melodious French air which seemed to bubble over with droll merriment. It took only a few moments for Mary to catch the lilt and rhythm of it, and to add her own joyful trilling accompaniment, wordless but effective. Thereafter they sang side by side in laughing accord, clear, uninhibited, neither in the least self-conscious, caring naught for the astonished stares of the villagers of Longforgan or the embarrassed frowns of the two Orkney servants who rode well to the rear as though to disassociate themselves from the unseemly performance in front.

After the village there was a long straight stretch of road before it reached the coast at Invergowrie, and with a flourish Patrick smacked his horse into a canter. Not to be outdone, Mary promptly urged her own mount to a round gallop, passing the man with a skirled challenge, hair flying dark behind, her already short enough skirt blown back above long, graceful legs. Shouting, the Master spurred after her, gradually overtaking, until neck and neck they thundered together, raising a cloud of brown dust all along a couple of miles of rutted highway, whilst cattle scattered in nearby fields, folk peered from cot-house doors and the grooms behind cursed and made pretence of keeping up.

Just short of Invergowrie they pulled in their frothing beasts to a trot once more, the girl panting breathless laughter and

97

pulling down her skirt. Patrick reached out, to run a hand down her flushed cheek and over her shoulder and the heaving curve of her young bosom.

'We are sib . . . you and I . . . are we not?' he said.

'Indeed, yes,' she agreed, frankly. 'Would it not be strange if we were not . . . since you sired me?'

'M'mmm.' Sidelong he looked at her, silenced.

She turned in her saddle. 'You did not think that I did not know, Uncle Patrick?' she wondered.

'I . . . I was uncertain. Your father . . . h'mmm . . . my brother, Davy Gray – he has never said . . . '

'Not to me. But I knew, years ago. Many made sure that I knew.'

'Aye, many would! But . . . ' He smiled again. 'God bless you – it was the best thing that ever I did, I vow!'

'A better would have been to wed my mother, would it not?'

It took him a moment or two to answer that. 'Perhaps you are right, my dear,' he admitted, quietly for him. 'I . . . I do not always choose the better course, I fear.'

'No,' she agreed simply. 'That I know also.'

Again the swift sidelong glance. 'You are like me, child, God knows. But . . . in some ways, curse me, you're devilish like Davy also! Like your, your Uncle Davy.'

She nodded seriously. 'I hope so, yes. For he is the finest man in this realm, I do believe. But . . . he is Father, not Uncle Davy. He, he fathered me, whilst you but sired me, Uncle Patrick. There is a difference, is there not?'

The Master of Gray looked away, his handsome features suddenly still, mask-like. 'Aye,' he said.

They rode in silence, then, through Invergowrie, and kept down by the shore-track thereafter to avoid the climbing narrow streets and wynds of hilly Dundee.

As they went, they could see men busily engaged in building up the broken town walls, and at the boat-harbour others urgently unloading vessels.

'It is an ill thing when people must fear their own folk, their own countrymen, because of the way that they worship the same God, is it not?' Mary observed. 'I do not understand why it should be.'

'It is one of the major follies of men,' her companion acceded. 'A weakness, apparently, in all creeds.'

'Yes. A weakness that, they say, you use for your own purposes, Uncle Patrick. Is it so, indeed?'

He puckered his brows, wary-eyed – for Patrick Gray seldom actually frowned. 'I must use what tools come to my hand, my dear.'

'For your own purposes, always?'

'For purposes that I esteem as good, child.'

'Good for whom, Uncle Patrick?'

'Lord, Mary – what is this that you have become? You talk like a minister of the Kirk, I swear! How old are you? You cannot be more than just sixteen – for I am but thirty-one myself! Here is no talk, no thoughts, for a girl. You should be thinking of other things at your age, lass. Happier things. To do with clothing and pretty follies. With lads and wooing. With courting and marriage, maybe . . . '

Directly she turned to face him, clear eyed. 'Like King Jamie, perhaps?'

Patrick touched mouth and chin. 'The King's wooing is of rather more serious import, my dear. So much may depend upon it. An heir to the throne, the peace and prosperity of the realm, the weal – perhaps even the lives – of many.'

Gravely, almost judicially, she inclined her head. 'That is what I thought, yes. That is why, Uncle Patrick, I sent word to the King about the Princess of Navarre.'

'You . . . what?'

'I sent word to the King. Through Vicky. Through the Duke of Lennox. Vicky does what I say, you see. I sent him word that the lady was ill-favoured and old and would bed with any. As the Lady Marie told Father.'

'Precious soul of God – you! It was you? You who turned James against the match? After all my labour, my scheming . . . !'

'Yes.'

'But this is beyond all belief! That you, *you* my own daughter, should think to do such a thing! And why? Why, in God's name?'

'Because it was not good. Surely you see it? The Lady Marie is true and honest. She would not lie – not to Davy

99

Gray. If the Princess is bad, and old, and ugly, then she should not be Queen in Scotland. King Jamie is but ill-favoured himself. With an old and ugly queen, would not the Crown be made to seem the more foolish? Weak, when it needs rather to be strong? If she is old, it might be that there would be no child, no heir to the throne. And that is important, is it not? Did you not just say so? Moreover, if she is but a whore, it could be that if a child there was, none would know who sired it. I think that would have been but an ill turn to Scotland, Uncle Patrick. So I sent word to Vicky. And that the little picture was ten years old, and a flattery.'

The Master of Gray let his breath go in a long sigh. He did not speak.

'I am sorry that you are angry,' she went on, reaching over to touch his arm. 'Do not be angry. Was what I did wrong?'

Slowly he turned to consider her, all of her, vital, lovely, pleading, yet somehow also compassionate, forbearing, so unassumingly sure of herself. Swallowing, he shook his head.

'I am not angry,' he said. 'And, Heaven forgive me, you were not wrong!'

Mary smiled then, warmly, nodding her head three or four times as though in confirmation of what she already knew.

They were not much more than half-way to Broughty Castle, but already they could see it rearing proud and seeming defiant on its little peninsula that thrust out into the estuary four or five miles ahead. Something of a fortress this, rather than an ordinary castle, the Grays had used it for generations, in conjunction with another at Ferry-Port-on-Craig on the Fife shore opposite, to command the entrance of the Tay, thus narrowed by headlands. Theoretically it was for the defence of Dundee and other Tay ports, but in fact had been used to levy tolls and tribute from all shipping using the harbours – a notable source of the Gray wealth. My lord's father, the fourth lord, had shamefully surrendered it to the English under Somerset nearly forty years before, during a disagreement with the Queen Regent, Mary of Guise; and my lord himself, two years later, had gained his limp and almost lost his life seeking to retake it. The damage done then, by cannon-fire, had never been fully repaired – hence the present crisis.

100

As man and girl rode on along the scalloped coast, presently Mary began to sing again, a sweetly haunting melody of an older Scotland still. Patrick did not join in now, but he eyed her, time and time again, as she sang, wonderingly, thoughtfully, calculatingly – and when her sparkling eye caught his own, he mustered a smile.

It was seldom indeed that the Master of Gray did not set the pace in any company that he graced.

They came to Broughty Craig two hours after leaving Castle Huntly, and found it as busy as an ant-hill, with men re-digging the great moat which cut off the headland from landward, shoring up timber barricades against the broken battlements, filling in gaps in the sheer curtain-walling with its many wide gun-loops. It was a more gloomy frowning place than Castle Huntly, less tall but more massive, consisting of a great square free-standing tower of five storeys, immensely thick-walled and small-windowed, rising from an oddly-shaped enclosure, almost like a ship, which followed faithfully the outline of the rocky headland itself, this latter also provided at its corners with smaller round flanking towers. Around three sides the sea surged, and under the stern ramparts the harbour crouched – the ferry harbour, which was another source of my lord's revenues, since none might come and go across the estuary to St. Andrew's, without paying a suitable tax. Other ferries were effectively discouraged.

The newcomers found David in the courtyard superintending the hoisting of heavy timber beams up the outer walling to the dizzy parapet-walk at top floor level, doublet discarded and sleeves uprolled like any labouring man. He stared at his spectacularly clad brother, astonished, and then curtly ordered him to wait, and safely out of the way, while the delicate process of hoisting was completed. Then, running a hand through his sweat-damp hair, he came over to them.

'What brings you here, Patrick?' he demanded. 'My lord is here. Within. Talking with your brother Gilbert, and the Provost . . .'

'What of it, Davy? May a man not call upon his father, on occasion? Even such a father as ours? And Gibbie – Lord, I have not seen Gibbie for years. Eight years. Ten. He will be a man now, also, of course.'

101

'He is laird of Mylnefield, and a burgess and bailie of Dundee.'

'All that? Young running-nosed Gibbie! It makes me feel old, I vow! Well, well – let us within.'

'Patrick – think you it is wise?' David sounded hesitant, uneasy. 'My lord – he is in no sunny mood. With all this expense . . . '

'The more reason that she should be gladdened by the sight of his missing son and heir – if not his firstborn, Davy! Besides, I can save our skinflint sire some of this foolish expense – ever the sure road to his heart! Come.'

Patrick led the way in at the door of the keep, Mary and David following. The girl slipped her hand within her father's arm.

'Uncle Patrick is not afraid, Father,' she murmured. 'So why should you be? He has faced more terrible folk than Granlord, I think.'

'It is not your Uncle Patrick for whom I am afraid, girl!' David answered briefly, grimly.

They heard voices from the great hall on the first floor, and mounted the worn steps thereto. The place was less large than might have been expected, owing to the great thickness of the walls, and only dimly lit by its small deep-set windows. Moreover it was but scantily furnished with a vast elm table in the middle of the stone-flagged floor, and a few chairs and benches. My lord had always least liked this castle of the many that he had inherited – partly no doubt on account of the shattered knee-cap, won here, that he had carried with him for forty years – and maintained it was only a keeper-cum-toll-gatherer and a few men, none of whom used this great central keep. It was cool in here however, at least, after the mid-day July heat outside – although the musty smells of bats and rats and damp stone caught the throat. Two men sat, with tankards in their hands but all attention, at the great table, and the third limped back and forth before them, declaiming vehemently.

At sound of the newcomers, my lord looked around, though he halted neither his pacing nor his harangue at first. Undoubtedly the dim lighting denied him identification – although the younger of the seated men got slowly to his feet, staring at the doorway. Probably it was this that made the nobleman glance again, and he perceived at least Mary Gray there, with Davy and the superbly dressed visitor. His heavy sagging features lightened, and if the growl did not go right out of his voice, it developed something of a chuckle.

'Ha – my poppet! My ain pigeon! Is that yoursel', lassie? What brings *you*, like a blink o' sunshine, into this thrice-damned sepulchre o' a place? Eh? And who's that you've got wi' you bairn . . . ?'

'Can you not see, Granlord? Is not this splendid?'

'Does blood not speak louder than words, my lord?' Patrick asked pleasantly. 'I rejoice to see you well. And active in, h'm, well-doing.'

'Christ God!'

'Scarce that, my lord – just your son Patrick!'

The older man groped almost blindly for the support of the table. His thick lips moved, but no sound issued therefrom. Mary ran to his side, to take his other hand.

Patrick and David came forward. 'It is some years, sir, since we have had the pleasure, is it not?' the former went on, easily. 'You wear well, I see. And is that Gibbie with you? Brother Gibbie – a man now, a sober, respectable, man, I vow – and scarce like a Gray at all, at all! Greetings, brother. And to you, Mr Provost.'

My lord smashed down his fist on the table-top. 'Silence!' he barked, though his voice broke a little. 'Quiet, you . . . you mincing jackdaw! You mocking cuckoo!' As Mary tugged at his arm, whispering, he shook her off roughly. 'Fiend seize me – what ill chance brings you here? How dare you darken any door o' mine, man?'

'Dare, sir? Dare? Why, I am a very lion for daring. That at least I inherit from my sire – if naught else. Yet!' Patrick smiled. 'I dare, my lord, because I would see you, have word with you – who knows, even possibly come to terms with you!'

'Never, curse you – never! I told you yon time – never did I want to see your insolent ninny's face again. I meant it then, by God – and I mean it yet!'

'My lord . . . ' David began, but Patrick silenced him with a gesture.

'My face, sir, may not please you – since it is vastly unlike

103

your own . . . which no doubt contents us both well enough! But, I had thought that you at least would wish to look on the face of your eventual heir. The seventh Lord Gray, to be. You did not grace his christening. So I have brought him to Castle Huntly, that you may see him there.'

'Then you may take the brat away again – and forthwith!' the older man returned. 'I want no more sight o' him that I do o' you, d'you hear? I ken you, you crawling thing, man! First you would come to me hiding behind a woman's skirts. Now, behind a suckling's wrappings. I'll no' . . . I'll no' . . . ' The Lord Gray all but choked to silence, his face congested, purple, his heavy jowls shaking. He staggered a little, and the hand which reached out for the table again trembled notice-ably.

Mary ran back to his side, to hold him, biting her lip.

The Master's slender ruffled wrist was gripped strongly, as in a vice. 'Enough,' David said, low-voiced but commanding. 'He will take a hurt. He is your father – and mine. Enough, I say.'

Patrick slowly inclined his handsome head. 'Very well,' he murmured. And louder, 'These family pleasantries over, then – I come to business, my lord. Private business, and pressing.' He turned to the two men at the other side of the table. 'Mr Provost – you will excuse us? You too, Gibbie, I think. Yes – go please.'

Both sitters rose, the younger, thin, dark-featured, long-chinned, frowning. 'Sir . . . Patrick . . . !' Gilbert Gray pro-tested. 'This is . . . this is insupportable! You'll no' treat me like a lackey . . . and in my father's house!'

'Lord, Gibbie – I treat you like I do the Provost, here. With great respect, but scarce requiring your presence in the private business, affairs of state, that I have to discuss with my lord. So – off with you both to somewhere else.'

The Provost, a fat and perspiring bald man, ducked and bowed and mumbled in alarmed reaction to the authoritative, indeed imperious, orders, moving hastily if sidelong towards the door. Gilbert Gray, almost involuntarily did likewise, but more slowly and looking to his father.

My lord was staring glassily straight ahead of him, breath-ing stertorously, aparently heeding none of them.

As they reached the door, however, Patrick suddenly stopped them with a snap of his long fingers. 'Stay, Provost – a moment. You may as well hear this first. Before you go. You may spare your worthy citizens their unnecessary labours, man. Their hammerings and stone-masonry and running to and fro. Likewise, my lord, your distressing activities here. There is no need for such extremities. All unnecessary. Huntly is not coming south.'

They stared at him, all of them.

'Tut – do not gawp! You have jumped at shadows. Your panic is superfluous. Save yourself further troubles, gentlemen. And expense. Huntly will not move. His outliers will retire on Aberdeen by nightfall. Already they will have turned back. There is no danger to your douce town of Dundee.'

'But . . . but . . . ?'

'How do you know this, Patrick?' David jerked.

'I have my sources of intelligence, Davy. As you know.' Patrick smiled. 'Moreover, the King and a great Protestant host, filled with holy and Reformed zeal, will be beyond Strathmore and Jordan . . . or the Esk . . . by this! I left His Grace at Perth yesterday noon, rumbling martial thunderings from lips and belly. So there is naught to fear.'

'My lord . . . honoured sir . . . ,' the Provost gabbled. 'Is this . . . is this sooth? You are assured o' it . . . ?'

'A pox, fellow – do you doubt my word! You?'

'Na, na – och, never that, sir! Never that . . . '

'Then be gone. And you, Gibbie. Every minute will save money, will it not?' It was perhaps noteworthy that though the Master of Gray dismissed his lawful brother thus cavalierly, he did not make any similar gesture towards his bastard half-brother. Nor, for that matter, towards young Mary. Turning his elegant back on the pair from Dundee, he addressed his father, who appeared to be recovering. 'Perhaps you should sit down, my lord,' he suggested. 'That we may discuss our business in . . . ' – he glanced around him distastefully – ' . . . in such comfort as this rickle of stones allows.'

'I have . . . no business . . . to discuss . . . wi' you!' my lord rasped throatily, harshly – 'Now, or ever.' He did not move from his stance by the table.

'Ah, but you have sir, I assure you. On a matter close to

105

your heart, I vow. Siller, my lord – siller! Sillibawbys, merks and good Scots pounds! Sink me – have I not already saved you a pretty purseful by this intelligence that I bring? You no longer need spend a plack on this rat-ridden ruin. Send all your drudges home. And let your pocket thank me – even if naught else does!'

From under heavy brows his father gazed at him, like a bull dazed and uncertain. 'This . . . is certain? About Huntly? And the King? We are safe, now?' he got out.

'Now – and before. You never were in danger. Huntly makes a demonstration – that is all. For, shall we say, a variety of excellent reasons. He never had any intention of descending upon the south. The King of Spain, God preserve him, has sent Huntly a consignment of gold ducats, and he must make pretence of using them to good effect. Moreover, Huntly does not love my lord of Bothwell, and considers that his wings needed clipping. This achieves it. So King Jamie marches valiantly north, and will enjoy a notable, a resounding victory – since none will oppose him. Oh, some Highland caterans will be slaughtered and a few Aberdeen burghers hanged, no doubt, for dignity's sake – but Huntly will speak loving peace with His Grace, and some few of the ducats will belike find their way into Jamie's coffers . . . '

'God's death – what mad rigmarole is this?' his father cried. 'Are you crazed, man?'

'Hardly, sir! Do you really think it? Indeed, I humbly suggest otherwise. For, you see, good is served all round is it not? Elizabeth of England, perceiving the great stresses and dangers King Jamie lives under, in preserving the sacred cause of Protestantism, must needs increase her contributions towards the upkeep of a stronger and truly loyal guard in this happy realm. The matter is vital – for the Reformed faith, you understand. Already, indeed, the couriers are on their urgent way to London, to that effect. Heigho – all things work together for good, as I say, do they not?'

My lord was speechless.

It was David Gray who spoke, in a whisper. 'So soon!' he said. 'So soon! We are back where we were, i' faith! Nothing is changed. The . . . the Devil is come back to Scotland!'

'Come, come, Davy – you flatter me! Besides, no harm is

done. Quite the reverse, I vow. Are not all advantaged – or nearly all? Which brings me, my lord, to the matter of our business – so that *we* shall be advantaged also. The matter concerns the Abbey of Dunfermline.'

'A-a-ah!' Lord Gray said, despite himself.

'Exactly! I intend, you see, to recover my commendatorship and the revenues thereof. George Gordon of Huntly has enjoyed them quite sufficiently long for any small service that he effected. He is proving stupidly obdurate, however. Always George was stupid – do you not agree? And our Jamie is something of a broken reed in the matter, I fear. Indeed, I suspect His slobbering Grace. So, I propose to sue George for Dunfermline in the High Court. And believe that, with a little forethought and judicial, er, preparation, I shall win. For Huntly has few friends amongst His Grace's judges – who are all good Protestants, of course!' Patrick sighed, a little. 'Unfortunately, such processes of law cost money. Siller, my lord – siller. A commodity of which I am, at the moment, somewhat short, more is the pity. Hence this approach . . . and your good fortune, sir.'

His father gaped like a stranded fish. 'You . . . you . . . ? Me . . . ? Siller . . . ?' With difficulty he enunciated consecutive words. 'Ha, you gon plain gyte, man? D'you think to win siller frae me? *Me*?'

'I do, naturally. And for good and excellent reason. I do not come to you out of mere, shall we say, family affection and esteem, my lord – admirable as are such sentiments. This is a matter of business, of lands and heritable properties. Heritable, I pray you note, is the significant word. Since, one day in God's providence, I or my son shall inherit from you the Gray lands, merest foresight and common prudence indicates that it is to you that I should offer Balmerino. So that, heigho, in the said God's time I shall have it back again! Balmerino, my lord – Balmerino!'

Lord Gray was so much moved that he groped his way round the table, Mary supporting him, to sink into one of the chairs. He never took his eyes off his beautiful son – although from his expression the sight appeared to afford him only extreme distress.

Well might the Master harp on that word Balmerino, of

107

course. Balmerino Abbey, or the ruins thereof, with its little town and port, lay almost exactly across the Tay estuary from Castle Huntly. Its lands were extensive and fertile; more important however, from Lord Gray's point of view, was the fact that owing to the shallows and shoals of the firth at this point, its port commanded the ship-traffic of the upper reaches of the estuary. Taken in conjunction with the Broughty Castle and Ferry Port toll barriers, it could completely dominate all trade, internal as well as external, along the entire causeway, with a judiciously-placed cannon or two. Long had the Grays looked across at Balmerino in North Fife with covetous eyes. Its possession could vastly increase their revenues.

Patrick answered his father's unspoken question. 'I have arranged with Sir Robert Melville an exchange of Balmerino for the Dunfermline pendicle of Monimail near to his own lands of Melville. When I win back Dunfermline, Balmerino will be mine. Or rather, yours, my lord – for one thousand silver crowns. A bargain, you will admit!'

His father uttered a groan of sheerest agony.

'You perceive, my lord, how necessary it is that I come to you, rather than to any other? Balmerino is worth a score of times more to Gray than to anyone else in the kingdom. Am I not a dutiful son, after all?'

'No!' the older man croaked. 'No! No!' he banged fist on the table time and again.

'But yes, sir. You would not throw away Balmerino for a mere thousand pieces of siller?'

His father was grimacing strangely. Undoubtedly it was the hardest decision of that nobleman's life, striking to the very roots of him. But he made it. 'Damn you . . . no! Never!'

Patrick was still-faced, curiously blank-looking for a moment. But only for a moment or two. 'I am sorry,' he said, then, shrugging.

"I . . . I vow you are, foul fall you!'

'But, yes. I would be as foolish not to be so, as are you in throwing this aside, my lord. Blinded by . . . by whatever so blinds you. I can get the money elsewhere, to be sure – but not so profitably for Gray.'

'Then get it, man – get it! For you'll no' win a plack frae me. All your days you've wasted and devoured my substance.

You'll do it nae mair. You can beg for crusts in the vennels o' Edinburgh, for a' I care, d'you hear? You and your woman and your brat can starve . . . '

'Oh, Granlord – no!' Mary cried.

'Here are but doubtful fatherly sentiments, my lord! You scarce ever doted on me, I think – but it seems . . . excessive. What new ill have I done to you since last we met, I pray?'

The other rose slowly to his feet, with something of dignity now. 'You butchered your Queen,' he said. 'You were the death o' the bonny Mary, that I loved well.'

There was complete silence in that dim and musty chamber, for seconds on end.

It was young Mary who broke it. 'It is not so, Granlord,' she said urgently. 'Not so. He went to save her, and could not. That is not the same. Queen Elizabeth it was who killed our Queen. Not Uncle Patrick. He was not able to save her. But then, neither was Father. Neither was Sir Robert Melville, who went too. None could.' Her young voice seemed to echo desperately round the gaunt vaulted cavern of masonry, pleading.

None of the men either looked at her nor answered the question behind her words.

'Why must you be so hard on each other?' she asked. 'So cruelly hard?'

'Mary – it would be better, I think, that you should leave us, child.'

'No. No, Father. Do you not see . . . ?'

My lord spoke through her pleas. 'Go!' he commanded – but not to the girl. 'Go, Judas – and never let me see your false face again! I want nane o' you – nane, d'you hear? Judas!'

The muscles of the Master's features seemed to work and tense. For once, there was little of beauty or attractiveness to be seen thereon, as glittering-eyed, ashen-lipped, he faced his father. 'For that word . . . you will be sorry!' he got out. 'Sorry!'

'Go . . . !'

'Oh, yes – I shall go. But first, I will have my rights from you. What you will not give in love and affection, even in decency, you will yield as of right. For I am Master of Gray

– heir to this lordship. I have never asked for it before – but I demand it now. I want my portion.'

My lord belched rudely. 'That for your portion, man!'

This crude coarseness seemed to have the effect of steadying the younger man, of enabling him to revert to something of his usual assured air of mastery of any situation. 'I think not,' he said, actually smiling again. 'The heir to Gray has certain rights, beyond the mere style. I have not sought them of you . . . '

'Any such you ha' forfeited long since. You ha' squandered my siller . . . '

'I refer, sir, not to your precious siller, but to more enduring claims. My patrimony. Properties. You have, I understand, settled Mylnefield on Gibbie. Brother James, I am told, has Buttergask and Davidstoun. William is in Bandirran. I am not wholly uninformed, my lord. Myself, I require the heir's portion.'

His father was breathing deeply, purpling again. 'Curse you – you'll get nothing! Nothing, I say. Knave and blackguard that you are! I . . . I . . . ' Of a sudden, my lord's heavy features seemed to lighten a little. 'Or . . . aye, I have it! That's it. Your portion, my bonny Master o' Gray! You have it, man – you're standing in it! *This* is your portion – all you'll get, while I am above the sod! Broughty Castle!' Hooted harsh laughter set the older man coughing. ' 'Tis yours, Patrick – all o' it, yours, by God!' he spluttered. 'See to it, Davy. The papers and titles – to Patrick, Master o' Gray, in life rent, Broughty Castle. The building only, mind. No' a stick or stone else. No' an inch o' land. No' a penny-piece o' the tolls. A rickle o' stones you named it, Patrick? Aye – then take it, and I pray to God it falls on your scoundrelly head and makes your sepulchre!'

Pushing Mary aside roughly, the Lord Gray stalked heavily past his sons without a further word or glance, and out of the arched doorway to the winding stairs.

Tears were trickling down the girl's face from brimming dark eyes, though she made neither sob nor sound.

'I shall build up these crumbling wall, I tell you – raise new towers and battlements. I shall root out these mouldering

110

boards and rotting beams. I shall open up these wretched holes of windows, and let in air and light. I shall hang these bare walls with Flemish tapestries and cover the floors with carpets from the East, and furnish these barren chambers with the finest plenishings of France and Spain and the Netherlands, such as not another house in this realm can show!' The Master of Gray was striding back and forward across the uneven bat-fouled flagstones of Broughty Castle's hall, set-faced, eyes flashing. 'I shall make of this stinking ruin a palace, I swear! A mansion which every lord in the land shall envy. Where the King will come to sup and wish his own. I shall make it so that Castle Huntly seems a hovel, a dog's kennel, by comparison, and its proud lord shall come here seeking admission on his bended knees! I swear it, I say – and swear it by Almighty God!'

'Uncle Patrick – don't!' Mary Gray said. 'Please don't. Please.'

David and the girl were watching the extraordinary, almost awesome spectacle of the most handsome man in all of Europe, the brightest ornament of the Scottish scene, the most talented gallant in two realms, in the grip of blind unreasoning bitter hurt and passion, tormented, distraught. Helplessly they watched him, listened to him, anguish and sorrow in their own eyes – for they loved him, both. Mary had never seen the like, although she had witnessed some shocking, savage scenes in that strange and contentious family. David had his arm around the girl's shoulders, holding her; he indeed had seen the like before – and it turned his heart sick within him.

Patrick Gray changed his tune. He stopped his pacing, and began to curse. Tensely, almost softly, but fluently, compre-hensively, he commenced to swear in breath-taking ingenious ferocity.

David Gray acted. Leaving Mary, he strode up to his brother, grasped him by both elegant padded shoulders, and with abrupt violence shook him as a terrier shakes a rat. 'Quiet!' he commanded. 'Quiet, I say. Patrick – be silent! Mary – by God, mind Mary!'

The evil flow was choked back, partly through sheer physical convulsion, partly by a real effort of will. Gasping and panting a little, the Master stepped back, and the scorching fury in his gaze at his half-brother faded. Slightly dazed-seeming, he moistened his lips and shook his head.

'I . . . I apologise,' he said thickly. 'My thanks, Davy. I . . . Mary, my dear – forgive me. If you can.' He looked over to her, and the change in his expression was quite extraordinary.

She came to him, then, wordless, to take his hand.

'I think . . . that I lost my head . . . just a little,' he said, jerkily. 'Unedifying in the extreme, no doubt. Davy . . . well, Davy knows me. Too well. But you, Mary lass, should have been spared that. It shall not occur again.'

'Granlord was very cruel,' she said. 'But he was hurt, too. He torments himself in believing so ill of you. In thinking you capable of so much evil.'

Over her head, Patrick's dark eyes met David's grey ones. 'And you, child, see me rather as an angel of light?'

'Oh, no,' she told him, simply. 'Not so. I know that you can do ill things. Uncle Patrick. Very ill. As in the matter of the Princess of Navarre. And the plot for the Catholics to gain the King and all Scotland, before the Armada invasion of England. But I am sure that you are not as my lord thinks. That you do much good, as well as ill. We all do ill things as well as good, do we not?' Seriously, she put it to him. 'I think that the good that you do, Uncle Patrick, will be better than most. Just as the ill is . . . is very ill.' For Mary Gray, that last was hesitant.

'Thank you, my dear,' the other said, shaking his head, and clearly moved. 'I do not know that many would agree with you!' And again he met his brother's level gaze. 'But thank you.' He raised her small hand, and brushed it with his lips. 'I believe that you are . . . very good for me. God keep you so. But . . . a moment ago, girl, you spoke of a plot? A plot, you said. Before the Armada of Spain. To gain the King and Scotland for the Catholics. This is . . . interesting.' His glance swivelled round to his brother. 'What did you mean by that, Mary?'

"Just that I saw your letter. The strange letter that you wrote to Father.'

'Indeed. It was not meant for such eyes as yours.'

'No. But I perceived that the writing was yours, Uncle Patrick. So I must needs read it.'

112

His brows rose. 'I see.'

'Yes. It was a very clever letter.'

'But . . . you saw it as a plot? A Catholic plot.' Still it was at David that he looked.

That man nodded.

'But it showed excellently well the way to save the realm,' the girl went on. 'Had the King of Spain triumphed in England. So . . . we told King Jamie, as you said. But that . . . that the Spanish Inquisition should not come to Scotland . . . ' Mary bit her lip. 'Lest the Office be set up on Castle-hill – that was how you wrote it, was it not? That there should be no chance of that ill thing, we told the King that it was the Protestant lords who should be assembled. First. Otherwise the same as in your letter, Uncle Patrick.'

The Master actually stopped breathing for many seconds together.

'Was that wrong?' she pressed him. 'It was not what you intended. We did you hurt in that, perhaps? But . . . we could not countenance a Catholic plot. Could we?'

'God . . . help me! What . . . ?' Patrick swallowed. 'What is this?'

David answered him, harshly, throatily. 'This is your daughter, Patrick. Your own flesh and blood. Risen up in judgment. Something that has stolen upon us all unawares. You could dispose of her mother as you would, you and my lord – but this is beyond you. Beyond us all.'

The other stared.

'Do not think ill of me,' Mary said – and it was to them both that she spoke. 'What I did was for the best. In all else it was as you advised, Uncle Patrick. And the King believed that all came from you. That you advised the mustering of the Protestant lords. So, you see, your credit stands the higher with him. He esteemed you Papist before – but this would cause him to doubt it. In that you are advantaged, are you not? It may be that he was the kinder to you at Holyroodhouse yon night, because of it. And why he attended Andrew's christening and stood godfather.' She nodded, as though to herself, satisfied. 'You see it, Uncle Patrick?'

It was Davy Gray who expostulated. 'Child – this is no way to talk! Subterfuge and guile and, and chicanery! Leave you

113

that to others, 'fore God!'

'It is but the truth, is it not, Father? So it has come to pass . . . '

Patrick interrupted her, laughing, in a sudden return to something of his old gay assured self. 'Ha – do not chide her, Davy,' he said. 'Here is a pearl beyond all price, indeed! The wisdom of dove and serpent combined! And all in the comeliest small head and person that we are likely to find in the length and breadth of this kingdom! Do not rail at what the good Lord has wrought!'

'You – *you* to talk thus?'

'To be sure. Why not? Since it seems that I may claim some of the credit! And I need all the credit that I may summon up, do I not, Davy? I think . . . yes, I think that Mary and I might run very well in harness. I must think more on this. For, i' faith, I'd liefer have our young Mary as my friend than my enemy!'

'That you will have always, Uncle Patrick,' the girl declared gravely. 'But it would be easier if you were a Protestant again, rather than a Catholic, I think.'

'In the name of Heaven . . . !' David Gray exclaimed.

'Exactly, Davy – exactly! But, come,' the Master said, in a different tone of voice. 'It is time that we were hence. I do not know whether my esteemed and noble father will be returning forthwith to Castle Huntly – but I would not wish Marie to be the object of his further attentions in his present state of mind.'

'God forbid!' his brother agreed. 'You left her at the castle?'

'Yes. I must get her away from there, and under some more hospitable roof.' Patrick looked about him, grimacing. 'Since I may scarce bring her here. Yet.'

David nodded. 'I am sorry,' he said. 'Sorry for all of it. But sorriest for Marie, who deserves better things.'

'Aye. Deserves a better husband belike?' Patrick shot a quick look at the other. 'A husband such as the upright Davy Gray, mayhap?'

'That is ill said, brother,' David observed, even-voiced. 'Marie deserves better than any man I know. Remember it, I charge you! Come, then – we waste time here.'

There was no sign of my lord or Gilbert Gray or the Provost of Dundee outside. Already the workmen had abandoned their various tasks and were leaving the place.

As the trio mounted and rode off over the drawbridge and the half-dug moat towards the village and harbour, Patrick turned in his saddle and looked back.

'A task,' he said softly, as to himself. 'A notable task. And expensive. But worth it, I think. Aye, worth it.'

'You mean to do it, then? Still? To go ahead with it, Patrick? Restore this great ruin?' David asked. 'That would be folly, surely?'

'Folly?' His brother smiled. 'Living is folly, and dying the only true wisdom, Davy, is it not? But there is folly – and folly! This folly might well make a fool of still greater folly. We shall see. But . . . I shall be obliged for those papers and titles that my lord mentioned, Davy – before he changes his mind!'

Chapter Six

DAVID GRAY paced the floor of his own little circular chamber in the north-west flanking tower of Castle Huntly, set-faced. Once again he held in his hand a letter – and once again it was in his brother Patrick's dashing handwriting. When he had recognised the writing, even when the missive was still in the courier's hand, his heart had sunk; for Patrick's letters seldom left their recipients as they found them, unmoved or uninvolved. This one was no exception.

It was addressed from the Laird of Tillycairn's Lodging, The Canongate, Old Aberdeen, and dated 27th July, 1589 – three weeks after the clash at Broughty Castle. This was no coded nor cryptic letter like the last, but it made its demands, nevertheless. It read:

'My excellent Davy,
    But a few days after we left you, His Grace summoned me here to Aberdeen. I was intrigued to know for why. I

115

have been reappointed to my old and useful position of Master of the Wardrobe – though not yet to the Council, as is my greater requirement. But that will come, no doubt.

The reason for my summons north would appear to be, not so much that His Grace and the Chancellor cannot bear to be without my presence, as that they seem to hold unwarranted and base suspicions as to my activities and whereabouts when I am not under their eyes! I wonder how they came to gain the whisper that I had hastened south to the house of my lord of Bothwell whenever I left them at Perth that day? A strange calumny, was it not? But with its own usages. Since now I am secure at Court – in fact, in the Wardrobe! Take note, Davy – *fama nihil est celerius!*

All here is triumph and rejoicing. Even the poor, damned Catholic rebels rejoice, so felicitous is the occasion and so clement the royal victor. As previously arranged. The Battle of the Brig o' Dee will, I doubt not, go down in our realm's history as unique – in that scarce a blow was struck, our martial monarch's very presence striking terror into the hearts of all Catholics, heretics, and enemies of Christ's true Reformed faith! Huntly, Erroll, Montrose and the others have yielded themselves up to gracious Majesty – who, I rejoice to say, agrees that mercy should temper justice quite signally. So all is contrition, love and merriment indeed – save for the good Chancellor, who would have preferred a few heads to fall – with our eloquent prince preaching the Reformed evangel with potent zeal. I, of course, am one of his most promising converts. As young Mary so shrewdly advises.

The which, Davy, brings me to my prayer and request. I would crave you to permit Mary to come to Court. I well know your own mislike of such, but I think, if you are honest – and always you are notably that, are you not? – that you will admit that she is as though born for the Court. Fear not for her safety. I shall watch over her well, I promise you, as though – why, as though she were my own daughter! She will, of course, lodge with us, and Marie shall cherish and protect her. You need have no fears on that score. Although, think you not, Mary may be well able to protect herself?

Do not dismiss this plea in selfish haste, Davy. There is much to commend it. Mary will be good for me, I think. There will be a Queen again in Scotland ere long, and Maids of Honour and Ladies in Waiting are already being selected. This comes within the province of my Lord Chamberlain – and I understand that Vicky is not without his own plans in the matter. So, dear brother and self-appointed keeper of my conscience, should you think to refuse to let Mary come, as I pray, consider well how a royal summons could *command* her to attend at Court. My way, I ween, is the more suitable. I swear that if she likes it not, or if it is anyways in her interest to leave, she shall return to your good care forthwith.

Consider for her, Davy – not for yourself. The Court returns south for Edinburgh tomorrow. A sennight at Holyroodhouse for a Council and the trial of the miscreants. Then Falkland and Majesty's beloved stags. Let it be Falkland for our Mary, brother.

I send my devotion to you all.

Patrick'

In a rounder and less spectacular hand was added, at the foot:

'Bear with us please, Davy dear. And guide Mariota to allow Mary to come. Even though it cost you both dear. Award the child her destiny. She might take it in her own hands, else.

Marie'

So David Gray paced his floor. He had got over the worst of it now, the pent-up fury, the hot resentment, the wrathful denial. David was just as much a Gray as either his father or his half-brother. The hurt, the pain, was with him still; but his head was cooler now, his reason functioning. Yet his expression grew the bleaker as he paced.

Could he hold her back? Should he? That was the question. Which way lay his duty to her? She was a child no more – but surely she yet required protection? More than ever, perhaps. And, God help her – what sort of protection would Patrick afford her? Marie, yes – but Patrick! And yet – did she have

117

a deal of protection here at Castle Huntly? Watch for her as he would? She came and went as she wished. She could twist every man and woman in all the Carse around her little finger. Including her grandfather. My lord would not relish this. Indeed, he would forbid it if he could. But . . . was that not to the point? The old man had always doted on her – but now did so unpleasingly. Lasciviously. As a woman, no longer as a child. And where women were concerned, he was without scruple. He was not good for Mary . . .

And if young Lennox worked up on the King to summon her? As Patrick might well put him up to if he did not think of it himself? There could be no holding her then against the royal command. Better surely that she should go freely, and in Marie's care, at least.

But Patrick! As sponsor for the girl into that wicked, deceitful and corrupt world? Patrick, the falsest schemer and liar and betrayer of them all! And her father, save in name. . . .

David came to stare out of his window. The leaves were already beginning to turn on the elms and birches, though not on the beeches and oaks, barely August as it was. So short a summer. Not that he saw any of them. He saw only a lovely, elfin face, great-eyed, wistful, grave, and true. And another, attractive also, smiling, handsome, and false. So like the other; so like.

It was the likeness that tipped the scales. Not merely the likeness of feature, of lineament. It was the inborn assurance, the air of breeding, the indubitable yet unpretentious quality of prescriptive right, that each wore like a casual easy garment. Something that was no more to be ignored than denied. Both had been destined by something more than mere birth for the great world of rule and power and influence. Who was Davy Gray the Bastard to say it nay?'

Sighing heavily, the man crushed that letter in his strong hand, and went downstairs to seek Mariota.

Mary Gray came to the royal burgh of Falkland on the eighth day of August. It proved to be a notably smaller place than she had imagined, a little grey huddle of a town, all red pantiled roofs, tortuous narrow streets and winding steeply-sloping alleys, crouching under the tall green cone of the easternmost of the Lomond Hills, and quite dominated by the turreted and ornate palace. This, although of handsome architecture, was itself of no great size for a royal residence, and the entire place, with the Court in residence, gave the impression of bursting at the seams. With David as escort, the girl had to force her garron through the throng that choked the constricted streets and wynds, a motley crowd of gaily attired lords and ladies, of lairds and clerics, members of the royal bodyguard and men-at-arms, grooms and foresters, hawkers and tranters, hucksters and pedlars, townsfolk, tradesmen and tinkers. People hung out of every window, as though being squeezed out by the press within, laughing and shouting to folk in the street, or across their heads to the occupants of windows opposite. Horses were everywhere, for the main business of Falkland was hunting, and followers might require three and four mounts in any hard-riding day. Hay and oats to feed the many hundreds of beasts crammed all available space, wagon-loads and sled-like slypes coming in constantly from the surrounding farms further jammed the congested lanes, together with flocks of cattle, sheep and poultry to provide fare for the suddenly trebled population. The bustle was indescribable, the noise deafening – more especially as the church bells were tolling clamorously, it was said for a witch-burning – and the stench was breath-taking, particularly of dung and perspiration and pigs, this warm August day. Mary was no stranger to the crowded streets of Dundee and Edinburgh, but this concentration in little Falkland was something new to her.

Pushing patiently through the press, David shepherded his charge, with her bundles of belongings, towards the lower end of the little town, where the palace reared its twin drum towers, its elaborate buttresses and stone-carved walls above gardens, pleasances, tennis-courts and the wide island-dotted loch. Mary, all lip-parted excitement and gleaming eyes, assumed that they were making for the palace itself, when her father turned his mount in at a narrow vennel called College Close, just opposite the great palace gates. Thence, through a dark and ill-smelling pend, they came into a sort of back court of small humble houses, jumbled together, in one of which they found the Mistress of Gray installed, with the baby

119

Andrew. It took Mary a little while to realise, even after the first fond greetings, that this was where she was going to dwell meantime, in this low-browed and over-crowded rabbit-warren. Not that she was foolishly proud or over-nice in the matter; it was just not what she had anticipated in this business of coming to Court.

The Lady Marie, strangely enough, was quite delighted with these lowly quarters. It seemed that King Jamie's passion for hunting was rued by his courtiers not only because of the everlasting cross-country pounding and prancing but on account of chronic lack of accommodation at Falkland, where earls had to roost in garrets and bishops crouch in cellars. The French ambassador was, in fact, lodging next door, and Queen Elizabeth's new resident envoy, Mr Bowes, across the tiny cobbled yard. Only the Duke of Lennox's good offices had got the impoverished Grays in here, this being the house of his own under-falconer, Patey Reid, whose acquaintance Mary had already made one day by Lindores Loch.

'My sister Jean is here with us also,' Marie told them. 'She is chosen one of the ladies to the new queen. She and Mary will share this tiny doocot of a room in here, under the roof – and no doubt will fill it with laughter and sunshine! For Jean never stops laughing, the chucklehead.' Her expression changed, as she turned directly to David. She laid a hand on his arm. 'So you have brought her, Davy,' she said. 'You have made your sacrifice – as I knew that you would. Never fear for her, Davy dear – we shall watch over your precious one.'

'That is my prayer,' the man said heavily. 'I require it of you, Marie, by all that you hold true and dear.'

'Yes. So be it.'

'You will send me word immediately should anything threaten her? Anything, or anybody. You understand?'

'I do. And I will, Davy.'

Mary came and clasped him, laying her dark head against his broad chest. 'Why do you fear for me so, Father?' she chided, but gently. 'Think you that I am so weak? Or so simple? Or very foolish? Or that I cannot think for myself?'

'No,' he jerked. 'None of these. But you are a woman, young and very desirable. Men, many men, will desire you. Will take you if they can. By any means, lass – any means.

And at this Court means are not awanting, examples evil, and consciences dead. Dead, do you hear? You must be ever on your guard.'

'That I will, Father – I will.' Mary smiled then, faintly. 'But so, I think, should be some of the men you name, perhaps!'

Laughing, Marie threw an arm around each of them. 'And that is the truest word spoken this afternoon, I vow!' she cried. 'Lord – I know one who already walks but warily where this wench is concerned! One, Patrick, Master of Gray!'

'Aye. May he continue to do so, then – or he will have me to deal with!' his half-brother declared, unsmiling still. 'Where is he, Marie?'

'Closeted with the English envoy. Across the yard yonder. As so often he is.'

'M'mmm. With Bowes? I see. Then you will give him my message, Marie. He will know that I mean it.'

'You will not wait, Davy? Stay with us? Even for this one night . . . ?'

'No. You forget perhaps, my lady, I am a servant and no lordling. My lord of Gray's servant. My time is not my own. My lord does not so much as know that we are here. He would never have permitted this – and it may be that he is right. I must be back to Castle Huntly this night – or Mariota will suffer his spleen . . . '

'Very well, Davy.'

They went down and out of the pend with him, to bid him farewell and watch him ride off with Mary's garron led behind, a sober, unsmiling, formidable man whose level grey eyes nevertheless gave the lie to most of what he appeared to be. There were tears in the Lady Marie's own eyes as she watched him go. Mary Gray's were not so swimming that they did not note the fact.

Coming down the narrow vennel from the street were three gallants escorting on foot a young woman whose high-pitched uninhibited laughter came before them to rival the pealing bells. One was but a youth, one a young man, and the third somewhat older; all were over-dressed. David's two horses, in that narrow way, inevitably forced them, from walking four abreast, to leave the crown of the causeway for the guttered

121

side of it, choked with the filth of house, stable and midden. Whereupon the two younger men shook their fists at the rider, cursing loudly, but the older took the opportunity to sweep up the lady in his velvet arms and carry her onwards – albeit staggering not a little, for she was no feather-light piece. Moreover neither his pathfinding nor his respiration was aided by the fact that he likewise took the opportunity to bury his face deep in the markedly open bosom of his burden's gown, so conveniently close. Whereupon the laughter pealed out higher than ever.

Davy Gray rode on without a backward glance.

Breathless and stumbling, the gallant precipitately deposited his heaving, wriggling load almost on top of the Lady Marie, and would have fallen had he not had the girl to hold him up. He sought to bow, but the effort was ruined by the eruption of a deep and involuntary belch; whereupon his charge thumped him heartily on the back, all but flooring him once more. The vennel rang with mirth.

'This, my dear, is my young sister Jean,' Marie informed, unruffled. 'Did I not tell you that she had an empty head but excellent lungs? Of these gentlemen, this, who is old enough to know better, is Patrick Leslie, the Commendator-Abbot of Lindores. The child there is my lord of Cassillis my nephew, and far yet from years of discretion. Who the other may be, I do not know – but he does not keep the best of company!'

'That is Archie, Marie,' the Lady Jean Stewart announced, giggling. 'Archie Somebody-or-Other. Very hot and strong! Like me!' She was a tall, well-made young woman, high-coloured, high-breasted, high-tongued, bold alike of eye and figure and manner, dressed somewhat gaudily in the height of fashion – an unlikely sister for the poised and calmly beautiful Marie. 'Who have we here?' She was staring now at Mary. As indeed were her three escorts.

'Somebody whom you are going to love, I think, Jeannie. Mary Gray.'

Mary sketched a tiny curtsy, and smiled. 'My lady.'

Impulsively the Lady Jean went up to her and threw her arms around her. 'Lord – how like him you are!' she exclaimed. 'You are lovely. I am crazed over him – so I shall be crazed over you, I swear!'

'Gray . . . ?' Leslie jerked. 'This, then, is . . . ?'

'Someone for such as you to meet only when you are sober, my lord Abbot!' Marie declared firmly. 'Be gone, gentlemen.' And, turning Mary around, with an arm about her shoulder, she led her forthwith back through the dark pend. Jean Stewart followed, laughing, leaving the three men gazing after them, distinctly at a loss.

Patrick Gray, roused by all the laughter and shouting, came out of another little house in the yard as they crossed the cobblestones, a tall bland-faced and richly-dressed gentleman at his side. Mary restrained her impulse to run into his arms, and dipped low instead to the gentleman, before searching Patrick's face from warmly luminous dark eyes.

The Master of Gray, who had been starting forward, like-wise restrained himself, actually biting his lip. Which was not his wont, for seldom indeed did that man require to amend or adjust his attitude, his comportment. Marie perceived it, with something like wonder.

'My dear,' he began, and paused. 'I . . . this is my brother's child. My half-brother, Mr Bowes. Mary Gray. Of whom I have told you. Come to Court. Mary – Mr Robert Bowes, Her Grace of England's envoy.'

'Ah? So! I congratulate you. Congratulate you both!' The tall suave man bowed, his smooth pale face unsmiling. Mary, meeting his glance, decided that his eyes were both cold and shrewd, and that she did not like him. 'Master Davy we know. And the Bishop of St Boswells we know likewise. His grand-daughter, I think?'

Patrick raised one eyebrow. 'You are well-informed, sir,' he observed lightly.

'As you say,' the other acceded. 'And as is necessary.'

'I believe that the Bishop of St Boswells would scarce thank you, sir, to remind him of the fact,' Mary said, without emphasis but seriously. 'Nor would such as I think to disagree with him.'

Patrick drew a quick hand down over his mouth, as his eyes gleamed. Lady Marie smiled, and her sister whinnied laughter.

'Indeed!' Mr Bowes said. 'Ummm . . . ah . . . is that so?'

Demurely Mary moved over to the Master's side, and rising

on tip-toe, kissed his cheek. 'I hope that I see you well, Uncle Patrick?' she asked.

The man tossed discretion overboard, swept an arm around her slender waist, and lifted her off her feet to kiss her roundly. 'Bless you, Mary lass – you see me vastly the better for the sight of you! Mr Bowes, I pray, will excuse us?' And nodding to the envoy, he reached out for Marie's arm also, and led them all over to their own little house.

Queen Elizabeth's representative looked after them thoughtfully.

All Falkland, it seemed, had been talking of the masque for days. Other intriguing matters occupied busy tongues of course – the King's unaccountable leniency towards the Brig o' Dee rebels, Huntly in especial, allied to his notable harshness towards my Lord of Bothwell; the rumours that Huntly was indeed a convert to Protestantism; the highly indiscreet behaviour of the young Countess of Atholl. The masque, however, maintained pride of place. It was being devised and was to be staged by the Master of Gray – and undoubtedly nothing like it had been seen in Scotland since those spectacular days of nearly ten years before when Esmé Stuart of Lennox Duke Ludovick's father, and the young Patrick, had ruled the land in the name of the boy King James. Details were being kept a close secret, but it was known that, weather permitting, it was to be held out-of-doors on the night of the ninth, and that outrageous requests had been made to shocked Reformed divines to pray that it did not rain. Who was paying for it all was a matter for much speculation – for the Master himself, having been stripped of all his properties at his trial, was known to be in dire financial straits, and the King certainly was much too fond of gold to waste any of it on such nonsense.

Mary Gray's arrival only the day previous would not have precluded Patrick from inserting her conspicuously into the scene somehow, had not Marie put her foot down firmly, declaring that, knowing her husband, this affair was unlikely to be a suitable launching into Court life for the girl, and that also, any so early thrusting of her into prominence might seem ostentatious and unseemly. Reluctantly he bowed to his wife.

In another matter he was adamant, however. Mary should

be dressed as she merited – or he was not the Master of the King's Wardrobe! One glance at the girl's best gown, extracted from her bundle, assured the need of his services, however gentle he was towards her susceptibilities in the matter, and however hard he was on the Lady Jean for her shrieks of laughter at the thought of anything so simple and plain being worn at Court. So, since time was short and the royal wardrobe not yet geared to the proper provision of clothing for women, the King's tailors and sempstresses were brought over to the falconer's house to adapt and cut down one of Marie's own dresses. Mary was almost overwhelmed by the situation – but not sufficiently to prevent her from selecting quite the least elaborate and unaffected of the choice before her, a creation of pale primrose satin, closely moulded as to bodice, with little or no padding on shoulders and sleeves, a high upstanding collar rimmed with tiny seed-pearls to frame the face, and skirts billowing out from padded hips, slit to reveal an under-skirt of old rose. Marie recognised the unerring instinct and taste, however much her sister might decry this as feeble and exclaim over more ambitious confections. The neckline provoked a further clash, Mary being quietly insistent that it was much too low for her, an attitude which both Jean and the dressmakers declared to be patently quite ridiculous in that bosoms were being bared ever more notably each season – and this gown was fully three years old. No prude, Mary neverthe-less maintained her stand, hinting that a little mystery at her age could be quite as effective as any major display, especially if display was otherwise the order of the night. Jean eyed her more thoughtfully, then. A yoke of openwork, diaphanous lace was therefore contrived, which had the desired effect, by no means hiding altogether the shadowed cleft of firm young breasts while at the same time intimating a suitable modesty – and which Jean cheerfully pointed out could conveniently be whisked out and discarded when the evening really got into its stride.

Marie smiled her slow smile from the background.

The evening sky was cloudy but, since rain withheld, Patrick declared this to be all to the good, providing a more effective dusk to screen preliminary activities and better to show off the fireworks. Patrick took a vociferous Jean away with him early, in noisy company. Mary, in due course, with Marie, found herself being escorted over to the palace gardens by the English ambassador and one of his gentlemen, Mr Thomas Fowler, a broadly-built Yorkshireman whose small round eyes lit up at the sight of the girl and who, while conversing with her politely enough in his strangely broad-vowelled lazy voice, almost seemed to devour her nevertheless with his busy unflagging gaze. Mr Bowes himself did not prevent his own glance from sliding very frequently in Mary's direction, the Lady Marie noted. The young woman's combination of modest discretion, youthful eagerness and calm assurance was as singularly engaging as it was unusual. She made no enquiries about the Duke of Lennox.

The gardens presented a kaleidoscopic and animated scene that set Mary actually clapping her hands, to the amusement of her companions. The shrubberies and fruit trees were hung with myriads of coloured lanterns of every hue and size and shape, and a double row of hundreds of pitch-pine torches blazed right down a long arboured rose-walk that led from the great gates directly to the lochside. Up and down this weirdly illuminated avenue, as well as on the grass and amongst the trees, the gaily-dressed crowd sauntered and eddied, presenting an ever-changing chequer-board of light and shadow, of pattern and colour and movement. Shining fabrics, gleaming bare shoulders, glittering jewels, and the motion of long silken hose, swaying skirts and glinting sword-scabbards, made a fairyland scene. Two great bonfires flamed at either end of the balustraded terrace between the long north front of the grey palace and the loch, casting ruddy leaping reflections on the dark water. Music drifted from hidden groups of instrumentalists near and far.

Mary, wide-eyed, seeking to miss nothing, yet careful to heed her escort's rather difficult conversation and suitably to greet those to whom the Lady Marie presented her, moved down to the loch, a broad shallow expanse of water, reed-fringed and dotted with many little islets. Here were tables laden with cold meats, cakes, sweets and fruits and flagons of wine and spirits – from which a pack of the royal wolf- and deer-hounds, as well as lesser dogs, were already being fended off by anxious servitors.

A fanfare of trumpets announced the King's arrival on the scene. James, clad in an extraordinary superfluity of velvets, fur, ostrich-feathers, gold-lace, filigree-work and jewellery, came down the steps from the palace, preceded by his own torch-bearers and heralds and followed by his great nobles, high clergy and ministers of state. Lolling his head in all directions, he waved an apple that he was munching towards sundry of the bowing and curtsying guests, but paused for none. Straight down across the grass to a sort of roundel or bastion of the lower terrace he hurried, throwing excited gabbled and unintelligible remarks over his grotesquely padded shoulders to his almost running retinue. At the roundel he gave his apple to the red and perspiring Earl of Orkney, his uncle and Marie's father, grasped a torch from one of the bearers, and promptly applied it to a large and ornamental rocket erected there especially on a wooden stand. Distressingly, in his trembling haste, James knocked the fire-work off its stand as he lit its fuse. Fumbling, he stooped to right it, thought better of it, and agitatedly signed to the torch-bearer to do so instead. That unfortunate hesitated in some alarm, but at his monarch's imperious urgings, gingerly picked up the spitting spluttering object, holding it at arm's length, to return it to its stand. Unhappily he held it fuse upwards, and thrust it thus on to the stand, leaping back therefrom immediately as though scalded. But even as James, voice rising in a squeak, pointed out the error, with a sudden whoosh the fuse ignited the charge and the thing went off. Sadly, of course, it went downwards, not upwards. It struck the paving of the roundel in a shower of sparks, and proceeded to dart and whizz and zig-zag furiously, unpredictably, like an angry and gigantic hornet, amongst the royal, noble and ecclesiastical feet, with notable effect. King James danced this way and that, cannoning into his supporters, seeking to get out of the way and the range of the erratic missile. Inevitably his entourage blocked the way of escape from the roundel – though not for long. Yelling with fright the King cursed them, and in as wholehearted and unanimous retiral as had been seen since the Rout of Solway Moss the flower of Scotland scrambled and scampered out from that corner of the terrace, stumbling over one another, leaping the fallen, some actually throwing

127

themselves over the balustrade, more than one landing in the shallows below with a splash. Fireworks were as yet something of an unknown quantity in Scotland, and this rocket a large one – indeed the signal rocket for the entire masque. The monarch and the torch-bearer vied with one another to be second-last or better still, out of that distressingly confined space, and had only partly achieved this object when the unpleasant pyrotechnic blew up with a loud bang, exploding a galaxy of coloured stars about the heads and shoulders and persons of the royal retinue. King Jamie's screech could be heard shrilling above the uproar, mingled with the yelping of one of the shaggy wolf-hounds which somehow had got a proportion of the burning phosphorus embedded in its coat, and went bellowing through the gilded throng into the night.

The noise was quite phenomenal, what with the shouts of the fleeing, the cursing, the plethora of commands, pleas and invocations, the baying of hounds and the vast and unseemly mirth of the scores not actually involved – in which, it is to be feared, Mary Gray's girlish laughter pealed high and clear.

Higher and clearer still, however, above all the babel and confusion below, rose the pure and silvery note of a single trumpet, turning some eyes at least upwards towards the topmost lofty parapet of the palace's flag-tower. Here a cluster of lanterns had been lit to illuminate the royal standard on its staff, and beneath it, standing balanced on the crenellated paparet itself, an extraordinary partially-robed figure, luminously painted, with gleaming helmet sporting wings, a staff with an entwined serpent in one hand and a voice-trumpet in the other, notably large white wings also sprouting from bare heels. This apparition, through the speaking trumpet, announced in high-flown terms to all mere mortals there below that he was Hermes or Mercury, messenger of the gods, and that to their unworthy earth-bound eyes would presently be revealed the fairest and greatest of all the heavenly host, Zeus himself, in search of love. Another ululant trumpet-note, and the vision pointed outwards, lochwards, commandingly, and thereupon faded into the darkness as his lights went out.

It is to be feared that less than the fullest of attention was paid to this supernatural manifestation, in the circumstances.

Indeed no great proportion of the company was able to hear what was said on account of the noise below, where a more terrestial potentate was providing his own commentary, and earls, lords, bishops and dogs were in loud process of reinstating themselves in their own estimation. Even amongst those who received the announcement from on high, it produced only a mixed reception, guesses at the identity of Hermes vying with the loud assertions of a dark-clad divine near the English ambassador's party that this was shameful, a work of the Devil, sheerest paganism if not what worse, popery.

In consequence, no very large proportion of the assemblage at first perceived the dramatic developments proceeding a little way out on the loch. Hidden lights came on, one by one, amongst the many islets about one hundred yards out, lighting up the dark water; and out from behind a long and artificial screen of reeds and osiers and willow-wands there floated a silver galley rowed by hidden oarsmen, ablaze with lights. On a raised daïs at the stern stood a tall slender woman, rhythmic-all brushing her long fair hair. It did not take a great many moments, thereafter, for this lady to draw most of the inattentive and preoccupied eyes in the sloping gardens in her own direction, for she was entirely naked, apart from a silver mask over her eyes, her body glowing greenish-white with luminous paint – although certain prominences were picked out in scarlet. Crouching at her feet but otherwise unclothed likewise save for masks, were three maidens, who stretched up willowy waving white arms towards their principal in adoration.

Music swelled from the islands as the silver galley moved slowly in towards the watching throng.

A great gasp swept the company, and out of it everywhere voices arose in wonder, admiration, speculation and condemnation. There was a notable surge down to the actual waterside, to shorten the distance between viewers and spectacle. The Kirk raised an almost unanimous shout of righteous indignation. King James sufficiently forgot recent misfortunes to call 'Bonny! Bonny!' out across the water in a cracked high-pitched voice. Everywhere men and women were disputing as to the probable name of the lady with the hair-brush. Mary, clasping her hands together, gazed raptly, almost forgetting to breathe. Nearby a group of men were loudly asserting that they could identify at least two of the masked maidens, offering detailed reasons for their beliefs, the Abbot-Commendator of Lindores being particularly vehement that he would recognise the high globe-like breasts of Jean Stewart of Orkney anywhere and in any light.

Another trumpet note from aloft presaged the announcement that Leda, Queen of Sparta and daughter to King Thestios of Aetolia approached. As a revelation this scarcely satisfied most of the company. The ladies present, at least, managed on the whole to withdraw their gaze in order to scan their neighbours to see, if they might, who was missing.

Then, as another and more orthodox rocket soared skywards from one of the islets, a great clashing of cymbals rang out, followed by much-enhanced musical accompaniment suddenly loud and martial, seeming to fill the night – not all of it immediately in time and key. And from behind every islet and the screen of greenery burst forth brilliant cascades of scintillating light, streams of blazing darts, fans of soaring sparks, shooting stars, flaring fizgigs that burst on high to send down showers of shimmering tinsel. Loud explosions succeeded, with lightning flashes, to drown the music and shake the very ground. On and on went this dazzling percussive display, to the amazement and delight of the watching crowd. Or perhaps, not quite all of it, for though the head-shakings of the divines could be taken for granted, Mary at least heard still another reaction. Just behind her, Mr. Bowes muttered to Mr. Fowler that this was altogether too much, that they might have known that the fellow would overdo it, and did he think that silver crowns grew on trees? To which Mr. Fowler replied something that Mary did not catch save for the last broad phrase to the effect that Sir Francis might not scan the account too close so long as the goods were delivered in good shape.

Mary neither turned round nor showed signs of listening.

As the bangings and thunderings mounted to a crescendo, quite battering the ear-drums and overwhelming all other sound, they were abruptly stopped short, cut away, finished quite; the sparkling, spraying fireworks also. And into the throbbing, almost painful, silence that followed, thin strains of sweet and gentle music gradually filtered. Out from the suddenly silent and darkened islands sailed into view a great swan, calm, tranquil, immaculate. The sigh that ran through the waiting gathering was as though a breeze stirred a forest.

The swan, lifelike, white as snow, graceful, with noble wings part-raised and arching, glowed with lights without and within. It might be perhaps five times life-size and appeared indeed to be coated with gleaming real feathers. Slowly, serenely, it came sailing shorewards, towards the waiting galley, its propulsion invisible, a mystery. The lady on the daïs turned to watch its approach, stilling her brushing, the maidens likewise. These were no more than thirty yards from the shore now, and receiving their mede of admiration, some gallants being actually up to their knees in the water the better to show their appreciation.

As the swan, unhurried, came up to the silver galley, the trumpet sounded once more, and Hermes announced his father Zeus, Ruler of the Heavens, Giver of Laws, Dispenser of Good and Evil, and Source of all Fertility. Up from between the arching white wings rose a glowing male figure, perfectly proportioned, poised, naked also save for a golden fig-leaf and a celestial pointed crown. Hair was lacquered silver to mould the head as in a smooth gleaming cap; at the groin too hair was silvered, otherwise body and face were clean-shaven. In one hand he held the dumbell-like symbol of the thunderbolt. No mask hid these beautiful, smiling and confident features. Patrick Gray was ever his own mask.

As the cymbals clashed again, Zeus leapt lightly from the swan up on to the daïs of the galley. Low he bowed to Leda, who drew back, while the arms of the kneeling damsels waved in undulations about them both. Then, as the music sank to a low, rhythmic and seductive melody, the man commenced an extraordinary dance sequence. With but a few feet of platform on which to perform, he moved and twisted and insinuated himself amongst the white shrinking bodies of the women, at once suppliant and masterful, coaxing, pleading yet assured. Sinuously, gracefully determined, fluid in movement but wholly masculine, he postured and spun and circled, in sheerest desire, yet in perfect tune with the tempo and mood of the languorous melody. The maidens' fluttering, waving arms reached up and out to him, seeking to draw him away, to protect their mistress, stroking at his legs and thighs and belly

131

in part-restraint, part-caress; but he would have none of them, spurning their silent urgings, his very body eloquently flicking away their anxious lingering fingers, concentrating all his frank and potent manhood on the more mature fullness of the tall, fair Leda.

One by one the younger women sank down level with the rush-strewn platform in defeat and rejection, throwing the central figures, pursued and pursuing, into high relief. And now the tenor and tone of the dance subtly altered. Pleading faded from the man's gestures, and command began to reinforce his coaxing. He was smiling brilliantly now, and every so often his fingers lighted on and loitered over the smooth flesh that no longer shrank from him. For the woman was cold no longer, but turning to him, commenced to respond to his vehement though still courtly advances. Quickly the movements of both grew more sensuously desirous, more blatantly lustful, above the bare backs of the low-bent girls, as the beat of the music mounted hotly. Tension could be sensed growing avidly amongst the watching company.

With every motion of man and woman working up to a controlled frenzy, the climax came suddenly. Holding up the golden thunderbolt that he had made play with suggestively throughout, Zeus twirled it in triumphant signal, pulling Leda to him by a hand on her swelling hips. Then he tossed the thunderbolt high, away from him, so that it fell with a splash into the water. The cymbals clanged and throbbed, and, a little belatedly presumably, firecrackers exploded their dutiful thunder. A cloud of pink smoke rose from the body of the galley, to envelope the daïs, billowing and rolling, while the throng peered and fretted impatiently. When it cleared at last, it was to reveal the three damsels sailing away in the swan, waving swan-like white arms in mocking salute and farewell, while on the galley the two principals were posed in close and striking embrace, the woman bent backwards, hair hanging loose, bosom upthrust, the man leaning over her, lips fused to hers, one hand cupping a full breast, the other holding aloft her mask. Despite its felicity, it must have been a difficult pose to maintain.

Loud and long sounded the applause, tribute and exclamation – with a certain amount of rueful complaint that Zeus's head still enfuriatingly prevented the face of Leda from being seen and identified.

In a final fanfare of trumpets, all the lights were extinguished somewhat raggedly, and the two luminous-painted bodies now glowed ghostly and indistinct. There came a woman's breathless squeal from the galley, and then the clear mocking note of the Master of Gray's silvery laughter floated out across the dark water.

Not a few eyes turned thereafter to look at the Lady Marie, Mistress of Gray.

She was smiling, and offering Mary a sweetmeat.

The great voice of Master Andrew Melville, Kirk leader and Principal of St. Andrews University, could be heard declaiming to the King that these last ill sounds were the most lascivious and ungodly of all the disgraceful display – to which James answered obscurely in what was thought to be Latin.

Torches now sprang into ruddy flame on the galley, and it was seen to be rowing directly towards the land. Its high curving prow grounded on the reedy shore, and hitherto unseen oarsmen, mighty ordinary-seeming, jumped out into the shallows to run out a wide plank as gangway from the daïs to the beach. Down this, hand in hand, and bowing, smiling, strolled Patrick Gray and the still unclothed lady – the latter, however, once again safely masked, indeed with a veil over her face also.

There was a near-riot as spectators hurried close, shouting questions, comment, witticisms, demanding the lady's name, making shrewd suggestions – all manner of suggestions. Only the torch-bearers and oarsmen kept a way open for the couple, less than gently, reinforced by Patrick's own laughing requests that they make passage to the King's Grace. Sauntering unblushingly, unashamedly forward, the pair made barefoot, and bare all else, across the grass to where James stood doubtfully, plucking at his lower lip.

'Och, Patrick – this is . . . this is . . . och, man, man!' His Majesty faltered, his darting glance afraid to linger on the lady's charms at such close range.

'This, Highness, is Queen tonight from another age and sphere and clime. Spartan indeed, as you will perceive – though thank the good God it is a warm night! Eh, my dear?'

133

'Sire!' boomed Master Melville. 'You canna tolerate this. This scandal. You'll no' give your countenance further to this disgraceful ploy, sir? This . . . this shameless strumpet!'

'The Lady Leda has naught to be ashamed of . . . that I can see!' Patrick rejoined lightly, but ignoring the divine. 'Can Your Grace discern any imperfection?'

'Eh . . . ? Na, na. Och – no' me, Patrick. Be no' so sore, Master Melville. Other days, other ways, mind. 'Tis but a dramaturgy, see you – a guizardry, no more. And a bonny one, you'll no' deny. Aye, wi' a right notable exode. Erudite, Patrick – most erudite. A credit to your scholarship, man. I'll say that.' James tapped Patrick's bare arm. '*Vita sine litteris mors est*, eh? Aye, and *hinc lucem et pocula sacra!*'

'Precisely, Sire. Therefore, *vivat Rex! Fama semper vivat!*'

Delighted, James chuckled and nodded. 'Ooh, aye. Just so. *Vivat regina*, likewise!' He glanced more boldly at the lady, in high good humour now. James dearly loved Latin tags, and much approved of those who would exchange them with him. 'So we'll hope that she'll no' catch her death o' cold, man. Do I . . . do I ken the lady?'

'Not so closely as I would wish, Sire!' Leda answered for herself, giggling behind a hand raised to lips to disguise her voice.

'Hech, hech!' James whinnied, reached out a hand, thought better of it, and coughed. 'Aye. Well. I'ph'mm.'

'I have a notion, Sire, 'tis the Countess of Atholl,' the Earl of Mar suggested, at the King's side. 'I wonder if her lord is sober enough to know? Where is he?'

'I think not. The hair is unlike. So is . . . so is . . . I would suggest the Lady Yester,' Lord Lindsay put in.

'Na, na, man,' Orkney objected, chuckling fatly. 'The Lady Yester's borne bairns, and this quean hasna, I'm thinking. I jalouse the Lady Borthwick.'

'Gentlemen, gentlemen!' Patrick intervened, but easily. 'How undiscerning you are! And how ungallant! Do none of you respect a lady's, h'm, privacy? Master Melville, here, I swear, is better disposed. Indeed he will be eager to assist, I think! May I borrow your cloak, sir?' Without waiting for permission, Patrick twitched off the good dark woollen cloak that the Principal wore over his sober habit, and flung it around the gleaming shoulders of the lady in almost the one graceful movement. 'Off with you, sweeting!' he said, and patted her bottom with genial authority.

As Principal Melville spluttered and protested, Leda dipped a brief curtsy to the King, kicked an impudent wave at the noble lords, and turning, ran off towards the palace in tinkling laughter, the clerical cloak flapping around her white limbs and seeming to make her distinctly more indecent than heretofore. Quite a pack of eager gentlemen ran after her.

'*Vera incessu patuit dea!*' Patrick murmured.

'Ho! Ha!' James guffawed. 'Apt! Right apt, 'fore God! Man, Patrick – it has been a notable ploy. Aye, and I'm . . . we are much diverted. We thank you. Your wit's none blunted, I warrant.'

'Your Grace is gracious . . . '

At the King's elbow Orkney spoke, low-voiced. 'It's a wit we could well do with on the Council, Jamie,' he said. 'We're no' that well founded in wit, yonder, I'm thinking!'

Mar overheard, and frowned, glancing at Lindsay and Glencairn. 'Your Grace . . . ' he began, but James overbore him.

'Aye , my lord – you are right. I was thinking the same. Certes, you are right. Patrick – we will have you on our Council again. Aye, we will. We'll welcome your advices there – eh, my lords? We ha' missed our Patrick's nimble wits and nimble tongue, to be sure. You are commanded, Master o' Gray, to attend our Privy Council henceforth, as before.'

'Your Grace is good – most generous. And I all unworthy . . . '

'Aye. Well. I'ph'mmm. Now – as to yon guizardry, Patrick. Wasna Leda mother to Castor and Pollux? Aye, and Helen. The fair Helen. You could ha' shown us these man. Another time, maybe – aye, another time. And I am wishful to see the swan. It was bonny . . . '

Presently the Master of Gray came strolling through the company that now concentrated largely on the laden tables, still naked save for his fig-leaf, but totally unconcerned. His progress was slow, for practically all the women present seemed intent on speech with him – whatever might be the reaction of their menfolk. His passage was accompanied, indeed, by an almost continuous series of shrieks, squeals and giggles, a situation which by no means appeared to embarrass him.

Almost breathless, he arrived at last at the little group which contained his wife and Mary, composing his laughing features to gravity, and carefully straightening both crown and fig-leaf with a flourish. 'Lord,' he exclaimed, 'never have I had to carry such weight of affection and esteem! Never to receive so many kisses and, h'm, even warmer tokens of enthusiasm, in so short a space! 'Pon my soul, I had no notion how many fair aspirants there were for the part of Leda!'

'No doubt but you will take note . . . for the future?' Marie observed gently.

'Exactly, my dear.'

'You were very adequate, Patrick. As always you are in such matters.'

'My thanks, heart of my heart.'

'But it would be a pity if you were to contract a chill in your exposed parts, would it not? Or to discommode or distress Mary here.'

'M'mmm.' Patrick turned to the girl – indeed his glance had all along tended to slide to her face. 'You . . . you were not outraged, my dear? Offended?'

'No,' she assured him simply. 'Should I have been? You are very beautiful so. I like you lacking your beard. But you should have stayed on your boat, Uncle Patrick.'

'Indeed?'

'Yes. You were king there, were you not? Here you are but a spectacle.'

Almost audibly the man swallowed, and Marie raised a handkerchief to her face. 'You . . . think so!' he got out.

'If your boat had come to the shore and waited, instead of you coming to King James, he would have come to you. On the boat. And all others after him. To touch you and be close to you both. It would have been a more fitting triumph I think. And the lady remained a queen and not become a trollop.'

'God save me!'

'Yes. Would you like a cloak, Uncle Patrick? I am sure that Mr. Fowler here would lend you his.'

'I . . . no. Not so. That will not be necessary.' The Master was clearly disconcerted. 'I thank you. I am not cold.'

'Nevertheless, Patrick, I commend Mary's advice,' Marie put in, seeking to keep her voice even and her face straight.

'Very well.' He was almost short. 'You, sir, have no complaints?' That was thrown at Mr. Bowes who stood a little back. 'Anent my procedures?'

That suave man inclined his head. 'It was featly done, sir. A notable achievement,' he said smoothly. 'Although . . . perhaps as much might have been achieved with less expenditure of costly fireworks?'

'Would you scrape . . . !' Patrick stopped, and then shrugged. 'At least it achieved its object,' he ended lightly again. 'I am restored to the Council.' And bowing sketchily to them all, he strolled away.

Bowes and Fowler exchanged glances, and drew a little way apart.

'Come, my dear – while any meats and wine remain,' Marie said, taking Mary's arm. 'You are a poppet indeed – an angel, straight from Heaven.'

'Who is Sir Francis, Aunt Marie?' the girl asked quietly, apropos of nothing.

'Eh? Sir Francis? Why, I know no Sir Francis, I think . . . save only, of course, Walsingham. Sir Francis Walsingham, Queen Elizabeth's evil Secretary of State. But he is far from here, thank God! Why, precious?'

'I but wondered.'

'So? There may be someone of that name. But . . . call me Marie, will you, my dear. I . . . I do not relish to feel so venerable.'

They had scarcely reached the now depleted tables when there was a stir, as all heads turned towards the palace once more. The occasion for this was a sound strange to hear these days in Lowland Scotland – the high wailing challenge of the bagpipes. Not a few smiling and carefree faces sobered abruptly at the strains – for little that was good was associated in Protestant and Lowland minds with that barbarous and wholly Highland instrument.

Out from a door of the palace issued first two pipers, clad in kilts and plaids of tartan, blowing lustily. Behind them came two very different-seeming gentlemen; one, large florid, proudly-striding, dressed in an extraordinary admixture of

Highland and Lowland garb, bright orange satin doublet, somewhat stained, tartan trews right down to great silver-buckled brogues, wrapped partially in a vast plaid, hung with dirks, sgian-dubhs and broadsword, sparkling with barbaric jewellery, and on his dead a bonnet with three tall upstanding eagle's feathers; the other, most ordinary-looking, small, stocky and young – Ludovick, Duke of Lennox, Lord High Chamberlain, quietly dressed for riding, and evidently not a little uncomfortable beside his huge and highly colourful companion. Six more to be presumed Highland gentlemen marched behind them, all swords, targes and tartan, and then two more pipers playing approximately the same skirling jigging tune – if that it could be called – as the first pair. Though toes could have danced to that tune, 'The Cock o' the North' as it was called, none of the company there assembled showed sign of any such inclination.

Only King James himself started forward a little, as though to go to meet the noisy newcomers, recollected himself, and stood still, grinning and mumbling.

Mary Gray, much interested, whispered in Marie's ear. 'Who is that? That very strange man with Vicky? I have never seen the like . . . '

'That is my lord of Huntly,' Marie told her. 'A sort of cousin of yours, my dear.'

'Oh! The turkey-cock!' the girl said, smiling delightedly. 'I see why Father called him that.'

George Gordon, sixteenth Chief of his name, Gudeman o' the Bog, Cock o' the North, Lord of Strathbogie, Enzie and Gight, of Badenoch and Aboyne, Lieutenant of the North, fifth Earl of Huntly and principal Catholic of the realm, came stalking down towards his King with every appearance of one monarch joining another, his great purple-red face beaming. Never did Huntly travel without at least this small court of duine-wassails and pipers, never did he make an entry other than this – even when, as now, he was theoretically being brought in ward, for high treason, from nominal imprisonment in Edinburgh Castle. Only when he was within a pace or two of James did he doff his bonnet – headgear never removed for any lesser man, nor even in church, it was said – and produced what was apparently intended as a bow.

138

'King Jamie! King Jamie!' the Gordon boomed, not awaiting the Chamberlain's official announcement. 'God bless you,
laddie! The saints preserve you! It does my auld heart good
to see you.' Huntly was no more than thirty-three, but looked
and acted as though twice that. He kissed the royal fingers,
and then closed to envelope James in a great bear's-hug,
kissing his face also. 'Man – what ha' you got on you?' he
demanded, in mock alarm. 'Mother o' God – you're puffed
and padded and stuffed so's I can scarce feel the laddie inside!
Dia – it *is* Jamie Stewart, is it no'?' He bellowed great laughter,
while all around fellow earls and lesser nobles, good Protes-
tans all, frowned and muttered.

The King tried to speak, but could by no means outdo the
bagpipes which were still performing vigorously at closest
range. Huntly would certainly not have his personal anthem,
The Cock o' the North, choked off before its due and resounding finish, so perforce all had to await, with varying expressions, until the instruments expired in choking wails.

James, strangely enough, was mildness itself, when he could
make himself heard. 'Man, George,' he protested, ' 'Tis the
latest. The peak o' fashion. Frae France. You wouldna have me
no' in the mode?' He was stroking Huntly's arm. 'Waesucks
– you've been long in coming, Geordie. I hoped I'd see you
ere this. Vicky – I told you to fetch him wi' all expedition, man
– expedition.'

'We were delayed, Sire. By Sir John. By my Lord Chancellor Maitland,' Lennox began. 'He was not for releasing my
lord, here. He said that it was ill advised.'

Huntly interrupted him. 'Precious soul of God! That
snivelling clerk! That jumped-up notary! To seek to hold me –
me, Huntly! Against your royal warrant. By the Mass, I'd ha'
choked him with his own quills if I could ha' won near him
for his guard. *Your* guard, Jamie – your Royal Guard! That
pen-scratching attorney, that . . . that . . . ' The Earl positively
swelled with indignation, like to burst.

The King patted and soothed him as he might have gentled
a favourite horse. 'Och, never heed him, Geordie – never heed
him. He's a sour man, yon. Thrawn. But able, mind. Aye, and
honest. Maitland has his points. Ooh, aye. He shouldna ha'
spoke you ill, mind. And he shouldna ha' questioned my royal

command. I'll speak a word wi' him as to that. But . . . never mind Maitland. It's good to see you, man. The pity that you missed the guizardry. The Master o' Gray's ploy. Och, it was right featly done . . . '

'No doubt, Jamie – no doubt.' Interrupting his monarch was nothing to George Gordon. 'But I *will* mind Maitland! I do mind Maitland, by the Rood! And I'll be heard, whatever! As all yon guard heard his insults! God's Body – he had his men lay hands on me! On me! Your men! The Royal Guard. For that . . . for that I'll hae my recompense! Mother o' God, I swear it . . . !'

'Och, wheesht, wheesht, man. Take it not so. It's no' . . . it's no' . . . ' James was plucking agitatedly at his slack lower lip. 'See you, Geordie – here's it. Here's your recompense, then. I appoint you Captain o' my guard. Aye – that's it. Captain o' the Royal Guard. Is that no' right apt and suitable?'

If the Earl of Huntly took his time to digest this unexpected appointment, his fellow nobles around the King did not. Almost as one man, if with many voices, they protested loudly.

'Your Grace – this is impossible! Insufferable!'

'Sire – you cannot do it! Huntly is tried and condemned for treason!'

'Damnation – this is beyond all! The man's a rebel . . . !'

'He is a Papist, Highness. You cannot put a Papist over your Royal Guard. It's no' to be considered.' That was the Earl of Mar, stepping close. The King's boyhood companion, son of the royal guardian, who had shared to less effect the alarming George Buchanan as tutor, he frequently dared to take even greater liberties with his sovereign than did his peers.

'Aye – but he's no' a Papist. No' any more, Johnnie,' James declared earnestly. 'I have converted him, mysel'. Aye. I have been at pains to bring him to see the blessed light o' the Reformed evangel. Have I no', my lord o' Huntly?'

'Ah . . . just so, Sire. Exactly, as you might say. Amen. H'rr'mmm,' the Gordon concurred, eyes upturned Heavenwards, and stroking a wispy beard.

'God save us all!' somebody requested fervently.

'A pox – here's madness!' a less pious lord declared.

'Huntly converted? Not while Hell's fire burn!' a realist maintained.

140

'Do not be misled, Your Grace,' Mar urged. 'My lord of Huntly, I think, but cozens you. He would but humour you . . .'

'Not so, Johnnie – not so. My lord wouldna deal so wi' me. We have reasoned well together. Aye, long and well. At Edinburgh Castle. He couldna confute my postulations and argument. Eh, Geordie? I am assured that he will now be as a strong tower o' defence to our godly Protestant religion. Aye.' The King cleared his throat loudly, placed one hand on Huntly's shoulder and the other raised high. He raised his voice likewise. 'Hear ye, my lords. I have fetched my lord o' Huntly here this day to declare to you his devoted adherence to the Reformed faith and to announce to you that I . . . that we are pleased to bestow on him the hand in marriage o' the Lady Henrietta Stuart, our royal ward, daughter to our former well-loved cousin Esmé, Duke o' Lennox, and sister to Duke Ludovick here present. Aye. In marriage.' James came to an abrupt end, coughed, and looked around him.

Into the silence that succeeded this announcement, pregnant and all too certainly disapproving, only one voice was raised, after a few seconds, a voice pleasantly melodious.

'How pleasant to be my lord of Huntly! How greatly to be congratulated.' The Master of Gray had returned, clothed, though with his hair still lacquered in silver. He spoke from just behind Marie and Mary – and probably only the former knew what anger and resentment was masked by those light and silky tones.

Or perhaps, not only Marie. Huntly himself turned around quickly. 'Ha – does that bird still sing?' he jerked. 'I'd ken that tongue anywhere.' He did not sound as though the knowledge gave him any satisfaction.

'The sweeter meeting for so long a parting, Cousin,' Patrick rejoined. It was the first meeting of these two since the Master's disgrace and banishment.

'Come, Patrick man,' James urged. 'Greet well my new Captain o' the Guard . . .' He was caressing the Gordon's hand.

'The King seems very loving towards my Lord Huntly,' Mary said.

'Loving is . . . accurate!' Marie returned dryly.

'Uncle Patrick, I think, was ill-pleased.'

141

'Ah – you perceived it also! He will be the less gratified.'

The Master of Gray's rearrival on the scene had drawn the Duke of Lennox's glance in their direction. Rather abruptly excusing himself from the King's immediate presence, he came hurrying.

'Mary!' he exclaimed. 'Mary Gray! You, here! I' faith, is it yourself?'

'Your eyes do not deceive you, my lord Duke,' she agreed, curtsying.

'But – here's joy! Here's wonder! When . . . ? How . . . ? I knew naught of this. Are you but new come? To Court? Your father . . . ? He allowed it? 'Fore God, you look beautiful, Mary! You look . . . you look . . . '

'Hush, Vicky!' She indicated the Lady Marie. 'Here's no way to behave, surely?'

'Ah. Your pardon, Mistress of Gray. I . . . your servant.'

'I doubt it, my lord Duke – when you cannot even serve me with a glance! Not that I blame you. You approve of Mary coming to Court? You approve of her looks? You approve of how we have dressed her? Indeed, like us, you approve altogether?'

'Yes,' he agreed, simply but vehemently. He sought to hold Mary's arm, as they stood side by side.

Gently but firmly she removed his hand. She smiled at him, however.

After a brief interval indeed with the King and Huntly, Patrick rejoined them. 'Ah, Vicky,' he said, nodding. 'My congratulations to the so happy bridegroom will scarcely extend to the bride, your unfortunate sister! And you I can scarcely congratulate on your errand to Edinburgh. If I had known . . . ' He shrugged, and took his wife and Mary by their arms. 'Come, my dears – the air further off is the sweeter, I vow!'

The Duke stolidly stuck to Mary's side. He seemed the merest boy in the presence of the other.

'This upraising of Huntly cannot but set back your plans, Patrick?' Marie said. 'As to Dunfermline. I am sorry.'

'It will make my course more difficult,' he admitted. 'James has kept it all devilish secret. He had need to, of course. If the Council had known, it would never have been permitted.

Had Maitland known in advance, Huntly would have been found dead in his quarters in Edinburgh Castle, I have no doubt! But . . . Captain of the Guard! It is a shrewd move. Now Huntly can surround himself with armed men, here in the Lowlands, as he does in the North. Until he is unseated from that position, Maitland cannot reach him.'

'Until . . . ? Who can unseat him, Patrick?'

'The Council can. And no doubt will, in due course. No Papist may hold any office of authority under the Crown save by the Council's permission.'

'But he has professed the Protestant faith. Did you not hear? The King says that he has converted him!'

'That, my dear, can be satisfactorily controverted, I think.' Patrick produced his sweetest smile. 'Matters of religion should not be turned into a jest, should they? Have you not said as much frequently, my love?'

His wife looked at him thoughtfully. Then she inclined her fair head in the direction of Lennox. 'Ought you not to be more discreet, Patrick?' she suggested calmly.

'Vicky? Lord, Vicky's all right. He is no more overjoyed at his sister being given to Huntly than am I, I warrant?'

'I was not asked,' the Duke agreed, frowning. 'James told me only to bring Huntly here.'

'And was the Lady Henrietta asked?' Mary put in.

'I cannot think it likely,' Patrick said.

'I doubt if she has so much as met him,' Lennox added.

'That is wrong, surely,' the girl declared, very decidedly. 'She should refuse such a marriage.'

'Ha!' Patrick smiled. 'There speaks a rebel. It is not hers to refuse, my dear.'

'I would refuse to marry any man save of my own choice,' Mary said quietly.

'So you are served due warning, Patrick!' Marie observed, laughing.

'Indeed? But then, Mary lass, you are neither a duke's sister nor a king's ward.'

'For which I am well pleased.'

'I would make you a . . . a . . . ' Lennox began, and then fell silent, biting his lip.

The Master of Gray looked at him keenly. 'What would

you make of her, Vicky?' he wondered.

'Vicky would forget that he is Duke of Lennox and near heir to the throne,' Mary answered for him. 'And that I am a land-steward's daughter.' That was firmly said. And in a different tone. 'Uncle Patrick – is the King my Lord Huntly's catamite?'

Even the Master of Gray gulped at such frankness. 'Lord, child!' he gasped. 'Here's no question to ask. In especial not at this Court! Sink me, I did not know . . . I would not have believed that you possessed such a word! Knew of such things . . . '

'The Carse of Gowrie is not the Garden of Eden, Uncle Patrick – nor is Dundee the end of the world. As I think you know well.'

'M'mmm.' Patrick glanced sidelong at his wife, who pulled a comic face. They had stopped by the lochside.

'I have heard it said that the King is so inclined,' Mary went on. 'If it is true with my Lord Huntly, then I think it is your plain duty, Vicky, to preserve your sister from him. And you, Uncle Patrick, to aid him.'

'Me . . . ?'

'Yes. Surely such is the duty of all decent men?'

'You see, Patrick,' Marie said. 'As a decent man, your path is now clear. Has anyone ever before flattered you so?'

'A pox!' the Master groaned. 'What sort of a reformer have I brought to this Reformed Court?'

'I will speak with James,' Ludovick said. 'But he is not like to heed me. And . . . Hetty has to marry someone. There are worse than Huntly, I think.'

Almost pityingly she looked from one to the other. 'Poor Henrietta!' she commented.

A herald came hurrying through the throng, seeking Lennox. 'His Grace requests your presence, my lord Duke, forthwith,' he announced.

As the young man moved off, reluctantly, Mr. Bowes, who had been hanging about nearby, came close, obviously desirous of speaking to Patrick without the Duke's presence. For once his smooth brow was distinctly furrowed.

'This of Huntly, Master of Gray, is the very devil!' he declared. 'I can scarce credit it. My princess will take this but ill, sir. Huntly is . . . anathema.'

'I am sorry for that, Mr. Bowes. We can but seek to do what we may in, er, rectification.'

'You must do that indeed. And without delay,' the Englishman said sharply.

'But, of course.'

Mary Gray considered them both, grave-eyed.

Mr. Fowler came, almost running. 'Excellency,' he said to Mr. Bowes, 'the French Ambassador. He is speaking close with the King and the Duke. He has news, I vow – important news. He is most exercised.'

Others apparently had heard the same rumour and were moving in towards the group around the King. Patrick and Mr. Bowes did not linger.

James was looking distinctly upset. Plucking at his lip, he was blinking at the spider-thin but painfully elegant figure of the elderly M. de Menainville, Ambassador of His Most Christian Majesty who, gesticulating vehemently, was pouring out words. Huntly and the other lords, their differences seemingly for the moment forgotten, were gathered close, intent, their expressions various.

Lennox detached himself from the group and came over to Patrick's side, 'It is the King of France,' he announced. 'He is dead. We brought the French courier with us from Edinburgh. With a letter for de Menainville. This was the tidings.'

'Indeed,' the Master of Gray said, inclining his head.

Mr. Bowes was a deal more exclamatory. Tonight, his suavity was being sorely tested. 'Dead? Henri? My God – here's a to-do! He is . . . he was not old . . . '

'In God's gracious providence, it is the way of all flesh!' the Master observed piously.

James was raising his hand for silence. 'My lords, my lords,' he mumbled. 'I . . . we are much afflicted. Sair troubled. Our royal uncle, His Grace o' France, is dead. Aye, dead. Our ain mother's gudebrother. We . . . we much regret it. Aye, deeply. We must mourn him.' Vaguely he looked around him. 'We . . . we'll ha' to see to it, aye.'

M. de Menainville said something very rapidly in French, eyes upturned to the cloudy sky. No one else knew what com-

145

ment to make – for Henri Third of France had been a weak and treacherous nonentity, wholly under the potent thumb of his late aged tyrant of a mother, Catherine de Medici, and an unlikely subject for grief on King James's part. Yet that the King was distressed was most patent.

The Master of Gray was nowise perplexed or in doubt. 'God save King Henri the Fourth – late of Navarre!' he called out mellifluously. 'Happy France!'

'Ah. U'mmm.' James caught his eye. 'Ooh, aye,' he said.

Hurriedly the French Ambassador demonstrated diplomatic agreement in a torrent of words and gestures.

There was a vibrant silence in that garden, as all eyes turned on the Master. He had had many triumphs in his day, as well as reverses – but this was quite the most unexpected, unheralded and peculiar, and quite undeniable despite its barrenness of all advantage save to his own prestige. If James had taken his advice not so long ago, a mere few months, he would now be betrothed to the sister of the King of France – who moreover had not produced an heir in seventeen years. The cause of their monarch's distress became apparent to all.

Orkney, blunt as always, put the thoughts of many into words. 'It's no' too late to hale back the Marischal frae Denmark, is it?' he suggested.

'Aye, bring him back.'

'Put off the Danish match.'

James was gnawing his knuckles. 'I canna,' he wailed. 'It's no' possible. It's ower later, ower late. I . . . we . . . the Chancellor . . . we sent my lord o' Dingwall to Denmark six days syne. To marry the lassie. By proxy. For me. It was . . . in view o' the delay . . . we deemed it advisable . . . ' The royal voice faded away.

Only a few had been privy to the Lord Dingwall's mission. Patrick himself had learned of it only two days before.

It was Patrick, for all that, who came to the King's rescue. 'It is unfortunate,' he agreed. 'But Your Grace could scarce guess that King Henri Third would thus meet an untimely fate. The Danish precaution was entirely understandable, all must admit.'

Gratefully James looked at him. 'Aye, Patrick – that is so.

We werena to ken. But . . . you were right, man. Waesucks, you were right!'

'It so happened that way, Highness, on this occasion. Another time . . . ' The Master shrugged, and smiled kindly. He had made his point – or had it made for him – for all that mattered in Scotland to perceive. And gained doubly in virtue by his forbearance from saying 'I told you so'. Undoubtedly his credit was well restored – and his position on the Council would be the stronger.

All recognised his triumph – even though not all rejoiced in it. Only Mary Gray expressed her foolish feminine doubts a little later when the company began to move into the palace banqueting hall for the dancing.

'Uncle Patrick,' she asked seriously, at his elbow. 'Are you not glad, really, that the Princess Catherine of Navarre is not to be queen in Scotland? Old and ugly and unchaste as she is?'

He looked down at her, and said nothing.

'And you said, did you not, that the King of France met an untimely fate? I do not understand why you should have said that.'

The man's face for a moment or so went very still, expressionless. Then he raised a hand to touch and pat his lacquered silver hair. 'Did . . . did I say that Mary?' he asked, tautvoiced.

'Yes. I thought it strange, when Vicky and the King only said that he was dead. Also, you were not surprised, I think. You knew already, did you not?'

'No!' he jerked, glancing around swiftly, to ascertain that none overheard them. 'God's eyes – how should I know, girl? And, a pox – what is it to you? Fiend seize you – I'll thank you to mind your own affairs!' When she did not answer or look up, he frowned. 'I am sorry. But . . . Lord, was I a fool to bring you here?' he demanded. 'To Court?'

'You may send me away again, if you will,' she pointed out quietly.

'No doubt. But . . . do you want to go, lass?'

'No, Uncle Patrick.'

'Then' – he mustered a smile again – ' . . . then, my dear, my strange, shrewd and damned dangerous daughter – be

147

assured to remain my friend, on *my* side, will you? For I would not like you as enemy, 'fore God!'

'How could I be that?' she asked simply.

Looking patient but determined, the Duke of Lennox came up to her. 'Mary,' he requested, 'will you dance with me?'

'Why yes, Vicky – in due course. But there is no music, as yet.'

'No. But . . . ' – he waved his hand over towards a group of smirking gallants and lordlings who stood and jostled each other – 'these are speaking of you. They would dance with you. All of them. Say that you will dance with me, Mary.'

'That I will.' She laughed, and patted his hand kindly. 'I will. But not *all* the dances . . . '

Chapter Seven

THE Court moved back to Edinburgh in only a few days. This was a surprise, and much sooner than had been intended – sooner undoubtedly than the King would have wished, for James much preferred residence at Falkland or Stirling or even Linlithgow to adorning his capital city of Edinburgh. Nevertheless it was the King's own sudden decision. The Earl of Huntly was to be married, and as quickly as possible – and Edinburgh, at Holyroodhouse, was unquestionably the right and most suitable venue for a near-royal wedding.

The urgency of Huntly's nuptials was of course by no means occasioned by the usual stress of circumstance, the bride and groom scarcely being acquainted with each other. The need was pressing nevertheless, from the royal point of view. The Gordon's abrupt rise to favour was far from being accepted by the Court in general and the Kirk party in particular – the man's natural arrogance by no means assisting. Despite James's assertions, Huntly's adherence to the Protestant faith was openly scouted. He was shunned, save by sycophants, and termed a Highland barbarian – though in fact he was no true Highlander. Most serious of all, somehow Sir John Maitland got to know of the matter the very next day – which indicated that somebody had despatched a swift courier to Edinburgh that selfsame night – and he sent an immediate and strongly-worded protest to James, declaring that he would resign the chancellorship forthwith were Huntly not at least dismissed from the office of Captain of the Royal Guard.

The King, though much distressed, was stubborn. He confided in the sympathetic Master of Gray that all misunder-stood and misjudged him. His elevation of Huntly was not merely out of affection for his well-loved Geordie Gordon, but for the betterment of the realm, the ultimate bringing together of the warring Catholic and Protestant factions, and the furtherance of the true religion. Without Huntly, the other Catholic lords, Errol, Montrose, Crawford and the rest, would be leaderless. It was a serious exercise in statecraft, the mumbling monarch stressed. Patrick declared that he fully understood and concurred, but advised caution, with perhaps some temporising and dissimulation in difficult circumstances. He was even notably civil to Huntly himself. James at least was appreciative. But on one issue he was adamant; the mar-riage with the Lady Henrietta Stuart must go forward at once. A wedding, by the Reformed rites, with the King's close cousin and personal ward, would establish Huntly's position in the regime more securely than anything else. The Master, as ever, bowed to the inevitable with commendable grace.

So all repaired across the Forth to Edinburgh, and Mary Gray found herself installed in the Earl of Orkney's rag-tag and raffish establishment in the neglected east wing of the palace of Holyroodhouse which had formerly been part of the old Abbey buildings. Patrick, as Master of the Wardrobe, was to have quarters in the more modern part of the palace, but as yet these premises were not ready for him.

My lord of Orkney's household was an unusual one – and as stirring as it was singular. A family man *par excellence*, he liked to be surrounded both by his offspring and his current bedmates – and the latter were apt to be only a little less numerous than the former. This friendly and comprehensive suite demanded a deal of accommodation, for Orkney's reproductive prowess was famous, indeed phenomenal, and the thirteen legitimate progeny were as a mere drop in the bucket compared with his love-children, of whom no final count was ever possible or attempted – and only a percentage of whom could, of course, be conveniently housed in their sire's vicinity. All who could, however, lived together in approximate amity, along with a contemporary selection of lady-friends. To term these last as mistresses would be inaccurate and unsuitable; for one thing, there were too many of them – they could hardly all be mistresses; for another, seldom were any of them old enough aptly to bear such a title; moreover mistress as a designation has overtones of dignity about it, of orderly arrangement – and assuredly there was nothing either dignified or orderly about the high-spirited, boisterous and lusty Orkney household. King James therefore, was thankful to turn over this decaying, rambling and far-out extension of Holyroodhouse to his chronically impoverished uncle, to be quit of him and his entourage – and to hope that the noise of it would not unduly disturb the more respectable quarters. It was noticeable, however, by the observant, that there was a not infrequent drift eastwards by some of the respectable, of an evening, for Robert Stewart was the soul of hospitality and prepared to share all things with practically all comers. How the Lady Marie, eldest of his legitimate brood, serene, fastidious and discreet, could have issued from this nest was a mystery to all who knew her. The Lady Jean, undoubtedly, was more typical.

The Master of Gray kept his own little *ménage* as separate as was possible – and spoke to his father-in-law forcefully and to the point on the subject of Mary Gray, whose youth and loveliness made an immediate impact on the roving eyes not only of Orkney himself but of the regiment of his sons, sons-in-law and less certainly connected male dependents; though so positive and uninhibited a family-circle was not to be held at arm's length very effectively. Not that Patrick need have worried, it seemed – for Mary promptly if unassumingly adopted the entire extraordinary household as her own, apparently taking it and its peculiarities quite for granted. Clad in a sort of unconscious armour of her own, compounded of essential innocence, friendliness, self-possession and inborn authority, she was uncensorious, companionable and happy. If individuals, in the grip of liquor or other foolishness, sought

150

to take liberties, she had learned well in her native Carse of
Gowrie how to take care of herself, if in a fashion not usual
amongst Court ladies – so that, indeed, only the second day
after their arrival, the Master of Orkney, heir to his father,
perforce went about with two long red scratches down his
smiling face, and moreover enjoyed having them tended and
cosseted by the forgiving donor into the bargain.

Huntly and the Lady Henrietta Stuart were wed only a
week and a day after the return to Edinburgh, almost in
unseemly haste. The bride, a pale quiet girl of sixteen,
appeared to be entirely apathetic, and made considerably less
impression than did her train of maidenly attendants, gathered
together at short notice, including the Lady Jean Stewart and
no fewer than four other high-spirited daughters of the King's
uncle, these being conveniently to hand, and not fussy about
religious allegiance – and all, it was pointed out, by different
mothers. Mary Gray was to have been recruited for the bridal
retinue, but surprised all by her refusal, polite but firm,
unusual an honour as this represented for one in her position.
Since she did not think that the marriage was right, she
pointed out, it would ill become her to assist at it, even in the
most minor capacity. From this peculiar attitude none could
budge her, try as Patrick and Ludovick might. The fact that
she seemed to be the only person at Court so concerned,
including the Lady Hetty herself, made no difference.

Neither the ceremony itself nor the festivities thereafter
were just as the King would have wished – whatever Huntly
himself felt, who appeared to treat the entire business in a
somewhat flippant and casual manner. Lack of time for due
preparation was partly responsible, together with the fact that
the royal treasury was ever insufficiently full for all the demands upon it – and James's own wedding celebrations, due
in a month or so when his bride should have been brought
from Denmark, must not be prejudiced. Huntly himself, of
course, was rich enough, richer than his monarch undoubtedly,
but he was perhaps understandably disinclined to go to any
great expense to entertain large numbers of his enemies –
which approximately would be the position, for his own friends
were in the main far away in the north, and, being Catholics,
unlikely to desire to attend any such heretical nuptials any-

way. Moreover, the costs of a great marriage were traditionally the responsibility of the bride's family – and the Duke of Lenox lacked wealth. If the entertainment had to be on a modest scale, however, at least there was no embarrassing cold-shouldering of the occasion, no undignified paucity of guests; the King saw to that by the simple expedient of commanding the presence of the entire Court at the ceremony, rather than merely inviting it.

He was less successful over the officiating clergy, unfortunately, for the Kirk was made of stern stuff. Principal Andrew Melville of St. Andrews, the acknowledged leader of the miltant and dominant Calvinist extremists, flatly refused, in the name of his Saviour, to perform the ceremony for such a notorious former enemy of Christ's Kirk and doubtful convert, and his reverend colleagues took their cue from him, so that even Master David Lindsay, the King's favourite divine and royal chaplain, found a convenient illness to excuse him. James had to fall back on Andrew Davidson, Reformed Bishop of St. Boswells and former holy Lord Abbot of Inchaffray – who, incidentally amongst other things was Mariota Gray's father and Mary's other grandfather, completely as he ignored the relationship. This prelatical celebrant was not just what the occasion demanded, admittedly – almost any of the sternly Calvinist divines would have been better – but at least he conducted the union on approximately Protestant lines and spared the restive congregation the usual two-hours sermon thereafter. Also, his rich crimson episcopal robes made a better showing against Huntly's barbaric tartan-hung and bejewelled splendour than would have the plain black gown and stark white bands of Geneva. The King himself gave away the bride, and surprisingly, the Master of Gray appeared as principal groomsman to his far-out cousin.

The banquet thereafter was a comparatively dull and sedate affair, Huntly's unpopularity, the King's role as host, and the inferior quality of the entertainment all combining to inhibit the traditional excesses of the bridal feast. Indeed, carefree horseplay was wholly non-existent, despite one or two gallant attempts by the Orkney faction, and even the public disrobing and ceremonial bedding of the bride and groom, normal highlight of the occasion, was dispensed with – for who would dare lay hands on the fiercely proud and unpredictable Gordon chief surrounded by his Highland caterans armed to the teeth? In consequence the thing degenerated into mere steady eating and drinking, interspersed with uninspired speeches which even the Master of Gray's barbed wit only spasmodically enlivened. So humdrum and disheartening was the cumulative effect of all this that something in the nature of a spontaneous migration eventually developed at the lower end of the hall towards my Lord Orkney's quarters, where no doubt more spirited celebrations were almost bound to develop as antidote and compensation. Soon only the inner and official group around the King and Huntly remained; the women, including the heavy-eyed bride, having been got rid of, these others settled down to an evening's hard drinking, with Highland toasts and pledges innumerable.

When Patrick was able decently to withdraw, the King being noisily asleep and Huntly becoming indiscriminately pugnacious, he strolled over to his own quarters, thankful for the fresh air, to find Orkney's wing in a vastly different state. The entire range of buildings appeared to shake and quiver with life and noise, not a window unlit, the place seemingly all but bursting with active humanity. Shouts, varied music, raucous singing, screams of female laughter, and an almost continuous succession of bangs, thumps and clattering, emanated from the establishment. Patrick had difficulty in even gaining an entrance, two unidentified bodies lying in close and presumably enjoyable union just behind the door, so that he had to squeeze in and step over jumbled clothing and active white limbs even to reach the stair-foot. Thereafter his progress up to his own modest attic chambers on the third floor took on the nature of an obstacle-course, the winding turnpike stairway providing a convenient series of perches, partially screened from each other, for sundry varieties of love-making, physical self-expression, intimate argument and bibulation, up, down and through which screeching girls were being chased by the more agile-minded. Few of the doors were closed, and within, the rooms were littered with wedding garments of many of the royal guests. Giggles, gruntings, and shrieks of not too urgent protest followed him all the way upstairs, and from somewhere indeterminate the great bull-like voice of the Earl and Bishop

153

of Orkney bellowed for wine, wine – to which no one appeared to pay the least attention. The servants, it seemed, were as fully engaged as were their betters.

Patrick found his wife and Mary sitting together alone in one of their three attic rooms – although one of the others at least was patently much occupied. Marie was stitching at a tambour-frame, and the girl rolling hanks of the silken thread into balls. The baby, Andrew, slept undisturbed in his cradle. They made somehow an extraordinary picture in that setting, so entirely normal and respectable did they seem.

The man began to laugh, quietly, with real mirth. 'God save us – virtue triumphant!' he exclaimed. 'Was ever such propriety so improperly enshrined! My sweetings – how do you do it?'

'What would you have us to do, Patrick?' Marie asked.

'Lord knows,' he admitted. 'Just what you are doing, I suppose. But . . . one thing I do know – we must get out of this den if we are to have any peace this night. Your peculiar family is in fullest cry, my love. Gather together some night clothes and blankets, and we shall seek shelter elsewhere for the nonce.'

'Gladly. But where? We cannot go traipsing the streets of the town at this hour. And the palace is full to overflowing.'

'Save for one quiet corner,' her husband pointed out. 'I warrant our unpopular Lord Chancellor Maitland's quarters in the north wing are not overcrowded. They will be a haven of peace, I vow.'

'Maitland!' Marie exclaimed. 'The Chancellor? Your worst enemy . . . ?'

'Whom worthy and righteous folk would say that I should love and cherish . . . would they not?'

She ignored that. 'But the man who worked your downfall? Who clamoured for your blood . . . ?'

'The same, my dear.'

Mary spoke, without interrupting her winding. 'I overheard my lord Earl of Moray say, but yesterday, that he believed that the Master of Gray was privily seeing a deal of the Chancellor.'

'The devil you did!' The smile was wiped off Patrick's face. 'Moray? Say it to whom?'

'To Mr. Bowes, it was, Uncle Patrick.'

'A pox! I . . . I . . . ' He paused. 'You have devilish long ears, girl! You overhear too much!'

'Great lords and gentlemen think not to whisper when only such as I am near,' she pointed out, equably as frankly. 'When I do hear your name spoken, Uncle Patrick, would you have me not to listen?'

'M'mmm. Well . . . I suppose not.'

'Is it true, Patrick,' Marie asked, 'that you are secretly seeing much of Maitland?'

'What if it is?' he returned. 'In my present pass, I cannot afford to be at odds with the Chancellor of Scotland.'

'Knowing you, I suppose that I must accept that. Just as you made common cause with Queen Elizabeth, who so shamefully had betrayed you. It is Maitland that I do not understand. What can *you* offer him, I wonder, in exchange for his good offices?'

'Tush, woman – leave statecraft to those who understand it! A truce to talk of this sort.' It was not often that the man spoke thus to her. His glance shot warningly in Mary's direction. 'Gather you together the night gear and wrap up Andrew, and I shall go and apprise Maitland of your coming . . . '

'No, Patrick. You may be prepared to toady to Maitland, but I will not be beholden to the man who sought the execution of my husband . . . and who tortured Davy Gray!'

'Toady . . . ? I mislike your choice of words, Marie – by God I do! And . . . Davy, eh? Perhaps the beating of Davy weighs even heavier against Maitland in your eyes than his impeachment of me?'

'Do you choose to believe so, Patrick?' That was calm, evenly said.

He bit his lip.

'It is none so ill here,' Mary intervened quickly. 'The noise will abate presently, to be sure. Already it is quieter than it was, I think . . . '

'Yes, there is no need to move,' Marie took her up. 'None are doing us hurt here . . . '

'*You* may be well enough,' Patrick rejoined. 'To you, after all, this is nothing new. You were reared in this extraordinary household. But with Mary . . . ! I would not have this squalor even touch the hem of her skirt! What goes on in this house . . . '

'You are become exceeding nice, of a sudden, Patrick? And there are more kinds of squalor than one,' his wife pointed out. 'I make no excuse for my father's habits, for I have ever condemned them. But are there not worse ills for Mary to observe than the mere lusty sins of the flesh? Lies, intrigues, back-biting, dissembling, dishonour, treachery? Statecraft, if you prefer the word!'

The man went very white, dark eyes blazing. 'I'll thank you to be silent!' he jerked.

'Silent, yes. I have been silent for too long, perhaps, Patrick. Silence is a quality much in demand for the wife of the Master of Gray – and I do not come of a notably silent family, as you have observed! There are times when it would serve you but ill to keep silent – and I think that this is one. I know all the signs, Patrick – I have seen them so often ere this. You are about to launch some dark and underhand plot, some scheming subtle venture, in which someone will be direly hurt . . . for the benefit of the Master of Gray! Is it too late to ask that you stay your hand, Patrick? Too much to ask you to renounce it?'

'What nonsense is this? Have you taken leave of your wits, Marie, for God's sake? With an obvious effort, he controlled himself. 'See you, statecraft is none so ill a business. It cuts both ways – works much good for many as well as some small hurt for a few. The realm cannot be served without it. My life it is. I am on the Privy Council again . . . '

'The Council will hear naught of this that you are now plotting, I warrant! Or your meetings with Maitland would not be secret.'

'It is better that way. For the weal of the realm. For the King's peace.'

'The realm! The King! Oh, Patrick – who do you deceive? Not yourself, and not me. Not even Mary here, I think.'

Mary looked from one to the other gravely, hurt in her eyes. 'Do not speak to each other so,' she pleaded. 'Please do not.'

Both reacted to that, and at once. Patrick took a pace towards her, changed his mind, and turning strode to the door and out, without another word. Marie rose from her frame, and

156

came to enfold the younger woman in her arms.

'My heart, my sweet Mary!' she cried. 'Forgive me. That was unkindly done. I was foolishly carried away. I do not know what made me behave so. I am sorry!'

Mary kissed her. 'Do not fret, Lady Marie,' she said. 'All will be well. I know it. Uncle Patrick must scheme and plot. As he says truly, it is his life. And he is very good at it, is he not? He will not stop it, I think. So . . . we must just scheme and plot also. So that whenever he makes a mistake, we may perhaps right it. You and I. Is that not best?'

Marie drew back a little, to stare at the girl, wonderingly. 'Oh, Mary my dear,' she exclaimed. 'Bless you. But . . . you do not know what you say. What you propose. What goes on in Patrick's handsome head.'

'I think that I do. I am very like him, you know – very like him indeed. My father – Davy Gray – says that we come out of the same mould. It may be that the same goes on in my own head. Good and ill, both.' She smiled, warmly. 'Is it not . . . convenient?'

'Lord . . . !' the Lady Marie said, shaking her head.

James was in high good humour. The hunt had found in the boggy ground around Duddingston Loch, a mere mile over the hill from Holyroodhouse; it would have been strange had they not, perhaps, considering the pains taken by the King's foresters to ensure that there were always deer in the royal demesne, however tame and imported – and however many Edinburgh citizens with a taste for venison must hang to discourage poaching. They had killed, after an excellent chase, up on the high ridge near Craigmillar Castle to the south, James himself striking the fatal blow. Moreover, his favourite goshawk, set at a pair of mallard from the loch against Johnny Mar's bird, had flown fast and true, stooped on the drake and brought it down cleanly, whilst Mar's hawk had gone bickering off after a heron to no advantage. So the King smirked and chuckled, railing his former playmate, and declaring that his fine Geordie Gordon should have been there to witness it – for Huntly, who had set out with the rest from the palace, had unfortunately been recalled by a messenger on seemingly urgent business, and had not as yet rejoined them.

It was almost certain that no further quarry would be found, save down in the great swampy area by the loch again, for this was no hunting country in fact, far too populous an area, too near to the city, for deer to lurk save in the marshy, reedy sanctuary west of Duddingston. The head forester, therefore, advised that they return downhill, and suggested that the scrub woodland around Peffermill was the likeliest place to try, with the wind south-westerly and the easten area already disturbed. James thought it would be better further west still, at Priestfield perhaps, but the Master of Gray agreed convincingly with the forester, pointing out the much more free run that they could have from Peffermill, leaving Priestfield for even a possible third attempt. The King's good humour, plus his intemperance for the sport, allowed him to agree.

It was Mary Gray's first royal hunt, this twenty-second day of August. Only the day before, James had made official announcement that, allowing for all contrary winds and possible delays, his special emissary the Lord Dingwall, acting as his proxy, should have wedded the Princess Anne in Denmark by now, and that therefore he, James, by the Grace of God, King, could be considered to be a married man, and Scotland to have a queen. That this queen was only the second daughter of the King of small Denmark, and not the sister of the childless King of mighty France, was a pity, but must be accepted philosophically. James therefore concentrated now on the youth – she was barely fifteen – and declared pulchritude of his bride, and asserted that he was madly in love. Contemporaneously with the royal announcement had come a proclamation from the Lord Chamberlain, publishing the names of the new queen's household. The Countess of Huntly would be principal Lady-in-Waiting, and amongst others, the Lady Jean Stewart one of the Maids of Honour, and Mary Gray an extra Woman of the Bedchamber. So now Mary held an official position at Court, and should begin to take a fuller part in its activities.

With Jean, she rode between Ludovick of Lennox and Patrick, up near the front of the colourful cavalcade, and even the King, who was apt to be more impressed by male good looks than by female, remarked on her fresh young beauty, and leeringly dug an elbow in the Duke's ribs and mumbled congratulatory jocularities. It was accepted by all, undoubtedly that she was Lennox's mistress.

Down the hill through the fields towards the low-lying marshland between Craigmillar and the great towering bulk of Arthur's Seat they streamed, the head forester and his assistants first, followed by a small detachment of the royal guard, then the King and his falconers. It was in the group of lords and their ladies, immediately behind, that Mary and Jean rode, thanks to the lofty status of their escorts. Further back straggled the field of fully three-score laughing, chattering riders, no great proportion of them vitally absorbed by the hunting, but only there because it was expected of them, it was the thing to do – and since it was their monarch's passion, because those who showed no interest in it might well offend the source of privilege, position and preferment. Some, having put in an appearance, would undoubtedly take the opportunity quietly to fall behind and make their way back to the city, rather than put in some further hours of pounding about the thickets and waterlogged unpleasantness of Duddingston Myres.

From the hamlet of Peffermill a causeway led out into the great green marsh area. The normal procedure would be for the hunt to wait here, while the foresters went in to try to find and rouse a skulking stag amongst the water-meadows, and force him out to hard ground for the sportsmen to chase. But James, timorous and hesitant in almost all else, was a paladin where hunting was concerned, frequently indeed himself doing the work of his foresters. Nothing would serve now, but that he and all others who called themselves men, should plunge into the morass and beat out the place thoroughly. Sighing and shrugging, his younger nobles and some of their more spirited ladies prepared to follow on. This had happened before. The dozen or so members of the bodyguard looked depressed.

As James clattered on to the causeway, past the last of the buildings, the millhouse itself, a stout figure came hurrying out, calling and waving and panting, apron still round a wide middle – no doubt the miller himself. The King frowned impatiently, and gestured a rebuff, for this was no time for petitions and the like. The Master of Gray, however, reined up and over to the man. He exchanged a few words with him before hurrying on after the others.

'Heed nothing, Sire,' he called out. 'Just some complaint of robbers and vagrants. As ever.'

The King waved back in acknowledgment.

Where the causeway forked, perhaps a quarter-of-a-mile in, was the obvious place to spread out. The foresters shouted to that effect, and James was ordering his reluctant guard to fan out left and right, with the group of nobles still a little way behind, when the green leafy place of tall reeds, alder spinneys and drooping willows suddenly seemed to erupt in noise and men. Out from the plentiful cover, as at a given signal, poured scores of unkempt and ragged figures, yelling, brandishing swords and clubs and daggers, some mounted, some on foot. The leaders notably were dressed in tartan and wore Highland-type bonnets.

'A Gordon! A Gordon!' range out on all sides. From some-where unseen, a single piper skirled the rousing notes of *The Cock o' the North*.

All was immediate chaos amongst the hunting party. The guard was already spread out on either side, dispersed. James all but fell off his handsome black Barbary in alarm, staring wildly about him. This was of all things, indubitably, what he most dreaded, victim already of many abduction attempts. His hoarse cries were almost like those of a trapped animal.

Only a small part of the hunt cavalcade could see what was going on, owing to the windings of the causeway amongst the scrub woodlands, and its narrowness stringing out the com-pany almost indefinitely. Indeed most, having few ambitions to act as bearers in a quagmire, were deliberately hanging back. Most of the lords in the foremost group, however, after a momentary hesitation, spurred on to the aid of their monarch, tugging at their swords. Even the readiest, however, must needs follow Patrick Gray who had his sword drawn almost as soon as the attackers appeared, and dashed forward with ringing cries.

'The King! The King!' he shouted. 'Save His Grace!' And then, 'Guard! Guard! Back here! To the King! Back to the King!'

The men-at-arms who had each more or less been riding at

the nearest of the assailants, were somewhat confused by these gallant orders. Some turned back indeed, some hesitated, others pressed on. Those who came back became entangled with the hurriedly oncoming lords – for the level and firm ground of the causeway was narrow, and space for excited horses and riders circumscribed to say the least of it.

Confusion indeed reigned all around, and not only on the side of the defenders. The attackers themselves appeared to be almost as uncertain in their assault, however vigorously brandished their weapons and fierce their cries. If there was a concerted plan of action, it was not evident. Men rushed and darted, wheeled and dodged and sallied, by no means all pressing in on the King himself. The clash of steel, the thudding of blows, the high whinnying of horses, all rose to mingle with the monotonous chant of 'A Gordon! A Gordon!' and to all but drown that turbulent clan's challenging battle-anthem on the bagpipes.

One of the noblemen, at least, did not aid in the confusion. Instead of rushing forward with his elders, the Duke of Lennox reined his mount right round and came plunging back to Mary's side. There he drew sword, and so sat, his pleasant blunt features tense, jaw dourly set.

Mary, flushing, leaned over to grip his arm. 'No, no, Vicky!' she whispered. 'Not here. Up yonder – with the King. You should be with him there.' Uneasily she glanced round at the few other women, clustered together there. It was not often that Mary Gray looked embarrassed. Fear did not seem to have touched her, as yet.

'James is well enough served,' Ludovick returned. 'All run to his aid.'

'But . . .' Mary, noting that set look, did not press him. 'At least, look to these ladies. Not me only,' she urged, low-voiced.

With no very eager or gallant expression, the young man tossed a look at the small group of flustered and alarmed women. He nodded. 'Back,' he told them, gesturing along the causeway. 'Back to the others. Toward the mill.'

Most of them, with only uncertain glances forward toward their menfolk, did as they were bidden. Mary, however, sat her horse, one of the Duke's own, unmoving, gazing ahead with keenest interest rather than apprehension. Jean, after a few moments' hesitation, elected to remain with her. Lennox placed his mount between them and the trouble in front.

It was very difficult to ascertain just what was happening, so congested was the causeway up there. The King, at any rate, seemed to be safe, back amongst a tight group of his nobles, and cowering in a state of near collapse. Fighting of a sort was proceeding at a number of points, so far without any noticeable casualties. The Master of Gray undoubtedly was foremost and most militant amongst the Court party, dashing hither and thither, sword waving, shouting instructions, urgings, threats.

The royal guard, although outnumbered and dispersed, appeared to be gaining the upper hand; at least, the attackers seemed notably averse to coming to grips with them. For that matter, there was a lack of close-quarters engagement all round. The famed Highland dash and ferocity was perhaps only largely vocal, after all.

Three rough-looking individuals, swathed in tartan plaids, came yelling down the line, their very third-rate horses splashing in the reeds and surface-water at the side of the causeway. At the martial gestures of the Earl of Mar and the Lord Yester, they drew away prudently and came on towards Lennox and the girls. The Duke, frowning and a little pale, prepared to take on all three.

More huntsmen were coming up from the rear now, however, bewildered but alerted by the women who had ridden back. The trio of bullyrooks presumably decided in the circumstances that a closer approach would be inadvisable, and contented themselves with standing where they were, shaking fists and weapons and chanting their slogan. Mary, when she perceived that they were not in fact going to attack, was not so frightened as to perceive some other things also; for instance that there was no sign of blood about these warriors, even on their swords; that their voices did not sound in the least Highland; and that under their plaids their clothing seemed to be quite Lowland and ordinary.

The winding of a horn from somewhere out of sight forward sounded high above all the shouting and clash. It had an extraordinary and immediate effect on the entire scene – indeed, not even the rockets of Patrick's pageant of Leda and the Swan were more salutory in their effect. On the part of the assailants, all fighting was broken off forthwith. With a unanimity and discipline that had been somewhat lacking in their advance, the attackers obeyed what was clearly a signal to retire. Men turned about in their tracks and went plunging back into the long reeds and waterlogged thickets of the myre, mounted and foot alike splashing away promptly and whole-heartedly, heading into the cover nearest to them like so many water-rats released near their chosen habitat. If the assault had been a failure, there was no foolish reluctance about conceding the fact.

No single victim was left behind to witness to the fury of the attack.

Patrick Gray made the only gesture at pursuit. He rode a little way after one of the mounted men who elected to flee along the fork of the causeway eastward. He soon came trotting back however, sword still in hand, and actually laughing. Mary, now alerted to such things, noted that his sword was unblooded also.

He found the lords clustered round their trembling sover-eign, congratulating him on his escape, inveighing against all traitors, dastards and poltroons, and preening themselves a little on prompt and effective action. Lennox and his two ladies rode forward to rejoin the group.

'All gone, Sire,' the Master of Gray called out, sheathing his sword at last with something of a flourish . . . 'Bolted like coneys for their holes! They will not return, I swear! You are not hurt? They did not reach Your Grace?'

Although James could not yet find words to answer, the others did, volubly. Loud and long were the assertions, ques-tions, demands. Everywhere the name of Huntly was being cursed and reviled.

Patrick appeared to doubt the general assumption. 'I cannot believe that this was my lord of Huntly's work,' he said, when he could make himself heard. 'He would never so move against His Grace's royal person! 'Tis highest treason! After all the King's love for him? No, no. Moreover, Huntly surely, had he planned such wickedness, would have worked it to better effect. These, I vow, were but feeble warriors . . . '

'They were Gordons, man! Did you no' hear them, 'fore

God? Huntly's own ruffians!'

'Who else leads Gordon, but Huntly? That curst tribe!'

'Tartan savages they were! Hieland cut-throats!'

'Aye. And were they any more valiant at Brig o' Dee? They fled then, the arrogant Gordons . . . '

'My lords,' Patrick declared, waving his hand. 'It may be as you say. But let us not judge too hastily. Huntly is not here to answer for himself . . . '

'No, by God – he's no'! Where is he, then? Why turned he back . . . ?'

'Aye – where is the forsworn Papist? He knew well no' to come hunting this day!'

Patrick shrugged elegant shoulders.

The King, unspeaking, was urging his tall horse through the press now, back, southward along the causeway toward Peffermill again, head down, eyes darting. He pushed and prodded his lords, to have them out of his way, all fear, hurt and suspicion. He answered none who addressed him, met no eyes, uttered no words although his thick lips seemed to be forming them. On he urged his mount, regardless of how many he forced off the causeway into the myre. In jostling disorder the strung-out hunt turned itself around and headed whence it had come.

Somehow Patrick Gray managed to draw ahead, and as they emerged on to the firm and open ground near the mill, went cantering towards the millhouse itself, authoritatively demanding wine and sustenance for His Grace the King.

James, still trembling almost uncontrollably, allowed himself to be persuaded to dismount, and shambled into the miller's house, supported by the Master of Gray and the Earl of Mar.

Lennox was about to follow the other great lords inside, when Mary laid a hand on his arm.

'Vicky,' she said quietly. 'Your sister, the Lady Hetty. How greatly do you love her?'

'Eh . . . ? Hetty?' He shrugged, French-style. 'I know her but little. She was reared in France, with my mother, while Patrick brought me here. We are . . . not close.'

'But she *is* your sister. I believed that you owed her a duty – to save her from being wed to my Lord Huntly. But now she is his wife, for better or worse, you owe her another duty, do you not?'

Uncertainly he looked at her.

'She is Countess of Huntly, now. If ill befall her husband in this, she must suffer also.'

'If Huntly is rogue enough to misuse James and attack his King's person, he must needs pay the price, Mary. The price of treason.'

She shook her head. 'Huntly may indeed be a rogue. But this roguery, I think, is not his. Here was no treason, Vicky.' Sitting their horses side by side, she spoke close to the young man's ear. 'Could you not see it? See that it was all a plot? But not of Huntly's making. Those were no true Highland-men, no true Gordons. It was no true attack. No blood was spilt, that I saw. All were too careful for themselves. None pressed close to the King. It was but play-acting, nothing more. I am sure. To bring down Huntly.'

'M'mmm.' Ludovick rubbed his chin. 'You think it, Mary? All that? The fighting, to be sure, was but half-hearted . . .'

'Yes. So the Lady Hetty must be warned, Vicky. And Huntly also. Before . . . before his enemies have their way. Before a great injustice is done.'

'But who . . . ?'

'My Lord Huntly has many enemies. He makes them apace. But that does not merit . . . this.'

Her companion frowned. 'Nor is he any friend of mine,' he pointed out. 'And if I go now, hasten back to the city and leave James, it will be noted. When Huntly is warned, in time to flee, it will be Lennox his new gudebrother who warned him. To the King's declared hurt.'

'That is true. I had not thought of that. Yes, you must stay. I will go. Give me something of yours, Vicky, that I may show to them. Lest Huntly does not believe such as myself. Your signet-ring – that he will recognise . . .'

'Aye – take it, Mary. If you think that is best. God knows if this is wise . . .'

'It is right. Fair. Is that not enough?'

'I do not like you to go alone . . .'

'Why not? It is but a mile or two. If I cannot gain entry

to Huntly, I shall ask the Lady Marie to aid me. All know her. Tell my Uncle Patrick that I felt weary. Upset by the stramash. And went back. Go in now, Vicky – to the King.'

Mary reined her horse round, waved to Jean, and rode off eastwards.

In the crowded millhouse, James sat crouched over a rough table, gulping and spilling small ale from a pewter tankard, pale but apparently recovering. Every now and again he reached out an uncertain hand to pat the arm of the Master of Gray standing close by, whom he evidently looked upon as his saviour. So far, the name of Huntly had not crossed his lips. Those around him, however, made up for his omission. On all hands were demands for the Gordon's immediate arrest, trial, even execution. After all, he was still technically under sentence of death for treason, from the Privy Council, for the Brig o' Dee Catholic rising. The King's personal pardon had never been officially confirmed by the Council, dominated as it was by the Kirk party. Only Patrick Gray raised a voice on Huntly's behalf – which may have been partly responsible for James's obvious gratitude and trust. He was pointing out to all, that he had recognised none of the Gordon lairds in the assault, when Ludovick came in.

'I agree with the Master of Gray,' that young man announced, jerkily. 'It may be that Huntly himself had no hand in this. Only, perhaps, his enemies!'

All eyes turned on him – and none more sharply than Patrick's. A chorus of protest and derision arose from the other lords.

'There speaks a prudent and generous voice,' the Master commended.

'And the Countess o' Huntly's brother!' someone added.

Something of an uproar followed. It faded only as a newcomer pushed his way urgently into the crowded low-ceiled room, clad in the royal livery – indeed, Sir John Home, lieutenant of the King's guard.

'Sire,' he announced. 'Instant tidings from my Lord Chancellor Maitland.' He laid a folded and sealed letter before the King. 'For your immediate eye, Highness.'

James picked up the paper gingerly in shaking fingers, held it away from him as though it might carry the plague, turning it

166

this way and that. Then, the seal still unbroken, he handed it to the Master of Gray, signing for him to open and read it.

Patrick did as indicated. The letter proved to have a second paper within it. He glanced at the contents, and his fine eyebrows rose and his mouth pursed.

James peered up at him, in mute question. As did all present.

'Your Grace,' he said slowly, almost hesitantly for that confident man. 'The Chancellor has . . . has come upon a letter. This letter. Intercepted it. From Huntly. It bears his seal, see you. It is to my lord of Livingstone. At Callendar. Requiring him to muster men and arms. Secretly. To be ready to march. In the service of the Holy Catholic Church and the true and ancient faith . . . '

He got no further before his words were drowned in a flood of furious outcry, passionate, continuous, demanding. Louder and louder grew the din, so that Patrick, shrugging, laid down the papers.

As though moved by a force outside himself, James rose unsteadily to his feet, and so stood for a few moments, ill-shapen features twisted and contorted with emotion, great liquid eyes heavy with sorrow, like some dog ill-used by its master. Then he raised a hand for silence.

'My lords,' he said, 'so be it.' His voice, now that he had found it at last, was stronger, more resolute, than might have been expected. 'Sir John Home, you will take my guard and apprehend and arrest George Gordon, Earl o' Huntly, forthwith. Wherever you shall find him. To be warded secure in the Castle o' Edinburgh. On charge o' conspiracy against the safety o' our realm and royal person, in highest treason. Aye. We . . . we . . . ' The unusually firm voice broke. 'Och, to your ill duty, man – to your duty. And may the good God ha' mercy on me, his silly servant!'

In the succeeding acclaim and fierce plaudits, the King turned to the Master again. 'Take me awa', Patrick – take me awa',' he pleaded. 'I'm no' feeling that well. I'm sick, man – sick to death. I want out o' here. Frae a' these loud men.'

'Assuredly, Your Grace. At once. We shall have you back at Holyroodhouse almost before you know it.'

'Na, na – no' there, man. No' there. Geordie might raise

the town against me. There's Catholics aplenty, and other ill bodies, in Edinburgh. He'll maybe try again. I'll need a strong place. A castle. Craigmillar's near – a big, bonny, strong place. I'll to Craigmillar, Patrick – I'll be safe there. In case o' more deviltry. Aye, take me to Craigmillar.'

'As you will, Sire . . . '

It was evening before Patrick Gray returned to his lofty chambers in Orkney's wing of Holyroodhouse. He seemed to be a little bemused, abstracted in his manner, for he quite forgot to kiss, as was his usual, either his wife or Mary or the baby Andrew.

'A busy day you have had, Patrick,' Marie said pleasantly. 'Brave doings, by all accounts – and James much beholden to you, I gather. So your credit stands the higher. My brother Robert tells me that the King has taken refuge at Craigmillar. I wonder that he permits his guardian angel to leave his side thus long to visit us here!'

Thoughtfully the man considered her. 'Do I detect some displeasure here, my dear?' he wondered.

'Why, no. Should it not be pride, rather, in my husband's bold championing of his King? His heroism? All testify to your gallantry, to your . . . preparedness! It seems that, once again, Patrick, your quick wits won the day!'

He stroked his now clean-shaven chin. 'You are too kind, Marie. And you will have heard – that Huntly escaped?'

'So it is said,' she nodded. 'You will have eaten at Craigmillar? Or shall I find you some supper?'

He began to pace the attic room. 'Someone warned him. I would give much to know who it was. Home rode straight from Peffermill to Huntly's lodging here, and found them gone. I have questioned him. They had been gone only minutes. Yet scour the city as he would, he found no trace of them. Some of his Gordon lairds they took – but not Huntly or his wife. Maitland sent men hot-foot along all roads to the north – but without avail. It is believed now that they slipped down to Leith, and took boat to Fife. They will not catch Huntly now, I think.'

'And that will upset your . . . plans?'

'Plans? Is that not a strange word to use? The King's safety

is what signifies. The ship of state upset – not plans of mine.'
He shrugged. 'For myself, it is of little matter whether
Huntly escaped or no. He is forfeit now. The forfeiture papers
are already signed.'

'Indeed? So soon? They were quickly drawn up, were they
not?'

'Maitland, my love, is ever efficient! And prompt. As he
was over my own forfeiture one time!'

'And as he was, it seems, over this letter of Huntly's that
was . . . intercepted. To Livingstone, was it not? Most timely.
Was it a forgery, think you?'

Patrick grimaced. 'Indeed no, Marie. You insult the
Chancellor! Maitland is never clumsy. It bore Huntly's own
seal. I noted, however, that it was undated!'

'Ah! Then . . . then it probably was old? Written some time
ago? Intercepted some time ago? Before Brig o' Dee, perhaps?'

'I commend my wife's intelligence! Let it be a lesson to us
all never to write treasonable correspondence in clear words,
my dear!'

Both were surprised, undoubtedly, by the little gurgle of
amusement from Mary where she sat at the window.

'I see,' Marie said, after a pause. 'So Huntly is forfeit.
But forfeit only. He is still powerful.'

'In the north, Marie – in the north, only. And Dunfermline
is in the south, is it not? Sweet and precious Dunfermline!'

Long the Mistress of Gray looked at her husband from level
grey eyes, and said nothing.

He turned away, to the younger woman. 'My dear, I missed
you after Peffermill,' he mentioned. 'Vicky said that you were
upset. I am sorry, Mary. But there was no need to be so.
None. I esteemed you in no danger.'

'Nor I, Uncle Patrick,' she assured. 'No danger at all.'

His eyes widened a little at that. 'Had I believed there to be
any, I would have looked to you, child.'

'Yes. I know that. You see, I looked to the King's head
forester. When I saw that he sat his horse unmoved, in all that
stramash, even with his arms folded, I knew that there was
no danger.'

The man swallowed. 'You watched him? The forester . . . ?'

'Yes. You see, I saw you speaking with him in the stableyard last night, and giving him money. Was I not wise to watch him, then?'

'Wise . . . ?' He drew a long breath. 'Wisdom, God help me, is over rife in this family, I think!' His brows came down. 'Then . . . then what upset you, child? If you were so assured?'

Her pink tongue just tipped her lips. 'I was upset . . . only for foolish woman's reasons. But I am so no longer. I am recovered quite.' Mary rose, and came to him, smiling her warmest. 'I am happy, now. Happy that my lord of Huntly escaped. And the Lady Hetty. Are not you, Uncle Patrick? Really? It is so much better that way. You escaped from Edinburgh to Leith yourself, once, did you not? Just in time, likewise.'

'Ah . . . yes,' he admitted. He blinked quickly.

'I watched you both go – you and Lady Marie. And my lord of Huntly aiding you.'

'H'mm. Yes. But . . . at a price, girl. At a price! It cost me Dunfermline!'

'It cost more than that,' she said. 'It cost my father, Davy Gray more than that. Perhaps you do not know, Uncle Patrick, what it cost him?'

Both of them were now gazing at her strangely, intently.

She looked up at him, smiling again. 'But that is all done with. Dear Uncle Patrick – forget Dunfermline! Forget Huntly! You are high in the King's favour, and all is well. Let us all be happy again!'

He searched the young, eager, lovely face upturned to his, wonderingly. 'A kiss from you, sweeting . . . and I count Huntly well lost! Perhaps Dunfermline, even!' he exclaimed.

'You shall have it.' Flinging her arms around him, she kissed him vigorously, whole-heartedly. Still clutching him, she held out a hand towards the Lady Marie. 'You too,' she pleaded. 'Come. Please do. Now we shall all be happy again, together – shall we not? Come.'

Marie looking from one to the other, bit her lip, hesitating, and then came. Patrick's hand went out to her likewise.

170

Chapter Eight

THE King of Scots walled himself up in Craigmillar Castle, high on its ridge south of the city, seeking security, if not peace of mind, within its outer bailey and inner bailey, its ditch and drawbridge and its massive keep – and would not stir therefrom. All who sought the fountain of honour, authority and government must seek it past three gatehouses, a guardroom and parapets bristling with armed men. Nothing would coax majesty without – not though it was the height of the hunting season, with the stags of the great park of Dalkeith nearby at their best and fattest. Hawks could be flown from Craigmillar's great grass-grown outer court, tennis be played and archery practised – but James was in no mood for such pastimes, and they were followed only by such of his unfortunate Court as found itself immured within the gaunt walls, sombre vaults and frowning towers of the castle.

James himself, after the first fright of the ambush and its implications wore off, and as fear of further repercussions began to fade, not unnaturally perhaps turned his mind more and more to distant vistas far beyond these safe but enclosing walls, and to contemplations more apt for a newly-married young man – even if only wed by proxy. He began to dwell upon the imagined person, parts and prospects of his bride, as a more rewarding thought than the perfidy of Geordie Gordon. Indeed, he shut himself up for most of days on end in a lofty turret chamber, where he could look out over the wind-whipped Firth of Forth estuary, past the rock of Bass and the Isle of May, to the grey North Sea, in the direction of far Denmark. Here, with a portrait of the Princess Anne that had been sent to him, he indulged in a positive orgy of synthetic emotion, an auto-intoxication of purely intellectual adoration for the Viking's princess of his imagination.

No doubt the sad and sudden termination of his pseudo-romantic relationship with Huntly was partly responsible. James, not notably masculine in himself, but brought up to condemn and fear his unfortunate and lovely mother, Mary

171

Queen of Scots, and educated by stern Calvinist divines who frowned on women – at least in theory – had ever sought his emotional satisfactions from his own sex, and all from older men than himself. The succession of favourites, however far they went in their relationship with this unlovely and loveless royal youth, had all proved to have feet of clay; all had used their intimacy with the source of privilege to gain for themselves power and wealth and domination. All had been brought down by jealous nobles. Disappointed, hurt, James, now twenty-two, turned, in at least temporary revulsion, to this new and exciting prospect – a young woman, innocent and fair and already his own, although unknown, who would give him what hitherto his life had lacked.

So, in escape from the reality of the present, he wrote to her innumerable letters which could by no means be delivered, in a strange mixture of passion, dialectics, philosophy, semi-religious ecstasy and gross indecency. He indited poems, large and small, and then decided upon a really major work, which history would rate as one of the literary masterpieces of all time. He studied erotica, consulted much-married men and women – the Master of Gray and his wife, embarrassingly, in especial – physicians, necromancers, herbalists, even mid-wives. He toyed with the idea of having a relay of ladies to bed with, both experienced and virgin, and of various ages and shapes, in order to practise upon – but decided eventually in favour of pristine innocence rather than expertise, for presentation to his sea-king's daughter. He grew pale and languishing and greater-eyed than ever – and kept his Master of the Warbrobe busy indeed in ordering and fitting the most elaborate and fanciful garb ever to be worn by a Scots monarch, for outdoors and indoors, day and night wear, most of it in a taste as bizarre as it was grotesque.

All of which was something of a compensation and source of infinite, if guarded, merriment to the royal entourage in more or less forced confinement within Craigmillar – although one or two of his Court perhaps perceived pathos therein, and discovered in their hearts some sympathy with this strange, complex, shambling creature, born in sorrow and treachery, separated from his mother almost at birth, who had known no true love in all his life, the pawn of arrogant scheming

172

nobles and harsh and dictatorial clerics.

The Gray family was inevitably much at Craigmillar – although its members continued to reside at Holyroodhouse, the distance between being but two or three miles. Patrick was in high personal favour again – although this, unfortunately, owing to James's almost complete temporary withdrawal from affairs of government, was not translated into any real political power, which remained more firmly than ever in the hands of the coldly astute Maitland. The King, in his present preoccupation with womankind, anatomy, and the like, saw a deal of his cousin Marie Stewart, finding in her a quiet sympathy, sensibility and frankness which he had hitherto overlooked. And since Lennox – whose defection at Peffermill did not seem to have been noticed by his royal cousin – was now, as Chamberlain, necessarily domiciled at Craigmillar, he sought to entice Mary Gray there at every opportunity – the Master by no means hindering him. With the new queen expected almost at any time, and her household, of which Mary was now a member, having to be prepared and made ready for her arrival, this proved easy and convenient enough, indeed to be expected – even though Duke Ludovick would perhaps have preferred that Mary did not take her sewing and embroidery duties quite so seriously, as did not the Lady Jean, for instance.

The relationship between Patrick Gray and Ludovick Stuart was interesting and not unimportant. Undoubtedly many about that licentious and idle Court believed it to be illicit and unnatural. They made a strangely ill-assorted pair certainly, the handsome, talented, quick-silver and accomplished man, and the plain, solid, rather awkward and ineloquent youth. But they had been good friends for many years – ever since, at the age of ten, young Vicky had been brought from France by Patrick, at the King's command, to succeed to his late and brilliant father's dukedom. The Master of Gray's part in the downfall and subsequent death of the same father, the usual kind informants had not failed to disclose to the young heir; but Ludovick, who had scarcely known his sire, had clung to Patrick. Indeed his early affection for the Master had grown to an admiration amounting almost to adoration, that nothing then or later could ever wholly upset.

It was a day of unseasonable battering rain and wind in mid-September, that Mary Gray sat stitching at the window of a small room in the main keep of Craigmillar. This chamber was one of three grimly functional apartments, all bare masonry, gun-loops and arrow-slits, set aside for the Master of the Wardrobe, and the unlikely repository of the fripperies and confections of the royal trousseau and plenishings. Shot-holes stuffed with scintillating fragments of cloth-of-gold and brocade, coarse elm tables littered with lustrous and colourful silks and satins, now mocked the severity of those frowning walls where once Mary, the Queen's half-brother Moray, her future husband Bothwell, and her Secretary Lethington, brother to Sir John Maitland, had secretly plotted, urged on the Queen's divorce from King Henry Darnley, James's father, and set alight the train that exploded at Kirk o' Field with Darnley's assassination.

Because outdoor activities today were precluded, and young men for the moment in short supply in the castle, the Lady Jean Stewart, supposedly also applying herself to the new Queen's needlework, but in fact gossiping, gesturing and giggling without cease, kept Mary company. Such was life for this true daughter of Orkney.

It was thus that her distant cousin Ludovick found them. Not infrequently he managed to escape from his duties to this little room. That on this occasion he would have been content for the Lady Jean to be neglecting her needlework elsewhere went without saying, but Lord Chamberlain as he might be, he was not the young man to order her hence. One attempt he did make, however.

'The Commendator of Lindores is at cards down in the Preston Tower. With Ferniehirst, Borthwick and, h'm, others. He might be grateful were you to rescue him, Jean.' That came abruptly, after a silent minute or two.

'If the Commendator prefers his silly cards to . . . to better sport, let him stay!' She shrugged. 'He is losing again, I suppose?'

'Aye, naturally.'

Mary looked out of the streaming window. 'Uncle Patrick plays also?' That was more of a statement than a question.

'Aye.'

Jean hugged her buxom self. 'Then the good Commendator-Abbot's goose is cooked! Serve him right, I vow – for he is plaguey mean. He would have his fairings at the cheapest, would Lindores – including me!'

'I have seen you less than dear, yourself!' Lennox said bluntly.

She did not so much as colour. 'You mistake, Vicky. You would, of course.' She glanced from the man to Mary. 'I am no huckster. I give for nothing – or else I play high. Like Patrick Gray. Lindores does not understand. He has the mind of a tradesman . . .'

'He would wed you, I think,' Mary observed.

'No doubt. But he is old, as well as mean . . .'

'He is less old than Patrick,' Lennox pointed out. 'He is not yet thirty, I think . . .'

'Patrick is different! Patrick will never be old. Patrick is wonderful. At cards as at all else! I dote on him . . .'

'So all the Court knows!' Ludovick grunted. 'As, indeed, do half the women here!'

'No less than yourself, perhaps, Vicky!' That was barbed.

'He is my friend,' the young man declared stiffly.

Jean Stewart skirled high laughter. 'None would deny it . . . !' She stopped, as the door opened. A head peered round, a large somewhat lop-sided head crowned by an absurdly high hat decked with ostrich-plumes.

Hurriedly all three rose to their feet, and the girls curtsied over their needlework, as the King shuffled in, large feet encased in loose slippers.

James ignored them. 'Vicky,' he complained querulously, 'I've been seeking you a' place. Man, you shouldna hide yoursel' away like this. You're the Chamberlain. Here's this wee man – the Provost, it is. Frae Edinburgh. About the reception ceremonies in the town. For Anne. My . . . my wife. The Queen, aye. He says you sent for him. You should be seeing him, Vicky – no' me. I'm busy. I'm in the middle o' a sonnet . . .'

'Your pardon, Sire. I did not know that he was come. You should have sent a page for me, an officer . . .'

'Och, I was for stretching my legs. I was ettling to find Patrick too. He's hiding away somewhere. A' folks hiding

away frae me. It's nae better than a rabbit-warren, this castle.
I thought on this wee room, wi' your Mistress Mary. Away
you down and see the man, Vicky.'

'At once, Your Grace.'

'Aye.' James did not follow Lennox out, but moved over
to the window, to peer through. 'It's wild, wild,' he declared.
'Ill weather for the sea. Wind and rain. It's no' right, no'
suitable.'

'You could play at the tennis in the Hall, Sire,' Jean said
helpfully. 'I have heard that my lord of Moray does so, at
Donibristle. Indoors . . . '

'Houts, woman – tennis!' the King cried. 'A pox on
tennis! It's no' tennis – it's Anne! Your Princess. My wife.
She's on the sea. Coming to me. In these accursed storms.
Waesucks – it's no' fair! The lassie – she'll puke. It's an ill
thing, the sea – sore on the belly. The great muckle deeps, see
you – they're like ravening wolves! Aye, wolves. Opening their
slavering jaws for my puir Annie! In this plaguey wind . . . '

'Do not fear, Your Grace,' Mary said earnestly. 'All will
be well, I am sure. The Queen will be safe. This is not truly a
storm. It may not be blowing out at sea, where the ships are.
It is from the west, you see – the other way.'

'D'you think I dinna ken that? So it blaws in her face, lassie
– it keeps her frae me! It blew a' yesterday, too. The Devil's
in it, for sure. I'll need to have prayers said . . . '

Jean actually giggled.

Furiously James turned on her. 'Quiet, girl! Will you laugh
at *me*? God's soul – I'll no' have it! Silence, d'you hear?'

Jean swallowed. 'It was just . . . prayers, Sir! Against a
puff of wind . . . '

'A puff! Fiend take you – here's no puff! A' night I lay and
listened to it, wowling and soughing round this castle. wheech-
ing and girning. I couldna sleep thinking o' the lassie's boatie.
And it's getting worse, I tell you. Aye, and you whicker and
snicker! Och, away wi' you, wench! Out o' my sight. I'll no' be
whickered at. Begone, you ill hizzy!'

Hastily the Lady Jean, flushing at last, backed out of the
room, dropping her embroidery in the process. At the door
she turned and fled, forgetting to curtsy. Mary, less precipit-

176

ately, would have followed her, but Majesty pushed her back into her seat.

'No' you, lassie – no' you,' he told her. 'Och, I canna bide yon Jean! Aye gabbing and caleering! Making sheep's eyes. Sticking out her paps at me! I dinna like it. I'll need to be getting her married off on some man. It's no' decent. She's aye like a bitch in heat. I'll have to think on it.'

'The Lady Jean has no evil in her, Sire,' Mary told him. 'I pray, do not misjudge her. She is but overfull of spirit.' She paused for just a moment. 'Although she would be better married, I truly think.'

'Aye. I'll consider it.' James looked at her sidelong, out of those great liquid eyes. 'And you, lassie? Are you no' the marrying kind, yoursel'?'

She smiled. 'Time enough for that, Your Grace. I am but sixteen years.'

'Ooh, aye. Though, mind you, my ain lass is a year younger. And you're ripe for it – 'sakes aye!' He looked her up and down judicially. Then he tipped forward his extraordinary hat, to scratch at the bulging back of his head. 'But . . . eh, now . . . Vicky. Vicky – the Duke o' Lennox – is young, young. And fair donnart on you, lassie. Mind, I'm no' blaming him that much! You'll be bedding wi' him, belike?'

'I bed with no man, Sire.'

'Eh? No?' The King looked surprised. 'I thought . . . I jaloused . . . ?'

'Then Your Grace jaloused but mistakenly,' she assured, but gently enough. 'Others, I have no doubt, do the same. I am very fond of my lord Duke – but that is all. We have been friends since we both were bairns – good friends. But that is all. I am my own woman, still.'

'Ummm.' James plucked at his sagging lower lip. 'You're . . . you're holding him off, then? For he's hot for you. I've watched him, aye. And, 'sakes, I'm fond o' Vicky, too, lassie.' He began to shuffle about the room, touching things. 'Vicky's near to me, near to the throne, see you. Of the blood-royal, aye. Mind, now, I'm a married man, and like to be making bairns o' my ain, he'll no' be next heir muckle longer. Na, na. But . . . but . . . even so, he's no' just . . . he's a duke. And . . . '

177

'Sire,' the girl interposed. 'If you are seeking to tell me that the Duke of Lennox is not for such as me to marry – then content yourself, for I know it well. When he weds, it must be to some great noble's daughter. And she must be rich – for Vicky has insufficient wealth. I know it all. Rest assured, Sire, I shall not seek to marry your cousin.'

'Aye, so. Good, good. Proper – maist proper. Nae doubt we shall find a good worthy husband for you. Ooh, aye – some honest decent laird, wi' broad acres belike. Some lordling, even – for you've the Gray blood after a' . . . '

'I thank you, Highness – but I am in little hurry. And when I do seek a husband, it would please me well to choose my own – by Your Grace's leave.'

'Och, well – we'll see, we'll see.' The King began as though to move to the door, but shufflingly, darting looks hither and thither, as though reluctant to go. Suddenly he turned round and came back to the girl, and looks and tone changed quite. 'See, lassie,' he said, almost diffidently. 'You've got a wise-like head on your shoulders, and a decent honest tongue. There's a wheen things you maybe could tell me – things I dinna just ken aright. About lassies . . . ' He coughed. 'I ken maist things, mind! – I'm no' just an ignorant loon. But . . . och well, she's about your ain age, and there's things I'll need to do wi' her . . . '

'I understand, Your Grace,' Mary said, soberly. 'Anything that I may decently tell you, I will.'

'Aye, well. I've never had a lassie, you see. Mind, there's some been gey near to it – ooh, aye. Bold brazen hizzies would ha' had the breeks off me if I hadna . . . h'mmm . . . ' He paused. 'Will it hurt, d'you ken? I mean, really *hurt*?'

'I take it, Sire, that you mean will it hurt the Queen, and not yourself? For I think, surely, that last is unlikely.' Only a single dimple in her cheek countered her gravity of mien. 'But I am told that so long as you are gentle, any slight hurt for the lady will be swallowed up quite in the satisfaction.'

'Eh, so? Uh-huh. Gentle. Is . . . is that possible. I mean . . . ?'

'I esteem it so, Sire. Firm, but gentle.'

'Aye. Well, maybe. Like . . . like with a new-broken colt?'

'Perhaps. But I would think with rather more of fond affection.'

'I've aye been fond o' horses,' the King said simply.

'Yes. I had forgotten.'

'She's young, mind. Anne. And will be a virgin, for sure. A pity it is that you will be a virgin too, lassie? It would ha' been better . . . You'll no' ken so much.'

'I am sorry. But I have good ears, I am told – and have heard not a little. Though, are there not plenty otherwise whom you may ask, Sire?'

'Aye, plenty! Plenty! But . . . God save me, I just canna bring mysel' to ask them, Mistress Mary! Yon Jean, now! She'd ken plenty, yon one! But she'd whinny like a mare at me. Her sister, even – the Mistress o' Gray. She's kind, and she's told me some bits, mind. But . . . you see, she's used wi' Patrick. And . . . and I'm no' Patrick! He's different frae me. We both have the Latin and Greek. We both have the poetry. But . . . we're different other ways. So . . . och, I just canna speak wi' her as I do wi' you.' James looked at her from under heavy drooping eyelids. 'Maybe . . . maybe we could do mair than just *talk*, lassie? Maybe . . . well, maybe you could come ben to my bedchamber, the night? I could arrange it that you bide here, at Craigmillar, the night. It's gey wet for going back to Holyrood. Aye, we'd learn a thing or two, that way . . . ?'

With all seriousness, Mary Gray appeared to consider this suggestion. 'You are gracious, Sire – and I am honoured. But I think, no. No. It would be better, more meet, I think, to await the Princess Anne – the Queen. That you should both learn of these things together. She will esteem you the more, that way, I think. *I* would . . .'

'But she needna ken . . .'

'If she is a woman, then she will ken, Sire.'

'M'mmm. You think it? Ah well . . .' James gave the impression of not knowing whether to be disappointed or relieved. He nibbled at his finger-nail. 'It's right difficult,' he muttered.

'I think, perhaps, you make too much of the difficulties, Highness,' she told him gently. 'After all, it has happened before. Many times.'

'Aye – but no' to me. No' to the King o' Scots. I am the Lord's Anointed, lassie – Christ's Viceroy. I am the father o' my people, see you – the fountain o' the race! It wouldna do . . .

it's no fitting, that I shouldna ken the way to handle a lassie
in a bed. You see my right predicament? I've heard tell it's no'
that easy, whiles, to get your mount to the jump, in time? And
I wouldna like to jump my ditch afront my mare! Maybe I'd
ha' been better wi' the Navarre woman, after a'. She'd ken the
whole cantrip good and well . . . '

'Never that, Sire. You chose aright, I swear. Never heed
about that first . . . ditch. There will be many such, after all.
And in your own chamber, I cannot think that the Princess
Anne will consider you as the Lord's Anointed or Christ's
Viceroy – but just as her own new young husband. Be assured,
she will not be critical of you, but only of herself.'

'You think it?' That was eager. 'Och, I hope so – I hope
so. Maybe . . . maybe if I was to indite a poem about it, for
her? Read it to her afore we bedded – maybe that would aid it?
I'm good at poems, you see – I ha' the pen o' a ready writer.
Aye. Even if I've no' just . . . no' . . . Och, well.'

Mary nodded. 'I understand. I am sure that the Queen will
greatly esteem your poetry. But, Sire – I would counsel you
to keep the poems out of the bedchamber, nevertheless. At
first. Women are but silly shallow folk, you see – and perhaps
Her Grace would liefer have just then kisses and fondling. I
think that would be my preference.'

'It would? Kisses and fondling.' He sighed. 'Aye, maybe.
Mind, it's maybe no' that easy to go about the business with
a lassie you havena met wi', till an hour or two before. I'm
doubting if it'll just come natural.' The King licked his lips.
'Now, it wouldna be that difficult wi' you, Mistress Mary –
now I ken you, you see.' A royal arm slid around the girl's
slender waist, and the long and delicate, if ink-stained and not
overclean fingers sought for and captured her own.

'The Queen, I feel sure, will not prove difficult, Your
Grace. She is young, and by her picture very bonny. And the
poems that you have written for her will have greatly moved
her, I vow. For few women are so . . . honoured. Your praise of
her beauty and grace, your avowal of your great passion – all
will move her. If indeed these are what Your Highness has
written?' And with the most natural movement in the world,
Mary turned to stoop and pick up a fallen hank of silken thread,
thereby disengaging herself deftly from her sovereign's clasp.

That hinted question as to the tenor and content of his muse was highly successful, in that James at once reverted to the ardent poet and wordily-confident lover of the past few weeks. He dropped the girl's hand to grope about in an inner pocket of his stained doublet.

'I've two-three sonnets here. By me,' he told her. 'Well-turned and euphonious without being ambiguous – if you ken my meaning, Mistress. Aye. One's notable – right notable. Here it's – this one.' He extracted one of a number of crumpled papers, and smoothed it out. 'Listen you here, lassie. I've no' just decided on its title, mind – but you'll no' deny its quality, I'm thinking.' Striking an attitude, James began to intone – and as he read, his hand came out again to recapture Mary's.

> 'The fever hath infected every part
> My bones are dried, their marrow melts away,
> My sinnews feeble through my smoking smart,
> And all my blood as in a pan doth play.
> I only wish for ease of all my pains,
> That she might wit what sorrow I sustain.'

Finished, eagerly he peered at her, to observe the effect.

Mary cleared her throat. 'Most moving, Sire. As I said. 'Twill move her, to be sure. You did say . . . pan? Blood in a pan . . . ?'

'Aye, pan. Pot wouldna just do. Chamber-pots, you ken. Nor goblet. Cauldron might serve – but och, it wouldna scan, you see. D'you no' like pan, Mary?'

'To be sure, Your Grace – pan let it be. It . . . grows on me, I think.'

'Aye. That's right. That's how I felt mysel', lassie. Now, heed you to this one. It's maybe no' so lofty in sentiment – but it rhymes brawly. Longer too.'

The King was still declaiming, and so engrossed in the business that he did not notice when a knock sounded at the door, nor yet relax his moist clutch of Mary's hand. The door opened, and Patrick Gray stood there, looking in, his scimitar eyebrows rising high. Mary looked over to him, and smiled slowly, tranquilly, with just the tiniest shake of her dark head to advise against interruption.

It was the Master's courteous applause, at the end, that informed the King that they were no longer alone. He flushed hotly, stammered, and dropped the girl's hand as though it had burned him.

'Bravo, Your Grace! Eloquence indeed! A royal Alcaeus . . . with our Mary as Sappho!'

'Eh . . . ? Och, no. No. It's you, Patrick man? You . . . you shouldna do yon. Creep up on me. No, no. And you mistake. I was just . . . just rehearsing a bit sonnet. For Anne, you ken. For the Queen. To hear the way it scanned, just. The lassie here . . . another lassie . . . about the same age, see you . . . listening . . . '

'So I perceived, Sire . . . '

'His Grace was much concerned about the wind and rain, Uncle Patrick – for the Queen's journey.' Mary came to the royal rescue. 'Telling me of his fears for the delay of the ships, he . . . he graciously thought to read over the poems welcoming her to his realm.'

'Ah . . . quite.' Patrick nodded gravely, though his eyes were dancing.

'Aye – the wind, the wind!' James recollected gratefully, turning to the window. 'It's wild – och, a storm it is. And getting worse. Waesucks – ill weather for journeying. And a lassie. It's the powers o' darkness, I swear – Satan himsel' working against me. He'll confound me if he can, I ken fine – for he's dead set against a' Christian monarchs. Ooh, aye. There was Anne's ain faither, King Frederick, met an untimous end no' that long ago. And even my late uncle o' France – cut off in his prime, even though naught but a Papist. By ill cold steel, I'm hearing.' James shivered. 'God rest his soul. Och, it's right dangerous labour being a Viceroy o' Christ – dangerous.'

'I cannot think that the present wind need unduly alarm you, Sire,' Patrick reassured. 'Nor, I esteem, are all crowned heads in hourly danger from His Satanic Highness. For, see you, your right royal cousin Elizabeth of England has well survived his spleen these many years!'

'Spleen!' James spluttered. 'Are you so sure it's spleen, man – in her case? A pox – I'm thinking it's his protection she's had, the auld . . . auld . . . ' He swallowed, and royally sought forbearance. 'Och, well – we maun just pray God will take her in His ain good time. Amen.' One pious thought led to another. 'Aye – prayers. We'll ha' to order prayers in a' churches o' the realm, Patrick. For the abatement o' these ill winds. Aye – forthwith. The Kirk owes it to me, its sure Protector. I'll see Master Lindsay about it, right away. Aye.' With sudden determination, the King shuffled to the door. 'I'll clip Auld Hornie's wings yet, by God!' At the open door itself, he glanced round. 'You needna bow on this occasion,' he announced with regal condescension, and hurried out.

For long moments Patrick and Mary eyed each other, thoughtfully – and seldom had they looked more alike. The man spoke first.

'So I have to congratulate you on another conquest, my dear! A notable one, indeed. It . . . it seems that I am ever underestimating you, Mary! Not, h'm, one of my commoner failings!'

'No,' she told him. 'Here is no cause for such talk, I think. Just a poor, wandering, lonely man in need of a friendly hand.'

'I noticed the hand!' Patrick agreed, laughing. 'Call it what you will, Mary – so long as it is *your* friendship and *your* hand that our Jamie seeks! Properly prosecuted, this may lead to great things. I confess, it had never crossed my mind . . . '

'Nor should it now, Uncle Patrick,' she interposed firmly, seriously. 'I pray you, build nothing out of this. For my sake, if not the King's. He was but carried away by his own rhymings, his own fears and hopes. It seemed that he needed help – and I sought a little to help him.'

'Precisely, sweeting. And let us hope that you will be enabled to help him again, and considerably. For James, you see, has not hitherto looked to women for his help. Dealing with kings, you know, can be to much advantage. But it requires much thought and planning – for they are not as other men. You must take my advice . . . '

'Dealing with kings, Uncle Patrick, it seems may not always be of much advantage – to the kings! It was cold steel that killed King Henri of France, it seems! And you were not surprised by the tidings, that night at Falkland. I wonder why?'

The man's features stilled in the extraordinary fashion that on occasion could change his whole appearance. It was as though a curtain had dropped over those lively laughing eyes. 'What do you mean, girl, by that?' he said softly, almost under his breath.

'Just that, Uncle Patrick, our dealings with kings may often best be kept privy to ourselves – do you not agree?' And when he did not answer, she smiled. 'Do not be angry. Did you win a lot of siller from the Commendator of Lindores? Leave him some, Uncle Patrick, please – for I think that he may well wed the Lady Jean. And she will need siller, too . . .'

Without a word he turned and left her there.

Alas for the efficacy of prayer even by royal appointment. The weather that autumn of 1589, whether devil-inspired or otherwise, did not moderate. Indeed it worsened, south-westerly gales blowing almost incessantly throughout the entire months of September and October. They were as bad as those which had dispersed Philip's Armada a year before, and of longer duration. The belated corn harvest was flattened and rotted, haystacks were blown to the winds, all round the coasts fishing-boats failed to return to their havens, and ordinary sober men shook their heads in foreboding.

The state of mind of King James bordered on chronic hysteria, in consequence. He shut himself away even more rigorously in the keep of Craigmillar, and even within the castle itself showed himself to few. He saw the entire climatic disturbance as a personal conspiracy against himself and his unseen beloved, and in a lesser degree and somewhat obscurely, against Christ's Holy Evangel, with which of course he closely identified himself. The Huntly business was all but forgotten; the irresponsible antics of the Earl of Bothwell, who, having won free from Tantallon, was as usual running wild in the Borders, no longer affected his monarch, it seemed; the normal machinations of mutually jealous lords left him apparently unmoved. He filled the long days and nights of waiting, particularly the nights, with alternate bouts of prolonged prayer, increasingly peculiar versifying, even deeper study into the supernatural and the black arts, with necromancers and reputed dabblers in these things sought out and brought to him from all over the land. Not to put too fine a point on it, the sovereign's mind appeared to many to be in process of becoming quite unhinged.

The rule and governance of the realm, in consequence, devolved almost wholly upon the Lord Chancellor, Maitland. This undoubtedly by no means suited many of those at Court; particularly Patrick Gray, who, despite his recent rapprochement with the Chancellor, found his wings considerably clipped – since his influence with that wily if upstart lawyer was inevitably a deal less effective than with the young James. As the weeks wore on, indeed, Patrick became very preoccupied indeed. He spent an ever-increasing proportion of his time in the company of the Duke of Lennox, it was to be noted.

With the continued non-arrival of the ships from Denmark, Mary Gray, for one, watched the King, Patrick and Ludovick, all three, with concern. James himself she did not often see, though when she did he was apt to dart strange, uneasy, almost appealing glances in her direction – glances which, she was well aware, Patrick seldom missed. For his part, the latter saw that Mary was very consistently at the castle; indeed, had not his wife put her foot down firmly, he would have had the girl lodging there. As Master of the Wardrobe he was, with the Chamberlain, the official most responsible for arrangements for the Queen's reception; the Queen's ladies, therefore, he kept under his own appreciative eye.

Ludovick, these long inclement days, tended to be moody and morose. A vigorous and active young man, with no great intellectuality or fondness for indoor pursuits and idle Court dalliance, or for that matter the card-playing which his friend the Master found so profitable, he fretted at the forced immurement within Craigmillar's thick walls. Out of patience with James, ill at ease with most of his fellow courtiers, a fair proportion of the time that he was not with the Master of Gray he tended to spend in the small room in the keep with Mary and her colleagues. There were distinct doubts as to whether Patrick wholly approved now, whatever had been his previous attitude.

On one such occasion, in mid-October, with Lennox watching Mary at her stitchery with more than usual stolid gloom,

185

the girl rallied him smilingly.

'Vicky,' she protested. 'You puff and sigh there like a cow with an overfull udder! Why so dolorous these days? I have not seen you smile in a week, I vow!'

'Eh . . . ? Well . . . in part because I never see you alone, Mary. Always other women are with you. That Jean. And Kate Lindsay. And the Sinclair wench. I do believe that Patrick arranges it so. Always working away at these clothes and trappings.'

'But that is why we are here, Vicky – our duty. You of all men should know it, as Chamberlain. Besides, are we not alone now, and have been these ten minutes? And all you have done is moon and scowl!'

'You are ever sewing and stitching. Never done with this sempstress's work. It's not suitable . . . '

'It is especial work, Vicky – close wear for the Queen's own person. It *is* suitable that her ladies should do it. It is all that we can do for Her Grace, in this pass. Save pray for her safety and speedy arrival.'

'Pray!' The young man all but spat that out. '*Mortdieu* – I've had my bellyfull of that! All this morning we were at it.' He jumped up, and began to pace the small apartment. It was unusual indeed to see Ludovick Stuart thus moved. 'Hours he kept us on our knees. Mine pain me yet! Though, on my soul, it was like no praying I have ever known ere this! He weeps and shouts at his Maker, *parbleu* – when he is not babbling about black arts and wizardry! All over a chit of a girl whom he has never even seen! 'Fore God, I believe – aye, I believe that his mind is going. That we may have to take steps, as Patrick says.'

'I think that is unfair, Vicky. That you are too hard on the King, by far. He is only distraught, surely.' Mary looked up at him thoughtfully, biting a thread with small white teeth. 'And . . . what does Patrick say? What steps are these?'

He frowned heavily. 'It is very secret,' he said, lowering his voice. 'Privy only to ourselves. Perhaps I should not tell – even to you, Mary. He said to keep it close.'

'Even from me, Vicky – who can keep a secret? And I know many of Uncle Patrick's secrets. Did he say not to tell *me*?'

'No. No, but . . . well, if you swear not to tell it to a soul,

Mary? Aye. Patrick, you see, fears for James's reason – and *mon Dieu*, he is right, I begin to believe! If the King's mind goes – goes completely, you understand – then it will be necessary to take steps. Great steps, and prompt. For the weal of the realm. He says that a Regency would have to be set up – to rule instead of the King. As a first step. It might be necessary even . . . even to find another king. Later, that is. Should this madness continue.' Lennox was speaking jerkily, and looking almost shocked at his own words. 'But first a Regency.'

Mary did not answer, but only gazed at him great-eyed.

'You see how it is, Mary? You understand? The country cannot be governed by a madman. There have been Regencies before, a-many . . . '

She nodded slowly. 'And who would be this Regent?'

He swallowed. 'Why me, Patrick says. I am next heir, you see. Since it could not be my cousin Arabella Stuart, in England. And . . . and . . . '

'I see.' Steadily she considered him. 'I see. So says Uncle Patrick?'

'Yes.'

Mary looked down at her sewing. 'Not all would welcome this, I think, Vicky. Even those who might be agreeable to turn against King James. Some would say that you are not old enough to be Regent, perhaps. Chancellor Maitland might say as much, I think.'

'Aye. Belike. But Maitland would not be told. He would be the last to be told. He likes me not, that man.'

'But, as Chancellor, first minister, must he not know? And act . . . ?'

'He would no longer be Chancellor,' Lennox told her simply. 'The Regent's first duty would be to appoint a new Chancellor.'

'Uncle Patrick?'

'To be sure. Who else?'

The girl's breath issued in a long sigh. 'Of course,' she said. 'Who else!' After a moment or two she rose to her feet and came over to him, to take his arm. 'Vicky – here are deep matters indeed. I do not wonder that you have been anxious, ill-humoured. But do you perceive how deep? Such talk now

187

is . . . treason! Uncle Patrick at least advised you well in this, that you should not speak of it to anyone. For your head's sake!'

The other's boyish features flushed. 'No, no – not that! Not treason, Mary! Lord – never say it! You do not understand. We must take thought – for the realm. For its safety and governance. We . . . we are high officers of state, members of the Privy Council. You are a woman – you do not understand . . . '

'I understand all too well, I think, Vicky. Men have died for less dangerous words than these. Some might call them betraying your king. Be careful, Vicky – think well. King James is shrewder than you take him for. He is far from mad, I do believe. Promise me that you will say nothing of it to anyone! And that you will tell me should the matter go any further. I do not fear so much for Uncle Patrick – for he has walked dangerously all his days. But, you . . . !'

Unhappily her companion nodded. 'As you will, Mary. I promise. I did not mean . . . perhaps it is too soon to consider these things . . . '

'And it would be better, Vicky, that Patrick does not know that you have told me. Much the best. You see that?'

'Aye. I shall not tell him.'

'Good,' she said. 'Poor Vicky – such anxieties but ill suit you. Statecraft is but little to your nature, I think.'

Heartily he agreed with her. 'You are right, i' faith! Would that I could exchange it all for the good clean air of Methven and the hills of Strathearn! Out of these accursed enclosing walls and crazy humours! And you with me there, Mary . . . '

The girl smiled, but kindly. 'Patience, Vicky,' she said. 'Though, to be sure, I would rather see you Laird of Methven than Regent of Scotland.'

'And you? How would you see yourself?'

'As Mary Gray, just. And your friend. Just that. Always that.'

He sighed, gustily.

During the next three days Mary sought to see the King alone – and found it more than difficult. James did spend most of his time alone – but shut in his own chambers with guards at every door. To have sought audience past these would have made the girl conspicuous and provoked comment inevitably – the last thing that she desired. And no amount of waiting about in likely places, or other like device, was of any avail.

It was on the last day of that week, after mid-day meal taken in the great hall in company with most of the resident courtiers but minus the royal presence, that, climbing the long winding turnpike stair to the Wardrobe rooms again, Mary's glance was caught whilst passing one of the narrow arrow-slit windows. Down below she had glimpsed an unmistakable shambling figure, pacing the flagged parapet walk that surmounted the walling of one of the secondary corner-towers, solitary though every now and again raising a hand in a repetitive gesture.

Only for a moment or two did the girl hesitate. That tower was an inner one, relic of the original smaller fortalice, sheltered from the wind, its top hidden from most of the castle's windows and courtyards – no doubt why James had selected it for privacy. Her Uncle Patrick had recently settled down to a game of cards, she knew, with carefully-chosen and wealthy companions. Ludovick was gone down to Leith, to superintend the repair of decorations erected for the Queen's reception and blown down by the gales. With a brief word to her two colleagues, the Ladies Jean Stewart and Katherine Lindsay, indicating that she had left something behind, Mary turned and ran light-footed down the steps worn hollow by mailed feet.

Darting along the bare labyrinthine mural passages that honeycombed the thick walling, up and down steps, she came to the foot of the little stairway of the tower where the King promenaded. An armed guard stood there. With entire authority she asserted that she was from the Master of the Wardrobe, with word for His Grace. Known by sight to all in Craigmillar, the guard let her past without demur. Another man-at-arms held the caphouse door at the stairhead – but he was no more obstructive; indeed the unexpected sight of a pretty, breathless girl commended itself to him sufficiently for him to whisper confidentially in her ear that His Highness being in a passing strange state, it behoved her to watch her virtue and perhaps close up the front of her gown – a liberty she forebore to rebuke as he opened the door for her.

189

James was shuffling up and down, up and down, over the counter-placed flagstones at the other side of the rectangular walk that crowned the tower within the crenellated parapet, lips moving, arms gesturing – whether apostrophising his Maker, declaiming poetry, or making incantations, was uncertain. Mary, lifting her skirts a little, went tripping over the stones towards him.

The King halted in mid-pantomime at sight of her, glowering blackly. Then, as she straightened up from her brief curtsy, and he perceived her identity, his features slackened to a grimacing smile.

'Och, it's yoursel' just, Mistress Mary!' he declared, in relief. 'You gave me a right fleg! I was thinking o' Anne, you see – o' the Queen. I wondered if I was beholding her drowned ghost . . . !'

'Oh hush, Sire – how could that be?' she returned. 'Your lady is safe and well, I vow, and no ghost. Moreover, not to be confused with the humble daughter of Davy Gray.'

'Aye. Aye, belike you're right. It was just a sudden notion, you ken.' James scratched at his straggling apology for a beard. 'But . . . what brings you here, lassie? You're alone, just? There's nane hiding behind yon door? I'm no' seeing a'body . . . we are not giving our royal audience to any. We would be private . . . '

'No, Sire – I am quite alone.' The girl hesitated, prettily. 'I . . . I came, Your Grace, to seek a favour.'

'Aye. Ooh, aye. A' folk do that,' the disillusioned monarch agreed, with a sigh. 'What is't you want then, Mary?'

She wrinkled her lovely brow. 'It is difficult. I am overbold, I well know. I should not ask it. But . . . I must needs dare turn to you, Sire, in my trouble. You see, I also am turning my foolish head to poetry. Although that is much too fine a name to give my poor verses. I seek to write an ode to your princess, Sire – a little song of welcome for your young Queen Anne from her most lowly Woman of the Bedchamber. I have got so far, poor as it is – but now I am stuck. Stuck quite, Your Grace, for a rhyme. So . . . so I dared come to you for help . . . '

James of Scotland was quite transformed with delight. Shining-eyed, stammering his pleasure, he turned to her, grasping her arm, her hand again. 'Hech, hech – is that s'so? Y'you are, Mary l'lass? Mercy on us – it's kindly in you, right kindly. Aye. I rejoice to hear it. No' that you're stuck, mind – for I ken what it is to be stuck for a rhyme. Many the time I'm stuck, mysel'. But . . . och, I'd never ha' thought it. And you but a bit lassie . . . '

'That is so, Your Highness. And my, my presumption is the greater in coming to you who are not only the King but so renowned and practised a poet . . . '

'Aye – but who better, who better?' he exclaimed. 'Wae-sucks – do I no' writhe betimes on the same slow fire mysel'?'

'Yes – that is my sole excuse, Sire. Here is my trouble. It is in the third verse. It goes thus:

> My voice I raise, my lyre I tune,
> to thee fair daughter of the seas,
> Thy coming cannot be too soon
> for this poor handmaid of thine ease;
> O end my weary waiting, please
> with solace of thy presence . . . *well* . . . boon.'

'Eh? Boon?' James repeated. 'Boon, you say?'

She bit her lip. 'Boon, yes. That is all that I can think of to end the verse. It is not very good, is it?'

'Boon.' The King scratched his head under the inevitable high hat. 'I canna see how it could be boon, lassie . . . thy presence boon. Na, na – it's no' right, some way.'

'No,' she agreed meekly. 'I know it. That is why I came to you. I cannot think of aught else.'

'Ummm,' he said. 'Oon's no' that easy, to be sure. To do wi' a woman's presence. Moon wouldna do, nor yet swoon. Mind, if you'd done it in the Scots, it would be better, Mary. Then you could ha' said doon or abune or goon. Aye, or her royal croon. Och, it's easier to make words rhyme in the Scots, I find.'

'Perhaps I should have done that, yet.'

'Aye. But maybe it's no' too late to change it a wee thing, here and there. Into the Scots. I ken it's an ill task for a poet having to change the words he's wrung oot o' his heart's blood – but och, whiles it has to be done, lassie. Now . . . wi' solace

191

o' thy presence boon' it was, was it no'? Aye. See you – if you were to change a wheen o' the rest o' the words into Scots, then you could set the last line the other way roond, and say "wi' presence royal my solace croon." '

'Ah – how true, Sire! Splendid!' Mary clapped her hands. 'Why did I not think of it? Not only does it rhyme, but it is better, much better.'

'Aye, I think it so mysel'. But mind, you canna just ha' the one Scots word to it, Mary. You'll need to go through a' the ode and change a bit word here and there to oor ain Scots usage. It'll no' be that difficult. What was the line before it . . . ?'

' "O end my weary waiting, please." '

'I'ph'mmm. I'm no' that rejoiced wi' yon "please", mind. "Waiting, please" is no' just perfect, maybe.'

'Indeed it is not, as I am well aware.'

'Aye. You could mak it "Gladden my weary waesome ees", belike.'

'Waesome ease . . . ?'

'Ees – eyes, you ken. Een would be righter – but, och, it wouldna rhyme. We'll no' mend that. Ees it'll ha' to be.

          "Gladden my weary waesome ees,
          Wi' presence royal my solace croon."

That's nane so ill.'

She moistened her lips. 'Indeed, Sire – it is truly most . . . most apt. So quickly to perceive the need and supply the answer. I am overwhelmed. But . . . I must not keep you further, must not trespass on your precious time, must not intrude more on your own royal muse . . . '

'Och, never heed it, lassie – I like it fine,' James assured. 'I'm right practised at it. Ooh, aye. See you – go you right through your ode frae the beginning, Mary, and I'll gie you a bit hand. Wi' the Scots. For the prentice hand's aye slower than the master's.'

'Oh, but that is too much, Your Grace. You are too kind . . . '

'Na, na. Let's hear it a' . . . '

So, hand in hand and side by side, the teetering unsteady monarch and the dainty girl went tripping round and round that battlemented walk, bobbing up and down over the flag-

stones gapped for drainage, reciting, inventing, weighing, if
scarcely improving the doggerel verses that Mary had so
hurriedly concocted, James eager, voluble, authoritative, his
companion appreciative and serious, the wind blowing her hair
about her face and her skirts about her legs. For anyone in a
position to overlook them, undoubtedly they would make a
curious picture.

It was only when the King had the pathetic little ode almost
transformed to his own peculiar satisfaction, that a thought
occurred to him that abruptly halted him in his wambling
tracks, his face falling ludicrously.

'Eh . . . but what o' the Master?' he demanded. 'What o'
Patrick Gray, your faither? Or your uncle, or what you ca'
him? Was it he . . . did he set you to this poetry, girl? He's a
right notable poet himsel', I ken. You're . . . you're no cozening me? Seeking to befool me wi' *his* verse . . . ?'

'Sire – my Uncle Patrick knows naught of this. It is my
own entirely.'

'But why came you to me when you could go to him,
woman? For help and improvement? Eh?'

'Uncle Patrick is much too throng with affairs, Your Grace,
to trifle with my poor rhymes. He is much too taken up with
other matters to think of poetry, at this time.'

Sidelong he peered at her. 'He is, eh? What takes up our
Patrick so?'

'In the main, matters of money, Sire, I think. Siller and
gold. In your affairs, and his own.'

'Moneys, eh? Siller and gold? And in *my* affairs, you say?
Hech, hecht – what's this?' The muse forgotten, James was
all ears. 'Out wi't, lassie. What moneys?'

She hesitated modestly. 'It is not perhaps for such as me to
speak of these matters . . . '

'Houts, lassie – ha' done! It's . . . it's our royal will that
you tell us o' the business. Aye.'

She bit her lip. 'As you command, Sire. Siller is much in
Uncle Patrick's mind, I fear. The cost of the arrangements for
the Queen – as Master of your Wardrobe. He and the Duke of
Lennox are ever fretting over it. And my Lord Chancellor
says that your Treasury is near empty.'

'Ummm,' James said. 'Aye, maybe. Siller's a right rare

193

commodity, to be sure. Aye, and Maitland's close, close, the man.'

'Yes. So Uncle Patrick ever turns his eyes southwards. To Queen Elizabeth. On Your Grace's behalf.'

'Eh ... ? He does? Elizabeth? Aye – my pension. She doesna pay it, the auld ... the auld ...'

'No. But you will recollect, Sire, that Uncle Patrick brought you a thousand gold pieces of it when he returned to Scotland. He believes that he can win more for you – for it appears that he understands this Queen passing well. So he writes letters, many letters, and much presses Mr. Bowes.'

'Aye, he's right close wi' Bowes, I do hear. Ower close, maybe. I dinna like yon man, mysel, wi' his smooth white face ...'

'Nor, I think, does Uncle Patrick, Your Grace. But as the Queen of England's envoy he must needs work with him on your behalf. For the increase of this pension ...'

'Increase! Waesucks – if she'd but pay the sum agreed, the woman! Since Patrick agreed it wi' her three years syne, for two thousand pieces each year, she hasna paid a quarter o' it! And she's been right gorged wi' gold and siller since then – maist pecunious. Yon man Drake and his pirates fair load her wi' Spanish gold and plate. Hundreds o' thousands. It's no' right, no' decent. I'm her heir and successor. It'll a' be mine when she dies ...' The impoverished heir of Gloriana all but brought himself to tears at the contemplation of the gross injustice done to him.

'Yes, Your Grace. Hence Uncle Patrick's efforts. He believes that he can gain you the money. The promised increase. Even more, perhaps. So he writes and writes. But ... but letters are poor things. If he could but see the Queen. Elizabeth. Speak with her. As before. Assuredly he would be the more successful.'

'Aye. I'ph'mmm. See her.' The King nodded, stumbling onward again. 'Aye. Maybe that is well thought o'. See her. An embassage ...'

'Yes, Sire. An embassage.'

'Aye. But ... did Patrick put you up to this, lassie? This embassage? Why did he no' speak o' it to me, himsel'? I had word wi' him but this morning.'

Mary sighed. 'I fear that he but thinks of the embassage as distant. Not immediate. He . . . he has other plans, meantime . . .'

'Other plans? What now – what now?'

'Plans of his own, Sire. I told you, he is much concerned about siller – in his own affairs as well as for Your Grace. Since his forfeiture and banishment he has had but little money, as you will know. My lord of Gray will give him nothing. He has great expenses. He is building again Broughty Castle, his portion. So . . . so he seeks to win back the Abbacy of Dunfermline.'

'No!' For once James Stewart was vehement, decisive. 'No' Dunfermline! I'll no' have it. I told him so lang syne. It's no' to be, no' suitable. If he sent you seeking Dunfermline frae me, Mary . . .'

'Not so, Your Grace. He does not know that I am with you. He would be but ill-pleased, I think, if he knew that I told you of it. But he is powerfuly set upon Dunfermline. He believes that it should be his, yet. That my lord of Huntly should not have it. Like a sickness it is with him, eating away at him. He even plans to take the Earl of Huntly to the Court of Session for it. And for that he needs more money.'

The King wagged his head in agitation. 'No' Dunfermline,' he wailed. 'It's no' like other places, you ken. It's the brawest property in a' the realm. When Patrick was forfeited, he lost it. He got it frae yon ill man Arran, some way. I canna just let him ha' it back. Would he ha' me look a right fool? Maybe I'll see what can be done for him wi' some other place, but no' Dunfermline. Na, na – it's no' to be thought of. Geordie Gordon doesna deserve to keep it, to be sure – but there's plenty wanting it! Johnny Mar. Aye, and the Earl o' Moray. Och, I'm thinking the Chancellor himsel's after it! I canna let Patrick have it. They'd a' be at my throat like a pack o' hounddogs!'

'I know it, Sire. So, surely, must my uncle. Yet he seems mazed about this matter. Not like himself. Foolishly determined . . .' She paused, as though suddenly an idea had occurred to her. 'Sire – there is a way that this could be resolved, I think. That Uncle Patrick may be turned away from it – and the others likewise. Give Dunfermline to your

195

new Queen, as a marriage gift. Then none can seek it.'

'Lord save us!'

'Yes. Would that not be best, Sire? Uncle Patrick would be weaned from his trouble. He could not sue the Queen, and waste great moneys. Your lady would take it most kindly – and you would have the spending of its revenues.'

Her companion had halted, blinking, licking his lips. 'Precious soul o' God, lassie – here's a notion! A right notable notion!' he exclaimed. 'Aye – Huntley's forfeit now. I can take it. For Anne. But . . . but Patrick? What o' Patrick? When he hears. He'll be fair scunnered at me! He'll plot and scheme against me, the man. He'll no' help me wi' Elizabeth and my pension, I swear . . . !'

'He will be very hot when he hears,' she agreed gravely. 'But . . . he need not hear until too late. If he was not here. If he went on this embassage to England at once. Before your lady arrives. And . . . ' She tipped her red lips with pink tongue prettily. ' . . . if he was to receive some compensation. Some small lands somewhere. And, perhaps, some part, some portion of the moneys that he wins for you from Queen Elizabeth? That would much sweeten him, would it not? Siller that he could use to build Broughty. In exchange for his hopes of Dunfermline. A thousand gold pieces, perhaps – if he could win Your Grace two thousand. Or three. That would be but fair, would it not? And greatly encourage him in his dealings with Queen Elizabeth.'

'Lord ha' mercy on us – who taught you to think this way, girl?' James whispered. 'Who taught you, a lassie, the likes o' this?'

Surprised, she considered that. 'I do not think that anyone taught me, Sire. Save Davy Gray, of course.' And suddenly she trilled a laugh, happily, at some thought of her own. 'Yes – it must have been Davy Gray. Dear Davy Gray!'

Wonderingly the King looked at her, shaking his head. 'Yon dour man . . . ?' he doubted. Then he changed his head-shaking to nodding. 'But you ha' the right o' it, Mary – 'deed aye. The embassage to Elizabeth it shall be – and at once. Aye, forthwith. Before . . . before my Anne comes, belike. We shall see to it. Our special envoy to the Court o' Saint James, the Master o' Gray – *celeriter*!'

The girl nodded her head, satisfied. 'I have always wished to see London,' she said. 'And to see Elizabeth the Queen.'

Chapter Nine

THE cavalcade had barely left Berwick Bounds behind it, and crossed into England, before the wind died away and the sun blazed down upon a sodden and battered world. Men and women threw aside their heavy soaking travelling cloaks, sat up in their saddles after long crouching, and positively bloomed and expanded like sun-starved flowers in the genial warmth and brightness, the first that they had known for months on end. It was the second day of October.

'This, I vow, will set King Jamie smiling again,' the Earl of Moray declared, stretching his arms out luxuriously as he rode.

'I hope that you are right, my lord,' Patrick Gray said. He had been laughing gaily, rallying them all, rivalling the new sun's own brilliance this cheerful morning, but fell sober again at the other's words. 'If the sun but shines in Scotland likewise . . . and if His Grace's mind is not itself permanently clouded over and agley.'

Moray looked at him sharply. 'You mean . . . ? You fear, sir, that . . . that . . . ? You are not suggesting that James is affected in his wits?'

'I hope not, God knows. It is my prayer that I may be mistaken,' the Master answered gravely. 'But . . . he has been acting very strangely. For too long. It is a great cause of anxiety. You have not been much at Court of late, my lord. Those of us in daily touch with him cannot fail to be aware of the danger, of the sad but steady deterioration of his powers of judgment, the abdication of his kingly responsibilities . . . '

'He frets excessively for his princess – all Scotland knows it. And always he has been strange in manner, fearful of spirit. But more than that I cannot believe . . . '

Mary Gray, seeking to pay due and respectful attention to

197

the feather-brained chatter of the Countess of Moray at her side, and yet to miss nothing of the conversation of the two men immediately in front, above the clatter of their horses' hooves, bit her lip.

'I do so believe it, my lady,' she said, straining her ears. 'Indeed, yes.'

' . . . for the good governance of the realm,' Patrick was saying. 'I fear – aye, i' faith, I fear for our land. Maitland rules, not James. If His Grace's condition grows the worse, then it behoves us all to take serious thought for the realm's weal, my lord. It will not serve to shut our eyes.'

'God save us!' The Earl's comely and attractive features reflected a simple consternation. 'I have heard naught of this, Master of Gray. No talk of it has reached me. I have been in the north, at Darnaway . . . ' He shook his fair head, at a loss.

Greatly daring, and with a swift apologetic glance at the Countess, Mary leaned forward to speak, and sought to make her voice low but penetrating. 'Hush, Uncle Patrick!' she said. 'If I can hear your words, so may others. And . . . and that is not to be desired, is it?'

Patrick turned in his saddle to stare at her, slender eyebrows raised. 'My dear,' he said evenly, 'what I say to my lord of Moray is for his ears alone, I would remind you.'

'Why, yes – that is why I speak,' the young woman nodded, with a darted look left and right as though to indicate that there were ears all round them – although in fact the nearest squire rode a good ten feet to the flank, and the men-at-arms in front still further away. 'If I overhear, others might. To great ill, perhaps.'

'You have over-long ears, girl – as I have had occasion to remark ere this!'

'Yes, Uncle Patrick – but so I have heard you say has Queen Elizabeth! Ears everywhere.'

'A plague, child! What's this? Would you teach me, *me*, how I should speak?'

'Ah, no. No – but my lord said that no talk of this sort had reached him at Darnaway.' Mary's colour was heightened and her breathing quickened. 'Forgive me – but I would but have you assure yourself that no talk of it reaches London either!

For – hear me, please – would not any such talk ruin all? If Queen Elizabeth was to question, even for a moment, whether King James was sound in his mind, to wonder if his wits were disordered, would she indeed cherish him further? Let you have the money for him? Do what you would have her to do, on this embassage? Would she even consider him heir? Heir to her England?'

Patrick had caught his breath. For a long moment he looked at the girl unblinking before, without a word, turning to face the front again.

Moray had gazed behind him also. 'Burn me, but she is right, Gray!' he exclaimed. 'The lassie is right. A knowing chit, eh? A head to her, as well as . . . other parts!' Still considering the girl, he smiled slowly, taking in all her flushed and eager young loveliness, looking at her with new and speculative eyes – eyes that did not once slide over in the direction of his wife at whose side Mary rode. 'Here is matter for thought,' he added, facing forward once more, and still smiling reflectively – for one who was not notably a reflective and thoughtful man.

The Countess of Moray slumped more heavily in her saddle, and fell silent for the first time since the weather had brightened.

James Stewart, Earl of Moray, had been selected personally by his royal namesake to be the second envoy on this embassage to the Court of St. James. It was always the prudent Scottish custom to send two ambassadors on any important diplomatic mission – lest one should perchance be tempted to betray his trust. Moray was a shrewd enough choice, whatever his companion's professed doubts about the King's sanity. Known as the Bonnie Earl, he was both popular and notably good-looking; not so brilliantly handsome and graceful as the Master by any means, but fair to look upon in a lusty, strapping and uncomplicated fashion, tall, broad-shouldered, and of a sort of rampant masculinity – and young. All important qualities where Elizabeth of England was concerned. A favourite of the Kirk party, he could be guaranteed to be suitably suspicious of the Master of Gray, whom few in Scotland believed to be other than Catholic at heart. Moreover he was very rich, in his wife's right rather than his own, and so could comfortably and conveniently pay for the entire embassage – always an important consideration with King Jamie.

Never, surely, was a monarch so well supplied with cousins as was James, thanks to the phenomenal potency of his maternal grandfather James Fifth, whose heart may well indeed have broken at being able to show only the one surviving legitimate offspring, and that a mere girl, the unfortunate Mary Queen of Scots – although unkind gossip had it that his untimely death at the age of thirty was rather the result of being worn out by extra-marital exercises. At any rate, his bastards were legion, and few indeed of the ladies of his Court seem to have eluded his attentions; not that he confined his favours to the aristocratic and highly-born, by any means – for had he not been known as The Poor Man's King? The Reformation and the breaking up of the vast Church lands, at this juncture, had been a godsend indeed, providing properties and commendatorships innumerable for the suitable support of this host. Moray was the son of one of them, another James, titular Abbot of St. Colme, later created Lord Doune. A young man of initiative as well as looks, the son had eight years before managed to obtain the prized wardship of the two daughters of his late uncle, the most important bastard of them all, James Stewart, Earl of Moray and former Regent of Scotland – and the very next day married the elder daughter, Elizabeth, and assumed the earldom. The late Regent, needless to say, had done very well for himself in three years of ruling Scotland in the name of Mary's infant son – and having no son of his own, his heiress brought her husband great lands and riches. In the eight years of their marriage, the new Moray had managed to dispose of much of these responsibilities, but in return had given her five children. Now, at the King's insistence, the Countess accompanied her husband to London, and Mary Gray went as her attendant.

Patrick Gray, after only a brief period of quiet, was soon laughing and gay once more – for he was never the man to sulk or brood. Indeed, as they rode southwards, presently he was singing like a lark, seemingly without a care in the world, to the amusement of Moray, the delight of his wife, and the embarrassment of much of their train – and encouraging Mary to join in, so that apparently he was going to bear no resent-

ment over her intervention. Her clear young voice rose to
partner his rich tenor, to while away the long miles. It was
noticeable that after fording the swollen River Aln, Moray
rode behind, beside Mary, and the Countess in front with the
Master of Gray.

That evening, at Morpeth, Moray was markedly more attentive to Mary than he was to his wife.

It was the following night, as the girl was preparing for bed
in the country inn just over the Yorkshire border, that he
came to her garret room, opening the door without any warning knock. Hastily drawing one of the bed-covers around
herself, Mary turned to face him. She did not cry out or
otherwise lose her head; indeed she did not even shrink back,
but after only a momentary hesitation actually moved towards
the man.

'My lord,' she said. 'I think that you have made a mistake.'

Moray's ruddily handsome features were flushed still further
by wine. 'Not so, my dear,' he denied thickly. 'Far from it, I
vow – as my eyes do assure me!' He grinned at her.

'Nevertheless, sir – you do much mistake. Your wife's room
is below.'

'I know it, moppet!' Moray advanced into the room, having
to stoop to get through the low doorway, his great frame seeming to fill the little coom-ceiled chamber. He shut the door
behind him, with no attempt to do so quietly, furtively. 'Let
her be. If mistake I made, it was in delaying so long down there
at cards with your . . . your uncle!'

Mary sought to keep her voice even, although the heaving of
the coverlet wrapped tightly around her told its own story.
'At cards – and wine, my lord!' she said. 'The wine, I fear,
has confused your wits.' She looked very small, standing stiff
and upright there before him. 'Else you would not be here.'

'Tush, girl – have done!' he exclaimed, and a hand reached
out to her, to grasp the cover and wrench it aside, baring one
white shoulder. 'You are good with words, I grant you. Let us
see how good you are otherwise, my dear!'

Still she stood, unmoving, her head held high, her dark eyes
meeting his steadily. 'It is pleasure that you seek, sir?' she
asked, huskily.

'Why yes, Mary – pleasure it is! What else? And pleasure I

201

shall have, I warrant – for you are passing pleasurable!' He laughed. 'Perhaps, i' faith, you shall win a little pleasure out of it also, lass – for I am none so ill at the business, so others have informed me!' He drew her irresistibly to him, and dragged down the coverlet further, stooping low to bury his face against the swell of her bosom.

She did not struggle, however stiffly she held herself. Her words continued, stiff also, level but emphatic. 'I cannot stop you taking me, my lord – since you are stronger than I am. But I can promise you that you shall have no pleasure in me.'

'Ha – think you so!' Raising his fair head, Moray chuckled in her face. 'Woman – do you not know that a little reluctance, a mite of resistance, but increases the pleasure? Certes, it is so, I promise you. For you also, perhaps. Come now, lass – enough of this foolery. I do not wish to hurt you . . . '

'*Your* hurt it is I fear, my lord. Your grievous hurt.'

'Eh . . . ? A pox – what is this? Here's no way to bed! Am I so ill-looking? And you, I swear, have fire in plenty in this body . . . '

'I would need to have, to warm you . . . when you are bedding with your death, my lord! A cold loving!' Low-voiced she said it.

'Fiend take me – death? What i' God's name mean you, wench?' The man stared at her, actually shook her. 'What fool's talk is this? Are you crazed, girl?'

'I think you do not know the Master of Gray very well – or you would not ask,' she said. 'Nor would you be in this chamber.'

'Gray? I know him well enough to have lost three hundred crowns to him at cards this night, damn him! I will have some return, 'fore God!'

'You will have your death, my lord – nothing surer,' she told him gravely. 'And I would not wish that. You are too proper a man to die so young, for such a cause. And your wife and bairns deserve better, I think.'

Astonished, perplexed, Moray drew back a little, the better to consider her. 'Burn me – never have I heard the like!' he muttered.

'I believe it, sir. But never, I think, have you sought to injure the Master of Gray. My father.'

202

'Ha!' It was the first time that Mary had publicly claimed the Master as her sire – even though few at Court had any doubts of the fact. The Earl rubbed his chin.

'He is fond of me – otherwise I should not be coming to London with you,' Mary went on, drawing the coverlet over her shoulder again. 'He has other plans for me, I think, than to be your plaything, my lord. And consider well what happened to others who have crossed the Master of Gray! My lord of Morton, the Regent, did so – and died. Ludovick of Lennox's father likewise – and is dead. My lord of Arran, the Chancellor – he fell, and is no more. Even my lord of Gowrie, they do say, his uncle . . .'

'God's curse!' Moray all but whispered, staring at her. 'What are you? Devils both?'

She answered him nothing, but looked him in the eye, unwinking.

He drew himself up to his full and impressive height, mustering a short laugh. 'Do not think that you frighten me, young woman!' he said.

'I think it not. You are a man, and bold. It is I that am frightened,' she answered simply. 'For you. I cannot think that I shall pleasure you, sir.'

The young Earl drew a long breath, opened his mouth to speak, and then shut it again almost with a click. He turned on his heel, strode to the door, threw it wide, and went stamping out.

Mary Gray sank down on her bed, trembling. Dark-eyed she looked through the open doorway. 'Forgive me, Uncle Patrick,' she whispered. 'God forgive me!'

For long she sat thus, motionless, before she rose and closed that door.

The next morning Moray was silent and withdrawn, and rode with his wife. Patrick, in the best of spirits, sought to draw him, and was rebuffed. He turned his attention to the Countess, and soon had that featherhead whinnying high laughter, to her husband's marked offence. Mary, save for being perhaps a little paler than usual, slightly darker about the eyes, was her quietly composed self. But when presently, as they skirted the low rolling Cleveland Hills, so much tamer than their Scottish

203

uplands, Patrick began to sing once more, it was not long before she joined her voice to his. Moray eyed them both askance.

So they pressed steadily southwards. By the time that they reached the flat lands of Lincolnshire, two days later, the Earl was himself again, prepared to chat and even laugh with Mary – as he should have been, for she was at pains to be most kind to him. Now it was Patrick Gray's turn occasionally to eye them both, thoughtfully.

They came to London eleven days after leaving Edinburgh – and smelt the stench of it for miles before they reached its close-packed streets and teeming alleys, Patrick explaining that there being little in the way of hill and sea breezes in this flat inland plain, the cities here must needs stink worse than their windy Scots counterparts. Wait until they reached the oldest and most densely populated area near the river, he warned them.

Mary, for one, although much excited and impressed by the vastness of the sprawling city, the noise and bustle of the narrow thoroughfares and dark field lanes, where every prospect revealed but deeper labyrinths of crazily crowding, soaring, overhanging and toppling tenements, taverns, warehouses, booths and the like, all built of wood unlike Edinburgh's grey stone masonry – Mary was soon all but nauseated by the smell of it, dizzy with the clangour and ceaseless stir of milling humanity, and suffering from a claustrophobia engendered by the endless tall inward-leaning buildings that all but met over their heads to shut out the sky and seeming about to fall in upon them. She did not wonder in the least, and was duly thankful, when Patrick's shouted enquiries elicited the information that Elizabeth – good Queen Bess, as they called her – was not presently occupying her palace of Whitehall, in the midst of all this, but was down the Thames at Greenwich some five more miles to the east, where presumably the air would be at least breathable.

As the now much extended Scots company of about fifty threaded and worked its slow way through the congestion and turned eastwards parallel with the river, Moray demanded of a substantial burgher standing in the doorway of a handsome house with an elaborate hanging sign, what all the church bells were ringing for, in the middle of a week-day afternoon. The man eyed him with astonishment mixed with both scorn and suspicion, and pointed out that no true and loyal citizen need ask such a question. Nettled at his tone, the Earl replied sharply that they were travellers from Scotland, and in the habit of receiving civil answers to civil questions.

'If that's where you are from, cock, then belike you should heed well those bells,' the other returned, spitting at their horses' hooves. 'You'll be heathen of some sort, if not traitorous and bloody Papists, for sure. Those bells, I tell you, ring for the joyful examining and burning of thrice-damned recusants, priests and Jesuits! Aye – and for four days they have rung without cease, by the Queen's command. And Bess, God preserve her, will keep them ringing for four more, I warrant!'

'You mean . . . men are being burned? Now? Catholics? For their faith? Their religion?'

'To be sure they are, simpleton – praise God! Two score but three burned yesterday – and they do say that one lived two hours from his disembowelling. Sweet Jesu, I wish I could ha' seen it!'

'Faugh, man . . . !'

As Mary blenched, Patrick leaned over to jerk her horse's rein and urge the beast forward – but not before she heard their informant declare that if they cared to ride round by the Bridewell they would see a row of Jesuits and Papists hanging by their hands all day in preparation for tomorrow's burnings – which should be most apt warning to all traitors, Scotchies and other enemies of the good Bess.

'Lord!' Moray exclaimed, as they rode on. 'Is this how they treat Catholics here. I' faith, the Kirk has much to learn, it seems!'

With a quick shake of the head Patrick glanced towards Mary. 'They are still afraid of Spain, with Guise and Philip in league, and Spanish soldiers as near as Brittany. There may be profit for Scotland in that same, let us not forget.' He changed the subject, abruptly for that man. 'There is the river, Mary. Down yonder lane. You just may see it. The first time that I came to see Elizabeth Tudor, we met her there. On the water. It was a notable ploy. Perhaps Davy . . . perhaps your father has told you of it?'

Despite the Master's spirited and graphic account of that adventure five years before, the girl hardly heard a word of it. Her ears rang much too full of the jangling of those church bells. It was as though she listened tensely to hear indeed what other sounds those bells hid and covered up. London seemed to be full of clamorous churches that afternoon. Even she sniffed at the tainted air, as though to test what dire elements it carried. Almost she wished that she had never contrived to accompany this embassage.

A mile from Greenwich Park, they were surprised to be met by a brilliant escort of gentlemen sent out to greet the Scots envoys in the name of the Queen. It appeared that Mr. Secretary Walsingham, that grim shadow on England's fair countenance, although reputed to be an ailing man, kept himself and his royal mistress as well informed as ever – so much so that the tall and slender, darkly-handsome man with the haughty manner but flashing smile, who led the party, knew even that he was going to meet the Earl of Moray as well as the Master of Gray. Since of deliberate policy no courier had been sent on ahead to herald their approach, this knowledge was the more remarkable.

'I rejoice to see you again, Patrick,' the spokesman declared, sketching a bow. 'Rejoice too that you are, I perceive, like to dazzle us, as ever! This will be my lord of Moray, of whom we have heard? Your servant, my lord. Her Grace sends you both greetings, and would welcome you to her Court.'

It was noticeable that the speaker's distinctly arrogant glance, whatever his words, slipped quickly away from both Patrick and Moray, quite passed over the Countess and lingered unabashedly on Mary Gray, in keen and speculative scrutiny.

'Her Grace is most kind, Walter. We are sensible of so great an honour – as of your own presence. This, my lord, is Sir Walter Raleigh, whose fame has reached even poor Scotland. And Sir Francis Bacon, if I mistake not? And h'm, others, of no doubt like distinction . . . if that were possible! So much brilliance, I swear, quite overwhelms us humdrum northerners. Gentlemen – the Countess of Moray.'

'Enchanted, your ladyship.'

'Your devoted and humble servitor, madam. And, er, the other, Patrick?'

'A young relative of mine, no more – attendant upon the Countess,' the Master informed briefly.

'Ah!'

'Relative? Precisely. How fortunate is her ladyship! Come, then . . .'

Mary Gray rode towards Greenwich Park surrounded by such a glittering galaxy of male elegance and wit as ought to have quite intoxicated her – had she not still heard through the gay chatter and heaped and extravagant compliments, the echo of those jangling bells.

The travellers were installed, not in Greenwich House itself, which like James's Falkland was small as royal palaces went, but in a goodly house in the town, near the park gates. Here Mary did not have to roost in any remote garret room, but was allotted what seemed to her far too magnificent an apartment on the main floor, intercommunicating in fact with the Master's own. The dandified courtier who conducted them to these quarters clearly took her to be Patrick's mistress – a misconception which nobody troubled to correct.

So commenced a strange interlude for the Scottish party, a period of waiting which was both amusing and galling, flattering and the reverse, superficially active and basically futile and frustrating. They were treated with the utmost cordiality and courtesy. Hospitality was showered upon them, invitations without number. Seldom was there not some lord or gallant calling upon them. Gifts of fruit and comfits and even flowers came to them from the palace daily, many with verbal messages of goodwill and greeting from the Queen herself. Life was an incessant round of festivities, receptions, entertainments, routs and balls. But at none was Elizabeth herself present – although at many she was expected to be just about to come, or had just left – and no actual summons to her presence was forthcoming from the palace. Moray grew restive, however content was his wife to bask in the sun of a social whirl such as she had never even contemplated – for Elizabeth's Court was the most brilliant in the world at this period – and Mary frequently questioned the Master on what all this delay portended. But Patrick himself was unruffled, serene, at his most attractive, all good humour and high spirits, making no hint of complaint. He explained to the girl that this was not untypical of Elizabeth Tudor. Although one of the greatest monarchs in Christendom, with a head as shrewd as any of her counsellers, she loved to demonstrate that she was all woman, to keep everyone about her on tenterhooks, to play the contrary miss even on her glittering throne. None must ever know just where they stood with Elizabeth, even her closest and oldest advisers. Patrick smiled, and added that he thought that perhaps she would particularly apply this contrariness to himself.

'To you?' Mary wondered. 'You mean – yourself? Not just to this embassage?' And at his nod, 'Why to you, Uncle Patrick? Can you be so important to the Queen of England?'

'Why yes, I think so, my dear. Overweening modesty was never my greatest failing!' Laughing, he took her hand.

It was late at night, the eighth night of their sojourn at Greenwich, all but morning indeed, after a great ball and masque at the house of the Earl of Essex, where Sir Francis Bacon had presented Mr. Burbage's players in a notable play by a new young man from the Midlands named William Shakespeare, entitled *Love's Labour's Lost* – vastly entertaining. Mary was sitting up in her great bed, all bright-eyed eager liveliness, with little of sleep about her, and the man sitting on the edge of the bed. Often he came in from his own room, day or night, to talk with her, clearly enjoying her company, frankly admiring her loveliness, caring nothing how tongues might wag. Nor was Mary any more concerned, never experiencing the least fear or embarrassment in his presence – however fearful she was over much that he did.

'This Queen is a cruel and evil woman, I think,' Mary said. 'How you can mean much to her – sufficient for her to play such games with you, to hold you off thus, yet to send these flowers and gifts – I know not. I do not understand it, Uncle Patrick.'

'I believe that you are a little unfair on the great Gloriana, child. I would not call her evil. And I conceive her to be no crueller than the rest of her delightful sex – yourself included, given the occasion, my dear! She is a queen, the reigning prince of this great realm, and statecraft, as I have told you ere this, demands stern measures as well as kindly, cunning as well as noble gestures. For Elizabeth, statecraft is her life. She *is* England, in a fashion that no Scots monarch has ever been Scotland. And . . . I have bested her more than once! Hence her present display of feminine contrariness.'

'You – *you* have bested Queen Elizabeth?'

'Why yes, my pigeon – I think that I have. And hope to again, bless her!'

Intently the girl looked at him. 'Did she not best you? Did she not once best you grievously? Did she not betray you shamefully to Chancellor Maitland? Deliberately. Causing you to be taken and tried for treason? Over the death of our good Queen Mary, whom she murdered? So that you all but lost your life?'

He stroked his chin. 'I suppose that is true, Mary. But . . . statecraft is a ploy in which one must learn to let bygones be bygones. Revenge and vindictiveness are luxuries that may not be afforded in affairs of the realm. Especially towards a reigning prince. I can nowise drag Elizabeth off her throne. Yet because she sits on that throne, I may achieve much of benefit. I would be a fool, would I not, to prefer to remember that it once suited her policy to be rid of me?'

'I see,' Mary considered him gravely. 'She might be so suited again.'

'Aye, she might.' He laughed, fondling her smooth bare arm. 'But enough of such matters – no talk for a girl lacking her beauty-sleep. We shall await Gloriana's pleasure, since we can do no other – and then seek to pit our wits against hers. For all dealing with Elizabeth is such – like swordplay. She has to be approached with a fresh and unprejudiced mind. But, you – you are not wearying, my dear? Finding your time to hang heavily? You, who have half of our ageing Elizabeth's pretty boys running after you, paying *you* court instead of her? I vow she will be sending for us soon, if only in sheerest desperation to be rid of you, my sweet!'

The young woman shook her head. 'I am not wearying, no. I like it very well,' she said frankly. 'But I do not flatter myself that the flattery of these gentlemen is more than that . . . nor their court more than a step towards winning into my bed.'

'H'mmm.' Patrick's stroking of her arm paused for a

moment. 'I' faith, you are . . . plain-spoken, girl,' he said, blinking a little. 'For your years. But . . . I give thanks at least that you are not swept off your dainty little feet by these gentry. Even Raleigh himself, I notice, seems over-eager. You are new and fresh, of course – a freshness that the Court ladies here notably lack. And devilish attractive, although I say it myself . . . !'

'Thank you. Sir Walter, I think, feels it necessary to conquer every new lady,' she said. 'He seeks to do so very spendidly. I would not wish to distress him that he has failed to conquer my heart – so long as that will content him. As I have told him.'

'On my soul, you have! Damme – that could be a dangerous hand to play! You think . . . you think that you can play it, lass? At your age? With such experienced gallants as these?'

'Why yes, Uncle Patrick – I think so. None of these fine gentlemen, you see, are one half so pressing as was Nick the stable-boy at Inchture. Or even the blacksmith's son of Longforgan.'

Swallowing audibly, the Master rose to his feet. 'Is that so?' he said, moistening his lips. 'I . . . ah . . . I perceive that I am but beating the air, my dear. Left far behind you. You must forgive me.' He took a pace or two away, and then came back to the bed. 'Moray,' he said, in a different tone. 'You have no trouble with Moray, I hope, Mary?'

It was the girl's turn to blink a little. 'Why, no,' she answered, after only a moment. 'My lord and I understand each other very well, I think.'

'I am glad of that,' he said. 'You must tell me if it should turn out . . . otherwise.' Patrick stooped to kiss her. 'Goodnight, my dear. Tell me . . . am I getting old, think you?'

Her soft laugh was very warm, as her arms went up to coil round his neck. 'You are younger than I am, I do believe, Uncle Patrick!' she said.

The very next evening they saw Elizabeth. They were all at a great entertainment of dancing and music given by the Earl of Oxford in the Mirror Ballroom of Greenwich House itself – for the Queen preferred her subjects, in especial such as basked in the light of her favour, to provide the festivities for her multitudinous Court out of their pockets rather than her own. An interlude of dancing apes, dressed male and female in the very height of fashion, was just concluding with the females beginning to lewdly discard their clothing, to the uproarious delight of the company, when a curtain of silence fell gradually upon the crowded colourful room. All eyes turned from the grotesquely posturing monkeys towards the far end of the mirror-lined apartment. Only a slightly lesser hush had descended when the apes had been brought in, and at first Mary Gray anticipated only another such diversion, and anyway could see little for the throng. Then, as everywhere women sank low in profound curtsies, and men bowed deeply, and so remained, she could see over them all. She caught her breath, dazzled.

The dazzlement was by no means merely metaphorical. The brilliance of what she saw actually hurt the girl's eyes – so much so that, initially, detail was blurred and lost in the blaze of radiance. Scintillating, flashing in the light of a thousand candles, and duplicated to infinity by the mirrors on every hand, a figure stood just within the doorway – a figure indeed rather than a person. It was only as Mary stared, scarcely believing her own eyes, that she belatedly perceived two facts; one, that there was a·pair of very keen and alive pale eyes glittering amidst all this brilliance; and two, that she herself was the only other person standing fully upright in all that assembly, and in consequence that those searching eyes were fixed full upon her. Down the young woman sank.

The tap-tapping of a sharp heel on the floor was the imperious signal that all might resume the upright. Elizabeth Tudor came on into the ballroom on the arm of her host Edward de Vere, Earl of Oxford, with an almost tense and deliberate pacing, as though she held herself in from more rapid motion, and on all sides men and women pressed back to give her clear and ample passage. Even now Mary could scarcely discern the pale thin features of the woman herself, so extraordinary was their framework. The Queen was dressed all in white satin, but in fact little of this material was to be seen, so thick encrusted was it with gems and jewels. Her gown was rigid enough to have stood upright on its own, so closely sewn was it with diamonds, emeralds, rubies, in clusters and galaxies and designs. Her great upstanding ruff, which forced her to hold her head so stiffly, was pointed and threaded with literally hundreds of small pearls and brilliants. Hanging from her neck were at least a dozen long ropes of great pearls. Her once-red hair, now covered with an orange wig, had a myriad of pearls large and small threaded on many of the hairs. Above it a pearl and diamond tiara was perched. Her fingers were so beringed that they could scarcely bend, and her wrists and forearms were sheathed in bracelets of white enamel studded with more gems. All this, coruscating and sparkling in the bright light, was so overwhelming on the eye as to leave the beholder dazed, dizzy. Its absurdity was on such a scale as to benumb the critical faculties.

Woe betide anyone, however, who equated that absurdity with weakness or vapidity of character, took such outward display as indicative of emptiness within. Elizabeth's passion for precious stones was a weakness indubitably, but there was strength enough in other directions to counter-balance many such. None who knew her were ever so foolish as to allow themselves to be deceived.

The Queen paced stiffly round the great and respectful company, throwing a brief word here, a thin smile there, once hooting a coarse laugh at some whispered remark of Oxford's, poking a diamond-studded finger into the padded ribs of my lord of Essex, frowning impatiently at one unfortunate lady who, when curtsying, slipped a heel on the polished dancing floor and thudded down on one knee. It was the respect, awe almost, which so much impressed Mary Gray – so different a reaction to that inspired by King James in his courtiers and subjects. Which the girl found strange indeed, for Elizabeth in her own way was almost an incongruous and ridiculous a figure, on the face of it, as was her distant cousin of Scotland. Fascinated, the girl watched.

Elizabeth moved hither and thither amongst Oxford's guests, but though time and again she came close to the Master of Gray and the Earl of Moray, always she veered off. Almost certainly she was deliberately avoiding them, for it was unthinkable that she did not know well of their presence there; Walsingham and his horde of spies, had for years seen to it that Elizabeth was the best-informed monarch in Christendom. Mary glanced at Patrick sidelong. The man was his smiling assured self – although Moray was much otherwise, flushed and plucking at his pointed golden beard.

The Queen circled back eventually to the little group that stood actually alongside the Scots party – Raleigh, Francis and Anthony Bacon and the Lord Mountjoy. With them abruptly she was a changed woman, vivacious, easy, swift in gesture, rallying the young men, her strange pale golden-green eyes darting. Mary, watching closely, was sure that those eyes flickered more than once over in their own direction, but no move, no hint of acknowledgement of their presence, was vouchsafed.

Elizabeth was now in her fifty-seventh year, and in the girl's youthful eyes, was showing her age, although her clear and absolutely colourless complexion was still extraordinarily free of wrinkles. She was not beautiful, nor had ever been; the long oval of her face, high aquiline nose, faint eyebrows and thin tight lips, precluded it; but when animated, there was an undoubted attractiveness in her features, a magnetism that was not to be denied.

Suddenly, with a ringing laugh, she turned away from the four young men, ordering Oxford to proceed with the evening's entertainment, presenting only her stiffly upright back to the Scots emissaries in the process, and went pacing off towards the head of the room amidst the consequent stir. Seldom could there have seemed a more deliberate snub.

'My God . . . !' Moray growled. 'This is not to be borne!'

It was the Master of Gray's laughter that rang out now, and more melodiously than had the Queen's. 'My lord – you are a notable performer at the glove and the ball, we know. But this is a more delicate sport – and he who holds his hand to the last round may win the game!' He by no means lowered his voice to make this comment, and undoubtedly Raleigh and the rest heard him, possibly even the receding Elizabeth herself.

Oxford gave a signal to the musicians in the gallery, and thereafter Elizabeth led the stately measures of the first dance with her host as partner. Couples were slow to be first to venture out in the Queen's company, and only two or three had in fact been bold enough to make a move when Patrick,

bowing to Mary, took her by the arm and swept gracefully out
into mid-floor with her. For a few moments, although others
were circling on the perimeter, only these two pairs were out
in the centre of the room, the target of all eyes. Patrick guided
Mary so that they passed very close indeeed to the Queen and
Oxford. Darkly smiling eyes met and held narrowed golden-
green ones, and then they were past. The Master chuckled in
the girl's ear.

'Heigho!' he said. 'Two can play this game. Let Gloriana
pretend now that our presence is unknown to her!'

'I think that Her Grace is not greatly going to love me!'
Mary murmured.

'Tush, lass – Elizabeth admires best those who stand up to
her . . . if so be it she does not chop off their heads! And she
can scarce do that to the King of Scots' envoys!'

After only a minute or two more of the dance, the Queen
abruptly adandoned it, indeed abandoned the ballroom
altogether, stalking off through the doorway by which she had
entered, Oxford hurrying in her imperious wake. Few failed to
notice the fact, Mary included.

'She has gone,' she told her partner. 'She is set against us,
quite.'

'Wait,' Patrick advised. 'She is not gone for good, otherwise the music would have been stopped, and we would be all
bowing and scraping. Wait you, moppet.'

They had not long to wait, in fact. The first bars of music
for the next dance were just being struck up when Sir Walter
Raleigh came to touch the Master on the arm.

'Her Grace commands the presence of my lord of Moray
and yourself, with your ladies, in the ante-room,' he said
expressionlessly. 'Come.'

'Indeed? We are ever at the Queen's commands, of course.
We were about to dance this pavane, however. Perhaps . . . ?'

'I think that would be inadvisable, Patrick.'

'Ah – you think it? Perhaps you are right. You agree, my
lord? Lead on then, Walter.'

Elizabeth was seated in a throne-like chair in a smaller
chamber beyond the ballroom, Oxford and Essex at her back.
As the visitors made the required obeisance, she smiled
graciously.

214

'Welcome to our Court and presence, once more, Master Patrick,' she said pleasantly. 'I see that you appear to be nowise disadvantaged from heretofore. I congratulate you on your . . . resurgence. I think, almost, that you are indestructible!'

'You are kind, Highness – as always. And more adorably beautiful than ever!' Patrick stepped forward, sank on one knee, took the proffered bejewelled hand, and raised it to his lips. 'It is like the summer returned to be put in Your Grace's presence once more.' It was noticeable that he retained a hold of the royal fingers.

The Queen looked down at him quizzically. 'You ever were a talented liar, Patrick!' she observed. She twitched her hand away from his grasp, then, almost flicking his face with the hard diamonds in the process. 'Impudent!' she snapped.

'Say, rather, overwhelmed and beside myself, Lady!' he amended gently, rising.

'I doubt it, sir – God's death, I do! But nor am I overwhelmed, I'd assure you! Be certain of that, my friend. If anyone is beside himself, I conceive it to be my peculiar cousin of Scotland, who can still consider you a worthy emissary!'

'On your own recommendation, Madam, I am grateful to say!' Smiling, Patrick half-turned. 'May I present to Your Grace my prince's other emissary – my lord the Earl of Moray, close kinsman to the King.'

'Aye, I have been noting him! A better-made man than you, Patrick – and more honest, I hope! Welcome, my lord – in ill company as you are!'

Moray, obviously uneasy, uncertain how to take all this, bowed stiffly over Elizabeth's outstretched hand. 'I present my prince's traist greetings and salutations, Your Grace.'

'To be sure, to be sure. No doubt. But not your own – eh, sir?' the Queen rejoined dryly. 'I have heard you named bonnie, my lord – and perhaps with some slight cause. At least you are bonnier than your late good-father and uncle, the previous Moray! For he was as sour-faced a knave as any it has been my lot to meet!' Elizabeth opened her mouth, and then clapped a hand to it in a seemingly impetuous and girlish a gesture as might be imagined. 'Sweet Jesu – a pox on my runaway tongue!' she declared, eyes busy. 'This will be his daughter? You must forgive an old woman's scattered wits, my dear.'

The Countess, flustered and speechless, curtsied, glance darting towards her husband, who seemed all but choking.

'Your Grace . . . !' that man spluttered.

'Yes, my lord?'

When the other found no words, and Patrick seemed about to intervene, smiling still, Elizabeth raised a hand to halt him.

'Tell me, my lord of Moray – how many bastards besides your father and goodfather did the late King James of pious memory produce? On ladies of noble blood, I mean, naturally – since the rest can be ignored. It was always been a question of some doubt with me. Once, I thought that I could count seventeen – but since I had no fewer than five named James amongst that total, I grew confused. Perhaps no proper count was kept?'

The Earl's good-looking ruddy features grew almost purple, but the Queen went on before he could speak.

'And this,' she said, turning to look at Mary now, 'is the wench of whom I have not failed to hear! An interesting face – is it not, Patrick? Even though it need not show its mislike of me so plainly! Your name, child?'

'Mary Gray, Your Grace.'

'Aye. It could scarcely be other! I wonder, Patrick – have I wronged you? Or . . . not wronged you enough?' She was patently comparing the two Gray faces, feature by feature. 'A fascinating problem, I vow! What do you find so amiss in me, child? Come – tell me.'

Mary shook her head gravely. 'I would not dare to find aught amiss with the Queen of England, Madam, in her own palace.'

'Ha! Minx! That is as good as to admit you mislike! What ails you at me? Out with it, I say. Be quiet, Master of Gray! Speak but when you are spoken to!'

The girl chose her words carefully, but with no sign of agitation. 'I but wonder, Your Grace, why so great and power-ful a princess should act so. Assuredly there must be a reason.'

Elizabeth's jewelled shoe tapped the floor. 'Act so . . . ?' she repeated. 'You, in your wisdom and experience, chit, conceive it that I act amiss as a princess? On my soul, this

216

intrigues me! And you seek a reason for my actions?'

'Why yes, Highness.'

'And have you thought of one?'

'No, Your Grace. Not yet.'

The Queen barked a brief laugh at that. 'Fore God – you are candid, at least! Like that other you once brought to my Court, Patrick – the natural brother that you miscalled secretary. Was not Davy his name? Aye, Davy Gray. He had the same critical eye, the same damned uncomfortable honesty! Unlike yourself, Patrick! And yet . . . and yet the likeness between you two, otherwise, is not to seek! A strange contradiction, is it not?'

'Not so strange, Highness – since Davy Gray had the upbringing of Mary here,' Patrick told her.

'Ah – so that is it? The upbringing, you say? But not, perhaps, the begetting?' She smiled, looking from one to the other. 'I perceive it all now. A remarkable situation. I see that you deserve my sympathy, child, rather than my just ire. To be such as you are, to have in you such opposing strains – to be Patrick and Davy Gray both! God help you!' The Queen leaned back in her chair. 'But enough of this,' she said, changing her tone. 'Is my young cousin of Scotland in good health? He has sent me no poems, of late. He is not sickening?'

'His Grace is much distressed, Madam, in awaiting his bride. The Princess Anne,' Patrick told her. 'These long continuing contrary winds and storms . . .'

'Ah, yes,' Elizabeth sniffed. 'Had he chosen the Princess of Navarre, as we advised him, he could have spared himself this. You led me to believe, Master of Gray, that you could convince him to that course. And you did not. I do not commend such failures, sir. Navarre is now France, and his sister heir thereto. Here was folly.'

'Admittedly, Highness. Nor have I ceased to point it out. But His Grace had reversed his decision before ever I reached Scotland. Indeed the selfsame day that I arrived there, the Earl Marischal was being sent to Denmark with betrothal gifts.'

'Your prince is advised by fools, I swear! How shall little Denmark serve him? I am much displeased, sir. God help this sweet realm of mine should he and his advisers ever have the ruling of it!'

At her back the two English earls made hurried and fervid protestations that the Queen should even for a moment consider the possibility of such a disaster. Elizabeth, if not immortal, undoubtedly would outlive them all.

Mary shot a troubled glance at the Master, whilst Moray frowned and tugged at his beard.

Patrick seemed nowise upset however. He laughed. 'So far distant an eventuality need scarce trouble us today, Your Grace,' he declared. 'By which time, who knows how much additional wisdom King James will have gained . . . and how much better advisers!' With something of a flourish, he tossed back the tiny scarlet-lined white satin cloak which hung from one shoulder of his padded doublet, to reach into a deep pocket therein. 'At least in this matter, Madam,' he went on, 'I deem that you will consider His Grace well advised – since I myself was consulted! From King James, Your Highness, with his esteem and devotion.'

Elizabeth's eyes narrowed and then widened, as she stared at what the Master held out to her. Too swiftly for dignity her hand reached out to grasp it. 'A-a-ah!' she breathed.

A great diamond, as large almost as a pigeon's egg, set in a coiling snake of amethysts, hung on a golden chain composed of delicately-wrought smaller serpents, each in its tail clutching a pearl.

The Queen, thin lips parted, held the jewellery up to the light, turned it this way and that so that it all flashed and glittered, as did the rest of her sparkling, shimmering display, stroking her finger-tips over the polished surfaces, weighing, assessing, gloating, her breathing heightened, her hands trembling a little.

'Whence . . . came . . . this?' she got out.

'It was one of the late Queen Mary's gifts from her first husband, the Dauphin of France,' Patrick answered easily, without the flicker of an eyelid. 'It was found in one of the houses of the deplorable lord of Morton, but recently.'

'It was . . . hers!'

'Aye. Who more fitting to have it than yourself, in consequence, Madam?'

Elizabeth's eyes met his for a long moment, her lips moving slightly. But no words issued therefrom.

218

It was Moray who broke the silence. He too delved into a pocket and brought forth a little gold casket, cunningly wrought to represent a beehive which, when its tip was pressed, opened on hinges to reveal a brooch sitting in a velvet nest within, in the lifelike form of a great bee, fashioned wholly in gold and precious stones.

'Also from King James,' he announced, but omitted to proffer with it any message of devotion or regard.

Almost absently the Queen took the casket from him with one hand, whilst in the other she still caressed the diamond and chain. 'I thank you, my lord,' she said, more or less automatically. 'You will thank His Grace for me, for his munificence . . . ' But her glance returned almost at once to the Master's face, to the first gift, and back again.

Moray cleared his throat. 'I shall do so, Highness,' he agreed brusquely. 'Now – as to the subject of our visit, it is our prince's request that you . . . '

'In due course, my lord – in due course,' Elizabeth interrupted. 'Not now.'

The earl blinked. 'But, Madam – we have waited . . . waited . . . '

'A mere day or so, my lord. Is King James in such pressing need that we must discuss his rescue at my good lord of Oxford's entertainment?' Suddenly the Queen was her commanding, assured self again. 'So do not I the state's business, sir. Anon, I say. I shall inform you of a suitable occasion.'

Before Moray could reply, Patrick spoke, quickly. 'We are grateful for this gracious audience, Highness, for your royal acceptance of these toys and of our master's fair wishes. We shall wait your further summonses assured of your kindly goodwill towards our prince . . . and even perhaps towards our humble selves?'

'Do that, Patrick,' Elizabeth agreed, cryptically. 'My thanks for these . . . tokens. I shall consider the quality of your advice to King James.' Her pale eyes flickered over them all – and came to rest on Mary Gray. 'You have given me food for thought,' she added. 'All of you. You have my permission to retire.'

They bowed, and backed out, Raleigh still with them.

Although Patrick might have remained to partake of more of Lord Oxford's hospitality, none of the others were so inclined. Moray was seething with ill-suppressed rage, and caring not that Raleigh perceived it.

When they were safely out of Greenwich House, and alone, the Earl burst forth. 'The bitch! The arrogant, grasping, ill-humoured bitch! Fiend seize her! This is not to be borne. To be insulted thus! Mocked at – by that barren harridan! I'll thole no more of it, Gray, I tell you. It's home to Scotland for us – forthwith. I'll not stay to be spat upon by yon Jezebel .. !'

'We must first perform what we came for, my lord . . . '

'How shall we do that, in God's name? She will have none of us, the harridan! She will snatch at your gifts, but give us nothing in return. She is set against us, man. Even you must see it. There is no profit for us or King Jamie here.'

'I think that you misjudge the matter somewhat, my lord,' Patrick declared, soothingly. 'I believe our case is less ill than you imagine. I know Elizabeth . . . '

'Then I do not congratulate you, sir! *You* may swallow her insults and play toady to her – but I will not. Not for King James, or Christ God Himself! I ride for Scotland tomorrow. We have wasted too long here already.'

'As you will, my lord. I cannot stop you. But I think it unwise. I have a card or two yet to play . . . '

'Play them then, sir – but play them without me!'

'I shall, if I must . . . '

Later, in the privacy of her own room, it was Mary's turn to speak. 'Is not my lord of Moray right?' she put to Patrick. 'This Queen will serve you no good. She hates Scotland, I think – or she would not treat its envoys so. She hates our King, her heir though he is. She basely slew his mother. Will it indeed serve any purpose to wait on her longer, Uncle Patrick?'

'Why yes, my dear – I believe that it may. Do not judge Gloriana too sorely. She is not just what she seems, as I have discovered. And recollect that we are the beggars – not Elizabeth. We desire much from her – and she knows it. She needs nothing from Scotland – save only peace . . . '

'And our Queen Mary's jewels!'

'M'mmm. Jewels are her weakness, yes – and thank God

for it! Jewels and young men.'

'She did not greatly esteem my lord of Moray.'

'She might have done – had he played her aright. For he is good to look at. But he was too hasty. I fear he has no gift for statecraft . . . '

'Why did you advise King James to send the Queen that great jewel, Uncle Patrick? Surely that was ill done? The good Queen Mary's, whom this Elizabeth murdered . . . '

'Hush girl – watch your words! In Walsingham's England, even walls have ears! And what you say is foolishness. Queen Mary has no further need of such. They are the King's now. And this was the finest – the most apt to please Elizabeth and bring her to think kindly of our embassage . . . '

'But your embassage is but to gain money from her – this pension. Surely the jewel itself is worth a great sum? To give it to her, when it is worth . . . '

'It is worth a great deal, yes – but only what men will give for it. In money. The King needs money, siller, not jewellery. No lord in all Scotland has sufficient to buy yon toy – even if he wanted it. Scotland is ever short of money, lass. It is the blight of the land.'

'I see. Only one of the blights, I think.' She shrugged slender shoulders. 'So you think that the Queen may be kinder to you hereafter?'

'That is my hope.'

'It may be so,' the girl said slowly, thoughtfully. 'I think that she may have misjudged you – as she said. I think that my presence with you has harmed you with her, Uncle Patrick – and I am sorry. No doubt she was informed that I was close to you. She would believe that I was your doxy, bedding with you – as I think do many. That she would not like, for she is foolish enough to desire that all men around her think only of herself, I do believe. But now – she has seen me, seen us together. She knows the truth of what is between us – for her eyes are sufficiently sharp. I think that she will relent, perhaps, towards you. If that is what caused her to keep us waiting.'

Stroking his chin, the Master looked at her wonderingly.

'You . . . you continue to surprise me, Mary,' he said. 'Where did you get the wits in that pretty head of yours? Heigho – it must have been from myself, I suppose, for your mother, though fair and kind, is scarcely so gifted! Yes – you may well be right. It may be as you say . . '

A knocking at the door of Patrick's adjoining room interrupted him, and drew him through thereto. A servant stood there, and beside him a messenger in the royal livery.

'The Master of Gray?' this functionary enquired. 'The Queen's Grace commands your presence in her private apartments forthwith, sir.'

'Ah! She does? Then . . . then, sir, the Queen's Grace must be obeyed of course. *Instanter*. Give me but a moment . . . '

Chapter Ten

PATRICK was led through a garden and pleasance to a small side door at the extreme east end of the palace where, after a muttered exchange, a guard admitted them. His guide then conducted him, by a maze of passages, to a brightly lit and luxuriously appointed chamber, where instruments of music, embroidery-frames, part-worked tapestries and other signs of feminine occupation were evident, but which at this midnight hour was empty. Beyond was a spacious boudoir, all mirrors, with walls upholstered in quilted satin, in which a single weary elegant paced to and fro. He raised an eyebrow at the Master, sighed, and holding up a minatory finger as though to restrain further progress, turned and opened one of a pair of double doors, knocked gently on the inner one, waited, and then slipped within. When he emerged again it was to beckon the visitor forward, though with no expression of approval. He said no word.

A puff of warm and highly-scented air met Patrick as he passed into the chamber beyond. Just within the doorway he paused and bowed very low – although he could barely distinguish at first what lay beyond, so dim was the lighting. Here was a small room, panelled severely in dark wood, but with a large fire of logs blazing on the hearth – which, apart from only a couple of candles, provided all the illumination. A great bed with canopy and rich hangings occupied much of the apartment, but it was unoccupied. On a couch by the fire, a figure reclined, clad in the loose and very feminine folds of a flowing bed-robe.

'Come, Patrick,' a voice invited, low, companionable, warm as the room. 'This is better, is it not?'

'Immeasurably, Your Grace,' he replied, as easily. 'I rejoice in it.'

'Aye. But rejoice not too soon, my friend, nevertheless,' the Queen warned. 'Do not stand there, man, you were not always so backward! Come, sit here by me – for the night is plaguey cold.' Elizabeth was ever concerned about the temperature.

She did not however move aside on the couch on which she was extended, so that the man, to sit down thereon, must needs perch himself uncomfortably on the edge. He chose carefully to sit approximately half-way down, part-turned to face the Queen.

'Cynthia, Moon Goddess, Queen of the Night!' he murmured.

'And a match for Patrick, Master of . . . Darkness!'

'Match, aye – what a match, Madam, there would be!'

'Bold!' she said, but not harshly.

For a few moments there was silence, save for the splutter and hiss of the burning logs. The Queen drew up her knees a little, so that they pressed into the skin-tight silken hose of the man's thigh. He did not move away – indeed he could not have done so without leaving the couch altogether.

'Your Mary Gray is . . . remarkable, Patrick,' Elizabeth said presently. 'I vow I must congratulate you! My good Moor, Walsingham, misled me, I fear. For once. How old is she?'

'This was her seventeeth summer.'

'Ah! Seventeen? You were an early menace to poor foolish women then, Patrick – as of course you would be!'

'Perhaps. Or else their victim. But here was one indiscretion of youth that I have no cause to regret.'

'No? You are proud of her, then? You would not have brought her here else, of course. Proud . . . but wise? I wonder, Patrick? That one is too like yourself for your comfort, I think.

223

Take heed for yourself, my friend – for there is a will as strong as your own. And wits as sharp, I'll wager. Your Davy, who so long sought in vain to honest you, may have forged here sweet steel to tame you!'

'I beg leave to doubt it. But I am flattered indeed at Your Grace's interest in my humble person and affairs! It augurs well . . . '

'Tush, man – do not build on it! I am only the more wary.'

'Hence, dear lady, this so privy audience? Such wariness is a delight, indeed . . . !'

Sitting up, she leaned forward, and raising her hand, slapped the man's face – a sharp blow and no playful tap. 'Delight in that also, sir!' she jerked.

Not only did Patrick not draw back, but he did not so much as change expression or tone of voice. 'I do, fair Dian – I do! As I must delight also in what my happy eyes behold!' And coolly, deliberately, he looked downwards.

The Queen's face was very near to his own – for she had not sunk back into her reclining position after her blow. As a consequence of her forward-leaning posture, her bed-robe gaped wide before her, wholly revealing bare breasts, small but firm and shapely for her years, if flattered somewhat by the rosy uncertain flickering firelight. She did not move nor speak, although her lips were parted.

So they sat, close together, considering each other, understanding each other.

At length Elizabeth leaned back again, with a little sigh, and though she raised a slender white arm behind her turbaned head, she made no attempt to close up the front of her robe. Undoubtedly she wore nothing beneath it. Relaxed, she lay thus, a faint smile playing about her thin mouth.

The man reached out and gently took her hand. She allowed him to stroke her long tapering fingers, occasionally to run his own up over her wrist and forearm. Once she shivered slightly, and for a moment his fingers gripped tight before resuming their unhurried stroking once more. Somewhere a clock chimed half-an-hour past midnight.

'Blessed no-words, Patrick,' the Queen murmured, at length. 'I hear ever such a flood, a plague of words. So few may ever keep silent in my presence. Though you – you are eloquent indeed even in silence, my friend!'

He smiled only, and raised her finger-tips, ringless now, to his lips, and kissed each individually before turning her hand over and kissing the narrow palm. His caresses moved on, over wrist and up white forearm, so that it was his turn to lean close indeed. She permitted him to reach the region of her elbow, and therefore to be within an inch or two of her pale bosom, before her other hand reached out gently but firmly to grip his ear, restraining him.

'Linger a little, Patrick,' she murmured huskily. 'The night is young, yet.'

He raised his eyes to hers. 'You are no woman to linger over.'

Elizabeth smiled. 'Impatient!'

'Very, Diana!'

'Then . . . in that case, I have you where I want you, Master of Gray! Pleading! On your knees.'

'Have you not always?' he asked, and slipped down from the couch to kneel beside her. Still she held on to his ear.

'I think not, Patrick. Your mind seldom pleads, I swear. Nor are the knees of your heart apt for bending!'

'They bend to you, fair one.'

She nipped that ear between finger-nails, almost viciously. 'For what does your heart and mind plead, Patrick? Your heart and mind, I say, not . . . other parts?'

'Why is not that evident, indeed, Diana? All my parts are at one in pleading for . . . all of the loveliness before me.' He leaned still closer, against the pain of that ear, so that the warmth of her body actually reached his cheek.

'Liar!' she whispered. 'What did you come for, man?'

'I came because you sent for me, and because of the love I bear you – in hope.'

'Dolt! Not now. Why came you to me, from Scotland?'

Patrick drew a long breath, 'My prince sent me . . . at my own urgent behest,' he said.

'For what purpose?'

'Not the purpose for which I kneel here, Lady.'

'I wonder! Think again, Patrick. You are here for money, are you not? For golden coin, and nothing more! Wait, man –

wait! And if you can come to the money more surely, more swiftly, through my woman's weakness – then so much the better!'

'Your Grace – you wrong me! I vow you do – most sorely.'

'I think not. You use all men – and women, also – for your own ends, Patrick Gray. Always you have done so. But you will not use me, by God! Up off your lying knees, man! If you must kneel, go kneel to my Lord Treasurer!'

Slowly, reluctantly, Patrick rose to his feet. But he did not move away from the side of the couch. Nor yet did his beautiful features show any sign of emotion other than sorrow and a gentle reproach, allied with a hint of wonder.

'You brought me here, to your privy room – only to tell me this?' he asked.

'That – and to test you, sir.'

'Aye – and to tease me, I think,' he added, slowly. 'To torment my manhood. They do say that such makes sport of a sort for some women – half-women. But not, surely not, for the Queen of the Night!' And he sighed.

Elizabeth sat up abruptly, and whipped her bed-robe tight around her. 'How dare you, sir!' she said. But she seemed more put out than angry, searching his face in the flickering firelight.

'I would dare much for your favour, Madam – to banish your suspicions of me.'

'And to win my money, rogue! That damnable pension!'

'The money I seek only for my prince,' he told her. 'For that I would dare but little. Your esteem and regard I seek, for myself – and for that I would indeed dare all.'

'All, Patrick?'

'All.'

'Then dare you to go back to King James empty-handed, my friend. Dare to tell him that he must earn his own gold. Dare to tell him that my heir must be a true man and not a beggar! Dare that, and earn my esteem and love, Patrick Gray!'

'Aye, Lady – that I dare do. I shall do, if it is your wish. And come again. Another day. Happy day. To claim my . . . reward! Joyfully.' He stepped back a single pace.

226

Keenly, warily, the Queen looked at him. 'You would do this? So readily?'

'Why yes, Your Grace. For *I* am no beggar – save of your heart's warmth. Of which I felt the divine breath minutes ago. I agree entirely that pleading for this promised pension but harms the dignity of King James. Mine also, if I were to descend to it. I am glad to be spared that.'

'So-o-o!' He had Elizabeth tapping finger-nails on the edge of her couch now. 'You surprise me, Patrick.'

'Why so, Your Grace?' Almost casually he asked it, and turned to stroll round the back of the couch, so that she must needs turn her head to follow him with her pale eyes. 'Did you deem me happy in mendicancy? Riches have never been a love of mine – and assuredly I cannot prostitute myself for them on behalf of another, even my prince.'

She was silent for a little, but her glance never left his face. 'I still cannot believe that you are so readily dissuaded, Patrick Gray,' she said, at length. 'I think that I know you better than that.'

He sighed. 'My sorrow, that you so judge me, Diana. It is but a woeful end to what might have been the night of nights! A sorry farewell to carry away with me on my long journey.'

'Journey? You would ride, then? Forthwith? Back to Scotland?'

'Why yes, Highness. This very day, since it is now past midnight. Why wait? Such is my lord of Moray's intention, already . . . '

'You are plaguey quick, man, to get away from me!'

'Not so. It will be like plucking the beating heart out of my breast. But better that than teasing and disenchantment here. The sooner that I dare my prince's wrath for you, as you ask, the sooner I may return – I pray, to your favour.'

'You think then that King James will permit you to return, in such case?'

Patrick actually laughed a little. 'Indeed it is next to certain, Lady,' he said.

'Why?'

'He is sore in need of siller, as we name it, for his marriage to the Princess Anne. For her Coronation, likewise. For the strengthening of his Royal Guard, that there be no more threats of abduction by lords who might seek to take him, or his queen, into their power. So, if the King gets it not from Your Grace, he must needs seek it elsewhere.'

Elizabeth snorted. 'And who else will give him so much as a single gold piece, man? Not the King of Denmark, I swear. James will be fortunate if he ever so much as sees his wife's dowry, from there!'

'Not Denmark, no. But it occurs to me that he might well turn to France. To King Henri, formerly Navarre.'

'Faugh, stupid – after rejecting Henri's sister Catherine of Navarre? There will be no French gold for James. Besides – would he send *you* again, Patrick, on such a mission? After returning empty-handed from this?'

'I think that he would, Madam. For only I have the information that he would need for success in it. Valuable information – that would make Protestant Henri look more kindly on my prince. And look askance elsewhere.'

'Eh? What information? What is this, sir?'

Patrick halted in his strolling round that bedchamber. 'Information that I have gleaned, Your Grace,' he said slowly. 'Information that will set Christendom agog! Notable information.'

'Well, man – well?'

'That the Queen of England is proposing to marry Protestant Lady Arabella Stewart, her cousin, to the Catholic Duke of Parma, Spain's Captain-General in the Netherlands, Butcher of the Low Countries!'

'Christ God!' the Queen exclaimed, almost in a croak.

'To be sure,' he nodded, smiling. 'Heigho, Highness – such information is worth . . . a king's ransom, is it not?'

Elizabeth was having difficulty with her breathing and with her words. 'How . . . fiend seize you, where . . . what a pox d'you mean . . . ?'

'I have it, Lady, from a most sure source. Your good Moor, Walsingham, is not the only one with an ear for information!'

'It is a folly! A lie . . . '

'Folly, mayhap – but no lie. Of this I am assured. On excellent . . . authority!'

'Sweet Jesu – when I find who babbled . . . !'

228

'Be not distressed, Your Grace. I would not have Gloriana distressed for . . . for all the gold in Christendom! If this is something that you would keep privy. None need know, other than myself. Have no fears . . . '

Elizabeth's voice grated. 'It is done with. A plan that came to naught. That might have healed the breach with Spain. It is past. A thing of Hatton's . . . '

'But still . . . dangerous, Madam. Still a matter that could greatly concern King Henri. Or other Protestant princes. Arabella is next heir to the Scots throne after Ludovick of Lennox, her cousin. And therefore to your throne also, Lady. Matched with Catholic Parma, the Executioner – who was carried in a litter over the mutilated corpses of thousands of Maestricht's citizens! Here could be gunpowder beneath the chancellories of Christendom, indeed!'

'Silence! Damnation, man – hold your tongue!' The Queen's slender fists were clenched, and she beat them on her knee. 'How you learned of this – you of all men – I know not. Heads will fall, as a consequence, I promise you! But . . . no word of it must be so much as breathed. You understand? That is my royal command.'

'I understand Your Highness's feelings in the matter, yes. I can be silent, Diana – silent as the grave itself.'

'Aye. As you had better be! And the price of that silence, Master of Gray?'

He drew a long breath. 'Why, fairest one – nothing. Nothing, at all. Or, at least . . . very little!' He moved back to the side of the couch again, and stood looking down at her. 'For love of you, Diana, I would keep silence at the stake itself!'

'See that I do not test you in that, in the Tower or the Bridewell – Papist!' she said. 'What is this very little that you want?'

'First, your smile in place of your frown, fair one,' he asserted. 'That before all.'

'All . . . ?' she repeated.

His little laugh was low-pitched, melodious and purely mirthful, as he sank down on his knees again, where he had knelt before. 'In certain matters, I am greedy indeed, Diana!' he told her, and reached for her hand.

'And I, sir, in those things may well be . . . parsimonious!'

she returned. But, after a moment's hesitation, she did not withhold her hand.

'That I will not believe,' he said, shaking his head. 'Let us essay the matter, Your Grace . . . ?'

Although Patrick was very quiet in entering his own chamber later that night, Mary heard him, and jumping out of bed came through to him.

'You have been long,' she said. 'Have you been with the Queen? All this time?'

'Aye,' he nodded. 'You should be asleep, girl.'

'What was this, Uncle Patrick? Why did she send for you? At such an hour. After dismissing us so?'

'Because she is a strange woman, Mary. Strange and cunning. And she thought that she could best me. Test me and best me. The Master of Gray!'

'And did she?'

'She tested me, yes. But I do not think that she bested me.' And he smiled.

She searched his face gravely. 'I would like to hear how that was done?' she said. 'You saw her alone?'

'Oh, yes. But now is not the time for the telling, lass. You should be sleeping. It is only a few hours to dawn – and we have a long day ahead of us. We must by no means sleep late.'

'Tomorrow? Why?'

'Because, my dear, I much respect Sir Francis Walsingham! The sooner that we are on our road back to Scotland, the happier I shall be!'

'Walsingham? Scotland? We are going home? Tomorrow? With my lord of Moray? After all?'

'Aye. Just as soon as I deem the Lord Treasurer to be out of his bed!'

'The Lord Treasurer? And Walsingham? I do not understand.'

'I hold, moppet, a note in the Queen's own hand, ordering the Lord Treasurer to pay me £2,000, being King James's increased pension. I have a notion that Walsingham would by no means approve – and as I say, I have a respect for him and his methods. I prefer to be well on my way back to Scotland before he finds out. And as you know, he is very well informed.'

'So-o-o!' the girl breathed out. 'You have done it! You have the pension – and doubled it! You have succeeded in your mission, after all? I wonder . . . I wonder how you did that, Uncle Patrick?'

'Shall we say that I used the gifts the good God gave me? Now – off to bed again, child, and let me to mine.'

Chapter Eleven

THE unexpectedly successful embassage arrived back in Scotland on the cold bright last day of October 1589, to a singularly surprising situation, notably altered from that they had left – indeed a situation without parallel in the country's history. The King was gone.

At Berwick-upon-Tweed, when the travellers first heard these tidings, they by no means believed them. But resting overnight at Fast Castle, the eagle's-nest stronghold on the Coldinghamshire cliffs of Patrick's freebooting cousin Robert Logan of Restalrig, they learned the truth of it. James had left Scotland eight days before. Word, it seemed, had eventually reached Leith that the Princess Anne's convoy of eleven ships, buffeted, battered and dispersed by contrary gales, after having been no less than three times within sight of the Scottish coast, had finally put back to Norway, abandoning all hope of reaching Scotland that season. James, quite desperate, had decided that there was nothing for a true lover, chivalrous knight and kingly poet to do, in the circumstances, but to set sail himself, go fetch his bride, and challenge the Devil and all his malign works of witchcraft in a heroic royal gesture that in due course would make the most splendid epic of all. Despite the astonishment, disbelief, alarm and unanimous disapproval of his advisers, the King was adamant – and urgent. He had ordered the most suitable ship in the harbour of Leith to be made ready for sea, and had appointed a Council of Regency to govern the realm during his absence, and on the 22nd of

231

October had set sail for Scandinavia, taking Chancellor Maitland with him, his chaplain Master David Lindsay to perform the marriage ceremony, and sundry others. By now, he might well be in Norway.

Even Patrick Gray was quite overcome by this extraordinary news. Eventually, however, he smiled, he chuckled, he began to laugh – and laughed until tears ran down his cheeks. The Earl of Moray was less amused, especially when Logan could by no means recollect his name amongst those nominated for the Council of Regency.

They set off for Edinburgh without delay next morning.

In the capital city they found a most curious state of affairs prevailing. James, in his delegation of authority, had been more astute than might have been expected. He had, with rather remarkable cunning, selected for various offices of government just those nobles who, because of mutual suspicion and rivalry, could be relied upon to counter-balance each others' influence and thus preclude any probable bid for power by a faction. Ludovick, Duke of Lennox, was to be viceroy and President of the Council of Regency; but lest any should seek to use that very young man too ambitiously, as Vice-President was appointed, of all choices, the madcap Francis, Earl of Bothwell, another cousin of James, whose fiery and unpredictable behaviour could be guaranteed to keep everybody on the alert. The chief military power was put in the hands of the Lord Hamilton, no friend of Bothwell's, and another contender for the heirship to the throne. Sir Robert Melville, a rather dull soldier but incorruptible, was appointed Acting Chancellor; but lest he be not sufficiently Protestant, Master Robert Bruce, chief minister of Edinburgh at St. Giles, was added to the Council with especial responsibility for the Kirk. And so on. Despite his hurried exodus, James undoubtedly had given these dispositions much thought. Perhaps he had been contemplating something of the sort for some time.

There were no special appointments for either the Master of Gray nor the Earl of Moray.

The Lady Marie welcomed Patrick and Mary back warmly. The Master of the Wardrobe's own quarters in the north wing of Holyroodhouse had at last become ready and available while they were in England, and Marie had removed there from her father's crowded establishment nearby. Here was space, privacy, comfort, with even a private stairway from the great courtyard, and a room for Mary's own use. After months and years of making do in cramped and inconvenient lodgings, Marie rejoiced in this domestic bliss, and asked no more than that her little household should settle therein quietly and enjoy it, during this unexpected interval of Court inactivity.

But it was not to be. Patrick Gray was not the man for settled and domestic bliss.

'I am sorry, my dear,' he told her. 'But this is no place for us, meantime. With the King gone, I should be but wasting my time in Edinburgh. There is much to be done elsewhere – especially at Broughty Castle. Many decisions await me there . . . '

'Not Broughty, Patrick!' his wife protested. 'Not that great gloomy, draughty pile! To dwell in! Winter is almost upon us . . . '

'It will be less gloomy now, Marie, I promise you. And the draughts somewhat abated, I vow. I love such no more than you do. But it is my house, my inheritance – thrown in my face by my father! I intend that he shall rue the day that he fobbed me off with Broughty!'

'Yes, Patrick – but we need not go to live there. Not yet. In winter. When we have this fine lodging here. You can visit Broughty, yes – to see how the work goes. But that need take only a day or two. We need not all go . . . '

'I fear that we need so, indeed,' he assured her. 'And get there as quickly and secretly as may be. Do you not realise, my heart, that I have here with me two thousand English pounds in gold? A vast fortune indeed. Half the lords in Scotland, not to mention lesser men, would sell their very souls for a tithe of it! That gold, and my life with it, must be protected, must it not? Once it becomes known that I have it – and Moray, I swear, will not fail to let all know that our mission has been successful – men with long knives and empty purses will be after it, and me. Nothing is more certain. So much ready money has scarce been seen in Scotland before. It must be placed in safety – and swiftly. And I can think of few places safer than in Broughty Castle, where only a few men might guard it against an army.'

'But it is the King's money, Patrick. Bestow it in the royal treasury . . . '

'A pox, Marie – that is the last place I would place it! Who has the keys of the royal treasury? My Lord Treasurer, the Master of Glamis, one of the biggest rogues in the land! No, that is not a temptation I mean to put in our friend Thomas Lyon's way! Nor in the way of any in the Council, God save me, with the King far in another land!'

'Ludovick would look after it. He is the King's representative, and honest.'

'Ludovick is young, a mere boy. He is honest, yes – but can be cozened. No – it goes to Broughty, and we go with it. Forthwith. This very night I shall go down to Leith to find a boat that may take us there. Safer, more secretly, than the long journey by land . . . '

'You are sure, Patrick, that you intend that all this gold shall come out of Broughty Castle again, into King James's hands, in due course?'

Patrick frowned. 'If that is a jest, Marie, it is but ill-timed,' he said coldly.

Mary Gray intervened, from the fireside where she had been listening quietly to this exchange. 'It will be good to be back in the Carse again,' she said. 'You will take me with you, Uncle Patrick? I shall go home to my mother and father at Castle Huntly. I am longing to see them again . . . '

A servant knocked at the door to announce the presence of the Duke of Lennox.

Ludovick came in hurriedly, breathlessly, having run up the stairs. His eyes, shining, turned immediately to Mary, before he recollected his duty to the Master of Gray and his wife.

'I was at Dalkeith, when I heard,' he declared, 'that you were returned. I came at once.'

'Ha – the ruler of Scotland in person!' Patrick exclaimed. 'My lord Duke, we are indeed honoured by your condescension in seeking out our humble abode.'

Ludovick's plain freckled features actually flushed a little. 'I came as soon as I heard,' he said, awkwardly. 'I rejoice to see you back. I . . . I have missed you greatly.' Once again his glance slid round to Mary.

234

The Master came across and put an arm around the younger man's shoulders. 'I will not ask, Vicky, which of us you have missed most!' And he laughed.

'Why, I . . . I . . . ah . . . ummm.'

The girl came to his rescue. She rose, and curtsied to him. 'How good to see you, Vicky,' she said. 'It was kind of you to come, and so quickly.'

'Mary!' he got out, and reached for her hand in a grab rather than in any viceregal gesture. 'You are well? So beautiful! I have wearied for you. It has been so long . . . '

'We have only been gone for a month, Vicky.'

'It has seemed more, much more.' Clearly the young woman's absence in England had had a great effect on the Duke, had served to confirm and crystallise his emotion with regard to her. A new urgency had come into his whole attitude.

Patrick did not fail to perceive it, and stroked his chin thoughtfully. 'I am sure that Mary is flattered, Vicky,' he said. 'But . . . you must have other matters on your mind, meantime? Matters of state. As President of the Council . . . '

'It is damnable,' the young man burst out, 'that James should saddle me with this. Men are at me all the time, to consider this and agree to that. It is papers and parchments and charters, every day – signing, always signing and sealing. Ink and sand and sealing-wax . . . !'

'Poor Vicky!' The Lady Marie smiled at him. 'When all that you want is a good horse between your knees, and hounds baying!'

'Aye. And . . . and . . . ' Ludovick looked at the younger woman.

'As well that Mary is going home to Castle Huntly then, perhaps.'

'Eh . . . ? Going . . . ? To Castle Huntly? You are not going away, Mary?'

'Why yes, Vicky. Meantime. It is time. I have not been home for three long months. I long to see my father and mother. And Granlord . . . '

'But your place is here. At Court. You are one of the Queen's ladies.'

'The Queen will not be needing me for months, to be sure.'

'But . . . you should not go. You have been away for toc

235

long, as it is. I . . . I . . . ' The Duke drew himself up. 'I could forbid you to go,' he said, thickly. 'I am Viceroy. I rule here, meantime.'

Mary's trill of laughter was spontaneous, mirthful. 'Do not be daft, Vicky!' she told him.

Immediately abashed, shamefaced, he looked down. 'I am sorry,' he mumbled. 'But . . . I do not want you to go.'

'I shall come back, never fear.'

'*I* shall come – come to you, then. To Castle Huntly. Or not to the castle itself, but nearby. You cannot stop me doing that, Mary – none can stop me. I shall leave Bothwell to read the papers and do the signing. He will like it well enough. I shall come to the Carse of Gowrie. Or to Dundee . . . '

'M'mmm – one moment,' Patrick intervened, carefully. 'I think, Vicky, that would be foolish. To hand over the rule to Bothwell. You owe the realm, and James, better than that. Bothwell is quite irresponsible. He might do anything. There would be trouble with Hamilton, for certain. No – you are Duke of Lennox and the King's lieutenant, and must bear the rule.'

The other set his chin obstinately. 'I go to the Carse if Mary goes,' he said.

'Then . . . then come to Broughty Castle with us, and bear the rule from there, Vicky.' Even Patrick Gray could scarcely keep the ring of excitement out of his voice. 'It is but a dozen miles from Castle Huntly.'

Quickly, searchingly, the Lady Marie looked at her husband, and then to Mary. She said nothing.

'That I should like very well,' Ludovick agreed.

'Sir Robert Melville's house in Fife is just across Tay from there. He acts Chancellor, they tell me? Nothing could be more convenient.'

'For whom?' his wife asked, somewhat tensely.

'For the Duke, of course, my dear. For the good governance of the realm. For Scotland,' Patrick answered easily. 'We go at once, Vicky – so soon as I can find a vessel to carry us. Secretly. For I fear for the King's siller that I have brought from Elizabeth. But you – you must come to Broughty later, with no undue haste. And not directly. Calling on sundry lords on the way – calling at your own house of Methven. It will

236

look better so. None must consider your visit to Broughty, your sojourn there, to be aught but casual, innocent . . . '

'Aught but innocent! There we have it!' Marie took him up. 'And if this is not innocent, then – is it guilty, Patrick?'

'Tush!' he exclaimed. 'You have the vapours, my love. You jump at shadows. Come, Vicky – accompany me down to Leith, to enquire of the shipmen. Then, if there is talk of me removing this money, the King's represenative himself will be known to be privy to it. The more reason for him to follow it to Broughty, i' faith!'

Reluctantly, after a longing look at Mary, the Duke followed the Master.

When they were gone, Marie went over to the baby in the crib by the window, and stood gazing down at it. 'I do not like it, Mary,' she said, shaking her fair head. 'I know that look in Patrick's eye. I fear more intrigue, more conspiracy. And therefore trouble. I see Patrick reaching out again for power . . . '

'He was made for power, Lady Marie. There is good in power, as well as ill. You will never stop Uncle Patrick reaching for it, I think. It is for us to be ever near him, to seek where we can that the power works for good. As we have done before.'

'As *you* have done, Mary. Lord, child – I believe that you were made for this power as much as was Patrick! And delight in it but little the less!'

The younger woman considered that gravely for a moment or two, and then shook her head in turn. But that was as far as her denial went.

And so, with scarcely believable ease and minimum of manoeuvre, Patrick Gray slipped quietly and inconspicuously into the rule of Scotland once again. Only a mere five months after the banished felon's uninvited return from exile, he was, temporarily at least, back in the saddle of supreme authority, operative if not titular – for he held the Viceroy of the realm in the hollow of his hand and took the decisions which Lennox promulgated. Scotland, for so long without a strong king or settled central government, swiftly if cynically recognised and accepted the familiar pattern of power, and all men with favours to seek and causes to further, concessions, exemptions, sanctions, positions, must come to seek them at Broughty Castle. In this Patrick was most effectively aided and advantaged by the very virtues of the acting Chancellor; Sir Robert Melville's unimaginative honesty, lack of ambition, and peaceable disposition, played into the Master's skilful hands. He went out of his way to seem to consult and defer to the older man, making many journeys himself and sending couriers daily over the Tay to the Melville house in Fife. He had his reward.

Moreover, despite his wife's fears, the Master of Gray was very good at the business. As had been the case three years before, when for the best part of a prosperous and peaceful year Patrick had largely controlled the destinies of his native land, so now, for those winter and spring months, Scotland was well-managed, discreetly guided, and comparatively tranquil. Admittedly Bothwell rampaged about the Borders, burning and slaying unchecked – but then, that was ever his habit, and neither James nor Maitland had found any method of stopping him. Huntly was feuding with his neighbours in the north, and taking the opportunity to devastate the Keith lands while the Earl of Marischal was still overseas – but that also was chronic, and at least he kept his activities well north of decent settled country. No doubt the far-flung Highlands seethed with strife and endemic clan warfare, but it was to the advantage of all good men that such barbarians should kill each other off as vigorously as possible. For the rest, a moderate calm prevailed, the grosser corruptions were discouraged, some notorious ill-doers were brought to justice, certain judges brought low, and the campaign against witches came almost to a full stop. There were growlings and snarlings from sundry nobles, inevitably, and carpings from the Kirk that Papistical influence was in the ascendant; but such broke no bones. And although tales were rife that a vast sum in English gold for the King was being salted away shamefully in Broughty Castle instead of in the royal treasury, the presence on the premises of the Viceroy himself largely tied the hands of any who might have sought to do more than talk. The Lord Treasurer, the Master of Glamis, at any rate, kept his distance – even though

238

that was not so very far off, in his castle of Aldbar, near Brechin.

Broughty Castle itself, and the little town that lay under its frowning walls, flourished in consequence as never before. Very considerable improvements had been made to the stern and battle-torn fortalice since the previous July, despite dire lack of funds, but now the place blossomed like the May. Suddenly there was no dearth of money – though whence it came was by no means clear. Broughty would never be a palace nor yet a ladies' bower; but at least it was made habitable, even moderately comfortable, timber outbuildings sprang up within the courtyard, whitewashed harling set the massive masonry gleaming, tapestries and hangings graced the bare interior walls – even a painted picture or two. Servants multiplied about the place, and from Dundee came a steady stream of furnishings, fabrics, provender and wines. And above the topmost tower fluttered proudly in the sea breeze no fewer than three standards – the silver lion on scarlet, of Gray; the fess chequery of Stewart quartered with the golden lilies of D'Aubigny and the red roses of Lennox; and the rampant lion of Scotland itself.

By no means could Patrick Gray force his father to come from Castle Huntly to see it all; but at least each day at noon an old cannon, put into commission for the purpose, thundered out a viceregal salute from the battlements, that must have been heard from one end of the Carse to the other and over half of Fife and Angus, proclaiming for all to hear that here on this barren rocky promontory, was authority, jurisdiction, rule.

There was much coming and going between the two castles, of course, even though Patrick would no more darken the door of the one than would his sire the other. Ludovick seldom let a day pass without covering the dozen miles of coastline. The Lady Marie was a frequent visitor at Castle Huntly, ignoring as best she might her father-in-law's jibes and jeers. Davy Gray went often to Broughty, and Mariota occasionally. As for Mary, she was almost as much in the one house as the other, a laughing lightsome figure, apparently reverted wholly to country ways again.

The trouble that Marie feared did not materialise.

The Duke's pursuit of Mary Gray was now frank, determined in a quiet way, and continuous. Though perhaps pursuit is no accurate description; attendance upon and following after would be more apt, for there was nothing of the hunt, nothing of attack and flight about their relationship. The girl remained wholly, if modestly, inconspicuously, in command of the situation, with Lennox the faithful, humble but persistent suppliant. He was quite without pride or self-esteem in the matter, not pressing his cause other than by displaying his devotion and seeking perpetually to be in her company, content to be her squire, her escort, her constant but undemanding companion.

That the young woman did not object to his company and attentions, she made no attempt to hide. She was kind, suitably respectful in public, not at all so in private, but considerate always. That he much preferred to be with her than to concern himself with affairs of state, she accepted – though not infrequently she gently urged him towards his duty, and sought to discuss with him the problems which he tended to avoid or dismiss.

There was talk, of course – much and scandalous talk. That the Duke should require a mistress was only to be expected; but with all the cream of Scotland to choose from, that he should select the ostensible daughter of a mere land-steward, and moon after her as though she were a princess, caused grave offence. That it was all a disgraceful plot of the Master of Gray's, of course, could be taken for granted; he was using this brat to enthrall Lennox and so control the realm.

If such talk worried none of the three principals, the same could not be said of Davy Gray.

One crisp sunny December afternoon, with rime almost as thick as snow upon the ground, my lord of Gray came riding into his courtyard of Castle Huntly, hoof-beats ringing metallically in the sharp frosty air. Davy Gray was crossing from the keep to his own sanctum in the north-west tower. My lord hailed him over peremptorily.

'*You* taught the wench this folly o' skating, Davy – this sliding about on ice. Bairn's play. I said it wasna suitable in a lassie, in a woman. I said she'd break a leg, or the like. But you kenned better – ooh, aye, Davy Gray ay kens better! Well, maybe you'll now change your tune . . .'

'Mary? She is not hurt? Skating? She has not broke . . . ?'

'No' her legs, no – it's mair like her maidenhead's in danger! If it's no' gone already!' the older man returned coarsely. 'She's out there on Sauchie Loch, clutching and hugging her precious duke to her, like any tavern trollop! I wonder we're no' hearing their skirling from here!'

The other eyed his father searchingly. It was not like Lord Gray directly to criticise Mary. 'I think that you are mistaken,' he said evenly. 'Mary behaves not so.'

'You say not? You give me the lie? Then go and look, man. Go to Sauchie Loch. She is sold to yon puppy Lennox. And it is Patrick's doing, God's eternal curse on him! The lassie is ruined, turned into a strumpet. And by yon evil devil in human shape that I had the mischance to beget!'

Davy Gray shook his head wordlessly. There was no profit in arguing.

'Dinna glower and wag your head at me, you ill limmer! It's the truth. I've been to Kinnaird. Going, I went to the smiddy with a loose shoe, and there was the pair o' them sitting by his fire watching yon great dolt o' a cousin o' yours, Don Affleck, fashioning two o' these skating irons for Lennox. God's body, but I gave him better work to do – and a flea in his ear in the by-going! But, coming back, here's them both sliding about the Shauch . . . Sauchie Loch, clasping and nuzzling each other!' My lord was having some difficulty with his enunciation. Abruptly his tone changed, and his flushed, florid and dissipated face fell ludicrously, the heavy, purple jowls seeming almost to quiver. 'Och, it's no' right, it's no' decent, Davy. She used to be my ain lass. She was canny and she was kind – my ain fair bit lassie, my ain troutie. You let her awa' to yon Court, to Patrick. You shouldna ha' done it. I told you. And now . . . now she's nae mair than a toy, any man's toy. Aye, and a broken toy at that, I'll warrant . . . ! A pox on you!' My lord, who had been drinking, was all but in maudlin tears as he stamped off. His son frowned after him.

Yet in only a few minutes that same son was making for the Sauchie Loch. It lay about half-a-mile away, between the castle and the village. It had been ice-bound for days, he knew – all fresh water had been frozen. After the winds and storms of summer and autumn, the winter had so far been one continuous frost, bright and still. King James would have cried witchcraft, indeed.

Sure enough, the man heard laughter ringing in the crisp air long before he reached the loch amongst the birch woods. It sounded clear, uninhibited and innocent enough, certainly.

He halted at the loch shore. They were out in the middle of some five acres of ice. There was some degree of truth in my lord's assertions as to hugging and clutching. The girl was holding the young man round the waist indeed, with both arms. But even as David watched, Ludovick's feet slid from under him and he went down on to the ice with a crash that would have been a deal harder had it not been for those encircling arms. There was much laughter once again, as she aided him to his unsteady feet. It was the Duke's turn to grasp his mentor.

As a turn, largely involuntary, in their erratic but hilarious progress, faced the pair in David's direction, the girl perceived her father standing there and raised a hand to wave. Even such withdrawal of support was enough to upset her pupil's precarious balance, and promptly his skates took the opportunity to slide away in almost opposite directions. Down he went once more, pulling Mary with him.

David was grinning before he recollected the unsuitability of all this, and switched to a frown instead. He paced out on to the ice, but carefully.

'Is not Vicky a fool, father?' Mary called out, as he approached them. 'He will not keep his feet together. I vow the skates should be on his bottom! Then we might do better.'

David did not relax his expression. 'Better still that you should consider my lord Duke's dignity – and your own repute, Mary,' he said sternly. 'Here is no way to behave . . . making a spectacle of yourself! You are not a child now.'

'No, I am not,' she agreed, but still smiling. 'Nor is Vicky.'

'Then remember it. This is unseemly. The realm's ruler should not be seen thus.'

'Is he being seen, Father? By any but you? And how shall it hurt the realm if its ruler laughs a little?'

'My lord saw you. And who knows what others. You can be heard afar off.'

242

'And that displeases you?'

He pursed his lips, for he was an honest man 'I . . . I fear it is unwise,' he said.

The Duke was approximately upright now, but still having to hold on to Mary. 'I thank you, sir, for your concern for my dignity,' he declared jerkily. 'Perhaps I do not esteem it so highly as you do.'

'That may be so, yes. But it is more Mary's name and repute that I think for, my lord Duke. As, I think, should you.'

The younger man, balancing uneasily there, frowned. 'As I do, Master Gray. Indeed . . . ' – he blinked rapidly – ' . . . indeed, I think of little else. She will scarce let me speak of it, but it is ever in my mind. I think so much of her name that, that . . . '

'That he would have me to change it!' Mary laughed. 'And I am very well content with it as it is, thank you! Whatever its repute.'

'Change it . . . ?' David repeated.

'I would change it to mine, sir. I would wed her – if she would have me.'

'God be good!'

'Exactly!' the young woman nodded, quite unabashed. 'So say I. And so would say all . . . '

'But it is I that ask you to wed me, Mary – not all! Not others. I care not what others say.'

'You must care what *I* say, Vicky, must you not?'

'To be sure, yes. But all the time you are thinking of others . . . '

'Myself also, I assure you.'

'See you,' Davy Gray broke in. 'This is madness! You cannot be serious, man – my lord. Such talk is complete folly. You are the Duke of Lennox, second man to the King himself in this land. You cannot wed such as Mary. You are too important a man . . . '

'If I am so important, may I not choose my own wife?'

'No doubt – but not the daughter of Davy Gray! It must be some great lord's daughter . . . '

'I do not desire some great lord's daughter. I have seen aplenty. I want only Mary Gray . . . ' In his emotion, Ludovick gestured with his arm – and it was almost his downfall again.

His precarious equilibrium upset, he would have toppled had not Mary tightened her grip and her father grabbed a ducal arm likewise.

The girl's laughter rippled. 'Perhaps Your Excellency should keep your mind on, on matters of immediate moment, sir!'

'Mary . . . !'

'Come,' David said, urging the younger man towards the shore. 'We cannot discuss such matters thus.'

'There is nothing left to discuss,' Mary declared, sighing. 'We have discussed it all overmuch already.' But she helped to steer the Duke towards the bank, nevertheless.

That young man laboured under an obvious handicap in expressing his point of view. 'I will wed none but Mary,' he announced, edging forward between them, with boyish set-jawed obstinacy.

'But . . . cannot you see my lord? It would not be permitted,' David pointed out. 'The King would not allow it.'

'James is not here. I am Viceroy. None could stop me.'

'Not even I, Vicky?'

'The marriage would be annulled when James came back,' David insisted. 'You are not yet of age. King and Council would invoke your lack of years, for certain. Think what it means. You are next heir to the throne. Should James die – should his ship sink in a storm, coming home from Denmark – you would be King, and your wife Queen! Mary Gray, daughter of a bastard of no account!'

'I care not. And if I am old enough to rule as Viceroy . . . '

'But others care, my lord Duke, *I* do! And Mary is not of age, either. She is under my authority . . . '

'While I am ruler of this realm, my authority is above yours, Master Gray!' the other announced heavily. They had reached the shore now. 'I can do what I will.'

'Vicky – do not be foolish,' Mary said, pleading a little now. 'What father says is true. You might insist on marrying me – but it would be done away with when the King returns.'

'James would heed me. He thinks kindly of me . . . '

'But he would not, *could* not, have me as good-sister! As good-sister to his new Queen. Wife to his heir. And consider Elizabeth of England. James is her heir, also – but only if she

244

so directs. Think you that she would for one moment agree to accept James if *his* heir was married to a commoner? Guidsakes, Vicky – I might then become Queen of England!'

That gave him pause for a moment.

'Elizabeth would insist on King James having the marriage annulled,' she went on. 'He would do it, for certain. And how would that leave me?'

'Then . . . then I must needs renounce my position. Give up my heirship to the crown. I care naught for it, anyway. That is what I shall do.'

'Dear Vicky – you would so do much, for my sake? You are kind. But . . . it cannot be. We cannot change the state into which we were born – either of us.'

'You are a peer of this realm, my lord – Scotland's only duke,' David said. 'You cannot renounce your blood. None could accept such a renunciation, since at any time you could change it again. I am sorry, lad. A man may not avoid his destiny, I fear.'

'Some would say that a man can *make* his destiny!' Ludovick asserted stubbornly. 'That I mean to do.'

Davy Gray shook his head helplessly. 'I am sorry,' he repeated. 'I cannot command your lordship's actions. But I can command my daughter, forbid her to see you . . .'

'And I can command her presence!' the other returned spiritedly. 'As well as Viceroy, I am Lord Chamberlain. Mary is one of the Queen's ladies, and all such are under my control . . .'

'And I say that she is not! Mary is under age. Until she is of full years, she is in my care . . .'

'Oh, a truce, a truce!' the young woman interrupted. 'If you could but hear yourselves! You are like bairns, both of you. I will not be pulled this way and that, like a bone between two dogs! I cannot marry you, Vicky – that is certain. But neither shall I be forbidden to see you, or . . . or any man! I mean to live my own life. Between you, I declare, you have spoiled a bonny day! I am going home. Alone. I seek my own company, only. If you must squabble thus, you can do it by yourselves.'

And tossing her dark head a little, Mary Gray turned and left them there by the frozen lochside. It was seldom indeed that young woman indulged in dramatics of this sort.

The men gazed from her slender back to each other, in sudden silence and discomfort.

It was her father who caught up with her, still some way from Castle Huntly.

'I am sorry, lass,' he said, taking her arm. 'I would not hurt you. That was unseemly, I grant you. Not well done. It is only my concern for you . . .'

'You need not concern yourself,' she told him. 'I can well look after myself.'

'So you think, Mary. But you are young. Too trusting . . .'

'Young? Do years matter so, Father? Can we not be young in some things, and old in others? You are older than Uncle Patrick in some things, but in others you are but a child, I think, compared with him. Myself, I do not believe that I am so very young in all things. Nor so trusting.'

'But in this matter of Lennox . . . ?'

'Vicky is the young one – not I! *He* trusts – not I! Poor Vicky!' She sighed. 'Where has he gone?'

'Back to the smiddy. For his horse. Then he returns to Broughty. Sir Robert Melville is attending him there tonight. With papers.' He looked at her sidelong. 'This is a bad business, Mary. That young man – are you fond of him?'

'I like him very well,' she answered quietly.

'M'mmm.' He frowned.

'He is true. Honest. He seeks little for himself. Save me! Indeed, he is not unlike yourself, Father. And not at all like me!'

Keenly he eyed her, but said nothing.

'Unlike the Grays,' she added, 'Vicky is no schemer.'

David shook his head. 'He has his virtues, no doubt. But better that you should not see him, nevertheless, girl. Further association can only bring you both sorrow.'

'That may be. But think you that *not* seeing him will spare us sorrow? Besides, I must see him. And frequently.'

'Must . . . ? Why?'

'Because . . . why, because of our Gray schemings! Because of Uncle Patrick. He uses Vicky. He would involve him in many things. Not all, I fear, to his advantage. I would not wish to see Vicky hurt, wronged.'

'You mean . . . you think that Patrick intends harm to the Duke?'

246

'No – for he is fond of him, too. But to Uncle Patrick, schemes, plotting, statecraft as he calls it, is more important than are people. You know that.'

'Aye,' the man agreed heavily. 'I know it.'

'Vicky's position is so important, it is inconceivable that Uncle Patrick would not use him. He has used him much already. I want to know of such things.'

'I see,' David almost groaned. 'This, Mary, is . . . familiar ground! I' faith, it is! What can you do, even knowing?'

'I can perhaps do a little, here and there. Vicky tells me all. He does not see it all, as I do. He does not understand Uncle Patrick as I do. Have I not some responsibility in the matter?'

'Lord knows! But it is not work for such as you, lass. All the dirty, plotting deceit and wickedness of Patrick's statecraft. You are young and fresh and wholesome – a mere girl. I should never have permitted that you go to Court. I blame myself. I should not have allowed you to enter that cesspool of intrigue . . . '

'And yet it suits me very well,' she told him. 'Perhaps I am not as you think me, Father. I do not find it all so ill.'

'Then I am the more afraid for you,' the man declared. 'I had hoped that the Lady Marie would have guided you, warned you.'

'As she does. We are close. Together we seek to aid the good in Uncle Patrick's works, and to hinder the ill.'

'You do?' They walked under the gatehouse arch. 'God of mercy – innocents! On my soul, d'you think that such as you can clip Patrick's wings? Outwit the nimblest wits in this realm?'

'*You* sought to do it for long, did you not, Father? With some little success? And we have certain advantages.'

He paced across the cobblestones, silent.

'You are not displeased? You do not think that we do wrong in this?'

'The Lord knows! Who am I to judge? But what can you do? Have you any notion, girl, of what you essay?'

'Why yes, I think so. We have been learning.'

'Learning . . . ? You mean that you have already been pitting yourselves against Patrick?'

'Not against him. Say rather *for* him. We are his friends.'

247

'As you will. He would scarcely thank you, nevertheless! What have you discovered? Is it plotting, again? What is he scheming now? He is strongly placed once more, God knows. Have you some knowledge of his intentions?'

They stood in the doorway of David's own small flanking-tower. 'He has schemes a-many, you may be sure,' Mary answered. 'Of some we have little knowledge. Some we believe to be good. But three in especial we fear may be dangerous. These we seek to counter, if we can. And it is through Vicky that we may best do so.'

'Dangerous to whom? Patrick? Or others?'

'Both, we think. One concerns Dunfermline.'

'Aye. He is still hot for that place. It is the sheerest folly. He will never regain Dunfermline Abbey. He talks of suing Huntly before the Court of Session, while he is out of favour. But I do not think that he can win the case – however much he may pay the judges. Too many men covert Dunfermline.'

'He cannot win it,' she agreed.

'He is being stupid about Dunfermline. And Patrick is not usually stupid. I think that some hatred of Huntly must be affecting his judgment.'

'And yet he is in close communication with my lord of Huntly.'

'Patrick is?'

'Messengers travel frequently between Broughty Castle and Strathbogie. Secretly. Jesuits. Priests in disguise.'

'Seize me – are you sure? Catholics again!'

'Yes. And Huntly is not the only earl with whom Uncle Patrick is dealing secretly. Messengers come and go to my lord of Bothwell, also.'

'That firebrand! Bothwell, eh? What should this mean?'

'We cannot be sure. But it is very close, secret.'

'And Lennox?'

'He knows naught of it. And I have not told him.'

The man, eyeing her, stroked his chin. 'Tell me, Mary – since clearly you do not miss much that goes on,' he acknow-ledged, 'have you heard Bothwell's name linked with Dun-fermline? Is he also one who desires that well-fleshed bone of contention?'

'I have heard that he has sworn to add it to his earldom.'

248

'Aye.' Davy Gray's breath came out on a long sigh. 'So that is it, I warrant! Patrick has not changed! I smell treason and treachery once more. And, God help me – how I hate the stink of it! There is to be another Catholic rising. Or at the least, the beginnings of one. Both earls will be implicated. And who knows how many others, who may be in Patrick's way. They need not all be Catholics. Bothwell is not a Catholic – a man of no religion. It matters not. Find out who are seeking to get hands on Dunfermline, and I wager they will be dragged in somehow. Then, when all is ready, the word of it will by some chance come to the King's ear! Or that of the Council, if before the King's return. Patrick will not seem to be the informer, to be sure – but his rivals for Dunfermline will be arraigned. For rebellion. Treason. The ground will be cleared, and the realm grateful!' The man's sigh was part groan. 'It is so familiar . . .'

'Yes.' The young woman's nod was quite brisk, and there was no groaning or sighing. 'That is how we conceived it, also. It must be stopped.'

'Stopped!' he repeated. 'Think you Patrick will effect all this and then stop it, on your plea or mine? He will deny all, and continue . . .'

'If it is as we believe, he will stop it – when he learns that Dunfermline Abbey cannot come to any of them. Or to himself, either.'

'What . . . ? Cannot come . . . ?'

'No. For it is to go to the Princess Anne. To the new Queen. As a wedding-gift.'

David stared at her, seeking ineffectually for words. 'Is . . . is this true?' he got out, at length; and at her nod, 'Patrick . . . ? He does not know it?'

'None knows it, I think. Yet.'

Her father swallowed. 'Save . . . save Mary Gray!'

'That is so. I it was who suggested it to the King. He was taken with the notion.'

'*You* did!'

'Yes. But the King was anxious about Uncle Patrick in the matter. He feared that he would be scunnered at him, he said. And might work harm. So he was to keep it close. Until the

Queen is here. But now – now it is time that Uncle Patrick should know.'

'Lord save us!' the other muttered.

A bellow rang out and echoed across the courtyard. From an upper window of the great keep, my lord of Gray leaned out, gesturing down at Mary. 'Come here, lassie!' he shouted. 'Here, I say. To me. Why stand down there? Where's yon gangling loon Lennox? Ha' you got him in there? I'll no' have it – cosseting and nuzzling in my house . . . !'

'He is not here, Granlord. He is gone,' Mary called back.

'As well he has! Then come you up here. You never look near me, Mary. A fine thing, in my ain house . . . '

'I am coming, Granlord. At once . . . '

'He is concerned for you,' David told her, as the older man withdrew his head. 'He fears that Patrick has sold you to Lennox.'

'And does Granlord believe that I could be sold to any man?' she laughed. 'He should know me better. As should you all, I think.'

'Aye.' Heavily David said it. 'I am doubting if I know you at all, girl, and that's truth! What of Patrick, then? And Dunfermaline. Are you to tell him what you have told me? That the Queen is to have it. And would he believe you?'

'*I* shall not tell him, no. He would be very angry. He would send me away from him. I could then do no more to serve him. And I would not have him hating me. That will not do. Vicky must tell him. Vicky receives letters from Denmark, from the King – long letters. At the next, he must go to Uncle Patrick. Privily. Tell him, as though he had learned it from the letter, that Dunfermline is now the Queen's property. He will believe that. He will be angry – but he cannot change the King's decree. He will halt this plot, it will no longer serve him. So you see, Father – I must not cease to see Vicky. For this, and for other matters. It is important. Besides, I want to see him. Even though I am not sold to him. I shall tell Granlord as much, also.'

Pressing his arm, she ran off, light-foot, across the frosted cobbles.

Davy Gray stood looking after her, long after she had disappeared into the keep of Castle Huntly.

Chapter Twelve

ALL Scotland that counted in the scheme of things flocked down to the Port of Leith that blustery first day of May 1590 – and most of Edinburgh, whether it counted or not. Two days previously a small fast ship had arrived from Denmark, with the information that the King and his bride were belatedly on their way home – and indeed the day before, the fleet itself had been sighted briefly off the mouth of the Forth, but owing to the sudden unseasonable south-westerly gale, had been unable to enter the firth, being blown northwards. Watchers now, however, reported the squadron straggling in distinctly scattered formation, off Aberlady Bay, and plans for the royal reception went into full swing.

The Duke of Lennox was very much to the fore, for in his capacity of Lord Chamberlain he was responsible for the arrangements – although in fact the Master of Gray had organised most of them. Ludovick did not desert Mary Gray, however, and indeed all the functionaries who sought the Viceroy and Chamberlain had to seek him in the cheerful and colourful enclosure below the Council House on the Coalhill, overlooking the harbour, where the Queen's ladies were assembled. He did not seem to be at all depressed about the imminent end to his viceregal powers and privileges.

In the four months that had passed since his spurned suggestion of marriage to Mary, the Duke had not been spared his problems and difficulties as nominal ruler of the land. He had been forced into opposition to his friend Patrick Gray on a number of issues – which had been unpleasant; though nothing like so unpleasant as the occasion when he had had to inform the Master that James had decided to present the Abbey of Dunfermline and all its lands and revenues to the new Queen as a bridal gift. The subsequent outburst of sheer fury and passion, quite unexampled in the younger man's experience, had shaken him to the core, so that for days afterwards he dared hardly look Patrick in the eye, even though that extraordinary man, once the cataclysm of his rage and disappoint-

251

ment was over, seemed to dismiss the entire subject from his mind, and reverted to his sunny normal with scarcely credible rapidity.

There had been some trouble with Bothwell, also. Disgruntled about something more than usually, he had been storming about the Borderland burning, slaying, and raping. This being more or less normal, despite being on a larger scale, would not greatly have mattered, but for some reason he had extended his depredations beyond the Debatable Land and over the Border itself into England – which Patrick Gray obscurely declared was done entirely to spite himself. At any rate, it produced angry representations from Queen Elizabeth, and demands for Bothwell's immediate apprehension and punishment. Which, of course, was quite impracticable, the Earl having more men – and wild moss-troopers at that – at his disposal than had the Crown of Scotland or any other noble in the kingdom save only Huntly. In consequence, Ludovick himself had had to make the humiliating journey to Hermitage Castle in wildest Liddesdale, not in any punitive role but rather with pleas to the devil-may-care Bothwell to be more discreet and to send an apology to Elizabeth – to both of which requests the other had laughed him to scorn. This had not been a pilgrimage on which the Master of Gray had found it convenient to accompany the Viceroy.

Huntly's rumoured new rising had fortunately not materialised; indeed, whether out of a suitable repentance or for some less creditable reason of his own, the Gordon had actually sent south his wife, Ludovick's sister Henrietta, to assist in the royal welcome – she was, of course, officially the Queen's principal Lady-in-Waiting.

The ladies in the roped-off area in front of the Council House built by the King's grandmother, the Queen-Regent Mary of Guise, made a laughing, chattering throng, as eye-catching and ear-catching as an aviary of tropical birds. It was perhaps amusingly appropriate, as certain of the gentlemen did not fail to point out, that this concourse of youth and beauty should be assembled before this especial house, for as it happened, no fewer than fourteen of the seventeen involved were in fact granddaughters of the said Mary of Guise's much respected spouse, King James Fifth – though not of her own.

Save for Mary Gray and two others, all were Stewarts, mainly daughters of illegitimate sons of that puissant prince. Queen Anne at least should not be able to complain about the lowly origins of her maidens, other than one.

The Lady Marie, Mistress of Gray at twenty-seven, was the oldest of them – she was not actually a member of the Queen's household, but was there to keep the others in order, since the limp and apathetic Countess of Huntly certainly would not be able to control all King James's other high-spirited cousins. After Marie, the oldest would be seventeen – and despite their status as Maids of Honour, knowledgeable gentlemen declared that there was not a virgin amongst them. Though, to be sure, there was room for error here, for undoubtedly they included Mary Gray in this category, as Ludovick's mistress, and were mistaken.

Patrick Gray brought to the enclosure a flushed small stout man, Nichol Edward, Lord Provost of Edinburgh, to report to the Duke of Lennox that despite stringent orders the Palace of Holyroodhouse was not ready for the royal couple, workmen having accidentally set fire to the anteroom of the royal bed-chamber. These dire tidings were just being assimilated when a shouting and clattering from up the Tolbooth Wynd turned all heads. Forging down through the narrow crowded street came a mounted cavalcade at the trot, steel jacked and morioned retainers laying about them vigorously with the flats of long swords, careless of who fell and who might be trampled beneath their horses' hooves. In the centre, a great banner streamed in the breeze.

'Sink me!' Patrick said, narrowing his eyes. 'I think that I recognise those colours. All too many quarter the royal arms of Scotland with a bend-sinister – but only one adds to them the white chevron on red of Hepburn!'

'Bothwell!' the Duke gasped. 'That man – here!'

The horsemen came prancing right to the enclosure, only pulling up when their foam-flecked mounts were directly against the rope barrier itself – their leader indeed jerking back his great roan so vigorously to its haunches that it reared pawing forefeet right above the heads of some of the alarmed young women, who pressed back screaming. Its rider laughed mockingly.

253

'I have been seeking you, my lord Duke,' he cried. 'I find you choose better company than I gave you credit for!' And he ran a scurrilous eye over the shrinking ranks of the ladies.

Lennox glowered at him, uncertainly. 'I . . . I bid you welcome, my lord of Bothwell,' he got out, reluctantly. 'I did not expect you.' Ludovick was little of the diplomat. He looked askance at the large contingent of Hepburn and Home lairds jostling behind the other, all clad for battle it seemed rather than for a royal reception, not to mention the fifty or so shaggy wild-looking moss-troopers who escorted them.

'My lord of Bothwell's known love and esteem for the King's Grace has brought him here hot-foot, Vicky,' Patrick said, easily, at his side. 'It could not be otherwise.'

'Ha, Master of Gray – whose friend are you today?' Bothwell asked coolly. 'On my soul, it will repay a man to know such a thing, any day of the year!'

'Why, my lord – your friend, of course. And the King's And, naturally, my lord Duke's. Indeed, I cannot for the life of me think of any that I would have as unfriend this May day . . . save only, of course, the King's enemies, who must always be mine!'

'Ha?' That was part-question, part-snort, as Bothwell searched Patrick's face. He threw himself down from his horse, tossing the reins to his banner-bearer. He was a tall, powerful young man, not yet thirty, with a high complexion, sandy hair and eyebrows, and vividly blue unquiet eyes – with little or nothing of the Stewart about him, although his father had been one more of James Fifth's bastard brood who had married the sister of the previous and notorious Bothwell, Mary the Queen's third husband. Two half-sisters of his were amongst the Maids of Honour, but he spared them no glance. He was dressed in his habitual steel and leather. 'I saw James's ships from St. Abb's Head, this morning, and came apace. In lieu of other business!' He jerked a laugh. 'I seem to have out-paced the ships!'

'Aye. These winds have been much against them. But they are close now. Your leal fervour, my lord, must be notably hot to bring you thus far so fast!'

The Earl hooted rudely. 'Say that I cannot delay to set eyes on the wench who has cheated me out of Dunfermline Abbey!'

he said, making no attempt to lower his strong, throaty voice.

The Master of Gray could not wholly repress his start. Closely he eyed the other, however suddenly expressionless his handsome features. 'Indeed, my lord? You . . . you know, then?'

'Aye. A letter was writ to me. Unsigned. It was not from you? The courier came from Dundee. I esteemed it from Broughty.'

'Is that so? M'mmm. Many people have been dwelling thereabouts, of late,' the Master said slowly. His glance slid from Lennox to flicker over the company at large.

'The men in the watchtower declare the King's ships just off the harbour-mouth,' a new voice announced. The high buildings that ringed the wharfside made it impossible to see seawards from the inner harbour.

'Lord – my good cousin Moray!' Bothwell exclaimed turning. 'Here's more joy!'

The Earl of Moray eyed him coldly. They were indeed cousins, like so many others present, but there was no love lost between them.

'Have your cannons to fire, then, Master Provost,' Patrick ordered the little stout man. 'Wait no longer.'

'But, sir – my lord,' Edinburgh's representative wailed. 'What o' the palace? What o' Holyroodhouse?' He was wringing plump hands. 'His Grace cannot go there.'

'Then he must needs go somewhere else, man. Lodge him here in Leith, meantime. In the Citadel, in the King's-work. That will suit. It is his own house. Where the Duke was going to lodge some of his new Danish friends. Have men array it suitably for the King and Queen. Bring more tapestries, linen, napery. See you to it . . .'

The Lord Provost hurried away, unhappily, while Moray, who was acting Captain of the King's Guard, perforce changed his arrangements for escorting the royal procession up to Edinburgh.

Bothwell cast his hot eye over the assembled women judiciously, an undoubted expert. It did not take him long to single out Mary Gray, and to inflict upon her a fleeringly comprehensive inspection and summing up, despite the frowns of the Duke of Lennox who moved closer. Mary met his gaze calmly, almost interestedly, making her own assessment. There was a tittering and stirring amongst the throng of young women. Though not handsome like Moray, Bothwell had his own magnetism, sheer blatant and aggressive masculinity, his reputation contributing not a little.

Patrick, his own eyes busy, spoke pleasantly, conversationally. 'My lord, it is devilish crowded along this street and pierhead, is it not? Might I suggest to you to move your, h'm, host some other where?'

'You might not!' the other returned, casually, without so much as raising his glance from Mary Gray.

Patrick's voice did not change its tone. 'Nevertheless, my lord, you would probably find it convenient to do so presently. The pilot will bring his Grace's vessel exactly opposite here, and there is to be some ceremonial and spectacle. Room will be required for it. The provosts and bailies of the city, and the good gentry of the Kirk will be coming . . . '

'Foul fall you – d'you expect me, Bothwell, to stand aside for such rabble?'

'Not so – not *you*, my lord, naturally. I hope that you will remain here to greet their Graces, with the Duke and myself. It is only your, er, line of battle. I fear that there will be no room for . . . '

'There is room for me and mine wherever I choose to stand in this realm, fellow!' the Earl shouted. 'Remember it. I'll not be pushed aside by any simpering, jumped-up wardrobe-master, d'you hear? By God's eyes, I will not!'

Patrick's beautiful face went as still and set as marble, and a sort of glaze came over those lustrous eyes. He did not speak.

A shudder went through Mary Gray as she looked at him, and she bit her lip. Unknown to herself her fingers dug deeply into Ludovick's arm.

Perhaps that young man was urged on thereby. 'Then be so by me, my lord,' he said, into the immediate hush, bluntly. 'I bid you move your bullyrooks.'

'Christ God!' Bothwell ejaculated, fist dropping to his sword-hilt. 'French puppy! Spawn of a boot-licking jacka-napes . . . !'

The rest was drowned in the crash of cannonry, as from the Citadel a few hundred yards away along the waterfront the

256

royal salute thundered out. Bothwell was left mouthing incomprehensibly.

None could have continued the dispute if they would, by any other means than actual blows. Most of the cannon from Edinburgh Castle had been brought down for the occasion, and the concussion in the confined space of Leith's tightly-packed tall tenements, was deafening and continuous. Everywhere men as well as women put their fingers in their ears, grimacing.

The gunfire achieved what Patrick and Ludovick had failed to do. The horses of Bothwell's cavalcade reared and plunged and sidled at the din, some backing almost over the edge of the pier and into the river. As the bombilation maintained with no sign of diminishment, the horsemen, for their own safety's sake, with one accord began to urge and guide their excited mounts away back up the crowded street, to put more distance between themselves and the source of the clangour. Angrily, the Earl looked after them.

Against this ear-shattering racket the final preparations to receive the happy monarch went forward somewhat incoherently. A number of black-robed divines came to take up a prominent position near the colourful band of young women, whom they did not fail to examine with every sign of disapprobation. The bailies and guild representatives of Edinburgh moved self-consciously into their appointed places, the nobility and gentry only grudgingly giving them passage. A small boy dressed, it was calculated, as an angel, was pushed by his red-faced mother into the very forefront of the assembly and there abandoned to the embarrassed care of one of the city halberdiers; his open-mouthed crying fortunately could not be heard for the gunfire, and the more copiously he wept the tighter his dignified guardian gripped him – while appearing not so much as to be aware of his humiliating presence. A garlanded doorway in a timber frame was brought by some workmen, who set it upon the cobbles of the pier – when no sooner were they gone than it blew down in the gusty wind. Everybody eyed it askance, but it seemed to be nobody's business to set it up again – certainly not that of the ministers of Christ's Kirk, nor yet that of the city fathers. Bonfires were lit at strategic points in the vicinity; unfortunately the nearest

257

one, at the harbour head to the west, appeared to be made of notably damp combustibles and produced little of flame, sent down vast clouds of thick smoke on the prevailing wind, to set the entire company coughing and mopping their eyes. As the fumes grew worse rather than abating, Patrick gave orders for the source thereof to be kicked bodily into the harbour.

'It is ever thus with King Jamie,' he shouted in his wife's ear. 'Heaven seldom smiles upon its ally, Christ's Viceregent!'

In the midst of all this, the mast-tops of a tall ship appeared above the lofty buildings seawards, from which the Royal Standard of Scotland streamed in the wind. Unfortunately, however, wait as the company would, the said masts seemed to draw no nearer. Eventually the agitated harbourmaster came hurrying to inform the Duke of Lennox that the King's ship had got as far as the outer harbour but by no means could make further progress against a direct head-wind, with no room to tack, into the inner harbour. Indeed she was dropping an anchor to keep her from being driven against the breakwater to seaward. What should he do? Should he launch small boats and bring off the royal party?

Ludovick looked unhappy. 'That will never do,' he declared. 'With the tide low, like this, it would mean His Grace climbing up a rope ladder to the pier! Twenty feet of it! And the Queen, too! No, no. Lord, that would never do!'

At his ear Patrick actually laughed. 'Is this not a problem for the Lord High Admiral?' he suggested, against the din. And he gestured at Bothwell, who still stood a little way apart.

That indeed was one of Bothwell's many offices – though one titular rather than military, even if productive of considerable revenues. When the situation was explained to him, he glared balefully at all concerned, but proffered no proposals.

'Might I suggest, my lord,' the Master shouted at length, 'that this is where all your horsemen could prove their worth? Ropes from the ship, and towed by teams of horses, would surely bring your liege lord safely into his own land!'

Plucking his small sandy beard, the Earl eyed him doubtfully, wordless.

'I see no other way. Do you, my lord Admiral?'

Cursing, Bothwell stamped off to collect his men.

So, after a prolonged and embarrassing delay, the royal

flagship, sails down, was warped into the inner harbour of Leith and alongside the pier, at the tails of some two score horses, a proceeding that set at least the vulgar populace of the port hooting with hilarity. As the vessel drew jerkily near, James could be seen standing on the high poop deck, in gorgeous array of gold and purple, alternatively wringing his hands, shaking a clenched fist apparently at heaven, and clutching his very high hat to keep it from being blown off. About him stood a number of gentlemen, but no ladies.

The cannonade redoubled its fury.

When at length the ship lay safely alongside the pier, and gangways were run out, the Duke, Sir Robert Melville acting Chancellor, and the Earl of Moray, were to go aboard to escort the royal couple ashore. But now all Bothwell's Borderers were milling about with their horses, disengaging them from their ropes, laughing uproariously, pushing aside ministers, bailies and all. The high officers of state seeking to thread their way through this mêlée, were inevitably delayed. The monarch himself, however, did not appear to find this awkward, and in fact came hurrying ashore himself the moment the gangway from his poop was down, apparently anxious only to get off the vessel. A few shambling paces on to the pier indeed, and he sank down clumsily on hands and knees, before thousands of astounded eyes, apparently to kiss the cobblestones.

Lennox hastened forward to raise him up, Patrick only a few paces behind. James fell on the Duke's neck, babbling incoherencies that were quite lost in the banging of guns. He drew back a little, to point upwards and vaguely westwards, and to shake his fist again, and then onee more to fall upon his cousin, stroking his face.

'Och, Vicky, Vicky!' he yelled. 'Out o' the jaws o' death! Och, it's good to see you. He near had me – aye, he near had me, I tell you! But I beat him! I beat him, Vicky!'

'Eh . . . ? Yes, Sire,' Lennox said, seeking to disentangle himself, much embarrassed. 'Who . . . ? Beat who, Sire?'

'Satan, man – Satan. Auld Hornie, himsel'. He's been clutching at me, all the way.'

'Satan . . . ?'

'Your Grace,' Patrick shouted into the King's other large ear. 'The Queen?'

259

James started, and whirled round. 'Eh . . . ? What's that? Dinna do that, I tell you! Och, it's you, Patrick man?'

'Yes. The Queen, Your Grace. Er . . . welcome. But – we wait to welcome the new Queen. Your own royal commands . . . '

'Ooh, aye – Anne!' James, in his highly excited state, had obviously completely forgotten his wife. Abruptly he turned, and pushing unceremoniously past certain of his train who were in process of following him ashore, hurried back on board.

A cluster of women were now to be seen standing amidships, with the spare and sombre, well-known figure of Chancellor Maitland in attendance. James grabbed quite the smallest person in the group by a hand, and came back with her, almost at a trot.

Even Patrick was taken aback at the extraordinary appearance of youthfulness of the new consort. Although now fifteen, and only a little more than a year younger than Mary Gray, she looked still a child. Padded and flounced as she was, in the height of fashion, her elaborate toilet only served to emphasise the slim immaturity of the body it covered. Her reddish-brown hair, dressed to stand high above her head, was much blown about by the wind. Nevertheless, as they came off the gangway, she contrived to look considerably more dignified than did her lord.

As the royal couple set foot on the pier, Ludovick, who had rehearsed all this thoroughly, bowed deeply, all the other men following suit, while the women sank low. Musicians were to strike up now – but whether they did or no was impossible to tell, in the continuing contributions of the cannoneers. Moray, as Captain of the Guard, gestured angrily but eloquently at one of his underlings to go and silence these enthusiasts.

James who, despite his written orders on the subject, patently had done no rehearsing himself, was for hurrying on still further, when most evidently his bride restrained him. They stood together on the pier, he fidgeting, she small head held high, while, following the example of the Lord Chamberlain, the great company raised itself slowly erect once more.

Precedence now fell to be strictly observed. As Bothwell came strolling up, Ludovick slipped forward to be presented

260

first the new Queen, by James himself so that he in turn could present others. Bothwell, close behind, ignored his jerky presentation and introduced himself arrogantly, coolly subjecting Anne to something not very different from his normal assessing scrutiny of the other sex, evidently without much satisfaction, James looking on with a strange mixture of pride and apprehension, clutching his hat. There was no occasion for converse.

Moray followed on, and then the great officers of state in turn, followed by many of the King's surviving illegitimate uncles led by Orkney, Marie's father. Then the senior nobility. The Countess of Huntly was the first woman to be presented. In this process, the Master of Gray came low on the list.

Mary Gray, from her position in the enclosure, watched the young Queen. A child, physically, she might be, but there was little else childish about her. She was self-assured, sharp-eyed, with a determined small chin and tight mouth. With no pretensions to beauty, she had a certain prettiness, and she bore herself well.

The Lord Provost was presented, the leaders of the Kirk, a clutch of bishops including Mary's grandfather of St Boswells, and then a long queue of lesser nobility and lairds. In the midst of it all, the cannonade stopped suddenly – to be succeeded by an uncomfortable and bemused silence.

Out of the shuffling, murmurings and whisperings, it was Patrick Gray's musical voice that was upraised. 'God save the Queen!' he called.

Raggedly at first, but steadying and strengthening, the chant was taken up. 'God Save the Queen! God save the Queen!' it rang out, the echoes being thrown back and forth amongst the tall tenements.

James nodded, smirked and rubbed his hands – and then began to pluck his lip and frown, as it continued. Perhaps he felt that an admixture of appeals to the Deity on behalf of the King also would have been seemly. He held up his hand.

Slowly the chanting died away.

'Aye,' he said, wagging his head. 'Just so. I'ph'mmm. Aye – we're glad to be hame. It has been a sair trauchle. The winds! The storms! The waves! Och, Satan opened his ill maw wide, wide to engulf us quite. Aye, he did his worst. But we are delivered out o' his clutches. Like blessed Peter, Galilee didna close ower us . . . '

Unfortunately, even at the best of times, James was no clear and resounding speaker. He was apt to mumble and splutter. In the open air, against three parts of a gale, and much moved about the dangers he had escaped, his eloquence was lost on all but those in his close proximity. Quickly, as a result, murmuring and chatter grew amongst the great company, until not even those nearest could hear a word. James appeared not to notice, until the young woman at his side perked his sleeve sharply, frowning, and his mouthings died away.

Patrick managed to catch the eye of one of the resplendently-clad herald trumpeters attached to the Lord Lyon King of Arms, and gestured to him. That man nudged his companion, and together they blew a shrilling fanfare.

This was the signal for Lennox to make a speech of welcome on behalf of the Privy Council. He had, however, forgotten every word of it, and the phrase or two of Danish, especially memorised, had quite gone.

'We . . . er, bid you welcome, Sire! And Your Grace, Madam. Welcome! To your realm,' he said, haltingly, into the succeeding silence. 'Very welcome.' He stopped, unable to think of anything else to say. The bawling of the small and almost naked boy shivering in the wind as an angel, came to his rescue. 'Provost!' he called. 'My Lord Provost!' He pointed at the infant.

Edinburgh's civic chief strutted forward, took the child from the halberdier who had clutched him manfully all this time, and dragged him towards the royal couple. Nearly there, he drew from beneath his robes of office a golden orb. This he thrust upon the youngster, before pushing him bodily towards the Queen.

The angel, intrigued by the round shining thing, stopped crying and walking both, and began to try to open it, turning it this way and that.

Smilingly Anne stepped forward, hand outstretched. The child shrank back, clutching his prize to him. Prettily the Queen coaxed him, to no effect. James, glowering blackly, pointed a peremptory royal finger, and then stamped his foot hard. The celestial messenger dropped his gift in fright, and

262

burst once more into wailing. The orb burst also, on the cobblestones, spilling out a handsome necklace of wrought gold links inset with pearls and emeralds.

Hurriedly before any of his courtiers could reach the spot, James himself stooped down to pick up the jewellery. Carefully he examined it, peering at the craftsmanship, holding up the stones to the light, assessing its worth – until Anne reached over and quite sharply twitched it out of his hands. She raised it to her young neck, squinting down at it with proprietorial satisfaction, and held it so. A man stepped out from the group of high personages close by, moving in front of Maitland the Chancellor and behind the Queen. He put out his hands to take the ends of the necklace from her fingers, and fastened them together deftly at the back of her slender neck. She turned to him quickly, surprised. It was the handsome Earl of Moray. Anne smiled warmly.

He bowed, but not low.

'So!' Patrick, further back, observed to Marie. 'Here is both an allegory and a lesson to be learned, I think!'

Before there could be any more unseemly and unprofitable time-wasting, the Kirk took charge. It had, indeed, been very patient. Andrew Melville, Principal of Glasgow University and fiery pillar of godly reform, a massive sombre figure with voluminous black Geneva gown and white bands flapping about him, stepped forth to announce in a rasping but powerful voice that had no difficulty in competing with wind or chatter, that Christ's true Kirk, recognising well the sins and follies that so readily beset those in high place – particularly women – greeted Christ's humble vassal James and the woman Anne whom he had brought back from a land where the truth was perhaps less firmly established than in this realm of Scotland, and prayed God that both might be delivered from the temptations to which they were all too vulnerably exposed, in fleshly lusts, carnal concupiscence, heretical doctrine, Popish idolatry, worldly converse and the curse of evil company. At this last, Master Melville glared round him at practically everyone present, especially the bishops. In token of which, he went on, he would now, in the Kirk's name, deliver an address of welcome.

Tugging at a forked beard, and fixing Anne with a fierce eye, he raised his voice to a higher pitch. Forceful, clear, vigorous, his sonorous periods rang out, cleaving the rushing air, throbbing in all ears. There could be no more doubting of the eloquence than the clarity – only, unfortunately for some, the said periods were entirely in Latin. Excellent Latin, needless to say, if delivered in a harsh Fife accent – all two hundred stanzas of it, a feast, a banquet of worth, edification and warning.

James paid due, indeed, appreciative attention to it all. Anne, whose education, is to be feared, had been neglected, did the epic performance less than justice, her sharp little eyes fairly soon beginning to wander. The Kirk did not fail to note, especially when more than once she yawned.

A right and proper atmosphere having thus been introduced, Andrew Melville launched into prayer. This was powerful stuff which could not fail to have a marked effect on his Maker, however incomprehensible it might be to most of the visitors. The real kernel and pith of the matter was still to come, however. With a wave of his hand, Melville summoned forward Master Patrick Galloway to preach the sermon.

Master Galloway, a noted divine, excelled himself, rising to the occasion untrammelled by notes or hour-glass, in an ever-mounting crescendo. His theme was the necessity of the obedience of wives to their husbands, and obedience of husband's to Christ's Kirk. After half-an-hour of it, Bothwell, who had been carrying on a loud-voiced conversation with some of his henchmen, abandoned the struggle, and with hooted laughter marched from the scene, followed by most of his party – and, sad to relate, not a few others who suddenly found pressing business elsewhere and took this opportunity to attend to it. After an hour, much of the crowd had melted away. Mary Gray, noting how pale the Queen looked, slipped under the rope-barrier, picked up a small drum that one of the city drummers had set down, and moved forward with it, braving the frowns of nearby clerics, to the group of wilting notables nearest the royal couple. There she handed it to Moray, whispering in his ear. The Earl, nodding, took it and carrying it over to Anne, threw his short velvet cloak over it, and motioned for her to sit. Thankfully the Queen sank down on it, eyed sidelong by her husband, who pulled at his ear, uncertain it seemed whether to be envious or scandalised.

Master Galloway thundered on.

At last it was over. There was to have been an elevating ceremony of Faith, Hope and Charity beckoning the King and Queen through the garlanded doorway to receive the keys of the city from the Lord Provost, but by unspoken consent – and since they would not in fact be going to Edinburgh today, after all – this was dropped meantime. With most of those who had been unable to escape hitherto rushing off incontinent for relief and refreshment to Leith's numerous taverns, it seemed that the royal welcome was completed. It but remained for the Master of the Wardrobe to acquaint the King of the unfortunate fire at Holyroodhouse and the consequence that the royal quarters would not be ready for Their Graces for a day or two. The King's-work, here in Leith, however, was prepared . . .

James threw up his hands. 'Fire!' he cried. 'Flames! Here, too! Even here he rages against me! In my own realm, my own house! He's aye clawing at me, clutching . . . '

'It was but some careless workmen, Sire . . . '

'It was Satan! It's aye Satan, I tell you. Reaching out for me. But he'll no' have me – God Almighty is my ally. The powers o' darkness winna triumph ower the Lord's Anointed!'

'Er . . . quite. Exactly, Your Grace. But, the Queen – she must be very tired. Her ladies await her, at the King's-work. Next to the Citadel. Just along the waterfront. Refreshment is there, Sire . . . '

'Aye, refreshment. Refreshment for the battle!' James muttered. 'Come, Annie – come you.'

But already the Queen had started out, on the arm of the Earl of Moray.

Chapter Thirteen

IT did not take Scotland long to discover that her new-married monarch had something on his mind more pressing than the cosy joys of matrimony. He had been in a strangely distraught

265

state before ever he set sail for Denmark; he returned, with his bride, even more preoccupied – though no longer distraught. Whether it was marriage that had done it, the months of absence from his own land, or discussions with curious foreign authorities, is not to be known – but he came back a man with a mission. He was going to get to grips with Satan, without delay.

Always James had been interested in and much aware of the supernatural. His lonely parentless childhood had been beset by devils, ogres and apparitions, all malevolent – many of them in the guise of steel-clad, hard-faced grasping lords. George Buchanan, his stern tutor and taskmaster, had been a student of demonology. The ministers of the Kirk who had borne heavily upon him all his days, were much concerned with the dark powers of evil. Now was the reckoning.

Despite all the other matters which clamoured for his attention, the King was much closeted in small dusty rooms, first in Leith and then in his own quarters at Holyroodhouse, with books, parchments, folios, on abstruse and difficult subjects such as necromancy, sorcery, Black Magic, wizardry, astrology and the like. No longer did he ink his fingers with much writing of poetry; now he was inditing more serious stuff. It was difficult for his officers and ministers to get in at him in these locked sanctums – and there was so much to be done; the innumerable matters of state that had had to be held over, awaiting the monarch's return; deputations to be received from all over the land; the due entertainment of the great company of distinguished foreigners, Danes in especial, who had come over with Anne; most important of all, the Queen's Coronation. James expended only grudging attention on all these.

The very night before the Coronation, indeed, with many of the details still to be arranged, Patrick Gray, responsible as Master of the Wardrobe for much of the ceremonial, prevailed on the Duke of Lennox to gain him the King's presence, somehow. Ludovick was in fact almost the only person for whom James would open his locked doors.

After much knocking and a certain amount of shouted reassurance, the King was persuaded to draw the bolts of his study in the south-west drum-tower of the palace, and peer round.

266

'What's to do now, Vicky?' he demanded querulously. 'Can you no' see I'm busy? And who's yon you've got there wi' you, man?'

'It is the Master of Gray, Sire. He has urgent matters for your attention. Regarding tomorrow's crowning.'

'Och, him! Patrick's aye at something . . .'

'Aye, Sire – but since he found the money to pay for this Coronation, he should be heard, should he not?'

'Humph! I'ph'mmm. Well . . . ' Grumbling, James let them in, and quickly shot the bolts again. 'He got a third part o' the gold himsel', did he no'? A thousand pounds! Bonnie payment for a' he did . . .'

'Was that not in lieu of his claim for Dunfermline Abbey?' the younger man asked bluntly.

'Tut, man . . .'

'Your Grace's generosity was notable,' Patrick intervened smoothly. 'I have no complaints. The difficulties now are otherwise. The most serious is the problem of the Queen's anointing. The Kirk is proving . . . obdurate.'

'There's nae problem in it, Patrick,' James answered testily. 'I have given my royal commands. The Kirk has but to carry them out in a seemly fashion. Waesucks – must I do their work for them? I hae other work o' my ain, 'fore God! That only I, the Lord's Anointed, can accomplish.' He pointed a stained finger at the tables littered with parchments and books. 'Have I no' plenty on my hands, man?'

Lennox looked askance at the disarray of papers. 'Inky work, Sire, it would seem! Is such not for clerks . . . ?'

'Clerks!' James all but squeaked in indignation. 'Could clerks wrestle wi' the Devil? Could clerks bind Satan in his ain coils?'

'Lord, James – are you drowning Satan in ink? Choking him with dust . . . ?'

'Dinna scoff, Vicky Stuart – dinna scoff! I'll no' be scoffed at, d'you hear? Belike he'll turn his assault on you, man, as well as me. I am binding Satan wi' words, see you – potent and mighty words. In the beginning was the word, mind. I, James, by the Grace o' God, am writing a book!'

His visitors stared from the King to each other and back again.

267

Apparently encouraged by the impression he had made, James nodded vigorously. 'A book. A great and notable work. On the wicked wiles o' Satan and his black kingdom. A book to undermine his ill powers and reveal his evil ways.'

'You . . . ?' Lennox swallowed. 'How may you do that, James? What even the Pope of Rome cannot do.'

'H'rr'mm,' Patrick coughed warningly.

'The Pope!' That was a snort. 'The Pope's ower near allied to the Devil himsel' to do any such thing! Forby, he hasna my advantages, as the Lord's Anointed. I am Satan's especial foe, see you – and his ways are revealed to me.'

'But . . .'

'You learned this in Denmark, Sire?' Patrick asked.

'I jaloused it before I ever went, man. You'll mind a' the storms that prevented my Annie frae coming to me? Yon was Satan's work. He wouldna hae me married and my royal line strengthened against him. A' the way yonder my ships were sore assailed. I was near the gates o' Hell. But I won ower. In yon Denmark, the winds dropped and the storms died. He couldna reach me there. A' winter there was scarce a breeze. But when I set sail again, the hounds o' Hell were quick after me, God kens! That very day the storms rose. Day and night the seas clawed at me. The deep opened its maw to engulf me. We were sucked in and spewed out again. Like yon Jonah. But I wrestled. I wrestled wi' Satan in person – aye, and wi' God too, in prayer. Notable prayer. And so we won back to this my realm. As an ill grudge, he set his flames to this house o' mine, but . . . but . . . ' Panting with his vehemence, the King paused for very breath.

Embarrassed, Ludovick looked at the floor. Patrick stroked his chin.

'And if you are convinced, Sire, that these unseasonable storms are the Devil's work, raised expressly against your person,' he said, 'how do you seek to bind him by writing a book?'

'Och, Patrick – where are your wits? You, of a' men, should see it. The Devil thrives in darkness, ignorance. He canna abide the light. The word is light. Do the Scriptures no' say so? The Good Book is the light that lightens the world. *My* book shall lighten Satan's ain world, Hell itsel'. To his undoing.'

'H'mmm. A lofty ambition, Your Grace. A Homeric task, indeed.'

'Do I not ken it, man? That is why I labour at it, day and night, thus – why I shouldna be disturbed wi' lesser things. I must mysel' read a' that's written. And I must test what I read. Try it. Aye, there will need to be a deal o' testing. I shall require your aid, belike . . . '

'Testing, Sire? What mean you by testing?'

'Ha – wait, Patrick man! Wait! You shall see. In good time. Aye, a' my realm shall see Satan tested. But no' yet. I'm no' ready yet. There's that much to do.'

'But . . . can you reach the Devil, to test him?'

'Satan works through men, Patrick. And women. As well as in winds and storms. Them I can reach.' James rubbed his inky hands, and actually chuckled. 'Ooh, aye – I can reach them.'

The Master of Gray searched his monarch's face intently, and said nothing.

'There is much to do at the Coronation also, Sire,' Lennox reminded. 'And on the morrow. This matter of the anointing. As Chamberlain, I must know . . . '

'Tcha! I told you – I have given my commands.'

'Unfortunately, Your Grace, the Kirk has other views,' Patrick pointed out.

'It canna. It canna. I am the head o' Christ's Kirk.'

'Yet the Kirk says that anointing with oil is a Popish practice. An idolatrous vanity. Master Robert Bruce says that he will not be a party to it.'

James gulped and giggled. 'He'll no' . . . ? He'll no' . . . ? Vanity? Idolatrous – the royal anointing! Guidsakes – is it no' what makes the monarch different frae other men? I am the Lord's viceregent – His Anointed. No subject will deny the anointing oil to my Queen!'

'Master Bruce says that he will, Sire.'

'Then Master Bruce is acting for Satan, no' Christ. Aye, that's it. Satan again, it is! He'd deny my Annie her royal due, and so hae my seed less than kingly. For his ain ends. Och, I ken him. He's but using Bruce. Tell you Master Bruce that he will anoint my Queen wi' oil, or I'll hae one o' the bishops to do it! That will scunner him! Or I could do it mysel'. Who is mair fitted to transmit the blessed unction than I who am already anointed? Tell me that.' James was trembling with emotion.

'Very well, Sire. It shall be as you say. Then there is the matter of where the bishops shall stand. And in what precedence. The Kirk would not have them in the ceremony, at all. It would put them after the last of the presbyters . . . '

'Soul o' God!' the King cried. 'Away wi' you! Hae them where you will. I'll no' be embroiled, d'you hear? Let them fight it out for themsel's. I hae God's work to see to – no' man's pride and folly. Away, now. Out wi' you both. I'll hae no more o' it. This audience is closed. Aye, closed.'

Patrick and Ludovick bowed themselves to the door, being all but pushed through it in the process. The latter eyed his companion ruefully.

'Heaven save us – do you think he's parted from his wits entirely?' he demanded.

Patrick took a little while to answer, as they went down the winding stairs. He was looking very thoughtful. 'I do not know, Vicky,' he said. 'It may be so – but the situation is not as it was, mind. He is married. Has been for six months. The Queen may well be with child even now – child herself as she is. She may soon produce an undoubted heir to the throne. So what we had in mind before will no longer serve . . . '

'What *you* had in mind,' the Duke pointed out.

The Master ignored him. 'It is . . . interesting. It behoves us to think carefully. Most carefully.'

'To what end?'

'Why – to the weal and benefit of the realm, Vicky. And us all. What else?' The other smiled his sweetest. 'You heard him. Testing, he said – trying. He would need our aid, he said. Know you any of the Devil's spawn to test and try, Vicky?'

Mary Gray, with Jean Stewart and Katherine Lindsay, stood or knelt around the thin white naked figure of Queen Anne, sponging and wiping and dabbing. Still in their fine gowns that they had worn for the Coronation ceremony, Mary's borrowed from the royal wardrobe, they busied themselves amongst the steam from the cauldrons of hot water, exclaiming, twittering consolations to their mistress.

Anne stood stiffly, on a pile of cloths and towelling, in the circular tower-room off the royal bedchamber which she was calling her boudoir – the room indeed directly below the King's study in the drum-tower. Pale, her lips tight, she was breathing hard – but even so her tiny budding bosom scarcely stirred. From most aspects, naked, she might have been a boy, so unformed in womanliness was her slender body. But her expression was neither childish nor lacking in definition. Her cold anger was remarkable in its still intensity. She answered nothing to her ladies' commiserations.

Mary reached for a new cloth, and hotter water. The oil was very hard to lift. It seemed to impregnate the very skin, as it had done the clothing. It seemed, also, to be of a singularly sticky and viscous consistency, and of a penetrating and un-lovely smell.

It would be hard to say who had won the battle of the anointing oil. Master Robert Bruce, of Edinburgh's High Kirk of St. Giles, faced with the King's furious commands and threats, and with bishops only too anxious to do the work for him, had at length consented, at the climax of the Coronation ceremony in the Abbey, to anoint with oil. But when the Countess of Mar, James's sour old foster-mother, had some-what opened the neck of the Queen's gown for the application, Bruce had roughly jerked the opening wide, to bare her pathetic padded bosom, and therein emptied the entire ampulla of oil. Thus, soaked and humiliated, Anne had had to wait through a further two hours of ceremonial, including another sermon, with the oil running down her body to her very feet, and ruining the splendid jewel-sewn dress and all below it.

A loud and impatient knocking sounded at the locked door on the other side of the bedchamber. Alarmed, the three young women looked from their naked mistress to each other. Anne gave no sign, made no move. Lady Jean giggled.

'The door, Your Grace . . . ?' she began. She was inter-rupted by renewed banging.

'Open!' the King's well-known thick voice cried. 'Annie – it is I. James. Your Jamie. Open, I say.'

The Queen shrugged thin shoulders. 'Let him in,' she said, in her stilted foreign accent.

Uncertainly the Lady Katherine went to open the further

door, flushing, whilst Mary reached for a robe to put round her mistress.

Impatiently Anne shook it off. 'Finish your work,' she directed shortly.

Jamie came pushing in, a paper in his hand. At sight of his unclothed wife amidst the steam, he halted, peered sidelong, and leered. 'Hech, hech,' he chuckled. 'Are you no' right bonnie that way! Aye, bonnie. I . . . I dinna like fat women.' He glanced over at his voluptuous cousin Jean, who sniggered.

'I care not how you like,' Anne said sharply. 'I am insulted. I am made a fool before all. In my country that man would die! He must be punished.'

'Houts, lass – wheesht you! Here's no way to take it. You mustna speak that way about ministers o' the Kirk. It was a mishap, just . . . '

'It was no mishap. The man Bruce looked at me, as he did it. He must be punished. And before all.'

'Na, na, Annie – it canna be. You hae it wrong. It was a victory, see you. The Kirk anointed you wi' oil, when it didna want to. What's a wee drappie ower much oil? Better than nane, lassie – better than nane. A victory for the Lord ower Satan. Christ's Kirk brought in . . . '

'I like not your Kirk, James.'

'Wheesht, girl – dinna say it! The Kirk's strong, power-ful . . . '

'More powerful than the King?'

'Na, na. But it doesna do to flyte it.'

'As it has flyted me! I think my lord of Moray to be right. He says that it is the Kirk that rules in Scotland, not the King!'

'Waesucks – Moray shouldna hae said that! It's no' right. The King o' Scots is head o' the Kirk. But it's a gowk that smites his ain left hand. The Chancellor and Council is my right hand, see you – but the Kirk is my left. My lord o' Moray should watch his words. Aye, and his ways! I'd thank you to see less o' him, Annie.'

The Queen's sniff, though eloquent, more aptly matched her childish appearance. She looked down. 'Are you finished? Is it all gone?'

'I think it,' Mary told her. 'I see no more.'

'Save on Your Grace's feet,' Jean pointed out. 'There is some even down between your toes!' That was a further cause for giggles.

'That can wait. My clothes.'

'Look, lassie – forget the oil for the nonce. See – I hae a letter here that tells me that a coven o' witches meets at North Berwick. A score o' miles, just down the coast. A right convenient place, eh? For raising storms against me. We passed it in the ship – you'll mind where yon great muckle rock rises frae the sea. The Bass. Ooh, aye – this could be maist significant.'

Anne did not so much as glance at his letter. 'I care naught for your witches,' she exclaimed. 'Is this time for such foolishness? I much more mislike your Kirk.'

'Och, hold your tongue anent the Kirk, Annie, I tell you! I need the Kirk to fight Auld Hornie. These witches and warlocks are belike his earthly instruments. And so his weakness. Satan's soft side, see you. It wouldna do to neglect this.'

But the Queen was not listening. With only her shift on she pushed aside the other clothes being held out for her, and hurried into the main bedchamber adjoining. The Ladies Jean and Katherine, after a glance at the King, followed her. Mary was left to clear up the towels and the steaming pots.

James tut-utted. 'Och, she doesna understand,' he said. 'She's ower young, belike. Mind, she's wiselike too, in some matters. Ooh, aye – she's no fool. But she's no' acquaint yet wi' the powers o' darkness, Mistress Mary. Och, it's no' to be expected.'

'No, Sire. It is not.' Mary looked up. 'Does Your Grace not fear this world of witches and warlocks is an invention? Of idle men? Or mischievous!'

'Guidsakes no, lassie! Witchcraft is a right serious matter. The Devil is never lacking his minions. And he's no' backward in this Scotland o' mine, I warrant! I hae been reading about witchcraft and the like. Plenty – aye, plenty. A' the signs are there. I must root them out.'

Mary bit her lip. 'Witches, I think – true witches – will not be easily found.'

'Hech, but you're wrong Mistress Mary. There's aplenty o' them – and I'll soon hae my hands on them, never fear. There's

273

a worthy bailie o' Tranent laid godly hands on one.' The King glanced at the paper. 'Seton, his name. He's put her to the question, maist properly, and she's given the names o' plenty mair. Waesucks – I'll hae her here and see what *my* questioners can do! Aye, I'll uncover the Devil's work, I promise you.'

She was silent.

'I'll get your . . . I'll get Master Patrick to help me. He has the kind o' wits to pit against Auld Hornie. They hae much in common, eh?' James whinnied a laugh. 'Nae offence, mind, Mistress Mary. Where shall I find the man? He's no' in his quarters.'

'I do not know, Your Grace . . .'

'This new folly of the King's?' the Lady Marie charged her husband. 'All this of witches and spells. Might not this cause much evil? Much cruel wrong?'

'Tell me anything that a king might do that could not?' Patrick answered.

'But this in especial. Anyone may cry witch. Proving innocence may be less easy.'

'No doubt. But that may have its advantages also, I think.'

'For whom, Patrick?'

'For those who would preserve the King's peace, my dear.'

'Preserve . . . ? You do not believe such nonsense? Such bairn's chatter about spells and incantations brewing unchancy storms?'

'The longer I live, my heart, the less I would declare what I believe and what I do not!'

'You do not speak plain, Patrick – so that I mislike it all the more!'

'You are a hard, hard wife to have, Marie Stewart!'

Mary joined in. 'This of North Berwick, Uncle Patrick? Can there be anything of truth in such a tale?'

'There could be. I have heard strange things of North Berwick ere this. That is what we must find out.'

'We . . . ?' his wife echoed.

'Why, yes. His Grace seeks some help in the matter. You would not have me deny my King?'

Marie sighed, and shook her fair head. 'I know you when you are this way, Patrick. There is nothing of worth to be had from you. But this I do know – if you are for aiding James in this foolishness, it is for your own advantage.'

'Say to *our* advantage, my soul's treasure. For are we not one? Doubly one, if such a thing were possible, since we were wed by both Catholic and Reformed rites! And, to be sure, for the advantage of many others also. That is the great comfort of statecraft. I find. Whatever is done must of necessity advantage almost as many as it injures!'

'I desire no advantage at the cost of others' suffering and sorrow, Patrick.'

'Think before you speak, my heart. All that you do, all that you are, all the food you eat, the very threads that you work in your frame there – all come of the sorrow, pain and toil of others. So our Maker made us. It is all a matter of degree. All acts of man have more consequences than one. There is black and white to every picture, to every man. I but seek to choose the lesser evil. The compromise between black and white.' He laughed aloud. 'Not for nothing am I named the Master of Gray!'

'I have heard your philosophy before, Patrick – and have seen where it has brought you.'

'It has brought me back to the King's right hand,' he told her lightly. 'Which minds me – whither I must now go . . . with your permission, ladies.' Bowing deeply, and throwing them a kiss each, he strolled out.

'God help me – why must I so dote on that man!' the Lady Marie exclaimed. 'When he is the most part knave, reprobate, as I know full well.'

'Because he is . . . Patrick Gray,' Mary answered her, gently, briefly, but sufficiently.

Chapter Fourteen

IT was not really dark enough to suit the King. But truly dark nights are rare in Scotland in July. It requires heavy cloud, storm perhaps – the sort of weather with which Satan had plagued James heretofore. Now, of course, night after night, there were clear pale skies and never a breath of wind. Satan's adversary was not surprised.

The royal party was congregated in a deep hollow of the sand-dunes at the west side of the great sandy bay of North Berwick. It was exactly half-past eleven, and the King was much agitated lest they be too late – for these affairs, he asserted, always started at midnight, the witching hour. But Patrick was adamant that they would spoil all by being too soon. The church was on what amounted to an island, a bare peninsula of rock jutting into the sea, offering only the one covered approach. To arrive there before all the coven had assembled would almost certainly end in their discovery, the abandonment of the meeting, and therefore the ruin of their plans.

'There is time yet, Sire,' he pointed out. 'We can cross this bay in but a few minutes. Let them be started.'

'Satan will see us coming, belike, and warn them.'

'If that be so, he could have warned them any time since we left Edinburgh, Your Grace.'

There were five of them in the royal party besides James; Lennox, Sir James Melville of Halhill who was Sir Robert's brother, Master David Lindsay the King's chaplain, and, much overawed by the company he was keeping, Bailie David Seton of Tranent. In a nearby and larger hollow was a score of the royal bodyguard, standing by their horses.

James was actually trembling with excitement. The great round timepiece which he carried shook as he consulted it, unhappily raising it to his ear in case it had stopped.

'Guidsakes, it's an unchancy business this!' he exclaimed, not for the first time. 'I pray the Lord God will see us right! It's His work, see you. Master David – will you gie us another bit prayer, man?'

Nothing loth, the divine obliged, his stern voice a little less confident perhaps than usual. Patrick nudged Ludovick in the ribs, and grimaced.

Their due devotion occupied them until midnight, the Kirk being equally strong on volume as it was on intensity. James was in major agitation, on the horns of the dilemma of offend-

276

ing God or being too late for the Devil, when Lindsay finally panted to a close.

Leaving the escort and horses, with strict instructions as to what to do on seeing certain signals and flares, the six men emerged from their hiding-place. They did not head straight across the open beach, but crept round the side in the shadow of the dunes. It was not dark enough wholly to hide them, but undoubtedly at any distance they would not be noticed. Patrick led the way.

Very soon he had to slow down. James, never very good on his feet, was stumbling and puffing. Melville and Lindsay were both middle-aged and found the soft sand heavy going. The bailie was a lean and hungry-looking character of a sour and sanctimonious expression, but nimble enough.

It was nearer the half than the quarter-past midnight when they reached the rocks wherein nestled the harbour of North Berwick and on which stood its ancient whitewashed kirk. High above the tide it crouched, amongst scattered graves that were scooped out wherever there was sufficient soil in pockets amongst the rocks. The place was silent, seemingly closed up – but from its windows a faint flicker of peculiar light glimmered.

'Up to the east end,' Patrick, who had prospected the site two days previously, whispered. 'Behind the altar.' He coughed, apologetically glancing at Master Lindsay. 'Behind the Communion Table. The windows are low. To see in. Keep away from the door, at the other end.'

They crept up over the rocks and between the hummocks of the graves. They began to hear faint sounds of music coming from the church.

Crouching under the easternmost windows, they gradually raised their heads, to peer inside.

The King's croaking gasp of alarm ought surely to have been heard within. Whatever any of them had been expecting, indeed, the sight that met their gaze was sufficient to catch their breathing – even Patrick Gray's. The church was almost full – fuller no doubt than the minister was accustomed to seeing it on a Sabbath. It was not a large church admittedly; there might however have been one hundred and fifty persons present. Of them all, fully nine out of ten were women. This

277

was entirely obvious, for though otherwise fully clothed, indeed seemingly dressed in their best, their bosoms were wholly bare. It made a quite extraordinary sight, all those breasts, large and small, young and old – a scene most aggressively, intimidatingly female. The few men, in fact, seemed quite pathetically humdrum and feeble, looking painfully normal save that they all wore hats in the pews, and highly self-conscious expressions.

Patrick had the temerity to hush his monarch, who was babbling something incoherent and disgusted about cattle; James never had been much of an admirer of the opposite sex.

The church was lit with a ghostly light, by candles – ghostly in that they burned with a blue flame, the candles themselves being black, not white. Four burned on the Communion Table, where a cross stood upside-down amongst a litter of flagons, obviously empty.

But it was towards the pulpit that all eyes were turned. There, flanked by two more of the black candles, stood an extraordinary apparition. Tall, commanding, clad wholly in black, with a cloak over tight trunks, a black mask over his features, a close-fitting hood over his head out of which rose two small curving horns, this individual was clearly reading aloud from a great book, by the light of the blue flames, although the watchers outside could only hear the murmur of his voice, deep-toned, sepulchral enough to be one of the luminaries of the Kirk.

The King chittered and mouthed. Master Lindsay groaned deep within him, and Lennox crossed himself. Patrick Gray was less affected.

'A pity that we cannot hear,' he mentioned.

However, the reading stopped almost at once, and the congregation rose and proceeded to turn round and round before the speaker, all in their own place, widdershins – that is, contrary to the movement of the sun – in a slow and stately fashion, the women six times, and the men nine, most peculiar. Then a young creature with fair hair, notably well-developed, came forward to the pulpit steps and producing a tiny instrument known as a Jew's-harp, proceeded to thrum and twang a strange and haunting melody with a catchy and mischievous lift at the end of each verse. The entire company sang to this in hymn-like fashion, solemn and dignified – save that at the

278

end of each stanza the women all lifted their skirts high and executed a skittish dancing-step and shook their breasts. The effect was quite original.

Although the chanting was slow and in unison, it was difficult outside to follow the actual words. That it was a travesty of some sacred cantata, however, was apparent. Repetitions of the strange phrase:

> '*Cumer go ye before, cummer go ye,*
> *Gif ye will not go before, cummer let me.*'

kept recurring. It was a pity that no sense could be made of this.

When this was over, the masked individual in the pulpit descended to the floor of the kirk, and moved forward to the table. There, with some ceremony, he removed his tight-fitting black trunks and hose before the assembly. And, lo – his flesh beneath shone as black as the rest of him. He thereupon hoisted himself up on to the table itself, clearing away up-ended cross and bottles to do so, and sat so that his sooty posterior projected a little way over the far or eastern edge, not a dozen feet from the wide eyes of the hidden watchers. Then he waved imperiously towards the congregation.

'Christ God save us!' James gasped. 'See his . . . see his . . . !'

'No tail, you'll note,' Patrick observed, more prosaically, to Ludovick.

Led by the young woman with the Jew's-harp, the company now formed itself into a long and orderly queue, and moved forward in single file.

The plump girl, rosy-cheeked and comely, came up to the table, turned widdershins six times once more before it, and then moving round to the rear, bowed low and kissed the outthrust black bottom. One by one the entire assembly filed up and followed suit.

Master Lindsay began to pray again, with muted fervour.

This lengthy proceeding over, and everybody back in their seats, the satanic Master of ceremonies pulled on his trunks again, and returned to the pulpit. He raised his left hand, made the sign of the crooked cross, and loudly announced the curious text:

'Many comes to the fair, and buys not all wares.'

This could even be heard by the watchers without. It was Patrick's turn to groan. He had never been an appreciator of sermons, and obviously one was now to follow.

However, this sermon was mercifully brief, though not loud enough to be intelligible outside. From the deliverer's manner and gesticulations it seemed to be a rousing affair, with perhaps even a certain amount of humour about it. It ended very abruptly, with the preacher suddenly producing a black toad from under his gown, and pointing thereafter towards the door, clearly urging some action upon the company.

His commands were obeyed with alacrity – so much so that the watchers had to go scrambling downhill amongst the rocks in undignified haste in order to avoid being discovered as the congregation came flocking out of the church, the King yelping his fright. Fortunately the crowd did not make for this eastern end of the precincts. Nor did they stream off landwards, however. Splitting up into groups, they went, laughing and joking, towards various parts of the rocky peninsula, spades and mattocks being picked up as they went. Two parties, all women, came uncomfortably near to where the King's party hid, and removing any remaining clothing which might have encumbered their upper parts, set about digging at a couple of graves quite close together amongst the rocks – which, by the darker soil rather than green turf which outlined their oblong mounds, were evidently of recent construction. The women took turns with the spades, and went about their task with vigour and gusto.

It was not long before something long and pale began to appear from the nearest of the graves – obviously a corpse in its white winding-sheet. Amidst skirling laughter and cackles, this trophy was unrolled, no attempt being made to lower voices or smother hilarity – the noise of the waves, of course, would cover the sound at any distance. In only a moment or two the stink had penetrated even the two-score yards to the watchers, that warm summer night.

The stench had no ill effects on the women however. With cries of delight and satisfaction they stretched out the body of what appeared to have been a youngish man not very long buried. Knives materialised from under skirts, and with these, certain of the party set upon the remains, encouraged by the others rapturously. Two went to work at the groin, and others at each of the hands and feet. Whether or not these were practised butchers it was impossible to tell, but before long they were holding up grisly objects in triumph, presumably toes and fingers as well as less public members. Roughly bundling up the ravaged cadaver, the others returned it to the grave, covered it over, and stamped down the soil.

The group at the next lair were equally busy; it was impossible, from the watchers' stance, to see what they had achieved, however.

Lennox licked dry lips, muttering his horror and disgust. 'Foul harpies! I could vomit!'

'Spare yourself,' Patrick advised him. 'They are not finished yet.'

'We have plumbed the depths of hell this night!' Melville averred.

'Wait you, Sir James!'

'*Deus avertat!*' James said. '*Quieta non movere!*'

Presently the twanging of the Jew's-harp sounded as a signal, and all the congregation began to wind up their activities and stream back to the church. It took some time for them all to finish their various tasks however, and an impatient shout, presumably from their sable leader, hastened the stragglers. At last all were inside again, and the door was shut.

Without delay the six men hurried back to their former vantage point.

Now a most fantastic scene was being enacted. The horned master of ceremonies had taken up his stance behind the Communion Table. In front of it an aged crone was extracting from a sack, held open by other women, a clawing and frightened black cat, oblivious apparently to the bites and scratches she received.

The unfortunate animal was placed on the table, and held down there. Strangely enough it lay almost completely still, gripped by the old woman presumably in such a way as to

281

render it nerveless. Then, from a horrible and gruesome pile of objects on the table beside it, certain choice items from the dead bodies were selected by the masked individual, and tied by the woman to the corresponding parts of the cat – finger-joints to the forepaws, toes to the rear legs, an ear round its neck, genitals round its middle.

Thus bedecked, the animal was returned to his sack, and the remaining trophies shared out amongst the congregation. This indeed was the only undisciplined incident of the entire per-formance so far, as the women fought and clawed at each other to obtain these most unattractive mementoes. What they would do with them beggared the imagination.

Thereafter there was a caricature of a benediction, with the master of ceremonies making rude signs with his raised fingers, and the assembly turned widdershins, chanting some sort of antiphon. This time the watchers had due warning, and were safely hidden before the company emerged into the open. Even so there was some alarm when, led by the tall black figure and the Jew's-harper, the crowd came surging in an easterly direction. However, they kept to the highest part of the rock, and were clearly not in the least concerned with searching for possible spectators. Seemingly they were heading for the ulti-mate point of the peninsula. Letting them get well past, the royal party followed on discreetly.

At the extremity of the headland the people clustered, while their leader made another of his orations, gesturing towards sea and sky. Unfortunately, since he faced in that direction, his words remained unintelligible from a distance behind. Never long-winded, however, he was soon done. Then the old woman with the cat descended alone to the tide's edge, and stepping gingerly on to something low, small and dark tethered there, sat down.

'Hech, hech – the sieve!' James exclaimed. 'Yon'll be her sieve, Seton man.'

'Nae doot, Your Majesty,' the bailie agreed. His unfor-tunate maid-servant Geilis Duncan, under severe pressure, had informed her determined questioners that the witches of North Berwick habitually sailed in sieves.

'It could be only a raft,' Lennox pointed out, reasonably.
'Houts, Vicky – wheesht!' the King decried. 'Dinna mock.'

To further chanting from the company, the crone and her cat were pushed out from the rocks, and whether by supernatural means or merely by the action of the outgoing tide, the strange craft proceeded seawards, unpropelled by oars or sail. It was not long before it faded from their sight, in the gloom. Soon after, there was an unearthly screech, from out on the water, high-pitched, penetrating, and then silence.

'Christ preserve us!' James prayed. 'Was yon the cat or the auld wife?'

'Here they come again,' Patrick warned.

Their business at the sea evidently completed, the crowd came trooping back. Once again the watchers had to hide. Now a distinctly different attitude seemed to prevail amongst the coven. The solemnity was gone. All was jollity and capering. Back at the kirkyard, the buxom harpist mounted up on to the back and wide shoulders of her horned master, and from this lofty perch, white thighs gleaming on either side of his dusky masked features, strummed her strange music while her cavalier jigged beneath her with an astonishingly light and graceful step, and all around the graves the company skipped and danced.

'See the wicked strength o' him!' the King whispered. 'Carrying yon big heifer like she was a bit birdie!'

'A notable physique,' Patrick agreed. 'Tall. Broad of shoulder. But with no great flesh to him. And a deep voice. H'mmm. Also, did I detect a slight lisp?'

Lennox looked at him sharply. 'I did not note it,' he said.

'No? Perhaps your ears are less sharp than mine, Vicky?'

The dancing continued, growing ever wilder.

A council developed around the King. Melville proposed that one or more of them should get down into some hidden corner, facing westwards, and light the signal flare which they had with them, to summon the Royal Guard hotfoot. To catch the entire coven before it could disperse.

'This will be the end of it,' he foretold. 'They will work themselves into a frenzy, and afterwards go home.'

'Think you . . . ? Think you . . . ?' James peered doubtfully, biting his nails. 'Is it no' ower dangerous? There's that many o' them. Our royal person . . . ?'

'We must smite them hip and thigh, Sire!' Master Lindsay

283

urged. 'As Samson smote the Philistines. It is no less than our duty.'

'Unfortunately we are unprovided with asses' jawbones,' Patrick mentioned. 'His Grace's safety must be our first consideration.'

Even Ludovick looked surprised; such caution was scarcely in character for the Master of Gray.

'You would not let them all go free?' Melville wondered.

'Why, no. I propose to wait here, and follow one or more of these beauties back to their lairs. Alone. Unseen. It should not be difficult. Then when we know who they are, where they live, the rest will be simple. And all with no danger to His Grace.' He paused, for a moment. 'No *further* danger.'

'Eh . . . ? Danger, Patrick? Mair danger . . . ?'

'That cat, Sire. We must believe that this curious proceeding of the cat was done for some purpose. And since it seems that Your Grace is Satan's immediate target, the purpose is against your own royal person, perhaps. I would counsel a speedy return to Edinburgh and the safety of the palace.'

'Against my person!' James stammered. 'You think it, man?' He gripped Patrick's arm. 'Another storm, belike? I didna like yon o' the cat. Aye, you're right, Patrick – you're right. It's a gey long ride back to Emburgh. Let's awa', let's awa'.'

'But, Your Grace, we cannot be sure that the Master of Gray will be successful in following these evil folk,' Melville pointed out. 'If he loses them, then all our vigil is fruitless.'

'Na, na – no' fruitless, Sir James. We ken a deal that we didna ken before. Certes, we do! Patrick has the wiselike head in these matters. And you'd no' hae me further endangered, man?'

'No, Sire. But . . . '

'Come, then. Sufficient unto the day is the evil thereof. Mind that. We mustna' waste mair time. Back to the horses. Will I send you some o' the Guard, Patrick?'

'No. I am better alone.'

'I shall come with you,' Lennox said.

'No Vicky – your place is with His Grace. One man will more easily follow these others unseen than will two.'

'You're no' feared, Patrick?' the King asked.

'It is not me that Satan seeks to overwhelm is it, Highness?'

'Waesucks – no! That's right. It's me. Aye – let's awa' frae here. Quick, now.'

'I shall report to you in the morning, Sire,' the Master assured. 'I trust that no storms develop on your road home . . .'

Mary Gray sat on the grass and played with a daisy, as Ludovick paced up and down on the turf before her, high on the green flank of Arthur's Seat that towered above the grey palace of Holyroodhouse and all the jumbled roofs of the burgh of Canongate. She watched him thoughtfully.

'You believe it – and yet you disbelieve?' she said. 'It was evil – but you could not quite credit it?'

'Some of it,' he nodded. 'Something did not ring true. I do not know. But I felt it . . .'

'You felt perhaps that they were not true witches, Vicky?'

'How can I tell? *Are* there true witches? Do they indeed exist? These women were shameful, disgusting. All that they did was ill. Devil's work it may have been. But . . .'

'But it was not the Devil who directed it?'

'I think not. Certainly the black man with the horns but played the part.'

'Yet the King believes that it was Satan himself?'

'To be sure. James went expecting to see Satan – and saw him. As did, I think, Melville and Lindsay.'

'But not Uncle Patrick, I warrant!'

'Patrick was strange. In many ways. It was almost as though he himself was play-acting.'

'Yes. I can believe that. Tell me, Vicky, what he did. What he said.'

'It was scarcely what he said and did. It was his manner, Mary. As though he knew what was to happen. Almost as though he was privy to it all.'

'He went to North Berwick two days before, to spy out the land.'

'It was more than that. He knew much more. He told us when there was more to come. Worse things to be seen. He seemed to be surprised by nothing. The evil of it scarcely seemed to touch him.'

'Perhaps because it *was* play-acting? Perhaps because he had arranged it so, for the King?'

285

'But why?'

'That I do not know. You said that the King was expecting to see the Devil. Uncle Patrick perhaps produced the Devil. For some purpose of his own. Always he has a purpose of his own. You say that he did not return with you?'

'No. That also I did not understand. When the others would have signalled for the Guard, he would have none of it. He held that there was danger for James. Until then he had not seemed to think it. All must hasten away – save himself. He would watch on, and follow some of these people to their homes. To discover who they were. I would have gone with him, but he would not have it. I found it strange.'

'Yet did not the Lady Marie say that Uncle Patrick was home before the King?'

'Aye, we were much delayed. By a sea-mist. Near the Salt-pans of Preston. Thick mist in which we could scarce see our horses' ears. James swears that it was the cat's doing – that Satan sent it instead of a storm. So that he should perchance ride over a cliff, like King Alexander of old. Patrick got none of it. He followed a man home to Kilmurdie, a place near to Dirleton, helped himself to one of the man's horses, and rode back to Edinburgh bareback. He took the inland road, by the Gled's Muir, and saw no mist, he says.'

'This man that he followed – he was not the one who played Satan?'

'No. That one had a horse waiting. Not far from the kirk. And a groom, Patrick said. So that he might not follow him.'

'He was of the gentry, then – if he had horses and groom. Did you not learn anything of him? Who he might be? Even masked as he was.'

Ludovick shook his head. 'It was not possible. Besides the mask, he was all over blackened. And the light was but dim. All that we could see was that he was a tall man, well made but not fleshy. And of much strength, for he danced with a young woman on his shoulders. He had a deep voice. And . . . ah, yes – Patrick said that he spoke with something of a lisp. Although myself I did not hear that.'

'Do you think, then, that Uncle Patrick knew this man? If it was play-acting, and he was the leader . . . ?'

'Who can tell? But I do not believe it play-acting in the true

286

sense, Mary. These people were practising evil, denying God, insulting Christ. And they were well versed in it. They had done it many times, to be sure. It may, as you say, have been arranged last night especially for James. But it was no mummery. It was a coven practising its wickedness – that I'll swear. It was most vile.'

The girl scanned his face. It was not often that Ludovick Stuart was moved to this extent. 'What will the King do now, think you, Vicky?' she asked, presently.

'Why, send for this man Hepburn, no doubt. To put him to the question. To see what he may tell. Of the others . . . '

'Hepburn . . . ?'

'Aye. The one that Patrick followed. To Kilmurdie. He is Hepburn of Kilmurdie – a small lairdship near to North Berwick.'

'Hepburn – that is my lord of Bothwell's clan.' Suddenly Mary Gray sat up straight. 'And . . . and Bothwell speaks with a slight lisp, Vicky! A lisp! And his castle of Hailes is but a few miles from North Berwick!'

They stared at each other.

'Bothwell is tall and strong and wide of shoulder,' she went on.

'Aye, and deep of voice, too, by God! Could it be? Could it? Always he was crazed, wild . . . '

Mary was silent.

'Bothwell!' Ludovick repeated, almost breathlessly. 'One of the greatest in the land. The King's cousin, also. Who could think it . . . ?'

'Perhaps only the Master of Gray!' she said, slowly.

'What do you mean?'

'I mean, Vicky, that the Earl of Bothwell insulted Uncle Patrick yon day at Leith, when the Queen came. That was a dangerous thing to do!'

Askance he eyed her from under down-drawn brows.

'He called him a jumped-up wardrobe-master, before all. I feared for him, even as I listened. Now, I fear the more!'

'But, if it be the truth . . . ?'

Mary got to her feet and set off downhill without another word.

287

Chapter Fifteen

QUEEN Anne, very small in the great four-poster bed with purple hangings, pointed imperiously. 'The comfits, Mary – give them here. Then you may go. And bring the candles nearer.'

'Yes, Your Grace,' Mary did as she was bidden. 'There is nothing else . . . ?'

From under the pillows embroidered with the crown and royal monogram, Anne drew a sealed letter. 'See that this reaches the lodging of my lord of Moray. Forthwith. And . . . not by one of His Grace's pages, nor yet my own. You understand, Mary?'

The girl inclined her dark head.

'Also, see that the Lady Jean is in her room, and abed, as you go. The last night that it was her duty to attend me she was not there when I rang the bell. She was gone, for long. Off like a bitch in heat after some man. And not to the Abbot of Lindores, I vow! I know her. See to it, girl!'

'Yes, Your Grace. And a goodnight,' Curtsying, Mary slipped out of the royal bedchamber.

The Lady Jean Stewart was not, in fact, in the room across the stairway occupied by the lady-in-waiting on duty. Mary went into the larger anteroom on the same level. Jean was not there either. Two of the King's pages were present, one sprawled asleep across a table, the other, a pretty boy with painted lips and rouged cheeks, lounged in a chair, a goblet in his hands, a lute at his feet.

'Master Ramsey,' she said 'know you where the Lady Jean may be?'

The youth yawned. 'Know I do not – nor care. But I might hazard a guess, Mistress!'

'Then go, if you please, where you guess, and request that her ladyship come back here.'

'Not I, wench. I have more to do than run sniffing after such game!'

'No? I think that you have not!' Mary considered him comprehensively, calmly. 'Besides, it is the Queen's express command. And I will thank you to mind your words, Master Ramsay. Where is His Grace?'

Ramsay grimaced and pouted, pointing a finger upwards. 'Where but, as ever, amongst his papers and books? A pox on all such dusty foolery!' Grumbling, he strolled off on his errand.

Mary followed him down the winding stone stairs, past the sleepy, yawning guards. She crossed the inner courtyard of the palace to another corner-tower, and mounting to the first floor, entered a room, spartan-bare and untidy, where a young man was in the act of removing his doublet.

'Your pardon, Peter,' she smiled. 'At this late hour. Is my lord Duke here?'

'Abed and asleep, Mistress Mary. We rode from Linlithgow.' The other's face had lighted up at the sight of her. 'But it is never too late to see *you*. Come – a glass of wine? Shall I wake the Duke?' Without saying so, he implied that that might be a pity.

'No – thank you, no, Peter. It is just a letter. To go to the Earl of Moray's lodging in the Canongate.'

Peter Hay raised his eyebrows at the folded paper. 'The King's seal – but not the King's hand o' write, I vow!' he commented. 'Blows the wind so?'

'I perceive no such wind, Peter. Will you carry this letter, please?'

'Must it go to my lord tonight, then?'

'I fear so. Forthwith, was the command.'

Lennox's page sighed, and reached for his boots.

When he had gone, Mary went to the inner door and quietly opened it. In the dim light of a single guttering candle, Ludovick lay naked on the top of his bed, on his back, arms thrown wide, while all around him his fine clothes lay crumpled as they had been cast down, littered anywhere. Lips slightly parted, curling hair disarrayed, breathing with little puffs, he looked more boyish than ever. One hand lay open, but in the other a yellow velvet ribbon was entwined round his fingers. Mary recognised it at once. It was one that she had used sometimes to tie up her hair, and had unaccountably lost a week or two before.

289

For a little while she watched him there, a faint smile playing round the corners of her mouth. Then quietly she tip-toed into the room, picked up all the scattered clothing, folded it neatly and placed it on a bench near the bed – having to displace a riding-boot, a crossbow-bolt, a pistol and an entanglement of fishing-line, in the process. This completed, she stood over the bed for a moment or two before, with a little quiver of sigh, she snuffed out the candle and slipped away, closing the door behind her.

Mary did not go to her own chamber in the Master of the Wardrobe's quarters, but returned across the courtyard to the tower that housed the royal private apartments. Climbing the corkscrew stairs again, she looked in at the ladies-in-waiting chamber, but Jean was still amissing. A further flight she mounted, to pause outside a shut door. Softly she knocked – and knocked again.

'What now, what now?' The King's voice sounded irascible.

'It is Mary Gray, Highness,' she said, as quietly as she might.

'Eh? Eh? Speak up. Who's there? What's to do?'

'Mary Gray, Sire. To speak with you.'

'Och, awa' wi' you, lassie. Tell the Queen I'll no' be long. Tell her to go to sleep. I'm occupied, see you – much occupied. Wi' important matters.'

'Yes, Sire. But this is important also. The Queen has not sent me. I crave word with you. Concerning this matter of witches.'

That ensured her admittance, albeit with much royal muttering. Carefully locking the door behind them, James, untidier even than usual, peered at the girl in the candle-lit confusion of parchments, books and papers.

'Well, lassie – well? he demanded testily. 'You shouldna be here, you ken. It's no' suitable. I'm no' sure that Annie would like it ... '

'That I have considered, Sire. But I believe it to be important.'

'You said it was anent the witches? Has Patrick found out mair ... ?'

'No. The Master of Gray has not sent me. I have heard that

290

the Earl of Bothwell is shut up in Edinburgh Castle, Sire. On charge of witchcraft?'

'Aye, the ill limmer! He is so, God be praised! I believe him to be Satan's lieutenant in this realm o' Scotland. A man sold to the Devil.'

'But, Sire, how can . . . ?'

'No buts, Mistress! I saw him at his wickedness. Wi' my ain two eyes. In the kirk o' North Berwick. A right terrible sight.'

'Yes. But did you not declare to the Queen, Your Grace, and to others, that it was the Devil himself that you saw there? How could it then be my lord of Bothwell?'

'Eh . . . ? Och, well.' James plucked at his loose lower lip. 'Belike it was Bothwell acting for the Devil.'

'Did you not tell the Queen that he had horns and claws and cloven hooves? How could that have been Bothwell?'

'M'mmm. Aye. But I saw his shape, girl. I heard his voice.'

'Yet you did not think that it was Bothwell then, Sire? You thought it was the Devil.'

'No. But . . . och, dinna harry me, this way. You canna talk so to the King, woman. It's no' respectful.'

'I would never show disrespect for Your Grace,' Mary assured him earnestly. 'I am but your humble and honest servant. I but seek your Highness's weal and honour.' That might have been Patrick Gray himself.

'As is right and proper,' James nodded sternly. 'Mind it, then.'

'Yes.' Then directly she put it to him. 'Do you believe that my lord of Bothwell *is* the Devil, Sire?'

'Houts, lassie – houts! Na, na – I wouldna just say that.' James was wary. 'No' just Auld Hornie himsel', maybe.'

'Then, Highness – if it was one or the other that you saw at North Berwick, I can assure you that it was not Bothwell. For he was in Edinburgh all that night. In bed in the house of the Commendator of Lindores.'

'Nae doubt that is what he *says*, Mistress.'

'He did not say it to me. I learned it otherwise. Perhaps the lady will speak for him.'

'Lady . . . ? His wife, mean you? Would she no' say aught to advantage him?'

291

'Not his wife, Sire. The lady with whom he spent the night at the Commendator's house in the Lawnmarket.'

'Guidsakes!' The King shambled round the table, touching papers here and there. 'Who was she – this woman?'

'I would prefer not to tell her name, Sire.'

'It's no' what you'd prefer or no' prefer, i' faith! I'm asking you, woman!'

'I believe that Your Grace also would prefer not to hear it.'

'Eh . . . ? How might that be?'

'She is the wife to another. To one close to your Highness. Notably close, it is said. Who complains that she is being neglected by her husband. In her wifely rights. Since coming to Court.'

'Oh! Ah . . . ummm. Ooh, aye. D'you tell me that, Mistress?' Eyes rolling in alarm, the King moved further away. 'Here's a right pickle! How d'you ken a' this, Mistress Mary? About Bothwell,' he added hurriedly.

'I made it my business to find out, Sire.'

'Aye – through that Jean Stewart, nae doubt. She beds wi' Patrick o' Lindores. But why, lassie? What interests you that much in Francis o' Bothwell? You're no' taken up wi' the rascal your ain sel'?'

'Far from it, Sire. Indeed I like him but little. But I would not have Your Grace's fame spoiled by the hurt of an innocent man.'

'Aye. I'ph'mmm. Would you no' . . . ? Well, well – we'll see. This requires thinking upon. Much thought.' James edged towards the door.

'Sire,' the girl said, a little breathlessly for her, 'do you not write any more poetry? It is a great wonder to have a king who is a poet. Your renown goes forth . . . '

'Och, I havena time for yon,' James interrupted. 'I'm ower busy dealing wi' this o' the Devil.'

'Could that not be what the Devil wishes you to do, Your Grace? That you serve him best by fighting him at his own game, with his own weapons? Perhaps by poetry and other things – kindly arts reaching to the hearts of men – you may do better. Injure his kingdom more.'

'Och, Mary lass – dinna haver! I'll no' beat Satan wi'

292

poetry. He needs harder knocks than that. Forby, I'm writing
a book. To open men's eyes to his wiles and deceits. Na, na –
I've no time for rhyming.'

Mary sighed. 'I am sorry. I had hoped that Your Grace
might have helped me again. With my own poor verses. You
were so good before. So clever. A true poet, you guided my
faltering lines . . . '

'You are writing mair verses, Mary? To the Queen? Annie's
no' that taken wi' poetry, I've found.'

'No. To . . . to another. I am finding it difficult. But with
your help . . . '

'Na, na. Go you to Patrick Gray, lassie – to your uncle. No'
to me. He's a poet, and he's far mair time, forby. He hasna this
realm to rule and Satan to fight. Off wi' you now, and let me
to my work. Begone, girl.'

Sighing again, Mary curtsied. 'I beg Your Grace's pardon,'
she said, and moved to the locked door.

Patrick Gray paced back and forth across the stone-flagged
floor, behind the table – the only man so to do. Which was
unlike that self-possessed individual. Indeed, he was probably
the man least himself in that sombre wood-panelled chamber
of Edinburgh Castle. His companions sat or lounged around
three sides of the great table, interested, concerned, bored or
lethargic – or plain drunk. One or two goblets were already
overturned, with the wine spilled and dripping on the floor.

In his high chair at the top, the King sat forward absorbed,
eager, avid almost. Seldom had any of those present seen that
strange young man so much alive, so keenly intent. A large
sheet of paper lay before him, with ink-pot and sand, and in
his hand he held a newly-sharpened quill, with others, used
and unused, lying by. The paper was one-third written upon
in James's spidery hand. Clerks sitting at another smaller
table clutched their pens much less earnestly.

'Sit you doon, sit you doon, Master o' Gray,' James said,
licking thick lips. 'Dinna be so impatient, man. We'll win to
the truth yet.'

'I doubt it, Your Grace – mightily I doubt it. By this
road,' Patrick returned without pronounced respect. 'If I am

impatient, it is at this waste of your royal time. Of all our time. Here is no way to . . . '

He stopped, both his speaking and his pacing, as a high-pitched screaming came through to them from some chamber beyond, bubbling, half-strangled. Broken and crazed it rose, three times, before sinking in a whimpering that presently failed to reach them.

The King rubbed his hands. 'Hear you that?' he charged them. 'We'll no' be long now, I warrant!'

'May the Devil so screech eternally in his hell, and all who favour and abet him!' Master Lindsay observed, piously.

'Amen, amen!' James agreed wholeheartedly. Hastily some others of the company added their assent.

'Christ's cause will triumph!' added the Chancellor, newly created Lord Maitland of Thirlstane by a grateful monarch. 'God's will be done.'

Patrick swung on him. 'How can you listen to that, my lord, and call it God's work or Christ's cause?' he demanded. 'I am a sad sinner, as none knows better – but I would not saddle the sweet Christ with such as this!'

'Tush, sir . . . '

'The Lord Christ scourged the wrong-doers out of the temple, Master of Gray,' Lindsay reminded him sternly. 'All evil must be scourged and beaten out of wicked men. Only so shall Christ's kingdom come. The punishment of evil-doing is God's work.'

'Punishment, sir? This then is punishment? For sins committed? I understood that this was a court of law. Duly instituted by the King. To try. To enquire into. No verdict has yet been pronounced. No decision reached. No sentence given. Is it not early for punishment . . . ?'

'Och, Patrick man,' James interrupted, 'you ken very well we must needs put them to the question. Likewise that Satan keeps their lips tight closed lest they tell his black secrets. Ooh, aye. Only by sic-like pains can we overcome his ill hold on them. It's full necessary, man. Forby, they're a' guilty as hell itsel'. You ken that fine. We saw it wi' our ain eyes. Waesucks – their punishment is well earned! We but require the evidence established according to the law. Is that not so, Sir William?'

Sir William Elphinstone, Senator of the College of Justice,

one of the three Lords of Session present, roused himself, peered, and hiccuped. 'Undoubtedly, Your Grace,' he said.

'Aye. We but seek the truth, Patrick. The truth we must have. You'll no' deny that? Guidsakes, man – it was yoursel' that uncovered for us this nest o' infamy and ...'

An animal squealing interrupted even the monarch, a sound grotesque and repetitive that seemed impossible to have come from human lips.

One of the more somnolent judges sat up, eyes open, suddenly interested. 'Fiend seize me – is yon the auld one or the young one?' he demanded. 'I'll wager you a crown it's the auld one, Dod.' Then recollecting the King's presence, he choked and stammered. 'Your ... Your Grace's pardon!'

James was not listening – at least, not to this. He was craning his head forward, a little to one side, staring directly at the blank wall of panelling, as though he would project himself entirely into what went on in that next chamber.

Patrick came directly up to the King's chair. 'Your Grace,' he urged, 'I pray you halt this, this savagery. No evidence gained thus is worth a packman's whistle. They will say anything.'

'Wheesht, man – wheesht!' With an almost physical effort, James brought himself back to present company. 'You err, Patrick. These toils are necessary and proper. The creatures will no' speak, otherwise. That we ken. Even at my royal command.'

'They will speak, Sire – have spoken. Only not what you would have them to say ...'

James straightened up in his chair. 'Houts, sir – that's no way to speak to me! I'll thank you to watch your words in our presence.'

'I think that you forgot yourself, Master of Gray,' Maitland said coldly from across the table. 'Recollect that you are not in your Wardrobe now!'

Patrick ignored him. 'Sire – these methods smack of Queen Elizabeth's Walsingham rather than of the King of Scots,' he charged – a shrewd stroke, for of all men James loathed and feared Mr. Secretary Walsingham, the greatest spy-master and inquisitor outside Spain.

Visibly the King drew back. 'Eh . . . ? Walsingham!' he

muttered. 'No' that . . . you'd no' say . . . '

The door of the adjoining chamber opened, turning all heads. A continuous chittering moaning sound was at once evident; as well as a most unpleasant smell. With these, in through the doorway, came a moon-faced fat man, bald, indeed hairless, as a baby, and as pink-and-white. In shirt and breeches, with sleeves uprolled, he came forward, bobbing a series of jerky bows at the King, sweat streaming from his cherubic features and soaking his shirt. Red blood too splattered the latter.

'Well, Master Broun – well?' James demanded. 'Ha' you been successful? Ha' you displaced the Devil and let in the fear o' God?'

'Aye, Majesty – mair or less,' the other answered. He had a high squeaking voice to match his face. 'But I'm thinking she'll no' tak mair, the noo. It's weak flesh, weak. It fails me, for a' my craft and cunning. Mair, at the present, and you'll get nae sense oot o' her, I fear – just mowlings and mewings nae better than a cat. Twice she swooned awa', Majesty. But I'm right nimble at fetching them back. I ken the ways o' their bodies. I'm skilled at searching oot their . . . '

'Enough of yourself, man!' the Lord Chancellor broke in. 'His Grace is not interested in your fell trade. Is the woman yet in her senses?'

'Aye, my lord. It's been a sair trauchle to keep her so. But she has her wits yet, in a manner o' speaking . . . '

'Then fetch her in, Master Broun,' the King ordered, 'fetch her in.'

The fat man backed out, and presently returned with two brawny guards half-carrying between them an extraordinary and distasteful apparition, a sagging and untidy bundle of trailing hair, limbs, and torn and soiled clothing. This twitching, sprawling spectacle they brought forward to the table – until, wrinkling his nose in disgust, the Chancellor waved them away.

'Further back, for a mercy!' he ordered. 'Further back, fools! A pox – how she stinks!'

'Ha – see you, Dod!' the Lord of Session Graham chuckled. 'I said it was the auld one . . . '

'Yon's no' the auld one, Johnnie,' Sir William Elphinstone

296

reproved. 'See her paps. The auld gammer couldna show the likes o' yon, I'll warrant! It's the young quean. Use your eyes, man.'

'Your Grace – this . . . this is beyond all bearing!' Patrick Gray exclaimed. 'You cannot countenance such barbarity!'

'Then stand you back, Master of Gray – if your stomach is over-nice!' Sir James Balfour observed dryly. 'I would scarce have believed one of your, h'm, experience to be so delicate!'

The King did not seem to hear any of them; nor did he appear to be ill-affected by either sight or smell. He had half-risen to his feet involuntarily, as though indeed he would have moved closer to the sorry creature that had been brought in to them, but he slowly resumed his seat, contenting himself with leaning forward over the table, slack lips working.

'Aye, aye,' he got out at length. 'So is ill pride fallen! Here's the end o' black shame and whoring wi' Satan!' He actually wagged a minatory finger at the unsavoury scarecrow. 'You're nane so vaunty now, Mistress! Changed days since you rode the Devil at North Berwick! Siclike are the wages o' sin, woman.'

Certainly the broken and repulsive eyesore before them was hardly to be accepted as the same comely and voluptuous young female who had played the Jew's-harp at North Berwick kirk and led the dance on the shoulders of the horned preacher. The worthy Lord of Session was scarcely to be blamed for mistaking her for the old hag whom they had interrogated with her, previously; hollow-eyed, her flesh turned grey where it was not discoloured with bruising, her tawny hair ragged, sweat-stained and matted with blood as a result of the twisting of a rope around her head – a favourite method of extracting the truth from witches – she looked as she had sounded, scarcely human.

'Can she speak, Master Broun?' the Chancellor demanded, doubtfully.

'Oh, aye. Fine, my lord. Naught wrang wi' her tongue. You should ha' heard her back there . . . '

'Quite, man – quite.' Maitland raised his voice, as though to bring the prisoner to her senses. 'Woman,' he said sternly. 'Hear me. You will now give answer to our questions. Honestly and respectfully. We will have no more lies and evasions . . . '

297

'Bide a wee, bide a wee, my lord,' James intervened, frowning. 'Wi' your permission *I* will question the creature.' He signed to the man Broun. 'Cover her up. She's no' decent. An offence, just.' Primly he tutted. 'Now, Mistress Cairncross – your attention, if you please. We maun hae an answer to these several points. *Imprimis* – do you admit that you are a sworn servant o' the Devil and the enemy o' the Lord God and His Kirk? *Secundum* – that the true and veritable reason for yon ill conventicle at North Berwick was the sore hurt and harm o' me, James Stewart, your liege lord, King o' this realm o' Scotland, and Christ's viceregent? *Tertium* – that you and your coven hae held the like wicked and abominable conventicles and practices at times previous, and in especial when I was aship at sea, wi' the object o' effecting storms and great waves to swallow me up. Aye, and mists too. Yon mist. And other siclike calamitous hurts. *Quartum* – was your captain, precentor and leader in all such abominations the Devil himsel', or a man in his dark service? A man, just? Aye, and *Quintum* – if a man, was he no' Francis Stewart, calling himsel' Hepburn, Earl o' Bothwell?' James scanned his paper, to make sure that he had missed no point. Then he jabbed his pen at the wreck of a young woman. 'Now, Mistress – that's clear enough, is it no'? We'll hae the first. You admit that you are a sworn servant o' the Devil? Eh?'

The faint mumbling and moaning that came from the prisoner slumped between the two guards was no different from what she had been emitting since being brought into the council-chamber.

'Tut, woman – speak up!' the King urged. 'I canna hear you.'

'Sire – she is in no state to speak to any effect. Your butcher has seen to that . . . !'

'Master o' Gray, I'll thank you to hold your tongue!'

'A mouthful of wine, Highness,' Melville suggested. 'To loosen *her* tongue.'

'Aye, gie her that, Broun man. A bit sup.'

While wine from a goblet on the table was being forced into the woman's slack mouth, Patrick brought the chair that he should have been seated upon, set it behind her and eased her down into it. Even so, the guards had to hold her up or she would have slipped to the floor.

'You are exceeding tender towards an idolatrous hellicat, Master of Gray,' the Chancellor observed.

'She is still a woman,' the other answered simply.

'So, sir, was His Grace's royal mother the late Queen Mary – was she not?'

'God's passion, Maitland . . . !' Patrick swung upon the Chancellor.

King James banged his hand on the table. 'A truce, a truce!' he squeaked. 'Hold your tongues, both o' you. Guidsakes – I'll no' have it! This is a court o' law, I'd mind you. Doing God's business. Aye, Now you, Mistress Cairncross – answer me. Admit to me that you are sold to the Devil.'

Wild bloodshot eyes flickered over the company, and returned shrinking, not to the King but to the baby-faced man beside her. A thick and unintelligible sound issued from her swollen lips – but she nodded her head, helplessly, hopelessly.

'Ha! And so we have it.' James beamed on her, on them all. Then he bent, to scratch his pen over the paper. 'The panel admits the prime complaint. Why couldna you have tell't us that before, woman – and saved a deal o' time. Now, *secundum*. Wasna yon ploy at North Berwick aimed against my ain royal sel'? Directed at me, the King?'

Again the mouthing and nodding.

'See you, my lords and gentlemen,' James looked round them, squaring his normally drooping shoulders, heavy head for once held high. 'It is as I said. Me, it is – me!' He beat on his padded chest. 'Me, James Stewart, that the Devil is fell set against. Me he fears. I ken it, fine.'

Heads bowed in due acknowledgment.

'Aye.' He consulted his papers. 'Well, then. Mistress Cairncross – the third point leads on frae the second. You'll no' deny previous conventicles o' sin? And nae doubt they'd be for the same ill purpose? The storms when I was on the sea? And when the Queen couldna win to me? These too were your detestable work? Your foul coven brewed these ills for me likewise, did they no'?'

The woman was nodding and gabbling before ever he had finished.

Triumphantly James turned to the Master of Gray. 'Did I no' tell you, Patrick? We win to the truth at last. Master Broun has well furthered the Lord's work.' He wagged his admonitory finger. 'You erred, Patrick – you greatly erred.'

Patrick Gray shook his head. 'What have we learned, Sire, that we did not know before? What does it advantage us to hear it again, wrung from a foolish country wench by torture?'

'It is evidence, man.'

'Evidence of what? Evidence of the frailty of human flesh against the rope and the screw? Naught else, I swear. The evidence that we need is from my lord of Bothwell. Question *him*, Your Grace . . . '

James nibbled at his pen. 'We canna do that, Patrick,' he interrupted. 'You ken it. Bothwell is a peer o' Scotland. Forby a member o' my Council, and a cousin o' my ain. We canna put him to the question like, like . . . '

'Like less fortunate of Your Grace's subjects!'

'A peer of this realm and member of His Grace's Privy Council may only be tried by that Council,' Chancellor Maitland intervened stiffly. The period of co-operation between these two had been only brief; now their mutual antipathy was as pronounced as formerly. 'As well you know, Master of Gray – who were in the same position not that long syne!'

'I have not forgotten, my lord. Nor what went before that peculiar trial – and the questioning of my half-brother, Davy Gray! And who performed that questioning. Davy was only a peer's bastard, of course – which no doubt makes a deal of difference. But I am not here talking about my lord of Bothwell's trial. I referred but to his questioning.'

'He has been questioned – and admitted nothing. You know it.'

'But not questioned as this wretched woman has been questioned.'

'Would you, *you*, have a noble of Scotland, and one of the highest in the land, thus mishandled, sir?'

'For so fresh-minted a noble as yourself, my lord, you are touchingly considerate for your new kind!' Although Gray's lip curled, he eyed the Chancellor keenly, thoughtfully. Maitland had never loved Bothwell, indeed had suffered at that

300

madcap's hands. If now he was taking Bothwell's part, then it must be for good and sufficient reason. This would obviously require watching.

That Bothwell appeared to have another unexpected friend present now became apparent. The Earl of Moray had hitherto taken no evident interest in the proceedings. Now he spoke up.

'Is it not the case, Sire, that Bothwell is known to have spent yon night you were at North Berwick, in Leslie of Lindores' house in the Lawnmarket? And there's a certain lady can prove it!'

Nervously, the King peered at him from under down-drawn brows. 'Eh . . . ? Say you so? Well, now. A tale, nae doubt – a tale. Did he tell you it himsel', my lord?'

'No, Sire. It was a lady who told me. But not *the* lady, mark you!'

All members of the court were now sitting up, with interest introduced into the occasion. Patrick's eyes were busy.

'This lady . . . ?' he began.

Elphinstone was leaning forward. 'Aye, the lady's name, my lord?' he demanded.

The King banged his hand on the table. 'Enough o' idle tattle and gossip!' he ordered squeakily. 'You, my Lord o' Session, should ken better. Aye, better. This is a court o' law.' He coughed. 'To proceed. Woman!'

The unfortunate prisoner had sunk into a partial coma during this exchange. Now she was roused roughly by the man Broun, into gasping attention.

'My fourth question, Mistress, if you please.' James pointed the pen at her. 'It is fell important, see you. Was yon limmer in the pulpit at North Berwick – aye, whose black arse you so shamefully kissed – was yon the Devil or man?'

Gnawing swollen lip, the young woman gazed around her like a trapped animal. This was not a question to which she could merely nod her head.

'Come, Mistress – out wi' it,' James urged irritably. 'You must ken – you who lewdly bestrode his wicked shoulders.'

Still she did not answer.

'What's wrong wi' you, woman?'

'She does not know what you would wish her to say – that's

what is wrong with her,' Moray shrewdly asserted. 'In your other questions, she knew.'

'It was a man, was it not?' Patrick put in swiftly. 'A man, acting for the Devil?'

Almost eagerly the prisoner nodded. 'Yes,' she said. 'Yes.'

'Now we have it. Aye, now we come to it,' the King said.

'Belike the wretched creature would have said as much for the Devil,' Moray observed. 'Put it this way. Tell me, woman. This man – it was the Devil in the guise of a man, was it not? A man in form, but the Devil in person?'

For a moment or two she hesitated. Then she nodded. 'Aye,' she whispered.

'You see, Sire!'

James frowned and tutted. 'I'll thank you, my Lord o' Moray, to leave the questioning to me. Aye – all o' you. D'you hear? To me. You but hae the woman confused. Mistress – see here. This man in the Devil's guise – was it my lord o' Bothwell, or was it no'?'

Desperately the unhappy creature looked from one to another of them. 'I . . . I canna say,' she got out.

'Waesucks, you can! And you shall. You are a right obdurate woman. Aye, obdurate. I'm right displeased wi' you. Was it Bothwell or was it no'? Answer me.'

'Sink me!' Moray exclaimed. 'So there's your evidence!'

'Aye, Bothwell has naught to fear here,' Chancellor Maitland agreed.

'It is as I said, Your Grace.' Patrick smoothly altered his stance. 'Such evidence is of no value to us. None of it. This last but means that Bothwell, if it be he, does not use his own name at such affairs. And who would expect him to?'

But James was not satisfied. 'I say she lies,' he declared. 'She kens the creature well enough, wi' his breeks on an' wi' them off! She kens him as carnally as he kens her, I warrant! Dinna tell me that she never asked his name. Woman – what is the man's name?'

She shook her head.

'Answer me, witch – answer me!'

'We . . . we but ken him as Jamie. Jamie, sir – the same as yoursel'.'

'Guidsakes, do you so!' The King was indignant. 'Jamie,

is it? Jamie what? What's the rest o' it?'

'Just Jamie, sir.'

'Havers, woman! Dinna tell me that you never spiered mair about the man whose arse you kissed. And who's had you times aplenty, I'll be bound! How d'you name him, eh?'

Dumbly she shook her head.

Exasperatedly the King wagged his pen at her. 'Master Broun – to your trade! See if perchance *you* can bring back her memory!'

The fat man grasped a handful of her hair, close to the head, and twisted it, and the already wrung and tortured scalp beneath. Half-rising in her chair to the agony of it, the woman emitted an ear-piercing shriek that rang the very rafters, and swooned away unconscious, dragging down even the expert questioner. Disgustedly he threw the inert body to the floor.

'Fiend tak her!' he exclaimed. 'She's failed me, at the last.'

'Is it not yourself that has failed *us*, fellow!' one of the professional judges complained. 'That's the end o' her, for a wager. We'll get no more out o' her. We're wasting our time.'

'Not quite the end o' her, my friend,' James corrected. 'That is still to come. Nor have we entirely wasted our time, I think. We've this ill woman's confession, added to the testimony o' our ain eyes, that she has committed the vile sin o' witchcraft – which is a burning matter. Aye, and that she and others contrived it against my ain royal person – which is highest treason, forby. You a' heard her. In consequence, this being a court o' justice duly constituted, we needna spend mair time on her. I pronounce her black guilty o' these maist abominable crimes and offences, and do hereby sentence her to just and lawful punishment.' He paused, licking thick lips. 'Aye. She shall be taken out the morn to the forecourt o' this my castle o' Edinburgh, and the good burghers o' this town and city summoned by tuck o' drum to witness. And before them a' she shall be worried to the half-deid, and thereafter burned wholly wi' fire. As is just, right and proper, according to the law o' this realm and the precepts o' Christ's Kirk. *Ex auctoritate mihi commisâ.*'

'Amen!' the Church, in the person of Master Lindsay agreed fervently.

303

'Correct, meet and due,' the law acceded, by the lips of one of the senators.

' 'Fore God – has she not suffered enough?' the Master of Gray demanded.

'Thou shalt not suffer a witch to live!' the King intoned. 'Would you deny Holy Writ, man Patrick?'

'I can recollect other Scripture, I think, less savage . . . '

'Tush, man – dinna bandy words. You're no' in a proper and seemly state o' mind this night, Master o' Gray – you are not. You've no' helped the assize. You've but hindered the course o' justice. Aye. But enough o' this. Our royal word is said, and sentence passed. Awa' wi' her, Master Broun. And then we will hear the other. Fetch in the auld wife.'

'In that case, Your Grace – have I your permission to retire?' Patrick asked. 'Since my presence is of no help . . . and my stomach will scarce stand more of this!'

'Aye – go then, Patrick. You may leave us. But I'm right disappointed in you – I am so. A weak vessel, you prove. Tried, I find you wanting, man – wanting.'

'I had believed that it was to be the Earl of Bothwell who was tried – not myself, Sire. Seemingly I was wrong. Your Grace . . . my lords . . . gentlemen – I bid you a good night. If that is possible after . . . this!'

Chapter Sixteen

LUDOVICK STUART came long-striding up the steep grassy hillside, breathing deeply. Mary Gray waved to him as he approached, from where she sat on a green ledge amongst the yellow crowsfoot and the purple thyme. But she did not smile.

'I thought . . . that I might . . . find you here,' he panted. 'I searched all the . . . palace for you. None had seen you. Jean said . . . Jean said that you would be with my page, Peter Hay. But I did not believe her.'

'The Lady Jean is of that way of thinking, Vicky. So works her mind.'

'Yet you are a deal away from the palace these days, Mary.'
He stood before her, hands on padded hips, his Court finery
as usual looking somehow out-of-place and alien to his sturdy
stocky figure. 'Is it ever here you come? All this way?'

'Not always. But often, yes.'

'And alone?'

'Alone, yes. Although sometimes the Lady Marie comes with
me. And little Andrew. To escape . . . to get away, for a
little, from, from . . . ' It was not often that that young woman
left her sentences unfinished or lacked due words – save
perhaps when she had occasion to play the part of an innocent
girl.

Involuntary both of them turned to look out across the
deep trough where acres and acres of jumbled roofs and spires
and turrets, part-hidden in the swirling smoke of a thousand
chimneys, climbed the crowded mile from the grey palace of
Holyroodhouse up to the great frowning fortress of Edinburgh
Castle on its lofty rock. If they did not actually see more and
different smoke drifting down from that grim citadel's forecourt, they did not fail to sense it, smoke tainted with a smell
other than that of wood or coals.

'Aye,' the young Duke said heavily. 'I also. Often I could
choke with it. The palace, the whole town, stinks of death.
Aye, and fear. I would be out of it all, Mary – away . . . '

'Yes,' she said. 'I knew that smell in London. Elizabeth's
fires at the Bridewell. I had not thought to smell it here in
Scotland. Madness, it is – cruel madness . . . ' She paused.
'Once I feared that it might be the Spanish Inquisition's fires
that would burn on the Castle-hill of Edinburgh! Now . . . !'

For three weeks the fires had blazed on the windy plateau
before the gates and drawbridge of Edinburgh Castle. For
three weeks the screams of the condemned had rung through
the crowded vennels and tall stone tenements of the capital.
For three weeks the citizens had daily been gorged with the
spectacle of justice most evidently being done, of strings of the
Devil's disciples being led in chains through the streets to the
wide and crowded castle forecourt, there to be part-strangled
publicly by teams of lusty acolytes and then tied to stakes to
burn, for the confounding of evil and the greater glory of God.
Day in, day out, and far into the night, the work went on, King

305

James himself personally supervising much of it, especially the examining, determined, indefatigable, confounding his arch-enemy Satan. There was no lack of material for his cleansing fervour; sufficiently questioned, almost all suspects could be brought to the point, not only of confession to the most curious activities, such as sailing the Forth in sieves, and turning themselves into hares, hedgehogs and the like, but also of denouncing large numbers of their acquaintances as equally guilty of these disgraceful practices. These, apprehended and similarly questioned in turn, could be brought to implicate ever greater numbers more. It was extraordinary how, once the rope was sufficiently twisted round their heads, names would come tumbling from their lips. The process was cumulative, the good work ever widening its scope and ramifications, growing like a snowball – to the notable enlargement and improvement of the King's monumental book on demonology. Seldom indeed had an author been so blest with the supply of excellent research material.

The citizens had long lost count of the numbers of culprits, after it had run into hundreds – mostly women, but with a fair sprinkling of men, and even children. Clearly the abominable cult and practice of witchcraft and warlockry was infinitely more widespread than anyone had dreamed. North Berwick and that part of Lothian had soon ceased to be the centre and hub of activities; the net was spreading far and wide over Scotland. To cope with the alarming situation, King James hit on the ingenious expedient of granting Royal Commissions throughout the land, with power 'to justify witches to the death' without further formality – stipulating only that all interesting occult revelations should be passed on to himself. Fourteen such Commissions had indeed been granted in a single day. There seemed no reason to suppose that the momentum would not further increase and the harvest expand.

The Earl of Bothwell meantime remained warded in the fortress, still not brought to trial – but warded as befitted his rank and standing, with his own suite of rooms and his own servants.

'Madness indeed,' Lennox agreed, thickly. 'I fear that Patrick may have been right, yon time. That James is indeed mad. Either mad or a monster. And yet, if he be so, so many

306

others are likewise. James leads, yes – but he has no lack of followers.'

Mary shook her head. 'I do not believe that he is mad. Nor yet a monster. I think that he is a man frightened. Fearful of so many things. Unsure. His head so full of strange learning that he cannot comprehend. If he is working a great wickedness, it is because he is what men's wickedness has made him. And he is so very lonely.'

A little askance the Duke looked at her. This sort of talk was beyond him.

'All kings are lonely,' the girl went on. 'But James is the most lonely of all. He has never known mother or father, brothers or sisters. Always he has been alone, close to none – but watched by all. Trusting none, and for good reason. Yet greatly needing others close to him. More than do many.'

'He has a wife now, Mary.'

'I cannot think that the Queen is the wife that he needed. She has a hardness, a sharpness. She will not pretend for him, as he needs – pretend that he is a fine gallant, a notable poet, a strong monarch.'

'And she has the rights of it – for he is none of them!' the young man said bluntly.

'No. But a wife could aid him to be more of them. A wife should aid her husband,' Mary averred. 'And James needs aid greatly. You, Vicky, are closer to him than is the Queen, I think.'

'Not I. I will be close to no man who delights in blood and torture and burnings.'

'But if you could help to wean him away from these evil things, Vicky? The Queen will not do it. She cares not, it seems. But he still thinks well of you.'

'Think you that I have not tried? He will not heed me, Mary. He treats me like a child – he who is but five years older than I. I am near eighteen years, see you . . .'

She smiled. 'But nearer seventeen! Do not forget that we are almost of an age, Vicky.'

'What of it? I am a man. Man enough to be Chamberlain of Scotland and Commendator of St. Andrews. To have been President of the Council. Man enough to marry . . . ' His expression changed. 'Mary,' he said urgently, 'enough of all

307

this of James. He will not change for me. And I cannot breathe at Court, these days – or in this Edinburgh itself. Nor can you, it is clear. Let us away, then – together. You and me. Marry me, Mary – and let us leave all this. Forthwith. Marry me.'

Troubled she searched his face. 'Vicky – why do you hurt us both? You know that I cannot marry you. You know that it is impossible. I am not for such as you. A great lady you must marry, with name and lands and fortune.'

'I wish only to marry you. How many times have I told you so? Come away with me, Mary – away from this Court, from cruelty and fear and the smell of death. From plotting and lies and intrigue. Come to my castle of Methven, on the skirts of the Highland hills, where we can be free and live our own lives. Together. I can find a priest to marry us – a minister. Tonight, if need be. Then it will be too late for James to say no. Too late for others to arrange my life for me!' That was eloquence indeed for Ludovick Stuart.

She reached up to touch his arm, her fingers slipping down to catch and hold his own. But she shook her head. 'You are kind, Vicky – most kind. I thank you for it. But it is not to be – however much we could wish it. We are born into very different degrees, different places in the world – and nothing that we may do will alter it. Besides, I cannot leave the Court. Not just now . . . '

'Why not? What keeps you here? You hate it. The Queen will do very well without you, I swear.'

'It is not that . . . '

'It is Patrick again, I suppose? Always it is Patrick Gray! This world turns round that man!' Ludovick ground his heel into the turf.

'Yes, it is he. While I can serve him, I must, Vicky.'

'Serve him! Think you that he needs *your* service? Or any? Think you that Patrick Gray requires any but himself? That he cares for any but himself? The Master of Gray is sufficient unto himself, now and ever. Damn him!'

Mary stared, and her hand slipped out of his. Never had she heard Lennox speak so; about anyone, but especially about Patrick. 'You are wrong, Vicky,' she protested. 'Grievously wrong. He needs friends also – much, he needs them. Against himself, most of all. He needs his wife. I think that he needs

308

even me. And you. Yes, you. Are you not his friend? Always you have been that.'

'Always I have been, yes,' the other repeated bitterly. 'But has he been mine? Is any man's friend, the Master of Gray – save his own? How say you – is he?' Almost the young man was fierce.

Mary looked away and away, and did not answer.

'I will tell you how much he is my friend,' the Duke went on, hotly. 'The King has commanded me to marry the Lady Sophia Ruthven! Aye, marry. And it is on the advice of the Master of Gray.'

The young woman sat up straight, now, stiffly, eyes wide. For a long moment she did not speak. Then her breath came out in a quivering sigh. 'So-o-o!' she said.

'Aye, so. His cousin. His uncle Gowrie's daughter. His mother's brother, Gowrie, the Treasurer, who was executed. Patrick has gained the wardship of her and her sister Beatrix. Did you know that? Profitable wardship. Beatrix is to be lady to the Queen, in place of Jean Stewart, whom Anne will have no more of. Jean is to marry Leslie of Lindores forthwith . . . and I am to marry Sophia Ruthven.'

'I see,' Mary Gray said, quietly.

'Do you see? All of it? *I* see, likewise! The Earl of Gowrie, you'll mind, lost his head and his lands, for treason. Six years ago. There are plenty say that the Master of Gray had a hand in that. His lands were forfeit. But he had lent much money to the Crown. Private money, expended by him as Treasurer – through the Master of Gray. A dangerous practice. They say that the Crown owed him £80,000! Though how much got past Patrick Gray's hands is another matter! It was when Patrick was acting Chancellor. So . . . Gowrie died. And now I am to marry his daughter.'

'Who has been telling you all this?'

'Who but his son, the young Gowrie. He is still not of age, and still has not the use of his father's estates. Or what is left of them. Gowrie was one of the richest lords in the kingdom.'

'I see,' she said again. For that young woman her voice was flat, level, but still calm. 'Sophia Ruthven. Why, if you must marry, my lord Duke, it might as well be the Lady Sophia. She is gentle and, and guileless . . . as well as rich.'

'She is sickly and plain, and scant of wits! But do you not see? I am but to be made use of! Married to me, Patrick and the King think to control her wealth. I, her husband, will be no trouble to them! Until her brother Gowrie is of age, they will have their hands on all the Ruthven wealth. The bills for £80,000 are not like to be claimed! It is but a covetous plot – with me the fool, the clot-pate!'

'You are sure that this is Uncle Patrick's work?'

'Young Gowrie says that it is. He is but fifteen years, but he should know. Patrick has been dealing with him. He is to be sent away to Padua. To the University there. For study. By the King's kindly command. But by Patrick's arranging, who was there but a year or so ago, in his exile. Has it not all every sign of the Master's hand behind it?'

'It may be so,' she admitted. 'But he could be acting your friend still, Vicky. Thinking for you, also. And for her, perhaps. After all, many a great lord would be happy to wed the Lady Sophia. So rich, and of so powerful and ancient a family. Knowing that you, Scotland's only duke, must needs marry some such, it may be that he seeks to serve you well by recommending Sophia Ruthven. She is his cousin. And his ward, you say – though that is new . . . '

'If it was a kindness to me, might he not have consulted me? *Me*. If I am to marry her!'

'He knows . . . ' She hesitated. 'He knows that . . . '

'Aye – he knows that I would only marry *you*. Which does not suit his plans.'

She sighed. 'He knows, as do all others save only you, Vicky, that that is impossible. Surely you must see it?'

'I see, rather, a man selling his friend. As some say he sold my father. Selling me to the King. Or, better, buying himself back into James's favour, through this marriage project. All know that James has been cool towards him since these witch trials began. Somehow his plot to bring down Bothwell has failed. Something has gone amiss. I know not what. And James frowned on him.'

'I think that I know,' Mary said evenly. 'Uncle Patrick has many faults, no doubt – but he has many virtues also. He is a plotter, but there is no savagery in him. He is not cruel. He could not stand by and see women tortured, I think that he

310

never actually believed in the witchcraft himself. He but sought to make use of the King's fear of it, for what he calls statecraft. He sought to bring Bothwell down, yes. But when he saw what hurt and evil was being visited upon these unhappy women, he would have none of it. He is sorry now, I believe, that he ever took a hand in the business . . . '

'It may be so. But that does not explain how Bothwell has escaped. What went amiss with the plot. There is more here than that Patrick mislikes these questionings and burnings. Bothwell must have more potent friends than was believed, arrogant and unfriendly as he is. James, it seems, is afraid to bring him to trial. Why? It is said that my lord of Moray spoke strongly for him. Had some information which saved him. Moray, who was Patrick's friend. And yours.' Ludovick looked at her directly. 'You have become very friendly with Moray, Mary, have you not? I have seen you much in his company, of late. I do not like the way that he looks at you.'

'Moray looks at any woman that way.'

'But you see over much of him.'

'He is much about the Queen. And I am the Queen's servant.'

He sighed. 'Well . . . know you what is at the bottom of it all? Why he turned against Patrick?'

'Perhaps he but seeks to save Uncle Patrick from a, a foolishness? The act of a friend indeed.' She changed the subject. 'When must you marry the Lady Sophia?'

'When? Why, never – if you will but come away with me. Marry me first. Once I am married to you, Mary, I can laugh at James's royal commands. And Patrick must needs think of a new plot to control the Ruthven siller!'

She shook her head. 'Do not cozen yourself, Vicky. It would not serve. The King, and the Kirk, would annul your marriage. Nothing would be easier. We are both under age. Nothing would be resolved.'

'Let them, then. Let them annul our marriage, if they can. But what matters it if we are beyond their reach? We shall go, not to Methven, but to the far Highlands. Clanranald is my friend. We could go to his far country, where James could never reach us. Better even, we could flee to France. I am a noble of France as well as of Scotland – the Seigneur D'Aubigny. I have lands and houses there.'

'You could give up all this for me, Vicky. All your high
position and esteem, here in Scotland? Your dukedom, your
Priory of St. Andrews, your castle of Methven, the office and
revenues of Lord Chamberlain? All – for Mary Gray, the
bastard?'

'Aye, would I! And more. All that I am and have. Did I not
promise you, long ago, that I would give up life itself for you –
swore it on my sword hilt. I meant it then, and I mean it now.
You only, I have wanted, always. None other and naught else.
You, my true love – the truest, fairest, most kind, most gentle
woman in this land. Or any land . . . '

'Hush, Vicky – hush!' The girl's voice actually broke as
she stopped him, and she turned her face away so that he
would not see how it worked and grimaced. 'You are wrong,
so wrong!' she exclaimed. 'I am not what you think, Vicky –
believe me, I am not! I am far from so true, so gentle, so kind.
I am two-faced and a deceiver. A dissembler. I am Patrick
Gray's daughter indeed, and like him in much. I also am a
plotter, an intriguer – so much less honest than you are. In
some ways the life of this Court that you hate suits me very
well. Here I can pit my wits against others, intrigue with the
best. You are deceived in me, Vicky. You must not esteem me
as other than I am.'

He craned his neck, to look at her curiously. 'I am not
deceived,' he declared. 'I have known you too long for that.
You are much that I am not, yes – clever, quick of wits. But
true. Unlike Patrick, true. But . . . why do you tell me all
this?'

'Because I would not have you believe that in not having me
you were in aught the loser.' That was level again, flat.

'Loser? Not having you? Then . . . you will not come away
with me? You will not marry me? Whatever I say? Whatever
I do? Wherever I go?'

'No, Vicky, I fear not.' She swallowed. 'Go you and marry
Sophia Ruthven. You could do a deal worse, I think. Keep the
King's regard and your high place in the realm. You need not
play Uncle Patrick's game thereafter.'

There was a silence.

'And that is your last word?' he said, at length.

'It is, yes. I . . . I am sorry, Vicky.'

'Then I am wasting my time.' He straightened up, then suddenly turned back to her. 'It is not . . . it is not Peter Hay? My page?' he demanded.

'No, Vicky. It is not. Nor any man.'

'Aye. Well . . . so be it. I bid you good-day, Mary.' Stiffly, awkwardly, ridiculously, he bowed to her on her grassy ledge, and swung away abruptly to go striding back down the steep green side of Arthur's Seat, whence he had come.

Mary Gray sat looking after him steadily, dry-eyed, tight-lipped, motionless. Motionless but for her hands, that is; her fingers plucked at and tore to shreds stalk after stalk of the tough coarse grasses that grew there, methodically, one after another, strong and sore on her skin as they were. Long she sat there, long after the tiny foreshortened figure of the Duke of Lennox had disappeared into the busy precincts of Holyroodhouse, before sighing, she rose and went slowly downhill in her turn.

Chapter Seventeen

LUDOVICK OF LENNOX did not flee to France – nor even to the distant Highlands. He remained at Court, although in no very courtly frame of mind, and in a few days the announcement was made from the palace that King James had been graciously pleased to bestow on his well-beloved cousin in marriage the hand of the Lady Sophia Ruthven, sister to the Earl of Gowrie and ward of the Master of Gray. The wedding would be celebrated shortly.

This was not to say that the young man was reconciled to his fate, however. According to Peter Hay, his page, he spent a large part of each night pacing up and down the confines of his bedchamber, unapproachable, disconsolate. Nor by day did his attitude typify the eager bridegroom. He spent an inordinate proportion of his time riding, tiring out horseflesh and himself by furious and otherwise purposeless galloping about the countryside, apparently with no other object than working off pent-up feelings and spleen – a notable change in one so normally level-headed and straightforward. He was barely civil to any with whom he came in contact – although he avoided as many as he could – including his monarch and cousin. The Master of Gray he sought to ignore completely. To the Lady Marie, whom still he appeared to trust, he confided that he was only remaining because he could not drag himself away from the vicinity of Mary Gray.

In Mary's company, however, he was only a little more civil than in others. Without being actually rude, he was aloof, abrupt, jerky, most obviously ill at ease, seeking her presence yet rebuffing her when he had gained it. She, for her part, sought to be no different from before with him, even kinder perhaps – but found this to be impossible. He would have none of it. Frequently she would catch him gazing at her with reproachful eyes, but when she made a move towards him he shied off like an unbroken colt.

That behaviour such as this on the part of so prominent an individual as the Duke of Lennox did not arouse more stir and comment than it did, might be accounted for by the fact that there was so much else to occupy the attention of the Scottish Court that summer of 1590. The witch trials went on, and had reached new heights of sensation with the naming, arrest and putting to the question of two ladies of some quality, Barbara Napier, sister-in-law of the Laird of Carschoggil, and Euphame MacCalzean, daughter of former Lord of Session Cliftonhall. That such as these should be implicated, sent a tremor of new and more personal excitement through all. At this rate, who was safe? Could any, save the most highly placed, be sure that the accusing finger might not next point at themselves? What had been a mere subject for gossip, speculation and some entertainment at Court, became suddenly a matter for serious thought, for discreet precautions, for assessing one's neighbours and acquaintance – even one's friends. Clearly the King's new obsession was becoming more than a joke.

Then there was the intriguing business of the Earl of Moray and the Master of Gray. These two seemed to be beginning to clash at all points – no one quite knew why. They had been esteemed as friends after the London embassage, but that obviousy no longer applied. Some said that the rift dated from Moray's unexpected support of Bothwell – who still lingered in ward, though comfortably enough; but the more popular theory was that it was over rivalry for influence with Queen Anne. The King's preoccupation with witchcraft, the black arts and book-writing, left Anne with much time on her young hands, and she was apparently of a nature to interest herself in sundry affairs of state – which by no means suited Chancellor Maitland. Those who deplored Maitland's power and influence, therefore tended to encourage the Queen in this, and something of a Queen's party gradually developed. In this, two men, Moray and Patrick Gray, were from the first preeminent. To both Anne turned for guidance, support, company. But it was noted by those particularly interested in such things that whereas in matters of statecraft, appointments and suchlike, she was apt to lean more heavily, naturally, on the experienced Master of Gray, in matters personal she seemed to delight rather more evidently in the younger Earl of Moray. After all, at thirty-two Patrick was twice her age, whereas Moray was nine years younger. Which, according to these acute observers, was a situation not to be borne by the handsomest man in all Europe, for whom women in general were to be expected to swoon and prostrate themselves. Another suggestion was that Moray, while dancing attendance on the young Queen, was interesting himself quite notably at the same time in her much more delectable tire-woman, Mary Gray – to the Master's disapproval.

Whatever the truth or otherwise of these intriguing theories, there could be no doubt that these two ornaments of the Court, the quite beautiful Master of Gray and the so bonny Earl of Moray, were no longer on the best of terms. They displayed this in very different ways, needless to say, the Master being exceedingly polite with only occasional viciously barbed remarks open to various interpretations, while Moray could be frankly scurrilous.

Then there was the Queen's supposed pregnancy to add spice to the situation. The Court was fairly evenly divided in opinion as to whether or not she was indeed with child. She showed no physical signs of it – but acted as though she was. King James himself, too, was for ever making knowing refer-

315

ences about an imminent heir, winking towards his wife, and somewhat crudely playing the expectant father. Certain close to the royal couple, however, asserted that it was all pretence – notably Jean Stewart, formerly Lady-in-Waiting, although she might indeed have been prejudiced.

There was much speculation, also, about Bothwell and his probable fate. He had been warded now for months without trial. It seemed to many that the King was in fact afraid to bring him to trial. Yet determined and persistent questioning brought to bear on others, had produced evidence quite sufficient to incriminate him – as indeed was scarcely to be wondered at – including two especially valuable testimonies, from a matronly dame named Agnes Sampson, known as the Wise Wife of Keith, renowned for good works, and from Doctor Fian, the schoolmaster of Tranent. Both these had testified, after due persuasion, that Bothwell had approached each of them with requests for the means whereby he might encompass the death of King James by witchcraft. Mistress Sampson said that she had produced the well-tried method of making a wax image of the monarch, which was passed round the coven, each saying in turn 'This is King James the Sixth, ordained to be consumed at the instance of a noble man, Francis Earl of Bothwell,' and thereafter melted in fire. Doctor Fian had aspired somewhat higher, and roasted alive a black toad in place of the King – much to his sovereign's subsequent indignation.

All this may have seemed a trifle elementary for someone so notably close to Satan himself – and moreover, markedly unsuccessful. But at least it was testimony to high treason, and many had died for a deal less – including, needless to say, the two informants. That, even so, Bothwell remained untried could only mean that he had friends sufficiently powerful to prevent the King from forcing the issue.

Mary Gray came to this conclusion rather sooner than did most, perhaps. Frequently she pondered the matter, and wondered how Patrick saw it all and how he might react. He had not taken her into his confidence, on matters of any import, for many a month.

It was Patrick himself however who brought up the subject with her on a notable occasion – or at least on the day thereof. It was indeed the day of Ludovick's marriage, in the Abbey

316

church of Holyrood, beside the palace. Mary, for perhaps one of the few times in her life, shirked an issue, and pleaded a woman's sickness as excuse for not attending in the Queen's retinue at the wedding, remaining in her own room when all others flocked to the ceremony. Few, probably, wondered at this, for she was generally esteemed to have been Lennox's mistress, and so might tactfully have absented herself; but Patrick Gray at least was surprised, knowing her quality. He was concerned enough to leave the marriage festivities early, and come back to the Master of the Wardrobe's quarters of the palace, where he found Mary on hands and knees on the floor of her own room, playing a game with young Andrew, now a lusty boy of eighteen months.

'Ha! So I need not have concerned myself for your health, my dear!' he commented, smiling down at her. 'You make a pretty picture, the pair of you, I vow – and far from sickly!'

'And you, Uncle Patrick, a most splendid one!' she returned, unabashed. 'I like you in black velvet and silver. And to see you smile again. You have smiled at me but little, of late.'

'M'mmm.' He eyed her thoughtfully, as she rose to her feet. 'You have not done a deal of smiling yourself, Mary, I think.'

She shrugged. 'Perhaps not. They have not been smiling times. But – the wedding? Did all go well? You are back betimes. There were no . . . hitches?'

'None – save that the bridegroom might have been at his own funeral, and the bride a ghost!' he told her. 'The feast now proceeding lacks something of joy and gaiety in consequence. I have seen wakes more rousing!'

'Poor Vicky,' she murmured. 'Poor Lady Sophia, also.'

Patrick stroked his chin. 'Do not waste your compassion on Vicky, my dear,' he advised. 'He is none so unfortunate. Amongst such as might marry the Duke of Lennox, Sophia Ruthven stands high. She has more to commend her than most. And as husbands go, Vicky I have no doubt, will serve her well enough.'

'No doubt,' she agreed, a little wearily. 'So all do assure me.'

He reached out to run a hand lightly over her dark hair.

317

'Mary, lass – you are not hurt, in this? It is not like you to avoid the wedding to feign sickness. I know well that you are fond of Vicky. You have been friends always – since that first day I gave him into your young hands at Castle Huntly. But you have always known, also, that this must happen, that he must marry. That he was . . . '

'That Vicky was not for such as me,' she completed for him, evenly. 'Yes, I have always known it. Do not fear, it is not for myself that I grieve. It is for Vicky. He is unhappy.'

'He will get over it – nothing more sure. He is very young – little more than a boy, indeed. Young even for his years. He has a deal to learn. High rank, high office, demands much . . . '

'All that I know well,' she interposed. 'I but preferred not to watch a marriage in which there was no fondness. You will mind that I did not attend his sister's to my lord of Huntly, either. Tell me – did Master Bruce preach a sermon? Did the King make a speech?'

'Both, woe is me! And belike we shall have to sit through it all tomorrow when Jean weds Leslie of Lindores.' He groaned. 'Ah, me – the folly of it! This flood of words that poor old Scotland drowns in! I heard Johnny Mar bewailing that he was not shut up safely in ward like Bothwell, so as to be spared further attendance at such!' He stopped, as though the name of Bothwell had given him pause, and took a pace or two across the room. 'I wonder, now . . . ?' he said slowly, looking out of the window.

Mary followed him with her eyes. 'You wonder about Bothwell – or my lord of Mar?' she asked.

'About both,' he answered. 'The way that slipped out, from Mar. I would say that he does not therefore esteem Bothwell to be in great danger. A small thing, but . . . '

'And do you so think, Uncle Patrick?'

'Why no. Not now – not any more.' He turned back to her. 'Why? Are you interested in Bothwell, moppet?'

'I have wondered much about him. He has been held so long imprisoned in the Castle, and not brought to trial. Despite the wicked deaths of so many others. Does the King no longer seek his life?'

'The King would have his head tomorrow, if he dared!' Patrick told her.

'That means, then, that my lord has powerful friends. As I thought.'

'The most powerful, it seems!' the man agreed grimly.

'The Chancellor? My lord of Moray? They were not formerly his friends.'

'More powerful than these.'

'More . . . ? But, are there such? The Kirk? Surely not the Kirk? Bothwell has been no friend to the Kirk.'

'More powerful even than the Kirk.'

'Then there is only . . . only . . . ?'

'Aye – only Elizabeth! Only the Queen of England. That good lady chooses to interest herself in Bothwell's fate.'

'But why? Did she not ever speak only ill of him? Call him a brigand? Write that he treated her borders like his own backyard?'

He shrugged. 'All true, my dear. But she is a woman, and may change her mind. She must have some reason – but I have not fathomed it. I have seen a letter from her to the King, urging clemency, saying that he is but a young man misled, that there is no real ill in him. She offers no reason for this change of face – but needs none. James dare not controvert her – if only for his pension's sake! That is why my Lord Chancellor has turned Bothwell's friend. Although I cannot think that it is Moray's reason.'

'So he will not die?'

'Not, at least, on this occasion, I fear!'

'How long then, will he stay in ward?'

'As for that I neither know nor care,' the Master said, with a snap of slim fingers. 'Until he rots, if need be! Not,' he added sardonically, 'that he is in any present danger of rotting, I believe.'

'No,' she agreed. 'I hear that he is very . . . comfortable.' Mary came over to take his arm. 'Uncle Patrick,' she said. 'Do you not think that you might serve yourself better, over my lord of Bothwell?'

'Eh? Better? How do you mean better, girl?'

'Better than now. Better than by leaving him there, to rot. You brought him low, did you not, for your own purposes? Now, raise him up again, also for your own purposes.'

319

He gazed at her, scimitar brows raised. '*I* brought him low . . . ?' he repeated.

'Yes. Over the North Berwick witchcraft plot,' she answered factually, calmly. 'Now you say that the King will not dare to try him. So that you can gain nothing more with him. Can you? In ward. Because of his powerful friends. But if his friends are so strong, why fight them? Become one of them, rather. Aid Bothwell now, Uncle Patrick. Once you told me that it was a fool who fought a losing battle. And also that in statecraft a man could not afford to keep up private enmities.'

Still-faced the man considered her, silent.

'Aid Bothwell now,' she repeated. 'He has paid sufficiently for what he said at Leith, yon time – has he not? And gain much credit with his powerful friends.'

Patrick was actually smiling again. 'It warms my heart to see you so!' he declared. 'To hear you. I' faith, it does.'

'Perhaps . . . but laugh at me at your peril!' she warned. 'For I am very serious. Does what I say not make good sense? By your own measure, Uncle Patrick?'

'I do not know – yet. It will require thought. But, on my soul, if you are for teaching me my business, child, will you not spare me this uncling? Uncle Patrick! Uncle Patrick! Will you uncle me all my days? Can you not call me but Patrick, as others do?'

'Why, yes, Patrick – I shall,' she agreed. 'If you will spare me the child. You scarce consider me a child, yet, do you?'

'By God, I do not! You are right, young woman. It is a bargain! No childing, and no uncling!' He folded his arms. 'Now Mistress Mary Gray – what would you have me do with Bothwell?'

'You could seek to have him released. Do better than these so powerful friends of his.'

'And lose more favour with the King? That I cannot afford, my dear.'

'Then . . . could you not aid his escape from ward? From the Castle. Others have won out of Edinburgh Castle ere this, have they not? With assistance. Secretly. Might it not be arranged?'

He tipped his lips with his tongue. 'You are . . . quite a little devil, are you not, Mary my pet?'

320

'You are not jealous?' she wondered seriously.

He laughed musically. 'Perhaps I should be! Instead, damme, of being . . . well, just a little proud!'

'Of me? Then, you think well of my suggestion?'

'Say that I see possibilities in it – no more,' he told her lightly. 'Possibilities, sweeting.'

'Yes,' she nodded, satisfied. 'That is what I thought. Now – go you back to the wedding-feast, Patrick. Or your absence will be noted . . . and the unkind will say that you are plotting some ill! Which would be very unfair, would it not?'

He took her chin in his hand, and considered her quizzically. 'Witch!' he accused. 'If our King Jamie seeks true witches, he has not far to look for one!'

Her lovely face clouded at his words, and she turned away. 'How can you jest about so terrible an evil?' she demanded.

'Why, girl, sometimes I jest that I may not weep.'

'Yes. I am sorry. Go then, Patrick – and thank you for your coming. It was kindly. Will you tell Vicky that I wish him very well?'

'Aye, if you say so.' He grinned. 'That should much aid his bridal night! A kiss, now, moppet . . .'

The officer unlocked the great door at the foot of the turn-pike stair, and raised his lantern to point down the further steep flight of stairs.

'Yonder is the room, sir,' he said, handing Patrick a key, and also the lantern. 'My lord may be abed by this. His man has left him for the night, and sleeps in the guard-room above, with my fellows. You will find me there when you are finished.'

'My thanks, Captain. I may be some little time.'

Patrick went down the remaining steps to the door at their end. Some perhaps misplaced courtesy made him knock theron before fitting the key to the lock. The door opened to a darkened chamber which the lantern revealed to be vaulted, fair-sized, and though walled and floored in bare stone, to be furnished in reasonable comfort. On a bed in one corner a man lay, in shirt and breeches, blinking and frowning at the light.

'A God's name, Wattie – what ails you?' he snarled. 'What do you want at this hour?'

'Here is no Wattie, my lord,' Patrick answered pleasantly, 'But another, more . . . effective.'

'Eh . . . ?' Bothwell sat up. 'What is this? Who, i' the fiend's name, are you?'

'I wonder that you are still so free with the Fiend's name, at this late date, my lord!' Patrick observed, laughing. 'I would have reckoned that you might have had your bellyful of him!'

'I know that voice,' the other cried. 'It's Gray, is it not? That ill-conceived and treacherous scoundrel, the Master of Gray?'

'Your tongue would seem to lack both accuracy and charity – but there is nothing wrong with your ears! Gray it is.' Patrick held the lamp high. 'I see that they have given you a better chamber than they gave me three years agone!'

Bothwell rose to his full height. If captivity had weakened his frame or blanched his cheek, it did not show in the lantern's light. Tall, muscular, hot-eyed, angry, he stood there, swaying slightly.

'Curse you!' he spluttered. 'You it is that I have to thank that I am here, they tell me!'

'How mistaken you are, my lord. That is wholly the King's doing, in his diligent assault on witchery and warlockry. Poor James – he is much upset . . . '

'Liar!'

Patrick shrugged. 'Have it your own way, my friend. But I would urge that you do not make my mission here tonight of no avail.'

'Aye, what are you here for – reprobate!'

'Your release, my lord – what else?'

That brought the other up short. 'Release . . . ?'

'Release, yes. Or, more exactly perhaps, your escape. At any rate, your abstraction from these present toils.'

Bothwell was staring at him. 'Mockery becomes you no better than does lying!' he said, but with less of conviction.

'I no more mock than lie. But perhaps you do not choose to leave the security of these four stout walls, my lord?'

'Fool!' the other jerked. 'Come – say what you came to say, and be gone!'

Patrick sighed. 'For one so ill-placed as yourself, I confess that I find you much lacking in civility. You are a hard man to be friends with, it seems! I am almost minded to leave you to your fate.'

'Out with it, man – out with it.'

'Very well. I am prepared to aid your escape out of this place. It can be done.'

'A trick, I vow!'

'No trick. What would it serve me to trick you in this?'

'I do not know. But I know that I do not trust you one inch, Gray.'

'Then remain here and die, my lord.'

'I will not die, I think. But why should *you* seek to aid me?'

'Why, that one day you may aid me in return, my friend.'

This frankness may have commended itself somewhat to Bothwell, for he considered his visitor with at least more attention. 'What do you want?' he asked.

'Let us leave that, for the moment. Say that I feel sure that you can be of more benefit to me out of ward than in it, my lord. Now – to get you out of here, I believe, three items only are required. A rasp, a rope, and a bold courage. The first two can be supplied. The third you must contribute for yourself.'

'My courage, sir, has never been called in question. A rope, you say . . . ?' Bothwell's eyes swung towards the two small barred windows.

'Aye.' Dryly the Master glanced in the same direction. 'It is a long drop, my lord. Some forty or fifty feet of walling, and then a couple of hundred feet of good Scottish rock. But a knotted rope of ample length, a clear head and a stout heart – and helping hands to aid you on the rock – and heigho, it will be your own Borderland for you again!'

The Earl said nothing.

Patrick strolled over, and raised his lantern to look more closely at the window bars. 'Aye – nothing here that a stout rasp will not cut through in an hour or so. Nor is the space so small that you could not win through. There should be no difficulty, my lord.'

'Save getting the file and the rope to me, here! The rope

in especial. How are you to get that past the guard, man? Enough rope . . . ?'

'It must needs be a very slender cord, I fear – but sufficiently strong, for it would be a pity if it broke, would it not?' The visitor's eyes gleamed in the lamplight. 'I fear that you must just trust the jumped-up wardrobe-master for that, my lord! Slender enough to be wound around a man's person many times, under his clothing as an officer of the King's Guard. He will bear also a rasp, of course – and a letter for you with the King's seal. Also an order to see you, bearing the signature of my lord of Moray, Captain of the Royal Guard!'

'But . . . a pox! Moray would never do that! Put his own head in a noose! For me?'

'I did not say that he would – did I?' The Master smiled. 'Just have a little faith in your treacherous scoundrel, my Lord Bothwell. I have achieved much more difficult tasks than this. Give me a few days – a week – for I would not wish this my visit to you to be linked with the business. That would serve neither you nor me, you will agree?'

Bothwell remained silent, suspicious.

'That is all, then, I think. Wait you for a week. Do not disclose to any, even to your man, that you think to be leaving these quarters. The letter will tell you when to assay the escape. Also where men will be waiting for you, with horses, below the rock. All will be dealt with, never fear.' Patrick laughed. 'And the rope will be long enough and strong enough, I promise you!'

'And the price, Master of Gray? Your price for this service?' Bothwell got out at last.

'That can wait. Let us not haggle and chaffer like hucksters. We neither of us are merchants, my lord – both men of the world. Say that I may seek *your* aid at some later date – and hope not to be rejected!'

Still the other did not commit himself. 'We shall see,' he said, cryptically.

'Undoubtedly. I give you goodnight, my doubting friend. When next we meet you will be a free man.' He sighed. 'Or a dead one!'

The King was all but in tears. 'It must ha' been Moray, I

tell you!' he cried, thumping his hand on the table. 'Here is the warrant, signed in his ain hand, to admit the bearer to visit the Earl o' Bothwell on the King's business. On *my* business, waesucks! It's treason, I tell you – blackest treason!'

The hastily-assembled members of the Council, such as could be gathered together at short notice thus early in the day, eyed their dishevelled monarch and each other with various expressions of unease, resentment and blank sleepiness. Most had barely got over the last night's potations, and were in no fit state to deal with high treason before breakfast. James himself was only part-dressed; after long studies later into the night than usual owing to the Queen's absence, on witchcraft and the writing of his book, he was blear-eyed and unbeautiful. Never apt for early rising save when hunting, today he had been awakened with the dire news of Bothwell's escape from Edinburgh Castle, and nothing would serve but an immediate meeting of his Council, assured that his royal person was in imminent danger.

'I cannot believe that my lord of Moray would be a party to this escape, Sire,' Sir James Melville declared. 'He is not a man for such ploys. He does not concern himself with affairs of the state. His interests are, h'm, otherwhere! He is no dabbler in plots and treasons. He spoke for my lord of Bothwell yon time, yes – but he was never Bothwell's friend.'

'Aye,' his brother Sir Robert agreed, and yawned.

'They are full cousins,' Chancellor Maitland observed briefly.

'Aye, but so are they both cousins o' my ain!' James took him up. 'God's curse – I've ower many cousins!' He flapped the paper with Moray's signature. 'This bears his name. None could ha' gained Bothwell's escape but through this officer o' my Guard he sent yesterday – the traitorous carle!'

'Who was the officer, Sire?' his uncle Orkney asked shortly. 'Have him in. We'll soon ha' the truth out o' him.'

'But nobody kens who it was, man!' James wailed. 'It wasna one of my usual officers. But dressed in my royal colours, mind. An imposter, just, I swear. Wi' this letter frae Moray. And Moray is Captain o' my Royal Guard!'

'An appointment, Sire, of which I never approved,' the Chancellor reminded, sourly. 'I ever say that such beautiful men are seldom honest!' And he shot a baleful glance at the Master of Gray sitting far down the table.

'At least he was a more honest beauty than the last Captain of the Guard – my lord of Huntly!' the Earl of Mar snorted.

James flushed. 'Is there no man I can trust?' he asked, broken-voiced.

Patrick spoke. 'Your Grace – might I see the pass-letter?' When the paper was passed down to him, he scrutinised it closely. 'It is certainly like my lord of Moray's hand o' write. Such is familiar to me – after our embassage to London. But . . . it could be a forgery, Sire.'

'Eh . . . ? How should it be a forgery, man?'

'There are not a few expert forgers in this town, I think – even in this Court! At my own trial, of unhappy memory, forgeries were produced to damn me – most admirable likenesses of my own writings. Were they not, my Lord Chancellor?'

'Sire – this is intolerable! The Master of Gray was condemned by his own writings, and the sure testimonies of others. Including Queen Elizabeth. Not by forgeries. Just as, I swear, this is no forgery. Why should it be a forgery?'

'Have him in, then. Ask him.' Orkney said impatiently. 'Where is Moray?'

'He's no' here,' James declared. 'He's awa' to Fife.'

'He is escorting the Queen to Dunfermline, my lord,' Patrick informed his father-in-law easily. 'To inspect the progress of her new house at the Abbey there. The house I myself started to build, one time!' He smiled. 'They left yesterday. Her Grace was very concerned to see the house. And my lord of Moray is entirely attentive to Her Grace's wishes, is he not? His Highness being . . . otherwise occupied.'

The King peered at the Master in new alarm. 'You're . . . you're no' saying . . . ? You dinna mean, Patrick, that she . . . that my Annie . . . ? That Moray . . . ?'

'No, so, Sire – of course not! Never think such a thing. The Queen is entirely safe with my lord of Moray, I vow. His love for her is most fervent, as we all know.'

James swallowed, and achieved only a croak.

Orkney hooted rudely.

'Moreover, have they not his Countess with them, Sire. Have no fears.'

'Yon addlepate . . . !' the King muttered.

'Sire – is not this profitless talk?' Mar interjected. 'Moray can wait. He will deny this signature, anyway. Is it not more needful to be considering Bothwell? What *he* will do. He will be an angry man – and he is crazed enough when he is not! I wager he will now be a man beside himself. And only Huntly can field more men-at-arms.'

'Aye – I ken, I ken!' James quavered. 'Is that no' why I called this Council? He'll be rampaging the Borders, now. Raising the Marches against me!'

'Or nearer – at Hailes Castle, raising Lothian and the Merse.'

'Or nearer still, at Crichton, ready to descend on this Edinburgh!'

'My lords – Your Grace!' Patrick protested. 'Bothwell only made his escape last night. He can raise many men, yes – but they are scattered. It will take him time. He is hot-headed – but despite some of the testimony we have listened to, he is but human! He cannot descend upon His Grace, whether from the Borders or Hailes or Crichton, today or tomorrow – if such is his intention. Men take time to assemble – as most of us know from experience. *We* have time, therefore – a week, at least.'

'Aye, maybe,' James conceded. 'But time for what, man Patrick? I canna trust my Royal Guard, after this. Can I assemble men as quick as can Bothwell? And whose men . . . ?'

'Have I not ever urged, Sire, that you should seek to enroll many more men? Not merely to increase the Royal Guard, but to have a force always ready. Your own men, for the sure defence of your realm. Other monarchs have such, and do not depend only on the levies of their lords . . . '

'But the siller, man – the siller! Where's it to come frae? To pay them. Elizabeth's that mean . . . '

'There is siller, Sire in your own Scotland – not a little. And there are means of winning it. But now is not the time for that . . . '

'I rejoice to hear the Master of Gray admit that, at least!' Maitland remarked.

Patrick ignored him. 'Increase your Guard, yes. Appoint a new Captain. Have the Provost call out the City Bands.'

'I misdoubt if I can trust them!'

'They hate Bothwell, Sire. He has ridden roughshod down their High Street too often . . .'

The Lord Chancellor intervened again. 'Highness – all this will be done, without the Master of Gray's advising. You may entrust your safety to my hands.'

'Ooh, aye,' James acknowledged doubtfully.

'Heigho – then all is settled securely!' Patrick laughed, pushing back his chair. 'All will now be well. We have the Lord Chancellor's word for it! Surely we need no longer delay our breakfasts, gentlemen?'

Uncertainly they all looked at each other.

'Na, na,' the King objected. 'What's been decided? I dinna ken what's been decided?'

Orkney guffawed. 'Why – that we adjourn. Maitland, here – a pox! I forgot. My Lord Maitland o' Thirlestane. My lord will attend to all. He kens our mind. To breakfast, then – before our bellies deafen us!'

The Privy Council broke up forthwith, however uncertain the monarch or frosty the Chancellor. As the members streamed out, Patrick stooped to the crouching King's ear.

'Sire,' he said quietly, 'the stags are fat and free of velvet in Falkland woods. You have been neglecting them! Overmuch study, overmuch witchcraft, overmuch work, is serving you but ill. Move the Court to Falkland, Your Grace, and chase the deer again, instead of warlocks. You are further from Bothwell there. The Queen then can watch her house abuilding at Dunfermline, without bedding away from your side. And my lord of Moray, at Donibristle, is under your eye. To Falkland, Sire! Leave this Edinburgh to my Lord Chancellor.'

James Stewart looked up, and almost eagerly he nodded his heavy head.

Chapter Eighteen

MARY GRAY pulled up her sweating, foaming mount, and peered from under hand-shaded eyes into the already declining October sun. This *ought* to be the valley, surely? She had forded the River Earn fully five miles back, at Aberdalgie, and the land was obviously falling away, in front, to the next strath, that of the Almond she had been told, with the Highland hills rising beyond. Methven was this south side of the Almond, all agreed. Where then was the castle? This green land of wide grassy slopes and identical rounded knolls was confusing.

Stroking the mare's soaking quivering neck, she urged the tired beast on. She herself was tired, but this was no time to acknowledge it. For almost five hours she had been in the saddle – for foolishly, she had got lost amongst the Glenfarg foothills.

Rounding one more of the grassy knolls a mile or so further, she heaved a sigh of relief. Ahead, the hillocks seemed to draw back to leave a broad open basin of fair meadowland, cattle-dotted, and gently rising pasture, wide to the south but hemmed in and guarded on the north by the frowning ramparts of the blue heather hills. And on a tree-scattered terrace between meadows and upland, bathed in the golden rays of the slanting autumn sunlight, stood a large and gracious house, its red stonework glowing like old rose.

At first sight of it, Mary found a lump risen in her throat. Often she had visualised Methven Castle, Vicky's home, the place that he had besought her so often to come and rule as mistress. In her mind's eye she had seen it as little different from all those other castles which she knew so well, Castle Huntly where she had been born, Broughty, Foulis, Craig-millar, tall frowning battlemented towers of rude stone, small-windowed, picked out with gunloops and arrow-slits, stern, proud, aggressive. But this was quite other, a smiling place of pleasing symmetry, of slender turrets and many large windows reflecting the sun. A sort of royal dower-house for generations, and never a grasping lord's stronghold, James had given Methven to Ludovick in a fit of eager generosity on his first coming to Scotland from France, as an eight-year-old boy. Like a magnet it beckoned to the lone rider now.

Nevertheless, as Mary rode into the fine paved courtyard on the north side of the castle, enclosed by wings of domestic buildings, she gained no sense of welcome, no feeling of reception of any sort. The house itself was nowise unfriendly, quietly detached, serene, rather; but of human reaction there was none. No grooms came churrying to her horse's head, no men-at-arms lounged about the yard, no faces looked out from the ranks of the windows. The great front door stood wide open, certainly, and white pigeons strutted and fluttered and cooed about the courtyard, but otherwise the place might have been deserted. Autumn leaves had drifted in heaps in many corners, and no single plume of smoke rose above any of the numerous chimneys.

Mary's heart sank, as she dismounted stiffly

Leaving her mare to stand in steaming weariness, she moved over to the open doorway. After a moment or two of hesitation, she raised her voice in a long clear halloo. Other than the echoes, and the sudden alarm of the pigeons, there was no response.

She stepped in over the threshold, into a wide vestibule. It was lighter, brighter, in here than in any of the houses that she knew, with their thick walls and small windows. At either end of it a broad turnpike stairway arose – two stairs, an unimagined luxury. Yet even in here dead leaves had blown. The great house was entirely silent; only the soft murmuration of the pigeons broke the quiet.

Somehow Mary could not bring herself to shout out again, inside that hushed place. Biting her lip, she was moving over to one of the stairways when she perceived a cloak thrown carelessly over a chair in a corner, most of it trailing on the floor. Her heart lifted at the sight. She recognised it as one of Vicky's cloaks, and certainly it was thrown down in his typical fashion. The familiarity of it, so simple a thing as it was, warmed her strangely. Kilting up her riding-habit, she ran light-footed up the winding stair.

From the wide first floor landing long corridors stretched

right and left, lit in patches by the yellow beams of westering sunlight slanting in from sundry open doors. The first such that she peered in at showed a fine panelled room, with a splendid painted coved ceiling in timber, depicting heraldry and strange beasts. The grey ashes of a dead fire littered the handsome carved stone fireplace, and the rugs of skin on the floor were scattered haphazard. At one end of a great table were the remains of an unambitious meal.

The next room was even larger, but was only partly furnished and gave no impression of habitation. The next door again was locked.

Frowning, Mary was for moving over to the other corridor, when she stopped. Faintly she heard a dog barking – or rather, the high baying of a hound.

Hurrying through the first room to its south-facing window, she peered out. Away to the south-west, across the water-meadows, a single horseman rode, flanked by two loping long-legged wolf-hounds. He rode at the gallop, high in his stirrups, hatless, towards the house, scattering the grazing cattle left and right. Mary knew that stance, that figure. Thoughtfully she considered it, before she went tripping downstairs.

Ludovick of Lennox came clattering into the courtyard, still at a canter. His glance lighted on the drooping mare, still standing there, and swung at once to the front doorway. At sight of the young woman waiting therein, his eyes widened, and he reined up his mount so abruptly that its shod hooves scraped long scratches on the paving-stones, showering sparks. Before the beast, haunches down, could come to a halt, he had thrown himself from the saddle and came running.

'Mary! Mary!' he cried, amidst the agitated flapping of pigeons and the excited yelping of his hounds.

The girl herself started forward, hands outstretched – and then halted. But no such discretion could halt the young man. Upon her he rushed, arms wide, to enfold her, to hug her to him, to lift her completely off her feet. His lips found hers, and clung thereto, as together they staggered back against the door jamb.

Mary did not struggle or protest in his arms. But when, panting for breath, he lifted his head for a moment to gaze into her dark eyes, before seeking her mouth again, she raised a

331

hand between their lips, so that it was her fingers that he must needs kiss. She did not trust herself to words.

'Mary, my dear! My dear!' he exclaimed. 'How come you here? From where? Are you alone? How good it is to see you. Oh, my dear – how good!'

'And you, Vicky – and you!' she whispered.

'It has been so long. An eternity!'

'Silly – a bare month. No more.'

'An eternity,' he insisted. 'Each hour a day, a month . . . '

Gently she disengaged herself from his closest grip. 'Here . . . here is no talk for a wedded husband, Vicky!'

He snorted a mirthless laugh. 'Whatever else I am, that I am not!' he declared.

'Hush, Vicky . . . !'

'It is the truth. But . . . how are you here, Mary? And alone? But one horse . . . ?' He still held her arms.

'Yes. Alone. I have ridden from Falkland. To see you.'

'Falkland! That is thirty miles. Forty . . . '

'More – as I rode it! Foolishly, I lost myself. In the hills beyond Glenfarg.'

'You should not have done it, Mary! A woman, alone . . . '

'Tush – I am not one of your fine Court ladies. I can look after myself. I had to come, Vicky. Matters go but ill.'

'When did they do other?' he asked, a bitter note in his voice, new to that uncomplicated young man. 'And why from Falkland?'

'The Court has moved there. Did you not know? After Bothwell's escape.'

'I heard that Bothwell had escaped from ward, yes. All the land knows that. But . . . come inside, Mary. You must be weary, hungry. What do I dream of, keeping you standing here! I will tie the horses for the nonce – and bait them later.'

'*You* will bait them . . . ?'

'Why, yes. I am alone here.'

She stared at him. 'Alone . . . ?' she echoed.

'I prefer it that way. I sent the servants back to the village. It is but a mile off. And Peter Hay has ridden to Edinburgh for me, two days agone. He carried a letter. For you . . . '

'But . . . ' She searched his face. 'The Duchess?'

332

'Sophia? She is not here.'

'But, Vicky – why? Where is she?'

'I sent her home. To Ruthven Castle. It is not far. Near to St. John's Town of Perth. It is better that way.'

Mary bit her lip. 'Oh, Vicky – I did not believe that you could be so cruel.'

'Is it cruelty, Mary? I think not. Sophia Ruthven has no more joy in this marriage than have I. And she is sick, very sick. She coughs. She is never done coughing. She coughs blood. She is better with her mother at Ruthven.'

The young woman was silent for a little. 'I did not know,' she whispered, at length. 'Did not know of her sickness. Poor lassie.'

'Nor did I. But Patrick knew. And the King knew, I swear. And yet . . . !' Scowling, he left the rest unsaid.

Unhappily Mary eyed him. 'I am sorry,' she said. 'So very sorry. But . . . does she not merit the more kindness? Need you have sent her away . . . so soon?'

'I deemed it kinder that she should go. She wished to go. She wanted nothing that I could give her. We did not once sleep together.'

'How much did you . . . offer her, Vicky?'

'God – would you have had me force her? You?'

She shook her head. 'Never that. Only a little of kindness, of patience, Vicky. You are man and wife. You took vows, in the sight of God . . . '

'Is that how you name what was done to us in yon Abbey of Holyrood?'

She drew a long breath. 'No. Perhaps not. Vicky – do not let us talk to each other thus. It is . . . not for us. Forgive me.'

'And me. This is folly. You are tired, Mary – and I keep you standing here. Come you inside.'

'We shall see to the horses together, first. I am none so tired. Not now.'

'What brought you here then, Mary?' he asked as they entered the great stables, empty save for two other horses. 'You said that matters went ill?'

'Yes. I need your help, Vicky. That is why I came. I am not so clever as I thought myself, I fear. I . . . I am frightened.'

So little in character was this for Mary Gray that Lennox

paused in his unsaddling, to stare at her. 'You?' he said. '*You* are frightened?'

'Yes. For what I have done. For what may happen because of what I have done. Because of my presumption. This time. I fear that I have been too clever, and a great evil may follow.'

'Patrick again?' he asked.

She nodded. 'I led him to effect Bothwell's escape. Yes, it was my doing. Thinking at least to aid one man, to undo one wrong. Perhaps even to help bring these evil witch-trials to an end. Hoping that with Bothwell free, the King might relent, might even be afraid to go on, to fear what Bothwell might do if he continued.' She looked away. 'Patrick said, did I think to teach him his business? God forgive me, I think that perhaps I did! If it is so, then I have my reward. For Patrick but used my conceit to bring down another. My lord of Moray.'

'Moray? And Bothwell? How comes Moray into this?'

'He is Captain of the King's Guard. Or was. Bothwell was the King's prisoner. He could be held responsible. But, worse – the escape was gained through a man dressed as an officer of the Royal Guard, and bearing an order supposedly signed by Moray, as Captain, to gain him admittance to Bothwell on the King's business. A forgery, of course. But ample for the occasion. Ample to poison the King's mind. Moray's denials count for little.'

'Who was this man? This officer of the Guard?'

'Nobody knows . . . or will tell. But he was dressed in the royal colours and livery. And only one close to the Guard could have gained him that. Or close to the Wordrobe!'

'I see. So Patrick cries down Moray, now? Why?'

'Not so. He is loud in Moray's defence. Too loud. Making excuse for him in this. But also in the matter of the Queen. It is for this last that I am frightened, Vicky. This of the Queen.'

'You fear for the Queen, Mary? Surely not that? Not even Patrick could . . . '

'The Queen, yes. Although not so much as for Moray. I fear for them both. Together. Patrick is very attentive to the Queen. But she has Dunfermline, that hateful place that he had set his heart on. He will never have it now – and I think

334

that he will never forgive her. And, sorrow – that was my doing also. It was I who urged the King to dower her with Dunfermline Abbey. To prevent Patrick from ruining himself to get it. I was clever again, you see – so very clever. So I bear responsibility for both, for Moray and the Queen, Vicky . . . '

'I think that you blame yourself overmuch, Mary.' He frowned. 'But . . . I do not understand. How comes the Queen into this matter? Of Moray and Bothwell? What do you fear for her, in it?'

'It is not that. It is that the Queen is seeing overmuch of Moray. From the first she has liked him well, as you know. But it becomes too much. In especial since coming to Falkland. And Patrick is effecting it so, I am sure. Falkland is not far from both Dunfermline and Donibristle, Moray's house in Fife. The Queen is ever going to Dunfermline, to see to her house building there, while the King is hunting or at his books and papers. Moray is in disgrace, and banned the Court meantime – but he is much at Dunfermline, and the Queen at Donibristle.'

'You think that they are lovers?'

'No. Not that. Not yet. But Moray is . . . Moray. And very handsome. And the Queen is lonely, and very young. And Patrick, I think, would have the King come to believe it. To Moray's ruin.' She sighed. 'I have spoken to him, of course. He but laughs at me, denying it. But as one of the Queen's women I see much. I see how he ever entices the Queen to Dunfermline, with new notions for her house, new plans for the pleasance she is making, for the water-garden, for new plenishings that workmen he has found for her are making. When she would have the King go with her, I have seen how Patrick works on him to do otherwise – a deputation to receive, a visit to Cupar or St. Andrews or Newburgh, new papers to study, or some notable stag spied on Lomond Hill. He is always with the King, closer than he has ever been. With Moray and Bothwell and Huntly banished the Court, the Chancellor still in Edinburgh, and many of the lords at their justice-eyres – aye, and you away here, Vicky – thus there are few close to the King to cross Patrick's influence. Only Mar, who is stupid. And Atholl, who is drunken.' She paused,

335

almost for breath. 'I fear greatly for Moray and the Queen,' she ended flatly. 'And I must blame myself.'

'You blame yourself for too much, Mary. This is Patrick's doing, not yours.'

'But I – I thought to outplay Patrick at his own game. That there is no denying.'

He carried an armful of sweet-smelling hay to the manger. 'Patrick is nearer to the Devil than ever was Bothwell!' he said.

Her lovely face crumpled as with a spasm of pain. 'Do not say that, Vicky!' she pleaded. 'Never say it.'

'It is the truth,' he declared bluntly. 'The man is evil.'

'No! Not evil. Not truly evil. My father – Davy Gray – said that he had a devil. I did not believe him. Yet he loved him – loves him still. Perhaps he is right – perhaps he has a devil. Perhaps he is two men – one ill and one good. There is much good in him, Vicky – as you know, who are his friend.'

'*Was* his friend,' Lennox corrected briefly.

'Was and are, Vicky. You must be. True friendship remains true. Even in such case.'

'May a man remain friends with evil, and still not sin?'

'I think he may, yes. Is it sin for me to love Patrick still, as I do. Not the evil in him, but Patrick himself.'

'He is your father . . .'

'I do not love him because he sired me. Davy I love as my father. I love Patrick . . . because he is Patrick.'

'Aye.' Ludovick sighed. 'So do we all, God help us! Come – into the house with us.'

'Then – you will come back with me, Vicky? To Falkland? To help me? To try to save Moray. And the Queen. And Patrick from himself. I know that you hate the Court, Vicky – but come.'

'Lord!' Almost he smiled. 'All that! So many to save! I will come, Mary – but cannot think to achieve so much. I am no worker of miracles, as you know well. Or you would be my wife here in Methven. But come I will – since you ask it. As you knew I would – or you would not have come, I think.'

'As I knew you would,' she agreed, gravely. 'Thank you, Vicky.'

Later, with a well-doing fire of birch-logs blazing and spurting on the heaped ash of the open hearth, filling the handsome room with the aromatic fragrance and flickering on the shadowy panelled walls, Mary sat, legs tucked beneath her skirt, on a deerskin rug on the floor, and gazed deep into the red heart of the fire, silent. It was indeed very silent in that chamber, in all the great house, in the night that pressed in on them from the vast and empty foothill country. The only sounds were the noises of the fire, the faint sigh of evening wind in the chimney, the occasional call of a night-bird, and the soft regular tread and creak of floorboards as Ludovick paced slowly to and fro behind her. They had not spoken for perhaps ten minutes, since she had cleared away the meal that she had made for them, and he had lit the fire against the night's chill.

The young man's voice, when it came, was quiet also, less jerky and self-conscious than was his usual. 'This . . . this is what I have always dreamed of, Mary. You, sitting before my fire, in my house. Alone. And the night falling.'

She neither stirred nor made answer to that. His steady but unhurried pacing continued at her back, without pause.

'You are so very small,' he mentioned again, presently, out of the shadows. 'So slight a creature to be so important. So small, there before the fire – so slightly made, yet so perfect, so beautiful. And so strong. So strong.' That last was on a sigh.

'I am not strong, Vicky,' she answered him, after a long moment, calmly, as out of due consideration. 'No, I am not strong.'

'Yes, you are,' he insisted. 'You are the strongest person that I know. Stronger than all the blustering lords or the frowning churchmen. Stronger than all who think that they are strong – the doctors and professors and judges. Aye, stronger even than Patrick Gray, I swear.' He had halted directly behind her.

She shook her head, the firelight glinting on her hair, but said nothing. Nor did she look round or up.

'Why should the woman that I want, and need, be so strong?' he demanded, his voice rising a little. 'When *I* am not strong? Why should it have been you . . . and me? In all this realm?'

'I do not know, Vicky,' she told him. 'But this I do know

'... that I do not feel strong this night.'

'You mean . . . ?' Looking down on her, he opened his mouth to say more, and then forbore, frowning. When she did not amplify that statement, made so factually, he resumed his pacing.

An owl had the silence to itself for a space.

'All men want you,' he said, at length. 'I watch them. See how they look at you. Even some of the ministers of the Kirk. Even James, who is fonder of men than of women. All would have you, if they could. Yet you look to care for none of them. You smile kindly on all. On many that deserve no smile – ill, lecherous men. But yourself, you need none of them?' That last was a question.

'You think that?'

'I know not what to think. I wonder – always I wonder. You keep your inmost heart . . . so close.'

'You make me sound hard, unfeeling, Vicky. Am I that?'

'No. Not that. But sufficient unto yourself, perhaps. Not drawn to men. Yet drawing men to yourself.'

'I mislike the picture that you paint of me. Is it true, then?'

'It cannot be – for I would paint you as the loveliest picture in all this world, if I could, Mary – if I but knew how.'

'Dear Vicky.'

'Mary.' Abruptly he was standing directly above her again, his knees all but touching her back. 'Have you – have you ever given yourself to a man? So many must have tried to have you. Have you let any take you?' That was breathlessly asked.

'Why no, Vicky. I have not.'

He swallowed, and was silent.

She turned now, to look up at him. 'Why do you ask? Do you fear that I am cold? Unnatural? That I find no pleasure in men, perhaps? And think that this may prove it?'

'No, no – never that, Mary. I am glad. Glad. I hoped . . . ' He paused. 'You see, neither have I ever had a woman.'

Slowly she smiled. 'No?'

'No.' Something, perhaps her faint smile, made him add, hurriedly, almost roughly, 'I could have had, Mary. Many a time. Many would have . . . that Jean Stewart . . . '

She nodded. 'I know it, Vicky. The Duke of Lennox need never lie lonely of a night.'

'But I do, Mary – I do!' he cried. 'There's the nub of it! And it is your doing.'

'I am sorry,' she said flatly.

The silence resumed, and Ludovick's pacing with it.

Presently, and very quietly, the girl began to sing, as though to herself, an age-old crooning song with a haunting lilt to it, as old as Scotland itself. Softly, unhurriedly, deliberately, almost as if she picked out the notes on a lute, she sang, eyes on the fire, swaying her body just a little to the repeated rhythmic melody. The song had no beginning and no end.

Gradually the young man's pacing eased and slowed, until he was halted, listening, watching her. Then, after a minute or two, he came to sink down on his knees on the deerskin beside her. His hands went out to her.

'Mary!' he said. 'Mary!'

Turning her head, she nodded slowly, and smiled at him, through her singing. She raised a finger gently to bar his lips. Her strange song continued, uninterrupted. The two wolf-hounds, that had sat far back in the shadows, crept forward on their bellies into the circle of the firelight, until they lay, long heads flat on outstretched forepaws, on either side of the man and woman.

A quiet tide of calm flowed into and over that chamber of the empty house, and filled it.

Her singing, in time, did not so much stop as sink, diminish to a husky whisper, and eventually fade away. Neither of them spoke. Ludovick's arms were around her now, his face buried in her hair. Presently his lips found her neck below her hair. In time a hand slipped up to cup one of her breasts.

She did not stir, nor rebuke him.

More than once words seemed to rise to his exploring lips, but something in the girl's stillness, the positive calm of her, restrained him. He held her close, while time stood still.

It was the sinking of the fire, the need to replenish it with logs, that changed the tempo. Lennox, after throwing on more wood, became imbued with a new urgency. His lips grew more daring, his hands roved wider. At last Mary stirred, sighing.

'Vicky,' she said, 'this way lies sorrow, hurt. For us both. You must know it.'

'Why, Mary? Why should it? We shall not hurt each other,

you and I. And we are not children.'

'Not children, no. But you have a wife, Vicky. I cannot forget it.'

He frowned. 'In name only. I have told you. And many men have wives . . . and others.'

'Yes, my lord Duke,' she said. 'And others!'

'Lord – I am sorry, Mary! I did not mean it that way.'

'No. But that way the world would see it, Vicky. Not that I greatly care what the world thinks of me. But I care what I think of myself. And of you. Moreover, I will not further hurt your Lady Sophia. In this house, where she should be.'

He shook his head, wordless.

'We must not think only for the moment,' she added.

'Moment!' he jerked. 'This marriage of mine is not for any moment. It may be for years – a lifetime! I cannot wait for that. I have warmer blood than that!'

'And you think that I have not?'

'I do not know. I only know that you are strong. So much stronger than I am.'

'Do not talk so much of strength,' she said, low-voiced. 'If I was so strong, I would not be here in this great empty castle with you now. I would have gone back, forthwith, late as it was. When I found you alone. Not to Falkland but at least to St. John's Town. Or even to the inn in your village here. If I had been so strong.'

Uncertainly he eyed her, surprised at her sudden vehemence.

'I have told you before, Vicky – I would not have you think me other than I am.'

'Will I ever know you?' he demanded. 'Know you as you are?'

It was her turn not to answer.

'Are you unhappy, Mary? Here. Alone in this house, with me?'

'No.'

'You are not frightened? Not of me, Mary? Never of me!'

'No, Vicky. I do not think that I could ever be frightened of you. Only of myself, perhaps.' She paused. 'So . . . so you will help me, will you?'

He stared at her, swallowed, and could find no words. But after a few moments his arms came out again to encircle her –

but protectively this time, and so remained, firm, strong.

Her little sigh might have been relief, relaxation, or even just possibly, regret.

Presently she settled herself more comfortably on the deerskin, leaned her head against his shoulder, and closed her eyes.

She did not sleep. But after a while Ludovick did, his weight against her becoming heavier. Long she crouched thus, supporting him, growing cramped, sore, although with no discontent thereat showing in her features. Indeed frequently a tiny smile came and went at the corners of her mouth. Sleep overcame her, at length.

Sometime during the night she awakened, stiff, chilled. Ludovick lay relaxed, arm outflung, but shivering slightly every so often in his sleep. The fire had sunk to a dull glow, and the hounds had crept close about them for warmth. Smiling again a little at the thought of forty empty beds in that great house, Mary carefully reached over to draw up another of the deerskin rugs that littered the floor. Settling herself as best she could, she pulled it over them, man, hounds and all.

Chapter Nineteen

AT first light they rode away from Methven Castle. They went first to the village nearby, where Ludovick knocked up his steward and left sundry instructions, and then turned eastwards for the Earn and Fife, going by unfrequented ways and avoiding Perth. They parted company some miles outside Falkland, so that Mary could enter the town alone and without arousing special comment. The Lady Marie knew of her errand anyway, and she had chosen an occasion when Patrick had gone on one of his many brief visits to Broughty Castle, to examine progress of his works of improvement.

Lennox's return to Court that evening, even without his new wife, evoked no great stir. James was glad to see him, in an absent-minded way. Patrick also professed himself to be overjoyed, when he got back from Broughty next day. Otherwise there was little interest, for the Duke had as few friends as he had enemies.

Thereafter began a strange and unacknowledged tug-of-war over the activities and influences and persons of James Stewart, Earl of Moray, and Anne of Denmark, Queen-Consort. Undoubtedly none of the principals knew anything of it. Nor did the King, though the effects were not lost on him, perceive the tugging, the stresses and strains of the warfare, the gains and losses sustained. Even Patrick Gray himself probably did not fully recognise the positive and consistent nature of the opposition to his plans. He could be amusedly sure that his daughter, wife and Lennox would disapprove of any obvious moves against Moray; but then, the Master's moves were seldom obvious. That Mary Gray was, in fact, little more obvious than himself, had not yet fully dawned upon him.

Moray was still banished the Court, but was living less than a score of miles off at his own house of Donibristle. Dunfermline was only five miles away, and Anne was as often there as at Falkland. Mary, as was to be expected, was usually with her – and so now was Ludovick Lennox who had never previously shown any notable interest in the young Queen. He was seldom far from her side, indeed – which did not escape the notice of the Court, and did not endear him to Moray any more than to Patrick, whatever Anne thought of it. James would remark, waggishly, that his good Coz Vicky seemed a deal fonder of the Queen than of his own Duchess – but few doubted that the stiff and unforthcoming Lennox was in fact more interested in the Queen's tire-woman than in Anne herself, Mary being sufficiently kind to him in public to give some substance to this assumption.

The Queen, therefore, although she saw much of Moray, seldom saw him alone. Lennox was as good as a watch-dog – and notably well-informed as to Anne's every move. Probably she believed that James had arranged it, and even Patrick may have assumed the same. As a situation, it verged on the comic.

Patrick sought continually to arrange matters so that the Queen should be thrown in Moray's way, and that the King might find them together in some incriminating circumstance.

Mary, Marie and Lennox, from their positions of strategic vantage close to the King, Queen and Patrick himself, sought to make sure that this did not happen. It could not have been achieved without Lennox, and him devoting almost his full time to the business. Patrick, in due course, came to realise this, even though attributing much of it to the King's instigation – and the rift between these two former close friends widened. And, in time, however successful the countermeasures, that rift began to worry Mary Gray almost as much as the fate of Moray. Thwarting the Master of Gray, however secretly, was a chancy activity, and like trying to damp down a volcano; there was no saying where one might cause another irruption to break out, in consequence, with who knew what hurt to others.

When, one day, Lennox came to her in the Commendator's House of Dunfermline Abbey, Mary saw the writing on the wall. Actually in this instance the writing was Bothwell's, in the form a letter just delivered to Ludovick, and of which that young man could make neither head nor tail. It was written from Hailes Castle in Lothian, and after professing the keenest regard for the Duke and asking after his health, declared that the writer understood that he, Lennox, was interested in the better running of the realm and the reform of certain notable tyrannies at present afflicting it, in especial the witch-trials which had become no more than a means for bringing down one's unfriends. Bothwell urged Lennox to band himself together with him and sundry other similarly well-intentioned lords, with a view to ending this reign of terror, and assured him that the time was almost ripe. He prayed that he might have an affirmative reply – as it was indeed the plain duty of all honest men in the kingdom to act in this matter.

'I cannot understand it, Mary,' Ludovick declared. 'This, from Bothwell. Why write this to me? I am no friend of his. I am against all bonds and plots. I have not great tail of men to help form an army. I am against this folly of the witches, yes. But I cannot see that Bothwell is the man to reform the government of this realm. And he has ever scorned me. Why should he approach me now? What can I answer him? I do not see the meaning of this letter . . .'

Mary looked out into the wet street. 'I fear that I do, Vicky,' she told him. 'And you should nowise answer it. This letter – do you not see? It is a trap. Burn it, Vicky – in case any other see it but ourselves. And pray that there are no more from whence it came! This may be Bothwell's writing – but I fear that it is Patrick's hand behind it!'

'Patrick's? Surely not!'

'Yes, Patrick's. Do you not see it? Answer this, show but the least interest in what Bothwell says, and you could be deep in trouble. Any communication with Bothwell, the King would take amiss. This, a bond with others, and against his precious witch-trials, he would name treason without a doubt. Aimed at himself . . . '

'James knows that I would never commit treason. That I would never league myself against him.'

'Are you so sure, Vicky? Remember that once you talked of deposing him, with yourself as Regent. Because you feared him mad. If he was to hear word of that . . . !'

'That was Patrick's project.'

'Yes. And there is the danger. Vicky – you have put yourself in Patrick's way. Because I besought you. But – whoever does that is in danger. I should have realised this before I sought your help. I have begun to fear something of the sort, these last days. Patrick's hand is behind this, I am sure. This way he could have you removed, out of the way. He may intend no more than that – but it could lead to worse things.'

'I cannot believe that this is Patrick's doing, Mary. How could he have Bothwell write to me?'

'Easily. Remember, he now can act Bothwell's friend and counsellor. Bothwell owes him his freedom. No doubt Bothwell *is* planning all kinds of treasons – he is ever at it. What more simple than for Patrick to have him include you in his crazy plans? One day a letter will come into the King's hands, from you to Bothwell, or from him to you, and you will be no longer dear Cousin Vicky but a treasonable plotter! This is a warning.' Mary stepped over to the fire, and thrust the letter into its heart.

'Suppose that I told James that it was Patrick who aided Bothwell to escape from Edinburgh Castle?' Ludovick said slowly.

344

'Would you? And think you he would believe you? Patrick would deny it – and you have no proof. Only my word. None would accept that. Even . . . even if I would agree to testify against him!' Her voice faltered just a little as she said that.

Helplessly he shook his head. 'What are we to do, then?'

'What we should have done ere this.' She quickly was her calm self again. 'I spoke of it before, with the Lady Marie, but we believed that it could wait. Have the King send Moray north, Vicky. He has great lands there – his own earldom of Moray. Convince the King that he is seeing overmuch of Queen Anne, here in Fife. Abet Patrick in this, at least! It should not be difficult. Have him banish Moray to his castle of Darnaway. Work on Mar and some of the other lords to support you in this. I do not see how Patrick can object. But do it secretly, so that the Queen does not come to hear of it, or she may prevail on the King not to do it. Then . . . you will be no more in Patrick's way in this matter.'

'Lord, Mary!' Brows furrowed, he stared at her. 'How do you do it? How do you think of these things. On my soul, it is a marvel! And yet so simple. So simple that I would never have thought of it. Where do you get such wits?'

'You know where I get them,' she answered him, her voice strangely flat. 'I heired them. They are my inheritance. Sometimes I wish to God that they were not!'

Long he considered her. 'I think that I do, also,' he said, at last.

'Yes.' She turned away. 'But you will do this? Speak with the King. Secretly. Plague him, if need be. He will do it, if only for the sake of peace. His mind is wholly on his book and his witchcraft. It is the best course. Better Moray banished to the north, but free, than languishing in a pit of Edinburgh Castle. Which is where Patrick, I think, would have him.'

'Aye. But why is it, Mary? Why does Patrick so hate Moray? He did not, formerly.'

'I do not believe that he hates him. Indeed, I do not believe that Patrick hates any man. It is never hatred, I think, which makes him act so, but something quite other. You may laugh at me – but I believe that the greatest evils that Patrick has done were done with no malice to any. Not to the persons he injures. Can you understand that, Vicky?'

345

His blank face was eloquent enough answer.

'It is so hard to explain. But I think that I have come to understand him. By looking deep into my own mind, perhaps. Patrick is not interested in *hurting* people. In especial he would not seek to injure poor people, ordinary folk – although many innocent folk may come to be hurt in the working out of his plots. He is a better husband than most, a good master, and one of the ablest rulers this realm has ever known. But he sees statecraft as a game, a sport. And all that influences the rule of the state, in power, position, even religion, as but pawns in that game. He is a gamester, in more than cards and horse-racing. His greatest sport is this – the game of power. As Moray excels at the glove and the ball, so Patrick excels in this greater sport. He knows that he is better at it than is any other. Any that cross his path in this, he must remove. It is a challenge that must be met, and overcome. It is not the man that he fights, or the woman, but the challenge. Do you not see it?' Urgently she put it to the young man, so urgently that she gripped his arm, all but shook it. 'Do you not see it?'

Doubtfully he eyed her. 'It is difficult, Mary. I see a little, perhaps. Patrick is not as other men, I do perceive. But this bringing down of others, so many, to their ruin, even their deaths – that is evil, surely? Only evil.'

'I know! I know!' she cried. It was seldom indeed that Mary Gray raised her voice thus. 'I do not say that it is not evil. But Patrick does not see it so. You asked me why he hates Moray. I do not believe that he does. But Moray has crossed his path, with the Queen. Moray's folly with the Queen could harm the realm. So Moray must fall. There may be more than that – I do not know. But that is enough, for Patrick.'

He shook his head. 'You are too deep for me,' he said. 'Too clever – you and Patrick both.'

Strangely enough that remark seemed to strike home at her. 'So clever,' she repeated, dully. 'Yes – too clever. I could be too clever. I was, before. I hope, I pray, that I am not being too clever. This time. But . . . we must do something, Vicky. We must do *something*.'

He nodded. 'That we must. And this appears the wise course. What you now propose. I shall see to it. Never fear.' He kicked at the floor with his toe. 'I am sorry, Mary. I did

346

not mean . . . that you thought yourself too clever. Never that.'

'I know it, Vicky. But it is true, nevertheless.'

'The Queen?' he asked, changing the subject abruptly. 'How is it with her?'

'All is well. Mistress Cunningham is curling her hair. Moray is there – but so are Lady Kate and your good-sister, the Lady Beatrix. All is well, for the moment.'

He sighed. 'I wish, Mary . . . !'

She completed that for him. 'Methven Castle will wait for you, Vicky,' she assured.

Although in the past King James had cared nothing for weather, so long as the hunting was good, this season his heart was not in hunting, and the November rain drove him back to Edinburgh. Bothwell seemed to have lain suitably low since his escape from ward, and it was to be hoped that he had learned his lesson at last. Even the Master of Gray seemed to consider that it would be safe enough to return to the capital. There was some talk of going back to Craigmillar Castle for security, or even to Edinburgh Castle itself; but none of the Council seemed to think that this was necessary, not even the cautious Maitland. Since Moray had been packed off to his northern fastnesses at Darnaway, a certain aura of peace had descended upon the Court. There was no denying it. The Queen was less upset than might have been expected. After only a day or two of sulks, she consoled herself readily enough with the Duke of Lennox and the Master of Gray – which allowed her husband to get on with the all-important issue of his book and his warfare with the Devil.

In this connection there was a grave, a shameful matter to put right. One of his special courts for trying the witches had actually acquitted the woman Barbara Napier – after he had forfeited her lands of Cliftonhall and bestowed them upon young Sir James Sandilands of Slamannan, his latest page, who was an extremely talented youth in certain ways, even if the ladies did not like him. In righteous wrath James had had the entire jury responsible arrested, brought to Falkland, and themselves thereupon tried on a charge of bringing in a false verdict, in manifest and wilful error, the King himself presiding. Faced with a fate exactly similar to that they should have imposed upon the high-born Mistress Napier of Cliftonhall, the jury sensibly and humbly confessed their fault, and clearly would not so err again. James was magnanimously pleased to pardon them. But others might do likewise, and it seemed clear that Christ's vice-regent should return to the centre of affairs forthwith – for it demanded eternal vigilance sucessfully to counter the Devil. The Justice-Clerk was instructed peremptorily to have the woman Napier re-tried and condemned, without further delay.

So to Holyroodhouse they all returned. The Queen, in lieu of the fascinations of house building and plenishing, fell back upon the cosy winter-time delights of possible pregnancy, and set her ladies to much making of baby-clothes.

Satan was not backwards in seeking to overturn King James's godly campaign. By a most unhappy coincidence, the same young James Sandilands, in an excess of youthful spirits, had the misfortune to shoot and kill a Lord of Session, Lord Hallyards, in the street soon after the return to Edinburgh. This greatly upset many of the judicial fraternity, some of whom even went so far as to demand that James should have his new page tried and punished. The King's indignant refusal undoubtedly had a deleterious effect on the witch-trials, which he had ordered to have precedence over all other matters juridical. He came to believe that the entire legal profession began to drag its feet in this vital issue – indubitably to Satan's glee.

As if this was not enough, there came a complaint from, of all people, George Gordon, Earl of Huntly. Although banished to his own countryside, he was still Lieutenant of the North – since there was nobody else up there powerful enough to control that barbarous land – and while besieging the Laird of Grant in Castle Grant, for some reason or another, had been attacked by the Earls of Moray and Atholl, coming to Grant's aid. No doubt only the fact that Moray was the King's cousin had produced this petition of protest from Huntly in place of a much more drastic and typical reaction. James was annoyed, justifiably. A plague on them all!

Mary no sooner heard of this than she imagined Patrick's hand behind it somewhere, pursuing Moray even two hundred miles into the Northland. He was in constant secret touch with Huntly, she knew. Atholl, a weak and unstable character, was married to the Lady Mary Ruthven – the same who was suspected of playing Leda to Patrick's swan at Falkland, and his full cousin as well as the elder sister of Ludovick's new wife. Patrick had used Atholl as his tool before this. Or it might have been a trumped-up clash arranged through Huntly himself . . .

In deep trouble, Mary Gray looked within himself. To such a state of suspicion, of irrational fears and dark imaginings, had she come. She saw Patrick's shadow everywhere, suspected his every action, sensed mockery behind every smile, tainting her love. It could not go on, thus. Either they must come to terms, or one must yield and go. And she did not see the Master of Gray conceding the game, the game that was his very life, to his unacknowledged daughter.

Chapter Twenty

ONLY five days before Christmas, with Queen Anne planning Yuletide revels on a Danish pattern and scale, something new and therefore suspect in Scotland, Patrick Gray surprised his wife and Mary by announcing that it would be suitable and fitting that he and his family should celebrate Yule in their own house of Broughty, not in this rabbit-warren of a palace. To Marie's protests that it was late in the day to think of this, that the journey at this season of the year would be most trying, and that Broughty Castle was indeed the last place that she would choose for festivity, her husband made laughing reply that she was obviously getting old and stodgy, and needed shaking up a mite; that the weather was excellent for the season; and that Broughty Castle was somewhat improved since last she had seen it. Moreover, would she not see her beloved Davy Gray?

He was in the best of spirits, anything but harsh, but adamant in this sudden whim. They would travel first thing the next morning. Mary was included in this arrangement.

349

While they would be sorry to miss her company, she could spend her Christmas at Castle Huntly if she preferred it. Evidently there was no question of her being left at Holyroodhouse, Queen or no Queen.

Sudden as seemed this decision, Ludovick would have accompanied them – but Patrick demurred. It might look somewhat blatant, he suggested, for so newly a married man. Moreover, Anne might well be sufficiently concerned over losing her Maid-in-Waiting for her Yuletide antics, without sacrificing her most faithful admirer and constant attendant into the bargain. The Duke of Lennox was not as lesser men, and must bear the responsibilities of his high calling.

They took two easy days to the journey, stopping overnight at Falkland. Mary was escorted to the gatehouse of Castle Huntly, but neither the heir thereto nor his wife and son crossed the threshold. My lord's shadow lay too heavily athwart it.

Mary was joyfully received, the unexpectedness of her arrival nowise detracting. My lord, three parts drunk, welcomed her like the prodigal returned. Mariota wept in her happiness. The young brother and sister shouted. It was left to Davy Gray to remark concernedly that she was looking pale, great-eyed, strained – not the same cool and serenely lovely young creature that she had been, although almost more beautiful.

Mary, for her part, was more glad to be home than she could say, more in need of its settled normalcy and security than she had realised – and especially her father's strong, reliable presence. Undoubtedly prolonged association with Patrick Gray enhanced an appreciation of David, his illegitimate half-brother.

The day after Christmas, in sunny open weather, Mary rode pillion behind her father the dozen miles to Broughty. Even at a distance, Patrick's hand was notably visible. After the French fashion he had harled the bare stone wall outer walls and colour-washed all but the actual battlements and parapets in a deep yellow, so that the fortress on its rocky promontory soared above the sparkling, blue and white of the sea like a golden castle, gleaming in the sun. The place was larger too, new building towering above the high curtain-walling that faithfully followed the outline of the small headland; the restricted site precluded any lateral extensions, so Patrick had built upwards, and again in the French style, with corner-turrets, rounded stair-towers, overhanging bartizans and conical roofs. Over all no fewer than six great banners fluttered in the breeze, proud, challenging.

'Patrick has done as he vowed,' David said, over his shoulder, pointing. 'Broughty is no rickle of stones, any more. It is a finer place than Castle Huntly now – finer than any castle that I have seen north of Tay. But the cost! He has poured out siller like water. Where does he get the money, Mary?'

She shook her head. 'A thousand pounds of Elizabeth's pension to the King he got – for fetching it, and as solace for Dunfermline . . . '

'That is as nothing to what has been spent here. You have not yet seen the inside. I cannot think where he has gained it.'

'He wins much at cards. And it may be that he has his hands on some of the Ruthven money already, with the wardship of the daughters. And he still has dealings with Queen Elizabeth.'

'Aye, then. To pay so well, what does he sell her?'

When they reached the castle, the reason for David's wonderings was amply clear. The place was transformed. From a bare echoing shell, it had become a palace. Tapestries and hangings clothed every wall, and not skins but carpets on every floor, brought from the East. Great windows had been opened in the thick walls to let in the light, fireplaces blazed with logs in every chamber, and candles in handsome candelabra turned night into day. Furnishings, bedding, silverware, pictures – nothing was stinted, nothing less than the best. Nothing in Holyroodhouse could compare with this. If Patrick Gray knew how to find money, he knew how to spend it also.

Questions and doubts, however, had to give way to greetings, admiration and festivity. Patrick was at his dazzling best, all laughter, wit and brilliance, like quick-silver. Even to Davy he was all affection, gaiety, frank brotherliness. As for Marie, with all she loved most gathered around her, she accepted this day as snatched from care, not to be spoiled. The others found themselves of a like mind.

It was evening when this pleasant interval of accord was

interrupted. A sudden great hullabaloo and outcry from outside, from the direction of the gatehouse and drawbridge, sent David striding to the nearest window. Quite a large company of horsemen were milling about just beyond the artificial ditch spanned by the drawbridge, which separated the promontory from the mainland, many of them with blazing torches held high, while two of their shadowy number held a shouted exchange with the porters on the gatehouse parapet.

'Ah – company!' Patrick's voice sounded softly at his brother's shoulder. 'A pity, perhaps, that they could not wait until morning. We were so . . . well content.' He turned back into the great vaulted hall. 'You will excuse me, my dears? It seems that I must go play host.'

'Who is it, Patrick?' Marie asked, tension coming back into her voice. 'At this hour? What can it be?'

'That remains to be seen,' he told her easily. 'Nothing for you to distress yourself over, at least. And there is victual enough here to feed a host.' He closed the door behind him.

Marie looked from Mary to David. 'So short a time,' she sighed. 'It is not . . . your father?'

'No,' David perked. 'It is a large company. But whoever it is, my lord it is not! He will never darken this door, I fear. Patrick has fulfilled the rest of his vow, yes – that he would make this rickle of stones a palace that the King might envy. But he will never bring his father here to his gate, begging admittance, as he swore. Some tasks are beyond even Patrick.'

'I would not be so sure,' Marie said, shaking her head. 'Do not underestimate him, Davy. But a few days ago he won from the King the appointment of Sheriff of Forfar – in place of his father. So that he is now justiciar of all this region. Why? Why should he saddle himself with all this duty and responsibility? It is not like Patrick to take on such tasks. He will require to pay a deputy, since I swear he has no intention of dwelling always here in the sheriffdom. So that he will make little out of it.'

David whistled soundlessly. 'My lord was much hurt at being dismissed the office. He has held it long – and is moreover an Extra Lord of Session. But . . . he does not know that it is Patrick who succeeds him. That will be the sorer blow.'

'Yes. But that is the least of it, Davy. Do you not see? What it means? He is now the law in this sheriffdom, the voice of the King. If any transgress that law, or the King's will, Patrick can summon the same to him. Here, to Broughty. To judgment. And they must come, or suffer outlawry, banishment. Including my lord of Gray – should some transgression be suggested!'

'God's mercy! This is ... this is ...'

'This is Patrick! He has not told me that this is his purpose. But I think that I know his mind.'

Mary spoke. 'If we could but bring them together. In love, not in hurt.' Her dark eyes were pools of trouble. 'Deep in his heart I believe that Granlord aches for his son. And Patrick does not hate his father – only what he stands for, I think. He must beat all who oppose him.'

'Perhaps,' David sighed. 'Think you that I have not tried? All my life I have tried. There is that between them neither will yield ...'

He stopped. Plain for all to hear came the thin wailing of bagpipes.

They stared at each other.

'Dear Lord!' David exclaimed. 'I know only one man who so loves that sound that he must have it even here and now! Huntly!'

'Huntly – here!' Marie looked startled. 'But, why? What could bring him here? So far from Strathbogie. That man ... !'

'I do not know. But this I do know – that wherever that turkey-cock gobbles there is trouble.'

'This . . . this could be construed as treason! Harbouring Huntly, who is banished to his own North ...' Marie faltered.

'This may be why we are here, nevertheless,' Mary suggested quietly. 'We came here to Broughty. So that Patrick might meet Huntly. Secretly.'

'I thought of it,' Marie admitted. 'But why bring us, then? Better without us, surely?'

'Patrick knew that he was coming,' Mary insisted. 'Or that someone would come.'

In doubt they eyed each other.

A moment or two later the door was flung open, and on a gale of sound Huntly strode in, a moving mountain of flesh, tartans, armour, jewellery and eagles' feathers, with Patrick behind him. He had not doffed his bonnet. Even Marie rose to her feet.

'Greetings, my lord of Huntly, to this house,' she said, somewhat thickly. 'In this season of goodwill and peace. We . . . we wish you well. You have not brought your lady wife?'

'Wife . . . ? God – no! I do not travel the passes in winter on women's work, Lady!' Huntly boomed. 'A blessing on your house.' His choleric eye lighted on David Gray, and he looked as though he might retract that benediction. 'You!' he barked.

'Aye, my lord,' that man gave back evenly. 'It is a far cry from Strathbogie.'

'My lord of Huntly has come south on important business,' Patrick interposed, pleasantly. 'On the King's business, indeed. He heard in Dundee that we were at Broughty, and came, assured of a welcome in any house of mine.'

'Young Jamie Stewart needs my services,' the Earl amplified, chuckling. 'He'll no' long manage this realm without Gordon!'

'But . . . only north of Dee, is it not, my lord?' Marie said. 'Coming south, thus, do you not endanger yourself? And . . . and others?'

'Wait you!' the other advised her shortly, cryptically. 'You will see.'

Marie inclined her fair head. 'No doubt.' She swallowed. 'Now, my lord – you will be weary, and hungered. If you will come with me, I shall see to your comfort. And your people also. How many . . . ?'

'There is no need, my dear,' the Master mentioned. 'I have already given orders. All is in train. If you will come with *me*, my lord . . . ?'

When the door closed behind her visitor again, Marie sat down abruptly. 'There is villainy here!' she exclaimed. 'I smell it. I hate and fear that man.'

'And yet, if such there is, then it would be Patrick who conceived it, not the Earl of Huntly.'

Surprised, the other two looked at Mary. It had always been the girl's part to uphold Patrick, to speak for him, to find excuse. This was a notable change.

'That is true,' David nodded. 'Huntly is a vain and stupid man, with not a tithe of Patrick's wits. If he is here, it is because Patrick moved him to come.'

'Yes. So that, if there is danger in it, hurt, Huntly himself is in more danger than are any of us whom Patrick loves,' Mary pointed out. 'We should, perhaps, be sorry for my lord.'

Marie suddenly buried her face in her hands.

Both of them went to her, Mary to kneel beside her chair, David to stand behind her, his hand on her bowed shoulder.

'Do not be downcast, lassie,' he said thickly. 'Naught may come of it – naught of harm. You have faced much worse than this – and smiled through it.'

'Oh, Davy! Davy!' she mumbled brokenly, reaching out to clutch his arm. But she kept her head down.

'My dear,' he said.

Mary looked from one to the other, but said nothing.

'I am foolish, Davy – oh, I know that I am foolish,' Marie declared. 'But I am tired, weary of it all. Weary of struggling, of fighting against shadows, of fearing what each day may bring, of living a lie . . . '

'*You* never lived or thought or told a lie, all your days, woman!' the man declared, deep-voiced, set-faced. 'I know you.'

'Do you, Davy? Do you? Even so?' She looked up at him, now, urgently. 'Oh, I wish that it was true! You do not know that even now I am living a lie – and to you. To you both. And endangering you, it may be, because of it. For there was danger, treason itself perhaps, in this house before Huntly came to it – and I did not tell you. There are Jesuits living here secretly – priests, emissaries, spies from France and Spain, sheltered here by Patrick . . . '

'Jesuits! Here?' David looked startled.

'Yes. It seems that they have been here for months. Coming and going. They use this house as a centre for their journeys and missions. They are thought of here as but foreign artists and craftsmen, employed by Patrick in the building and plenishing of this castle, working in paint and plaster and glass and tapestry. Some indeed do so. They can come and go secretly by boat, at night. None can observe them, on this sea-girt headland. They could scarce have it better arranged.'

'Aye, that I see,' David sighed. 'So Patrick still paddles in that mire! I had thought that in this, at least, he would have learned his lesson. What does it mean? That still he hopes to restore the Catholics to power in Scotland? Is that why Huntly is here – the greatest Catholic of the realm? Is Patrick truly a Catholic himself, at heart, Marie?'

'God knows – for I do not!' she cried. 'Patrick's heart lies well buried. I know not what he is, or what he believes, deep down. Or where his heart lies. Even after these years . . . '

'Save that he loves *you*, Lady Marie,' Mary put in quietly. 'That you know.'

Slowly, steadily, the older woman turned to look at the younger. 'Do I so, Mary?' she asked, at length. 'Do I know that, if driven to it, he would not sacrifice me also, to his scheming? Use me, like all others, as but a pawn in his game. Has he not done so, indeed?'

Mary shook her head. 'Not to your hurt. Not of intention. He loves you. Indeed he loves all three here. Each differently. That we do know, if naught else.'

'He has used me full often, for his gain and my risk,' her father jerked. 'And you also, girl, I think. Let us not cozen ourselves. Enough to have Patrick ever cozening us . . . '

More shouting from the gatehouse stopped him. There was no such outcry as formerly, but clearly some new visitor was demanding admittance this busy Yuletide night, against the gate-porters' doubts. David stepped over to the window again.

'But the one man, I think,' he reported, peering out into the dark. 'It is hard to see. Only the gatehouse torches to light him. Some messenger for Patrick, no doubt. Aye – there clank the drawbridge chains. They are letting him in.'

'Wherever Patrick may be, messengers come day and night,' Marie said, shrugging. 'At least, this one comes openly at the gate, and does not slip in at a secret postern, from the sea.'

It was a little time before voices sounded from the echoing stone-vaulted passage without, one of them urgent, excited. The door opened to reveal a travel-stained, mud-spattered and dishevelled young man, blinking in the light, with Patrick behind him.

'Vicky!' Mary exclaimed, and started forward, before she recollected herself.

Lennox came to her without hesitation or ceremony, and undoubtedly would have embraced her before them all had she not drawn back. Only perfunctorily, then, at her warning gesture, did he pay his respects to his hostess and nod to David.

'Vicky has strange tidings. From Edinburgh,' Patrick mentioned easily. 'Most . . . interesting.'

'I' faith, I'd call it more than that!' the young man burst out. 'It was treason. Rebellion! Only by a mercy was the King saved.'

'Precisely,' Patrick nodded. 'As I said – distressing.'

'The King? Rebellion? Not . . . not Huntly?' Marie gasped.

'Huntly . . . ? No. How should it be? It was Bothwell. He struck yesterday. On Christmas Day. At Holyroodhouse. With many men. They came at darkening. Wild mosstroopers and broken men. How many I do not know – but they swarmed like rats over the palace. We were all at the Queen's revels, in the banqueting hall. Save James. And Maitland. James had gone back to his books and papers, tiring of the Danish play. The Guard was keeping Yule in my lord of Orkney's quarters. Mar, the new Captain, was with the Queen. As was I. We found ourselves to be locked in the banqueting hall, with Bothwell's bullyrooks guarding the doors. I won out through a window, to reach the Guard. But they were for the most part drunken, or . . . or . . .'

'Aye – we know how it would be!' That was Davy, briefly, as the other paused, partly for breath. 'What of the King?'

'Aye – what of the King, Vicky?'

'He was locked in his room. In his own tower. The guards on the stairs had the wit to lock the great double doors at the foot of the tower, when they heard the din and clash. They shouted to the guard on Maitland's tower, across the court, to do the same. Bothwell had not considered that – or else his men were slow. No doubt he thought to find James with the Queen and the rest at the revels in the hall. The great doors held. One is a yett of iron. So they could not get at James. So little a thing saved the King.'

'Saved the King . . . ?' Marie echoed, appalled. 'But, what would Bothwell have done, Vicky? What was his purpose? You do not think that he would have harmed the King? Done him a hurt?'

'I do not know. Some said that he would have slain him. In revenge for imprisoning him, and naming him devil-possessed. All know that Bothwell is half-crazed . . . !'

'Nonsense!' Patrick intervened. 'Whoever so said is equally crazed. How would it serve Bothwell to kill the King? He would turn all against him. It is but the old game. He who holds the King holds the power.'

'He may have thought to make himself king in James's place,' Ludovick claimed. 'He is of the royal house. Closer than am I, save for the illegitimacy . . . '

'But that is all-important. And others are closer still, but with the same taint. Marie's father. Moray. No, no – he would but hold the King. Get rid of Maitland and the others. Be assured of that.'

'James feared for his life, nevertheless. Still does.'

'James always does that! Bothwell is not so great a fool. He would have all against him if he slew the King. Including Elizabeth, who presently aids him. But . . . how stands the position now, Vicky? How do they, now?'

'James is in Edinburgh Castle, safe. Bothwell's Borderers could not gain entry to his tower. I roused such of the Guard as I might. There was much fighting.' Ludovick flushed slightly, stumbling over his words. 'I . . . I killed a man! It was him or me. He had a whinger. Swording. He near had me. I could not get my sword out of him. It was fast held. He had a black beard. Blood running down it . . . ' His voice tailed away.

'Vicky!' Mary came to his side, to hold his arm. 'Dear Vicky – I am sorry!'

With an obvious effort the young man recovered himself. 'They were too many. We could not hold them,' he went on, jerkily. 'We were driven back. I got away. Took one of their horses. I won past their picquets. Into the town. I went to the Tolbooth. Roused them there. Had the bells rung – to summon the lieges. To bring out the Blue Blanket. Turned out the Town Guard. We had the church bells ringing. The burghers took long about it – but the apprentices rallied quickly. With them, and the Town Guard, I went back to the palace. And with some lords lodging in the town. Four score of us, perhaps – or a hundred. At first we could do little, against Bothwell's men who held the gates. But when the burghers and the crafts came, with their Blue Blanket, to save the King – then they could not hold us. They came in thousands – half the town. Shouting for the King. We forced the gates. The mosstroopers could not stand against so many. They fled. But I heard Bothwell shouting that he would be back. That he would burn the city, and hang the provost and bailies. So the provost hanged eight of the Borderers that they had caught. In front of the palace. As a warning . . . '

Panting, the Duke took the glass of wine that Mary was holding out to him, and gulped it down unsteadily. His features, under the grime of long and hard riding, were lined with weariness.

'You would seem, Vicky, to have been most . . . adequate,' Patrick murmured. 'Quite the paladin! And Bothwell notably ineffective. A bungler. So the town mob saved James, did it? I had scarce thought that he was so popular! Or is it just that they mislike Bothwell more?'

Lennox raised his brows. 'They but did their duty to their liege lord, as leal citizens, did they not?'

'Ah, yes. Of course, bless them!' The Master, though he spoke lightly, was clearly somewhat preoccupied, his mind not wholly on this exchange. 'And now the position is . . . ?'

'The townsfolk carried James up to the Castle. He was in great alarm. He could scarce speak. I saw him safe bedded there. Then I took horse forthwith. To ride here. To tell you.'

'Vicky! You did not sleep first? You have not rested, since that evil fighting? You rode through the night? And all day . . . ?' Mary was shocked.

'It was necessary. It is a long ride. I have worn out three horses. I had to come, Mary. All is confusion at Court. Bothwell is not far away. Only at Crichton, they say. Gathering more men. He can raise thousands, from the Border valleys and Lothian and the Merse. He said that he would be back. None knows what to do. James is safe for the nonce – but all the realm is endangered. I could think only of coming here, to you . . . '

'What of the Chancellor? My lord Maitland? Is not all in his capable hands?' Patrick wondered.

'He is a clerk, no more! As you know. He blames all, but does nothing. Save pray! He is at the Castle likewise, but helpless. None need him, anyway. Mar talks loud enough, but knows not what to do. You, Patrick, I thought . . . you always know what to do . . . '

'I am flattered by your faith and confidence, Vicky. We must see what can be done, yes.' The Master laughed. 'Heigho – is it not most fortunate, most convenient, that we have here at Broughty, by purest chance, the one man in this peculiar realm who can out-man Bothwell! In the circumstances, my lord of Huntly might be described as a God-send, might he not?'

'Huntly? He is . . . he is not here? At Broughty? Huntly himself . . . ?' Ludovick stared.

'Huntly, yes – your own potent good-brother! He is indeed. He arrived but an hour ago. Did you not see his troop's horses thronging the courtyard? Huntly has honoured us at an auspicious moment, it seems.'

'But he is banished! In disgrace!'

'Whom the King has banished, he can unbanish! Especially if the disgraced one can produce five thousand armed men to counter Bothwell's mosstroopers and rievers!' Patrick smiled, and patted the younger man's shoulder. 'Tomorrow I shall ride for Edinburgh – though in not quite such haste as you have ridden here, Vicky. I shall acquaint our liege lord of his great good fortune! All shall be well, for the best, never fear. I warrant that Jamie Stewart will fall upon my undeserving neck – and summon Huntly back to favour and the Court *instanter*!'

Mary Gray was considering Patrick long and thoughtfully. So much that had been unexplained now fitted neatly into place. She turned her head, to catch the grey eye of Lady Marie. Then she found David looking from one to the other of them. None spoke, nor required to speak.

Lennox, bewildered, ran a hand over his brow. 'I do not understand,' he faltered. 'This of Huntly . . . ?'

'Never heed it, Vicky,' Mary advised. 'You are done – tired, hungry. Come with me.' She took him by the hand.

He nodded, and went like a child.

360

Chapter Twenty-one

ON 29th December 1591, King James signed a decree ending the banishment of his trusty and well-beloved councillor and Lieutenant of the North, George Gordon, Earl of Huntly, Lord of Strathbogie, Enzie, Badenoch and Aboyne, and summoned him to Court at the Castle of Edinburgh with all haste, duly accoutred and equipped for the sure defence of his sovereign lord and fast friend, James R. And on the first day of January 1592, the Cock o' the North rode in through the West Port of the city, with a mere token tail of two hundred Gordon swordsmen at his back, and the hearty assurance that there were plenty more where these came from, and indeed on the way. The citizens looked on askance, silent; the Kirk groaned in spirit; Mr. Bowes, the English envoy dispatched an urgent courier to Walsingham. But the Catholics rejoiced, and the sentinels up on the grim walls and turrets of Edinburgh Castle relaxed a little their anxious southwards vigil. Bothwell, reading the signs aright, turned and retired to his castle of Hermitage, deep in the Border fastnesses.

So Huntly strutted the stage again, and Edinburgh resounded to bagpipe squeals, strange Gaelic oaths, and the skirls of women outraged or prepared to be. The Court, after an interval, moved back thankfully to Holyroodhouse, and Catholic lords unseen for years, like Erroll, Crawford, Montrose and Seton appeared thereat. Bishops and prelates crept out from their holes and corners; Chancellor Maitland sank back like a snail into its shell; the witch trials came to an abrupt halt. Patrick Gray stood, debonair and smiling, close to the King's ear – none closer.

The delicate scales of Scottish politics teetered to a precarious balance, once more. None anticipated that they would do so for long, however assured seemed the urban Master of Gray. Men watched and waited.

James, temporarily lacking witches to justify, was at something of a loose end. He had ever been rather more fond of horseflesh than the human variety, and the death of his Master

Stabler, one John Shaw, and the loss of some of his favourite mounts in the Bothwell raid, caused him great concern and presently a return to poetry. He wrote a sonnet to commemorate the Stabler's gallant end, the first gesture towards the Muse in a full year, and roused himself to such heights of indignation and passion in the process that nothing short of some sort of demonstration and physical action against the perpetrator of the outrage would relieve his emotions. After consultation with the Master of Gray he first held a ceremony to divest Bothwell of his great office of state, that of Lord High Admiral, and promptly bestowed it upon the reluctant and embarrassed Duke of Lennox who so gallantly had brought the citizens of Edinburgh to the royal rescue. And secondly he mounted an expedition to the Borderland, January though it was, to display to that unruly and disobedient area who ruled in this realm of Scotland. With a mixed but strongly armed force consisting of the Royal Guard, Gordons, city levies and retainers of various lords, James in person made a hurried excursion southwards. Admittedly he confined his attentions to the East March, whilst Bothwell was known to be at Hermitage in the west, and after burning a few peel-towers and hanging some rievers and mosstroopers who were always the better for such firm treatment, hastened back to Edinburgh before Bothwell could do anything substantial about it – much to the disappointment of Huntly who was congenitally in favour of such entertainment, of Johnny Mar who enjoyed being Captain of the Guard, and even of Ludovick, who felt that a demonstration of the royal authority was overdue, whatever the risks. But James was adamant. A four-day expedition was quite adequate; moreover he had fallen into the Tyne in crossing that rain-swollen river of the Debatable Land, and was in dire alarm at catching cold in consequence.

Patrick Gray had excused himself from this martial adventure, on grounds of pressure of work. Nevertheless, the King's company was not half-a-day on its way when he took horse, with his hard-riding cousin Logan of Restalrig as companion, and headed southwards into the hills himself, although in a rather more westerly direction. He was back two days later, tired but good-humoured, only a day before his sneezing monarch.

James, despite aches and shivers, was much uplifted in spirit by this warrior-like gesture, and from his foot-baths and doctorings issued strong and manly pronouncements on the stern duties of kings and their subjects and the inescapable punishment and doom of all malefactors, especially those in high places. In some glee he sent a long letter to his royal cousin of England, acquainting her of his escape from enemies unfortunately supported by those who should know better, and of his strong measures against Bothwell on their mutual frontier, at which he was sure she would rejoice – mentioning, in passing, that his long promised English dukedom had still not materialised and would not this be a most suitable occasion for its bestowal? Patrick Gray enclosed a more cryptic covering-note of his own.

In this uplifted and magnanimous mood, the King was pleased to reconsider a petition to which he had hitherto been determinedly opposed, despite Patrick's generous and disinterested pleas. The Countess of Moray had unfortunately died, back in November, of some unspecified female ailment, and Moray had requested royal permission to come south to Donibristle to bury her – for in her sickness she had not accompanied her husband to the north and his banishment. Now, on Patrick's representations that it would please the Kirk, which was becoming ever more restive under increasing Catholic advancement – for Moray had ever been a favourite in that quarter – and moreover might help to keep Huntly from becoming so arrogant as to be unbearable, James relented. Moray might return to Donibristle, but no further; he must not cross the Forth or come to Court. The Queen, although she listened to their conversation, made no pleas of her own.

Mary, back at her duties in the Queen's household, watched and wondered.

On the last day of January, she overheard Patrick telling Anne that the new tapestries in the Flemish style that he was having woven for her were finished and it only required Her Grace's own decision as to which rooms of her house at Dunfermline each would best enhance. A short visit to Fife, perhaps . . . ? Mary's heart sank within her. She might have known. Was there to be no end to it? Were they back where they had been, so soon? Patrick was inexorable, to be diverted by nothing and nobody. Or was she but imagining evil, treachery? Seeing menace in the most innocent of actions? Had she reached the stage of suspecting Patrick's every move, however much she claimed to understand him? If so, how much was her vaunted love worth? She was weary, weary of it all; she could shut her eyes to that no longer. There it was, then; she was weary, but Patrick was not. The day that Patrick Gray wearied of his sport, his game with men, he would be dead. She knew it now.

Weary, imagining things, or not, she went to Ludovick forthwith and told him what she had heard and what she feared. If the Queen decided to go to Dunfermline would he be sure to go with her, scarce leave her side, she demanded.

'Again?' he sighed. 'I had thought to have finished with that. I find her passing dull, Mary. And all will say that I but follow you, who will be in Anne's train. That it is you that I follow, not her.'

'Let them say it. Better that they should. Indeed, I could entice you to do so. Before others. Before the King if need be. Persuade you. So that your coming will seem the less strange.'

'And have yourself named courtesan!' he exclaimed, frowning.

'Why not? I am so named already, I have no doubt. I care not, so long as *I* know what I am. And you do, likewise. If that I am to be called, let the name have its uses.'

'Its uses,' he repeated. 'As have I!' That was just a little bitter.

She touched his arm. 'Poor Vicky,' she said. 'I am sorry . . . '

The good burghers of the grey town of Dunfermline scarcely glanced at the young man who cantered a tired horse through their narrow streets. They had seen many much finer fish than this, of late, since the young Queen had come to lodge in the Abbot's House – even this very afternoon. Only the fact that the horse was a fine one and was tired, obviously having been ridden hard, attracted any attention; a courier with tidings for the Queen, no doubt.

The young man brought tidings, certainly – but not for Queen Anne.

Reining up in the stableyard of the Abbot's House, beside

which the Queen's fine new lodging stood all but completed, Ludovick of Lennox gazed about him urgently. A few other horses stood therein, hitched to rings and posts; but not what he had looked for – no large troop, nothing hard-ridden like his own beast. Frowning and biting his lip, he jumped down and ran indoors, shouting for Mary Gray and not the Queen.

He found her lighting lamps from a long taper in the former library of the Lord Abbot, for already the short February afternoon was dying towards dusk.

'Vicky!' she exclaimed, surprised but welcoming. 'How good! You are back. So soon!' It was the 7th of February, and he had only been gone from Dunfermline for three days, summoned back to Holyroodhouse expressly by the King at, they had suspected, Patrick's instigation.

'No. I am not.' He came to her, but anxiously rather than with his usual impetuous eagerness. 'Mary – is Huntly here?'

'Huntly? No. He was. But he is gone.'

'When?'

'An hour ago. More. Why, Vicky?'

'Did he ask for Moray?'

'No. He called merely to pay his respects to the Queen, he said. As he passed through Dunfermline.'

'Going where?'

'I do not know. He may have told Her Grace. Ask her, Vicky. Is it . . . bad news?'

'And Moray? He is not here, then?' This curt questioning was unlike Lennox.

'He was here yesterday. And the day before. But not today, no. You think that Huntly is looking for Moray?'

'I know it. He carries a decree from the King for Moray's arrest. For high treason.'

The girl drew a long breath. 'So – it has come to that!' she said. 'After all.'

'I would to God that was all!' he jerked. 'Mary – will Moray be at Donibristle? Now?'

'I would think it, yes. I do not know – but it is likely. His house . . .'

'Did Huntly take that road, then? The sea road, for Fordel and Aberdour?'

'I did not watch his going, Vicky.'

'No. The stable-boys may know. But . . . why ask? Whatever road he took, he will have gone to Donibristle. Nothing surer. As therefore must I. At once. Pray God I may be in time.' Already he was making for the door.

'In time, Vicky? For what? To warn Moray? It will be much too late, I fear. And what else can you do?'

'I do not know. But if I am there, it may be that Huntly will hold back. From his worst intent.' He was striding out now, down the long corridor towards the courtyard, Mary having almost to run to keep up with him. 'I may yet save Moray's life.'

'His *life*!' the girl gasped. 'What do you mean?'

'I believe that Huntly means to slay Moray, not arrest him!'

'Slay? Oh, no! No!' That was a wail.

'Yes. I cannot wait, Mary. To tell you all, now. But I believe it is so. And that James knows it, God forgive him. Aye, and Patrick also.'

'Never! Not that. You must be mistaken, Vicky . . . '

'Would that I was. But I heard the King's parting words to Huntly. Saw his look. Patrick's also. We were hunting. This morning. At Barnbougle. It was to be secret. Huntly rode direct from the hunt. I wondered at it. Then Peter Hay told me that he had heard one of Huntly's lairds saying to another that Moray would not live to see another day. He said Huntly had sworn it.'

'But . . . but . . . ' Helplessly, Mary shook her head. 'Why? Why, Vicky?'

'Reasons a-plenty – of a sort.' They had reached Ludovick's horse, now, where it stood steaming. 'Huntly has a blood-feud with Moray. From the days of his father, brought low by Moray's uncle, the Regent. Half the earldom was Huntly land once. And James becomes ever more jealous of Anne. Patrick has worked on him all too well. Now that Moray's wife is dead, he fears still worse things. That his wife may be stolen from him. Even his heir, possibly. And so the realm. You know James. It is crazy – but no crazier than the witches and Bothwell.' The young man hoisted himself up into the saddle. 'I must be gone.'

She laid a hand on his knee, as though she would restrain him. 'Moray may not need your warning, Vicky. He has men of his own. Huntly had but two or three gentlemen with him.'

'Aye – when he called here! As when he left the hunt. But at the Queen's Ferry I learned that forty men-at-arms had awaited him there. So all was arranged beforehand. If he did not bring all these here, he must have left them somewhere in the town. Hidden. And at the Ferry, Huntly had given orders, in the King's name, that no ferry-boat, or other craft, was to sail across to Fife today. After him.' Ludovick snorted a mirthless laugh. 'It required siller, and my fine new authority as Lord High Admiral, to get across myself! Think you now that Moray is in no danger?'

The young woman shook her head. 'I know not what to think. Save . . . save that there is danger for you also in this, Vicky. Must you go? What can you do? One man . . . ?'

'You know that I must, Mary. I can do no less. Huntly is married to my sister. You would not have me fail to do what I can?'

She sighed. 'No. No. But . . . take care, Vicky. Oh, take care.'

Lennox bent to pat her hand, then dug spurred heels into his beast's flanks.

Ludovick smelt the tang of smoke on the chill east wind before ever he saw the fitful glow of fire. The evil taint of it caught at more than his nostrils and throat. He flogged his weary mount the harder.

He saw the dark loom of the sea, and the red glare of flames at the same moment, as he breasted a low ridge, the one against the other. The house of Donibristle stood on a pleasant grassy headland of the Forth estuary midway between the burghs of Inverkeithing and Aberdour, six miles from Dunfermline. A tall narrow tower-house, rather than any castle, Moray's father had built it here instead of on the island itself, a couple of miles off-shore, when his royal sire had granted him the abbacy of St. Colm's Abbey; it was a deal more convenient than being marooned out there on Inch Colm amongst the seals and guillemots. Moray's widowed mother, the Lady Doune, still made it her home. But would not, it seemed, after this night.

Appalled, Lennox stared. There was no doubt that the flames came from the house; he could just glimpse the lofty outline of it intermittently against the glare, though the smoke and the dusk confused sight. This was worse than he had feared.

He spurred headlong down to the lower ground, through copse and farmland. He passed groups of cottars gazing, horror-struck. Soon, above the drumming of his horse's hooves, he heard on the wind the hoarse shouts of men. Then a woman's thin screaming.

At a gateway to the demesne itself, two mounted guards came rearing out of the shadows of trees to bar his progress, Gordons with broadswords drawn.

'Back! Back! Halt, you!' Highland-sounding voices cried. 'In Gordon's name – halt!'

'Aside, fools!' the younger man flung at them. 'I am Lennox. The Duke. Stand aside.'

His authoritative tone seemed to impress one of the sentries, but not the other. With a flood of Gaelic this individual blocked his way, sword point flickering wickedly in the ruddy uncertain light of fire. Ludovick had to pull back his mount to its haunches, and drag its head round.

'Knave! Idiot!' he shouted. 'Out of my way! I am from the King,' he lied. 'Do you not know me – your lord's good-brother, the Duke of Lennox?'

That last appeared to penetrate, and they let him past, if doubtfully.

With those flames as beacon, he rode on, down to the little headland. With a measure of relief he perceived as he drew close that it was not exactly the house itself that was burning – although it probably would be, very shortly. It was brushwood heaped high all around its stone walls that was blazing, and busy figures, black and devilish against the red, were running to and fro, adding fuel to the conflagration – pine-tree branches, hay from the nearby farm-steading, implements and furnishings from the farm itself, anything which would burn and smoke. The smoke, without a doubt, was as important as the flame. Moray was in process of being smoked out.

These stone towers, with iron-grilled outer doors, stone vaulted basements, and lower windows too small to admit a man, were all but impregnable, save to artillery. But smoke, skilfully applied, could render them untenable. The glass of

368

lower windows, and especially of stairway arrow-slits, smashed, and fire applied judiciously, with fierce heat to cause a great updraught of air, and the tower became little less than a tall chimney for sucking up billowing clouds of smoke. None within would be able to endure it for long. Huntly no doubt was an expert on the subject.

Nevertheless, Ludovick knew some relief. At least, since they were still piling on fuel, Moray was presumably still untaken and safe, however uncomfortable. There might yet be time.

Above the crackling of the fire, Lennox began to distinguish the louder reports of spasmodic shooting. Then, against the glare, he perceived occasional brighter flashes from the topmost windows of the house, especially from the watch-chamber that surmounted the stair-tower. Moray was fighting back, then – no doubt trying to pick off the hurrying figures that were feeding the flames. Shots, too, came from various dark groups on the ground, scattered around the house, firing arquebuses, hackbuts and dags at the upper windows.

Throwing himself off his horse, Lennox hurried to the first of these groups. Somewhere nearby a woman was sobbing hysterically.

'Where is Huntly?' he demanded. 'My lord of Huntly – where is he?'

Only one man so much as deigned to glance at him. 'Who asks, cock-sparrow?'

'I am Lennox. The Duke. Chamberlain of this realm. I ask in the King's name.'

The other cleared his throat. 'Och, well. I'ph'mm. Yonder's himself, my lord. By the horses. There, at yonder tree . . . '

Ludovick ran forward. To windward of the blaze he could distinguish Huntly's tall and ponderous figure now, steel half-armour on top of the tartans which he had worn for hunting. He stood with some others just back from gunshot range of the house.

'George!' Lennox cried, panting a little. 'What . . . what folly is this? Have you taken leave of your wits?'

'Precious soul of Christ!' The big man whirled round. 'Vicky Lennox! How a God's name came *you* here?'

369

'Following you. From Barnbougle. In haste. Praying that I would be in time.'

'Eh . . . ? Aye, you are in time, a plague on it! The fox is still holed up in his cairn! But we'll have him out soon, never fear. A curse on him!'

'No!' the younger man cried. 'Not that, George. You must stop it . . .'

'Stop it? Are you crazy, Vicky? Who says so?'

'I do. Listen to me, George. You cannot do this. This evil thing . . .'

'Sink me — what brought you yapping at my heels, boy?' Huntly demanded frowning blackly. 'Has our Jamie changed his mind, then? So soon?'

'Yes! Yes — that is it.' Ludovick clutched at any straw. 'I have come from him. From the hunt. No harm is to come to Moray. No harm, d'you hear?'

'I hear pap-sucking and belly-wind!' the other snorted. 'Think you that I am a bairn like yourself? If James Stewart cannot remain of one mind for two minutes on end, Gordon can! Gordon will do what Gordon came to do!'

'No, George — you shall not! You are not in your North now. The King's rule runs here — not Gordon's!'

'Faugh!' Huntly hooted his opinion of the King's rule. 'Besides, I have your King's decree to take Moray. Here in my pouch. Signed with his own hand.'

'To take. Not to harm. Not to burn, to shoot . . .'

'Think you not so?' The other grinned.

'No, I tell you! The King at least has come to his senses in this. You are not to do it.'

'If the fool resists the King's orders, he must take the consequences.'

'Not this. Not burning, slaying. Not murder. Moray is of the blood-royal. You cannot do it.'

'No? You watch me then, boy. Watch Gordon!'

'I say no! In the King's name. I am Chamberlain and High Admiral of this realm. I command that you call off your men. Douse those fires.' Ludovick's voice cracked a little as it rose.

'And I am Gordon — and no man commands in my presence! Nor do puppies bark! Out o' my way, loon — this is man's work, not laddie's!'

'I warn you, George – if harm befalls Moray . . . '

'Hold your fool tongue, boy!' the other snarled, and turned away.

Donibristle House seemed now to be a roaring inferno. How any survived, even in the topmost storey, was a mystery, for clouds of smoke were belching out of all the broken upper windows. Yet shots continued to be fired from some of the same windows.

An outbreak of shouting from round at the west side of the house, where the smoke was thickest, attracted attention. Soon one of his Highland swordsmen came running, to inform Huntly that two of the defenders had bolted from the tower by leaping out of a third-floor window on the roof of a range of outbuildings and so to the ground, under cover of the smoke blown to that side on the east wind. Both had been caught, however, and were now suitably dead. Apparently they were mere craven Lowland hirelings.

Huntly reacted swiftly. If two had done this, others might also. Moray himself, perhaps. They would scarce win out any other way, now. The place would repay watching. The Earl led his group of lairds thither. Lennox, ignored, followed on.

In the lee of the building, the heat and smoke was highly unpleasant. Soon they were all coughing, with eyes smarting and running, complaining that they could see little or nothing.

In the event it was their ears which warned them. The shooting from the tower seemed to have stopped. That could mean either that the remaining defenders had been overcome by the fumes, or that they might be seeking to make their escape.

'Watch you, now!' Huntly shouted to his minions. 'We'll have the tod out now, I vow!' He drew his broadsword with a grim flourish.

'George – put back that sword!' Lennox exclaimed tensely. 'For Henrietta's sake, if naught else.'

'Glenderry!' Huntly commanded. 'Keep you an eye on my lord Duke. I hold you responsible for him. I will have no interferences – you understand? Use what force you must, should he be foolish. See you to it.'

'I' faith, if your bullies lay hands on me, George, they shall suffer! And you also. I swear it!' Ludovick cried. 'I swear likewise, that if you harm Moray, in capturing him, you will pay a dear price . . . '

'Quiet, fool! Enough of your babe's puling. See to it, Glenderry . . . '

A volley of shouts interrupted him. Fingers, weapons, were pointing. Dimly to be distinguished in the swirling smoke, men had appeared on the outhouse roof. This was itself now ablaze. Even as they stared, part of it fell in with a crash and a shower of sparks – and one of the men with it. His screams shrilled high – and then ceased abruptly. There were still three left, four, crouching desperate figures, crawling on the steep flame-spouting roof.

From as near-by as they dared approach, watchers mocked them and skirled, swords ready.

In a window higher in the tower, a man appeared framed, a fearsome spectacle, ablaze from head to foot. Arms flailing wildly, he leapt out and down, for the roof a dozen feet below. Blinded, no doubt, by smoke and pain, he misjudged, struck only the edge of the guttering, and plunged another twenty feet to the ground, there to lie still. The impact extinguished some of his fire, but not all.

Huntly hooted. 'This is better than Patrick Gray's fireworks!' he chuckled. 'The pity he is not here to see it.'

'Christ God – save these men!' Lennox shouted. He would have rushed forward, but strong arms held him on either side.

The men on the roof were jumping now – a long jump. Broadswords, dirks, flickered redly in the lurid light, to receive them should they survive. Taunts, challenges, rang out.

Then a kilted warrior came running round the south front of the house, calling for Huntly. Two men had won out of a window on the east side, he reported breathlessly. By a rope of sorts. Proper men, richly dressed. Buckie thought that one could be Moray himself.

Huntly delayed not a moment. For his bulk he was extraordinarily nimble on his feet. Bellowing for men to follow him, he rushed off round the house, cursing furiously.

His minions streamed after him. Ludovick, sensing that the men who were holding him were straining to do likewise, dragged forward also. They all went, running.

A single swordsman awaited them at the other end of the

house. He pointed southwards, seawards.

Strung out, stumbling in the darkness, tripping over stones and obstructions, they raced on, armour clanking. The house stood a mere couple of hundred yards back from the shore. The beach was narrow, stony.

Panting hugely, Huntly came to the edge of the sea-grass, where a group of men stood, dark against the faint luminosity of the sea.

'Fiend seize me – where are they?' he demanded, spluttering. 'Buckie – why in God's name are you standing there?'

Gordon of Buckie, a dark hatchet-faced man, broadsword in one hand, dirk in the other, grinned. 'Never fear, my lord,' he answered, and pointed. 'See you there. I but waited for you.'

All stared whence he gestured. Over there, a little way to the east, amongst the rocks and reefs of the shore, something glowed dully red.

'By the Rood!' Huntly gasped. 'You mean . . . you mean . . . ?'

'Aye – yonder he is. My bonnie lord o' Moray. Singed a mite – but all fowl are better so to pluck and truss, are they not? He conceives himself to be hidden . . . '

'You are certain that he it is, man?'

'To be sure, yes. He was well illuminated as he ran, my lord!' Buckie chuckled. 'His hair burned but indifferently – but the plume of his helm flared like a torch. As good as a beacon. Yon is the stump of it you see, I wager. Wiser he would have been to throw it into the sea.'

'He is not alone, your man said?'

'No. Another is with him, there. Him they call Dunbar, the Sheriff of Moray, I think. Sore hurt, I believe. Else Moray might have fared better, for he is an agile carle. He was aiding him . . . '

'Aye. Come, then. Let us finish the matter.'

'George Gordon!' Lennox cried, from the rear. 'Moray is to suffer no hurt. No further hurt. I charge you, in the King's name. Before all these. Heed well . . . '

'Mother o' God! Does that cockerel still crow?' Huntly threw back over his plaided and corseleted shoulder. 'Quiet, loon!'

373

Down they streamed towards the tell-tale glow of smouldering stump of proud horse-hair helmet-plume. Too late its owner realised that his position was discovered. Springing up, and by his height and splendid stature revealing himself to be Moray indeed, the fugitive looked as though he might seek to bolt still further along that rock-bound shore. Then glancing down, presumably at his wounded companion amongst the weed-hung boulders, he straightened wide shoulders, shrugged, and raised his voice.

'I am the Earl of Moray,' he called. 'I yield me.' And he threw his sword from him, towards them. It fell amongst the stones with a ringing clatter.

The chorus of shouts that greeted his gesture might have come from a pack of wolves, Huntly's own fierce vituperation high amongst them.

Down upon the unarmed man the yelling crew rushed. Moray stood waiting. Above the shadows of the rocks his upper half was clearly illuminated in the glare of the burning house. He wore no armour, other than the helmet. His fine clothing was blackened and soiled. His long fair hair, that normally fell to his shoulders, was burned away unevenly almost to the edges of the helmet.

Too late he perceived that his surrender meant nothing to his attackers; that there was no mercy for him here. He turned, and started to run towards a black crevice amongst great rocks – no cave, but perhaps some shelter and shield from flanking blows; but Gordon of Buckie, fleet of foot, headed him off. Leaping boulders like any deer, his broadsword lifted, and he brought it slashing down upon the Earl's shoulder and back.

With a choking cry, Moray whirled round, his fine frame bent, twisted to one side, to lean against a rock, gasping. He thrust out both hands, empty – although one drooped limply.

Buckie drew back his sword, laughed aloud, and lunged forward again with his full force, to run the other right through the belly.

Coughing, vomiting, groaning, Moray sank to the stones, the steel still transfixing him.

Yelling, the others came surging round the prostrate Earl. But as they stared down at the convulsive figure, their cries died away. Even Huntly was silent.

Not so Gordon of Buckie. 'There is your tod, Huntly!' he cried out. 'Your fox out of its cairn. Is it Huntly's fox – or only Buckie's? Where's your steel, my lord? Your steel?'

His chief drew a deep breath, clenched his teeth, and raising his sword, hacked it down, right across the dying man's upturned face.

The moaning shudder which followed that ghastly blow was not only Moray's.

Ludovick's shocked cry of horror died away as a thick uncouth sound came from the riven mouth itself, that spouted blood blackly over the stones. Out of the jumble, words came with infinite difficulty, slowly, one by one.

' . . . Huntly . . . you Hieland . . . stot! You ha' . . . spoiled . . . a better . . . face . . . than . . . your own! May . . . God . . . '

A great spate of blood came gushing, and the voice choked and gurgled, not to silence, but to incoherence.

As of one accord the company fell upon the twitching, writhing body, flailing, slashing, stabbing, with dirk and broadsword and whinger.

Lennox was violently sick on the shingle of the beach.

Chapter Twenty-two

SCOTLAND seethed like a cauldron on the boil. The bonnie Earl of Moray was dead, slain foully by Huntly, by the King, by the Master of Gray, by the Catholics. Moray was of the kirk's persuasion, if less than zealously. From every pulpit in the land thundered furious denunciation, protest, demands for retribution, fierce attacks on the King. Moray, the idol of the faithful, must be avenged. The Papists must be crushed. Huntly must die. Parliament must assemble and express the people's horror and detestation.

Moray, of course, had been a notable performer with the football, the boxing-glove, the tennis-racquet and the golf-club. Even Mary the Queen's death at the hands of Elizabeth, five years before, had not aroused such a clamour.

James dared not appear in the streets of Edinburgh for fear of being hooted and jeered at, even having refuse pelted at him. Moray's hacked and battered corpse was brought to the family burial ground at Leith for public display in the kirkyard there, by his mother, displaying her own singed grey hair and refusing burial for her son until she was granted vengeance. A Campbell, daughter of MacCailean Mhor himself, Earl of Argyll, she was not one to be content with half measures.

On Patrick Gray's advice James persuaded Huntly to ward himself in the West Lothian fortress of Blackness Castle, meantime. It was not truly a warding, of course, for Huntly swaggered there in style with all his men, indeed kept up almost princely state within its extensive walls and went out hunting in the adjoining woodlands, inviting James as his guest. But it did enable the King to declare that he was taking steps, and that justice would be done. He also announced that he had evidence linking Moray with Bothwell's treasonable attempts, and that was why Huntly had been sent to arrest him. This scarcely satisfied many, needless to say, but it made a gesture towards public opinion. More effective, again on Patrick's advice, was James's announcement that he had sent Lennox hot-foot after Huntly as soon as he had heard rumours that the Gordons might carry out the arrest over-vigorously. Unfortunately, the Duke had arrived too late. Moray had resisted lawful arrest, fired on Huntly from his tower, and largely ordained his own fate.

Since there was nothing to be gained by bringing the King into lower public estimation than he enjoyed already, Ludovick kept quiet. He did not leave James, or Patrick Gray either, in any private doubt however as to his opinions and feelings. The rift between them widened.

Lennox had gone back to Dunfermline that dire night, eventually. On hearing his news, Queen Anne had taken to her bed, and had there remained for almost an entire week. She ate little or nothing, permitted only her closest women near her, and received no single visitor – save, strangely enough, at the end of the week, Patrick Gray. He came to comfort her, and to urge a prompt return to her husband's side, pointing out that this separation did not look well in view

of the popular slanders anent herself and the late lamented
Moray. All who had the privilege to know Her Grace realised
how baseless was such talk, how true and leal was her devotion
to her royal and loving spouse; nevertheless, undoubtedly
monarch and consort being parted at this difficult time was
arousing comment and speculation. Also it would much please
her devoted admirers, Patrick Gray in especial, if Her Highness
would restore to them the sun of her presence at Holyroodhouse.

Anne agreed to consider the matter.

It was as Patrick left the royal bedchamber that Mary Gray
awaited him.

'Can you spare me a moment, Patrick?' she asked, even-
voiced.

'Why, my dear – need you ask? Always I can do that, and
more. It is my pleasure.'

Without answering, she showed him into an anteroom, and
closed the door behind them.

Ruefully he eyed her. 'Do I sense, moppet, that in some
way I have transgressed? Displeased you? Of what am I to be
convicted, now?'

She turned to face him. 'Any displeasure of mine matters
nothing,' she said. 'If your conscience does not convict you,
how shall I?'

'Conscience?' he repeated. 'Ah, me – a chancy and
unreliable witness! What is conscience, my heart? An irrational
sense of guilt, largely affected by what one ate for supper the
night before? Regret for aspects of failure? One is seldom
conscience-stricken, I find, over successes! Fear of consequences? I am suspicious of too active a conscience, Mary.'

'Words, Patrick,' she gave back, levelly. 'Easy and fine
words. Always you have them in plenty. But words will not
serve to bring back my lord of Moray to life. Words will not
undo what has been done.'

'Why no, lass. But should not you address your homily to
Huntly? He it was, I understand, who unfortunately made an
end of the so popular Moray. Not your erring sire.'

'Was it? she asked flatly.

He raised slender brows at her. 'That was my impression.'

'But not mine, I fear. Would that it was. Nor Vicky's.
Huntly's was only the hand that struck the blow, I think.

377

Your's was the mind that planned it so, was it not?'

His beautiful features, that so nearly mirrored her own, went completely expressionless. '*I* think that you go too fast, my dear,' he said softly. 'Too fast and far.'

She shook her head. 'I have watched you working for months to pull Moray down. As you have pulled down so many. You conceived him as in your way. Now he is dead. Whether you ordained his killing or no, I think that you knew that Huntly intended his death. And did naught to stay him. I see blood on your hands, therefore.'

'You see phantoms! Vain imaginings, girl,' he returned, more sharply now. 'You, in your wisdom, think this and think that! How can you tell what I know or plan or intend? How could I know that Huntly intended the death of Moray – if he did?'

'Vicky saw his parting from you. At the hunt. He heard the King's instructions. You were at the King's side. Vicky said . . . '

'Aye – Vicky! Always it is Vicky! That young man that I cherished is, I fear, become a viper in my bosom! It seems that I shall have to deal with Vicky.'

'No!' she cried, alarm widening her eyes. 'Not that! Never Vicky . . . '

'Then tell him to keep his fingers out of my affairs, Mary.' Patrick recovered his smile. 'With all suitable parental diffidence, my dear, I would suggest that you might even do the same! For your own sweet sake, if not mine!'

'You . . . you are warning me, Patrick?' she put to him. 'Warning me off?'

'Why, not so, my heart. I would do nothing so unseemly. I but plead with you not to meddle in affairs beyond you, lest you burn your pretty little fingers. Which I would not like to see. You cannot label that a warning, I vow!'

'No? Then let me offer you a similar plea, Patrick,' she said, calm again. 'Do not seek to bring any more men low. Cast down no others. You used Huntly to bring down Moray. Now, brute-beast as Huntly is, I fear for him. As I fear for Bothwell still. Sometimes, I even fear for the King himself!'

Their eyes met, and held. He did not speak.

'Oh, Patrick,' she exclaimed, in a different voice. 'Will

378

you not stop it? Make an end of it. For Marie's sake. For little Andrew's. And Davy's. And mine. Who love you. Will you not?'

He drew a long breath. 'You dream, girl,' he said. 'You deceive yourself.'

'No. For I know you, you see.'

'How do you know?'

'I know you, because I know myself. We are none so different, perhaps, you and I. So, I beg you, I entreat you, I urge you – hold your hand. Lest . . . lest . . . '

'Aye,' he said, eyes narrowing. 'Lest what?'

'Lest I forget that I am your daughter. And do . . . do what I conceive to be right. My duty, Patrick.'

Long he looked at her, searching her lovely elphin face, staring deep into her dark eyes, as though to probe to the very core of her being. Then abruptly, without another word, he swung about and left her there, striding to the door and out.

She stood alone, trembling a little, gazing blindly at the open door.

Anne returned to Holyroodhouse two days later, and Mary with her. James made a great show of welcoming her, riding out with half his Court as far as the Queen's Ferry, to escort her to the city and the palace. To emphasise their happy conjugal bliss a touching ceremony was organised at the West Port, where carefully selected representaives of the citizenry presented the allegedly pregnant young Queen with items of baby-wear, and James made a speech in Latin, with droll obscenities in Greek and Hebrew, initimating the joys and privileges of fatherhood, and the realm's felicity in anticipating the arrival of an heir to the throne. He even patted his wife's stomach, in an excess of enthusiasm – although it had to be admitted that Anne, pale and drawn and unsmiling, had never looked slimmer.

Unfortunately the cosily domestic atmosphere engendered by this scene was rather spoiled by the appearance in the crowd of some rude fellows leading a horse on which was displayed a man-size picture of the Earl of Moray. It was no ordinary picture this, for the Lady Doune had had it painted of her son lying outstretched on the ground, naked save for a loin-cloth, and most obviously and unpleasantly dead, his body hacked, slashed and punctured with major realism. Queen Anne all but swooned away at the sight of it – indeed she would have fallen from the saddle had not Patrick Gray ridden alongside to catch and support her bodily. From immediately behind, Mary Gray spurred her mount forward at the same time, and across the Queen's swaying person man's and girl's eyes met for an instant, tensely.

James, ever affected drastically by the sight of blood, even painted blood apparently, gobbled in horror, dug spurs into his horse's flanks, and slapping high hat hard down, went galloping off down towards the Grassmarket, scattering the crowd right and left, and leaving wife and entourage behind.

The royal procession took a deal of reorganising thereafter.

The ball which had been hastily arranged for that night at Holyroodhouse, was as hastily cancelled on account of the Queen's indisposition.

In the weeks that followed, the bonnie Earl of Moray continued to make a greater impact on the affairs of the realm in death than ever he had done in life. Various determined folk saw to that. The Kirk promoted him to the status of Protestant martyr, and inspired true believers to make pilgrimage to the kirkyard at Leith, where his unburied body still was on gruesome display, with an armed guard of the faithful on duty day and night to ensure that the King's men did not spirit it away or unsuitably inter it. Parallel with this beatification of the martyr of Donibristle, came a steady series of demands to the King and Privy Council that rigorous steps should be taken against Huntly; Catholicism should be proscribed and made a penal office; and Parliament called to enact laws to make Presbyterianism the official church government for all time coming, and to remove all bishops, abbots and commendators from the seats they held in Parliament.

The Lady Doune was tireless in keeping her son's memory not so much green as red. She paraded the streets, not only with her painting, but with Moray's rent and blood-stained shirt as banner, picqueting the Holyroodhouse gates day after day. She involved her brother Argyll and much of Clan Campbell in the business. It was said that she kept re-singeing her own and her daughter's hair, to counteract the healing effects of time.

As well as oratory, art and pageantry, poetry and literature also seemed to gain new life out of the death of Scotland's posthumous hero. The country was flooded with printed verses, songs, lampoons and pamphlets on the subject, extolling the virtues and beauties of the deceased, his royal blood, proclaiming that he was the Queen's true love, and hinting that in the circumstances the hand behind Huntly's was not far to seek. Since printing was a new and expensive process, the quantity and distribution of these compositions held its own significance.

Mary Gray, watching the Master these days like any hawk, came to the conclusion that for once he had made a grievous miscalculation in his statecraft, had quite failed to estimate public reaction to Moray's death. Until, that is, one day the Lady Marie showed her a scrap of paper which she had found in the pocket of one of Patrick's doublets, given to her for cleaning. It was in his own handwriting, and consisted of a couple of verses of a typical – if better composed than usual – panegyric on Moray, insinuations of the King's guilt, and demand for vengeance. Certain words had been scored out here and there and improved upon, in the same hand. And Maitland's name was included amongst those who were to be held responsible for the tragedy.

Obviously here was much food for thought.

James was forced, in varying degrees, to bow to pressure. A judicial enquiry was at last ordered into the allegations against Huntly – and in due course and not unnaturally, found that nobleman innocent of any greater offence than over-zealousness in discharge of his appointed duty. With Gordons innumerable parading Edinburgh streets, hands on dirks, such a verdict was entirely realistic. The Cock o' the North emerged from Blackness Castle vindicated, and after a single high-spirited demonstration in Edinburgh, sensibly set out for his own North, where Protestant lords like Atholl, Forbes, the Marischal and Grant had been at play while the cat was away.

The Lowlands heaved a premature sigh of relief.

Lord Chancellor Maitland, who had been keeping much in the background of late anyway, came to the conclusion that overwork was affecting his health, and with the King's permission retired to his house of Thirlestane in the Borderland for a vacation of unstipulated duration. No acting-chancellor was appointed but the Master of Gray, with all his wide experience, was at the realm's disposal at all times.

A Parliament was called for June, to consider the Kirk's demands on church government, bishops and the like, and other weighty matters. One of these, curiously enough was a claim put forward by the Master of Gray against the royal treasury; a notably large claim amounting to the peculiar sum of no less than £19,983 – pounds Scots, of course, since there was nothing like that sum in gold or English pounds in all the land. This claim, it transpired, was reimbursement and interest allegedly due to the Master for private monies expended on the nation's business during his previous period of acting-chancellor six years before. The King had signified his assent to this substantial requisition – indeed there were rumours that he was much more deeply involved, and that the whole thing was merely a plot on the part of Patrick and himself to lay hands on a deal of ready money that had recently accrued to the treasury through a spate of fines and forfeitures, to share it between them. Be that as it might, the Lord Treasurer, the unco-operative Master of Glamis, had his reservations, and the matter was to go before the Parliament.

Embalmed now, the corpse of the Earl of Moray remained unburied at Leith, a symbol and a challenge.

With Huntly safely out of the way and fully occupied in the North, Bothwell re-emerged from the wilds of Liddesdale, and took up his threat against the King more or less where he had left off. He was said to be at Crichton, at Hailes, in the Merse with the Homes, at Fast Castle with Logan of Restalrig. True or false, peaceable folk groaned in spirit.

It was only a day or two before the Parliament that Lennox came seeking Mary Gray in the Queen's quarters of the palace. Without ceremony he extracted her from the company of her colleagues, and taking her by the arm led her into the privacy of a tiny turret chamber.

'Sakes, my lord Duke!' she exclaimed. 'You are exceedingly ducal today! Should I be honoured? I so seldom see you now. You are so ducally busy. Closeted with my lord of Mar, with Master Andrew Melville, consulting with the Earl of Atholl, and, they say, with Chancellor Maitland away at Thirlestane.

Even, whisper it, while you are down in those parts, with Bothwell himself . . . !'

'Who said that?' he jerked. 'Patrick?'

'Why, no. Patrick no longer honours me with his confidences. I had it from the Master of Orkney, the Lady Marie's brother. He hears most of what goes on at Court, I have found.'

'I'd liefer you discussed my affairs with others than that lecherous clown, Mary,' he said stiffly.

Surprised, the girl eyed him. 'Vicky – this is strange, from you. He was but idly gossiping. About all and sundry . . . '

'What else did he gossip to you? About me?'

'So! There is something in it all then, Vicky? I did not believe it . . . '

'Well?'

'He said that you were set on being named second man in the kingdom. By this Parliament. Next heir to the throne. I could not credit that. It did not sound like you, Vicky. Do not tell me that it is true?'

'Aye,' the young man said heavily. 'It is true. In some measure. Not that I care anything for such, myself. As you well know. It is but to forestall the Lord Hamilton. He is known to be going to claim that position. His great-grandmother was a daughter of King James the Second. Why he is making the claim, I know not. But it is feared that he has ill designs. I am closer to the Throne than he, so this has been projected. That Parliament should name me as next heir, lacking issue of the King. Lest Hamilton and his friends make trouble . . . '

Mary all but moaned. 'More of it!' she whispered. 'This . . . this sounds like Patrick again, Vicky. Is it? Is he behind this intrigue? I vow it was never the King's doing. It smells of Patrick!'

'No. He has no hand in it. He has few dealings with me, now. He may be behind Hamilton's claim – I know not. But not this of mine. It is Atholl who led me to it. And Master Melville. The Kirk party do not trust Hamilton. It appears that they trust me. They believe that they can carry sufficient votes in this Parliament . . . '

'Yet Patrick is seeing a deal of my lord of Atholl, these days.

And he dined with Master Melville but two nights ago. Oh, Vicky – have naught to do with it! I suspect it. I do so . . . '

'It is but for the good of the realm, Mary. It is only a gesture. To give Hamilton pause. Anne will have a child – even if she is not pregnant yet. Besides, it is gone too far for me to withdraw now. And it but states the truth. That I am the next heir if James lacks children – as we have always known.'

'It is dangerous,' she insisted. 'I feel it, I sense it. Do not lend yourself to plots and intrigues, Vicky – whosoever concocts them. They are not for you.'

'I am Chamberlain and Admiral of this realm, Mary. I have been Viceroy. I cannot shut my eyes to what concerns its weal . . . ' Abruptly he abandoned the lofty and dignified tone that came so unnaturally to him, and was at once his normal, urgent and unaffected self again. 'Mary,' he declared, 'heed none of all this. Not now. It is not important. For us. It is not what I came to tell you. I . . . I . . . Mary – Sophia is dead!'

'Sophia Ruthven! Your . . . your wife! She is dead? Oh, Vicky!'

'I have just had word. Her mother, the Lady Gowrie, is new come from Ruthven. She was buried four days back. Of a flux of blood. A consumption.'

'I am sorry, sorry. She was so young. So unhappy. To die alone! You had not even seen her? Her mother did not send for you?'

'No. She did not want me. Her mother says it, and I know it. We meant nothing to each other. You know it, also. I am sorry for her, Mary – sorry that she suffered so. But she was ill when we were wed. She should never have been married. Now she is gone. I cannot mourn her – else I make myself a hypocrite. I think her better dead, indeed, than as last I saw her – coughing in her pain, weeping in her misery . . . '

The young woman nodded, sighing. 'I know, Vicky. I am sorry – for you both. It was a hard thing for both of you. But worse for her. Always it is worse for the woman. A bad marriage, a marriage without affection and trust, is for a woman utter woe and disaster.'

'Is that what *you* fear, Mary?' He took her shoulder, and turned her to face him. 'Do you fear a bad marriage? To me?'

'To you, Vicky? No – no, not that. That is not what I fear. How can I fear the impossible? *We* cannot marry . . . '

'But we can. I am free, now. To marry again. To marry you, Mary.'

Unhappily the young woman shook her head. 'You are not, Vicky – you are not! Nothing has changed. You must see it. Do not shut your eyes. Do not be blind to what all others can see. We can never marry, you and I. A moment ago you were reminding me of who and what you were. Great Chamberlain of Scotland. Lord High Admiral. Next heir to the throne. How can you be all these, and marry the daughter of Davy Gray, the land-steward?'

'All know that you are in fact the Master of Gray's daughter. His mother was Gowrie's sister. So you are indeed cousin to Sophia, once removed.'

'Removed by a great gulf. Not legitimate. Either I am the steward's daughter, and honest. Or I am illegitimate. Neither will make a wife for the Duke of Lennox. That is certain. The realm, whose weal you would serve, would not allow it. Ever.' Her voice quivered. 'Accept it, Vicky. As I do. I thank you for your . . . your devotion. Your love. And for asking. But do not ask it again, I beseech you. Never again. For, for I cannot bear it!'

It was Mary Gray's turn to cut short an interview. She turned in a swirl of skirts, and ran from that little chamber, blindly enough to collide with the door-post as she went.

Chapter Twenty-three

THE Countess of Atholl was vastly unlike her recently deceased sister Sophia Ruthven. Much the eldest of Lady Gowrie's children, she was a bold piece in more ways than one. That she it was who probably played the part of Leda to Patrick's swan at the Falkland pageant, was doubted by none on the score of boldness at least. This early summer morning, however, she was playing a part still bolder than in any pageant. An extra

Lady-in-Waiting to the Queen, who yet lodged, not in the palace of Holyroodhouse itself, but in her mother's house in the Abbey Strand close by, she was one of the very few persons who held a key enabling her to use the small postern gate which led in through the old Abbey precincts to the palace itself. This morning she brought in by this her usual route two servitors wearing the Atholl colours and bearing large baskets filled with delicacies for the Queen's Grace. One of the bearers, although he stooped notably, could be seen to be an exceptionally tall man.

Such guards as were on duty at that hour yawningly saluted the Countess and betrayed no interest in her servants. Most of the palace's occupants still slept deep, only two or three hours abed indeed after a great ball and masque held therein to mark the penultimate day of the momentous sitting of the Estates of Parliament; this had been a brilliant function in the organisation of which the Master of the Wardrobe had excelled himself, despite the stresses and tensions of the moment. If Lady Atholl looked a little less challenging-eyed and provocative than usual, she had her excuse, for she had, as ever, taken a major part in the procedings and had not been to bed since.

Life seemed to be stirring only in the kitchens and domestic quarters of the great rambling establishment, and the trio made their way, without meeting others, towards the drum tower from which were reached the royal apartments. At the great doors in the tower's foot, a double guard of four men was even reinforced by a fifth – no less a person than the Captain of the Royal Guard himself, John, Earl of Mar. The Countess found a brief smile for him. With only an inclination of his head, he turned and led the way upstairs, the guard remaining at their posts.

Halfway up the winding turnpike stair, the couple paused, by mutual consent, to glance through the window overlooking the main forecourt of the palace. Down there a large addition to the guard was in process of being posted at the gates and along the flanking walls, many men, fully armed. Two figures, conspicuous as not being in the livery of the Royal Guard, stood out, recognisable as the Earl of Atholl and the Duke of Lennox. Both kept glancing up and back towards the drum-tower windows. Mar and the Countess moved closer to the glass so that they might be seen. They raised their hands.

There were brief nods from the two noblemen below, as they turned away.

The first floor landing opened on to two apartments, the royal pages' room and that of the ladies-in-waiting. In the first, two young men slept, one on a bed, the other, fully clad, sprawled over a table; this latter was Thomas Erskine, a cadet of Mar's own family. Quietly the Earl closed the door and turned the key in the lock.

The Countess listened at the second door. This was locked on the inside, as well it might be with the royal pages so close; but the duty Lady-in-Waiting who slept beyond it was her own youngest sister, the Lady Beatrix Ruthven.

Exchanging nods, Mar and Lady Atholl proceeded quietly up the second stairway, the two servitors still following.

The same arrangement of two doors prevailed on the second landing. These each admitted to anterooms, and off these opened the King's and the Queen's bedchambers. These were by no means the finest and most convenient bedrooms in the palace, but James, not without reason, was much concerned with security, and had selected these carefully with that in view. Although Anne's boudoir had still another anteroom beyond, which communicated with a further corridor of the palace, the King's own apartment was only reachable by this one door. None therefore could approach him save past the guard at the stair-foot and his pages on the first floor. Above was only his study in the top of the tower.

The Countess carefully opened the door of the Queen's anteroom. It was in a state of untidiness from the night's festivities. The door to the bedchamber beyond was closed. Quietly she abstracted the key from the inside of the anteroom door, transferred it to the outside, closed the door and locked it. Then she dipped in a mocking curtsy, first to Mar and then to the taller of her two attendants, and with a whisper of skirts slipped away downstairs without a word said.

The tall man straightened up. He cast off the voluminous but somewhat tattered cloak and hood of the Atholl colours which had masked both figure and features, and stood revealed, in splendid half-armour, as Francis Hepburn Stewart, Earl of

Bothwell. From the basket, beneath the sweetmeats, he drew out and buckled on his sword.

Mar beckoned, and cautiously opened the door of the King's anteroom. Peering within, he signed the others forward.

They moved inside, the third man revealing himself to be Mr. John Colville, a professional diplomat and one of the original Ruthven raiders, high in the Kirk party despite being an associate of Patrick Gray's.

Tip-toeing to the royal bedroom door, Mar listened thereat. He shook his head. With the utmost care, he tried the handle. It was locked, as anticipated, from the inside. James was unlikely ever to forget such a precaution.

The three men drew back. Mar took up a position close to the window, where he could watch the forecourt below. The other two examined the arras which hung against the stone walls, in case it should be necessary to slip behind it for cover from view. They waited, silent.

They were not long inactive. Quite soon there were sounds of stirring from the next room. Then a bout of spluttering coughing. The trio exchanged glances at the unmistakable sound of a chamber-pot being filled. Then, after some more movement, there was a loud thumping on the floor-boards beyond the door. This was the monarch's method of summoning his pages from the room directly below.

Motionless the three men stood, watching the door.

After some more thumping, the King's voice was raised in querulous shouting. 'Tam! Tam Erskine, you ill loon! Here! To me. A plague on you, you lazy limmer! Here wi' you!'

A pause. Then they heard cursing from within, and the turning of the key in the lock. The door of the royal bedroom was flung open.

James came shambling out, to halt suddenly as though transfixed, as Bothwell stepped forward into the middle of the anteroom. The King made an extraordinary figure. He was naked from his bed, apart from a dressing-robe thrown hurriedly over his sloping shoulders, and his hose which sagged down to his ankles. In one hand he clutched certain of his underwear. Never an impressive figure, he showed now to less advantage than almost ever before. A wail escaped from his slack lips.

'Eh . . . ! Eh . . . ! Christ God – Bothwell!' he gasped. 'Fran . . . Francis Bothwell!'

The Earl removed his hand from his sword-hilt to sweep off his bonnet in a deep bow, smiling but unspeaking.

The King's great liquid eyes rolled and darted. Panting, he took a single step, almost involuntarily, towards the window.

Mar moved back a pace or two, so that his broad person filled the narrow embrasure. At the same time, Colville hurried from his stance by the inner wall, and slipped past the King and into the bedchamber. It was essential for their purpose that James did not reach either of the windows, to shout to or otherwise alarm the guard in the forecourt below.

James stared from Mar to Bothwell, and back. 'Johnnie!' he choked. 'You, Johnnie! Johnnie Mar.' Then his voice rose in a bubbling yell. 'Treason!' he cried. 'Treason!'

A shade anxiously Mar glanced out and down, to see whether this dread shout had reached the massed ranks of the guard confronting the palace gates. There was no sign of alarm below, however. He raised a hand to Lennox and Atholl, who still stood there, waiting to calm and reassure the soldiers, if necessary.

Bothwell spoke, the first word of any of the conspirators. 'Not treason, Your Grace. Far from it. We but seek your good. And the good of your realm . . . '

'Liar! Traitor! Devil! 'Tis treason! You seek my life. I ken it – fine I ken it, Francis Stewart!' Wildly the King glanced behind him, to find Colville standing there within the bedroom doorway. 'Waesucks – I am betrayed! Betrayed!' he all but sobbed.

'Not so, Highness,' Mar declared urgently. 'Would *I* betray you? This is but a necessary step. To ensure your royal safety. There may be trouble. Fighting. The Papists are stirring, assembling. This Parliament has been sore on them. It is even bruited that Huntly is returning. I have the guard protecting the palace. But who knows who are your enemies within, Sire? The Hamiltons. Morton. Crawford. *We* are all good Protestants, but . . . '

'False! False!' James exclaimed. But it was at Bothwell

that he gazed, as though fascinated by those piercing, vividly blue eyes under sandy brows. Seeking to cover his nakedness in some degree, he backed against the wall. 'Satan's tool! Satan's right hand . . . !'

Bothwell grinned. 'Scarce that, Sire – or I could have arranged this a deal more conveniently by witchcraft! I come but to seek your pardon, indeed, for breaking my ward. To stand trial before my peers on the witchcraft charge, if so be that is your royal wish. And to protect Your Grace from the evil that threatens from the Papists and those who would endanger your throne.' All this, the Earl announced with an expression of mockery quite at variance with his words. 'Your Grace has cause to thank me, not to fear me.'

James gnawed at his lip, in an agony of doubt.

'It is the truth, Sire,' Mar assured. 'Fear nothing . . . '

There was a diversion. Footsteps sounded on the stairs and the landing outside, and the door opened to admit a party of gentlemen. The royal eyes widened at the sound and sight of them, and he started forward in sudden hope, forgetting his precarious modesty and all but leaving his bed-robe behind him. He faltered, stopped, one trembling hand out appealingly, the other seeking to draw together his robe and cover at least his loins with the clutched underwear.

Ludovick of Lennox came first, followed by the Earl of Atholl, the Lords Ochiltree and Innermeath, the Master of Orkney, Sir James Stewart of Eday and Sir Robert Stewart of Middleton. They all bowed to their unclothed monarch, but kept their distance at the other side of the room.

James's expression underwent a series of swift alterations, as sudden relief was banished by uncertainty, perception, renewed fear and alarm, almost despair. He recognised that every man who had come in was a Stewart, of his own house. But they had none of them come to his side. All stood ranged behind Bothwell, even Lennox. Almost, it might have seemed, they left a gap amongst them for their dead kinsman Moray.

The King tried to speak, his thick lips working. 'Vicky . . . !' he got out, at length.

That young man inclined his head slightly, but said no word.

James looked from one to the other, and back to Bothwell,

and a new gleam of hope dawned in those tell-tale eyes. He had
his own intelligence, and perceived, panic-stricken as he was,
that Bothwell could not have assembled all these fellow
Stewarts in order to murder their royal relative before their
eyes. Out of a strong sense of self-preservation, and no little
cunning, he summoned an excess of courage of a sort, deliberately changing his whole attitude and bearing. He addressed
Bothwell only, in as loud and declamatory a voice as he could
muster, dropping his underwear and drawing himself up, to
hold wide his robe, so that his nakedness should be displayed,
not hidden.

'Do your worst then, my lord,' he declared strongly, even
though the words trembled. 'I am wholly in your power.
Take your King's life. You, nor your master the Devil, shall
have his soul!'

Bothwell was scarcely to be blamed if he stared, so unlike
James Stewart was this.

'Strike, man!' the King went on, warming to his part. 'I
am ready to die. Better to die with honour than to live in
captivity and shame. Aye, better. Stay . . . stay not your steel,
Francis.'

That this was sheerest play-acting all knew well, for James's
horror of cold steel was common knowledge.

But the performer had met as keen a play-actor as himself.
Bothwell, recovering from his surprise, glanced round at his
supporters. Then he drew his sword with a dramatic flourish,
and as James involuntarily cowered back at the sight of it, he
threw himself forward. But somehow he had his sword whipped
round now, and he sank to his knees before the other, presenting the hilt to his monarch.

'Here is my sword, Sire,' he cried, to the shrinking King.
'Take it and use it on me, if you truly believe me traitor! See –
I bare my neck.' He bent his head and pushed up his sandy
hair with his left hand. 'Strike shrewd and fair, Your Grace,
if you deem me ever to have harboured a thought against your
royal person.'

James gobbled and blinked and wagged his head, hoist with
his own petard. He could no more have used sword on Bothwell, or on any man, than he could have flown in the air. On
the other hand, to do nothing, to indicate that Bothwell did

not deserve death, was to condone all, besides displaying the greatest weakness. He temporised.

'False!' he mumbled. 'Nay, kneel not, man – and add hypocrisy to treason. You ha' plotted my death. I . . . I call upon you now to execute your purpose. Aye, your purpose. For I'll no' live a prisoner and dishonoured.' That was declared with rather less conviction than before.

'Nor will I, Highness,' Bothwell assured, straightening up a little. He kissed the hilt of his sword theatrically, and thrust it almost into the King's hand once more. 'Here shall be the end of your distrust of Francis Stewart! Us it now – or trust me hereafter.'

'Waesucks! I . . . I . . . ' In his predicament, James looked appealingly at the others, especially at Lennox.

That young man, in some measure, answered the appeal. Nodding, he spoke, if stiffly. 'Your Grace, I counsel you to raise up my lord of Bothwell. We are convinced that he intends no treason. If his manner of entry here offends you, how else could he have gained your face? He can serve you well in this pass, we are assured. Heed him, Sire.'

Something like a growl of agreement came from the assembled Stewarts.

James, thankful no longer to have to look at the kneeling Earl and his outstretched sword, released a flood of disjointed eloquence. 'It's no' right. It's no' suitable. This violent repair to me. To our royal presence. Is it no' dishonourable to me? Aye, and disgraceful to my servants who allowed it? It was ill done. Am I no' your anointed King? I am twenty-seven years of age, mind. I am no' a laddie any mair, when every faction could think to make me their ain property. You hear me? It is ill done.'

All eyed him steadily. None spoke. Bothwell had risen to his feet again. He returned his sword to its scabbard, with a noticeable screak and click. Play-acting was over.

The King did not fail to perceive it, and drooped puny shoulders, drawing his robe around him again. 'What . . . what would you have, my lords?' he muttered, almost whispered.

'Your goodwill and trust, Sire – what else?' Bothwell declared, briskly now. 'Your realm is in poor state. We shall order it better for you. These are true and leal men, of your

392

own house. Trust them, if you still do not trust me.'

'Aye,' James sighed.

'Much must be done, and swiftly. Now. Before this Parliament breaks. That it may show the consent of the realm. And of the Kirk.' Bothwell paused, and waved a hand to Colville. 'But we can consider this while Your Grace dresses. Tom Erskine shall attend you forthwith. I would advise that you attend the morning session in person, Sire. To announce certain concessions. And decrees. We shall support you.'

'This morning? Aye.' There was a hint of eagerness in that. James darted a glance towards the window. 'Aye. This morning.'

Bothwell read his thoughts. 'Your Highness will be entirely secure, rest assured,' he said, with a thin smile. 'I have five score horsemen to escort you thither. And a thousand men in the city. All will be well.'

The King all but groaned.

Mar led the way into the royal bedchamber, taking care however to resume his stance at the window. James looked from him to Lennox.

'Vicky . . . ?' he began. 'Och man, Vicky!'

Ludovick inclined his head, but kept his boyish features stern, unrelenting.

'Where . . . where is Patrick? Where is the Master o' Gray, my lords?'

'In his bed no doubt, Sire,' Ludovick answered. 'We have not concerned him in this matter.'

Once more Bothwell smiled, briefly. But he made no comment.

Thus, simply, quietly, without a drop of blood shed, the fearsome, devil-possessed and unpredictable Earl of Bothwell took major if temporary control of the realm of Scotland, after more spectacular attempts innumerable. There was no clash, no active opposition. A deputation of the citizens of Edinburgh, hearing rumours from the palace, did present themselves at the gates, and by the mouth of Provost Home asked if the King required their aid, perchance? James, only too vividly able to imagine his fate during the period of waiting for any such succour, sadly dismissed them. Thereafter, he rode in the

393

midst of a strong escort of mosstroopers, Bothwell on one side, and happily the Master of Gray on the other, to the Parliament Hall, where he made a short and largely unintelligible speech conceding practically all that the Kirk party demanded, removing episcopal and prelatical seats from the legislature, and promising compensation for Moray's family, preferment for his young son and heir, and vengeance on his killers. More ringing and heartfelt cheering than he had ever known followed the monarch out into the High Street, with Bothwell doffing his bonnet right and left, and Patrick Gray singing gently beneath his breath.

A special court of the Privy Council, consisting of Bothwell's peers, the Earls of Atholl, Argyll, Mar, Orkney, Glencairn, and the Marischal, considered formally whether he could be said to be guilty of treason or conspiracy. The accused tactfully absented himself from the proceedings, but his men surrounded the court in serried ranks. After a fairly brief deliberation their lordships acquitted Francis Hepburn Stewart on both counts, and commended him to the King's grace and assured benevolence. The next day, therefore Bothwell's peace was proclaimed by the heralds at the Cross of Edinburgh, amidst much jollification and free liquor for the citizenry. The matter of the witchcraft charges, which came into a different legal category altogether, were sensibly postponed until some suitable future date.

The Earl of Bothwell invented a new title for himself – Lord Lieutenant of Scotland – with Patrick's acclaim, though Lennox and others tended to look askance at it. The Kirk set up a Committee of Security to assist in the governance of the realm. Along with a number of others, Sir Robert Cockburn of Clerkington, the Secretary of State and Chancellor Maitland's son-in-law, was summarily dismissed. Patrick Gray, with typical sense of duty, made himself responsible for his office, meantime – this despite the fact that an ungrateful Parliament had not wholly accepted his claim for the £20,000 Scots, but had feebly passed it on to a special committee to consider.

On the subject of titles and offices, the Duke of Lennox found himself relieved of that of Lord High Admiral, in favour of its previous holder. He was allowed to remain Chamberlain, however.

The Earl of Moray remained unburied. His mother, as well as being a Campbell, was a woman of distinctly sceptical and disbelieving character.

Scotland watched and waited, as it had done so often before.

Chapter Twenty-four

PETER HAY, Lennox's page, came up the winding stairway of the King's tower two steps at a time, his spurred riding-boots stamping and jingling, his sword clanking – despite the edict that no swords were to be carried within the palace. Mary Gray and the Lady Beatrix Ruthven were descending, the former carrying a tambour-frame and the latter a box of threads, for the Queen's embroidery. They met at the first floor landing.

'Mistress Mary! Here's well met,' the young man exclaimed, somewhat breathless. 'I was looking to see you.' Recollecting, he doffed his distinctly battered bonnet. 'Your ladyship,' he acknowledged perfunctorily to the other and still younger girl. 'I'd hoped I'd find you, Mistress Mary . . . '

'Why, Peter – what's the haste?' Mary asked, smiling. 'What's to do? I thought that you were at Hailes, with the others? And you are all muddy. You . . . ' Her eyes widened, and the smile left her lovely face. 'Peter – there is blood on your hands! What is it? What has happened? Is something . . . wrong?'

'Well . . . no. No, naught is wrong.' He said that without conviction, however. 'A mishap, that is all.' His glance flickered towards the interested Lady Beatrix. 'I bear a message for the Queen. From his Grace. From Hailes Castle. He sent me, for young Ramsay is sick and Erskine gone to my lord of Angus, at Tantallon. I am to escort the Queen to Hailes Castle. Forthwith. The King is to stay there long. Hunting. For some days. But . . . but I wanted to see you first, Mistress Mary . . . '

'You are not hurt, Peter? That blood . . . ? Nor, nor any other?'

395

'No. It is nothing. Not *my* blood.' He looked again towards Beatrix Ruthven. 'Can I have a word with you, Mistress Mary? Before I see the Queen?'

The younger girl laughed. 'Give me the frame, Mary. I will tell the Queen that you will be with her presently. And shall not mention Master Hay! Her Grace is in the Orangery,' she told the page.

'Thank you,' Mary acknowledged. 'I shall not delay long. Come, Peter.' She turned, and led the way back upstairs to the apartment of the Ladies-in-Waiting.

Hay closed the door behind him, and stood looking at her. His clothing was spattered with mud, and flecked with foam from a hard-driven horse. There was a tension about him that was unusual and not to be mistaken.

'What is it, Peter?' Mary demanded. 'There *is* trouble, is there not? It is not Vicky? The Duke?'

'No. He is well enough. With the King and Bothwell. It is . . . other.' Putting a hand into the deep pocket inside his riding-cloak, he drew out a bundle of papers, letters, all mud-stained and dirty, some still sealed, some opened. Laying them down on the table, he pointed to the topmost, opened, soiled and crumpled. 'No doubt I should not show you these,' he said, 'but you have a better head than any I know. Besides, you are in some way concerned. You can tell me what to do.'

Frowning, she looked from the young man to the untidy papers and back. 'What is this? What have you done?'

'I was sent back, from Hailes. With a half-troop as escort. To fetch the Queen,' he explained, jerkily. 'Crossing the Gled's Muir, this side of Haddington, we came on trouble. Fighting. Or the end of it. A bad place it is, for cut-purses and broken men – miles of it, wild and empty. These were robbers – some of Bothwell's own damned mosstroopers, I shouldn't wonder, running loose. Lacking employment. Six of them. They had waylaid and cut down two men. Travellers. They were ransacking their bags. One was opening these letters when they saw us. They bolted as we came up. We were too many for them. They threw down the letters as they went. No doubt they got the purses. Other things, maybe.'

Mary's eyes were on that topmost letter. 'I know that handwriting,' she said tight-voiced. 'And those seals, broken as they are.'

'Aye. As do I. They are the Master of Gray's,' the other agreed grimly. 'One of the travellers was dead. The other died as we sought to put him on a horse. His blood, this is. Run through again and again. The one better dressed I recognised. He was a creature of Sir Richard Bowes, the English envoy. I have seen him about the palace here. The other would be guard and servant. Couriers, clearly. Heading south. For England. With letters and dispatches for the English Court. For my lord of Burleigh and Sir Edward Wotton.'

Mary shook her head. 'How cruel! How wicked a deed! God rest their souls. But . . . ' Stepping forward she picked up the top letter. 'This, of Patrick's, was with them?'

Hay nodded. 'It was within an outer paper. Both opened. The outer was in a different writing. And with plain seals. Addressed to the Lady Diana Woodstock. In care of the Lord Burleigh, Lord Treasurer, at the Palace of Saint James, London. This other was within it. I knew the hand. I have seen many letters from the Master to the Duke. It was sealed with the Gray seals. They had been broken, also.' He paused. 'I can well guess to whom it is written!'

'Yes.'

'Read it.'

Troubled, the young woman searched the other's face, before, clearly reluctantly, she conned the letter. It read:

'Dearest and Fairest Lady,

I acknowledge, with devotion and gratitude, the last sum of £500 remitted by the usual source. I have put it, like that which went before, to good and effective use. I think that you will not deny it. Unlike certain other doles which of your kind heart you see fit to dispense, these remittances are put to excellent purpose, for your causes as for mine. As I take no doubt but that your good Master Bowes, newly knighted, will sufficiently inform you.

Now I hasten to acquaint you that all is well, very well, in the great matter which we planned. The ineffable Bothwell fell most sweetly into the trap, and now struts the stage, calling himself Lieutenant of Scotland, no less. Believing that all the event was his own doing, he now works mightily and happily his own doom. Meanwhile, as foreseen, he works also our ends for us, most obligingly. The Papists are put down. Parliament may no longer be packed with mock bishops and prelates. The Hamiltons are in fullest flight. It will rejoice you to know that the unmentionable Maitland is at last unseated, and I have plans to keep him so. Cockburn, his lumpish good-son, likewise. Your siller is well spent, Lady?

As for your esteemed young coz, he is, I promise you, learning his lesson. I am in a position to know, for he places his fullest confidence in your unworthy servant, privily informing me of his secret mind, little knowing who was the architect, with your aid, Fairest Dian, of his present humbled estate. He will flirt no more with Huntly and Spain, of that rest assured. Nor will he again allow any lord to dominate your mutual borders, once Bothwell is down. So your peace is buttressed on two fronts. I continue with his instruction, and shall not spare the rod, like a good tutor, should need arise. As advised.'

Thus ended the first sheet of paper. Mary looked up, to meet the other's gaze. Her dark eyes were clouded, as though with pain. She said nothing.

'Read on,' Hay urged, handing her a second sheet. 'This was within the first.'

Almost as though it might burn her, Mary took it. This read:

'I used the threat of Hamilton's desire for second place in this kingdom, with the ire at Moray's death, to unite the Stewarts and bring all this about, Madam. Alackaday, perhaps I something wronged poor Hamilton, who has insufficient wit I fear to desire anything thus vigorously, other than a wench and a flagon. But the fact is that our friend the young Duke is more truly smitten with that same sickness. He supported the enterprise the more readily in that he desires to see the Hamiltons laid low and his own claim to second place and heir established. Indeed, it goes further than this. I have reason to know that, once his claim is accepted – Parliament has remitted it to the next sitting – he plans to have your poor coz proclaimed insane and crazed, and unfit to reign. Himself then as Regent. Then, later, King in his stead, no less. I fear that the lad has grown over-ambitious. Can you, great Diana, contemplate Esmé D'Aubigny's son as heir to England? But fear you not. I shall deal with Master Vicky in due course. I have my plans prepared.

A further dispensation of your liberality would much aid me, I would mention.

Meanwhile, may the good God prosper all your affairs, as they now prosper here, and grant you health and well-being to match your wit and beauty. Until these poor eyes feast upon your loveliness again,

I remain, sweet lady, your humblest and most devoted servant and adorer,

P.'

'Well?' Hay demanded, when he saw that she had finished reading.

Mary moistened her lips, but for once had no words.

'You see what he says? What it means? It is lies – all lies. You know it, as do I. He knows it also – the Master of Gray. But it could mean my Duke's head, nevertheless.'

'It . . . is . . . ill . . . done,' the girl said slowly, each word standing alone.

'It is worse than that, by God!' the young man cried. 'This is as good as an assassination! Written to Elizabeth of England, who hates the house of Lennox. She will inform the King. Nothing is more sure. Higher treason than this could scarce be thought of. And all lies. My master no more desires the throne than, than . . .'

'I know it,' Mary said quietly. 'This shall not be.'

Something about her voice calmed him. 'What can we do?' he asked.

'I shall do what I should have done, long since,' she told him, levelly. 'God forgive me that I have waited this long.'

Doubtfully he eyed her.

'Patrick is still at Hailes, with the King?' she asked.

399

'Yes.'

'I shall see him, then, tonight. You said that you escort the Queen there, forthwith? This afternoon?'

'Yes. But what can you do?'

She did not seem to hear him. 'Peter,' she went on, 'take these letters to Sir Richard Bowes. All save this of Patrick's. Tell him what happened.' She leafed through the other letters. 'These are no concern of ours. Do not tell him of this one. If he knew aught of it, and asks you, you know nothing. The robbers must have taken it. You understand?'

'Aye. You will keep it?'

'Meantime, yes. And, Peter – when you have taken us to Hailes, I think that I may have a further task for you. If you will do it? Weary as you will be . . . ?'

'Anything, Mistress Mary,' he assured her.

'My thanks. Now, to the Queen. And then, while she prepares to ride, to Sir Richard Bowes' lodging.'

'Aye. You know what you will do?'

'God granting me the resolution, I do,' she said. 'Come.'

In a stone garden-house of the pleasance of Hailes Castle, in the gorge of Tyne, the only place it seemed in that crowded establishment where she could be assured to privacy, Mary Gray turned to face her father, pale, set-faced.

'This will serve I think, Patrick,' she said.

'I should hope so!' Patrick, although he laughed, considered her shrewdly. 'I warrant half the Court is watching this so secret assignment! And debating the wherefore of it. As I do also, moppet, I confess. Rejoice as I do in your company therefore, my dear, I bid you be discreetly brief. In here. Lest your reputation suffers – and I, I am labelled even worse than I am! A man who would corrupt his own daughter!'

'Would that was all that you could be labelled!' she told him flatly.

'Eh . . . ?' Startled now, he stared. 'What a plague do you mean by that?'

'I mean, Patrick, that I have come to know you for what you are. At last. I can no longer blind myself.'

Still-faced, he waited, unspeaking.

'Davy warned me,' she went on, in a curious, unemphatic,

factual voice. 'Others also, to be sure. Times a-many. But I believed that they wronged you. Deep down, they wronged you. I believed that I knew you better – because I knew myself. And loved you. We were out of the same mould, you and I. So that I understood you, as others did not. I saw the gold beneath the tarnish. But it was I who was wrong. There is no gold there. Only . . . corruption!'

Taut-featured now as she was herself, he stood motionless, scarcely seeming to breathe. Only his delicate nostrils flared, as a spirited horse's will flare. As did her own, indeed. Never had they seemed more alike, those two. 'Yes?' he said.

'You betray all with whom you have dealings,' she told him, and the unemotional, level, almost weary certainty of her utterance made the indictment the more terrible. 'You betray always, for love of betrayal. Davy said that you were a des-troyer. I know now that you are worse than that. A destroyer can at the least be honestly so. A lion, a boar, a wolf – these have their parts. But you – you seek men's trust and love, in order to destroy them. You charm before you betray. You, Patrick, are not even a wolf. You are a snake!'

'God's passion!' Blazing-eyed the Master took a step to-wards her, fists clenched, knuckles white. Almost it seemed that he would strike her. Only with a tremendous and very apparent effort of will did he hold himself back. Panting, his words came pouring out, his voice no longer musical and pleasingly modulated but harsh, strident, staccato. 'How dare you! You young fool! What do *you* know? In your in-sufferable ignorance! None speaks me so – you, nor any. Do you hear? Christ – you, of all!'

She stood, head up, unflinching, meeting his furious gaze, not challenging or defiant, but with a calm resolution, sorrow-ful but sure. She actually nodded her head. 'I know – because this time you have betrayed yourself,' she told him. 'This time it is your own words that condemn you. Written testi-mony.'

That gave him pause. He drew a deep quivering breath. 'What mean you by that?' he asked thickly.

'I mean that you have gone too far in betrayal. Even for my indulgence, Patrick. I did not believe that you had betrayed Mary the Queen, to her death. Now I do. For I have proof

401

that you have betrayed the King. And intend to do so further. You betrayed Moray, again to his death. Bothwell here, also. The Hamiltons. Even Huntly, and your Catholics. For money. For power. For revenge. For amusement, sport, no less! And now, God forgive you if He can, you have betrayed Vicky.'

'A-a-ah!'

'I warned you,' she went on inexorably. 'At Dunfermline. I warned you to cast down no more men. If you touched Vicky, I said, I would no longer forget my duty.'

'Vicky!' He spat out the name. 'That young blockhead! For him you speak me so! For that ducal dolt you would discard me? *Me*, your father! He has turned your silly head.'

'Not my head, Patrick,' she corrected. 'My heart, perhaps, but not my head. The head that I heired from you. The heart, I pray God, I heired from my mother!'

'You insolent jade! You interfering hussy! Foul fall you – are you out of your mind? Are you, girl . . . ?' The man's words faltered, however, as something of the quality of his daughter's strange certainty tempered the heat of his fury. 'What is it? Out with it! What lies has Lennox been spilling into your foolish ears?' he demanded.

'None,' she told him. 'I have not seen Vicky for three days. The lies, Patrick, are all your own! Written lies. In your letter to Queen Elizabeth.'

His lips parted, and he drew a long breath, but spoke no word.

'That evil letter will not reach Elizabeth,' she went on. 'It was . . . intercepted. I have read it . . . '

'Great God! Who . . . ? Who intercepted it? Who has seen it?' Patrick grasped her arm in his sudden urgency. 'Where is it, Mary? Not . . . not Bothwell? Or the King . . . ?'

'Would you be here, a free man, this night, had either of these seen it?'

He moistened his lips. 'Who then? I warn you, girl – do not seek to cozen me!'

'Who intercepted it matters not, Patrick. Only one other, and myself, have seen it . . . as yet.'

'Where is it, then? Who holds it?'

'I hold part of it.'

'Part? Only part?'

402

'There were two sheets, you will recollect. Within the plain outer paper. Written with your own hand, and sealed with your seal. That in which you betray Vicky, I hold. The other is ... elsewhere.'

'Elsewhere ... ?' He swallowed. 'Damnation – where?'

Mary shook her head. 'Where you cannot reach it.' Her voice quivered now. 'Patrick. I have brought you here to say goodbye.'

He stared at her. 'What nonsense is this? You mean that you are leaving Court? Going back to Castle Huntly? I' faith, it is not before time, I think! It was my folly ever to have brought you.'

'*My* going is of no matter. It is yours that is important. *You* are leaving Court, Patrick. Leaving Scotland. Forthwith.'

'Christ – are you crazed? What a plague means this? Have you clean lost your senses, girl?'

'It is my sorrow that I have been lacking my senses for so long, Patrick. That I forbore to put a halt to your evils long ere this. As I could and should have done. Because I loved you. Because I believed that there was good in you – that there *must* be good in you. How wrong I was! It is ...'

With an impatient gesture of his hand he interrupted her. 'Enough of this puling folly! Think you I must stand and listen to your childish insults?'

'You must do more than that, Patrick. You must go. Leave all.' Almost without expression she spoke. 'I warned you. If you touched Vicky, I told you, with your, your poison, I would set my hand against you.'

'So! You esteem Vicky Stuart higher than you do me, your father?'

The word was long in coming. She raised her head until her small chin was held high. 'Yes,' she said at last, simply.

Something seemed to crumple in the man, then. He turned away from her, to gaze out of that little summer-house to the towering bulk of the great castle, stained with the reflection of the sunset, his beautiful features working spasmodically.

In her turn, Mary's own hard-won resolution cracked a little. 'Oh, Patrick,' she cried, her voice breaking, 'why, oh why did you do it? How could you? To Vicky, who was like a son to you. Or a brother. Whom you brought to this land, from France. Who worshipped you. Who used to esteem you little less than a god. How could you so turn on him? To write those lies about him to Elizabeth. Knowing that she hates and fears the house of Lennox, which is too near to her own throne. Knowing what she would do. That she would be certain to tell King James.'

'Vicky has been riding too high,' the Master jerked, thickly, still not looking at her. 'He presumes. He interferes. Since Moray's death he has set himself against me . . . '

'With cause, has he not? Did not *you* kill the Earl of Moray, Patrick – even though it was Huntly's hand that struck the blow? You planned his death?'

'Not his death. Only his fall.' The Master sighed. 'Moray had to go. For the sake of the realm. He had stolen the Queen's affections. The greatest evil could come of that. For Scotland. Even for England. Can you not perceive it? For doubts as to the father of James's heir could keep him out of Elizabeth's throne. Many in England are against his accession, in any case. Elizabeth herself is hesitant. Moray had to go.'

'His death was ordered by Elizabeth? And paid for with her gold?'

'Not his death. His fall and disgrace. Banishment, perhaps. Until James should have an undoubted heir. Huntly went too far.'

'So you betrayed Huntly, through Bothwell? You plotted Bothwell's attack on the King. Now you are betraying Bothwell. Again with Elizabeth's money. He is working his own doom, you wrote. You released him from Edinburgh Castle for this! And the Lord Hamilton. He is broken and disgraced, put to the horn, for no other reason than that you could use his name to unite the Stewarts to aid Bothwell's attempt against the King . . . '

'Lassie! Lassie!' Patrick Gray interposed, almost wearily. 'Can you not see? Can you not understand? The rule and governance of this unhappy realm is balanced as on a sword's edge. The throne is insecure, and has no power, no strength. Any blustering lord can command more men than can King James. The country is at the lords' mercy, torn with strife and jealousy and hatred. Catholics and Protestants are at each others' throats. War is ever around the corner – civil war, bloody and terrible. Then thousands would die – innocent, poor folk. That is what I struggle and scheme to save this land from, always. Better that an arrogant lord or two should die, than that. Can you not see . . . ?'

'I see only betrayal and bad faith, deceit and lies. Even though you name it statecraft.'

'Aye, statecraft! What else? The ship of state is an ill craft to steer when its master is a weakly buffoon and its crew pirates with every man's hand against another. For the sake of the realm, of our people, I have set *my* hand to steer this ship, Mary – for want of a better man, or a surer hand. Can you name any that could do it better? So I am a Catholic one day and a Protestant the next. One day I support Bothwell, the next Huntly – when either gets too strong. I cherish the Kirk – and when it becomes overbearing and would weaken the throne, I bring in the Jesuits and Spain. Elizabeth's gold I use, yes – but for Scotland's weal. The throne must be supported, buttressed, always. Somehow. For only it stands between the lords and the people. How may a king like James be sustained, save by setting his enemies against each other? How think you that James has kept his crown all these months? By my wits, girl – *my* wits!'

'Yet you betray James also, to Elizabeth!'

'Betray! What fool word is this that you prate like a parrot? One day, Mary, with God's help and these wits of mine, Scotland and England shall be one realm, with one monarch. Strange fate that it should be drooling Jamie Stewart! Then there shall be an end to wars and hatred and fighting. That united realm shall be great and powerful enough to hold all Europe in check. Spain shall no longer threaten it. Nor the Pope. Nor even France. Law and justice shall rule it, from a strong and wealthy throne, with nobles tamed and a church less harsh. To that end I work. For that I plot and scheme, raise men up and bring them low – that James's throne may survive until then. I would have thought, Mary, that you, of all people, would have had the head to see it! For that greater good, we must suffer the lesser evils . . . '

'Such as achieving the destruction of your friends? Causing the deaths of those who trust you? Selling one who is as good as a son to you?'

405

'Tcha! God in Heaven, Mary – can I not make you understand? Are you blind?'

'No, I am not blind, Patrick. Not any more. You have blinded and dazzled me for too long. I see clearly now. I see that my father . . . that Davy Gray was right. He said that you had a devil. I believe it, now. I believe now that even Granlord was right – that you were the death of our Queen Mary. And . . . and I swear, Patrick, that you shall not be the death of Vicky Stuart! All for the weal of the realm!'

'Tush, child – I wish no hurt to Vicky. Only a warning . . . '

'You accused him of highest treason, to Elizabeth – of having James declared insane, and himself made Regent. Then King in his place. Knowing that Vicky has no thought of power or rule. Knowing too that Elizabeth must tell James. And that, hearing it, he could scarce do less than have Vicky's head, for so great a treachery and threat. And none to know that you, his friend, were behind it!' The young woman's dark eyes flashed now. 'For that, Patrick, no words will suffice. Only deeds.'

'And what deeds, pray, do you intend to perform, Mary, to suffice your maidenly ire?' The Master's scimitar brows rose mockingly. 'Perhaps I deceive myself – but I believe that I may just be able to withstand your direst darts, my dear!'

She shook her head, but sadly, with nothing of triumph. 'The deed is done, Patrick,' she said. 'Past recall. You are too late to save yourself.' Mary looked out at the last of the sunset. 'Tonight, possibly even at this moment, a trusted messenger hands the first sheet of your letter to my Lord Maitland, the Chancellor, at Thirlestane Castle in Lauderdale. He will know well what to do with it.'

'Merciful Christ!' For once that melodious voice was no better than an ugly croak. 'Maitland! You did that? You sent the letter to Maitland? Maitland, of all men! My chiefest enemy . . . '

'I sent it to the Chancellor of this realm. He still is that. Whose duty it must be to take action upon it. I cannot believe that he will fail to do so. And promptly.'

Appalled, aghast, the Master searched his daughter's face. 'Do . . . you know . . . what you . . . have done?' he demanded, from a constricted throat.

'I do. I did it of set purpose. This is what the Chancellor requires. To raise himself up again. And to bring you down. It cannot fail to do so.'

'It cannot fail to lose me my head, damn, burn and blister you! In that letter I said . . . I said . . .'

'You said that you would not spare the rod, on King James. That you were the architect of his present humbled state. That he informed you of his secret mind, which you then disclosed to Elizabeth. I cannot think that this is less than treason.'

'And that you, Mary Gray, sent to Maitland! And you talk of betrayal!' The words rose to a cry that verged on the hysterical.

'I am the daughter of the Master of Gray,' she told him quietly, her voice so very flat in contrast to his. 'Perhaps betrayal therefore comes naturally to me, also!'

'Precious soul of God! This – from you!'

'Yes, Patrick. But at least I only hold the noose before your eyes. I do not put it round your neck and draw it tight! As you have done to others. I have left you with time to escape. Maitland is no young man. He will not ride through all the wild hills between Lauderdale and Hailes at night. You have time to reach the Border before he can act. England. From whence comes your gold and your orders. You will be safe there, will you not? Your fond Elizabeth will cherish you. Or may she no longer esteem you when your usefulness here is past? That you must needs discover.'

He said nothing.

'Perhaps you will fare better in France? Or Spain?' the girl went on, in the same inflexible voice. 'You will not lack employment, I feel sure. Meantime, a fast horse will take you to Berwick and over Tweed in three hours and less.'

'You . . . you are very thoughtful.' Somehow he got it out. 'But have you, in your lofty wisdom, considered Marie and the child? Whom you also have professed to love – God help them!'

'Marie knows all. I spoke with her before leaving Holyroodhouse. Even now she will be on her way to Berwick, with Andrew.'

'She will? Sink me . . . !'

'Marie agrees with what I have done. She said that I was to tell you so. That she believed it to be for the best. She longs to see an end to this evil. She has tried to halt you, but you would not heed her. It required your own flesh and blood to halt your course, Patrick – another such as yourself. So . . . this is goodbye.'

'You think, you believe, that you have halted me? A chit of a girl! You conceive Patrick Gray held by such as you? Lord – was there ever such insolent folly!'

Sighing, she shook her head. 'You have no choice,' she said. 'You *are* held. By noonday tomorrow, if you are not out of this realm, you will either be warded for treason and trial, or else outlawed, put to the horn. Your letter reveals your betrayal of all. You cannot flee north – for will Huntly or the Marischal save you now? In the south, Bothwell will hunt you down. Will Hamilton in the west spare you? Or the Master of Glamis? Or Mar? You are held, quite. When you penned that letter, Patrick, you wrote your own doom. When you turned on Vicky, you signed it.'

The man opened his mouth to speak, and then closed it again. Mary Gray had him silenced.

'Goodbye, Patrick,' she said then, huskily, unevenly.

He drew himself up, to look at her, to consider her all, every delectable inch of her. And looking, his expression changed, eased, softened. 'Mary, Mary!' he all but whispered. 'What have I done to you? What have we done to each other? You and I? God pity us – what are we? So close, so close – yet we destroy each other.'

'I do not know,' she answered, emptily. 'Save that we are the Grays – and fate is hard on us.'

'A-a-aye!' That came out on a long sigh. He held out a hand, open, empty, pleading. 'May I kiss you, child? Once. Before . . . before . . .'

'Yes – oh, yes!' she cried, and without hesitation flung herself upon him, eyes filling with tears. 'Yes – for I cannot but love you. Always.'

For long moments they clutched each other close, convulsively, passionately, murmuring incoherences. Then abruptly, almost roughly, the man thrust Mary away from him, swung

408

about, and hurried out of that pleasance-house, slamming the door behind him.

The girl sank to her knees over the carved stone bench and sobbed as though her heart would break.

Chapter Twenty-five

IT was grey morning before Mary saw Lennox. The previous evening she had deliberately avoided all contact with others, after coming in from the summer-house, even pleading a headache to excuse herself from her duties with the Queen, and retiring early to the bed which she was to share with the Lady Beatrix Ruthven, to hide herself if not to sleep. Now, darker-eyed than ever and just a little drawn and wan, she sought out the Duke in the little high turret chamber which was all that Bothwell had found for him in that crowded house.

Surrounded by his usual untidy clutter of clothes and gear, the young man was in his shirt-sleeves, brushing dried mud from his tall riding-boots, as the girl knocked and entered.

'Mary!' he exclaimed. 'I sought you last night – when I heard that you had come. With the Queen . . . '

'I was tired, Vicky. I went to bed.' She glanced around her. 'I see that Peter Hay is not back yet – since you clean your own boots.'

'No. It is strange. Where he is gone, I know not. He came with the Queen, and then . . . '

'It was my doing, Vicky. He went on an errand. For me. He rode to Lauderdale. Last night. To the Chancellor's house at Thirlestane.'

'To Maitland? Peter? For you? Sakes, Mary – what is this?'

'It was necessary. Something that I had to do. It . . . it is an ill story, Vicky.' Involuntarily she was picking up and smoothing out and tidying the strewn clothing of that little apartment, as she spoke. 'Patrick is gone.'

'Patrick? Patrick Gray? Gone? Gone where? What do you mean – gone?'

'Gone away. Left Scotland. Last night.' Listlessly she said it. 'He rode for Berwick.'

Astonished, he regarded her. 'But why? What is this? Is it some new plot?'

She told him, then, baldly, in jerky broken sentences. She did not spare Patrick, nor yet herself. Starkly, she declared what she had done to her father, and why.

Ludovick heard her out with growing wonderment, his blue eyes devouring her strained face.

'I' faith, Mary – here is a marvel!' he declared. '*You* did all this? You brought him low. Unaided. And . . . by all that is wonderful – you did it because of me?'

'Yes,' she admitted, simply.

He stepped forward, to grip both her slight shoulders, to stare down at her. 'But . . . what does it mean?' he demanded. 'What does it mean, that you should do this? Tell me, Mary.'

'It means many things, Vicky. But, for you, it means that my eyes are open. That I have made my choice. At last.'

'Mean for me . . . ?'

'Yes. You have been very patient. So faithful.'

He moistened his lips, although his grip on her tightened. 'I do not understand you, Mary. Speak me plain, for God's sake! What do you say?'

'I say that you were right, Vicky, and I was wrong. Not only about Patrick. About the life of the Court. About what is best for us, what is good and right and fair. I mean that I am done with courts and kings and queens. Done with deceits, intrigues and glittering follies. I want no more of it. I have finished with this life, Vicky – finished.'

'You mean that you are going home? To Castle Huntly?'

'No. Not unless I must. I had thought to go to another castle than that. To Methven Castle, Vicky.'

'What . . . !' Mary! What are you saying? Dear Lord – what are you saying?'

'I am asking that you take me away, Vicky. Will you take me away from it all? To your quiet green Methven. There to stay, to abide. You and me, together. As you have wished for so long . . . '

She got no further. The young man's arms enclosed her, swept her up off her feet, crushed the breath from her lovely body, held her fast, while he gabbled and gasped endearments, joy, praise and utter foolishness – when he was not closing her soft parted lips with his own urgent ones.

So different an embrace than that of the night before.

At last, breathless and panting, even trembling a little, Ludovick released her at least sufficiently to allow her to speak.

'My heart! My love! My sweet Mary!' he cried, 'So you will marry me, at last? Oh, my dear – we shall be wed. Soon. At once. Here is the most joyful day of my life. Here is . . .'

Shaking her head, but smiling, Mary extricated one hand, to raise it and place a forefinger over his eager mouth. 'Not so fast, young man,' she told him, tremulous only in her breathing. 'A truce, Vicky – one moment! Hear me, please.' And as he began to nibble at her finger, her face grew grave. 'I will not marry you, Vicky. I cannot. You are still the Duke of Lennox, the King's cousin. And I am still Mary Gray, the bastard. Nothing is changed, there. If we marry, in despite of the King and the Council, our marriage would be annulled forthwith. They would part us. They must. You must see it? So long as we do not marry, none will part us. None will see shame in a duke taking a mistress; but to marry out of his rank and style – that would be unforgivable!'

'But . . . but . . . I care not . . .'

'But nothing, Vicky. My mind is made up, quite. You want me. I want you, likewise. Take me, then. Take me to Methven with you. I shall be your wife in all but name. I shall keep your house for you. I shall cherish you always. I shall bear your children, God willing. But . . . I will not be Duchess of Lennox.'

'Heaven save us – this is beyond all!'

'No. Heed me, Vicky. I have thought long and deep on it. In God's eyes we may be man and wife, I pray – but not in man's. I shall cleave to you, never fear. Always. I shall keep your from the life of the Court as much as I may – for it suits you nothing. But some business of state you must perform, for you are born to it. In that I shall not interfere – for I have learned my lesson. I . . . I . . .' She swallowed. 'I shall endeavour not to be jealous when you marry again – as assuredly you shall. You must. To some lady of high degree.

To produce an heir to your dukedom...'

'Damnation, Mary – have done!'

'Hear me,' she commanded. 'I shall need help, then, Vicky – for I am only a weak woman. And she, whoever she may be, must have her rights. Although she must know, before she weds, that I am what I am.'

'A plague on it!' Almost he shook her. 'Do you know what you say? What this makes you? A courtesan, no more. That is what all will name you. Lennox's courtesan!'

'Why not? That is what I shall be, indeed. There are worse things, I think. Can you not stomach the title, Vicky – for me? Is it too high a price to pay for our happiness? Tell me – is it?'

Helplessly he stared at her. 'God knows,' he muttered at length. 'I do not.'

'God knows, yes,' she agreed, firmly, decisively. 'And there you have it. God knows what we are to each other – and I care not what any other says or thinks. So long as we are together, you and I. You will take me to Methven, Vicky, my love? On these terms. It is a compact?'

He drew a long breath. 'Aye,' he said. 'If that is your will, Mary.'

'I shall make it yours also, my heart,' she whispered.

Past Master

BOOK THREE

PRINCIPAL CHARACTERS

In Order of Appearance

(Fictional characters printed in *italics*)

Robert Logan of Restalrig: Adventurer; cousin of the Master of Gray.

Mary Gray : illegitimate daughter, publicly unacknowledged, of the Master of Gray.

Ludovick, 2nd Duke of Lennox; second cousin of King James and near heir to the throne. Lord High Admiral of Scotland.

Patrick, Master of Gray: son and heir of 5th Lord Gray. former Master of the Wardrobe, Sheriff of Forfar and acting Chancellor of Scotland. Condemned for treason, banished 1587, returned two years later, again fled country 1591.

King James the Sixth of Scots: son of Mary Queen of Scots and Henry Lord Darnley. Contender for the throne of England to succeed Elizabeth.

John Erskine, Earl of Mar: Keeper of Stirling Castle; boyhood companion of the King.

Lord Robert Stewart, Earl of Orkney: one of King James the Fifth's many bastard sons. Former Bishop of Orkney, uncle of the King and father of Lady Marie, Mistress of Gray.

Queen Anne: formerly Princess of Denmark, wife to King James Sixth.

John Maitland, Lord Thirlestane: Chancellor of Scotland.

Master Patrick Galloway: a prominent minister of the Kirk.

Master Andrew Melville: Moderator of the General Assembly, Rector of St. Andrews University; Kirk leader.

William Douglas, 6th Earl of Morton: a powerful nobleman.

Francis Hepburn Stewart: Earl of Bothwell: son of one more of James the Fifth's bastards, and nephew of Mary Queen of Scots' third husband, Bothwell.

Henry Frederick, Prince of Scotland: infant son of James and Anne. Died young.

George Keith, 5th Earl Marischal: Hereditary Marshal of Scotland.

5

Archibald Campbell, 7th Earl of Argyll: Chief of Clan Campbell, Justiciar of the West.

Master James Melville: nephew to Andrew Melville; a prominent divine.

The Lady Marie Stewart: wife of the Master of Gray.

David Gray : illegitimate eldest son of the 5th Lord Gray, half-brother of the Master; land steward and schoolmaster.

Sir Lachlan Mor Maclean: Highland chief and famous fighter.

Donald MacDonald, 10th Captain of Clanranald: important Highland chief.

Sir Christopher St. Lawrence: one of Queen Elizabeth's sailors.

Donald Gorm MacDonald of Sleat: leader of the Clan Donald Confederacy, claimant to the Lordship of the Isles.

Sir George Home: a favourite of King James, later Earl of Dunbar.

Sir George Nicolson: English envoy at the Court of Scotland.

The Lady Jean Campbell, Mistress of Eglinton: later Duchess of Lennox.

Patrick, 5th Lord Gray: the Master's father.

James Elphinstone: one of the Octavians; 4th son of 3rd Lord Elphinstone; later Secretary of State, and Lord Balmerino.

The Lady Henrietta Stewart, Countess of Huntly: sister of Duke of Lennox; wife of the Earl of Huntly.

John Ruthven, 3rd Earl of Gowrie: a young nobleman, Rector of University of Padua, son of former Lord Treasurer.

Alexander Ruthven, Master of Gowrie: brother of above.

Sir Thomas Erskine: a courtier, kinsman of Earl of Mar; later Lord Erskine of Dirleton.

John Ramsay; a favourite page; later Sir John.

Dr Hugh Herries: the King's physician. Created Sir Hugh Herries of Cousland.

Patrick Leslie, Lord Lindores: a courtier.

Andrew Henderson: chamberlain to the Earl of Gowrie.

Sir Thomas Hamilton: (Tam o' the Cowgate) Lord Advocate, later Earl of Haddington.

Sir Robert Carey: English courtier, son of Lord Hunsdon, a cousin of Queen Elizabeth.

Sir Charles Percy: brother of the Earl of Northumberland.

Chapter One

The servant, intending to show the hulking, travel-stained visitor into the lesser hall of Methven Castle, was shouldered roughly aside, and throwing the door wide, the newcomer stamped within, tossing his sodden cloak to the other and shaking the raindrops from his half-armoured person like a dog. Robert Logan of Restalrig was not the man to stand on ceremony, even with dukes.

A few strides inside, and he halted on the deer-skin strewed floor, to stare past the young woman who seemed to be that pleasant and comfortable room's sole occupant, peering into the corners already shadowed by the early February dusk of a wet day, as though he would root out, with his keen glance, anyone lurking therein.

Calmly the girl considered him, as she stood, a slight but shapely figure, beside the wide open fireplace where the birch logs sizzled and spluttered beneath the great stone-carved coat-of-arms.

'Well, sir,' she greeted him evenly. 'So it is *you*! Not a messenger from the King's Grace.'

The newcomer dismissed that with a flick of the wrist. 'A device, no more,' he jerked. 'To gain entry without names. I do not want my name shouted the length and breadth of Strathearn, lassie. H'mm,' he coughed. 'Mary? Mistress? Or my lady? How do I call you, these days?'

'Mary Gray will serve very well, sir,' she answered him coolly. 'But Mistress if you prefer it – since mistress is a true description of my situation. What may I do for you?'

'He's no' here? Where is he, lassie? Lennox. The Duke. Where is he?'

'My lord Duke is from home, sir.'

'Fiend take him, then! I've ridden far and fast to see him. And secretly. Where is he, Mary?'

She did not answer at once, considering him closely, thought-

7

fully, with her lovely dark eyes. She was very lovely altogether, that young woman, with an elfin fine-wrought beauty of feature, a slender but full-breasted figure, and a natural grace of carriage and inborn serenity of bearing which was as disturbing as it was fascinating to men.

'What is your business with the Duke?' she asked, at length.

Logan grinned. 'I said that I came secretly, did I no'? My business is private, lassie. Even from Lennox's courtesan!'

She nodded, accepting that. 'You are alone? You seldom ride alone. I think, sir? Usually with a band of cut-throat moss-troopers.' That was said no less calmly, factually, than the rest.

The man laughed, nowise offended. The Laird of Restalrig indeed was not a man who offended easily – nor could afford to be in sixteenth-century Scotland.

'No need for my brave lads this journey, Mary. When will Lennox be home? I know that he was here two days back. And that he has not been to Court in Edinburgh since Yule.' That was sharp.

'You are well informed, sir. My lord Duke is but at St. John's town of Perth. He will return tonight. At any hour. He could have been here by this.'

'Ha! Then I shall await him. Here. In comfort. With your permission, of course, Mistress!' He chuckled, unbuckling his steel half-armour. 'You will not deny me some small hospitality, Cousin? To stay a hungry and thirsty man who has ridden ninety miles and more this day. You will pardon my mentioning it – but you show no haste to sustain me!'

'I have never known your appearance herald aught but ill tidings,' she answered. But she moved to pull a bell cord hanging amongst the rich arras, to summon a servant.

He laughed again. Logan was a great laugher, an unfailingly cheerful rogue. He sat down on a settle, unbidden, to pull off his great heavy thigh-length riding-boots.

'You do me injustice, Coz,' he declared. 'Often my news is good indeed – for the right folk! As I swear it is on this occasion, lass.'

'I doubt it,' she said. 'You are apt to be too close linked to ... my father!'

He looked up, and his fleering grey-blue eyes met her dark

8

glowing ones. The grin died on his florid fleshy features.

'I'ph'mmm,' he said.

The servant reappeared, and was told to bring victuals, cold meats and wine.

The young woman paced over to the rain-blurred window that looked out over the fair prospect of green Strathearn, water-meadows and wide pasture-lands lifting and lifting through rolling foothills to the great heather bastions of the Highland Line, all grey and indistinct today under the thin curtains of the rain.

'You say that you have ridden ninety miles,' she said, without looking back. 'Edinburgh is little more than fifty, from here. So you have not come from Restalrig. Your castle of Fast would be near to ninety, I think. In the Borderland. Near to Berwick.'

'You are quick,' he acknowledged.

'If *you* come, in haste, and secretly, from that airt, then I cannot but fear the reason for your mission, sir. Vicky . . . the Duke, is not apt to be concerned with doings from those parts. Berwick and the Border only spell trouble. *He* is not one of those who accept secret doles and gold from Queen Elizabeth!'

'He is fortunate, no doubt, in not requiring to do so,' the other said lightly.

'No man, I think, requires to be a traitor to his country,' the girl gave back. 'Even the Master of Gray!' She turned round to face him. 'It *is* he that you came from, is it not? From my father? It is on his behalf?'

Restalrig drew a large hand over his mouth and chin. 'On whose behalf I come, Cousin, is my affair.'

'If the matter concerns my father and my . . . concerns the Duke of Lennox, then it concerns me also, sir. Though God knows I want none of it! It *is* Patrick, is it not? My father?'

'You are hard on him, lassie. Must you hate him so?'

'I do not hate him. Would that I could! My sorrow is that I love him still. But his works I hate, yes.'

'His works are for the good o' this realm, most times, girl. Statecraft. Patrick Gray can save Scotland. As he has done before. And, Deil kens, Scotland needs saving, in this pass!'

Her sigh had something almost of a shudder behind it. 'Has it come to this again?' she cried. 'So soon!' It was not often that Mary Gray allowed the tranquil assurance of her demeanour

9

to be disturbed thus. 'Patrick's works are evil. You know it. If he seems to save the realm on occasion, it is only for his own ends. And at the cost of untold misery, treachery, deceit. I say better far for the realm not to be saved – not by the Master of Gray!'

He padded across the floor to her in his hose. 'What so ails you at him, Mary? Has he ever done you hurt? God – I'd say it ill becomes any woman to speak so of her sire! However he conceived her! He loves you well, I swear.'

'I have told you – I love him also. To my grief, my shame. But I shall never trust him again. I have learned my lesson, learned it sorely but surely. A year ago and more I sent him away. Drove him away. Forced him to leave Scotland . . .'

'*You* did? Patrick Gray?'

'I did.' She nodded, with a quiet certainty, an authority almost, that sat but strangely on a young woman of only nineteen years. 'I forced him into exile. Never heed how. When his wickednesses became too great to be borne – even by me, who had condoned so many, God forgive me. When he turned against Vicky. When he would have betrayed the Duke. Who was almost as a son to him. You understand? Understand why I must know what now is toward? I *must* know.'

The other scratched his head. 'I canna tell you, lassie . . .'

'I thought, in my foolishness, that we should have peace from him. From Patrick. From his plots and schemings and treasons. That, banished the realm, he would no more endanger Scotland. Nor Vicky. Nor others. A year ago. Eighteen months. So little a time of peace! And now . . . ! Where is he, sir? Where is my father?'

Logan shrugged. 'That isna for me to say.' He turned away – and in doing so his eye took in the significance of a piece of furniture in the shadows to the right of the window. He stepped over to peer down.

'Ha!' he exclaimed. 'What have we here? Guidsakes, girl – what's this?'

It was a wooden cradle into which he looked. Within it lay a tiny infant that stared up at him with wide dark eyes, silent.

Mary Gray came at once, to kneel down by the cradle and smile into it gently, warmly. 'That is Johnnie,' she said, nodding simply but proudly. 'Johnnie, my heart! My little pigeon! My troutie! Three months old. Is he not an angel from heaven?'

At the change in her, so sudden, so complete, the great hulking man looked almost embarrassed, ill at ease. He grinned, and then guffawed. 'Shrive me!' he cried. 'Some, I'd swear, would call him otherwise!'

She did not look up, nor even alter her tone of voice. 'The bastard son of a bastard mother?' she said calmly. 'That is true. But what of it? He is no less an angel. And he is mine.'

'And my lord Duke's!'

'Why, yes. Of course.'

'Oooh, aye! Johnnie Gray, eh. My new cousin!'

'Not so,' she said. 'John Stewart. His father would have it so. Bastard he may be, in the eyes of men. But he is John Stewart of Methven also. Already. This castle and all its demesne is settled upon him. John Stewart of Methven, sir – not Johnnie Gray. And the King's cousin as well as yours!'

'My God!' Logan stared at her. 'Is this truth? You are none so blate, lassie! You do things in style, I'll say that for you!'

'There is nothing of my doing in it. All was his father's doing. On the day after I gave birth, he brought the papers to show me. All signed and witnessed and sealed.'

'So-o-o!' Logan looked round him at all the quietly comfortable splendour of that hall. 'All this is yours! Mary Gray's. All this – Methven Castle, one of the finest houses in the land. All yours – Davy Gray the land-steward's brat!'

She shook her dark head. 'Not mine. His. John Stewart of Methven's.'

Robert Logan of Restalrig was right about his cousinship. Both cousinships were true, as cousins go in Scotland, a country where clanship was always important. The Lady Agnes Gray, daughter of the fourth Lord Gray, sister of the present Lord and aunt of the Master, his heir, had married Logan's father. So he was a full cousin of Patrick, Master of Gray, and half-cousin of the latter's illegitimate daughter Mary. As for Ludovick Stewart, second Duke of Lennox, he was in second-cousinship to King James the Sixth. His father Esmé, the first Duke, was full cousin to Henry Stewart, Lord Darnley, who married Mary Queen of Scots and became James's father. For lack of closer relatives he was accepted as next heir to the throne of the so-far childless monarch.

Servants brought in food and drink for the visitor, who fell to without delay or ceremony. Mary picked the baby out of the cradle and moved about the great room with him in her arms, crooning softly. They made a pleasing picture, the beautiful girl, her exquisite finely-chiselled patrician features flushed with the bloom of tenderness and mother-love, and the solemn great-eyed infant. But Restalrig had no eyes for other than the viands set before him. More than once the young woman paused and looked at him, lips parted to speak, and then moved on again.

The faint sound of clattering hooves and shouting from the courtyard at the other side of the house, turned both their heads. In a few moments the door opened again to admit another man, preceded by two lanky steaming wolf-hounds, soaked and muddy. Long-strided he came across to enfold Mary and the baby in a boyish impetuous embrace without so much as a glance at the visitor – who indeed rose to his feet only belatedly, and still chewing.

The newcomer was a young man, younger-seeming even than his twenty years, of medium height, stocky but markedly up-right of bearing, with an open freckled countenance, blunt-featured and pleasantly plain. He could make no claims whatso-ever to either good looks or aristocratic distinction – in marked contrast to that of the girl he so eagerly saluted. Carelessly dressed in comfortably old clothing which had never been more than moderately fine – much less fine even than Restalrig's, who was no dandy – Ludovick Stewart seemed an unlikely character indeed to fill the role of next heir to the throne, second Duke of Lennox, Lord High Chamberlain of Scotland, Commendator-Prior of St. Andrews, Seigneur D'Aubigny of France and former Viceroy of the Realm.

'We have a guest, Vicky,' Mary said warningly, wiping a smear of mud from the baby's face. 'The Laird of Restalrig – who you will remember, I think. Related to . . . to my family. But here, I understand, for reasons less frank!'

Quickly the young man looked at Logan, and back to the girl. 'Indeed!' he said. 'M'mmm.'

'My lord Duke,' Logan said, nodding briefly. 'Your servant.'

'And yours, sir.' Lennox's manner was civil but stiff, wary, and little more courtly than Restalrig's. 'I have not seen you for some years, I think.'

'True, my lord.' The other grinned. 'I but little frequent His Grace's Court, I fear.'

'That I understand. Myself, I care little for it. But . . . this is a matter of taste. Whereas with you, sir, I believe, it is more than that. The last meeting of the Privy Council which I attended put you to the horn, did it not? For conspiring with the King's enemies? And declared you rebel also, for robbery, rape and assault, if I remember aright!'

Restalrig's grin was succeeded by a scowl, and his fleshy jowl thrust forward noticeably. 'You have a fair memory, my lord Duke. But also, no doubt, some knowledge of the justice of His Grace's Council! I seem to mind your own self being in trouble with them, two years back, over the Bothwell business! But never heed. It is no matter.'

'It matters, sir, that a pronounced rebel should be received in my house.'

'Tcha! I came secretly. None knows that Logan of Restalrig is at Methven. I have word for your private ear.'

'If it is treasonable word, sir, I had better not hear it.'

'Treason is a word for clerks and frightened fools! In affairs of the realm, only to lose is treasonable!'

'He comes on Patrick's behalf, Vicky, I fear,' Mary put in, urgently. 'He will not tell me what it is. But I am sure that it is Patrick again. And if it is, then it is better, I am sure, that you should not hear it. Should not listen to him.'

Frowning, the young man looked from one to the other. 'Is this true, Restalrig?' he demanded. 'That you come on behalf of the Master of Gray?'

'My instructions are that what I have to say is said in your ear alone, my lord.'

'Vicky – either do not hear him or let me hear him also! If it is my father's words he brings to you, then it is *my* concern. You know it.'

'This is no women's business, my lord Duke . . .'

Lennox interrupted him. 'If I hear you, it is in the Lady

Mary's presence – or not at all, sir. She . . . she is my other self, in all matters.'

The other snorted. 'God save us!' But Logan was no fool, and perceiving the expression on the young Duke's face, he shrugged. 'Och, well – so be it! If Mistress Gray can hold her tongue . . .'

'You will refer to her, sir, as the Lady Mary.'

"Ho! I will, will I? Mary Gray, the . . . ! A-well, a-well – if that's the way o' it! Aye, then – the lady is right, my lord. I bear you word from Patrick Gray. Privy word. Important word. Word that could hang men . . . and save Scotland.'

'Where is he? The Master? We heard that he was in London. Then Rome . . .'

'He is in my house at Fast Castle, my lord.'

Mary and the Duke exchanged glances.

'Back in Scotland!' the girl exclaimed. 'So soon! So near!' She clutched the baby tighter to her, as at a threat. 'Endangering his own life. And others'!'

Restalrig barked a laugh. 'Patrick's no' the man to shy at a small whiffle o' danger! No' that he's in danger so long as he bides in Fast. It'll take more than the Chancellor Maitland and the Council to winkle him out o' my house! Or King Jamie, either. I'm at the horn, am I no', and biding there secure? They'll no' touch the master o' Fast Castle. Folk ha' tried it before this – and learned differently!'

'You are not in Fast Castle now!' Lennox reminded.

'I' faith – that is true,' the other nodded. 'But Patrick is my friend, see you. As well as my cousin. A man must take a risk for his own blood, his friend. Or no?' He looked from one to the other.

'What does he want with me?' Ludovick asked heavily.

'He wants you, my lord Duke, safe in Fast Castle before the morning's light.'

'God in Heaven! Are you mad, man?'

'Save us all . . . !'

'With fresh horses, I can have you there before cock-crow. Ninety miles. Hard riding – but you are no shrinking lily, my lord. And I have already ridden that ninety here. None will see you, by night. Ride back tomorrow night. None will know that

14

you have been to Fast.'

'Why should I do any such thing, sir?'

'Patrick would speak with you. Urgently. And since he may not come here . . .'

'But, dear God – I cannot do this! Is *he* crazed, or you? I am Chamberlain of this realm, one of the King's ministers. Of his Council. I cannot wait secretly upon one banished the realm as an enemy of the King! It is treason for the Master of Gray to be back in Scotland, at all. For me to ride to him at Fast would be treason likewise. He knows that.'

'Nevertheless, my lord, that is what he's sent me to bid you do. He said – "Tell the Duke that the Protestant cause, the throne itself, may hang on this. And the English succession".'

Mary Gray emitted something near to a groan. 'This again! The same fell game!'

'This is no game, lassie! You ken the state o' the realm. Near enough to outright war, wi' our slobbering King pulled a' ways! A blow is to be struck that will topple Jamie into the Catholics' arms first of all. And then off his throne. And that will mean real war. Civil war. Aye, and invasion too.'

'I understood that you were of the Catholic persuasion yourself, sir?' Lennox charged him.

The other shrugged. 'You may say, like Patrick, that I dinna take religion ower seriously. Not to discommode me. That I'm fine and content to worship God in my ain way, and let other folk do the like. A plague on them both, I say . . . wi' due respects to your Dukeship that's of the Kirk party!'

'M'mmm . . .'

'There is nothing new in all this,' Mary put in, wearily. 'It is all as it was – ever the same. My father has been playing the Protestants against the Catholics and the Catholics against the Protestants for years. There is nothing new here, that should send the Duke hurrying to Patrick's beckon . . .'

'Aye, but there is. That's where you're wrong, Mary – there is. Patrick said to say that it was life and death. For the King. Aye, and for yourself, my lord Duke. Because you're near the throne. He says both your deaths have been decided upon.'

'Vicky!' The girl stepped close, to clutch the Duke's wrist with her free hand. 'Sweet Jesu – no!'

'Heed nothing, Mary,' Lennox told her, encircling mother and child with a damp arm. 'Nobody is going to kill me. It is but one of Patrick's alarums. My death would serve no cause, benefit none. I take no part in any of their affairs, neither Catholic nor Protestant. Besides, no one would dare...'

'Not even the Earl o' Bothwell?'

'Bothwell! But ... Bothwell is of the Kirk party. A Protestant.'

'Patrick says that Bothwell is about to change sides. To turn Catholic. And Bothwell, like yoursel', my lord Duke, is the King's cousin – though on the wrong side o' the blanket. A right bold and fierce man!'

'By the Powers – Bothwell!' There was no doubt about the Duke's perturbation now. Yet he shook his head. 'I do not believe it!' he declared. 'Bothwell has always been a Protestant ... if he has any true religion at all. Devil-worship and witchcraft, perhaps. But to turn Catholic – no!'

'If religion matters little to him, and this changing could give him the sure rule of Scotland, think you he'd scruple? Patrick says that he is changing – and have you ever kenned Patrick Gray wrong in his information?'

Mary Gray had, but not often – and she was in no state to contest Restalrig's claim. 'Why should he, Bothwell . . .' She swallowed. 'Why should he seek Vicky's hurt? Or the King's?'

The other shrugged. 'It's no' me you've to ask that, lassie – it's Patrick. I'm but his messenger in this, see you. To bring the Duke to him.'

'It is but a device. This threat to Vicky. To entice him to Fast Castle. To seek to entangle him once again in Patrick's evil affairs. Do not go, Vicky. Even if it is true about Bothwell, if you stay quietly here at Methven, far from Court, you can be of no danger to him. Why should he seek your death?'

'But James, Mary – the King? Is my duty not to the King? If *he* is threatened? Am I not sworn, as a member of the Council, to defend him, my liege lord, with my life? If Patrick *has* discovered some desperate plot against the King, am I not in duty bound at least to hear of it, for James's sake?'

'He canna come near to the King himsel',' Restalrig pointed out. 'He is banished the realm. Outlawed. He needs an ear close to Jamie's. That the King will heed. If his warning is to be in time. And there's no' much time, he says ...'

Lennox took a few paces away from the girl, and back, staring at the floor. 'I believe that I must go, Mary,' he said, at length.

She emitted a long quivering sigh, but inclined her lovely head.

'I shall hear him - no more. Do not fear that he shall cozen me, carry me off my feet, Mary. I know Patrick for what he is ...'

'Would that I could come with you, Vicky! Two heads are even better than one, in dealing with my father! But . . . Johnnie, here. Nursing the child, I cannot leave him.'

'Nor would I let you ride ninety miles through a winter's night, lass ...'

'I *could*, Vicky. You know that I could.'

'May be. But you will not. This is not for you.' He turned to Restalrig. 'When do we start, sir? I have fresh horses.'

'The sooner the better. Give me an hour, my lord. It will be full dark by then ...'

'You will be careful, Vicky? Oh, you must be very careful! Watch Patrick. Do not let him deceive you, charm you, hood-wink you ...'

Chapter Two

For fully an hour none of the three men had spoken – save to curse their weary drooping mounts when the all-but-foundered brutes slipped and stumbled on the rough and broken ground, benighted and water-logged. Coldingham Moor was no place to be in the dark, at any time – but especially not at four o'clock of a winter's morning, with a half-gale blowing sleet straight off the North Sea in their faces, and after having ridden across five counties.

Though he had no fondness for Logan, Ludovick Stewart's opinion of the man's toughness and vigour could hardly have failed to have risen during those past grim hours. Although of middle years and notorious for gross living, he had led the way, and at a cracking pace, right from Methven in Strathearn, across South Perthshire, Strilingshire, the three Lothians and into Berwickshire, on a foul night, and having already ridden the entire journey in the opposite direction. Not once, despite the thick blackness of the night, had he gone astray to any major extent.

The last lap of that long journey was, as it happened, the most trying of all. Coldinghamshire, that ancient jurisdiction of the once princely Priory of Coldingham, thrusts out from the rest of Berwickshire eastwards like a great clenched fist, where the Lammermuir Hills challenge the sea. At the very tip of the resultant cliff-girt, iron-bound coast, amongst the greatest cliffs in the land, Fast Castle perches in as dizzy and savage a situation as can well be imagined, an eagle's eyrie of a place – and a particularly solitary and malevolent eagle at that. No other house or haunt of man crouched within miles of it on the bare, lofty, storm-battered promontory.

Even high on the moor here, amongst the whins and the outcropping rocks, Ludovick could hear the roar of the waves, a couple of miles away and four hundred feet below. Heads down, sodden cloaks tight about them, soaked, mud-spattered, stiff

18

with cold and fatigue, they rode on into the howling black emptiness laced with driven sleet. The Duke imagined that hell might be of this order.

He was jerked out of what was little better than a daze by his servant's beast cannoning into his own, all but unseating both of them. He had been aware that his horse had been slipping and slithering more consistently, indicating that they had been moving downhill. Taking a grip on himself, and shouting at the groom, Ludovick brought his black under control.

Only a short distance further, Logan halted. Indeed it appeared that he had to halt, poised on the very brink of nothingness.

'Care, now,' he announced, having to shout above the sustained thunder of the seas which seemed to be breaking directly below them – but notably far below; as though all before had been the merest daunder. 'Dismount and lead.'

Himself doing so, he picked his way along a narrow twisting ledge of a path, steep hillside on one hand, empty drop on the other. It was a place for goats rather than men and horses.

They came to a naked buttress of the cliff, a thrusting rock bluff round which it seemed there was no passage. Down the side of this their path turned steeply, and then abruptly halted. They faced the abyss.

Logan pointed in front of him, eastwards, seawards – but in the almost horizontally-driving sleet Lennox could see nothing. Then the other drew a small horn out from his saddlebag, and blew a succession of long and short blasts on it. Waiting a few moments, he repeated this, and at the second summons a faint hail answered him from somewhere out in the darkness. This was followed presently by a creaking, clanking noise, and the rattle of chains.

'A drawbridge!' Ludovick exclaimed. 'I' faith – it is *here*?' He was peering into the murk. Vaguely, monstrously, something loomed up there, he believed, blacker than the surrounding blackness.

With a rattle and thud the end of a drawbridge sank into position almost at their very feet. This seemed to be little wider than the path itself; never had Lennox seen so narrow an access.

'Hold to the chain,' Logan shouted. 'The wind. Bad here.'

That was no over-statement. As they followed their guide out on to the slender gangway, which echoed hollowly beneath their feet, the wind seemed to go crazy. It had been blowing gustily hitherto, but consistently from the east; now it seemed to come at them from all sides – and especially from below – tearing at them, buffeting, shrieking and sobbing. It was presumably some trick of the cliff-formation and of this detached projecting pinnacle on which the castle must stand. Certain it was that without the single, swinging guard-chain to hold on to, the men would have been in grave danger of being swept right off that narrow cat-walk. Even the horses staggered and side-stepped, having to be dragged across in their nervous reluctance. Although Ludovick did not make a point of looking downwards, he was aware of a paleness far below, which could be only the white of the breaking seas which roared in their ears and seemed to shake that dizzy timber gallery. The salt of driven spray was now mixed with the sleet and rain which beat against their faces.

At last they lurched into the blessed shelter of an arched and fortified gatehouse, with solid level rock beneath their feet, and a relief from the battering of the wind. Rough voices sounded, hands took their horses' bridles from them, and flickering lamps were brought. The bare dark stone walls of Fast Castle may not normally have spoken of kindly welcome, but that night they were as a haven of peace and security for the reeling travellers.

Lennox, shown to a draughty small chamber in the main keep, where the arras swayed and rustled against the walling and a candle wavered and guttered, throwing off his wet clothing and donning a bed-robe, bemusedly considered that he had seldom sampled a fairer room. When Logan himself brought in food and wine, his guest partook of only token portions before collapsing on a hard bed and sleeping like the dead.

It was nearly noon before Ludovick awakened, but even so he did not realise the time of day, so dark was it still in his little chamber, with its gloomy hangings and its tiny window only half-glazed, the lower portion being closed by wooden shuttering. The storm still raged apparently, and little of light penetrated the small area of glass, not only because of the heavy overcast sky but because the air was thick with spindrift.

When the young man had prevailed upon himself to rise, and went to the window to peer out, he could see nothing through the streaming glass. Opening the little shutters, he stooped and thrust out his head – and all but choked in consequence; it was not so much the violence of the wind that took his breath away – it was the prospect. He hung directly over a boiling cauldron of tortured seas, riven and torn into foaming, spouting fury by jagged reefs and skerries, just about one hundred and fifty feet below – hung being a true description, for the masonry of this tower rose sheerly flush with the soaring naked rock of the precipice, which itself bulged out in a great overhang, sickening to look down upon. Ludovick's window faced south, and by turning his head he could see, through the haze of spray and rain, the vast main cliff-face that stretched away in a mighty and forbidding barrier three hundred feet high separated from his present stance by a yawning gulf. In other words, this castle was situated half-way down that cliff-face, built to crown an isolated and top-heavy pillar of rock that was itself a detached buttress of the thrusting headland, on as cruel and fearsome stretch of rock-ribbed coast as Scotland could display. How anyone could have achieved the task of building a castle here in the first place, apart from why anyone should wish to do so, was a matter for uneasy wonder. How many unhappy wretches had dropped to their death on the foaming fangs beneath, in the creating of it, was not to be considered. Lennox well remembered King James himself – who, of course, had only viewed the place from the sea – saying once that the man who built it must have been a knave at heart.

Noting, however, that despite the grim aspect and evil reputation of this robber's stronghold, not only had he survived a particularly heavy sleep therein but that while he had been thus helpless his clothing had been taken, dried and brought back to him, along with adequate wherewithal to break his fast, Ludovick dressed, ate, and went in search of company. Descending two storeys by a narrow winding stone stairway in the thickness of a wall-corner, wherein chill winds blew at him from unglazed arrow-slits and gun-loops, he came to the Hall of the castle on the first main floor. It was a small poor place compared with the great hall of Methven, bare and stark as to furnishings but better lit than might have been expected by four windows provided with stone seats, and with a great roaring fire of sparking driftwood blazing in the huge fireplace which took up most of one wall. Here he encountered the Lady Restalrig, Marion Ker, Logan's frightened-eye young second wife, whose nervous greeting to her ducal visitor and swift self-effacement thereafter, seemed perhaps suitable behaviour on the part of the chatelaine of Fast Castle.

Ludovick, gazing into the fire, was wondering at the reactions of any young woman brought to live in such a place, when a voice spoke behind him from the doorway.

'My dear Vicky – here is a delight, a joy! On my soul, it is good to see you! It was a kindly act indeed to ride so far to see me, through so ill a night. I hope I see you well and fully rested?'

The young man swung round. He had looked for this, been prepared, anticipated the impact of the Master of Grey, knowing so well the quality of the man. Yet even so he was somehow taken by surprise, confused, immediately put at a disadvantage. This was so frequently the effect of Patrick Gray on other men – although on women it was apt to be otherwise. The Duke found himself mumbling incoherencies, not at all in the fashion that he had decided upon.

It was partly the complete contrast of the man with his surroundings the so obvious unsuitability of everything about Fast Castle as a background for the Master of Gray. Exquisite without being in the least effeminate, laughing-eyed, friendly as he was entirely assured, vital and yet relaxed, the handsomest man in all Europe stood in that harsh, sombre, savage place, and was somehow almost as much a shock to the beholder as had been that plunging, throat-catching prospect from the bedroom window. Even his cordial, courteous and so normal words, spoken in light but pleasantly modulated tones, seemed as much at odds with the true situation as to be off-putting.

Smiling, hands out, the newcomer stepped forward to embrace Lennox to kiss him on both cheeks, French-fashion – for Ludovick had been brought up in France, and it was the Master who had brought him as a boy of ten from that country to Scotland, on his father's death. The younger man coughed, stiffened within the other's arms, and found no words adequate to the occasion.

'Eighteen months it has been, Vicky? Twenty? Too long, at any rate. Too long to be separated from my friends. How often I have thought of you, sought news of you, wished you well. In strange and foreign places. But, heigho – that is now over. A happiness, I vow, a good omen indeed, that the first man that I should meet on my own native soil again, apart from my host and cousin Restalrig, should be my good friend Vicky Stewart, Lord Duke of Lennox!' Patrick Gray had stepped back a pace, though still holding the other by the shoulders the better to smile upon his friend in warm affection.

That was such an astonishing misconstruction of the situation as to set the younger man blinking – and to make his protest sound even more abruptly ungracious than he had intended. 'Dammit, Patrick – I am here only because Restalrig dragged me, under threat of God knows what dire disasters! As well you know.'

'Ha, lad – ever the same forthright, honest Vicky! It does me good to hear your plain, frank candour again. After all of these months with dissemblers and sophists in half the Courts of Europe. Now I know that I am home again, in truth!'

Helplessly, Ludovick stared at him. He knew that he was being unreasonably, unprofitably boorish – and knew too that part of this boorish hostility stemmed from the very fact that this man was so devilishly and winsomely like his own Mary. He had tended to forget just how alike they were, and marvelled anew that so beautiful a man could be so essentially masculine, virile, while his daughter, so similar in looks, bearing and calm assurance, should be all womanly woman. Patrick Gray, clad now, as ever, in the height of fashion but less spectacularly than sometimes, as befitted a courtier on his travels, had reached the age of thirty-four, although he looked even younger – certainly too youthful-seeming to have a grandson like little John Stewart of Methven. Yet the Duke saw the resemblance even to his child, with a sinking heart. The man was of medium height, of a lithe and slender grace of figure and carriage, his features finely-moulded and clean cut, enhanced by brilliant dark flashing eyes beneath a noble brow. His black wavy hair was

23

worn long, but carefully trimmed, and the smiling lips were somewhat countered by a wicked curved scimitar of moustache and a tiny pointed beard.

'You are home, Patrick, only in that you have somehow managed to set foot on this outlandish doorstep of Scotland,' the younger man said harshly. 'You are still banished the realm under pain of death. Nothing is changed. And you must know that, in insisting that I come here to meet you, *my* head is endangered likewise!'

'Tut, Vicky – you are too modest, as always. No one is going to have the Duke of Lennox's head, for any such small matter – least of all our sovereign and well-beloved monarch, your cousin! He loves you too well, my friend, as well he might. And secretly, you know, I do believe that he in some small measure loves me also! Poor Jamie is ever a little confused in his loving, is he not?'

'What . . . what do you mean by that?'

'Merely that our liege lord is apt to be pulled in different ways than more, h'm, ordinary mortals! A matter which his enemies seldom forget – so that it falls to his friends not to forget either.'

'And you count yourself that? A friend of the King?'

'Why yes, Vicky – to be sure. Albeit a humble one. Is that remiss of me?'

'After . . . after all that you have done?'

'After all that I have done,' the Master nodded, easily. 'So much done, or at least attempted, for the weal of James Stewart and his realm. So much endeavoured, over the years, to guide and draw the frail ship of state on a sure course through the perilous seas of statecraft – with alas, so many failures. But, heigho – my small successes also, Vicky. *You* will not deny me them? When His Grace was away in Denmark winning himself his bride, we ruled Scotland passing well together, you and I, Vicky. Did we not? You acting Viceroy. I acting Chancellor.'

'I did what you told me, Patrick – that was all. No more than a tool in your hands. And who gained thereby? You, and you only.'

'Not so, Vicky. You gained much also, in experience, in public esteem, in stature. And the realm gained, in peace and prosperity, did it not? So James gained, since he and his realm are one – as he will assure you most vigorously! But enough of this,

24

my friend – such pry talk of days past is no way to celebrate this happy occasion. Especially since I now come to prove my friendship for King Jamie in much more urgent fashion. But first, lad – tell me of Mary. Here is what I long to hear. How does she fare? I learned that you had taken her into your own keeping. No doubt a convenient arrangement – although bringing its own problems! And the child . . . ?'

'Mary is well. And content,' Lennox interrupted shortly. 'She sent . . . greetings. She is as she wishes to be. And the child. A boy. Like to herself in looks. We are very happy.'

'How fortunate. How excellent. Felicitous. All the satisfactions of marriage – without the handicaps! At least, for yourself, my lord Duke!'

'No!' the younger man cried. 'It is not that. Not that at all, Patrick. You mistake – as do all. I would have married Mary. I prayed, pleaded, that she would marry me. But she would not. She would have it this way – this way only. Her mind was set on it. Still it is – for I would marry her tomorrow, if she would do so. But she will not. She says that because I am Duke, and close to the throne, it is not possible. That she could not be Duchess. That the King and the Council would end it, annul the marriage, declare it void – because of her . . . her birth. We are both under age. They would separate us, she says – where they will not separate us, as we are.'

'I see. She is probably right. Yes – I think there may be a deal of truth in that.'

'It is a damnable position!' Lennox declared. 'I care nothing for the succession, or for this matter of dukes and position at Court. I hate the Court and all to do with it – save only James himself. I want nothing of all this. Only Mary for my wife, and to live my own life at Methven . . .'

'No doubt, Vicky. But, alas, we are not all the masters of our own fate. Born of the royal house of Stewart, you are not as other men, whether you wish it or not. It has its handicaps, yes – but its great benefits likewise. These you must hold, use and pursue to best advantage.'

'But that is not my desire. Why, because I am my father's son, must I live a life I do not want to live? Why must I concern myself with affairs of state when they mean naught to me . . . ?'

'I' faith – and there you have it, man! Affairs of state may mean naught to you – but *you* mean a deal in the affairs of state! That indeed is one reason why I am here. That you may be spared from certain of their more violent attentions!'

'Aye – what folly is this . . . ?'

'Folly indeed, Vicky – but dangerous folly.' The Master seated himself on a bench at the side of the fire, and gestured to the other to do likewise. 'There is notable violence afoot– and you, I fear, are intended to be part of it. You and the King, both.'

'Restalrig said something of this. That is why *I* am here. He swore that the King was endangered. So I came. In duty. To James. As no doubt you intended.'

'As I hoped, yes.' Gravely the other nodded. 'For if the King is to be saved, and you with him, I need your help.'

'A plot? A conspiracy?'

'You could name it so, indeed. Though it is more than that. A strategy, rather – part of a great strategy. To turn Scotland Catholic again, to isolate England, and to bring Bothwell to power and rule.'

'That mad-cap! You believe it serious?'

'When Bothwell makes common cause with Huntly, all Scotland must need think it serious!'

'Huntly! But . . . they have always been enemies.

'Ambition can make strange bedfellows.'

Lennox did not require the other to elaborate on the menace, if these tidings were true. The Earl of Huntly was his own brother-in-law, even though there was little love lost between them, and Ludovick well knew both the arrogant savagery of the man, and his military strength. Chief of the great northern clan of Gordon and hereditary Lieutenant of the North, he was probably the most powerful nobleman in Scotland, and a militant Catholic. He boasted that he could field five thousand men in a week, and, with his allies, double that in a month – and he had proved this true on many an occasion. Only two other men in all the kingdom could produce fighting-men on this scale. One was the Earl of Angus, head of the house of Douglas – and his religious allegiance was to say the least doubtful, though he had leanings towards Catholicism; but he was a hesitant man of no strength of character. The third was Francis Hepburn Stewart, Earl of Bothwell, who controlled, after a fashion, a vast number of wild Border moss-troopers as well as his mother's free-booting Lothian clan of Hepburn; moreover, he was married to Angus's sister. An alliance between these three could have fifteen thousand men in arms within days, without even calling upon friends and supporters for aid.

The young man moistened his lips. 'If this is true...'

'It is true, Vicky. I have seen a letter from Bothwell to Huntly. All is in train.'

'They would rise in arms? These two? Against the Protestants? Against the King?'

'Aye. And more than that. They will discredit the King first, and so weaken the Protestant cause. And that is not the worst of it. James, unhappily, has played into their hands. You recollect the bad business of the Spanish Blanks?'

The Duke's eyebrows rose. He had hardly expected the Master of Gray to mention that wretched and treacherous affair, since he was believed to have had a controlling hand in it. 'Who could forget it? But that spoiled the Catholic cause, not the King's.'

'Wait, you. Those were blank letters, sheets of paper already signed by Huntly, Erroll and other Catholic leaders. Angus too. With their seals attached. Sent to the King of Spain, for him to fill in his own terms for the invasion of Scotland in the Catholic interest – a stupid folly if ever there was one. Their courier, George Ker, was captured, and the blanks with him. Put to the torture, he revealed all. Or, at any rate, much! That was a year and more ago. All Scotland knows this. But what Scotland does not know is that more than the blank letters were found on George Ker. There was also a letter from James himself to Philip of Spain. Asking on what terms Philip would send men to Scotland to help put the Kirk in its place!'

'God be good! no! That I do not believe!' Ludovick cried.

'It is fact, nevertheless. George Ker himself told me. He who was carrying the letter. I saw him in Paris. James was most foolish. But he is much browbeaten and bullied by the Kirk, as you know. He has to play one side against the other, to keep his throne. He should not have committed himself in writing –

27

that was a major blunder. But then, His Grace has been but ill-advised, of late.' The Master smiled slightly. 'Since I left Scotland and his side.' That was gently said.

Lennox answered nothing, as his mind sought to cope with the duplicity, the bad faith, which all this implied, amongst those in the highest positions in the land.

Gray went on. 'It was the Kirk authorities who captured Ker and his letters. They have not revealed that they hold this letter from James to King Philip. Not to the world. But they have, I assure you, to James himself! Melville and his other reverend friends hold this letter over our hapless young monarch's head like a poised sword! In order that he may do as they say. And it has served them well, of late – as you must agree. The King has truckled to them in all things. Hence the Catholics' fury. The Kirk goes from strength to strength, in the affairs of state. All goes down before the ministers and their friends. They threaten James with the letter read from every Protestant pulpit in the land! And worse – excommunication! If he does not play their game.'

'Excommunication! By the Kirk! The King?'

'Aye. And that dread word has poor Jamie trembling at his already wobbly knees!'

'I knew naught of this ...'

'My dear Vicky – I think that you have been further exiled from Holyroodhouse at your Methven in Strathearn, than I have been in London, Paris and Rome!'

'And gladly so! I hate and abominate all this evil scheming and deceit and trickery, that goes by the name of statecraft! Give me Methven ...'

'Ah-ha. lad – but it is not Methven that you are to be given! But something less pleasant. The Duke of Lennox, unfortunately, must pay heed to all this, whether he would or no. Bothwell and Huntly have planned shrewdly – indeed so shrewdly that I needs must think that there is some shrewder wit behind all this than the furious, half-crazed Francis Stewart of Bothwell, or that turkey-cock, George Gordon of Huntly! Through Ker, the courier – who of course is in their pay – they know the contents of the King's letter to Philip of Spain. They intend to have it shouted abroad from one end of Scotland to the other.

The Kirk will have to deny it – or lose its hold over James. Either way, the King's credit will suffer greatly. So the Protestant cause will be divided – King's men against Kirk's men. And Bothwell and Huntly, with Angus and the other Catholics, will strike.'

'With their thousands of men? War?'

'That too. But first, rather more subtly, I fear. James, discredited and isolated, will be struck down. Assassinated. Whether by dirk, poison, or strangling like his father Darnley, I have not yet discovered.'

'Precious soul of God!' Ludovick was on his feet, staring. 'Assassinated! Murdered! You . . . you are not serious, Patrick? Not that! Not the King! They would never dare . . .'

'You think not, Vicky? James would have had Bothwell burned for witchcraft had *he* dared. Huntly slew James's cousin, the Earl of Moray, with his own hand.'

'But not the King!'

'Why not? His father, King Henry Darnley, your uncle, murdered at Kirk o' Field. His mother, Mary the Queen, harried, imprisoned, executed. James Third murdered at Sauchieburn. James First murdered at Perth. What is so sacred about our shauchling Jamie?'

'But how would the King's death aid them? Bothwell and Huntly? Neither of *them* can aspire to the throne. Bothwell is a Stewart, yes – but his line is illegitimate.'

'Aye. And here we come to it, my friend. Here is the beauty of it all. Our youthful Queen Anne at last, after so many alarms and make-believe, is with child. As all know. She is due to be delivered very shortly. In a month. Less. Hence my haste to come here, to have you brought here – for the time is short indeed. All the plans are laid. Within days of its birth, the child will be seized, captured. Held by the Catholics. And proclaimed King. Or Queen, if it is a girl. For James will be dead – having been murdered the same night. And Bothwell will rule in his name, as Regent. And in the King's name, the Catholic armies will march.'

Ludovick shook his head, wordless.

'Moreover you, my dear Vicky, unfortunately have to die also. None greatly hate you, I think – but you stand in the road of these men. You would still be next heir to the throne – and since

29

a new-born babe is but uncertain of survival, you could be dangerous. A figure round which opposition might rally. You are a Protestant, well spoken of by the Kirk. They might set you up as alternative Regent. Or perhaps even as King. So you too must die. At the same time as James. And Bothwell, son of one of James the Fifth's many bastards, will rule this holy Catholic realm secure. Indeed, I have heard that he intends to divorce his wife, and marry the widowed Queen Anne. A thoughtful gesture! Especially as, that same eventful night, and possibly successively thereafter, she is to be bedded. H'mm forcibly. In order that she may conceive another child. Er, promptly. By Bothwell – but reputedly by James. A nice precaution, in case the first child dies. To ascend the throne. A useful second string to Bothwell's bow. You will perceive that nimble wits are here at work, Vicky?'

Lennox's appalled youthful face was a study. 'This . . . this is the work of devils!' he whispered. 'Fiends of hell, rather than men. It must not be! It must not be! What would you have me to do?'

'Bring me to the King, Vicky. Without Chancellor Maitland's knowledge. Maitland is my enemy, and will thwart me before all else, if he can. If he knew that I was in Scotland, he would have me imprisoned forthwith. And then done away with, before word could reach the King's ear. I am still banished, on pain of death. So all must be done secretly. And swiftly. For there is little time.'

'How can I do this, Patrick? James lives in fear, dreading attempts on his person. Since Bothwell's last venture. He is guarded at all times. With the Chancellor ever close. You know that . . .'

'I know that he trusts you. That you have his ear at all times. Also that my brother James is still a Gentleman of his Bedchamber. And that the Earl of Orkney, my wife's father and the King's uncle, will aid you.'

'If I tell James. What you have told me. Then he will be warned. Can take the steps necessary. Without . . . without you having to be brought to him . . .'

'Would he believe you? And if he did, how would he behave? I vow he would weep and take fright. Go straight to Mait-

30

land and babble all in his ear. And that sour and desiccate lawyer would counsel inaction, saying that it was all a plot of *mine?* I know them both. Nothing would be done that could halt these resolute and powerful men. Moreover. I have told you but the broad strategy. The vital details are still to be told.' The Master nodded in most friendly fashion. 'And by me alone. No, no, Vicky – I fear, in all modesty, that you need Patrick Gray. Unless you flee the country, without me, you and James both, I have no doubt, will be dead men within the month.'

Helplessly the young man looked at the handsome, sympathetic and wholly assured face of the man who lounged there across the wide hearth. 'Mary said . . .' he began, and stopped.

'Ah, yes – what did Mary say?' That was quick.

'She said that I must be careful. Not to let you deceive me, hoodwink me, charm me.'

'M'mm. She did? Ever she had a pretty humour, that one! But, Vicky – even Mary, I swear, would not wish her child an orphan!'

The Duke turned to pace the floor. 'What is to be done, then?'

'Have my good-father. Orkney, hold one of his deplorable entertainments. In his Abbot's quarters at Holyrood. To celebrate some family event. A birthday, a betrothal, anything! He has sufficient offspring, God knows, lawful and otherwise, to arrange such at any time! The King to be invited. Coaxed by some means – pretty boys, a witch to question, a request to recite some of his terrible poetry! Anything. Maitland will never show his thin nose in such a company. An ascetic, he loathes Orkney and all his hearty brood. As do the Kirk divines. So I shall win into the King's presence unknown to my enemies. For the rest – never fear.'

'But I do fear, Patrick. Once before, you'll mind, I aided you to the King's presence, from banishment. And lived to regret it.'

'Lived to doubt me and misjudge me rather, Vicky – to my sorrow and your loss,' the other corrected, gently. 'Allowed your mind to be poisoned and your trust in me cruelly slain. This time, even if you doubt me, you will continue to *live!* The poison and the slaying being . . . otherwise.'

Ludovick sighed. 'Very well. But, I warn you Patrick – do not fail me in this. Or, 'fore God, I promise you that you will fail

31

no others hereafter!'

'On my soul Vicky – such suspicions are unlike you! Banish them from your mind. Myself it is that takes the risks. Has this not struck you? I need not do this. I need not come to the rescue of James and yourself. As it is, I am putting myself in your hands entirely. I trust you with my life, see you. Come, lad – here's my hand on it! Now – tell me about my grandson. A pox – what a thought! That Patrick Gray should be a grand-father ... !'

Chapter Three

The ancient Abbey of Holyrood, nestling beneath the soaring bulk of Arthur's Seat, had witnessed many a stirring scene in its day, with so much of Scotland's turbulent history apt to take place in its vicinity, even within its walls. Of late years the character of these scenes had tended to change – for the times themselves had changed, the Reformation had come to Scotland, and abbeys and the like were not what they had been. Indeed the magnificent Abbey church, formerly as great as any cathedral, was now largely demolished and reduced to form a royal chapel and a parish kirk. But the monastic buildings still remained, to the east of the handsome new palace of Holyroodhouse which King James the Fourth had erected at the beginning of the century. These, centring round the old Abbot's House, were now the residence of the man who, after the Reformation, had been granted the secular control of these valuable church lands, as Commendator-Abbot – Robert Stewart, one of the numerous illegitimate sons of King James the Fifth, a brood for which the newly-seized ecclesiastical properties had come as a godsend indeed. Robert Stewart had done notably well out of it all, becoming in due course, as well as Abbot of Holyrood, Bishop of Orkney and later Earl thereof. Now an elderly man but by no means palling of his vigorous appetite, he lived here, surrounded by a vast number of his children, legitimate and otherwise, grandchildren, mistresses current and pensioned-off, and general hangers-on. No one, least of all Earl Robert himself, ever knew the total population of the Abbey precincts at any given time – or greatly cared. Undoubtedly, in numbers, it was the largest private establishment in Edinburgh, certainly the most raffish, and probably almost the most seedy also – for Orkney's revenues were never up to the strain their lord put upon them. Nevertheless, it was a most cheerful and lively household, a haven of refuge, if not peace, for all and sundry, where tolerance and liberality and licence were the rule, and

33

few questions were asked so long as visitors were of a hearty disposition and uncensorious.

Not infrequently, of course, it became something of an embarrassment to the palace to the west which, however it turned its back on it, could never quite disassociate itself from the uninhibited, decayed and rambling establishment next door. Not that the King himself suffered much in the way of embarrassment – for James, whatever his shortcomings and peculiarities, was far from prudish or conventional; the offence was felt by his spiritual advisers of the ruling Kirk party and their more devoted adherents, and especially by the sternly Calvinist Chancellor Maitland, first minister of the realm and recently created Lord Thirlstane. Strait-laced as he might be, however, he was hardly in a position as yet to do more than frown caustically upon his sovereign's reprobate uncle.

Robert Earl of Orkney's eldest legitimate daughter, the Lady Marie Stewart, was wife to the Master of Gray.

Tonight, that of the 13th of February 1594, the Abbot's House with its appendages was truly bestirring itself, so that its ancient and ill-maintained fabric seemed to be all but bursting at the seams. Every window was alight, every door open, every chimney smoking. The very walls seemed to throb and quiver with noise and hilarity, music, shouting, laughter and female squeals emanating from every corner and precinct. Numbers of the citizenry of Edinburgh, with a well-developed instinct for free entertainment, thronged the nearest public stance in the Abbey Strand, looking, listening, questing the air, hopeful for spectacle and scandal.

The Duke of Lennox waited, in a fret, near the main door on the inner or courtyard side, just across from the tall frowning bulk of the palace which, notably less well-lit tonight, appeared to stare haughtily in the other direction from its randy, rackety neighbour. Ludovick was in a fret for a variety of reasons. He was waiting to receive the King – and was not at all convinced that James would in fact put in an appearance; when he had last seen him, that afternoon, the monarch had mumbled merely that he *might* come, that he would see, that it was gey cold, and that he was busy working on a new ode to celebrate the forthcoming birth of an heir to the throne – all of which, from James

34

Stewart, might mean anything or nothing.

Moreover, Lennox, as yet, had seen no sign of the Master of Gray. After persuading Orkney to arrange this jollification, he had sent a trusted courier to Fast Castle, giving the details – and had since heard nothing of Patrick Gray.

If however, the two principal guests were thus doubtful as to appearance, there was one who was not, but whose presence added to the Duke's anxieties – Mary Gray herself. Mary, still suspicious of the entire proceedings, had insisted on coming from Methven for this occasion, to confront her father, bringing the baby with her. She was somewhere in this rambling building – and to have had to leave her unattended in this houseful of roystering, lecherous men, a young, beautiful and defenceless woman unfortunately with the reputation of a courtesan, was not a situation which Ludovick could contemplate with equanimity – despite the girl's assurances that she could well look after herself, having indeed lived in this household at one time, with the Master and his wife.

Finally, however much he tried, the Duke could not remain wholly unmoved by what was so frankly going on in a sort of open alcove flanking this door, designed presumably as a porter's lodge; quite unconcerned by his pacing and frowning presence only a few feet away, a young woman in there, of ripe charms, her clothing so disarranged as to be almost discarded, was generously, indeed enthusiastically, sharing her favours with two youths, who pulled her this way and that on an alternating basis, to a panting commentary, interspersed with her giggles. One of the young men was David Stewart, fifth or sixth legitimate son of the Earl, whilst the other was almost certainly one of his bastard brothers; and the lady appeared to be one of their father's latest mistresses. Ludovick found their antics a little upsetting; there was neither door nor curtain to the alcove, and try as he would he could not prevent his eyes from straying frequently in that direction. He wished that they would go and pursue their unseemly love-making elsewhere.

He debated with himself not for the first time, whether or not he should go over to the palace, to discover the King's intentions. But he was reluctant, however foolishly, to leave this house with Mary in it; moreover he could not be certain that James might

35

not come from the palace at all. It was all most irritating that he must hang about like this – especially since assuredly it was the host's duty to welcome the monarch, either in person or through one of his sons; but neither Orkney nor any of his crew had shown the least inclination to break off their various pleasures on this or any other account, and the Duke had felt bound to do the honours, for decency's sake. Not that decency was an attribute that anyone would look for in this house.

The inevitable clash of interests appeared to be coming to a head in the alcove, two more revellers arrived to watch and advise, and Ludovick, though not a young man normally much concerned with his dignity, was deciding that he could no longer linger here, when the clank of steel sounded from outside. Five men appeared at the door, two in front in half-armour and morion helmets and the colours of the Royal Guard, bearing halberds, two following in velvets and satins and a third guard bringing up the rear. Ludovick bowed low.

'Y'Grace,' he said briefly.

The King, stumbling over the steps up to the doorway, did not actually speak, although his thick loose lips were moving, shaping words. He may have nodded his head to his cousin – but James's head, much too large-seeming for his body, was always apt to loll and nod, especially when he walked. He came shuffling indoors, between the in-turned figures of his escort, tapping the worn flagstones rhythmically with the ferrule of a long white staff almost as tall as himself and decorated with a bunch of much tattered black ribbons. Clearly he was in the throes of composition.

James, King of Scots, was certainly an eye-catching figure. Now aged twenty-eight years, he looked a deal older, a slack-featured, slack-bodied, knock-kneed shambling man, ridiculously over-dressed in enormously high hat braided with silver and sprouting orange ostrich plumes, padded and stuffed crimson velvet doublet and trunks slashed with emerald-green satin, hose sagging about spindly legs, and high-heeled shoes of pale blue with huge bows and jewelled buckles. Around his neck was a great ruff, sadly stained and crumpled, and hanging about it a series of golden chains with crosses and charms, with over all a short purple cloak, lined with cloth-of-gold.

His companion was a big, burly man of similar age, high-complexioned, haughty-eyed, richly clad although his garb seemed quiet beside that of his liege lord – John Erskine, Earl of Mar, Captain of the Royal Guard, Keeper of Stirling Castle and the King's boyhood playmate. At James's back he nodded to Lennox, and grimaced.

The King may have been a poor physical specimen and unprepossessing as to feature, with a lop-sided face and a tongue too large for his mouth that caused an almost permanent dribble; but there was nothing wrong with his eyes. Indeed, they were his only good feature – great, dark, liquid eyes, almost feminine in appearance, expressive and with their own shrewdness however much they rolled and darted. And now, however preoccupied he appeared to be with his muse, his glance quickly perceived the performance in the porter's closet, and despite Lennox's attempt to usher him along the stone-vaulted corridor towards the main hall or refectory, he shuffled over, to peer in at the spectacle with keenest interest.

'Fornication and all uncleanness,' he mentioned thoughtfully. He poked with his long staff. 'Yon's Davy Stewart – a bonny lad, and strong. Strong. The other – houts, I canna just place him by the parts I can see!' James sniggered. 'Who is he, Vicky – who's this?'

'I do not know, Sire. Heed them not – they are all drunk. Will Your Grace come this way?'

'Drunken with wine, aye. Chambering and wantonness. Ooh, aye. On such cometh the wrath o' God. And they're gey young for it, I reckon. The lassie I dinna ken.' The King wrinkled his long nose distastefully when he perceived that the young woman at least had eyes for him there, and was indeed smiling up at him. 'She's a great heifer, is she no'? Shameless! Shameful!' He wagged his head, and his glance darted at Mar. 'Hech, aye – here's a right paradox, Johnnie, a conundrum. Can she be both shameful and shameless at the once? How say you – can she?'

Mar shrugged. 'I have not Your Grace's gift for words,' he said shortly. 'I'd name her a dirty bitch and h' done with it!'

'Shameless and shameful.' James muttered to himself. 'Aye, I could use that...'

'Sire – may I conduct you to my lord of Orkney?' Lennox

37

urged, and the King allowed himself to be escorted along the dimly-lit and echoing passage. In dark corners and recesses couples clung and wrestled and panted, and if James seemed disposed to linger and peer, his companions marched him along to the great hall from which light and music and shouted laughter streamed forth.

It was a lively and colourful scene that met their gaze, from the arched doorway of that abbey refectory. Three sides of the huge apartment, where hundreds of candles flared and wavered and smoked, were lined with tables where men and women sat or sprawled or clutched each other, amongst a litter of broken meats, flagons of wine and spilled goblets. There were many gaps at the tables, some represented by snoring figures who lay beneath. Dogs, great deerhounds and wolfhounds, were successfully taking over the remains of the repast unmolested either by the diners or the servants, themselves apt to reel, who still plied a proportion of the guests with fresh flagons. In the central space a group of gipsy fiddlers played vigorously, and to their jigging music a dark, flashing-eyed girl, diaphanously clad only in veiling, danced sinuously, voluptuously, to a great solemn dancing bear, which lumbered around her suggestively graceful posturings with a sort of ponderous dignity. And along the table-tops themselves, a man stepped and picked his way amongst the platters, bottles and debris, himself tripping a step or two of the dance now and again, skipping over some diner fallen forward with too much hospitality. He was a portly, florid, elderly man in disarrayed finery, who played a fiddle the while in tune with the gipsies, though occasionally using the bow to poke shrewdly at certain of the ladies below him – the Lord Robert Stewart, Earl and Bishop of Orkney.

It took the Earl – or anybody else, for that matter – some little time to notice the newcomers. When he did, he produced a great resounding crescendo of screeches from his fiddle, and flourished the instrument, to end by bowing low over it in an exaggerated genuflection which drew all eyes capable of being drawn in the direction of the doorway. What he said was of course lost in the general hubbub. He did not descend from the table-top. The lady and the bear continued to dance.

James had no eyes save for the bear, his expression registering a mixture of alarm and unwilling admiration. Indeed he backed a little against his companions each time the brute turned in his direction. Quite clearly he had no intention of advancing further into the hall until the creature was safely out of the way.

When, presently, the young woman reached a climax of hip-twisting, stomach-gyrating and bosom-shaking ecstasy, and thereafter slipped in close actually to embrace and rub herself against the burly upstanding shaggy animal, and its great fore-paws closed around her twitching, fragile-seeming form as the music sobbed away to silence, the King all but choked.

'Waesucks! Look at that!' he cried, in agitation. 'Look at the lassie! And yon horrid brute-beast. Och, foul fall it – the nasty great crittur! It'll . . . it'll . . . och, save us all – this isna decent!'

'It is but a ploy, Sire. There is no danger,' Mar assured. 'The gipsies tame these brutes from cubs. They come from Muscovy or some such parts. She'll come to no hurt – not from the bear, leastwise!'

James shook his heavy head. 'She shouldna ha' done that,' he declared, frowning. 'I didna like that. Na, na – it's no' right . . .'

With the musicians for the moment silenced, and the girl dis-entangling herself from the bear without difficulty and mincing off, the creature resuming all fours and waddling after her meekly enough, Orkney from his raised stance lifted his richly-seasoned voice.

'Our gracious lord! Most noble and revered liege and suze-rain. Welcome to my humble house and board, Sire! Come, Majesty, and honour this poor company.' The Earl, whether deliberately or by accident, ended that with a notable belch.

With an eye on the disappearing bear, James nodded, and began to move forward. 'Aye, my lord – but no more o' yon, mind. No more wild beasts, see you.' Compared with his uncle, he had a singularly squeaky, and thick uneven voice.

Most of those in possession of their wits had got to their feet, or approximately so, though not without some stumbles and collapses. A place was cleared for the monarch and his two companions at the centre of the high transverse table at the head if the chamber, Orkney arranging this with the aid of his fiddle-bow. The officer of the Guard who had accompanied the King detached himself and made a circuit of the tables, knocking off the hats of such revellers as had so far forgotten themselves as to remain covered in the presence of the Lord's Anointed.

James had difficulty with his stave, as he sat down, not knowing quite what to do with it and apparently reluctant just to lay it on the floor. Eventually room was made for it to lie along the table itself – where unfortunately its bunch of ribbons lay in a pool of spilt wine. Lennox hoped that it was a good omen that the King had brought that staff tonight; it had been a present from the Master of Gray, brought on the occasion of his last return from banishment, as unauthorised then as now, five years before.

James, waving aside the food and drink set before him, drew out from within his doublet a crumpled bunch of papers, which he spread carefully on the table before him. At sight of them Orkney groaned, and hastily signed to the musicians to strike up once more.

'My new ode, my lord,' the King revealed, patting it proudly. 'More properly, an epode. Aye, an epode. To the new prince, Duke of Rothesay, Earl of Carrick and Lord of the Isles. Or, alternatively, to the Princess of Scotland, as the case may be. I'ph'mm. Just some wee bits of changes, here and there, will serve. Near finished, it is, but for a verse or two. Aye, and it goes excellently well, I warrant you. I have seldom wrought better verse. I will read it . . .' He looked up in annoyance as the gipsy players broke into full fiddle. 'A plague on that ill squawking!' he exclaimed, and flapped a paper at the musicians as one might shoo away a wasp. 'I say that I'll read it. I am prepared to honour this company wi' the first reading o' this most royal epode! Hush them, man – hush them.'

'Your Grace – perhaps later?' his uncle said urgently. 'When all is quiet. When the servants ha' removed the meats, the eating over.'

'Tush, man – am I, the King, to wait for scullions and lackeys? And these scurvy Egyptians wi' their caterwauling!'

'No, Sire – not so. I but suggested that it would be mair seemly suitable, to hear your verses later. After you've partaken o' my providing.' Orkney's voice was rich, thick, and just a

40

little slurred. He was not drunk – he was seldom actually drunk; equally seldom was he sober.

'I'm no' hungry. Nor thirsty.'

'A pity, Sire. But the maist o'my guests are both! To read this . . . this effusion now, could be but casting pearls before swine, I say.' He had a little difficulty with that phrase. 'I had thought, later. When all are eaten. In a small privy room, maybe . . .'

'No' here? No' to a' the company? But I *came* to read it, man! It's a right notable rhapsody . . .'

'No doubt, Jamie – but it's no' a' folk who can take in the like, see you. There's a wheen o' them here'd no' appreciate it. There'd be no keeping them quiet. Better to have but a few. In a small room. Presently.'

The King was offended. 'We are displeased. Much displeased,' he said. 'Vicky Stewart said I should read it.' He gathered up his papers, and pushed back his chair. 'Where's this room then, my lord?'

His uncle seldom allowed anything to upset him, but now he looked a little flustered. Then he shrugged, as James rose, and got to his own feet, beckoning a servitor to his side. All who were conscious of the fact, and able, must rise when the King rose, and in the confusion Orkney jerked a word or two to the servant. Then, picking up a candlestick, he conducted his nephew along behind the table, towards a door to an inner chamber. Mar and Lennox followed, and in some doubt not a few of the top-table guests left their womenfolk to do likewise. The royal guards took up positions at the doorway.

It was only a small room indeed into which the monarch was shown, containing a table, a few chairs and benches, and little else. There was no space here for much of an audience, and Orkney in fact turned back all at the door save Ludovick and Mar. James had promptly taken a chair, and was smoothing out the distinctly tattered and now wine-wet sheets of paper on the table, before he perceived how select was to be the company.

'What's this? What's this?' he demanded. 'Is this a', man? To hear my epode? Waesucks – but Vicky and Johnnie and yoursel'?'

'You'll no' want a rabble, Sire?' his uncle said. 'It's quality

41

you'll want, I'm thinking – no' quantity.'

'Better this way, Your Grace,' Lennox assured. 'Here is no matter for the crowd, the multitude.'

Mar, who was not of a poetic turn of mind, muttered something unintelligible but resentful.

James, despite his disappointment, was already peering at the first lines of his precious work, lips savouring the opening words.

'You'll need mair light, Jamie. Bide a wee,' his uncle urged. 'I've sent for mair candles.'

'Aye, it's gey dark in here. Mind, I ken the most o' it by heart. But...'

They all looked up as another door opened at the far side of the room, and a cloaked figure came in bearing a silver-branched candlestick, unlit. This man came over to the table, and proceeded to light his candles from that already burning there. Then he set the illumination down beside the King, and stood back.

James promptly returned to the perusal of his papers without a glance at the newcomer. It was probably the other removing his dark cloak, and the consequent glow of light from that quarter, which caused the King to turn round – or it may have been the silence which had suddenly descended upon that little chamber and which could be felt almost like something physical – a silence which was broken by a choking sound from the Earl of Mar.

James stared, mouth open, jaw falling, at the resplendent vision which the candlelight revealed. A wavering hand, paper and all, came out in a part pointing, part holding-back gesture.

The newcomer, tossing aside the cloak, and running a hand over his carefully-cut long black hair, bowed deeply, with arm-flourishing elaboration. 'Your excellent and dearly-esteemed Grace's most very humble servant!' he said, smiling brilliantly.

James gobbled, clutching at his chair and half-rising, eyes rolling in alarm. 'P'Patrick!' he got out thickly. 'Patrick Gray! Guidsakes! Patrick, man – you! What's this? What's this? Mercy on us – you!'

'None other, Highness. Patrick Gray returned to your royal side, in love and duty. From far and foreign parts. Seeking your gracious clemency – and rejoicing to see you well. To see

42

that I am in time. Aye – and bringing Your Grace an even more valuable token of my love and devotion than on . . . that last occasion!' The Master sank down on one knee beside the royal chair.

James continued to stare, slack lips working, long tongue licking. The suppliant looked quite the most splendid and immaculate figure seen in Scotland for long, dressed in white satin doublet and extraordinarily short trunks, slashed in gold, his spun silk hose sculpturing a lengthy leg as graceful as it was masculinely strong. The high upstanding collar of his padded doublet was edged with a chaste row of black pearls, and the Knight's Cross of the Order of St. Lazarus hung at his chest. High-heeled white shoes with jewelled buckles completed a dazzling appearance.

'This is an outrage!' Mar declared forcefully.

The monarch turned to look helplessly at Lennox and Orkney. 'But . . . but you canna do this, Patrick!' he quavered. 'It's no' proper. You're banished the realm, man! I've no' recalled you. The Council banished you. You behaved treasonably against me, Patrick – treasonably!'

'Only in the opinion of some men, Sire – never in my heart. That is not possible. Only in the prejudice and mistaken views of such as my lord of Bothwell and his friends.'

The King plucked at his lip. The name of Bothwell always perturbed him. 'Aye – but others too, Patrick. Maitland – my Lord Thirlestane, the Chancellor. He told me you were writing ill letters to Elizabeth o' England. Aye, and taking her gold. Plotting against me . . .'

'Never, Sire. The plotting and treasons are otherwise – as I have come to reveal to you. I left your realm because my enemies – and yours, Sire – had become too strong for me. I have returned to thwart them. And to save you,' Patrick had risen to his feet.

'Na, na – it's no' just that simple, Master o' Gray,' James declared, recovering himself somewhat. 'You canna just flout the decisions o' King and Council this way, I'd have you ken. Eh, my lords?' He looked round at the two earls and Lennox, all members of that Privy Council. 'Banished is banished, is it no'? Banishment canna just be terminate when the . . . the felon would have it so!'

'That is so,' Mar said heavily. He had never greatly loved the Master of Gray.

'Precisely, Sire. I am the last to dispute it. *You* only can terminate my banishment. You, the King. So I have come to you. If you will not do so, I abide the consequences. Either to return to outer darkness whence I came, from the sun of your presence. Or, if my presumption in coming here is too great, to pay the penalty for offending, with my life. But, to save *your* life, I had to come, Highness.'

'Eh? What's that? Save . . . save my life? What a pox . . .?'

'You are in deadly danger, Sire. From wicked and powerful men. I have uncovered a devilish conspiracy against you. But . . .' Patrick Gray glanced about him. 'As well that so few are here to hear me. Leal men. I'd be happier in even a more private place . . .'

'A cell in the Tolbooth, sir! Or better still, in the Castle!' Mar intervened grimly. 'Suitable enough for a forsworn traitor! As Captain of the King's Guard, *I* am responsible for His Grace's safety. And I'll see to it, never fear.'

'While you live, no doubt, my lord!' Gray returned briefly. 'Recollect that my lord of Moray was also Captain of the King's Guard!' That name upset both Mar and the King, as it was intended to do, for the Bonnie Earl of Moray's death had been horrible, and James could not wholly deny complicity. The Master pursued his advantage.

'It will require more than your Guard, my lord. The dagger even now points at the King's heart. Cold steel seeks his life's-blood – and swiftly. You do him no service to counsel that . . .'

* He got no further. As he was well aware, the very words that he had used were enough to arouse the King to desperation. James was on his feet now, even though unsteadily. All his life he had had the utmost horror of cold steel, a terror at the sight or thought of spilled blood – believed to have been born in him when David Rizzio, his mother's Secretary, was savagely butchered in the Queen's presence a month or so before her son's birth. Now he was gabbling incoherently.

Patrick waited, as Mar cursed, Ludovick sought to soothe and reassure the King, and Orkney considered his son-in-law from shrewd if blood-shot eyes.

'Out with it, Patrick,' the latter said, above the hubbub. 'What is this? What scoundrel thus dares to threaten the King's Grace? You'll no' make such charges without good cause, I'm thinking?'

'Indeed no, my Lord. Have I Your Grace's permission to proceed?'

James was still standing, and the others therefore had to be on their feet likewise. He had grabbed up his precious papers from the table, clutching them to him. Only after considerable coaxing by his uncle and Lennox, did he allow himself to be guided back into his chair. It was Orkney who signed to Patrick to continue.

The Master, amidst many interruptions and displays of royal horror, consternation and positive gibbering panic, recounted the gist of what he had told Ludovick at Fast Castle, with one or two elaborations relating to the scale of Spanish aid expected by the Catholics, the circumstances of the courier, George Ker's revelations to Patrick, and the names of other Catholic lords believed to be in the conspiracy – Seton, Sanquhar, Maxwell and Fleming. But he also made certain omissions, saying nothing about the proposed rape and remarriage of the Queen, and making only an oblique and disguised reference to the King's indiscreet letter to Philip of Spain, thus only hinting at the Kirk's blackmailing tactics on James – although, that the latter picked these up shrewdly enough despite his agitation and alarm, was evident by his quick, furtive and appealing glances at the speaker.

When Gray was finished his account of the plot, the monarch was reduced to tearful and hand-wringing impotence, a pitiful sight. Orkney was silent and very thoughtful. Not so the Earl of Mar.

'I do not believe it!' he cried. 'Bothwell is a crack-brained hothead – but he would never stoop to the death of the King! I would believe much of Huntly – but not this! He is your good-brother, my lord Duke. What think you of this tale?'

Ludovick shrugged in French fashion. 'I know not. But after Huntly's slaughter of Moray, I believe that little is beyond him. You will recollect that *I* did not choose him as my sister's

45

husband!'

That had been James's doing, it was thought on the advice of the Master of Gray. The King chewed his trembling lower lip, blinking great liquid eyes.

'All this depends on the word of George Ker, does it not? That perjured rogue!' Mar went on. 'Should we believe such a renegade?'

'Not at all, my lord,' Patrick said. 'I made a most searching inquiry, when I heard of it. All of which confirmed the conspiracy. For instance, I have sure word that the Pope has promised Huntly a large sum in gold, to assist the project.'

Mar spluttered. A fervid Protestant, he was ever ready to pounce on the villainy of the Pope of Rome. '*That* I'll credit!' he said. 'But not this of murdering His Grace.'

'Whether or no they would go such lengths, the rest sounds like enough,' Orkney observed. 'This of seizing the child. Bothwell was but recently shouting it abroad that His Grace was of unsound mind. Declaring the same again, and holding the child, he could take rule in its name. And with the Pope's backing, the other Catholic powers, as well as Spain, would accept him. That would be an ill business, whatever else.' The old Earl was half-drunk and slurred his words slightly, but then that was his normal state, and presumably left his wits but little affected.

'God forbid!' James mumbled. 'We must take steps. Aye, steps. Forthwith.'

'Undoubtedly, Sire,' Patrick nodded. 'Stringent and vigorous steps!'

'Aye. But what, Patrick man – what?'

'That is a matter for the Council,' Mar asserted.

'Assuredly. The Council,' the Master agreed, 'Which is yourself. And the Duke, here. And my lord of Orkney. And, of course, amongst others, the Lords Bothwell, Huntly, Angus, Erroll, Seton, Fleming, Maxwell and so on! A notable company. May I wish the Council's deliberations most well?'

'No! No!' James cried. 'Folly! It's no' for the Council. There's no trusting the Council. Waesucks – who *can* I trust?' That was a wail.

'You can trust the Kirk,' Mar asserted. 'The Kirk will aid you.'

'Will it?' Patrick wondered.

At his tone, they all looked at him.

'Of course it will,' Mar said. 'The Kirk is as the King's right hand.'

'Then I think perhaps His Grace may be left-handed! Perhaps he writes his letters with his left!'

'Eh...?'

James stared at the Master in new and different alarm. 'Patrick, man...!' he faltered.

The other made a reassuring gesture. 'I refer to letters of which the Kirk should not know. Letters of state, which are no business of the godly divines!'

'You talk in riddles, sir,' Mar objected. 'To what end?'

'Patrick means letters . . . letters to the like o' my good sister o' England, Elizabeth,' the King intervened hurriedly. 'Eh, Patrick?' He could be as quick as any, on occasion. 'The like o' that, you mean?' There was pleading, there.

Gray smiled warmly. 'Exactly, Sire – the like o' that! I but point out to my lord of Mar that the Kirk's interests and those of the Crown may not always coincide. As in our Auld Alliance with France, for instance.'

'To be sure! Quite so. Just that. Precisely.' James babbled his relief. 'Patrick's right. Aye. The Kirk is no' to be relied on implicitly. No' in such-like a matter, Johnnie.'

'To whom will you turn, then, if not to Council nor Kirk?'

James tugged at his wispy beard. 'God kens! The Estates o' Parliament. Call the Estates. The folk, the lieges, will aye support their King!'

"How long will that take? Weeks. A month. And the child due any day.'

'The Chancellor. Maitland. He'll ken what to do...'

'That whey-faced clerk! This will be no work for clerks – if the Master of Gray speaks truth!' Mar was no great lover of his fellowmen.

'Aye, but he has a good head on him, Johnnie,' James protested. 'Maitland's a canny chiel. Long-headed. He's no fool, Maitland...'

'Perhaps my lord Chancellor may be just a little too long-headed for the present business,' Patrick intervened, mildly enough. 'For the normal affairs of state, I have no doubt he serves you admirably. But in countering violent men, armed uprising, as my lord of Mar says he may be something lacking. More especially as he is already linked with Huntly...'

'Huntly!'

'Maitland and Huntly! Never!'

'You jest, sir! That Calvinist capon and the Catholic rooster!'

This time his hearers were united in their incredulity. The Master had gone too far. To name the sober, Lowland, Protestant Chancellor in the same breath as the swashbuckling, arrogant Papist Cock o' the North, was almost to mock the intelligence of his companions. Ludovick, strangely enough, felt almost disappointed in his former friend and guardian.

'No jest – as Moray found out to his cost, my friends.'

'Moray? What has Moray to do with Maitland?' The King's voice quavered again.

'Your Grace does not know? Perhaps ... perhaps, then, I should not have spoken? Forgive me, Sire. Forget my chance remark.'

James chewed at the back of his hand, eyes switching from one to another of the nobles, in most evident and unhappy quandary. The shocking and shameful murder of the handsome Earl of Moray, cousin of the King, by Huntly, had been the most unpopular act of the reign – for Moray had been the people's darling and beloved of the Kirk. James's jealousy of the sporting Earl, and his accusations of his tampering with the affections of the young Queen, were known to all, and his implication in the tragedy doubted by few. The sternly upright Chancellor Maitland however, had stood by the King, and with Patrick's help James had weathered that storm – even though Huntly had weathered it even more successfully. Now, it was clear that the unfortunate monarch was torn between his natural desire to have the whole wretched affair buried and forgotten, and to learn whether there were indeed aspects of it all which had escaped him and which in consequence might lighten his own burden of guilt.

James was of an inquisitive soul, and curiosity prevailed over apprehension. 'What's this? What's this, Patrick? Yon was a bad business. I was right displeased wi' Huntly. He overdid it

'– aye, he much overdid it, yon time. But what's this o' Maitland? Out with it, man.'

'As Your Grace wishes. I would have thought that you would have been informed of this. The Chancellor was behind Huntly in Moray's death.'

'Why?' Mar jerked. 'What had Maitland to gain from that?'

'Much. Nor is he finished yet, my lord. All men, they say, pursue some quarry in their lives. With some it is pleasure; with some, knowledge.' Patrick made a small bow towards the King. 'With some, women; with others, position and power. Maitland pursues wealth. Already he has amassed much, gained great estates. But he seeks ever more. And these days, not in small handfuls but in great. Who are the wealthiest men in the land? Huntly, Angus, Hamilton and Argyll. The Gordons and the Douglases are too strong for Maitland. As are the Hamiltons. He has set himself to bring down Argyll, and gain the Campbell wealth.'

'He mislikes Argyll, yes. But what of that? What has it to do with Moray's death?'

'Moray's mother was old Argyll's daughter, my lord. Moray had the guardianship of young Argyll, the control of his great lands. Since his death, they have passed to the control of two of the young Earl's uncles – Sir Colin Campbell of Skipness and Sir John Campbell of Cawdor.' The Master snapped his fingers. 'I would not give that much for the lives of these two gentlemen!'

All gazed at him, with varying expressions of disbelief, perplexity and horror.

'This is but a conjecture, sir – a surmise,' Mar declared. 'Maitland does not have it in him to fly so high!'

'You think not?' Patrick turned to the King, smiling. 'Have you ever known my information amiss, Sire? This I am assured of.'

There was silence in that small chamber. Ludovick marvelled at the man. Since coming into the room he had managed to undermine almost the entire fabric of the realm. How much of what he said was fact, only time would tell; but meanwhile he had succeeded in creating suspicion and doubt about practically every powerful man and group in the land. It had been a masterly performance, such as only the Master of Gray could accomplish. And the immediate result was not hard to foretell.

'What is to be done then, Patrick?' Orkney demanded. 'You will have your notions as to that, I warrant!'

'Aye, Patrick – what am I to do?' James bleated. 'Maitland's my Chancellor! I need him, man. And the Council's no' to be trusted. And the Kirk ... the Kirk ... !'

The Master nodded briskly. 'Three steps, Your Grace. The Queen to be guarded surely night and day. In a strong place. What is your strongest castle? Stirling? My lord of Mar is Keeper thereof – also Captain of your Guard. Put the Queen in Stirling Castle under my lord's care, forthwith. So shall mother and child be secure. Eh, my lord? Thereafter you to be keeper of the young prince or princess until this danger be overpast.'

'That is wise, yes,' Mar nodded.

Ludovick almost found it in himself to smile. So the difficult Mar, who hated Huntly and despised Maitland, was won over.

'She's near her time, Patrick,' James mumbled. 'I misdoubt if she can travel to Stirling.'

'In a litter, Sire. With care, and well happed-up, she will do very well, I swear. There are a few days yet, are there not?'

'Aye. But ... och, well. I'ph'mm.'

'Secondly,' the Master went on, 'We need men. Many men. And quickly. Not scores or hundreds. Thousands of men. Or the threat of them. Huntly and Bothwell and Angus have the largest followings – but there are others none so far behind. One is waiting, ready to hand – Argyll. He can field three thousand Campbells.'

'He is young. But a laddie ...' the King pointed out.

'All the better. He will play your game with the less trouble. But he is nineteen – of an age with my lord Duke, here, almost. That's none so young. At nineteen I was . . . heigho – never mind! This way, you shall halt Maitland's scheming also. Give young Argyll some high appointment. He will be flattered, and grateful. You will have three thousand Campbell broadswords – that have been itching in their scabbards since Moray's death – for a start. To add to your Royal Guard.'

'Shrewd,' Mar acceded, judicially.

'Who is next, with numbers? Apart from the wilder Highland clans of the north-west, who would take time to bring to your side. The Kennedys. The King of Carrick – young Earl of Cass-illis. He can bring out two thousand, at least.'

'Hech – but he's younger still, Patrick! He'll be but sixteen.'

'His aunt was wife to my lord of Orkney, here. And his mother a sister of your Treasurer, the Master of Glamis.'

'Aye. Aye. But could we persuade the Kennedys to arms, man? They are an ill lot. And no' that kindly towards their King.'

'*I* could persuade them, Sire, I believe. And if you get the Kennedys, then you get Eglinton's Montgomeries and Glen-cairn's Cunninghams also! They are all linked by bonds and marriage. Another three thousand!'

Orkney chuckled, but said nothing.

'That brings me to my third step, Your Grace. Countermand my forfeiture and banishment, Sire, I pray you. Forthwith. That I may serve you in this matter. If you will so honour me, give me back my position of Master of the Wardrobe. It allows me to remain close to your royal person. An advantage. Which, h'm, is both my joy and my leal duty!'

Mar drew a long breath, and stared up at the groined ceiling.

James looked at the Master from under down-bent brows licked his lips, and then looked at the others. 'Aye,' he said. 'Ooh, aye. Let it be so, Patrick. Just that.'

It was as easy as that. Almost an anti-climax. No contrary voice was raised. Patrick Gray had anticipated accurately.

He had anticipated thoroughly also. From out of his dazzling white satin doublet, he drew a folded piece of paper and a neat little ink-horn and quill. Opening the paper he put all on the table before the King. 'Since it would be unsuitable to disturb the Chancellor at this hour of night, Sire – and since the Sec-retary is his nephew Cockburn – I thought it might be helpful to have this ending of my outlawry written and signed. By now, no doubt, not a few will know that I am here, in Edinburgh. So, if Your Grace will but add your royal signature to these few words . . . ?'

James, for whom the written word held an importance that was almost a fascination, was already scanning the paper, his lips forming the words as he read, '. . . restored to his former positions, privileges and offices . . .' he muttered.

'Modest and humble as they were,' the Master mentioned, easily. 'Including, of course, my Sheriffship of the shire of Forfar.'

'Ah! Umm. Well . . .'

'I thank Your Grace.'

With a sigh, the King fumblingly dipped quill in ink-horn and appended his signature, the pen spluttering.

By the time that the King's party came back into the hall, organised entertainment had been superseded by private, however much some of it might savour of public display. Pandemonium in fact reigned. Whether or not the host had been any restraining influence, his absence appeared to have removed all semblance of order. Two of his ladies, considerably underclad, had taken up his position on the table-top, and were attempting to emulate the bear-dancer's act, to the music of a gipsy fiddler standing on the King's chair, a young lordling, with one of the sheepskins from the floor around his shoulders, performing the bear's part with much pawing and embracing. Further down the table active love-making was in process, at various stages, to the uncaring snores of the sleeping or the encouraging advice of those too drunk to stand but not drunk enough to sleep. Horseplay of sundry sorts was going on all over the great chamber, guests, members of the establishment, entertainers and servants apparently equally involved.

The most popular activity, however, judging by the amount of attention received, was taking place on the raised dais at this top end of the room, behind the high table, where two gallants were fighting a spirited duel with naked swords over a young woman whom they had penned into a corner there, while a third young man egged them on with the King's white staff. Strangely enough, despite the vigour and drama of the sword-fight, and the shouted comments of the onlookers, it was the young woman herself who drew all eyes, so at odds was she with the scene around her. Seemingly wholly unconcerned with what was represented by the swording, the noise, and all else, she was gazing calmly over that chaotic hall, with a detached interest that had as little of shrinking alarm in it as it had of proud self-assertion. Even her dress was out-of-place – though by no means in the way that was the case with many women present; she was clad, not in any finery but in a plain dark pinafore-gown of olive green, that was almost prim, lightened by the white collar and sleeves of a linen under-blouse. For all her air of demure modesty and quiet reserve, she was the loveliest, proudest-borne and most alive figure in that room. She was Mary Gray.

The scene affected the royal party in differing ways. The King, at sight of naked, gleaming steel, blanched and flapped his hands wildly, exclaiming. The Duke of Lennox let fly an oath, and went striding forward. And the Master of Gray came to a halt, and stood completely still, staring at the girl, lips slightly parted below that crescent of moustache.

Mary turned her head and perceived the newcomers. Her dark eyes locked with those of her father. After a moment or two, she moved, coming straight towards him, even though her route inevitably lay close to the sparring, panting swordsmen. With quiet assurance she raised her hand a little to them, spoke a word or two, and without pausing came on. The duellists obligingly moved to one side, sensibly slackening the vigour of their clash, even grinning in drunken fashion. One of them was Patrick, Master of Orkney, the old Earl's heir, and the other the Lord Lindores, a son-in-law.

Mary reached Ludovick first, as he hurried to her, but though she held out a hand to him, touched his arm, she moved on. To the King she curtsied gravely, from a few paces off. Then she turned to her father, searching his face.

He had not ceased to gaze at her. So they stood, so uncannily alike. There might have been no one else in all that noisy, chaotic room.

Only Ludovick knew how last these two had parted. It had been in dire, tragic emotion in a garden-house of Bothwell's castle of Hailes in Lothian, twenty months before, with the girl informing her father that she had deliberately betrayed him, sent proof of his most treasonable activities to his prime enemy, the Chancellor Maitland, and warned him that he had only hours to get out of Scotland before the Chancellor would seize him on a capital charge, whereafter nothing could save him from the headsman's block. None had witnessed that scene between these two – but Mary had told Ludovick something of it, for it was for his sake that she had done it, to save him from the evil consequences of the Master's plotting. The distress of mind which forced that terrible action, long put off as it had been, had deeply affected and changed Mary Gray; it was to be seen whether it had in any way changed the man who at the age of fifteen had conceived her.

Patrick it was who acted. He did not move, but slowly his hands rose, open, towards her, arms wide. 'Mary!' he said, throatily, huskily.

She ran, hurling herself into those arms, to clutch him convulsively, to bury her dark head against his white padded shoulder. 'Patrick! Oh, Patrick!' she sobbed.

He held her to him and kissed her hair, eyes moist, hushing her like a child.

Watching, Ludovick bit his lip, frowning blacker than he knew.

The King, although somewhat preoccupied by the still naked swords so close at hand, and also by the insolence of a gipsy standing on his chair and one of Orkney's sons purloining his staff, could not find it consistent with his royal dignity to stand waiting in public while this private reunion was enacted, however touching. But he had a soft spot for Mary Gray, whom he conceived to be one of the few people who really appreciated his poetic outpourings, and was disposed to be lenient. He moved over, to tap her on the heaving shoulder.

'Mistress Mary,' he said. 'Waesucks, Mistress – I think you forget yoursel'. In our presence. Aye – this isna seemly, lassie.'

For a brief moment the Master's dark eyes blazed. But he restrained himself. As for the girl, she stepped back, raising her head, uncaring for the tears on her cheeks.

'As you say, Sire. I crave Your Grace's pardon. It has been a long parting.'

'I'ph'mm. No doubt.' And then, relenting. 'I've no' seen you for long, Mistress. How's the bairn? Vicky's bairn?'

'Well, Sire. Very well, I thank you.'

'You should be more about my Court, lassie. You and Vicky.

54

No' hiding away in yon Methven. I . . . I miss you. Aye, I miss you both. See to it, I say.'

'But, Your Grace . . .'

Patrick spoke quickly. 'Highness – this, I swear, is well thought of. That Mary should return to the Queen's side. She can no longer be a Maid-in-Waiting, it seems, as she was! But if Your Grace was to appoint her a Woman of the Bed-chamber, she could serve all notably well in this pass. Close to the Queen, at all times, and with a child of her own. She is quick, sharp-witted . . .'

'Aye, to be sure. She couldna be a Lady-in-Waiting, no. But an extra Woman o' the Bedchamber. Aye, we could have her that . . .'

'But I do not wish . . .'

'Wheesht, lassie – it's no' for you to wish this or that! This is our royal will, see you – for the good o' Her Grace and the realm. So be it. Aye. Now – come, Johnnie. Attend me back. I'm needing my bed. There's ower much clatter here. It's a right randy crew! Vicky – get me my stick. Yon ill limmer Robbie Stewart's got it. There's nae respect here. Come . . .'

'May I wait upon you in the morning, Sire?' the Master said. 'With plans. For your urgent attention?'

'Aye, do that, Patrick – do that. A good night to you. Aye – to you all . . .'

As they straightened up from their bows and curtsies, Mary signed to her father to follow her, while Ludovick trailed reluc-tantly after the King. At a side door she turned.

'This way, Patrick – I have a small room in the bell-tower.'

He climbed the narrow winding turnpike stair after her, up and up, to a tiny high chamber under the old abbey belfry, sparse and bare, and only large enough to hold the bed, a chest, the cradle, and little more. In it the gorgeous Master of Gray looked like a peacock in a henhouse. Arm around the girl's shoulder, he stepped with her over to the plain wooden cradle.

'Ha! A darling! A poppet!' he exclaimed, peering down at the wide-eyed, wakeful but silent child. 'And handsome! On my soul – he's not unlike my own self!'

'In looks, Patrick – only in looks, I pray!'

Soberly he looked up at her, saying nothing.

'How is Marie? Dear Marie?' she asked, then. 'And Andrew? He will have grown . . . ?'

'They are well. Both. And none so far off. In Northumberland. At the house of a friend – Heron, of Ford Castle. Marie is with child again, bless her! And young Andrew is a stout lad. Near eight. But not so like me as this of yours . . .'

'Patrick,' she interrupted him, with a tenseness which was not at all like Mary Gray. 'Pay heed to me. You have gained your way with the King again, it is clear – as I knew that you would. You are to be accepted back to Scotland, at Court, banishment past. Once more. I . . . I cannot be glad of it. I fear for us all.'

'Shadows, my dear – you imagine shadows, and start at them.'

'Aye, shadows, Patrick. Shadows of your casting. You are, as always, good to see, good to look upon. In one way, you warm my heart. But the shadows you cast are not good. They are cold.'

He sighed. 'Are you not a little unfair to me, Mary? I have made mistakes, yes – done certain things which I would wish undone. But I have done much otherwise. I have saved this realm more than once. Spared it from war and bloodshed. Preserved the King. I come to do so again . . .'

'Patrick – for sweet mercy's sake, do not palter and quibble! Not with me. Let you and I, at least, speak each other frank. We are too close to do other, too alike to make pretence. I know how your mind works – because my own works in the same way. But, pray God, to different ends! You . . . you learned that, when last we spoke, Patrick. To your hurt. And to my own. I crossed you then – sore as it hurt. I would do the same again.'

Slowly he spoke. 'Are you threatening me, Mary?'

'I am warning you.' Her hand reached out to grip his arm. 'Patrick – understand me. If I can understand you so clearly – then surely you must be able to understand me? We are of the same mould and stamp, you and I. Heed my warnings, then. For your own sake, and mine. And for Marie's, and Andrew's – aye, and Vicky's, and this child's also. For we have both great power to hurt and harm those we love!'

'Love!' he exclaimed. 'A strange love this, which knowing nothing yet threatens and counters me . . .'

'I know enough, knowing *you*, to feel already that cold shadow which you can cast, Patrick! I feared this, and would have stopped you coming, if I could. Although I longed to see you, God knows! No – hear me. Let me say my say. Now that you are here, I must give you my warning. Do not entangle Vicky in your schemes again. That before all. Do not injure or betray the poor silly King...'

'God help me, girl – it is to save him that I am come!' the Master cried. 'Aye, and Vicky too. This conspiracy is against *them*...'

'Aye – that I believe! But, Patrick – from what Vicky has told me of it, the same conspiracy is far too clever, far too deep-laid, far too intricate for my Lords Bothwell and Huntly to have contrived. Or any of their friends. Any man in all this realm ... save Patrick Gray!'

He drew a long breath, looking at her steadily. 'You believe that?'

'I believe that,' she nodded. 'Oh, some of it – much, perhaps – may be based on a true design of these wild and arrogant lords. They are capable of great villainy, great ambitions. But not of the cunning interweaving of artifice, the subtle stratagems, the close-knit scheming perfection of this master-plot! That would demand a mind infinitely more talented – with the evil talents of the Devil himself!'

'On my soul – I do not know whether to be flattered or affronted!'

She ignored that. 'This I see clearly. What I do not know is your object. Your main object, Patrick. Whether it is all just a device to win you back from banishment into a position of power, with the King much dependent upon you? And having gained this, little more will come of it? Or whether there is more than that? That you have worked up this conspiracy in order to betray it, so that there will be great upheavals, great troubles, which you may seek to control for your own ends? I wish that I knew.'

He swallowed. 'This is extraordinary!' he declared, turning to pace the two or three steps which was all that tiny chamber would allow. 'Are you out of your mind, Mary? What sort of creature did I beget on your mother those twenty years ago?'

'One too like yourself for your own comfort, perhaps! Or her own! One who can plot and plan also, if need be. And, as you have learned, betray! So heed me well, Patrick. For I have much more to scheme and fight for. More than formerly.'

'As . . . ?'

'Ludovick. Our son, John. John Stewart of Methven. All that Methven means to me . . .'

'You call that much, Mary? Mistress to Vicky, Duke though he be! To be cast off at will? Damme, child – I could make you better than that! With your looks and wits, and my influence, you could and should go far.'

'I desire no better than Vicky and Methven. His love – and its peace. These I have. I am secure in Vicky's heart. He would marry me – but I know this to be impossible. I know what I want, Patrick. I do not want position at Court. You will not make me one of the Queen's ladies again. For your own ends . . .'

'That is a royal command, girl. You cannot ignore or avoid it. You must obey – you have no choice.'

'I shall obey for a short time. Till the child is born. Then I shall take leave of the Queen. She will let me go. She does not love me greatly. Nor I her. So heed me. Do not seek to entangle Ludovick or myself in your schemes – or you will find me a more certain foe than Chancellor Maitland!'

'And what are you now?'

'Your daughter, Patrick, in bastardy and unacknowledged – who would love dearly to be your friend.'

Chapter Four

So Patrick, Master of Gray, returned to the left hand of the
King of Scots – and it was not long before all Scotland was aware
of it. The new hand bearing on the helm of the ship of state was
not to be mistaken, a firm hand, assured as it was flexible – but
flexible as is a Ferrara rapier blade.

The Chancellor, of course, remained the right hand of the
Crown, the official agent of authority. That Lord Maitland of
Thirlestane did not relish the return of his long-time foe went
without saying: but he was too shrewd a man to fail to perceive
that for the meantime he had been out-manoeuvred, and that he
must bide his time if he would restore the situation. He made
no secret of his distrust and dislike of the Master – but he did
not deliberately put himself in the other's way or seek to provoke an open clash.

This situation was much facilitated by the immediate removal of the Court to Stirling. The very day after Patrick's
arrival the move was made. James had always preferred Stirling
to the Capital. He had been brought up there, in the castle of
which Johnnie Mar's father had been Keeper; from there he
was closer to his beloved Falkland, where this most unmanly of
monarchs yet doted on the manly pursuits of the chase – hunting,
hawking and coursing. Maitland, however, a Lothian man, had
in the past years centred nearly all the agencies and offices of
government, that were not there already, in the Capital; he was
now more or less tied to Edinburgh – where also the Kirk
leadership was ensconsed. All this the Master knew well, and
had allowed for.

King, Queen and Court, therefore. travelled the thirty-five
miles to Stirling, in the waist of Scotland, leaving the Chancellor
and his minions behind. The young Queen, although nearly
five years married, was still not nineteen, and looking somehow,
with her great belly, even more physically immature than ever,
however shrewd of eye and sharp of tongue. She rode, com-

plainingly, in a horse-litter, with her ladies on palfreys all around her, a colourful, chattering, giggling throng. The King, all clumsy and excessive attention – for though he lacked enthusiasm as a husband, he had been anxiously awaiting this heir and proof of his manhood for years – kept close by. The Duke of Lennox also rode with the ladies, to be near Mary Gray, who carried her baby in a wicker pannier behind her. Mar, however, and most of his nobles, kept as far away as possible – with the Master of Gray circulating around all groups of the strung-out cavalcade, throughout the entire protracted journey like an elegant but genially authoritative sheep-dog. He was noticeably more welcome with the ladies than with the men. And he was very urgent that the escort of two hundred men-at-arms of the Royal Guard should maintain a tight circle at all times round the Queen's litter – although it seemed unlikely indeed that any kidnapping attempt could have been organised so quickly after this change of programme, and anyway it was notorious that members of the Royal Guard were usually the first to be suborned in any major conspiracy.

The journey was accomplished without either attack or premature birth, and the great fortress-castle of Stirling, towering above the climbing grey town and shaking its fist at all the frowning bastions of the Highland Line, received them into its security. But even before they reached it, Patrick Gray went to work, having a messenger despatched, in the King's name, to the young Earl of Argyll at his Lowland seat of Castle Campbell at Dollar, a dozen miles away, to summon him forthwith to his monarch's side. In the event, the young man was at Stirling soon after the King, and after being kept waiting for an hour or two was highly astonished to have James inform him in a fractious and preoccupied fashion – for he was distracted by the loss of a couple of sheets of his poem which must have been left behind at Holyroodhouse – that he was herewith appointed Lieutenant of the North, in the place of the Earl of Huntly, and was to be given a commission of fire and sword against that nobleman and his treasonable Catholic associates. More than this the bewildered youth could not get out of the King – whereupon Patrick took him in hand, explained the position privately and approximately, informed him that Maitland was plotting his downfall and the seizure of his lands, but that he, Gray, was his friend and had engineered this situation in order to bring to justice the murderers of the Earl of Moray, Argyll's cousin and guardian. This was the opportunity for which Clan Campbell had been waiting. MacCailean Mhor, to give him his proud Gaelic patronymic, set off for his West Highland fastnesses there and then, eyes glowing, to raise the clan, on the Master's assurances that he would inform his Campbell uncles, his present guardians, of what was toward.

Next day Patrick himself set off south-westwards, for Ayrshire, to inveigle, if he could, the Kennedys and their allies the Montgomeries and the Cunninghams, into the prompt armed service of the King. He promised that he would be back in three days at the latest.

Curiously enough, however, riding alone, once he was well clear of the Stirling vicinity, he turned his horse's head southeastwards rather than south-westwards, towards the Border hills.

That same afternoon, whether as a result of the journey from Edinburgh or merely because of the fullness of time, Queen Anne's pains began. A strange young woman, she had had a number of false pregnancies, over which she had made the maximum fuss, setting her household by the ears; throughout the long period of this true pregnancy she had been difficult and demanding; but now, with the actual birth-throes upon her, she discarded all this, became calm and quietly assured, dismissed all her feather-headed and chattering ladies except the diffident young Lady Beatrix Ruthven who was her close friend and confidante, and Mary Gray whom she apparently trusted in an extremity, and sent for the midwife. To Mary she awarded the unenviable task of keeping her unsuitably interested and vocally anxious husband out of her chamber as much as possible.

Mary, therefore, spent much of the rest of the day and evening in an ante-room of the Queen's bedroom, discussing and indeed concocting poetry with King James, conceiving this to be the surest way of distracting his attention from what was going on next door. New stanzas were added to the natal epic – some of which pleased the royal composer so greatly that nothing would do but that they should be taken through forthwith and read to the labouring Queen, despite her evident lack of appreciation. James was also much interested in Mary's feeding of her own baby, which took place at intervals.

Inspiration in verse was still not quite exhausted when, at last, a child was born late that evening on the 17th of February 1594 – a son, somewhat weakly and small, but with none of the dire disabilities or deformities which the King, in moments of stress, had confessed to Mary as dreading, convinced as he was of the personal vendetta of Satan against himself, as Christ's Vicar and Vice-regent here upon earth.

James's relief and delight knew no bounds. Quite ignoring his exhausted wife, even before the child was properly wrapped and bound, he insisted on taking and parading the new-born Prince Henry throughout the castle, showing him to all whom he could find to look, courtiers, men-at-arms and servants alike, to the wailing not only of the infant but of the midwife and wet-nurse also. Mary, with Ludovick, accompanied the monarch on this tour, and indeed after some time she managed to prevail upon the exultant father to let her comfort the limp infant at her own breast. It demanded considerable dissuasion to prevent James from carrying out his heir to inspect the great bonfire which he had given immediate orders should be lit on the top-most tower of the castle, as signal to all the realm that a Prince of Scotland was born. If, throughout this perambulation, Ludovick was told once by his gleeful royal cousin that his eye was now put out, that he was fallen from high estate and no longer heir to the throne, he was told a dozen times. That the younger man was far from downcast, indeed even relieved, strangely enough did not commend itself to the other, either.

No one about the Court achieved bed until the early hours of the morning.

Next day brought to light a rift within the lute. James had had a nightmare. He had dreamed that the new prince had indeed been seized and spirited away from him, his mother playing a leading part in the abduction and going off with the kidnappers. Nothing would do now but that the precious infant should be delivered forthwith into the sure care of the Earl of Mar, to be kept in the most secure inner fastness of the fortress, with his wet-nurse. Queen Anne's indignation and protest at this decision was fierce but unavailing. She had already reverted from her excellent birth behaviour to the tantrums of the pregnancy period, and had taken a violent dislike to the wet-nurse, loudly declaring that the woman was a coarse and low-bred slut and that she should not be allowed to suckle the heir of a hundred kings. Mary Gray was to suckle the prince, she asserted, and although that young woman protested that she had her own child to feed and had not enough milk for both, the Queen was adamant. When confronted with James's fiat that the infant was to be put into Mar's keeping there and then, there was a major and unedifying scene, which ended with the King insisting on his decision, but agreeing that meantime Mary should act as foster-mother, despite the latter's objections.

So willy-nilly, Mary found herself in the situation, absurd as it was unwanted, of ostensible foster-mother to the new prince, temporary link between the indignant Queen and her offspring, and repository of the sovereign's confidences. A new wet-nurse was found for the infant, of course – for despite the royal desires, even commands, she would by no means agree to taking over the nursing of the prince herself and handing over her own son to another's feeding. James and Anne were more openly estranged than ever they had been, the Queen pouring out her troubles in the reluctant ear of the Duke of Lennox especially – whilst the nation, by royal decree, made holiday in public rejoicing, ringing church-bells, lighting beacons and composing loyal addresses.

This was the state of affairs to which Patrick Gray returned after two days – undoubtedly to his entire satisfaction. Whilst sympathising with everyone's problems, he had an air about him as though matters could hardly have been bettered had he arranged them himself.

All was well with the Kennedy project, he reported. While the young Earl of Cassillis was under age, and his uncle and Tutor, Kennedy of Culzean was unpopular, the leadership of that war-like clan had been assumed by the Laird of Bargany, head of the next most senior branch, a forceful and ambitious man who had readily responded to the Master's approaches on the royal behalf, on promise of pickings from the estates of the Catholic Lords Maxwell and Sanquhar. Moreover Bargany's

sister was Countess of Eglinton, mother of the boy Earl, chief
of the Montgomeries. This latter family was linked with the
Campbells of Loudoun, the south-western branch of the great
Clan Campbell. These also the Master had called upon. One
thousand men of Ayrshire would be ready to march within the
week, two thousand in a fortnight, and more if required. With
Argyll's Campbells and the Border moss-troopers of the King's
firm friends the Homes, a force was being born sufficient to
meet the Catholic threat.

This news was well received – but the difficulty now was for
anyone to maintain a belief that any such threat really existed.
As the days passed and no action developed, no signs of subversion appeared, men began to doubt. The Chancellor had
always pooh-poohed it all; now he sent messages to James
declaring that it was all a fantasy, an alarum perpetrated by the
wicked Master of Gray for his own ends. Indeed he strongly
advised the King to forbid this unwarranted and dangerous
assembling of armed men forthwith, as a menace to the security
of the realm. Who could tell what ill uses they might be put to –
especially the cateran and barbarous Campbells? It was always
easier to raise the Devil than to lay him again.

Patrick smiled, unruffled, at all this. Was his information apt
to be mistaken, he demanded? It would be ignored at peril. Let
His Grace call a parliament, he advised, at which the Catholic
lords should be summoned to appear for trial of treason, of conspiring against the realm with the King of Spain, and with
plotting against the King's life. Since Bothwell was still ostensibly a Protestant, let him be summoned on a different charge
– that of receiving English support against his liege lord, of
accepting English money and arms to equip his forces illegally
assembled. That, which was truth, Patrick assured, as he knew
on best authority, should serve the case. The alleged conspirators, if they were indeed innocent, would come to the
parliament to proclaim their innocence. If they stayed away,
they as good as admitted their guilt – and anyway could be proceeded against as disobeying the King's summons. Even Maitland, who was a great parliament man, and the Kirk leaders
whose policy was to strengthen their temporal power through
parliament, could not disagree with this advice. It would take

at least a month to organise and stage a meeting of parliament, because of the distances to be travelled and the arrangements to be made. Patrick privately assured the King that things would, in fact, come to a head before the parliament could meet, and urged that the forces which he had been conjuring up for the royal protection should be maintained in immediate readiness to move.

Maitland was commanded to proclaim an assembly of the Estates of Scotland in parliament, and send out the summonses in the King's name.

Chapter Five

It was, it is to be feared, a long time since Patrick Gray had attended divine worship as authoritatively laid down by God's true and Reformed Kirk – more especially in that temple and citadel of the faithful, St. Giles' High Kirk of Edinburgh. Yet not only had he gone to considerable trouble to attend there that showery April morning, but it was solely because of his efforts that the great church was crowded with so many other worshippers, to hear Master Andrew Melville expound the word of God, that hardly another could have been squeezed inside – in that he had persuaded King James to come all the way from Stirling for the occasion. He now sat, uncomfortably, on a bare, hard and backless bench, to the left of the King's stall, with Lennox on the right, and considered himself fortunate to have a seat at all, for most of the attendant courtiers had to stand, the Kirk being no respecter of persons. In a three-hour service this could be an excellent test of faith. Every now and again throughout the vehement and comprehensive praying of Master Patrick Galloway, he raised the head which he should have kept suitably downbent, and looked quizzically at the soberly-clad, dark-advised and stern-featured man who sat so rigidly upright in his accustomed place below the pulpit – John Maitland, Lord Thirlestane, Chancellor of the realm. Only once those steely eyes rose to meet his – and there was nothing quizzical or remotely amused in their brief but baleful glare.

King James fidgeted. He always fidgeted, of course, but this morning he excelled himself, for he was more nervous even than usual. Matters had reached a thoroughly alarming stage, and he doubted very much whether he ought to have allowed that difficult and demanding limmer Patrick Gray, who was too clever by half, to bring him here at all. Likely he should never have left Stirling, where he was safe.

James, in his fumbling, dropped his high hat on the floor for the third time, and the clatter of the heavy jewelled brooch that

66

held the orange-yellow ostrich-feather in place drew a quick frown from Master Galloway in his wordy assault on the Almighty. Picking the hat up, James scowled. He had a good mind to clap it on his head, kirk or none. Only in church, out of practically every other waking occasion, did he uncover. He even kept his hat on in his own bedchamber quite frequently, and had been seen by Mary Gray wandering into the Queen's boudoir, more than once, dressed in a bed-robe and nothing else but a high-plumed bonnet. All men must uncover in the King's presence; but here, in the kirk, the proud black-gowned divines behaved as though he, the King, was uncovering for *them?* James sighed gustily, and shuffled his feet. He nudged Lennox with his elbow.

'Is he no' near done yet, Vicky?' he whispered loudly. 'Man, I'm fair deeved wi' him!'

Master Galloway raised his harshly sonorous voice a shade higher, louder, praying for all sorts and conditions of men, especially those in high places who so grievously failed to recognise their responsibilities to God and man, who lived for their own pleasures, bowed down to idols, tolerated the ungodly wickedness of Popery, and hindered Christ's Kirk in the true ordering of His ways upon earth. He came to a thundering finish which certainly ought to have reached and affected the Deity.

With a sigh like a sudden stirring in the tree-tops, in profound relief the congregation straightened bent shoulders, relaxed stiff muscles, and eased their positions generally. Some of the women sat on stools which they had brought with them, but most of the great company stood upright on the flagstones, and now moved and stirred in their need.

The King looked along at the Master of Gray. 'Now?' he demanded. 'Will I do it now, Patrick?'

'No, no, Sire. Not yet. It must be *after* the sermon, to have fullest effect. The folk must go out with *your* words in their minds – not Melville's.'

'Ooh, aye.' That was acknowledged with a distinct sigh.

Patrick himself would have much preferred to get it over and to be able to escape the sermon – but that would not serve their purpose.

Andrew Melville came stalking to replace Master Galloway in the pulpit, black gown flying, white Geneva bands lost beneath his beard. Here was a man to be reckoned with - and none knew it more surely than Patrick Gray. Now in his fiftieth year, tall and broad, with a leonine head of grey hair and beard as vigorous as the rest of him, he had the burning eyes of a fanatic but also the wide sweeping brows of a thinker. Melville was indeed the successor and disciple of John Knox, but a man of still greater stature, mentally as physically. Like Knox he was an utterly fearless fighter for what he esteemed to be God's cause, but possessed of a bounding intellect and not preoccupied with the problem of women as to some extent was his predecessor. He had been regent of a French college at twenty-one and professor of humanity at Geneva a year or two later. At home, appointed Principal of Glasgow University at twenty-nine, five years afterwards he was Principal of St. Andrews. Now he was Rector there, Moderator of the General Assembly, author of the *Second Book of Discipline* and all but dictator of the Kirk of Scotland. He it was the hater of bishops, and not Knox, who had managed to establish the Presbyterian form of church government upon Scotland.

Patrick Gray had no doubts that he and Andrew Melville could never be friends; but certainly he was more than anxious not to have the strongest man in Scotland as his foe. Hence this visit to St. Giles.

After gazing round upon the huge congregation in complete silence for an unconscionably long time, to the King's alarm, Melville started by startling all and quoting as his text; 'But the thing displeased Samuel when they said, Give us a king to judge us. And Samuel prayed unto the Lord.' He could not have known that James was to be present, for no word had been sent from Stirling. Whether therefore he totally altered the subject of his discourse for the occasion was not to be known, although it seemed that way; certainly what he had to say was very much to the point, suitably or otherwise. He preached on the position of temporal princes in God's world.

From unexceptional beginnings, mainly historical, he traced the sins and follies and limitations of the kings of the earth from earliest recorded times, to the Israelites' demand for a monarch, on through the degenerations of the Roman emperors and the barbarities of the Dark Ages, to the glittering vanities of the Renaissance and on to the religious interference of the princes of the present-day – with many a shrewd swipe at the bastard and Anti-christian kingship of the Popes of Rome in the by-going. It took him a long time, but even so he held the great concourse enthralled, by the flow of his knowledge, his eloquence, his unerring sense of drama, his sheer story-telling. Even James was absorbed enough in the brilliantly selected sequence and exposition to apparently swallow for the moment the consistent implication of tyranny, malpractice and disobedience to God's ordinances of his own order of kings throughout the ages. He had dropped his hat again early on, but thereafter let it lie.

And then, after a full hour of it, Melville abruptly changed his entire tone, manner, and presentation. Throwing up his hand to toss back the wide sleeve of his gown, he suddenly pointed his finger directly at the King – who shrank back in his stall, eyes rolling, as though he had been struck. There sat the King of Scots, he cried, his voice rasping, quivering with power, to whom belonged the temporal rule of his vassals, under God. But woe to him who misused that rule. For King James himself was only God's silly vassal. There were two kings and two kingdoms in Scotland. There was Christ Jesus and His kingdom the Kirk, whose subject King James was, and of whose kingdom not a king, nor a lord, but a member. And they whom Christ had called and commanded to watch over His Kirk, and given his spiritual kingdom, had sufficient power from Him and sufficient authority to do so, which power and authority no Christian king nor prince could or should control.

James, under this abrupt and unexpected attack, gobbled and gasped, half-rising in his seat, and holding up a trembling hand before him, as though he would hide the preacher from his sight. All around him his courtiers stared, frowned, and murmured. Somewhere a woman giggled hysterically, although the mass of the congregation stood as though electrified, their eyes riveted on the speaker. The Master of Gray sat forward on his bench, admiration, assessment and concern struggling within him. To an anxiety about the time – for he had relied on the fact that of late years Melville's preaching had tended to become comparatively brief, in contrast to that of most of his colleagues – was added anxiety about the effect of it all on the King, and the direction which the man might take from here.

Master Melville seemed to be incensed by James's feeble rising in his seat. Both hands raised now, he declared in a terrible voice that he spoke from the most mighty God. Where the ministry of the Kirk was once lawfully constituted and those that were placed in it did their office faithfully. he cried, all godly princes and magistrates ought to hear and obey their voice, and reverence the majesty of the Son of God speaking in them. But did King James so do? Did he not rather accept and solicit devilish and pernicious counsel, desiring instead to be served with all sorts of men, Jew and Gentile, Papist and Protestant? Melville glared now, not so much upon the open-mouthed monarch but upon the angry, embarrassed or perturbed men around him – and, it seemed, most especially upon the Master of Gray.

Patrick looked back at him, and gravely nodded. But he was more tense than he looked. Much depended upon the next words – and on James not becoming so flustered and upset that he forgot his part.

Leaning forward, Melville altered his demeanour and attitude once more. Now, while still authoritative, dominant, he was understanding, forgiving, even confidential. The King was young. Those who advised him were the greater sinners. He paused, for moments on end. Urgency charged that eloquent voice. The inevitable consequence of the King heeding such corrupt counsel was upon him, upon the realm upon them all. This day, this very hour, the hosts of Midian were on the march. The Papists, the legions of the Whore of Rome, were in descent upon the faithful. He had sure word that those sinful and violent lords, Huntly, Erroll and Angus were even now on the man h south from their ungodly domains, with a great army. Nearer still, just north of the Forth, was the young Earl of Argyll, hot-headed and misguided son of a pious father, with a heathenish Highland host. Worst of all, that apostate son of the Kirk, the Earl of Bothwell, was reliably reported to have ignobly forsworn himself and turned Papist, and was marching north from the Border, with English aid, to the scathe of the realm and the Kingdom of Christ. The Devil himself was this day abroad in Scotland.

As alarm, almost panic, swept the congregation, the great voice quelled and overbore the rising disturbance, as the preacher lifted clenched fists high above his head.

'Now is the time to draw the sword of the Lord and of Gideon!' he thundered. 'Time for the Kirk and all the men to arise and put their armour on. Let them gird their brows with truth, and don the breastplate of righteousness! Let them take the shield of faith and wear the helmet of salvation! Let them draw the sword of the Spirit! In the name of God the Father, God the Son and God the Holy Ghost!'

Something like a sobbing wind arose throughout the great church as he finished, a wind that set the tight-packed ranks of worshippers swaying like a cornfield. Voices rose, men shouted, women screamed. A form of bedlam broke loose – while the man who had provoked it gazed around and down at it all, stern, alert but confident, assured that he was wholly in command of the situation even yet.

Strangely enough of all that excited throng, Patrick Gray was probably the only other man as calm as the preacher. Whilst others stormed and exclaimed, he sat back now, relaxing. All was well. It was better, much better even than he had hoped. His planning and manipulation had succeeded. One day he would preach his own sermon on the snare of the fowler!

King James was on his feet in much agitation, his hat clapped back on his head. He was wringing his hands. 'What now? What now, Patrick?' he demanded. 'Och, man – all's awry! They'll no' heed me now. He's ca'd the ground frae under me . . .'

'Not so, Your Grace,' the Master assured. 'Far from it. Rather has he prepared the ground for you. Now is your opportunity. Do as we agreed. Proceed, Sire, as arranged. All will be well.'

'But . . . but, they'll never hear me in this stramash! It's ower late . . .'

'They will hear and heed you,' Patrick turned, to catch the eye of one of the trumpeters who accompanied the King on all public occasions, and signed to him. 'I pray Your Grace to remember well the words we decided upon,' he advised, but easily. 'And to recollect your royal dignity.'

The high blaring summons of the trumpet neighed and echoed, piercing the hubbub like a knife, even as Melville raised his own hands to regain control. The sudden surprise on the man's face was noteworthy. Everywhere folk were galvanised by the authoritative sound. Men stilled, voices fell. By the time that the last flourish had died away there was approximate silence in St. Giles once more. Into it the Master of Gray's voice, so musical, so pleasantly modulated, after the vibrant harsh intonations of the preachers, spoke calmly, almost conversationally, but clearly enough for all to hear.

'Pray silence for His Grace. King James speaks.'

'Aye,' James quavered. 'That I do. That we do,' he amended, to use the royal plural. 'We would speak to you. We are much concerned. It's a bad business – bad! We are sair grieved. He's right, the man – Master Melville's right. In this. No' about my lord of Argyll, mind. But the others. There's revolt and rebellion afoot. It's yon Bothwell's doing. He's an ill man – I aye said he was an ill man. I had him locked in my castle o' Edinburgh here, yon time. He was let out, some way . . . I was right displeased . . .'

Patrick coughed discreetly, and glancing along at him, the King swallowed, and wagged his great head.

'I'ph'mm. Well – Bothwell's joined forces wi' the Catholics, foul fall him! He's been colloguing wi' the English ower the Border, this while back. We've kenned that. Now, yesterday, he crossed back into our realm o' Scotland in insolent and audacious rebellion. Wi' many Englishry. And a host o' his own scoundrelly folk frae Eskdale, Liddesdale and the like. To attack his lawful prince. That's . . . that's treason maist foul!'

A murmur swept the congregation. All eyes were fixed on the awkward, overdressed figure of the Lord's Anointed.

'We have instructed my Lord Home and the Laird o' Buccleuch to hold him. Meantime. At Kelso. To gie us time. The Earl o' Cassillis marches frae the west wi' his Kennedys, to intercept. But it's a gey long trauchle, frae Ayr and yon parts. He'll likely no' be in time, at Kelso. The Homes and the Scotts will no' hold Bothwell that long, I doubt. So . . . so, my friends, I jalouse we're like to hae the wicked rebels chapping at the gates o' Edinburgh-toun in two-three days' time! Aye . . .'

James flapped his hands to quieten the surge of alarm which gripped the concourse. His voice squeaked as he raised it to counter the noise.

'You'll no' want that limb o' Satan and his wild moss-troopers rampaging through your bonny streets! Like Master Melville says, it's time for a' true and leal men to arise. Aye – that's the Kirk, and the toun, the train-bands and the guilds. A' sound men. And mind, no' just to guard the toun's walls. Na, na – to issue forth. A great host, to contest Bothwell's wicked passage. Wi' my Royal Guard to lead it. And cannons frae the castle. The sword o' the Lord and Gideon, right enough!'

Quite carried away by this unaccustomed belligerence, James had difficulty with the tongue which, always too big for his mouth, tended to get grievously in the way in moments of excitement. Master Galloway and one or two other divines had moved over to Chancellor Maitland's stall below the pulpit, and were holding a hurried whispered consultation, Melville bending down from above to take part.

Patrick touched the King's arm. 'Excellent, Sire,' he encouraged. 'A little more Protestant zeal, perhaps! Assail the Catholics. A, h'm, holy crusade! And explain Argyll.'

James raised his voice again, but could be no means make himself heard against the hubbub he had aroused. Patrick had to signal the trumpeter to sound another brief blast, before the royal orator could resume.

'Wheesht, now – wheesht!' he commanded. 'I'm no' finished. I canna hear mysel' speak. Aye, well –that's Bothwell. But there's the others – the main Catholic host. Coming frae the North. Geordie Gordon o' Huntly, Douglas o' Angus, and the rest. They're further off, mind – still but in Strathmore, I hear. No' at Perth yet. But there's mair o' them – a great multitude. Aye, a multitude o' wicked men. Descending upon us, the . . . the Lord's ain folk!' James stumbled over that; he was not entirely convinced that the Kirk held open the only clear road to salvation, nor yet that the Lord personally sponsored men, or groups of men, subjects, others than His own anointed Vice-Regent the King. 'They tell me there's eight or ten thousands o' them. Wae-sucks – we'll no' need to let them join wi' Bothwell! That's

73

the main thing. That's what Argyll's at, see you. He's brought his Campbells frae the Highlands. They're moving into Fife, the now. Like Master Melville said. That's to keep Huntly frae crossing Forth. They're on my side, *our* side, mind – they're to stop Huntly. If they can. So . . . so . . .' His thick voice tailed away uncertainly.

'The crusade, Sire,' the Master prompted, in an urgent whisper. 'Your royal oath!'

'Ooh, aye. Here's work . . . here's work, I say, to do. The Lord's work. It's a crusade, see you – a crusade against violent and wicked men, Satan's henchmen. To that crusade I, James Stewart your liege lord, call you. I . . . I will lead you, and all true men, in person. Aye, in person. Against the troublers o' the realm's peace. Rally you, then – Kirk, tounsfolk, gentle and simple all. I say – rally to me, and I . . . I . . .' The King, swallowing, in an access of enthusiasm, raised his hand on high. 'I swear to God Almighty, on my royal oath, if you'll a' arm and march wi' me to the field, I'll no' rest until I have utterly suppressed and banished these limmers, these ill men, these rebellious Catholic lords and traitors, frae my dominions. On my oath – so help me God!'

Patrick Gray was on his feet almost before the King finished. 'God save the King!' he cried. 'God save the King!'

All around, the cry was taken up in a roar of acclaim. Everywhere men stood and shouted. Even Ludovick, who had been a somewhat cynical spectator of the entire performance, rather than any participant, found himself on his feet, applauding. The ministers, though clearly concerned by the way in which the initiative had been taken from them, could not but approve of this public royal commitment to their cause, whatever the underlying meaning. Only one man in all that church seemed to remain unmoved, stiffly unaffected by the dramatic proceedings – Chancellor Maitland. He sat still in his stall, frowning, while the din maintained. Patrick Gray caught his steely eye for a moment, before noting Melville's preliminary attempts from the pulpit to restore order, he turned to make for the great main doorway. He waved to those around the King to do likewise, and nothing loth they began to move in the same direction. James was not going to be left behind, and seeing the King going, most of the congregation felt impelled to leave also. Everywhere a surge towards the various doorways commenced.

Andrew Melville, a man practical as he was eloquent and able, raised a hand and pronounced a hasty benediction.

Outside, in the jostling, milling throng in the High Street, Patrick found his sleeve being tugged. A rough-looking, sallow-faced man in dented half-armour, had pushed his way close – Home of Linthill, one of Logan of Restalrig's cronies.

'Fiend seize me – I've been trying to get to you this past hour!' he jerked. 'Restalrig sent me with word. From Fast. Bothwell has jouked my lord and Buccleuch at Kelso. Coming down Teviotdale from the West, he cut ower by Bowden Muir and Melrose, and up Lauderdale. He camped on the south side o' Soutra last night.'

'Damnation!' Patrick exclaimed. 'By now, then, he'll be in Lothian! Within a few miles . . . !'

'Nearer than that! I came in from Fast by way of Haddington, Musselburgh and Duddingston. I saw the tails o' his rearguards.'

'His *rear*guards, man . . . ?'

'Aye. He was making for the sea, folk said. For the Forth. At Leith.'

'Slay me – Leith!' The Master clenched his fists. 'The fox! It's Huntly. He's driving through, to link with Huntly. With all haste. 'Fore God – he's much cleverer than I thought! Or somebody is! But . . . at this speed he cannot have his entire host? You cannot move an army at such pace.'

'No. He left his main force in the Borders, to front my lord and Buccleugh. He has but the pick o' his horse. Moss-troopers frae the West March dales – Armstrongs, Elliots, Maxwells. Cut-throats and cattle-thieves. Six hundred o' them. But bonny fighters.'

'Aye. So that's it! Here's a pickle, then. Six hundred of the keenest blades in the land to face – and only the Royal Guard and a pack of townies to do it. But we've got to keep him from joining Huntly. Either crossing Forth himself, or holding Leith, for Huntly to cross.' He frowned as a new thought struck him. 'But . . . why Leith? If he's for holding Leith it could be that Huntly's sending part of his force by sea. It could be, by

75

God! He has all the fisher-craft of Aberdeen and Angus to use. Sink me - could it be that? We shall have to have Bothwell out of Leith . . . !'

'What's this? What's this?' King James was plucking at his other sleeve. 'Here's the Provost, man. I'm telling him he's to assemble the toun. Forthwith. We . . . we march the morn. That's what you said, Patrick . . . ?'

'That is what I said, Sire,' the Master nodded grimly. 'But I was wrong. We march sooner than that, I fear. Much sooner.'

'Eh . . . ? Hech - what's this, man? What's this?'

'I have just had word, Sire, that Bothwell is at Leith. He has eluded Home and Buccleuch, in the Borders. Ridden hard, with six hundred men, over Soutra, and is even now at the port of Leith.'

'Leith! Waesucks - *Leith*, d'you say?' James wailed. 'Bothwell at Leith! Guid sakes - it's but two miles to Leith, man! It's no' possible. I'll no' credit it! No' Leith . . .'

'I fear it is true, Sire. We shall have to act accordingly. And swiftly . . .'

'Stirling!' James ejaculated, thickly. 'I must get back to Stirling. Aye, to Stirling. I should never ha' left Stirling. This is your doing, Master o' Gray. You shouldna ha' brought me here. I told you it was dangerous. It was ill done, I say . . .'

'It was necessary, Sire. Necessary that you won the Kirk and the town of Edinburgh to your side. There was no other way. Just as it is necessary now that you stay here. That you do not flee back to Stirling . . .'

'Wi' yon Bothwell but two miles off! And him ettling to murder me!'

'He is not attacking the city, Your Grace. Not yet. It is Leith that he has made for. It must be to take the port. To hold it. Perhaps Huntly is sending a force by sea. We must not let him land at Leith. Bothwell must be driven out. He has but six hundred men, I hear. A few minutes past you swore your royal oath before all in the church that you would lead them, and all true men. In person, against these rebels . . .'

'Aye - but that was different, man. Different. That wasn't to-day. That was for the morn. To march for the Border. To join Home and Buccleuch and other lords. Wi' their host. Och, I'd march wi' them, mind. Some way. Ooh, aye. But . . . no' this! No' a battle wi' Bothwell today. At Leith. On the Sabbath . . .'

'Someone must needs do battle with Bothwell today, Sabbath or none, Highness – or your cause is lost!'

'Aye – but no' me mysel', Patrick! It's no' safe. No' seemly . . .'

'His Grace is probably right,' the Duke of Lennox intervened, from behind the King. 'He ought not to be hazarded in this. He would be safer back at Stirling. If someone is required to lead a force against Bothwell, I will do it. In the King's name . . .'

'Don't be a fool, Vicky!' Patrick snapped – a very different man this from the languid and ever-amused courtier. 'Can you not see? Only the King's presence can muster a force out of these townsmen. There are but two hundred of the Royal Guard – and half of them are left guarding Stirling Castle! Kennedy of Bargany has three hundred riders outside the city, at Craigmillar – but that is all. Save for what the Kirk and the town can give us. Cassillis and the main body of the Kennedys are somewhere crossing the Border hills from Ayr. Argyll's Campbells are at Loch Leven, entering Fife. Both too far off to be of any use to us in this pass. Only the presence of the King himself will produce a host to attack Bothwell. And attacked he must be.'

'God save us a' . . .' James cried.

'What's to do, Your Grace? What's amiss?' a new voice interposed, sternly, strongly, as the powerful and authoritative figure of Andrew Melville reached group around the King, after cleaving his way through the press. 'What's this talk of Bothwell that I hear?'

'Wae's me – he's at Leith, man! Leith, d'you hear!'

Other voices broke out in amplification.

Patrick Gray, looking at the confident, dedicated and commanding man before him, made a swift decision. A gambler by nature, he assessed all in a moment, and staked the entire issue on a single throw. 'Sir,' he said, touching the other's black sleeve. 'We must act. Without delay. Or the Kirk's cause is lost equally with the King's!'

'I had not known, Master of Gray, that you were concerned for the Kirk's cause! Indeed I esteemed you Papist!'

'I have been esteemed many things, sir – even by those who should have known better! But that we can discuss on another occasion. I am concerned for the Kirk's cause because it is identical with the King's cause today, the realm's cause. To all of which you are committed, Master Melville, as much as am I.'

The other eyed him steadily for a little, ignoring the royal gabblings and the other voices upraised around them. 'Well, sir?,' he said at length. 'What would you?'

In terse clear fashion the Master briefly outlined the position, paying Melville a compliment by neither elaborating or explaining. The divine heard him out in silence.

'You desire, then,' he said slowly, 'that the Kirk joins forces with you and such as you, in violence and strife?'

'I do. The Lord whom you preach used violence and strife to cleanse the temple, did he not? And joined forces with publicans and sinners against those who threatened *His* cause. You said back there, sir, that now was the time to draw the sword of the Lord – for all true men to arise. I believe that you meant that, and did not but mouth empty words. As do some. I do not believe that you are a man of words only, not deeds. Or that the Kirk will stand by and watch Bothwell, for his own ends, seek to turn this realm Papist again.'

'In that you may be right. But the Kirk's action, and mine, may not be as your action, sir.'

'Only one sort of action will prevail to drive Bothwell out of Leith this day!' Patrick returned strongly. 'Drawn swords in the hands of resolute men. Or do you believe that words, mere words, will turn him?'

Melville inclined his lion-like head. 'No, I do not. So be it. This once. What is required?'

'Every able man and youth who can handle a sword or a pike, to assemble in the King's park of Holyroodhouse, forthwith. Or as swiftly as may be. Two hours – no more. We cannot spare more. In the name of the Kirk. And the King. Bellmen and criers through the streets, with your ministers. To tell the folk. The kirk bells to ring. Royal trumpeters. To get the folk out. You, Sir Provost – the Watch. Have it out. The Town Guard. The train-bands. The guilds. Have the bailies and magistrates out, to lead the townsfolk. In the King's name. Armed to

the fight. Before Holyroodhouse. You have it? In two hours –
no more.'

The little stout Provost of Edinburgh began to stammer his
doubts, but Melville cut him short. 'How many men are required?'

'Every man that we can muster. Bothwell has only six hundred, I am told – but they are seasoned moss-troopers, cattle-
thieves who live by the sword.'

'Very well. And you, sir?'

'I go to the castle. His Grace agreeing. There is the garrison.
And cannon. The Royal Guard is at the palace – such as is not
here. Vicky – my lord Duke – ride you to Craigmillar, where
Bargany and his Kennedys lie. They had to be kept out of the
town. Bring them to Holyroodhouse. Provost – riders out
hot-foot to all nearby lairds, Protestant lairds. In the name of
King and Kirk.'

Melville nodded. 'The Kirk will be there,' he said levelly.
'What of the King?'

'His Grace has sworn his royal oath before all men,' Patrick
said, with entire confidence. 'To lead in person. It is unthinkable that any should doubt the King's word.'

All looked at the unhappy James. Not meeting any glance, he
stared down at the cobblestones of the High Street, fiddling
with the buttons of his doublet. 'M'mmm. Eh, eh. I'ph'mm,'
he mumbled. 'Ooh, ay. Och, well . . .'

'Exactly, Sire. No other course is consistent with your royal
honour. I shall not leave your side . . .'

Melville smiled thinly. 'Just so, Your Grace. Thou hast said!
Master of Gray – I will await the King at Holyroodhouse. In
two hours.'

Patrick inclined his head – but his eyes held those of the other.
Here was a man with whom he could work; or do battle.

Chapter Six

'A great host, Sire,' the Master of Gray said, striving to sound enthusiastic. He had been seeking to edge the King 'further away from the solid phalanx of Bargany's contingent of three hundred tough Kennedy horsemen, who insisted on making loud and ribald comments on the appearance and fighting qualities of the rest of the assembly spread over the green meadows at the foot of towering Arthur's Seat. 'They have mustered well. Many men.'

'Iph'mm,' James acceded doubtfully. 'Many men, aye. But . . . will they fight? Eh? *Can* they fight, man? Against Bothwell's limmers!'

'It is for that they have assembled. To fight they must intend, at least! And . . . I sense much holy zeal!'

'D'you no' reckon the zeal's more for the Kirk than for me, Patrick? I dinna like the looks o' some o' them.'

'Let us hope that Bothwell will think the same, Sire! What matters it who the zeal is for, so long as they fight Your Grace's battle?'

Andrew Melville and his clerical colleagues had certainly proved persuasive recruiters. A vast, if far from disciplined mob milled and seethed between the grey palace and the abrupt slopes of the hill, armed with almost as much variety as was the range of age and appearance – with pikes, swords, daggers, bill-hooks, sickles, axes, staves and knives bound to poles. Half the city appeared to be present – though which were volunteers and which mere spectators was difficult to ascertain. There was much brandishing of these weapons and much shouting, it being doubtful how much of it was Godly exhortation and acclaim and how much native quarrelsomeness, high spirits and horse-play. There was, and could be, no real order of formation maintained – although the many black-gowned ministers who pushed everywhere amongst the crowd, seemed to be trying to impose their own ideas of military, or at least militant, comportment.

Women and children permeated the assembly, and looked as though they were by no means going to be left behind when the time came to march.

The Duke of Lennox had been urging for some time that such order should be given forthwith. A certain amount of internecine strife had already broken out between the warlike townsmen and their traditional oppressors, the Town-Guard, and Ludovick had been seeking to aid the Provost and magistrates to restrict this within modest limits; the apprentices, who were out in force, clearly had other ideas, and, grievously outnumbered, the Town Guard had now formed a tight square around the civic dignitaries, and the Duke had been sent to beseech the King either to send his own Royal Guard and the Kennedys to their aid, or to order an immediate march on Leith as distraction.

Patrick Gray had demurred. Let the Town Guard solve its own problems, he argued; the last thing that they wanted was for the King's Guard to make itself unpopular with the populace. Moreover, they must await the arrival of the cannon from the castle, which should make for a great access of enthusiasm and aggressive spirit. Also, so far, very few parties of retainers and men-at-arms had appeared from lords and lairds near the city and they, being horsed, were badly required.

Andrew Melville came striding up to the royal party, beard, white Geneva bands and black gown all streaming in the breeze. 'We must up and move, Your Grace,' he declared strongly. 'The good folk get restive. Let us wait no longer.'

'Aye. But . . . the cannon . . . ?' James, nibbling his nails, looked at the Master.

'A little longer, Master Melville,' Patrick said. 'We would be foolish not to await the cannon. The sight of them, I swear, will greatly encourage these people of yours. Also, the garrison from the castle who brings them are to bring with them all the armoury of pikes and halberds. Hundreds of them. These we much need. They should have been here by this but the oxen that draw the cannon are slow . . .'

There was a diversion, as the thunder of hooves drew all eyes eastwards. Round the foot of the hill, from the higher ground at that side, came at the gallop a gallant cavalcade, about one hundred strong, banners flying, steel glinting, armour clanking. The great leading banner showed the famed Red Heart of Douglas.

At sight of that dread emblem there was next to panic amongst much of the crowd, for the Douglas reputation was as savage as it was ancient and the Earl of Angus, one of the chief rebels, was head of the clan. But the knowledgeable sighed with relief, recognising the ensign of the Earl of Morton, from Dalkeith five miles away, of the Protestant branch of the house.

Morton himself, elderly, portly and purple, clad in magnificent and old-fashioned gold-inlaid armour, led his superbly equipped and mounted cohort up to the King's position, scattering lesser folk, volunteers, guild-members and ministers alike, right and left, his men roaring 'A Douglas! A Douglas!' in traditional fashion. James shrank back before the flailing hooves of Morton's charger, as the Earl pulled the beast back. in an abrupt, earth-scoring halt, on to its very haunches.

'You need Douglas, I hear, my lord King?' the old man bellowed. 'I came hot-foot with these. Twice so many follow. What's to do, eh? What's to do?'

'Aye. Thank you, my lord. Aye, my thanks,' James acknowledged from behind Patrick. 'It's Bothwell...'

'Bothwell! That bastard's get by a Hepburn whore!' Morton cried, caring nothing that the bastard involved was one of the King's own uncles. He dismounted heavily, throwing his reins to an attendant, and clanked forward, roughly pushing aside the two divines, Melville and Galloway. 'Out o' the way o' Douglas, clerks!' he barked.

'Sir!' Master Galloway protested. 'Have a care how you go...'

'Quiet, fool!' the Douglas standard-bearer ordered, coming behind his lord.

'But... I am minister of the High Kirk of St. Giles...!'

'I carena' whether you're the Archangel Gabriel, man! No daws squawk where Douglas is!'

Andrew Melville stroked his beard, but said nothing.

Patrick hastened to close the breach. He had helped substantially in bringing low the previous Morton, the terrible one-time Regent of Scotland, and had no love for the nephew. But this unexpected adherence now was a major access of strength. 'My lord,' he cried. 'You are welcome, I vow! A notable augury – Douglas joins the King and the Kirk! Master Melville here has nobly rallied the faithful. Brought out this great host of the people, to assail Bothwell . . .'

The Earl snorted. 'That rabble!' He spat. 'Clear them out of the way, I say! Before Bothwell does. They encumber the decent earth!'

'My lord of Morton,' Melville said, quietly but sternly. 'I mislike your words and your manners. You speak of the people of God! Fellow-heirs, with yourself, of Christ's mercy. By the looks of you, you will need that mercy more than most. And sooner than some!'

'Devil burn you!' Morton swung round, to stare at the other. 'You . . . *you* dare speak me so! God's Passion – I'll teach you and your low-born like to raise your croaking voice in Douglas's presence! By the powers . . .'

Patrick was tugging at the King's sleeve. 'Quickly!' he whispered. 'Stop him, Sire.'

'Eh, eh! Hech, me! My lord! My lord o' Morton – ha' done. We . . . we command it. Aye, command it. You also, Master Melville. Ha' done, I say. This'll no' do, at all.' James's thick voice shook, but he went on. 'It's no' suitable. In our royal presence. Eh . . . ?' Patrick was prompting at his side. 'Aye. We need you both – greatly need you. Our cause is one. We canna have bickering and brabbling . . .'

A commotion to the north drowned his words. Shouting arose, there and was taken up by the huge concourse, as with a great groaning and squealing of wooden axle-trees, three massive iron cannon, bound and hooped, each drawn by a train of a dozen plodding oxen, lumbered from the cobblestones of the Canongate on to the grassland of the park. Such a thing had not been seen since Flodden. Everywhere men surged forward, to admire and exclaim. Even Morton forgot his spleen, to stride off to inspect the monsters. Folk were shouting that here was Mons, good buxom Mons, the most famous piece of ordnance ever forged.

Gratefully Patrick seized the opportunity. He slipped over to Melville's side, spoke a few sympathetic words, and urged immediate superintendence of the issue of the garrison's hundreds of pikes and halberds to the people. Then he besought the King to mount his horse and have the Royal Standard unfurled above his head, to a fanfare of trumpets. No speeches this time – for not one in a hundred would hear him. Then, the move to Leith at last.

So, presently, that strange, discordant, sprawling horde set off on its two-mile march, surely the most unlikely army ever to issue from the Capital behind the proud Rampant Lion of Scotland. First rode an advance-party of fifty Kennedys, to clear the way and act as scouts. Patrick had been anxious about the Kennedys and the Douglases coming to blows, and conceived this useful and honourable duty as in some way countering Morton's arrogant assumption that he and his must remain closest to the King. Then came the hundred of the Royal Guard, preceding the King's Standard-bearer and the Lord Lyon King of Arms. James himself followed, with Morton only half a head behind on the right and the Duke of Lennox on the left, flanked by Douglas horsemen, four deep. Next a motley group marched on foot – including, strangely enough, the Master of Gray, despite tall riding-boots and clanking spurs; when he had discovered that Andrew Melville and the other Kirk leaders intended to walk all the way to Leith, refusing to be mounted where there followers were not, he promptly handed over his horse to a servant and marched with them. The little fat Provost also puffed and panted with this party, as did certain deacons of guilds, magistrates and other prominent townsfolk. Then came Bargany and his remaining two-hundred-and-fifty horse, followed by a mixed assortment of mounted men to the number of another hundred or so. Thereafter the castle garrison, with the ox-drawn cannon, followed by the great mass of the people, starting with companies and groups which kept some sort of order, armed with pikes and bills, but quickly degenerating into a noisy and undisciplined mob, to tail off eventually in a vast following of onlookers, women, children and barking dogs. How many the entire strung-out host might add up up to it was impossible to guess – but it could be computed that there were over five hundred horse and perhaps a thousand footmen who might generously be called pikemen, with three or four

84

times that of miscellaneous approximately armed men, apart from the hangers-on who far outnumbered all.

This straggling multitude progressed – since it could hardly be said to march – in a general northerly direction, by way of the Abbey Hill, the flanks of Calton Hill, the village of Moutrie, the Gallow's hill where the bodies of offenders hung in chains, and on down the long straight track of Leith Loan past the hamlet of Pilrig and the outskirts of Logan's property of Restalrig. The bare two miles took the best part of two hours to cover, largely because of the desperately slow pace of the plodding oxen drawing the heavy cannon over the churned-up mud of the uneven route. Indeed, the impatient apprentices, who started by helping to push the lumbering artillery at bad patches, presently took over from the oxen altogether, and the last part of the journey was completed at a slightly better pace. By which time the entire incoherent column had spread and strung itself out sufficiently to make it barely recognisable as a unified force.

The Kennedy outriders kept the leadership posted as to the situation ahead. Quite early on scouts came back with the word that Bothwell, after taking Leith with little or no resistance – for the town walls, once stronger than those of Edinburgh itself, had been broken down during the religious wars of Queen Mary's reign and never rebuilt – had now moved out of the port itself to the east, to take up a defensive position amongst the fortifications in the open area outside the town known as Leith Links. Later information confirmed that he was still there.

The news could be both good and bad. He was evidently not sallying forth to challenge the King's force; on the other hand, he was not retreating – and these fortifications, earthworks thrown up to protect Leith and the Capital from an expected English landing by sea fifty years before, were defensively very powerful.

As the leaders of the royal force neared the broken walls of Leith, James became ever more agitated. He was a good horseman, strangely enough, although his slouching seat was deceptive, but, though twice the man mounted that he was on his shambling feet, he was still no warrior-king. Without Patrick Gray at his side to sustain him, and unappreciative of Morton's bellicose confidence, he kept looking back wistfully, most clearly desiring to be elsewhere. Ludovick Lennox presently fell behind to speak to the Master, to declare that if he did not come forward to take the King in hand again, there was likely to be a crisis.

So, his usually immaculate appearance notably soiled and mud-spattered, Patrick took to horse once more and resumed his nursing of the monarch's slender militancy.

In sight of the town's belatedly closed gates and gapped walls, they swung away right-handed, eastwards. They could see the green mounds of the earthworks on the Links, now, about half-a-mile away, between them and the sea. A few figures could be distinguished on the summits of the ramparts, but there was no sign of an army. Bothwell's troops could be hidden behind the grassy banks easily enough.

The King's relief at not being able to see his enemy was comic. Patrick was more concerned at not being able to see the sea, which the banks and the town between them hid.

'We must send a party to keep watch from the Signal Tower, Sire,' he declared. The environs of Leigh were flat, with no hills to offer vantage-points, and a tall watch-tower was a prominent feature of the harbour works, for observing the approach of shipping. 'If Bothwell is waiting here, it may well be to help in the landing of a force coming by sea. We must be warned of any such.'

'Aye, Patrick – Aye.' James obviously had an idea. 'I could do that, man. *I* could watch in the auld Signal Tower. Fine I could. And keep you informed here . . .'

'No doubt, Sire. But your royal presence with this host is entirely necessary. All would be at each others' throats without you, I fear – or away home to Edinburgh! Others we can spare – not the King!'

Silent, James rode on.

They were about four hundred yards from the first of the ramparts when the scene was suddenly and most dramatically transformed. All along the summit of that lengthy line of earthworks horsemen appeared, in a well-concerted movement, to stand there, side by side, upright lances glistening in the sun, pennons fluttering. The line was only one man deep but it was almost half-a-mile long, and the effect was impressive in the ex-

treme – and daunting to more than King James. The advance of
the royal horde came to a ragged halt.

Seeking to soothe the sovereign's near panic, Patrick pointed
out that there was no immediate danger. The ground between
the forces was cut and scored by trenches and holes, out of
which the soil for the ramparts had been dug – now mostly
filled with water. No cavalry charge across this was a practical
proposition, from either side. Bothwell could not come at them,
in his present formation, any more than they could get at him –
save with footmen, who were certainly not likely to be anxious
to throw away their lives in any head-on assault. And the range
was too great for musketry. They had one advantage, however,
denied to Bothwell. They had artillery. When the cannon came
up, the situation would be changed.

Only slightly reassured, James was in a fret for the arrival of
the guns. Confusion prevailed along the royal line – if line it
could be termed. Some bold spirits pressed forward, to shake
weapons and fists at the long still array of horsemen quarter-
of-a-mile away – but more pressed back. There was a deal of
shouting, some unauthorised and wild musket-fire, and considerable prayer, both offensive and defensive. Morton, without
consulting anyone else, ordered his Douglas horsemen into a
spectacular earth-shaking, lance-shaking, gallop, up and down
the front, back and forward, shouting slogans, banners flying –
but not coming within three hundred yards of the enemy. The
main mass of townsmen, still coming up, kept pushing in
amongst those in front, and then, discovering the situation,
pushing back again.

In contrast to these highly mobile and fluid tactics, the enemy
remained rather alarmingly motionless, grimly sure of themselves. Only in the centre of the long front was there any
movement at all, where, under the red and white banner of
Hepburn a small group of dismounted men were clustered.

Kennedy of Bargany, a stocky, bull-necked middle-aged man,
and veteran of innumerable feuding affrays in his own lawless
Carrick, rode up to Patrick, and after hooting his contempt of
the King's force in general, and disparaging Morton's antics
with his Douglases in particular, suggested that he should seek
to outflank Bothwell with as much of the cavalry as could be

spared. The fortifications ended at the very walls of Leith on the west, and nothing could be done there; but they must peter out somewhere to the east, amongst the open sand-dunes, and the enemy line could be turned from that side.

Patrick agreed – although the riding away of a large part of the cavalry might have a disastrous effect on the foot. On the other hand, to wait there doing nothing in the face of that grim line of moss-troopers was equally bad for morale. Bargany's move might at least cause Bothwell to break his threatening frontal formation.

Andrew Melville, from a consultation with some of his clerical colleagues, came to announce that the shepherds of Christ's Kirk had not marched all this way to stand inactive before the Philistines. The Lord's battles were not won so. Let them advance and come to grips. The Kirk would lead if the King would not.

Both these proposals appalled James. Patrick however saw virtue even in the latter, suitably modified – since almost any action, in the circumstances, was better than this inaction, which was in danger of turning their unwieldy host into a useless panic-stricken mob. Something to keep the crowd interested and occupied, whilst they awaited the cannon, was essential. Any head-on assault would be suicidal – but if part of the cavalry riding off to the east was balanced by a movement of foot to the west, order might be maintained and the impression given of some assured strategy. He urged Melville to lead some portion of his Kirk following in a flanking move to the west, towards the point where these ramparts joined Leith town walls. The said walls were broken and tumbled, and it ought to be possible to infiltrate through the streets and possibly work round the back of the enemy line. This, taken in conjunction with the Kennedy move, should at least worry Bothwell – whilst leaving the front clear for the cannon when at length they could be brought to bear.

Melville conceded the sense of this, and he and his fire-eating clergy went to harangue their more fervid supporters, while Bargany, with his own people and the miscellaneous horse, rode off eastwards, to the jeers of Morton's breathless warriors, now returned from their exercises in the full face of the enemy.

As the faithful surged off to the west, quite a proportion of the main body electing to trail after them, Morton transferred his scorn and abuse to these, asserting that they were deserting the field as he had known they would, but that honest men were well rid of riff-raff of the sort. The King's Grace was in a bad way when he had to call on such to fight his battles for him – and Westland Kennedy bogtrotters little better! Let His Grace but wait until the Douglas reinforcements arrived, and they would sweep Bothwell and his scoundrelly Borderers into the sea without more ado.

The Master of Gray gravely acknowledged that this, of course, would be the ideal consummation, and to be looked forward to by all. But meantime they must be content with less epic gestures – and if his lordship would be so good as to use some of his horse to go back and help expedite the arrival of the dilatory cannon ...

Whilst King, Duke and upstart courtiers were being informed in no uncertain terms of the unsuitability of any suggestion that Douglas should be looked upon as agency of any sort of haulage and traction, a substitute for draught-oxen, happily a rumbling and creaking from the rear announced the arrival of the ordnance at last. The effect upon all was extraordinary. The crowd seemed to forget its fear of that ominous waiting rank of steel-clad horsemen fronting them. Everywhere men actually pressed forward as the pieces were trundled up. Even James himself was partially transformed. He dismounted, and went to pat Mons Meg, the largest of the monsters, stroking the great barrel as though it was a restive horse. His well-known hatred of cold steel did not seem to apply to forged iron. Perhaps something of his great-grandfather James the Fourth's strange and ill-rewarded enthusiasm for artillery – and James the Second's before that – had descended to their unlikely successor.

The cannon were set upon the nearest thing to an eminence that could be found thereabouts, and the castle garrison set about the laborious process of loading, priming and preparing to fire. James himself was eventually proffered the burning, spluttering rope, to have the honour of firing the first shot from Mons – but he preferred to leave it to the master gunner, and retired a fair

89

distance back and to the side, clapping his beringed hands over his ears and tight-shutting his eyes.

The report thundered out with a most satisfactory crash, shaking the earth, belching forth flame and black smoke, sending echoes chasing amongst the tall lands of nearby Leith, and setting the sea-birds screaming and Morton's horses dancing. A great cheer arose from the throng – despite the fact that the ball smashed into a ditch fully one hundred and fifty yards short of the enemy, throwing up a huge fountain of mud and water. The second piece did not go off properly, most of the blast seeming to blow backwards rather than forwards, to the alarm of those nearby, and the ball only went a short distance in a visibly drooping arc. The third however went off with another tremendous bang, and though nobody detected where the shot went – certainly no enemy were seen to fall – enthusiasm was restored.

The loading and priming process recommenced.

Whilst they waited, the crowd continued to cheer. At the same time, activity was to be observed in the centre of Bothwell's line, with men mounting and riding here and there. Patrick spoke low-voiced to Ludovick.

'We have stirred up Francis Hepburn at last, Vicky. Now we shall see some action. If he elects to come straight at us, see you to the King. He cannot charge us, over that broken ground – but he could ride through in column. He far outnumbers Morton's horse. I do not think that he will do it, mind – although he would only have to face one salvo of cannon, for he would be on us before they could be recharged. But if so, get the King out of it swiftly, eastwards to Bargany. At all costs he must not be captured, whatever else happens.'

"I'd prefer some stouter role ..."

'Don't be a fool, Vicky! The King is the ultimate prize. Lose him and all is lost in this unfortunate realm ...'

Mons roared once more. Earth and sand flew up from the base of the green rampart on which the Borderers were ranked. Horses could be seen to rear and plunge. Loud and shrill was the delight of the onlookers.

A trumpet neighed tensely in the middle distance in front. And like puppets pulled by a single string, the entire extended array of Bothwell's moss-troopers turned around to drop away out of sight behind the embankment, as suddenly and completely as they had first appeared.

'Now how do we get at them?' Lennox demanded. 'Our shots cannot reach them behind yonder.'

'No. But he cannot just sit there, with our two forces working round behind him. Moreover he throws away his great advantage, in his cavalry . . .' Patrick stopped, to raise a pointing finger. 'See there!' he cried.

Although the height of those ramparts hid men and horses both, they were not quite high enough to hide something else – the proud red-and-white banner of the Hepburns. The top half of this could still be seen, clearly outlined against the pale blue of the sky over the sea. And it was streaming out, not hanging limp – moving fast, eastwards. And not only the banner; keen eyes could just distinguish, behind it, lesser movement in the same direction, small pennons and the tips of lances, going at an equal pace.

'What now, Patrick? What now?' the King wondered, as voices shouted these tidings.

'Bothwell moves east, Sire. Fast.'

'Aye. But where, man? And why?'

'That we must wait to discover. The Kennedys are there.'

'He'll no' round on us, that way?'

'Not without Bargany warning us. Have no fear, Sire. There is no lack of time. And my lord of Morton will guard you well!'

There was a distinct unease now amongst the royal host, with nothing for the cannon to fire at, and Bothwell on the move, while much of their own strength was dispersed. When, presently, a single horseman came galloping towards them from the east, in obvious urgency, something like alarm gripped a large proportion of the concourse. There was a notable tendency to drift in the other direction.

The messenger, one of Bargany's men, panted out his news in his singsong West Country voice. Bothwell was gone! He and his whole company had ridden out of the fortification area at a point where he had been able to avoid the Kennedys, and headed south by a little east, at fullest speed. Bargany was following, keeping him in sight – but there seemed to be no likelihood of his turning, of seeking to make some circling attack on the King's rear. He gave every sign of being in full flight.

At first it seemed as though nobody took it in. Only gradually did it begin to dawn. The Battle of Leith Links was over. Without a drop of blood shed, without a single casualty on either side, as far as it was known, the day was won and lost. The forces of the Lord had triumphed. They had blown the trumpets, and down had come the walls of Jericho. Patrick Gray began to laugh softly to himself.

King James was the last to be convinced that the immediate danger was over. He was sure that it was all a cunning stratagem on Bothwell's part to take him unawares. And then, when presently another messenger from Bargany arrived to say that the enemy were now past Restalrig and fleeing due south on a line to take them east of Arthur's Seat, the King was prepared to accept that the threat for the moment was over, he nevertheless became convinced that this merely meant that Bothwell intended to attack Edinburgh itself, while its protecting forces were absent and thus cheaply win the Capital. While Patrick doubted the likelihood of this, not believing that Bothwell's mind would work in that way, he had to admit that it was a possibility, however much Morton scoffed and others expressed more polite disbelief.

Few here were indeed to take fears seriously now. Most people there at Leith Links went slightly mad, in their relief, laughing, singing and dancing. Some even remembered their previous praying, and one or two went so far as to get down on their knees on the grass and thank the Kirk's God for this happy reward for their valour and petitions – which reminded Patrick to send a messenger to inform Andrew Melville's company of the changed situation.

The King refused to be impressed or lulled by the general jollification. That Devil-possessed man Frances might be yammering at the door of Holyroodhouse, or planning to take over the castle that lacked its garrison, he claimed. Nothing would do but that they hasten back to Edinburgh forthwith. The problems of getting the excited and now carefree crowd in hand again, of collecting the missing Kirk contingent, and of re-establishing connection with Bargany, did not concern him. Patrick must see to that.

Patrick pointed out that the threat from the sea, which presumably was behind this business of Bothwell, was still to be faced. He proposed that the cannon and their crews should be left to take up a good position guarding the entry to the harbour of Leith, to prevent a landing, and that the Kirk's leaders suitably instigate their followers in the port to rise in arms to defend the town. Melville could see to that and then come on after the King to Edinburgh. Meantime fast couriers should be sent off to the south to try to find Lord Home and Scott of Buccleuch, to inform them of Bothwell's movements. Home of Linthill, Logan's messenger, had told Patrick that he understood his chief and Buccleuch to be hurrying north, on hearing of Bothwell's original sortie. By this time they might not be far from Edinburgh. They might just possibly catch Bothwell between them.

All this took longer to arrange than it ought to have done, against the holiday mood of the vast majority; but presently the faces of most of the host were turned towards the Capital, whilst on in front making no attempt to linger with the many, Morton's Douglases with the small remainder of the mounted men and courtiers, rode hard and fast, and, strangely, in the lead and most urgent, was now the newly victorious King of Scots.

Another line of battle, another confrontation of armed forces – this time on the long ridge of Edmonstone, south of Edinburgh and near to Dalkeith, in Morton's territory indeed, and much more the traditional battlefield than Leith Links. More professional and military, too, the loyalist array. The King's hard-riding party could see them lined up along the ridge in reassuringly solid-looking formation as they themselves rode out of the valley behind Craigmillar, somewhat wearily. That these others up above must be a deal more weary did not strike all. These were Home's and Buccleuch's men – not the main force, but a strong detachment of perhaps a thousand horse under the Lord Home himself, who had hastened up from the Borders after Bothwell, and had now, almost by accident, come face to

93

face with their quarry as he returned south towards his own main army.

Bothwell, it seemed, had not in fact designed to attack Edinburgh. Now he stood at bay on this flat ridge of Edmonstone, so near where greater battles had been fought earlier in that troubled century, at Pinkie and Carberry, the latter indeed where his predecessor, the former Bothwell, had taken his last leave of the lovely Queen Mary nearly thirty blood-stained years before. James's company after having rejoined Bargany and his Kennedys on the Borough-muir of Edinburgh, had been brought this information, and now rode to join Lord Home.

But on this occasion, also, actual hostilities, the clash of arms, was to elude the diffident monarch. His column reinforced by another two hundred Douglases, met in Leith Loan, was barely half-way up the long sloping farmlands of Edmonstone when a convulsion seemed to seize the ranked men on the skyline. Abruptly the solid phalanx broke and scattered, chaos and confusion succeeded comforting and substantial order, shouts and trumpet-calls and clangour came thinly down on the breeze. King James drew rein in haste, only to resume his advance again, with caution, when the sounds of strife were clearly receding over the brow of the hill.

Arrival at the summit revealed no fighting, but a deal of disarray. Also an angry and discomfited Lord Home, whose greeting to his sovereign was somewhat perfunctory in consequence. Bothwell, it seemed, after having shown every sign of riding off the field, as though to continue his retiral southwards, had suddenly swung round and made a flanking attack on Home's force from the side, at speed, his manoeuvre hidden by a slight rise in the ground. Thus he had been able to bring almost his whole force to bear against only part of Home's. With sad results. A dozen men were dead – all on Home's side – more were wounded, and Home himself had had a narrow escape, so narrow indeed that his personal trumpeter, close at his side, had been captured. Surprise achieved, Bothwell had returned to his former position half a mile away. Home did not say so, but probably a glimpse of the King's force, approaching up the north side of the hill, had caused him to draw away. Added to all this distressing mishap was, apparently, the fact, vouched for on all hands, that Bothwell's men had fought shouting as slogan 'For God and the Kirk!' The enemy, clearly, was not lacking in initiative when he did not have to face artillery.

While Morton was authoritatively describing to Home how *he* would have dealt with the situation, and Patrick was assessing the military possibilities, a diversion occurred. A small party, under a white flag rode out from the now familiar extended front of the Bothwell line, and came to just within hailing distance of the loyalists. A trumpet blared.

'My lord Earl of Bothwell's compliments to my Lord Home,' a voice called. 'He has, by inadvertance and chance, collected a poor cornet and his trumpet, who claims to be the property of the Lord Home. Not being in need of so sorry a fellow he returns the creature herewith, and two rose nobles in generous recoupment. If the Lord Home considers this to be insufficient indemnity, my lord requests that they meet, alone, in personal match, here between the arrays, to settle the matter.'

Out from the little party then rode, distinctly sheepishly, the missing trumpeter, towards his own folk.

King James, now feeling comparatively safe with some fifteen hundred horsemen around him, actually began to tee-hee with mirth at this sally – to the grave offence of Lord Home, who was after all his most senior and experienced soldier. Home's answer of a salvo of musket-ball shot through the white flag was probably fair enough.

'Bothwell was ever a madman,' Ludovick commented. 'What does such a caper serve?'

'It serves two purposes, I think,' Patrick answered. 'For time, first – time to observe our strength, and to assess. He is no man's fool, is Francis Hepburn Stewart. And his spirit, it seems, is nowise damped.'

'Perhaps. Should we not therefore now attack? We must outnumber him by three to one . . .'

'I wonder, Vicky? Contrary to the opinions of some, I am a man of peace. I am but little fonder of bloodshed than is our liege lord. It would be better to end this day without actual blows, if it may be so. And if I interpret this latest gesture of Bothwell's aright, he now intends to retire. He would not have thought of it, I believe, had he intended to attack. It allows him to leave the field with a flourish – and who would deny him that, so long as he returns south whence he came?'

'But . . . our task is to roundly defeat him, to bring him low, not to let him go unscathed!'

'We shall not roundly defeat him, by any means, Vicky, if he does not intend to fight. In this situation, commanding some of the finest horsemen in this land, and in open country, he has but to signal them to disperse – and that will be the end of it. With foot it is different, but cavalry in open country cannot be defeated if they choose not to fight. Home, I think, will reckon the same.'

Whatever Lord Home's assessment of the situation – and he showed no signs of preparing to attack – was little to the point. Almost immediately after the return of his white-flag party, Bothwell's trumpets rang out, to be followed by rounds of mocking cheering from his moss-troopers. Then, unhurriedly and in perfect order, the long line of horsemen swung round and merged into a column-of-route formation, and so trotted off southwards behind the Hepburn banner in most final fashion.

Home sent scouts to the highest vantage-points around, to ensure that there was no circling back – but that is as far as his counter-measures went. No major protest was raised from the loyalist ranks at this policy of strategic inaction, least of all from the King of Scots.

A party of Douglas horse were despatched to trail the invaders southwards, to make certain that they left the district – which, being Morton's domains, he did not contest. In an access of relief, James thereupon dramatically knighted Kennedy of Bargany for courageous service on the field of battle. On this happy note, horses' heads were turned towards Edinburgh, the sunset and supper.

It had been a momentous Sabbath. Patrick sent a messenger ahead of them to proclaim victory and to have the church-bells acclaim the King's triumphant return to his rescued Capital.

Chapter Seven

The Chapel-Royal at Stirling Castle was packed tight as any
barrel of Leith herrings. A small place, built only a few years
before by King James to replace one that had fallen into ruins,
it had been designed only for the devotions of the monarch and
his suite, and was quite inadequate and unsuitable for any
major ceremonial. But here the ceremony must be, for still, on
no account would the King permit that his precious son and heir
be carried over the heavily-guarded threshold of Stirling Castle.
So willy-nilly, into this meagre space must be packed not only
much of the Protestant aristocracy of Scotland, but the host
of special envoys and representatives of the Courts of Europe
invited for the occasion – for James was, these days, much uplifted with satisfaction, pride and self-esteem, and was determined that the world should not be backward in recognising
the good cause he had for it.

Despite all this, however, and her lowly status, Mary Gray had
one of the best positions in that seething crowded church, up at
the chancel steps, between the altar and the font. This was not
so strange, for she held in her arms the principal and centre of
interest of the entire affair – the scarlet-faced and distinctly puny
Prince of Scotland; by the King's command, if not the Queen's.

The trouble was that Mary had already held the infant for
over twenty difficult minutes. James had insisted that his son
should be in good time for his christening, that all might have
the opportunity of admiring him – an understandable paternal
ambition had, in fact, the crowd in the chapel been of a density
to see anything other than their nearest neighbours; or had he
ensured that the ceremony started approximately up to time.
As it was, the situation was on the verge of getting out of hand,
and deteriorating rapidly.

In the heat of that August day, the Chapel-Royal was like
an oven. Even Mary, normally so cool and fresh, was pink and
breathless. The baby, in its tight swaddling clothes, was turn-

97

ing from scarlet to crimson, and seemed to be near apoplexy with bawling – even though, with the noise made by other people, the child's cries were next to inaudible.

Mary, exhausted, limp, and isolated by the throng from all assistance, almost fell on his neck when the Duke of Lennox came, elbowing his way through the crush to her side.

'Oh, Vicky,' she gasped, 'God be praised that you have come! The child – he is all but crazed. The heat! The noise! This long waiting . . .'

'I am sorry, my dear. It is the Queen. She is beside herself. She forbids that the christening goes on if the child is not baptised Frederick first, after her father of Denmark. And only then Henry. The King insists that it be Henry first, as compliment to Queen Elizabeth, after *her* father. That the boy may one day be King in England also. Elizabeth must be conciliated, he says. Neither will yield – Henry Frederick or Frederick Henry!'

'The folly of it! They are no more than stupid wilful children themselves! They care nothing how the bairn suffers! Tell the King that the child will be ill, Vicky. Endangered. They must delay no longer . . .'

'Already I have tried,' he told her. 'But you know Anne!'

'Can Patrick not help?'

'Patrick is soothing the Kirk. And Elizabeth's special ambassador, Sussex. He esteems this an insult to his Queen.'

'Ask Patrick, nevertheless.'

Whether Patrick Gray's doing or not, a flourish of trumpets sounded from outside, fairly soon after Lennox's departure, the signal for the royal entry. Obviously, however, it was quite impossible for the procession to come in by the main door and up the aisle, as arranged. Instead, the small vestry door near the chancel was thrown open, and through its narrow portal the official retinue had to squeeze – with a certain forfeiture of dignity. The Lord Lyon King of Arms, his heralds and trumpeters, preceded the other high officers of the realm, who bore the Sword of State, the Sceptre, the Spurs and so on. Then came Lennox as Lord Chamberlain, followed by the youthful Earl of Sussex, resplendent in pearl-sewn velvet, and carrying a towel with which most evidently he did not know what to do. At his

back and jostling to see which could be hindmost, and therefore
senior, came two clerics, one in sober black and Geneva bands,
one in gorgeous cope, alb, stole and mitre – Master David
Lindsay, the King's chaplain, and Cunningham, Bishop of
Aberdeen. Two young women then appeared, edging through
side by side, one nervously giggling, the other red-eyed with
weeping – ladies in waiting.

There was a space, and then the Queen sailed in head
high, set-faced and frowning blackly, the two pages who held
her train having to follow at the trot. She was a small creature,
slim as a boy, with sharp-pointed features, reddish hair, and a
darting eye. She had had a certain pert prettiness when first she
came from Denmark five years before, but at nineteen this was
no longer apparent. She was clothed in royal purple, which went
but doubtfully with her red-brown hair.

King James came in with the two pages – indeed he all but
trotted with them, looking anxious, clad in sufficient magnificence for three men. The Master of Gray slipped inside last of
all, to close the door. After only a moment or two, however,
he turned back and opened it again.

Queen Anne, ignoring the Lord Lyon's indication of where
she should stand, made straight for Mary Gray, to snatch the
protesting infant from her, glaring.

Although this was not the arrangement, Mary gave up her
burden with relief, curtsying. It distressed her that the Queen
should look upon her as an enemy nowadays, as one of those
who kept her from her baby. The fact that Mary had no wish
to act as a sort of governess to the young prince, and indeed
longed only to get back to her own life with Ludovick and her
son at Methven, did not help her with Anne, who saw her now
only as the woman who was supplanting her with her child.

The King, gobbling with apprehension, hastened forward to
remonstrate. He actually laid hands on the child – whereupon
the Queen clutched him the tighter, suddenly became a tigress
with her whelp. It looked as though a tug-of-war might develop,
when the Master of Gray sauntered up, smiling, to murmur
soothingly to the King and then to turn his fullest charms upon
Anne. What was said could not be heard by others because of
the baby's yells and the chatter of the congregation. But some-

how Patrick convinced the Queen, however reluctantly, to hand over the squirming, yelling bundle to the young and far-from-eager Earl of Sussex, who held it gingerly, dropping his towel in the process. James himself stooped to pick this up, hovering around Elizabeth's envoy in agitation. Hurriedly Patrick signed to Lyon, who nudged the nearest trumpeter. The blast of the instrumentalists thereafter drowned all other sounds in that constricted space.

As the reverberations died away, with only the baby un-affected apparently, Master Lindsay, having taken up his position in front of the altar, but facing the congregation, made it very clear whose service this was by plunging into headlong and vigorous prayer. Unprepared for this, it took a little while for the assembly to adopt an attitude of silent devotion, es-pecially those visitors from furth of the realm unused to Scottish customs. The King it was, waving his towel and shushing loudly, who succeeded in gaining approximate quiet from all but his son.

It was a long prayer, a monologue adjuring the Deity to be on watch and take particular care for this infant from the fell dangers of idolatry, heresy, Popery, Episcopacy, witchcraft and other like devilries, to which the bairn looked like being most direly exposed. That neither the Almighty nor anyone else make any mistake about the danger, he went into considerable detail on the subject. Sussex squirmed with his burden, and shot agonised looks all round, which met with only darts of sheer venom from the Queen, whilst James punctuated the praying with vehement amens – which, if they were intended to bring it to a premature close, were notably ineffective.

At length Master Lindsay had to pause for breath. The Bishop seized his opportunity. Straight into the baptismal rite he swung, his voice sonorous but mellifluent after the other's vibrant harshness, presently holding out his arms for the child. Never did a proxy godparent deliver his charge more promptly.

Thus started, things went with a swing, almost a rush, Bishop Cunningham apparently being unwilling to surrender the initia-tive even for a moment. Responses were taken for granted, inessentials jettisoned, and the office repeated at a pace which could scarcely have been bettered or even equalled, yet without a single slip of the tongue or scamped intonation – a piece of epis-scopal expertise which was much admired.

The Bishop was slightly less successful, however, at the actual moment of christening when, after a quick glance at the Queen and then the King, he signed with the holy water and rather mumbled. Many there were, including the monarch himself, who declared stoutly thereafter that he enunciated 'Henry Frederick – Frederick Henry'; but Mary Gray for one was quite sure that he in fact said 'Frederick Henry – Henry Frederick'. But then, the Bishop of Aberdeen was susceptible to young women; moreover he was near enough to the Old Faith still to consider Elizabeth Tudor a dragon and her father Henry the Eighth as Antichrist himself.

If it was possible, the Bishop actually quickened his pace. Dexterously balancing the infant between the crook of his arm and the edge of the font, he dived a hand within his cope, to produce a small silver phial, to the accompaniment of a rich flood of words, and proceeded to anoint the child's head with oil therefrom, in the name of the Trinity. King James's dark eyes gleamed triumphantly, there were gasps from certain of the congregation, and Master Lindsay started forward, hands up-raised. But it was all over too swiftly for any intervention, and the episcopal eloquence slowing down, the Bishop handed the prince back to Sussex, and sinking his mitred head towards his breast, tucked ringed hands within the wide sleeves of his cope and, reverently contemplating the floor, sank his voice away into private whispered intercession.

Thereafter, as the Queen suddenly darted forward to snatch the child from Sussex, the much more assuredly Reformed Master Lindsay sternly, angrily, took over again, and after more resounding prayer and a lengthy reading from the Scriptures, showed every sign of being about to preach a sermon. Mary Gray looked desperately at her father, who nodded, and signed to the Lord Lyon. At the first opportunity thereafter the trumpets blared out once more in joyful and sustained flourish. The trumpet, Patrick reflected, was the undoubted prince of instruments.

Not waiting for any benediction, the Queen turned and hurried for the open vestry door, baby in her arms, taking her train-bearers and ladies by surprise. But not her husband. Moving with unusual swiftness, James reached the door first, and with a sort of dignity bowed, and quite firmly took the infant from her. Holding the prince proudly if inexpertly, he shambled out first into the sunshine. He hurried round to the front door of the Chapel-Royal, to display his son to the congregation as it emerged.

The move to the Great Hall thereafter was not a stately procession, as planned.

The King, still clutching the baby, was entering the Hall, one of the noblest apartments in the land, where refreshments were laid out for all, when he remembered to give orders for the firing of the cannon.

This martial touch, a subtle reminder of James's recent successful campaigning, was on a scale hitherto unknown in Scotland. Pieces had been brought specially from Edinburgh to reinforce the local artillery, and the resultant uproar was breathtaking. The castle, Stirling itself, the entire Carse of Forth shook and trembled to it, and the mountain barrier of the Highland Line threw back the echoes. Inside the Great Hall, as time went on, women grew pale, rocked to and fro, and neared hysteria, while strong men held heads in hands and stared glassily ahead – for of course no conversation was possible, no two consecutive words were to be distinguished. The great cannon and culverins, the smaller sakers and falconets, and the host of lesser pieces, skilfully synchronised, ensured that not for one second was there a pause in the assault upon the eardrums – a triumph of the cannoneer's art, undoubtedly.

The heir of Scotland screamed on and on, while his mother wept, and Mary Gray, after having pleaded in dumb show with Ludovick and Patrick to try to have the hellish din halted somehow, slipped away to her own quarters of the castle, to soothe young John Stewart of Methven.

Eventually James, who had taken the precaution to bring woollen plugs for his ears, grew tired of it, and sent a thankful messenger to halt the clamour – to the great relief of the Lord High Treasurer, the Master of Glamis, amongst others, who though now somewhat deaf could still count the cost of such expenditure of costly gunpowder.

To the dizzy and all but concussed company, the monarch then gleefully announced that although the main celebrations were being reserved for the evening, when there would be a banquet with masque and guizardry, withal of deep moral meaning, present delights were not quite completed. He thereupon turned to the Lord Home, who had carried the Sword of State, demanding the said weapon – which caused some small upset, for it was of the awkwardly huge two-handed variety, suitable only for heroes like the original owner, Robert the Bruce, and Home had left it standing in some corner. When produced, James found it exceedingly difficult to handle, his wrists not being of the strongest, but refusing proffered alternatives, and tucking it under his arm like a lance, he advanced upon his son held in his mother's shrinking arms – to the alarm of more than the Queen. Poking at the infant with its enormous blade, approximately on the shoulder, he cried out,

'I dub ye knight, Sir Henry! Aye, Sir Henry Stewart! That is ... Henry Frederick. You'll no' can arise, my wee mannie, as a knight should – but no matter. Aye. Now, Johnnie – Johnnie Mar. The spur, man.'

The Earl of Mar stepped forward, holding out one of the symbolic spurs. As he bore down upon Queen and babe, Anne made as though to hide the child from him, for she had conceived a great hatred for Mar, the prince's governor. The touching with the spur, therefore, was only a modified success, especially as its spikes got entangled with the infant's christening robe, to the mother's loud protest.

The Lord Lyon, however, came to the rescue by making impressive announcement of the new knight's styles and titles, crying.

'See here the Right Excellent, High and Magnanimous Henry Frederick, Frederick Henry, by the Grace of God, Knight, Baron of Renfrew, Lord of the Isles, Earl of Carrick, Duke of Rothesay, Prince and Great Steward of Scotland!'

This over, and the child's health and well-being pledged by all, James suddenly wearied, as he was apt to do, and began to look around him.

'Mistress Mary,' he called, querulously. 'Where are you? Vicky – where's your Mary Gray? Where is she, man?'

'She has gone, Sire. To see to our own child, I think.'

'Then she shouldna ha' done, Vicky. She hadna our royal permission to leave. We are displeased. Aye, right displeased. Fetch her back. Here to me.'

'As you will, Sire.'

'No – wait, now. We havena the time. It's no' suitable for us to wait on the lassie. Take you the bairn to her, Vicky.'

Ludovick, faced with the unenviable task of abstracting the infant from its mother's embrace, went about the business but hesitantly. Seeing which, James himself hurried over, took his son from his wife's protesting grasp, and handed him to Lennox.

'Off wi' him. And watch him well, mind. The bairn's no' to be wearied, see you. I'll no' have him unsettled.'

'As you say, Sire.'

'Aye. Well – I shall retire. I'll need to prepare for the masque. Anne! Fetch Her Grace, Patrick man. Lyon – your trumpets . . .'

'How does it feel, Patrick, to sit and watch all dancing to your tune? To move men like pawns in a game? To watch all that you have contrived come to pass?'

'Not all, my dear. Most perhaps, but not all,' the Master amended lightly.

'Does it make you happy?'

'Happy? What is happiness, Mary? If you mean am I contented – I am not. Nor elated. Nor proud. Say that I see a good beginning, and am encouraged and hopeful.'

'I think perhaps that you even deceive yourself, Patrick – as well as others!'

'But not Mary Gray! Eh? Never Mary Gray!'

She did not answer that. Father and daughter were sitting together in quite a lowly position at the banquet in the Great Hall – Ludovick being required to take his due place up at the dais table near the King, amongst all the ambassadors and chief guests. The Queen was not present, pleading a headache – and undoubtedly James was in better fettle for her absence.

'You accuse me of deceit, Mary,' her father said conversationally. 'Because, on occasion, I do not tell *all* the truth – all that I know. But where is the virtue in a surfeit of truth? Look around you this August night. What do you see? The King merry, and safe. The new prince secure. The realm as near at peace as it has been all this reign. Bothwell abandoned by Queen Elizabeth and skulking a fugitive in his Border mosses. Indeed Elizabeth godmother to the precious child, her cousin Sussex bringing rich gifts and sitting at the King's side – and the English succession that much the nearer. All this, and more, that might not have been. And you see naught in it but deceit!'

'The English succession!' she took him up. 'That, to you, is all-important, is it not? Paradise! The Promised Land itself! Why, I have never understood.'

'I should have thought that wits so sharp as yours would require no telling. Only when the two realms are united under one king, will our land have settled peace, Mary. Only then will Scotland open and flourish as she should, with hatred past and opportunity before her. Always, the threat of England's might has constrained us, hedged us in. Always there has been an English party in Scotland, betraying the nation...'

'*You* say that! You who have betrayed so much and so many? Who have accepted so much of Elizabeth's gold...!'

'Aye. I say it. For I have chaffered with Elizabeth for Scotland's sake, not to line my own pockets, girl! As do the others. What you name my betrayals have been done that Scotland might survive. Always I have laboured and contrived that this realm should survive in the face of all that would tear it apart, sufficiently long for King Jamie there to be accepted also as King in England...'

'And Patrick Gray a power in two kingdoms!'

He sighed. 'You are hard on me, lassie. In some ways, those bonnie eyes of yours, that see so much, are strangely blind. You see me as crazed for power. That I have never been. As hungry for wealth. That I do not seek, save to carry out my purposes. As pursuing vengeance on those who counter me...'

'I see you as a puppet-master, Patrick – with men and women as your puppets. Aye, and kings and queens and princes. Even Christ's church! Puppets that you discard at will, caring not that they have hearts and souls! The puppet-show alone matters to you, not the puppets. Can you deny it?'

He was silent, then, for a little, his handsome face without expression.

As so often was the way it went, Mary could not withhold her love and pity – although pity was scarcely a word that could be used in respect of the Master of Gray – from this extraordinary sire of hers. Her hand went out to touch his arm.

'I am sorry, Patrick. Sorry that I should seem to think so ill of you. But... I cannot forget what you have done.'

'You speak out of ignorance, Mary. You do not know one tenth of the circumstances.'

'Perhaps not. But the tenth is more than sufficient. I would not wish to know more.' She paused. 'Though that, I think, is not wholly true. I would much like to know, Patrick, how your present triumph was achieved?'

'I do not take you? You have seen what has been...'

'Do not cozen me, Patrick. Credit me with some of those wits you spoke of! Do not tell me that much of all that has happened was not planned months ago. Before ever you came to Fast Castle. Someone planned it, surely. And neither Bothwell nor Huntly has the head for it. Moreover it has worked out only to *your* advantage...'

'And the King's.'

'Perhaps. But King James did not plot it, that is certain. Was any of it true, Patrick? Was the realm ever in real danger? Did Bothwell ever really design the King's death? And the capture of the prince? This move to Stirling – was it not all that you might draw the King away from the Chancellor Maitland? Did Bothwell ever intend to attack Edinburgh? Was the threat no more than a device that you might gain the Kirk to your side? You that I think are a Catholic at heart! I think that I see your hand behind Bothwell in all. But Bothwell is now a fugitive – whilst you, that was a banished outlaw, now guide the King's hand!'

'On my soul, girl, you attribute me with the powers of a god!'

'Not a god, Patrick!'

'Are you finished, my dear?'

'You have not answered any of my questions.'

'Save to say that all are nonsense. Something has disordered your mind, I fear. Childbirth, perhaps?'

'Is it nonsense that you devised this threat to the prince, for your own ends? To separate him from his mother? In order that the King and Queen should be thus at odds – and you have the greater hold over both?'

''Fore God, girl – you are bewitched! Spare me more of this, for sweet mercy's sake! You are, I think, clean out of your mind!'

Mary uttered a long sigh. 'Perhaps I am, Patrick. It may be so. Sometimes I tell myself that I am. Indeed, I would wish with all my heart that it is so. And yet . . .' She shook her head, and left the rest unsaid.

He considered her, and then patted her hand. 'There is ill and good in all of us,' he said, more gently. 'Allow me some of both! Even the Kirk is prepared to do that! Is my daughter less generous than Master Melville and his crew?'

'The Kirk! The Kirk would be wise to take care with the Master of Gray, would it not?'

'The Kirk must learn who are its friends. I have spent much time and labour this day aiding the Kirk. Convincing the King that he must allow the Kirk some part in the christening – for he would have had only the Bishop. Ensuring that the Bishop was discreet – and swift. Soothing Master Lindsay over the anointing oil. It is only because of the shameless and heretical Master of Gray that the righteous representatives of the Kirk are sitting here tonight.'

'And is that greatly to the Kirk's advantage? Or just to your own?'

'To the Kirk's, equally with the realm's. And therefore mine. And yours. In this pass the Kirk must be seen to act with the King. If that fails, they will go down both.'

'Is that true, Patrick? Is there any true threat remaining? Was there ever? Are not the Catholics everywhere held? Their day done?'

'Lassie,' Patrick lowered his musical voice to a murmur. 'Believe me, the Catholic threat is not gone. Was never so great, indeed.'

'You mean Huntly, still? The Catholic North. And Bothwell?'

'A greater threat than Huntly or Bothwell. Not a word of this to others, Mary – for none know it yet. Not even to Vicky, I charge you. But I have sure word that the King of France has turned Catholic.'

'Henry! That was Henry of Navarre? The Protestant lion!

Champion of the Huguenots! Never! That I do *not* believe.'

'Be not so sure, girl. Henry is under great pressure. He must unite his France – and the Catholic party is much the stronger. The Emperor, the Pope, Philip of Spain – all are pressing him hard. France, weakened by internal wars, needs stronger friends than little Scotland.'

'Even if this was true – why need it threaten Scotland?'

'Because it is only France that has restrained Philip. From doing as Huntly pleads, and invading Scotland. He cherishes an old claim – that Mary the Queen left him the throne of Scotland. He has feared France and our Auld Alliance – that France would attack Spain if he attacked Scotland. But should Henry turn Catholic, will he hurt Catholic Spain in favour of Protestant Scotland?'

Mary was silent. At length she spoke.

'You have known this for long? This of Henry?'

'For only a few days. But . . . I was expecting it.'

'How is it that Patrick Gray always knows such things before his King and the Council?'

'Because, my dear, I make it my business to know. Information, knowledge, is valuable. Especially in this game of statecraft. I have always paid much silver that I could ill afford in order that I might know of important matters a little sooner than do others. Many times I have proved the money well spent.'

'Even when it was Elizabeth's money? As when, at Falkland five years ago, you knew even before the French ambassador that the previous king had died? I remember that – and how you turned the knowledge to your own advantage. It was then, I think, that I first began to perceive what sort of man was the Master of Gray!'

He smiled thinly. 'I shall forbear to thank you for that! But I was right then, was I not? As I shall be proved right now . . .'

A commotion turned all heads towards the great main doorway. Through this was entering an astonishing sight, a magnificent Roman chariot, painted white, drawn by a single gigantic Moor, naked but for coloured ostrich plumes, ebony skin gleaming, mighty muscles rippling, and a grin all but bisecting his features. The chariot was heaped with fruit of various kinds, and standing amongst it were six divinities most fair. These were young women of most evident charms, garbed significantly but scantily, to represent Ceres, Liberality, Faith, Concord, Perseverance and Fecundity – the last as naked as the Moor save for three tiny silver leaves no larger than those of a birch-tree. This, the Lady Lindores, formerly the Lady Jean Stewart, Orkney's second legitimate daughter and Patrick's sister-in-law, had always been a warm and roguish piece, like most of her kin; now she was grown into a most voluptuous young woman, challenging as to eye, body and posture. She held in one hand a cornucopia which seemed to spill out the fruits to fill the chariot, and cradled in her other arm a doll fashioned in pink wax, baby-sized, with open mouth towards her full thrusting breast.

The King's cry of delight was undoubtedly mainly for the Moor and the fact that he could alone draw the chariot – for James was never really interested in women. He shouted, and clapped his hands, jumping to his feet – which meant that every-one else must likewise rise.

'Your work, I think?' Mary said. 'It has all the marks of your devising.'

'You are too kind,' Patrick told her. 'It was His Grace's notion. As his Master of the Wardrobe, it falls to me to, h'm, interpret the royal wishes in such matters.'

'I do not believe the King would have thought of displaying the Lady Jean so – who has been four years married and still no child!'

'A small conceit!' he nodded. 'You are not jealous, my dear? Would you rather that I had chosen you?'

'Even you, Patrick, are insufficiently bold for that! Perhaps you might more aptly have used me as Perseverance!' She smiled faintly.

He laughed. 'I should have thought of that. I vow you well earn the part, where I am concerned! Why, Mary? Why do you do it?'

'Because I am your daughter. Does that not answer all?'

'And so you must reform me? A hopeless task, I fear, my dear.'

'Say that I seek to out-persevere my sire.'

'You are a strange creature, lass.'

'Bone of your bone, Patrick. Blood of your blood.'

The Moor was drawing the chariot round all the tables of the Banqueting Hall, whilst the ladies thereon handed out fruit to all who would partake. Few refused such fair ministrants; many indeed sought more than their fruit. The King rewarded the Moor by feeding him sweetmeats, but after a sidelong askance glance, he ignored the lovely charioteers altogether.

Soon James was gesturing vigorously towards the Master of Gray, who in turn nodded to a servitor near the door. Shortly afterwards a thunderous crash shook the entire castle, guests, tables and plenishings alike leapt, and black smoke came billowing in at the open doorway. There were cries of alarm and some screaming – until it was seen that the King was rubbing his hands and chuckling gleefully. Then a great ship surged in, a true replica of a galleon, a score of feet long, all white and gold but with the muzzles of ranked cannon grinning black through open gun-ports. The tall masts had to be lowered to win through the doorway, but once inside they were cunningly raised, the central one to a full forty feet, to display a full set of sails of white taffeta, emblazoned with the Rampant Lion of Scotland and finished with silken rigging. No men were in evidence about the vessel, but when it was approximately in mid-floor out from beneath it emerged, with a swimming motion, no less a figure than King Neptune himself, complete with crown, trident and seaweed hair, who after a few capers, turned to bow deeply towards the ship.

King James cheered lustily.

'This, I may say, is *all* His Grace's devising,' Patrick mentioned. 'Spare me any responsibility. It represents his triumph over the sea, no less. And his epic Jason-like quest to claim a sea-king's daughter. Now he lauds the voyage rather than the bride!'

An anchor was cast to the floor in realistic fashion, and out from the entrails of the vessel streamed a dozen boys, entirely unclothed save for caps of seaweed, bearing all sorts of fish and shellfish moulded in sugar and painted in their natural colours, for the delectation of the guests. Neither sweetmeats or boys lacked appreciation.

'I go now,' Patrick whispered. 'To prepare for what follows. If you are wise, my heart, and can tear yourself away from this spectacle, you will brave the royal wrath and come with me. You will not regret it, I swear!'

'How so ... ?'

'Our liege lord is not finished yet! Come.'

They were not quite in time. Slipping out behind the tables, father and daughter were nearing a side-door when the cannonade started. The model ship could only support comparatively small pieces firing blank shot, but even so, within the four walls of the Banqueting Hall, and only feet away from the crowded tables, the noise was appalling, causing the earlier bombardment to seem like a mere pattering of hailstones. Thirty-six consecutive detonations crashed out, the chamber shook, bat and bird droppings fell amid clouds of dust from the roof-timbers, and acrid smoke rolled and eddied everywhere, while men cowered and cringed, women stuffed kerchiefs into their mouths, threw skirts over their heads or merely collapsed, and even Neptune's youthful assistants scuttled from the scene as their fine vessel shook itself to pieces.

Up at the dais table, James was on his feet again – but this time nobody noticed, or rose with him. He was slapping his thigh and shouting his merriment – having of course come provided with his ear-plugs – a picture of uncouth mirth.

'Since Leith,' Patrick bellowed in Mary's ear, 'Majesty has become aware of the delights of gunpowder. Would that I had realised the price of victory!'

The girl nodded. 'I go to soothe my child. And his!' she cried, and fled.

When Mary returned to the Hall some time later, it was to find the King absent but armed guards permitting no guests to leave the chamber nevertheless, anxious as were many to do so. A sort of dazed torpor had come over most of the company – although some determined drinking was going on, as a form of elementary precaution, no doubt, against promised further regal entertainment. The air was still thick with throat-catching fumes.

Ludovick hurried to Mary's side.

'Would to God we could escape from this madhouse!' he

groaned. 'Oh, for Methven, and you alone! And Johnnie, of course. This is Bedlam, no less! James grows ever the worse. You are all right, my dear? I saw you go out . . .'

'I went to Johnnie. And the little prince. Patrick knew what was to come, and advised that I go. Both bairns were awake, the prince screaming but Johnnie quiet. They are now asleep.'

'You were wise to go. And fortunate! It was beyond all belief So sore was my head that I could not see. Besides the smoke. I was blind. Nor I only. Young Sussex was sick. All over the Countess of Northumberland – though I think she scarce noticed it. He is but a frail youth. And James has been paying him attentions, stroking him like a cat, which must alarm him. What tales he will take back to Elizabeth, the good Lord knows! He asked permission to retire – but James would have none of it. None must leave. He has quick eyes, even though they roll so! He even saw you leave, my dear, and would have had you brought back. But I told him that you would be going to see to the prince. He is but a step from madness, I do believe.'

'Hush, Vicky!' Mary laid a finger on his lips, glancing around them. 'Such talk is dangerous. You know it. We learned that before. Nor is it true, I think. The King is not mad. He is strange, yes. And capricious. But he is clever too. Quick with more than his eyes. Shrewd after a fashion. And frightened – always frightened. He was born frightened, I think – as well he might be! We owe him pity, Vicky – compassion. As well as loyalty.'

'Always you were generous, Mary. Kind-hearted. I still think him mad – or nearly so. After the cannons, he read us this poem that he has been writing for the christening – that you have been aiding him with. Even so it was a purgatory! And endless! Save that it was better than the guns.'

'He means kindly . . .'

'Does he? I think otherwise. He is but puffed up with foolish pride. And he shows scant kindness to his wife. The Queen sent for me to attend her, a little back – but James would not hear of it. I must wait, we must all wait, to witness his next triumph! It is a great secret. Has Patrick told you what it is?'

'No. He but said that the King aimed to surpass himself. You know how Patrick would say that. But little of this night's doings are his work, I think.'

'Do not be so sure, my love...'

A fanfare of trumpets cut the Duke short. There was the clatter and stamp of hooves on the stone floor outside, and then into the Hall itself pounded three riders in wild career, scattering servitors right and left.

The wildness was not confined to the canter of heavy horses indoors; the riders were wilder still. Amazons they were intended to represent, undoubtedly, complete with long streaming hair, brief green skirts, and great flouncing breasts in approximately the right positions. Nevertheless, these were most obviously men, and identifiable men – indeed Scott of Buccleuch had not troubled to shave off his red beard, and with his long black wig and massive hairy limbs, made a fearsome sight. The other two were younger and less fiercely masculine – the Lord Lindores, formerly Prior of the same, Lady Jean's husband, painted and powdered with lips red as cherries, and Orkney's favourite illegitimate son, lately made Commendator-Abbot of Holyrood in place of his father, a graceful hairless youth adorned with the largest bosom of all.

Round and round the Hall this trio rode their spirited steeds, to mixed affright and acclaim, colliding with tables, upsetting furnishings, scoring and splintering the floorboards with iron-shod hooves. Armed with short stabbing spears, they made playful jabs at all and sundry, uttering eldrich whoops and falsetto cries. The Abbot's breasts, phenomenally nippled but unstably anchored, slipped round until he was able to hold them securely, one dome on either side of his left shoulder. Even the pale Lord Sussex smiled faintly.

A second blast of trumpets heralded more hoof-clatter, and in at the door rode, less precipitately, a figure in full armour, helmeted and visored, splendidly mounted and couching a long lance. This anonymous paladin was clad at all points as a Christian Knight of Malta, wearing no blazon and carrying no banner. But there was something familiar, even under the unbending armour, about the slouching seat and lolling head. Moreover, he was mounted on one of the King's favourite Barbary blacks. The Earl of Mar led a dutiful cheer, and everyone rose to their feet.

James trotted round the great room, graciously waving his

guests to their seats. The circuit made, he turned his attention to the Amazons, digging in his spurs.

As has been indicated, James was at his best on a horse, despite his peculiar posture. He rode straight at the Laird of Buccleuch. There was little room for manoeuvre in that place, and a high standard of horsemanship was demanded to remain even in full control of the beasts. In the circumstances, Buccleuch's avoidance of the royal lance-tip was masterly, especially as he made it seem a very close thing, and his return gesture with the short stabbing spear hopelessly wide of the mark.

This set the tone of the encounter. The Amazons dodged and jinked and ducked, however much their mounts slipped and slithered on the timber floor, and ferociously as they yelled and skirled, their counter-attacks were feeble and ineffective, even allowing for the inadequacy of four-foot spears against a twelve-foot lance. Not that the said lance was always accurately aimed either, but at least James wielded it with all the vigour of which he was capable.

It became evident that the object was to defeat the Amazons by separating them from their bosoms. That this was not entirely achieved by the royal lance-point was neither here nor there. To the plaudits of the company the trio were reduced to huddled shame and abasement – whereupon the enthusiastic monarch set about removing their long tresses also, a still more ambitious and hazardous procedure which soon had the demoralised Furies dismounted and running from the Hall, casting all trace of their femininity from them in shameless panic.

Thereafter, left victor, the King threw up his visor, and pantingly launched into a lengthy harangue and explanation. Because of his excitement and his breathlessness, and the hollow boomings of his helmet, his words were even less clear than usual, his Doric broader. But it seemed that what had been witnessed was an allegory of much significance and moral worth. The Amazons, it appeared, as well as representing undisciplined and assertive womanhood in general, also were to be identified as the evil harpies Witchcraft, Heresy and Treason, from whose grasp he, James, with God's help, was in process of freeing his realm. As the Viceroy of Christ, with the armour of faith and the lance of righteousness, he would smite these daughters of Satan hip and thigh.

James was warming to his theme when a servitor pushed his way to where Ludovick was standing, with Mary.

'I come from the Queen's Grace,' he said, low-voiced. 'She orders that you attend her forthwith, my lord Duke. By her royal command.'

'Command . . . ?' The young man bit his lip. 'James will not like this. Why should she want *me*? But – I cannot refuse her command.'

'No. You must go. The poor Queen – I am sorry for her. But she has her own dangers, Vicky. Be careful with her . . .'

Patrick returned soon after Ludovick had left the Hall.

'You are elevated and informed, I hope, Mary?' he murmured.

'I am a little weary,' she answered.

He looked at her quickly. 'I don't think that I have ever heard you admit as much, before. Do not say that our puissant monarch is too much for Mary Gray! But it is near done now, lass. And the final act will revive you, I swear!'

'There is more to come?'

'A last tit-bit. That only His Grace would have thought of. Meanwhile, let us see if we may anywise shorten this homily.'

Patrick waited until the King's next needful pause for breath. Then he nodded to his man at the door. Just as James was about to recommence, music struck up from outside, fiddles, lutes and cymbals. A protesting royal gauntlet of steel was raised, but it was too late. In filed a column of sweet singers, the former Neptune's acolytes, now decently clad in black, reinforced by a number of older vocalists and instrumentalists. They were chanting the hundred and twenty-eighth Psalm, in fourteen-part harmony.

The King, whom life had made a realist of sorts, accepted the situation, and switched from declamation to lusty psalmody:

> For thou shalt eat of the labours of thine hands
> O well is thee, and happy shalt thou be . . .

he boomed from within his helmet, waving to all his astonished guests to raise bodies and voices in vigorous worship.

'James, by the grace of God, King. Protector of Christ's Kirk here on earth!' the Master of Gray observed. 'Look at Master Melville, my dear! And Lindsay. And Galloway. They are smiling, all. For the first time this night. The day is saved. The True Faith triumphs. King and Kirk are one, after all!'

'*You*, then, did have a hand in this, also?' Mary charged him.

'I? I do not even know the words of the psalm,' he said.

> The Lord shall bless thee out of Zion: and thou shalt see
> the good of Jerusalem all the days of thy life ...

the King shouted, strongly if tunelessly:

> Yea, thou shalt see thy children's children, and peace
> upon Israel ...

Chapter Eight

Falkland was the smallest of the royal palaces, and the little grey-stone, red-roofed Fife town which huddled round it, beneath the green Lomond Hills, as ever when the King was here, was bursting at the seams, every house, cottage, room even, taken up and overflowing with the host of nobles, envoys, courtiers, ministers, their families, retainers and servants. On this warm evening of early September, everyone seemed to have surged out of the crowded houses into the narrow streets and wynds, the gardens and pleasances and encroaching woodlands, for air and space. Ludovick Stewart, hot and tired after his long ride, pushing his way through the throng with only a groom in attendance, frowned at the milling crowds distastefully, wrinkled his nose at the stink, and cursed again the fate of birth which enforced on him a life for which he had no desire, amongst people with whom he had little sympathy, when all that he wanted was to live quietly, simply, at Methven with Mary. It was all wrong, and the sort of grudging affection he had always had for his cousin the King was suffering under the strain. He had hoped and expected that now that there was a prince, and he was no longer heir to the throne, the situation might have improved. But things were in fact worse, with James demanding ever more of his time and company – whilst yet finding fault with him constantly.

Just across from the palace gates, he was held up by a herd of bullocks being driven down to the slaughter-houses by the waterside, and further congesting the already crowded streets of the little town. The feeding of the Court here was ever a major problem, for Falkland was a hunting palace, set down in an area of forest, marsh and wilderness with no farming country nearby, and the influx of hundreds, even thousands, presented great difficulties of commissariat. Yet it was James's favourite house, and once the stags were in season and the threat of attack apparently receded, nothing would do but that the move from the confining fortress of Stirling twenty-five miles away must be made. But not for the prince; that precious babe's safety was not to be risked outside the castle walls. Therefore Mary Gray must needs remain at Stirling also, plead as Ludovick would. Hence his almost daily rides of fifty miles, and his monarch's oft-expressed complaint.

Before ever he reached his modest room in the palace, Peter Hay, Ludovick's page, met him.

'The Queen again, my lord Duke,' he announced. 'You are to go to her. At once, she says. For hours she has been having me seek you.'

Lennox groaned. 'What ails her now? What does she want with me, this time?'

'I do not know. But she is most strong. I was to bring you to her forthwith, she said. She is in her bower . . .'

'She can wait until I have washed, at least,' the Duke growled. 'Where is the King? Still hunting?'

'Yes. Since morning.'

When, presently, Ludovick presented himself at the Queen's apartments however, Anne had him kept waiting for a full half-hour in an ante-room, making the stiffest of talk to her ladies and ill concealing his impatience – for he was both hungry and tired. At length a bell tinkled to admit him to the presence.

The Queen stood with her back to him, facing a window of her boudoir looking out on the palace gardens. 'You have been long, Ludovick,' she said, without turning. 'Too long. On my soul, you pay a deal more respect to that by-blow of Gray's than you do to your Queen! I have been left alone all this day. Must you be off to Stirling all and every day, sir?'

'Had I not gone to Stirling, Ma'am, I would have been required to go hunting with His Grace.' That was gruffly said, it is to be feared.

'Aye – chasing stupid deer! The folly of it. Always chasing deer!' Anne's voice, still with traces of its guttural Danish accent, was accusing, petulant.

Lennox did not comment on that. 'You sent for me, Your Grace?'

'Yes, how is my child? How is the Prince Frederick?'

'Well, Highness. Never better.'

'Is that all you have to tell me? To say to me? His mother!'

Ludovick was not a hard-hearted young man and he did sym-
pathise with Anne in her unhappy situation with regard to her
baby. He cleared his throat. 'The child seemed happy. Contented.' Perhaps that was not the right thing to say to the
deprived mother? But what could he say about an infant, that
was merely a bundle of swaddling clothes and a pink screwed-up
face? 'He is fatter a little, I think. Mary looks well to him.' That
also might not be what she wished to hear? 'You need have
no fears for the child, Highness.'

She did not directly answer that. When she spoke, however,
her voice was quite changed. It had become soft, girlish, almost
playful. 'Ludovick,' she said, 'come and sit here by me. I have
tidings for you.' She sat down on a cushioned window-seat.

Without enthusiasm he had moved forward obediently before
she half-turned towards him on the seat, and he perceived
how she was dressed. Embarrassed, he faltered.

The Queen wore a long bed-robe of blue silk, but underneath
it she was bare to the waist, below which there was some sort of
underskirt. The robe was hanging open, and Anne was making
no attempt to hide her body. Always she had had a figure more
like a boy's than a woman's; but motherhood had developed her
breasts. They were still small, but pointed. It seemed that she
was proud of them, for the rest of her remained slender to the
point of thinness.

When she saw the young man hesitate, Anne smiled. 'Come,
my lord Duke,' she urged. 'Have you no compassion for me,
left alone all the day?'

'I . . . I am sorry,' he said.

She sighed. 'I am sorry also. I am no less a woman for being
a queen, see you.' When still he stood irresolute, she pointed,
imperiously now. 'Sit!' she commanded.

He lowered himself, almost gingerly, on to the very edge of the
window-seat. This however brought him very near to the Queen's
person. He sat back, therefore, into the corner; but even so, they
were very close together.

Now that she had him there, Anne herself seemed to know
discomfort, and turned to stare out of the window. She was less
than a practised charmer. She had recently celebrated her

twentieth birthday, although in manner and outlook she was old for her years. Sharp-featured, with darting pale blue eyes beneath her reddish-brown hair, with a determined small chin and tight mouth, she could lay few claims to beauty. But Ludovick perceived that she had indeed taken some pains with herself this evening, for as well as the sudden flush over her normally pale complexion, there were distinct traces of deeper colour on her cheeks, there was a dusting of dark shadow at her eyes, and her lips were carmined – as indeed, he realised, were the nipples of her breasts. Nothing of this recognition added to the man's ease.

They seemed to have nothing to say to each other now. Small talk had never been Ludovick Stewart's speciality. To look at her he found upsetting; to stare out of the quite small window brought his head altogether too close to the Queen's; so he gazed stolidly into the room – which, littered about with women's things, and with the door open to her bedroom beyond, failed to soothe likewise.

'Your Mary,' Anne jerked, at length. 'Mary Gray. She is very fair. And sure of herself. For such as she is.'

'She is . . . Mary Gray!' Ludovick answered briefly.

'She is like her father. Perhaps too much like her father.'

He did not answer.

'Your wife. Who died. Gowrie's daughter – the Lady Sophia Ruthven. She was a poor creature, was she not?'

She had roused him now. 'She was not my wife,' he answered hoarsely. 'I scarce knew her. We never lived together. We were forced to wed. But that did not make us man and wife. It was but a device. Of . . . others.'

She nodded. 'Many marriages are so.' Anne sighed. 'Queens' in especial.'

He cleared his throat. 'Perhaps, yes. You said that you had tidings for me, Ma'am?'

'But yes. They will interest you, I think, Ludovick. I have to-day had word, sure word, that Maitland is ailing. The Chancellor.'

Lennox looked at her now. 'Ailing? You mean, seriously?'

'Very ill. A sick man – and like to remain so. To worsen. He has left Edinburgh for his house in Lauderdale. And is never likely to come back again.'

'So-o-o!' The young man thought rapidly. He could not remain unaffected by the news, any more than could almost anyone else in Scotland – even though it was not necessary to be so undisguisedly gleeful as was the Queen. Maitland was not a popular figure, cold, sour, dry; but he was the most effective administrator Scotland had known for generations, and he had had the day-to-day running of the country in his hands for so long that his removal must needs in some measure concern all.

'You are sure? He is none so old a man. Fifty? No more . . .'

'The word is sure,' she nodded. 'Maitland's day is over.'

'His Grace? What says His Grace to this?'

'James does not yet know.'

Lennox raised his eyebrows. Who would inform the Queen before the King? And why? All knew that Anne hated Maitland. She had disliked him from the first, when he had accompanied James to Denmark to fetch her to Scotland. Then there was the business of Musselburgh. The rich regality of Musselburgh, with its revenues from coals, fisheries and salt-pans, had been given long ago by David the First to the Abbey of Dunfermline. Maitland had managed somehow to get these detached and into his own hands soon after the break-up of the old church lands. The Abbey of Dunfermline had been conferred upon Anne by James, as a wedding-present – but Maitland had clung to Musselburgh despite all her attempts to regain it. Lastly, since the Master of Gray had returned, it was whispered on all hands that Maitland had been behind the murder of the Earl of Moray by Huntly – and Anne had been fond of the bonnie Earl.

'Your Highness is sure that this is truth? If the King has not been told . . . ? It may be but some tale. Mere idle talk.'

'The Master of Gray's tales, Ludovick, are seldom idle, I think!'

'Ummm.' So here was Patrick's hand again. He might have guessed it. In which case the matter was serious, whether strictly true or not. And Patrick had come to tell the Queen; for some good reason of his own, no doubt. And the Queen had sent for himself. 'His Grace will be much concerned,' he said.

'His Grace will be better served, lacking Maitland! He is an evil man. Hard and cruel. The realm has too long suffered under his grip, Ludovick.'

'At least his grip was firm, able. As Chancellor he was strong. Who will succeed him?'

'Need any succeed him? Meantime. Should not James take more the rule into his own hands? Lest another become too strong. The Kirk – the Kirk would clamour that the new Chancellor should be of that party. Possibly the man Melville himself! Then the Kirk would indeed rule the King, as well as the kingdom. The King must rule. To that he is born. Should not the chancellorship be left in . . . in abeyance?'

Thoughtfully Lennox considered her. These words, these deliberations on a new problem of state, were not those of the twenty-year-old Anne herself, that he was sure. They could only be Patrick Gray's, using the Queen. Which meant that he was on the move once more. And it was not very difficult to perceive his direction.

'I see,' he said.

'My lord of Mar also would wish to be Chancellor,' the Queen went on. 'That would not be wise. He is not the man for it, and too greatly sways the King even now.'

That was true, of course – despite the fact that Anne looked on Mar as almost as much her enemy as was Maitland, since James had put the young prince in his keeping.

She reached out suddenly, to touch the young man's arm. 'Ludovick – it is our opportunity,' she said eagerly. 'To aid His Grace in the proper rule of this realm. James is timorous. He lacks judgment in many things. He is foolishly trusting. He needs our aid, Ludovick. Together, and with one or two others of goodwill, lacking Maitland we could take the rule in Scotland. For its good. And His Grace's good. Do you not see it?'

He drew back as far as he might into his corner. He could not well shake off the Queen's hand from his sleeve, any more than he could rise and leave her without permission. He was as uncomfortable over her intimacies as he was over her suggestions. Seldom, if ever, had Ludovick Stewart been so embarrassed.

Anne tightened her grip. 'Do you not see it, Ludovick?' she repeated, her voice a strange mixture of coaxing caress and impatience. 'Maitland has so long managed this realm that none other is ready to take his place. Save only Melville and the Kirk. That must not be, or there is an end to the Throne, to us all. But Queen and Duke acting together, behind the King. With others to aid us. With the Prince Frederick back in my care. Against such the Kirk could not prevail. Nor any other faction.'

'All this, Your Grace, according to the Master of Gray?'

Anne hesitated, searching his blunt features. 'The Master would aid us, no doubt...'

'Aye, no doubt. Or we should aid him. Or serve to shield him, rather...'

'But ... he is your friend, is he not? Your Mary's father. You assisted him to return, after banishment.'

Heavily Lennox sighed. 'All true,' he admitted. 'But ...' He shrugged. 'Let Patrick be. But myself – I am not your man for this, Highness. I wish the rule over none. I have no love for statecraft...'

Quickly she caught him up. 'Then, is not your love for me, your Queen, sufficient, Ludovick? Will you not aid me, for true love's sake? And therefore, of course, James.' She moved closer, so that her knee now pressed against his. 'Always you have been my friend. When others were not. When boorish lords and haughty clerics scorned me, a weak woman, you were kind. Always you were kind.'

'Majesty, it was but ... it was but ...' He swallowed. 'I am your friend, yes. Your true servant. But...'

'You like me well enough? Not only as a princess, but as a woman?'

He was intensely aware of her nearness – as well he might be. She was leaning forward, her gown hanging open, so that her pointed breasts were within inches of his hand, the perfume and faint woman-smell of her in his nostrils, the warmth of her leg against his own. He was no prude, nor cold, nor afraid of women; but Anne held no appeal for him. Yet, even had she not been the Queen, he could not have told her so, could not so grievously have wounded any woman.

'Your Highness is very fair. Very comely. And kind also –

most kind. I am honoured by your regard. But this of rule and power is not for me.'

'You were Viceroy of the realm once, were you not? When James was in my country?'

'Aye – in name. But only that. Patrick Gray decided all. He it was who ruled. I but signed my name to his edicts. And liked not all of them! I swore that never again would I do the like!'

'You are older now, a man, when then you were but a youth. A notable man, and strong – born to high things. You would not fail me? I need a man on whom to lean, Ludovick. James . . . he is scarce a man, I sometimes think! No woman, queen though she be, can stand alone. Even Elizabeth Tudor! And, God knows I am more woman than ever she was! This heart that beats in my breast, is it not a woman's heart? A frail and tender woman's heart that must needs serve a queen – and needs the more a strong man's sure support. Hold it, Ludovick, and see, feel . . .' She reached for his hand, and drew it to her left breast, holding it there. 'Tell me – does it say naught to you?'

Into Lennox's embarrassment and alarm flooded a great pity. He did not snatch his hand away – although neither did his fingers move to fondle her warm flesh. The recognition flashed upon him that here was a woman denied, starved of that dual love that was her due, the true love of both her husband and her child. That she had never before seemed to be a passionate woman – as Mary Gray, despite her inherent serenity, was passionate – might but mean that she had not been fully awakened. For she was young, his own age exactly, although he had been apt to think of her as older. He would not hurt her if he could help it. Yet . . . how to free himself of this tangle?

'Your Grace's heart is warm. And true,' he got out, hoarsely. 'It beats . . . it beats stout and sure, I vow, for those you love. For His Grace. The child. Your friends. Even myself, perhaps. I . . . all must rejoice in it. As I do. But – my, my devotion, my support, must be in humbler things than you ask, Highness. For affairs of state I have no inclination, no aptness. You named me strong – but I am not strong. Save only in my thews and sinews. In joust and tourney, or even battle – then I'd be your champion, with sword or lance . . .'

'And that you shall be, Ludovick!'

'But this other is not for me. If Patrick Gray again would steer the ship of state, let him...'

He broke off as upraised voices sounded beyond the boudoir door. The Queen still clung to his hand, but she too had her head turned and raised. A woman's voice rang out high and clear.

'Your Grace...!'

Lennox was just in time to jump to his feet, pulling his hand free, and taking a stride or two forward, when the door was thrown open and the King came in, his mud-spattered riding-boots scuffling.

'Annie! Annie – a white hart!' he cried. 'White – all white. We killed at yon Hainingshaws. Far out. A great bonnie beast, wi' a notable head. Never have I taken a white hart. I ran it miles – och, miles...' James's excited thick voice faltered and died away as he saw Ludovick. Then his great rolling eyes darted to his wife, and he screwed them up against the evening light that flooded in at the west-facing window. He perceived how the Queen was dressed – indeed she made no attempt to hide her comparative nakedness nor to draw the bed-robe closer. 'What's this? What's this?' he gobbled.

The younger man bowed. 'Your Grace,' he jerked. 'You have had a good day?'

'Vicky! Anne, woman! What's this? What's to do here?'

'Nothing is to do, James', the Queen told him coolly. 'Save that you stamp into my bower as though you were still hunting your deer! In mud and...'

'Wheesht, woman! What is Vicky Stewart doing here? Eh? And you this way? Look at yoursel', Anne! You're no' decent! Cover yoursel' up, woman – cover yoursel', I say!'

She stood up, drawing the robe around her, but turning a disdainful shoulder on her husband. 'Ludovick and I have been discussing the illness of the Chancellor – that is all,' she said.

'Wi' your paps hanging out!' he cried. 'Fine that! You'll no' tell me...' James paused. 'Eh? The Chancellor, did you say?'

'The Chancellor, yes. Maitland. He is an ailing man. He has gone to Thirlestane, and is not like ever to leave it.'

'Waesucks! Maitland! Hech, hech – sick? Sick to death? Na, na – it canna be. No' Maitland.'

She shrugged. 'Believe it or not.'

'Why . . . why was I no' informed, then?'

'You were away chasing your deer! All the day. The Master of Gray came from Edinburgh. At midday. Since you were not to be found, he came to me.'

'Patrick! It's *his* word?' The King tugged at his wispy beard. 'This is bad, bad. The Chancellor's the chief minister o' the realm. If Maitland has to yield it – who then? There's no' that many could play Chancellor! Guidsakes – here's a right coil!'

'Need there be a Chancellor? Always? Could not you rule your own realm? Are you dependent on such as Maitland to manage the kingdom?'

'Eh? What's that? No Chancellor?' James stared at her. 'Well, now . . .' He shook his head. 'Where's Patrick? I maun see him. Vicky – fetch you Patrick here.' Then James recollected. 'But . . . hech, hech! Bide a wee! No' so fast, man. First tell me – aye, tell me what you were doing here? Wi' Anne yon way. In her bower. The two o' you. Aye. Vicky Stewart – tell me that!'

'There is nothing to tell, Your Grace. The Queen summoned me here, on my return from Stirling. To tell me of this. This matter of Maitland. Yourself being absent . . .'

'Aye – absent! There you have it, Vicky! Mysel' being absent!'

'I but meant that the tidings being notable, Her Grace would discuss them with someone. Someone close to you, yourself being away . . .'

'Aye, close. Gey close! My being away! So she takes off her clothes, the better to discuss the matter wi' Vicky Stewart! Ooh, aye – fine I understand!'

'Not so, Sire. You greatly err, I swear!'

'Na, na! I'm no more a bairn than you are, Vicky. And there's nothing wrong wi' my eyes, mark you!'

'You are wrong nevertheless, Sire. On my honour . . .'

'Your honour? Och, well – your honour could be no' that reliable, Vicky! I've had a notion o' this, mind, this while back. Aye, I've seen you slipping off to Anne. Many's the time. Colloguing together.'

'I have been the Queen's friend, yes . . .'

'Friend! Aye, more the Queen's friend than the King's, I

jalouse!' The more Ludovick protested, the more furious James grew. 'I'll teach you to cuckold your liege lord!'

'James – a truce to this! You ill serve your own honour when you so assail the Queen's!'

'Say no more, Ludovick,' Anne urged. 'Here is only folly. Madness.'

'*You* would name me mad, woman!' James all but screamed. 'You, now – who bore my bairn!' He gulped, slobbering, seeking to win under control the tongue which was too big for his mouth. 'If . . . if it *was* my bairn! Aye – whose bairn was it? Was it mine, or his?' A trembling finger pointed from one to the other of them, as the King sobbed out his dire question.

The Queen swung round abruptly, without a word, and almost ran to her bedroom. The door slammed shut behind her.

The bang of it seemed to bring James more or less to his senses. He stared at the shut door in silence for a few moments, and then glanced sidelong at Ludovick, from under down-bent brows. 'Aye,' he said. 'Och, well.'

'Have I your permission to retire, Sire?' the younger man asked stiffly.

'Ooh, aye. Go. Aye, leave me.'

'I ask permission further, Sire, to leave the Court. To retire to Methven. Forthwith.'

'Eh . . . ? Methven? Na, na – wait you, man. That's another matter.'

'Your Grace cannot desire my presence here, believing me false. Nor do I wish to remain at Court.'

'*Your* wishes are no' the prime matter, Vicky. You're High Chamberlain, I'd remind you. On my Privy Council. Aye, and Lord Admiral o' this realm. At my pleasure.'

'It is my pleasure, Sire, to resign these offices.'

'Ha – hoity-toity! No' so fast, no' so fast! I'll maybe ha' need o' your services yet, Vicky Stewart. If Argyll finds Huntly ower much for him, likely the Admiral o' Scotland will need to go aid him!'

'And gladly, Sire. That would much please me. As you know, I would have gone north with Argyll two weeks ago had you permitted it.'

'Umm. Well – we'll see. But you're no' to retire from Court

lacking my permission, mind. And you're no' to take your
Mistress Mary away from Stirling. I require her there. Mind
that, too. You understand, Vicky?'

Lennox bowed stiffly, curtly. 'Is that all, Sire? Shall I send
the Master of Gray to you?'

'No. No' now. I would be alone.'

Ludovick went storming through the palace to his own room.

'A fresh horse,' he shouted to Peter Hay. 'And food. Ale.
In a satchel. I ride for Stirling forthwith.'

'Stirling? But . . . you are new here from Stirling!'

'Back to Stirling I go, neverthless. See you to it – and quickly.'

'Yes, my lord Duke . . .'

128

Chapter Nine

The King of Scots sat in the Hall of Scrymgeour the Constable's castle of Dudhope, in Dundee town, biting his nails. Down either side of the great table the members of the hastily called Council sat, looking grave, concerned or alarmed – those who were sober enough to display any consistent expression. Eight o'clock of an October evening was no time to hold a Privy Council.

Alone, down at the very foot of the table, sat a beardless youth almost as though he was on trial, drumming fingers on the board – Archibald Campbell, seventh Earl of Argyll. James glowered everywhere but at him.

'They slew a herald wearing my royal colours!' the King muttered, not for the first time: This, of it all, seemed most to distress him. 'Huntly killed my herald! That's more than treason, mind – that's *lèse-majesté*!'

'It is the work of wicked and desperate men, fearing neither the ordinance of God or man, Sire!' Andrew Melville declared strongly. 'They must be destroyed. Rooted out, without mercy. In the past Your Grace has been too merciful.'

'The destroying and rooting-out would seem to be on the other foot!' the Lord Home snorted. 'Who will now do the rooting, Master Melville? The Kirk?'

'Aye, my lord – the Kirk will root right lustily! Have no fear. Pray God others may do as much!'

'If Argyll's six thousand Highlandmen ran before Huntly, how does the Kirk propose to destroy him, sir? By prayer and fasting?'

'My lord!' young Argyll protested from the foot of the table. 'My Highlanders did not run. They stood their ground and died by the hundred. Cut down by cavalry – Huntly had horse in their thousands. And mown down by cannon – Your Grace's cannon, which Huntly held as your Lieutenant of the North!'

'Ooh, aye,' the King said vaguely. 'The ill limmer!'

'We shot his horse under him. We killed his uncle, Gordon

of Auchindoun. Also Gordon of Gight. We sore wounded Erroll ...'

'But you lost the day, man – you lost the day!'

'My lord of Forbes, with the Frasers and Ogilvies and Leslies, was to have joined me. They were but a day's march away. We were waiting them at Glenlivet when Huntly attacked. With cavalry and cannon ...'

'Hear you that, Master Melville? Cavalry and Cannon!' Home taunted. 'That is what you face. On, the godly ranks of the Kirk!'

'Curb your tongue, scoffer – ere the Lord curbs it for you!' Melville thundered. 'Christ's Kirk will triumph!'

'Undoubtedly,' the Master of Gray intervened soothingly. 'So pray we all. Meantime, the Council must advise His Grace on his immediate action. May I ask my lord of Argyll if he knows whether Huntly pursues?'

'I think not. But how can I tell, sir? When all was lost, I was ... Tullibardine and others dragged me off the field. By main force. My Uncle Colin of Lundy was sore wounded at my side. Campbell of Lochnell my Standard-bearer, dead. I would have stayed – I would have stayed ...' The young man's voice broke.

'Surely, surely, my lord,' Patrick nodded. 'None doubt your hardihood. We but would learn if Huntly is like to descend upon us here at Dundee. Whether he follows close? Or at all?'

'No. No – I do not believe it. Huntly lost greatly also. My Uncle John said he must surely lick his wounds awhile. And with Forbes and the others only a day away. We withdrew northwards after, after ... towards Forbes. My people were scattered. I sent to gather them. Sent Inverawe back to Argyll for more men. Left my uncle, Sir John of Cawder in command. Then hastened south to inform and warn His Grace.'

'Then, no doubt, were Huntly indeed hot on your heels, Sir John would have sent word. We should put out picquets to watch all approaches from the north – but I think we need have little fear of surprise. We can therefore plan how the situation may be retrieved.'

'That is so, Patrick,' James nodded sagely.

'We must back to Edinburgh,' the Earl of Morton roused

himself to declare, hiccuping. 'This is when that mis-miscreant Bothwell will strike. Back, hic, to Edinburgh, I say!'

'Not so,' the Earl Marischal countered. 'The capital is well enough defended. Most of the realm's cannon is there. Your Grace should advance, and raise the loyal north against the Gordons and Hays. Aye, and against the Douglases of Angus!' Keith, the Earl Marischal's estates, of course, were in the north; whereas Douglas of Morton's were south of Edinburgh.

'The north is more loyal to Gordon than, hic, to the King, I think,' Morton sneered. 'How many men will my Lord Marischal provide?'

'A thousand – given time to raise them.'

'We'll no' can go north, Your Grace,' the Master of Glamis, the Treasurer, protested. 'If Huntly can defeat six thousand Campbells how shall we face him wi' this? We should remain here, at Dundee. Mustering our strength. All leal men to assemble here. Within the month. Then, in strength, march against Huntly. Not before.' The Glamis lands lay close to Dundee.

'Wait a month and let all Scotland see Huntly set King and Kirk at naught!' Melville cried. 'Here is craven counsel, I say! In a month Bothwell could have railled again – raised new forces in the Border. The King of Spain could send men instead of gold. Papists everywhere would rise, acclaiming Henry of France's apostasy and Huntly's victory. Delay, my lords, can only hurt our cause, Christ's cause. The King set out on this progress to show the north who ruled in Scotland. I say let him continue. Let us march north tomorrow, trusting in God and the right! Take the bold course, Sire – and led by the Kirk your people will support you.'

Into the hubbub of challenge and mockery, Ludovick Stewart raised his voice. It was his first intervention. 'I agree with Master Melville,' he said. 'To go back now would be to concede defeat before all. This battle will have cost Huntly dear. Let us strike now while he is still not recovered. We can confront him within two days. From here.'

James plucked his thick lower lip. He did not look at Lennox, any more than he did at Argyll. In the month which had elapsed since the scene in the Queen's boudoir at Falkland, there had been a notable stiffness between the cousins. The King would not allow the other to retire from Court, but he behaved towards him almost as though he was not there. On his part, Ludovick was rigidly, coldly correct, and that was all – at the Court but not of it. All knew the cause of the trouble – the Queen's ladies-in-waiting left none in doubt – and whispers inevitably magnified the entire business dramatically, so that most had come to assume that Anne had indeed been Lennox's mistress; indeed the English envoy wrote to his own Queen to that effect. This progress to the north had, in consequence, come as a most welcome break to Ludovick.

'Aye, well,' James said. 'Maybe. I'ph'mm.'

The Master of Gray nodded. 'There is much in what all have said, Your Grace. I would humbly suggest that something of all should be done. Have my lord of Morton, and perhaps the Laird of Buccleuch, return south to strengthen the defences of Edinburgh. Call a muster here at Dundee. No doubt the Treasurer will be glad to remain here and see to it.' He raised a single eyebrow in the direction of the Master of Glamis, an old enemy. 'Although I think it need not take a month. For the rest, let us march north forthwith, as Master Melville advises. Before Huntly rallies again after this battle. My lord Duke is right – Huntly cannot fail to be ill prepared for us at this juncture. His victory was dear won, it seems. Erroll is out of the fight. Auchindoun, the best of the Gordon leaders, is slain. Angus is a weakling. Moreover, my lord of Forbes and the loyal northern clans have not yet been engaged. With my Lord Marischal and his Keiths, and the reassembled Campbell host of my lord of Argyll, we should outnumber Huntly three to one.'

'But not his cannon!' Home pointed out.

'Our strategy must be to give him no opportunity to use his cannon, my lord. We all know that cannon have their drawbacks. They are cumbersome, slow to move, and require a set target. At Leith, once Bothwell moved, our cannon were of no service to us. We must offer Huntly no target, seek not to bring him to battle, but to harass him at every turn. Attack not Huntly himself, but the Gordon and Hay lands of his lairds and supporters. So that they leave him to go defend their houses. Thus, too, shall we provision ourselves whilst cutting off *his* provisions.'

That was shrewd pleading. At the thought of the easy pickings, under royal license, of a hundred fat Gordon lairdships, many eyes gleamed and lips were licked. Only the Treasurer's voice was raised in opposition.

'How does the Master of Gray, Sire, ensure that his old friend Huntly obliges us thus kindly?'

'Your Grace – if we play our cards aright, he has no choice. He cannot move the Gordon lands and castles, that have been his pride and strength. Nor can he defend them all, or any number of them. We shall make them his weakness rather than his strength. We shall not fight my lord of Huntly and his host, we shall fight his broad provinces of Aberdeen and Buchan and Moray and the Mearns – and watch his army melt away like snow in the sun! I assure you . . .'

He was stopped by the great shout of acclaim.

Ludovick Stewart had great difficulty in making himself heard. 'I had not meant, Sire, that we should go to war against a land, an entire countryside. These are your people, as well as Huntly's. Your Grace's subjects . . .'

'They are rebels, young man!' Melville declared sternly. 'And Papists to a man. In arms against both God and the King! They must be rooted out, as were the Amalakites . . .'

'They are Christian men and women, sir. Fellow-country-men, fellow-subjects of your own.'

'We are well aware, my lord Duke, that Huntly is your sister's husband!'

'To my sorrow and hers! That was a marriage arranged otherwhere!' He shot a glance from the King to the Master of Gray. 'On Huntly I would make war, yes – but not on the homes of his people!'

James frowned. 'Aye, but it's no' you that's making the war, Vicky Stewart! It's me. I, the King, make the war.' He wagged a finger. 'Me it is they rebel against, mind – no' you! They slew my herald, Red Lion. That's tantamount, aye tantamount, to an attack on my own royal person. It's no' to be borne.'

'Then we march, Sire? Northwards?' the Earl Marischal demanded.

'Och, well. I'ph'mm. Aye, it seems so, my lord, does it no'?'

'God be praised!' Melville exclaimed.

Patrick Gray caught Lennox's eye, and almost imperceptibly shook his head.

Perhaps two-thirds of the way up the long, long ascent of Bennachie, Ludovick of Lennox drew rein, to rest his weary sweating horse, and behind him his straggling column of something like one hundred men-at-arms thankfully did likewise. All Aberdeenshire seemed to slope up, from every side, to this thrusting central isolated cone of Bennachie, and if the Duke's magnificent Barbary black was weary and flagging, the lesser mounts of his followers were all but foundered. And not only the horses; the riders also were drooping with fatigue. Few would elect to go campaigning with the Duke of Lennox again, were they given the choice.

This land of Aberdeenshire was vast, so much more widespread, richer, populous and diverse in aspect than Ludovick had realised. They had been in the saddle since daybreak, and now it was mid-afternoon, and most of the intervening hours they seemed to have spent climbing, climbing towards this green rock-crowned pinnacle of Bennachie. There had been distractions, of course, diversions, turnings-off from the line of general advance; but these, in the main, Ludovick would have preferred to forget – if he could.

This was the second day of the advance into the great Gordon territories, and they were not yet within twenty-five miles of Huntly's inner fastnesses of the upper Don basin, of Strathbogie, Formartine and the Deveron. But yesterday, whilst still south of the River Dee, Ludovick had had his bellyful of the royal progress, and had urgently sought permission to lead instead one of the scouting forces which probed ahead of the main army, seeking contact with the enemy – since he could by no means bring himself to recognise as the enemy the occupants, men, women and children, young and old, of the innumerable houses, towers and castles, small and great, which were the object of the kingly wrath and the Council's policy, rebels as they might be named. Sickened, after witnessing the fate of a dozen such lairdships, belonging to Hays and Douglases and other lesser allies of Gordon, on the mere outer fringes of Huntly's domains, and finding his protests of no

avail, he had chosen this scouting role of the advance-guard,
hoping for clean fighting, honest warfare, in place of sack,
rapine, arson and pillage, in the name of Kirk and Crown.
Allotted a company mainly of Ogilvy and Lindsay retainers
from Angus, with a leavening of more local Leslies and Leiths,
his task, along with other similar columns, was to ensure
that there was no unknown enemy threat ahead of the more
slowly advancing and widely dispersed main punitive force of
the King. The high pass between the two peaks of Bennachie,
and its secure holding for the King, had been his day's objective.
    Their route here had been devious indeed, despite the way
that all the land rose to this proud landmark – for in this vast
rolling countryside it was not sufficient just to press ahead;
always they had to scour the intervening territory to left and
right, to ascertain that there were no concentrations of men
hidden in the far-flung ridge-and-valley system, with its spreading woodlands, and to link up regularly with other columns
similarly employed. Groups of armed men they had encountered
now and again, and some had even shown tentative fight – but
these were small parties and obviously merely the retainers of
local lairds, concerned to defend their homes. Although it was
no part of his given orders to do any such thing, the Duke had
further used up considerable time and effort in seeking out the
towers and mansions in his area of advance, which might be
linked with the Gordon interests, to warn their occupants of the
fate which bore down upon them so that they might at least
have time to save their persons, families, servants and valuables
by fleeing to some hiding-place. These warnings had not always
been well received nor acted upon; nor had Ludovick's men-at-
arms considered the giving of them a suitable and profitable
employment.
    Now, turning in the saddle and gazing back eastwards and
southwards over the splendid landscape which sank, in the
golden October sunlight, in great rolling waves of tilth and
pasture, moor and thicket and woodland, between Dee and Don,
to the level plain of the distant, unseen sea, Ludovick stared,
set-faced. From on high here, the fair land seemed to spout
smoke-like eruptions from underground fires. There were the
dense black clouds of new-burning brushwood and thatch;

the brown reek of hay and straw; the murky billows, shot with red, of mixed conflagration well alight; and the pale blue of old fires, burning low. All these smokes drifted on the south-westerly breeze to mingle and form a pall of solid grey that hung like a curtain for endless miles, as though to hide the shame of the land. Directly behind themselves, the fires did not start for perhaps five or six miles – though even so, it meant that the main force, still unflagging in its enthusiasm, was closer than Ludovick had imagined; but elsewhere the smokes were considerably further forward, almost level, if more scat-tered – indicating that not all of the advance-parties were, like his own, failing to further the good work in their necessarily more modest way.

Lennox, by now, well knew the significance of those different-hued burnings. The thick black represented thatch torn from cot-house roofs and laid against the walls of stone towers. These little fortalices of the lairds, with their stone-vaulted basements, gunloops and iron-barred small windows, were almost impossible to reduce without cannon, even for a large force, short of starving out the occupants; but they could be rendered untenable by the knowledgeable. Masses of dense-smoking material, heaped all around the thick walls almost as high as the narrow arrow-slit windows to vaults and stairways, and set alight, would soon produce, with the fierce heat, a strong updraught of air. This, sucked through the unglazed or broken windows into the interior of the house, especially the winding corkscrew stairways, could in a short time turn any proud castle into what was little better than a tall chimney. No occu-pant could endure this for long; all must issue forth for fresh air, or suffocate. The yellow and brown smoke was corn and hay barns burning. Other fuels produced their own coloration.

Silently the Duke pointed to where, perhaps eight miles south by east of them, in the area of their own march, a fire larger than the others was spouting dense black-brown clouds at the foot of the lesser Hill of Fare. The dark young man beside him, John Leslie, Younger of Balquhain, appointed as his guide and local adviser, nodded.

'Midmar Castle,' he said. 'Where we were at noon. Gordon of Ballogie's house. An old man. He said he would not leave, you'll mind. He would have done better to heed your warning, my lord.'

'He gave us food and drink. His wife was kind. And there were two girls, bonnie lassies . . .'

'Aye, his son George's daughters. Janet is . . . friendly. George is with Huntly. Yon will bring him home, I warrant!'

Ludovick said nothing. His thoughts went back to the only other occasion, three years ago, when he had viewed a castle in process of being smoked out – that grim February night at Donibristle on the north shore of Forth. Then Huntly himself had been the incendiary, and the victim, the Earl of Moray, unable to stand it longer, had leapt from a window, hair and beard alight, to run to the sea, and on the beach had been over-taken, run through by Gordon swords, and slashed across his handsome face by Huntly's own, Ludovick helpless to restrain it. Some would therefore call this but justice – save that it was not Huntly himself who now bore the brunt of it, but old men and girls, his innocent people.

Sighing, the Duke turned away. 'We shall move on up to the pass between the hill-tops,' he said. 'We shall secure that, and plan its defence. Then send out parties beyond, to ensure that there is no enemy near. To inquire also the whereabouts of my Lord Forbes's force. Is there a house convenient nearby where we may pass the night?'

'There is Balfluig, my lord,' Leslie answered. 'A Forbes house – but it is five miles beyond the pass.'

'Too far. We must be close at hand. Encamped, if need be, in the pass itself. An enemy column stealing through here could play havoc amongst the King's scattered forces.'

'Aye. But we need not all spend a cold night on the hill, my lord. I have just minded – there is a house nearer, *this* side of the pass. The House of Tullos. It lies yonder, maybe a mile or so more to the north, unseen in a fold of the hill. A snug place.

'Seton is laird – and married to a daughter of Gordon of Tillyfour!'

'Gordon!' Ludovick frowned, biting his lip. He was coming to dread the sound of the name. 'Another of them?'

'Aye – and Papists all.'

The Duke sighed. 'Then, they fall to be warned. But first the pass.' He looked wearily up the hill.

'Send a party up there, my lord. To the pass. No need for you to go. It has been a long day. Let us to Tullos. Our lads will soon inform us if there is aught amiss up there.'

'No,' Ludovick decided. 'That pass is important. Of all this country, there alone could Huntly slip through a force unobserved. I cannot leave it to others to see to. I must go prospect it. You, Leslie, go to this Tullos. My compliments to its laird. Take a score of the men. Say that we come peacably – but that tomorrow he would be wise to seek some sure hiding-place for his people. This night, if he will have us, we'll bide with him – and pay for our entertainment. If not, we shall spend the night in the pass well enough. It is for him to say, in his own house ...'

'But they are rank Papists, my lord!'

'I was born a rank Papist, sir – as, little doubt, were you! So speak them fair. I want no trouble. Remember our task – not to punish Catholics but to seek out Huntly. See to it, friend. I will come later.'

So Ludovick rode on up the long hill, with the majority of his men, whilst Leslie and a lesser company trotted northwards over the slantwise sheep-dotted pastures.

The pass between the Mither Tap and the Millstone Hill of Bennachie was a narrow defile of bracken, heather and rocks, one thousand feet high, breaking the long barrier of hill which so effectively divided the great shire of Aberdeen, the largest single area of fertile land in all Scotland. Because of its situation, with the land dropping away steeply on all hands, a comparatively few determined men could hold it against an army. Ludovick approached it very cautiously, quite prepared to find it held. But it proved to be clear. Also the onward slopes seemed to be devoid of life save for the scattered peacefully-grazing cattle which obviously had not been disturbed for long.

There was no lack of cover in the place, with great boulders and outcrops littering the sides of it, and Ludovick chose positions for his men, strong positions. He was not concerned with hiding their presence. Better indeed that the enemy should know that the pass was held against them, and so not attempt any passage thereof. Ludovick was by no means looking for trouble. He gave orders therefore that his men should gather fuel – dried heather-stems, roots, bog-oak, anything which would burn - to light fires and if possible keep them burning all night, so that they might be seen from afar. He sent pickets out to spy out the land ahead and appointed watchers and sentinels on the actual flanking hill-tops and ridges. Not until all was to his satisfaction did he leave, to ride back downhill towards the House of Tullos.

He saw the smoke almost as soon as he came out of the defile, and recognised that it came from the direction Leslie had taken. Set-faced, he spurred his jaded horse.

He never doubted that the fire was at Tullos. The smoke rose out of a sort of corrie, or fold in the hill – and Leslie had mentioned only the one such house. This was thick black smoke – like thatch again. It could scarcely be that - but whatever it was boded no good. Smoke, to Ludovick Stewart, now represented only sorrow and shame.

As he neared the cleft in the hillside he could hear the crackle of fire, interspersed with shouting. The quality of that shouting, coarse laughter, taunts and jeers, darkened the Duke's features.

Riding over the lip of the corrie, Ludovick saw that it was altogether a bigger and better place than he had anticipated. In a wide green apron on the lap of the hill sat a pleasant whitewashed house backed by trees. Flanking its sides and rear was a farm-steading, barns and cot-houses, while an orchard slanted down in front to where a fair-sized burn was dammed to form a duck-pond, the whole looking out south by east over the prospect of a quarter of Aberdeenshire. The house itself was quite substantial, of two storeys and an attic, L-shaped, with a circular stair-tower in the angle and squat round corner-turrets at the gables. It had a stone-slated roof – but the roofs of the outbuildings and cot-houses were reed-thatched. It was this that was burning.

The shouting came from behind the house. Hastening there, Ludovick came to a cobbled yard between house and farmery. It was thronged with people, mainly his own men-at-arms, their horses feeding on heaps of hay thrown down at the windward side of the burning buildings where the drifting smoke would not worry them. The men were much and noisily engaged. None even noticed the Duke's arrival.

Ludovick spurred forward to see what went on within the circle of shouting troopers. Apart from these, there were two groups of people in the centre of the courtyard. One contained a middle-aged, heavily-built man, a buxom woman, a boy in his teens and a girl still younger. These, plainly but decently dressed, were all held fast by soldiers, being forced to watch the proceedings. One of the man's eyes was practically closed up by a blow. The other group was larger, obviously servants and farm-hands huddled together in cowering fear. The women's clothing was noticeably disarranged and torn. They stared at what went on in the centre.

There a peculiar proceeding was being enacted, whither was directed all the shouting. Two people were being forced to kneel on the cobbles, gripped by men-at-arms – a comely young woman and facing her a young man in rent and soaking blood-stained shirt, with blood trickling down from his hair. These were notably alike in feature, and looked as though they might be brother and sister. Between them, on a stone mounting-block, stood a carved wood crucifix perhaps eighteen inches high. Nearby was a half-barrel of water.

The young man and woman were being forced to fill their mouths with the water, and then to spew it out over the crucifix. At least, that was their tormentors' intention. In fact they were spilling and ejecting it anywhere but upon the cross. For their obstinacy they were being kicked their arms twisted and mugfuls of the water thrown in their faces, to mingle with the girl's tears and the young man's blood.

Appalled, seething with anger, Ludovick drove his black horse straight into the press of the men. 'Fools! Oafs! Animals!' he exclaimed. 'Stop! Enough! Have done, I say!'

Leslie came pushing towards him, gesticulating. 'My lord, my lord!' he cried. 'I couldna help it. They'll no' heed me. I've told them . . .'

Ludovick ignored him, shouting at the men around the crucifix. He in turn was ignored.

Leslie reached for the black's bridle, and held on to it. 'They'll not heed me,' he insisted. 'I can do nothing with them. But it's Seton's own fault. He resisted us. They're all stiff-necked, inso-lent. One o' his people drew a sword on us . . .'

'I told you. You were to speak him fair. There was to be no trouble. You were in command. You are responsible.'

Leslie looked half-frightened, half-defiant. 'They are not *my* men. I never saw them before this day. They scoff at me. One in especial – yon red-headed stot Rab Strachan . . . !' He looked very young and inadequate there amongst all that passion and violence – although he was possibly a year or so older than Lennox.

'Here – take my horse!' Ludovick threw him the reins, and leapt down. He pushed his way through the throng, elbowing men aside. He came to the central space.

'I said stop that!' he snapped. 'Unhand these two – d'you hear! At once.'

Men turned to stare now, and the shouting died away. But the comparative quiet only emphasised the crackling roar of the burning roofs, with its own inflammatory effect on the tempers of men. Even the heat engendered inner heat. Lennox himself was affected by it. He could hardly control his voice.

'You . . . you louts! Sottish numbskulls!' he yelled, when none answered him. 'Do as I say.'

None moved. None released their grip on the unfortunate pair at the crucifix, or on those forced to watch. Then a big and burly red-haired man deliberately stooped, to scoop up a mugful of water from the barrel and throw it hard in the girl's face.

Blazing-eyed Ludovick strode up to the fellow, and slapped him across the face, twice, right and left, with the palm and back of his hand. 'Brute-beast!' he jerked. 'Miscreant! Obey, fool!' He swung round, to grasp the shoulder of one of the troopers who held the young woman, and flung him aside. 'I said unhand her, scum!' He stooped, to take the girl's arm.

It was the warning in the kneeling young man's eyes that saved him. Ludovick twisted round, just in time to avoid a savage, swinging clenched-fisted blow from the red-headed Strachan.

He side-stepped, rage boiling up within him, his hand dropping to his sword-hilt. Then he mastered himself somewhat, and drew back a little in distaste. The last thing to be desired was for him to become involved in a brawl with his men. 'How

141

dare you!' he cried. 'Stand back, man! All of you – do as you are told. Back to your horses. Back, I say!'

'No' so fast, your Dukeship – no' so fast!' the man Strachan declared thickly, standing his ground and scowling. 'Why so hot? Eh? What ill are we doing, sink me? We're but justifying thrice-damned Papists!'

'Aye,' one of the others supported him. 'Where's the harm? They're a' doing it. The others, Shauchlin' Jamie, the King, himsel'! Why no' us? Doon wi' the sh-shtinking rebels, I say!' Like the other, he spoke indistinctly. Obviously they had been drinking; presumably they had found liquor in the house.

There were hoarse shouts of agreement from all around.

'Silence! You dare to raise your voices to *me*! Lennox!' Ludovick glared round at them all. He reached for the young woman's arm again, and raised her up. She stood trembling and sobbing at his side. He twitched off the short riding-cloak that hung from one shoulder, to drape it around her near nakedness – at which mocking laughter rose from his men.

The red-head pointed. 'See – that's it!' he hooted. 'He wants the bitch for himsel'! Our Dukie wants her . . .'

'Hold your idiot tongue! I am Chamberlain and Admiral of this realm. You will obey my orders. And without question. Or die for it! 'Fore God – this is the work of felons! Savages! And dolts! Leslie – here! Take this girl, and this young man. Into the house. Forthwith. And release the laird and his lady. I will deal with these fools. Come . . .'

As without enthusiasm John Leslie came forward, some of the soldiers barred his way. An angry murmur arose. Leslie was fairly easily dissuaded.

'Here's idolatry!' Strachan shouted. 'They're Popish idol-ators. Bowing down to idols. The Kirk says we're to root them oot. Aye, and the King, too! He says it. If the Duke o' Lennox doesna ken better, he needs teaching, I say!'

There was a great shout of acclaim.

'Would he have us bear wi' images and idols? Eh?' The man spat in the direction of the crucifix. 'We'll teach him . . .'

'You imbecile! You ignorant clod!' Ludovick turned, and snatched up the cross. 'This is no idol. This is the simple symbol of your Saviour. Of Christ, who died on such a cross.

For you and for me. For this girl and this man likewise. For Protestant and Catholic alike. We are all Christians, are we not? Christ died on the cross for all men – not just for some. For the mistaken, for sinners – aye, even for fools like you! And you spit on His cross!'

'It's an image!' Strachan insisted heavily. 'Made wi' men's hands. A graven image . . .'

'It is a symbol. As is the King's crown. As is that blazon you wear.' He pointed to the blue and white fesse checky, the arms of the House of Lindsay, painted on the man's breastplate of steel. 'A sign. Of something that means much. If you spit on Christ's cross, you spit on Christ Himself!'

'Talk! Just talk – and accursed Papist talk at that! You'll no' cozen us, laddie, wi' your ill talk – Duke or nane! Images are images, and them that bow doon to them, damned! They've to be rooted oot . . .'

'Likely he's a Papist himself!' a small dark man shouted shrilly. 'They say his sister's married on Huntly!'

'Aye, like enough. Sold to the Whore o' Rome!'

'A buidy Catholic – like a wheen ithers aboot the King!'

'Doon wi' the fell Papists!'

As the uproar mounted, Ludovick handed the crucifix to the wounded youth who now stood at his side. Then grimly, silently, deliberately, he drew his sword from its sheath. The weapon came out with the creaking shrill of steel. It was but a thin high sound, but it seemed to cut through the hubbub of angry voices as though with the slender blade's own keenness.

The shouting died away, to leave only the roar and crackle of fire and the jingle and stamp of restive horses.

Lennox gestured to the brother and sister to follow him, and moved forward directly towards the house, sword-point extended before him.

In the face of that flickering steel men fell back. When one, bolder than his fellows, seemed to hold his ground, the blade leapt out like a striking snake, and the fellow jumped aside cursing – but discreetly.

The Duke, with the two youngsters close at his heels, came up to where Seton of Tullos, his wife and the other two children were held fast.

143

'Free them,' he jerked at their captors, reinforcing his command with a flick of the sword. To Seton himself he bowed briefly. 'My apologies, sir. I am Lennox. All this is directly against my orders. Madam – believe me, I am sorry.'

Neither the laird nor any of his household made any reply. They stared from angry hostile eyes, in hatred.

'Into your house,' Ludovick directed tersely. 'All of you. Take your people. Lock your doors. Quickly. But . . . be gone by morning, if you value your lives! To some hiding-place. When the King comes.'

As they turned to go, without a word, it was the bloody-headed youth again who warned Lennox. 'Sir . . . !' he said, glancing back urgently.

Ludovick swung round. The man Strachan had drawn his own sword, and was advancing upon him menacingly.

When the fellow saw that he was observed, he raised his voice. 'Hey, lads – come on!' he yelled. 'We'll teach this Romish duke to name us names! To call us fools and savages. God – we will!'

He gained much vocal support, and a few of his companions crowded behind him, but only one actually drew his sword.

Ludovick smiled now, thinly, grimly, his blunt boyish features much altered. Flexing his blade purposefully, he moved in to meet them.

The red-head, nothing loth, came at him fiercely, heavily, at one side, his colleague, the same dark wiry man who had announced Lennox's relationship to Huntly, dancing in in bouncing fashion on the other. Ludovick made a swift assessment. He seemed to make directly for Strachan, but just before they closed he swung abruptly to the left and lunged at the small man. Taken by surprise his opponent skipped backwards, and a second quick feint by the Duke sent him further back still, blinking. Ludovick swung on Strachan.

This one had not half the speed of his friend, but he had a furious determination. His vicious slash at Lennox would have cut him down there and then, and for good, had it struck home – and indeed the Duke only avoided it by instants and inches. The backhand sideways stroke which he flashed in return only rang upon the other's steel breastplate.

Ludovick leapt clear, his glance darting round the circle of the other men-at-arms. He saw no sympathy for himself in their eyes – but none had drawn their swords. Reassured, he turned his full attention on his two immediate assailants.

He allowed Strachan to rush him, almost scornfully side-stepping and warding off the jabbing thrust with a parry and twist of the wrist. Then, as the man stumbled past, he beat him insultingly across the back with the flat of his blade, and in a single complicated movement switched to the dark fellow, his point flickering and flashing about like forked lightning. Before even this agile customer could win clear, his sword-hand wrist was slashed and spouting blood and only the tough leather sleeve of the hide jerkin he wore beneath his breastplate saved his entire arm from being ripped up. With a yelp of agony he dropped his weapon, and stumbled back clutching his wounded wrist.

Lennox turned back to the red-head. That individual, though still gloweringly angry, was wary now, as well he might perceiving something of the quality of the Duke's swording. Ludovick had learned the art, from boyhood, at the hands of the Master of Gray – who was possibly the finest swordsman in all Scotland. Not for him the lusty but crude cut-and-thrust of men-at-arms. Moreover his blade was much lighter and more manoeuvrable than that of the heavy cavalry sabre used by the troopers. Strachan's only advantage was in his slightly longer reach and the fact that he wore leather and steel against the Duke's mere broadcloth.

Ludovick undoubtedly could have dealt with the big man, alone, in a very short time. But his intentions were otherwise. He was not merely fighting Strachan; he was concerned to re-impose his authority and control over his mutinous soldiery. So they should be taught a lesson, through this over-bold red-head.

Therefore he sought to play with the man, and to make it obvious to others that he was so playing – a dangerous game for both of them. Round Strachan he skipped and gyrated, flicking, darting, feinting with his sword, pinking the leather jerkin, tapping the steel breastplate – and avoiding the other's ever more wild rushes. What he was doing must have been apparent to all – he hoped with the desired effect.

There was one effect, however, which Ludovick had not bargained for. Strachan, perhaps, had a close friend amongst the watchers; or it may have been the dark man's friend. A shout from Leslie, in the background, saved the Duke – but only just. A thick-set bull-necked man had picked up the wounded trooper's sabre, and now sprang at Ludovick with this held high.

It was almost disaster. Flinging himself out of the way of the descending blade, the younger man all but impaled himself on Strachan's sword. The point of it indeed ripped through his doublet at the back of the shoulder, to come out again at the front, fortunately merely grazing the skin. Not so fortunate was the fact that for the moment it transfixed him, skewering through his tightly-buttoned doublet. He lost his balance, toppling.

Although this mischance had the effect of temporarily disarming Strachan, it also left the Duke wide open to the other man's attack. Desperately he took the only course left open to him – he hurled himself down at the red-head's knees, encircling them with his left arm. The force of his unexpected attack and the other's own impetus, brought them both to the ground with a crash. The third man, unable to halt his advance in time, cannoned into and fell headlong over them.

Great was the confusion. Ludovick, however, had the small but significant advantage in that he was not taken by surprise. He had done what he did deliberately. While the others scrabbled and floundered he, despite the handicap of the sword through his doublet, was purposefully wriggling himself free. He still clutched his own sword, and as the stocky man, on top, struggled up, the Duke, with a great effort twisted himself into a position where he could reach up and bring down the pommel of the weapon hard on the back of the other's neck. Grunting, the fellow sagged, and slewed sideways.

Somehow Ludovick got himself out from under them – and staggering to his feet abruptly found himself in command of the situation. Strachan now had no sword, and on top of him the other man was dazed, moaning. Panting, Lennox tugged out the skewering blade from his shoulders, and so stood, a weapon in each hand.

He stared round at the circle of watching faces. None of the others had drawn sword. No eye met his own. All gazed fascinated at their two colleagues helpless below him.

Ludovick's sigh of relief was lost in his deep breathing. For long moments he stood; there was no hurry now.

Then he sheathed his own sword, making something of a play of it. But as the stocky man was unsteadily rising to his feet, the Duke quite leisurely leant over and brought down the flat of Strachan's weapon on the man's wrist, not hard enough to break the bone but enough to make the unfortunate drop his sabre with a cry of pain. Ludovick kicked the weapon out of the way, and then, stepping forward, slapped the man across the face and pointed peremptorily over towards the horses. He stood blinking for a moment, and then turning, tottered away, mumbling.

A sort of corporate sigh issued from the ranked spectators.

Strachan was now on all fours, looking up at the younger man with fear in his eyes.

'You I should kill,' Ludovick said slowly. 'You are not fit to live. Can you think of any reason why I should spare you?'

The man gulped, but found no words.

'Speak, oaf! Can you, I say?'

'N'no, lord.'

'Nor can I. Save, I suppose, that Christ died for you, as I said! Is that sufficient that *I* should spare you?'

Hope dawned in Strachan's eyes. He began to gabble. 'Aye, lord. Ha' mercy, lord. Aye – spare me, for sweet Christ's sake! Spare me, my lord Duke!'

'If I do, it is not I who spare you, but Christ's cross. Which you spat upon! Yoo hear? Christ's cross. Remember that, always.' He looked up. 'And you all. Remember it, and take heed.' Then he held out his hand. 'Here is your sword, man.'

The other stared at the sabre proffered him, scarcely comprehending. He did not even put out his hand to take it.

Shrugging, the Duke tossed the weapon to him, and turned on his heel, ignoring him thereafter. 'Leslie,' he called. 'Have all men mounted forthwith. Then up with them to the pass. Do not wait for me. I go speak to Seton.'

There was a general move towards the horses almost before Lennox had finished speaking. The incident was over.

Another house, another godly assault, more faith, fervour and fury. And again Ludovick Stewart groaned in spirit. But this time he had to restrict himself to groaning, and that inwardly. For the assault was by no means confined to unruly men-at-arms; the highest in the land were involved, from the monarch downwards.

It was two days after the affair at Tullos – and no battle had taken place. There had been isolated scuffles between small parties on both sides, but the main forces had not been engaged. It seemed evident now that Huntly dared not attack the King, indeed did not even dare to take vigorous defensive action. For this house which was now being assailed was none other than his own great Castle of Strathbogie, for centuries the headquarters of Gordon power in the North.

At first, on arriving at Strathbogie, there had been a sort of constraint about everyone, despite the sense of jubilation and assurance, ever growing, which these days possessed the King and his army. Strathbogie was so vast a place, so proudly assured itself, as to daunt even the boldest – although Ludovick's advance-party had duly sent back word that it was not in fact even occupied much less being defended, and there was no sign of an enemy force within a dozen miles. It had taken some little time, when the royal force came up, for the sense almost of awe to wear off, in the face of this mighty establishment which spoke so eloquently, however silently, of enormous wealth, entire authority, almost unlimited power, in a way that none of the royal castles and palaces seemed to do. This was no military fortress, towering on top of a frowning rock like Edinburgh or Stirling; it was not even in a notably strong position within the spreading parkland and water-meadows at the junction of Bogie and Deveron – and the very lack of these obvious defensive precautions spoke of the complete confidence of the Gordon chiefs, Cocks o' the North for centuries, that here amongst their Grampian foothills in the centre of a million acres of Gordon-dominated territory, they were entirely, perpetually secure. This Strathbogie was not so much a castle or palace as a city in itself, surrounding and building up to the great central mass of masonry which was the citadel, tall, commanding, serene. That all this should be utterly devoid of life this October day only added to the sensation of eeriness, as of something wholly assured, infallible that but waited to strike.

James himself, these last days, had become a man transformed, as the certainty grew upon him that his coming had changed Huntly from being a rampant and ever-present menace to something like a wary fugitive. Strathbogie abandoned before him had seemed like the crowning of his efforts. Nevertheless, when he had walked through the empty halls and corridors of the Gordon citadel, he had been much affected, doubtful again. Even the riches littered there in such profusion – plenishings and furnishings, tapestries, plate, pictures, gold and silver ware – although they had him licking his lips and ordering all to be packed up and sent to Holyrood, Falkland, Stirling or Linlithgow, nonetheless made him uneasy. That any man could go and leave all this behind him, wealth grievously unsuitable for any subject, somehow oppressed him. It must argue vastly more elsewhere, to be sure.

But now James was confident again, restored in spirit. The first blasts of gunpowder had done that; there was something so positive and vigorous about gunpowder, and the King had developed an extraordinary faith in it. Not that it was proving very effective at Strathbogie as yet. Many of the surrounding buildings were tumbling down nicely – but the main central range was altogether too massively built, with walls ten to twelve feet in thickness, with iron-hard cement; it would require ever greater charges of explosive, ever bigger bangs. But meantime there was ample good work to be done on a different scale, much faithful effort requiring direction.

The Kirk needed no egging on, at all events. Led by Andrew Melville, the covey of ministers who accompanied the army and acted as local recruiting-officers, had all along marched and campaigned like troopers, fighting vehemently where opportunity offered, strong in the Lord's work. Melville had actually borne a pike throughout. Now he was zealously demonstrating to an admiring group how that horror of horrors, the Popish chapel of Strathbogie, could be demolished with greatest effect.

The King was more concerned with the castle itself. As well as cavities to be made in the great walls, for the explosive charges, there were battlements and parapets to be toppled, windows to be torn out, stone carvings to be defaced. He had to keep an eye also on the unending stream of men who emerged from the castle, ant-like, bearing idolatrous images, shrines and pictures, as well as doors, panelling, tables, benches and other non-valuable plenishings, to feed the flames of two huge bonfires which burned in the large main courtyard – for of course it was necessary to ensure that nothing of real worth was destroyed.

Ludovick, already roundly rebuked as faint-heart, backslider and appeaser of evil, who had been pacing restlessly, unhappily, to and fro near the King, turned to go and seek the Master of Gray whom he had noted earlier entering the castle pleasance. He found him, stretched out in a garden-house, making the most of the October sunshine, a picture of relaxation and ease.

'Patrick,' he cried, 'can you not do something to halt this folly, this destruction? This senseless violence. It is like a plague, a pestilence, sweeping the land!'

The Master yawned. 'My dear Vicky,' he said, 'why fret yourself? What's a little burning and knocking down of masonry? It relieves feelings which might well burst forth in worse things.'

'You sit there and say that? When the King himself leads the folly, pointing the way for others. And when on you lies much of the responsibility!'

'On me? Shrive me – how could that be?'

'Was it not you who advised James to this course? Destroy the Gordon homes, you said, so that Huntly's army may melt away. Do not fight battles, you said – burn roofs instead, and Huntly cannot strike back. Well, you were right. Huntly is beaten without a battle. But not without cost. The price paid is a king and people with the lust of destruction. Are you proud of your handiwork, Patrick?'

The other shook his handsome head. 'On my soul, Vicky, you astonish me! Since I made your education my own concern, I must indeed be at fault. I would have thought that your judgement would better this. Has it not occurred to you that in this sad world we cannot always have perfection? That ill exists and will not be wished away – so that the wise man makes the best that he can out of it, and does not weep and wail that all is not excellence...'

'Spare me a homily, Patrick – from *you*!'

'Someone else said that to me, not so long since. Our Mary, I think. The saints forbid that Patrick Gray should take to preaching! Could it be a sign of premature age? I shall have to watch for this! Nevertheless, may I point out, my good Vicky, that I feel I scarce deserve your censure, for seeking to make better what might have been infinitely worse. Is it not infinitely more desirable that stone and lime should be dinged doun, wood and gear burned, than that men should be slain? That was the choice. Huntly had to be defeated if James's crown and realm was to be saved. Enough blood has been spilt at Glenlivet – but that would have been as nothing to the bloodshed that must have followed had this course not been taken, whoever won. I do not like bloodshed, Vicky, however ill my reputation. And of all bloodshed, civil war is the most evil...'

'What do you name this? Ludovick swept an eloquent arm around to encompass all smoking Aberdeenshire. 'Is this not civil war most damnable?'

'No, lad – it is not. I have seen civil war. In France. The same weary, sad folly, between Protestant and Catholic. And it is much . . . otherwise. The dead choking the rivers, men, women and children, stinking to high heaven! Cities in ashes. Forests hanging with corpses. Disease and famine rampant. By the Mass, I will do much to keep such from Scotland! This . . . this is a mere punitive expedition by the King. A corrective display, that serves to enforce the royal authority, and at the same time leads to the disintegration of the Gordon host. Only material things are being destroyed in this. They can be replaced. New houses will go up, new sacred carvings be contrived...'

'You name it but material things when men and women are forced to deny their faith at the sword-point? When terror is called God's work? When the price of safety is to renounce belief?'

'Would you prefer that it should be battle, then? Slaughter and blood? Thousands dying for these same beliefs? Is my way not the better?'

The Duke was silent.

'These days will pass, Vicky, and men will be but little the worse for the heat and fury. But dead men will not live again. It is ever the way with religion...'

"Fore God – you, a Catholic at heart, talk so! I noted you swore by the saints and the Mass, back there. I cannot understand you, Patrick.'

'Am I a Catholic at heart?' the other wondered. He waved a lazy hand around. 'Might I suggest, lad, that you moderate your voice, if not your words? The phrase could almost be construed as a charge of highest treason hereabouts! Let us not add fuel to the already well-doing fire! Say that I am an undoubted but doubtful Christian, and leave it at that! That I value the substance higher than the form – unlike most alas!'

'So you will do nothing to halt this wickedness? You, who are as good as Chancellor of the realm, and can sway the King more than any other man!'

'You flatter me now, I vow! And I am not convinced of the wickedness. This Strathbogie is but a house, when all is said and done. Huntly is the richest lord in all the land – much richer than our peculiar liege lord James. He has enriched himself at the expense of many. Even at *my* humble expense, when he cost me Dunfermline Abbey! A little wealth-letting will hurt only his pride – of which he has over-much. And pride is a sin, is it not? So we do him little disservice . . . !'

'On my soul, you are impossible!' The younger man swung about and went stalking back whence he had come.

After a few moments, the Master rose unhurriedly and went sauntering after the other.

Back at the courtyard the work went merrily, enhanced by the infectious enthusiasm of Andrew Melville, who, having seen the demolishment of the chapel well under way, had now turned his attentions to the secular challenge. He was attacking the citadel walling with intelligence and vigour, as an example to feebler folk. Using an ordinary soldier's halberd, he was picking and probing shrewdly at the mortar around the masonry of a gunloop, an effective method of making a cavity large enough to take a major charge of gunpowder.

James was examining a handsome carved-wood chest which he appeared to have rescued from the bonfire. Beside him stood a protesting black-robed divine, comparatively youthful, his gown kilted up with a girdle, and long dusty riding-boots showing beneath. A group of grinning lords stood around, watching.

'It's a bonny kist, man,' the King insisted. 'Right commodious. It could be put to good and godly use.'

'It is stained with the marks of idolatry.' The minister pointed to a carved panel containing the intials I.H.S. flanking a cross. 'Evil cannot be countenanced in the hope of possible good to follow, Sire.'

'Ooh, aye. But this is no' a' that evil, maybe! Just the letters and a bit cross. There's . . . ha . . . there's a cross in your own coat-armour, Master Melville!'

'I do not use or acknowledge such vanities, Sire!' the young preacher declared. This was James Melville, nephew of Andrew, and no less positive in his views. 'There must be no truck with sin. Idolatry is sin, and these things are idolatrous.'

'Oh, no' just idolatrous,' James contested. 'A thing's no' idolatrous until it's worshipped, man.'

'No! No Sire I say! An idol is an idol, whether you or I worship it or no! It should be hewn down and broken in pieces and utterly destroyed, according to the word of the Lord!' The utter blazing-eyed authority of the statement set the King biting his nails – but still tapping at the oak chest with the toe of his boot.

From the rear Ludovick spoke up. 'You, a minister of Christ's Kirk, then name the cross of Christ an idol?' he demanded.

'Christ's true cross, no sir. Vain and paltry representations of it, yes!'

'That true cross exists no more. Is not its symbol to be reverenced?'

'The only honest symbol of Christ's cross is in the hearts of his elect, sir! No other is to be acknowledged. All images are false.'

'Yet you reverence the image, the symbol, when it represents the reality which is absent, do you not? Even you and your like! You acknowledge the signature on a letter, do you not? It is not the reality, only the symbol. The seal on a document, proving it valid. On your ordination papers, sir. That also you acknowledge, do you not? Representing due authority. His Grace, here – his crown. The image of that crown represents

153

the King's power when he is absent. Much is done in its name –
must so be done. Do you spurn the royal crown?'

'Aye, Vicky – you have the rights o' that!' James said – one
of the few words of commendation addressed to the Duke in
weeks.

'I do not worship crown, seal or signatures!' James Melville
declared stiffly.

'And I do not speak of worship. Only reverence. Respect. You,
who name yourself reverend, should know the difference.'

There was a murmur of amusement from the listening lords,
few of whom loved the ministers.

'These are different, quite,' the other jerked. 'I deal with
God's affairs, not men's.'

'Then I think you are presumptuous, sir! God made you a
man, and set you in the world amongst other men. Is it not said
that the sin of presumption is grievous? Almost as grievous as
idolatry?'

The King all but choked with a sort of shocked delight.

'Sir – beware how you mock the ministers of the Lord!'
James Melville exclaimed hotly.

'I do not mock,' Ludovick assured. 'I am full serious. More
serious than you, I must believe, when you name this poor
block of wood God's affair!'

James slapped his knee, and hooted. 'Man, Vicky – I didna
ken you had it in you!' he cried – though with a quick glance over
towards Melville senior, who was still picking away at the
Strathbogie masonry.

'My lord Duke is a man of hidden depths, of many surprises,
Your Grace,' the Master of Gray observed conversationally.
'He has been opening my eyes to a number of things! He takes
Holy Writ seriously! An uncomfortable habit – eh, Master
Melville?'

'Such jesting is unprofitable, sir.'

'Ah, but I do not jest. Nor, I think, does the Duke. I could
almost wish that he did, indeed! He actually believes in the
practice of mercy – as distinct from the mere principle thereof!'

Warily both the King and minister eyed him. Ludovick himself opened his mouth to speak, and then closed it again.

'He has been telling me, Sire, that he considers that with the triumph of the fall of Strathbogie, the policy of spoiling the Gordons has reached its peak and pinnacle. He holds that when this good work is finished . . .' The speaker raised a single eyebrow at the Duke in warning. '. . . When this is finished, further spoliation will but set back Your Grace's cause. A view which may possibly hold some truth, perhaps. Further measures against these people, after the notable downfall of Huntly's principal stronghold, might well savour of the futile, of flogging a dead horse. Moreover it might turn the folk sour – all the North-East. They must fear the King, yes; but the Duke's point, I think is that they should not *hate* Your Grace.'

Ludovick stared, at a loss.

'Eh . . . ? You mean . . . ? No more?' James looked from one to the other.

'So my lord Duke proposes, Sire. And he may well be right.'

'Would you leave the task half-finished, man?' the Earl Marischal demanded.

'Aye, why hold your hand now? When all the North is as good as ours?'

'Because a king is a king to all his subjects – not just to some few,' Lennox asserted strongly.

'But these are rebels. my lord – the King's enemies.'

'They are all His Grace's subjects, nevertheless. However mistaken.'

'The man, be he king, lord or common, who sets his hand against evil and then turns back, is lost, condemned in the sight of God!' James Melville exclaimed. 'Remember Lot's wife!'

'Ooh, aye,' James said.

'From such fate you must pray the good Lord to preserve us, my friend!' Patrick Gray agreed, smiling. 'But may it not turn on the question of what is evil?'

'There you have it!' Ludovick said strongly. 'A king who pursues vengeance on his subjects, even rebellious subjects, instead of showing mercy, I say does evil. Master Melville, I think, will not deny *his* own Master's words. "Blessed are the merciful, for they shall obtain mercy!" '

The young divine raised a declamatory hand. 'Mercy on sinners, yes! But on their sin, never!' he shouted. 'The sin must be rooted out. This Northland is full of the sin of idolatry, heresy and all uncleanness.'

He drew a greater measure of growled support for that than was his wont – from lords growing rich on Gordon pickings.

Perhaps it was his nephew's upraised voice which reached Andrew Melville. He left his labours at the wall-face and came striding over to the group around the King, still clutching his halberd, dust and chips of mortar further whitening his beard and flowing hair. All there were the less at ease for his arrival – save for Patrick Gray, who hailed him in friendly fashion.

'Well come, Master Melville,' he greeted. 'Yours is the wise voice we require, to be sure. Like dogs at a bone we worry and snarl, discussing good and evil, expediency and mercy. We deeve His Grace with conflicting views. My lord Duke of Lennox holds that mercy will now best become King and Kirk. Others say . . . otherwise.'

'To halt now, with Popery still rife in the North, would be weakness,' the younger Melville asserted, with certainty.

'Yet the Duke holds rather, does he not, that mercy is a sign of strength?'

'I do not play with words!' Andrew Melville announced shortly. 'What is debated?'

'Simply, sir, with Strathbogie fallen, whether His Grace should go on after lesser and lesser things, as though unsure of victory? Or proclaim victory to all by calling a halt here. By offering mercy to all who return to the King's peace and the Kirk's faith. Not to flatter Huntly by chasing him further into the trackless mountains; but to show him to all as no longer a danger, his teeth drawn. To turn back at the height of victory rather than to go on and possibly, probably, fail to catch Huntly. This I conceive to be the Duke's advice.'

As his nephew began to speak, Andrew Melville held up his hand peremptorily. 'The Duke, sir – but what of your own? The Master of Gray is not usually lacking with advice. What say *you*?'

'Aye, Patrick,' James nodded. 'What's your counsel, man?'

'This exchange was between the Duke and Master James Melville, Sire. I only interpolated, perhaps foolishly. But if you would have my humble advice, it would be somewhat other. A mere matter of degree. I would say neither go on nor go back. Turn aside, rather, to the good town of Aberdeen. It has long had to bear Huntly's arrogance; let it now know the King's presence and clemency. The Kirk there has suffered much. Hold a great service of thanksgiving, I say, in the High Kirk there, for victory over Huntly and the Catholic threat – the provost, bailies and all leading men to attend.' Patrick, though ostensibly speaking to the King was looking at Andrew Melville. 'Some days of rejoicing, feasting, and then Your Grace returns south in triumph.'

Melville was considering the speaker keenly, calculatingly. Here was strong pressure. Of all Scotland's major towns Aberdeen was weakest for the Presbyterians. Not only was the old religion still well entrenched here, but even amongst the Reformèd, episcopacy was strong, reinforced by the University with its pronounced episcopal tradition. The Bishop of Aberdeen was no lay lordling, no mere secular figure enjoying former church revenues, as were so many; he was the most powerful prelate remaining in Scotland – and the Kirk had not forgotten his anointing-oil at the christening of the infant prince. Any opportunity to advance the Kirk's prestige and power in Aberdeen was not to be dismissed out of hand.

'A service of thanksgiving, sir, would be apt and suitable,' he said slowly. 'Provided that it was performed in meet and worthy fashion.'

'Who more able to ensure that than the esteemed Moderator of the General Assembly of the Kirk? And, h'm, the Rector of the University of St. Andrews!'

Since Andrew Melville held both of these offices, the matter was unlikely to be challenged in present company. The masterstroke, of course, was the anticipation of St. Andrews University being in a position to lord it over its upstart rival in Aberdeen itself. This could do no less than clinch the issue as far as the Kirk was concerned.

'It would appear, Sire, that such a course is worthy of consideration,' Melville advised, with dignity.

'Aye. But . . . to leave Huntly. At large. Undefeated . . .'

'In all that matters, Sire, he is defeated now,' Patrick as-

157

sured. 'We know that he has retired into the mountains. Your Grace cannot follow him there. We cannot bring him to battle now, even if we would. October is almost past. You cannot campaign in the mountains in winter. Indeed the campaigning season is all but over.'

'That at least is so,' the Lord Home agreed.

'So Aberdeen will serve you well in all ways, Sire. Deny it to Huntly. When you return to the south, leave it well garrisoned. Huntly will miss its protection this winter. There will be near-famine, I think, in this land, for the corn is everywhere un-gathered and wasted, and the beasts scattered. If Aberdeen is held for the King, where can he shelter and feed his men? And if its port is denied him, and other smaller havens along the coast, he can receive no help from Spain or the Pope. Is that not so, my Lord Marischal?'

Grudgingly the Earl agreed.

'Aye, well,' James sighed. 'Maybe you're right.'

'It is important that Your Grace returns south shortly, before the hard weather. When the passes may be closed by snow and flood,' the Master went on. 'It will, of course, be necessary to appoint some wise and sober royal representative, Sire, who may govern here in your name. My lord of Argyll is still Lieutenant of the North in room of Huntly – but he is returned to his Argyll, er, licking his wounds. Some other will be necessary.'

'Eh? Umm. Aye.' James looked vague. 'Argyll could be fetched back.'

'He requires time to recover himself, I think. He is young. Glenlivet hit him sore.'

'My Lord Marischal then, maybe . . . ?'

'An excellent choice, Your Grace – save in that the Keiths are the inveterate enemies of the Forbeses. My Lord Forbes, I fear, would not supply men for my Lord Marischal. Which men Your Grace sore needs. I suggest that the wisest choice would be my lord Duke.'

'Eh? Vicky . . . ?'

'I have no wish for such a position,' Ludovick announced shortly.

'Have you no' . . . ?'

'No, Sire. I wish to return south as soon as I may.'

'Aye. Aye, Vicky Stewart – I dare say that you do!' James's eyes narrowed. 'That I could well believe.'

'If the Duke has pressing interests in the south, Sire, on which he is set, I of course withdraw the suggestion,' Patrick said. 'Now who else might serve . . . ?'

'You may withdraw or suggest as you will, Master o' Gray – but *I* decide!' the King declared strongly. 'Mind that. There's times you are presumptuous – aye, presumptuous, Patrick! The Duke o' Lennox will bide here if I say so. As I do. He'll take rule in the North, here, when I go. Wi' the Earl Marischal to aid him. And my Lord Forbes too. That will be best. We shall hold a right Council to confirm these matters, sometime . . .' His voice trailed away. Then he turned to the castle. 'Aye, when we've dinged doun Geordie Gordon's house! This Stra'bogie still stands! There's work to do here. We're no' just finished yet! Master Melville had the rights o' it – Master Andrew! To work, my lords and gentles. We've had enough o' talk. Aye – and this oak kist, here. Lay it aside. A' Gordon's gear's confiscate to the Crown. *I'll* decide what's to be burned and what's no'!'

All bowed low, and none lower than the Master of Gray.

It was some time before Ludovick had opportunity for a word with Patrick Gray alone, amongst the fury of destruction which followed.

'Mary says that you have a devil,' he charged him. 'I say that you *are* one! What you did, back there, was devilish!'

'I think you . . . exaggerate,' the other replied, easily.

'Could I?' Ludovick considered him heavily. 'To use others, so cynically, so shamelessly, you can have no respect, no regard, for them, for anyone. Are men and women nothing to you but pawns to be moved on a board?'

'Tush! The state, this realm, consists of men and women, Vicky. There is no steering it save by moving them.'

'But not as you do it. Not by esteeming men as less than animals.'

'Here is wild talk. Who have I ever used so?'

'Myself. The King. Even Melville – although I would scarce

159

have thought it possible. Any and all you manipulate. Strip naked of all dignity, to win your own way . . .'

'*My* way! Shrive me – has it not been your way that I have been winning, this day?'

The Duke shook his head. 'Never that. Always your own. You but used my desire to have done with this burning and destruction, to smooth your own way. You had decided this of Aberdeen long before – that was clear. You twisted Andrew Melville round your finger for the same ends. James you made a mock of, as ever. And then you persuaded him to appoint me Lieutenant here in the North!'

'And who better? That your own policy of mercy be carried out . . . ?'

'Do not seek to cozen me with such talk, Patrick. I am no longer a child. You want me to be kept here. You want to take Mary away from me – that is your aim. So you would keep us separate. So you entangled me with the Queen! Think you I did not know you were behind that? So I am to be as good as exiled here . . .'

'On my soul, Vicky – this is too much! Even from you. You do not know what you say! I warn you – do not try me too hard! Others have done so, and regretted it.'

'Think you I care for your threats? I tell you this, Patrick. You will not part Mary and me. You will not, I say! We love each other. We are as one, belonging one to the other. It is not something which you will understand. But it is true. None shall part us. You hear?'

The other was moments in answering. 'Do you think that only you understand what love means, boy?' The Master's voice, normally so assured and controlled, actually quivered as he said that, 'Great God in His heaven – if you but knew . . . !'

Without another word, Patrick Gray swung abruptly about and left an astounded Ludovick Stewart standing there amongst the smoking ruins of Strathbogie.

Chapter Ten

Mary Gray came to Castle Campbell soaked, her hair plastered about her face, her riding-cloak heavy sodden with rain. But it was warm rain, and for this she must be thankful. At least the winter's snow and frost and sleet seemed to be over at last, and the passes to the North would be clear, or at least clearing. Although floods also could cut off that mountain land.

She urged her reluctant mount up the steep climbing track between the wooded ravines of the twin burns of Care and Sorrow towards the tall, frowning castle. It was not any lengthy and punishing journey from Stirling – a mere dozen miles – but the beast was a poor broken creature, though the best that she could hire secretly, out of her slender resources. She was less conspicuous so mounted, anyway, than on a horse from the royal stables, and she believed that she had escaped notice, at least as anything but a countrywoman returning home from Stirling market.

She was challenged, of course, at the outer bailey gatehouse, and here she had to play a different role.

'I am the Mistress Mary Gray, daughter of the Master of Gray,' she called to the porter. 'Seeking my lord of Argyll.'

That gained her admittance with little delay – for it would have been a bold man who would have risked offending unnecessarily the Master of Gray that spring of 1596, in Lowland Scotland. The drawbridge was already down, and Mary rode across it, having to withstand nothing more daunting than the speculative stares of men-at-arms and murmured asides as to her chances with their peculiar lord.

The inner bailey was not even guarded and she rode straight under the archway into the main courtyard. The rain had driven everyone indoors, and the place seemed to the girl as cheerless and unwelcoming as its name and reputation. When the first Earl had bought it, exactly a century before, on appointment as Chancellor of Scotland and requiring a house nearer

Stirling than his traditional seat of Inveraray on far-away Loch Fyne, it had been called Castle-Gloume, or just The Gloom. Set on a spur of the Ochils above the township of Dollar, sometimes spelt Doleur, and set between these burns of Sorrow and Care, even its wide prospect of the Carse of Stirling and the Forth estuary, and the change of the name to Castle Campbell, did not altogether counteract the sombre feel of the place.

The girl was ushered into Argyll's presence, not in any of the main chambers of the great beetling central keep, but in a small room in a flanking tower of the courtyard, where he was writing letters before a blazing log fire. Archibald Campbell, seventh Earl, was a strange, studious, unsmiling young man to be chief of so pugnacious and influential a clan, dark, slight and wary – and his experiences at the Battle of Glenlivet almost six months before had by no means heightened his spirits. Mary Gray he knew slightly, as must all about the Court.

His surprise at seeing Mary there was not lightened by any access of gallantry. Far from a lady's man, he tended to avoid women. Clearly he would have preferred to be undisturbed at his writing.

'I am sorry if I trouble you, my lord,' the girl said. 'I would not do so, you may be sure, were the matter not urgent.'

Belatedly he laid down his pen, nodding. 'How may I serve you, Mistress Gray?' he said briefly.

'By hearing me out, my lord,' she told him frankly. 'A hard thing perhaps to ask of any man, with a simple woman!'

He blinked at that, eyeing her more warily than ever. Mary Gray was ever a problem and challenge to men, even to those not attracted to her physically; her modest quietness of dress and manner were so much at odds with the innate assurance and calm authority of her whole bearing, so unlooked-for in a young woman of her age and in her peculiar position. 'I would not name any of the Master of Gray's kin simple!' he returned. But he waved her to a settle near the fire. 'You are wet. Your cloak...'

'It is nothing. I am no fine Court lady to shrink at a little rain,' she assured him. But she laid her cloak across the end of the settle, to steam in front of the blaze, and deftly touched up and tidied her soaked and wind-blown hair. Without sitting down, she turned to him. 'My Lord – I learned only yesterday that you had come back from the West, from Argyll. At last. I came as quickly as I could.'

He frowned. 'Why, Mistress?'

'Because I have been waiting for you. For long. Months. To come from Inveraray. I know that the passes have been closed ... but the waiting has been weary work.'

'You waited for *me*?' Argyll was not the man to make the obvious jests over her avowal.

'Yes. Since you are the King's Lieutenant of the North.'

He waited, searching her lovely face. 'What of it?' he said, at length.

'My Lord – the Duke of Lennox has been held at Aberdeen all these long months. Acting for you. He would be home. And I would have him home.'

Argyll stared at her. 'You are ... you are ... !' He coughed.

'I am the Duke's concubine, yes. His mistress,' she agreed calmly. 'No more than that. I can make no claims upon him. But still he wishes to return. And dearly I would have him back.'

The very simplicity of that set the young man's dark head shaking. 'But ... this is the King's business!' he protested. 'A matter of the state. Not for, for ...'

'For such as myself to meddle in? It may be so. Perhaps I am remiss. But I know the Duke's mind in the matter.' She sighed. 'I have indeed spoken to the King.'

'You have!'

'Yes. And the Duke has written letters. But he will not heed.'

Argyll picked up the pen again, and nibbled at its feathering. 'In that case, why come to me? The Master of Gray? Your ... your sire. He now all but rules in Scotland. He is the man to petition, to be sure.'

'My father, I fear, considers the Duke well placed in Aberdeen!'

'M'mm. Indeed! Well, dear God – what can *I* do?' the other demanded. Despite his sober and serious manner, he seemed very young – at nineteen, a year younger than herself, and in all but years infinitely her junior.

'You can do much, my lord – if you will. You can go there. To Aberdeen. To take up your rule there.'

Argyll threw down his pen and got to his feet, to pace about the little room. 'That is not possible,' he said. 'What you ask is not possible, Mistress Mary. I could not go there now – even if I wished it. I was made Lieutenant of the North a year ago, in name only. Well I knew it. In order that my Campbell broadswords could be used against Huntly. It was an appointment of the Master's – your father. The King would never have thought of it. A scratch of the King's pen made me Lieutenant – at Gray's behest. Another scratch made the Duke Lieutenant in my place.'

'If you will pardon me – no, my lord. Not so. The Duke's position is only as *acting* Lieutenant. *You* are still Lieutenant of the North. He writes to me that his commission appoints him until you, my lord, resume your duties. Why my father planned it so, I do not know. But no doubt he had his reasons.'

The young man shook his head. 'I cannot go. But even if I could and would, it is clear that the Master – and therefore the King – would not have it so. I would be stopped forthwith.'

'Not if you went quietly, swiftly, secretly. As you have right to do. You are Lieutenant, the Duke but your deputy. You could be in Aberdeen in two days – and the Duke back here before the King and Council knew aught of it.'

'God be good – and to my cost! Do you know what you ask? You would have me to offend the King and your father! For what? For the sake of your fond lust for Ludovick Stewart! Does he esteem me fool enough so to pander to him ... !'

Calmly, quietly, the girl spoke. 'Ludovick did not send me, my lord. He knows nothing of my coming to you. Nor would he approve, I think. Before you say more ill of him, I pray you, hear me out – as first I asked. None would esteem you fool, my lord – least of all myself. There is more need for you to go north to Aberdeen than merely to allow the Duke to return to his son and mistress!'

He paused in his pacing at that, to peer at her. 'I cannot go, I tell you – be it for one reason or another. I have other and pressing work to do. But ... what is it you speak of? This need that I go to Aberdeen?'

It was the girl's turn to pause, and move a little. She turned to face the fire. 'My tidings will hurt and displease you, my lord,' she said slowly. 'I am loth to tell you. But you ought to know them, I judge. And you cannot know them – or you would scarce be here at Castle Campbell this night!' She looked at him over her shoulder. 'You were betrayed at Glenlivet, my lord.'

'What . . . ? What do you say? Betrayed?'

'Yes. Shamefully betrayed. That you should lose the battle.'

'Christ God! What is this? What do you mean, woman? How betrayed? And by whom?'

'By those you trusted. By your own people – some of them. Aided by . . . others. You were not intended to win that battle, my lord.'

Appalled he gazed at her. 'It is not true . . .' he got out, thickly.

'I fear that it is,' she assured him sadly. 'I would not lie to you.'

'Who, then?' he demanded.

'I do not know all the names. But . . . too many of them were Campbell!'

'No!' he cried. 'Never! That I will not believe.'

She went on steadily, if unhappily. 'All the names I do not know. But some I do. Campbell of Ottar. Campbell of Lochnell . . .'

'That is false, at least! Lochnell was my own kinsman. My Standard-bearer. And he died by my side.'

'By a chance shot, my lord. He nevertheless was one of the ringleaders in selling the battle to Huntly. He was near enough kin, was he not, to see himself as Earl in your place? His death, perhaps, was just – since he caused many others to die. Then there was Campbell of Glenorchy . . .'

'Another cousin. He commanded the van. Here is folly!'

'Aye – folly! Campbell of Ardkinglas, too. Others were Campbell of Inverliver and MacAulay of Ardincaple. Likewise John, Lord Maxwell, who is linked to you in some way. All conspired that the battle should be lost. That Huntly should attack early. That my Lord Forbes should be misinformed, and fail the rendezvous. That one of your arrays – I know not which –

should take the wrong glen and so miss the onset . . .'

'That was Glenorchy, yes. Leastwise . . .'

'All was arranged, my lord. Huntly was not to be beaten. Only checked. Your own life was to be forfeit – but something miscarried. Probably the chance death of Lochnell at your side . . .'

'Lord have mercy! But why? Why, woman? Why should men act so? My own people?'

She shook her head. 'Can you not better answer that? Why do men do these things? Lie and cheat and betray? For gain, or for power, is it not? Most, no doubt, desired to see your great Campbell lands and wealth differently divided! Under a new lord. But others, behind them, would be playing a deeper game. The game they call statecraft – which is of all sports the most evil! The balance of power! In that sacred name, all wickedness may be allowed, all vileness accepted!'

'How could Huntly achieve this?'

'It was not Huntly's achievement, my lord – though Huntly benefited. It is all a balancing, see you. Huntly must not be brought too low, and the Catholic cause fail utterly, lest Campbell and the Kirk grow too strong! The scales must ever balance!'

Argyll was considering her wonderingly now. 'How do you, who are a mere girl, know all this?' he demanded. 'Did Lennox tell you?'

'The Duke does not know, I think. Besides, I have not seen him for six months and more. Few indeed know this. For if the Kirk had learned of it, all would have been lost.'

'Aye – the Kirk! The Kirk would have given much to know this, I warrant! But *you* know it! If you did not learn it from the Duke, it could only have been . . . !' He left the rest unsaid.

'My lord,' she said steadily, levelly, 'how I learned this matter is my affair only. You I have told, that you might be warned. Since your life is still in danger, I think. But I ask that you keep my secret. For not only I might suffer, in consequence.'

He nodded, sighing. 'I understand.'

'So you must go north. For some of these men are still in Aberdeen, with your Campbell host, are they not? Glenorchy and Ardkinglas? Moreover, your uncle, Sir John Campbell of

Cawdor, is threatened, I understand. He is in command there, is he not?'

'Yes. But why should my Uncle Cawdor be threatened?'

'Because he is your Tutor, your lawful guardian, is he not, until you come of full age? And if you were to die, my lord, it is thought that he would have next claim to the earldom.'

'Fiend seize me!' Almost as alarming to Argyll as these revelations themselves was their quiet, factual enumeration by this young and innocent-seeming girl. He stepped close to her. 'Tell me,' he said tensely, 'is it Maitland who is behind all this? The Chancellor? As they say he was over the death of my cousin Moray, my former guardian.'

She shook her head. 'I think not. He would be useful, to take the blame of it, if need be. But he is a sick and dying man. Maitland's is not the hand, I think.'

'Then . . . ?' He eyed her from under down-drawn brows, and all but groaned. 'Mistress Mary,' he whispered, 'you frighten me!'

'That I can understand,' she agreed. 'I also am frightened. Will you go, then? To the North?'

'I cannot!' he cried, turning away again, and clutching the loose furred robe which he wore. 'Not now. It is impossible. I return to Inveraray tomorrow.'

'But . . . you only came from there two days ago!'

'Yes. But I must go back. I have received word of trouble, sure word. Only today. I must return to my own country at once. In the morning. That is why I write these letters.'

Mary sought to swallow the flood of her disappointment. 'Is it so urgent? This trouble. More so than the other?'

'Aye, it is. The Clan Donald is on the move. From the Isles. There was some word of it before I left, but I did not esteem it serious. Now I hear that it is. There is something much amiss. A great fleet of MacDonald galleys is moving south from Skye, growing as it comes. I am Sheriff of Argyll, as well as Earl. Also Justiciar of the Isles. I must go. Indeed, I am recalling my host from Aberdeen. I may need my broadswords nearer home!'

'Why should that be? The MacDonalds – it is not you they move against? Who do they threaten?'

'When the war-galleys sail from the Isles, there is no saying where they will attack! I do not think that they intend war with me. But my lands of Islay and Jura and Kintyre are on their road, and they may be tempted to raid them in the by-going.'

'On their road to where, my lord?'

'To Ireland. To Antrim. This is the word I received this morning. Donald Gorm of Sleat and the other chiefs of the Clan Donald Confederacy have decided to take part with the Irish in their revolt against Elizabeth of England's power. You will know that the Earl of Tyrone and O'Donnell have risen in Ulster, and are seeking to throw off the English yoke. Now this host from the Isles is sailing to their aid, it seems.'

'But why? The Islesmen have never loved the Irish. They are all Catholics, but...'

'They have been bought. With gold. From Spain and the Pope. That rogue Logan of Restalrig is with them. He brought it. The gold. So Maclean of Duart writes me...'

'Restalrig! Robert Logan!' Involuntarily Mary Gray's hand rose to her mouth. 'This is ... this is ...' She bit off her words thereafter.

'Aye – that forsworn scoundrel! A Papist and as big a rascal as any in this realm – although he is banished the realm, and outlawed! If he is in it, the matter is serious. It's an ill day when that one crosses the Highland Line!'

The girl stared into the fire. 'This could not be linked with Huntly?'

'No. I think not. Huntly is still in the glens of Mar. A hundred miles and more from our Western Sea. Moreover, the Islesmen hate him. As Lieutenant of the North he has borne hardly on them for long years. Clan Donald would not readily play Huntly's game, I swear!'

'All this, then – the Isles and the remote Highlands of the North-West – comes under the rule of the Lieutenant of the North?'

'Why, yes. In so far as it can be reached and ruled, at all! The North is all the North, not only the North-East. All the Highlands and Islands should be his concern.'

'I had not understood that.' She looked thoughtful. 'So meantime Vicky – the Duke – could be held in some measure responsible for this of Clan Donald?'

'Eh? Responsible? No, no – that would be beyond reason. No man can control the Isles from Aberdeen. But it is in his bailiwick.'

Mary hardly seemed to be listening. 'This MacDonald host. This fleet of ships. It is now at sea? Making for Ireland?'

'No – that is not the way the Islesmen work. Or there would be little danger to the Campbell lands. They move down the islands, gaining strength as they go, drawing in others, extorting tribute, lifting cattle and victuals, taking women. It is a sport, with them. Then, when they are ready and their enemy has grown careless, they sail across the narrowest seas to fall upon them. It may take them months. They will aim to win more than Spanish gold, if I know them!'

'I see. You go to halt them, then, my lord?'

'Halt them? Not I! As well seek to halt a torrent in spate! I go to protect my lands and people. From the plague that may strike them. Meantime, I write my news to the King. To my Uncle Cawdor. And . . . ' He paused. '. . . to my Lord Maxwell! Whom you say betrayed me!'

'Yes.' It would have been dark in that room now with its small window, without the flickering firelight, as the wet March evening closed down around Castle Campbell. 'My lord,' she said, 'it is time that I was gone. It will be full dark soon, long before I can reach Stirling. I am sorry that you cannot go to Aberdeen. But at least you are warned. Of what was done against you, and what may still be planned.'

'Yes. I thank you for that. I would aid you if I could.'

'I understand.'

'You came alone? I will provide an escort, at least, for your return.'

'It is not necessary. Indeed I would rather not . . .'

'A woman, riding alone? At night? And the country unsettled thus?'

'Very well. But they must leave me before Stirling. I came secretly and I would return secretly.'

'Why?'

'Would you not agree that the fewer who know that Mary

169

Gray rode to visit the Earl of Argyll in his castle, the better?'

'M'mmm. Aye, perhaps you are right, Mistress.' He held up her cloak for her. 'The Master, then, does not know that you are here?'

'The Master is at Forfar, where he is Sheriff. Holding justice ayres.'

'Ah. Your cloak, I think, is near dry...'

The Master of Gray did not lodge within Stirling Castle, which might have had its inconveniences on occasion, tightly guarded as it was. He rented instead a modest house in the Broadgait of the town, where it climbed the hill to the castle. It was here that Mary Gray presented herself later that same wet night, asking of the astonished servant to see the Lady Marie.

She was shown into a warm and comfortable room, mellowly lit, where before a cheerful fire a woman rocked a wooden cradle with the pointed toe of her shoe while she knitted something in white wool. It was a homely and domestic scene indeed for the house of the notorious Master of Gray.

The woman, who had been crooning gently to the cradled baby, looked round smiling as Mary was announced - and then rose quickly, grey eyes widening, at sight of the girl's bedraggled and mud-spattered appearance.

'My dear, my dear!' she cried, starting forward. 'What is this?' What's amiss?'

'Nothing, Marie – save a little mud and rain! Leastwise...' Mary kissed the other. 'It is shame to be troubling you. So late.'

'You coming is never trouble. Not to me. You know that, Mary, my sweet. But this is an ill night to be abroad. Come to the fire...'

Firmly but without fuss, the younger woman was taken care of and cherished, her wet clothing removed, things of her hostess's given her to wear instead, a hot posset sent for, and food provided – all before Mary was allowed to declare the object of her untimely visit.

The Lady Marie Stewart, Mistress of Gray, was like that. Only recently returned to her husband's side from Ford Castle in Northumberland with her new baby, she was a person as practical and forthright as she was fair. Now in her early thirties, well built and fine-featured, with her broad brow, grey level eyes and sheer flaxen hair, she was a very beautiful woman – an extraordinary daughter for Robert Earl of Orkney, though less extraordinary niece for the late and lovely Mary, Queen of Scots. Eldest legitimate child of the Earl, she seemed to be not only quite untainted by all the peculiarities of her Stewart ancestry, but by her upbringing in the raffish Orkney establishment. For that matter, she was almost equally unlikely a wife for Patrick Gray.

'Now,' she said, when she had Mary settled and cosseted to satisfaction. 'I'll have your explanation, young woman!'

'I have been to Castle Campbell, Marie,' the girl told her. 'And to no avail. My lord of Argyll will not go to Aberdeen.'

'You went, Mary? That was rash. But who am I to talk, who would have done the same myself! But . . . Argyll then, was not to be moved? Even by what you told him? Of the treachery?'

'I told him, yes. He was much distressed. At first would not believe me. But there is no winning him to Aberdeen. He returns to his own Argyll tomorrow, Marie – there is more trouble. More wickedness. More than we knew. Much more.'

The Lady Marie searched the younger woman's lovely face, and said nothing.

'Have you heard Patrick say aught about the Isles? The Hebrides? And Clan Donald – the great Clan Donald Confederacy?'

'No, I think not. It is a far cry to the Hebrides, Mary.'

'Yes. But I fear . . . I greatly fear it may not be too far for Patrick! Marie – Argyll has word that thousands of MacDonald clansmen are making for Ulster, to aid the Irish rising against Queen Elizabeth. Paid by Spanish gold. And the gold was brought to them by Logan of Restalrig!'

'Robert Logan!'

'Yes. Had it been almost any other . . . ! Marie – you told me that he was here, some time ago? Secretly.'

'It was a month ago, perhaps. Yes, soon after I returned here. He came one night. He was closeted with Patrick most of the night. And gone by morning. You think . . . ?'

'How much of Patrick's ill work has Logan done for him?

He is the tool most apt to Patrick's hand. Did you learn anything of what he was here for, that night?'

The other gave a small laugh – but with little of mirth in it. 'Aye – you may be sure I asked Patrick! And for once he told me, with seeming frankness, secret as it was. He was in excellent spirits was Patrick that morning! It was gold that Logan had brought! Much gold!'

Mary Gray let out her breath in a long quivering sigh.

'Wait, my dear,' Marie told her, in a tight voice. 'It was not Spanish gold that Logan fetched – at least, so Patrick said. It was from Elizabeth! English gold pieces!'

'Elizabeth! English gold! For Patrick? Not the King's pension, at last?'

'Not the King's pension, no. James knows nothing of this.'

'Then what . . . ?'

The two young women stared at each other across the cradle wherein the Master of Gray's infant daughter gurgled contentedly, to the hiss and splutter of the burning birch-logs.

'Oh, no – not that!' Marie said, at length. 'Even for Patrick! Not so bare-faced as that!'

'You think not? No other would think of it – but Patrick might well. Playing his eternal game of balancing the scales of power. He saves Catholic Huntly from the Protestant host which he himself assembled. He could use Protestant Elizabeth's money to hire legions to aid the Catholic cause. It would all be of a piece.'

'But why aid the Irish? Will that not only inflame Elizabeth's ire against the Scots? Which cannot be Patrick's desire. All he works for, he says, is the English succession.'

'That I do not know. But it may be that it is not for Ireland that the MacDonalds make, at all. That could be but a feint. Suppose they were really to aid Huntly? Coming south, merely to turn to march east. To move in behind the King's forces, and cut off the North – all the North. Ludovick would be trapped!'

'How would that advantage Patrick, my dear? He does not want the Catholic threat to be wholly lost, I think, for fear that the Kirk grows too strong, and silly weak James goes down before it. But it is the Protestant cause which he upholds in the end, surely? He must, because of the English succession.

Only a Protestant prince will ascend the English throne after Elizabeth.'

'With Patrick, who can tell his true aims? At heart, I am sure that he is more Catholic than Protestant.'

'At heart, Patrick is only . . . Patrick" his wife said, heavily.

'That is true. But it serves us little here . . .' The girl leaned forward. 'Marie – together we have halted some of Patrick's wickednesses before. We must do so again, if we can. For his own sake, as well as others'. Will you do me a notable great favour? Only you could do it – and only you could I ask. Will you take the Prince for me? And my Johnnie too? So that I may go to Vicky?'

The Lady Marie swallowed, seemed about to speak, and then changed her mind.

Mary went on. 'I know how much I ask. It will be a great burden to you, with your own baby, and little Andrew, to look to . . .'

'That would be the least of it, my dear! The King . . . !'

'The King will be angry, yes. But he admires you, is a little afraid of you, I think. And you are his cousin. And the Master of Gray's wife. He will at least agree that I left his child in good hands! You can face him, Marie, as none other could.'

'And face Patrick, too!'

'All Patrick needs to know is that I have grown weary of my separation from Vicky, and have decided to end it. Patrick contrived that separation, and knows that I would have gone long ere this had the King allowed it. Time and again I have asked His Grace, pleaded with him. But he will not hear of it. I must stay with Prince Henry. Patrick it was who had me appointed to this position, for his own purposes, against my wishes. He need not be surprised that I rebel, at last.'

'His surprise, I think, will be that his wife aided you in your rebellion!' the other said, a little ruefully.

Mary bit her lip. 'I am sorry,' she said. 'Selfish. But . . . so much hangs on it.'

Marie sighed. 'So be it. But have you thought of the difficulties, my dear? How it is to be contrived? With the Prince close-guarded in the castle.'

'You will do it, then? Oh, Marie – you are good, good!'

'I will do it, yes – for you. There is not much that I would not do for sweet Mary Gray.'

'I am not sweet.' That was levelly said. 'I am a hard and sinful woman – and near as great a schemer and plotter as my sire.'

'My dear – that you say so makes you sweeter still!'

Mary shook her head. 'No. It is true. But . . . as to tonight, I have thought of how it may be done.'

'Tonight? Mercy, girl – *tonight*, you say?'

'Yes – it must be tonight. Every hour is precious, now. And only at night could it be done as I plan it.'

'But, Mary – a night of wind and rain, like this! And late . . .'

'So much the better for my purpose. Wind and rain are kindly things compared with what we fight against, Marie.'

The other considered the young, eager but strangely assured and authoritative creature before her for a few moments. 'You are your father's daughter, of a truth!' she said. 'Go on.'

'I plan it thus. You come back with me to the castle. With a servant. This child under your cloak. We tell the guards that you accompany me because of the hour, and the rain. Your cloak should be kenspeckle, if it is possible – different from mine. That the guards may recognise it later. Letting all know that you are the wife of the Master of Gray. So we gain my lodgings in the Mar Tower, where sleep the Prince and my Johnnie. There should be no trouble – the guards know me well. Then I leave you with the bairns, wearing your cloak. I am smaller than you – but only a little. The rain will well excuse me being close-hooded. The guards will look to see you return, and with your cloak and your servant, in the dark and rain none will question me, I wager. I return here – and then take my journey north.'

Marie drew a long breath, and then nodded. 'Yes. It will serve, I have little doubt. I must needs take up my quarters in the castle, then? Leave this house. Until you return.'

'No, Marie dear – not until I return. I do not intend to return! Not to being governess to the Prince. The King must find another governess. Why not the Countess of Mar? She lives there, in the same tower. She sees the child each day. Her husband is his governor. Henry is weaned now. There should be no difficulty in a change. If Lady Mar will not, there must be many others the King could call on.'

'So, as well as offending the King, and my husband, I must needs now find a new governess for the Prince, before I can return to my own house, and the said husband's side!'

Mary bit her lip, and did not answer.

Marie leaned over to touch the girl's arm. 'Never fear,' she said. 'I will brave them all! But I am still suckling my baby. That may cause difficulties. If I could but bring the two bairns here...'

'I think the King would never permit that the Prince should leave the castle. He so greatly dreads an attempt to seize the child.'

'We shall see. But you – what of yourself, Mary? This talk of journeying to the North. Who is to take you?'

'I need no one to take me. I can well look to myself, Marie – have often done so. If I may borrow one of Patrick's horses, to take me to Castle Huntly? There, Davy Gray will set me on my way to Aberdeen. If I start by daybreak, I shall be at Perth by midday and Castle Huntly before evening. Then another day to Aberdeen.'

'Alone?'

'Why, yes. I have gone far alone, many times. Have no fear for *me*. I was reared a land-steward's daughter, you'll mind – not a dainty lady!'

'I do not think Davy Gray will let you ride alone to Aberdeen,' the other said. 'Davy Gray! It is two long years and more since I saw him. You will tell him of my, my devotion, Mary?'

The girl nodded. 'That I will. He will rejoice to hear of it, I know well . . .' She smiled. 'You are very fond of Davy Gray, Marie, are you not?'

'Yes,' her hostess said simply.

'I know that he is . . . like-minded. Sometimes I think . . .' She paused.

'Do you, Mary?'

Again she smiled. 'Yes. Sometimes I think that I may think too much! But, Marie – the time! It is late. There is much to do...'

'Very well, my dear. I am at your service. First, let me find a cloak...'

Mary Gray's plan worked without a hitch. The guards, well knowing the Prince's governess, admitted her and her two companions to the castle without question. With most of the Court having to lodge outside the fortress walls, they were used to much coming and going. The baby hidden under the Lady Marie's handsome white riding-cloak fortunately did not cry or whimper and attracted no attention. The only remarks passed were disgusted comments on the wretchedness of the night. In Mary's quarters at the top of the Mar Tower, the tire-woman who aided with the little Prince was dismissed to bed. Within half an hour Mary was returning as they had come, wrapped in the white cloak, with the old servitor, after a sore-hearted parting from a calmly sleeping Johnnie Stewart of Methven – their first real parting. The guards at the gatehouse made no remarks, and Mary came without incident back to the house in Broadgait.

Well before daybreak, well mounted and equipped for the road, she was on her way north. The rain had stopped.

Chapter Eleven

David Gray, land-steward to the fifth Lord Gray, rode quietly, almost stolidly, at Mary's side, saying little but listening to the girl's talk and nodding occasionally. He was a stocky, plain-featured man now in his late thirties, rather taller than he seemed because of his width of shoulder. Hair showing no grey above his somewhat heavy brows, strong-jawed, muscular, simply-dressed, he looked very much of a man of the people – and a strange man for the lovely, delicately-built and patrician-seeming young woman to be calling father, in aspect as in age.

Always Mary Gray had called him father, an address she had never used to her true sire. David Gray, eldest child, though bastard, of Lord Gray, and only six months older than his legitimate half-brother Patrick, had at sixteen married Mary's mother bearing Patrick's child when the latter would and could not. He had brought up Mary as his own – and indeed, in his undemonstrative way, loved her even more deeply than the three later children of his own begetting. Mary Gray admired him above all men.

'They are no closer, then?' the girl was saying. 'No less at odds? I had hoped, prayed, as time passed, that they would come together. Slowly, perhaps, at first. But as Granlord grew older . . .'

'No,' the other said. 'It is not so. If anything the breach is wider, deeper. I have sought to do what I could. But it is of no avail. My lord will hear no good of Patrick. And Patrick will make no move towards his father. There is a hardness as of steel that nothing will break.'

'It is so wrong, so stupid! They are like foolish, wilful bairns. Patrick is much to blame, of course – but I believe that Granlord is more at fault. Patrick once would have come to terms with his father.'

'Aye. But the terms were to be his wn! My lord will never

177

forgive him for his betrayal of the Queen. Of Mary Stewart. Never!'

'Nor will you, I think, Father?'

He shook his head. 'Who am I to forgive or not to forgive? To judge at all? I failed the Queen also. If I failed her less than Patrick, it was because I had less opportunity.'

'No! No – you must not speak so!' she told him. 'It is not true. You might fail in your task – as might all men. But you would never fail anyone who trusted you. Especially Mary the Queen. Not Davy Gray!'

He was silent.

'So now,' she went on, 'Patrick and his father hide from each other in separate castles a dozen miles apart, frightened that they may cross each other's paths! Have ever you heard such folly!'

That was indeed the position between the Lord Gray and his heir. While Patrick was holding his justice ayres in this his sheriffdom of Forfar, he stayed in his strong castle of Broughty on its jutting rock in the Tay estuary, while his father abandoned his house of Castle Huntly a few miles away to retire to Foulis Castle amongst the Sidlaw Hills. That the son had been granted the sheriffdom in place of his father, some years before, by no means assisted amity.

Mary herself, of course, was also avoiding the Master of Gray this breezy spring morning, keeping well clear both of Broughty Castle and of Forfar town in her ride north. She could scarcely hope that her sire would be as understanding as was her foster-father over this expedition of hers.

David Gray, though scarcely approving of the girl's project, had done what he could to aid her in it. He and her mother, Mariota, had welcomed her warmly to her old home at Castle Huntly the previous evening, and knowing their Mary had made no major attempts to dissuade her from her chosen course. The Lady Marie had been right, of course; David Gray would not hear of his daughter riding to Aberdeen alone, and now accompanied her himself on the seventy-mile journey.

They went by Auchinleck and Guthrie and Brechin, through a bare treeless land of rolling pastures, heath and isolated grassy hills, and they were thankful that the weather had improved, for it would have made grim travelling with no cover from wind and rain. By midday they were back to the coast at Montrose, and thereafter were never far from the white-capped sea. In the late afternoon they passed near the Earl Marischal's great castle of Dunnottar on its thrusting promontory, before riding down into Stonehaven. After that it was barely two hours more to the Dee, through a cowed and ravaged country, with Aberdeen town rising beyond. Saddle-sore and weary, and depressed by the evidences of men's passions and savagery which they had ridden through, the travellers were thankful indeed to reach the end of their journey.

And now Mary had reason to be grateful for David Gray's presence – for Aberdeen in 1595 was something of which she had had no experience, an occupied city in a conquered country-side. The place was full of soldiers and men-at-arms with not enough to do, men but little amenable to centralised authority and discipline, being in the main the retainers of individual and often jealous lords and the clansmen of fierce Highland chiefs. A woman riding alone through the crowded evening streets of Aberdeen would have been fair game indeed; even with David's masterful dourness they made a difficult and sometimes alarming progress. Only by dint of much shouting of the name of the Duke of Lennox did they gain passage.

The Duke's headquarters were in the Bishop's palace in the Old Town, and this being to the north of the city, reaching it presented the greater problem. When eventually they arrived, it was to discover that Lennox was away investigating some disturbance in the Skene district, but was expected to return before nightfall. Fortunately Master David Lindsay, the King's Chaplain, one of the group of ministers appointed to the Council of Lieutenancy, well knew Mary in Stirling – he it was who had conducted the Prince's baptism service, and was now much enjoying occupying the hated Bishop of Aberdeen's palace; while strongly disapproving of ducal concubines, he recognised that Lennox would expect the lady to be well treated.

When Ludovick duly arrived, therefore, himself somewhat tired and travel-worn, it was to find his visitors washed, fed and refreshed. At sight of Mary sitting in smiling anticipation at the table in his private room, he was quite overwhelmed. Never one for ducal dignity or any sort of public or private pose, he shouted aloud his joy, and ran across the chamber to pick her up bodily out of her chair and hug her to him in an embrace which would have done no injustice to any bear, gasping incoherent questions and exclamations in the process of covering her face and hair with kisses. It was some time before he even realised that David Gray was also in the room.

That sobered him only a little, although from boyhood he had always been slightly in awe of this strangely humble man with the almost legendary reputation for competence and effectiveness, the only man of whom Patrick Gray was said to be afraid. Still clutching Mary to him, he more or less carried her over to where David stood, to take the other man's hand and wring it warmly.

David Gray was no more enamoured of Mary's peculiar relationship with the Duke than was Patrick or other members of the family – than indeed was Ludovick himself; but he recognised that they loved each other deeply, in fact looked upon each other as man and wife in the sight of God. He knew that any such unsuitable marriage for one so close to the throne would be immediately annulled by King and Council, undoubtedly. Faced with this fact, therefore, and out of his great love for Mary, he had accepted the situation with the best face possible, and sought to disguise his heartache for the girl.

After the first brief and disconnected explanations, and while Ludovick ate the meal which the servants brought him, Mary told him of the treachery to Argyll, and how she had sought to use her knowledge of it to persuade the Earl to come and take up his still official appointment as Lieutenant of the North. Long before she was finished this part of her story, Ludovick had his chair pushed back, his food forgotten, and was striding about the room in indignation and near-despair.

'I need not ask you,' he interrupted the girl, at length, 'whose hand was behind this infamy! There is no lack of dastards and betrayers in this Scotland of ours, sweet Christ knows! But only one, I swear, who would think of such a thing as this! Of such extreme perfidy. It is his doing, I say, as though all signed and sealed with his own hand!' He swung on David Gray. 'You, sir

– have you any doubts as to who was responsible? For this evil betrayal of Argyll?'

'None,' the other answered gravely. 'Although no doubt my brother would justify it to you in most convincing fashion!'

'Aye – for the King's and the realm's weal! Necessary, for the good steering of the ship of state! That, to Patrick, is justification for all. Hundreds may die, men behave worse than brute beasts, good faith be spat upon ... !'

'I do not excuse any of it, Vicky, God knows,' Mary interrupted, 'but Patrick *does* care about bloodshed. Of that I am sure. I think that he truly believes that much of what he does is to spare worse things. Worse bloodshed. It may be folly, but it is his belief.'

'Aye, I have heard him at that, Mary! He is the chirurgeon! A little judicious blood-letting, here and there, to save a life! But it is ever Patrick who wields the knife, who chooses the victim!'

'Yes – but Vicky, had he not arranged the betrayal of Argyll, had he allowed the battle to go on, would there have been less bloodshed or more? Might there not have been a great deal more? In a full battle between two armies, as was planned, might not thousands have died? Instead of a few hundreds. Not only Gordons. As many and more Campbells might well have been slain in a true battle as in that rout which he contrived.' She shook her head, as the men stared at her. 'Oh, I may be wrong, wicked, to think such things. I may be too like Patrick, my own self! But – if we would contain and counter him, halt him in any way, we should at least seek to understand how he thinks, *why* he acts as he does! Is that not so?'

Ludovick did not answer, but David Gray nodded slowly.

'There is something in that,' he conceded. 'Your understanding of Patrick's mind, lass, might well be the strongest weapon that can be brought against him.'

'Not against him, Father! I do not fight against Patrick,' the girl asserted strongly. 'Patrick himself I love, despite all. I have no choice. It is his schemes and plots and acts that I hate.'

'Is a man to be judged apart from his actions, then?' the Duke demanded.

'I think so, yes. We can see and judge of his actions. But the man himself, what is in him, what he fights against, what moves him – do any of us know? And if we do not know, how can we fairly judge?'

'Save us, Mary – you are as bad as the ministers! As Melville and his kin!' Ludovick complained. 'If a man does evil, again and again – that is enough for me.'

'Do we not all do evil, again and again, Vicky? In some degree. In the judgment of different people. I know that I do. I am doing it now, in being here at all ...'

'Enough, Mary – enough! This is hair-splitting! When *you* accuse yourself of evil-doing, enough nonsense has been talked! I am a practical man. Actions to me speak louder than words. What are we to *do*? That is important.'

'No more hair-splitting then, Vicky. For it is action that has brought me this long road. The dire need for action. The betrayal of Argyll is bad, but it is past – whatever may yet come of it. There is more than that to concern us. A matter more urgent. There is trouble in the North-West. In the Isles. I believe Patrick to be behind this also. And so long as you act Lieutenant, it is your responsibility also, is it not?'

Puzzled, he eyed her. 'What do you mean? Trouble in the Isles ... ?'

'Sit down and eat, while I tell you,' she said.

Once again, long before Mary was finished her account of the bribing of Clan Donald – or he was finished his repast – Ludovick was up and pacing the floor. He could not sit, or for that matter stand still, over what he heard. Continually interrupting exclaiming, demanding, he made so much poorer a listener than had David Gray the day before.

'You think, then,' he charged, at length, 'that Patrick does this to aid the Catholic cause? To hold his damnable balance? To spite Elizabeth? Or what? Where's the reason for it? The Argyll treachery is simple, compared with this.'

'Who knows? Patrick's reasons are seldom simple or straightforward. There may be a number not all evident.'

'If this is indeed Patrick's work?' David put in. 'That is not yet certain.'

'If Logan is in it, I'll wager it is!' the Duke said. 'Logan carrying gold! Who else would he be working for?'

'If it was Spanish gold, as the rumour has it, he might be working for the Catholic party itself, rather than Patrick. For Huntly. Or more possibly Bothwell, since he comes from the Borders.' The other turned to Mary. 'You say that the Lady Marie knew naught of this? Had heard nothing?'

'No. Save only that Logan had been to Patrick's house in Stirling secretly, a month ago. Bringing *English* gold. Or so Patrick said.'

'It looks damning,' Ludovick said. 'And whether it is Patrick or other, the position is full of danger. It must be dealt with. When the Clan Donald Confederacy is on the move, and the war galleys sail, it behoves all men to take heed. Especially the Lieutenant of the North!'

'So thought I,' Mary agreed. 'Whether they move to aid the Irish, assail the Campbell country, or turn east, leaving their galleys, to cut you off here in Aberdeen, they signify peril. Peril for you, Vicky – if not for all Scotland.'

He nodded. 'I must find out what is intended. What is behind it all.' He looked from one to the other. 'How is it to to be done? Who can I turn to? The Western Highlands and Isles are a world to themselves, speaking a different language. Who can tell me what goes on there?'

'Who sent the word of this to Argyll?' David asked. 'Did he tell you that, Mary?'

'Yes. It was Maclean, he said. Maclean of Duart.'

'Maclean? Sir Lachlan? Why, he led one of Argyll's arrays at Glenlivet! The man who came best out of that sorry business.' Ludovick paused. 'Unless . . . ? Save us – this couldn't be linked to the other? More treachery? I do not know the man. He was gone back to his own country before I came here. Is he another false knave, another Judas?'

'I did not know that he was at Glenlivet . . .' the girl faltered. 'You think . . . you think that this could be some further device? Against Argyll? Part of the same conspiracy?'

'I do not know. How can we tell? It may be all lies. A plot to entangle Argyll. On my soul, I am so confused by plots and trickery and deceits . . .'

'Wait you,' David Gray interposed. 'Lachlan Mor is a fighter, not a schemer, I think. You say that he came well out of Glenlivet? It is what I would expect...'

'You know him, then?'

'I have met him, yes. In the old days. He is a man to be reckoned with. No cat's-paw. He is chief of his name, and a giant of a man. Some would name him rogue, no doubt – but it would be roguery in no petty fashion. Patrick told me once that he received a pension of four hundred crowns each year from Queen Elizabeth to keep the narrow Hebridean seas open to her ships, and to recruit Highland mercenaries for her armies in Ireland.'

'Plague on it – and you call him no schemer! Is he not but another traitor...?'

'I think he would not consider himself that, my lord Duke. These island chiefs scarce look on themselves as vassals of the King of Scots. They esteem themselves to be petty princes, all but independent. You'll mind it is less than a hundred years since James the Fourth put down the Lordship of the Isles – in name, at least. Before that, these chiefs held their charters and paid their tribute to the MacDonald lords, as sovereign, not to the King. They allied themselves to whom they would. Some still think so. Sir Lachlan will go his own way. But he fought bravely against the King's enemies at Glenlivet, did he not? With Argyll.'

'It may only have seemed that way. Foul fall them all – I do not know what to think!'

'This at least you may be sure of,' the older man told him. 'Lachlan Mor hates the MacDonalds. They took from the Macleans the island of Coll and part of the Rhinns of Islay. They have been at bloody feud for years. Indeed, he and Angus MacDonald of Sleat were both forfeited by the King for refusing to obey his orders to make peace. Still are, I should think. So, since this news concerns the MacDonalds, I think it will be true, and no mere lying device. He will make it his business to know what the MacDonalds are doing, you may be sure. What they intend. That he may counter them. Not for the King's sake. Nor the Protestants'. Nor Argyll's. But for his own. If you would know what goes on in the Isles, my lord – send to ask of Sir Lachlan Maclean.'

'Aye. You are right. But – better than that,' the Duke said, grimly. 'I shall go myself.'

Mary nodded. 'That is what I would say also, Vicky. Go yourself.'

'Is that wise?' David asked. 'Can you do it, my lord? Can you leave here for so long? It is a far road to the Isles. You rule here, in the King's name . . .'

'I rule there also, in the King's name, do I not? Supposedly, at least. Rule, action, may be required. And swiftly. If I must wait here whilst couriers make the journey to and fro, I may be too late. This authority which I have, and do not want, might there serve some good purpose, I think. Here the Marischal and Forbes and the ministers, the Council of the Lieutenancy, have power and authority in plenty. They do not need me. Indeed they would liefer have me gone, I know well – for I restrain them grievously! They consider me weak, afraid to act, over merciful. I have had months of them . . .' He clenched his fists. 'All winter, month after month, I have been held like a trussed fowl in Aberdeen. I have had enough. Here is opportunity to win free. If James does not like it, he may appoint a new Lieutenant!'

'Well said, Vicky! And I shall come with you.'

They looked at her askance.

'My dear, this is no work for a woman,' Ludovick said 'Journeying over the roughest bounds of the realm. Amongst the wild clans . . .'

'Are the clans and the Islesmen like to be more wild than the rude men-at-arms of proud lords? Has journeying ever troubled me?' she demanded. 'Besides, this is best for me. I came to be with you, Vicky. I hazarded much to be so. I cannot go back to Stirling meantime. Nor to Methven. The King would soon hear of it. He will be very angry. He may even send for me, here. Better that I should be gone where he cannot reach me, until his wrath is cooled. It may be that he will have cause to be grateful to us hereafter, Vicky, when he may forgive.'

The Duke could never out-reason Mary, even when he desired to do so. He part shrugged, part nodded. 'You may be right. And Heaven knows, I would be loth to lose you now!' He turned to David Gray. 'And you, sir? Do you come with us?'

The other shook his head. 'I am a man *under* authority, not having it, my lord. I cannot come and go as I please. I must return to Castle Huntly tomorrow.'

'Must you, Father?'

'You know that I must, lass. I cannot spend days, weeks, stravaiging amongst the Highland West. With my lord at Foulis, Castle Huntly and half the Carse of Gowrie is in my charge alone. Besides,' he smiled, faintly, 'you came all this long way to be with my lord Duke – not with me!'

In the morning, then, leaving the Earl Marischal in command at Aberdeen, they rode across the Brig o' Dee and took the road south, as they had come, now a party of a dozen – for though the Duke would have preferred to have ridden alone with Mary, it was inconceivable that the King's Lieutenant of the North should range unescorted about the land; he took a group of tough Campbell gillies, under young Campbell of Ardoran, conceiving these to be of more use in the Gaelic-speaking West than any larger troop of conventional men-at-arms. Like them, he and Mary were mounted now on shaggy, short-legged Highland garrons, essential for the country they would have to cover.

At Brechin, nearly forty miles to the south, they parted from David Gray in mid-afternoon, to turn west, by Tannadyce and Cortachy, making now for the great mountain barrier that frowned down upon these Braes of Angus. Their more direct route, of course, would have been up Dee, through Mar, and over into Speyside and so down Laggan into Lochaber and the Western seaboard – but Huntly, after a fashion, held all the upper Dee and the hill country of Mar. Hence this more southerly route.

They could have spent the first night at Cortachy Castle, whose laird, Ogilvy of Clova was a loyal supporter of the King, and kinsman to the Lord Ogilvy; but Ludovick had no wish for his identity and whereabouts to be known and reported, and was determined to avoid all castles and lairds' houses, even though this was bound to add to the discomforts of the journey. Mary would have been the last to complain. So they passed well to the south of the castle, and pressed on into the sunset, climbing steeply now into the skirts of the high hills, to pass the night in the great Wood of Aucharroch at the mouth of Glen Prosen. The Campbells, experts at living off the land, produced a couple of fine salmon out of the river to add to the provender they had brought with them. Eating this by the light of the flaring, hissing pine-log fires amongst the shadowy tree-trunks, sitting at Ludovick's side, Mary felt happier than she had done for many a long month. They slept, wrapped in plaids, in great contentment.

In the morning they started really to climb, and went on climbing all day, with only occasional and minor descents into the transverse glens of Isla, Shee and Ardle, through the vast, empty, trackless heather-clad mountains which formed the towering backbone of Scotland. Even though the sun did not shine and the going was hard, it was a halcyon day wherein fears and anxieties could be dismissed, if not forgotten, banished in the limitless freedom of the quiet hills. The larks trilled praise without end, the grouse whirred off on down-bent wings, and high above them eagles wheeled their tireless circles in the sky. The air was keen, but heady with the scent of heather and bog-myrtle and raw red earth. The world could once again be seen as a clean, simple and uncomplicated place. Although the travellers covered less than half the mileage of the previous day, by nightfall they were in Atholl, lodging in the hut of a cowherd high on the roof of the land between Garry and Tummel. Save for this silent but smiling man, they had not spoken to a soul in thirty miles.

Two more days they took to cross the breadth of the land, climbing, descending and climbing endlessly, skirting great lochs, fording foaming torrents, ploutering through bogs and peat-hags. Young Ardoran was invaluable as guide, leading them heedfully to avoid the settled haunts of men. This was not only to avoid recognition of the Duke, but was a normal precaution for Campbells travelling clan country where they could be by no means certain of their reception. The next night they bedded down on a sandy island in the middle of the rushing, peat-brown River Orchy. On the afternoon following, the second day of April, they smelt salt water and the tang of seaweed on the westerly breeze, and presently came down to the great sea-loch of Etive, to gaze out over the magnificent prospect of the isle-strewn Sea of the Hebrides.

Mary sat her garron enthralled. Never had she dreamed of anything so lovely, seen so much colour, known such throat-catching sublimity of beauty. The sea was not just all of a single shade of blue or grey, as she had known it hitherto, but as though painted with a hundred delicate variations of azure and green and purple and amber, reflecting the underlying deeps or shallows, the banks of gaily-hued seaweeds, multi-coloured rock and pure white cockle-shell sand. Into or out of this thrust mountains and headlands to all infinity, dreaming in the sunlight under sailing cloud galleons; and everywhere were islands, great and small, by the hundred, the thousand, proud peaks soaring from the water, cliff-girt and sombre, smiling green isles scalloped with dazzling beaches, tiny atolls, abrupt stacks, scattered skerries like shoals of leviathans, weed-hung reefs and rocks ringed with the white lace of breaking seas. No one had prepared the girl for all this wonder. She drank it all in, lips parted, speechless with delight. Even Ludovick, less susceptible, was affected. The Campbells merely hailed it as signifying journey's end.

Ardoran led them down to the very shore of the wide Firth of Lorne where, on a jutting promontory a tall castle stood – Dunstaffnage. They were in Campbell country now, with need for anonymity over, and Campbell of Dunstaffnage was close kin to Argyll himself; indeed the place ranked as one of the Earl's own strengths, and its keeper was hereditary captain thereof rather than true laird.

They were well received, and slept in beds for the first time since leaving Aberdeen – even though the master of the house seemed less impressed by the presence of the King's ducal Lieutenant than by his comely young woman companion.

He was full of anxieties and rumours about the Clan Donald activities. They were swarming south like locusts, he declared, eating up the islands as they came. Donald Gorm of Sleat, Angus of Dunyveg and Ruari Macleod of Harris, were said to be leading the sea-borne host; but now Clanranald had joined the enterprise, with MacDonald of Knoydart, MacIan of Ard-namurchan, and other mainland branches of the clan, and was ravishing and plundering his way down the coastline by land. Much of Lochaber and the Cameron country was already overrun, as were the Maclean lands of Ardgour. Only the Appin Stewarts lay between them and Campbell territory. MacCailean Mor, Argyll himself, was back at Inveraray, calling in men fast. It was to be hoped that he would make haste to send some of them, many, north here to Dunstaffnage, for it lay full in the route of the MacDonalds, the first major Campbell stronghold which they would reach.

In the circumstances, the Captain was disappointed that his visitors were set on moving on across the Firth of Lorne and the Sound of Mull – for even such small reinforcement would be welcome if the MacDonalds came. He tried to put them off by warning them of the dangers of the narrow seas, of freebooting MacDonald galleys, of strange winds and currents. When he saw that they were determined, however, he provided them with a boat – not his one galley, which he could by no means spare at this juncture, but a seaworthy, high-prowed fishing-craft for eight oars, which Ardoran's gillies were competent to handle.

That night Mary Gray saw her first Hebridian sunset, and laughingly but determinedly denied Ludovick's urgent arms until its last fiery glories died in smoking purple.

In the sparkling morning they put to sea from the little haven under the castle walls. Their course was due west, and with a southerly breeze they were able to hoist the square sail to aid the oarsmen. They bowled along in fine style, at first, the boat dipping spiritedly to the long Atlantic swell. The rowers chanted a strange endless melody as they pulled, age-old and haunting in its repetitive rhythm. Soon Mary found herself joining in, humming and swaying to the lilt of it. This bright morning, it seemed scarcely to be believed that their journey was being made against a threat of war, bloodshed and treachery.

The Maclean territory was the large island of Mull, third in size of the Hebrides, and Sir Lachlan's seat of Duart Castle perched on a rock at the end of a green peninsula thrusting into the sea at the north-east tip of it, dominating all the narrows of the strategic Sound of Mull, the Firth of Lorne and the Linne Loch, so that no vessel might sail the inner passage of the islands should Maclean seek to challenge it. Queen Elizabeth never paid her pensions for nothing.

Duart Point lay some nine sea miles from Dunstaffnage, no

lengthy sail. But there had been something in their late host's warnings as regards tides and currents at least, for amongst all these islands and peninsulas, representing really the tops of sunken mountain ranges, the tide-races, over-falls and undertows were quite phenomenal. The rowers presently found that once they were clear of sheltered waters, the incoming tide, sweeping down the Sound of Mull and circling the tip of the Isle of Lismore, was largely countering their efforts and the effect of the sail. They had to pull even harder to make any substantial headway, and Mary and Ludovick soon were doing most of the chanting, the oarsmen's contributions being reduced largely to gasps. The mountains of Mull seemed to keep their distance.

Never did nine miles seem to take so long to cover. Not that Mary, at least, could arouse any impatience, so well content was she to feel herself part of that fair painted seascape. She could not really conceive the continuous scanning of the horizon by Ludovick and Ardoran, for the menace of Clan Donald galleys, to be more than play-acting. After leaving a few inshore fishing-boats behind, no single other vessel was to be seen in all that sun-filled prospect – although admittedly, as Ardoran pointed out, a hundred might lie hidden behind the myriad islands.

At last the towering rock of Duart, with its castle perched high above the waves, became distinguishable from its background of the blue mountains of Mull. But barely had they descried it than out from behind the tip of Lismore, the long low green island which had formed a barrier to the north of them for hours, swept another vessel at last. A groan went up from the straining Campbells as they saw it.

'Is that . . . a galley?' Ludovick demanded, a little breathlessly. He had never seen such a craft.

Ardoran nodded, grimly. 'A galley it is, God's curse on it! Och, they have been just lying in wait for us.'

Certainly the ship appeared to be making directly for them. It was a long, low, dark, slender vessel, with soaring prow and stern, rowed by double banks of lengthy oars and having a single raking mast set amidships supporting a huge square bellying sail. It was the centuries-old pattern of the Viking-ships, scarcely altered, which had terrorised these same northern waters then and ever since, lean greyhounds of the sea, the fastest craft that sailed. At either side the blue water boiled, leaving clouds of drifting spray, where the double lines of oar-blades lashed it in urgent oscillation.

'How many oars?' the Duke asked.

'Each side a score. To each oar, two men. On this. Larger galleys there are than this.'

'What do we do now?' Mary wondered.

'What *can* we do? That craft can move five miles to our one,' Ludovick said. 'We can only wait, and parley.'

'Parley!' Ardoran snorted. 'Much parleying will the Mac-Donalds be offering us! Strike first, and parley with the corpse – that is the style of them, whatever!'

'They may not be MacDonalds . . .'

'That is a war-galley. Whose else would it be if not Clan Donald? Or their friends.'

The long-ship came up on their quarter at a great speed, with a notable bow-wave snarling in disdain at either side of her lofty prow. A device was painted in bold colours on her huge sail, but because the wind was southerly and the galley bore down on them from the north-west, the sail was aslant and the device undecipherable. Ranked warriors lined her sides, steel glinting in the sunlight. If there were eighty oarsmen, there must have been at least as many fighting-men.

The galley swung round the smaller boat in a wide arc, fierce faces inspecting them.

Ludovick stood up. 'We must put some face on this . . .' he muttered. Raising his voice, with as much authority as he could muster, he shouted. 'Who are you? And what is your business? Answer me!'

There was a general throaty laugh from the larger vessel.

A young man spoke from the prow, in good English. 'We but come to meet and greet you, my lord Duke. You are welcome to the Isles.'

Ludovick all but gasped his surprise. 'A pox! How . . . how knew you? What is this? Who are you?'

'My name is Maclean, lord – and little takes place in all the Isles that Maclean does not know. Especially so important a matter as the coming of the King's Lieutenant, the Duke of Lennox – God preserve him!'

'Maclean?' Ludovick frowned. 'You mean – from Duart?'

'None other. Where my father waits to receive you.'

'You are Sir Lachlan's son?'

'Lachlan Barrach, yes.'

'But, how . . . ?' The Duke stopped. There was no sense in shouting his questions at such range, to the hurt of both throat and dignity. The young man, although his words were polite enough, had a fleering note to his voice. He was dressed in a long tunic of untanned calf-hide, brown and white, which almost covered his kilt, and he carried his broadsword on a wide shoulder-belt studded with silver-work and jewels which glittered in the sun. A single tall eagle's feather adorned his bonnet. He made a tall, swack figure, and knew it.

'Come aboard, my lord,' he invited, all but commanded. 'A poor craft that is to be carrying a duke. And his lady. We'll take you to my father.'

Something of mockery in his tone made Ludovick refuse, although the other's suggestion was sensible. 'We are very well in this,' he gave back. 'But you may take us in tow.'

They were near enough to observe the quick frown on young Maclean's darkly handsome features. Ludovick chuckled. He thought that would touch the fellow. For a proud galley captain to have to return to port towing a small and humble fishing-boat would be a tough mouthful to swallow.

The other hesitated, pacing the tiny foredeck as his men with their oars skilfully held the great vessel almost stationary against the tide-race.

'Well, sir?' Ludovick shouted. 'Are you unable to tow the King's Lieutenant?'

With what looked like muttered cursing, the other turned to give curt orders. The galley spun round almost on its own axis, to present its pointed stern to them, and a long rope came snaking over to the smaller craft. Grinning, Ardoran tied it fast.

Mary, dark eyes dancing, touched Ludovick's arm. 'That was well done, my lord Duke!' she murmured. 'Another word that may be whispered round these Isles!'

'Aye. But how did they know? About me? How *could* they know?'

'That I cannot tell you. But . . . no harm is done. As well that your coming should create a stir, surely?'

If Lachlan Beg Maclean felt in some measure humiliated, he sought to make up for it in his own way. Despite the contrary tide, he most obviously called for the very maximum of the galley's speed, urging his rowers to their most vehement efforts. The vessel positively leapt over the sea – and the small boat behind seemed to alternate between almost leaving the water altogether and plunging its nose deep into the waves of the other's creaming wake, in crazy career. Never had any fishing-boat moved at such a pace before. Tossed about like peas in a pan, the Duke's party were quickly soaked by the water they shipped and by the continuous clouds of spray which enveloped them from the galley's oar-splashing. Unable to make their protest heard above the lusty chanting of nearly two hundred throats in front, they were glad to run down their sail and huddle together beneath its canopy.

In such fashion, they came to Duart.

Chapter Twelve

Maclean's castle of Duart which, because of its position and
site might have been expected to have certain affinities with
Logan's Fast Castle, had in fact no similarity. Where the latter
stronghold, clinging precariously to the Berwickshire cliffs, was
a harsh and savage place, a secret, almost furtive, this Hebridean
fortress was proud, assured, open flaunting itself indeed on its
rock in confident challenge. It was much larger also, something
of a citadel, its lofty retaining walls enclosing all the summit
of its rocky knoll, the great square keep within massive and
towering high to lofty battlements, the stonework rude but impressive. An enormous banner streamed in the breeze from its
topmost tower. And inland from the castle, nestling below it on
the low-lying greensward of the peninsula, was an entire town of
cot-houses and huts, over which hung a blue haze of peat-smoke.

Young Maclean had to moderate his pace on nearing his land-
fall, and the newcomers were thankful to be able to emerge from
beneath their sail and relax somewhat. Indignation was fairly
quickly submerged in wonder at what they saw.

Most castles had a portcullis, included in their gatehouses, to
raise and lower a drawbridge over a moat; Duart had its version of this device facing not towards any approach road but to
the open sea, its massive double chains plunging directly down
into the water itself. Ardoran explained that these great chains
were anchored to a projecting reef far out, and though they hung
slack just now, could by a pulley system be drawn taut to stretch
just above the surface of the sea right across the intervening
channel, and so effectively bar to shipping the only passage round
the east of the great island of Mull – for the deep water channel
here ran close in around Duart Point, and beyond the reef referred to was perilous shoal water strewn with rocks and skerries.
The fate of any vessel reaching this upraised barrier and refusing to pay Maclean's toll, could be envisaged very clearly; the
black snouts of cannon thrusting from the crenellations of the
castle parapets were very eloquent.

There were other evidences of Maclean's persuasiveness. What at first had looked like a forest of bare tree-tops rising from behind a spur of the castle-rock, as they rounded the Point proved to be the masts of over a score of galleys anchored in neat rows in a sheltered little bay tucked in to the north-west. On the boat strand behind this possibly a hundred small craft were drawn up.

The visitors were not unimpressed.

It was the sound of piping which drew their attention from these indications of naval strength up to the high castle-keep itself. There a group of kilted musicians paced round and round the battlements, blowing lustily. It was not at these, nevertheless, that Mary pointed mutely. Projecting from the keep's sides, just below parapet-level, were booms, long poles of wood. From these hung things that swung and twirled in the breeze – men. There were three hanging from one pole, four from another, two from a third. Altogether the girl counted sixteen corpses dangling there – and that did not include any who might hang at the unseen sides of the building.

The sight affected more than Mary. The Campbells eyed each other uneasily, and Ludovick fell silent.

His silence was neither here nor there a few moments later, when galley and tow turned into the haven behind the castle. This evidently had been a signal. Cannon fire crashed out from the battlements above, to set the seabirds screaming and the mountains around echoing and re-echoing. How many guns were fired, and how often, was uncertain in all the reverberation, and by King James's standards it was no doubt quite a modest bombilation; nevertheless it was as the greeting of one prince for another. After Davy Gray's observations, Ludovick did not fail to recognise the significance of it.

Ardoran cast off the tow-rope so that they might row to the shore with some dignity – the maintenance of dignity being obviously of prime importance amongst these people. They were watched in silence from the anchoring galley.

Men came hurrying down a path from the castle, led by an enormous young man with a shock of fiery red hair, dressed in full Highland finery of great kilt and plaid. Despite all his magnificence however he strode straight into the sea as the Campbell boat grounded forefoot in the shallows, and came splashing out to its side, careless that the skirts of his kilt floated wide on the water. Reaching the boat he extended great arms over the side to grasp Mary where she stood waiting, and with no more greeting than a wide grin, swept her up as easily as though she had been the merest child. He turned to carry her ashore under one arm, before she or anyone else could make effective protest. Seeing others wading out to the boat, Ludovick, sensing their intention, hastily lowered himself over into the water. It came well above the tops of the thigh-length riding-boots which he wore. So he splashed to land, his own man still.

The red-head, who yet clutched Mary's arm, laughed aloud. 'You should have waited, my lord Duke!' he cried. 'Necessary it was, of course, to bring the lady first. If you had but had patience...'

'I have been having patience for the past hour, sir!' Ludovick told him grimly. 'So you also know who I am? How comes this? I sent no word.'

'That is nothing,' the other said, still laughing. 'We know here at Duart what Dunstaffnage, or any other Campbell, dreams on his bed of a night! How much more when the Duke of Lennox comes seeking boat to the Isles!'

'I see. You keep spies in other men's houses, sir! And presumably fast boats to carry their tales through the night?'

'Spies...?'

'Informants, then!'

'To be sure, informants is a better word, entirely. Information is an excellent thing, is it not, my lord?' The big fellow chuckled – a cheerful soul it seemed. 'Och, we can never be having sufficient of it, to be sure. Holy Writ says something of the sort, does it not? It is information, I think, from some good informant, that brings the King's Lieutenant here to Duart, this day?'

'H'mmm.'

Mary gently disengaged herself from her captor's grasp. 'You also are a Maclean?' she asked, smiling a little.

'Are not we all, lady? But I am Hector. Hector Ruari Younger of Duart. And you... you are very fair, whatever!'

'I thank you,' she said gravely, although Ludovick frowned. 'For your information, I am Mary Gray, mistress to my lord Duke.'

Grinning, the big man looked from one to the other assessingly. 'Come,' he said. 'I'll be taking you to my father.'

He turned and led them up the steep climbing path to the castle, gallantly offering Mary his arm – and when she declined its aid, masterfully taking her own. There was only room for two abreast on that track, so perforce the Duke had to come up behind, water squelching about inside his thigh-boots unpleasantly. By half-way, the martial figure of Lachlan Beg had come up and taken his place at his side, no word spoken.

So they came to the outer bailey, crowded with armed clansmen who watched, silent, a distinctly daunting company. Here two more pipers met them, and turned to escort the little party, marching before them and striking up a lively air. Thus they crossed the slantwise naked rock to an inner bailey, where other men stood waiting. These were more elaborately dressed in finer tartans, and bore themselves proudly – obviously gentlemen and minor chieftains of the clan. They offered no sort of greeting, but fell into place behind the four and the pipers, to pace across the inner courtyard.

In the open arched doorway of the central keep itself, directly below those hanging figures high above, a single man stood, tall deerhounds at his side. It was quite a lofty arch, but even so this man stooped slightly, and not from age or infirmity. He was quite the largest individual that either Ludovick or Mary had ever seen, dwarfing even the burly Hector Ruari, as all others there. He must have been at least seven feet tall, and broadly built in proportion, with huge shoulders and a great barrel of a chest. His features were leonine and ruddy, his blue eyes keen but strangely pale, and his plentiful hair which had been notably blond and was now silvering, fell to his shoulders. He wore a red tartan doublet, a long embroidered waistcoat, and tartan trews cunningly cut on the slant to clothe his tremendous thighs and calves close as a glove right to the ankle. His expression was stern, but he smiled gravely as his eldest son came up with Mary, to step aside and allow Ludovick to approach him first.

The bagpipe music died away in bubbling groans, both above and below, and only the screaming seabirds continued their accompaniment.

'Duke of Lennox – I rejoice to see you,' the chief said, his voice curiously light and musical for so vast a man. 'I bid you welcome to my humble house. A pleasure it is to receive the representative of King James.' He turned to Mary, and bowed a little – thus emphasising that he had not bowed to the Duke. 'And you, lady – all that is mine is at your service.'

Ludovick cleared his throat, and spoke almost as carefully as did the others. 'Sir Lachlan – your fame is known to me, to all. I have come far to see you. *I* rejoice to have reached Duart safely. I have noted your . . . arrangements for my reception!'

'Had you sent word of your coming. Duke of Lennox, I would have received you more fittingly! But perhaps King James's Lieutenant must be discreet in how he visits one whom King James and his Council have seen fit to forfeit!' The English was as perfect as his every word was significant, however gentle the slightly sing-song intonation of the North-West.

The other schooled his features to expressionlessness. 'Your services to His Grace, I am sure, will outweigh any such unfortunate edict, sir,' he answered slowly in turn. 'I came secretly for other but good reason. That others should not know of my visit, and that I might travel the faster. The matter that brought me is urgent.'

The big man nodded. 'The matter of Clan Donald, I have no doubt. I can think of no other that would bring the representative of James Stewart to Duart, Duke of Lennox!'

Ludovick inclined his head. 'That is the reason, yes. And is it so strange that the King's Lieutenant should be here – when, Sir Lachlan, I understand that you receive Queen Elizabeth of England's representative almost yearly!'

There was silence then as they eyed each other, and all others watched and waited. Now at last they knew where they stood. Lennox had served notice that he knew of Maclean's English pension, and indicated clearly the chief's duty and service to his own monarch; the other had evidenced his resentment at the sentence of forfeiture passed upon him over his feuding with the MacDonalds, and hinted at his refusal to acknowledge overlordship of any sovereign by his persistent use of the term King James instead of the King. Notable also was his refusal to accord the customary my lord to Ludovick – or, no doubt, to any man.

The giant seemed in no hurry for further speech. For his part, the Duke bit back the words that sprang to his lips, and instead raised his head to contemplate the corpses hanging there against the blue of the sky.

'Mainly MacDonalds!' the chief observed, briefly. Then he turned to Mary again. 'This lady – how do I receive her, Duke of Lennox?' he asked, in a different tone.

'As my wife, sir.' That was crisp.

'Very well. Her sire is known to me. The Lady Grizel awaits her. I bid you both enter my house.'

Involuntarily, Ludovick heaved a sigh of relief, as possibly did others. The pipers took up their refrain once more, but remained to pace and blow outside as Sir Lachlan led his visitors into the echoing vaulted corridors of Duart Castle.

Mary was delivered into the motherly charge of the Lady Grizel Cunningham, who greeted her in friendly fashion. Maclean was unusual in this also, that he had married a Lowland wife, a daughter of the Earl of Glencairn, from Ayrshire. Undoubtedly she pined for the gossip of her own kind. Ludovick was taken to a chamber on the second floor, where three Highland servants awaited him. One was a plump, sonsy smiling girl, and after the merest flickered glance at his guest Maclean dismissed her casually.

'A meal awaits you below, when you are ready,' he mentioned. 'Anything which you require, these will serve you. They speak your tongue.'

'I thank you, Sir Lachlan. You are . . . thoughtful!'

The magnificent meal over at last, Maclean filled a great drinking-horn with amber liquor, sipped it, and then passed it to the Duke. 'Your good health and good fortune, sir,' he said. 'And now – to our business.'

The Lady Grizel rose, at her cue, glancing at Mary Gray. But though that young woman smiled and nodded, she did not rise in turn.

'If it is permitted, I would remain, to listen,' she said, greatly daring. Her expression was modesty itself, however.

Maclean and his sons stared – although Hector Ruari, who had hardly taken his eyes from the girl's face throughout the repast, looked well content, as did the youngest of the family, Ian Ban, a lanky lad of eighteen. There seemed to be no Maclean daughters.

'The Lady Mary is much interested in affairs. Interested – and wise,' Ludovick said. 'She is, h'm, the Master of Gray's daughter!'

'Ah!' Maclean nodded and shrugged in one. 'I have met the Master.' He made no other comment.

A little uncertainly the Lady Grizel left them.

Ludovick barely touched his whisky although the others, even the young Ian Ban, were drinking deeply. 'Sir Lachlan,' he said, 'the Lady Mary it was whom my Lord of Argyll told of your message. Regarding the Clan Donald. At Stirling. Conceiving it my business, she rode hot-foot north to Aberdeen, to inform me. I set out for Duart the very next morning.'

'Then you have not come from Stirling? From King James and the Council?'

'No. *I* am the Lieutenant of the North. The responsibility is mine. To discover the truth of this matter. To learn what action may be necessary.'

Keenly the other searched his face. 'James Stewart does not even know that you are here?'

'No. Leastways, not of my telling.'

'And the Master of Gray? He knows naught of this, either?'

'The Master has his own sources of information. Who can tell what he knows or does not know? But . . . he has learned nothing of this from me.'

The big man looked at Mary.

She shook her head. 'I have not seen my father for two weeks. He is at his justice ayres. At Forfar.'

'You would pass Forfar, would you not, riding to Aberdeen, lady?'

'I did not turn aside to call on him, sir.'

Maclean stroked his clean-shaven chin thoughtfully. 'That is what you meant, then, Duke of Lennox, when you said that you came secretly?'

'In part, yes. This matter is so uncertain, so delicate, that we decided that none should know of it until we learned the truth.'

'God be good!' Lachlan Barrach burst out. 'There is little uncertain or delicate here, I swear! Donald Gorm and Angus of

Dunyveg are at Rum and Eigg and Coll and Tiree, sword in hand! And Clanranald and his kin ravage Morvern and Ardgour – Maclean lands. They all but surround Mull, in their arrogance! What is delicate there, sir . . . ?'

His father signed him to silence. 'If the Duke of Lennox esteems it delicate, Lachlan, then no doubt he has good reason?'

That was a question, and Ludovick felt that too much questioning was coming from Lachlan Mor. 'Sir,' he said, 'you are well informed. It is clear. Have you learned where this Mac-Donald thrust is aimed? Is it to aid Huntly? Against the King? Or against Argyll, perhaps? Or even yourself . . . ?'

'I believe it to be aimed at Ireland. To aid Tyrone and O'Donnell.'

'That is the word you sent Argyll, yes. But is it so indeed? Why should Clan Donald aid the Irish?'

'For gold. Spanish gold.'

'Aye. But . . . even so? Would the Spaniards be so eager to spend their gold for that?'

'They ever seek to weaken England. A great uprising in Ireland would force Queen Elizabeth to send ever more men to hold down that country. And so weaken England.'

'M'mmm.' Ludovick glanced at Mary. He could scarcely declare that they in fact believed the gold to be English, not Spanish, and so demolish the other's theory.

'Spanish gold might be equally well spent, might it not, aiding Huntly in place of the Irish?' Mary suggested diffidently. 'If Scotland could be turned Catholic again, would that not serve Philip of Spain no less?'

The big man looked at her consideringly from those pale eyes. 'I think not. That would take a deal longer. Besides, Donald Gorm is assembling more and more galleys in the havens of Coll and Tiree. From all over the Isles. What purpose would these serve were he aiming at the mainland, to aid Huntly?'

'He is? You are certain of this?' Ludovick demanded. Coll and Tiree were the outermost isles of the Inner Hebrides, and surely would never be selected as an assembly place for any attack on the mainland.

'Think you that I would not know such a thing!' the chief gave back haughtily. 'That I am not watching them like a hawk?

I have men, galleys, fishing-boats, watching every move that they make.'

'Yes, yes – I understand. But why do they need more and more galleys? Out there?'

'To carry the mainland branches of the Confederacy to Ireland – Clanranald, Glengarry, Knoydart. Keppoch, and the rest. These, being mainly inland clans, have no galleys – or but a few. They gather there for a swift descent on the Irish coast – where no word may reach the English fleet. Small craft can bring out the others to Coll and Tiree. These galleys are for the open sea crossing. And the assault on the Ulster coast.'

'I see. Yes, it could be so. The English ships – where are they? Of that, no doubt sir, you are equally well informed?'

'Naturally. Save for a small squadron, off Dublin, they are massed in the south. Elizabeth fears aid to the Irish from Spain and France – not from Scotland. I have sent word – but it has a long road to travel. It could be weeks before the main English might can reach these waters.'

Mary drew a quick breath, as though to speak, and then changed her mind.

'Then what is to be done?' Ludovick demanded. 'Such an attack on Ireland could be almost as ill a blow at Scotland as at England. It would anger Elizabeth against James. It would enhearten the Catholics everywhere. And if it was successful, France and Spain and the Pope could use Ireland to invade Scotland just as readily as England. More so, i'faith! Possibly to attack England through Scotland.'

'I rejoice that the Lieutenant of the North perceives it so!' Lachlan Mor said grimly. 'Argyll, and those others I have warned, but consider the danger to their own lands, it seems, should the MacDonalds turn eastwards against them. Naught else concerns them.'

'And you? You take the longer view, sir? You see the danger to the realm? And would act, if need be?'

'I shall act, Duke of Lennox. Even though your King James and his Council proclaim me forfeit. Though I act alone!'

'You would so act, I think, not out of love for the realm, Sir Lachlan, but for Queen Elizabeth! And out of hatred for Clan Donald! Is it not so?'

The other looked at Ludovick steadily, unwinking, but did not answer.

'Maclean acts as Maclean sees fit!' Lachlan Barrach declared strongly. 'In the Isles, that is enough.'

'Does it so greatly matter *why* the MacDonalds are halted, so long as halted they are?' Mary Gray asked. 'Maclean's cause, the King's cause, even Queen Elizabeth's cause, could all be at one in this.'

'Well said!' Hector Ruari approved. 'The lady has the rights of it.'

His father nodded. 'So I see it. So I act. My galleys lie ready, beneath these walls. Throughout Mull my people wait. I could strike tomorrow. But . . . what can King James do? Can he lend a single blow to the onset? The cause may be one – but effecting it would seem to be all for Maclean!'

'That is it, by the powers!' his younger son cried.

Ludovick spoke slowly, carefully. 'There is much, I think, that the King may do – through his Lieutenant of the North. I hold fullest powers to act in the King's name. To raise men, to command service, to exact provision, gear, arms, horses. To take over houses, shipping. All in the King's name.'

Lachlan Barrach's snort and his father's level stare demonstrated how much they thought of such powers, and how much attention would be paid to them in the Highlands and Islands.

But the Duke leaned forward over the table urgently. 'Wait before you scoff!' he charged. 'What if, in the King's name, I lift the sentence of forfeiture? If I accredit Sir Lachlan Maclean of Duart to act in the same King's name against the still forfeited Clan Donald, now in open revolt? If I authorise Maclean to demand men, seize boats and take victuals, commanding the aid of all leal subjects of the realm, under pain of treason? Does that not play a different tune?'

He had their attention now. The turning of the forfeiture into a royal commission of fire and sword against the MacDonalds, which was what Lennox's proposal amounted to, was a dramatic and notable inducement. The royal power in this area was negligible – but Maclean acting in the name of such royal power was a different matter altogether.

'Would King James and the Council agree to such?' Lachlan Mor demanded shrewdly.

Ludovick considered his finger-nails. 'Is that important?' he asked, in turn. 'They might not, I admit. From prejudice and lack of knowledge of the true position. They might seek to repudiate what I had done afterwards – were we unsuccessful. They would not, if we were successful, I think. But either way, that need not trouble us now – for it would take much time for them to hear of it, and then to do aught concerning it. Meantime, I am the Lieutenant, and have full and undoubted powers to act as I think best in the King's name and service. The responsibility is mine, Sir Lachlan.'

The older man eyed him steadily. 'There is much in what you say, Duke of Lennox,' he admitted at length. His glance slid over to Mary. 'This, I say, is uncommon like the work of the Master of Gray!'

'Like, may be – in some measure,' Ludovick conceded. 'But it is not, sir, nevertheless. I propose what I believe is best for the King and the realm. Do you agree to it? Your forfeiture cancelled? And you to act to prevent the Clan Donald's descent on Ireland – or anywhere else indeed – in the King's name?'

'Aye. But on one condition. You must act with me. At my side. For I will not act under King James's authority. *With* his authority – that I can use. Maclean will act with King James's Lieutenant – not *for* him!'

'I understand. It shall be as you say. If you will bring me paper and pen, I shall write it so, that there be no mistake. We can agree the words together.'

'Aye, so. Duke of Lennox, I think we may work well together!' The big man smiled faintly. 'And while you use pen, sir – write you to MacCailean Mor, to Argyll, commanding men and galleys. Not to sit close defending Campbell lands, but out here, to assail King James's enemies! And quickly. A score of galleys and two thousand men, shall we say, for a start?'

Ludovick drew a hand over his mouth. 'That is . . . apt!' he said. 'I shall do that. There are others too that we can summon?'

'To be sure. MacDougall of Lorne. MacNeil of Barra. MacQuarrie of Ulva. Stewart of Appin. And lesser men.'

'Very well. Let us to work. There is no time to be lost ...'

'I am proud of you, Vicky,' Mary said. 'You have done splendidly. You have held your own all day, in the face of this proud and wily chief. And you have gained what you set out to gain, and more.'

'What *we* set out to gain, Mary. I could not have done it without you. As well you know. Yours is the mind behind all this. And I think that Maclean knows it likewise! Often when he seems to be speaking to me, it is you that he watches. I have seen it. He is no fool.'

'And you have shown him that you are not, either, Vicky. You have achieved much – more than I had looked for. If only we are in time.'

'Aye. There's the danger. Time. Will the MacDonalds give us time? Time to assemble these forces that I have written for? Time to bring them to bear?'

'Sir Lachlan believes that Donald Gorm and his main force will wait for Clanranald and the others. The inland clans. And these are still on the mainland. To carry them out to Coll and Tiree will take time – thousands of men.'

'Yes.'

They lay on their bed of plaids laid on layer upon layer of the shaggy hides of Highland cattle, and tried not to listen to the creaking of the chains that hung two storeys above, with their grisly burdens, swinging in the night wind. It had been a taxing, busy and eventful day. Sleep eluded them.

Tossing, Ludovick sighed. 'I still cannot see Patrick's purpose,' he said. 'In this of Ireland. Granted that he seeks to hold a balance between Catholic and Protestant. In Scotland. Where is the sense in using Elizabeth's money to send forces to Ireland? To aid Huntly, I could have understood. Even to assail Argyll, and so weaken myself and the King's forces at Aberdeen. But ... Ireland! This is to aid the Catholic cause at large – the Pope, Spain, France. Why should he do that? We know that, Catholic though he may be at heart, his concern is with Scotland. That his abiding aim has always been to see James succeed to Elizabeth's Protestant throne, to rule one united kingdom. How can this serve that aim?'

The girl did not answer for a while. When she did, she spoke very thoughtfully, picking her words. 'I have much considered this. Sought to put myself inside Patrick's mind. Remembering that his mind is never simple, never obvious. I think that I may have found an answer. I may be wrong, but at least there is sense in it. To hold the balance between Catholic and Protestant will be a matter of much delicacy. We know that. Because of the betrayal of Argyll, we are apt to assume now that Patrick must be ever working against the Protestants. But it could be otherwise. It could be again Huntly's turn to be worked against. Wait, Vicky – hear me! Suppose that Huntly himself had been seeking the aid of the MacDonalds? It could be. They have not been friends – but then neither have the Irish and the Mac-Donalds been friends. They are all Catholic, and the Clan Donald Confederacy is the greatest single force left in Scotland, is it not? Suppose that Huntly offered Donald Gorm the Lord-ship of the Isles back again, if he would aid him in gaining the power in Scotland? But for King James the Fourth, Donald Gorm *would* have been Lord of the Isles, would he not – an independent prince in all but name? Might he not swallow that fly?'

'M'mmm. Perhaps. Go on.'

'Suppose, then, that Patrick learned that such was planned. And decided that the combination would make Huntly too strong – as it well might. How could he stop it? While still having MacDonald think that he was acting in the Catholic interest, against the Protestants and King James? Why – by this very thing! By paying him with gold, said to come from Spain. To go to the aid of the Irish Catholics. Against Protestant Elizabeth. If the MacDonalds are fighting in Ireland, they cannot be aiding Huntly.'

'Dear God! But . . . to use Elizabeth's gold for it! If he did . . .'

'That would please Patrick more than anything, I swear! And since this of Ireland is unlikely to lose Elizabeth her throne, he may consider the money well spent on James's behalf! A patriotic duty, no less!'

'Save us, Mary! This is too fantastic!'

'Is it any more fantastic than so many other plots and intrigues that Patrick has devised? Only on a greater scale ...'

'No. It is too much! But the wild imaginings of your mind, my dear ...'

'Perhaps.' She was suddenly quiet-voiced, lying back. 'But remember, Vicky, that I heired part of that mind from Patrick Gray!'

It was long before they slept, that night.

The day that followed was a strangely idle one, considering the urgency of the situation. Having written his letters, and despatched them by Maclean couriers, to Argyll and other chiefs, there was nothing more that Ludovick could do meantime save await the response to his summons. As for Maclean, he was all poised for action anyway, and only awaited tidings, information, from his many and far-flung scouts and spies. So there was little to be done in the great castle on Duart's rock. After all the travelling of the last days, Mary especially would have been glad of the interval, to rest and relax – but the atmosphere was not conducive to relaxation. There was a tension in the air, a waiting as for something to explode, a sense of violence on leash in all around, save only the Lady Grizel, which precluded rest and ease.

Maclaine of Lochbuy, chief of the most important subsidiary of the clan, sailed in in a galley that afternoon, a fiery-seeming and harsh-spoken man of early middle years, who had very little English and made no secret of the fact that he was but little impressed by the Duke of Lennox. He brought word that he had eight galleys, as well as smaller craft, lying manned and ready in Loch Buy, and that MacQuarrie of Ulva was assembling his small clan.

All that day Hector Ruari Maclean was hardly away from Mary's side. While his father and brothers, and Ludovick with them, spent most of the time down amongst the men at the township and about the galleys, he made it clear that he was more interested in the entertainment of their guest than in war-like preparations. Mary, however, who had had much experience of admiring and pressing young men, forceful as they might be, had no difficulty in looking after herself and keeping the jovial Hector approximately in his place.

The news which reached Duart late that evening was unexpected. Clanranald and the mainland MacDonalds had turned back, to north and west, leaving south Lochaber and the threatened Appin area, and streaming back into Morvern and Sunart – to the relief and congratulation of the Stewarts and Campbells. Lachlan Mor was very thoughtful at hearing this, dismissing scornfully any suggestion that it could be on account of any menace to the rampaging MacDonalds posed by the said Stewarts of Appin and the Campbells. He interpreted it as meaning changed plans on the part of Clanranald – which probably meant urgent instructions from Donald Gorm.

The air of tension was by no means lessened when Mary and Ludovick retired for the night.

They were awakened early and rudely. Horns were bugling loudly, alarmingly, above them, presumably from the castle battlements. It was apparently just dawn. Even as they sat up, questioning, young Ian Ban Maclean opened their door excitedly to announce that his father required the Duke of Lennox's presence below forthwith. He added that it was action, at last.

Wisely dismissing any offence at this peremptory summons, hastily Ludovick threw on some clothing. Mary, wrapped in a bedrobe, insisted on accompanying him. Down in the Great Hall, they found Lachlan Mor, his sons, and some of his chieftains, already assembled and in urgent discussion. Maclean made an even more striking, almost awesome, figure than usual, clad now in a long coat of antique chain-mail, which made him seem taller and more massive than ever, a huge two-handed sword slung behind his back with its hilt thrusting up at the back of his silver-blond hair, his head being covered with a great winged helmet. He had the appearance of some ancient semi-legendary hero of centuries before.

There was nothing legendary or theatrical about his manner or voice, however, as he swung on the new arrivals. 'Duke of Lennox,' he jerked, his sibilant voice crisp. 'The time for talk is past! Clanranald goes too far! He has had the insolence to set foot on my territory – on Mull. Yesterday, late, he and part of his host sailed from Loch Aline, in Morvern. In small craft. To join Donald Gorm at Coll. This north-westerly wind that has blown up has much hindered their passage up the sound.

Last night they turned in to land. But not to their own side. Not to Sunart or Ardnamurchan. To mine! They are landed at Tobermory Bay – a thousand of them, and more. On Maclean's land!'

The whereabouts of this temporary landing seemed of less significance to Ludovick than was Clanranald's ultimate destination. 'On their way to join Donald Gorm? At Coll? You are sure of this? That must mean, then, that they are ready. To cross to Ireland. For all these thousands, on small islands like Coll and Tiree, would soon starve.'

'No doubt. But . . . we shall see that they never reach Coll and Tiree, to starve there!'

There was a growl of agreement from the others.

'You do not wait for Argyll and the others, then?'

'I do not! Here is an opportunity not to be lost, whatever! I strike at once. Clanranald's force is split. There are not boats enough to carry them all out to Coll, at once. He can have few galleys – only birlinns and small craft. We sail as soon as my men are embarked. If you would come with us, hasten.'

Ludovick nodded. 'I shall not delay you.'

If the Duke did not get away quite so quickly as he anticipated, it was mainly, strangely enough, because of Mary. She was all arguments and pleas to be taken also. From protests as to unsuitability and inexpediency, he had to progress through prophecies of encumbrance and danger, to firm refusal, before she yielded her claims that she would be perfectly safe, in no man's road, and would keep hidden in the ship. But for once Ludovick overruled her vehemently. She would remain in Duart Castle, he declared. She might think like a man in some things, travel like a man – but when it came to warfare she must remember that she was a woman. When Mary saw that he was determined, she gave in with good grace – but nothing would prevent her from coming down with the men to the boat harbour, to see them off.

They sailed, just as the first lemon-yellow bars of the sunrise sent slantwise rays between the purple-tinged night clouds above the eastern mountains.

Chapter Thirteen

Ludovick Stewart, though essentially a man of peace, with no love for strife and clash, could by no means deny the excitement and elation of that early morning dash up the long Sound of Mull. Twenty-three galleys in all, long, dark and menacing in the strange half-light, unhampered by any smaller and slower vessels, slipped out of Duart Bay and headed due north-west, directly into a stiff and steady wind. No sails were raised, in consequence, and the host of oarsmen strained at their long sweeps with fierce and sustained vigour, to send their leanly sinister craft surging against wind and seas. Fortunately the tide was nearing full ebb, for otherwise, in the narrow two-mile-wide sound, twenty-five miles long, even these greyhounds would have been held as though in leash. As it was, vying with each other – although none ever drew ahead of Lachlan Mor's galley – they raced up the dark mountain-girt channel at a stirring pace, each craft's position picked out by the stark white of its bow-wave, the steady lines of oar-splashes, and the creaming wake. Snatches of the panting, moaning chant which rose rhythmically from each vessel could be heard between the gusts of the wind.

It was cold out on the water thus early, and the breeze searching. Ludovick almost envied the rowers their task and exercise. He stood on the tiny forecastle of Sir Lachlan's craft, with Ian Ban and two or three of the clan's chief men, Hector and Lachlan Barrach captaining their own ships. A film of salt spray and spume stroked his face continuously, for these vessels seemed not so much to ride the seas as to cut through them.

There was twenty miles of narrow seas between Duart and Tobermory, from the south-east to the north-west tip of Mull, and the galleys raced to cover it in ninety minutes or less. It was Maclean's aim to reach Clanranald before the other put to sea again. This breeze would be apt to delay the departure.

'But would you not better wait until they *are* at sea? In their small boats?' Ludovick put to his host, with vivid memories of their own helplessness, in the Campbell fishing-boat, before the swift might of Lachlan Barrach's galley. 'At sea, you would scatter them like a flock of sheep before wolves.'

'Scatter them, aye. But that is not Maclean's intention, my friend! I go to smite and destroy the MacDonalds, not to scatter. Once they are in their hundreds of small craft, there will be no bringing them to battle. Some we would hunt down, to be sure, but most would escape us amongst the islands. Eagles cannot fight finches!'

'How do we do, then?'

'We smite them by land as well as by water,' the big man said grimly. 'I will teach the Sons of Donald to take heed for the Sons of Gillean!'

By the time that the sun was fully risen clear of the Argyll mountains, and dazzling all the sound behind them with its sparkling brittle radiance, Sir Lachlan was scanning the Mull coastline on his left front keenly. Many small headlands thrust out from it but, well ahead, there was one taller and more massive than its neighbours.

'Yonder,' he pointed to Ludovick. 'Rudha Seanach. There we land. Behind it opens the bay of Tobermory. One mile.'

'You attack overland?'

'Aye. My main strength. The galleys will land us. Then go on. Tobermory bay is wide – but its mouth is all but closed by an island. Calve Island. A sheltered anchorage – but I will make it a trap! The main entry, to the north, is but a quarter-mile wide. That to the south is much narrower – a mere gullet. Stop these with my galleys, and Clanranald is bottled up. He must stand and fight.'

'I see. Yes. But . . . would it not serve to scatter and disperse the MacDonalds? To spare his, and your own, men? This battle and bloodshed. I say that would serve our purpose. There is no need for a great slaying.'

The chief considered him coldly. 'Maclean does not engage in play-acting, Duke of Lennox!' he said briefly. 'In especial against Clan Donald.' And he turned away abruptly, to speak to his shipmaster.

As they neared the headland of Rudha Seanach, keeping fairly

211

close in-shore now, a single small boat put out from the shadow-slashed coast there to meet them, making straight for Sir Lachlan's own galley. It brought Maclean of Tobermory himself, a dark, wiry man in stained tartans, who swarmed up a rope into the larger vessel with the agility of a monkey. He it was who had sent Lachlan Mor the news in the first place. Now he came to announce that the MacDonalds' camp was astir but that they were not yet embarking, no doubt giving time for the strong wind to subside – as he prophesied it would. They might, however, be awaiting the next tide. Himself he had offered no resistance to the invaders the previous night. In fact, on word of the host of craft approaching, he had slipped quietly away from his house, leaving servants to say that he was from home. Clanranald, he was sure, was unsuspicious of attack.

Lachlan Mor was well satisfied. He turned his ship directly into the little bay beneath the high headland.

Skilfully steered and rowed, the leading galley gently grounded its forefoot on the shingle of the beach, and Sir Lachlan, despite his years and heavy chain-mail, was first over the side and into chest-high water. Ludovick could not do other than follow, gasping at the cold.

Soon armed men were streaming ashore by the hundred. All save a few of the galleys' fighting-men, as distinct from the oarsmen, were landed, to the number of some seven hundred. Sir Lachlan, with Hector Ruari and Ian Ban, Maclean of Tobermory and other notables, was already striding up the rugged hillside of the ridge which lay between them and Tobermory's bay. Ludovick was thankful for the exercise, at least, to set the blood flowing in his veins.

The galleys were still all lying huddled close in the inlet below, when the climbers neared the top of the ridge. Lachlan Barrach had been left in command of the ships.

Cautiously the Maclean leaders approached the crest, the main mass holding back. Utilising the rocks and bushes, they crept up, to peer over.

The basin of the bay of Tobermory was still half in shadow. It was large, as Maclean had said, fully a mile across, with fairly steep sides heavily wooded, curving round to two headlands. Between these lay a long, low, green island, substantially blocking the entrance. To the south, the passage looked little wider than a river; to the north it might be four hundred yards, but was narrowed by a thrusting sand spit.

The entire area, land and water, presented a scene of activity this early morning. The bay itself was full of craft, mainly small but with two or three galleys and birlinns amongst them. There was much coming and going of rowing-boats out to these. On land there was considerable movement, mainly down to the shore. It looked as though camp was now being struck.

'Good! This is well!' Lachlan Mor declared. 'We shall leave them a little longer. There is no hurry now, at all, at all! Signal your brother to wait, Hector.'

The red-head slipped down below the skyline, to stand up and wave his plaid in the direction of the galleys below, a prearranged notification.

'You wait? For more men? Further aid?' Ludovick inquired.

'No. Not that. Clanranald has more men than I have, yes. I but wait for more of them to embark. So we shall lessen his advantage.'

They lay watching while the sun rose higher, and more and more of the MacDonalds transferred from the shore to the boats. Obviously they were not going to wait for the tide. As had been foretold, and as often happens, with daylight the night wind was dropping. At length Maclean was satisfied.

'Now!' he said. 'Sign him to start, Hector.'

Lachlan Barrach, below, was quick to recognise his brother's second signal. It was only a few moments before oar splashes could be seen, and the galleys began to move seawards.

As soon as he saw the leading vessel rounding the point of Rudha Seanach, with a bare mile to go to the south channel and Calve Island, Lachlan Mor rose to his feet, right on the skyline as he was. Reaching back over his shoulder, he drew the great two-handed sword strapped there in a single magnificent sweep, to hold it aloft.

'Brothers!' he shouted, in the Gaelic. 'Sons of Gillean! There is your prey. Come and kill!' And he flung the sword round in a flashing arc, to point northwards, downhill.

A roar rose from hundreds of throats, as the impatient multitude surged forward.

After that, as far as Ludovick was concerned, all was chaos and confusion, in an onset totally unlike anything he had experienced hitherto. In that yelling, shouting rush downhill, he was quickly overtaken and passed by more enthusiastic and lighter-clad runners, broadswords held high – though even so, mail-clad as he was, Sir Lachlan with his vast strides kept the lead. No doubt the continuous shouting, since it was led by the chief, was more than just barbarous sound and fury, and intended to confuse the enemy as to numbers; it certainly had the effect of confusing the Duke, its rageful uproar preventing him from thinking, from using his brain coherently at all. It was only later that he could piece together the happenings of the next hour or so into any comparatively clear pattern.

Clanranald and the other leaders of the MacDonald host were still on shore when the Macleans appeared on the skyline to the south and came charging down upon them. With most of their men embarked, it was obviously their best policy to embark likewise, rather than to stand their ground. This they were proceeding to do when the topmasts of the galley fleet were perceived above the low sandhills and grass banks at the southern end of Calve Island, most evidently blocking the south channel. A general movement of boats towards the north channel followed, in consequence.

But it was too late. The Maclean galleys were there first, and all escape by sea was precluded. Clanranald's horns bugled the recall.

Getting his scattered host back to the shore again, however, and in fighting trim, was no easy task. It demanded time – and time was a commodity in short supply indeed that morning. Their numbers much masked by the woodland, but sounding a fearsome array, the Macleans bore down on the beach at a furious pace.

Clanranald could only turn now and face the onslaught as best he might, with a bare third of his force, hoping that others would reach him quickly. But this was to reckon without Lachlan Barrach. Only a comparatively few of the Maclean galleys were required to block the entrances to the bay; with the others, braving the hazards of navigation in the confined and shallow waters, he drove in and bore down upon the trapped craft, large and small, his cannon crashing out their dire contribution. The MacDonald boats darted hither and thither in complete disorder.

No real battle eventuated, however many minor skirmishes developed. The MacDonalds were brave and indeed terrible fighters, but in the circumstances they could make no coherent stand, no unified defence. In the face of Lachlan Mor's headlong charge, those around Clanranald were borne back, overwhelmed and driven into the sea.

Ludovick's own part in it all was scarcely glorious. By no means in the front rank of the Macleans, after having tripped over tree-roots, fallen in a burn and floundered through bog, he found himself carried down over the shingle of the beach and into the water itself. There, in a wild melee of struggling men, he was knocked over by combatants, much at a disadvantage over keeping his feet on the slippery wet stones in his heavy riding-boots. He was staggering up when he was attacked by a black-bearded MacDonald wielding a dirk which already dripped blood. Trying to shorten his sword for in-fighting in the crush of men, Ludovick defended himself as best he could, whilst seeking space to use his weapon to fuller effect. Before he could succeed in this, the MacDonald's steel struck sparks on the simple breastplate which Ludovick wore, and slid along it to rip open the left shoulder of his doublet and the skin beneath it. As the man stumbled forward with the impetus of his blow, Ludovick desperately smashed down the hilt of his sword on the fellow's back neck. He collapsed into the water.

Reeling, the Duke was carried along in the press of struggling fighters, dazed now and not very certain who was friend and who was foe in the tartan-clad and largely bare-chested throng. Recognising both his danger and his uselessness, he turned to try to force his way back to dry land – and was promptly knocked down by a furious Maclean in consequence, fortunately with only a random blow from the flat of the sword. On all fours thereafter he dragged himself up on to the shingle of the beach and so crouched, clutching at his shoulder.

He was still huddled thus, unheeded flotsam on that beach of battle, when horns beginning to bray from near and far announced Clanranald's surrender and the end of hostilities. All

fighting did not cease forthwith, especially out amongst the
boats and on Calve Island where many of the MacDonalds had
landed to offer a more effective defence than in swaying small
boats. But all major resistance collapsed, and the day was lost
and won.

If it was not a great battle at least it was a most notable victory,
and Clan Donald's pride, the fiercest in Scotland probably, took
its greatest humbling for centuries. As well as Clanranald's,
Lachlan Mor accepted the surrendered swords of three of his
uncles, of Donald Gorm's brother, of MacDonald of Knoydart,
MacIan of Ardnamurchan, and other celebrities. Undoubtedly
not a few MacDonald clansmen escaped into the interior of
Mull, but some eleven hundred were taken prisoner. Of corpses
there were astonishingly few, considering the noise, cannonade
and fury – although the sea might have hidden some; but there
were large numbers of wounded, most of whom bore their
injuries with astonishing philosophical calm.

Ludovick's own inclusion in this total seemed to raise him
greatly in the estimation of all. Happily, although painful, his
was merely a surface cut and far from serious. Yet even Sir
Lachlan appeared to consider that he had gained much stature
in consequence.

Maclean, indeed, was in fine fettle altogether, giving praise to
his people, courteous to his captives, genial towards all. Not
wishing to burden himself with large numbers of prisoners, he
appropriated the weapons, equipment and anything else which
his people fancied of the bulk of the MacDonald fighting-men,
and then turned them over in batches of one hundred or so to
his various galley captains, with orders to take, land and release
them in isolated parts of the Clan Donald coastline of Ardamur-
chan, Moidart and Morar. All chieftains, lairds and gentleman,
of course, he held for ransom. Keeping the captured galleys and
birlinns for himself, he distributed the small craft amongst his
clansfolk. All this seen to, he re-embarked, with his principal
prisoners, for Duart.

Scudding down the Sound of Mull with sails set and the
wind behind them, they made a swift and triumphant return.
Ludovick took the opportunity to speak with Donald, tenth
Captain of Clanranald, a fine-featured youngish man of proud

carriage, who bore his humiliating defeat with dignity. His line, although it had never been that of the later Lords of the Isles, claimed nevertheless to be the senior stem of the great Clan Donald and of the dynasty of the mighty Somerland. He acknowledged Donald Gorm of Sleat as *de facto* leader of the Confederacy, but by no means as his chief.

Whilst he was far from voluble or forthcoming, Clanranald did admit, in response to Ludovick's questioning, that this Clan Donald adventure was indeed aimed at Ireland and the aiding of Tyrone and O'Donnell. Without conceding that he personally had soiled his hands with money, he agreed that gold was involved, gold from Spain. When the Duke suggested that the gold was in fact from England, the other showed that he was slightly better acquainted with the specie than he had indicated by acknowledging that the actual coins were English gold crowns, for convenience, but that they had of course come from the King of Spain. No other source, obviously, had occurred to him. He also admitted that Logan of Restalrig had acted as inter-mediary, and had in fact recently called upon him at Castle Tiorrim on his road south from Donald Gorm in Skye. Ludo-vick could get no more out of him, save that his captors need not imagine that this small reverse would seriously upset Clan Donald plans, for Donald Gorm had a force of at least eight thousand men assembled out there amongst the Isles, and would avenge this day's work in suitable fashion.

So they came back to Duart Castle, with cannon firing and cheering. For the ceremonial entry, the captive chiefs were chained together like felons, and their banners dragged in the mud behind them – although, as soon as they were safely inside the castle walls the chains were taken off and they were treated almost as honoured guests. Apparently there was a Highland form to be observed in such matters.

The Lieutenant of the North, the only member of the castle party to have been wounded in the engagement, found himself elevated to something of the status of hero, a situation which, after due modest disclaimer, he found it best to accept with good grace – especially from Mary, who cherished him with a concern worthy of a man at death's door.

In the midst of it all, Maclean's courier to Argyll arrived

back from Inveraray. He brought word from the Earl that he would answer the Duke's call for men and ships as effectively and quickly as possible – but that he was much exercised over another and more personal matter. His uncle and former guardian, Sir John Campbell of Cawdor, had been murdered – here in his own Campbell country. On Argyll's instructions he had been bringing the remainder of the Campbell host back from Aberdeen, to face this MacDonald threat, and the journey nearly over had ridden ahead to his own house in Lorne, where he had been shot dead through a window.

Ludovick and Mary eyed each other sombrely at this news. The cold hand of fear reached out to touch them again.

It took two weeks and more to assemble the force and fleet which Lennox had called for to assail Donald Gorm, largely on account of continuing high winds from the north-west which made navigation on this beautiful but dangerous seaboard hazardous indeed – but also, of course, because of the lack of enthusiasm on the part of the chiefs involved. For this latter reason too, the host which did eventually gather was a deal smaller than had been hoped for, amounting to no more than four thousand men in all, with some twenty more galleys and a number of birlinns.

Fortunately the same unfavourable winds had been equally so for Donald Gorm and his MacDonalds, out in the further isles, holding up his reinforcements likewise as well as precluding his sailing for Ireland. Clanranald's prophesy that the defeat at Tobermory and consequent loss of support would not dissuade him from the enterprise, appeared to be confirmed; the advance was only being postponed.

Maclean was for immediate action, despite odds – but Ludovick insisted that they should wait for Argyll. There were above a thousand Campbells in their company, but Argyll himself delayed, intent on discovering who had slain his uncle. Urgent messages went from Duart that he should leave this inquiry until later.

In the end, coincident with a marked improvement in the weather, the long anticipated tidings arrived. Strengthened by a further contingent of Macleods from the Outer Isles, Donald Gorm had sailed from Coll and Tiree, south by west, in a great fleet of some sixty galleys as well as many other craft. And as, furiously, Maclean ordered his host to prepare to put to sea, a flotilla came sailing up the Firth of Lorne, led by a galley with its sail painted with the bold gold-and-black gyrony-of-eight of the Campbells and the proud banner of MacCailean Mor himself flying at its masthead. Argyll had come at last, with five hundred more broadswords.

The Earl, it turned out, had brought more than that. In his own galley, specially fitted up with comfortable cabin-space fore and aft, came his lady-mother, the Countess Agnes. Also his young brother, Colin Campbell of Lundie. It was an indication of the state of mind prevailing in this proud house, in this era of treachery and murder, that the Earl had not dared to leave mother and brother behind, even in his castle of Inveraray. The death of Cawdor, after all the others, left only this young Colin as sure heir to the earldom and chiefship. One by one those close to Argyll had been eliminated. He was now taking no risks.

Mary Gray, of course, had been agitating to be taken on this important voyage also, the more so as it might well be a prolonged one. Hitherto her pleas had been unsuccessful. The arrival of the Countess Agnes however put a different complexion on the matter. Argyll would not hear of his mother being left behind at Duart, a young man now trusting no one but himself; and if the Countess was to sail with them, Mary claimed that there was no valid reason why she should be forbidden. Argyll, grateful to the girl for what she had revealed to him that day at Castle Campbell, and seeing her as company for his mother, backed her plea, offering to take her in his own vessel. Ludovick, actually delighted to have her company, could not refuse, however much Maclean might scoff at the idea of women in war galleys.

When the combined fleet, therefore, sailed from Duart only a couple of hours after Argyll's arrival, Mary shared the stern cabin of the Earl's galley with the Countess and her maid, while Ludovick, as before, accompanied Lachlan Mor. In the event of battle, it was agreed that Argyll himself would transfer to another Campbell galley leaving this craft to keep well out of danger's way.

They drove down the Firth of Lorne, a magnificent sight in

the gold and shadow of the evening sunlight, the largest fleet seen in these narrow waters for many a long day – over forty galleys and a dozen birlinns, but nothing more slow such as might hold them back. The MacDonalds had a sizeable start, but they had somewhat further to sail, and would be delayed inevitably by the craft, slower than the galleys, which they were having to use as additional transports. Almost certainly they were making for the Irish rebel stronghold area of Ballycastle in Antrim, and Maclean hoped and anticipated that they would keep fairly close in to the Scottish coast, amongst the islands, until opposite the northern tip of Antrim, lie anchored in some remote and sheltered bay overnight, and then in the early morning make a swift dash across the North Channel, the shortest direct crossing – this in order to avoid losing any of their slower vessels during the night, and also to avoid being spotted by the watchdogs of Elizabeth's navy which patrolled these Irish waters continuously. The one great danger which Donald Gorm had to fear was to be caught by a squadron of English ships of war and galleons, in a position where his superior speed and manoeuvrability could not save him – for compared with these the galleys were cockleshells and could be sunk with ease by the others' vastly greater fire-power and longer range. Sir Lachlan was going to take the risk of sailing all night, even through these dangerous reef-strewn seas, in order to steal a march on his enemy.

The wind, though much moderated, was still north-westerly. This, for the sake of speed, meant that Maclean should take the most southerly course possible, once out of the Firth of Lorne – that through the narrows of the Sounds of Luing and Jura. Donald Gorm, who would probably reach the same waters via the Sound of Islay – and it was no part of Lachlan Mor's strategy to engage in a stern-chase and open battle with sixty MacDonald galleys as against his own forty. He required surprise to aid him outnumbered as he was, and planned accordingly. Emerging therefore from the comparatively sheltered waters of the Firth, instead of south he swung round almost due west, half into wind and seas – to the immediate reduction of their speed. Passing to the north of the jagged fangs of the Garvelloch Isles, dipping and tossing and leaving behind a drifting cloud of spray from a couple of thousand lashing oar-blades, they made directly for the open sea.

Nearing the long island of Colonsay, and night coming down, Maclean signalled for all his galleys to close in, reef sails, and reduce speed. From now on the most intense care was demanded of every captain. Few commanders would or could have risked this endeavour, for there was still some twenty miles of rock- and skerry-infested waters to be covered, including the far-flung menace of the Torran Rocks, before the final isolated reefs of Dubh Heartach were reached and they could turn due south in clear deep sea. For over fifty ships to thread this vicious maze in formation, in darkness, demanded a discipline and standard of navigation ill at odds with the wild appearance of this clan host. Led by Sir Lachlan's own galley, the vessels must proceed three abreast and only one ship's length behind the trio in front, each guided by the white splashes of its leaders' and neighbours' oars. Course-changing would be ordered by a code of signals blown on horns and passed back from ship to ship. Hector Ruari and Lachlan Barrach alone were exempted from these strict commands; almost as expert as their father, they were to act as sheep-dogs for the convoy, to watch for stragglers, round up and warn off, as necessary – an onerous task indeed in the darkness.

Ludovick, fascinated by it all, could by no means curl up in a plaid and sleep, as advised by Maclean, but stood hour after hour on the heaving forecastle of the leading ship, chilled as he was, while admiration for the older man's brilliant seamanship, swift decision and uncanny instinct, grew upon him. Time and again his heart was in his mouth as sudden spouting seas to left or right hissed and snarled dire danger. But not once did Sir Lachlan show hesitation, alarm, or even anxiety. The lives of up to five thousand men depended upon his sole and instant judgment, but he revealed no hint of strain or excitement.

Mary, for her part, was no more prepared to sleep, whatever the comforts available. She found the Countess a proud and haughty woman younger-seeming than might have been expected considering that, before she had married the Earl's father and former Chancellor, she had been the widow of the famous

Earl of Moray, Regent of Scotland and eldest half-brother of Mary the Queen – a child-wife she must have been, surely, for the Regent was dead twenty-five years. She was a Keith, daughter of the fourth and sister of the present Earl Marischal. Full of her woes now, she was apparently more outraged by the blows to Argyll pride than distressed by loss or danger. Mary discovering the more sympathy for the Earl and his brother, preferred their company up at the galley's prow. Their vessel, of course, was deep in the centre of the flotilla, sandwiched between others, with responsibility only for maintaining position – but even so the situation absorbed the girl. She knew no fear, but recognised the danger, savouring the spice of it. Peering into the blackness ahead and around, and seeing only the vague outline of the ship in front and the wan white of oar-thrashed water, listening to the hissing rush of the waves, the whine of wind in cordage, the creak of timbers and oars, and the gasping refrain of the rowers, she knew a strange exhilaration that desired only that this should go on and on, that it should not stop, a feeling that she and the sea and the night were one. Even when young Colin Campbell, shivering, went below, and Argyll urged her to do likewise, she shook her damp head and remained standing at his side, wrapped in a wet plaid, hair plastering her face, licking the salt spray from her lips. Although they scarcely exchanged a word throughout, some affinity developed there between the girl and the restrained, sombre, dark-browed young man, an affinity unexpressed and unstressed, yet which would hold Archibald Grumach Campbell, in some measure, for the rest of his life. Frequently, inevitably, with the lurching of the ship, they staggered against each other; sometimes she grasped his arm for support, sometimes he held her firmly.

It was nearly midnight before an eerie winding of horns from front to rear of the fleet proclaimed that they were past the unseen pillar of Dubh Heartach and its savage outliers, and a change of course of almost ninety degrees was ordered. No more navigational hazards now lay between them and the north coast of Ireland, sixty miles south. The same formation was still to be kept, but with much more space allowable between ships. Sails were hoisted and speed picked up, reliefs of rowers taking over. Tension relaxed everywhere.

Just before she went below, Mary turned to the silent Argyll standing by her side. 'My lord,' she said, 'that was good for us, I think. Clean danger, not foul. That was living, was it not?'

He nodded, wordless.

'All men are not betrayers,' she added. 'There is courage and strength and honesty in men. Aye, and faith – much faith. Deceit and treachery – these, in the end, must fail. The good, the true, *must* prevail. I know it. Something . . . something in this night tells me so.'

For a little he stared straight ahead of him. Then slowly he inclined his head. 'It may be so. I hope so. I thank you, Mary Gray.'

She touched his arm briefly, and left him there.

As she lay in her dark bunk thereafter, it came to her that this unsmiling lonely youth, whom men already were calling The Grim, had not asked her why and what made her speak as she had done, how she had come to her conclusion. He had somehow understood and accepted. Which was more than Ludovick Stewart, for instance, would or could have done.

Chapter Fourteen

Probably it was the comparative quiet and the lack of motion which wakened Mary. The Countess and her maid still slept. She rose, tidied herself, and slipped out into the grey light of early morning.

It was a strange sight that met her gaze. All around her, men slept, slumped over their oars, curled on every bench, littering every inch of space in the crowded galley. And on every hand the galley's sister-ships lay sleeping also, tight-packed in neat rows in a small bay, gunwale to gunwale, stem to stern, a concentrated mass of timber and armour and sleeping clansmen, motionless save for the slight sway that was the echo of the Atlantic swell. Close by, to the south, a rocky beach rose in broken redstone cliffs, backed by grassy hills of an intense greenness, even in that dove-grey morning light. The bay was sheltered, irregularly shaped, and perhaps half a mile at its mouth, and of approximately the same depth. Seaward, perhaps five miles to the north, on the edge of the slate-grey horizon, the long black line of a low island showed.

The girl's impression that all the Highland host slept, exhausted, was soon corrected. On their own ship's forecastle two or three men stood, wrapped in their plaids, silent – and when she looked around her, she perceived that on every vessel men thus stood, on watch. She perceived also that all these seemed to divide their attention between two points – or rather, three – forward, where Sir Lachlan's galley lay broadside on to the bows of the first row of ships, giving it greater opportunity to manoeuvre, and east and west to where on the green summits of the headlands which enclosed the bay, two dark columns of smoke rose high in the morning air. That these were signals of some sort could hardly be doubted. They were obviously preoccupying the attention of the silent watchers.

Mary could by no means make her way forward to the forecastle over the sprawled bodies of some hundreds of Campbells,

224

but she climbed the ladder to the after-deck which roofed in the Countess's cabin. There, amongst more sleeping men, including the galley's captain, one man sat, hunched in a corner but awake – Archibald, Earl of Argyll, MacCailean Mor himself. He might have been there, waking, all night by the set look of him.

'My lord,' she whispered, 'Do you not sleep?'

He shook his dark head. 'I am no great sleeper,' he said. 'Besides, we shall have more to do than sleep presently, I think.' And he nodded towards the smoke signals.

'Where are we? Is this Ireland?'

'Aye. A small bay to the west of the great bay of Ballycastle, on the north coast of Antrim. Yonder, to the east, is Kinbane Head. Here we await Donald Gorm. But . . . it seems we have been discovered.'

'Those smokes? Are they to warn the MacDonalds that we are here?'

'Who knows? But they are surely to warn someone. O'Neill and O'Donnell have sharp eyes, it seems. For we crept in in darkness. The fires have been lit but a score of minutes.'

As they watched those ominous black columns that drifted away on the north-west breeze, there was a certain stir amongst the watchers on each vessel nearby as a small rowing-boat wove its way in and out amongst the closely-ranked galleys, a man therein shouting up to each one, in the Gaelic, as it passed.

'What does he say, my lord?' Mary demanded, as it came near.

'That Maclean orders all captains to be ready to sail at his signal. He has sent ashore a party to deal with those fires.'

As the bustle of waking men stirred the fleet, a single man came climbing up from the small boat into Argyll's galley. It proved to be the Duke of Lennox himself. Embracing Mary frankly, openly, he turned to the Earl.

'I came to apprise you of what is toward, my lord,' he said. 'It would be wisest, I think, if you would now move to another ship of your array, and keep close to Maclean, so that this galley with the women may remain hidden and secure. There may be fighting shortly.'

The other nodded. 'Are Donald Gorm's ships sighted?'

'No. Not that we may see from here. But perhaps from the high ground. These smokes may mean that watchers on the headlands have seen them, and seek to warn them of our presence. Or it may be only that the warning is for Tyrone and O'Donnell themselves, inland. Ballycastle, their main stronghold, is but some five or six miles south by east of here. That is why here it is that the MacDonalds must come.'

'Then . . . it may not be a warning at all?', Mary put in. 'If these watchers look for a Highland fleet, will they not be likely to take us for the MacDonalds? So these signals may be but a sign to the Irish chiefs that his friends are come.'

'Yes. It could be so. We cannot tell. Maclean has landed a party to go up there and discover the matter. When we have their report, we may have to move swiftly.'

'Move from this bay?'

'Aye, if need be. This place, though it hides us well from sight from the sea, could be a death-trap for us. As was Tobermory Bay for Clanranald. We are here to hide from Donald Gorm, to sally out and attack him when he is unready, approaching Ballycastle Bay, and knowing nothing of our presence. But if he is warned that we are in here, he could bottle us up. We would be lost.'

'Maclean did not foresee this?' Argyll demanded.

'He did not look to be observed so soon. Not in this remote bay of Kinbane. He knows this coast well. There is empty moorland and bog behind here, for miles, he says – savage, waterlogged country where no men live. It is strange that it should be watched, guarded.'

'It may be only because the Irish look for Donald Gorm?'

'How could they know when he would come? He has been many weeks preparing . . .'

While they were discussing it, a considerable outcry developed from the detachment which Maclean had sent ashore. They had climbed up the rising ground of the eastern horn of the bay, Kinbane Head itself, making for the nearest fire, and had reached an intermediate summit, a spur of the headland. Here they had halted suddenly, and begun to wave and gesticulate wildly, their shouts sounding thinly on the morning air. Obviously they had seen something which excited them greatly.

'Donald Gorm! They have spied his fleet!' Mary cried.

'I think not,' Argyll said, in his unemotional, factual way.

'They would have shouted before this, in that case. If they can see the MacDonald ships now, they could have seen them before – for they have but moved on to a knoll yonder. They would not have waited. No, it is because they can now see down beyond. Eastwards, into the next bay. Into the main Ballycastle Bay, or whatever lies beyond that cape. It is something down there that they have seen.'

'You are right,' Ludovick nodded. 'It must be that. Perhaps it is an encampment, there. Of the Irish . . .'

Whatever they had seen, the scouting party considered it of sufficient importance to abandon their mission to the hilltop. They came hurrying downhill again, sending two racing emissaries ahead.

Argyll, anticipating trouble, went below to arm and to inform his mother and brother that he would be moving to another Campbell galley meantime. Ludovick waited, for the small boat to come back for them.

While still they waited, the word flew like wildfire round the fleet, from ship to ship, that it was not Donald Gorm at all that was spied – it was the English! A large squadron of English ships of war were in the main bay, just around the headland. So said the running scouts.

Men's excited discussion of these tidings was interrupted by a peremptory blaring of horns from Maclean. Sir Lachlan, waiting for no one, had his oarsmen pulling already, and was signalling all craft to make for open water immediately. Even as they wondered at his precipitate haste, eastwards they saw the topsails of the first English ships appearing above the thrusting base of the headland.

There was no question now of Lennox getting back to Maclean's galley, or of Argyll transferring to another meantime. Already there was urgent movement all around them, with ships manoeuvring for space and position in the constricted space.

More English ships appeared as the leading galleys headed for the mouth of the bay. Argyll's vessel, delayed until it had space to use its oars, had just begun to move when a cannon crashed out its angry message. A great spout of water rose out of the sea just ahead of Lachlan Mor's ship.

'God be good – the knaves! The fools!' Ludovick exclaimed.

227

'What do they think they are about? We are their allies . . .'

'No doubt they also mistake us for the MacDonalds,' Mary said.

'But they cannot know about Donald Gorm.'

'Even so, they must esteem us foes . . .'

Unswerving, Sir Lachlan drove his galley straight ahead. His urgency to get his ships out of that trap of a bay was now vindicated and explained.

Six English ships were now in view, large ships all, one of them a great galleon, a proud sight with all sails set. Even as they watched, this tall ship, with its rows of black open gun-ports, swung round directly into the north-west wind, and suddenly seemed to explode in orange flame and black smoke, as a tremendous broadside thundered out.

Undoubtedly this was intended as a demonstration of might and authority rather than an actual attack, for the galleon was the furthest away of the English ships, and all the shot fell well short of Maclean's craft, throwing up a vast wall of water, scores of feet in height.

Sir Lachlan, now in the mouth of the bay, could have swung hard to port, to the west, and drawn clear away – for, sailing into a wind, of course, his galley, with all its oars, had possibly three times the speed of the fastest English ship dependent wholly on sails. But he did not do so. He continued on his course, directly towards the Englishmen – though from his stern he signalled for the remainder of his fleet to veer to port, westwards out of that corner of the bay.

'He will be blown out of the water!' Ludovick cried to Argyll, who had now reappeared, in armour. 'He is sailing right into their guns.'

Lachlan Mor was no suicide, however, determined as he might be to give his fleet every opportunity he could to win out of the trap. He hoisted a large white flag to his masthead, part of an old sail – surely the first time that any vessel of his had worn so sorry an emblem – and for good measure draped another approximately white sail over his sharp prow.

No further broadsides were fired from the English vessels, but the leading ships turned a few points more north by west, to cut across Sir Lachlan's bows, clearly attempting to head off and draw within range of the escaping galleys beyond. Three more tall ships had now appeared round the headland, making nine in all.

'My lord,' Ludovick exclaimed, to Argyll. 'Direct your captain to sail us after Maclean. Not with the others. I must get to those English fools!'

'Even in this women's galley?' the Earl asked, thin-voiced, brows raised.

The Duke bit his lip. 'Aye – even so,' he said. 'I must, man! They may not heed Maclean, a Highlander. But they must surely heed me. The King's cousin! The Lieutenant! Sweet Jesu – am I not Lord Admiral of Scotland?'

'Aye. But how to let them know it, my lord Duke?'

'Only by going to them. There is no other way. It is necessary.'

The Earl nodded. Turning, he shouted the required orders, in Gaelic, to his captain.

The big galleon, obviously the flagship of the English squadron, was now moving in to meet Maclean, although the other craft were making what speed they could against the wind to head off at least some of the galley fleet. The leading two fired the bows cannon, but these were lesser guns with shorter range than those of the galleon, and their shot fell far short.

It was clear that most, if not all, of the Highland ships would escape.

Because Argyll's vessel was, as it were, going against the tide, by having to cross diagonally the route taken by the other galleys, its progress was infuriatingly slow – at least to Ludovick Stewart. He paced the after-deck impatiently, urging speed.

'Do not fret, Vicky,' Mary soothed. 'The big ship is not firing on Sir Lachlan.' She had been told to go below, but with good sense had spiritedly declared that if their ship was going to be shot at and sunk, she would much prefer to be on its open deck than trapped beneath.

'One shot, now, is all that is needed, and Maclean is finished!' he told her. 'Those great cannon could smash his galley, at such distance, like an egg-shell.'

'Sir Lachlan knows that. But still he goes on. The English are not savages. They will respect his flag-of-truce.'

'I hope so. I pray so.'

'Even though they believe us to be MacDonalds they will surely parley...'

'Why should they believe us to be MacDonalds? How could they know of the MacDonald threat, Mary? How could they have learned of this?'

'That I cannot tell you.'

'And how is this great squadron of ships up here? Maclean said that all the English ships of war were being kept in the south, for fear of an invasion from France or Spain. That only small scouting craft kept watch in these waters. And Maclean should know. He deals with Elizabeth, and makes it his business to know all that goes on in these waters. Yet . . . here are these great ships. Nine of them. Come this day, of all days!'

Wordless, Mary shook her head.

The galleon had now hove to, and Lachlan Mor's galley was almost up with it. Most of the Highland fleet had made good its escape from the bay and was fanning out north-westwards into the open sea; but some few vessels were trapped, and were in fact turning back into the bay under the threat of the English guns.

Argyll's craft, also with a scrap of sail hoisted as a white flag, now bore down fast on the two leaders' ships. Ludovick could see Maclean standing in his prow, hand to mouth, shouting to the galleon. Lennox urged Argyll to draw in still closer to the great ship, closer than was Maclean, despite the gaping mouths of all those rows of cannon.

On the towering aftercastle of the English flagship, a colourful group of men stood, most handsomely dressed in the height of fashion, an extraordinary sight to see at this time of the morning on a war-vessel at sea. One of these, a tall, slender, handsome black-bearded man, dressed in what appeared to be crimson velvet, save for the yellow satin lining of his short cloak, had been conducting an exchange with Sir Lachlan through a voice-trumpet. Now he swung on the newcomers.

'Who a God's sake do *you* say you are – in the Queen's name?' he demanded, in a voice weary as it was haughty. 'If you can speak the Queen's English!'

Argyll and Ludovick exchanged glances. The latter raised hand to mouth, to shout back.

'Sir – I mislike your manners, as I mislike your cannonry! Towards lawful users of these waters, and friends of your Queen. Aye, and towards your betters, sirrah! What do you mean by opening fire on the ships of the King of Scots?'

'Insolent!' the Englishman snapped back, at least the weariness going out of his voice. 'Have a care how you speak, fellow – or I shall be sore tempted to send you and your oar-boat to the bottom of this bay! Your name and business in these waters, coxcomb?'

'Within a score of miles of the Scottish coast, no Scot requires to state his business to an Englishman, sir!'

'Fool! Trifle no more, or . . .'

'Very well. I trifle no more. I am the Lord High Admiral of Scotland, Ludovick, Duke of Lennox, Lieutenant of King James's Northern Realm . . . and in cousinship to your Queen, Elizabeth Tudor!'

There was a choking sound into the voice-trumpet, and then a sudden and profound silence from the tall ship's aftercastle. Heads thereon drew close together.

Mary touched Ludovick's arm, smiling. 'Vicky,' she murmured, 'sometimes I love you even more than usual!'

The Duke pressed home his advantage. 'Come, sir – who are you who crows so loud in other folk's yards? And what is *your* business here?'

'H'mmm.' They could hear the elegant clearing his throat. 'I am Sir Christopher St. Lawrence, commodore of this special squadron of Her Grace of England. Here on Her Grace's business. An especial mission.'

'And does that business and mission include opening fire on your Queen's allies, sir?'

'My apologies for that, my lord Duke. A, h'm, an accident of war! No more. We mistook you for . . . another.'

'So! You shoot first, sir, and make your inquiries after? Is that the English way?'

'I am sorry, my lord . . .'

'Then, Sir Christopher – signal your other ships to halt their hounding of my galleys forthwith! Quickly, man – before blood is shed!'

'Yes, my lord Duke. At once . . .' Sir Christopher St. Lawrence turned to give orders to one of the brilliant young men at his side. As he did so, another man, much more soberly dressed, indeed in old and dented half-armour, came hurrying across the aftercastle to him, having just climbed up from the main deck, urgency in every line of him. With almost equal urgency, Mary Gray grasped Ludovick's wrist.

'Vicky – look!' she whispered. 'See you who that is? Who has just come up? It is Robert Logan! Logan of Restalrig!'

'Eh . . . ? Dear God – you are right! Logan! Fiend seize him . . . !'

Astounded, they stared at each other, minds groping for what this could mean.

Sir Christopher, after listening to Logan, was hailing them again, but in their preoccupation they missed much of what he said.

'We must get to the bottom of this,' Ludovick muttered. Suddenly he came to a decision. Raising his voice again, he cried. 'A plague on this shouting! My throat is raw! Lower a ladder, sir – I am coming aboard you.' He turned his back on the Englishman. The Duke of Lennox could play the haughty autocrat with fair verisimilitude also when occasion demanded.

Argyll, who had not spoken throughout this exchange, nodded to Ludovick. 'Well spoken, my lord,' he said quietly. 'You, I think, make a better Lieutenant of the North than ever I would do!'

'Arrogance ever rouses me,' the other jerked, almost apologetically. 'My lord, can your captain bring this craft sufficiently close in for me to board that ship?'

Expertly the galley was manoeuvred so that its high stern eased in gently to touch the galleon's quarter, and was held there by skilful oar-work. A rope-ladder was dropped to her from the high aftercastle. As Ludovick reached for it, Argyll moved close, declaring that he would come with him.

Climbing up the swaying contrivance, the Duke was aided over the side by eager hands, to be greeted with much respect by St. Lawrence and his gentlemen. Even so, he could not but be aware of his humdrum, not to say unkempt appearance compared with that of these elegants – and was the haughtier in consequence. Logan, he noted, had disappeared.

Sir Christopher St. Lawrence, a man of early middle years, was now all suave good humour and aplomb. He expressed renewed regret for the misadventure, as he termed it, but smilingly indicated that he had not expected to discover the Lord Admiral of Scotland in what he had taken to be a Highland pirate galley. From his inspection of Ludovick's person, the younger man also gained the impression that neither had he expected such a dignitary to be a carelessly-dressed and undistinguished-looking twenty-year-old.

Somewhat curtly the Duke introduced MacCailean Mor, High Chief of Clan Campbell, Earl of Argyll and Justiciar of the West, who, at two months younger still, was perhaps equally unimpressive as to appearance.

St. Lawrence's greetings to the Earl were brief, for he was already looking beyond, behind him. 'And the lady, no doubt, is the beautiful daughter of the Master of Gray?' he said, bowing deeply.

Ludovick turned. He had not known that Mary had followed them up the ladder – although he should not have been surprised. She, at least, was no disappointment to the eye, neither unkempt nor insignificant, despite the simplicity of her dress – indeed looking as lovely, fresh and modestly assured as though specially prepared for the occasion. The murmur amongst St. Lawrence's young men was eloquent tribute.

Ludovick nodded. 'The Lady Mary Gray,' he said, crisply. 'My help-meet and close associate in all things.'

'Ah yes.' There was a second round of bows and protestations of service from the impressionable gallants.

Lennox cut short the civilities. 'Sir Christopher,' he said, 'there is much that requires explanation here – and time may well be short. Why are you and your squadron here, may I ask?'

'That is easily answered, my lord Duke,' the other said, shrugging. 'Although, these being the waters of my Queen's realm of Ireland, I need offer no excuse for sailing them – even to the Admiral of Scotland! But that apart, I am here to intercept and put down a wicked and treasonable invasion of the said realm of Ireland by renegade Catholic subjects of your King. MacDonalds from the Isles. For them we mistook your galleys.'

Ludovick rubbed his chin. 'Then we are on the same errand,

sir. But, that you should know of this attempt is . . . interesting.'

'Our Queen is not uninformed of what goes on even in your islands, my lord!'

'Certainly she expends much gold on the business! But your knowledge, in this case, is very exact, Sir Christopher, is it not? And I saw that you had on board your ship a certain subject of my prince – Robert Logan of Restalrig!'

The other paused for a moment. 'That is true,' he agreed.

They eyed each other searchingly.

'I think that we might discuss this matter more privately, later,' the Duke decided. 'But meantime, sir, since we look for Donald Gorm of Sleat and his MacDonalds to appear at any moment,' he glanced seawards, 'it would be wise to make our plans. Sir Lachlan Maclean of Duart, in the first galley there, commands. Kindly summon him aboard, sir.'

The older man, however little he could have enjoyed this assumption of command, gave orders as required with a fair good grace.

When Maclean arrived, he was in no mood for civilities either. His resentment against the English was strong – but some of it seemed to spill over on to Lennox and Argyll also. However, his main concern meantime was for an end to this idling about in open waters, with the Clan Donald liable to be on them at any time. He demonstrated no joy that St. Lawrence was here seeking Donald Gorm likewise, but he agreed that they co-operated at least to the extent of getting back into Kinbane Bay at once, and hidden.

The English did not seem to like the use of the term hidden, esteeming it as undignified. Their combined forces, St. Lawrence pointed out, with his gun-power and the Scots' speed, should be more than ample to ensure that no MacDonalds ever returned to their barbarous islands. What need was there for hiding?

Ludovick intervened to declare that the objective was not to kill MacDonald but to prevent an invasion of Ireland and a Catholic triumph. If Donald Gorm could be turned away, sent back to Skye without battle, so much the better. To that end they should plan.

St. Lawrence eyed him askance.

In the end it was decided that each fleet should put back to its former position, the Scots hidden in the small bay, the English lying in a corner of the large. From whichever direction the MacDonalds eventually came, this should trap them. If Maclean remained undiscovered, he would hold back until St. Lawrence opened fire.

On an impulse, Ludovick decided to remain on board the galleon. He felt that he might be able to exert some slight moderating influence on the Englishmen should it look like becoming a massacre. Moreover, he wanted an interview with Logan. Mary would stay with him, but Maclean and Argyll would go back to their own craft.

Whether St. Lawrence appreciated the continued presence of his self-invited guests, he entertained them royally. As they headed back behind the promontory of Kinbane Head, into Ballycastle Bay, he took the young people down to his own great cabin immediately below the aftercastle, and breakfasted them as befitted any Lord High Admiral and his lady. No more convincing example of the benefits of adopting a lofty and overbearing attitude could have been demonstrated.

Ludovick and Mary did not have to use any great wiles to gain information from their host. He seemed to know the Master of Gray well, at least by repute, and undoubtedly was the more disposed to talk to the daughter. He admitted frankly enough that it was thanks to the Master that he and his squadron were here. The Master had discovered this Catholic plot to aid the Irish rebels, sent word of it to Queen Elizabeth, and then had sent this Logan to bring them down on the Islesmen. The Master had long been a good friend to the Queen, undoubtedly, and one of the most notable men in Europe. Sir Christopher acknowledged it a privilege to meet his daughter.

For once that daughter was less than adequate to the occasion. Set-faced, she mumbled something almost inaudible, and toyed with her food.

The Duke of Lennox was silent also, and the Englishman looked from one to the other keenly.

'You were not aware that the Master has sent this information, my lord?' he said.

'No, sir,' Ludovick answered briefly – since it would have

been futile to pretend otherwise.

The other fingered his small black beard. 'I wonder why . . . ?'

Mary, recovering herself, spoke quickly. 'No doubt my father sent the word to you after my lord had set out for the Isles. This expedition has taken some time to mount, sir.' It was important that St. Lawrence should not suspect that the project did not have the royal blessing.

'Is that so?'

'Yes,' the Duke put in. 'As you will well perceive, sir, it is necessary to hunt galleys with galleys. His Grace's ordinary ships would not serve to catch galleys, any more than these vessels of yours! So the Isles had to be scoured for such ships. And most had already been collected by the MacDonalds. This took time . . .'

'No doubt. But it is strange that the Master did not inform *us* of your expedition, my lord! Logan at least knew naught of it.'

'M'mmm.'

'Robert Logan was in the Isles himself until but recently,' Mary said. 'He cannot have had time for any close contact with my father. No doubt only messages, letters, passed between them, and this matter was not mentioned.'

As explanation, this did not seem entirely to convince Sir Christopher. But fortunately at this moment shouts from above announced the sighting of sails on the northern horizon. Their host hurriedly left his cabin and guests.

'Oh, Vicky!' Mary said, her voice quivering. 'This is . . . this beyond everything! Treachery upon treachery!'

'It is unbelievable!' Ludovick exclaimed.

'No.' She shook her head. 'Not unbelievable. Not when you think of it. Not for Patrick. Indeed, perhaps I should have thought of it. For here is the fine pinnacle and perfection of betrayal! In the cause of balancing power. He uses Elizabeth's gold to bribe the MacDonalds against Elizabeth; then informs Elizabeth that the MacDonalds move against her, so that she may destroy them!'

'But, dear God – why? Not, surely, merely for the reward . . . ?'

'No – although, no doubt, rewards he will gain. But if thus he can have the MacDonald power destroyed, there is none

other to whom Huntly can turn. Yet the Catholics will still believe him their friend. As, of course, will Elizabeth. Patrick gains
on all hands, trusted by all. At no cost to himself.'

'Not to himself. The cost is eight or nine thousand Mac-
Donalds!'

'Vicky – we must save them! Somehow!'

They hurried aloft.

Donald Gorm was approaching from the north-west, having
used the bulk of the long island of Rathlin to mask his descent
upon the Irish coast. It could not have been better from St.
Lawrence's point of view, for it meant that the invaders would
not see into the west side of Ballycastle Bay, and so would have
no warning of the English squadron's presence there until the
last moment. How soon they discovered Maclean's fleet of
galleys would depend very much upon the MacDonald's angle
of approach. But strategically the situation could hardly have
been improved. The fires on the headlands had now been extinguished – for these, it transpired, had been lit by English
parties, to give warning to St. Lawrence. All unsuspicious,
therefore. Donald Gorm bore down on his fate.

From the galleon, of course, nothing of the developing situation could be seen; but St. Lawrence had pinnaces out, lying
below the very point itself, to signal back information.

Ludovick, adopting his most hectoring and authoritative
tone, left the English commander in no doubt that the approaching MacDonalds, although misguided, were nevertheless
King James's subjects, and must be treated with no more
severity than was necessary to cause them to turn back. Any
undue violence and bloodshed would undoubtedly be construed
as an attack upon the dignity and privileges of the King of
Scots – who of course was Queen Elizabeth's heir. This warning
was not enthusiastically received. Ludovick hoped that Maclean,
for his part, would be content with the moral defeat of his hereditary foes, rather than seek any blood-bath. His behaviour over
the Clanranald business gave some grounds for this, probably.

The waiting, inactive, anxious, was trying. When, however,
action did develop, it was not heralded by the anticipated appearance of MacDonald galleys round Kinbane Head, but by the

237

crash of a single cannon. This, after a few moments' pause, was followed by others, but only in scattered, haphazard shooting, not in a concentrated cannonade.

Angrily, St. Lawrence ordered his squadron to move out into open water. 'Curse him! God's wounds – the fool has warned them off!' He swore.

Mary caught Ludovick's eye. Perhaps Lachlan Mor drew the line at allowing Englishmen to massacre fellow-Islesmen, even MacDonalds?

The great English ships, wholly dependent on sails and wind, seemed to take an unconscionable time to beat out of the bay. When they did reach a position where they could gain a wide view, it was to discover an astonishing situation. The sea seemed to be littered with galleys, score upon score of them, oar blades flashing in the new sunlight, swirling, weaving, darting round each other in a milling mass, in negation of any order or formation. Occasionally a cannon would boom out, but this seemed to be more in the nature of a conventional accompaniment to all the urgent movement than any determined attack – an impression reinforced by the fact that no crippled or sinking vessels were in evidence. It was clear, at least, that both fleets were involved – but that was all that was clear in the position. All else was a confusion, a positive vortex of ships, in which it would have required much more expert watchers than any in the English squadron to tell Maclean galleys from MacDonald.

St. Lawrence could scarcely contain his wrath. 'Dolts! Numbskulls! Knaves!' he exclaimed. 'Here's the folly of all follies! Look at them! I can do nothing. Nothing! I cannot fire, lest I hit friend instead of foe. If you can name Maclean friend – which I much misdoubt! Beshrew me – I do not even know which is which!'

'Why so eager to fire your cannon, if the matter may be resolved otherwise?' Ludovick demanded. 'They are not child's playthings, sir! Men's lives are at stake.'

Although St. Lawrence could not fire, he and his squadron drove straight on into the mêlée of ships. It could now be seen that the slower transports of Donald Gorm's fleet had been sent in a tight group northwards again, under escort of the birlinns, as far from danger as possible.

'Make for Sir Lachlan's galley,' Ludovick urged St. Lawrence. 'Yonder, with the ship painted on its sail. Demand a parley. There is naught else to do.'

This indeed seemed to be the case, and even Sir Christopher could think of no other practical course in the circumstances. He set bugles blowing on his flagship and bore down as best he could on Maclean's craft. Sir Lachlan made it easy for him, coming to meet the Englishmen.

Ludovick hailed him. 'Maclean – we must have a parley,' he shouted. 'With Donald Gorm. Where is he? Which is his ship?'

'That with the great banner and the eagle prow. You would parley?'

'Of course. What else is there to do?'

'This is madness, man!' Sir Christopher put in, through his voice-trumpet. 'Play-acting! Mummery! What are you at? You have ruined all, I tell you!'

Maclean ignored him.

'Donald Gorm will talk, I think, Duke of Lennox,' he called. 'He is held. He saw us in the bay, coming from this side. We had to issue out, or be trapped. I have sought to break up this array ...'

'Aye – to be sure. You could do no other. Come with me, to Donald Gorm.' Lennox turned to St. Lawrence. 'Sir Christopher – steer for that galley with the great banner. And I'll thank you for less talk of madness and play-acting!'

The Englishman looked daggers but said nothing.

The play-acting jibe was not far from the truth, of course, for there was no actual fighting going on, and even the demonstrations of cannon-fire had died away. It was stalemate, and all knew it.

Donald Gorm MacDonald of Sleat proved that he perceived this as clearly as anyone else, by waiting in his more or less stationary galley for the other two flagships to come up with him. Surrounded by a group of spectacularly colourful chieftains, he stood on his forecastle, silent.

Ludovick was in a fever of anxiety lest wrong words should be spoken at this stage, for the proud MacDonalds would be sore and touchy, and much evil could yet eventuate this day. He was about to hail the other, before they were suitably close, to forestall any arrogant bluster on the part of St. Lawrence, when Mary touched his arm.

'The trumpet,' she murmured. 'Sir Christopher's trumpet.'

'Ah, yes.' He turned and stepped over to reach out for the voice-trumpet which St. Lawrence held in his hand. 'With your permission, sir, this will aid, I think.' Firmly he took the instrument from his host's reluctant fingers.

The device was a great help, lending the shouter confidence and authority, as well as easing his vocal strain. 'This is the Duke of Lennox, Lieutenant of the North and Admiral of Scotland,' he called. 'I would speak with Donald MacDonald of Sleat.'

A voice came back, coldly. 'MacDonald of the Isles is here, and listens.'

'The position must be clear to you all. You cannot now land on this coast to aid the Irish. We can do battle. But whose advantage will it serve? It is time to talk.'

There was a brief pause. Then in sing-song English came the answer. 'Talk, then. Donald of the Isles hears.'

Ludovick bit his lip, as, at his side, Sir Christopher smiled thinly. He surely could look for some co-operation from the Mac-Donalds in this situation? Their spokesman was a tall bearded man in vivid tartans; but each time before speaking he bent to have word with a short squat clean-shaven man beside him, plainly clad in half-armour, leather jerkin and small helmet.

'Are you Donald Gorm?' Lennox demanded.

'No. Donald of the Isles does not shout,' he was informed briefly.

Ludovick flushed, the more so at St. Lawrence's bark of mirthless laughter. A hot answer was rising to his lips when the girl again touched him.

'Be patient, Vicky,' she whispered. 'They have been sore hit. All their hopes dashed. Agree with him. On the shouting. Invite him to this ship. As your guest. He is proud. He will not wish to seem fearful to do so.'

'Tell him that I have forty cannon trained on him!' Sir Christopher cried, from his other side. 'They will make him shout – for mercy!'

Frowning, the Duke raised the voice-trumpet again. 'I dislike shouting also,' he declared strongly. 'I invite Donald of Sleat aboard this ship. That we may discuss this matter like gentlemen. His safety and free return is assured – upon my honour!'

Long seconds passed, and then there came the answer. 'Donald of the Isles accepts your invitation.'

'It is as though the fellow was a prince!' St. Lawrence snorted.

'As he considers himself to be, sir. He would be Lord of the Isles, a prince indeed, but for the stroke of a pen. And the authority of that pen he does not recognise!'

The MacDonald galley nudged in alongside the big ship aft. Two Highlanders leapt aboard, to aid their chief, but the stocky dark man ignored them and mounted alone, with marked agility. Two of his chieftains came after him.

It was strange what an impression of strength, contained force and quiet dignity the newcomer made. It was easy to see why he was known as Donald Gorm, *gorm* meaning blue; for he was so dark as to be almost swarthy, and his shaven square chin was blue indeed. He was not really a small man at all, however short-seeming, being in fact immensely broad and of a compact masculinity, with no fat to his curiously squat person. A man of early middle-age, he stood there on the English ship, silent, assured, self-sufficient, as though a victor awaiting the formal surrender of his foes.

Ludovick bowed slightly. He gestured towards his companions. 'This is Sir Christopher St. Lawrence, commodore of the English ships. And the Lady Mary Gray.'

Sir Christopher turned away, and stared into the middle distance. Mary sketched a curtsy, and smiled.

Donald Gorm inclined his head. 'Roderick MacLeod of Harris, and Angus MacDonald of Dunyveg,' he mentioned, deep-voiced.

The two chiefs made no sort of acknowledgement.

Ludovick swallowed. 'Perhaps Sir Christopher will invite us below to his cabin? Where we may discuss our problems more suitably?' he suggested.

The Englishman frowned blackly. But before he could raise his voice, Donald Gorm spoke.

'No, sir,' he said, with a decisive shake of his head. 'What is to be said may be said here.' His English was good but careful. And final.

'As you will.' Lennox glanced over to where a slight commotion heralded the re-arrival of Lachlan Mor, uninvited. Ludovick was unashamedly glad to see him.

'Sir Lachlan – come!' he exclaimed. 'We seek to resolve this situation. Fighting between us, I say, would be foolish. Is indeed scarcely possible. And would gain nothing, for neither side could win a clear victory . . .'

'I could crush these galleys with my cannon as I would crush eggs!' Sir Christopher declared scornfully. 'Why this talk of no clear victory?'

'Some of them, no doubt, sir. A few. While they remained within your range. But since they can out-sail you with ease, most would elude your guns. And so long as they remain amongst Sir Lachlan's ships you cannot fire. On the other hand, they cannot attack you either. Nor can they do what they came to do – land to aid the Irish. We can prevent any large landing, and destroy the ships of any who do land. Is that not all true, gentlemen?'

None could deny it. But that did not mean that it could be just accepted and agreed, there and then, nevertheless. Too much of pride and prestige was involved.

Donald Gorm himself said little; he appeared to be a man of exceedingly few words. But his two companions, Angus of Dunyveg and MacLeod of Harris, said much, the former in diabolical English and the latter in Gaelic, both of which Maclean had to translate. Their main points seemed to be that they outnumbered the combined opposition by more than two to one; that they were without doubt the finest fighting-men on the seven seas; that the English cannon might damage a few of their vessels, but that they could twist and turn their galleys in mere moments and so avoid the enemy broadsides; that they would cut off and board the slow English ships one by one, as hounddogs pick off stags from a herd; and that Maclean knew Clan Donald's mettle too well to dare become involved in any close fighting.

Sir Christopher's angry denials, taunts and challenges, though well-sustained and insulting, never quite reached the stage of breaking off the discussion and ordering the Islesmen off his ship. For his part, Ludovick found himself become a mediator more than anything else, while Sir Lachlan, when he was not translating, contented himself with comparatively mild and modest assertions as to his prowess and powers.

Fairly soon deadlock seemed to have been reached on the diplomatic front, equally with the strategic.

Ludovick was racking his brains to think up some face-saving formula which would allow both sides to step back, with dignity more or less intact, from the positions thus taken up, when Mary Gray, with every appearance of extreme diffidence, made a suggestion.

'My lord Duke – sirs,' she said, hesitantly. 'Forgive me if I speak both foolishly and immodestly, a woman meddling in men's affairs. But it seems to me that here is occasion for a compromise. An honourable compromise – a treaty, indeed. A treaty between Donald and the Confederation of the Isles, on the one hand, and the representatives of the King of Scots and Queen of England on the other. Whereby each acknowledges the other's potency and right, and each agrees that all should return whence they have come, unmolested and with full honours and unassailed authority. Leaving the situation as it was before this morning's light. Such treaty would harm the repute of none. And it would absolve the Clan Donald from its undertaking in this Irish adventure, with . . . with whoever they made the compact!'

Donald Gorm had been eyeing the girl keenly. 'A treaty!' he said slowly. He inclined his dark head. 'There, perhaps, is the first sense spoken this day!'

'I sign no treaty with rebels!' Sir Christopher announced, flatly.

As Angus of Dunyveg, blazing-eyed, began to make hot reply, Ludovick held up his hand.

'These are subjects of the King of Scots, sir – so how can they be rebels to you! As the King's Lieutenant, *I* shall decide who is rebel and who is not! Moreover, there is no need for you to sign anything, Sir Christopher. As senior here, Admiral of Scotland, in alliance with your Queen, I only sign.'

'As well, my lord! For I will not! Here is weakness and non-

243

sense, also, by God's death!'

'And yet, sir, I think were my father here, this is what he would counsel,' Mary put in, quietly.

That produced a sudden silence, as men considered its implications according to their knowledge – as was the intention.

The young woman went on, looking at Donald Gorm now. 'He is not here – but his emissary is, his associate. Logan. Logan of Restalrig. He is here. Ask him.'

The dark man stared. 'Logan! Logan of Restalrig! Here? On this ship ... ?'

'Yes.'

The other swung on Ludovick, on Sir Christopher. 'Is this true? A prisoner ... ?'

'It is true. But no prisoner,' St. Lawrence said. 'He led us here. He it was who informed us of your coming ...'

'*Diabhol*! Here is treachery, then!' Donald Gorm actually took a step backwards, as though nearer to his own ship. 'We have been betrayed.'

No one spoke.

'This man – Logan. Fetch him here. To me.' the Mac-Donald chief commanded, tight-voiced.

Sir Christopher looked him up and down. 'No!' he said bluntly.

'Sir – I insist!'

'On my ship, MacDonald, only I may insist! Mark it!'

As angry Highland hands slipped down to broadsword hilts, Ludovick intervened. 'Gentlemen – such talk aids nothing! Whatever Logan may have done, and wherefore, alters nothing of the situation. This treaty – is it agreed?'

Donald Gorm searched Lennox's face with those intensely alive dark eyes, and then nodded. 'Very well. Be it so. But a few words will suffice, whatever. That all go whence they came, with full honour. If honour is a word that may be used towards those who deal in treachery!'

Ludovick nodded, ignoring that last sentence. 'Sir Christopher – paper and pens, if you please ...'

A single sentence was all the wording necessary for the body of their compact, all perceiving that the fewer words the better. The title however was more difficult, and seemed to be the most important part as far as Donald Gorm was concerned. He declared that the word treaty must be used – obviously the term assuaged his wounded pride somewhat, that he should be making a treaty with the King of Scots and Queen of England. As, of course, Mary had intended that it should. He wished also that the term 'Donald of the Isles' be used; but this Ludovick could not agree to, since it implied that he was indeed Lord of the Isles, a title now incorporated in the Crown of Scotland. A compromise, again suggested by the young woman, of 'Donald, of the Confederation of the Isles' was eventually accepted. Under that heading and the single sentence that followed, Donald and Ludovick signed side by side, with Sir Lachlan adding his name just below.

With a stiff bow to Lennox, an inclination of his head to Maclean and an eye-meeting lingering glance, even the glimmered beginnings of a smile, to Mary Gray, Donald Gorm of Sleat turned about, ignoring Sir Christopher altogether.

In silence they watched him and his companions return to their own ship.

It took some time for that eddying confusion of vessels to disentangle, but at length the watchers saw the Clan Donald armada pull away north-westwards, to join up with its birlinns and transports to the west of Rathlin Island. Maclean's fleet drew off a little way to the east, only Sir Lachlan's own galley remaining close to the galleon.

Ludovick turned to St. Lawrence. 'We now may go our several ways, I think, Sir Christopher. Your duty is done. There will be no invasion of Ireland. The Islesmen are gone.'

'They may turn back.'

'No. They will not do that, I warrant. Donald Gorm will not go back on his word. Besides, he conceives himself to have been betrayed. By those he compacted with. He will return to his own Skye, now.'

'My galleys will shadow him all the way, to see that he goes,' Maclean added grimly.

'Before we leave, however, I would have word with Robert Logan,' Ludovick added.

The Englishman looked doubtful. 'To what purpose my lord?'

'For my own purposes, sir! Must I, the Admiral of Scotland,

explain my purposes to *you*? Logan is a Scots subject – and an outlawed one! Bring him to me.'

Shrugging, St. Lawrence left them.

'What can you do?' Mary asked, low-voiced. 'He will not give up Logan to you.'

'I do not want him. But I can at least confront the fellow. Question him . . .'

'To what end? We know who gives Logan his orders. None of all this is of his conceiving, I am sure.' She glanced at Maclean, who was hailing someone on his own galley. 'Talk with him here, before others, will serve us nothing. It could be dangerous. Be content, Vicky. We have spoked Patrick's wheel, and saved the MacDonalds. Avoided bloodshed. It is enough, is it not?'

It had to be. When at length Sir Christopher returned, it was to announce that Logan was nowhere to be found. At Ludovick's protest, blandly the Englishman suggested that he must have slipped away into one of the Scots galleys. Three, after all, had been alongside his ship.

There was clearly no answer to this. Lennox had to seem to accept it.

Their leave-taking of St. Lawrence was formal, less than cordial. His young men were clearly much disappointed in Mary Gray. As a parting thrust, he requested that his respects be paid to the Master of Gray – and to Logan of Restalrig when they found him.

Back in Maclean's galley, Sir Lachlan considered his two passengers quizzically. 'Whose day was this, think you?' he wondered.

Ludovick rubbed his chin. 'I do not know,' he admitted.

'*I* know,' Mary said quietly. 'It was Scotland's day. Whoever lost or failed or gave way, Scotland gained. No one of the King's subjects has died, I think. The realm's honour is saved, and the Protestant faith suffered no hurt. It might have been much otherwise. King James should rejoice.'

'Should, perhaps – but will he?' Sombrely the Duke turned to gaze away eastwards, towards Scotland.

'It must be our task to make him see it,' she answered. 'We can do it, I believe – with the help of Sir Lachlan Maclean and my lord of Argyll.

Chapter Fifteen

Wonderingly, Mary and Ludovick looked around them at the narrow crowded streets of Stirling town, as they rode behind Sir George Home and a detachment of the Royal Guard. No one was either jeering or cheering, but the citizenry was obviously out in force, and showing a lively interest in their passage. Young Home was being fairly affable, but that might be only sympathy – although, as one of the most insufferable of the King's youthful favourites, sympathy was not much in his line. The Provost of the burgh had met them at the Drip Gate – a highly unusual circumstance. Was all this to confirm their fears or relieve them?

Home had arrived at Methven Castle at midday, with the royal summons – and the travellers had only reached that pleasant sanctuary, from the Isles, the day before. They had assessed this as ominous indeed, for the King was not usually so well served as to information, and they took it to mean that Patrick Gray was behind it, had been watching and waiting for them, and that this demand of their immediate presence at Stirling was his doing rather than James's. Moreover Home had been commanded to bring them both, Mary as well as the Duke, which struck her as alarming. A royal command they could not disobey, but they had ridden the score or so of miles to Stirling in some trepidation. This was not the way that they had planned to make their return to Court – indeed, Mary had intended to stay at Methven and avoid the Court altogether if she could, save for a quiet and unannounced visit to the Gray house in Broadgait, to collect young Johnnie and have a word with the Lady Marie. The inevitable interview with her father, thereafter, could as well be held at Methven as anywhere else, private as it must be.

Outriders of the Guard had hurried ahead, and at the great gatehouse of the fortress on its rock they were met by no less a person than the Earl of Mar himself, Keeper of Stirling Castle. He was barely civil – but then, that was quite normal with Mar, and he and Ludovick had never loved each other. They were to be conducted into the presence of the King forthwith, was all that he told them, and curtly.

He led them to the Lesser Hall of Audience, the second greatest chamber of the castle, whence came the sound of music. Mar told them to wait at the door, and himself went within. In the few moments which they had before he re-appeared, they spoke to each other low-voiced.

'This is no ordinary summons,' Ludovick murmured. 'James himself is in this. It is not all Patrick's doing. I fear he must be very wrath. Our letters cannot have moved him.'

Lennox had written lengthy letters to the King, in advance of his return, sent by swift couriers, one from Duart Castle and one from Inveraray, whence they had sailed on with Argyll on their long road to the south. These had informed James of what had happened – or at least, some of it – and made clear the gain to Scotland's cause and reputation of the confrontation off Ireland. They had prevailed on Sir Lachlan and Argyll to write also, separately, claiming the entire affair as a victory for the King and for the Protestant religion. The Master of Gray's name had not been mentioned in any letter, although his daughter's hand had inevitably featured fairly prominently.

'It is my fault,' the girl said. 'The King will not lightly forgive me for deserting Prince Henry, and for leaving his Court secretly . . .'

'No, no – that is nothing,' the Duke shook his head. 'A mere peccadillo compared with what he will hold against me! I have left the North-East without his knowledge. Taken liberties with his name and authority. Conducted a campaign in the Isles without reference to him or the Council. Aye, and annulled Maclean's forfeiture. But – it was necessary, God knows . . . !'

Mar threw open the door in front of them. 'Come,' he said.

The music had died away. In silence they followed the Earl into the crowded hall, and up between the long tables towards the raised dais at the further end. Never had either of them felt such culprits, somehow. Scotland's Lord High Admiral certainly was sensible of nothing of the confidence which surely ought to go with that high office that May afternoon.

At the dais-table, King James was dressed with great elaboration and deplorable taste. On his immediate right was a stranger, a courtly-looking individual with peculiar hooded eyes, richly but discreetly clad. On his left sat, surprisingly, the Earl of Argyll, who could have returned to Castle Campbell only the day before. And next to the Earl sat the Master of Gray, at his most dazzling. The Queen was not present.

James, sprawling forward over the table, high hat somewhat askew on his oversized head, watched the couple's approach intently, plucking at his lower lip. Patrick was smiling brilliantly.

The King waited until the newcomers were close, bowing and curtsying at the other side of the table, before he spoke.

'Aye, Vicky,' he said thickly. 'My lord Duke. I rejoice to see you. And you Mistress Mary. Welcome back to my Court, after your much journeyings and labours.'

Bowing again they waited warily.

'We have awaited your comings with interest. Aye, with interest,' the monarch went on, as though reciting a rehearsed piece. 'It has been long since we have seen you. Long.' He nodded portentously.

'Yes, Sire.'

'You have been right active. Both o' you. We havena failed to note what you were at, Vicky.'

'My royal mistress also has not failed to take note, my lord Duke,' the dark stranger at the King's side put in.

'Ooh, aye. Vicky – here's the new English envoy. Sir George Nicolson. New up frae London. We are dining in his honour, see you.'

'I vow it should be in the Duke's honour rather, Your Grace. And . . . this lady's,' the Englishman asserted. He actually rose, and bowed to Mary.

'Aye, to be sure. I'ph'mmm. But bide your time, man! We are coming to that.' James coughed. 'Vicky. Mistress Mary. It is our pleasure, our royal pleasure and desire, to express our thanks. And gratitude. To you both. Aye, both. For your services to the realm. In this business o' the Isles. And the Irish. It was well done. As our Lieutenant. Wi' the help of my lord of Argyll. And yon man Maclean. Aye, it was well done. We heard tell you were wounded, Vicky? In battle . . . ?'

'It was nothing, Sire. No more than a scratched shoulder . . .'

'Hail the Duke of Lennox! And Mary Gray!' Patrick's voice rang out.

Cheers arose from all over the hall.

Ludovick and the girl exchanged glances.

The King tut-tutted, indicating that there were limits beyond which, in the royal presence, acclaim became unseemly. 'Aye, well,' he said, tapping the table. 'Because of the service you have done the realm, we are disposed to overlook, aye, overlook certain . . . certain matters. Irregularities – certain irregularities. You'll both ken what I mean?'

'I thank Your Grace,' Ludovick replied. He took a deep breath. 'But I would point out, with your royal permission, on behalf of the Lady Mary as well as myself, that these irregularities as you name them, were entirely necessary. Otherwise we could not have done what had to be done.'

'Aye, some o' them, no doubt. Vicky – some o' them. But we'll no' pick that bone the now! Come you and sit in – both o' you. I'd hear your tale. My lord o' Argyll here has told me some o' it. And we had your letters. But, waesucks – Elizabeth o' England seems to ken mair than me about it!' And he frowned in the direction of Sir George Nicolson.

Places were made for them at the dais-table, one on either side of Argyll, the Duke next to the King and Mary next to her father.

Patrick kissed her warmly. 'My dear,' he said, 'how good to see you again. And how beautiful you are! To be good, beautiful and clever, is given to few of us!'

She found herself scarcely able to answer him, trembling with a strange emotion, torn between revulsion and fascination, shrinking and affection. She muttered something, staring down at the table.

'I vow I must needs be proud of my daughter,' he went on. 'Since it is undoubtedly your guiding hand that is to be seen behind all. This was far beyond our Vicky. I, h'm recognise the Gray touch, my dear!'

'So, to my sorrow, did I!' she got out.

He ignored that. 'Did you enjoy your first visit to the Hebrides? I understand the prospects there to be magnificent, in a barbarous way. Myself, I have never been further west than Dumbarton. The people, I believe, are quite extraordinary. Little better than savages. You were, I think, over-rash to venture amongst them, Mary.'

She glanced to her right. Argyll was involved in the King's converse with Ludovick. On Patrick's other side, his father-in-law, the Earl of Orkney, was fully occupied with and all but fondling a handsome lady whom Mary did not know.

'They are far from savages,' she said, her voice low but tense. 'I would that you *had* travelled in the Isles, and learned to know them. Then, perhaps, you might not have sought to throw thousands to their deaths, for a whim, for one of your wicked plots!'

He blinked. 'Plots? Save us, girl – what's this now? Thousands to their deaths? Have you taken leave of your wits again?'

Wearily she shook her head. 'Spare me, and yourself, the denials, Patrick,' she urged. 'We know each other too well. I have traced your hand in this all the way. None other, indeed, could have conceived it all! Think you that Robert Logan could have thought of it himself? Such double betrayal!'

'*I* am not Logan's keeper!' he said, shrugging. 'If you think to see me behind him in this business, you mistake, I assure you. Even you, Mary, bewitched as you are bewitching, can trace no possible link, I swear! It is all in your head, child.'

'You forget Sir Christopher St. Lawrence, Patrick, I think!'

She heard his quick intake of breath. 'He admires you greatly,' she went on, almost in a whisper now. 'He esteems you one of his Queen's best friends! He sent his respects and grateful thanks. He did not know, of course, that the gold you paid Donald Gorm and Clanranald was Elizabeth's. English!'

She saw his knuckles gleaming white as his fists clenched there on the table, and for a little he did not speak. But when he did, his words were calm, controlled, reasonable.

'It is a great sorrow to me, my dear, that you are forever discovering evil, plotting, treasons, behind all that I do – and more that I do *not* do! It has become something of an obsession with you, I fear. It cannot but poison the well of our mutual fondness, unfortunately – and I am very fond of you, Mary, as you know full well. A pity, too, to spoil this happy occasion.

This welcome back to the Court...'

'Yes, Patrick,' she interrupted. 'Why did you do it? Plan this welcome for us? It is your doing, I know well. The King would never have done it, to be sure. He is none so pleased with us. He has not forgiven either of us, that is clear. You arranged this, convinced the King to do it did you not? Why? When we have spoiled your plot...'

'You have spoiled nothing of mine, girl. Save, with your accusations, the pleasure of this day. Can you not cred't me with a father's affection and regard?'

'In some matters, yes. But not this. You did not move the King against his will, and swallow a rebuff to your plans, out of fatherly regard and affection! Even for me, Patrick! I think that you must be afraid. Afraid that we are in a position to hurt your schemes further, perhaps? To talk. Is that it, Patrick? You would keep us quiet, lest we tell King James what we know? Or the Kirk? Or even Queen Elizabeth, through her envoy?'

'A pox, Mary – what next? This is beyond all! You but dream, child. For I tell you that you know nothing, in this. Nothing which could injure me with the King. Or the Kirk. Or Elizabeth. You only guess, conjecture, surmise. And make nonsense! You can show nothing of proof, establish nothing. Think you that any would believe your insubstantial phantasies against the word of the Master of Gray?'

'Yet you did send word to Elizabeth that the MacDonalds were moving to aid Tyrone. That can be proved.'

'To be sure I did. When Logan sent *me* word of it, my duty was clear. Such folly would have greatly damaged the King's good name in Elizabeth's eyes. So I sent her warning. It was necessary. I am thankful that I was in time.'

She gazed at him, speechless now. He was armoured, impregnable, with an answer to everything. Suddenly she was very tired. She shook her head, and the faintest droop might have been discerned in her shoulders.

He smiled, as suddenly, warmly. 'Poor Mary! Dear Mary! As I said, you are good and beautiful and clever. But I fear that you lack just a little in judgement! A small matter, that years will no doubt mend. Experience, my poppet.' He actually patted her arm. 'In time, sweeting, that will come. Meantime, however, it would be less unnatural, would it not, if you sharpened your pearly teeth on other than your sire! And, probably, more successful!' Sighing humorously he leaned back a little in his chair. 'Ah, me – little of reward I get for all my efforts on your behalf over those bairns! The devil of a task I had with our peculiar monarch over that puny princeling of his – especially with the bawling brat turned up in my own nest, as it were! I tell you, there had to be plotting and scheming then, if you like! To soothe the King, to find a new governess for the child, to win back my own wife to my bed! Heigho – you set this Court by the ears then, Mary Gray! As well, I think, that you had me for a father!'

She considered him, for her, almost helplessly. 'Does nothing reach you, Patrick – reach past that clever, mocking head of yours into your heart?' she demanded. 'No prick of conscience, ever? How it can live with your head, in one body . . . !'

When he only smiled for answer, she sighed, and went on, level voiced. 'How is Johnnie? Marie would see to him well, I know.'

'Your Johnnie thrives. He laughes and eats and laughs and sleeps and laughs. A true philosopher, and excellent company. He seems to have much of his grandsire in him! He and I esteem each other highly.'

She bit her lip. 'Where is he? Here, in the Mar Tower still? With the Prince Henry?'

'Ah, no. He is with us in our house in the town. We had to stay in the castle until new arrangements could be made for the ever-wailing prince, since the King would by no means hear of him being taken out. You may be sure that I wasted no time in relieving Marie of that infant's burden, for I mislike being shut into this place, and I find Mar's close company insupportable. Lady Mar is now the child's governess – and she is welcome to him.'

'Poor sad bairn! You would think that he had no mother! Will not the King relent? Allow the Queen to have her son?'

'Not James! He believes that she would but use the child against him. Hand him over to some faction seeking power. As indeed she might for Her vixenish Grace becomes ever more concerned with power, and meddling in affairs of state.'

'She but turns to that, no doubt, lacking her child. Could you not mend this matter, Patrick? Since you now control most other matters of the realm. It should not be beyond your powers? Although perhaps you do not wish it mended – since I think it is your aim to keep King and Queen separated? That you may wield more power, playing one against the other, as you play Catholic and Protestant, Kirk and Council, noble against noble.'

'Ha – more phantasies, girl!'

'Are they? Who was it held that to divide is to govern? Davy Gray says that it has been *your* guiding principle always. And I believe him. You are a notable divider Patrick! You cannot deny it.'

'Davy was ever prejudiced. Full of honest worth, but lacking judgment. A common complaint! You both mistake. My aim is not to divide but to balance. It is not the dividing that governs, it is the holding of the balance. Only so may a weak king and a torn realm be governed – by holding a delicate balance. No light task, I may say. Someone must hold it if Scotland is to survive.'

'Ever it comes to that – the excuse for all! For that, you would do anything...'

She stopped, as along the table King James beat on the wood with an empty goblet, for silence.

'My lords,' he called out. 'Hear me. I have now listened to more o' this matter. From the Duke. This o' the Islesmen and the Irish. It was a notable ploy – aye, notable. Acting as our Lieutenant, the Duke has achieved much. In conjunction with the ships o' our good sister Elizabeth o' England, the forces o' rebellion have been vanquished. Or, leastways, dispersed. Aye, dispersed. A right happy eventuality. Mind, I'll no' say it wouldna have been better if he had informed us o' what was to do. It would have been more seemly...'

Patrick Gray cleared his throat with some vigour.

'Aye. Umm.' James glanced along the table at the Master, his great expressive spaniel's eyes rolling. 'That is so. In consequence o' all this, it behoves us to look with increased favour on our good cousin o' Lennox, young as he is. Aye, young. Anything that has been amiss, we can justly blame on his youth, I say – for mind, he's no' yet of full age.' James paused, as though

254

to let that fact sink in. 'So, my lords, it is now our pleasure to show our thanks to the Duke by more than words, just. In token o' his services to this realm, I now release him frae his duties as Lieutenant o' the North. The which will revert to my lord o' Argyll here. Instead, I appoint him to be Governor and Keeper of my royal fortress o' Dumbarton Castle – as was his father before him. Also President o' my Privy Council.'

He paused, and there was some polite applause, while James wiped his ever-wet lips with the sleeve of his doublet. For his part, Ludovick looked doubtfully along at the Master of Gray and Mary. That man smiled and nodded in genial congratulation.

James resumed. 'Further, it is our royal will and pleasure to advance our good cousin Ludovick, Duke o' Lennox, in other fashion likewise. Aye, as is suitable and seemly. That he may more meetly carry out the duties o' Lord President and High Admiral o' this realm. I therefore – he being no' yet o' full age, o' the royal house – do hereby bestow on him in matrimony the hand o' the Lady Jean Campbell, relict o' the umquhile Master o' Eglinton and daughter o' the umquhile Sir Matthew Campbell o' Loudoun, one o' the greatest heiresses in this my realm!' And the King leaned forward to leer along the table at the lady who sat at the other side of his uncle the Earl of Orkney.

The great room seemed positively to surge with the sensation. Seldom indeed could a royal pronouncement have produced such startled effect. Everywhere, despite etiquette, voices were raised in astonished and excited comment and exclamation. The piquancy and drama of the situation required no explaining to even the least informed.

Mary Gray had listened to the King as though in a dream, a nightmare. Scarcely able to grasp the reality of it, she crouched there dazed, a pulse beating in her head.

Ludovick had half-risen from his seat, fists clenched, wild of eye, the picture of angry protest, seeking for words.

James flapped him down, imperiously. 'Sit, man – sit!' he ordered. 'I'm no' done yet. Wheesht, you!' He raised his voice. 'It is my will and command that this marriage shall take place without delay. In the shortest possible time. Aye. In my royal presence and at my charges. And now – Lady Jean!'

'Sire!' Ludovick cried. 'This is not possible! Hear me . . .'

'Quiet, I say! It is more than possible, Vicky – it is my royal command. And here's the lady . . .'

The Master of Gray had risen, and slipped round to aid the Lady Jean from her seat. He now brought her along behind the chairs, to the King. She curtsied low to James, murmuring something – but her glance was on the Duke of Lennox.

Jean Campbell was a tall, well-built young woman, just a little less than strapping, with a proud carriage, strong and striking features, a wide sensual mouth and a firm chin. Six or seven years older than Ludovick, she was obviously nobody's fool – and by no means young for her years. Magnificently gowned, comporting herself with a nice mixture of assurance and modesty, despite the distinctly awkward position into which she was thrust, she looked what she was, a woman of experience, strong character and hot appetite. Beside her Ludovick Stewart seemed almost younger than his score of years.

Desperately the young man looked from her to the King, along to Mary, and back again.

'Houts, man – where's your manners?' James demanded, ponderously playful, poling the Duke in the ribs. 'Have you no civilities to show the lassie?'

Ludovick got to his feet, and bowed briefly, curtly.

'My lord Duke,' the young woman said, smiling faintly. 'Yours to command!'

He stared at her, shaking his head and biting his lip. Then he swung on the King again. 'Sire – your permission to retire, I pray. With . . . with this lady. There is much to say, to discuss. Not meet to do before all these . . .'

'Na, na, Vicky – no' so fast! Be no' so hot, man!' James chuckled now. 'A fast change, hey? One look at the lass and he's for off wi' her, for privy chambering! Na, na – sit you, man. And you, Lady Jean. See – the Master's brought a chair for you. We're no' done yet. Later. Aye, later, you'll get to be alone wi' her. Ooh, aye – plenty time for that! Meantime there's the matter o' my lord o' Argyll, who also deserves well o' us. And the reversal o' forfeiture on Sir Lachlan Maclean to pronounce . . .'

Quietly, Mary Gray rose from her seat, and without seeking

the royal permission or saying a word to anyone, head down, moved swiftly over to a side door behind the dais-table. If the King saw her, he made no comment. A guard at the door opened it for her, and she slipped out.

Hitching up her skirts and almost running, the girl hurried out into the great paved Upper Square of the castle, and down the steps cut in the living rock, past the Chapel-Royal and the Inner Barbican to the cobbled ramp which led down to the great gatehouse. Men-at-arms, palace officials and servitors looked at her in surprise, but she scarcely saw them, saw anything, in her anguish of mind. The guards at the gatehouse knew her well, of course, and let her through. Her feet drumming on the drawbridge timbers, she ran out, and down the open marshalling-ground towards the town, a slender figure of distress.

Up the stairs of the tall narrow Gray lodging in the Broadgait she stumbled. The door was not shut this fine May evening. Within the Lady Marie was aiding a tire-woman to settle young Johnnie in his cot beside that of her own baby daughter. Into the older woman's arms Mary flung herself, panting, sobbing as though her heart would break.

Never before had Marie seen the girl lose control of herself, her normal quiet serenity and innate composure shattered. She held her close, stroking her dark hair, soothing her with gentle crooning words, like one of the children, while at the same time she gestured for the maid-servant to leave them alone.

'Oh, Marie! Marie! I have lost him! Vicky,' she gasped brokenly. 'They have taken him from me. I have lost Vicky, Marie!'

'No, no, my dear. Not lost him. Not Vicky. I am sure not. Hush, my love, my sweeting. Hush you.'

'I have! I have! He is to be married. The King said so. In front of all. To the Mistress of Eglinton. Forthwith. A royal command. I have to leave him. Leave Methven. Oh, Marie ... !' That ended in a wail.

'My precious Mary!' The other almost rocked her in her arms. 'This is a wicked thing. Shameful. But ... do not despair, my dear. It may not be quite so ill as you fear ...'

Mary broke away from her. She darted to the cot, and snatched up her little son, to cover his smiling round face with salt kisses, and then to clutch him to her fiercely, possessively. Over his small head she stared at the other.

'This is Patrick's work!' she cried, almost accusingly.

The Lady Marie shook a sorrowful head, but did not answer.

'It is! I know it. His revenge for us having interfered in his wicked plot. The King would never have thought of it. He has agreed to it because of that folly of the Queen. When he accused Vicky of being her lover. But he would never have thought of this. It is Patrick – the thinking of it and the way it was done, there before all the Court! Where we could do nothing – Vicky could do nothing. It . . . it *stinks* of Patrick! Can you deny it?'

She did not give her friend opportunity to deny or admit it. 'This is Patrick's love for me!' she exclaimed, chokingly. 'He brought us here – for this! He has ever sought to come between Vicky and me. He does not love me – he hates me!'

'Ah, no, Mary – not that! Patrick does love you – that I swear. Whatever else, that is sure. This may be his doing indeed – though I have known naught of it. But even so, he loves you . . .'

Mary was not listening. She paced the floor, hugging and kissing her child. 'Johnnie! Johnnie dear!' she gulped, thickly. 'My bonnie baby, my own darling! What are we to do? Oh, what are we to do? Your father – they have taken your father from us!'

Marie Stewart watched her, her grey eyes sombre, hurt in all her lovely features. This abandon was so unlike Mary Gray as to be alarming in itself, over and above the grim circumstances which produced it. But presently to hurt was added firm decision. She moved over to the younger woman and put an arm around her, propelling her quite strongly to a chair by the smouldering log fire.

'Come, now – sit Mary. Calm yourself, my dear. You must, and you can – for you have the strongest will I know. Stronger even than Patrick's, I do believe! Yes it is. This is not like Mary Gray! You must be yourself. I shall fetch you a posset. As I did last time that you were here. You remember? Then you were anxious, fearful, also – but strong. Fighting. The Mary I know. As you must be again, my sweet. For Johnnie's sake. For

Vicky's sake. Even for *my* sake – for we have a compact, you and I, have we not? That we shall fight and counter, where we may, the evil Patrick does. That we must still do. Only we can do it – his wife and his daughter!'

Her words, and the firm level tone in which they were spoken, affected the younger woman, calming and at the same time challenging her. Gradually she relaxed.

'See – I shall make the posset here beside you,' Marie went on. 'Tell me it all . . .'

Ludovick Stewart shut the door of the ante-room, and turned, leaning his back against it. They were alone, at last. Heavily he gazed at the young woman.

The Lady Jean spoke first. 'Well, my lord Duke – do I so repel you? Am I so ill-favoured, so repugnant, that you must needs treat me like one of the Furies?'

He moistened his lips. 'I am sorry. It is not you. Not you yourself . . .'

'But it is, my lord. Me. Me that it seems you have to marry! Aye – and you that *I* must! Which is a minor matter perhaps – but of some small consequence to me!'

'Then fear no more, ma'am, for I shall not wed you. Nor you me! We shall not quarrel over that!'

She looked him up and down frankly, assessingly. 'I did not esteem you a fool, my lord,' she said. 'Nor am I, I'd have you know. I know that we must wed – as do you. Since it is a royal command. I am a ward of the Crown, and you are under full age. We cannot shut our eyes to it. We have no choice in the matter. For me, I may say, if I *had* my choice, it would be . . . otherwise.'

Ludovick started to stride about the little room. 'Royal command!' he repeated, almost snorting. 'What is a royal command but the mere spoken word of my havering, spineless cousin James Stewart! It is not the voice of God Almighty! What he has said he can unsay. Many's the time I have heard him do so.'

'Perhaps, my lord. You know the King better than do I, no doubt. But he will not unsay this command, I think, given before all the Court and the ambassadors of other princes. How could he, without losing all respect? Moreover, what would the

Master of Gray say?'

'Aye – the Master of Gray! Little need to question whose hand is behind James in this! Curse him!'

'Hush, my lord! That is a dangerous thing to say in Scotland today, is it not? Besides, the Master is something of a friend of mine!'

He paused in his pacing, to stare at her, narrow-eyed. 'Ha! Is that so, indeed?'

She nodded. 'As you are of his, he assures me.'

'Then he is a liar, ma'am – amongst other things!'

She shook her head at him. 'It seems that I am to have a rash husband indeed! And, my lord, since we are fated to be bed-mates, must you be ever calling me ma'am? As though I was your mother! I am older than you, yes – but even so I am no more than twenty-six years. Even though I have a daughter of five.'

'You have a daughter . . . ?'

'Yes. Does that offend you?'

'No. No – but . . .' Ludovick, with an effort, took a grip on himself. 'Lady Jean,' he said, 'listen to me. I do not wish to hurt you, God knows – but while you may accept this marriage, I cannot! It could never be aught but a travesty, a hollow pretence. I am already married, in all but the name. To Mary Gray. I love her. We look on each other as husband and wife. We have a child, a son.'

'All this I know,' she said, quietly now. 'I am sorry also. But . . . it alters nothing. You are not married to Mary Gray. And if you were, the King would have it annulled. Your child by her cannot heir your dukedom. We might have a son who could.'

'Damn the dukedom! It is Mary Gray that I want. And our son Johnnie. Not to provide heir to the dukedom . . .'

'But you can have both, my lord. Why all the pother?' She shrugged strong shoulders at him. 'Think you I care about your mistress? Many husbands have mistresses. I shall not keep you from your Mary Gray.'

He came up to her, frowning. 'You say that? What is there in this marriage to advantage you?' he demanded. 'Why do you seek it, woman?'

'I do not seek it. Indeed, I would have chosen very differently, had it been possible. But I have learned – as should you, my lord – that where circumstances may not be mended they are best accepted with a fair grace. I was not asked if I would wed the Duke of Lennox – I was told that I must. So I make the best of it.'

Despite himself, Ludovick rose to that. 'So you do find some merit in me as husband?'

'Oh, yes. I have seen worse-made men! And clearly you *are* a man, and no painted boy, like so many around the King. That I could scarce have stomached! Then, I shall be a duchess – the only such in this land. That will not be without its advantages, I think. I shall be able to queen it over many proud countesses who now look down their noses at me – including my haughty good-sister the Countess of Eglinton, who hates me. A prospect no woman would despise! I suppose that I might even be the Queen, one day – although that might be a better dream than a reality! All that – and I might think of more. For instance, having a husband who would not be like to watch me with too doting and jealous an eye . . . !'

'Sink me – you are frank, at least!'

'Yes, sir – as I hold that you should be also. In our state there is virtue in frankness, is there not? For yourself the marriage will not lack advantage. A wife who will make no great demands upon you. The use of great wealth . . .'

'I do not want your money, woman!'

'So you say now, my lord. But perhaps, when it is there to your hand, you may find otherwise. Moreover, I am a Campbell, and to be allied to that clan might serve a man very well – even a duke! Where broadswords are needed.'

'You need not think to buy me with fighting-men, either . . .'

'I do not seek to buy you. We are sold already, both of us! I but look for what gain there is for us in it.'

'But . . . God's mercy! You may accept all this as sure, settled – but I do not. *I* am no ward of the King. I shall be of age in September. Four months, no more! Thereafter none can force me to anything.'

'Which is no doubt why His Grace hastens the wedding! The more proof that he is determined in this.'

'If I was to bolt. To go away. Where James could not reach

me. Back to the Isles, perhaps. Before any wedding. Until September. Then I could not be forced. James would be angry – but could do nothing . . . '

'Think you that this has not been thought of?' she interrupted. 'They have been preparing this for weeks, see you, awaiting your return. I cannot think that you will be allowed to leave the walls of this Stirling Castle until you are safely wed, my Lord Ludovick!'

'You mean . . . ?' Almost he made for the door, there and then, but restrained himself. 'You think that I am a prisoner, then – to crown all?' he cried.

'If I was the King, you would be.'

'But – this is monstrous! Beyond all bearing. And you?'

'I also, I have little doubt.'

He strode to the door now, and threw it open. In the stone corridor outside no fewer than five guards stood about, armed, alert. They eyed him stolidly.

'Take me to the King,' Ludovick barked, with all the authority he could muster. 'I would have word with him.'

'His Grace has retired for the night, my lord Duke,' one of them answered. 'He gave orders that he was not to be disturbed.'

'This is important. Business of state.'

Nobody spoke, or moved.

'The Master of Gray, then. Bring me here the Master of Gray.'

'He has left the castle, my lord.'

Ludovick bit back a curse.

'If your lordship wishes, I will conduct you to your room,' the young officer went on, stiffly.

'No – I am not staying at the castle.'

'On His Grace's express command, my lord, you are! A room is prepared for you.'

'And for me?' Jean Campbell asked, at the Duke's back.

'Yes, ma'am. Your rooms are . . . together. In the Albany Tower.'

'How . . . thoughtful!' the young woman murmured.

'If you will follow me, my lord Duke . . .'

Patrick Gray strolled into his modest house in the Broadgait, humming tunefully to himself. At sight of the two women sitting by the fire, his face lit up with pleasure.

'So you have the runaway, Marie my dear!' he said. 'I thought that she might possibly be here, come to see young Johnnie and yourself.' He came over, to pat Mary's hunched shoulder. 'The trouble this young woman is to me!' he sighed, but humorously. 'Do you know what she did, Marie? She up and left the royal table without permission! Without so much as a nod at His Grace! Our liege lord, when he discovered, was like a clucking hen . . .'

'Patrick!' his wife interrupted. 'Spare Mary this, for a mercy! She is sore-hearted and in no mood for your witticisms. Nor, indeed, am I!'

'Nor was His Grace, if you will believe me! But let it pass. Mary is sad? I feared she would be. Indeed, it could scarce be otherwise. But it will pass, my dear – it will pass. This marriage of Vicky's was bound to come. The Dukedom of Lennox must have a legitimate heir.'

'Patrick – will you stop it!' his wife exclaimed. 'Have you no heart?'

'Heart, my love? Need *you* ask that . . . ?'

'Where is Vicky?' Mary asked levelly, without intonation.

'He is still at the castle. There is much for him to see to.'

'He sent me no message?'

'Not by me, my dear. Would he know that you were here?'

'He would know where I would come.' She raised her head to eye him directly. 'Is he held? In the castle?'

'Hardly held, lass. He will be stopping there meantime, I should think . . .'

'Yes. I should think so also! You will not let him leave, I warrant! In case you do not see him again until he is of full age! It is only till September. Why will you not be honest with me, Patrick? If, indeed, honesty is something of which you are capable!'

'Mary, my child – you are distrait, downcast. Do not take it so hard. You must have known that Vicky would marry again. He was married before, to Sophia Ruthven, poor creature . . .'

'That you arranged also. That, as well as separate us, you

263

might lay hands on her great wealth. How much will you gain from the Mistress of Eglinton?'

'God save us, girl – what do you take me for?'

'For what I have long known you to be, in my heart – the greatest rogue in this realm! Caring not who you hurt, or how many, so long as you gain your own selfish wicked will!'

The Lady Marie bit her lip, but said nothing.

'You, h'm, exaggerate, my sweeting!'

'Do I? Is it possible? To exaggerate? About the man who got my mother with child – and then left her for Davy Gray to take the blame, care for and marry? The man who betrayed Mary the Queen to her death? The man who brought down Vicky's father, his friend? Who betrayed the Earls of Moray, Arran, Bothwell, Huntly and God only knows how many more? Aye, who would have sold Vicky, on false charges to Queen Elizabeth, had I not halted it! And who now has betrayed the whole Clan Donald? Do I exaggerate, Patrick? Is there indeed anyone who you have *not* betrayed? Or would not . . . ?'

He did not answer her, did not speak. White to the lips, teeth clenched, he swung on his heel and strode for the door, without a glance at either of them, out of the room and out of the house. They heard the click-click of his high-heeled shoes as he ran down the outer stairs to the street, and then silence.

After a few moments staring after him, Mary turned to look at the Lady Marie. At the stricken face she saw there across the hearth from her, she gulped and sprang from her seat.

'Oh, Marie! Marie!' she cried, hurling herself over the intervening space, to sink on her knees beside the older woman and clutch her convulsively. 'What have I done? I am sorry! Sorry! I have hurt you. Oh, fool that I am – I have hurt *you*! Forgive me, Marie! Can you forgive me? You, in all the world, I would not wish to hurt.'

'There is nothing to forgive, my dear – nothing,' the other said, stroking the girl's dark hair. 'It was all true, I have no doubt. But . . . did you have to say it all!'

'No,' Mary whispered. 'No, I did not! It was ill done. But then, I am Patrick's daughter you see! Of the same black blood!' Abruptly she got to her feet. 'I must go, now,' she said.

'Go? What do you mean, Mary? Go – at this time of night?'

'I must go away. From this house. I cannot stay here. This is his house, Patrick's house. I cannot remain in it, after what I have said. Or my son. And what he has done. You must see it, Marie.'

'It is my home too, Mary.'

'Yes. All the more reason why I must go. I come between you and your husband.'

'No. You are wrong. But – where can you go? Back to the castle?'

'No – I cannot go there. Not now. They would not allow me to be with Vicky, I know. And they might take Johnnie from me. As they took Henry from *his* mother!'

'It is too late for you to ride back to Methven tonight . . .'

'Not too late, no. I care not where I ride, by night or day. But I cannot go to Methven either. It is not for me, now . . .'

'Do not be too proud, my dear. It is your home.'

'No. Not now. It is where Vicky must take his wife. My home is with Davy Gray and my mother, at Castle Huntly. There I will go.'

'But, child – you cannot go all that way tonight!'

'Not now, no. Tonight I know where I shall go. Where I went last time that I was here. When I left Johnnie with you. I shall go to Castle Campbell, at Dollar. My lord of Argyll will take me in. Archibald Campbell and I understand each other, I think. That is where I shall go. If you will lend me a horse again, Marie? And a plaid to wrap Johnnie in. Please, Marie. My mind is made up . . .'

And so, a couple of hours later, in the grey half-light of a northern May midnight, Archibald Grumach Campbell was awakened, with the somewhat startling information that a young woman and her baby had come to Castle Campbell, seeking shelter and his charity. She had sought only some corner, and would not have his lordship disturbed – but since she was, it seemed, the Mistress Mary Gray, daughter of the Master, the gatehouse porter reckoned that he should be told.

Pulling on a bed-robe, the young Earl hurried below. He did not have much to say to his untimely guest, but as he conducted her up the winding stone turnpike stair, calling to sleepy servants for food, wine, firing and the like, he held her hand in his.

Chapter Sixteen

The wedding was celebrated in the Chapel-Royal of the castle, by Master David Lindsay, the King's chaplain, before a select but highly interested, not to say intrigued, congregation. If it seemed a very rushed affair, everyone recognised the reasons therefore, many comments being made that they were at least not the usual ones for hurried marriages.

Ludovick made a sullen and unco-operative bridegroom, refusing even to dress at his best. He had not been allowed to leave Stirling Castle in the eight days which had elapsed since his arrival there, and had been forced to perceive that he had no option but to submit, with whatever ill grace. Obviously he would be married even though he had to be brought in chains to the ceremony. The King's decision was law, and there was nothing that a minor could do to invalidate it short of putting himself physically beyond the hands of the authorities.

He had ample time and opportunity, at any rate, to consider the situation, in the fretting confinement of those late May days. At first he had been puzzled to understand James's determination in the matter. Patrick's motives were clear – revenge for interference in his affairs, and to separate Ludovick and Mary; also, almost certainly to gain control of some part of the bride's wealth. But, although vengeance and gain to some extent might also influence the offended monarch, more than that was surely involved. He had had only the one interview with the King in the interim, and that not alone; but he had talked with various others. He had come to the conclusion that James's urgency to have him married was largely on account of the Queen. James actually believed Ludovick to be a menace to him, not only in the Queen's affections, but that, unwed, he was in a position to marry her if James himself was removed, and so to control the child Henry or even make himself the King. So he was to be wed, and not to any great lord's daughter who might conceivably push him towards the throne, but to the heiress of a simple knight, however influential. That the King could be so mistaken in the assessment of the situation would have been laughable had it not been tragic – but no doubt Patrick Gray had carefully nurtured these delusions.

As a consequence, the Queen had been brought to the wedding, and the duchess-to-be was already appointed to be her principal lady-in-waiting, that the lesson be well and truly rubbed in.

The days of waiting had at least somewhat improved the Duke's opinion of his unwanted bride. Inevitably he saw a lot of her, for their apartments were side-by-side and they had to share a single public room. This could have been quite intolerable, for Ludovick at least, with most women; but Jean Campbell was understanding, tactful after a forthright fashion, and cheerful without being aggressively so. Her philosophical treatment of the whole affair was entirely practical, even humorously resigned. Since there seemed to be no way out of their entanglement, he might have had a much worse partner in it.

She at any rate had dressed for the occasion, and was now looking very fine in richly jewelled brocade. Since it was a second marriage for both of them, the dispensing with many of the frills and extras was entirely seemly. It gave the greater opportunity, however, for Master Lindsay to preach a really notable sermon, on the sins, follies, and temptations of those in high places, the dangers of wealth and the pitfalls of pride – more than making up for any brevity in the actual ceremony. As an exhortation to those about to enter upon holy matrimony, it was salutory.

James himself gave the bride away, and the Master of Gray acted groomsman – as was suitable for one who had brought the boy from France to Scotland ten years before. He it was who produced the ring as required, and, when Ludovick himself showed no interest in it, placed it on the lady's finger for him. If the Master did not actually say the responses it was not because the groom did so himself; they were taken as said. Ludovick and Jean were duly pronounced man and wife, in the sight of God and according to rites of the Kirk and the law of Scotland.

The reception thereafter was a brilliant affair such as Patrick delighted to organise, with a wealth of pageantry, masque and allegory – to be paid for, no doubt from the lady's deep purse. James had written a poem for the occasion, mercifully brief.

Ludovick came face to face with the Queen for the first time in many months. She eyed him searchingly and then beckoned him close, conspiratorily.

'I know that this is none of your doing, Vicky,' she declared in a penetrating whisper which neither the King nor the Lady Jean nearby could fail to hear. 'You are leal and true to me, without a doubt. Believe me that I trust you.'

Embarrassed, Ludovick coughed. 'Your Grace – I, ah . . . I am ever your servant, of course, I, h'm, rejoice to see you.'

'I understand, Vicky.' She pressed his arm. 'We shall speak together on another occasion. Not now.'

James looked at them sourly, but said nothing.

Patrick strolled up, and having skilfully involved both King and Queen with the new English envoy on the ever-burning question of Elizabeth's non-payment of James's pension, drew Jean Campbell over to Ludovick's side.

'A word in your pretty ear, Duchess,' he said – the first to accord her her new title. 'And yours, Vicky. You will be glad, I vow, that having both of you been wed before, you can be spared the unseemly business of the public bedding – a mercy indeed! Nevertheless, I hear that there is a move afoot to escort you presently to your bridal chamber. I thought that perhaps I should warn you.'

Ludovick snorted. He could scarcely bear the close proximity of the Master, and had to hold himself from abruptly turning his back on the man. He would have preferred to ignore any remark he made – but this information penetrated his hostility.

'A plague on them!' he exclaimed, hotly. 'Let them but try!'

'I think, nevertheless, we ought not to have a scene,' his bride said, sensibly. 'That would be unsuitable.'

Patrick nodded. 'I thought you might wish to slip away quietly. Not perhaps to the Albany Tower. Away from Stirling altogether. It is too late for Methven tonight, but perhaps . . .'

'We do not go to Methven tonight or any night,' the Duke snapped.

'No?' Patrick raised his brows.

'No. Mary is at Methven.' That was flat.

'Ah. H'mm. Well no, Vicky – she is not, I fear. She is . . . otherwhere.'

'Eh? Where is she? Do not say . . . do not tell me that she is taken also! That you have held Mary as you have held me here?' Blazing-eyed he swung on the other man.

'Tut, man – do not be so plaguey hot! *I* have not held you, anywhere! And Mary certainly is not held. She has, er, gone where she will.'

'Where?'

'I am reliably informed, Vicky, that, curiously enough, she went to Castle Campbell. To our young friend Argyll. The very night you parted. I take it that she established some sort of association with him on your, h'm, travels!'

'I do not like the way you said that,' Ludovick jerked.

'Dear me – do you not? I assumed, since she went to him, that they must have become friends. Forgive me if I mistake!'

'If Argyll took Mary to Castle Campbell, it would be to shelter and protect her. We became friends, yes. In the Isles.'

'Ah, yes. Quite. Only, Argyll did not take her. Mary went there by herself. Late that night. Leaving my house to do so, where she was surely sufficiently sheltered and protected!'

'Ah! Then, Patrick, I commend her choice!'

'Indeed. I wonder at that. But perhaps, as a married man now, you see matters differently! At any rate, there is nothing to prevent you and Jean going to Methven now.'

'But there is. Methven Castle is no longer mine. It is Mary's home. More than that, it is made over altogether, by charter, to our son John Stewart of Methven, in her care. I do not take this lady there!'

Patrick stared. 'You mean . . . ? That you *meant* that nonsense? About putting the barony in the name of the child? You have left yourself without a house!'

'*I* do not do all with intent to deceive!' the younger man retorted. 'I provided for Mary and the child – as was my least duty. Would you have me to other – to your daughter?'

'Then . . . you have nowhere to go now? Nowhere to take your wife, man!'

'Should that concern *me*?' Ludovick smiled, albeit mirthlessly. 'Though to be sure, have I not Dumbarton Castle now? From my generous liege lord. There will be a house there, I've no doubt – and myself the new Governor!'

The Lady Jean intervened. 'Why all this talk of houses to go to? I have houses and lands a-plenty. And if you do not wish to live in Cunningham or Kyle, we can buy a house near to Stirling.'

'Aye. Are you not fortunate in your wife, Vicky? But, to-night? Where will you go?'

'I am content with His Grace's provision,' the Duke said. 'We both are well enough suited. In the Albany Tower. Would you have us spurn the royal hospitality? We shall continue to enjoy it.'

As Patrick, looking from one to the other, was about to speak, the young woman caught his eye.

'We shall do very well there, meantime,' she said, nodding. 'Do not concern yourself further, sir. If you can but aid us out of this hall unnoticed, we shall be in your debt . . .'

And so, presently, in the confusion attendant upon the exit of a troupe of tumblers and acrobats and the setting up of a tableau representing the Marriage at Cana of Galilee, with water being poured in at one end of a barrel and red wine being tapped off at the other, the bridal couple managed to make their discreet departure. They crossed the crowded Upper Square, where servants, men-at-arms and performers were at their own noisy merry-making under the May night sky, to the Albany Tower that had been their prison. Their eyes met as Ludovick opened the door for his Duchess to enter.

Upstairs, at first floor level, was the large public room which they had used in common that past week. Ludovick paused at the door there, but the young woman continued on up the winding turnpike stairway. When she perceived that he did not follow her up, she turned and looked back.

'Which chamber do we use, Ludovick?' she asked. 'Yours or mine?' That was calmly, factually put.

Much less calmly, he cleared his throat. 'Which? Why, both. I assumed that we would be using both. As we did before . . .'

'But we are not as before, Ludovick. We are now man and wife.'

'In name, yes. But . . .'

'In fact. We are as truly wed as any man and woman in the land. And will remain so. There is little sense in shutting our eyes to it.'

'There is more in marriage, woman, than a few mumbled words in a kirk!'

'True. That is why I ask – which chamber!'

He frowned, tapping a toe on the stone landing. 'Mistress . . . Jean I prefer to bed alone! If you please.'

She looked down at him thoughtfully. 'What you mean, I think, is that you would prefer to bed with your mistress. With Mary Gray.'

His head jerked up, at that. 'Very well. Put it so, if you will. I would prefer to bed with Mary Gray!'

She nodded. 'That I well believe and understand. And, as I said, I shall not keep you from seeking to do so again. But this day you married me, Jean Campbell. I am your lawful wife, the Duchess of Lennox, and this is our bridal night. Do I have to demand my rights, Ludovick?'

When he did not answer, she went on. 'I am not hot for you – think it not, my lord Duke! I too would prefer to be . . . elsewhere! In a certain small castle in Kyle. But I am in Sterling Castle, not Kyle – just as Mary Gray is not here, but apparently in some other man's house. We have to take life as it is, Ludovick – not as we would wish it. Be we dukes and duchesses, or lesser folk. We are wed, the two of us, and must accept it.'

'You are a great accepter!' he charged her.

'I have been well trained in it! You, it seems, have not. Facts, even hard facts, are best accepted – and can be made thereby the softer, I have found.'

'So you have said before. You are welcome to your convictions – but mine are otherwise!'

'You would deny facts? Deny that we are man and wife . . . ?'

'I deny nothing – save that it is any duty of mine to go to bed with you this night!'

'No? But suppose the boot had been on the other leg, sir? How then? How many women are left in no doubt that it *is* their duty, God ordained, to lie with their husbands, this first night, or any night, of their marriage? Still – let that be. Did you marry me with the intent that we should never bed together?'

Biting his lip, he kicked at one of the stone steps. 'H'mm. I . . . ah . . . no. Not so. But that is . . . well, it is for the future. Not tonight. Tonight it is different. Too soon . . .'

'Is that a man speaking? Or a mouse?' she exclaimed. Then the young woman quickly changed her tone, coming indeed a couple of steps down the stair. 'See, Ludovick – it is better thus. Tonight. We are not children. We know that in matters of this sort there can easily be difficulties, barriers, stumbling-blocks. Put off, delay or shy at it, and it becomes the more difficult, the harder to come together . . .'

'God be good, woman – you make it sound as though we were horses to be broken to bit and bridle! Of a mercy, spare me more of this!'

'Very well,' she said, shrugging. 'Lord – what have I married? My late lord, to whom I was wed at fourteen, was a stallion! Now, I am tied to a gelded palfrey!'

Flushing hotly, Ludovick flung into the room in front of him, and slammed the door shut.

For a considerable time he paced up and down there, scarcely aware of what he did. Young, vigorous and far from undersexed, the woman's strictures hit him hard. What right had she to speak so to him? Right or reason? Excuse? It was beyond all bearing that, just because, for their own unholy purposes, the King and Patrick had forced this match upon him, he should be faced with this ridiculous quandary. The fact that, from one point of view, Jean had the rights of it, made it the more damnable. What was a man to do, in the circumstances? The situation would not get better, as she said. Was he fated to battling with her on this of all subjects . . . ?

Ludovick found a flagon of wine, and drank deeply.

He waited for quite some time longer before leaving the room and going upstairs. He did not slam the door behind him on this occasion; indeed he all but tip-toed up the steps.

Ignoring the part-opened door of the young woman's room, he went into his own chamber – to find Jean Campbell sitting up in his great four-poster bed, a robe around her shoulders. The light from the small window at that hour was not good, and she had a single candle burning nearby. She smiled at him, but said nothing.

He halted uncertainly, perplexed. 'I . . . I do not congratulate you!' he got out, at length.

'No? Is it part of a husband's duty at such a time? I shall survive the lack, I think! You have been long in coming, Ludovick.'

He did not answer that, but moved over to the bed, to stand nearby looking down at her. The robe she had only loosely thrown about her, and it was clear that she wore nothing beneath.

'Why do you do this?' he asked. 'You say that you are not hot for me. Would you have me believe that?'

She shrugged, and one white shoulder slipped out from the robe. 'Believe it or not, as you like. It is both true and untrue, I think. I am not hot for *you*, Ludovick Stewart, in especial. But I am a woman not unappreciative of men – and I have been widowed over long! Moreover, this is my wedding-night. Does that answer serve you, my lord?'

'Aye,' he said, on an exhalation of breath. 'You are frank now, by the Powers! I vow I prefer it to all the talk before. Of what is best for me, the duties of marriage and the like.'

'I thought that you might,' she allowed, low-voiced but smiling again. She beckoned him closer. 'Come!' she said.

He ignored her invitation. 'That does not change matters,' he asserted heavily.

'No? Why do you look at me so, then? Your eyes betray you, my lord Duke! I think that you are a man, after all!'

'A man can have more attributes than the one,' he got out, from lips that were somehow awkward, mumbling, reluctant. 'A man is will, as well as body. Loyal. Able to keep himself . . .'

'Yet you vowed, a few hours ago, before all men, to keep *me*! Must I trade words with you? Bicker and argue? Here and now, at this pass? What ails you, Ludovick? Am I so ill-favoured? Others have not esteemed me so, I tell you! But, Lord – enough of words!'

With a toss of her head she threw off the robe and kicked

273

back the bed-clothes, to sit there naked before him, in invitation and challenge both.

She was very desirable. A big woman in every way, generously made, she was none the less rousing on that account, although she lacked, for instance, Mary Gray's perfection of proportion and subtler loveliness. There was indeed nothing of subtlety about Jean Campbell's great thrusting breasts, strong arms, rounded belly and massive thighs. But she was all woman nevertheless, urgent, essential, demanding.

Ludovick all but choked at what he saw and sensed, and despite himself took that final pace forward which brought him to the side of the great bed. As he did so, the girl reached out to grasp his arm, to pull him bodily down on top of her.

Once his hands were on her robust and vehement flesh, there was of course no further holding back. In a mounting, ungovernable surge of fierce, dominant desire, he took possession of her with a masterful passion which no other woman had ever roused in him.

Sobbing, Jean abandoned herself.

When the storm was past and they lay spent, relaxed, she was the first to speak.

'I shall not call you mouse again! Or gelding!' she murmured, idly combing a slack hand through his hair. 'Not that I ever truly thought you such. Or even King James could not have forced me into this marriage.'

He grunted. 'It was all lies, then? All your talk.'

'No. Not lies. I meant what I said. That it is best this way. Best for us both. Since it must come to this, better sooner than later.'

'It came to this – because you made it so!' he said, shaking his head free of her hand.

'Ha! Who is now the liar?' she demanded. 'Your eyes, your hands, your body, all your manhood belies your words, Ludovick. You wanted me, whatever you said. Do you think a woman does not know? Aye – and now you keep your eyes shut lest they, and all the rest, do so again! As will be so. You know, and I know. You fight the wrong enemies, husband! Open your eyes, Ludovick Stewart. And unclench your fists. Why waste your fine strength? I can use it . . . !'

Chapter Seventeen

Mary Gray, in the act of setting and pressing the oat-sheaf firmly against its neighbours to complete the stook, raised her head to glance ruefully over to where young Johnnie Stewart, on plump but unsteady legs, was doing his tottering best to pull apart the last stook that she had built. The smile died on her lips, however, as her eyes lifted, to narrow against the golden blaze of the declining September sun, westwards towards the frowning red stone castle which towered half a mile away on its rock above the wide levels of the Carse of Gowrie.

'Company, Father, I think,' she called. 'Armour glinting. My lord does not ride at such speed these days ...'

Davy Gray straightened up from the back-breaking task of gathering the cut swathes of oats into great armfuls, and binding these together with a twisted rope of their own long stalks. He followed her gaze.

'Gilbert, it may be, from Mylnhill? Or William from Bandirran? To demand that my lord's steward does this or that for them! To borrow men or beasts. But neither of them, you may be sure, to set dainty hand to my lord's corn!'

The girl smiled, but said nothing. David Gray's scorn for his younger legitimate half-brothers was best treated as a joke.

She made a delightful, vital and lightsome picture, standing there in the harvest-field, all glowing health and essential femininity, flushed with her exertions, browned by the sun, her bare arms powdered by the oat-dust, flecks of chaff and straw caught in her dark hair. Dressed with utter simplicity in a brief white bodice which clung lovingly to her young rounded excellence of figure, skirt kilted up to the knees, with legs and indeed feet bare, she had never looked more enticing – and never less like a lady of the Court.

David Gray considered her fondly – as he had been doing off and on as he worked, for he found it hard indeed to keep his eyes off her. She loved the satisfying and fundamental work

275

of the harvest-field, as he did, and they were seldom happier than when they were so employed together. The past summer months had been happy ones for the man – and, he thought, after the first weeks, to some extent for the girl also; peaceful, uncomplicated, undemanding. She had slipped back into the old life of Castle Huntly, after the years of absence, as though she had never been away – save that now she had her little Johnnie with her. And Castle Huntly had been the sweeter for her return, the old lord more bearable to live with – for Mary had always been the apple of that irascible tyrant's eye – and her mother Mariota rejoicing to have her back and almost like a girl again, for there were only the fifteen years between their ages.

'Two riders only,' she reported. 'And in a hurry. I hope they do not bring ill-tidings . . .' She stopped, stiffening in her posture. 'Dear God,' she whispered, 'I think . . . I think I know . . .' She bit her red lip.

Quickly he looked at her, and back to the advancing horse-men. 'Aye,' he nodded, frowning. 'He it is, I think.' Heavily he said it. 'Och, lassie . . . !'

One rider came spurring ahead, his magnificent horse lathered with hard riding – Ludovick Stewart.

He was off his mount and running to her before ever the brute had halted. Stumbling amongst the swathes of cut corn in his tall heavy riding-boots, he flung his arms around her and swept her up bodily off her feet.

'Oh, my dear! My little love! My heart's darling!' he panted, the words tumbling incoherently from lips that sought hers. 'Mary, my own, my precious . . . !'

She clung to him, returning kisses almost as fierce and vehe-ment as his own, trembling in his arms.

Nearby Davy Gray moved slowly over to take the unsteady toddler's hand, and to watch them sombre-eyed.

When eventually Ludovick set her down, the girl's lashes were gleaming wet with tears. She tried to speak, but could not against the spate of his endearments and emotional release. She could only smile and shake her head helplessly.

At last he paused for very breath, but even so Mary could find no words to express the chaos of her feelings. It was David

Gray indeed who spoke, and brought her back to realities.

'My lord Duke,' he said, levelly. 'I am glad to see you well. And honoured, of course, by your presence But is your coming here wise, seemly or proper?'

Ludovick looked at him over Mary's head. 'I think so,' he said. 'I believe so.'

'Yes, Vicky,' the young woman cried, although she still clung to him. 'Why did you come? Oh, why did you come?'

'It was necessary. I had to come, my dear. And ... 'fore God – I should have come long ago!'

'No! No!' she said. 'You know that is not so. You have had my letters...'

'Letters!' he exclaimed. 'Aye, I've had your letters, Mary. Letters that have had me near to weeping! Oh, they were kind, and I cherished them. But what are letters compared with your own self? In especial, when they tell me to keep away from you!'

'The letters spoke truth, nevertheless, Vicky. Oh, you must know it, my dear? You should not have come.'

'I came for good reason. Although I yearned to see you, Mary, I would not have come. Not now. But for my lord of Gray. Your grandfather, I came to see him. But he is not at the castle. They told me that you were here, in the fields...'

'What of my lord?' David asked sharply. 'Why should he bring you to Castle Huntly?'

'This morning, sir, at Falkland, I saw an edict of the Privy Council, signed by the King. It ordered the arrest of Patrick, Lord Gray, on pain of treason. On a charge of rebellion. The said arrest to be executed forthwith. By the Sheriff of Forfar!'

'Rebellion...!'

'Arrest? Granlord? Oh no, Vicky – no!'

'Yes. Arrest, in the King's name. I thought it right to come in haste. To warn him.'

'But, dear God – Granlord has not rebelled! He has done nothing against the King. What folly is this...?'

'I do not know. I would not have thought my lord to be engaged in anything smacking of treason or revolt. I believed him to have taken no part in affairs of the realm for many years. The warrant but charges rebellion. Anstruther, Clerk to the Council, showed it to me – for I, for my sins, am now Lord President thereof. No details are set forth. I made excuse to James that urgent matters called me to my Priory property at St. Andrews, and came forthwith.'

Mary swung on the older man. 'Granlord has not been doing aught? In plotting or the like? You would know, Father, if he had? It is not true, is it?'

David Gray stroked his pronounced clean-shaven chin. 'Not rebellion. Against the King. Of that I am sure,' he answered slowly. 'But . . . he has been seeing a deal of certain ministers of the Kirk, of late. In Dundee and St. Andrews. Always he was of the Kirk party, of course, though taking no great part in its affairs. But of late he has talked much of the Kirk. I took it to be but an old man's concern for his latter end! But, who knows? He has twice seen Master Andrew Melville at St. Andrews. And Master James, his nephew, was here but two weeks since.'

'But there is nothing of rebellion in that!'

'No. But a clever man might make it seem so, in certain circumstances, to the King, perhaps.' He paused. 'I note that the Sheriff of Forfar is named in this!'

Mary drew a long breath, but said nothing.

Ludovick nodded. 'That is why I came hot-foot!'

'No – he would not do that!' the girl cried. 'Even Patrick would not act so to his own father!'

'He did not hesitate to betray his own daughter!' the Duke said heavily. 'Why should he balk at his father? They do not love each other, Mary. He ousted my lord from the sheriffship, did he not?'

'I cannot believe it, Vicky . . .'

'Whether this is Patrick's doing, or other's, *we* must do more than talk about it,' David jerked. 'You thought, my lord Duke, that there was need of haste?'

'The thing was secret, and had been hurried before two or three members of the Council – all creatures of Patrick's, as it happens. He rules Scotland now, does the Master of the Wardrobe, openly – the more so since Maitland is dead. So that, when he acts secretly, as here, I believe he will act the more swiftly . . .'

'Maitland dead? The Chancellor . . .'

'Had you not heard? He died at Thirlestane two weeks ago. Loudly repenting of his sins, I'm told! And there is to be no new Chancellor. Patrick has convinced James to rule without one. Which means, in truth, to rule through the Master of Gray. James has written a poem declaring this, indeed. An epitaph. He read it out to the Council, choking with laughter. A welter of words, but saying that he was resolved to use no more great figures or chancellors in his affairs, but only such as he might chide or hang.'

'You do not think, then, that Patrick himself covets the Chancellorship?' Mary asked. 'He acted Chancellor before.'

'No, no. He is far too cunning for that. The Chancellor is responsible. He can be called to account. He must bear the burden of his policies. Patrick prefers the power without the responsibility. He moves from behind, not in front...'

'Aye,' David interrupted. 'See you – I think I know where I may find my lord. If I may take your horse, my lord Duke, I shall ride fast. To warn him. You and Mary have matters to discuss, I have no doubt.' He handed the bronzed and chuckling little boy to his mother. 'I shall see you at the castle later – if your lordship has not already gone!'

Ludovick looked after the strong and effective figure of the land-steward as he vaulted into the saddle, supple as any youth, and wheeled the beast round, to spur away westwards.

'He does not like me greatly, does Davy Gray!' he said, shaking his head.

'No, no – he esteems you very well, at heart, Vicky,' the girl asserted. 'It is but your position that troubles him. Always it has been that. That you are a great lord, a duke. He cannot see that our . . . our closeness can bring us anything but pain and sorrow.' She controlled the quiver in her voice. 'As seems may indeed be true!'

He shook his head strongly. 'No – it is *not* true! We have had great happiness together, Mary – and will have again. I know it. Swear it. And, look – this young man here is the sign and surety of it! Johnnie is the token of our closeness, Mary – and has not brought us pain and sorrow. Has he?' Ludovick took the child from her. 'Save us – how he has grown! Eh, my fine warrior? You are a son to be proud of, John Stewart of Methven!'

The young woman looked from the face of the man to that of the child, so close, and back again. She sighed, wordless.

Signing to the man-at-arms to ride on ahead, Ludovick settled his son firmly on his right arm and shoulder, and taking Mary's elbow in his other hand began to walk her towards the distant castle. They went slowly across the golden rustling stubbles, bare-footed and heavy-booted.

'Vicky,' Mary said, 'If Granlord is taken and warded, how could this serve Patrick?'

'I do not know,' he admitted. 'I thought that you might. You it is that has the sharp wits. That best perceives his schemes. And what is behind them. Could it not be just spleen? Revenge? They have been long at odds.' He spoke stiffly, stiltedly, well aware that his talk would not long postpone what had to be said otherwise.

'Patrick does not act for spleen and spite,' she answered. 'He always has reasons for what he does . . .'

'*You* can say that? After how he spited us? *There* was spleen enough, I say!'

'I do not believe that he did it just to spite us, Vicky, nevertheless. He was determined to part us, yes – but not out of mere spleen, I think. Oh, I believed so at the first, and was bitter, bitter. But I have thought much on this, and now . . .'

'Mary! Do not tell me that he was worked on *you*! Changed you? Turned you against me? Is that what your letters meant? Keeping me away. Mary – say that it is not true . . . !' He had stopped walking, to stare at her.

'Or course it is not true, Vicky! How could you think it? Be so foolish? Dear heart – you are my very life! How could I turn against you . . . ?'

'Yet you have kept me away, Mary. All these months. Would not have me here now . . . ?'

'Only because I must, Vicky. Surely you must see it? You are married, now. You have a wife. A duchess. All is changed.'

'A duchess, may be! But a wife? You call this marriage, Mary? Two people forced at the King's command to go through the marriage ceremony! Is that being wed? Does that make us man and wife, in truth?'

'I fear it does, Vicky. Certainly in the eyes of men. Perhaps in God's eyes also – since you took the vows in His house . . .'

'I took no vows! I did not open my lips in yonder Chapel-Royal! I was there only because I was forced to be there. And for no other reason.'

'But you live with her, as man and wife, do you not? You . . . you have bedded with her, Vicky?'

He swallowed. 'Ay, I have. I have, Mary – God forgive me! I tell you . . .'

'I do not think that you need God's forgiveness for bedding with your wedded wife.'

'I do, Mary – I do! I did not mean to. I suppose that I am weak, weak. It was not my wish. At least . . .' He hesitated, frowning blackly. 'How can I make you understand? It is difficult, when two people share the same house, the same rooms . . .'

'I do understand. It is . . . as it must be, had to be. But, surely, you must see that all is changed? For us, Vicky. I cannot . . .' Her voice shook a little. 'I cannot *share* you with your duchess!'

Ludovick rubbed his chin on his small son's curly head, eyeing the young woman sidelong. 'It is only you that I want, Mary. Only and always you. It is you alone in my heart.'

'Your heart, yes – but not in your bed!'

He shook his head. 'Then . . . then I must deny Jean Campbell my bed, also. It will be difficult – but I must do it. If you will but come back to me, Mary . . .'

'No, no! That is not possible. Do you not understand, Vicky? I cannot, I will not, dispossess your lawful wife. It would be most wrong, sinful, shameful. It is not to be thought of.'

He wrinkled his brows in some bewilderment. 'But, Mary!' he protested. 'I do not understand. These years we have been together, you would not marry me, often as I pleaded. You said that the marriage would be broken by the King and Council, and that you were content to be called my mistress. You have been named Lennox's courtesan – and cared nothing. Yet now, mistress in name, you will not be mistress in fact! There is no sense in it . . .'

'No doubt you are right, Vicky, I am foolish, wilful. But that is how I feel. I am sorry . . .'

He gripped her arm tighter than he knew. 'See you – do you not remember that day at Hailes Castle in Lothian, Bothwell's house? Three years ago. The morning after you had forced Patrick to flee Scotland. Have you forgotten what you said to me then? You said that you had made your choice, and that your eyes were open at last. You said that I was to take you away, away to Methven. To be with me, you and me together. You said that you would not marry me – for they would part us if we wed. You said that you would cleave to me always, bear my children – but as mistress, not wife. Aye – and do you remember what else you said? You said I was to help you not to be jealous! Have you forgotten that?'

Silent, she hung her head.

'You said that you would try not to be jealous when I had to marry again. You said I would assuredly have to marry. Some lady of high degree. To produce an heir for the dukedom. You said that she must have her rights. But that you might be weak, and jealous, and I must help you then. But that you would cleave to me always. That was our compact, Mary, was it not?'

She put her hand in his, nodding. 'I said it all, Vicky,' she admitted. 'I remember.'

'But now . . . ? Now that it has come to the test, you say differently?'

Again she nodded.

'Mary – I have never known you like this! To go back on your word ...'

'I said that I might be weak. I . . . I am weaker than I thought, I fear.'

'No! Always you were the strong one. Stronger in will than anyone I know. Much stronger than I am. For you to act so is not just weakness. It must mean that you have changed. Changed towards me! Have you changed, girl! Do you no longer love me?'

'I love you, yes, Vicky. More, I think, than ever. I believe that I always shall. But . . . I find that I cannot do what I thought to do. To share you. To have only a part of you. To take what your duchess leaves. Oh, I know it is wrong of me, wicked – just sinful pride. But I *am* proud – shamefully proud. I have tried and tried to fight it. But I cannot. Not now, Vicky. Perhaps . . . . perhaps later. Give me time. Please try to understand, to bear with me.'

When it was the man's turn to be silent, she clutched his arm urgently. 'Vicky – feelings are not things which we may command – deep feelings. Even if I was to come back to you, to live with you again, it could not be the same. There would be a barrier between us. No doubt it is different for men. But for me, I could not forget the other woman.'

'Then . . . Patrick has won? He has parted us, possibly for ever!'

'No! Not that. Do not say it, Vicky. In our love he cannot part us. It is only in this of living together. Give me time. It may be that, in time, it will be different . . .'

Unhappily they walked side by side for a while, nearing the tall, arrogant castle. At length Ludovick spoke.

'At least, Mary,' he pleaded, 'go back to Methven. Live there. It is your home, now . . .'

'How can you say that? It *was* our home. But all is changed there also. It is your house, and therefore your wife's . . .'

'No. Nothing is changed at Methven. It is not my house. You'll mind well that I settled it on this child. John Stewart of Methven. His it is. He should be living in it. With you. For in settling it on him, it was to *you* I gave Methven in truth. Until Johnnie is of age, Methven is yours.'

'You are kind, Vicky – generous. But . . .'

'Here is no generosity. It is but what we planned. For Johnnie. Because you have changed, and let pride rule you, will you deny the boy his rights? Here he is but a child born in bastardy. At Methven he is laird of a great estate. If you cannot think for me, Mary, think for Johnnie.'

'All that is but ink and parchment. His lairdship is only in name . . .'

'Not so. It is fact. All is his. All rents and revenues are paid in his name. The moneys wait and grow for him. I have touched nothing of them since . . . since we parted.'

'But . . . your wife? What of the Duchess Jean, Vicky? How can she be dispossessed by her husband's bastard?'

'Jean is not concerned in it. She knows that Methven is Johnnie's, not mine. She has never been there, nor will I ever take her. I have bought another house, in Monteith. There we are living. Methven Castle has stood empty all these sad months.'

283

'It has? Empty? You have never gone there?'

'*I* have, yes. To look to affairs. That all should be ordered aright for you and Johnnie. But only that. I have never spent a night under its roof. Nor shall, until you are there with me.'

Helplessly she spread her hands. 'There it is, Vicky! Do you not see? Until I am there with you, you say. If I go to Methven, with Johnnie, I could not keep you out, even if I would. And if we are living together in the same house, then . . . oh, you must see what would happen!'

'I see that we might yet find some peace and happiness together.'

The girl sighed, looking up at the castle towering above them, the living rock and then seven storeys of red masonry seeming to grow out of it.

'Let us talk no more of it now, Vicky,' she said, almost pleaded. 'I am sorry . . . but you must give me time . . .'

Before ever they had climbed to the level of the courtyard, they heard the stamping of horses' hooves and the raised voices of many men. Apparently the Lord Gray had returned. Involuntarily they both quickened their pace.

More than this they heard, as they crossed the flagged court within the curtain walling, where the score or so of men-at-arms of my lord's bodyguard were wiping down and unsaddling their sweating horses; out from the doorway of the great central keep of the castle, an angry voice was declaiming loudly, harshly. The young people exchanged glances, and Mary reached over to take the child from Ludovick.

They found Patrick Gray senior stamping up and down the great hall of Castle Huntly in a fury, bellowing like a bull; indeed he was bull-like in ever way, a massive, heavy man, gross of body and florid of feature. Although no more than in his late fifties, he looked much older, the marks of lifelong dissipation strong upon him; but though sagging jowls and great paunch spoke of indulgence and physical degeneration, there was no hint of weakness about the thrusting bullet head, the jutting jawline and the keen, shrewd, pig-like eyes. A more unlikely father for the exquisite and beautiful Master of Gray would have been hard to imagine.

He was shouting now at Davy Gray as he paced his hall,

every now and again emphasising his harangue by smashing down his great ham-like fist on the long central table as he passed it. The lofty stone-vaulted and otherwise empty chamber seemed to shake and quiver to his fury – yet the sole recipient of all this wrath and invective appeared to be by no means overwhelmed by it. The situation was far from unusual, of course, even though on this occasion the older man was more than normally roused. Davy Gray, the land-steward and schoolmaster, had since early youth been whipping-boy and butt for his potent father's lashing tongue – and despite his bastardy and employed position, refused to be daunted by it much more successfully than had any of his legitimate half-brothers. In fact, Lord Gray had long relied upon this early by-blow of his for the efficient running of his great estates and the management of his household. At heart, the arrogant lord knew well that though he was proud, this modest-seeming, self-contained offspring of his was prouder.

At sight of the newcomers, Gray paused only momentarily in both his pacing and his diatribe, to point a finger at them which trembled with ire, not weakness, and forthwith to launch into a vehement denunciation of the King, the Privy Council, the Court, and all connected with it – including, it seemed, the Duke of Lennox – as abject fools, weaklings, and knaves, at the beck and call of that epitome of all ill, iniquity, impiety and infamy, the son and heir whose name he seldom allowed to pass his thick lips. On and on he ranted, growing ever more purple in the face, until sheer lack of breath and evident dizziness forced him to pause and to put out his hand to the table, this time to support and steady himself rather than to pound and beat.

Mary it was who spoke into the quivering silence, gently. 'Granlord,' she said, 'you have cause to be angry, there is no doubt. It is wicked, shameful. But this is but a poor welcome to your house for my lord Duke, surely? Who has hastened here, at cost to himself, to warn you.'

It was only a mild rebuke, but no one else of my lord's household or family would have dared to administer it. Her grandfather glared at her, lips working, but no words coming. After a moment or two he transferred his glare to Ludovick, and that seemed to help.

'Young man . . . !' he got out, with something of a croak. 'Young man . . . !'

'My lord,' the Duke said, 'it is my sorrow to be the bearer of ill tidings. But I would not have you taken unawares.'

'Would you no'? That's kind, aye kind, my lord Duke! But I'm no' that easy taken, see you, awares or otherwise!'

'H'm. Nevertheless, sir, I would urge that you make haste to leave this house. To seek some secure hiding-place where they will not find you.'

'So I have been pressing,' Davy Gray declared. 'I say that he should be off without delay. Up into the hills. He would be safe up in Glen Isla or Glen Prosen. None could come at him there . . .'

'God's death, man – would you have me skulk and slink? Like some Hieland cateran! Me, Gray! On my own lands. And from one o' my own brood, base, unnatural hell-hound though he be! Enough o' such talk!'

'Granlord – you must heed us,' Mary pleaded. 'You are to be arrested. In the King's name. What for, I know not. But they will come here seeking you. Vicky thinks very soon. They must not find you here. For you cannot resist the King's officers . . .'

'Can I no'? Fiend seize me – I'll show them who rules in the Carse o' Gowrie! Think you that accursed scoundrel that Satan spawned on my wife will send me fleeing to the hills? Think you that the minions o' shaughling, idiot Jamie Stewart can lift Gray out o' Castle Huntly? Devil burn them – let them try!'

'But Granlord dear – do you not see . . .'

David Gray's voice, level, almost toneless, but somehow with a quiet vehemence and power that was fully as potent as his father's raging, overbore the girl's. 'My lord,' he said sternly, 'Hear me. Great swelling words will serve you nothing in this pass. You are accused of rebellion. The King and Privy Council have issued a commission against you. Whether on Patrick's prompting or otherwise. If you have not rebelled, little can be done against you. If you are from home, gone to travel your hill country properties, that cannot be held against you. But if you are here, and you resist those who come in the King's name – than that *is* rebellion. Worse – if you seek to hold this castle against the King, it is treason. No cursing will alter that. With your men-at-arms you may hold out against the King's forces for a time. But you cannot remain holed-up here for ever. When you do go forth, the King is still King. And you are in treason and rebellion undoubted.'

That was a long speech for the laconic David Gray, and it was some tribute to the unstressed force behind his words that his puissant sire for once heard him out without scornful interruption. From under heavy bull-like brows he glowered upon this bastard of his, chin outthrust, silent.

Mary, still holding her child in her arms, ran forward to grasp her grandfather's arm, his hand. 'Do listen,' she urged. 'Go while there is yet time. You should not have delayed thus long, Granlord. It is . . .'

Even as she spoke, all their eyes turned towards the windows of the hall which overlooked the courtyard, whence came a renewed noise of horses' hooves and shouting. Ludovick, nearest to one of the windows, was across to it in a few swift strides, to peer out and down.

'Too late!' he announced grimly. 'Here are the King's officers. It is young George Home again. And James Elphinstone. You have waited overlong, my lord!'

'Slay and burn them . . . !'

'No, no!' Mary cried. 'There is still time. You can still escape. By the privy stair. The wicket-gate. Down the cliff path . . .'

'Tut, lassie! Wheesht! Enough o' your womanish havers!' the old lord growled. 'Peace, for God's sake! Think you Gray is the man to scuttle from Gray's castle, like any rat? Before a wheen Court jackdaws! Foul fall them – if they come chapping at Gray's door, Gray they shall see!'

'No, Granlord! Oh, this is folly!'

'Out o' my way, girl!' Roughly her grandfather pushed her aside, and marched for the door with his limping stride.

Biting her lip, Mary turned to Ludovick, and thrust young Johnnie at him. 'Take him, Vicky. I must go after my lord. I must stop him, if I can. From worse . . .'

'I shall come also.'

'No. Not you. They must not see you here, Vicky. Or it will

be known. The King will hear. That you came to warn him . . .'

'I care not.'

'But *I* do. You must stay with Johnnie.'

She turned after Davy, who was following his father down the stairs to the courtyard door.

The emissaries from Falkland had dismounted, leaving perhaps a dozen armed men sitting their horses and looking doubtfully at four times their numbers of Gray's retainers who lounged about the cobbled yard. At sight of Lord Gray standing in the keep entrance, they quickened their pace, a slight sallow man of early middle years, and the over-dressed and somewhat effeminate-seeming George Home of Manderston, the King's favourite.

'My lord of Gray,' the latter said, inclining his fair head just sufficiently to indicate that he did not feel the need to bow. 'I am George Home, Groom of the Bedchamber to His Grace. And this is James Elphinstone of Invernochty. We require you to attend us, in the King's name. To the Castle of Broughty.'

Gray opened his mouth, and shut it again, his whole bulky person seeming to quiver with ill-suppressed rage. At his back Davy Gray stared stolidly.

Elphinstone spoke, less offensively. 'My lord, it is our misfortune to bear a Privy Council commission against you, signed by His Grace. It requires us to bring you before the Sheriff of Forfar, at Broughty Castle, forthwith.'

'Broughty . . . !' the older man burst out. 'My own house o' Broughty! God's eyes – jackanapes! Daws! Prinking ninnies! Dare you come here and name Broughty to *me*, Gray! Prate to me o' the Sheriff o' Forfar – who was Sheriff for twenty years! Burn your bones – is James Stewart gone clean mad, to send the likes o' you to Castle Huntly! If he esteems me so ill, of a sudden, at least he could have sent *men* to me!'

'Beware how you speak, my lord!' young Home cried, taking an involuntary step backwards at the virulence of the old lord's fury. 'We are the King's representatives . . .'

Elphinstone held out a folded paper with a red seal dangling therefrom. 'Here is our commission, sir. Charging you with rebellion. Read it, if you doubt our authority.' He stood well back from Gray, however, who would have had to step forward some paces to take the document.

'Keep your bit paper!' the older man snorted.

At his back, Davy spoke low-voiced. 'My lord – this will not help your case. Abusing these will hurt only yourself.'

'Quiet, you! If puppies and lickspittle upstarts think to require this and require that o' Gray, in the Carse o' Gowrie, in all Angus, by the foul fiend they'll learn differently!'

'Granlord!' Mary exclaimed desperately at his other elbow. 'Why . . . why do you play Patrick's game for him? Oh, should you not rather play your own?'

'Eh . . . ?' That reached him, piercing the armour of his prideful wrath, as she intended that it should. 'Patrick's game . . . ?'

'Yes. This is what he hoped for, no doubt. This charge of rebellion – it can be but a stratagem, a device. To rouse and anger you. But if you play his game, resist these officers from the King, refuse to go with them to Broughty – then he has made his false charge of rebellion come true. Do you not see it? You are rebelling *now* – which is what Patrick wants you to do!'

'A pox! Would you have me truckle to such as these? Painted bed-boys and up-jumped clerks? Go their meek prisoner to my own house o' Broughty . . . ?'

'Go to Broughty – yes. But not a meek prisoner. Go as Lord of Gray, on Gray land, to a Gray house. Go to face Patrick there – if that is where he is. You have your men-at-arms – more than these. Ride with them. So you do not disobey the King's command – but you show who is lord here in the Carse.'

He stared at her for a moment, and then slapped his great thigh and bellowed a hoot of laughter. 'Precious soul of God, girl – you have it! Aye, you have it. Mary, lass – you have a nimble wit for a woman, I swear! So be it. I ride to Broughty. And if these . . . these Court cuckoos choose to ride with me, let them! Aye – you hear that, witlings? I go see the Sheriff o' Forfar in my castle o' Broughty. You may ride with me, or no', as you choose. Davy – have my guard out again, every man o' them. Quickly. We'll go see the Master o' Gray – may he roast in hell eternally!'

Doubtfully David looked from his father to the perplexed envoys and then back to Mary. She nodded.

'And horses for us also,' she added quietly. 'This is a family matter, is it not?'

It was almost dark as they approached Broughty Craig, which thrust into the sea five miles beyond Dundee town, its castle glowing pale and gleaming with lights as it seemed to rise out of the very waters of the widening estuary of Tay. It had been a gloomy crumbling fortress of a place, semi-ruinous and bat-haunted on its little promontory, until a few years before, my lord in a savage gesture of finality had bestowed it upon his son and heir as his inheritance, his single and sole patrimony out of the vast Gray lands, this rickle of stones on a rock in the sea, with not an acre, a tree or a penny-piece else, as ultimate reckoning between them. Patrick had sworn then that he would make his father rue that day, that he would turn the ruin into a palace which would far outshine Castle Huntly, that men's eyes would turn to Broughty from far and near, and that its former proud lord would come seeking admission on his bended knees. He had largely fulfilled that angry vow. Broughty Castle had been restored, extended and remodelled beyond all recognition, externally and internally. Its walls soared high to dizzy battlements, turreted, corbelled and embellished in the French fashion, rough-cast over naked stone kept dazzling with white-wash. Plenishings, furniture, tapestries, pictures, gleaned from all over Europe – even carpets, a thing scarcely known in Scotland – graced its many chambers. Patrick had very quickly prevailed upon the King to deprive his father of the Sheriffship of Forfar and to bestow it upon himself, so that Broughty became the seat of jurisdiction of all Angus, where men must turn for justice and favour. And during James's long absence in Norway and Denmark, when he went to fetch his bride, Patrick as acting Chancellor, with the young Ludovick as Viceroy, had ruled Scotland from here, with the royal banner and those of Lennox and Gray all flying from its topmost tower – to the unutterable fury of his father, who not only had sworn never to set foot in the place again but at great inconvenience had frequently had to make long detours inland in order to avoid even setting eyes on its soaring, flaunting whiteness.

Now, for the first time in five years, the Lord Gray approached Broughty Castle.

It was a strange cavalcade. In front, with his trumpeter and standard-bearer, my lord rode under the great streaming white lion on red of Gray, setting his usual headlong pace. In close-packed ranks behind him came no fewer than seventy men-at-arms, the greatest number that he had mustered for many a day, some of them only doubtful warriors, herd-boys, farm-hands and the like. Following on, having some difficulty in keeping up, after their long ride from Falkland, came the two King's officers and their much smaller band of armed men. And lastly rode David Gray, Mary, and the Duke of Lennox with his two attendants. Ludovick had insisted on accompanying them, declaring that, if on no other account, as President of the Council he was entitled to see this affair to the end.

The castle was practically islanded on its rock, but the draw-bridge, was down, and cantering through the huddle of small fishers' and ferrymen's houses, that clustered round the harbour, Lord Gray thundered across the bridge without pause, lashing porters and servitors out of the way with the flat of his drawn sword, his trumpeter at his back keeping a loud and imperious if somewhat unmelodious summons the while. Across the inner court, striking sparks from the flagstones, he clattered, to pull up his massive powerful white stallion to a standing, pawing halt in front of the main arched doorway of the keep.

'Gray, to see the Master!' he cried, above the noise of hooves behind him. 'Fetch him, scum! Have him here, to me. Quickly. Off with you, filth! Ordure! Do you stand gawping at Gray?'

The alarmed and uncertain men who stood in the doorway scuttled off, none hindmost.

'Blow, damn you!' the old man commanded. 'A plague – what do I keep you for? To belch and wheeze? Blow, fool!'

However breathlessly and brokenly, that trumpeter blew and blew, and the white enclosing walls of Broughty echoed and reverberated to the shrill neighing challenge.

Lord Gray sat his restive mount in towering impatience.

No one came to receive the visitors.

Wrathfully Gray stared up and around at the castle's many lit windows, shaking sword and fist, while the exhausted musician's efforts grew weaker and more disconnected.

Still no sign or movement showed about the buildings around them.

'Dear God – he will burst his heart!' Mary groaned to Ludovick. 'He is too old for these mad rages.' She began to push her way through the press of horsemen in that crowded courtyard.

But her grandfather's scant patience was exhausted. Cursing steadily, he flung himself down from his horse, and went storming indoors, sword still unsheathed. Behind him, dismounting in haste, hurried the two courtiers, Mary, Ludovick and David.

'Foolish! Foolish!' Mary declared, almost sobbing. 'He has thrown away his advantage.'

Because of the formation of the rock site, the hall of Broughty was at courtyard level, not on the floor above as was usual. Stamping along the white-walled, sconce-lit corridor therefore, my lord had no stairs to climb to reach its door, which stood slightly ajar, more light streaming therefrom. With a great kick of his heavy riding-boot he flung it back with a crash, and limped within.

The Master of Gray, dressed in the height of fashion in silver satin slashed with maroon, pearl-seeded ruff and lace at wrists, lounged at ease at a small table with two other gentlemen – his sheriff-depute and one of his brothers, James Gray, who like Home was a Groom of the Bedchamber to the King. A decanter of wine, glasses – not the usual goblets – and playing-cards littered the table. At sight of the old lord, these two started to their feet, but when Patrick remained sitting, his brother, looking uncomfortable, sat down again.

'Ha, my lord and presumed progenitor!' the Master greeted, smiling genially. 'It is you, is it? I thought it might be. I heard a bellowing and braying somewhere. I vowed it must be either yourself or a cattle drove! Come in. I rejoice to see you at Broughty, at last. A great joy, long delayed. But . . . dear me – why the ironware? You do not have to *break* your way into my house with swords, I do protest!'

It is to be doubted whether his father actually heard any of this, so astonished was he at the transformation which had over-taken the hall of Broughty Castle. Formerly it had been but a great vaulted barn of a place, ill-lit with tiny windows, damp and gloomy. Now the windows were large and many, such naked stone as was to be seen on the vaulting was washed a warm rosy pink; colourful arras hung to cover the walls, and a notable Flemish tapestry dominated the far end of the chamber. Carpeting, rugs and skins of animals hid the floor flagstones, and instead of the usual massive table to run the length of the room, with benches, many small tables and richly carved chairs, settles and couches dotted the apartment. In two great fire-places cheerful log fires flamed and crackled, while candles innumerable blazed from branched silver candlesticks and wall-brackets. Never had the lord of Gray seen anything like it.

Patrick waved a friendly hand. 'Ah, Davy ! More joy! And Mary!' He actually rose to his feet at the sight of the girl. 'This is a delight indeed. Is it not, Jamie – a family gathering.' Then abruptly his expression changed, as he perceived Ludo-vick standing behind the others in the doorway. 'So-o-o!' he ended, on a different note. 'My lord Duke also! This is . . . interesting! I wonder . . . ?'

He got no further. Lord Gray recovered his voice, although it quivered a little.

'Silence!' he exclaimed. 'Hold your lying, treacherous tongue! Dastard! Ingrate! Mountebank! Have done wi' your mockery. We'll talk plain, for once, knave!'

'Gladly, sir – gladly. Talk is so much more comfortable than shouting. I must confess that I never could match you at bellow-ing! But come inside, do. Poor Vicky is having to peep and peer behind you! Sit here, where we may talk in comfort. Wine . . . ?' He resumed his seat.

'No! Any fare of yours would choke me!' The older man stamped into the room nevertheless, the others following him. 'I am here for but one reason – to discover what new wickedness you brew with the King! This, that these popinjays prate of . . .'

'Then, to some extent we are at one, my lord – since the wickedness which these King's envoys speak of is also my concern, as Sheriff of this shire. But – is it not what new wickedness *you* have been brewing, sir? So it seems to the Privy Council, at least. I hope, of course, that these inquiries will prove it all to be a mistake, a mere indiscretion on your part...'

'God damn you, Patrick! I warn you – do not think to ensnare *me* in one of your foul plots!' His father crashed his sword hilt down on one of the small tables, and a porcelain vase thereon jumped, to fall to the floor and smash in fragments. 'I warn you – keep your traitor's hands off me. Or I tell what I know. To the King and Council. To the Kirk. To all. O' many matters that will gar you grue! Of your base betrayals. Mary the Queen. Gowrie the Treasurer, Esmé Stewart, this lad's father – *your* friend, whom the King loved! Of Moray and Arran and a dozen others. Keep your dirty hands off me, I say, or you'll rue it!'

The Master raised his hands and brows, and glanced around him, a man perplexed. 'On my soul,' he said sadly, 'it looks to be as I feared. Your wits are becoming affected, my lord – you dream, imagine, wander in your mind. I thought it must be so. A sad state of affairs, sad – for you are not so devilish old.' He sighed. 'And yet . . . and yet, perhaps it is better so. It would account for so much. Yes – that is it. How this folly of yours may be explained...'

'Fiend seize you! You dare . . . you dare accuse me! To doubt *my* wits! Nincompoop – you!' His father was all but choking, heavy features darkening alarmingly.

'Patrick! Granlord!' Mary cried, starting forward to stand between them. 'Stop! Oh, stop! This is . . . this is shameful! For sweet mercy's sake, do not so misuse each other. Patrick – can you not see what you do...?'

'Bless your heart, Mary – of course I see. Fortunate indeed that I do! I see that our, h'm, noble relative cannot be held to be fully responsible for his words and actions. For the present. No doubt it will pass – a temporary aberration. Unfortunate – but not uncommon as we grow older. Better, at all events, than rebellion and treason against His Grace!'

'Treason?' his father croaked. 'Fool – I leave treasons to you! I have done naught against His Grace, as well you know...'

'Oh come, come, my lord! Or . . . is your memory going likewise? All too much evidence has been laid before the Council. Have you forgotten how close you have become with certain ministers of the Kirk?'

'A pox! Is it treason now to worship God? In this Reformed realm?'

'Ha – a point indeed! Some I could name, of the Old Religion, have been asking that for some time! But the charges of rebellion do not rest on your worship, my lord. Nor on colloguing and engaging with such as our good and worthy parish pastors here in the Carse. It is black crows of a different feather who endanger the realm. In Dundee and St. Andrews. Notably the Melvilles, Andrew and James. And . . . others.'

'Melville? Andrew Melville is of the Council himself! Moderator o' the General Assembly. Rector o' the University. God be good – is it rebellion to deal wi' such?'

'Not, h'm, necessarily! Not yet. Though, who knows how soon it might become so? Our fiery prophet of the New Order becomes increasingly indiscreet. Increasingly hostile to His Grace . . . '

'To yourself, you mean – you and your Papist friends! Everywhere you are bringing them creeping back. The Kirk, the true religion, is threatened. It must be stopped, before . . . before . . . '
The older man's choleric words died away.

'Yes, my lord?' Patrick's voice was silky. 'Pray proceed.'

His father swallowed, glaring, but said no more.

'Yes. Perhaps you are wise to leave it there, my lord. Masters Andrew and James are gathering round them an obnoxious covey of corbies indeed. Who not only seek but caw loudly about the downfall of the King's realm and the setting up in its stead of a Kirk-state, where ministers shall rule, not King and Council. To this ill company you, unfortunately, are no stranger, my lord.'

'Have I no' always been o' the Kirk party? Never a secret Papist like yourself!'

'You flatter me! I fear that my hold on religion is less certain than yours. I have ever been a sad doubter, where dogma is concerned. A sorry case! But . . . here we are not concerned with faith and creed. We are concerned, my lord, with rebellion, treason and matters of state. For your friends have overstepped the bounds of religion and dogma. In especial one – Master

David Black, of St. Andrews!' That name was shot out.

Lord Gray opened his mouth, and then closed it almost with a click.

'I see that you are sufficiently lucid in your mind to take my point!' Patrick went on. 'Master Black, aided and abetted by others in higher places, who should know better, has gone too far. Even for our forgiving liege lord and a patient Presbyterian Council. He has publicly declared all kings and princes to be bairns of the Devil, with Satan the head of both Court and Council, and called for the overthrow of the throne and the setting up of the supreme rule of the Kirk. Can you deny it?'

'What is it to me what Black preaches from his pulpit?'

'Much, I fear. When such as the Lord Gray, Andrew Melville and others, see a deal of a hitherto inconspicuous preacher who mouths such sentiments, it behoves the Council to take heed. More than that, had this loud-tongued clerk contended himself with public outcry against his own prince, he might have been dismissed with a warning. But he has seen fit to declaim against Queen Elizabeth of England likewise, naming her an atheist. This has been reported to her by her ambassador Nicolson. She takes it ill, and has even sent up her old envoy, Sir Robert Bowes again, to take order with His Grace. Elizabeth demands redress, restitution, threatening much. Do you understand, my lord?'

There was silence in the great room save for the noise of the fire and the heavy breathing of the older man. All eyes were fixed on him.

'I do not,' he got out thickly. 'Burn you – what has this to do with me?'

'Master Black has been summoned before the Council. He has refused to appear, and left St. Andrews. He is to be taken into custody, to answer for his preachings. Our information is that he has crossed Tay to Dundee, in this my sheriffdom. And I have further information, with sworn witnesses to testify, that you my lord spent three hours closeted with him in Dundee town but two days ago!' He paused, and then snapped out. 'Where is David Black?'

The old lord stared back at him, fists clenched, wordless.

'Come – tell me. You must know. We have combed Dundee for him. He is not there. Where is Master Black hiding, sir?'

'Curse you – think you I would tell you? You! If I knew.'

'I think you would, yes. If you have any wits left at all! For I'd remind you that I am Sheriff of Forfar, under express command of the King to find this preacher. To refuse to aid the King and Council in such a matter is flagrant and deliberate treason, sir! As well you know. Whatever you have done or have not done hitherto, if you refuse to tell me now, before these witnesses, then I declare you are guilty of treason.'

'May . . . you . . . burn . . . in . . . hell . . . eternally!' Word by individual word the father spoke the shocking thing to the son, dropping them like evil stones into the pool of silence.

There was a choking sob from the girl.

At her side Ludovick Stewart raised his voice, to break the appalled hush. 'So it is Andrew Melville's turn to be pulled down, Patrick? The same sorry business. Build up, use, and pull down! You no longer need the Kirk?'

'The Kirk, or part of it, is seeking to pull down the King, Vicky.'

'Is it? I have not heard of it. Only that the ministers protest that the Catholics are coming back.'

'Aye – there you have it!' Lord Gray burst out. 'This is naught but another Papist plot, you may be sure. Erroll and Angus are back in the north, from France. None molests them. Huntly's Countess is back at Court, sharing the Queen's naked bed – aye, and gaining more o' the Queen's kisses than does her husband, they tell me! The shameful hizzies! Is there wonder that the Kirk cries out on such lewd abominations!'

'Tcha – spare us such talk, my lord!' Patrick said, frowning. 'In front of our Mary. Aye – and the Duke. The Countess of Huntly is Vicky's sister, after all! Had you forgot? And 'tis all a, h'm, mere matter of hearsay.'

Ludovick looked straight ahead of him, tight-lipped.

'Hearsay, is it? There's folk to swear to it. Aye, and is it to be wondered at, wi' the King himself no better?' Angrily scornful, Gray glanced over at George Home and his companion. 'These gentry will tell us, maybe, if Jamie Stewart's unnatural lusts are but hearsay! Eh, my pretty boys?'

'Enough, sir! In my house, I insist on it!'

'Na, na! I'm no' finished wi' my hearsay yet, man! I've heard tell that but three nights ago Huntly himself landed secretly in Scotland again. From the Continent. At Eyemouth, they say. In the Merse. Huntly's back!'

'Eyemouth!' That was Ludovick, turning to stare from Mary to Patrick. 'Eyemouth is but a mile or two from Fast Castle. Logan's house. Lord . . . !'

'Tush! Vapours and rumours!' The Master dismissed the matter with a wave of his hand. Neverthless those who knew him best detected a hint of discomfort in his normal complete assurance. 'Some of our spiritual guides and shepherds see Catholics behind every stone! Smell a Popish plot in every Court breeze . . .'

'Do *you* deny that Erroll and Angus are back, whether Huntly is or no?' his father interrupted. 'And lesser Papists with them?'

'I do not. They have given assurances of their repentance. Seen the error of their ways. Expressed themselves contrite and willing to receive all instruction in the Reformed faith. To support Presbyterian chaplains in their houses. His Grace has been gracious. Wisely, I think. He has shown mercy. For these are our fellow subjects. Are they not, my lord Duke? You were concerned for this, I mind. And they have already suffered much for their adherence to the unpopular faith. They are, of course, now confined to their northern estates, warded in their own castles. And with my lord of Argyll strong in Aberdeen, as Lieutenant of the North, they can do no harm. For princes to show mercy and forbearance, with strength, is commendable, is it not . . . ?'

'Hypocrite! Dissembler!' Lord Gray shouted. 'You prate of mercy and forbearance, knowing what you know! What you yourself devised! When it is all a covetous, grasping plot for money! Aye, Patrick – I know what you are at. You and the King. The treasury is empty. Elizabeth isna sending gold, any more. You are spending silver like water. And so you are desperate for money. You sought money from the Kirk – and when it wouldna give God's ordained tithe into your clutching hands, you turned to the Catholics. They are *buying* their way back. Huntly, Erroll, Angus and the rest. Pouring gold into your coffers that they may once again harry the land and flaunt their idolatrous worship . . .'

'Have done, sir!' Patrick actually rose from his seat. 'Who

now can doubt that you are crazed? Deranged? Only a madman would conceive such charges. If your Kirk friends have told you this, taking advantage of your senility . . .'

'God's Passion, you . . . you . . . !' His father gulped for breath, for air, as well as for words.

'On my soul – that I should have sprung from such a doited fool!'

'Patrick!' Mary's voice rose almost shrilly. 'No! Stop! For the love of God – stop! You will kill him. He is your father. You are blood of his blood!'

'Aye – it is enough, Patrick.' That was David Gray, speaking for the first time in this encounter, levelly, but strongly, authoritatively. 'Have you not enough on your conscience? Be done with this evil play-acting – for that is all it is . . .'

'Sakes, Davy – do you name high treason and the commands of the Privy Council play-acting? *You* should know better. This peculiar sire of ours has been dabbling in pitch. As well indeed that he is proving himself to be clouded in mind. That I may attribute his folly, to the King and Council, as mere dotage . . .'

David moved forward slowly, deliberately. 'I said enough, Patrick!' he repeated. There was something infinitely menacing about the stocky plain man's advance upon his elegant half-brother, as about his few quiet words. 'Do you require that I should teach you your lesson again? After all these years. Before these?'

At the sheer fist-clenched and jaw-outthrust threat of the other's approach, the Master backed a pace, his fine eyes widening. He forced a laugh. 'Ha – use your head, Davy! As I do. Can you not see it, man?' His words came much more quickly than usual, almost breathlessly. 'Aye – and my lord's head, likewise! We must use the fact that he has lost *his* head, to save it! That his wits are gone . . .'

The clatter of Lord Gray's sword falling to the floor as its owner brought up both hands in strange jerking fashion to his thick throat, drew all eyes. The older man was staggering, mouth agape, eyes protruding, heavy features the colour of mahogany. Thick lips tried to form words but failed. Great choking gasps shook him. Then his leg-booted knees buckled beneath him, and the heavy gross figure fell with a crash like a stricken tree.

In the confusion that followed it was Mary who took swift command, running to kneel beside her prostrate grandfather, loosening his doublet and neck-cloth, wiping his foaming mouth, demanding space and air. The old lord was unconscious quite, twitching and stertorously breathing.

His three sons, after a little, picked him up as the girl cried that he must be got to bed and a leech summoned to bleed him. Staggering under the awkward weight of him, with Ludovick's help, they were making for the door and the main turnpike stairway to the sleeping accommodation of the upper chambers, when Patrick directed them otherwise, pointing to a smaller door at the side of the great hall fireplace, declaring that this was better, easier. Here, behind the arras, a narrow straight stair led within the thickness of the walling, down not up. It was the usual laird's private access to his wine-cellar, which could thus be kept locked away from thirsty servitors. Down this constricted dark flight of stone steps, stumbling and with difficulty they bore their groaning, snoring burden, Mary and George Home bearing candles before and behind.

In the cellar at the foot, Patrick directed them out through a door into a dark vaulted passage, and gestured towards another stairway at its end. This again led down. Mary alone had breath to protest – but she was once more told briefly that this was best, that all was in order. Broughty Castle's foundations no doubt followed the uneven surface of the thrusting rock on which it was built; nevertheless, here they must be nearly underground.

Down this second flight they lurched, to another damp-smelling corridor where the candles revealed a row of four heavy doors ranged side by side. Nothing more typical of a castle's dungeons could have been imagined. Patrick, turning a great key in the lock, opened the second of these, and signed the others in.

Mary at least was surprised. A lamp already burned in here. The place was no more than a small vaulted cell, otherwise lit only by a tiny barred slit window high in the arch of the vault at the far end. But despite this, there was comfort here, a small fireplace whereon logs smouldered, a bed and other furnishings, rugs on the stone floor, even two or three books on a desk.

They laid the unconscious man on the bed, and Mary and David busied themselves in getting off his harness and outer clothing.

When they had done all that they could for the sufferer, and must await the physician whom Ludovick had gone to fetch from Dundee, the girl found that only Patrick and David remained in the chamber. She looked from one to the other.

'You planned this, Patrick, did you not?' she said quietly. 'All arranged for. Nothing overlooked.' And she gestured around her.

Her father shook a faintly smiling head. 'Now, now, Mary – even you will not credit me, I think, with arranging my lord's bodily condition, his health and sickness!'

'I would not swear to that!' she told him. 'You knew well that he had over-much blood. When last you spoke with him, years ago in this same house, you made him ill with your baiting. You have not forgot that, I swear! Tonight, with your wicked talk of dotage and senility, you as good as drove him to this. Why?'

'A marvel! *You* answer that, my dear, since you are so clever!'

'I think that I can, Patrick. You swore to humble Granlord over this Broughty – swore it before Davy and me, that day. You have done much to bring it about – but you could not get my lord to come here, to force him to acknowledge your triumph. Now, with this charge of rebellion, you have got him here at last. But that does not content you. You must make him eat the very dust at your feet – your own father! You itched to see him locked up here, in the very deepest dungeons of the castle he flung at you! Did you not? You prepared this cellar for him – but you could not be sure that you could win him here without using force. And he has more than seventy armed men fretting in your courtyard. So you devised to get him here otherwise – and succeeded! By working upon his anger and rageful choler. Deliberately. Time and again I pleaded with you to stop . . .'

'Nonsense, girl!'

'Is it nonsense? You cannot deny that, knowing how it must infuriate so proud a man, you continued to taunt him with being witless, wandering in his mind . . . ?'

'For his own sake. Can you not see? That he might escape the full consequences of this charge of rebellion and treason.'

'Which you arranged likewise, did you not?' She waved her hand. 'And this chamber, this cell! Down in the rock itself. It is a pit, a prison. You made this ready for him – not one of the rooms which you would give to a guest, where there is light and air. For the Lord of Gray, whose castle this was . . .'

'Are you as blind as he is, child? Do you not see that, as Sheriff of Forfar I must obey the King's edict? In name at least. To ward him and charge him. I must seem to do my duty. Imprison him. Then go plead his failure of wits before King and Council. If I install him in any honourable room in this house, who will take my warding seriously? Will he? My lord? Will he abide quietly in any proper chamber? I tell you, it had to be down here. But I have made it comfortable for him. More so than most of the rooms of his own house. Than ever was *my* room at Castle Huntly. I have sought to think of all things . . .'

'Aye, Patrick – you have thought of all things!' David repeated heavily. 'God forgive you, if He can!'

'You too! God grant me patience, you mean!' The Master swung about, and thrust out of that cell.

Later, with the blood-letter at his unchancy trade, and the Lord Gray still unconscious, Ludovick Stewart came to the girl in the vaulted passage outside the sick-room.

'Mary,' he said, 'the hour is late. Come away now. You are weary, pale as a ghost. There is no more that you can do here. Come away. With me.'

She shook her head. 'I must stay here.'

'Why? What good can you do? You will not budge Patrick in his course. You should know that, by now!'

'Granlord needs me, Vicky . . .'

'I need you likewise. More than he does.'

'That I cannot believe, Vicky. Want. Desire, perhaps. But not need. Any more. Granlord *needs* me. I must stay with him here, meantime.'

'*I* cannot stay in this house, Mary. Patrick does not want me, and makes it plain. Nor do I wish to bide under his roof. Besides, I must get back to Court, to Falkland . . .'

'Yes. And to your wife.'

He frowned. 'I did not say that. But James will look for me.'

At the stiffness in his tone and bearing, Mary bit her lip. Her hand reached out to his arm. 'You are hurt, Vicky. I am sorry. Oh, I would not wish to hurt you, my dear. But . . . I cannot help myself. It must be this way. At least, meantime. Try to understand.'

'I do not understand you,' he told her flatly.

'Then . . . then, Vicky, at least forbear and forgive. For love of me.'

He paused, and then swallowed. 'I can try,' he said. 'For love of you, Mary, I can attempt anything. But, you? How of your love of me?'

'My love of you is sure. Certain. For always. For my life and beyond my life. That you have, my beloved.'

'And yet – this!'

'This, yes – to my sorrow. Now go, Vicky, Go – before my heart is broken quite.'

Hard he stared at her, almost glared. 'I shall come back,' he said, tight-lipped. 'I must. I cannot leave it so. I must come, hoping. Believing. That one day you will change. See it all differently. Need me as I need you . . .'

'No more, my heart – for sweet pity's sake! For I cannot bear it.'

He took a step forward, as though to take her in his arms, and then thought better of it. Set-faced, sighing, he bowed swiftly, jerkily, and turned blindly away.

Even so, it was the young woman who spoke the last word, hesitantly, faltering. 'Vicky,' she got out, from constricted throat. 'Is she . . . is she kind? Warm with you? A . . . an able lover . . . ?'

He did not so much as glance back, dared not, but made for the narrow mural stairway almost at a run.

Chapter Eighteen

In all his affairs, save only one, the world wagged well for
Patrick Gray. And, it must be admitted, for Scotland likewise –
in consequence or as a mere coincidence. With no new Chancellor appointed, and Maitland's lieutenants quietly got rid of,
the Master of Gray now guided the King in all matters, and
through him ruled the land. He did so well, efficiently and tactfully, without seeming to push himself forward – so that James
himself, it is probable, scarcely realised how firm was the hand
that controlled his own, how hollow a façade was the personal
government by divine right of which he was so vocally proud.
Patrick claimed no other Court position than that of Master of
the Wardrobe still – which of course gave him the readiest
access to the monarch's person at all times. He also had his seat
on the Privy Council. These were sufficient for his purposes.
And, for Scotland, the ship of state sailed a comparatively steady
course, however strong and warring the underlying currents.

The religious dichotomy which had bedevilled the land for
half a century was brought once more to a state of precarious
balance, by effective however peculiar means. The Kirk, while
still apparently paramount, had its vaunting power and political
pretensions curbed. The law was invoked against certain of the
activities and pronouncements of ministers; dissension was
created amongst the ranks even of the elect by the introduction
of bishoprics of the King's appointment. Andrew Melville was
got rid of by a judicious linking with Masters Black, Davidson
and others, some of whom were, it was whispered, in fact *agents
provocateur* in the King's pay. He found his closest associates
arrested on charges of treason, and was manoeuvred into a
position where every word that he spoke was weighed and tested.
Like a wounded and baited lion eventually he could stand no
more, and lashed out against earthly tyrants who set themselves
up against the supremacy of Christ, quoting passages of the
Basilikon Doron, King James's own book, as yet unfinished,

written for the future instruction in kingship of Prince Henry. How Melville obtained knowledge of these passages was a mystery, for they could only have been supplied by someone very close to the King; but they served their purpose. The royal wrath was unleashed in a flood. Melville fled the land.

In matters of administration the realm was being served more effectively than almost ever before. No Lord Treasurer was appointed in place of Patrick's old enemy, the Master of Glamis, one of the first to be disposed of. Nor was there appointed a new Secretary of State, a post formerly held by Maitland's nephew. Instead eight new men were brought in, without specific title, to handle, under the Privy Council all the business of the realm. All were able, reliable, and of comparatively humble origin, the most prominent being James Elphinstone, a son of the Lord Elphinstone – and all were associates of the Master of Gray. They became known as The Octavians – and Scotland had never before known their like. They made an interesting contrast to Robert Logan of Restalrig, who now returned swaggering to Court banishment annulled.

Another swaggerer to return at almost the same time as Logan, and from the same direction, was George Gordon, Earl of Huntly, forgiven by a gracious and forbearing monarch. Melville's sentence of excommunication upon him was solemnly revoked by the Kirk – for was he not daily receiving instruction from a patient Presbyterian catechist? His grim murder of the popular Earl of Moray now conveniently laid at the door of the late Maitland, Huntly strutted and postured as effectively as ever – and with good cause, for James had ever a weakness for him. He was reappointed Joint Lieutenant of the North, with Argyll. His wife being the Queen's closest companion, he had his feet well planted in both Court camps.

That there were indeed two distinct camps at Court was now undeniable, even by James himself. The Queen was as open and frank in her political manoeuvrings as she was in her contempt of her husband and hatred of Mar, her son's governor. Moreover she was showing much interest in Catholicism and was said to be closeted frequently with Jesuits – these, some suggested, being supplied by the Master of Gray. However unkind this might be, Patrick did in fact make a point of remaining on good terms with the difficult and unpredictable Anne – to James's relief, who evidently felt that he could leave this awkward personal problem, like so many others, in the Master's capable hands. Despite the fact that she was allegedly pregnant again, seldom indeed now were the monarch and his consort seen together. Despite the usual questions and rumours anent the paternity of this putative embryo, James made no accusations, against Ludovick or others. Anne, indeed, although she still carried on an occasional arch exchange with the Duke, now appeared to be more interested in the company of young women than young men – which suited her spouse.

One hitherto unfailing source of trouble faded most fortunately from the Scottish scene – Francis Hepburn Stewart, Earl of Bothwell. After Glenlivet and the collapse of the Catholic cause in the north, this fire-eater, excommunicated, fled to Orkney, there apparently to take up the trade of pirate. He was less successful in this profession than might have been expected, however, and soon found his way to the Continent, where quite suddenly, at Naples, he died in somewhat mysterious circumstances. It is safe to say that few mourned him.

The Master's more private affairs fell out in almost equally satisfactory pattern. His father, never fully recovered from his providential stroke at Broughty, remained in his cell at the castle for months on end, a changed man – scarcely a man at all indeed. In the end Patrick packed him off back to Castle Huntly, the suddenly feeble and querulous old man being not worth fighting. Mary had taken up her residence at Broughty, unasked, to look after him – another good reason for getting all charges against his father dismissed and sending him home.

With Mary herself the situation was somewhat improved, in that she was making little or no trouble, refraining from meddling in his affairs, however damnably reproachful and unforthcoming she might be when they met. By arranging that the King sent Ludovick away on prolonged embassages, one to the Court of Elizabeth and one to that of France, this source of friction and disharmony was removed – for the meantime at least.

All this was satisfactory. But there was one fly in the ointment. Financially, matters were far from well. This was nothing new in Scotland, of course, where money had always been the scarcest of commodities. But in the circumstances it greatly hampered Patrick Gray, tying his hands at every turn, hitting him both in matters of state and person. The cream was just not there to be skimmed. Good government was more expensive than the almost non-government of the previous era. It is always more difficult to get contributions out of people in time of peace and comparative prosperity. The Kirk and the nobility saw no need to dip hands in pockets – and the ordinary folk had never had to.

Patrick and his Octavians were busy on schemes of taxation, after the English model – especially directed at the burghs, the craft-guilds and the mass of the people, who were prospering as never before. But this was a long-term prospect, and immediate funds were urgently necessary. The raising of a permanent and sizeable body of royal troops solely at the disposal of the Crown, was a first priority – but there were numerous other clamant demands for public works which no private purse was going to defray. Long years of misrule and misapplication of moneys had left the Exchequer not only empty but in serious debt; eighty thousand pounds was owed to the late Earl of Gowrie's heirs alone, moneys advanced by him at a time of the Crown's grievous need, and unrepaid.

All Patrick's not inconsiderable wits, these days, seemed to be bent on this intractable problem. If only Queen Elizabeth would die, and in dying make it clear that her heir was indeed her distant cousin of Scotland, the entire matter would be solved – for the English Treasury bulged indecently. Yet she had not even paid James his agreed pension for years. The King of France, having turned Catholic, was disinclined to aid his impoverished partner in the now somewhat blown-upon Auld Alliance – though this was the ostensible reason for Ludovick's mission to Paris. King Christian of Denmark, on approach, proved to be in even greater financial embarrassment than was his brother-in-law. Patrick toyed with the idea of making a personal visit to London. But his successes with the Virgin Queen in the past had been largely attributable to a delicate blending of sex, wit, and blackmail; it was doubtful whether the ageing lady, with no gift for growing old gracefully, would still respond to such treatment.

It was with a certain trepidation then, even for Patrick Gray, that he turned his speculative eye still further afield. There was one unfailing and acknowledged source of great wealth in the world, hitherto quite untapped. Admittedly it would take a very bold, quick-witted and agile man to tap it – but was there not just such a man in Scotland?

After considerable cogitation and some little research, on an afternoon of October 1598, in the modest quarters of the Master of the Wardrobe in the Palace of Holyroodhouse, Patrick sent for James Elphinstone of Invernochty.

Elphinstone came in haste. Third son of the impoverished third Lord Elphinstone and of a Catholic Drummond mother, he was a peculiar man, abler than he looked, and younger. He had a diffident, almost retiring manner, unusual in his class, and a deprecating smile. But he had a good brain and a trained mind, having been bred to the law. Indeed he had been made a judge, a Senator of Justice at the age of thirty; the reason for his reaching such eminence so early was as mysterious as for his sudden deprivation of the office a year or two later. Now he served the Master of Gray as the senior of the Octavians.

'James, you look weary,' Patrick greeted him pleasantly. 'You are working too hard. That is foolish. The realm's cause requires diligence, yes – but hardly such desperate devotion. A glass of wine? You need it by the colour of you.'

'There is much to do, Patrick. Pleas. Petitions, Causes. Tax schedules...'

'No doubt. But you must find others to aid you with these. You are too valuable a servant of His Grace to so squander your talents.'

The other looked swiftly, almost uneasily, at the speaker, and made no comment.

'Too much toil is not only wearisome, James – it is to be deplored, avoided at all costs. Do you not agree? For it defeats its own end. The keen mind – and God knows there are few enough of them! – can become blunted, lose its cutting edge, by the dull grind of unremitting labour. Myself, I always seek to play rather more than I work – for the work's sake. I believe it to be a sound principle.'

Elphinstone sipped his wine, and waited warily.

'It occurs to me,' Patrick went on conversationally, 'that successful as has been our experiment in, h'm, fourfold responsibility, the time may be near when a change might be made, with profit. It seems to me that while His Grace's affairs may well proceed satisfactorily without a Chancellor, or even a Lord Treasurer, yet in matters of administering the state, some single man should bear the principal authority. Bear the authority, I say, rather than do the work. You will note, also, that I speak of administering, not of policy. Does your experience not lead you to agree?'

The other blinked rapidly. 'It might well be so,' he temporised.

'It is possible that the office of Secretary of State ought to be revived. And filled. You, James, might make an excellent Secretary of State, I think – if you could be prevailed upon not to work so devilishly hard!'

His visitor's sallow face flushed, and he swallowed.

'It might possibly be arranged,' the Master observed, and then paused. 'You are a good Catholic, are you not, James?'

Pleasantly, almost casually, as this was said, the colour drained away from Elphinstone's features. Tensely he sat forward, gripping his wine-glass. 'Not . . . not so!' he got out. 'I am not active in religious matters. I leave that to others. I have not, perhaps, leant strongly towards the Kirk. But . . .'

'Tush, man – we can talk plainly, here in the Wardrobe! Your lady-mother is of a strong Catholic family, the Drummonds of Inchaffray. Your cousin Drummond is Bishop of Vaison, is he not? Close to the Vatican. You receive Jesuits in your lodgings, on occasion. As, of course, do I – though perhaps for different purposes!'

The older man looked down. 'If I have been indiscreet, I will rectify it. I assure you, Patrick, that you . . . that His Grace need have no doubts as to my behaviour and loyalty. The Protestant cause is entirely safe as far as I am concerned . . .'

'M'mm. I am glad to hear that, James. That is as it should be, in this godly Reformed realm. It would be quite insufferable, would it not, if the monarch's principal Secretary of State should be known to be an enemy of the Kirk?'

'I am not, Patrick. Never have I lifted a finger against the Kirk. I swear it ...'

'Quite. No doubt.' The Master lounged, toying with his glass. 'Nevertheless, you know, there could be advantages in the situation also, James. *Your* situation. So prominent a Catholic family, the Drummonds. Even His Holiness himself, I dare say, will know of your name, fame, and, er, inner faith!'

'His Holiness ... ?' the other faltered.

'Exactly. His Infallible Highness the Supreme Eminence. The Holy Father. The Pontiff and Vicar of Christ ... or Satan's Principal Disciple and the Keeper of the Whore of Rome. Depending upon the point of view!'

'It is possible that the Pope may know of my name, my family. But that is all. I swear it. He cannot esteem me as more than, than ...'

'A good Catholic at heart, as I said. And that is all that is required, I think. Sufficient for our purposes, James.'

Bewildered Elphinstone gazed at him. 'I do not understand,' he said. 'What is required of the Pope? What purposes?'

'The most common requirement of all, James – man's universal need. Gold. The filthy mammon of unrighteousness – of which, if you ask me, the Holy Father has accumulated an embarrassing superfluity! He should be grateful for the opportunity of disposing of some small proportion of the wicked burden of it all! To us. To, h'm, further the cause of the one Church, Holy, Catholic and Apostolic, in this far northern realm of Scotland. Is that not so?'

'You mean ... ? You mean that you will ask the *Pope* for money?'

'Tut, man – not I. I am but the Master of the King's Wardrobe. It is not new clothing that we need in Scotland! Besides, I have – whisper it – sought money from His Holiness before! With but indifferent success. No – the request must come from a loftier source. The highest, indeed. And if it is endorsed, amplified, buttressed and given some detail and explanation by His Grace's new Secretary of State, so much the more impressed will be His Holiness as to the possibilities, the lively possibilities, of the re-establishment of the good and true faith in this sadly lapsed Scotland. With consequent suitable and substantial contributions from the Vatican vaults to aid along this happy development.'

'God, Patrick – you think to gain the gold we need from the Pope!' That was a whisper.

'Why not? All know that the walls of the Vatican are in sore danger of falling with the weight of gold, jewels and the like within! For centuries wealth has been pouring in from all Christendom. Notably, of late, from the Spanish Indies, with the Dons making sure of heaven. Absurd that this small corner of Christendom should fail in good and godly government for lack of a moiety of the Pope's gold! If His Holiness is sufficiently impressed by the probability of success in Scotland, he will loosen his purse-strings, I vow. For Scotland today could mean England tomorrow. Elizabeth cannot live for ever. And a King of Scots soon to become also King of England...'

'But King James is no Catholic. Why should the Pope credit such a possibility?'

'*You* will convince him, my dear James. As will ... others! By many notable signs and portents. And one of the most notable will be that His Grace is appointing the good Catholic James Elphinstone – h'm, we might say *Sir* James Elphinstone, possibly – to be his Secretary of State! Think you that this would not be a convincing sign, in itself?'

There was silence in that small panelled room for a space. At length Elphinstone spoke. 'I do not understand,' he said. 'How can His Grace be brought to this?'

'Leave you His Grace to me, James.' The Master smiled. 'Indeed, I think you may safely leave all to me – save your signature on the letter to His Holiness! Is it agreed?'

The other let out a long breath. 'I ... I can but bow before your superior knowledge and experience, Patrick,' he said. 'But ... I confess that I am surprised. For this Papal gold you are prepared to turn Scotland Catholic again?'

'A pox, man – what's this? Do I mis-hear? Or have I mistook my man? I had not thought you stupid.' Patrick stretched, and lifted easily to his feet. 'A stupid Secretary of State would not do, at all, I'd remind you! Who said anything about turning Scotland Catholic...?'

The ante-chamber was warm, too warm, and there was an aura of women about it which amounted almost to an odour, a little too strong even for Patrick Gray, admirer of the sex as he was. Two young women sat therein, amongst a surplus of furnishings, one working at a frame, the other sitting at a virginal. He exchanged pleasantries with them even as his finely chiselled nose wrinkled a little.

The inner door opened, and the satisfying, almost challenging figure of the Duchess of Lennox emerged on a further waft of heat, her high colour heightened by the temperature.

'Her Grace will see you, Master of Gray,' she announced formally – but raised her brows at him as she said it, making a tiny grimace. Instead of waiting at the inner door, she came over to escort him thither.

As he strolled beside her, the man raised a hand to run his fingertips lightly up and down the inside of the Duchess's bare arm. ''Tis a wicked waste, I vow, Jean – you, in this assembly!' he murmured in her ear.

'Who put me here, Patrick?' she asked, in return.

'Did I do you an ill turn, then?'

'I have made no complaint, have I? As yet.'

'Nevertheless, I must do what I may to console. To compensate, Jean.'

'Further?'

'Further.' He nodded, glancing down appreciatively at her magnificent and frankly displayed bosom.

She smiled, and threw open the inner door. 'The Master of Gray seeking audience, Your Grace,' she called.

The Queen's private boudoir was like a hot-house, despite the October sunshine. Anne sat over at the window-seat, clad in the flimsiest of bed-robes, her pale, distinctly foxy features red at the cheek-bones, her quick glance busy. Beside her sat another young woman, taller, fairer, but strangely colourless. She rose, as Patrick was shown in, as though to move away – but the Queen held out a hand to keep her close.

The visitor bowed low. 'Highness,' he said, 'I am, as always, dazzled by your presence. And rejoiced at my good fortune in being admitted to it.'

'Flatterer, as ever, Patrick!'

'But, no, Madam. There are times when flattery is impossible. As now.' He inclined his head briefly to the other woman. 'Lady Huntly – your devoted servant.'

'And what is it in my poor power to do for the influential Master of Gray, Patrick?' the Queen asked, a little breathlessly. 'Since I cannot conceive of this visit as being purposeless.'

'If I could but answer that, Your Grace, as my heart dictates! But since it is not permissible . . . ' He paused and sighed – but at the same time glanced over towards Huntly's wife, Ludovick's sister, who was looking at him with her peculiar lack-lustre eyes. 'I must needs fall back on matters of mutual concern, in the realm's affairs – while still basking in the sun of your royal presence. But, h'm, somewhat close affairs, Highness – for your private ear alone.' And again he looked towards the other woman.

The Lady Henrietta Stewart, Countess of Huntly, was only two years older than her brother, but made him an unlikely sister. Brought up in France, and hardly knowing Ludovick, she had been sent for by the King ten years before to be married to George Gordon at the age of fifteen, an odd marriage which had produced little of co-habitation, for most of these years the wife had spent at Court while the husband was in more or less active rebellion elsewhere, or else in exile. Yet the lady appeared to be anything but the strong-willed woman determined to lead her own life – such as was Ludovick's wife; on the contrary, the most distinct impression that she gave was of negativity.

'I have no secrets from Hetty,' Anne declared sharply, and again her hand reached out to the other.

Patrick inclined his head, and shrugged slightly at the same time. 'As you will, Highness. As well that it is the Lady Hetty, and none other, however, in this instance.'

'What do you mean, sir?'

'Merely that her ladyship's discretion is well known – and here discretion is essential. Moreover, she is of course also known to be of the Old Religion – which is relevant to the matter.'

The two women exchanged quick glances.

'What matter?' the Queen jerked. 'What is this, Patrick?'

'Nothing to distress you, Highness – be assured,' the Master told her, soothingly. 'No sudden crisis. I have been meaning to speak with you on the subject for some time. And this seems an apt opportunity...'

'Come to the point, sir! What do you want?' That was sharp. 'You seek my aid, do you not?'

'It would be my joy to be even more indebted to Your Grace than I am now,' the other answered smoothly. 'But in this instance, the boot is rather on the other leg! The matter in case refers to, shall we say, two interests which I know to be very close to Your Grace's warm heart. Have I your royal permission to sit down?'

Eyeing him closely, the Queen nodded, unspeaking.

'In the past, Madam, knowing your interest in religious and, h'm, moral questions – comparative theology I believe, the savants call it,' Patrick went on genially, 'it has been my privilege and pleasure to find for your information learned men with whom you could discuss these profound but no doubt enthralling issues...'

'Say Jesuit priests, man, and be done with it!' Anne interrupted tersely.

'Very well, Highness – Jesuit priests. I do not know what stage you have reached in your investigations into these matters – but if you feel that the time has come for carrying them a stage further, the opportunity seems now to present itself. Also, there is the matter of your son, Prince, er, Frederick Henry.'

The Queen sat forward abruptly at mention of that name – and for the first time Patrick wondered whether there might not be something in the current rumours that she was pregnant again. Slenderly, almost boyishly built, she had scarcely shown signs of the previous infant's presence until close indeed to her time of delivery, so that up till the last moment most of the Court had assessed it all as but one more of her innumerable and much advertised false alarms.

'What of Frederick?' she demanded urgently.

'Just that he is now five years of age, and his instruction in matters religious, as in other things, ought properly to be considered. Does Your Grace not agree?'

'God be good – do not play with me, Patrick Gray!' the Queen exclaimed. 'Do not presume to mock me, I warn you! Nor to cozen me. I am not such a fool as is my husband! You know

314

well how dear is my wish that my poor child should receive true and honest instruction. Not pedantic vapourings such as his father writes for him in that stupid book. Nor the heretical ravings of the Kirk's zealots . . . !'

'H'rr'mm.' Patrick glanced around him expressively, warningly. 'As well, Madam, that your ladies are beyond doubt trustworthy!' he told her. 'Nevertheless, if I may be so bold . . .'

'Would you seek to muzzle me, your Queen, in my own bower?'

'Ah, no. Far from it. Only remind Your Grace that there are more effective ways of obtaining one's ends than stating them loudly enough for enemies to hear!'

'What do you mean? Come to the issue, Master of Gray. Where does all this talk lead us?'

'It leads us, Highness, to the Vatican.'

The indrawn breaths of both women were ample testimony to the impression that he had made.

He went on. 'In strictest secrecy, I have reason to know that an approach is to be made to the Pope. On a matter of state. A special courier will be entrusted with this most delicate mission. This courier, however, could carry more letters than one! I have long known and sympathised with Your Grace's distress at being unnaturally kept apart from the young prince. Here, I submit, is an opportunity for you to alter this sad situation. The state, the realm, requires the Pope's aid in a matter of policy. If Your Grace was to write to His Holiness urging that he insist to the King that the young prince be brought up, if not in the Catholic faith, at least in full knowledge thereof, with a grounding in the elements of the true religion – then I think that King James and the Council might be hard put to it to refuse. Or to deny due and natural access to the prince's lady-mother.'

The Queen was clasping and unclasping her thin hands, eyes glistening. 'You think this? You believe this? Is it possible . . . ?'

'More than possible – almost certain. If you ask this of the Pope, he cannot refuse you, since it must coincide with his own wishes and policy. It must be his anxious desire that the Prince of Scotland, who will one day be King of England also, should be on the way at least to being a good Catholic. Is it not so?'

'Glory be to God – I had never thought of that! Hetty – do you hear?' The Queen turned, with hands out, to her pale-eyed friend. 'My son. Do you understand?'

'It could be a notable endeavour, Your Grace,' the Countess said more cautiously, in her flat voice. Patrick eyed her thoughtfully.

'I shall write the letter. Now. At once,' the Queen declared. 'You will guide me, Patrick in what I should say?'

'Gladly, Highness.' He stroked his chin. 'It would be as well I judge, if you were to encourage His Holiness, at the same time, with some intimations that the Catholic interests in Scotland are by no means in eclipse. If you were to mention that the Catholic earls are all returned from exile and in good favour again. That many of the faithful are in high office, including James Elphinstone, who is much in the King's confidence. That your Jesuit friends come and go unmolested . . .'

'Yes, yes. And the Master of Gray himself, who is the key to all, is favourable to the true religion!'

'Ah no, Madam – to state that would be injudicious, I fear. To my sorrow. In the past, I have had the misfortune to seem to be at odds with the holy Clement, on occasion. My dealings with Queen Elizabeth have no doubt been misrepresented to him. I am told that he once asked why I was not excommunicated! In the circumstances your plea would carry more chance of success without my name being mentioned.'

The Countess of Huntly emitted a curious brief snigger, and then was as silent as before. Undoubtedly she blamed her marriage, and possibly other things, on the Master of Gray.

Patrick nodded towards her, while still addressing the Queen. 'It might be as well, Your Grace, if the Countess also addressed a letter to the Holy Father. As the wife of Scotland's premier Catholic nobleman. She might inform His Holiness, for instance, that the King is considering the bestowal of a notable mark of his favour on my Lord of Huntly, an increase in his already lofty stature. And therefore of her own!' He paused significantly. 'With other reports of royal, h'm, tendencies, it might well impress the Vatican.'

The Lady Henrietta opened her mouth, but seemed to decide against speech.

'Is this so, Patrick?' Anne demanded. 'I have long besought James to honour Hetty. But he would not.'

'It may come about this way. Your Grace, and you, Lady Hetty, may rest assured that I will do what I can in the matter.'

'Excellent! Then – the letter . . .'

'I will pen a few words to aid you, and have it sent to Your Grace forthwith. Meantime, I think that I need not stress that none must know of this. Any of it. Even your other ladies.'

'Have no fear, sir . . .'

Although Patrick Gray dined with the King that night, in the company of Nicolson the English ambassador, Mar and Huntly, he made little mention of affairs of state and none of any gesture towards the Vatican. It was the following afternoon that he ran James to earth in the royal stables, where he was rapturously admiring a magnificent pure white Barbary mare, running his hands over the creature's shining flanks and cooing and drooling with delight.

'Look at her, Patrick!' the King commanded. 'Is she no' bonny? Two years, no more. The finest bit horseflesh I've seen this many a day.'

'No doubt, Your Grace, a handsome animal. Have I not seen her somewhere, before . . . ?'

'Aye. She was Huntly's. Geordie brought her back frae France wi' him. You'll have seen him riding her.'

'But she is now in your royal stables, Sire?'

'Aye. Is she no' a notable gift, Patrick? Geordie Gordon gave her to me in a present. Was that no' right kindly o' him?'

'My lord is very good.' Patrick sighed. 'He is fortunate in being able to afford such gestures.'

'Ummm,' the King said.

As James continued to fondle the mare, and point out her excellence Patrick said not a word. At length his liege lord turned on him. 'Man – what ails you?' he demanded. 'You're byordinar glum! Soughing and puffing . . . !'

'Your pardon, Sire. Think nothing of it. I have had some ill news from England, that is all.'

'Eh? Frae England? What's ill there, Patrick?'

The Master raised his eyebrows towards George Home who,

as so frequently these days, was in close attendance on the King. James flapped a hand at the young man, as though shooing away a hen.

'Off wi' you, Doddie,' he ordered. 'We hae matters to discuss.' Then, to Patrick. 'What's amiss, man?'

'It is the Queen's health, Sire. Reports on Her Grace of England's state are not encouraging, I fear.'

James leered. 'Is that a fact? Guidsakes man, 'tween me and you, is that cause for a long face? The auld Jaud's had her day. Ower long a day! They could do fine wi' a new bottom sat on the throne o' England, I say!'

'Quite, Sire. Undoubtedly. It is what we have worked for, all these years. If it was only Her Grace's bodily health that was failing, I could contain my distress! But her mind also, they tell me, is growing enfeebled. And since she has not yet named you finally and certainly as her heir, there is danger in this.'

'Hech, me! D'you say so!' Anxiously the King licked thick lips. 'But she'd no' go by me now, man? Who else is there?'

'It is not so much the danger of her naming another, Sire. But if Elizabeth's mind goes, altogether, before naming you – there is the danger.'

'But, Patrick – who else could they choose? Yon Arabella Stewart's a right glaikit crittur – and no' near it in the blood as am I. Vicky Lennox is nigh as near it as she is. Waesucks – it's no' that? You're no' telling me that there's any thinking on Vicky as King o' England, in place o' me!'

'No, no, Sire – that at least I think you need not fear! The trouble is otherwhere. The only other claimants who have any possibility even of being considered, are the Infanta Isabella of Spain and Edward Seymour, Lord Beauchamp, great-grandson of Henry the Eighth's sister Mary. These two, separately, scarce menace Your Grace's position. But combined, it could be otherwise.'

'Combined, man? How could that be? The Infanta is married to the Archduke Albert. Beauchamp couldna marry her, Forbye, he's a Protestant and she's a Catholic.'

'Not that, Sire – not marriage. My dread is that their *support* might be combined. The Infanta's claim is supported by the English Catholics – and there are not a few of them. But neither

Queen nor Council nor yet the mass of the people would have her. Beauchamp is a different matter. The late Queen Mary Tudor considered his aunt, Jane Grey, near enough to the crown to have her executed. But he is a man of straw and unpopular ...'

'What, then?'

'My tidings, Sire, that distress me, are these. There is a move afoot, they say, that the English Catholics should transfer their support from the Infanta, whom they recognise as having no hope, to Beauchamp, under a secret agreement that he should turn Catholic. That is the danger that lengthens my face, Your Grace!'

'Christ God, man – no! It's no' true! They couldna do that to me – James o' Scotland!' In his agitation, the King grasped Patrick's arm and shook it vehemently. 'No' for a crooked carle like yon Beauchamp. It's shamefu' even to think on it!'

'Shameful, yes, Sire – but possible. The Infanta's and Beauchamp's support combined could be no light matter. And if sustained by the Pope and the Catholic powers . . . with many who mislike the Scots, in England ...'

'Fiend seize me, Patrick – what's to be done, then? What's to be done?'

The other took a pace or two away, over the stable cobblestones, and back. 'I have been thinking on this, Your Grace. Seeking to find a way out. It seems to me that the solution of the matter lies with the Vatican. The Pope. As supreme leader of the Catholic world, he could change all. If he was to tell the English Catholics *not* to lend their support to Beauchamp, then there is no longer a problem.'

'Aye – but how is that to be done?'

'If His Holiness was to be convinced that Your Grace would be a better King of England, from the Catholic point of view, than would Beauchamp ...'

'But, man, he kens fine I'm no Catholic. I've ay been the Protestant monarch.'

'Even Protestant monarchs can turn, Highness – as witness Henry of Navarre, now of France! And Beauchamp is also a Protestant – so far! Not, of course, that I am suggesting that Your Grace should turn secret Catholic – God forbid! But if it could be made clear to the Pope that, unlike Elizabeth, you would be kindly disposed towards Catholics. That you would work with them, and with the Pope himself. That you are the least prejudiced of princes...'

'Ooh, aye – but how to convince the Pope o' this? Eh?'

'If you were to send a letter to His Holiness. By special courier. Secret, of course – since it would never do for it to be known that the King of Scots was in communication with the Tyrant of Rome! A letter which would leave the Pope satisfied in his mind that you were very favourably disposed towards his people...'

'Och, Patrick man – yon Pope's no fool! D'you think he'd no' ken? If I was to write to him of a sudden, yon way. Fine he'd ken I was wanting something. He'd soon sniff it out what we were at.'

'Therefore, Highness, you must indeed seem to want something from him. Something other than your true requirement. And something, if possible, that further confirms your goodwill. Your acknowledgement of the Papal authority in its own sphere. But yet that does not commit you to anything dangerous. For instance – you might write to him hoping that he might be graciously pleased to create a Scottish Cardinal.'

'Eh...?' James blinked at him, mouth open.

'A Cardinal, Sire. A Prince of the Church. It is long since there has been such appointment, of a Scot. But a Scottish Cardinal could be most useful, in dealing with the other Catholic powers – and most of Europe is still Catholic. So Your Grace might well make such a suggestion. And the Pope would esteem it as grace, I am sure!'

'On my soul...!'

'It would cost you nothing, commit you to nothing. Yet the impression on His Holiness would be great, I swear. Especially if it was supported by one or two other indications of Your Grace's open mind in such matters.'

'But... but...' Helplessly the King scratched his head. 'Who, Patrick? Where are we to find a man to name? We havena any...'

'I think I know just the man, Sire. One Drummond, Bishop of Vaison. A prominent cleric, much in favour at the Vatican. By birth a member of the Inchaffray family – and indeed uncle to our good James Elphinstone. The Lord Elphinstone married a Drummond of Inchaffray.'

'You tell me that! Och, my goodness me! But . . . it's a notion, Patrick – it's a notion. Elphinstone, you say? Well, now. Yon's a canny chiel, James Elphinstone. Right eident and diligent. His uncle? But . . . wouldna this Drummond, this Bishop, wonder why for I should be naming him, Patrick? Would it no' smell right strange? Since I've never heard tell o' the man? Would he no' maybe go to the Pope and say there was a twist to it, some way . . . ?'

'I have the answer for that, Your Grace. You must seem to honour James Elphinstone. Make him Secretary for State. It is necessary that this position be revived. The work demands it – work that Elphinstone is already doing. There should be one senior of the eight men who serve you so well – if only to sign the papers. He is the only one of noble birth, and the hardest worker. Make him Secretary of State. Perhaps knight him. Then, Sire, it will seem to the Bishop, and to the Pope, that it is but *he* who presses his uncle's name with you. All will be credible, natural.'

'Guidsakes, man – you think o' everything!'

'I but seek to serve Your Grace to the best of my limited ability. Unlike my lord of Huntly, I cannot present you with costly gifts. Only the products of my poor wits.' He paused. 'As to the same lord, it occurs to me that you could show your appreciation, Sire, of this kindly token of affection, as well as of probable future benefits to come – for the Gordon is passing wealthy – by bestowing upon him some token of your own, some suitable token. In the state of the Treasury, it must cost you nothing. But Your Grace is the fountain of honour. And honours cost you but the price of a piece of parchment and some sealing-wax!'

'Hey – what's this, now? I'd like fine to honour Geordie Gordon some way – but how can I? He's an earl already, and Lieutenant o' the North again. I couldna raise him to be duke, for he's no' o' the blood royal . . .'

'No, that is not possible. But the English whom, pray God, you will soon be ruling, have found a new title, midway between. That of marquis. Higher than earl but less than duke

– taken from the French. You might create Huntly Scotland's first marquis. At no expense to yourself.'

'M'mmm. Uh-huh. I could, aye. Marquis, eh? Think you Geordie would like that?'

'I am sure that he would. He likes strange titles, and revels in calling himself Cock o' the North and Gudeman o' the Bog! He would be suitably grateful, I feel sure. But, what is more important, I think that the Pope in Rome would be the more impressed. With your magnanimity towards the Catholics. In having bestowed this signal honour on your foremost Catholic subject.'

'Aye – that's so. There's something to that, maybe. Marquis o' Huntly! Cardinal Drummond! Aye – and no' costing me a penny-piece! Man – where did you get your wits, eh? No' frae that auld donnert father o' yours!'

'Perhaps it was from the Ruthvens, Majesty. My mother was Barbara Ruthven of Gowrie.' He looked suddenly, directly, levelly, at his monarch. 'Gowrie – to whom the Treasury owes so much money!'

'Ech? Hech, hech! Och, man Patrick. H'rr'mmm.' Hastily coughing and looking away, the King changed the subject. 'Where's . . . where's this place? Vaison, did you say? Where the man Drummond's Bishop?'

'I have not a notion, Sire. Somewhere in France, belike. But we shall find out. Shall I pen some small points to aid you in your letter to the Pope?'

'Do that, Patrick – do that. Aye.'

'Then, with your royal permission, I shall to my desk, Sire . . .'

Reasonably satisfied, Patrick Gray bowed out of the stable.

Chapter Nineteen

King James thrust his chair back violently from the head of the long table, so that it scraped harshly on the Council-chamber floorboards, and started up, to stamp the great room with his shambling, unsteady gait, ramming down his ridiculously high hat more securely on his head. Everywhere, turning eyes to the ceiling or to each other, the entire Privy Council had to rise likewise and so stand in their places while their sovereign paraded. This sort of thing was becoming almost routine at Council meetings, unfortunately.

'Ignorant fools! Presumptuous dolts! Numbskulls!' The King had difficulty in getting the words round his oversized tongue, and, as always when he was excited and upset, his voice went into squeaks. 'They'll pass this folly and that! The Estates o' the Realm will have this done and that done! Ooh, aye. But they'll no' pass my stints and taxations. They'll no' put their hands in their pouches. It is resolved to do this, and resolved to do the next thing – but, waesucks, never a cheep o' where the siller's to come frae! I tell you, my lords, it's no' to be borne! They refuse my right clamant demands. They delay and hold over the right fair and necessary taxes and imposts that Patrick . . . that the Master o' Gray has devised. They say the realm must be strong and I must build up an army. But who's to pay for it? Do they think I'm *made* o' siller?'

Happening to be passing the bulky person of the Earl Màrischal, James poked him strongly in the back. 'You, my lord – do you think the like?' he cried. 'How much have you given to my royal Treasury o' late? Eh?'

A little startled by this unexpected attack, the Keith chief gulped. 'I . . . I sent five hundred crowns no more than three months back, Sire . . .'

'Five hundred! What's five hundred crowns frae half The Mearns? And you, my lord o' Cassillis? What has Carrick sent? Tell me that. What o' the broad lands o' Carrick?'

'I am gathering what I can, Your Grace. But at this season it's no' easy. After the harvest, may be ...'

'Harvest! Houts, man – I canna wait till harvest! This is June. I may need ten thousand men any day – and you say wait till after harvest! A hundred hands are clawing out at me for siller – and you say wait for harvest! You are as bad as the Estates yesterday, my lord!'

A Convention of the Estates, the Scottish parliament, had held one of its infrequent meetings the previous day, the 26th of June 1600. Presented with an excellent and comprehensive scheme of taxation, broadly-based, fairly-designed, it had temporised, hedged and voted for delay – whilst enthusiastically adopting the Octavians' projects of good government and public works. The King himself had presented the demands, and had been mortified by the rebuff.

He stormed on, waving his hands. 'It's no' right. It's no' right, I say. That the King o' Scots should be thus vexed and constrained. For lack o' money to rule and govern his realm. And to support his just and lawful claims to another realm – England! My lord o' Atholl – what o' you? When last did *you* put your hand in your pocket, for your king?'

Emboldened perhaps by the fact that he was himself a Stewart, a far-out cousin of the monarch, Atholl spoke out. 'Sire – my duty is to protect you, to support you at need with armed men – not with pounds and shillings. I am an earl of Scotland – not a merchant!'

The murmur of acclaim that greeted his assertion was faint but eloquent – and significant. James gobbled in anger. 'My lord ... my lord ... !' he got out thickly, and then turned helplessly to look for aid from Patrick Gray.

That man, standing near the foot of the table, close to Sir James Elphinstone the Secretary of State, did not fail him. 'Your Grace,' he said, mildly, easily, 'perhaps my lord of Atholl, in his remote mountain fastness, has not perceived that times have changed? That the sword no longer rules in Scotland. That a tail of blustering men-at-arms is no longer the standard authority in this realm. It is four years, five, since Your Grace last called upon any of your lords for fighting men. All of you ...'
He amended that. 'All of us, my lords, have had these years

of peace, to tend our lands and mend our affairs. Do we owe nothing to His Grace for these years when he has made no call upon our duty? When he has maintained the King's peace with but little aid from us? Is the continuing good government of the realm no concern of ours? Are swords all we are good for, my lords?'

There was silence in that Council-chamber of Edinburgh Castle. Many men frowned darkly, but none spoke.

'Aye. Well said, Master o' Gray', James commended thickly. In the lowered tension, he shuffled back to his great chair at the head of the table, and sat down. Thankfully all followed suit. 'The Master speaks truth,' he went on, banging on the table for quiet. 'He does right well to reprove you, my lords. For it's little enough the most o' you have contributed, this while back, out o' the great lands you hold o' me, the King. Mind you that! You hold your lands o' *me*. At my pleasure. You'd scarce think it, whiles. Wi' the most o' you. But no' o' the Master himsel'. Na, na. I tell you, this past year and more, the realm couldna have been managed lacking the Master putting his hand in his pouch. His own pouch, mind. God kens where he got it, but . . .'

'God . . . and the Pope!' a voice said quietly, from half-way down the table.

There was a stir, with exclamations, muttered charges and counter-charges.

The King was slapping the table again. 'My lord! My lord o' Gowrie!' he cried. 'Watch your tongue, I say! It ill becomes you – aye ill. To make sic-like observes. And against your cousin! You, but who yesterday raised voice against me in the Estates.'

'Not against you, Sire. Never that. Against your advisers, only. Upon a demand for more moneys that your subjects have to give – your poorer subjects. And for a purpose which all true men must conceive to be dishonourable.'

Clearly, firmly, and unflurried, the youthful voice answered the King. The speaker was a man of only twenty-one years, good-looking, fine-featured, well-made – John Ruthven, third Earl of Gowrie and sixth Lord Ruthven. Son of the late Lord Treasurer Gowrie, who had been executed fourteen years before for alleged treason after a murky Court intrigue, he and his family had long been under official royal displeasure – for had it not been to Ruthven Castle that the young King James had been kidnapped and held prisoner for nearly a year, in the lawless 1580s. After his father's execution, the young Earl, with his brother, at the age of fifteen, had been sent abroad, and had spent six years at the University of Padua – to such good effect that he was now in fact Rector of that great seat of learning. He had been back in Scotland only since April, and was already making his presence felt. The day previously he had been the only great lord actually to raise his voice against the King's demand to the Estates for one hundred thousand crowns as an immediate levy on the burghs and lesser barons and lairds.

James was all but speechless. 'Dis . . . dishonourable!' he croaked. 'You! You, to say the like! You, son o' a beheaded miscreant! Grandson o' yon black devil who knifed Davie Rizzio in my own mother's presence! You . . . !'

Only Gowrie's clenched fists betrayed how he disciplined himself. 'Sire, my father's and my grandsire's actions are not my affair. And were dearly paid for. My father's in money as well as blood – for did Your Grace not accept a loan of eighty thousand pounds no less, from his hands? As Treasurer. Which moneys have not yet been repaid . . .'

Again there was near uproar in the Council.

It was not the excited clamorous voices which prevailed, but the young Earl's calm and measured statements. 'What I hold to be dishonourable,' he managed to resume, 'is the policy of raising an army to invade England. This costly threat to enforce Your Grace's claims to the throne of Queen Elizabeth . . .'

'Have done, I say!' James interrupted him furiously. 'Do you dare so decry your prince's legitimate endeavours? We a' ken why you're so kindly concerned for Elizabeth! We ken that you spent two months at her Court on your way home – aye, often close-chambered wi' the Queen hersel', we've heard! No' for nothing, my lord – no' for nothing, I'll be bound! Meddling in matters that are no concern o' yours. To your prince's prejudice – aye, prejudice.'

'Not so, Sire . . .'

'Silence! You will remain silent, sir! This, I'd remind you, is *my* Privy Council – no' yours! Learn you how to behave! My lords,' James declared agitatedly, great eyes rolling as he looked round at all of them, 'the situation o' my royal succession to England is serious. Most serious. Elizabeth is auld and crabbit, and daily grows less clear-like in her mind. She refuses most contumaciously to name me heir. I have ay been her true heir, a' these years. You ken it, she kens it – a' true men ken it. But she'll no' say it, the auld . . . the auld . . . !' He swallowed, but even so, a deal of the royal saliva was lost.

'I had' done a' that man can to bring her to the bit, my lords,' he went on. 'Cecil, her Secretary, and Willoughby, likewise. But to no avail. The stupid auld woman has it in her head that if she once names her heir, she is as good as a corpse! Heard you ever the like? Hersel' a sick and failing husk, and England lacking the sure knowledge o' who'll be on her throne to-morrow! It's wicked, my lords – wicked! And as a consequence, the land is fu' o' plots and schemes. To put this on the throne, and that! God kens a' the claimants there are now sprung up – wi' no' least title o' right to them! There's even a party, they tell me, for Vicky Stewart here, Duke o' Lennox . . .'

Ludovick, sitting at the King's right hand, as nominal President of the Council, had sat silent throughout – as indeed was quite customary when he attended at all. Now he spoke, briefly but strongly.

'Your Grace knows very well, as do all others, that I have no interest in the throne of England, or any other throne. Indeed, if all England, and your royal self, offered it to me in gift, I would refuse it without a second thought. I seek nothing of kings and rule and courts.'

'Aye. I'ph'mm. Just so.' James looked sidelong at him. 'But that's no' the point, Vicky. The point is that on account o' Elizabeth's right stubborn silence as to the succession, there's folk scrabbling for her throne like hound-dogs for a bone! That throne is mine by right, in blood, in reason, and in the policies o' our two states. And, as God's my witness, I shall have it! These two kingdoms shall be united under my reign – to the glory o' Almighty God and the peace and prosperity o' both peoples!'

There was even some applause for this resounding affirmation of faith, led by the Master of Gray.

Encouraged, the King went on, leaning over the table. 'You a' ken, my lords, how we'll benefit – *you'll* benefit. It's to your most notable gain. No more wars. Peace on the Border, for a' time to come. A share in England's wealth, my lords. Appointments at my English Court. Offices o' profit and honour. Broad English lands in my gift. Trade for your burghs and merchants. Aye . . .' That goodly catalogue, ending in a long royal sigh of contemplation, had not only James Stewart licking his lips.

'It's near, my friends – near!' the King went on eagerly, if wetly. 'It could be the morn's morn. Ours! But . . we maun be prepared to *take* what's ours, if others seek to steal it frae us. If Elizabeth doesna name me heir, before her death, there'll be plenty seeking to get sat on her throne the moment she's awa'! Seeking, wi' armed force. They're no' a' like Vicky Lennox, here! There'll be war, my lords. I must have a Scots army standing ready on the Border, a stronger host than any the others can raise, to march south the instant moment the word o' Elizabeth's death is brought. No less will serve to win me what is mine. And for that, my lords, I must have siller. Much siller.'

Now, he had most of the Council with him, or at least interested. White-faced, set, Lord Gowrie stared straight ahead of him. Ludovick looked down at his finger-nails, expressionless. Certain others frowned or murmured. But by and large the general air of hostility was abated.

'I must have that hundred thousand crowns I asked the Estates for, and more,' James told them, nodding portentously. 'And at once. If no' frae them, frae you, my lords! You'll get it back, mind – ooh aye, you'll get it back. Wi' interest. Once I'm in yon London. You can do it fine and easy, if you set your minds to it – you ken that. Some, mind, ha' been right generous already. My lord Marquis, in especial . . .'

Huntly, who had seemed to be asleep, opened his eyes, nodded casually in the direction of his monarch, a crooked grin on his big red face, and shut his eyes again.

'Aye. And the Constable, my lord of Erroll, has done right nobly likewise.'

There was some throat-clearing at the especial mention of these two Catholics. James nodded again.

'Others, o' maybe a different conviction havena yet seen fit to do the like,' he added.

Ludovick almost opened his mouth to observe that his Protestant wife's deep coffers, at least, had been most thoroughly and consistently raided – but thought better of it.

'So there it is, my lords,' the King declared. 'If you would have your prince King o' England – wi' a' that will mean to you – then waesucks, you'll just ha' to find me the siller! And forthwith. I must raise and equip an army, without delay. How many ha' we got there now, Patrick? And in what-like state?'

'Sir James, I think, can best tell us such details, Sire.'

The diffident but efficient Secretary of State kept his eyes down-bent on his papers, even though he did not require to consult them. 'You have four thousand and three hundred men enrolled, Your Majesty. Some three thousand trained and equipped. But horses only for eleven hundred. More horses are coming from the Low Countries, and arms from France. But ... these are not yet paid for, Sire.'

'Aye. And I need at least ten thousand, my lords!'

Into the murmur of talk which arose, Patrick Gray raised his melodious voice again. 'Your Grace – may I point out our especial need? I hear noble lords saying that they will supply men, rather than money, as formerly. But this will not serve. Bands of men-at-arms, my friends, are not sufficient for His Grace's purpose, however many. This host must be disciplined sternly. To stand and wait. Possibly for months, even years. It must obey no orders but the King's. If it has indeed to march into England, it must do so under strict control – for it must not assail or offend the English people, the King's new subjects. You know your men-at-arms, my lords – we all know them, all too well! They will not serve, in this.'

None could controvert him.

'Moreover, it is not only the soldiers,' he went on. 'There are many in England who will support the highest bidder! Unprincipled gentry, no doubt – such as none here would countenance!' He smiled round them all, genially. 'Such disbursements and subventions, to carefully chosen persons in the English Court circle, although costly, will afford most handsome interest. But, alas, His Grace's coffers are empty, scraped clean as a bone. As is my own humble purse.' He nodded with entire goodwill in the direction of his cousin Gowrie. 'God – or even the Pope, my lord – are but unchancy contributors, I fear, and the widow's cruse would appear to have run out!'

There was a laugh at that, for young Gowrie was known to be of a notably religious turn of mind, almost a Puritan indeed, and the Biblical reference apt. The statement also was literally true, although the speaker hoped that only he and Elphinstone knew how true. The Pope's largesse, which had so largely kept the protestant ship of state afloat this past year and more, had now dried up. His munificence had amounted to more even than the hundred thousand crowns demanded of the Estates. But in the continued absence of any sign of Scotland turning Catholic or King James making any public pronouncement towards that end, His Holiness was now limiting his benevolence to promises – even if princely promises. Two million crowns, no less, would be despatched from Rome the moment that James published liberty of conscience for all subjects of the two kingdoms, and moved his forces over the Border for London. Patrick Gray, of a night, was apt to dream longingly of that two million.

'Aye, my lords – that's the way o' it,' James took him up. 'I've been Elijah ower long. I charge you a' to reckon up forthwith what moneys you can raise out o' the lands you hold o' me, and inform the Secretary here. Aye, and dinna be grudging, my friends – if you'd have me remember you kindly in London-town! Then awa' wi' you and gather together the siller. Is it understood?'

If the depth of silence was the measure of the assent, then there was no misapprehension in the Privy Council

The curiously unsteady yet for once determined royal glance made a slow circuit of all the faces at that table, until it came to that of the Earl of Gowrie, and there halted. For seconds on end these two eyed each other, as all men watched – and it was the monarch's regard which dropped first.

'Aye.' James jerked. 'Mind it! I say, mind it.' He got to his teetering feet. 'This Council stands adjourned. God preserve you my lords!'

As the others rose, he was already making for the door.

Patrick Gray was there first, nevertheless, to open the door wide, having signed Elphinstone back. 'Magnificent, Sire,' he murmured as the King lurched by. 'I am lost in admiration! Only – Your Grace omitted to mention the Duchess of Lennox's contributions, as I suggested. It would have been wise, I think.'

'Guidsakes – I clean forgot! It was yon Gowrie – yon ill limmer, Gowrie! A curse on him! To owe the likes o' him a' that siller! Eighty thousand Scots pounds! In this pass. It's scarce to be borne, Patrick – scarce to be borne!'

'As Your Highness says – scarce to be borne,' the Master repeated evenly, and bowed to the royal back as the Guard outside escorted the sovereign hence.

Ludovick Stewart stroked the dark curly head of the six-year-old son at his side – and quickly the boy broke away and darted across to the edge of the tiny terrace garden carved so cunningly out of the cliff below towering Castle Huntly, keeping his small square shoulders stiffly turned away from the visitor.

'See you that!' the man complained. 'He scarce knows me – his own father. Is that right? Is that proper, Mary?'

The young woman bit her lip. 'It is near two years since he has seen you, Vicky. Do not blame him ...'

'I do not blame Johnnie,' the Duke answered her. 'It is you that I blame. It is not his fault that he and I are all but strangers, Mary – it is yours. You who keep us apart. Will you not, for his sake if not for mine, come back to me? Back to Methven, at least. His heritage. Where we can be together at times, if no more than that. It has stood empty, waiting, all these long years. It is all that I live for, I swear.'

Troubled deeply, she eyed him. He had never seen her look so lovely, in her simple country gown, with the basket of cut flowers on her arm. Now twenty-five, Mary Gray was in the fullest bloom of fair womanhood, of an exquisite beauty of feature and figure to tear at the man's heart, patrician grace and carriage in every line of her however humble her attire and modest her demeanour.

'Not ... not in front of Johnnie, my dear,' she murmured, low-voiced. 'I beg of you – not now.' She moved a little away over the short turf of the narrow terrace in the warm July sunshine. 'You have ridden far today, Vicky?'

Shortly, abruptly, he answered her. 'Only from Falkland. The

Court is there again. Since four days. I crossed the ferry at Erroll. No great distance, as you know.' He glanced down at himself, frowning. 'It seems to be my fate ever and only to come to you thus, covered in dust, booted and spurred, smelling of horses...'

'Do you think I care for that – so long as I see you?' she asked, reaching out to touch his arm lightly.

'You can say that – when still you keep me from you!'

'To be sure – for I did not cease to love you, my dear, when we were forced to part. You should not visit me here – that is certain. But when you do, can I help it if my heart all but bursts at the sight of you?'

'Mary...!'

Quickly she went on, before he could make too much of that. 'It is twenty long months since last you came to Castle Huntly, Vicky. That black day when... when...'

He nodded. 'I have been far since then. In London. And Paris. Burgundy. The Low Countries. Sent on embassages, now here, now there. Sent, I do believe, to get me out of the King's sight, out of Patrick Gray's sight – even out of *your* sight!'

'No!'

'But, yes. Who knows, perhaps out of Jean Campbell's sight, also!'

'Your wife...!'

'I prefer to call her my duchess!'

Mary drew a deep breath. She turned, to call the boy over to her, to hand him the basket of flowers. 'Johnnie – take these up to Granlord's room. Tell him that I shall come to see him very soon. Talk with him, Johnnie. Tell him of the martin's nest you have found in the cliff, here...'

'How is he? The old lord?' Ludovick asked, as the boy ran off.

'A broken, done old man,' she answered, sighing. 'But the empty shell of what he was. He seldom stirs from his chamber, high up at the battlements. Staring and staring out over the Carse all day. Lips moving but not speaking. He will see only Davy and myself. And Johnnie. And even us he does not seem to know, at times. Oh, Vicky – how terrible a blow Patrick struck him, that day!'

'Aye. When Patrick strikes . . . ! God only knows – perhaps I should never have come, that day. To warn him. Perhaps it would have been better, kinder, to have let the matter take its course. He would have resisted the arrest – Lord Gray. There would have been fighting. And that would indeed have been treason. But he would have gone down like a man.'

'No. You did what was right. And generous. This would have happened anyway – this of Granlord. The bad blood has been working its ill between them for long. All my life. Indeed, it may be that my life was the cause of it all – my birth that raised the wicked barrier between them. Sometimes of a night I lie and think of that, Vicky . . .'

'That is folly, lass. Those two would have clashed on any and every issue. And sooner or later Patrick would have struck. As he always strikes – unexpectedly, like a scorpion, a snake, a viper! As, I fear he will strike again . . . !'

Tight-lipped she turned to him, eyes asking, but wordless.

He nodded grimly. 'Aye, it is Patrick that brings me here again – since I must needs have an excuse to come to you,' he told her bitterly. 'Patrick, and the King. I fear now greatly for another man – Gowrie. I fear for him, Mary.'

'The Earl of Gowrie? John Ruthven? The Lady Beatrix's brother?'

'Yes. And your cousin. The Lady Gray, Patrick's mother, was sister to Gowrie's father, was she not?'

'I scarce know him, nevertheless, Vicky. Always he has been away. Abroad. I had heard that he was back, that is all.'

'He is back. And putting himself in Patrick's way, the King's way. Honest and fearless, but not knowing what he does, what he hazards. I have tried to warn him – but he will not heed me.'

'You think . . . you think that Patrick means him an injury?'

'I know it. Is not anyone who opposes Patrick in danger? Gowrie opposes his policies openly. He condemns the English succession policy. He openly refuses to contribute to the King's levy. He cares not what he says, so long as he believes it right – noble behaviour but dangerous, fatal. *You* know it. We have seen so often what happens to those who run counter to Patrick. Gowrie is in deadly danger. I am sure of it. I see all the signs. I have sought to tell him. Twice I have spoken to him.

But to no avail. There is so little to point to, for Patrick is never obvious. And Gowrie does not know him. He was only a child when he left Scotland, six or seven years ago. He does not know that he is dealing with the Devil himself!'

Patrick's daughter gulped, but said nothing.

'Gowrie, I think, conceives me as but a fool, or worse. He sees me as close to the throne, a tool of the King's party, warning him off. To keep him quiet. Also, he does not love me, on account of his sister, Sophia. My first wife – if you could name her that. God knows, I had no responsibility for her death! But the family think the less of me, in consequence. I spoke to the other sister, the Lady Beatrix, your friend. But to no better avail. I urged that she tell him to leave Scotland. To go back to Padua. He is a scholar, Rector of the University there. But she herself does not know the danger, as you and I know it. And her brother is noways close to her, almost a stranger to her, seeing her also as of the King's company, a lady-in-waiting to the Queen. So . . . I come here, Mary.'

'But what can I do, Vicky?'

'You, and Davy Gray. I thought that Gowrie might listen to you, perhaps. Patrick's daughter and brother. You might persuade him. You are clearly not of the King's company . . .'

'Davy is away. Visiting Granlord's properties in The Mearns.'

'You are the more important in this. Gowrie is at his townhouse in Perth. He left Falkland yesterday. If you would ride there, with me, to speak with him. It is not two hours riding. He might listen to you, Mary – for all men listen to you! You are related to him. You can speak of Patrick as no other can . . .'

'You are asking me to . . . to witness against my father? To this stranger?' That said low-voiced.

'I suppose that I am, yes. That he may possibly be one less stain on your father's name and conscience! As I fear he will be, otherwise.'

She said nothing.

'Mary – if, by speaking to Gowrie, you can save an evil deed being done, should you not do it? How would you feel, my dear, if you withheld, and later Gowrie was brought low by some wicked intrigue? *I* am no friend of his – but that is what I ask myself. That is why I am here.'

'Very well.' She raised her head, decision taken. 'I shall ride with you. Vicky. First, I must see to Granlord. Then, in an hour, I shall be ready...'

Accompanied by two of Ludovick's grooms, presently they rode through the July afternoon the fifteen miles along the fertile cattle-dotted Carse of Gowrie to Saint John's town of Perth. So long it was since the girl had ridden at this man's side, that at first she could only delight in it, despite the object of their journey. To begin with she was almost gay – and Mary Gray, like her sire, could be sparkling gaiety itself. But as they neared Perth, following the narrowing Tay by Seggieden and Kinfauns a silence descended upon them.

'Mary,' the Duke said, after a long interval. 'How long is this to go on? How long will you keep me away from you? Hold me off? Is there to be no end to it? When we love each othe1. When our son sees his father only as a stranger? It has been three years now – three endless years.'

'I am sorry, Vicky,' she answered him, almost in a whisper.

'You said the same two years ago! You said to wait. I have waited, Mary – God knows how I have waited! How much longer must I wait?'

'I do not know. I only know, my heart, that I cannot share you. Not with any prospect of joy or peace between us. I am sorry. I know that it is my grievous fault – wicked pride, no doubt. But I know myself sufficiently well to be sure that if I made myself come to you, shared your bed again, there would be always that other between us! The true trust and dear unity would be gone, my love – broken. And that I could not bear. We would be less happy than we are now. Believe me, it is so.'

'Then, shrive me – what is there to wait for? Do *you* wait for a miracle? For Jean to die, maybe? Do you wish her dead ...?'

'Ah, no! Do not say that. It is not true. I am a wicked proud woman, Vicky – but not so vile as that. I swear it! No – I ask you to wait for something in myself. Some change ...'

'I would seek a divorcement – since it was no true marriage. But the King and the Kirk would never hear of it.'

'No. For it was true enough marriage to produce a child,

335

Vicky. You have a daughter, I hear. Is she ... is she fair? A joy to you?'

'No. I scarce know her. I am unfortunate with my offspring, am I not? Her mother keeps her close. I seldom see the child ...'

'Vicky – is that fair to the bairn?'

'I know not. I would not have the child to suffer – although she has been a sickly creature from the first. But Jean hides her away. We can hardly be said to live together, you understand. Have not done so for many months. She goes her way – and goes it boldly, as I know – and I go mine. Though, to be sure, mine is a more lonely way than is hers! We see each other about the Court – that is all.'

'Oh, Vicky – what a tangle it is!'

'No such great tangle, Mary. Nothing that we could not cut through this very night – had you the will for it!'

She lowered her head, and they rode on unspeaking.

Crossing the bridge of Tay into Perth town, they were quickly at Gowrie House, which indeed faced the river, its gardens running down to the water's edge. It was a great rambling establishment, turreted and gabled, forming three sides of a courtyard, with one wing flanking the street of Speygate. With the tall Kirk of St. John, it dominated the town – as indeed had done its family for long. The young Earl had been but a week or two back in Scotland when he was appointed provost of the town and chief magistrate.

The visitors were first received by the Earl's brother, Alexander, Master of Gowrie, a cheerful, smiling youth of nineteen, who had been playing tennis with a page. Obviously much taken with Mary Gray, and suitably impressed by the eminence of the Duke, he led them by many corridors and stairways to a moderate-sized room off a great gallery on the second floor, evidently a library. Here his elder brother was surrounded by books and parchments strewn on tables and floor, and was dusting and arranging them. Although he evinced no great joy at the interruption of his task, he greeted his guests courteously, requesting the Master to have wine and refreshments set before them, and explaining that the house had been long standing unoccupied and that he was concerned to discover what of value might be in his father's library.

336

Ludovick was little of the diplomat, and came quickly to the point. 'This, my lord, is the Lady Mary Gray, mother of my son – who would be my wife if I had been able to have my way. She is natural daughter to the Master of Gray – and therefore your own cousin in some degree. I have brought her here because I believe that what she can tell you is of the highest importance to your lordship.'

Gowrie looked at Mary keenly, thoughtfully, and inclined his head. 'I am honoured by your interest,' he said quietly. 'I have not failed to hear of the lady. But how do my poor affairs so greatly concern her, my lord Duke? Or indeed, yourself!'

'Myself, I have already spoken to you. To but little effect, I think. The Lady Mary may be more successful. I pray so.'

'My lord,' the young woman said earnestly. 'My position is difficult, unhappy. When you have heard me, you will absolve me, I hope, from any charge of meddling, of undue interest in your concerns. I am a woman of no position or importance – but I have this one qualification, that I know my father, the Master of Gray, very well. Sometimes to my sorrow!'

'Whether this is a cause for congratulation or for sympathy, madam, is for you to say. For myself, I have had few dealings with the Master, cousins though we be – nor have ambitions for more!'

'Anyone who takes any hand in the affairs of this realm, has to deal with the Master. Whether he knows it, or not, my lord! If you run counter to the King's present policy – as I am told that you do – you run counter to the Master of Gray. And that can be dangerous!'

'Is it so? All must agree with His Grace's every notion, then – or risk my cousin's righteous displeasure! Is that the way of it? A dire matter!'

At the young Earl's tone of voice, Mary shook her head. 'I am sorry,' she said. 'Be patient with me. Small disagreements, minor dissensions, would not matter. But you, my lord, I understand to oppose the King on a great issue – the issue nearest to his heart. The English succession. The matter above all others which over the years my father has worked for. You are against the finding of this money, as the Duke tells me, for the raising and providing of an army, to hold in support of His Grace's

337

claim. You may well be right – indeed, although my poor woman's opinion is of no value to any, I would think also that this is not how the succession should be assured. But this is scarce the point . . .'

'You will forgive me asking it,' Gowrie interposed stiffly. 'But what *is* the point? If the rights and wrongs of the matter are not!'

'It is hard, sore, for me to say it, my lord – but that because of this course, you are in real danger, I fear.'

'Danger, madam? Of what? And from whom?'

'From the Master of Gray. Of what, I cannot say. My father is not one to make his moves apparent, to be guessed at. But this I do know all too surely, that those who oppose him in major matters are always in danger. Most real danger. It has been proved too often to be in doubt, my lord.'

'A most convenient reputation for the Master to cherish!' the other commented coldly. 'None must oppose him – or they suffer terrible but undisclosed dangers! A valuable celebrity, fostered and published by his household and friends!'

'Do not be a fool, Gowrie!' Ludovick burst out. 'We are not here on the Master's account, but on yours. We fear – we more than fear, we are certain – that some move will be made against you. What we know not – but I have observed all the signs . . .'

'You would have me jump at signs and shadows, my lord Duke? I note your warning, and shall be on my guard. But I cannot esteem such shadowy fears to have any justification. I do naught that any other member of the Council has not a right to do – to oppose the expenditure of moneys on a policy which was before the Estates. It is no more than my duty, if I conceive the policy wrong. As I do. Are all who voted against it in the Estates likewise in danger of the puissant Master's ire?'

' 'Fore God, man – can you not see this as it is? Not as you would wish it to be? It is not some mere taking of sides in a debate on the state's policy. It is a direct attack on the King's most cherished project, his lifelong ambition. And today the Master of Gray is behind all the King's projects, and moreover believes this succession to be the greatest good that Scotland can achieve. At the Estates, it was your voice raised that turned the tide against the King's tax. And in the Council you could not but see how hot was the King against you for it. Since then you have stated that you will give nothing towards the levy which is being demanded of all great land-holders. No others have seen fit to say as much. Others may hedge and delay and seek to win out of it. But you, of all men, ought not to have cried your refusal to the heavens.'

'Why me, of all men, I pray?'

'Because, my lord, the Crown owes you for eighty thousand pounds! That is why. And no debtor on this round earth could love the man to whom he owed such a sum!'

There was silence for a few moments. For the first time, Gowrie seemed in any way affected or concerned. The Master and a servitor came in with food and drink, and no more could be said until the latter at least was gone. The Earl dismissed his brother also.

'I have not demanded any immediate repayment of these moneys,' he told them, presently. 'Knowing, indeed, that I would not get them. Am I now expected to throw good money after bad?'

Ludovick shrugged. 'I care not if you never give James another silver piece. But to oppose him openly, and to lead others to do the same, is folly.'

'Such is to break no law. What can they do against me?'

'My lord – you do not know my father or you would not ask that!' Mary Gray declared. 'If you stand in the way of anything to which he has set his hand, he will find a way of pulling you down. Many have discovered that, to their cost . . .'

'*My* father did!' Ludovick interrupted harshly. 'His close friend. I now know that he brought him low, to his ruin and death. His own father, the Lord Gray, he has recently dragged down likewise, without shame or compassion, for his own ends. And *your* father, my lord – what of him? The first Gowrie – Greysteil. He was beheaded on a charge of treason, was he not? After making a secret confession, under promise of pardon, and so brought to his doom. Whose hand was behind that, think you?'

'That was on account of the Ruthven Raid. Patrick Gray, they told me, worked for his pardon. That was Arran's work, was it not?' The Earl stared.

'Arran scarce moved a hand, in statecraft, without Patrick behind him. He was Chancellor only in name. The business bears all the marks of the Master's hand.'

'I'll not believe that. His own mother's brother!'

'Who gained the administering of your great Ruthven estates while you were under age, my lord? Who had your sister Sophia married to me – bairns, both of us? And why?'

The other plucked his chin, looking from one to the other of his visitors.

Mary was wringing her hands. 'My lord,' she said, 'this of your father, I do not know. I was too young. It may not be so. But . . . there have been others, I fear, in plenty. Patrick . . . Patrick is a strange man. He has great qualities – but he can be the Devil incarnate! He is, many will say, the most able and clever servant that any King of Scots has known. The realm has never been better ruled, most will admit. But he has no least scruple, where his path is crossed. I urge you, I pray you – do not fail to heed us. Do not dismiss your warning . . .'

'In God's name – what would you have me to do?'

It was the Duke who answered, 'Go back to Padua,' he told him tersely. 'Before it is too late.'

'Shrive me! Padua! Do you jest? Leave Scotland . . . ?'

'Aye, my lord. Just that. Leave Scotland – while there is yet time.'

'This is nonsense! Unthinkable! I shall return to Padua in due course. Next year, it may be. For my affairs there are still to settle. I am still Rector of that University. But not now. I am but three months home! Think you I will go running, like some whipped cur? From the Master of Gray. I – Gowrie!'

'It is not only from him – from the one man. It may be from the whole power of this realm. Which he may use against you. Do you not understand? It is for your own safety and weal . . .'

'Is it, my lord Duke? Of a truth? Is it not perhaps for Patrick Gray's weal, rather, that you come? Perhaps a device to get me out of his way, at no cost? Are you sent to scare me off . . . !'

Ludovick jumped to his feet. 'Have a care, sir, what you say!' he exclaimed. 'Lennox is no lackey of the Master of Gray, or any man, I'd have you know! You will not speak to me so . . .'

'Nor will *you* frighten me with bogles!' Gowrie also rose. 'I will not be threatened...'

'Vicky! My lords!' Mary cried, 'Not this – I beseech you! Be patient – there is so much at stake. Hot words will serve nothing...'

'No words will serve with my lord of Gowrie, I think!' the Duke asserted. 'I, for one, will waste no more on him.'

'For that, at least, I am grateful, sir!'

'Come, Mary...'

'Is our journeying to be quite fruitless, then?' the young woman asked, helplessly. 'Will you not be warned, my lord? Perceive your danger...?'

'I perceive, of a truth, that Patrick Gray would have me out of his path! That, at least, is clear,' Gowrie said, moving after Ludovick towards the door.

'You will take heed, then? Take precautions...?'

The Earl did not answer. They went down the stairs singly, the Duke hastening in front, Gowrie next, and Mary lagging in the rear. At the outer door, where the grooms waited with the horse in the stone-flagged courtyard, the girl turned again to the stiff younger man.

'You will do something?' she urged. 'Be guarded well? Ready to fly if need be...?'

'I shall pleasure myself by keeping away from Court, at any rate,' he told her, distantly. 'I have lands in Atholl which I have not seen for long. There I may visit. But I fly for no man...'

With that they had to be content, and took their departure with only bare civilities.

As they clattered over the cobblestones of Perth, Ludovick alternately raged against the stiff-necked folly and blind self-sufficiency of the man they had set out to succour, and apologised for having brought the young woman on this thankless errand. Loudly employed thus, he did not at first hear when Mary presently called urgently to him – and by the time that she had succeeded in attracting his attention and directing his gaze where she indicated, it was too late.

'Amongst that throng of drovers and Highlandmen,' she called. 'Around the alehouse. It was Logan! Logan of Restalrig.

I swear it was he! Looking at us. He turned and hurried off. When he saw I perceived him. Down that vennel. It was Logan, Vicky!'

'Restalrig! Here, in Perth? That bird of ill omen! You are sure?'

'I would not mistake that face. It has cost us too dear, in the past.'

'Patrick has had his outlawry annulled. He hangs about the skirts of the Court. I have never seen them together, but . . .'

'Should we go back? Tell the Earl? Warn him?'

Ludovick snorted. 'Warn that one! Tell him what? Think you he would thank us for the information that one of Patrick's bravoes is in his town? Besides, it may have nothing to do with Gowrie.'

Preoccupied and with no hint of gaiety left to them, they crossed the bridge over Tay and turned their beasts eastwards for the Carse.

Chapter Twenty

The Duke of Lennox drew rein, and the steam from his panting, sweating mount rose to join the mists which, on this still August morning, had not yet had time to disperse, caught in all the shaws and glades of the great marshy forest of Stratheden. He cocked his ear – but could hear only his horse's snorting breathing and the hollow thud of hooves on sodden ground as his falconer came cantering up behind him.

'I thought that I heard the horn,' he called back. 'Did you hear aught, Pate?'

'No, lord. No' a cheep.'

'It is early to have killed. But we are on the wrong track, that is clear. The brute must have circled round to the north. Do many follow us ... ?'

Thin and high, from some distance off, a hunting-horn sounded.

'North, as I jaloused. By west, some way. It has made for higher ground, then – swung away from the river. A pox on it – the King was right!'

'Aye, His Grace is right canny when it comes to the stags, lord. He seems to ken the way a hunted beast will think, will turn.'

They could hear other riders who had followed the Duke's mistaken lead approaching now. Ludovick pulled his spume-flecked black's head round to the right, and spurred on, to pick his way amongst the alder, birch scrub and hollies, northwards.

There did not sound to be many behind him. Most must have followed the King when, about two miles back, the stag and baying hounds had taken the south flank of a wooded hillock, and James had pulled off to the north. He shone at this, did their peculiar monarch; in the forest, with deer to chase, he was a different man, with a sheer instinct for the business that was more than any mere experience and field-craft. His heart was in it – to the woe of most of his Court.

It would not be much after nine now – and they had been in the saddle for almost three hours. Small wonder that the numbers riding were small, despite royal disapproval – and most of these resentful. A man had to be an enthusiast indeed to be up day after day at five of the clock, wet or fine – and no women, however ambitious or spirited, would face it. Ludovick himself, in his present restive and fretful state of mind, made no complaint. He too was fond of the hunt, the vigorous action of which gave scant opportunity for gnawing thoughts, broodings and repinings, the long days in the saddle which left a man too tired to care overmuch for his lonely nights, to pine for the presence which meant all to him.

Riding north now, in answer to the horn's summons, to what must be an early kill, with the headlong pace of the chase slackened, Ludovick could not keep the sore and aching thoughts at bay – more especially as it was not so very far from here that once, on just such a morning and occasion as this, he had contrived a meeting between Mary Gray and the King, which had led to the return from his first exile of the Master of Gray, and so to a co-operation between them, the Duke and the land-steward's reputed daughter, that culminated in their loving taking one of the other. The contemplation was bitter-sweet indeed.

The intermittent winding of the horn guided him in time to the more hilly ground that lifted towards the foothills of the Ochils between Strathmiglo and Balvaird, where the trees grew smaller and stunted and gave place to whins and thorn. Here, on an open grassy terrace, about six miles from Falkland and the palace, the stag had been cornered, almost prematurely, in a re-entrant of outcropping rock, and brought down, a big beast with a magnificent head but too much weight to its forequarters. A score or so of horses were being held by grooms and falconers, deer-hounds were pacing about with lithe grace, and men were grouped here and there.

But although Ludovick rode straight to the spot beside the rocks where the chief huntsman was kneeling, busy at the bleeding and gralloching of the quarry, James was not there; which was strange, for desperately as he hated and feared the sight and presence of blood and naked steel, the King never appeared to find any displeasure in this messy business of the gralloch – and indeed was apt to offer pawky advice to the operator, with proprietorial interest in the slain, and sometimes even to lend a hand himself. On this occasion, however, the royal victor was not crowing about his prowess, as usual, but standing some distance away, talking to a single individual. Another little group, including the Earl of Mar, George Home, and John Ramsay, the present favourite page, stood nearby, presumably beyond hearing, watching. And the remainder of the hunt stood further off, all eyeing the King, not the ceremony of the gralloch.

Ludovick was not so enamoured of his cousin's company and presence as to hasten to his side. But a movement of the King's ungainly form suddenly revealed to the Duke the slender figure of the man he spoke with. It was Alexander Ruthven, Master of Gowrie – whom Ludovick had not set eyes upon since that day at Perth a full month before. Frowning, he moved over.

Johnny Mar told him that the Master, with a cousin, Andrew Ruthven, had come up behind them as the stag turned at bay. They had certainly not started out on the hunt with the rest. He had requested to speak with the King apart. Some request for office or position, no doubt – one more pretty boy, the Earl suggested, with a scornful glance at Home and young Ramsay.

'He came seeking the King, then?' Ludovick asked. 'It was not the King that sent for him?'

'Would he be like to send for the fellow in the heat of a hunt?'

Presently James, who seemed much interested in his conversation, perceived the Duke's presence and beckoned him forward.

'Hech, hech, Vicky – you missed it! Aye, missed it! You were smart enough, back yonder. You should ha' held to me, man.' The sovereign chuckled his triumph. 'But, see – here's Sauny Ruthven, Gowrie's brother. He's come tell me that my lord his brother has something for me, at Perth. Aye – maist interesting.' And he shot a quick glance at the handsome young Ruthven.

'Indeed, Sire,' Ludovick said flatly.

'Aye. It's . . . it's right kindly intentioned. He would have me ride there, forthwith. To Perth.'

'*You*, Sire? Ride to Perth? Now? At Gowrie's behest?'

'Aye. You see, it's this way, Vicky. Gowrie has yon ill loon the Master o' Oliphant, some place in Perth. Him that's at the horn. You ken I've been to take order wi' him for long, and couldna lay hands on him. Now he's done this new vile and proud oppression in Angus, and he'll have to pay for it. Guidsakes, yes. He's lying in Perth...'

'Even so, Sire, I see no reason why you, the King, should go in person to apprehend him. To call off this hunt and ride a dozen miles just to act sheriff! Send a party. Send Gowrie authority to arrest Oliphant himself – although he needs it not, for he is provost of the burgh.'

'Na, na, Vicky – I maun' go mysel'. He's an unco proud and agile rogue, this. He's old enough to be Gowrie's father and would befool him, to be sure. It'll need the King himsel' to put the King's justice on yon one.

Mystified, the Duke shrugged. 'As you will, Sire – but I cannot see the need of it.' He looked doubtfully at young Ruthven. 'Has my lord of Gowrie not sufficient stout fellows in Perth town to apprehend old Lord Oliphant's son?'

The young man coughed. 'I fear not, my lord Duke. It's a kittle matter...'

'Aye, just that,' the King said brusquely, finally. 'Kittle, aye. We'll ride. But no' a' this throng. Vicky – do you and Johnny Mar select a number decently to company me. And pack the lave back to Falkland. Bring you my Lords Lindores and Inchaffray. And Sir Thomas Erskine and Jamie Erskine. Ummm. And Geordie Home and Johnny Ramsay, there. Aye, and the physician-man, Herries. Och, aye – wi' yoursel's, that's aplenty. See you to it. Come you, Master Sauny...'

So presently a reduced and somewhat bewildered company of sportsmen thus nominated, with the Duke at their head, were pounding after their liege lord on the twelve-mile ride to Perth, while the others were left, ruefully or gratefully as it might be, to escort the single trophy of an abortive day's hunting back to wondering Falkland town.

James had waited for none, and superbly mounted on the splendid white Barb which had been Huntly's gift, was already well in advance, young Ruthven being hard put to it to keep up with him.

They went, by the little valley of the Binn Burn, down into the steep winding defile of Glen Farg, forded the river thereof down near the mouth of the glen, and thereafter went thundering at a fine pace across the level haughlands of the great River Earn, mile upon mile, scattering cattle and raising squattering wildfowl from the scores of pools and ditches. It was not until Bridge of Earn itself was reached that Ludovick caught up with the King, who was now somewhat held back by the Master's tired horse. It was always a mystery how James, who looked so ill on a horse, like a sack of meal in the saddle, in fact rode so well and tirelessly. His great-grandfather, James the Fourth of sad memory, had been the same.

He seemed to be in excellent spirits, despite this extra-ordinary interruption of his beloved hunting. 'No' far now, Vicky,' he called out. 'But three miles beyont this brig, ower the side o' yon Moncrieffe Hill. We'll soon ken the rights o' the business, now!'

'There are doubts, Sire? Of the rights of it? Anent the Master of Oliphant?'

James rolled his great eyes, from Ludovick back towards Ruthven, who was beginning to fall behind. He pulled his white over closer to the Duke's side.

'It's no' Oliphant, Vicky – no' Oliphant, at all! Yon was but a device, see you. Necessary, you understand, to keep the matter close. And it is a right close matter.' The King had dropped his voice, so that the other had great difficulty in hearing him. Yet he sounded notably pleased with himself, almost gleeful. 'Right close. Weighty. Aye, o' great consequence.'

Ludovick looked at him keenly, wordless.

'I can tell *you*, Vicky – but no' a word to the others, mind. It's no' a matter to be shouted abroad, this! Guid kens it's no'! There's gold in this, Vicky – yellow gold! Gowrie and his brother ha' gotten their hands on a mannie wi' a pot o' gold!'

'What!'

'Gold, I tell you! A byordinar strange discover. Last night, it was. Sauny Ruthven, here, came on this mannie. Out in the fields some place, beyond Perth, he says. A right mysterious carle, muffled to the nose in a cloak. Ruthven had never seen the like. When he challenged him, the crittur was fair dismayed,

347

and began to run. But Sauny's young and quick. Forby, the stranger was sair weighted down. Sauny got a hold o' him, and off wi' his cloak. And, man, under it he had this pot o' gold. A great wide pot, full o' gold pieces! Have you ever heard the like?'

Lennox's almost open-mouthed astonishment was answer enough.

'Aye, then. A most notable employ, you'll agree, Vicky? Sauny was right exercised. So he haled the carle to Gowrie House, wi' his pot, and has him secure in a bit privy chamber there. Then, at cock-crow, he's up and on the road to gie me the tidings. What think you o' that Vicky Stewart?' All this in a confidential if gabbled undertone, with much glancing over padded shoulders and around.

'But . . . but . . . !' Ludovick had seldom had more difficulty in finding words. 'You don't tell me . . . Your Grace isn't riding to Perth on such a, a bairn's gullery? A fable!'

'Ah, but we maun discover the matter aright, Vicky. Sauny has the man lockit up for us to see. To question. And his gold wi' him. Foreign gold it is, too – all Spanish coin, Sauny says. It will be a Jesuit priest, belike – a Jesuit, wi' moneys to raise a rebellion.'

'Sire – Jesuit plotters, I'll swear, don't travel the country carrying pots of gold pieces under their oxters! This is the sheerest invention . . .'

'How d'you ken what they do, Vicky? What do *you* know o' Jesuit priests? They peddle Spanish gold – we a' ken that. They maun carry it some way. Why no' in a pot?'

'But . . . Sire, this is madness! Never have I heard so unlikely a tale! And if it were true, why bring the King all this long road to Perth, to see the prisoner? Surely the man could have been brought to you?'

'Och, well – there might ha' been a rescue, see you. The carle was for taking the gold some place, mind. His friends in the business will be right put out. They'd likely try a rescue. The gold's safer at Gowrie House.'

'If any gold there is!'

'You . . . you misdoubt the business Vicky'

'I do, Sire. As I say, I cannot think of it all as other than a fable. A madness. But for what purpose . . . ?'

They rode on in silence for a little, and it was noteworthy how the King slackened his pace. The Master of Gowrie was almost up with them again when James spoke to his companion in a hoarse whisper.

'Madness, heh? Are you thinking, maybe, that Sauny Ruthven's gone clean mad? Is that it, Vicky?'

At the sudden change of tune, Ludovick blinked, shaking his head. 'No. No – that was not my thought. He seems sufficiently sane. The madness, if such there is, would seem to be elsewhere!'

'Ummm.'

They were now topping the shoulder of Moncrieffe Hill, with the fair valley of the silver Tay spreading before them, and the grey roofs and walls of the town of Perth huddled directly below. Young Ruthven, who had drawn level, on the other side of the King, sought permission to ride ahead the remaining mile or so, in order to warn his brother of his liege lord's approach, that he might welcome him suitably. James agreed, and the youth spurred on.

The rest of the party had now reached them, and were speculating on the possibility of resistance to arrest on the part of the Master of Oliphant, and likelihood of sword-play – for all were practically unarmed, clad in green hunting costume, and bearing only dirks and hunting-knives; indeed the page, John Ramsay, was the only member of the company equipped with a whinger, or short sword. James made no attempt to reassure them, or to admit that Oliphant's capture was not the real object of the journey. His only expressed concern was with the dinner that he was likely to get at Gowrie House.

The royal party was through the gates of Perth and into the narrow streets before the Earl of Gowrie and his brother, with two or three hastily gathered representatives of the town, came hurrying to greet the King. It was a somewhat stiff and formal encounter, for unlike the Master, the Earl was no dissembler and showed his feelings all too clearly. James indeed was the more affable of the pair, affecting a heavy jocularity. Neither made any reference to the object of the visit, in front of the company. Gowrie, after a single brief bow and exchange of cold glances with Lennox, ignored the Duke's presence.

Gowrie House was as empty-seeming and bare as at Ludovick's previous call, and gave no impression of being prepared for a royal occasion. The Earl explained that he was but two days back from his Atholl property, and that his mother and main household was at Dirleton Castle, his Lothian seat, where he intended to join her in a day or two. He hoped that the King would bear with him if he had to wait a little while for a modest dinner, himself having already dined early. There was a grouse or two in the larder, and he would have a hen killed . . .

This seemed to Ludovick almost as extraordinary a situation as that indicated by the story of the pot of gold. It looked, indeed, as though the Earl had not expected the King's visit, and was in fact upset and embarrassed by it. Could it be that his brother had not told him of his ride to Falkland? Or even, perhaps, of the mysterious captive in the privy chamber?

As strange as all this was the fact that, despite all the urgency and speed of their coming here, neither James nor young Ruthven now showed any hurry to go and inspect the prisoner or his treasure. James sat in the pleasant if somewhat overgrown garden, sipping wine and holding forth on the history of the former Black Friars Monastry on which this house was founded, to any who would listen to him, while hungry huntsmen, who had not eaten for nearly seven hours, waited with less patience. Ludovick, low-voiced, asked once when the King was going to investigate the matter they knew of but was waved away with a royal frown, and told to bide in patience like the rest of them.

This supposed reference to the delayed meal raised a growl of feeling, particularly from the Earl of Mar who was a great trencherman.

Admittedly the Gowrie House kitchens seemed to be singularly unequal to their task, that day, for although it was just after twelve-thirty when the visitors arrived, it was after two o'clock before Gowrie himself came to announce that some humble provender now awaited them in the dining-hall. In the interim there had been not a few comments on the well-known Puritan habits and frugality of his young lordship, one of the wealthiest men in the kingdom – criticisms which were by no means stilled by the eventual sight of the provision made for them within.

The Master was presumably giving a hand in the kitchen, for he had not shown himself since their arrival.

The King was served at a small table by himself, the Earl waiting upon him personally – and if he did not fare sumptuously, he at least did better than did his supporters; Master Herries, the royal physician, who had been bred for the Kirk, remarking that a miracle of the loaves and fishes was sore required in Saint John's godly town of Perth.

At least it did not take long to demolish the meal. Even James, who was a dawdler with his food, had finished and was back to sipping wine, when young Ruthven appeared at last, and approached the royal table, to say something in the King's ear.

The monarch rose, as of course did all others. He began to accompany the youth towards the door, but when Ludovick and others started to follow, he waved them back peremptorily, declaring that Master Sauny had something private to show him, above. They should all go out into the garden and await him there. He passed through the hall doorway, making for the main stair.

There was a sniggering murmur from sundry of the company. The Master was a personable youth, and the King's peculiar tastes were only too well-known. Ludovick glanced at Gowrie himself, who seemed to be unconcerned and only glad that the problem of feeding his many visitors was disposed of.

In the garden there was considerable debate about the real object of this peculiar visit – since it seemed apparent that the apprehension of the Master of Oliphant was, to say the least of it, scarcely preying on the mind of the monarch. On the other hand, it did not seem likely that any mere assignation with young Ruthven would have brought James all the way to Perth, especially with such a tail of followers – when all could have been achieved a deal more effectively at Falkland. Ludovick said nothing.

Some of the guests were wandering about the garden, seeking to supplement their dinner by eating cherries off the trees, when Thomas Cranstoun, Gowrie's equerry, came to announce to the Earl that he was told that the King was away. Had left the house by the little Black Turnpike, as he called it, a narrow winding turret stair that led down from the corner turret that overlooked both street and garden, at second floor level.

Gowrie, staring, interrupted him 'Away? What do you mean, man – away?'

'They say, my lord, that His Grace came down the Black Turnpike, went to the stables, mounted his horse and rode away. He is even now riding across the South Inch.'

There was not a little commotion at the news. Men started up, and led by Gowrie, hurried round to the stables, calling for horses to follow the King. Doubtfully indeed Ludovick followed on. It was highly unlikely that James had done any such thing. His disbelief was confirmed, when he reached the stable-yard and saw the King's white horse still standing beside his own black.

He turned, to point this out to Gowrie, who was questioning the gate porter, this man asserting that nobody had in fact issued through this main gate, and that the back-gate was locked and he had the key here in his lodge. Gowrie, at Ludovick's announcement, frowned.

'Stay here, my lords,' he called. 'I will go up and discover the verity of all this.' He hurried off.

Mar and some of the others were already mounting, but the Duke declared that he was quite sure that the King had not gone, that it was all some stupid mistake started by a servant. Nevertheless, he was uneasy. The entire affair was so strange and indeed nonsensical that there was obviously more behind it than met the eye. He did not wish to break the royal confidence by enlarging upon the ridiculous story of the pot of gold.

Gowrie had just come hurrying back, saying that he could see no sign of the King or of his brother in the long gallery or elsewhere upstairs, and that it looked as though they must indeed have ridden forth, when there was a dramatic development. There was the sound of a window being thrown open directly above them, and then the King's voice sounded, high-pitched, excited, and even more indistinct than usual.

'Treason! Treason!' it cried. 'Help! Vicky! Johnny Mar! Help! I am murdered!'

At least, that is approximately what most thought had been cried, for there was no certainty about it. Not unnaturally, for as they all stared upwards at the small window of the round turret, it was to see the King's agitated and indeed contorted face thereat, with a hand at his throat, his mouth – whether his own hand or another's was impossible to tell at this angle. James was hatless and his thin hair awry.

Immediately, of course, there was pandemonium, as men shouted, cursed, threw themselves down from horses, and rushed for the house door. Ludovick ,who had not been mounted, led the way. He ran indoors and leapt up the main stairway. At the second-floor landing, above the hall, he came to the door of the same long gallery off which had opened the library where he and Mary had had their interview with the Earl a month before – and from the far end of which the turret chamber must open. The door was locked.

Mar and the others came panting up as the Duke beat upon the door's panels.

Ludovick was desperately looking round for something to use to force or break down the heavy door. A small ladder lying on the landing, for access to a loft trap-door, was all that he could see. Grabbing it, he and others began to better it against the timbers. But without avail. The ladder's wood was less solid than that of the door and broke away.

'Hammers! Axes!' Mar shouted. 'God's death – find axes! Where's Gowrie?'

'It's a plot! A trap! Gowrie will be in it.'

'The other stair,' Ludovick cried, as he continued with his battery. 'The Black Turnpike! The turret stair. Try that . . .'

Lord Lindores and some others ran off downstairs again, to seek Gowrie, axes and the small back stairway.

Some were still down in the courtyard, including Gowrie himself, who seemed to be completely bewildered by the sudden crisis and clamour. Sir Thomas Erskine, a cousin of Mar's, after shouting encouragement to the King above – whose face had now disappeared from the turret window, but whose shouts could still be heard suddenly swung on the young Earl.

'Traitor!' he cried. 'Traitor! This is your work!'

His brother, James Erskine, a Gentleman of the Bedchamber, leapt forward to grab Gowrie at one side, Sir Thomas at the other. The Earl did not resist them at first, only crying out that he knew nothing of it all, what had happened and what it meant.

The gate-porter and other of Gowrie's servants could not stand by and see their lord mishandled. They flung themselves upon the Erskines and freed Gowrie. That young man, seeing Lindores and others come running upon him, from the house, backed alarmedly out into the street, panting. Then, in a sudden access of courage or fury, he ran back, snatching out the gate-porter's sword from its scabbard and crying that he would take charge in his own house or die in the doing of it. His equerry, Cranstoun, now also drew sword, and men fell back before their flickering blades as these two raced for the turret stair nearby.

Meanwhile, at the head of the main stair, Ludovick was still battling fruitlessly with the locked door. Somebody brought a heavy poker from the hall fireplace, and this, when inserted between door and jamb, using the broken ladder as fulcrum, looked as though it might effect an entrance. He thought that he could hear shouting from within as well as from without, which led him to believe that the King's murder was, at least, as yet incomplete.

Mar had arrived with a mattock from the garden, and somebody else with a great lump of stone with which to assail the lock. All the door's attackers, however, got much in each other's way, and Ludovick's curses were not all for the stoutness of the timbers and lock. In the event, while still the door withstood their efforts, shake as it did, they heard a great outcry from within, the sound of many upraised voices. Clearly an entrance had been gained elsewhere.

A few moments later the hinges of the door began to give, before the lock, and furious blows soon had it swinging open drunkenly from the top. Staggering, the batterers struggled through into the long gallery.

At the far end, where the turret room opened, men were milling about. King James was one, dress in disorder, wild-eyed, blood on his sleeve. He was clutching the arm of John Ramsay his page, and of all things appeared to be trying to catch a hooded hawk which was fluttering about trailing its chain. Ramsay had had the bird, the King's favourite goshawk, on his wrist all day. The same Ramsay, the only member of the King's party who had been equipped with a sword, now bore this naked in his hand – and no two glances were needed to see that it was bloodstained. One other drawn sword was in evidence. It was no longer the Earl who carried it, however, but Sir Thomas Erskine. And this sword was bloodied also. Lindores and others, who had followed Gowrie and Erskine up the small back stairway, were in agitated movement around the monarch. One man knelt on the floor – Herries the physician.

Ludovick ran forward to the King's side. 'You are safe, Sire? Unhurt?' he panted.

James was far too excited to answer, or even to hear. But it was evident that the blood spattered upon his person was not his own, and that however distressed he was not seriously injured. He was gabbling incoherently, now stroking Ramsay's arm, now making ineffectual grabs at the blinded, bewildered hawk, and now pointing back into the turret chamber.

Ludovick was about to hurry therein when he all but fell over the kneeling Herries – and was brought up short by what he saw when he glanced down. The physician was examining a body on the floor, twisted and crumpled – that of John Ruthven, third Earl of Gowrie. As the Duke stared, he had a vivid mind-picture of another body that he had once gazed down at, some years before, in similar conditions, state and posture, and another earl likewise – that of James Stewart, Earl of Moray, the Queen's friend. The Earl of Gowrie was not so handsome as the bonny Earl of Moray – but he was equally dead.

Feeling sick, Ludovick mumbled, 'Who . . . who did this?'

At his side, Lindores answered him. 'Ramsay. Johnnie Ramsay. We came up the wee stair. The King named him traitor. Gowrie. Said had he come to do what his brother hadna been able to do? Gowrie had his sword, but when the King cried on him he dropped his point. Ramsay ran him through. Aye, through the heart. A shrewd stroke, by God!'

'God!' Ludovick echoed. He stared from the body to the gabbling monarch, to the young, brilliantly smiling Ramsay with the reeking weapon, and back to the corpse on the floor. 'And the other?' he faltered, all but whispered from dry lips. 'His brother? The Master?'

Lindores jerked an eloquent head towards the turret room,

355

from the window of which James had called for help. The Duke strode therein.

The little room was bare, empty – but the floor-boards were shockingly splashed and befouled with gouts of blood. At one side, a lesser door stood open, also blood-smeared. From this the narrow turnpike stair descended. And lying asprawl on the steps, head downwards, arms outflung, was the body of Alexander Ruthven, the Master, hideously butchered.

As Ludovick gazed, a groan escaped his lips. At his elbow Lindores, who had followed him in, spoke.

'We came on him as we came up. He wasna dead then – though sair stricken. Tam Erskine finished him off wi' the man Cranstoun's whinger. He was struggling wi' the King, Ramsay says – this Sandy Ruthven. Another man too. Ramsay was right quick to find this bit stair. He was the first here. Aye, and ready wi' his blade, seize me!'

'Aye. Ready with his blade!' the Duke repeated slowly, grimly, and turned back towards the gallery, heavy at heart.

Somebody had caught the ridiculous goshawk and it was now secured again at Ramsay's bloody wrist. Everyone was talking loudly, the King loudest of all, in a jumbled, breathless stream, recounting the dire nature of the attack upon him, declaring the wicked and vile treachery of the Ruthvens, and making much both of his own courageous resistance and the valour and vigour of his deliverers, Ramsay and Sir Thomas Erskine. It was noticeable that it was on these two that he showered his encomiums, the two who held dripping swords in their hands, touching and fondling them – James Stewart, who had never been able to abide the sight of either blood or naked steel. Noticeable too, to the Duke at least, that Erskine received almost as much praise as young Ramsay, despite the fact that he had done little more than the rest of them in rescue, other than apparently wantonly stabbing at both Ruthven brothers' bodies after they had been laid low by the martial page.

Ludovick did not join in the flood of excited exclamation, congratulation and question. His mind was busy in a number of directions, somewhat numbed as it was by the sudden and ghastly tragedy. He looked at the flushed and grinning Ramsay, a slender youth of no more than eighteen, and it came to him that he had not seen him in the garden with the others, after the meal. With that hawk on his wrist, he would have been apt to catch the eye.

Perhaps, even in his elevated state, the King noticed his cousin's silence, for he suddenly turned to him – and the glance he gave him was strange indeed, sly almost, with triumph and something that might have been fear commingled.

'Vicky – are you no' blithe to see me? Safe delivered? Frae this most vile attack. And conspiracy – aye, conspiracy. Did the Almighty no' confound my enemies quite, and deliver them into my hand? Should we no' a' give thanks? Wasna Johnny Ramsay here raised up as a tower o' strength against the wicked? Aye, strength and fury.'

'He was certainly sufficiently furious, with his sword! Your Grace's safety is cause for rejoicing, yes. But was it necessary that they should be slain? That both the Ruthvens should die?'

'You ask that! O' traitors? Treacherous miscreants! Yon Sauny had hands on me, man – violent hands. On me, the King!'

'He attacked you, Sire?'

'Aye. Wi' most murderous intent.'

'But he was not armed, Sire. He wore no weapons.'

'Eh? Eh? Hech, man – what o' that? He put his hands on me, to my throat. He could ha' throttled me, could he no'?'

'But why should he seek to do any such thing? What would it serve young Ruthven to throttle the King? Alone with you in this small room? Do you believe, Sire, that he brought you here to strangle you?'

'How should I ken, Vicky? But he laid hands on his King.'

'So Ramsay found you so, and slew him out of hand? Unarmed as he was?'

'Aye. But . . . but there was another man. Another man in it. And he was armed, Vicky. A right savage and terrible man. Standing there!' James pointed vaguely into the turret room.

'So you were *not* alone with the Master?'

'No. There was this other. When we came in here. I dinna ken who he was. Armed. Wi' mail beneath his coat. Eh, Johnny?'

'That is so, Sire. A stranger. Wearing mail,' the page answered promptly.

'So Ramsay slew the unarmed man, and left the armed one!

What then, Sire? Where is this stranger now?'

'Houts – how should I ken that? He went off. In the stramash. I didna see where. I was right put about...'

'If he went off, he could only have gone down the turnpike stair here – since the gallery door was still locked. From the inside. Others came up that stair, but moments later. Did they see this man? Sir Thomas? Herries? Did you see him?'

Nobody could claim to have seen the mysterious stranger. But Erskine declared that he could have left the stair at the first floor landing and gone to hide elsewhere in the house.

'Aye – search the house!' James cried. 'Let no murderous plotters escape!' As some ran off to do his bidding, he turned on Ludovick. 'I mislike this, Vicky Stewart – aye, I mislike it! You sound more concerned for Sauny Ruthven than for your sovereign lord! When I'm new escaped frae the jaws o' death, here's you putting me to the question like a common felon! I'll no' have it!'

'Your pardon, Sire. I but seek to learn the full extent of the matter. For Your Grace's further safety and, h'm, repute.'

'You choose an ill time, then! Aye, and you werena so timeous, back there! In coming to my rescue, Vicky Stewart! I could ha' been throttled quite, for a' *your* haste!'

'H'rr'mm.' The Earl of Mar, who had been equally held up by the locked door, intervened. 'We couldna get in, Sire. The door was steikit. But there's no profit in this. We've more to do than talk, I say. The main matter is that this, this carrion's dead!' And he spurned the fallen Gowrie with his boot-toe. 'But there may be more to it than this. A further attempt against Your Grace. These two would not be the only ones. We'd be safer out o' this town o' Perth, I'm thinking.'

'Aye, you're right. That's more wise-like talk than the Duke's, my lord! But first, my friends – let us give thanks to God for His most notable mercy and deliverance. On your knees, sirs, as becomes guid Christian gentlemen.' And leaning on Erskine's arm, the monarch got down on his knock-knees beside the crumpled body of his slain host. All, however reluctant and embarrassed, must needs get down with him, Ramsay the slayer, hawk on wrist, with the rest.

At this precise moment the bells of St. John's Kirk began to

ring, to be followed almost immediately by other bells. 'See you
– the very bells canna contain themsel's, my lords!' James declared, uplifted. 'Shall we let them outdo us in thanks to our
Maker?' And composing his voice to its most pious, the King
addressed the most high protector of kings and support of
princes, thanking Him for a truly miraculous deliverance and
victory. He acknowledged that he had most evidently been
preserved from so desperate a peril in order to perfect some
great work to God's glory. Developing this theme enthusiastically, he went into a sort of court of enquiry, there on his knees,
as to what this work might be, coming to the eventual conclusion
that it must be the bringing of both the peoples that the Almighty
had entrusted to his care, the Scots and the English, to a proper
understanding of how they should be governed in unity, in
church as in state.

How much more detailed the revelation afforded by this
curious act of worship would have grown, only James and possibly his Maker knew. But the thick and unctuous voice was
now having to compete with more than the clangour of bells;
another sound arose, which grew louder and more strident
rapidly, and set all men glancing uneasily towards the windows
At length, carried away by his devotions and visions as he was,
the King became aware of it, and faltered to a stop. It was the
sound of many voices, upraised, the voice of a crowd and undoubtedly an angry crowd.

Hardly had the royal words ceased than men were scrambling
to their feet and hurrying to the windows at the end of the
gallery and in the turret, which overlooked the street of the
Speygate. A mass of townsfolk were approaching, filling the narrow thoroughfare, and being added to every moment by others
flooding out from each wynd and vennel, townsfolk in an ugly
mood, most evidently.

'The bells werena just for thanksgiving, then!' Mar commented grimly.

'They've heard!' Herries exclaimed. 'Somebody has told
them. That the Earl is dead.'

'He was provost here. The Ruthvens – they have a great
following in this town ...'

'The gate!' Ludovick interrupted sharply. He ran to the

turret window, pushing aside others there, to lean out and look down. The courtyard gate still stood open to the street. Neither the porter nor any of the Gowrie servants were to be seen. Two or three townsmen stood out there, gazing in, but nobody appeared to have entered as yet.

One or two of the royal party's grooms were standing about the yard. 'That gate! Shut and bar it!' the Duke cried to these. 'Haste you. Do not stand gaping there! Get it shut – if you value your skins!'

He was only just in time. The startled grooms had barely got the massive double doors closed and were sliding the heavy greased oaken beams out of their deep sockets to bar them, before the crowd was surging and seething at the other side, yelling and banging on the timbers. In the forefront of the throng were the gate-porter himself and two others in the Ruthven colours.

There was no doubt as to the hostility of the mob, nor of the reason for it. To the accompaniment of much fist-shaking and brandishing of weapons, the shouts of 'Murderers! Assassins!' and the like arose. Some stones came up, and broken glass tinkled to the floor.

Ludovick held up his hand for silence, trying to speak to the crowd. But they would not listen to him, although he shouted that he was the Duke of Lennox, Admiral of the Realm, and that the King himself was within. At length he desisted. The gate remained secure, and the high courtyard wall would keep out intruders so long as they did not bring ladders to scale it.

Turning back, he discovered the King to be a changed man, his exaltation gone and replaced by a trembling, mumbling fear. 'Tullibardine!' he kept repeating. 'Where's Tullibardine?'

'Your Grace must needs speak to them,' Ludovick urged 'They will perhaps heed you, the King. If you show yourself, it may quieten them. Gowrie was popular, good to his people. They have heard that he is foully murdered ...'

'Na, na – I'll no' can speak to them, Vicky. No' to yon yowling limmers! I canna do it. If Tullibardine would but come, wi' his Murrays ...'

'The Lord Murray? What of him? Why should he be here, Sire?'

The King darted a glance at him, nibbling his nails. 'His house is no' that far away, is it no'? He has plenty o' men, to come to my aid.'

'He cannot know that you need help. His house is miles away. You must speak to these folk, Sire. Quietly. Firmly. Tell them that there has been attack upon your person. But that you trust the burghers of Perth. Say that all is now in order. Command that they retire to their homes. They will not heed me, but you they may obey.'

With the greatest of reluctance James was led to the turret window. At sight of him, however, the yells and jeers redoubled, and he shrank back at once, and nothing would bring him forward again.

'Murderer!' someone screamed. 'You murdered the faither! Now you murder the sons!'

'Come down, son o' Seigneur Davie!' another mocked. 'You've slain an honester man nor yoursel'!'

'Aye – gie us our provost. Or the King's green coat shall pay for it!'

James retreated to the farther side of the gallery in an agony of apprehension. Mar went to the window and leaning out shook his fist at the mob.

'Fools that we were, to ride unarmed!' he stormed. 'Wi' two-three hagbuts we'd send these curs scuttling to their kennels!'

But they had no firearms, and only two swords to the entire party. A search of Gowrie House might discover one or two more – but clearly they were not going to be in a position to withstand an attack by the townsfolk. It would be only a question of time, with the crowd in this temper, until they found their way over the courtyard wall.

'The back gate?' Ludovick suggested. 'The gate His Grace was said to have left by.'

A visit of inspection was made to this rear exit, only to find that a smaller crowd was congregated behind this high wall also. But Ludovick learned from the terrified Cranstoun, the Gowrie equerry, held close by some of the King's people, that there was a third way out of the establishment – the river gate, a seldom used postern at the bottom of the garden which opened on to the river bank. A boat or two lay there, for catching the Tay salmon.

Investigation revealed nobody in sight outside this gate, save a couple of small boys playing by the waterside. But the boats were small and would not take the entire royal party save in relays – and without their horses. The King, in consequence, although anxious to be anywhere but in Gowrie House, would not hear of making a bolt for it and having to entrust himself to his own two feet across the river. He was, in fact, now rapidly nearing the stage where it would be impossible to do anything with him.

It was at this impasse that an alteration in the quality of the noise and shouting from the streets revealed a new development. From the house windows the cause of this could not at first be ascertained but soon it became evident that the crowd was now becoming agitated on another score – its own safety. Which could only mean that it was being assailed somewhere by another and possibly more powerful faction. Presently the clattering of shod hooves on cobblestones proclaimed that the newcomers were mounted. The packed throng in the Speygate began to surge and eddy and thin out.

Then a large troop of men-at-arms, their armour glinting in the watery late afternoon sunshine, came into view from the south, the other direction from the river, forcing their way with the flats of their swords. A banner at their head fluttered blue with the three white stars of Murray.

'It's Tullibardine!' Mar cried. 'God save him – I have never loved John Murray but I'll shake him by the hand this day!'

'Aye,' the King muttered. 'Aye. He's no' before his time, the man!'

Ludovick turned to consider his cousin pensively.

Soon John Murray, Lord Tullibardine, was sitting his horse beneath the turret window, in the midst of his tight steel-clad company, but with the Perth crowd still in evidence all round and beginning to raise their voices again. Clearly he was not happy about his position and not wishful unduly to provoke the townsfolk – who, after all, outnumbered his troop twenty to one. To his invitation that the King should come down and be escorted to safety through the streets by the Murrays, James would by no means agree. He would not even allow the great gate to be opened to allow either Sir John in or himself out. Instead, it was arranged that he should now slip quietly out by the river gate, to be rowed across Tay, and there to be met by half of the Murray company whilst the rest maintained their present position in front of the main gates as a blind.

So, at last, the King of Scots left Gowrie House, furtively, in fear and in scowling silence. He was in ill temper with all, even with Lord Tullibardine his rescuer – and as for the Duke of Lennox he did not so much as address a word to him all the weary ride back to Falkland. Not that that young man was in any cheerful or conversational mood himself, having a sufficiency of dark thoughts of his own to occupy his mind.

In one of the King's few remarks, however, that now wet and gloomy evening, Ludovick did take a keen and silent interest. They were nearing Falkland, Lennox riding close behind James, when the latter beckoned one of the escorting Murrays, Sir Mungo, to his side, and spoke low-voiced, urgently. Ludovick could not hear just what was said, although he did distinguish the word Dirleton. Neither did Murray hear, however, and the monarch had to raise his voice.

'I said, I have a task for you, Mungo,' he declared, and this time the Duke missed nothing. 'Take fresh horses frae my stables at Falkland, and ride you, wi' some o' your lads, this night. For Dirleton. In Lothian. The auld bitch, Gowrie's mother, and her two other sons, are biding at their castle o' Dirleton. I want them, Mungo. They're just laddies – but the ill blood's in them. Young vipers frae the same nest! Arrest them a' – the Countess, too. In the King's name. Before they get word o' this, and flee. You understand, Mungo? We'll make an end o' the Ruthvens. It's an ill night for riding – but you'll be none the poorer for it, man, I promise you!'

'Yes. Sire. Dirleton. Near to North Berwick. I know the house. But it is a far cry – twenty-five miles to Stirling, thirty-five more to Edinburgh. Then twenty beyond. Perhaps better by early morning light...'

'No – tonight, man. Tonight, I said. Ride to the Queensferry. Rouse the ferrymen. In my name. That will save near thirty miles.'

363

'Very well, Your Grace...'

Ludovick hurried straight to his quarters in the Palace of Falkland, demanding his page, Peter Hay – which young man had to be ravished from the company of some of the Queen's ladies.

'Peter – you have some fondness for the Lady Beatrix Ruthven, I understand?' the Duke said, without preamble. 'Aye – then you have opportunity to serve her, poor lassie. The Earl and the Master, her brothers, are dead. Foully slain. Ask me not how – not now. You must ride forthwith. Secretly and fast. For Dirleton Castle, in Lothian. To her mother and the two young boys, her remaining brothers. They are in gravest danger. Tell the Countess to flee with them. To England, or where she will. But at once. Before morning. They are to be arrested. You understand? Sir Mungo Murray is on his way to take them. In the King's name. If he does, God help them! You must reach them first. Ride to Dysart – that is quickest. Ten miles only. Get a boat there, fishermen, or others. To put you across Forth. Here is money. If you have trouble, demand it in the name of the Lord Admiral. But ... as secret as you may, or we both may suffer for it! Have the boat to put you in at the little landing behind Fidra Isle. Thence it is but a mile or so inland to Dirleton Castle. Ride at once, Peter – and you should be there much before Murray. He goes by the Queensferry. And Beatrix Ruthven will have cause to thank you ...'

Chapter Twenty-one

With but surly assent, Sir David Murray obeyed Ludovick's peremptory command and ordered the half-troop of the Royal Guard to turn in, with their burden, towards Castle Huntly, from the Dundee road.

'The man's as good as dead, my lord Duke,' he said. 'You'll no' save him. And it was the King's command to bring him to Falkland forthwith.'

'He must have the chance, I say. To live. I take responsibility for this, sir. Besides, what use to the King is a dead man?' That last was purely rhetorical. The Duke knew as well as did Murray that Harry Younger was indeed of more use to the King dead than alive – for so at least he could not talk. That is why he now lay unconscious, bleeding from many stab wounds, tied like a gralloched stag on his own lathered horse that was led behind one of the guard.

The deed had been done perhaps three miles back, nearer Dundee. Younger, a far-out cousin of the Ruthvens, had been summoned to Falkland. But the very next day, the King, impatient, had sent this half-troop under Murray to fetch him from Dundee. Ludovick, seizing the chance and excuse to pay even a brief visit to Castle Huntly, and also hoping that he might be able to question the man before the King did, had volunteered to accompany the party – to no one's enthusiasm. They had met Younger himself, near Invergowrie, riding alone from Dundee to obey the royal summons. Murray had immediately treated him as a dangerous malefactor, insisting that he be bound there and then with ropes. Although Ludovick had declared vigorously that this was not necessary, Younger had taken fright, as well he might, and spurred off, apparently making a dash for the fastnesses of the Sidlaw Hills. Murray had engaged the Duke in altercation while the troopers raced after the fleeing quarry. When Ludovick had eventually caught up with them, in a corn-field, it was to find Younger lying below a stook,

365

little better than a corpse. That it had been all arranged so was not difficult to perceive.

The Duke's presence gained them entry to Castle Huntly without delay, and Davy Gray came hurrying to meet them as they rode into the courtyard. One glance at the bleeding body on the horse and he took charge in his curt and efficient way, having the victim carried carefully into a chamber of one of the flanking towers, sending a groom hotfoot to Longforgan for the physician, and shouting for Mariota his wife to come and aid him and for Mary Gray to provide refreshment for the Duke and Sir David.

Ludovick's meeting with Mary therefore, the first since their abortive ride to Perth together, was again not as he would have wished it. He took her aside, as soon as he decently could do so, and left Murray to consume his regalement in his own company.

'Oh, Vicky!' she burst out, whenever they were alone. 'Here is evil! That poor man – he cannot live. He is almost gone, now. What wickedness is this? How come you to be in it? Here, in the Carse?'

Briefly he told her, stroking her dark hair and holding her to him.

'So it is more of this of Gowrie!' she whispered. 'That shameful savage work! That terrible sin is not done with, yet!'

He shook his head. 'Far from it, I fear, Mary. Gowrie's and his brother's deaths were only a beginning. There will be much ill done yet, before the cup is full, I believe.'

'But why, Vicky? Oh, why? What does it all mean. Has the King run mad indeed? I know so little of it. Only what you told me in your letter. And the common talk. How does all this murder help the King?'

'It is that bloodshed breeds bloodshed. Mouths must be closed. Some men bought to keep them quiet. Others quieted thus! Having set his hand to evil, James must needs continue in it, lest men learn the truth. This man died, I think, because the mysterious armed stranger whom the King says was in yon turret at Gowrie House with the Master, has to be found. To colour the King's story. I do not believe that any such man existed – therefore a dead man, a relative of the Ruthvens, is

366

better witness than one who could still talk! Especially if he can be said to have fled, in guilt, when being taken before the King!'

'Dear God – so this man had done nothing? Was wholly innocent?'

'So I believe. As innocent as was Cranstoun, the equerry, who was executed. As were Craigengelt, Gowrie's steward, and the gate-porter. All arrested, tortured and hanged. Even Gowrie's old tutor, broken with the boot, to have him confess to a plot against the King, of which he could know nothing even if it had ever existed – which I do not for a moment credit. And there will be more – never doubt it!'

'But, Vicky – *why*? Why do you say there will be more?'

'Because the King's name and fame is at stake – and James perceives it. That is why he ordered bonfires to be lit on half the hills of Scotland, in celebration of his great deliverance! Why he ordered every church in the kingdom to hold services of thanksgiving, and the fifth day of August to be in all time coming a day of public rejoicing in the realm. Most of the Kirk has refused to obey, since all honest men cannot but doubt the King's story. So he is in fear and fury. And when kings are so, no man is safe. Any minister refusing to hold the thanksgiving service is now forbidden, under pain of death to preach in any pulpit – or even to come within ten miles of Edinburgh! Summonses of treason are issued against the two children, Gowrie's remaining brothers. Also their mother. Thank God that they escaped in time, to England! The very name of Ruthven is proscribed, forbidden to be used, written or spoken. Even the turret chamber in Gowrie House is pulled down and demolished. All to cover up James's guilt.'

'You are so certain, Vicky? That there is no truth in the King's story?'

'As certain as that I stand before you, Mary. I dare not say it to any but you – or my own head would roll, close to the throne as I am. It was a plot, yes – but *against* the Ruthvens, not by them. A plot in which a few carefully chosen men were concerted. With the King. Men who have been well rewarded indeed – and whose mouths are successfully stopped! One of them is in this house this moment. It was partly for that reason that I came with this company today.'

367

'You mean Sir David Murray?'

'Aye. The Murrays were in it. They ever envied the Ruthvens. Why else has this one been given the great Gowrie lands and lordship of Scone? For, of course, all the Ruthven estates and moneys are forfeit and confiscate. Why has Sir Mungo Murray been given Ruthven Castle – so long as he names it by another name? Tullibardine himself gets the Perth lands, Gowrie House and the Sheriffship of Perthshire. All this, that they do not talk. Explain how it was that they rode into Perth that afternoon a month ago, three hundred strong, in time to rescue their King – when they should not have known that he was not still hunting at Falkland? The Murrays were in it – although they were a little late! James was asking where Tullibardine was an hour before they appeared!'

'So false? All these?'

'Aye – and more than these. Sir Thomas Erskine, a kinsman of Mar's gets Dirleton Castle, the plum of it all. Aye, he is a great man now, the Lord Erskine of Dirleton no less! Which is strange, for he seemed to play a secondary part to young Ramsay – who is now, of course, Sir John Ramsay, with a handsome pension for life! I have not yet discovered why Erskine was the most favoured – when he only stabbed fallen, dying men! Perhaps Herries, the physician, could tell me – save that he also is now knighted, and laird of the fat barony of Cousland! Others too will remain silent for similar reasons.'

The girl shook her head. Then, staring out of the narrow, iron-grilled window, she spoke from tight lips. 'Vicky – in all these names there is one that you have not pronounced. Patrick's! Does it mean . . . is it that, for once, after all, Patrick is not one of them? It was against Patrick that we warned the Earl of Gowrie – not the King. Were we wrong? In all this, what of my father? What of Patrick Gray?'

'Well may you ask, Mary – what of Patrick Gray! Despite the fact that his hand is behind the King's in almost every matter of state, most men would say that Patrick is not concerned in this evil. At no point, that I have heard, does his name come into it. He was not there, nor at the hunt – for he seldom hunts. Indeed he had left Falkland for Broughty the day previous. I have not heard that he has gained anything of the Ruthven riches. And yet ... and yet ...'

'And yet what, Vicky? You believe otherwise?'

'Aye, Mary – I do. Leastways, it is not so much belief as instinct. Somewhere behind it all, I sense Patrick's hand. It is not just that we feared it ...'

'Might it not be? We feared it, yes – and so we must discover it – ? But – it may not be so, Vicky. After all, it is not like Patrick's work, all this. So bungled, so evidently false, so lacking in the subtlety with which he always acts.'

'I wonder. May not this be, rather, the greatest subtlety of all? That it may seem all to be the King's own doing. That Patrick himself must seem most assuredly to have no hand in it. That, this time, there be no whispers, no questions, no fingers pointing at *him* ...'

'But is that not *too* clever, Vicky? Are we not in danger of making him into a demi-devil, a nightmare? Seeing him in every shadow ... ?

'Perhaps. There is that danger, yes. Often I tell myself so. But certain aspects of this matter, not in its carrying out but in its results, do point to Patrick, say to me that he *ought* to be concerned in it. Not only that nothing of great import touching the King happens without him knowing, if not arranging it. He has not sought at any point to halt this wicked course – as surely he would have done had it lacked his approval. But there is more than that. Queen Elizabeth, out of it all, has turned towards James. She has sent him the kindest letter, in her own hand, that she has written for long years. She declares her joy at his escape from death, assassination, and her horror of the attempt. And though she ends by warning him against anticipating her own funeral and intriguing with her courtiers regarding the succession, she does imply succession and signs herself His Grace's loving sister and cousin. This is esteemed to be a great step towards the English throne – goal of Patrick's policy. Elizabeth, ever since she ordered our Queen Mary's death, has been haunted by a terror of the violent death of princes. It is her great weakness, I think that Patrick played on it.'

'It could be, heaven knows! But also it could have happened otherwise.'

'It could – although we were looking for him to arrange something against Gowrie. That eighty thousand pounds of debt can now be forgotten, and much Ruthven silver added instead to the empty Treasury. There is that, also. But there is something else – something strange, which has the smell of Patrick to it. You remember how you spied Robert Logan at Perth, yon day? I told you how he was back at Court, his horning annulled. Now he is at the horn again, and fled abroad, a ruined man, all his goods and lands being forfeit to the Crown. For being art and part in the conspiracy of Gowrie!'

The young woman stared. 'But . . but . . . ? If there *was* no conspiracy? What can this mean? How can this point to Patrick, Vicky? Logan was ever Patrick's man. Does this, if it is true, not point against Patrick having plotted the business?'

'You think so, Mary? Remember Patrick's power in the land. He could have halted this new outlawry against Logan, had he wished – just as he had the old outlawry annulled. He has not done so. Why?'

'Perhaps Logan *was* intriguing with Lord Gowrie? On his own part, not Patrick's. For he was always a rogue . . .'

'Consider this, my dear. Just days before this new horning was proclaimed, and he disappeared to France or wherever he is, Logan signed deeds of sale of his estates. All except Fast Castle. And to friends of Patrick's. Elphinstone the Secretary got Restalrig, for eighteen thousand merks. And George Home the Berwickshire properties for forty-five thousand. Which moneys have not yet been paid. Nor ever will be, I reckon – since Logan and all his possessions are now outwith the law! You see what this means, Mary?'

She wrinkled her brows. 'Can it be . . . ? Can it mean that Patrick has deserted his henchman? Has thrown Logan to the wolves?'

'Aye – but more than that. It means that Patrick was privy to what was to take place regarding Gowrie – for he must have had Logan's part and implication arranged beforehand. And the sales of the lands drawn up. For all was done within a day or so of Gowrie's death. Patrick *must* have known.'

'Oh, Vicky! Can it be so?' She drew a long, quivering breath. 'It can, of course. How well we know that it can! How familiar the pattern.' Wearily she asked it. 'What was Logan's part? What was he supposed to have done, in the plot?'

'He was to have had a boat ready to carry the King captive, in Gowrie's power, to Fast Castle. To be held there, while Gowrie and his friends ruled the land in his name. The Ruthven Raid of 1582 again! Only, this time, a fable, a chimera without foundation, backed by forged letters. So one more is added to the list of those whom Patrick has betrayed – his own creature and tool! And I shall be surprised indeed if the revenues of Logan's lands – and that includes much of the town of Leith – despite the names of those who seem to have bought them, do not find their way into Patrick's pocket!'

Mary almost groaned. 'This, at least, sounds like my father!' she said.

The Duke nodded. 'Logan is scant loss. But, Mary – I said I feared that the evil was by no means finished yet, the cup not full.' He took her hand in his. 'I believe that there is much yet to come. Innocent folk still to suffer. It may be that I can do some little to halt it. With your help, my dear. As we have done before. I want you to help me. You, who are better able than any other. You cannot do so here, at Castle Huntly. Come back to Court, my heart – and work with me.'

Almost in panic, it seemed, for that usually so serene and assured young woman, Mary Gray looked at him. 'No, Vicky – ah, no! Not that. Do not ask me . . .'

'You are afraid? It is not like you, Mary, to be timorous, frightened.'

'I am afraid,' she nodded.

'Of what? Of whom? Not of me?'

'No – not of you. Of myself.'

Sombrely he gazed at her, for a moment. 'I think that you are wrong, Mary – all wrong. But . . . even so, be afraid for someone else, I say. Be afraid for Beatrix Ruthven, for one. She is your friend, is she not?'

'The Lady Beatrix! She . . . is she in danger also?'

'Need you ask? She is Gowrie's sister, still unmarried, and the last Ruthven left in Scotland. Only the Queen's protection has saved her hitherto. For the Queen declares openly that she disbelieves this of a conspiracy. She refuses to dismiss her lady-in-waiting. But . . . I fear for Beatrix. The King rages at her whenever he sees her. Declares that she poisons the Queen's mind against him. She is a simple creature, and requires a wiser head to advise her. Wiser than the Queen, or that sister of mine, Hetty. And I do not trust my . . . the Duchess. You could help her, Mary.'

She said nothing.

'And you could watch Patrick. As you have done before. As only you can do. You . . . you have hidden away here, Mary, for long enough.

She looked down at the stone-flagged floor. 'You think that?' she said, almost below her breath. 'Think that I hide myself here?'

'Yes, I do.' That was blunt, almost harsh.

Mary gulped. 'But . . . I cannot live with you. That is not possible. And the Queen would not have me back, even though I wished to go . . .'

'You can go back to lodging with Patrick. I saw the Lady Marie, his wife, before I came here. She said that I was to bring you back with me. She said that I was to tell you that she loved and needed you, sorely. That wherever they lodged, room awaited you. And Johnnie. She said that I was not to come back without you.'

'Marie said that? Sweet Marie! Dear Marie! But – Patrick . . .?'

'He *is* your father.'

'But . . .'

Davy Gray came seeking them, grim-faced. 'Your prisoner is dead, my lord Duke,' he said. 'It was too late for aught we could do. Here was dastard's work, I think.'

Ludovick nodded. 'Well may you say so. God rest his soul. And God forgive the men who decided that his life was worth less than a black lie! Have you told Murray?'

'Aye. And he seemed no' ill-pleased, the man.'

'No doubt. Since he is little better than a hired assassin! A knightly cut-throat! Although he that hired him has the greater charge to answer.' He shrugged. 'At least I may spare myself the displeasure of his further company. He may carry his trophy back to his master at Falkland lacking my aid. I will go tell him so – and we shall breathe the sweeter air for his absence! Mary

372

will give you the bones of the matter, sir.' And the Duke strode off to get rid of the unwelcome guest.

When he came back, presently, it was Davy who addressed him, heavily.

'I hear, my lord Duke, that you are to have your way! Or something of it. That Mary is going back to that den of iniquity, the King's Court. It is against my wish and counsel. But she is her own woman – not mine. Nor, my lord, any other man's! I'd mind you of that!'

'I do not need reminding, sir.' Ludovick could not keep the surging elation out of his voice. He turned to the girl. 'Mary – you have decided? I thank God!'

'Vicky – be not too thankful! I warn you – I have not changed my mind. I come only because my conscience will not allow me to stay here. That I may serve perhaps to counter a little of Patrick's wickedness, once more. That, if possible, I may aid the Lady Beatrix. I do not return as your mistress, Vicky. You understand? I shall not permit that you see overmuch of me . . . or I of you! However great the temptation. And it will be a notable temptation, God knows – for I love you fully as hotly as you love me, my dear. But on this condition I come, and this alone – that even though tongues wag, as indeed they will, we remain . . . we remain . . .' Her voice broke.

He inclined his head. 'As you will, Mary.'

'You have a wife. And at Court. I will cheat no woman. Slight none – nor be slighted. Is . . . is it a compact, Vicky?'

'It is a compact, my dear. At least I shall see your loveliness, hear your voice, share the same air you breathe. And hope – always hope.'

'That, at least, it is not in me to deny you, Vicky,' she said.

Chapter Twenty-two

The Parliament Hall in Edinburgh was crowded to suffocation point. But the smell of humanity and not over-clean clothing was sweet nevertheless, compared with that other stench. Ludovick, all but nauseated by both what his eyes and his nose told him, was astonished that the King seemed not at all affected, in either sense, and indeed leaned forward in his chair of state, avidly drinking in the scene and all that was said, apparently oblivious of the stink. It might have been noticed that, earlier, the Master of Gray, making an appearance at the door, had taken one glance at the packed assembly, wrinkled his fine nose in disgust, and straightway left the hall.

Not only King James was sitting forward now. There was a stir of urgent interest throughout the entire great chamber, as the Lord Advocate, Sir Thomas Hamilton, the gross, coarse but shrewd Tam o' the Cowgate as his monarch delighted to name him, called what all understood would be the key figure of this strange trial, to the witness stand.

'I call Andrew Henderson, lately chamberlain to the accused,' he rumbled. 'Andrew Henderson to the stand, to testify, I say.'

Then came a murmur of disappointment from all around. Here was anti-climax indeed. An utterly unknown name, a mere nonentity, a house-steward! Rumour had been busy with all sorts of impressive identities for this so important witness, found after long searching, the mysterious stranger on whose testimony it was believed the King's case would be established. Even Ludovick himself was surprised. He had never so much as heard the name of Andrew Henderson.

Nor was the man, whom the guards now ushered in, any more impressive than his name and style. A small, tubby, ruddy-featured individual, with sparse, receding hair and anxious, indeed hunted expression, he came in, bowing obsequiously to all whom he could see, all but prostrating himself before the burly

374

figure of the Lord Advocate – but curiously, quite overlooking the King, the only hatted person present, in his chair at the side of the court – until, that is, Hamilton roared out his omission, pointing an imperious finger, when the little man doubled himself up in his agitation, to the titters of the crowd. He was thereafter hustled to the witness-stand.

After administering the oath to the trembling man, Hamilton declaimed, 'You are Andrew Henderson, until the fifth day o' August last chamberlain and house-steward to the accused John, Earl o' Gowrie, at Gowrie House in Saint John's Town of Perth?'

'Aye, sir. Aye, my lord. That is so. Aye.'

'You recognise and identify the panel? Aye – both o' them?'

'Eh . . . ? What's that? I . . . I dinna take you, my lord?'

'Recognise, I said. Identify. Your master. The accused. And his brother. Look, man – and tell the court.' And again the Lord Advocate threw out a pointing hand to accompany his bellowed command. This time he pointed to another corner of the cleared central well of the hall, flanking the witness-stand, so that Henderson had to turn to peer – and turning, all but choked in strangled horror, the blood draining from his ruddy face. It appeared indeed that he could have slid to the floor had not the guards grabbed and supported him.

At the bar of the court, two figures sat – or, at least, were propped up – the grey face of one seeming to grin toothily in hollow-eyed mirth, the other to sleep, the decomposing bodies of the brothers John and Alexander Ruthven, former Earl and Master of Gowrie, dead for fourteen weeks.

Henderson, being for the moment in no state to make coherent answers, his recognition was taken for granted, and Sir Thomas declared in sonorous tones that this Andrew Henderson, apprehended at Gowrie House on the 5th of August last and confined in the Tolbooth of Edinburgh since, on charge of treason as having been art and part in the murderous and desperate attempt on the life of their beloved sovereign Lord James, by the grace of God, King, Protector of Christ's Holy and True Kirk, the said Andrew Henderson had of his own free will and decision sent a letter from the said Tolbooth to Master Patrick Galloway, Minister of the Gospel, declaring that he it was who was the armed and mail-clad man present with Alexander, Master of Gowrie in the turret-chamber of Gowrie House, on the occasion of the wicked and treasonable attack upon the King's Majesty. In consequence of which letter, a deposition had been taken from the said Andrew Henderson, and thereafter His Grace had been graciously pleased to waive and revoke the aforesaid summons for treason against him in order that he might give proper and lawful evidence, according to the laws of this realm, at this the trial of the said John and Alexander, formerly Earl and Master of Gowrie.

Ludovick could scarcely believe his ears. Was anyone expected to believe this masquerade and mummery? Was this the best that they could do? Was this frightened little man the savage and terrible armed stranger who had allegedly played so strange a part in that turret-chamber? Henderson, the house-steward! Who had escaped so mysteriously down the Black Turnpike? And if Henderson, what of Harry Younger? That unhappy individual seemed to have died entirely in vain.

The Lord Advocate having given the witness time to recover from his shock, now began his examination. But Henderson was clearly not of the stuff of heroes, and was much too overcome by the grisly presence of his late master's corpse to make a satisfactory witness. He mumbled and mowed, mis-heard and mistook, and ever his eyes were drawn round to the horror at the bar of the court. Eventually, in disgust, Sir Thomas had to content himself with perfunctorily asking the witness to confirm its truth, and accepting any sort of reaction, gabbled incoherences, nods, blank stares or complete silence, as confirmation.

The story he pieced together was little more convincing than was the witness. Henderson deponed that on the early morning of the 5th of August last he had ridden to Falkland from Perth with the Master of Gowrie, to seek interview with the King. The Master had informed His Grace that he had captured a suspected Jesuit priest with a hoard of gold pieces, and desired His Grace to come to Gowrie House to put the prisoner to the question. When the King agreed to do this, he, Henderson, had ridden on ahead with all speed, to inform the Earl that His Grace was on his way.

There was a stir of interest throughout the hall. This was the first public reference to the curious wayfarer with the pot of gold. Ludovick looked across the court, to find the King's eyes fixed upon himself. James had never told the rest of the courtiers this tale; as far as others knew, it was some hope of catching the elusive outlawed Master of Oliphant that had decoyed the King to Perth. This item of testimony, then, presumably had been put in to keep him, Lennox, quiet. Ludovick was puzzled. Also, he was sure that he had not seen the man Henderson at Falkland, or at the hunt – or indeed ever before in his life. And if the Earl of Gowrie was thus informed of the King's coming, why had he made no provision to entertain the royal party?

Sir Thomas Hamilton continued with his reading of the deposition. The Master of Gowrie, soon after his arrival with the King, had ordered Henderson to arm himself and wear a pyne-doublet, or vest of chain-mail, under his coat, and had then taken him to the turret-chamber and there locked him in. Later, after dinner, he had come back, bringing His Grace, and again locking the doors behind him. His Grace had mistaken him, Henderson, for the Jesuit priest, but the Master had delayed no longer with play-acting. Laying hands on the King's person, he had cried out that he was now in his power, that this man was armed and ready to use his weapons, and that the King must do as he was told. Henderson here had inserted a telling touch of dialogue. 'Sir, you must be my prisoner,' the Master had declared. 'Remember on my father's death!'

King James thumped his staff on the floor at this quotation, apparently much moved. The Lord Advocate bowed towards him, as though in receipt of applause. The Lord President Seton and his fellow Lords of Session on the Bench, nodded in shocked concern.

The witness, seemingly enheartened by the impression his composition was making, gained a better possession of his faculties and even went so far as to interject that he had not known that it was His Majesty that he was to be armed against, that he had indeed understood that he was to apprehend some Highlandman.

'Ha! So you've found your tongue, my mannie!' Tam o' the Cowgate commented. 'You'll maybe answer my questions now, more like an honest Christian! Will you tell the court what was the Master of Gowrie's intention in laying hands upon his liege lord's sacred person?'

'It was to capture and carry off His Majesty, sir. Aye, carry off. To hale him awa' to the Laird o' Restalrig's house. To Fast Castle, on the Border. The same as his father did, mind, lang syne, when he held the King's Grace at Ruthven Castle. That was . . .'

'Silence, man! Have a care of your words. You have used a name that is forbidden and proscribed by law!' Sir Thomas turned to the King, and then to the Bench. 'Your Grace – my lords – I crave your indulgence for this witness. This once. He was carried away by the thought of the odious attack on Your Grace.'

Graciously the King waved a hand, and the judges inclined sage heads.

'So the King's Grace was to be captured and taken to Fast Castle? There to be held by the prisoners at the bar and that outlawed rogue Robert Logan, formerly of Restalrig? How was this to be achieved, man?'

'Eh . . . ? In a boat, my lord.' Henderson was flustered again. 'He . . . His Majesty was to be bound fast. And carried down the Black Turnpike. To the side gate. There two men were waiting wi' horses . . .'

'Two men? What men?'

Henderson hesitated, and glanced at the King. 'Hugh Moncrieff, sir. And Patrick Eviot. They had the horses at the side gate,' he said, in a rush.

'Hugh Moncrieff and Patrick Eviot. Aye – we'll no' forget their names! But you didna take to horse, with His Grace a prisoner? Why?'

'The King, sir. He got to the bit window. And shouted. The Master pulled him back. Then the laddie . . . the young gentleman Ramsay. He came up the turnpike. Into the turret yon way. He had a whinger in his hand. He ran the Master through.'

'That door was open, then? The turnpike door wasna locked?'

'Eh . . . ? I . . . ah . . . I dinna ken. No. No, it couldna have been . . .'

From across the court the monarch's own thick voice spoke. 'Locked frae the *outside*, man – the outside! Johnnie Ramsay turned the key and came in.'

'H'rr'mmm.' The Lord Advocate, with a darted glance towards the Bench, bowed hurriedly to the King, and resumed, 'And you, man? What did you do then?'

'Me, my lord? I wanted no part in it. No. no. God kens I was innocent o' any o' it! As John Ramsay sworded the Master, me, I ran out the way he had come in. Doon the turnpike and awa', afore any should take me. Out the gate and into the town.'

'Aye – a right heroic course! That is a' you have to say relative to the matter? In which case...'

'I never kenned there was to be aught against the King in it, sir. I thought...'

'Quite, quite. But the court isna interested in your thoughts, my man. You may stand down.' Sir Thomas seemed suddenly, perhaps understandably, anxious to be done with the witness. 'Take him hence,' he directed the guards.

As Ludovick watched the stumbling, unhappy Henderson bowing himself out, he marvelled that in fourteen weeks, and with half of the realm to choose from, James had not been able to produce a more eloquent witness and at least more convincing liar. After all, almost anyone would have served equally well, and many better, to represent the unknown and terrible stranger in the turret.

Even though it was only to bear corroboratory evidence, as Hamilton now declared, the next witness was indeed more eloquent. Master Patrick Galloway was called, and strode through the hall in his black gown, to mount the witness stand as though it was his own pulpit. He scarcely allowed the Lord Advocate to enunciate his identification questions before he lurched forth into full and resounding flood.

Yes, he was Patrick Galloway, as all men knew, shepherd of Christ's erring sheep, and chaplain to His Grace. Yes, he it was who had been God's chosen messenger and humble emissary in this matter, in that it was to himself that the wretched Andrew Henderson, tool of the traitors before them, had decided to confide his part in the foul and shameful conspiracy against the King's Majesty, writing to him the letter which proved him to be the armed accomplice of the vile plotters now arraigned at the bar to receive the court's verdict on their wickedness – God Himself having already pronounced and carried out *His* verdict on their sinful bodies, and no doubt now dealing justly and terribly with their thrice-damned souls.

Master Galloway proved himself to be a bolder as well as more fluent witness than the other, by pointing a long and jabbing finger directly at the two Ruthven corpses, and plunging into a thunderous condemnation of their enormities, concentrating more especially on the elder brother, who admittedly had been somewhat neglected hitherto, declaring that not only was he a would-be regicide and traitor, but an incarnate devil in the coat of an angel, a studier of magic and a conjuror with devils, many of whom he had at his command – a revelation which had James rubbing his hands and the company agog. Thereafter, completely ignoring the Lord Advocate's attempts to get a word in, he proceeded to curse the accused, jointly and severally, in detail and in general, their name, their forebears, their kin and memory, comprehensively, scorchingly, breathlessly, hand raised high. Lack of breath, indeed, alone seemed to bring the denunciation to a close. And without a glance at Hamilton, the judges or even the King, he stepped down unbidden from the stand and stalked out, head high, beard bristling.

As the crowded hall seethed and surged in emotive reaction, Sir Thomas, who himself would not have been where he was had he not been something of a showman, perceived that to call other and lesser corroboratory evidence now would but lower the temperature and create anti-climax, wound up briefly and succinctly by resting his case upon their lordships' sure judgement and demanding the maximum penalty within the court's power to impose.

The Lord President raised his hand to still the clamour, and with scarcely a glance at his fellow judges, proceeded in a broad and matter-of-fact voice to read a previously written judgement. The court, after full consideration of the evidence, found the said John and Alexander, sometime Earl and Master of Gowrie, guilty of highest treason. It passed sentence of forfeiture to the Crown upon all that they had possessed whatsoever, and declared their posterity infamous. The court further ordained that their bodies be taken forthwith to the Cross of Edinburgh and there hanged upon the common gibbet. Thereafter the said bodies were to be drawn and quartered at the said Cross, and the heads befixed upon the top of the Tolbooth, and their several members taken to the towns of Perth, Dundee and Stirling there to be affixed in the most patent places. God save the King.

James rose and nodded all around, grinning. Then patting his high feathered hat more firmly on his head, he commenced his teetering walk to the door. After a few paces, however, he paused, and looked across the well of the hall.

'Vicky,' he said loudly. 'I'm for the Cross. Come you wi' me, man.'

Stiff-lipped, Ludovick answered him. 'Sire – I pray you to excuse me. I fear that I have a delicate stomach!'

'Aye, Vicky Stewart – I'm thinking you have. Waesucks – sometimes ower delicate, I do declare! For a leal support o' the Crown. Come you, I said. Can you no' see they're a' waiting on us?'

Despite the short notice, the Master of Gray had worked wonders, and not even Nicolson, the English ambassador, always critical, could report that the evening was not a notable success, either the banquet or the masque and ball which followed. It seemed incredible that all should have been organised and arranged in two days – but there was no question that this was so, for the Queen's unexpected delivery of a second son had been a matter of weeks earlier than anticipated – some said brought on by shock at her husband's gleeful and graphic announcement to her of the disposal of the bodies of the Gowrie brothers; although this was probably a mere malicious canard set afoot by the same people who said that Her Grace had been over-fond of Alexander, the young Master. Be that as it may, the birth of the new Prince Charles had taken place the self-same night as that in which the unfortunate Ruthvens were dismembered and their heads spiked up atop the Tolbooth, not far from Holyroodhouse, to the cheers of the crowd – and old wives gloomily foretold that the young prince would be bound to suffer some derangement in consequence, some preoccupation with beheadings and dismemberments possibly.

Undoubtedly only Patrick Gray could have carried out the King's command to have this great entertainment two nights thereafter. It was a double celebration, to mark the birth of a second son, and to commemorate the King's miraculous escape from the Gowries. The Queen, of course, could not take part, but this was perhaps as well, for the royal partners were scarcely on speaking terms – this time over Anne's sustained refusal to dismiss the Lady Beatrix Ruthven, who lived more or less a prisoner in the Queen's apartments, afraid to venture out, Anne still declaring to all who dare listen that she believed nothing of her husband's story of the conspiracy, trial or no trial. However, James, after the banquet, had paraded the thronged Great Hall of Holyroodhouse with the new and bawling infant in his arms. Moreover he had at his side for most of the evening the seven-year-old Prince Henry, Duke of Rothesay, a weakly and frightened child, ridiculously over-dressed in velvet and sham jewels. The Scottish succession appeared to be assured; undoubtedly the English one was advanced thereby.

The entertainment, if scarcely up to Patrick's highest standards, was commended on all hands, the motif and theme being the royal fondness of the pursuits of the forest. Almost half of the vast hall was transformed into a forest glade, the trees and bushes – since it was mid-November – being evergreens and fir, hung with fairy lanterns. In and out amongst the greenery nymphs and satyrs flitted, roguishly enticing adventurous guests to sample their varied charms, embraces and delights. In the centre was a clearing in which arose a turfed mound, perhaps six feet in height, mounted by rustic steps, on the summit of which was an ingenious fountain, contrived in the form of a great bowl in which stood four naked figures, two male and two female, holding up pipes from which spouted red wine, pumped up by hidden, busy workers beneath the mound. From this happy source all might drink who would – and the surplus overflow splashed down into the bowl over the feet of the living statuary, and back into circulation.

Against this background were staged throughout the evening the usual tableaux, spectacles, charades, dances, feats of skill and mimicry, of a catholicity and cheerful variety, from flauntingly pagan to highly moral, to suit all tastes. A bearded Kirk divine, for instance, preaching furiously to a congregation of sketchily clad nymphs and goat-men, himself fully dressed in Geneva black gown and white bands in front but wholly unclothed behind, preceded an appearance of Sylvanus, the Wild Man of the Woods, uttering congratulatory verse to the royal parent and the new prince in stanzas both subtle and broad. And following on this came a mermaid with a ten-foot tail blowing Satan in front of her with puffs of wind, so that the crown-topped ship behind might come safe into Leith haven – a commentary on King James's single venture into heroics and the dangers of his journey to fetch his bride from Denmark.

Watching this last, and well back in a corner of the huge apartment, three people stood somewhat apart – the Duke of Lennox, the Lady Marie Stewart, Mistress of Gray, and Mary Gray. It was the first Court entertainment which Mary had attended for years, and despite her state of mind and all the circumstances, she could not but respond to it all in a pleasurable excitement. This was reflected in her sparkling eyes and vivid, alive loveliness; dressed in one of the Lady Marie's gowns, she was, as ever, drawing almost as many eyes as was the display. In consequence, Ludovick stood by in a fever of mingled pride, love and frustration. He saw so little of her, even now – for he could scarcely haunt the Master of Gray's quarters, where she lodged; and since she held no official position at Court and eschewed the giddy round, opportunities for meeting were not frequent, consistently as he sought to contrive them. Tonight, even, she would not have come, had she not been assured that the Duchess of Lennox, being in attendance on the Queen, would not be present.

'I wonder whether James ever senses the malice behind Patrick's masquerades and confections?' the Lady Marie murmured. She was drawing her own meed of attention, both as a maturely handsome woman of quiet but assured beauty, and also as wife of the powerful Master of Gray. 'How he ever seems to flatter – but always there is the sting, the mockery, their veiled contempt. As here. The mermaid playfully banishing the King's dread enemy, Satan, with such ease. The allusion that his fears were of naught, his terrors groundless. And yet, James seems to approve of it all. Look how he chuckles and simpers!'

'James, I swear, sees more than we credit, nevertheless,' Ludovick said. 'He has a shrewdness of his own that even Patrick would be wise to heed. A fool and a buffoon, he is, in some ways; but in others he is clever enough. Knowing. And a monster, God knows!'

'Softly!' Marie warned.

'Who is the mermaid?' Mary asked.

'The daughter of my new Lord Balmerino. Lately Sir James Elphinstone, the Secretary of State.'

'She is well-made. And fair.'

'Not as you are, Mary. She is not fit to hold a candle to your sun. Indeed, I cannot think of any other who is!'

She touched his arm lightly. 'You are prejudiced, Vicky! But leal. And . . . lacking something in tact!'

Marie smiled. 'I say he is honest. Which is more than are most men. Moreover, I agree with his judgement.'

Ludovick was not listening. He had stiffened, his rather square and far from handsome features set. Weaving his way through the chattering, colourful throng, smiling, tossing a word here and there, but most evidently making for this retired corner, came Patrick Gray at his most brilliant.

Mary touched the Duke's arm again, but this time with a different pressure. The two men were now apt to avoid each other, even when in the same room.

'On my soul, what need is here for spectacle and lesser delights, when you two are present to be admired!' Patrick greeted the ladies. 'I might have spared myself a deal of trouble. Vicky – you choose excellent company, I'll say that for you.'

The younger man bowed, curtly, stiffly, and said nothing.

'Your spectacles and delights are very successful, nevertheless, Patrick,' his wife said. 'All appreciate and applaud. Even . . . His Grace.'

He considered her. 'You think, perhaps, that His Grace might have reason to do otherwise, my dear?'

'I think that you should not mock him so obviously.'

'Obvious! Sink me – here is damnation indeed! To be obvious – that is anathema. I must be failing, I fear. You slay me, my heart, if you name my small efforts obvious. My aim, as you should know, is to make my point by what I leave unsaid, rather than by what I say.'

'Aye!' That was Ludovick, brief but eloquent.

'I am glad that my lord Duke agrees with me in this small issue.'

'You can tie us up in words, Patrick, always – or, at least, Vicky and myself. With Mary it is otherwise! But heed me in this. It is dangerous, I think, even for you, so to mock and disparage the King.'

'Who says that I mock and disparage His Grace – save only you, sweeting?'

'It would be strange if you did not – since you do all others!' Ludovick said. 'To their sore cost.'

'Folly, Vicky, mocks and disparages itself. Digs its own pit . . .'

'Patrick,' Mary intervened. 'Have you spoken to the King about the Lady Beatrix? To urge that she be spared further hurt and hounding? You said that you would . . .'

'His Grace is very obdurate about that unfortunate family, my dear. He will hear no good of any of them. An interesting subject for philosophical inquiry. I fear that the daggers of my uncle Greysteil and his father, when they let the life out of David Rizzio in Queen Mary's presence, let something equally unpleasant into the unborn James. After all, the Italian was probably his father – since Henry Darnley was scarce capable of begetting offspring. And so the debt is worked off. The sins of the fathers . . .'

'But Beatrix can do the King no harm. An innocent girl.'

'That is not the point, Mary. She is Gowrie's sister, Greysteil's daughter, the old lord's grand-daughter. James sees her only through a veil of blood.'

'Nevertheless, you could save her if you would, Patrick. You *must* save her.'

Her father stroked his scimitar of moustache thoughtfully. 'I said that I would do what I can. I can make no promises . . .'

'What would they be worth, if you did?' Ludovick demanded. 'Since I have no doubt but that you were behind the fall of her brothers! However carefully you hid your hand. To talk of the sins of the fathers is surely sheerest hypocrisy.'

'Have a care what you say, Vicky!' That was very softly

spoken. 'I will stand only so much – even from such as you. Do not try me too hard.'

'Do you assert that you, who move the King in all affairs, knew nothing of this great matter? In which so many were engaged – the Murrays, the Erskines, Ramsay and the rest?'

'None of these are associates of mine. You exaggerate, as do others my influence with the King. Do you not realise that there is a great part of his affairs in which I have neither influence nor interest? Thank the good God! Has it not occurred to you that this was a business which he *would* keep from me? Since the Ruthvens were kinsmen of mine.'

'Robert Logan was also a kinsman of yours!'

'What do you mean by that?'

'I mean that Logan is, or was, your jackal. You have used him in your unsavoury plots ever since I can remember. Since he was so deep engaged in this conspiracy – so the high court of Parliament declares – could you still know naught of it? A singularly uninformed Patrick Gray!'

'On my soul, you would try the patience of a saint in heaven! Think you that Logan lived only to do my bidding? He was a rogue with a hand in a hundred ploys. I neither knew nor desired to know a tithe of them.'

'Leave Logan, then. But there is one side of it all which I think you will find it hard to claim ignorance of. Queen Elizabeth was much put about. As she was meant to be, no doubt. She wrote a long letter to James very shortly after the murder of the Ruthvens; speaking in detail of much that had happened. James showed me the letter, with much relish. Therefore, she had been most fully informed. And swiftly. James himself did not write to her. He sent Captain Preston, of the Guard in due course, to acquaint her. But she knew it all before Preston left Falkland. Do not tell me that Her Grace of England has other correspondents at this Court more prompt than the Master of Gray!'

All three of them waited while Patrick looked away, craving forgiveness, to consider the progress of the current display, pointing out that unfortunately he had duties as Master of Ceremonies which must in some measure preoccupy him. When he turned back to them, he was smiling, wholly himself again. Mary, at least, noted the fact as significant.

'Now – let me see. What was it? Ah, yes – Queen Elizabeth. Her Virgin Grace, Vicky, has a quick-witted and thorough ambassador to this Court, with ample means to gain information for his mistress and to transmit it swiftly to her. Elizabeth is well served. There he stands, the nimble Master Nicolson, talking with my lord of Mar. I warrant that by daybreak tomorrow a swift courier will be on his way to London bearing word of what is done here tonight; whether His Grace was pleased or displeased; which royal favourite is receiving preference; the weight of the new prince and his likelihood of survival. And much else. Aye, much – including, I have no doubt, tidings anent the Duke of Lennox.'

It was Mary who took him up, quickly. 'What do you mean – the Duke of Lennox?'

'Why, my dear, merely that His Grace proposes once again to show his entire confidence and trust in his ducal cousin, by sending him to Elizabeth's Court at London as his envoy residentiary and ambassador in attendance.'

'Ah, no!'

'What? Ambassador? Resident? Me?' Ludovick jerked. 'I'll not go!'

'No? Against a royal command? Come, come, Vicky – you know better than that. You know that if your liege lord is determined on it, you cannot refuse and yet remain in Scotland. And consider the virtues of it, man – Gloriana's brilliant Court, instead of this dull company which you claim to like so little . . . !'

'This is *your* work, Patrick! You are seeking to have me banished the realm . . .'

'Tut, man – do not talk nonsense! His Grace requires an especial envoy, close to himself, with authority to deal with the various factions in England, that all may unite to call for his succession on the Queen's death. The faction of the Earl of Northumberland, Raleigh, and the Lord Cobham, in particular – in opposition to the Secretary Cecil and Howard. These must be brought to favour strongly our monarch's translation to the English throne – as Cecil and Howard do. And who more suitable to convince them than the Duke of Lennox?'

'Patrick, must this be?' his wife asked, almost pleaded. 'Would not another serve equally well?'

'Even the suggestion is unjust to Vicky, my dear! Besides, consider the chance it offers him to spy out the land! All England is the prize. When King Jamie does move south, think of the glittering prospect for his cousin and close supporter, the Duke! Of this land flowing with milk and honey. Here is a most happy opportunity to prepare the way for his own translation, to consider what offices, lands and houses he will have. Elizabeth cannot last long now. 'Fore God – most men would give their right hand for this so timely survey!'

'I desire nothing from England. You know that well,' Ludovick declared. 'My only hope for the English succession is that, once James goes to London, he will leave me here free to live my own life. That is all I ask of him.'

'Wait, my friend. Wait until you have considered well what England has to offer! Now – you will excuse me? I must go act midwife to the infant Moses – Charles, born amidst the Queen's bulrushes – lest Pharaoh's daughter makes a botch of it!'

'Patrick,' Mary said, as he made to move away. 'If I have spoken little, it is not that I am unconcerned. You have now the power and authority which you have always desired. Do not, I pray you, now play God's right hand as well as the King's! Lest you be struck down in your presumption. It seems that there is a danger of it.'

He paused, to eye her closely, sombrely, for a long moment. Then, without a word he turned and left them.

The girl emitted a long tremulous sigh. 'Vicky, Vicky – what have we done?' she whispered. 'Were we fools indeed to match ourselves against the Master of Gray?'

Neither of her companions answered her.

Chapter Twenty-three

Mary was right indeed. Patrick Gray had now the power which he had always sought, almost unlimited power, as Scotland moved into the fateful and eventful seventeeth century. And seldom can a man have been more suited to wield power, more competent to use it, more modest in its sway. Since power over men must by its very nature be a living force, and never a mere dominance and control, weighty and inert, which holds the seeds of its own destruction, its successful handling demands the finest, surest touch. The balance of political power is as vital in its own essential quality as in any outward expression and application. The forces which go to produce it, frequently diametrically opposed to each other, must be kept counterpoised as though on a knife's edge, if the delicate balance is to be maintained.

At such balancing Patrick Gray was the past-master. Power was his life, his goal, almost his religion – power itself, not as with most ambitious men, what power could bring him. He was not concerned with gaining wealth as such, or position, or adulation, or fear. He saw himself as born, and able, to wield power, pure power, and to wield it surely, economically, justly. Utterly without scruple as to how the power was obtained, the power itself was sacrosanct, not to be abused. Behind the extraordinary, shambling, uncouth figure of King James, the realm had never known so scrupulous a ruler.

His policy, of course, was aimed at the achievement of still greater power. Scotland was to be well-managed, prosperous and justly governed, not only because such was implicit in the correct use of power and aided the maintenance thereof, but in order that this should be seen and understood south of the Border, so that nothing should prejudice or hamper the overwhelming call to vastly enhanced power in London. King James was but indifferent material with which to work, not the most attractive monarch for the English to desire – but the Master of

389

Gray set himself to see to it that he *was* perceived as the infinitely desirable successor to the failing Elizabeth by all who mattered in England. To this end all was aimed. It happened that the policy demanded, meantime, effective good government in Scotland.

The interim was longer than any expected. Elizabeth, although nearing seventy, never robust and now a sick woman, had the spirit of a lioness, and clung to life tenaciously. Nor would she so much as countenance the possibility of her demise by naming her successor. Patrick, who knew her so well, had long recognised that she would never so oblige them – even though James himself kept trying to cajole such admission from her, to the end. Patrick's policy was concerned with others – those who surrounded the Queen, and those in opposition to them. He went to work on the susceptibilities, ambitions and the judgement of all in the major factions in England, patiently, systematically, but subtly, brilliantly, by building up his picture of a wise and liberal monarch ruling a contented and prosperous realm, who was the only possible choice as successor to their famous Queen; he offered future privilege, position and reward for present support; and he even reversed the accustomed flow by sending money south, to carefully selected key figures who would use it to best advantage – being something of an expert on the matter of subsidies. This despite the continuing grievous shortage of money in Scotland. A host of Scottish envoys, representatives, informers and spies descended upon England, sounding, probing, subborning, intriguing, under the cloak of the ultra-respectable and patently honest Duke of Lennox, whose lack of both guile and concern about the issue was obvious to all. And all the time, discreetly back from the Borderline, troops waited, in every town and burgh – not so large an army as Patrick would have liked to see, but sufficient to form a swift and ruthless striking-force to spearhead the move on London should more subtle methods fail.

The provision of the necessary funds for all this continued to be one of Patrick's greatest headaches, in a land where money always had been the scarcest of commodities; his success in the matter was probably one of his greatest triumphs, in consequence. The Pope's contribution, although now reduced, was still valuable. At one time it seemed as though His Holiness was going to dry up altogether, in disappointment of any sure evidence of Scotland's return to the true faith. Patrick had to sacrifice Elphinstone on the altar of expediency as scapegoat. The Vatican, in an effort to step up the pressure, published the King's letter suggesting the elevation of Bishop Drummond to the cardinalship, complete with James's incontestable signature – and Elphinstone, as Secretary, had to be made to confess that he had composed this letter and inserted it amongst other documents for signature, so that it was signed inadvertently by the King. However, skilful diplomacy turned even this mishap to good effect, secret assurances being sent to the Pope of James's increasing tendences towards Catholicism to the extent that he was suggesting that he might send his son and heir, Prince Henry, in a year or two's time, to be educated either in Rome or at the Court of Philip of Spain. Mollified and encouraged, the Vatican, noting that Queen Anne was now as good as a Catholic, resumed its subsidies – and Patrick Gray prayed for the speedy translation to a higher kingdom of Elizabeth Tudor.

It was one of his innermost personal satisfactions and proof that his machinations went undetected by the said Elizabeth and her Treasurer, at least, that to retain the good offices and services of Patrick Gray at this same juncture, an award of four hundred crowns a year was sent north, in order to 'aid in the suitable education of Andrew, son and heir of the Master of Gray' – a sum that continued to be paid indeed until the death of the Queen.

The Gowrie business had proved entirely successful, both in its direct and indirect results. Even despite the large grants of Ruthven lands to those who had aided in the matter, there was still a large surplus of the forfeited properties to come to the royal treasury – as well as the cancellation of the deplorable £80,000 debt. Moreover, the King's late colleagues in conspiracy, the Murrays, Erskines and the rest, could now be persuaded effectively to contribute quite large sums, on account of their new holdings and in anticipation of further benefits in England. Even better, the nobility at large, having seen what had happened to Gowrie who had been most outspoken in refusing to contribute to the nation's needs, now hastily chose the wiser and patriotic course, and dipped reluctant hands deep into pockets, their own and even more so, their vassals'.

One other small side issue of the Gowrie affair, which might have proved unfortunate, was happily disposed of by Gray wits – in this case partly by Mary Gray's wits. The King was still hot against the Lady Beatrix Ruthven's continued presence at Court, in the Queen's entourage, and the royal spouses were indeed more fiercely at odds on this subject than on any other. But it was obviously only a question of time until the unfortunate young woman paid the penalty of being sister to the Gowrie brothers, since she could not remain a captive in the Queen's apartments indefinitely. Mary was much worried on her friend's account.

One afternoon she ran Patrick to earth in the new bowling-green being constructed at Holyroodhouse, after considerable searching; for although her father should have been the busiest man in the kingdom, and bogged down in paper-work and affairs, in fact he appeared to be one of the most idle of men, with little of consequence to do much of the time – so adept was he at ensuring that others contributed the necessary labour to put his schemes, ideas and decisions into effective action. No man, he held, with the burden of major decision on him, ought to impare his faculties by dull toil and labour.

'You are the fairest sight these eyes have lighted on this day,' he greeted her, smiling. 'But since you seek me out thus, I fear the worst! What sin have I committed, my dear? What have I done now?'

She shook her head. 'It is not what you have done, Patrick. It is what you have *not* done. I asked you, besought you, to aid the Lady Beatrix. You have not done so.'

'Are you so sure? How do you know, Mary, what I have done? Beatrix does not suffer any hurt. She remains in the Queen's household. No steps have been taken against her. Why are you so sure that I have done nothing to aid her?'

'Because, if you had set your hand to the matter, it would have been to better effect. The Master of Gray does not deal in half-measures! The Lady Beatrix is no better than a prisoner, in fear for her life. The King smokes against her, declaring her to be the last of a viper's brood! Only the Queen's protection saves her. But how long can that last? The Court moves to Falkland soon. It is close quarters at Falkland – little space for any. When the Lady Beatrix leaves the Queen's apartments here at Holyroodhouse, will she ever see Falkland? Does the King not but wait for that?'

'I fear that you misjudge His Grace, my dear – you who used to play his friend, to speak for him when others decried. Was not this fair ear the repository for many a slobbering confidence?'

'I have learned King James's true nature, to my cost. He is a tyrant, a murderer!'

'A pox, girl – watch what you say! Even I could not save you if word of that sort of talk was carried to his ears.'

'To be sure. It was for less than that that he murdered Lady Beatrix's brothers!'

'Have a care, Mary, 'fore God! It is not like you to be so witless. You cannot, must not, accuse the King of the death of the Gowrie brothers. They sealed their own fate when they conspired against James . . .'

'Patrick – need you lie to me? Here, where none can overhear us. You know, as do I, that it was not the Ruthvens who conspired. But the King . . . and his advisers!'

'Idle tales, Mary. The slanders of false and malicious tongues.'

'No. The truth. Which can be established as the truth. Proven.'

It was as though a mask had been drawn over her father's handsome features, so still did they become. He leaned forward a little. 'What do you say?' he asked slowly. 'Proven? What do you mean?'

'I mean, Patrick, that the Lady Beatrix can establish that the conspiracy was on the part of the King – not of her brothers. She has the proof of it.'

'Impossible!'

'No – proof. And possessing this, she has the wherewithal to bargain for her life, has she not? The price of her silence. That is why I have come to you, Patrick. To bargain for my friend!'

He waited, silent.

'Days before that wicked deed was done, Master Herries the physician, who is now Sir Hugh, of Cousland, was with Beatrix. They are friendly. She railed at him, because of his bound

393

gouty foot, declaring that he was but a feeble physician who could not heal himself. He told her then that she would be singing a different tune very shortly. That certain folk close to her would be sore needing the services of the King's feeble physician, and not like to receive them. That a day of reckoning was at hand, and her proud house would be brought low. He had been drinking . . .'

Beneath his breath Patrick Gray said something indistinct but very vehement.

'So you see, Patrick, Herries knew beforehand that the Gowries were to fall. What happened at Gowrie House was no chance.'

'Here is no proof. No certain warranty. The babbling of a drunken fool . . . !' Although that was equally vehement, the Master sounded just a little less assured than usual.

'I think that others would see it differently. Since few believe all the King's story – even after the trial.'

'Who has she told? Other than you?'

'None. As yet. I said to tell none until I had spoken with you. Conceiving that she would be in a better situation to bargain. You see, Patrick – I have much faith in your ability to reckon up the true values of any situation! Where your advantage lies. No merchant, no huckster, I swear, has a clearer understanding as to when to come to terms . . .'

'Bargain! Terms! Can you not see, child? That this is a matter of the direst danger? For Beatrix Ruthven. I concede nothing as to its worth, its truth. But spread abroad, this story could do much damage. That I grant you. Therefore the wretched girl is in the greatest peril. If the King hears of this – *when* he hears of it – she will fall to be silenced. Forthwith. That is certain, inevitable.'

'Exactly. So I came to you. The King may act swiftly. But not before Beatrix can speak. Tell the Queen. And the others of the Queen's ladies. Then, what advantage in silencing her? I come to gain her life by her silence. Not . . . not her silence by her life!'

He stared at her, through her, for long, scarcely seeing her. Then he paced away from her, over the green turf. When he came back he was his assured self again.

'Very well,' he said, nodding. 'We can be agreed on this, I think. For her own sake, for the sake of the realm, Beatrix Ruthven must be silenced. And silenced for all time. She must not change her mind, after a while. She must never be in a position to give evidence in this matter. Or to call on Herries to give evidence. That is the heart of the matter. And there is only one way to seal her lips effectively – short of her death. She must wed Herries.'

Mary drew a quick breath, started to speak, but changed her mind.

'As his wife, she cannot bear testimony against him – even if she would. By good fortune, he is unmarried. It is none so ill a match for her, now that he is knighted and given Cousland . . .'

'He is old enough to be her father!'

'What of it? That is nothing. Many of the best marriages are such. And you say that they are friendly.'

Mary looked down, swallowing. 'Better, I suppose, to marry Herries than to die. But . . . is there no other course?'

'Not that will keep her quiet. As she must be.'

'Will he agree?'

'Give me but two minutes with Hugh Herries, and he will be running to offer his hand!' the Master declared grimly. 'This must be arranged swiftly, quietly. The King must hear naught of it, at this stage. Go back to Beatrix, Mary, and tell her. And no word, otherwise, to a living soul.'

'But the King . . . ?'

'Leave the King to me.'

And so the thing was done, the crisis was past. The Lady Beatrix became the Lady Herries, and with a suddenly chastened and sobered husband retired from Court to live on the former Ruthven estate of Cousland in Lothian. King James even gave them a wedding-gift – but quietly they were also given the word that he never desired to set eyes on either of them again. The Queen, curiously, mortally offended, said the same – but at least one stumbling-block between the royal partners was removed.

Mary Gray lay awake many a night wondering whether she had done rightly.

So the months passed. The tidings from England were good. Queen Elizabeth was failing steadily, in mind it seemed as well as in body. She had sent her favourite, Essex, to the block on a charge of treason, and was now grieving crazedly for him, often sitting alone in a dark room mourning and lamenting. Her judgement, which had so long been her own and England's pride, was impaired; she was rewarding close servants by allowing them to tax articles in general use, even salt and starch – to the indignation of Parliament and the people. She would sit about on the floor and refuse to move. At the opening of Parliament her robes of velvet and ermine proved too heavy for her, and staggering, she had only been saved from falling by the peer who stood nearest her in his arms.

Her cousin twice removed and would-be successor, rubbed his hands. It would not be long now.

The Duke of Lennox came back to Scotland unannounced and unbidden – and was warmly greeted by neither his wife nor his liege lord. Only Mary Gray rejoiced to see him – but even she still failed to give him the welcome on which his heart was set. Ludovick Stewart was a man at odds with the world.

At least he had had the wit to bring with him a letter from Lord Henry Howard, with which to soften the royal wrath. Lord Henry, brother to the Duke of Norfolk, was a fox, and closest associate of Sir Robert Cecil, the Secretary of State, who was ruling England in the Queen's name. While the peculiar Cecil was circumspect to the point of primness in his communications, Howard was allowed to be otherwise. James was so pleased with this letter that he read it aloud at a banquet to the assembled Court – to the vast embarrassment of Nicolson the English ambassador; and just in case any of his hearers had missed the significance of it, he read the part which he liked especially a second time. It went:

'You are the apple of the Eternal eye, most inestimable King James, whom neither death nor life nor angels nor principalities nor powers, shall separate from the affection and vows the subjects of this fair realm, next to the sovereign possessor, have vowed to you; the redoubtable monarch of whose matchless mind I think, as God's lieutenant upon earth, with the same reverence and awe which I owe to God himself when I am on my knees.'

While, shocked, some muttered about blasphemy, none could

deny that when Cecil's right-hand man wrote in such terms, the signs were propitious to say the least of it. Although Ludovick himself was revolted by the contents of the letter he had brought, the same nevertheless served to make King James applaud the bearer instead of berating him and sending him back to England forthwith. He kept quiet. Keeping quiet, and waiting, it seemed, was to be his role in life – and his cross and burden.

So the months went by.

Chapter Twenty-four

The reeling horseman on the foundered and indeed dying mount clattered alone up to the gatehouse of the Palace of Holyroodhouse, and all but fell from the saddle. The guard had heard those uneven hoofbeats on the cobblestones of the Abbey Strand in the silence of the night, and were waiting expectant.

'The King! The King's Majesty! Word for the King's Majesty.' The man's voice was as uneven as had been the sound of his approach, and, added to his English accent, made his words barely intelligible. But there was no doubting the urgency of his demand, or who he desired to see, as he slid, panting, from the horse and staggered up to the gate.

'His Grace is abed lang syne, sir,' the officer of the guard announced. 'Here's no time o' night to see the King! Who are you from, man?'

'Eh . . . ? Who . . . ? Abed?' Stupidly the newcomer peered at the speaker through the interlocking iron bars of the great gate, swaying drunkenly. In the light of the flickering torches he made a sad sight. His once-fine clothing was so befouled by rain, mud, sweat and horse's saliva as to be an offence to eye and nose both, and his unshaven features, although obviously comparatively youthful, were grey lined with fatigue, like those of an old man, and caked with the dried blood of a grazed cheekbone. 'Carey,' the apparition managed to enunciate. 'Carey – for the King's Majesty. I . . . I . . .'

His thick words were interrupted by a crash. Behind him the legs of his steaming, trembling mount had suddenly buckled and splayed, and the brute toppled to the cobbles in sprawling collapse as its heart gave out.

The young man scarcely turned to look. 'The fourth,' he muttered. 'Fourth. No – fifth. Fourth or fifth – God knows!'

They had the gates open for him now, and were just in time to save him from following his horse to the wet ground. The officer, supporting him on his arm, led him into the palace forecourt.

They were turning into the warmth and light of the guard-room, where a blazing fire kept the chill of the wet March night at bay, when the visitor resisted and held back, with un-expected strength and vehemence considering his state.

'The King,' he exclaimed again. 'I demand the King. His Majesty's presence. Take me.'

'His Grace is asleep, man. I darena wake him up at this hour...'

'Fool! You dare not *fail* to wake him, I say! I am Carey. Sir Robert Carey. From Richmond. From the Court of England. I must see the King.'

'Will it no' keep till the morn...?'

'No. Now, I say, Forthwith.'

The guard-commander shrugged, and still holding Carey's arm, moved on. He ordered two of his men to hurry ahead, one to waken the duty page and one to inform the Master of Gray.

Up the winding stone stairs of the most northerly of the drum towers he conducted the stumbling Englishman. At the first-floor landing, a sleepy-eyed grumbling youth was dragging on some clothing in the pages' room. The officer demanded a goblet of wine for the stranger before the page went upstairs to arouse the King.

'Tell His Grace that it is Sir Robert Carey. From England. On matters exceeding urgent.'

'Son to the Lord Hunsdon. Cousin to Queen Elizabeth.'

The page returned sooner than might have been expected. 'His Grace will see Sir Robert Carey,' he announced. 'Follow me.'

Up a second turnpike stair they went, to the next landing, where two armed guards stood on duty. They crossed an ante-room, and the page knocked on the door beyond. As they waited, swift footsteps brought the Master of Gray to their side, fully dressed and quite his usual elegant self, despite the hour. He greeted Sir Robert briefly, brows raised in unspoken question, and dismissed the guard-commander, just as the King's voice bade them enter.

James was sitting up in his great canopied four-poster bed, a comic picture, clutching a bed-robe round his nakedness, with a tall velvet hat, hastily donned and askew, replacing a discarded nightcap, presumably in pursuit of dignity. As always when upset or concerned, his heavy-lidded eyes were rolling alarmingly, and he was plucking at his lips. The page had lit three candles from the dying fire. The room was hot and stuffy.

'Hech, hech – what's this? What's this?' he demanded. 'It's no' . . . ? Man, it's no' . . . ?'

'Sir Robert Carey, with tidings for Your Grace,' Patrick said.

Carey, evidently revived by the wine, ran forward to the royal bed and threw himself down on his knees beside it, reaching out to grasp the apprehensive monarch's hand. 'Sire!' he cried. 'Twice, thrice King! Humbly I greet you! Hail to the King! King James, of England, Scotland, France and Ireland! God save the King!'

'Guidsakes!' James said, jaw sagging. 'Och, well now. Mercy on us.'

Swiftly Patrick was at the kneeling Englishman's side. 'This is certain, sir? Sure?' he demanded.

'Certain.'

'You have a writing? A proof?'

Carey put his hand into the bosom of his stained and soaking doublet, and drew out a glittering ring. Silently he handed it to the King.

James gobbled. 'I ken this!' he cried. 'Aye, fine I do. I sent this to her . . . to Elizabeth. One time. It was my mother's ring – Mary the Queen's ring.'

Patrick knew it also, since he it was who had handed it to Elizabeth Tudor, years before. He dropped on one knee, beside Carey, and took the monarch's hand, that still clutched the great ring, to carry it to his lips.

'Your most royal Majesty's humble, devoted and right joyful servant!' he murmured.

'Aye,' James said, on a long bubbling sigh. 'Aye, well. So . . . so she's awa'? At last! God be praised for a' His mercies!'

'Amen!' Rising to his feet, Patrick smiled slightly. 'May Her Grace rest in peace perpetual.'

'Ooh, aye. To be sure. Indeed aye. Our beloved sister and cousin.'

Carey remained kneeling. 'My sister, the Lady Scrope. A lady of the bedchamber. She drew the ring from Her Majesty's finger, Sire. As her last breath faded. She threw it to me. Out of the bechamber window. I was waiting beneath. All the night. It was a compact, between us. That I might bring it to you. The tidings. I have ridden night and day . . .'

'When, man? When was this?'

'The night of Wednesday, Your Majesty. No – it was Thursday morning. Three of the clock.'

'Thursday? And this is but Saturday night!' Patrick exclaimed. 'Four hundred miles! In three days and two nights?'

'I killed four horses. Or five. I have not stopped. Save once. When I fell. And must have slept awhile where I lay. Near to Alnwick, in Northumberland, I think.'

'Expeditious,' the King commented sagely. 'Maist expeditious. Aye, and proper.'

'I . . . my sister and I esteemed that Your Majesty should know. Be informed. At the earliest moment. I sought the honour. To be Your Majesty's first subject to greet you. First English subject, Sire.'

'A worthy ambition, man Carey. I'ph'mmm. Meritorious. You'll no' suffer for it – we'll see to that!'

'I thank you, Sire.'

'Sir Robert – the succession?' the Master of Gray said. 'The Queen's death is established. That is, h'm, very well. But – was aught said of the succession For, if not, it behoves us to act fast.'

'Waesucks, aye!' James's voice quavered again. 'What o' that, man? Was it decided?'

'Yes, Sire – your royal succession is assured. The Queen decreed it. In the end. Before she sank away. Earlier in the night. I was there present, myself. In the bedchamber. With other cousins. When she was evidently sinking, they questioned her. The Secretary, the Archbishop, the Lord Admiral. To name her successor. She said – and it was the last words she spoke, Sire, "My seat has been the seat of kings, and none but a king must succeed me".'

'Aye. Maist fitting and due,' Majesty nodded.

'Is that all?' Patrick demanded. 'No more specific word? Naught of the Lord Beauchamp?'

'She had said before that she would have no rascal's son in her seat. When he was named.'

'But, for her successor, she spoke no actual name?'

'After she had said this of only a king in her seat, they put names to her. The King of Spain. She showed no sign. The King of France. She did not move. Then they said the King of Scots. Her Grace started. She heaved herself up on her bed and held her hands jointly over her. Above her head. In the manner of a crown. Then she fell back. From then, Sire, to her last breath, she neither spoke nor moved. Three hours and more. While I waited below, booted and spurred.'

James nodded, beaming now. 'Explicit,' he said. 'Full explicit. The auld woman had some glisks and glimmerings o' sense to her, after all! Aye – though she was a fell time about showing it. So – a's by with. England's mine. England's mine, Patrick – d'you hear? I'm rich, man – rich.'

Patrick bowed, unspeaking. He turned to Carey, who at last had risen from his knees. 'What of Cecil? And the Council? What of a proclamation?'

'I heard Cecil say to the Archbishop, sir, that the succession of King James would be put to the Council so soon as it could be assembled, in the morning. And the proclamation issued thereafter. That same Thursday morning.'

'So I've been King o' England for two days, no less - and didna ken it! Guidsakes – you wouldna think it possible! It's a right notable thought. I could indite a poem on it – aye, a poem. An opopee. An ode. I'll do that, Patrick – get me papers and pens. Here's occasion for notable rhyming.'

Carey stared, as Patrick bowed and murmured. 'Excellent, Your Grace. But . . . at this hour?'

'To be sure. What has the hour to do wi' the divine creation? The ardent excogitation? Paper, man. And have the bells to ring. The Kirk bells. A' the bells. To be rung until I command that they cease. Aye, and bonfires . . .'

'Sire – might I suggest a small delay? Until the English Council's word arrives. Sir Robert's tidings are joyful and welcome. But they are those only of a private subject, however excellent.

It would be seemly would it not, to await the proper messengers of your Privy Council in England? And to inform your Scots Council before the public rejoicings.'

The King's face fell, and he darted a glance that was almost venomous at the speaker. He shrugged. 'Aye. Maybe,' he conceded shortly.

'Do you wish Her Grace to be informed, Sire?'

'Anne? Na, na – no hurry for that. She'll but haver and bicker on it. Soon enough for her, the morn.'

'Very well. I shall call a meeting of the Council for tomorrow?'

'Aye, do that. And see to Sir Robert here. Now – paper and pens, man...'

Chapter Twenty-five

The ranked cannon on Berwick's massive ramparts thundered out as never they had thundered before, it is safe to say, in all the Border fortress's long and turbulent history. Never had the cannoneers been so reckless of powder, and never before had those serried ranks of north-pointing English muzzles belched blankshot. The echoes rolled back and forth across the winding Tweed and all the green plain of the Merse, tossed hither and thither by the distant encircling hills. To their accompaniment the great company approached the ancient grey-walled, red-roofed town by the glittering sea, which had for so long been the most bitterly grudged bone of contention between the two hostile nations.

It was as good as an army which flooded down from the Lamberton ridge to the north – although a very different army from the steel-clad host which had for so many months kept its silent vigil along the Border, and now was at last dispersing unrequired. This company, although fully a thousand strong, represented the very flower of Scotland. Not since King James the Fourth had led his resounding chivalry to disaster and extinction at Flodden Field exactly ninety years before, had so much brilliance, colour and circumstance come to the Border. Some would go on, across Tweed, and some would turn back, men and women both.

King James the Sixth and First was apparelled for the occasion. Seldom indeed can a man have sat a horse for a long journey happed in such sheer yardage of velvet, cloth-of-gold and satin-ribbon, not to mention the ostrich-plumes, gold chains and sundry decorations. If he did not outshine all his entourage, it was not for want of ornament. His Queen, some way behind, amongst her ladies, was much less adorned – and still in evil humour because her children had been left behind in Edinburgh in the care of the Earl of Mar.

The King rode between Sir Charles Percy, brother of the Earl of Northumberland, and Thomas Somerset, son of Lord

Worcester, the English envoys who had brought north the official news of Queen Elizabeth's death, and the call to her throne from the Privy Council, three days after Sir Robert Carey's spectacular dash. Carey himself, promised a peerage and a pension, rode just behind with the Master of Gray and sundry English notables. The Duke of Lennox, who should have been close at his cousin's and monarch's side, was nowhere near – not even with the Queen's party where rode his Duchess, but far in the rear with Mary Gray, the Lady Marie and her children.

It looked as though even the weather of Scotland was glad to be getting rid of her peculiar sovereign, for the sun shone, the clouds sailed high and the air was balmy indeed for early northern April. This was as well, for the lesiurely progress southwards of this enormous cavalcade would have been a sorry business in bad weather. It was only the second day of the long journey, of course, which so far had been something in the nature of a triumphant procession, with cheering folk in every burgh and village, lairds hastening to provide stirrup-cups and lords greater hospitality; it remained to be seen whether the welcome of the southern kingdom, climatic and otherwise, would be as heartfelt as this northern farewell.

At least there was no doubt about Berwick's greetings and reception. The town had not had time to prepare the masques and spectacles seemly for the occasion – for James had wasted no time in shaking the dust of Scotland off his feet, this being but the 6th of April, he having set out only five days after the official news had arrived at Edinburgh; but, apart from the cannonade, Berwick's entire population showed its appreciation of its new situation, its release from the centuries-old condition of being almost a perpetually besieged city, by packing the narrow streets so tightly that it was almost impossible for the royal party to win through them. At the Scots Gate, the Governor and Marshal of Berwick, flanked by the Wardens of the Marches from both sides of the Border, awaited the monarch of them both – and who thereupon, with droll humour, dismissed them from their ancient offices, as no more necessary in his united domains. The Mayor then handed over the keys of the town – and what was still more welcome, a purse of gold – and commenced to read a lengthy peroration which the King presently interrupted, referring to the worthy as Provost and declaring that what he wanted to do was to inspect the cannon which had made such 'extraordinary exellent displosions'. Up on the ramparts which walled in the town, he started up the cannonade once more, himself gleefully discharging some of the pieces and commanding that there was to be no let up of the noise until all their powder was exhausted. Then, tiring of this, he set off through the crowded streets, to shouts of 'God save King James', his vast following making their difficult way through as best they might, down to the lower part of the town, near the river and harbour, called Ravensdowne, where at the Governor's House immense hospitality was prepared.

It was late in the afternoon before all was ready for the great moment, and the royal cavalcade somehow managed to re-assemble, to convoy the royal traveller down to the bridge to cross Tweed into his new realm of England. The river here at its mouth is quarter of a mile in width, and the long, narrow and spidery bridge of timber, patched and mended from shatterings innumerable by storm, flood and war, represented a tenuous link indeed between the two kingdoms. The sight of it, hitherto hidden by the tall enclosing walls of the town, brought suddenly home to many just how significant was the occasion – brought indeed a lump into many a throat.

Many, the greater proportion of the company, were turning back here and there was a great taking of leave and saying of farewells. A large concourse was to be seen awaiting the monarch's arrival at The Spittall, on the other side of Tweed. A couple of hundred or so would accompany James all the way to London. Others would cross the river to but set foot on English soïl and say their farewells there. Of this last group Mary Gray was to be one.

While this marshalling and leave-taking was going on, still to the intermittent booming of a few remaining cannon, a single horseman came cantering across the long bridge from the far side, his hoofbeats drumming hollowly on the timbers. It proved to be a young man dressed in the height of fashion, who jumped off his beast and sank on his knees before King James, holding out a large key in his hand.

'Your most gracious Majesty, serene exemplar of learning, humanity and piety, the heart's desire of all true Englishmen,' he cried in fluting tones. 'I am John Peyton, son to the Lieutenant of the Tower of London, the most humble of all your servants. Here is the key to that said dread Tower, Majesty, England's citadel, which I have ridden post to present to you ere you set foot on England's devoted soil.'

The Scots around the King coughed and looked embarrassed at such unseemly and magniloquent language; but James himself appeared to find nothing amiss with it. Smirking and nodding, he took the key, patting the young man's head, and on impulse told him to stay on his knees. He turned to Ludovick, at his side, demanding his sword, and taking it, had some trouble, with the large key in his hand, in bringing it down on the young man's shoulder.

'Arise, good Sir John . . . John . . . Eh, what's the laddie's name?' he asked, in a stage whisper, peering round.

'Peyton, Sire – Peyton,' Somerset said hurriedly. It was the Englishmen's turn to look embarrassed.

'Aye, well – arise Sir John Peyton. Vicky – here, take this key, man. It's ower heavy . . .'

That was but the first of three hundred knightings on the way to London.

'Come, Sir Percy. Come Somerset, man,' the King commanded, beckoning for his horse. 'Aye, and you too, Vicky. Escort me across this unchancy brig. It's gey long and it's gey rickmatick, by the looks o' it. You'd better go first, Vicky. Aye, you too, Percy. See it's safe for me. I dinna like the looks o' it . . . !'

'It is quite safe, Sire, I assure you,' Sir Charles Percy told him. 'I have crossed it many times. Heavy cannon cross it . . .'

'Aye, maybe. But go you ahead, just the same. It's a right shauchly brig, this. You should ha' done better for me, man!'

Ludovick looked back unhappily to where Mary stood; he had intended to cross the bridge at her side, with parting now so near. She waved him on, indicating that she would see him at the other side.

It was no doubt inevitable, indeed possibly essential, that the long bridge should sway somewhat in the middle, constructed

of wood as it was and with a dog's leg bend two-thirds of the way
across to counter the swift current of the tidal river. But long
before they were that far, James was complaining loudly,
bitterly, exclaiming at every shake and shiver. Presently indeed
he commanded a halt, and hastily got down from his horse,
pushing the beast away from him in case its weight should add to
his own danger. He would have turned back there and then, on
foot as he was – but it was pointed out to him that they were
more than half-way across now, with less distance to go forward
than back, and that the bridge behind them was crowded with
folk. Insisting that Ludovick led the two horses and kept well in
front, the King, clutching Sir Charles's arm on one side and the
parapet-rail of the bridge on the other, placed the remainder of
the way almost on tiptoe, staring horrified at the jabbly wavelets
beneath him, thick lips moving in mumbled prayer.

Thus James Stewart entered into his long desired inheritance. He made the last few yards to English soil at a sort of
shambling run, and reaching *terra firma*, sank down on his
velvet-clad knees dramatically and kissed the ground – to the
alarm and confusion of the great gathering here awaiting him,
who did not know whether to come forward, remain standing,
or kneel likewise. The Earl of Northumberland and the Bishop
of Durham, leaders of the welcome party, after a hasty whispered consultation, moved forward and got down on their own
knees beside the monarch, who, with eyes tight shut and lips
busy, was colloguing with his Maker and apostrophising the
Devil in the same urgent breath. The throng stared, enthralled.

When he opened his eyes and found others kneeling beside
him, James tut-tutted in displeasure, but used their shoulders to
aid himself to rise. Then perceiving that one was in holy orders,
he forestalled the address of welcome by launching into a stern
and voluble denunciation of a people and nation who expected
their prince to take his life in his hands and come to them across
a death-trap like that.

'It's no' right or proper, I tell you!' he declared, wagging a
finger at the unfortunate Bishop. 'I . . . we are much dis-
pleasured. Yon's a disgrace! We might ha' been submerged in
the cruel waters – aye, submerged. It wabbles, sir – it quakes.
It'll no' do, I say. It is our command – aye, our first royal com-

mand on this our English ground – that you'll build a new brig. Aye, a guid stout brig o' stone, see you. That'll no' wabble. Forthwith. See you to it. Our Treasury in London will pay for it.'

'It shall be done, Majesty. Most certainly. A start shall be made at once. And now, Sire, here is my Lord of Northumberland. He humble craves permission to present an address of welcome...'

Ludovick, standing by with the horses, like any groom, found Mary at his side. He thrust the reins into the hands of the nearest bystander, and taking the girl's arm, led her through the press some little way, to where, at the waterside, they might speak alone.

'Did ever you see such a to-do about nothing!' he demanded of her. 'Such a pother and commotion to make, in front of his new subjects! What they will think of him...'

She smiled. 'At least they will not *say* what they think, it seems – as some might, in Scotland! The English are most flowery speakers. I think King James more like to drown in a flood of flattering words than the waters of Tweed!'

'Aye – but he revels in their flummery. The more fawning and fulsome, the better! But . . . Mary, we are fools to waste time and thought on James Stewart, here and now. When we are so soon to separate. What are his follies and troubles to ours, who love each other and yet must be ever apart? You are sure? Determined? Even now. You will not change your mind? Come south with me? At least, with Patrick and Marie. To London. Even for a little time. You might like it well.'

'No, Vicky. Here I turn back. Here is where I belong. I have been to London, you remember. With Patrick, when he went to see Queen Elizabeth on the matter of the King's pension. I liked it well enough – but I could not bide there. I pined for our own hills, for the great skies and the caller air...'

'As did I. As I shall. But . . . I will return, Mary. And quickly. Nothing shall hold me. Once I have seen James installed on his new throne, I shall be back, hot-foot – that I swear by all that is true and holy. James may forbid it, threaten me with the Tower if he likes! But I will win back to you. To you. And swiftly. Back to Scotland.'

She gripped his arm. 'Do that, Vicky,' she said simply. 'I

shall be waiting.'

'You . . . you will welcome me back?'

'Oh, my dear – can you ask that? I shall barely live until I see you again.' Her voice was unsteady.

'Mary – you can say that now? At this pass! After all the years wherein you have held me from you?'

'From my body only, Vicky – never from my heart. You know that.'

'I know only that I am the most unhappy of men, Mary. To have tasted of heaven, and then to be cast out – while told still that my heaven is there, waiting, yet with me locked and barred from it! For the sake of . . . what?'

'For the sake, I fear, of *me*, Vicky. Myself. What I am. Oh, I am sorry. I am foolish, I know well – stubborn and proud also. And my folly was never more clear to myself than at this moment!'

'You mean . . . ?'

'I mean that I am seeing myself for what I am. And knowing not whether to weep or to laugh. I now know myself to be but a very frail and feeble woman, Vicky . . .'

'That you could never be!'

'My dear – you will discover! Soon, I pray.'

'Soon, aye. Before summer is in, I shall be back to you. I will come with the swallows. Swift, like the swallows. Would I had their wings. To Castle Huntly, in the Carse . . .'

'No, Vicky. Do not come to Castle Huntly.'

'No?' His face fell.

'No. Come to Methven. Back to our own fair Methven, in Strathearn. Johnnie's Methven. I . . . I shall await you there.'

'Mary! Mary!' Uncaring who watched them, the Duke grasped her, pulled her to him. 'My dear! My heart! You mean it? Is it true? You are going back to Methven . . . ?'

'Yes, Vicky. Johnnie shall go back to his inheritance. At last. And I with him. To await his father. And my love. There, beneath the blue Highland hills, we shall count the days . . .'

'But . . . thank God! Thank God, I say! But, why, Mary? I mean, what has changed you? At long last?'

She pointed, above the heads of the crowd, to where the Queen's mounted company was now debouching from the bridge. 'Yonder is my reason. So simple, so shallow. That makes a mock of all my fine talking and lofty airs, Vicky! Your Duchess. Leaving Scotland. There is all your answer.'

'Because Jean goes? To London. You will come back to me?'

'Yes. Simple, is it not? Now you know the deeps of a woman's nature! This woman – who has for so long prated of high-sounding precepts and principles. Because your wife will be four hundred miles away, I will return to your side, Vicky! Your Scots wife! I had a word with the Duchess. She spoke me very fair, I cannot deny. She will stay with the Queen. The move to London pleases her well. She will be a great lady there, indeed. She will not come back – any more than, I think, will the King. But *you* will – and I shall be waiting for you.'

He drew a long breath. 'Heaven be praised! I ask no better of life than this! Jean is no wife to me, Mary. She never has been. You are all the wife I have, or desire.'

'Not wife, only mistress, my dear. I have discovered myself to be less proud, less high-souled, than I believed. Your mistress I am content to be – so long as your Duchess is not wife to you. And stays four hundred miles away! It is no noble confession – but at least I see myself, at last, for what I am.'

'You are my heart's blood, my delight, my life, my all!' he said, deep-voiced.

'Then . . . I am content.'

Silent now, merely holding each other fast, they stood, at peace, until querulous royal shouts for Vicky the Duke reached them, and they made their reluctant way back through the throng.

James had had enough of speeches of welcome, and was for pressing on. Final leave-takings were in progress, and already the Queen's entourage was moving off.

'Vicky – where ha' you been?' the King demanded. 'You shouldna jouk off that way. You should be at my side, man. It's yon lassie again, I'll be bound! Mistress Mary. Aye. Well, you'll be quit o' her now – for she's no' coming with us. Na, na. There's some we'll manage fine without, in London!'

'She had no thought of coming, Sire. She goes back. With my lord of Argyll.'

'D'you say so, Vicky? Mysel', I reckoned she'd be going back

411

wi' her begetter, Patrick Gray!'

There was a sudden indrawing of breaths and silence from all near enough to hear. Men stared from the King to each other.

James licked his lips, eyes rolling, and whinnied a peculiar excited laugh. He looked round to where Patrick stood behind him. 'Aye, Master o' Gray,' he said. 'I'm thinking this is where we part company!'

Blank-faced, the blood draining from his handsome features, Patrick stood, lips parted, as though stunned. For moments he, the most eloquent man in two kingdoms, found no words. None other spoke.

'I . . . I do not understand, Your Grace,' he stammered out, at length.

'No? Do you no', Patrick? Yet it's simple, man – simple. *I* go on to this London – and you turn back. You understand now, my mannie?'

Patrick's fine nostrils flared, his eys narrowed. 'Your Grace means that you wish me to return to Edinburgh. Meantime. To complete some business of the state there, before coming to London?'

'No – my Grace doesna mean any such thing. We left a' things well arranged in Edinburgh, you'll mind. Ooh, aye – Edinburgh will manage fine.'

'Then, Sire, I repeat – I do not understand you.'

'It's no' like you, Patrick, to be so dull in the uptak! Most times you're quick enough – aye, ower quick, by far! What's come ower you, man?'

'I think, Sire, that I must ask that of your royal self!'

'Oho! Testy, eh? Vaunty! Paughty! To me, the King! Aweel, Patrick – I needs must discover you the matter, since you'll have it so. And now's as good a time as any. You are a rogue, Master o' Gray – and I've aye kenned you were a rogue! But I needed a rogue, see you. A great rogue, to berogue the lesser rogues around me! And I had them in plenty. Ooh, aye – it's a great place for rogues, is Scotland! But I intend to leave them there, Patrick man – no' to take them with me! The English are honester folk – eh, my lord Bishop? My lord o' Northumberland? And if they have a rogue or two in London-town – waesucks I'll find me one o' their own breed to berogue them! I'll no' need the

412

likes o' you in London, Patrick, Master o' Gray! Now you understand me?'

So quiet were all those about King James, that the shuffling of his feet and the tinkling of ornaments on his person sounded clearly.

Patrick Gray said nothing. He looked his monarch in the eye until the royal gaze faltered and fell. Then he bowed low, but with a thin smile and the elaborate flourish of sheerest mockery. Thereafter he turned his back on the King.

'My horse!' he called out. 'And quickly. I mislike the stink of this place!'

'Master o' Gray!' James cried, his voice quavering with anger. 'I've no' finished wi' you, yet. Wait you. You're . . . you're deprived o' your offices, man. You understand! You are no longer my Sheriff o' Forfar. And there's no wardrobe to master now, in Scotland! D'you hear . . . ?'

But Patrick Gray was not waiting. Without another glance round, he strode over to his horse, and mounted, the beast's head turned towards the bridge and Scotland. 'Where is my wife?' he asked of the silent watchers. 'Where is Marie?'

'Here, Patrick, my dear. Here . . .'

King James plucked at his lower lip, watching. Then his frown faded, and he actually chuckled. '*Alea jacta est*!' he said, and dug the Bishop of Durham in the ribs with his elbow. 'Or, more properly *Jacta est alea?* Aye. Is that no' apt, man? Apt. Hech, aye – Caesar crosses the Rubicon, and I cross Tweed! *Aut Caesar aut nullus*!' He looked round to discover how many recognised his learning and wit. Disappointed in what he saw, he sniffed. 'Come, Vicky – to horse,' he commanded.

Ludovick, aiding his cousin to mount, looked over to where Mary Gray stood watching. Their eyes met, and as though of a single volition turned to consider the receding elegant figure of the Master, already upon the bridge. When their glances returned, and held for a long moment, it was as though a spate of unspoken eloquence flowed between them, sombre and joyous both. Then the Duke mounted, raised his hand high, and spurred after the King.

It took some considerable time thereafter, because of the delay imposed by the constriction of the narrow bridge, for Mary and the Earl of Argyll to come up with Patrick Gray – by which time he had won free of Berwick town on the long road northwards. He was riding at a fast trot, the Lady Marie at his side, his children with the servants and all their baggage falling behind, apart from any other group or company.

Without a word spoken, Archibald Campbell drew back a little, as they neared the Grays, so that Mary might overtake them alone. The girl thanked him with her glance, and cantered ahead.

Patrick was staring fixedly in front of him as Mary rode up at the other side from his wife. He made no sign or greeting as she came up. The two women exchanged looks, but did not speak.

So the trio rode on in silence.

It was fully a mile further on before Patrick spoke, abruptly. 'Who was the greater fool?' he demanded.

Neither of the women presumed to answer him.

'That is what cuts deep,' he went on tight-voiced, as though to himself. 'Not the insult. Not the loss of place and position. Not the ingratitude, even – although he would not now be riding to London had it not been for what I have done. It is the knowledge that I have been fooled by a fool! How could it be?'

Slowly Mary replied. 'Perhaps, Patrick, only a fool *could* have fooled you? Perhaps it required that.'

He turned in his saddle to consider her and what she said. Then he actually laughed, a short bark of a laugh. 'Aye,' he said, 'it may be so.'

It was the girl who spoke next, as abruptly, briefly. 'And now?' she asked.

'Now, yes. What, you may well ask, Mary. This, at least – I am done with statecraft.'

'I thank God!' his wife said, deep-voiced, at his other side.

'You may say that my task is done,' he went on, still as though to himself. 'For years I have worked for this day. To make a unity of these two realms. To end the shadow of war and hatred between them. It is done – whether I go to London or not. That work is finished. I should rejoice, perhaps – like you, Marie? For, heigho – am I not a free man? At last!'

'I have prayed for this day, Patrick, for long years,' Marie said unsteadily.

'Have you, my dear? Is that how you love me?' He did not say that harshly, however.

'Yes, it is. God bless James Stewart, I say! We can now start to live again. Live as man and wife should, in trust and sanity . . .'

'In a stone tower on a bleak rock in the Tay! Can you think to roost in Broughty Castle, Marie my love?'

'You know that I can. I can live anywhere with you – so long as it is *you*, Patrick. And not . . . the Master of Gray!'

'Was he so ill a husband?'

'He was, I sometimes think, the Devil himself!'

Into the silence that followed, Mary spoke again. 'Why Broughty, Patrick? Why not Castle Huntly? Where you belong. My lord is but a shadow. A shadow that is fading fast. It is too late to alter that. But you will be the Lord Gray before long. *That* task is just beginning. Lord of great lands and many folk. Is it always to be Davy Gray's burden? Davy – who is so excellent a steward. And a father. But . . . no lord of Gray!'

'Dear Davy!' Marie said.

'Aye – there you have it!' Patrick nodded, smiling wryly. 'Dear Davy! Davy dear! Dare I take my wife back to Castle Huntly – who loves Davy Gray?'

'I love Davy Gray, yes – always have done and always will. But not as I love my husband!' Marie said simply. 'You may safely take me to Castle Huntly, Patrick. It is my hope that you will.'

'It is my hope also,' Mary agreed. 'For I go to Methven. With Johnnie. There to await Vicky. It is Methven for me.'

'Oh, Mary dear – I am glad, glad!'

'So that is the way of it, lassie, in the end? You have it all plotted and planned and arranged! The daughter of the Master of Gray!'

'That is the way of it, Patrick. In the end.'

Slowly he said it. 'Tell me then, girl,' he wondered, looking at her sidelong, 'Who spoke back yonder at the bridge-end of Berwick? James Stewart? Or Mary Gray?'

'Say that a higher voice than King James spoke there, Patrick – for it was time.'

'God saving King James?'

'Rather, I think, God saving Patrick Gray!'

415

FOOTNOTE

The history-books tell us that Patrick, Master of Gray, the handsomest man in Europe, the Machiavelli of Scotland, retired from public life after the Union of the Crowns in 1603 – save to sue the Crown in the Scottish courts for the sum of £19,993 for certain services rendered, and to win it; some historians have wondered why. That he succeeded his father as 6th Lord Gray in 1608, and died three years later in comparative obscurity. Let the history-books have the last word, then, as is only right and proper.

In 1612, Sir John Stewart of Methven, illegitimate son, by mother unnamed, to the Duke of Lennox, was, at the age of nineteen, appointed Constable and Keeper of Dunbarton Castle.

NIGEL TRANTER

THE BRUCE TRILOGY

In 1296 Edward Plantagenet, King of England, was determined to bludgeon the freedom-loving Scots into submission. Despite internal clashes and his fierce love for his antagonist's goddaughter, Robert the Bruce, both Norman lord and Celtic earl, took up the challenge of leading his people against the invaders from the South.

After a desperate struggle, Bruce rose finally to face the English at the memorable battle of Bannockburn. But far from bringing peace, his mighty victory was to herald fourteen years of infighting, savagery, heroism and treachery before the English could be brought to sit at a peace-table and to acknowledge Bruce as a sovereign king.

In this bestselling trilogy, Nigel Tranter charts these turbulent years, revealing the flowering of Bruce's character; how, tutored and encouraged by the heroic William Wallace, he determined to continue the fight for an independent Scotland, sustained by a passionate love for his land and devotion to his people.

'Absorbing . . . a notable achievement'

The Scotsman

HODDER AND STOUGHTON PAPERBACKS

NIGEL TRANTER

THE JAMES V TRILOGY

In 1513 – two hundred years after Robert the Bruce routed the English and restored his nation's pride – King James IV of Scotland lies slaughtered on Flodden's field. With Scotland in a state of turmoil, his seventeen-month-old heir lies at the mercy of ruthless rival factions.

Two men have been entrusted with the new king's welfare: loyal and steadfast David Lindsay and David Beaton. Sons of lowland lairds, they struggle in their role as royal protectors. For there are many who would seek to supplant or control the boy-king James V – his stepfather, the power-hungry Earl of Angus, is one; Henry VIII of England, his greedy eyes never far from the tempting realm of Scotland, is another. Even the boy's mother, Margaret Tudor, plots against her son.

And as he grows up, the young and handsome James V proves to be impetuous, hot-blooded, interested more in wine and women than matters of state. The two Davids have preserved him so far but the threats to James and his country seem to grow by the year . . .

In this fascinating trilogy, Nigel Tranter paints a vivid picture of a turbulent period, an unruly, perplexed and endangered nation, and an attractive but weak-willed king.

'Colourful, fast-moving and well written'
The Times Literary Supplement

HODDER AND STOUGHTON PAPERBACKS